The explanation of culture change: models in prehistory

The explanation of culture change: models in prehistory

edited by

COLIN RENFREW

Professor of Archaeology
in the University of Southampton

Proceedings of a meeting of the
Research Seminar in Archaeology and Related Subjects
held at the University of Sheffield

Duckworth

First published in 1973 by
Gerald Duckworth and Co. Ltd.
The Old Piano Factory
43 Gloucester Crescent, NW1

ISBN 0 7156 0673 5

Typeset by
Specialised Offset Services Limited, Liverpool,
printed by
Unwin Brothers Ltd., Old Woking, Surrey.

CONTENTS

Preface

Archaeology today is changing with astonishing rapidity. Along with the increased recovery of material through land developments or by improved recovery techniques, and with all the information yielded by new analytical methods and the procedures of data handling, the very nature of archaeology as a field of study is undergoing a profound transformation.

To speak of a 'crisis' in archaeology, or a 'methodological revolution' is now a commonplace. Indeed elements in the now-conventional approach of earlier generations are very widely seen as altogether inadequate today. Yet despite a measure of agreement over the inadequacies of these long-unquestioned procedures and beliefs of the received archaeology, of the subject as so long and unhesitatingly taught, there is as yet no clear and generally accepted view of just what new concepts and procedures should replace them. Some suggested elements provoke fairly widespread agreement: for instance the belief that statements can only be regarded as meaningful if they are, at least in principle, testable. Other steps towards the goal of archaeology as a 'scientific' discipline – for instance the view that the subject should be organized into a series of very general nomothetic statements or scientific laws – are much more discutable. Quite clearly such deep and basic rethinking about the very nature of archaeology is not yet at an end.

At the suggestion of Peter Ucko, the founder and guiding force of the Research Seminar in Archaeology and Related Subjects, a three-day meeting of the Seminar was held on 14th, 15th and 16th December 1971 at the University of Sheffield to hold discussions on the theme The Explanation of Culture Change: Models in Prehistory. Its aim was to bring together archaeologists, anthropologists, geographers and interested contributors from other fields, from both sides of the Atlantic, in order to discuss afresh both the aims of archaeology and the new approaches and methods of research which are themselves changing and shaping those aims. Kindly acting as Chairman of sessions, B.W. Cunliffe, A. Forge, P.J. Fowler, S.

Gregory, R.M. Loynes, R.D. Martin, R.J.C. Munton, A. Rosenfeld and P.J. Ucko stimulated some vigorous, even sharp, discussions at the meetings. Abstract and general problems, such as the nature of explanation, the role of law, and the place of systems thinking in archaeology were discussed. Individual sessions were devoted to themes particularly relevant to the understanding of change in past societies – to population and land use, to social organization, to trade and communication. A further session considered the effect that our procedures of gathering the basic data have upon the explanations that are formulated, and of these upon the gathering procedures themselves. A separate discussion examined the interpretation of artifact variability in the palaeolithic period. Together the papers constitute the most comprehensive review yet undertaken of this central question in prehistoric archaeology: the precise nature of its aims and objectives.

As is the practice with these seminars, the papers were circulated beforehand and this book consists of these papers, revised by their authors in the light of the discussions which took place, together with one or two additions also arising from the discussions. Edmund Leach kindly accepted an invitation to conclude the Seminar with a final address, and his trenchant and provocative text makes a splendidly partisan and open-ended conclusion to the book.

This is as it should be. It is too early yet to reach a definitive view as to what precisely the agreed procedures of prehistoric archaeology should be, or on the limits of inference and of potential research in this field. The discussion continues – as it continued after the meetings of the Seminar – and these papers accurately reflect the position which it has reached at the present time. I am very optimistic that, while we may not yet have produced all of the right answers, we are at least now asking some of the right questions.

Among the most lively – and frequent – interlocutors at the meetings were Professor François Bordes and Professor Lewis Binford. Their differing interpretations of artifact variability in the middle palaeolithic are fully examined in their respective papers. We include here, with their permission, a drawing made by Bordes and Pierre Laurent and given to Binford in 1968, as a graphic and less serious comment upon these differences and on the 'functional' view in prehistoric archaeology.

Colin Renfrew
Sheffield
January 1973

Grotte à la Cuisine. A graphic comment by Francois Bordes on the 'functional' approach to the explanation of variability in palaeolithic data (cf. Section 3).

Acknowledgments

All the archaeological staff of the Department of Ancient History in Sheffield, namely Andrew Fleming, Paul Mellars, Patricia Phillips and Jane Renfrew, were active in the organization of the Seminar, which owed much to the support of Professor R.J. Hopper. It was sustained by the efforts of our research students, Clive Bonsall, Mrs Linda Hazelhurst, John Hedges, Ruth Jones and Scott McCracken as well as several undergraduates, and by the University Television Unit under the direction of Janos Reeves. The typing of the papers was undertaken by Mrs D. Ridding, and much of the organization by Mrs P. Sykes, Mrs D. Spurr and Mrs E. Hudson. Susan Johnson, of the Institute of Archaeology, London, compiled the index. Throughout the planning and organization, the advice and support of Peter Ucko was crucial: so far as possible the meeting was modelled upon the two previous three-day meetings of the Research Seminar in Archaeology and Related Subjects organized by him with the support of Professor G.W. Dimbleby and (for the second) Dr Ruth Tringham, and held at the Institute of Archaeology in London. The papers of both these meetings have also been published by Duckworth as books – *The Domestication and Exploitation of Plants and Animals* and *Man, Settlement and Urbanism.*

List of Participants

(asterisks indicate contributors of papers who were unable to participate in person)

J. Alexander (Department of Extra-Mural Studies, University of London)
A. Ammerman (Institute of Archaeology, University of London)
P. Ashbee (University of East Anglia)
G.W.W. Barker (St John's College, Cambridge)
L.R. Binford (University of New Mexico)
F. Bordes (Laboratoire de Géologie de Quaternaire et Préhistoire, University of Bordeaux)
M.M. Borillo (Centre National de la Recherche Scientifique, Centre d'Analyse Documentaire pour l'Archéologie, Marseille)
L. Bourelly (Centre National de la Recherche Scientifique, Centre d'Analyse Documentaire pour l'Archéologie, Marseille)
W.M. Bray (Institute of Archaeology, University of London)
P. Burnham (Department of Anthropology, University College, London)
J. Carnochan (School of Oriental and African Studies, University of London)
H.J. Case (Department of Antiquities, Ashmolean Museum, Oxford)
*L.L. Cavalli-Sforza (Stanford University, Stanford)
*J. Chappell (Department of Geography, S.G.S., Australian National University, Canberra)
*J.L. Chartkoff (Department of Anthropology, Michigan State University, East Lansing)
D. Collins (Hampstead, London)
R.A. Crossland (Department of Greek, University of Sheffield)
B.W. Cunliffe (Department of Archaeology, University of Southampton)
N. David (Department of Anthropology, University College, London)
R.M. Derricourt (Department of African Studies, University of Fort Hare)
*P.M. Dolukhanov (Institute of Archaeology, Leningrad)
J. Doran (SRC Atlas Computer Laboratory, Chilton, Berkshire)
C. Doumas (Archaeological Museum, Santorini)

A. Ellison (Department of Archaeology, University of Cambridge)
J.D. Evans (Institute of Archaeology, University of London)
A. Fleming (Department of Ancient History, University of Sheffield)
A. Forge (London School of Economics)
P.J. Fowler (Department of Extra-Mural Studies, University of Bristol)
D.H. French (British Institute of Archaeology, Ankara)
P. Gathercole (Museum of Archaeology and Ethnology, Cambridge)
McG. Gibson (Department of Anthropology, University of Arizona, Tucson)
J. Goody (St John's College, Cambridge)
S. Gregory (Department of Geography, University of Sheffield)
L.M. Groube (Department of Prehistory, I.A.S., Australian National University, Canberra)
N. Hammond (Centre of Latin-American Studies. University of Cambridge)
D.R. Harris (Department of Geography, University College, London)
J. Harriss (Pembroke College, Cambridge)
C.B. Haycraft (Gerald Duckworth and Co., London)
F. Hole (Department of Anthropology, Rice University, Houston, Texas)
R.J. Hopper (Department of Ancient History, University of Sheffield)
J. Keighley (Institute of Archaeology, University of London)
*L.S. Klejn (Department of Archaeology, University of Leningrad)
R. Layton (Department of Anthropology, University College, London)
E. Leach (King's College, Cambridge)
R.M. Loynes (Department of Probability and Statistics, University of Sheffield)
E.W. MacKie (Hunterian Museum, University of Glasgow)
R.D. Martin (Department of Anthropology, University College, London)
*R.G. Matson (Northern Arizona University, Flagstaff)
C.B.M. McBurney (Department of Archaeology, University of Cambridge)
P.A. Mellars (Department of Ancient History, University of Sheffield)
D.H. Mellor (Philosophy Faculty, University of Cambridge)
P. Mortensen (Institute of Prehistoric Archaeology and Ethnography, Aarhus University)
R. Munton (Department of Geography, University College, London)
C.M. Nelson (Department of Anthropology, University of Massachusetts, Boston)
*E. Neustupný (Archaeological Institute of the Czechoslovak Academy of Sciences, Prague)
B.J. Orme (Department of Anthropology, University College, London)

C.R. Orton (Sutton, Surrey)
B. Ottaway (Department of Archaeology, University of Edinburgh)
A.P. Phillips (Department of Ancient History, University of Sheffield)
*F. Plog (University of California, Los Angeles)
*R. Pollnac (University of Missouri)
W.G.L. Randles (Eaubonne, France)
K. Randsborg (Institute of Prehistoric Archaeology, University of Copenhagen)
W.L. Rathje (University of Arizona, Tucson)
C.L. Redman (New York University)
C. Renfrew (Department of Ancient History, University of Sheffield)
J.M. Renfrew (Department of Ancient History, University of Sheffield)
V. Reynolds (Department of Sociology, University of Bristol)
A. Rosenfeld (Department of British and Mediaeval Antiquities, British Museum, London)
M.J. Rowlands (Department of Anthropology, University College, London)
*J.R. Sackett (University of California, Los Angeles)
A.G. Sherratt (Department of Archaeology, University of Cambridge)
B. Soudský (Institut d'Art et d'Archéologie, Université de Paris I, Sorbonne – Panthéon)
G. Sterud (State University of New York at Binghamton)
E.G. Stickel (Department of Anthropology, University of California, Los Angeles)
M. Tosi (Istituto Italiano per il Medio ed Estremo Oriente, Rome)
P.J. Ucko (Department of Anthropology, University College, London)
W.F. de la Vega (Centre National de la Recherche Scientifique, Centre d'Analyse Documentaire pour l'Archéologie, Marseille)
J. Virbel (Centre National de la Recherche Scientifique, Centre d'Analyse Documentaire pour l'Archéologie, Marseille)
P.J. Watson (Department of Anthropology, Washington University, St Louis, Missouri)
*R.A. Watson (Department of Philosophy, Washington University, St Louis, Missouri)
R. Whallon Jr. (Netherlands Institute for Advanced Study, Wassenaar)
R.D. Whitehouse (Southgate, London)
J.J. Wood (Northern Arizona University, Flagstaff)

Section 1: The explanation of culture change: central concepts

GENE STERUD

A paradigmatic view of prehistory

> This scientific revolution . . . was the product of a fundamental change in men's basic attitudes. (Sackett 1964)

> This new way of scientific thinking, with its emphasis upon uniformitarianism and evolution, enabled the discoveries of Pengelly and Boucher de Perthes to be accepted readily, whereas only a generation before, when the immutability of species and catastrophist diluvianism were the orders of thought, the discoveries of Schmerling and MacEnery had passed unnoticed or been rejected with scorn. (Daniel 1950:66)

Although a modicum of archaeological work had been performed in the century prior to the publication of *The Origin of Species* (1859), it was the intellectual and scientific environment engendered by the Darwinian revolution which provided the impetus for the development of a formal discipline of prehistory in the Old World. Particularly, it was the discovery of *time*, in the order of millennia, plus the definition of evolutionary *process* (social as well as biological), which permitted the establishment of a scholarly community committed to the documentation of this vast, hitherto unsuspected antiquity. Darwinism, in fact, made such an inquiry not only possible but necessary, for, if biological evolution was a reality, there had to be some evidence in support of this in the earth (Daniel 1950:66, 67). Thus prehistoric archaeology became an important contributor to and a prime beneficiary of the Darwinian revolution of a century ago, in spite of the fact that Darwin did not himself immediately acknowledge the authenticity of Boucher's finds (Daniel 1959:174, 175).

The present paper is an examination of the origin and development of this discipline through the perspectives of a model of change recently advanced by a philosopher of science, Thomas S. Kuhn (1962; 1970a). Kuhn offers a framework for understanding the nature of scientific development from the initial establishment of a common body of theory with its acceptable standards of measurement to and including that point when the long-accepted frameworks no longer suffice and the science takes on a new or revised set of standards. In doing so, he also includes some bases for prediction. If it is possible to apply his basic ideas to the rise of prehistory, then it may also prove to be possible to recognize the seeds of change sufficiently well to predict impending changes in our approaches to the study of the past.

Arguing that sciences develop through partial or wholesale replacement of theoretical structure rather than the widely proclaimed change-by-accumulation, Kuhn traces several stages of this development. These can be summarized simply as 'pre-paradigm', 'first paradigm' and 'new paradigm' periods. A paradigm here represents an internally consistent body of theory, including mutually acceptable tools and standards of measurement, held by a scientific community. A scientific community is composed of the practitioners of a scientific speciality who are characterized as having undergone similar educations and professional initiations, learned their constellation of beliefs, values and techniques from the same source (textbooks and lectures produced by the previous generation of adherents), and producing work which is considered by the community or school to be worthwhile. Within such a community there is a common recognition of areas of research which promise to add to the scope and precision of the current paradigmatic structure (Kuhn 1970a:43-51, 174-8; Masterman 1970:59-89; Kuhn 1970b:266-77; Hägstrom 1965).

The 'pre-paradigm' period is that posture of the science wherein there are a number of viewpoints and interests, each having some claim upon a portion of the total field. At this point in time there is no single, accepted view which spans the entirety of the field of interest. Instead, a number of competing views, each with a variant of a theory, emphasize a particular observational speciality which relates most closely to its theoretical orientation and which it can best explain. Although each variant makes contributions to the totality in the form of methods, techniques and conceptual ideas, in the absence of a common and uniform body of belief acceptable to all, the worker is forced to build up the theoretical foundations anew each time a contribution is made to the field. Since any scientific endeavour requires some body of theory or belief, explicit or implicit, during this 'pre-paradigm' period, a wide range of facts and ideas could appear to be equally relevant and different workers, using essentially the same 'facts', could arrive at quite different interpretations and explanations (Kuhn 1970a:10-18).

When one of the 'pre-paradigm' schools triumphs, it results in the disappearance of other variants. Accordingly, the triumphant school has emphasized some special portion of the totality and although it need not explain all of the facts and problems that confront the science, it must appear better than the other competing factions. The result of this successful competition is Kuhn's 'first paradigm' period. In addition to marking the disappearance of the unsuccessful competitors, the 'first paradigm' positively establishes a unified conceptual framework which sets the trend of future research. This period is often marked by the establishment of professional journals and scientific societies and the presentation of textbook summaries which incorporate the research to date supporting the paradigmatic body of belief as well as providing the basic means of orientation for the novice. Once the new paradigm is firmly entrenched, the textbook serves as the medium through which the theory and assumptions of the current paradigmatic structure are conveyed to the reader. Inasmuch as the whole scientific community is grounded in this theory, it is now unnecessary for each worker explicitly to revert to first principles. He can instead concentrate upon brief, specialized papers geared to the level of his professional colleagues. In other words, the theoretical framework is now implicit in the kinds of work being produced (ibid.:19-21).

The scope of research is narrowly directed and takes its essential meaning from the framework of established belief held by the scientific community. The members of the community 'see themselves and are seen by others as the men uniquely responsible for the pursuit of a set of shared goals, including the training of their successors' (Kuhn, 1970a:177). Kuhn's term for the type of research conducted during the period marked by an established paradigm is 'normal science' and consists of the articulation of problem areas which the paradigm earmarks as being important and worthy of investigation. It is the existing paradigm which supplies the theoretical fabric. At the outset of a new paradigm period, the success is largely a promise of future accomplishments, rather than a *fait accompli*. In the beginning only limited demonstrations are available to its advocates. Normal science is thus concerned with the empirical verification of the claims of the theory. This involves a demonstration of the application of the paradigm as well as attempts to improve on the precision of a previous application (Kuhn, 1970a: 23-34). Much of the work is in the form of 'puzzle-solving', i.e., the solving of problems which, based on the existing paradigm, can be assumed to have solutions and which are deemed worthy of being undertaken by the scientific community. Conversely, problems which may earlier have been considered as worthy of interest would now be rejected out of hand. Much of the end-product of normal science is the achievement of an anticipated outcome in a new way, thus validating the underlying theory. Normal science is the activity which occupies nearly the entire attention of most scholars (scientists) and is rightly described as the 'mopping up' operations which follow the establishment of sets of predictions which a new paradigm presupposes (ibid.: 24, 35-42).

This aspect of the scientific process *is* highly cumulative in nature in that it represents the steady extension of acceptable research into new and previously untested territories (ibid.:95). The commitment of the entire 'school' to the further documentation of the common belief system results in an inevitable willingness to defend these commitments, sometimes at considerable cost. This will often take the form of suppressing novelties which 'are necessarily subversive of its basic commitments' (ibid.:5). Since the paradigm, as established, did not claim to explain everything, it left the door open for novelty to creep in. It is at this point of structural instability that one may look for the roots of change.

Novelty, called 'anomaly' by Kuhn, often goes unrecognized if it is nonrecurrent. However, where anomalous events, which are produced inadvertently in the course of normal scientific activity of extending the scope and precision of the body of theory, occur repeatedly, they become an increasing cause for concern by the paradigm's adherents. Discovery of the breakdown of scientific expectation is the first step in a process which leads to paradigmatic change. The recognized anomaly triggers off an exploration of the area of theory-breakdown.

> When . . . the profession can no longer evade anomalies that subvert the existing tradition of scientific practice – then begin the extraordinary investigations that lead the profession at last to a new set of commitments, a new basis for the practice of science. (ibid.:6)

There seems to be, in fact, a very strong conservative tendency on the part of the scientist to suppress the production of alternative explanations. This unwillingness to change can be due to the costs involved. By this is meant time, energy and psychological adjustment involved in a substantial change in the paradigmatic orientation. Scientific work proceeds most efficiently through the skilled use of the tools already available for the task. 'As in manufacture, so in science – retooling is an extravagance to be reserved for the occasion that demands it' (ibid.:76). The degree of involvement or commitment to the existing paradigm on the part of the scientist works against change. The assimilation of a new idea is not merely an additive adjustment. It requires that he begin to see nature in a new and different way (ibid.:53). This attitude has been afforded a name, 'Graves' Law', which states: 'The greater the professional stake in the use of a particular research procedure, the less able (or willing) will a colleague be to recognize (or admit to) its particular limitations.' (Graves, Graves and Kobrin 1969:334; see also Martin 1971:2).

In spite of resistance, paradigmatic crises do arise and it is these crises and their resolution, that ultimately result in the emergence of a new paradigm, that Kuhn calls 'Scientific Revolutions' (Kuhn 1971:91).

Once an anomaly has become a serious source of contention, the state of crisis has begun and a period of 'extraordinary science' commences. Advocates of change appear increasingly in print in professional periodicals attacking the established paradigm. Supporters of the latter reply in order to justify their long-held positions. This is sometimes difficult since much of the theoretical groundwork for an established paradigm may have been laid down during a prior generation and accepted without criticism by this generation of scientists. They received their training in the 'normal' manner via textbook summary rather than having had to work out all of the proofs themselves. In addition, since normal science can often be carried on without direct reference to the underlying proofs, most rules, assumptions and conceptual parameters can be left implicit. Only during such a period of crisis is it necessary for the scientist to make his theoretical justifications explicit. The majority of scientists are inclined to doing 'normal science' and such a voyage into the world of scientific philosophy is an adventure in an uncertain terrain, and one which many would prefer to avoid (ibid.:87).

It is the most committed senior members of the community who come out most strongly in support of the *status quo* and at times use their senior position to place pressure on their opponents. The less strongly committed, and those bringing their experiences from other disciplines, are more willing to inaugurate change:

> Almost always the men who achieve (the) fundamental inventions of a new paradigm have been either very young or very new to the field whose paradigm they change . . . these are the men who, being little committed by prior practice to the traditional rules of normal science, are particularly likely to see that those rules no longer define a playable game and to conceive another set that can replace them. (ibid.:89, 90)

Moreover, once the opposing camps are established, there is little ground left for agreement since each debates its case within the structure of its own paradigm. With differing viewpoints, the arguments tend to be circular and at cross-purposes. The period of crisis represents an interim in which no single paradigm really governs the situation. The final resolution of these opposing belief systems may involve a long drawn out period during which time each attempts to work in its own way. Time, however, is on the side of the challengers, and if the crisis is not resolved via compromise or the grudging acceptance of a new or altered world view, the victory is eventually achieved by default as the older members retire or pass away. In the former case where a settlement is reached by the majority, those members of the scientific community who refuse to be bound by this altered paradigmatic system are simply read out of the field. Their works are no longer seriously considered (ibid.:17-19, 93).

Thus, in a very real way, a change in a paradigm, and the rejection and abandonment of a previous one, represent a revolutionary alteration of a world view. Scientific research that was once considered valuable loses its meaning. There are new sets of priorities and the work of 'normal science' focuses upon a series of new puzzles deemed worthy of solving and which promise to add scope and precision to the new paradigm.

No paradigm-directed scientific school ever depicts the entirety of a situation or attempts to deal with all of the attributes of a question. The necessary abstraction from the totality of those issues deemed meaningful forces exclusion of other facets of the situation. Thus, when the paradigm changes after a revolution, it is clear that scientists are indeed working in a new and altered perceptual world, not simply in the same world augmented by an increment of accumulated ideas.

The 'change-through-accumulation' explanation which has accompanied the development of prehistoric archaeology is evident in the various historical accounts of the 'growth' of archaeological research (Daniel 1943, 1950, 1967; Heizer 1969; Leakey and Goodall 1969) as well as in the historical summaries which are to be found in textbook treatments of prehistory (Clarke 1968:4-11; Hole and Heizer 1969; Gavela 1963; Kivikoski 1961; de Sonneville-Bordes 1961). As already mentioned above, textbook syntheses serve as the vehicles for the perpetuation of a current paradigm and are re-written after each scientific revolution (trace, for example, the ideas relating to the neolithic contained in Lubbock 1890; Pumpelly 1908; Clark 1952; Childe 1954; Braidwood 1967; Binford 1968a). Through their consumption of the existing views of the past, students and professionals alike 'come to feel like participants in a long-standing historical tradition' (Kuhn 1970a:137, 138). This is enhanced by the extraction from all past events of just those works which can be recognized as contributing to the present paradigm.

> Partly by selection and partly by distortion, scientists of earlier ages are implicitly represented as having worked upon the same set of fixed problems and in accordance with the same set of fixed canons that the most recent revolution in scientific theory and method has made seem scientific. (ibid.: 138)

The result is a linear progression of history and a cumulating body of theory and method climaxing in the present 'modern' position of our discipline. It is not accidental that the historians of prehistory have selected 'significant' landmarks in the development of the field (see, for instance, Heizer 1969:vii; Daniel 1967: preface).

The potential application of some of Kuhn's basic ideas to the changes which have taken place in prehistoric thought is quite great. For example, it is tempting to view the condition of prehistory prior to 1859 as coinciding with Kuhn's 'pre-paradigmatic' period. Indeed, there were several partial approaches to and explanations of the archaeological record. The Three Age System was a model for a means of orientation for a great number of antiquarians. The system was, however, not everywhere well-received (Daniel 1950:79-85). In

England, for example, the antiquarian was pre-occupied with the documentation of a pre-Roman Celtic prehistory, complete with its Druidic priesthood, thought to mark the earliest traces of European man (Daniel 1967:21-3; Sackett 1964; Piggott 1966). Much of this concern was incorporated into the gentlemanly pastime of curiosity-collecting and associated with leisured dilettantism (the English version being the 'virtuoso').

Elsewhere, other interests held the attentions of the student of man's past. With the age of the earth and man restricted to no more than 6,000 years, the Genesis account found the support of a large audience. It was reasonable, within such a perceptual world, that explanations of prehistoric finds should resolve around 'thunder-stones', 'vis plastica', 'fairy arrows', 'elf shot', and the like.

Out of these competing views emerged a variant which combined the recognition of sufficient time and an evolutionary concept for the organic world. Man became a part of nature and inherited a long past. This 'new look' permitted the formation of a discipline devoted to the documentation of prehistoric man and his cultures.

> Who can deny that by demonstrating that man and culture evolved from humble beginnings, the archaeologists of the last century effected as revolutionary a change in man's view of himself and of his place in nature as have Copernicus, Darwin or Freud? (Trigger 1970:36)

Within this cognitive framework, several schools developed. Each pursued a documentation of man's past within the same general body of belief; their differences could be best identified with the portion of the totality that they explored. Those scholars concerned with the palaeolithic adopted many of the methods of palaeontology and geology which had contributed to the initial recognition of man's past. Other investigators, focussing upon the neolithic and bronze age periods, incorporated a methodology as well as several techniques widely used by historians. This essentially historical orientation may be explained at least partially in terms of the heightened interest on the part of these workers, devoted to the more recent periods of prehistory, with the tracing of the ancestry of their own nations:

> Many Europeans took to the spade simply because of their own national origins: the French sought for traces of the Gauls, the English for ancient Britons, the Germans for the old Teutonic tribes, and so on . . . (R.J. Braidwood, in Daniel 1967:7)

It is within these two schools of prehistoric research that one sees the basis for the work that was to pre-occupy the prehistorian for the following century. Restricting our attention to the latter of these two schools, we can trace some of the elements of a newly established paradigmatic system. Although the 'new' field of prehistory did not solve all of the problems or explain all of the facts of the past, it did provide the appearance of being able to do so. The initial phase of this 'first paradigm' period was marked by considerable explicit theorizing, the establishment of a terminology for the field and the working out of a systematic method for classifying the artifactual remains. The credit for the latter is usually afforded to the Swede, O. Montelius, although there is some question as to his exact role in the establishment of the 'Typological Method' (Montelius 1869, 1884-91, 1900, 1903; H. Hildebrand 1869, 1880; Almgren 1965-6) with a number of variations being added by other early European methodologists (Müller 1884; Reinecke 1899; Nordman 1915; Lindqvist 1919).

Once the fundamentals of this paradigmatic body of belief were sufficiently well-known, one finds a diminution of explicit theory and the prehistorians settle down to the work of 'normal science', which in this case meant the conducting of excavations in many regions and the gradual development of a chronological framework consisting of periods and sub-periods, as defined by their characteristic material remains. Montelius, for example, developed a six-stage framework for the Scandinavian bronze age and linked it, through the extension of his 'method', to surrounding regions. No longer was it necessary for these prehistorians to preface their more-specialized work with references to the underlying theoretical bases. This was now accomplished by the production of textbooks and general syntheses which provided the novice with the necessary framework.

It seems to this writer that the 'first paradigm' period of European prehistory is still essentially operative. The one fact that strikes the American-trained archaeologist when be begins to work in Europe on prehistoric problems is that there is remarkably little 'explicit' discussion of theory, methodological assumptions and/or challenges to the established approaches to prehistoric research. At least in terms of the 'historically-oriented' typological methodology, the foundations were laid very early by Montelius and continue in use. Nor is this simply my intuition; E. Neustupný has recently remarked:

> Those who believe that archaeology is in a state of crisis may put forward strong arguments in favour of their thesis. Almost all that is of importance in archaeology has been known since the beginning of this century. This applies not only to the methods and theory (the concepts of typology, associated finds, archaeological cultures, etc.) but also to the results. It is true that many gaps have been filled, especially in some parts of the world, but this has not influenced the discipline as a whole. Thus, for example, in Central Europe, which is certainly one of the regions best known archaeologically, there has been little progress since the times of G. Kossinna, J. Pelliardi, O. Menghin, L. Kozlowski and the young J. Kostrzewski. The chronological schemes of O. Montelius and P. Reinecke for the Bronze Age are still used, and new cultures, if there are any, are mostly the result of mere subdivisions of earlier ones. (1971:35) (see also: Thomas and Ehrich 1969: 143; Spaulding 1960:83)

That the great majority of prehistorians continue to be guided in their research by the 'tradition-bound' patterns which were established in the closing years of the last century is, I believe, certainly demonstrable. The preoccupation with the general problems of a chronological nature (to the exclusion of other concerns) is one evidence of this.

While the majority of researches in European prehistory continue to follow the pattern of 'normal science', producing results according to the 'traditional orientations', in some areas of prehistoric investigation, anomalies have occurred which have had the effect of altering segments of the total field, resulting in new configurations of conceptual categories.

An excellent and current example of the appearance of anomalies and their ultimate effect upon an existing paradigm within one limited area of European prehistory can be found in connection with carbon-14 (C-14) dating.

After the initial development of the C-14 dating method, there was a considerable amount of debate as to the accuracy of the method. The method, newly developed, did not carry with it the claim of absolute perfection but eventually the great majority of prehistorians accepted the assumptions and some of the limitations of the method. Basic to this acceptance was the belief that the concentration of C-14 in the atmosphere was essentially constant and therefore the determinations represented a fairly accurate age of the object tested. A number of European prehistorians expressed their strong disbelief in the accuracy of the method and the well-known 'long' (C-14) chronology and 'short' (typological) chronology were developed and archaeologists were divided into these two camps. The latter has dwindled into a small band of holdouts and there has been an eventual widespread acceptance of the validity of C-14 dating from European prehistory and a subsequent use of such dates in outlining the course of prehistoric development (e.g. Clark 1965:45-8).

As with all paradigmatic models, the existing theory does not solve all problems but merely gives promise of possibly doing so. Therefore, anomalies can arise. In the case of C-14, it was early recognized that there were serious differences between historical dates and C-14 determinations. As early as 1961, the author recalls a public lecture at which Dr W. Libby remarked upon the inexplicable deviation of C-14 dates from historical dates in Egyptian archaeological contexts. From about 3000 B.C. there is an increasing variance between the two sets of determinations. At the time Libby jokingly remarked that he was hopeful that the Egyptologists were wrong. A similar response was made by de Vries during the early 1960s. Following upon the establishment of C-14 dating by Dr Libby, de Vries set himself the task of refining the problem areas and the scope of the method's utility. At a public lecture to a group of Egyptologists at Uppsala University, chaired by Professor Säve-Söderbergh, de Vries himself noted this discrepancy and his remarks paralleled closely those of Dr Libby (personal communication). This indicates how easily an anomaly can be coped with initially creating little serious concern. The concern, however, did increase. The Egyptologists attempted to trace the errors to their historical chronologies (Smith 1964).

The investigation of such a recurring novelty, which could not easily be disposed of, became the central theme of research for some members of the disciplines involved. The result was a collaboration by several radiocarbon laboratories and dendrochronologists in a study of the Sequoia and Bristlecone pines which has demonstrated the existence of systematic variances; the carbon-14 dates from 1500 B.C. and earlier are 'systematically younger' than the tree-ring dates (Olsson 1970).

At present, the debate continues over the cause of the variations and the question of the applicability of a sequence established in California to the rest of the world.

The effect of the 'provisional' resolution of this anomaly has been more than just an accumulation of a greater amount of knowledge of European prehistory. An entirely novel interpretation of the absolute chronology of prehistoric Europe has been presented. Incorporated in this chronological revision are several strategic events (e.g., the early appearance of metallurgy in the Balkans; an early date for the Tartaria tablets; a lengthening of the neolithic in Europe and the requisite re-evaluation of the nature of the megalithic tombs, the neolithic 'temples' of Malta and the British henges) (Renfrew, 1970a). This is no mere accumulation of historical fact; it constitutes a revision in our thinking:

> The new dates should not simply change our chronologies. They render meaningless so much that has been written in recent years that there must have been serious inadequacies in our whole approach to the past, not simply in our chronology. (ibid.:209)

The 'inadequacies' alluded to here revolve about an approach to the explanation of prehistoric culture change in Europe and the Near East which sees all major developments and innovations diffusing from the Near East into Europe. This attitude has been an integral part of our thinking for a century but, with the increased attention being given to the nature of the relationship between these two regions as a result of the recent C-14 work, explanations such as 'diffusion', 'influences', 'contacts', or 'migrations' are being rejected as too imprecise. Demands are being voiced for 'more detailed analysis of the actual mechanisms involved' (Renfrew 1970b:897-900; 1971a:72; 1971b:12-15; Clarke 1968:24-32; Harriss 1971:38-55). With an acceptance of the bristlecone pine calibrations, whereby the implications of this dramatically different vision of prehistoric Europe gain the approval and acceptance of the 'scientific community', the result must be a new belief system for European prehistorians and, hence, a new paradigm for this particular area of prehistoric research.

While British prehistorians are obviously playing a leading role in altering this basic approach, other parts of Europe remain deeply committed to the traditional chronologically-oriented goals. For example, the seventh Congress of Yugoslav Archaeology, May, 1966, devoted a lengthy session to 'Periodization in Archaeology'. This dealt with the division of the neolithic into two or three divisions and the question of whether such divisions should be pan-Yugoslavian or regionally separate; the sub-divisioning of the local bronze age; and included a scheme for the periodization of prehistory in all of Europe, dividing prehistory into 'first' (palaeolithic and mesolithic), 'second' (neolithic), and 'third' (bronze and iron age) epochs (Tasić 1967).

The recent evidences of efforts to break out of this trajectory in England, and recurrent statements of archaeologists working in various parts of Europe indicating discontent with the existing pattern, suggest that the seeds of change are in the air. Note, for example, the series of recent articles in the journal *Antiquity*, each dealing with the aims and directions of prehistory (Trigger 1970; Neustupný 1971; Isaac 1971). Trigger, sensing a change in the values of the younger generation of archaeologists, expresses the belief that this shift to a new set of problems, with an accompanying change in methodology, has important 'implications for the general orientation of prehistoric archaeology' (op. cit.:26). Neustupný, noting the existence of a period crisis in archaeological research, outlines some of the recent development in methodology, and concludes that 'There is no doubt that the present archaeological generation, old and young, is living in a period of *revolutionary changes* in its discipline' (op. cit.:39). Isaac, too, discusses several new methodological directions in which archaeologists are beginning to probe. In terms of Kuhn's crisis state in paradigmatic change, it is noticeable that these suggestions are being offered by a younger generation of scholars or those whose early training has been in some other field. Even in those cases where senior scholars find it possible to adjust to changing ideas, it is only with considerable difficulty that this is accomplished (Martin 1971:2). Nor is it accidental that a number of the new directions stem from developments which are taking place in the Americas, where prehistoric research is certainly in the midst of a crisis state, and where a strict 'historical approach' is much less in evidence (Taylor 1948:23-42; Ehrich 1970:673-6; Hammond 1971). Two very influential volumes, Clarke (1968) and Binford and Binford (1968), although pursuing somewhat different aims, have become characterizations of this change in orientation. Ehrich (1970:679) has drawn attention to the effect of American research upon Clarke's *Analytical Archaeology*, demonstrating that, of the 22 examples cited by Clarke, 14 of these were written by American scholars.

This increasing awareness, on the part of scholars from one country and 'school' of thought, of the work of other schools is seemingly another sign of imminent change. Illustrative of this is the independent development of seriation techniques in the United States and in England. An examination of the references cited in each of these areas impresses one with the fact that there was little if any important interaction between them (Brainerd 1951:312, 313). Only recently has this isolation broken down and meaningful interchange of information taken place (Renfrew and Sterud 1969:276, 277; Gelfand 1971:273, 274).

The development of new directions necessitates the explicit exposition of the essential theoretical and methodological bases for such changes. This has meant that certain goals previously considered important now assume a much reduced emphasis. One would expect, following Kuhn's model, that there would be a shocked and embittered response to the suggestions of new goal-orientations. Again referring to articles recently published in *Antiquity*, the J. Hawkes article (1968) seems to be a 'classic' example of such a plea for the maintenance of a 'traditional' humanist approach and a recognition of the threat to this long-established paradigm by the method and theory espoused by the 'statniks' and science-oriented archaeologists. One should expect such defences of the established paradigm to increase, leading to a crystallization of the older and newer viewpoints, and a more explicit statement of the essential theoretical systems of both the older and the newer camps. Whatever the specific outcome of present experiments into new areas of inquiry, there can be no question of returning to the state of the discipline of the past, even the most recent past. The result must be a somewhat altered 'world view' on the part of the prehistorian. His research aims will be altered. New questions will be asked and new methods will be developed to pursue the newly legitimatized and agreed-upon goals.

One important feature of Kuhn's theory is the possibility of providing the discipline with the grounds for prediction. Prediction is essentially based upon the recognition of signs of impending change. In the case of an imminent crisis certain indications are present long before the critical state is reached. These include: recurring anomalies which cannot be brushed aside; increased concern on the part of certain members of the 'community' for the exploration of these novelties; explicit inquiry into the fundamental bases of the current theory structure; increasingly explicit responses on the part of the strongly committed members of the scientific community, involving a 'philosophical look' at the long-standing 'implicit' bases of their positions with a view to justifying their career-long commitment to a certain form of 'normal scientific' research.

Whether or not one cares to examine the current state of prehistoric research within the theoretical framework offered by Thomas Kuhn, it is difficult to ignore the indications that many of the traditional concerns of prehistoric archaeology are being subjected to critical scrutiny. The present research seminar is itself an indication of a shift in the direction of new sets of priorities. The recognition of a breakdown of scientific expectation, most evident in the inability to achieve greater insights into the events of prehistory, in spite of greatly refined data collection and analysis techniques and a rapidly accumulating body of archaeological data, has caused many prehistoric archaeologists to search for different means for understanding the world of the past. The adoption by a number of the participants of a more explicitly scientific approach, the search for laws or law-like regularities, and the insistence upon explanations which derive from the scientific examination of the contextual record already sets them apart from the more traditional researcher content to rely upon traditional theory and method. This is most apparent in the contributions of E. Neustupný, F. Hole, F. Plog, P. Watson, G. Stickel and J. Chartkoff, and J. Wood and R. Matson (this volume; see also Harriss 1971; Binford 1968b; Watson, LeBlanc and Redman 1971). It is readily apparent that the participants in the current seminar do not comprise a representative cross-section of active prehistorians; the average age (in terms of years of active research) of the participants is predictably something less than that of the profession as a whole; many senior members of the profession are conspicuous by their absence. Noteworthy too are the recurring (but independently conceived) usages of such terms and phrases as: traditional methods, questioning of aims and methods, increasing concern, precise, explicit, systematic, scientific, processual, nomothetic, hypothesis testing, etc.

The immediate effect of the present scrutiny of traditional methodology must be an 'increasingly explicit and self-conscious' goal orientation (Trigger 1970: 26) while a predictable long range result may well be the 'enforced obsolescence of much of traditional theory and method' (Binford 1968b:27). What is certain is that the prehistorian, by adopting a more explicitly scientific approach and seeking answers to questions hitherto not considered meaningful, will be toiling in a new and altered perceptual world. It would appear that this will become the 'hallmark' of a new paradigm for prehistory.

REFERENCES

Almgren, B. (1965-6) Das Entwicklungsprinzip in der Archäologie – eine Kritik. *Tor.* Sweden, Meddelanden från Institutionen för Nordisk Fornkunskap vid Uppsala Universitet.

Binford, L.R. (1968a) Post-Pleistocene adaptations. *In* Binford, S.R. and L.R. (eds.) *New Perspectives in Archaeology* 313-41. Chicago, Aldine.
Binford, L.R. (1968b) Archaeological perspectives. *In* Binford, S.R. and L.R. (eds.) New Perspectives in Archaeology, 5-32. Chicago, Aldine.
Braidwood, R.J. (1967) *Prehistoric Men.* 7th ed. Glenville, Illinois. Scott, Foresman.
Brainerd, G.W. (1951) The place of chronological ordering in archaeological analysis. *American Antiquity* 4, 301-13.
Childe, V.G. (1954) *What Happened in History.* Revised ed. Harmondswoth, Middlesex, Penguin.
Clark, J.G.D. (1952) *Prehistoric Europe, the Economic Basis.* London, Methuen.
Clark, J.G.D. (1965) Radiocarbon dating and the spread of farming economy. *Antiquity* 39, 45-8.
Clarke, D.L. (1968) *Analytical Archaeology.* London, Methuen.
Daniel, G.E. (1943) *The Three Ages: an Essay on Archaeological Method.* Cambridge, University Press.
Daniel, G.E. (1950) *A Hundred Years of Archaeology.* London, Duckworth.
Daniel, G.E. (1959) The idea of man's antiquity. *Scientific American* **201** no. 5, 167-76.
Daniel, G.E. (1967) *The Origins and Growth of Archaeology.* Baltimore, Penguin.
de Sonneville-Bordes, D. (1961) *L'Age de la Pierre.* Paris, Presses Universitaires de France.
Ehrich, R.W. (1970) Current archaeological trends in Europe and America: similarities and differences. *Journal of World History, UNESCO.* 12, 4,670-81.
Gavela, B. (1963) *Praistoriska Arheologija.* Part I, Text. Beograd, Naucna Knjiga.
Gelfand, A.E. (1971) Seriation methods for archaeological materials. *American Antiquity* **36**, no. 3, 263-74.
Graves, T.D., Graves, N.B. and Kobrin, M.J. (1969) Historical inferences from Guttman Scales: the return of age-area magic? *Current Anthropology* **10**, 4, 317-38.
Hägstrom, W.O. (1965) *The Scientific Community.* New York, Basic Books.
Hammond, A.L. (1971) The new archaeology: toward a social science. *Science* **172**, 1119, 1120.
Harriss, J.C. (1971) Explanation in prehistory. *Proceedings of the Prehistoric Society* **37**, 38-55.
Hawkes, J. (1968) The proper study of mankind. *Antiquity* **42**, 255-62.
Heizer, R.F. (1969) *Man's Discovery of His Past.* Palo Alto, Peek.
Hildebrand, H. (1869) Den äldre jernåldern i Norrland. *Antikvarisk Tidskrift* **II**. Stockholm.
Hildebrand, H. (1880) Studier i jämförande fornforskning. I. Bidrag till spännets historia. *Antikvarisk Tidskrift* **IV**. Stockholm.
Hole, F. and Heizer, R.F. (1969) *An Introduction to Prehistoric Archaeology.* 2nd ed. New York, Holt, Rinehart & Winston.
Isaac, G.L. (1971) Whither archaeology? *Antiquity* **45**, 123-9.
Kivikoski, E. (1961) *Finlands Förhistoria.* Helsingfors, Centraltryckeriet.
Kuhn, T.S. (1962) *The Structure of Scientific Revolutions.* Chicago, University Press.
Kuhn, T.S. (1970a) *The Structure of Scientific Revolutions.* 2nd ed. Chicago, University Press.
Kuhn, T.S. (1970b) Reflections of my critics. *In* Lakatos, I. and Musgrave, A., *Criticism and the Growth of Knowledge.* Cambridge, University Press. 231-78.
Leakey, L.S.B. and Goodall, V.M. (1969) *Unveiling Man's Origins.* Cambridge, Mass. Schenkman.

Lindqvist, S. (1919) Den svenska folkvandringsstilens uppkomst. Rig. Stockholm.

Lubbock, J. (1890) *Pre-historic Times.* 5th ed. New York, Appleton.

Martin, P.S. (1971) The revolution in archaeology. *American Antiquity* 36, no. 1, 1-8.

Masterman, M. (1970) The nature of a paradigm. *In* Lakatos, I. and Musgrave, A., *Criticism and the Growth of Knowledge.* Cambridge, University Press. 59-89.

Menghin, O. (1931) *Weltgeschichte der Steinzeit.* Vienna, A. Schroll.

Montelius, O. (1869) *Från jernåldern. I.* Stockholm.

Montelius, O. (1884-91) Den förhistoriska fornforskningens metod och material. *Antikvarisk Tidskrift* **VIII**. Stockholm.

Montelius, O. (1900) Typologien eller utvecklingsläran tillämpad på det mänskliga arbetet. *Svenska Fornminnesförenings Tidskrift* **X**, Stockholm.

Montelius, O. (1903) *Die Alteren Kulturperioden im Orient und in Europa. I. Die Methode.* Stockholm.

Müller, S. (1884) Mindre bitrag til den förhistoriske archaeologins methode. *Aarbøger før Nordisk Oldkyndighet.* Køpenhavn.

Neustupný, E. (1971) Whither archaeology? *Antiquity* **45**, 34-9.

Nordman, C.A. (1915) *Kritik av typologien i Nya Argus.* Helsinki.

Olsson, I.U. (ed.) (1970) *Radiocarbon Variations and Absolute Chronology.* Nobel Symposium 12. Uppsala, Sweden.

Piggott, S. (1966) *Celts, Saxons, and the Early Antiquaries.* Edinburgh, University Press.

Pumpelly, R. (1908) Exploration in Turkestan: Expedition of 1904: Prehistoric civilization of Anau. *Publication of the Carnegie Institution.* no. 73.

Reinecke, P. (1899) Studien zur Chronologie des ungarländischen Bronzealters. Prähistorisches aus Ungarn und den Nachbarländern. *Beiblatt der Ethnologischen Mitteilungen aus Ungarn*, Band I, no. 1.

Renfrew, A.C. (1970a) New configurations in Old World archaeology. *World Archaeology* **2**, 199-211.

Renfrew, A.C. (1970b) Revolution in prehistory. I. *The Listener* 897-900.

Renfrew, A.C. (1971a) Carbon-14 and the prehistory of Europe. *Scientific American* **225**, no. 4, 63-72.

Renfrew, A.C. (1971b) Revolution in prehistory. II. *The Listener* 12-15.

Renfrew, A.C. and Sterud, G. (1969) Close-proximity analysis: a rapid method for the ordering of archaeological materials. *American Antiquity* **34**, no. 3: 265-77.

Sackett, J.R. (1964) The origins of palaeolithic archaeology. *Unpublished manuscript.* UCLA.

Smith, H.S. (1964) Egypt and C-14 dating. *Antiquity* **38**, 32-7.

Spaulding, A.C. (1960) Statistical description and comparison of artifact assemblages. *Viking Fund Publications in Anthropology*, no. 28. 60-83.

Tasić, N. (1967) Materijali IV. *Kongres Arheologa Jugoslavije, Herceg-Novi, 1966.* Beograd.

Taylor, W.W. (1948) *A Study of Archaeology.* Carbondale, Southern Illinois University Press.

Thomas, H.L. and Ehrich, R.W. (1969) Some problems in chronology. *World Archaeology* **1**, 21, 143-56.

Trigger, B.G. (1970) Aims in prehistoric archaeology. *Antiquity* **44**, 26-37.

Watson, P.J., LeBlanc, S.A. and Redman, C.L. (1971) *Explanation in Archaeology.* New York, Columbia University Press.

FRANK HOLE

Questions of theory in the explanation of culture change in prehistory

Change, a phenomenon readily recognized in human history, has intrigued scholars in numerous disciplines for many years. In view of this interest it is useful now to assess current archaeological theories of change. In my view, our theory on change is weak because we have not made necessary operational definitions of important concepts in terms of the properties of the phenomena under dicussion and the goals we wish to achieve. If we recognize these weaknesses we can remedy them by devising and implementing well-defined experiments or observational studies.

The title of this seminar contains five crucial concepts: explanation, prehistory, culture, change and models. The remarks that follow consider each concept in turn.

Explanation

What people accept in explanation of observed phenomena differs widely among the disciplines. In essence any explanation involves a statement of the causal relationships between a factor or set of factors and an observed outcome. What is considered explanatory depends on a person's conception of what explanation is and the stockpile of theories he has at his disposal. Thus, 'God's wrath causes plagues' and 'rats carrying germs into filthy crowded slums causes plagues' are both explanatory statements in terms of different systems of thought. In the history of thought conceptions of what explanation is and theories that will account for observed phenomena have changed.

In regard to explanation we have witnessed a growing split in recent years between archaeologists with humanistic interests and those who consider themselves scientists. The split has stemmed from the fact that different scholars base their statements of explanation on different premises and in consequence offer different 'explanations' for the same phenomenon. The question of who is right cannot be answered as long as there are no universally accepted criteria for judging the explanatory statements. Under these circumstances the worth of an explanation has traditionally rested on the esteem of its advocate and the persuasion of his literary style. As others in this seminar have discussed at length, to correct this problem there is a growing interest among archaeologists in science and scientific method. In truth, most scientists are little concerned with the philosophy of science; rather they are preoccupied with the pragmatic set of procedures that lead directly and economically to the desired results. This is the scientific method. I know of no clearer expositions and better illustrations of its power than an article by John Platt, 'Strong inference', and the essay that stimulated Platt, 'The method of multiple working hypotheses', by Chamberlin. Platt's statements of the procedure follow:

1. Devising alternative hypotheses;
2. Devising a crucial experiment (or several of them), with alternative possible outcomes, each of which will, as nearly as possible, exclude one or more of the hypotheses;
3. Carrying out the experiment so as to get a clean result;
4. Recycling the procedure, making subhypotheses or sequential hypotheses to refine the possibilities that remain; and so on.

Steps 1 and 2 require intellectual inventions, which must be cleverly chosen so that hypothesis, experiment, outcome, and exclusion will be related in a rigorous syllogism . . . It is clear why this makes for rapid and powerful progress. For exploring the unknown, there is no faster method; this is the minimum sequence of steps. Any conclusion that is not an exclusion is insecure and must be rechecked. (Platt 1964:347)

While this is standard scientific procedure, Platt points out that many scientists do not follow it rigorously. Why? Because they become method-oriented rather than problem-oriented. Or, as Chamberlin asserts (1965:755), they fall in love with their pet theory and become dominated by it. 'The mind lingers with pleasure upon the facts that fall happily into the embrace of the theory, and feels a natural coldness toward those that seem refractory . . . There springs up, also, an unconscious pressing of the theory to make it fit the facts, and a pressing of the facts to make them fit the theory.'

Finally, in regard to explanation itself, he paraphrased Karl Popper: 'There is no such thing as proof in science – because some later alternative explanation may be as good or better – so that science advances only by disproofs. There is no point in making hypotheses that are not falsifiable, because such hypotheses do not say anything: it must be possible for an empirical scientific system to be refuted by experience' (Platt 1964:350).

Employing the principles expressed by Platt and Chamberlin, our task is to postulate relationships among variables that can be tested using data derived from prehistory or other sources. The strategy is to 'study the simplest system you think has the properties you are interested in' (Platt quoting Levinthal 1964:349). Explanation then consists of the hypothesis which cannot be excluded after it has been tested along with alternative hypotheses. A given explanation thus represents the best we can do with the present evidence.

This definition of explanation is different from some archaeologists'. For example, following Hempel and Oppenheim, Hill asserts:

> . . . the deductive 'cover law' model holds that phenomena are only satisfactorily explained when their occurrence can be deduced (predicted) from a lawlike generalization . . . any satisfactory explanation is a general as well as a particularistic one. Given the specified conditions, the phenomenon to be explained can always be expected to occur – because the processual relationships stated in the law imply it of necessity. It was agreed [by the members of the seminar Hill described] that this formal model of explanation should be employed whether the cover-laws have been tested and accepted or not. In the present state of our knowledge, the testing of many of our explanations will show their presumed cover-laws to be false – but such testing is the only way to begin to build acceptable laws and higher-level theory. (1971:407)

There are several things to be said about Hill's statement. First, to adopt the view that explanation will result in prediction, while reasonable as stated, may cause the unwary to expect the same results time after time when certain conditions have been met. The proposition may appear to read, if A then B. Perhaps this is intended, but if we accept the possibility of indeterminacy, we should also be prepared to state, if A then B with a certain probability. In other words, we may have to predict the outcome in a probabilistic rather than in a deterministic sense.

A second point may seem trivial but it is not: if we say, if A then B, we may not say, if B then A. Thus while we may use the presence of B to infer A, we may not use B to prove the presence of conditions A. We recognize this as a common logical trap yet we may all fall into it upon occasion. If I understand Hill (1971:408) correctly he suggests that if we have an adequate 'cover-law' we can ignore the absence of artifactual evidence and assume the condition. 'The most difficult variables to measure are those involving information (including communication), but it was agreed that in most cases we do not have to measure these; we can simply assume that responses to extra-systemic inputs require the transmission of information as well as decision-making processes within the system.' This is fair enough but as stated it remains an inference based on analogy rather than a tested hypothesis. One does not explain by assuming a predicted outcome.

As a friend of mine is fond of saying, 'ideas are to use, not to believe'. It seems to me there is an imminent danger of believing one's cover laws, especially when they have not been tested and when the one in question is only one of a long series of assumptions. How does one really test a cover law that he pulls out of a sheaf of similar related and untested cover laws? Where does one begin? I submit that one may easily (as Chamberlin suggested) find supporting data (or bridge gaps with inferred data) since the testimony of antiquity is ambiguous. As evidence that this tendency is insidious, one looks long to find an archaeologist who has tried assiduously to disprove even simple alternative hypotheses (let alone cover laws) that might explain a phenomenon; rather archaeologists I have read have found evidence to support their theories.

While the members of the seminar that Hill reported 'opted for a "systems" framework', they agreed that there are 'no ready-made, published statements of systems theory that are adequate to explaining change in cultural systems' (Hill 1971:407). One wonders what an adequate theory would entail. We might make the reasonable proposition that it will consist of many cover-laws of different magnitude and of different layers in a hierarchy. But what is the fundamental theorem and can it be tested? Perhaps more to the point, can we test the proposition that system theory is the appropriate model for explaining cultural change? What are the alternatives and can they be shown inadequate?

To develop a system of theory relating to cultural change will probably be no easier than, let us say, inventing calculus. If this is even close to the truth, perhaps most of us would be better off attempting to establish some more minor advances of the type that will be discussed below, using rigorous scientific procedure.

Prehistory

To study prehistory completely requires multidisciplinary perspective, especially when we consider explanations, for there is very little in the archaeological record that provides explanations until we reach the historic eras. Rather we must depend on ancillary fields of inquiry for both data and theory: geology, palynology, zoology, biology, anthropology, sociology, economics, geography and ecology are commonly employed in archaeological studies. To appreciate the role of archaeology in the study of man's development we must recognize five of its fundamental aspects or properties.

1. Archaeological evidence is an incomplete record of man's activities. While it may not be as incomplete as it may seem to the unimaginative, it is hard to imagine that it will ever inform us as fully as we would wish on many crucial matters. It may never inform on some. So it is vital to determine what archaeological data can and cannot permit us to do.
2. Because the number of archaeological contexts adequately

reported for our purposes is small, sampling error must be considered whenever we base our conclusions on known data. The size of our samples would be considered woefully inadequate for many statistical studies.

3. As Piggott (1965:2), quoting Rhys Carpenter, suggests, archaeological evidence is inevident. What we see the data to be is what we are prepared to see, whether we employ analogy, statistics, or cover laws.
4. Prehistory is a record of 'firsts' in human activity: the invention of a new technique, the acquisition of effective language, the emergence of complex societies, etc. Things were different in a fundamental sense after each 'first'. Prior to the inventions or discoveries, behaviour must have been somewhat different; therefore the rule of principles of behaviour that we devise may not apply.
5. Archaeology is terribly inefficient. Two consequences are suggested. First, archaeology should not be used for purposes that it alone cannot serve. A case in point may be the theoretical study of culture change. If there are regularities in human behaviour some of them may be more readily and accurately observed among living peoples than dead peoples. Second, we must devise and employ methods (e.g. sampling, mechanical aids for digging, processing and analysing) to make archaeology more efficient.

It is clear from the foregoing that while prehistory is vital to a study of some changes, its record suffers from inherent defects that will make the winning of substantial advances toward explanation (i.e. through the testing of hypotheses) a slow and difficult process.

Culture

Archaeologists are accustomed to talking of archaeological cultures and culture change, the evidence for both of which is conventionally accepted to be in artifacts. It is useful therefore to consider both culture and artifacts. While culture is a basic concept of anthropology, it embraces a wide variety of ideas and in consequence is not a very useful working concept. Studies of culture area, structure and function, kinship, values, ethnohistory and the ecology of social organization employ definitions of culture tailored to serve the various ends. The question is not *what culture is* but *what set of concepts are of value to us* in studying a particular phenomenon – like change. Gordon Childe has defined one such set of concepts.

> An archaeological culture is an assemblage of artifacts that recurs repeatedly associated together in dwellings of the same kind and with

> burials of the same rite. The arbitrary peculiarities of all cultural traits are assumed to be concrete expressions of the common social traditions that bind together a culture. Artifacts hang together in assemblages, not only because they were used in the same age, but also because they were used by the same people, made or executed in accordance with techniques, rites or styles prescribed by a social tradition, handed on by precept and example and modifiable in the same way. (Childe 1947:51; also 1951:30-3)

Clarke (1968:666) echoes this definition, but in other references (e.g. 658, 659, 661, 654) in *Analytical Archaeology* he also asserts that 'culture is an information system'. The utility of this concept, as he rightly asserts, has yet to be demonstrated, although it may be the proper framework for modeling culture systems in terms of information theory and the like.

A number of archaeologists have considered culture, taken in its broadest sense, to be adaptive. The underlying idea is that man's culture, (behaviour, artifacts etc.), is his way of coping with biological, environmental and social problems. Man adapts himself to situations. In this sense, artifacts and forms of society are essentially tools to deal with environmental situations. While few would doubt the validity of this concept, it is an *ex post facto* judgement that usually takes the form 'if a culture did something it must have been an attempt at adaptation'. The success of the strategy can be judged by the continued existence of the culture but there is no good way to judge how effective the adaptation was except in terms of what eventually happened to the culture. The hypothesis that culture is adaptive cannot ever be excluded and is, in consequence, of little value.

It is a quite different thing to define culture as Childe did and to define it as an information or adaptive system. The first was an essentially pragmatic approach that enabled Childe to categorize his artifactual data. The latter definitions state behavioural relationships with no necessary implication that they will be evidenced in artifacts. They are general propositions about culture – in a sense high level cover-laws – whose validity is untested (but hardly questioned) and whose implications as far as artifacts are concerned need further thought.

Assuming that we have two points of departure, hypotheses about change and artifacts, how do we test hypotheses?

There is concensus among archaeologists that artifacts are tangible remains made or used by man, 'fossilized' evidence of human behaviour. It follows that we *may* (but not necessarily will) be able to infer behaviour from the artifacts. There are three general kinds of behaviour on which artifacts may inform: technological, sociological and ideological (Binford 1962:219-20). All artifacts are considered to relate to one or more of the three kinds of behaviour. When an archaeologist finds artifacts he may then examine them in terms of their relevance to these categories, thus establishing a structure for his analysis. The next step, however, depends on the archaeologist's conception of how artifacts relate to the behaviour in question. It is here we find widely differing analyses with consequent confusion and non-comparability of results. Since we are dealing here with the most elementary units of archaeological study, upon which all other analyses depend, an extended discussion of the problems is in order.

The first question is, what do we want to do with the information we get from analysing the artifacts? If we are interested in change, for example, what is changing? In order to determine this we need an accurate picture of the phenomenon we are studying at several points in time. Only in this way can we define what we mean by change and establish the context within which it took place.

Most archaeologists begin with sites and artifacts and attempt to explain what they have found. One may also begin with a cover-law hypothesis and see if one can test it with excavation or analysis. The two approaches are complementary, however, for one can hardly explain what one has found without some theory, and one cannot test hypotheses without data. Thus, no matter which situation stimulated our inquiry, we must deal in the first instance with the relations between artifacts and the behaviour we are seeking to explain. In my opinion *this is precisely the point at which archaeology is weakest.* Rather than an explicit set of theory we have a set of procedures: typology, numerical taxonomy, attribute analysis and the like. And even worse, since we must work with what we have, we tend to grasp at straws, hoping that such artifacts as exist will somehow inform us on the behaviour that we question. Neither established procedures nor the artifacts at hand necessarily result in information that is meaningful in terms of the cultural categories we wish to understand. Does, for example, Bordes' taxonomy necessarily provide the kind of data that are useful in the multivariate analyses performed on the Mousterian by the Binfords (Binford and Binford 1966:238-95)?

How then does one determine what kind of analysis will yield necessary information? Let us examine artifacts for a moment. While they may inform on cultural matters, artifacts have certain properties that must be understood before we can accurately assess their potential contribution to the problems at hand.

The fact that artifacts are made of animal, vegetable or mineral has some effect upon the finished product either in its ultimate form or in the range of objects that can be manufactured. One must ask to what extent the material affects the object and whether the material used can inform on something besides technology, e.g., trade. An analysis of technological changes must deal with the question of how the raw material affects the object while a study of the limits of archaeological cultures or the operation of cultural systems must consider the sources of the material.

Discussions during the seminar made apparent that we need a set of explicitly stated theories pertaining to relations between artifacts and culture. However, such theories may be restricted to such relatively simple matters as the relationship between raw material and the form of a chipped stone tool. As Professor Bordes illustrated, one can make a tool that appears the same in form and chipping from a variety of raw materials. The theory stating the relationship between *raw material* and *form* thus is: *Raw material has no significant effect upon the form of a chipped stone tool.* The important implication is that one may not explain variability in form by reference to differences in raw material. So stated, and following ample testing, the theory becomes extremely useful and eliminates at one stroke much fruitless discussion. In this example it matters not that raw material *does* have *some* effect on finished stone tools because the present theory as stated can be shown to be correct. Another theory or set of theories must be advanced to take account of other relationships between raw material and stone tools. The point is that the problem is simplified by explicit statement. Ultimately a set of theories can be developed to cover all the technical relationships between raw material, chipping techniques and the tools that result. These will include fracturing properties of stones, their value for different kinds of tools and the like. The development of such a body of theory will make it possible to differentiate what are purely physical factors from those that pertain to tradition, function and aesthetics. One might reasonably expect to be able to develop this body of theory in a year or so of thoughtful work.

Artifacts have size and shape as well as evidence of workmanship, chipping, cutting, polishing, baking etc. These are often called attributes, some of which are relevant to particular goals. Since it is not possible to analyse all possible attributes of an artifact, one must made a decision. Here again we are confronted with the problem of how any attribute relates to the problem at hand.

Artifacts occur in finite quantity and are found in a spatial and temporal context. Theory must relate artifacts discovered to what we take to be the totality of a site; to the manner in which their distribution in contemporary space relates to behaviour; and we must be able to state what their temporal context is in relation to both themselves (e.g., an occupation level) and to other sites.

Many of the interesting problems of change concern such things as the size and structure of human populations. 'How can we explain the emergence of urbanism or the state form of government?' If we take the position that artifacts and their relationships are the basic data of archeology, how do we use them to test hypotheses concerning the broader questions of social change? What kind of archaeological data can we use? Let us consider changes in the size of populations. The principal artifacts we have at our disposal are the size and number of sites of the same age of known cultural affiliation. To take the last point first, what constitutes cultural affiliation? Childe's definition of an archaeological culture is used most often, but is it valid for our purposes? What do ethnologists say about this? As far as I know the culture area approach in which tribes were compared on the basis of traits shared never produced the kind of information ethnologists were seeking. It is exceedingly difficult to define the limits of a culture (e.g. tribe) on the basis of tangible traits, even including those which would readily perish in archaeological contexts. Moreover, even if some traits serve to limit useful population aggregates, the chances that these will be preserved archaeologically may be remote. To assume then that the archaeological culture is equivalent to the kind of social grouping we need to define to test theories about change is certainly misleading.

One may, however, decide that an area which is suitably delimited by natural boundaries (e.g. a drainage area or valley) will constitute the unit of analysis. One can then treat population changes within this area, ignoring specific and, one hopes, minor cultural differences. We have done precisely this in our study of the Deh Luran plain and even in the larger nearby region of Khuzistan (Hole, Flannery and Neely 1969; also see Gumerman 1971).

Assuming then that we wish to study only gross changes in population size, we have two major problems. First, what characteristic of sites relates to population size? Most archaeologists use a rough formula that relates site size or number of rooms in the site to total population, but the relationship between these has seldom been tested in modern contexts, let along in prehistoric ones. The amount of space used by people is surely a cultural as well as geographic artifact. Some people live packed into small tightly clustered houses while others are spread all over the place. The number of people per room varies as does the amount of open space in a site. How do we assess these matters for sites that have not been excavated? In Southwest Asia we know there is a great deal of variability today and there may have been a similar amount in the past. The variability is so great as to render population estimates meaningless unless we are to tolerate threefold errors.

A purely archaeological problem is 'how much of the site was occupied at any given time?' or 'how big is the site?' Few sites in Southwest Asia have been surveyed to accurate dimensions and fewer still tested to determine the limits of occupations at different periods. The size at any particular period of a site that was occupied for 1000 years (at least in this area) is very hard to assess on the basis of surface survey. There are instances where wht appears to be a large site had a single structure from one period while it may have been a bustling village at another time. Perhaps the most systematic attempt to delimit occupation areas on all sites in question was carried out by James Neely in Deh Luran (Neely 1970), but the results, while vastly superior to previous estimates, are still somewhat ambiguous.

A final archaeological problem is to date the sites relative to one another. The overall size of population during any interval along a span of hundreds of years will be hard to pinpoint precisely, because the artifacts that signal archaeological periods may not indicate time more precisely than a few hundred years. This is obviously ample time for a single biological population to occupy several villages, and consequently be counted several times in the population estimates. I scarcely need add that some sites may go undiscovered and consequently lower the population estimate. We cannot assume this will offset the potential increases noted above.

In short, we need both studies of the nature of the occurrence of artifacts themselves and studies of the relationship of artifacts to cultural phenomena, so that we can establish a legitimate set of procedures that will enable us to work with our primary data in meaningful ways. Whether we are looking at projectile points or sites, we must recognize that they have intrinsic properties that vary independently of the cultural phenomena we are seeking to explain. Their physical properties may result in characteristics that we will confuse with cultural factors; they may be hard to date because of our limited analytic techniques, and they may be preserved or not in ways that are unpredictable so that it will be hard to relate quantity to the total population.

Change

In the title of this seminar, 'change' has been linked with 'culture'. I have already remarked that culture is too imprecise a concept to convey any accurate message. What we must do is talk about technological change, change in settlement pattern, change in social organization or in the various subsystems of culture. These are aspects of culture but are not culture in its widest sense and it does no good to confuse the issue; we must be as specific as possible.

The questions thus are: 'What changes?', 'What do we accept as evidence of the change?', and 'What hypotheses of change concerning the categories under consideration can we devise to explain the observed changes in prehistory?' In other words, what is our theory about the link between observed changes in artifacts and processes of change in particular areas of behaviour (not processes of culture)?

We are accustomed to break things down for analysis and it will be useful to do this for change. How many different kinds of things might we call change? Do these various kinds of change invite us to use different explanatory concepts? Change implies time although synchronic variability and differentiation must be given their due as well. Change through time may take the following forms.

1. From one equivalent kind of artifact to another, e.g., tin cans to aluminium cans.
2. From simple to complex, i.e., greater differentiation.
3. From one style to another with no apparent change in kind or complexity, e.g., clothing.
4. From one roughly equivalent kind of artifact to another, e.g., spears to arrows, ox-carts to trucks.
5. Increase or decrease in variety or technological complexity (evolution and devolution), e.g. in Europe from middle to upper palaeolithic, thence to mesolithic.
6. Changes in quantity, e.g. in population.
7. Discontinuities (replacement) or striking changes in rates of change.
8. To this list we can add, 'systemic change as opposed to homeostatic alterations in "state" ' (Hill 1971:406).

Synchronic differentiation may be expressed as horizontal change.

1. Over an area, changes in the proportions, style or manufacturing technique of artifacts.
2. Functional areas within single sites or settlement systems.

It seems to me there is enough variety in the listing above to preclude the use of a single set of explanations; rather each kind of change takes place within a context that must be understood in terms of some theory about how such changes take place. Once again we are faced with the need to study the relevant evidence as it has been developed in a variety of fields and to demonstrate to our satisfaction that the artifactual evidence we have at our disposal is suitable for making the interpretations we seek. When we have done this we may find that we need to devise new techniques of excavation or survey as well as of analysis.

The foregoing has assumed that the explanation of change can be found in the tangible archaeological record; however, it is clear that intangibles may also be important. How are we to assess the impact of changes in the effectiveness of communication, social organization, and economy; or changes in religious belief and values. Do any of these relate to changes in strictly material things and if so, how?

The foregoing has also assumed that the explanations of change may be found in exclusively 'cultural' factors, yet scientists in many fields often invoke random processes in which individual stages depend only upon previous stages and suitable randomizations to account for certain kinds of change. How do we handle this culturally? What is our baseline? How do we deal with changes brought about by changes? How too, do we handle the accidental: catastrophe, earthquake, flood or plague? The point is that the context of our studies may fluctuate and the variables may require different weights at different times. Finally, as I suggested earlier, we may want to consider indeterministic as well as deterministic processes, in which case, in view of the rather small sample of archaeological contexts at our disposal, we may have a very difficult time excluding alternative hypotheses.

The point I should like to make is not that we sound the trumpet of defeat because the problem is imponderable but that we ponder the problems in as many of their ramifications as possible. Then if we wish to exclude random processes or the effects of plague we can do so for explicit reasons. If we are looking for explanations we cannot afford to ignore possibly relevant factors.

Models

Models or hypotheses express the relationships among the variables that comprise our theoretical framework. The degree to which an archaeologist follows scientific procedure can be readily observed in the kind of models he uses. Clarke's (1968:33) discussion outlines the different kinds of models. We are concerned here with what he calls 'symbolic models' (hypotheses) that express relationships between variables in terms of deterministic, probabilistic or stochastic models, and with 'analog' models that relate modern situations to events in the past on the assumption that the contexts are similar enough that the same processes are operating. The latter are especially useful and unquestionably dangerous: useful because we cannot see in the dark and dangerous because often we cannot recapture the prehistoric context accurately enough to know whether the situations are analogous in the sense we think they are. Analog and symbolic models both have their legitimate uses, the latter being more elegant and usually of lesser scope, while the former are easily comprehended and wisely used. It is to the manner in which models are used that I should now like to turn.

To be of value, a model or hypothesis that states relationships among variables must have been tested and found acceptable, or it must be testable. It is in this regard that Chamberlin's multiple working hypotheses and Platt's strong inference are brought to play. In addition to Platt's list of procedures it cannot be stressed too strongly that the hypotheses one devises must take into account all of the variables one thinks are relevant. If an hypothesis cannot control some of the crucial variables, then it should be restated, perhaps in simpler form.

Scientists usually have some data at hand that they wish to explain; at this seminar, changes in various kinds of archaeological data. Our Western orientation in science disposes us to ask why?, with the expectation that causal factors can be found. Our anthropological disposition also turns our thinking toward cultural factors. Any finding that links cultural causes to observed data is likely to be appealing and may be considered sufficient, especially if we can find a high correlation between the supposed cause and effect. But the archaeologist must also consider whether the effects he observes archaeologically could have resulted by chance as well as by deterministic processes. A case in point is that rank-size correlations may result from growth being related to initial conditions: if things grow at a rate proportional to their size, large things get larger faster than small things.

The immediate question concerning a model is not whether it is true but whether it is false. One can often find, especially with judicious juggling of evidence and exhaustive correlations, that there are significant relationships among some variables. The question is whether these relationships really tell us what we think they do. Did the test give clean results? Unless we test possible alternatives we are likely to find we have set up a self-fulfilling prophecy whose outcome was never in doubt.

These points are almost trite but I make them because archaeologists in my experience have plunged into a time-consuming analysis knowing full well ahead of time that it had little expected validity. 'We have to start somewhere' is the rationale. Not surprisingly they have sometimes come up with correlations whose confidence levels were uniformly high – so high that one wonders why by chance they did not get some bad ones. Too good a fit between model and data is as suspect as uniformly uninspired results. The point is not that we must begin somewhere, but that we must start from a reasonable point. Unless we do so we cannot build on the results. At this point in the development of scientific archaeology we hardly need a host of spurious results to confuse the issue.

When models are based on studies made by economists and geographers, we will find they have a strong Western bias, even though we are sometimes told the models hold true around the world. Certain variables probably do relate in a systematic fashion in all cultures, but even if they do, are we to seriously suppose that prehistoric peoples behaved in the same way as even the primitives today? For example, are we to suppose that market motivations and transportation problems were weighted in the past as they are today? When did markets begin and when did man begin to view his time as a valuable commodity? In other words when did economic matters weigh heavier than other factors?

We may not find the answers to such questions readily, but there is no reason to stop short of seeking our goals. When we consider a prehistoric situation we must ask ourselves the following questions:

1. What do we know? What are our available data and what can they potentially tell us?
2. In view of what we know about the 'cultural' context, what kinds of processes can we imagine are possibly operative?
3. If any of our hypotheses have been tested in a modern context, can we assume the same conditions in our pre-

historic context (e.g. similar social, economic, political situations)?

4. If any of our hypotheses have been tested in a modern context, how closely did they conform with the actual situation and what factors were used to explain the deviation? Are these factors present in the prehistoric context?
5. Is there anything we know right now that invalidates any of our assumptions or renders any of our hypotheses false?
6. Can the hypotheses be stated more simply for easier testing and more rapid exclusion?

Models or hypotheses are necessary to give our thinking structure and to lead us as quickly as possible to devise the means for their testing. It would seem most appropriate at the present stage of archaeological development to devise hypotheses that will lead to tests of the very basic kinds of information we will require when we consider explanations of matters like 'systemic' change. We are still very much in need of basic data but these data in their raw form are still ambiguous. If we can clear away some of the ambiguity we will find that the data speak more clearly.

Concluding remarks

I have attempted to identify the kinds of things we need to know before we can carry out explanatory studies effectively, and have outlined some of the procedural steps and theoretical considerations I think are crucial if we are to achieve useful results. The argument is that we can do better if we will devote as much time to thought as to methodological manipulations. At the moment we have better analytic tools at our disposal than we have theory or data to use them.

After thinking through the implications of what I have said, I have come to the somewhat reluctant conclusion that the frontiers of archaeological theory are in studies of modern situations that serve to elucidate the relationships between what we may find archaeologically and the cultural or other processes that explain or even relate to them. Surely, if we can model the crucial relationships that we call culture processes, we ought to be able to test them more economically and accurately using data from contemporary life. Moreover, we will find a much greater array of test situations over which we can exert some control than we can ever hope to find in prehistory. One interesting implication of this relates back to what I said about archaeology: it records the development of man. At some points in the past the processes we find explanatory today may not have been operative. Can we discover these? If we can perhaps we will then be able to make some meaningful distinctions relating to man's overall cultural development.

From many points of view, it would be preferable for theoretically-oriented archaeologists to quit digging altogether, or to concentrate on situations for which there is excellent ancillary evidence, such as recent historical sites. Deetz' work at Plimoth Plantation (Deetz 1967), where he has unusually complete data on families and their material possessions, and his study of stylistic changes on gravestones (Dethlefsen and Deetz 1966), are cases in point. The recent studies by archaeologists of living peoples who are presumed to be illustrative of practices in the past directly through analogy (see Orme this volume), or who illustrate relational principles such as area of site as related to population (Cook and Heizer 1968, Naroll 1962), or the use of ethnographic remains as archaeological evidence (David 1971), are also most useful.

Archaeology is only one of several disciplines that study man and his works; a problem that cannot be solved archaeologically may be solved in a related discipline. The crux of the problem facing us in the future development of archaeology is to identify the essential elements we wish to understand and to pursue the testing of hypotheses in whatever discipline is the most appropriate. In this sense, there can hardly be a science of prehistory; rather we must conceive of a broad-based multi-disciplinary study of man. If scientific inquiry thus leaves archaeology a minor role in testing hypotheses about cultural matters, it clarifies its unique and valuable role in reconstructing the course of human development once we understand what the shaping factors are and were.

REFERENCES

Binford, L.R. (1962) Archaeology as anthropology. *American Antiquity* **28**, 217-25.

Binford, L.R. and S.R. (1966) A preliminary analysis of functional variability in the Mousterian of Levallois facies. *Recent Studies in Paleoanthropology*. Special Publication, *American Anthropologist* **68**, 2, part 2, 238-95.

Chamberlin, T.C. (1965) The method of multiple working hypotheses. *Science* 148, 754-9, reprinted from *Science* (os) **15**, 92 (1890).

Childe, V.G. (1947) Archaeology as a social science: an innaugural lecture. *Institute of Archaeology, Third Annual Report*. 49-60.

Childe, V.G. (1951) *Social evolution*. New York, Henry Schuman.

Clarke, D.L. (1968) *Analytical Archaeology*. London, Methuen.

Cook, G. and Heizer, R.F. (1968) Relationships among houses, settlement areas, and population in aboriginal California. *In* Chang, K.C. (ed.), *Settlement Archaeology*, Palo Alto, California, National Press. 79-116.

David, N. (1971) The Fulani compound and the archaeologist. *World Archaeology* 3, 111-31.

Dethlefsen, E.S. and Deetz, J. (1966) Death's heads, cherubs and willow trees: experimental archaeology in colonial cemeteries. *American Antiquity* 31, 502-10.

Deetz, J. (1967) *Invitation to Archaeology.* Garden City, New York, The Natural History Press.

Gumerman, G.J. (ed.) (1971) *The Distribution of Prehistoric Population Aggregates.* Prescott, Arizona, Prescott College Anthropological Reports No. 1.

Hill, J.N. (1971) Seminar on the explanation of prehistoric organizational change. *Current Anthropology* 12, 406-8.

Hole, F., Flannery, K.V. and Neely, J.A. (1969) *Prehistoric and Human Ecology of the Deh Luran Plain.* Ann Arbor, University of Michigan, Memoirs of the Museum of Anthropology, No. 1.

Hole, F. and Heizer, R.F. (1969) *An Introduction to Prehistoric Archeology.* New York, Holt, Rinehart and Winston.

Naroll, R.S. and Von Bertalanffy, L. (1956) The principle of allometry in biology and the social sciences. *General Systems* 1 76-89.

Neely, J.A. (1970) The Deh Luran region. *Iran* 8 202-3.

Orme, B. (1971) Archaeology and ethnography. (This volume).

Piggot, S. (1965) *Ancient Europe.* Chicago, Aldine.

Platt, J.R. (1964) Strong inference. *Science* 146, 347-53.

HUMPHREY CASE

Illusion and meaning

Research is the heart of an academic discipline. It transcends synthetic writing largely drawn from secondary sources, such as the 'scissors-and-paste' method of writing history (Collingwood 1970:257), however critically drawn or valuable educationally; it is more than cataloguing and more even than the hard skills of verifiable recording in the field or the laboratory. These important, self-sufficient and scholarly activities are peripheral to research. Academic critics of archaeology rightly categorize them as techniques which do not themselves form a discipline.

A discipline must have at its heart research which is descriptive, verifiable and demanding. The archaeological record is evidently 'referable to human behaviour' (Binford's words at the Research Seminar). Archaeological research therefore must go beyond retrieving and listing the human record to the more challenging task of describing human behaviour. The evidence in the record and the arguments concerning the behaviour must be verifiable and explicit. Thus, from its nature, research demands of those given to it not only mastery of taxonomies and techniques, derived from study of original material and command of secondary sources, but also the judgement appropriate to a humane discipline: in this context, historical sense.

Traditional and new archaeology

The creative instinct behind the new archaeology is to strengthen the subject as a discipline by broadening and deepening the range of verifiable description which a historical sense can use.

I take the field of research with which I am most familiar: the onset of the neolithic in West Asia and Europe. The traditional method of study has largely been stylistic classification of artifacts, which may be both monuments and relics. But a range of monuments (with settlements, and economic and ritual sites) has rarely been discovered in any one region; and relics have generally been rather unevenly classified, with pottery receiving most attention. Lately, systematic classifications of stone industries have given a better balance to research, not only because they have introduced a new variable but because the industries are more prevalent than monuments and potentially more various in themselves, and are at least as prevalent as pottery and likely to have been more basic economically. But even when fuller ranges of monuments have been discovered in many regions and excavated to affirm better associations of relics which will then be more evenly classified, the arguments which it would be possible to draw from such a small number of relatively undescriptive variables would still be few and lead to conclusions of only limited historical value.

Not only would the range of variables be small but the approach itself would be tangential. Monuments and relics have been studied because they are conspicuous and attractive works of man; but they are plainly somewhat indirect evidence of the neolithic, if by that term we imply the establishment of mixed farming by stone-using peoples. The most direct evidence for that lies in animal and plant remains, which are being studied altogether more seriously in the new archaeology. These studies in themselves of course are not at all new, although present day techniques and conceptions are sometimes new or revised: in Britain, for instance, reputable excavators have recorded the results of such studies in appendices, since Pitt Rivers. Nor are they newly esteemed: twenty years ago, Clark (1952:7) showed the opportunity prehistory offers of studying the relationships between culture, biome and habitat in an eco-system (a conception he borrowed from Evans-Pritchard); such relationships were demonstrated in Zeuner's teaching at London, and the Biologisch-Archaeologisch Instituut has flourished for decades. What is new is the deliberate re-direction of systematic research away from culture towards the effects of culture in biome and habitat, – a policy summarized best by Hole and his collaborators (Hole, Flannery and Neely, 1969:5-8).

Let us take excavation as an example of this re-direction. The field-work to discover sites and their priority for excavation may be quite different. The logistics too and techniques of excavating need to be greatly changed with the systematic introduction, for instance, of flotation to collect micro-specimens such as seeds and unfused epiphyses. The spectrum of relics recovered by flotation or sieving may then differ significantly from that revealed by traditional excavating, by including larger quantities, let us say, of microliths or very small sherds or beads (Keighley gives an example in this volume).

The samples of all kinds thus produced (or capable of being produced) may be so large that they can only be selected and analysed statistically; it is not necessarily a matter of preference;

there may be no choice. (But the researcher should also take advantage of the repetitive nature of the analyses to watch for traits not capable of being programmed, of the kind to which Beveridge advised scientists to be alert, 1964:27ff.) The success or failure of statistical analyses may be seen in whether they permit concise and informative verbal answers to the researcher's questions, thus: 'The assemblages of pottery are significantly different', 'The major use of banded flint was in phases when the settlement expanded' or 'This grave has conflicting dating characteristics'. Such answers form the raw material for historical judgements; and they can be verified repeatedly by other researchers from the same data.

It must be strongly emphasized that this kind of answer is an indication of success or failure in analyses of all kinds of trait (not simply those derived from culture); thus, in analyses of plant and bone remains, of soil, pollen, or of implement-utilization and in the many programmes of trace-analyses of materials selected or made by early man. Those who use scientific techniques in archaeology are from the very nature of their task engaged in the contribution of data towards a humane discipline – to whatever degree it may be debatable as to whether those who devise scientific techniques for use in archaeology are properly archaeologists or scientists.

In the same search for the effects of culture on biome and habitat, the new archaeology has increasingly sought examples in ethnography of measurable tasks capable of being performed in the recent past with somewhat similar equipment to early man's, and examples as to the variety of social organizations which may support such tasks. The techniques of so-called experimental archaeology (re-enactment of inferred farming practises for example) are partly aimed in the same direction.

In all these and other ways (including location analyses) variables have been multiplied and made more accessibly verifiable, and have become potentially more descriptive. With their aid, the researcher's questions may now be designed, as Childe foresaw (1958:2-3), to provide answers of deeper historical meaning. For instance: What was the environment of early man? What did he select from it to use or domesticate? What was his farming practice? Did he adapt it to one type of environment only? Or vary it to suit others? Did he improve it in the course of time? And thus adapt it to changes which he had himself induced?

To complete the research, the traditionally studied monuments and relics with their attached chronology may next be placed in context with the answers to these questions and used to provide further and historically more precise answers to such questions as: What was the normal unit of farming society in the region at the time? How was it organised? What did it achieve? Were some units more specialized than others? What was the function of ritual monuments? How did any of these units differ from those in neighbouring regions? Here intensified research in systematic human biology (into that part of the biome most intimately associated with culture) may permit still closer cultural definitions.

Thus, in the new archaeology, culture far from being diminished is enhanced. On the one hand, determinism is scarcely needed; whereas, paradoxically, in the traditional approach with a one-sided emphasis on culture, any reference to the environment can hardly fail to be deterministic. On the other hand, monuments and relics remain an essential part of the syntax of a new language of interpretation and must still be mastered – especially since not all deposits will preserve human or animal bones or plant remains or either, and some difficulties may continue to reside in distinguishing domesticated and wild animals from butchered remains. Thus, struck stone and to some degree pottery may remain the most prevalent and accessible traces of the onset of mixed farming in Europe and West Asia, and monuments the best evidence for communal enterprise. But relics and monuments will have been demonstrated in new contexts; and thus,even as isolated finds, given a deeper potential meaning.

My illustrations are drawn from the West Asiatic and European neolithic and their appropriate contexts; needless to say similar meaning can be given to any type of archaeological assemblage within its appropriate context, whether saucer-brooches or red-figure vases.

Illusion and culture change

Archaeology is a recent development. With only a short tradition behind us, we may be tempted to be rashly optimistic about the new archaeology by not recognizing that replacement of the traditional by the new is a very familiar process in reflective activity (of which archaeology is a youthful part), where innovations have succeeded each other irresistibly through the centuries. For example in literature and art, complicated changes of style and technique compiled from the talents of individual writers and painters (which historians and critics codify in schools, groups, movements and so on) have one after the other through the centuries reflected new views of reality to which individual writers and artists have themselves to some degree contributed, and beside which the traditional views have been found no longer to have any urgent meaning. The same is plainly also true of those reflective activities which take a more reasoned view of reality, history (Collingwood 1970:14ff; Oakeshott 1933:99ff) and science (Beveridge 1964). We should hold quite a deluded evolutionary opinion if we assumed that the old writers or artists were necessarily less perceptive or competent than the newer ones or that the patriarchs of history or science were necessarily stupid or unobservant in comparison to their successors. This seems indeed most unlikely. It is rather that what were urgent views of reality to them have become illusions or partial illusions to us.

A view of learning as a kaleidoscope of partial illusions will not surprise University teachers (or indeed their pupils). For example, while writing the first draft of this paper, I opened the *Oxford Magazine* more or less at random and read, 'A chemistry lecturer needs in effect to take Schools every five years or so if he is to teach current chemistry at all. In the arts the difficulty is not so much that the frontiers of knowledge are advancing rapidly as that the perspective is changing. We ask different questions about the Greeks from those that Gilbert Murray did, because we ourselves are different, with different interests and different sympathies . . . ; our pupils ask different questions again . . . Aristotle, viewed as proto-Ryle . . . Tacitus seen as super-Syme . . .' (Lucas 1970:110).

The present moment being instantly gone for ever, any reflection is with greater or lesser immediacy a record of the past; and we can all find ready instances to show that it is not only the remote past which attracts illusions (or has attracted them, as the first example I now give demonstrates).

Proneness to illusion is immemorial. One of the most extensive and enduring edifices of learning of our civilization was the Greek conception of Egyptian hieroglyphs as a symbolical system of writing: a system in which abstract notions and ideas could be expressed by means of concrete pictures of material objects, each hieroglyph held to be identified with a philosophical concept or demonological manifestation (Iversen 1961). This hypothesis, arising from a wish to explain Egyptian thought in Greek terms, was fully accepted, despite the fact that when it was forming, correct knowledge of hieroglyphic as a phonetic system of writing was not yet dead. The illusion that the Egyptians, a most practical people, were the originals of mystic and occult knowledge passed on Greek authority into Roman learning, lasted through the Middle Ages, and from the Renaissance onwards permeated speculative thought about the past, attracting a vast bibliography. It has been powerful enough to survive vestigially into our own day, whether in the fantasy of *The Magic Flute*, belief in the power of mummy-wheat to sprout, or speculations concerning Tutankhamun's tomb; and while drafting the final version of this paper I read that the *Titanic* foundered because a mummy was in her manifest.

Another example: the Alfred Jewel has rested in the Ashmolean Museum for over 250 years, an unemended complex of primary data. Yet over the decades and centuries each wave of scholarship has more often than not produced speculations plausible only to itself, unrelated to those before, with factual observations distorted by the hypotheses asserted. As an example of innumerable illusions of only a generation ago, we may take the beautifully excavated pits and puddling-holes (as we now see them) of Central European Linear Pottery Culture settlements, explained with plentiful ethnographic allusions as being the houses themselves, *Kurvencomplexbauten.* We can recognize that alongside contemporary social beliefs and evolutionary concepts it would have been difficult to see them otherwise. The peasant inhabitants of the settlements being illiterate were therefore incompletely evolved; being unevolved, they were therefore stupid and incapable of formal design in their personal lives; and being peasants, they would with all the more reason live in hovels with the corn in barns. And as an example from today, we seem reeling yet from the apparent collapse of great lengths of the pre-bristlecone pine radiocarbon chronology in a ruin of diffusionists and Argonauts – of a complex of illusions that ironically fitted an imperialist viewpoint.

Why this sequence of illusions? In archaeology we are tempted to believe it is because of our incomplete knowledge; we may perhaps feel that as the new archaeology fills some gaps, so our judgements will become more stable and truthful. The data on which we form our judgement may indeed become more stable and truthful (being more fully verifiable) but this is unlikely to be so of our judgements. This instability is at the heart of culture change: early man changed his culture indeed, but we change ours through which we observe him, and change it through observing him. It is not only that our data are meaningless unless we ask selective questions of them, but that the answers to our questions are little better unless we project our own vision on them – on experience which would be incomprehensible if we did not give it our own meaning: and it is the same vision which guides us both in collecting data (however scientifically) and in asking questions of them.

In Hulme's analogy (1960:177) we can only fold the tangled mass of reality flat, to see its parts separately. We see within the limits of our perceptions; and Gombrich's insistence that ' "perceptions are not disclosures"... we can only guess, and our guesses will be influenced by our expectations' is relevant far beyond the field of illusionist art where he applied it (1968:210). Indeed we can be no more successful than the illusionist painter has been in re-creating nature. The most he can do is to present an acceptable code of it, within the conventions of his epoch. The same for archaeologists. Our view of the past is likewise partial: an illusion of the whole deceptively constructed. We waste emotion deploring 'an inefficient state of affairs . . . certainly not peculiar to archaeology nor indeed to non-scientific subjects . . . that as much effort is spent in correcting the errors of' previous research 'as in gaining new understanding' (Doran 1970:294).

As Kendall found in seriation, 'one is driven to look for . . . procedures, the efficacy of which will be a matter of faith rather than knowledge' (1969:72), or Richards in such a different pursuit as analysing the technique of reading, 'However much evidence we amass, we still have to jump to our conclusions' (1967:14). The new archaeology shares the imperfection of all branches of learning in having to jump to its conclusions: by making hypotheses, testing them, rejecting them, advancing others and so on, unceasingly. It cannot generate data any other way. This process, according to Beveridge (1964:46), 'is the most important mental technique of the [scientific] investigator'. Hypotheses, he reminds, may be fruitful and yet found absurdly false; or in a seemingly irrational way the experiments they stimulate may not provide expected data but chance discoveries of more importance (1964:27ff). However produced, data are likely to be distorted; and the hypotheses themselves ephemeral, since they deeply influence a scientist's range and capacity in observation. Beveridge quotes the view that even Mendel's results show unmistakable evidence of having been biased in favour of the expected result (1964:108). Gombrich reminds us that even Leonardo da Vinci drew features of the human heart that apparently Galen made him expect, but which he cannot have seen (1968:72). 'Vesalius . . . could hardly believe his own eyes when he found structures not in accord with Galen's descriptions' (Beveridge 1964:107).

Myth, legend and judgements

We do best to recognize that the procedure of research is analogous to the deductive process: our historical judgements are by their nature provisional hypotheses delivered to our colleagues or to our own research to test. We can be consoled that we cannot generate data another way, and that data even if distorted and fragmentary accumulate and may be refined in serving the hypotheses of succeeding generations. We can now be trained to read hieroglyphic, hieratic and demotic Egyptian; our knowledge of early metallurgy is greater than some decades ago.

The past is an inescapable dimension. If we are reflective, we cannot but form views of it. The most we can claim for our judgements is that they have verifiable foundations (like Constable we will lay a violin in the grass to show we are right in our conviction that it is green); and we can claim that our judgements when 'conceived in tolerance and an experimental spirit' (Quine 1963:19) satisfy most of our categories of thought. But we might be greatly deceived if we assumed that our near or distant ancestors and fellow human beings, without comparative scholarship or scientific instrumentation, did not or could not form views of the past as truthful to their categories of thought and obedient to its disciplines, as intense or relatively complex as our own views – or indeed as fertile in change. Such views of the past we term myths and legends. Within the scope of our mental categories and their requirements of verifiable data, archaeology is of the same nature: a body of myth and legend for our times, as inspiring, consoling, entertaining and fugitive as those of the past. This opinion does not question its academic standing, for even the severe pursuit of ontology finds myths eventually (Quine 1963:18-19). And it implies an authentic social role for archaeology; and far from losing it to wild speculative freedom, demands the careful, instinctive, inherent discipline of all reflective work.

To draw another analogy from landscape-painting, the 'lasting and sober existence' which like Constable we try to give to 'one brief moment caught from fleeting time' may have a measure of truthfulness, but in the very act of translating that moment into our own medium we will have distorted it with our creative vision.

Conclusions: contextual archaeology

How then are we to exercise our judgement with tolerance and an experimental spirit to satisfy most of our categories of thought? Some of those adhering to the new archaeology seem to think that we should look for the stimuli which have conditioned human behaviour and try to codify them as laws. These laws would form a body of predictive inferences, both to explain future observations and to be tested by them, to enlarge or modify the boundaries of predictability, and so on. Childe was wisely Delphic about this procedure (compare 1958: 5 and 7). It can be a useful sorting process; the objections to over-insistence on it are not so much that the archaeological record has insufficient variables, as that the procedure implies an incomplete view of man's behaviour, however appropriate to apes (as Reynolds argues in this volume). In the trinity of culture, biome and habitat, the centre of culture and much of its outline would be rashly cut away. Such research would be verifiable but hardly descriptive.

Collingwood's opinion lay towards the other extreme: historians (by definition including archaeologists, 1970:212) should study reflective acts, acts done on purpose; and in studying them should endeavour to re-think the past. This procedure would plainly be helpful in archaeology when considering, for instance, questions of learning and language in the palaeolithic, and it has inspired much valuable technology in later periods. But the ethnographic record puts a question-mark against it: the reasoning of early man may have been different from our own, say not only in making implements (as in Childe's imagined version, 1956:171) but also in using them, and a large unverifiable part of the archaeological record may have resulted from unreflective, accidental or compulsive acts. (And compare

Iversen's view of the differences in Egyptian and Greek reasoning. 1961:39ff.)

I do not think there is a way between these two narrowing alleys. But a compromise stand, which seems to fit our present situation, can be taken on Oakeshott's assertions (1933:14, and see Lowther 1965): 'It is a presupposition of history that every event is related and that every change is but a moment in a world which contains no absolute *hiatus.* And the only explanation of change relevant or possible in history is simply a complete account *of* change.' Thus explanation of change is unattainable; but the fuller we make our account, the closer we may come to explanation, little by little, inevitably even unwittingly.

The process to be aimed for is manifold. First, the researcher must be tolerant and experimental in using taxonomies and techniques derived both from his own studies of original material and from secondary sources – taxonomies and techniques which may be diverse and conflicting and the more subtle and alive in their contributions for being so. Next, in research the collection of data should be aimed at contexts rather than sequences, and be intensive rather than extensive – towards greater and more complete detail. Data should be collected and recorded with the help of very sufficient technical resources and sorted in a convenient way for a whole network of mental processes to be applied to them: Intuitive insight (Beveridge 1964:68ff), inductivism (indispensible for sorting), deductivism (indispensible for checking), historical imagination (Collingwood 1970:231ff), arguments from particular to particular, and interpretative arguments of many kinds. These qualities and processes may enrich, confirm or deny each other and involve repeated re-checking of the data or repeating or modifying earlier stages of collection or sorting. The researcher must master networks of this kind (see Iversen 1961 on Champollion, and Beveridge 1964), and through them aim to write the completest possible historical account in diction approaching as near as possible to that of everyday. Hard and subtle meanings can thus be conveyed as Childe (1958), Collingwood (1970), Gombrich (1968), Quine (1968, loc. cit.) and Richards (1967) show. (We may all sometimes feel with the exasperated Blake 'that what is Grand is necessarily obscure to Weak men'. Technical terms may provide convenient abbreviations, but their unchecked use forms jargon, the temptation to which may be especially strong when we realize that plain language would soon exhaust our opinions, that our research is not new but quite traditional, not clear-cut but inconclusive, and transient not enduring. Jargon may then spread like algae on a polluted lake stifling insight and the experimental urge.)

Such aims for archaeology seem to fit quite well to the framework of reality in which we work. Superficially, for instance, they satisfy our need for quantitative verification, to which we have been educated both by history and science and by that bombardment of specifications which is inescapable in technocratic society; more profoundly, they gratify our requirement ultimately to justify learning to society, and they reflect our concern for our own environmental predicament through our interest in that of early man. Intensive excavation, for example, will not only obtain the utmost of data for the syntheses of future researchers, but leave unexcavated as much as possible of our heritage as can be saved for their improved techniques. (But research-excavations are the proper concern of professional institutions alone: a lesson from Pitt Rivers which is plainly hard to learn.)

We may call the embodiment of these aims *contextual archaeology*, which alone deserves to be considered a new archaeology – new in relation to *cultural archaeology* in the way that cultural archaeology (as associated generally and above all with Childe) was new in relation to *period archaeology* (as associated most closely in Europe perhaps with Montelius and Reinecke).

These aims for archaeology, while being firmly based on primary data, justify too moving from a puritanical obsession with them, a clinging attitude which sometimes characterized traditional archaeology. As an example of freer activity: since our ancestors manifestly travelled by sea, we are right to argue as to the kinds of boats they used, even if none survive, provided we argue contextually. We may argue in the same way about Thom's inferences about the system of mensuration, the geometrical lay-outs and the astronomical alignments of British early bronze age stone 'circles' of the 2nd or late 3rd millennia B.C. (Thom 1967), and need not fear the metaphysical. For instance, field-workers know that empirical plans are best laid out on the ground by pacing; and the measurements listed by Thom fit to a mean which is in fact a comfortable pace for an adult man, (2.72 feet), or three quite normal human feet. It is unnecessary therefore to assume, as Thom does, that a hypothetical standard (the so-called megalithic yard) was widely reproduced, although a standard would have been needed within any single site and its reproducibility would have been quite within the capabilities shown by early bronze age metal-workers. As to the lay-outs, the functions of Pythagorean triangles could have been accidentally, instinctively and repeatedly discovered in experiments with pegs and ropes by those manifestly familiar with circular plans (and are likely to have been so discovered in antiquity).

Similarly, if we admit the astronomical plans (and few have Thom's competence to verify them even partially), we may enquire about their purposes. May they not have been two-fold? Firstly, practical: through the sun and moon to determine and codify highly important dates, when to begin the spring cultivation for example, or when the stock would calve; and through the first-magnitude stars (before the days of watches or striking clocks) to indicate the progress of the night, especially in winter. And secondly, in the monumental forms, to satisfy metaphysical needs: to give early man a consoling and fortifying illusion of control over the earthly environment and the celestial sphere, induced by persuading himself that, since the stones appeared to fix the movements of heavenly bodies and the procession of the seasons, they also had some control over them, could bring them back to the same place again and make the natural world behave in a satisfactory and predictable way. Possessions of these qualities may be reflected in the behaviour of megaliths in folklore, where they move at certain times and seasons, whisper together, have such mysterious power that they cannot be counted and need refreshment with food and drink.

Acknowledgments

I am grateful for advice from my colleagues Mr D.A. Hinton and Dr P.R.S. Moorey and discussions with them during the drafting of this paper; and for discussions with many members of the Research Seminar during its progress.

REFERENCES

Beveridge, W.I.B. (1964) (1950) *The Art of Scientific Investigation*. London, Heinemann.

Childe, V.G. (1956) *Piecing Together the Past: The Interpretation of Archaeological Data.* London, Routledge and Kegan Paul.

Childe, V.G. (1958) Valediction. *University of London Institute of Archaeology Bulletin* 1, 1-8.

Clark, J.G.D. (1952) *Prehistoric Europe: The Economic Basis.* London, Methuen.

Collingwood, R.G. (1970) (1946) *The Idea of History.* London, Oxford University Press.

Doran, J. (1970) Systems theory, computer simulations and archaeology. *World Archaeology* 1, 289-98.

Gombrich, E.H. (1968) *Art and Illusion: A Study in the Psychology of Pictorial Representation.* 3rd ed. London, Phaidon.

Hole, F., Flannery, K.V. and Neely, J.A. (1969) *Prehistory and Human Ecology of the Deh Luran Plain.* Ann Arbor.

Hulme, T.E., ed. Read, H.E. (1960) (1924) *Speculations: Essays on Humanism and the Philosophy of Art.* London, Routledge and Kegan Paul.

Iversen, E. (1961) *The Myth of Egypt and its Hieroglyphs in European Tradition.* Copenhagen, GEC GAD.

Kendall, D.G. (1969) Some problems and methods in statistical archaeology. *World Archaeology* 1 68-76.

Lowther, G.R. (1965) Idealism and prehistorical studies. *Atti del VI Congresso Internazionale delle Scienze Preistoriche e Protostoriche* 2 (Sezioni I-IV), 3-7. G. Sansoni ed. Rome.

Lucas, J.R. (1970) Apology for Greats. *Oxford Magazine* 1 Hilary, 109-11.

Oakeshott, M. (1933) *Experience and its Modes.* Cambridge, University Press.

Quine, W. van O. (1963) (1961) *From a logical point of view:* 1-19. New York. Harper and Row.
Richards, I.A. (1967) (1943) *How to read a Page.* London, Routledge and Kegan Paul.
Thom, A. (1967) *Megalithic Sites in Britain.* Oxford, Clarendon Press.

PATTY JO WATSON

Explanation and models: the prehistorian as philosopher of science and the prehistorian as excavator of the past

There has been much recent discussion of archaeological theory in the two *Antiquity* journals (*Antiquity* proper and *American Antiquity*; Bayard 1969; Binford 1962, 1964, 1965; Fritz and Plog 1970; Hawkes 1968; Isaac 1971; Kushner 1970; Martin 1971; Trigger 1970) and at numerous professional meetings in both the Old and New Worlds. Some of these dicussions have even been crystallized in books (Binford and Binford 1968: Clarke 1968; Watson, LeBlanc, and Redman 1971).

The present international conference – focussing as it does on explanations and models, some of the matters central to the controversy over theory in prehistory – seems to be an ideal situation in which to review the basic issues and to attempt to reach some consensus. In order to further such an attempt I outline what appear to be the major points of debate and suggest solutions.

As discussed more fully elsewhere (Watson, LeBlanc, and Redman 1971; Watson 1971a, 1971b), the basic issues centre on the kinds of questions we ask of our data and the standards applied to evaluate the adequacy of possible answers. At the most fundamental level, the debate lies within the realm of epistemology, and several archaeologists have become conversant to a degree with various relevant aspects of the philosophy of science (for example, Fritz and Plog 1970, Martin 1971, and Spaulding 1968). This is a very healthy situation, if not carried too far. The writings of several philosophers of science (such as Brodbeck 1962; Hempel 1942, 1965, 1966; and Rudner 1966) are extremely pertinent to fundamental considerations about the nature of science, that in turn bear on two questions: *Can* prehistoric archaeology be an explicitly scientific discipline? *Should* prehistoric archaeology be an explicitly scientific discipline?

To date, answers to these questions by various archaeologists have ranged from a clarion yes, it can and should (Fritz and Plog 1970, Martin 1971) to a ringing no, it cannot (Hawkes 1968, Bayard 1969) or a modified no, it can but should not (Trigger, 1970, 1971). However, in my opinion there is no uncertainty as to the logical answer to the first question: Yes, certainly prehistoric archaeology *can* be a science; empirical data of any kind can be treated scientifically. Disagreement on this point results from misunderstanding as to what science is, particularly with respect to such issues as experimentation, objectivity, and the nature of scientific laws. A treatment of some of these points as regards geology, but easily translateable to archaeology, is provided by R. Watson (1966 and 1969); see also Hempel (1942), and Watson, LeBlanc, and Redman (1971: chs. 1, 2 and 6). The essence of science is the application of a particular logical framework to a particular subject matter; science is not delimited by use of computers, test tubes, Pearson's *r*, calipers, or lab coats.

The controversial question is whether archaeologists *should* use an explicitly scientific approach. I believe we should because it is the most efficient means of attaining knowledge of any empirical subject matter. (I do not consider here the arguments of those who say we should not because it detracts from the dignity of man, or we should not because man has free will and his behaviour is not determined as are objects of science. I believe these views to be wrong or misguided, but this is not the place to debate them.) To judge from the nature of the topic for this conference and the interests of those participants known to me, I assume that there is no serious disagreement on this level. There is plenty of room for debate and discussion at the next stage, however – deciding how we go about this – because here we go beyond the philosophers of science. We ourselves must work out the details of the generalized logical framework and fit it to our own particular data. It is up to us to determine which propositions we can consider as given (for instance, 'culture change is primarily caused by migration, diffusion, or a combination of the two', 'culture change is caused primarily by demographic response to the physical environment', 'culture change is primarily a result of sociopolitical evolution', etc.), and which propositions should be more closely examined, broken down to essential components, formulated as hypotheses or sets of hypotheses, and subjected to test. It is also up to us to decide what shall be regarded as adequate confirmation for those hypotheses and what kinds and quantity of results shall be regarded as satisfactory disconfirmation of the hypotheses.

Moreover, if we are to operate within the scientific framework we should explicitly accept and use scientific terminology, or at least understand how our terminology relates to that framework. This would help a great deal in cutting down confusion surrounding the use of words like explanation and model.

As an illustration of this last point, I can refer to the Halafian period in Near Eastern prehistory. We want to explain the relatively sudden spread of the Halafian painted pottery style, from Lake Van to the Mediterranean, from as far north as Elazig in Turkey to

Samarra in Iraq. How should we go about it? First we assess all the known evidence: chronology, site distribution, depth of deposit, nature of artifactual and other cultural debris associated with the characteristic printed pottery, etc. This will result in our arriving at some primarily inductively derived hypotheses about the nature of the culture that left these remains. The hypotheses can be formulated as a series of hypothetical explanations of the Halafian, e.g.:

1. The Halafian simply represents the diffusion by trade, or trade and copying, of a particular painted pottery style from a specific series of sites or a specific region.
2. The Halafian resulted from relatively rapid migration of human groups.
3. The Halafian is the result of gradual population growth and expansion.
4. The Halafian represents the chiefdom stage in precivilizational Mesopotamia: the elegant pottery plus the tholoi and various other items, such as the characteristic incised pendants, being part of a complex of luxury or status items marking the communication lines among local headmen (LeBlanc 1971: Chapter VI; and Service 1962).
5. The Halafian resulted from activity of small, resident groups of occupational specialists – possibly an ethnic minority – moving out from one or a few large centres.

The next step would be to choose the most likely of these or other possible explanations, derive test implications from them (including some critical tests to discriminate between equally likely possibilities), and then proceed to collect data necessary to check the implications.

For example, if 1 is the best explanation, then we should expect to find very little, if any, similarity from site to site in categories other than the fine ware, which would be expected to show remarkable stylistic homogeneity over great distances. Coarse ware, chipped stone, ground stone, architecture, physical remains and social organization of the villagers, subsistence pattern, and so on should vary considerably from one site to another outside the heartland. Within the heartland, resemblances between sites will be quite close in all categories.

However, if 2 is correct, physical remains of the villagers will be markedly similar over the entire extent of Halafian painted pottery, and cultural categories besides the fine ware will show close resemblances grading out from the heartland or place of origin.

If 3 is correct the general situation would be like 2, but the chronological interrelationships of the sites would be different (sites in the heartland would be definitely older than more peripheral sites, even though typological similarities would be close).

If 4 is correct, then there should be marked similarity among all

Halafian sites in the complex of items presumed to be status markers (painted pottery, tholoi, incised pendants, etc.), but considerable variation or no resemblance in other items. There would be little or no genetic resemblances in physical remains from one part of the area to another, but there would be clear indications of social stratification within at least the larger Halafian sites and possibly indications of hierarchical ordering among the sites themselves.

If 5 is correct, the general situation would resemble 1 and would be difficult to distinguish from it. Stylistic and technical aspects of the painted pottery would be even more homogeneous over the entire area, and careful sampling and excavation of individual sites should reveal the residences and workshops of the resident fineware potters. Within any one site, variations of the fineware would be less than would be true if any of the other explanations is the correct one.

The above is not an exhaustive list of possible explanations nor is the discussion of even these five complete, but should be sufficient for purposes of illustration.

Each of the sample hypothetical explanations could be referred to as a separate explanatory model, or some persons might regard 2 and 3 as two examples of a single demographic or populational model, or 3 and 4 as two examples of a general evolutionary model (biological and social respectively) whereas 1 is, of course, a diffusionist model. The whole example illustrates an explicitly scientific model of, or approach to, culture change as contrasted with the mystical model that might be exemplified by some theologically-based explanations of culture change.

No matter how the word 'model' is used, the logical structure of the whole procedure should remain clear: we are seeking an explanation of a particular phenomenon by reference to confirmed or assumed lawlike generalizations about the diffusion of material culture (hypothetical explanation 1 above), the nature of social evolution (4), the consequences of certain demographic processes (2 and 3), or of particular forms of social organization (5) among human groups. Archaeological theory consists of a body of lawlike generalizations, some of which relate ancient objects, architectural remains, etc. and their spatial distributions within a site to the behaviour patterns of extinct human groups. Others pertain to the processual dynamics of human groups in similar circumstances anywhere at any time (i.e., the mechanisms and effects of diffusion, migration, population expansion, social evolution and so on). However, there is a great deal of work to be done to confirm and to establish archaeological general laws in the first realm – that of behavioural correlates for material culture – and work in the second realm – laws of cultural process – is barely begun (although some examples are available, a few of which are relevant to the Halafian illustration: Carneiro 1970, Leone 1968, Naroll 1956, Sahlins and

Service 1960, Service 1962).

In summary, the controversy concerning archaeological theory should now be beyond the initial philosophy-of-science stages. It is clear that, logically speaking, the empirical data of archaeology can be treated in an explicitly scientific manner. But the questions asked of those data are not agreed upon; should they be essentially or predominantly particularistic or ideographic (reconstructing and explaining particular events or sequences in the prehistoric past) as in the Halafian example? Can we agree that there is a sufficient body of archaeological and social scientific general laws so that we can achieve valid explanations of our data? Or should we – at least temporarily – concentrate on nomothetic studies, formulating as hypotheses and trying to confirm the necessary first order archaeological general laws, while hoping that at least some ethnologists, social anthropologists, geographers, sociologists, historians, and other social scientists will be interested in working on and co-operating in the formulation and testing of hypothetical general laws concerning cultural processes? I believe we ought to emphasize nomothetic concerns now, not because I think prehistory should necessarily always be a predominantly nomothetic pursuit, but because I think we are a long way from attaining that corpus of accepted archaeological laws just referred to. Moreover, there is undeniable potential for immensely increased information from our data if we explore these new theoretical and methodological questions, while applying new and better methods to old questions like the explanation of culture change. The prehistorian as philosopher of science emerged in the 1960s; the 1970s should be devoted to the operationalizing of theory by the nomothetically-oriented prehistorian as excavator of the past.

REFERENCES

Bayard, D.T. (1969) Science, theory and reality in the 'New Archaeology'. *American Antiquity* **34**, 376-84.

Binford, L.R. (1962) Archaeology as anthropology. *American Antiquity* **28**, 217-25.

Binford, L.R. (1964) A consideration of archaeological research design. *American Antiquity* **29**, 425-41.

Binford, L.R. (1965) Archaeological systematics and the study of cultural process. *American Antiquity* **31**, 203-10.

Binford, S.R. and L.R. (1968) *New Perspectives in Archaeology*. Chicago, Aldine.

Brodbeck, M. (1962) Explanations, predictions and 'imperfect' knowledge. In Feigl, H. and Maxwell, G. (eds.), *Minnesota Studies in the Philosophy of Science*, Volume III, 231-72. Minneapolis, University of Minnesota.

Carneiro, R.L. (1970) A quantitative law in anthropology. *American Antiquity* **35**, 492-94.

Clarke, D.L. (1968) *Analytical Archaeology*. London, Methuen.

Fritz, J.M. and Plog, F. (1970) The nature of archaeological explanation. *American Antiquity* **35**, 405-12.

Hawkes, J. (1968) The proper study of mankind. *Antiquity* **42**, 255-62.
Hempel, C.G. (1942) The function of general laws in history. *The Journal of Philosophy* **39**, 35-48.
Hempel, C.G. (1965) *Aspects of Scientific Explanation and Other Essays in the Philosophy of Science.* New York, The Free Press.
Hempel, C.G. (1966) *Philosophy of Natural Science.* Englewood Cliffs, Prentice-Hall.
Isaac, G.L. (1971) Whither archaeology? *Antiquity* **45**, 123-9.
Kushner, G. (1970) A consideration of some processual designs for archaeology as anthropology. *American Antiquity* **35**, 125-32.
LeBlanc, S.A. (1971) Computerized, conjunctive archaeology and the Near Eastern Halaf. Ph.D. Dissertation, Department of Anthropology, Washington University, St Louis.
Leone, M.P. (1968) Neolithic economic autonomy and social distance. *Science* **162**, 1150-1.
Martin, P.S. (1971) The revolution in archaeology. *American Antiquity* **36**, 1-8.
Naroll, R. (1956) A preliminary index of social development. *American Anthropologist* **58**, 687-715.
Rudner, R.S. (1966) *Philosophy of Social Science.* Englewood Cliffs, Prentice-Hall.
Sahlins, M.D. and Service, E.R. (eds.) (1960) *Evolution and Culture.* Ann Arbor, University of Michigan Press.
Service, E.R. (1962) *Primitive Social Organization.* New York, Random House.
Spaulding, A.C. (1968) Explanation in archaeology. *In* Binford, S.R. and L.R., (eds.), *New Perspectives in Archaeology*, 33-40. Chicago, Aldine.
Trigger, B.G. (1970) Aims in prehistoric archaeology. *Antiquity* **44**, 26-37.
Trigger, B.G. (1971) Reply to 'Trigger and prehistoric archaeology'. *Antiquity* **45**, 133-4.
Watson, P.J. (1971a) The aims of prehistory and the search for explanation in archaeology. Paper read at the 36th Annual Meeting of the Society for American Archaeology in Norman, Oklahoma, May 1971.
Watson, P.J. (1971b) The future of archaeology in anthropology: culture history and social science. Paper contributed to a symposium on 'Archaeology's Future: Roles and Relevance', 70th Annual Meeting of the American Anthropological Association in New York, November 1971.
Watson, P.J., LeBlanc, S.A. and Redman, C.L. (1971) *Explanation in Archaeology: An Explicitly Scientific Approach.* New York, Columbia University Press.
Watson, R.A. (1966) Is geology different? A critical discussion of *The Fabric of Geology. Philosophy of Science* **33**, 172-85.
Watson, R.A. (1969) Explanation and prediction in geology. *Journal of Geology* **77**, 488-94.

DESMOND COLLINS

Epistemology and culture tradition theory

Explanation involves the formulation of generalizations. It is part of the pursuit of understanding, or in other terms the search for truth. The branch of philosophy which deals with these matters is called epistemology.

Two views of the epistemology of science

Induction is claimed to be the derivation of general laws from individual observations or facts. The idea was extensively developed at the end of the sixteenth century by Francis Bacon. He viewed scientific conclusions as the logical results of accumulating revelant observations which, regarded without prejudice or bias, led inexorably and logically by the process of induction to the truth. If error crept in, it was because the facts used were wrong or because the scientist had not freed himself completely from prejudice. This formulation would be accepted widely today as a valid description of science.

There is no possible quarrel with the objectives of induction. It would be marvellous if it were possible to establish the truth in this way. The problem is that in practical terms nobody had ever been able to visualize the mechanisms whereby observations could lead logically to a general law. Even more crucially, on rational grounds the induction of truth is clearly not supportable. This had been shown already with great cogency in the eighteenth century by David Hume; he and later philosophers have repeatedly pointed out that no single or finite number of observations could ever logically suffice to 'prove' the truth of any generalization or law. To put the matter baldly, proof by induction is a myth.

When the impossibility of such proof is pressed, a common line of retreat is to say that induction establishes only probability. But this claim likewise has never been substantiated, and so long as induction insists on a logical process leading from particularization to generalizations, the nature of this process must be clarified.

A second approach to the pursuit of truth in science has been called the method of Conjecture and Refutation or more formally Hypothetico-Deductivism. Its most prominent advocate today is Sir Karl Popper (see especially Popper 1959 and 1963). The view, however, is in part much older. Recognizing the existence of certain problems, 'deductivism' offers no surer or more rigorous way of arriving at a solution to these than conjecture, and it concentrates on the testing of these conjectures, by deducing implications from them and comparing these with reality or observational data. Above all it offers ways of deciding the relative merits of competing theories.

It is essential that the conjectures (hypotheses or laws) should be potentially testable, before the failure to refute them is chalked up as a success. Testability in fact is Popper's criterion for demarcating scientific theories from metaphysical theories. For a theory to be scientific one must be able to think of an observation which if in fact made, would refute or falsify the theory. If a solution to a problem is testable and after thorough testing still stands up, then we begin to have very great respect for it. But it has not become certain (or even probable); it is tested, and temporarily test successful or corroborated.

Much that passes for critical discussion in science is derived from inductivism and thus has no validity. Some of these misconceptions are listed under inductivism in the table below.

Concept	*Inductivism*	*Deductivism*
Status of scientific knowledge	Certain (or probable)	Hypothetical
Source of theories	Induction	Conjecture
Prematurity/ Anticipation	Deadly sin	Essential step
'Probability' of theories	Increased by induction	Inversely proportional to testability
'Supporting arguments'	Parts of the process of establishing truth	Some tests of a theory or its desirability

It is particularly worth noting that if at some stage in research supporting arguments are advanced for a theory, and later these are shown to be false, this does not show that the theory is false – merely that it was not tested by the supposed arguments.

In the light of deductivism it is evident that laws, theories and conjuctures are very similar concepts. Models and processes have the same logical status. If they are claimed to be true, they must be submitted for testing. If they are merely descriptive, they explain nothing. Explanation is a much used concept (but we should remember that the idea of a cause is viewed by many philosophers as somewhat comical). An explanation involves a general theory (from which the explicandum must be deducible) and one or more initial conditions. Both the theory and the initial conditions in turn will need to be 'explained', and the result of pursuing this will always be an infinite regress (or series of further explanations required).

The epistemology adopted by a scientist in general and by a student of culture in particular is of vital importance. If he insists he has none or fails to consider this question, his chances of avoiding error are small. If he embraces inductivism, this can hardly fail to mislead him. If he could in some other way justify a claim to have proved his researches or achieved anything superior to a hypothetical status to his work, he will be one of the most important philosophers in the history of the world. More likely he will find the deductivist framework useful; but he must remember that it is not immune from critical discussion – on the contrary it is about critical discussion.

The evaluation of theories

Many objections which have been raised against theories, such as their conjectural origin, lack of proof, inadequate or even inaccurate supporting arguments, assumptions, improbability and prematurity, can be seen in the light of epistemological analysis to be quite irrelevant to the truth. But there are a number of valid points of criticism that can relevantly be raised. The most important are inconsistency, test-failure and untestability. If the first two criticisms are valid, the theory must be rejected as untrue or else modified. If the third is valid, the theory must be regarded as metaphysical and non-scientific. In addition there are a number of other related criticisms which could never refute a theory, but are useful in deciding between the desirability of competing theories. Among the most important are explanatory content (or breadth of application) and simplicity. I suspect these are expecially important in archaeology.

The detection of inconsistency in a theory or system of theories lies within the realm of logic. Testing theories is the job of the scientist. Test-failure is refutation; test-success however must not be confused with verification, for no single or finite number of successful results constitutes proof, but only corroboration. Passing many severe tests constitutes a higher degree of corroboration than passing fewer less severe tests.

Testability is one of the most important notions in science, if not the most important. It is also one of the most difficult. For a theory to qualify as testable or falsifiable 'the class of its potential falsifiers must not be empty' (Popper 1959: 86), or in less technical language the theory must state that certain observational results will not actually be found, even though (outside the framework of the theory) such observations would seem quite possible. If the prohibited observations are unequivocally made, the theory is refuted. An example may help. Newton's Law of Gravitation requires that the attraction between bodies is proportional to the product of their masses and inversely proportional to the square of their distance apart. The theory therefore forbids the attraction to have any value other than this. It is one of the most useful and tested theories in science. It is also probably wrong to a minor degree, thus illustrating that the value of a theory does not necessarily vanish if it is wrong.

Testability has degrees (strong and weak testability) and it also has kinds (logical and actual); here we might mention historical testability, which would be straightforward observation at the time but subsequently becomes much less direct and quite difficult or even impossible. Also many theories are only partly testable. The synthetic or neo-Darwinian theory of evolution illustrates this problem all too well. Its testability revolves mainly around that part of the mechanism that can be observed today (Campbell 1966:9) and it is doubtful if any deduction bearing on whether evolution in fact occurred in the Pliocene or Cambrian can be made from the central theory, which is a strong enough 'prohibition' to be conclusively testable. Take an example from the evolution of the horse, such as the number of toes present in its Oligocene ancestor. An Oligocene fossil horse with too many or too few toes would refute a theory, but only a particular version of mammalian phylogeny, and its logical bearing on the central theory would be minimal.

Culture tradition theory

I conclude with a brief and tentative outline of a theory of culture change, which is specifically offered for critical discussion. The culture tradition theory recognizes a set of forces causing or favouring perpetuation of the pattern of culture unchanged – the continuity factors. A second set of forces causes or favours cultural innovation – the change factors. The factors are listed below to facilitate three lines of discussion. First, are any valid factors omitted? Second, are any of those listed demonstrably not operative? Third, can any be usefully quantified?

AI Factors causing continuity or replication of culture pattern.

1. Motor-reflex conditioning in individual's making of artifacts and other material culture; (also the 'mental template' method).
2. Culture transmission from elder to novice by instruction or copying.

AII Factors favouring continuity of culture pattern.

3. Conservatism; genetic, cultural or a combination of both.
4. Elimination by natural selection of individuals, families or communities which deviate 'unadaptively' from culture tradition.

BI Factors causing innovation.

1. Invention, often a rational conscious response to a problem.
2. Non-replication, or failure to accurately reproduce the culture tradition.

BII Factors favouring inventiveness.

3. Large neotenous brain and concomitant increased memory potential favouring faster rate of inventiveness than small brain.
4. Developed culture (especially developed language, large store of knowledge and increased culture contact) favouring faster rate of inventiveness than rudimentary culture.
5. Large total population has more inventions than small population. This does not affect the individual rate of inventiveness, except by means of factor B4.
6. Boredom, favouring 'trend-seeking'; also affects adoption of innovations.

BIII Factors favouring successful adoption of innovation.

7. Adaptiveness of innovations.
8. Major change of circumstances such as environmental catastrophes, upsetting the equilibrium of the group, and facilitating change.
9. Widening of communication and culture contact (travel, printed word, broadcasting etc.) replacing monopoly of culture transmission from elders of the group. This may cause relaxation of conservatism A3. Dramatic recent increase of population may remove natural selective pressure in force in A3 and A4.
10. Recent conscious sponsorship of change by commercial interests.

It is suggested that the kind of equilibrium achieved varies from period to period. A recurrent factor is the opposition between the younger generation favouring change and the older generation favouring stability; this opposition is already found in non-human primates. Between 1 and 2½ million years ago change is so slow that no cultural evolution can be recognized in a span of around a million years. During the Middle Pleistocene, phases of culture change can be distinguished at intervals closer to 20-50 thousand years. The first great acceleration in culture change had evidently already occurred. During the last 25 thousand years of the Pleistocene (i.e. during the upper palaeolithic or leptolithic) the interval of detectable change is nearer 1-5 thousand years. A second great acceleration had occurred. With the advent of metal using and urban communities clear culture change is detectable at intervals of under a millennium (perhaps around 100-500 years). I do not underestimate the difficulties in quantifying this change interval. With the scientific revolution of early modern times, the change interval becomes shorter again, and this decrease has presumably continued in the last 100 years.

Thus the forces of culture tradition, which are presumed to explain the consistency of the archaeological record, are weaker in the modern world than ever before. We naturally turn to non-literate peoples (as the biologist turns to animal species in their wild state) to test whether the mechanism is rightly understood. But we should never underestimate the strength of culture tradition even today; the immense surviving prestige of inductivism is a salutary reminder of how a logically unsound and pernicious philosophy can survive for several hundred years in a supposedly rational community, and still not have lost its hold.

REFERENCES

Campbell, B. (1966) *Human Evolution.* London, Heinemann.
Popper, K.R. (1959) *The Logic of Scientific Discovery.* London, Hutchinson.
Popper, K.R. (1963) *Conjectures and Refutations.* London, Routledge.

D. H. MELLOR

Do cultures exist?

The question whether cultures exist turns as much on the concept of existence as on that of a culture, and it illustrates an important general question about the social sciences. This is, roughly, whether their theoretical entities can be taken as seriously as those of physics. This question in turn bears on the current debate about the use social sciences can properly make of the methods of the physical sciences.

We seem to know what societies are made of (viz. people!) before we start theorizing about them; physicists lack such conveniently *a priori* knowledge of the makeup of physical things. Their discoveries can consequently add to our ontology in a way that those of social scientists apparently cannot. It has been held on these grounds (e.g. Watkins 1957) that such 'social individuals' as cultures are mere fictions or logical constructions and so cannot be governed by autonomous laws, e.g. the laws of historical development postulated by Marxists. My object here is to investigate the supposed ontological asymmetry between physical and social sciences which gives rise to such conclusions, taking the concept of a culture as a convenient exemplar.

The term 'culture' is variously used in archaeology, anthropology and related subjects. I shall use it not of artifact assemblies (*pace* Childe 1956), but of groups of prehistoric people characterized, roughly, by what artifacts they left and where, and not otherwise directly accessible to our observation. (The argument will not be affected if archaeologists who find this use of 'culture' too heretical substitute another term.) Not all such groups are cultures in this sense, but all cultures are such groups. Now no one doubts that artifacts exist, and I take it that the existence, in the same sense, of prehistoric people is equally undoubted. The question is whether cultures also exist in this sense.

I take the concept of existence to be the same in the social as in the physical sciences. Naturally the sense of saying that electrons exist differs from the sense of saying that cultures exist. That follows from the different meanings of 'electron' and 'culture'; it need not follow from different senses of 'exist'. Indeed I hold in general that there is only one concept of existence, applied equally to such diverse entities as God, numbers, ideas, ghosts, tables, electrons and cultures. I cannot argue this general point here (see, e.g. White 1956; Quine 1953), merely make a persuasive pass with Ockham's razor.

The temptation to invoke different concepts of existence (e.g. in Nagel 1961: pp. 145-52) results from the very different properties of the entities I have cited, and the consequently diverse methods needed to show whether they exist. Proving that there is no real square root of −1 has little in common with collecting evidence for the nonexistence of dragons. That is because numbers and animals have such different properties. Animals, for instance, have spatial and temporal boundaries: dragons, if there were any, would occupy some places and times and not others. Numbers, on the other hand, if they exist at all, exist everywhere and at all times. It makes no sense to go looking for numbers in the way one might go looking for dragons, because numbers have no properties that could let them show up in one place rather than another.

So one may be tempted to say that numbers exist in a different sense from animals. But given that the sufficiently different senses of 'number' and 'animal' make it needless to say this, it is obviously undesirable. Superfluous concepts of existence raise spurious problems about how they are related. They make plain questions of existence seem ambiguous. Take the question whether the sun has an odd number of planets. It may be taken equally as about the existence of planets or about that of their odd number. Yet these ways of taking the question plainly do not give it different senses.

No one minds talk of different 'modes' (e.g.) of existence where this means merely that things of different kinds have different properties and so are detectable in different ways. One may allow those Gods, numbers and people that exist at all to have different modes of existence in that sense. What one may not allow is that dragons, Hamlet or the real square root of −1 exist, only in different modes. We know, in each of these cases, what properties these supposed entities would have. Applying the appropriate techniques of detection we find that nothing has these properties. (I use 'has' here, and 'exists' and 'there are (is)' generally, tenselessly, in accordance with most logical usage. In tensed terms, I mean here that nothing has, had, or will have these properties.) There are no large scaly fire-breathing winged creatures with tails; no person exists whose biography could be used to 'correct' the soliloquies of Shakespeare's play; no real number has −1 as its square. These last three assertions are plainly true, and plainly unambiguous. It is not that dragons, Hamlet and real square roots of −1 have a different mode of existence, or subsist, or exist in a different sense. They simply do not exist at all; there are no such entities.

We have, of course, the concepts of these things. We know what something would have to be like to be a dragon. (How else could we know there are none?) But the concept of a dragon is not a dragon; any more than the concept of Hamlet is a person or that of a number is itself a number. The existence of a concept does not confer any amount, kind or mode of existence on its instances (with the doubtful and much debated exception of the concept of God).

I have laboured these points especially to bring out the intimate relation between existence and truth. To deny that dragons exist is to say that there is nothing of which what we believe about dragons is true. There is no real number of which it is true that -1 is its square. There has never been a person of whom it is true to say that he respectively did and said anything like the acts and speeches Shakespeare attributes to Hamlet. In all these cases existence is a necessary condition of certain truths; and the same truths in consequence are a sufficient condition of existence. If what we believe about dragons were true of anything, that thing would be a dragon (since that, for us, is just what it is for something to be a dragon). Dragons, consequently, would then exist. Similarly, of course, for Hamlet and the square root of -1.

We see then that the mere conception, or characterization, of a thing in no way suffices for its existence. To be convinced of that we must be convinced that the characterization is true of something.

Two questions, therefore, must be asked of a scientific theory in order to settle its existence claims. The first is: what statements does the theory assert? That is, what must we suppose to be true if we are to accept the theory? The second question is: what do these statements, if any, refer to? That is, what do they purport to be about? Then the theory may be taken to assert the existence of whatever the statements it claims to be true are about.

This may seem an excessively simple way to settle the ontology of a scientific theory. In fact neither question is as simple as it may seem. The first question is complicated on two counts. First it has been controversial whether scientific theories make statements at all, either true or false. Secondly, even supposing a theory to make statements, it is controversial whether its use involves any commitment to their truth. The second question is complicated by the difficulty of deciding just what it is that theoretical statements, if any, in science are about. I take these questions in turn.

The question has been long debated whether scientific theories make statements, that is whether they can be true or false. The alternative view is that they are to be assessed in terms of usefulness rather than in terms of truth and falsity. This view is usually called 'instrumentalism' because of its conception of scientific theory as an instrument, essentially for summarizing and predicting observations which could in principle be made and stated without it (see, e.g. Nagel 1961: chapter 6). I shall not here discuss instrumentalism further, largely because I think it false. I do not of course deny that theories can be useful; I deny only that the concept of usefulness enables us to dispense with that of truth. On the contrary, it is generally its truth which makes a theory useful. In any case, an instrumentalist could not maintain a consistent interest in the present topic. Instrumentalism precludes any interesting ontological discussion about theoretical entities such as cultures. Their assumption in archaeological theory, like that of electrons in physical theory, would be nothing to an instrumentalist but a useful fiction. If all supposed theoretical entities in science are merely useful fictions, *a fortiori* those of archaeology are; but that tells us nothing interesting about specifically archaeological items. The present question is whether social sciences in general, and archaeology in particular, can add to our ontology in the way the physical sciences are supposed to. That is, granted a realist (i.e. non-instrumentalist) view of physical theory, if only for the sake of argument, can it be sustained for archaeological theory, and what are its consequences therein?

I shall assume therefore that theories in both physical and social sciences are advanced as making statements about their respective subject matters, whatever these may be. The second part of my first question is whether adopting such theories involves accepting the truth of these statements. I hold the increasingly heretical view that it does. Of course we know that theories cannot be conclusively verified by experience. We know also that they cannot be conclusively falsified, because of the extensive, if not limitless, possibilities of explaining away conflicting evidence with auxiliary hypotheses and modifications of the theory. All this is even more plainly true of the statistical theories that predominate in the social sciences. No single observation or series of observations will conclusively refute or establish the truth of a statistical theory. One might consequently suppose that adopting and rejecting such theories as a result of making observations is not done on grounds of truth or falsity at all.

The chief objection to that conclusion is the lack of any alternative rationale in general for adopting and rejecting theories. Suppose one said vaguely that theories are adopted because their statements provide convenient 'working hypotheses' and rejected when they cease to do so. If we try and distinguish this view from instrumentalism, we may still ask: in what does the convenience of a working hypothesis consist? Presumably in the reliability of the predictions derivable from it. Suppose such a prediction is that if experiment E is done, the upshot will be observation O (or a probability distribution over a set of possible observations O_1, O_2, . . . O_n). But that prediction is only reliable to the extent that the corresponding hypothesis 'if E, than O' is true.

No doubt our evidence for the truth of interesting theories is usually very flimsy, and working hypotheses are entertained tentatively and modified by 'conjecture and refutation'. But the same is true of the reliability of interesting theories. The inevitable lack of evidence for a successful theory detracts not from its truth but from the force of our claim to be certain of its truth. So we adopt theories tentatively at first and are prepared for further experience to make us modify them or give them up. That is, we assume their truth tentatively and are prepared to be shown wrong in that assumption. What is tentative, however, is our assumption, not the theory's truth.

Again of course we often use false theories in special situations where we know their consequences to be true. This knowledge may be direct or backed up by the true theory that has superseded a false one. Thus we go on using Newtonian mechanics for convenience in almost all everyday situations. We know it to be reliable there, even though false in general, and that indeed follows from relativity theory. But to know it reliable there is to know its relevant consequences true, and that this follows from relativity is pertinent only if we in turn believe relativity to be true. Truth, in either case, is still the test of usefulness.

The tentativeness with which scientific theories are accepted tends in any case to be overrated by philosophers of science. Many theories in physics, once quite speculative, have ceased to interest philosophers because they have become as well established as the most mundane facts. The theory behind radio transmission is so reliable that its truth is no longer seriously in question. Nor, for that very reason, is the existence of its most characteristic theoretical entity, the radio wave. *How* we can know all this, on the basis of our limited sensory input, is a problem as yet unsolved in the philosophical theory of knowledge. But the difficulty of this problem arises from the very certainty of the knowledge, and equally certainly casts no doubt upon it.

The immediately relevant point, however, is that tentativeness in a theory is a sign of lack of evidence, not of lack of truth (or falsity). Evidence may be even harder to come by in the social than in the physical sciences, and archaeological theories, among others, may be correspondingly more tentative. But that affords no reason to suppose them less capable of truth and falsity than are the theories of physics.

I have dealt rather briskly with the first of the two questions I said must be answered in settling a theory's ontology. I have done so partly from conviction and partly because these topics, although somewhat controversial, are neither novel nor likely to illuminate the differences between archaeology and physical sciences. They might have done so when physical knowledge was supposed to be peculiarly reducible to incorrigible knowledge of sensations. It might then have been held, as it cannot now, that physical theory could claim truth, and thus reality for its entities, which social theories could not. I show below that lack of conclusive evidence is not to the point; but even if it were, any difference between physical and social sciences is one of degree, not of kind. (It is debatable anyway whether archaeology is any less securely based in experience than modern cosmology or nuclear physics.) Our chief concern is with the differences in what archaeological and other theories can be taken to refer to. In what follows I take for granted that theories of both kinds can be true and hence can refer to something.

Ontological debate in the social sciences has been overshadowed by debates about method. That societies are really 'nothing but collections of people' has indeed been asserted by so-called 'methodological individualists' (see, e.g. Watkins 1953, 1957). This claim about what societies are has been less disputed by so-called 'holists' than a corresponding methodological claim (Dray 1967). The latter is, roughly, that intelligible explanation in social science must in principle be translatable into terms of motives, actions and interactions of individual people. Our present concern, however, is first with the sense and then with the truth of the ontological claim, and its corollary that societies in general (and *a fortiori* cultures in particular) are mere fictions or logical constructions out of the people who are their members.

A common analogy with physics is useful here, but needs careful handling. It is easy to conceive of a society as made up of people in the way a gas was classically supposed to be made up of discrete molecules. People and gas molecules no doubt interact differently, but that does not affect the ontological comparison. There is nothing to a classical gas but its molecules. The laws governing the gas's macroscopic behaviour we will suppose both statable and derivable completely in terms of the laws governing its molecules' microscopic behaviour. Thus everything physics takes to be true of such a gas can be translated into truths that refer only to its molecules. The truth of the kinetic theory then only requires reference to gas molecules. Reference to macroscopic samples of gas is redundant.

Now it may seem convenient to put this fact, if it is a fact, by saying that gases do not really exist, only their molecules do so. Eddington, with his notorious 'two worlds' (1927: Introduction) put a similar conclusion in this way and has been followed in this by a number of philosophers since (e.g. Sellars 1961). But this way of putting it, however convenient it may seem, must be resisted. If gases *are* collections of gas molecules (as the translation project must require), and molecules exist so collected (as the adequacy of kinetic theory requires), then *a fortiori* gases exist. If Eddington's everyday table is in reality nothing but a swarm of fundamental particles, then it still exists, as just such a swarm. Similarly, a society that is nothing but a specified collection of people must still exist while they exist and are collected in the way specified.

The question of existence must be more carefully posed, therefore, if we are to exclude trivial answers. We are not interested in listing every kind of existent, everything that is or may be referred to in a true statement. If any archeological theory is true, cultures will certainly and trivially occur on our list, as will both gases and gas molecules. We want a list of kinds of what we might call 'basic things', of which things of all other kinds may be supposed to be made. Gases, it seems, are not basic things; are cultures? We need not enquire, of course, whether anything else is made of cultures, merely whether cultures are made of anything else. The question that concerns us is whether people and everyday physical objects between them provide enough basic things for the references of all truths about cultures. Whether truths about people and everyday objects are in turn reducible to truths about the more basic things postulated by physics is not immediately to the point.

I used simple kinetic theory to provide an ontological analogue of society, but it is not clear that the analogy was put the right way round. It is spatially plausible enough: molecules occur within gases much as people occur within societies. But that is not really the point. The question is: what impact, if any, does accepting an archaeological theory have on our list of basic things. In comparing social and physical theories we should presumably make their theoretical entities analogous to each other. Cultures, that is, should be made analogous to the molecules of a gas, not to the gas itself. And the analogue of the gas should then be an individual member of a culture. Or should it?

We see now a complication, which casts further doubt on the use of the physical analogue. The pertinent feature of a gas in relation to kinetic theory is that it is observable independently of the theory. The role of the theory, and of the molecules it postulates, is to explain the independently observable behaviour of the gas. The role of archaeological cultures, however, is not to explain the independently observable behaviour of their members. Prehistoric people are not observable independently of the archaeological theory; on the contrary, they are postulated by it to explain assemblies of artifacts. It is the latter which are in this respect analogous to macroscopic samples of gas.

We must take care, therefore, not to be misled by irrelevant analogies. One such arises from the prejudice that gives ontological priority to the smaller spatial parts of an object. That was the prejudice tacitly appealed to in my initial analogy. A gas sample may seem to be nothing but molecules because molecules exhaust its material spatial parts. Other items may of course be present within the gas without being part of it (e.g. electromagnetic radiation). People similarly exhaust the material spatial parts of a society, although other material objects occur within it (and may even be practically essential to its existence).

The principle I explicitly appealed to was that all truths about gases should be translatable into truths about gas molecules. This principle coincides for a gas with the 'spatial parts' prejudice. The coincidence is a consequence of a further regulative principle (or prejudice) in favour of explaining the behaviour of objects in terms of that of their parts (see Schlesinger 1963: chapter 2). If we add the deducibility criterion of explanation, namely that what is explained must be deducible from what explains it, we arrive at the translation principle. The deducibility criterion is highly debatable in general, but it is satisfied in the gas case, if imprecision is allowed for (see Mellor 1965).

It should be clear, however, from our preliminary discussion that the translation principle is what directly settles ontological questions. It is not the sizes or spatial relations of supposed entities that matter, but the need to refer to them in making true statements. The relevance of criteria of explanation is only indirect. They may constrain what true statements about cultures archaeological theory may propose in order to explain artifact assemblies. Whether cultures are basic things will then depend on whether reference to them in such statements is eliminable (e.g. by more complex reference to their members). The fact that cultures are not spatial parts either of their members or of artifact assemblies is immaterial.

One point of difference from the gas example, however, is very material. Gases may be wholly describable in terms of gas molecules, and so eliminable in their favour from our list of basic things. Assemblies of artifacts, on the other hand, are certainly not wholly describable in terms of cultures. For one thing archaeological explanation is largely nondeductive, so that even archaeological descriptions of artifacts are not wholly translatable into terms of the cultures that produced them. Now this might conceivably (though most implausibly) be a merely transient defect in archaeological theory. Much more importantly, artifacts have many properties which archaeology does not even attempt to explain (for example, most of their physical and chemical properties). Even a deductive archaeology would still leave many truths about artifacts unstatable in its theoretical terms. Archaeology therefore cannot hope on its own to reduce artifact assemblies to the status of logical constructions out of its own theoretical basic things. It might hope to do so in alliance with a sufficiently advanced physics; but such a physics might then well be nibbling at the ontology of people which archaeology presupposes and eventually eliminate the need for reference to any purely archaeological entities.

Pending this unlikely development, archaeology plainly must have people among its basic things, because of the way its field of study is marked out. To decide that a given object was not man made or manipulated is to remove it from the scope of archaeology. Were it to turn out that no prehistoric people ever existed, the whole of archaeology would prove false. Cultures may be distinguished one from another in terms of artifacts; they are all alike supposed to be composed of people. The supposition is not, of course, incidental; it is essential to the explanation of artifacts. Plainly the only way a culture can make a beaker is for one or more of its human members to make a beaker.

An economical ontologist contemplating archaeology might still wonder then whether it really needs culture as well as people and artifacts, given that the first is not needed as a basic kind of thing for the other two. For if talk of artifacts and their makers is not completely translatable into terms of cultures, perhaps the converse is true. Let us consider some more ontological principles.

A preference for the spatial parts of things is not the only basis of our inclination to give people ontological priority over groups of them. Another basis is epistemological. Recall that the existence of something purportedly referred to by a statement is only needed for, and provided by, its truth. We can only be certain of the existence of things about which we can make some certainly true statements. Now the statements we are concerned to make in the sciences, in physics as much as in archaeology, are not made certainly true by being necessarily true. They may be true or they may not, and in the last resort we have to decide which on the basis of some sensory experience that we take to be relatively indubitable. It is the object of an experimental scientist in any field to relate his theories to some such experience. He will try to devise experiments and observations whose unmistakable results are as sensitive as possible to the truth or falsity of the theory being tested, and as impervious as possible to any extraneous influence. When we say that people and gases are more readily and directly observable than either molecules or cultures, we refer to the relative ease of attaining this object in the former case. By and large observation can settle the truth of statements about people and gases much more readily, and subject to less questionable assumptions, than it can settle the truth of statements about molecules and cultures. Yet we think we know the truth of some statements about molecules and cultures. (If we did not, I have argued, they would set us no ontological problems.) How is this more theoretical knowledge possible?

The early, and overoptimistic, answer of the logical positivists was to suppose the translation process I have cited reversed. They supposed observation to be the only source of empirical (as opposed to logical and mathematical) knowledge, and scientific (as opposed to metaphysical) theories they supposed to be both empirical and knowable. Appearances to the contrary, therefore, such theories could not really refer to unobservable things like molecules and cultures. These apparent references were regarded as compendious ways of referring to the multiplicity of observable things whose properties they explain. In terms of these observables, then, all theoretical entities must be definable.

Logical positivism, thus crudely characterized, had variants, distinguished by the kinds of things admitted as adequately observable. The most stringent admitted only immediate sensory experience of such items as patches of colour in one's visual field. Only these were sufficiently indubitable to be acceptable as 'sense-data' and hence as basic things for the whole ontology of knowable natural science (see, e.g. Russell 1917; Ayer 1936). Scientists of positivist leanings were by and large less (and less consistently) sceptical, and prepared to take ordinary macroscopic objects as their basic observables. So, under positivism's 'operationalist' guise in physics, the content of all physical theory was supposed translatable into statements about the results of manipulating balances, clocks, meter rules, and the like (see e.g. Bridgman 1927). These, consequently, by our translation principle, were supposed to provide a basic ontology adequate for all physical theory. Far from gases being constructions out of gas molecules, it was the latter that were regarded as dispensable constructions out of the former. In psychology, the 'behaviourist' version of positivism gave its doctrines an explicitly ontological form (e.g. Watson 1925, Ryle 1949). Minds, and mental processes, it said did not exist, precisely for the reason that nothing irreducible to statements about behaviour could be shown to be true by observation. Whatever we can rightly claim to know of mental activity must therefore, for a behaviourist, be so reducible, and minds consequently must be mere fictions, logical constructions out of patterns of behaviour.

All this is now past history, because it has become clear that (i) no informative statements of the results of observation are absolutely indubitable, (ii) even if they were, statements about ordinary macroscopic objects (which are even more dubitable) are not reducible to them, (iii) statements about the theoretical entities of physical science are not reducible to statements about ordinary macroscopic objects. The demand must be given up that scientific knowledge be indubitably grounded in sensory experience. We must therefore equally give up the claim that either sense-data or ordinary macroscopic objects provide adequate reference for all scientific knowledge.

It nevertheless remains true that observation provides an inimitable check on claims to scientific knowledge. The more directly observable we suppose a kind of item to be, the less problematic are claims to knowledge of truths about it and hence to knowledge of its existence. Now on any currently conceivable scientific theories of human perception, we can generally observe people more directly than we can observe groups of them, just as we can observe gases more directly than we can observe their molecules. We are rightly convinced by this that people and gases are more certain to remain in our ontology than either molecules or cultures.

This need not mean that gases must either be or remain in the *basis* of our ontology, among the things of which all others may be supposed made. Successive physical theories may assert gases to be composed of different kinds of particles or other entities. Our more secure knowledge of gases tells us only that there must be some such composition, and that providing it is a *sine qua non* of any acceptable physical theory. It is still most likely that no such theory will ever list gases themselves among its basic things; that it will always provide translation into its own terms for everything we more certainly know about gases.

(I neglect, in the above, the considerable ability of physical theories to correct as well as to explain longer standing knowledge of physical laws. The point has, if anything, been overstressed in recent literature: given due weight, it does not affect the present argument. See e.g. Mellor 1965, 1969; Popper 1957a.)

What follows from all this about cultures? Cultures are not as directly observable as gases, but we see from that example that this need not affect their standing as basic things. It means only that particular hypotheses about cultures must be held more tentatively than the gas laws and are more subject to revision and rejection. But while such a hypothesis is held, however tentatively, those who hold it must take any culture it refers to to exist (i.e. have existed, see p. 60).

It is clear, moreover, that none but the most naive hypotheses about cultures could be reducible to the statements about artifacts which provide the evidence for them. In the first place, the serious postulation of a culture is bound to have consequences beyond what can be tested archaeologically. No one supposes that the members of a culture laid down all their artifacts, or confined themselves to laying down artifacts to the exclusion of breathing, eating, sleeping, breeding and other archaeologically undetectable activities. And of the artifacts a culture did lay down, no one will suppose that all must have survived, let alone been discovered and correctly identified.

Postulating a culture therefore entails many truths untestable by archaeology, as well as many possible archaeological discoveries which will in fact never be made. In the same way, postulating a table entails many truths untestable by viewing it (e.g. about its weight) as well as many possible views of it which are in fact never seen. These latter facts have been taken to be fatal to positivist attempts to reduce talk of tables to talk of views of tables. The former are equally fatal to an analogous reduction of culture talk to artifact talk. For one thing, the reduction in each case requires adding admittedly possible but in fact nonexistent items to the inadequate number of actual artifacts and views available. The objection to that is simply that merely possible artifacts are not available for this purpose (or any other), precisely because they do not exist.

One must beware of possibilities in ontology. It is all right to say that more things of some kind might have existed than do exist. It is dangerous to say that there is a possibility of more of them and quite wrong to say that they exist as possibilities. The last version is either unintelligible or false. If intelligible, it either involves self-contradiction (saying that the things both do and do not exist), or different senses or modes of existence (see p.60 above). Otherwise it postulates entities at once obscure and useless for the purpose. A possible but not actual artifact, for example, if one can conceive such a thing existing, is no substitute for a real one; certainly no known cultures ever produced any. Dragons, similarly, might exist even though they do not, but that does not mean that there are somewhere in the world such things as 'possible dragons'. There are no more possible dragons in the world than there are real dragons, viz. none. And there are no more possible artifacts in the world than there are real artifacts. In particular there are none available to replace cultures as the referents of archaeological truth.

Another reason why cultures are not reducible to artifacts is that the relation between the two is essentially statistical. That is, a given culture is credited only with a statistical distribution of artifacts. Even allowing for artifacts unmade, destroyed and undiscovered, no postulation of a culture would prescribe *exactly* the observed distribution. It will be compatible with an unlimited number of vaguely specified 'similar' distributions. This is not just to cover our experimental error in locating artifacts. The identity of no man or culture can be supposed to turn on such accidental behaviour as the precise laying down of an axe. So a culture can no more be completely defined by its actual traces than the bias of a coin can be completely defined by the results of its actual tosses.

It is obvious then that cultures are not definable by or reducible to their archaeological traces. It is also true, though perhaps less obvious, that they are not definable in terms of their members. We have observed that it is essential to archaeological explanation that cultures are composed of people. But that is not what distinguishes one culture from another, or cultures from other human groups. Nor is the content of archaeological theories provided by independently specified differences in their members' characteristics. There is no analogue of the kinetic theory's postulates governing their behaviour, from which that of their culture is derivable. I have already remarked the commonplace that we have no access to such specific knowledge of prehistoric peoples independent of the archaeological theories that postulate them. Nor has the development of social psychology and anthropology yet provided adequate grounds for postulating such knowledge on the independent basis of knowledge of modern societies. Moreover in modern societies we do have access to the individual members, and yet our knowledge of them does not enable us to deduce what is known of the societies they form. And if present societies must thus be admitted as ineliminable basic things, how much more must prehistoric ones be.

It may be argued that this conclusion merely reflects the limitations of our present knowledge. As we discover more about people, past and present, are we not bound to suppose a stage when all our knowledge of groups is derivable from our knowledge of their members? Not unless we beg the question by assuming *a priori* that group facts are just facts about their members. It is just as possible that knowledge of groups may perennially outstrip what can be inferred from knowledge of their members. That is speculation. When asked now what kinds of basic things there are, we can only answer in terms of what we know now. And it would seem that those who know archaeology must put cultures on that list.

REFERENCES

Ayer, A.J. (1936) *Language, Truth and Logic.* London, Gollancz.

Beck, L.W. (1950) Constructions and inferred entities. Reprinted in Feigl, H. and Broadbeck, M. (eds.) 1953. *Readings in the Philosophy of Science.* New York, Appleton-Century-Crofts.

Bridgman, P.W. (1927) *The Logic of Modern Physics.* New York, Macmillan.

Binford, L.R. (1968) Archaeological perspectives. *In* Binford, L.R. and S.R. (eds.) *New Perspectives in Archaeology.* Chicago, Aldine.

Childe, G. (1956) *Piecing Together the Past.* London, Routledge.

Clarke, D.L. (1968) *Analytical Archaeology.* London, Methuen.

Dray, W.H. (1967) Holism and individualism in history and social sciences. *In* Edwards, P. (ed.). *The Encyclopaedia of Philosophy*, vol. 4. New York, Macmillan.

Eddington, A.S. (1927) *The Nature of the Physical World.* London, Routledge.

Gardiner, P. (ed.) (1959) *Theories of History.* New York, The Free Press.

Hempel, C.G. (1969) Conceptions of cognitive significance. *Aspects of Scientific Explanation.* New York, The Free Press.

Mandelbaum, M. (1959) Societal facts. Reprinted in Gardiner, P. (ed.) *Theories of History.* New York, The Free Press.

Maxwell, G. (1962) The ontological status of theoretical entities. *In* Feigl, H. and Maxwell, G. (eds.) *Minnesota Studies in the Philosophy of Science, vol. 3.* Minnesota, University Press.

Mellor, D.H. (1965) Experimental error and deducibility. *Philosophy of Science* 32, 105-22.

Mellor, D.H. (1969) Physics and furniture. *In* Rescher, N. (ed.) *Studies in the Philosophy of Science.* Oxford, Blackwell.

Nagel, E. (1961) *The Structure of Science.* New York, Harcourt, Brace and World.

Popper, K.R. (1957) *The Poverty of Historicism.* London, Routledge.

Popper, K.R. (1957a) The aim of science. *Ratio* 1, 24-35.

Popper, K.R. (1963) *Conjectures and Refutations.* London, Routledge.

Quine, W. van O. (1939) Designation and existence. Reprinted in Feigl, H. and Sellers, W. (eds.) (1949) *Readings in Philosophical Analysis.* New York, Appleton-entury-Crofts.

Quine, W. van O. (1953) On what there is. *From a Logical Point of View.* Cambridge Mass., Harvard University Press.

Russell, B. (1917) The relation of sense-data to physics. *Mysticism & Logic.* London, Allen and Unwin.

Russell, B. (1919) *Introduction to Mathematical Philosophy.* London, Allen and Unwin.

Ryle, G. (1949) *The Concept of Mind.* London, Hutchinson.

Schlesinger, G. (1963) *Method in the Physical Sciences.* London, Routledge.

Sellars, W. (1961) The language of theories. *In* Feigl, H. and Maxwell, G. (eds.) *Current Issues in the Philosophy of Science.* New York, Holt, Rinehart and Winston.

Spaulding, A.C. (1968) Explanation in archaeology. *In* Binford, L.R. and S.R. (eds.) *New Perspectives in Archaeology.* Chicago, Aldine.

Watkins, J.W.N. (1953) Ideal types and historical explanation. *In* Feigl, H. and Broadbeck, M. (eds.) *Readings in the Philosophy of Science.* New York, Appleton-Century-Crofts.

Watkins, J.W.N. (1957) Historical explanation in the social sciences. Reprinted in Gardiner, P. (ed.) *Theories of History.* New York, The Free Press.

Watson, J.B. (1925) *Behaviourism.* London, Kegan Paul.

White, M. (1956) The use of 'exists'. *Towards Reunion in Philosophy.* Cambridge Mass., Harvard University Press.

Wisdom, J.O. and Brown, R. (1970) Situational individualism and the emergent group-properties. *In* Borger, R. and Cioffi, F. (eds.) *Explanation in the Behavioural Sciences.* Cambridge, University Press.

WARWICK BRAY

The biological basis of culture

Man, even Homo sapiens, is an animal, bound by many of the limitations which affect all other animals and subject to the biological pressures which constrain living organisms in general. His skeletal and physiological evolution shows no sudden biological discontinuities and must have been accompanied by equally slow and gradual changes in behaviour, though little of this can be reconstructed from the fossil record. This continuity leads one to ask whether the differences between man and non-man are merely those of degree, or whether at some stage of his development man crossed an evolutionary threshold to become a new *kind* of animal.

What sets man apart from other creatures is the quality of his culture. There are nearly as many definitions of culture as there are anthropologists (Kroeber and Kluckhohn 1952; White 1959a), but most authorities accept that it is a socially transmitted pattern of learned, rather than biologically determined, behaviour. There is also agreement among biologists and ethologists that instinctive (genetically-programmed) responses can still be recognized in human behaviour and that, conversely, elements of 'cultural' behaviour can be recognized among present day animals and must have been present at a much earlier state of their evolution.

The differences between human and non-human behaviour are largely those of emphasis. Short-lived creatures (with little time, and limited capacity, for learning) require swift and effective instinctive reactions. In man, as in other species with a long period of infancy during which to learn complex, 'cultural' behaviour, instinctive reactions play a less important part than reasoned, flexible responses based on intelligence and experience. In neurological terms, endocrine control of behaviour through the lower nervous centres has in higher mammals largely been replaced by cortical control. Thus, the complex societies of certain insects and the 'dance language' of bees are instinctive phenomena, whereas human forms of social organization and language are transmitted by cultural means from one generation to the next.

Cultural behaviour, in the rather limited sense of this definition, can be observed in most branches of animal activity. Some animals use, and may occasionally make, tools. As a tool-user man is in the company of such diverse creatures as the sea otter, the Egyptian vulture, the baboon and one of the Galapagos finches, while toolmaking of a rudimentary kind has been observed among bower birds, captive orang utans, and both wild and captive chimpanzees. It must be emphasized that 'culture' (in the form of tool-making) had appeared by the Australopithecus level of hominid evolution and preceded the biological stage at which Homo took on the morphological characteristics and brain size of modern man. The difference between human and animal tool-making is one of degree. Human tool-making activity is characterized by greater complexity, greater forethought, and above all by greater commitment. As Bartholomew and Birdsell (1953:483) have pointed out, 'man is the only mammal which is continuously dependent on tools for survival'.

Many animal species have created societies, and it can be argued that social organization among animals serves much the same adaptive purpose as it does among human communities (Kummer 1971). Even the so-called 'higher feelings' are not unique to man, for certain animals seem to have both emotional attitudes (Tax and Callender 1960:266) and aesthetic values (Dobzhansky 1962:215).

My colleagues in cognitive psychology and anthropology would argue that the possession of language is what sets man apart from the rest of the animal kingdom, not merely because human language is more complex and effective than any animal system of communication but because of the part it plays in the formation of the *constructs* and *construct systems* which characterize human thought processes (Leach, this volume; Shotter 1970, 1971). This is true as far as it goes; no non-human system shows a comparable capacity for symbolization and abstract thought, and we may here be dealing with a difference of kind rather than of degree (White 1949: Ch. 2. Hockett 1960). The fact remains, however, that both the biological capacity for speech and the psycho-linguistic qualities of Homo sapiens are the product of a long and continuous evolution – which brings us, unhelpfully, back to the central problem of where (if at all) can the line be drawn between non-human and human behaviour?

Cultural behaviour, of animals and humans alike, evolves with time, and ethologists have been able to study the processes of innovation and social transmission among several species of animals.

In the colony of macaques at the Japanese Monkey Centre, alterations in feeding habits came about as a result of what can only be called acculturation or diffusion (Imanishi 1957; Miyadi 1959). The habit of eating wrapped sweets was first taken up by juveniles (against their parents' wishes), and eventually passed to mothers who in turn transmitted it to dominant males, from whom it spread to the other males in the community. From innovation to acceptance, the process of adoption took three years. In another band, the habit of wheat-eating was introduced by a dominant male and was rapidly transmitted to the females and juveniles.

Another innovation, this time more akin to an independent invention, was made by certain members of the tit (*Parus*) population of Britain, who discovered how to peck through the caps of milk bottles left on doorsteps. Data collected by Fisher and Hinde (1949) showed that the practice originated in several different places and was socially transmitted through the population within a few years.

Case studies of this kind illustrate the continuity between the cultural behaviour of man and that of his animal relatives. But continuity is not the same thing as identity, and some biologists prefer to think that human evolution has been transformed into something which is unique, and therefore different in kind from ordinary biological evolution.

The critical factor is culture. Huxley puts his finger on the difference when he observes that biological evolution depends mainly on the self-reproduction of matter, whereas psycho-social (i.e. cultural) evolution depends on the reproduction of mind. Redefining culture in these terms, he suggests that it 'consists of self-reproducing or reproducible products of the mental activities of a group of individuals living in a society', and concludes that 'the capacity for cumulative transmission of experience marked a critical point in the evolutionary process – the passage from a biological to a cultural mode of evolution' (Huxley 1955: 16-22).

If Huxley is right, there is no reason why organic evolution should provide a valid model for cultural change. This paper will argue that Huxley's conclusions are wrong, but will use his remarks as the basis for a discussion of some points of contact between biological and anthropological theory.

Biological models and the new archaeology

One of the preoccupations of the New Archaeology is with the laws of cultural change. As one convert from traditional archaeology has recently expressed it, 'Our ultimate goal in anthropology and archaeology is to formulate laws of cultural dynamics; to seek trends and causes of human behaviour; and . . . to make probabilistic predictions' (Martin 1971:5). This in fact is not a single goal: elucidation of the laws governing cultural change is a very different thing from understanding the causes of human behaviour, and it is noteworthy that most recent archaeological theorizing has been concerned with the former rather than the latter problem.

Several of these attempts to formulate laws of cultural dynamics employ concepts derived from mathematics and from systems theory (reviewed in Doran 1970). One such is the model provided by Clarke (1968), who sees culture as an information system and stresses its self-regulatory nature. Clarke suggests that a culture passes through a succession of distinct states, the sequence of which depends on the past history of the culture and on the influence of the environment (both cultural and physical) with which it interacts. Regulatory mechanisms, including feedback, strive to keep the system in one of a set of possible states of equilibrium. The capacity to remain stable when the environment fluctuates derives from the flexibility, in terms of potential responses, which is inherent within the culture. This is an equally good model for biological change, and could just as easily be expressed in the terminology of genetics. It also represents, in an unusually sophisticated form, the challenge and response view of history.

Realization that cultural change is – at least in part – the product of interaction between man and his environment has also led to an increasing concern with ecological factors, though too many archaeologists have fallen into the trap of environmental determinism summed up by the belief that 'changes in the ecological setting of any given system are the prime causative situation activating processes of culture change' (Binford 1964:440). This quotation is rather unfairly lifted from its context, and elsewhere in the article Binford takes pains to emphasize that man exists in a socio-cultural environment as well as an ecological one. It can, however, be objected that this neat, self-contained scheme virtually denies acculturation and diffusion as agents of change (see also the criticisms of Kushner 1971) and makes the additional assumption that all changes are in some way adaptive. Many cultural changes have no obvious adaptive value. Innovations in burial rites, pottery decoration, aesthetics and verse forms (to give just a few examples) are clearly not the outcome of ecological pressures. If they are adaptive at all, the adaptation takes place at a psychological and social level; as a social animal, man must accommodate to his psychological environment, the 'climate of opinion', as well as to his ecological environment.

More serious, however, is the way that any simple cause-and-effect model begs the question of what is responsible for the changes in the setting, and tends to ignore the complex, reciprocal interaction between man and his environment. Ecological stresses do indeed generate technological responses, but these innovations bring about changes in the ecological balance which in turn demand further technological action. The same processes can be recognized in psycho-social adaptation too. Feedback types of model take account of this by recognizing that man is a part of his own environment.

On the credit side, the ecological approach and the New

Archaeology have provided many valuable studies. One of these is particularly relevant to the theme of this paper, for it was designed to test a series of evolutionary assumptions by means of ecological and archaeological fieldwork in the Valley of Oaxaca, a key area for Mesoamerican prehistory (Flannery, Kirkby. Kirkby, Williams 1967). The initial hypothesis was that those areas of Mesoamerica in which the greatest variety of agricultural techniques could be assimilated were able to retain their nuclear status, while those in which only the older techniques could be applied gradually lost their influence and assumed a marginal role. The archaeological results supported this suggestion. The inhabitants of the Valley did in fact successively assimilate dry-farming, infield-outfield systems, floodwater farming, pot irrigation, canal irrigation and hillslope terracing. Each innovation allowed new ecological zones to be brought into cultivation and opened up new demographic and social possibilities, allowing the Valley states to maintain a permanently nuclear status.

The theoretical impetus for the Oaxaca project has its biological parallel. Compare, for example, the archaeologists' original hypothesis with this statement by a geneticist:

> Under these conditions [an environment offering various alternative possibilities] a population which contains several adaptive genotypes will be better off than a genetically uniform one, and natural selection will favour diversity, polymorphism, the presence of genotypes suited for different aspects (ecological niches) of the available environment. (Dobzhansky 1962:222)

Taxonomy in biology and and archaeology

Many of the taxonomic problems which bedevil archaeology today were anticipated several years ago in biology – in the 'new systematics' of the 1940s and, more recently, among the numerical taxonomists whose work has had a strong influence on schemes of archaeological classification (Clarke 1968: Ch. 12).

Biologists distinguish two trends in organic evolution: branching evolution (speciation) and upward evolution in the direction of ever more complex levels of organization (e.g. from single-cell to differentiated creatures). Upward evolution is not to be equated with specialization. Where specialization leads up an evolutionary blind alley, progressive evolution (such as the change from reptilian to mammalian forms of birth process and temperature control) is generalized and open-ended, allowing still further change to take place.

The same trends can be recognized in cultural evolution, and the biological models have their equivalents in archaeology and anthropology.

1. *'Progress of Humanity' schemes*

Darwinian evolution and stratigraphic palaeontology provided a scientific basis for what had long been a subject of philosophical speculation. The 19th century historical-developmental schemes of writers like Tylor, Spencer and Morgan, assumed a single, universal and unilinear progress from a stage of savagery to one of civilization – though the best of these schemes admitted that both organic and cultural evolution show instances of regression from complex to more simple levels of organization, and that simpler lineages might persist alongside more advanced ones. The criteria of human progress were usually taken to be technological improvement (as in the Three Age System and its derivatives; see Daniel 1943), more efficient means of subsistence, or increasingly complex levels of social organization.

Since Childe (1929:vi) introduced a spatial component with his definition of an archaeological culture as a 'complex of regularly associated traits' with a limited distribution in space and time, most schemes have been of the multilinear type. But the notion of stages of increasing technological and social complexity is still very much alive: in the works of Childe himself (1942:252), in the functional-developmental schemes of Julian Steward (1953, 1955, 1960), in the evolutionary schemes of L.A. White (1947, 1959b) and of Sahlins and Service (1960), in the sequential 'stages' proposed by Willey and Phillips (1962: Ch. 3) for American prehistory, in Braidwood's (1960) 'levels' of achievement, and in the official Marxist doctrine that human society passes through pre-clan, clan, and class stages.

2. *'Family Tree' schemes*

Cultures and organisms exhibit two simultaneous kinds of change. One kind of development, *anagenesis* (phyletic evolution or successional speciation) takes place when gradual change occurs in a single line of descent until the final product is so different from the original that it merits a separate species name. Once this has happened, the ancestral species is in effect extinct. The second type of change, *cladogenesis* (divergent speciation), occurs when a single line of descent splits up into separate local populations, which develop in their own ways until they are so unlike each other (and the ancestral stock) that each has become a separate species. Cladogenesis can only take place where there is some discontinuity, usually a separation into inbreeding groups which respond to different selective pressures in relative isolation.

At the taxonomic level, the concept of *series* was developed by Rouse and Cruxent (1963:23-6) for the study of pottery styles, but it can be extended to other categories of artifact or to whole cultures (compare the concept of tradition discussed by Willey and Phillips

1962:34-9). A series undergoes both change through time (anagenesis) and differentiation (cladogenesis) into regional variants which may themselves eventually become new series, just as biological races develop into species. In a given area, cultures or styles belonging to one series may replace those of another, in much the same way as better adapted plant or animal species replace less effective forms. The Rouse-Cruxent scheme allows for a series to be modified by the adoption of traits from another series (i.e. acculturation), and admits that parallel development may take place without any cultural diffusion (i.e. that similar challenges tend to evoke similar responses). This last phenomenon has good analogies in biological evolution, for example in those mammalian lineages like the whales and dolphins which have returned to the sea after a period of land life and, through a process of selection, have taken on many of the external characteristics of fishes.

Rouse and Cruxent conceived the notion of series as a taxonomic, purely descriptive scheme, and (like all seriational models) it does not in itself explain the causes and mechanism of development. The archaeologist is still left with the problem of identifying the stresses (within the culture-system or outside it) which provide the stimulus for change.

One of the most overt attempts to combine a family tree type of taxonomy with an evolutionary and adaptive model of culture change was provided by Alan Bryan (1965) in his study of the earliest American stone industries. Bryan believed that a 'basic', generalized, percussion-flaked assemblage, with leaf-shaped projectile points as the diagnostic artifacts, was innovated during the early part of the last glaciation and then, during the later Wisconsin, began to differentiate into two branches (the Fluted Point and Parallel-Flaked traditions) which themselves underwent both anagenesis and cladogenesis. These technological changes took place 'in response to opportunities to concentrate upon hunting certain species of large mammals in different but ecologically similar environmental regions' (Bryan 1965:11). In biological terms, different ecological-environmental opportunities brought selective pressures to bear, and this encouraged adaptive radiation. The extinction of these technologies came when the particular game species disappeared, that is when the technology was no longer adapted to the environment.

Some of Bryan's archaeological conclusions have not withstood the test of time, and it must be emphasized that not all pre-agricultural cultures depended on the hunting of large game. The ecological-evolutionary model can, however, easily be extended to include cultures with every type of subsistence base. What is important is that Bryan has provided the kind of model which is testable against new evidence and can form a basis for problem-orientated research.

Another concept which culture historians might profitably adopt from biology is that of *clines* (Mayr 1942:94-8). Biological populations adjust to gradations of climate and environment by making small adaptations. Among plants, for example, 'altitude races' are fairly common, while in certain mammals changes in blood composition take place to compensate for the lack of oxygen at great altitudes. Similarly, the size of warm blooded vertebrates tends to increase in colder situations as an adaptive measure to reduce heat loss. These changes can be measured quantitatively. For instance, the linear dimensions of puffins increase by over 1% for each degree of north latitude, so that birds from north Spitzbergen are nearly double the bulk of those from Brittany, at the southern end of the species range (Huxley 1963:52). This increase is gradual and continuous; the birds are therefore classified as a single species.

In a similar kind of way, adaptive modifications (in subsistence, technology and behaviour) occur when a single culture is distributed over a graduated range of ecological environments. Returning to the biological analogy, if only Breton and Spitzbergen puffins had been observed, there might have been a temptation to classify them as separate species. There is an obvious moral here for archaeologists and anthropologists faced with assessing the relationship between cultures on either side of an unstudied area.

In biology there are many examples of clinal characters which seem to change quite independently of environmental gradients and are presumably not adaptive in any ecological way. Non-adaptive gradation can be seen in cultural as well as genetically-determined traits, for example in the changes of vocabulary and syntax which arise whenever a single language is spoken over a wide area.

The fundamental problem in all taxonomic schemes is to decide where to draw the dividing lines. Since some races are always on the point of becoming species, there must always exist borderline, transitional cases. The taxonomist, whether dealing with cultural or biological phenomena, must accept that the dividing line between borderline specimens is inevitably an arbitrary one. This was spelled out by Mayr (1942:16) when he suggested that within a species a local population should be granted subspecies status only when 75% of the individuals (or of the available sample) are separable, on the basis of their diagnostic features, from specimens of the most similar subspecies. Clarke (1968:198) is thinking along the same lines when he defines a subtype of a 'specific' artifact type as 'a sub-population with a high-level of affinity, perhaps 60-90%, uniting the individuals within the whole'. This suggestion has not won universal acceptance, but the call for some kind of agreed criterion, however arbitrary, should be heeded. In practice each archaeologist and anthropologist has tended to go his own way and, since the nomenclature is often intended to indicate the degree of relationship between the named classes, the outcome has usually been confusion.

The processes of change

Taxonomy describes and arranges the products of evolution but is not itself concerned with explaining or interpreting the processes involved. To decide whether the analogy between cultural and biological evolution is a valid one, we must also examine the mechanics of change.

Innovation

Biological innovation occurs through genetic mutation, which is random and non-purposive. No matter how beneficial a mutation may be, it cannot be produced to order by the organism's own efforts. In human behaviour, innovation comes about through discovery and invention, with diffusion playing a secondary role as a transmitter of innovations from one segment of the population to another (see *Combination and hybridization,* below). Discovery has been defined as the recognition and appreciation of some existing phenomenon (e.g. the medicinal qualities of penicillin) whose value had not previously been obvious. The biological equivalent of this kind of culture change is not mutation but *adaptive radiation* (see below).

The true analogy is between mutation and invention. Genetic mutation can take place only through the modification of already existing material. Similarly, all inventions derive ultimately from the existing body of knowledge, and usually consist of minor alterations to already existing forms (e.g. the application of pneumatic tyres to cars and bicycles, or the gradual modification of Christian doctrine over nearly 2,000 years).

Herskovits (1945:151) defines invention as 'purposive discovery' (in contrast to random mutation), but does not say what he means by the word 'purposive'. This is something for philosophers to ponder. Anthropologists themselves are divided, the anti-purposive school believing that, once technology has reached a particular stage, certain inventions are virtually inevitable (White 1949:168, 210). Clarke, in his information-system model of culture, takes a still more extreme view, arguing that internal innovation derives from the chance re-networking of existing components (Clarke 1968:60, 89) and that much of what seems to be 'goal-seeking' behaviour is an inherent property of the system itself (ibid.:52).

Selection and adoption

Once the innovation has been made, the parallels between cultural and biological change are close. In biological evolution, mutations which render an organism better adapted to its environment give the possessor a reproductive advantage over his competitors. Differential fertility, favouring the new gene, causes it to become established, and it may eventually come to replace its allele in the gene pool of the population as a whole.

Most inventions and discoveries, like most genetic mutations, are either neutral or harmful in the conditions of the moment, conferring so little advantage that they are not adopted by society and do not become established in the culture pool. As in biological evolution, the advantageous innovation appears only in a few members of the population, though cultural selection will encourage its rapid spread. In some circumstances it may oust its less efficient competitor. Thus, pneumatic tyres appeared at first in only a few designs of bicycle but soon became established in the bicycle population as a whole and almost brought about the extinction of the less well adapted solid tyres.

Adaptive radiation

In biology, adaptive radiation takes place when innovations which confer selective advantage under one set of circumstances prove capable of modification to suit a variety of local conditions, thus allowing colonization of new habitats. It may happen that the new, improved form replaces existing but less efficiently adapted forms. In industrial terms, an invention or discovery turns out to have a wide variety of applications (e.g. the use of the wheel for transport, pottery-making, cutting of timber, and transmission of power through gears). Many technological improvements consist of finding new uses for existing principles, and the biological analogy is with adaptive radiation rather than mutation (Barnett 1942; White 1949:168-210).

Preadaptation

Closely linked with the idea of adaptive radiation is the concept of preadaptation. Mutation followed by natural selection may lead to modifications which have no adaptive value at the time, but which turn out to be essential for some quite unforeseen change in the future. An organism which has the necessary preconditions for a particular change is 'preadapted' to that change. For instance, the group of fishes which moved to the land and gave rise to all terrestrial vertebrates had the following preadaptations for land life: an internal skeleton which prevented them from collapsing once out of water, fins already adapted to locomotion on land, and a respiratory system which allowed them to take oxygen from the air.

Similarly, the early protohominids were preadapted for culture by their possession of a well developed brain, a hand suited to complex manipulation, and a palate which allowed the development of speech. There must also have been psychological preadaptations (e.g. sociability) not recognizable from skeletal evidence.

Preadaptation permits some kinds of change to take place, and conversely the lack of preadaptation makes certain changes impossible (advanced astronomy, for example, had to wait upon the development of optics).

Biological evolution does not, and cannot, plan ahead. The lung fish of the previous example were not consciously preadapting themselves for terrestrial life. They were in fact trying to preserve the status quo by remaining adapted to life in shallow pools which frequently dried up. In spite of its appearance of purpose, cultural evolution is as blind as biological evolution in that the eventual consequences of adaptations bestowing short term advantages cannot be foreseen. As Steward (1960:182) has pointed out, the makers of the agrarian revolution certainly did not realize that they were preadapting human culture for civilization – any more than the makers of the industrial-technological revolution could have anticipated the atomic bomb and the ecological debate of the 1970s.

Stabilization

Biological evolution does not proceed at an even rate. An initially rapid rate of change slows down once the innovations become established and a new equilibrium is achieved between the organism and its environment. After a period of rapid adaptive radiation, the potential of the innovation is exhausted: all industrial applications of the invention have been recognized, all feasible ecological niches have been colonized. Huxley (1955:6) has noted that every line of biological improvement seems to reach a limit and to be incapable of evolving further. The same kind of cycle can be observed in technological evolution (cf. Spaulding in Willey and Phillips 1962:15), and probably also in psycho-social evolution. Once the limit has been reached, further improvement can only come about when a cultural or biological order which has not fulfilled all its latent potential makes a breakthrough to a new, higher level of organization.

Breakthrough

In biological evolution major breakthroughs from one stabilized pattern to another (e.g. from Reptilia to birds and mammals) are always uncommon events, and usually involve an element of preadaptation. 'In the early stages, a new group, however successful it will eventually become, is few and feeble and shows no signs of the success it may eventually achieve. Its breakthrough is not an instantaneous matter, for it has to be implemented through a series of improvements which eventually become welded into the new stabilized organizations' (Huxley 1960:250).

In cultural evolution the breakthroughs are what Childe called 'revolutions' (neolithic revolution, urban revolution etc.), and they bring about the new levels of sociocultural integration which constitute the 'stages' of the Human Progess types of scheme discussed above. As comparison of these schemes demonstrates, all authorities agree that major cultural breakthroughs were few (though there is no unanimity about the exact number), while the archaeological evidence indicates that Childe's revolutions were in fact slow and gradual processes of cumulative improvement.

Extinction

Biological selection favours the better adapted lineages *within* a species, but at the same time it discriminates between entire species in a situation of competition. The losers either become extinct, or forfeit their positions of dominance. The same processes can be seen in cultural change. Entire cultures and sub-cultures either become extinct or are reduced to marginal status relative to the expanding, improved cultures. Within individual cultures, patterns of social or technological behaviour correspond with the lineages of the biological analogy: thus oil and electricity have largely come to replace steam as a source of industrial energy, and may themselves eventually be replaced by nuclear power, which at present is still at a sub-breakthrough stage. The older technology still persists, but is becoming increasingly marginal. It is a fact of both biological and cultural evolution that, once an improved form is established, the previous one, even when well adapted, cannot stand the competition and is replaced. In both kinds of evolution, the new dominant form may evolve in situ or may come in from outside.

Polymorphism and variability

Genetic polymorphism is a prerequisite for adaptation by an organism to a changing environment. Similarly, the truly progressive cultures are those which are not merely adapted, but which also remain adaptable. Diversity is necessary to preserve the ability to respond to situations which we cannot yet forsee, any more than bacteria could have forseen the introduction of antibiotics into their environment and the need to evolve resistant strains. The cultures and organisms which are at risk are those which have mortgaged their long-term future by over-specialization to achieve short-term advantage, and in doing so have lost their flexibility. In the terminology of industry, 'the more specific the product, the more vulnerable is the plant to technological obsolescence' (McCarthy 1971:441).

Palaeontology demonstrates that those orders which make major breakthroughs generally start low down on the branching system of their group, and are the ones in which specialization has gone least far. The fish which came onto land were not those best adapted for life in water, but those which had retained more generalized characteristics and had not specialized too much for efficiency in swimming. Similarly, a man as an organism is relatively unspecialized, or (more correctly) is specialized in his ability to adapt.

Genetic drift

This becomes an important factor when a small part of a larger population becomes geographically and reproductively isolated – for instance, when islands are cut off by rising sea levels, when small groups of colonists hive off and lose touch with the parent population, when individuals or small parties are driven off course and cannot regain their homeland. This isolation has both biological and cultural consequences, and the genetic model has already proved useful in the interpretation of archaeological data (e.g. Dunn 1970).

When the newly isolated population is small enough, the 'founder principle' begins to apply (Mayr 1942:237). The colonists will carry with them only a fraction of the total gene pool (or culture pool) of the parent stock. This in itself will lead to a reduction in genetic/cultural variability, but the reduction will be reinforced by inbreeding. Biologically, this causes a reduction in genetic variability by encouraging homozygosity, so that in a population originally carrying two alleles at a give locus one is likely to be accidentally eliminated (Mayr 1942:234-37). In cultural terms, the behaviour pattern of a small, isolated community receiving no innovations from outside will tend to become more homogenous, and is unlikely to include alternative ways of doing the same thing.

Combination and hybridization

In cultural evolution, internal change is accompanied by inter-cultural borrowings (diffusion, acculturation). It is sometimes claimed that the analogy between cultural and organic evolution breaks down at this point because biological species can rarely produce fertile hybrids, whereas each individual culture is capable of borrowing from (interbreeding with) any other.

There is another, and I believe more valid, way of looking at this problem. Biologically man is a single breeding species with various races and sub-races. Similarly, human culture is basically of one type (characterized by tool-use, language, elaborate social forms, etc. – and presumably by psychological traits as well), though there are many variants on this basic theme. The dividing lines should not be drawn between individual human cultures, but between human culture on the one hand and animal culture on the other. All men can interbreed; all varieties of human culture can borrow from each other.

In both processes, the exchange of material (genetic or cultural) allows innovations which have taken place in separate lines of descent to be brought together, so as to create new and viable units and to maintain variability within the population as a whole.

The relationship between cultural and biological change

As long ago as 1864, in a paper in the *Anthropological Review*, Alfred Russell Wallace maintained that 'Natural selection, in working towards the genesis of man, began to follow a new path and make psychical changes instead of physical changes'. The implication is that cultural evolution has largely replaced biological evolution as the principal force affecting the development of man, or, in Huxley's phraseology, that there has been a 'passage from a biological to a cultural mode of evolution'.

These opinions, although supported by several eminent scientists, overstate the case. Mere possession of culture did not bring biological change to an end (witness the skeletal changes in man since he became a cultural, tool-using animal at the Australopithecus stage), and recent centuries have seen such major biological events as the extinction of entire populations (e.g. the Fuegians, Tasmanians, and several American Indian tribes). Genetic mutation is as inevitable today as in the past, and continues to offer new material for selection.

However, the existence of culture has brought about some important modifications in the course of human development. The most obvious of these is that change is now much more rapid in the cultural than the biological field, so that cultural rather than genetic change has become the main adaptive mechanism by which man responds to, and attempts to overcome, the pressures exerted upon him by his environment. There is, however, one basic distinction between natural and artificial (cultural) selection. In the words of a physical anthropologist, 'Natural selection solely and always favours relative efficiency in reproduction. Artificial selection may, and usually does, favour other and conflicting goals (and here they are goals)' (Simpson in Hockett and Ascher 1964:151).

Where genetic modification tends to produce specialized adaptations (long legs for speed, fur for warmth), cultural modification tends to generate flexibility. Man can exist in a greater diversity of habitats than any other creature; he can fly faster and higher than birds, can live underwater like fish, and can kill more efficiently than any other predator. And he can do these things *at will*. Even the physical range of his senses has been increased by instrumentation, though this may not be accompanied by a corresponding improvement in the fineness of his cognitive discrimination.

Culture exerts its biological influence by altering the adaptive value of individual genes. Because of man's advanced technology, there is little advantage to be gained from specialized structural modifications which favour greater strength, speed, resistance to cold etc. – though there is still selective pressure in favour of educability and cultural competence, which are, at least in part, genetically determined. These cultural factors have enabled man to retain and profit from a fairly unspecialized skeleton, the shortcomings of which are made good by culture, itself the product of a highly specialized brain. It is ironical that, at a time when culture has enabled mankind as a whole to remain a non-specialist organism, the very complexity of this culture condemns individual members of the species to a life of increasing specialization in only a small range of the available activities. In advanced civilizations, the cultural specialization of the individual has come to replace the biological specialization of the species as a whole.

Although the human skeleton has hardly changed since the emergence of Homo sapiens, we lack equivalent information about man's genetic history. There is no reason to suppose that his genetic makeup has remained constant or that genetic selection has ceased to operate in ways not reflected in the phenotype. Genetic selection maintains equilibrium by modifying the organism to fit the environment. This kind of selection is still taking place in man, but to an increasing extent he is reaching an accommodation by manipulating the environment to suit his own needs.

Since the environment which exerts selective pressure on the human genotype is largely man-made, and is changed as a result of cultural activities, there is a feedback relationship between biological and socio-cultural evolution. The relationship between tool-use and skeletal change during the early stages of hominid evolution has been analysed by Washburn (1960) and by Bartholomew and Birdsell (1953). The present day socio-cultural factors which act on the genotype, rather than the phenotype, belong mainly to the following categories:

1. Total population size. As Dobzhansky (1962:299) puts it, 'Some of the most radical changes in human environments arise from there being more and more humans'.
2. The degree of inter-population mobility. See Harrison (1971).
3. Control and regulation of childbirth. By such measures as infanticide, birth control (Medawar 1960:72-87: Muller 1960), genetic engineering (Muller op. cit.), or by social attitudes and/ or tax structures which penalize (or encourage) large families.
4. Assortive mating. On the basis of such things as skin colour, race, religion, language, educational attainment, social class,

wealth, socially-conditioned preference for a particular type of body build or ideal beauty, etc. Other social factors (e.g. exogamy or endogamy, and the degrees of consanguinity permitted in marriage) also affect the mating pattern (see, for instance, Dobzhansky (1962:234) on the genetic effects of the Indian caste system, and Medawar (1960:57) on those of polygamous marriage).

5. Disease. Haldane (1949) has discussed the changes in the pattern of disease brought about by urban life and long-range mobility. Modern medicine has also played its part by allowing survival to reproductive age of individuals with genetic defects which would once have caused early death.
6. Alteration of mutation rate, through exposure to drugs or radiation.

Genetic changes have brought about increased ability for adaptation by cultural means, and this cultural adaptation has changed environmental conditions in such a way that new selective pressures have arisen, leading to further genetic changes in the population.

Biological and cultural change serve the same end (to maintain the organism in equilibrium with its environment), and the fact that change is a continuing process merely serves to emphasize that a completely stable balance is never achieved. Not only are biological and socio-cultural adaptations imperfect in themselves, but the environment is also in a state of continuous change. Some alterations in the environment are induced by the organism itself, but others are independent of it and – like 'acts of God' in insurance terminology – are outside its control altogether. Instead of a once-and-for-all adaptation, we get a continuous trial-and-error oscillation around an unattainable and continuously shifting state of equilibrium.

In both biological and cultural change, innovations which upset the balance still further are selected against, and those which offer short-term advantages (i.e. which bring the system closer to equilibrium in the conditions of the moment) are adopted and transmitted. Along with the 'favourable' innovations are transmitted many neutral ones which have no adaptive value at the time, although they may include some which decide the fate of the species in the changed conditions of the future.

The one basic difference lies in the nature of this transmission. Biological evolution is Darwinian; cultural evolution is, to some extent, Lamarckian in that it allows acquired characteristics to be transmitted to future generations. Unlike all other organs, the brain can accept instruction directly from the environment, and its acquired characteristics (in the form of accumulated experience) are passed on by cultural rather than biological means, by education instead of copulation.

This cultural mode of transmission permits a very rapid rate of change, since devices like language, writing and radio enable an individual to influence many people with whom he has no genetic contact. (Even with artificial insemination, 2,000 offspring is regarded as a good effort by a bull, but the same figure represents a pretty small edition of a book). Through culture, the behaviour of a single individual may have a disproportionate effect on the course of psycho-social evolution but, since each person is a reflection of the culture within which he grew up, there is no problem about fitting 'great men' into a processual view of history.

In spite of the difference in the mode of transmission, cultural and biological evolution are so inextricably linked in a reciprocal, feedback relationship that they must be considered parts of a single system. This is especially true today, when culture and technology have given man the power to control his future genetic evolution, and when genetic engineering on a massive scale is seriously advocated by some biologists (Muller 1960). Cultural evolution has added an extra dimension to biological evolution, but has by no means replaced it.

Conclusions

As Martin pointed out, the New Archaeologists expect their models to generate 'probabilistic predictions' of a kind which can be tested (Martin 1971:5). The truth (or otherwise) of any biological prediction will not be apparent in the prophet's own lifetime, but the biological model of culture change does indicate some of the potentialities and dangers of present trends.

The optimists can argue that civilization is not dead yet, and that the complexity of present day culture offers a rich basis for further innovation and change. As Julian Steward (1960:180) has observed, advanced civilizations provide a greater range of adaptive possibilities than do less complex societies.

This is true enough in the short run, but what of the long-term prospects? On the debit side, the rapid spread of the technological-industrial pattern of civilization is eroding the world's cultural variety and at the same time making the environment ever more homogenous. Both kinds of over-specialization lead to an unsafe degree of dependence. For flexibility in the face of future, and unforeseeable, pressures, a diversified environment is as important as a diversified culture. The Irish and Scottish potato famines of the last century show what happens when the agricultural environment is dominated by a single food crop, and some ecologists and plant-breeders have now begun to appreciate the dangers of the Green Revolution which is replacing numerous local races of wheat, rice and potato by a few imported varieties (Chedd 1970; Ugent 1970). In the same way, the virtual collapse of the urban, 'civilized' way of life during an electricity blackout illustrates the dangers of over-reliance on one or two sources of energy.

In the biological record, the breakthroughs to new levels of organization were not made by the highly specialized, temporarily dominant, orders..If, as the prophets of doom predict, the 'advanced' civilizations are destroyed by their own technologies, or when our dominant technological-industrial culture peacefully reaches its evolutionary limit, the next breakthrough will have to come from below. The more 'primitive' cultures of today may turn out to be the progressive cultures of tomorrow.

Acknowledgment

Peter Ucko and John Shotter suggested many improvements to the original version of this paper, but neither of them should be held responsible for its present form.

REFERENCES

Barnett, H.G. (1942) Invention and cultural change. *American Anthropologist* **44**, 14-30.

Bartholomew, G.A. and Birdsell, J.B. (1953) Ecology and the protohominids. *American Anthropologist* **55**, 481-98.

Binford, L.R. (1964) A consideration of archaeological research design. *American Antiquity* **29**, 425-41.

Braidwood, R.J. (1960) Levels in prehistory: a model for the consideration of the evidence. *In* Tax, S. (1960), 143-51.

Bryan, A.L. (1965) Paleo-American prehistory. *Occasional Paper No. 16, Idaho State University Museum.*

Chedd, G. (1970) Hidden perils of the green revolution. *New Scientist* **48** (724), 171-3.

Childe, V.G. (1929) *The Danube in Prehistory.* Oxford, Clarendon Press.

Childe, V.G. (1942) *What Happened in History.* Harmondsworth, Middlesex, Penguin.

Clarke, D.L. (1968) *Analytical Archaeology.* London, Methuen.

Daniel, G.E. (1943) *The Three Ages: an Essay in Archaeological Method.* Cambridge University Press.

Dobzhansky, T. (1962) *Mankind Evolving: The Evolution of the Human Species.* New Haven, Yale University Press.

Doran, J. (1970) Systems theory, computer simulations and archaeology. *World Archaeology* **I** (3), 289-98.

Dunn, F.L. (1970) Cultural evolution in the late Pleistocene and Holocene of southeast Asia. *American Anthropologist* 72, 1041-54.

Fisher, J. and Hinde, R.A. (1949) The opening of milk bottles by birds. *British Birds* **42**, 347-57.

Flannery, K.V., Kirkby, A.T.V., Kirkby, M.J. and Williams, A.W. (1967) Farming systems and political growth in ancient Oaxaca. *Science* **158** (3800), 445-54.

Haldane, J.B.S. (1949) Disease and evolution. *La Ricerca Scientifica* 19 (Suppl.), 68-76.

Harrison, G.A. (1971) Human variation and its social causes and consequences.

Proceedings of the Royal Anthropological Institute for 1970, 5-13.
Herskovits, M.J. (1945) The processes of cultural change. *In* Linton, R. (ed.) *The Science of Man in the World Crisis*, 143-70. New York, Columbia University Press.
Hockett, C.F. (1960) The origin of speech. *Scientific American* 203 (3), 88-96.
Hockett, C.F. and Ascher, R. (1964) The human revolution. *Current Anthropology* 5 (3), 135-68.
Huxley, J.S. (1955) Evolution, cultural and biological. *In* Thomas, W.L. (ed.) *Yearbook of Anthropology, 1955* 3-25. New York, Wenner-Gren Foundation for Anthropological Research.
Huxley, J.S. (1960) The evolutionary vision. *In* Tax and Callender (eds.) (1960), 249-61.
Huxley, J.S. (1963) *Evolution in Action.* Harmondsworth, Middlesex, Penguin.
Imanishi, K. (1957) Identification: a process of enculturation in the subhuman society of Macaca fuscata. *Primates* 1, 1-29.
Kroeber, A.L. and Kluckhohn, C. (1952) Culture, a critical review of concepts and definitions. *Papers of the Peabody Museum of American Archaeology and Ethnology* 47 (1).
Kummer, H. (1971) *Primate Societies: Group Techniques of Ecological Adaptation.* Chicago, Aldine-Atherton.
Kushner, G. (1970) A consideration of some processual designs for archaeology as anthropology. *American Antiquity* 35, 125-32.
Martin, P.S. (1971) The revolution in archaeology. *American Antiquity* 36, 1-8.
Mayr, E. (1942) *Systematics and the Origin of Species.* New York, Columbia University Press.
McCarthy, Callum (1971) Universities and the future. *New Scientist and Science Journal* 50 (752), 440-2.
Medawar, P.B. (1960) *The Future of Man.* London, Methuen.
Miyadi, D. (1959) On some new habits and their propagation in Japanese monkey groups. *Proceedings, 15th International Congress of Zoologists*, 857-60. London.
Muller, H.J. (1960) The guidance of human evolution. *In* Tax, S. (ed.) (1960), 423-62.
Rouse, I. and Cruxent, J.M. (1963) *Venezuelan Archaeology.* New Haven, Yale University Press.
Sahlins, M.D. and Service, E.R. (1960) *Evolution and Culture.* Ann Arbor, University of Michigan Press.
Shotter, J. (1970) Men, the man-makers: George Kelly and the psychology of personal constructs. *In* D. Bannister (ed.) *Perspectives in Personal Construct Theory*, 233-53. Academic Press, London and New York.
Shotter, J. (1971) Understanding 'understanding'. MS. Dept. of Psychology, Nottingham University, March 1971.
Steward, J.H. (1953) Evolution and process. *In* Kroeber, A.L. (ed.) *Anthropology Today*, 313-26. Chicago, University Press.
Steward, J.H. (1955) *Theory of Culture Change: The Methodology of Multilinear Evolution.* Urbana, University of Illinois Press.
Steward, J.H. (1960) Evolutionary principles and social types. *In* Tax, S. (ed.) (1960), 169-86.
Tax, S. (ed.) (1960) *The Evolution of Man:* vol. 2 of *Evolution after Darwin.* Chicago, University Press.
Tax, S. and Callender, C. (eds.) (1960) *Issues in Evolution:* vol. 3 of *Evolution after Darwin.* Chicago, University Press.
Washburn, S.L. (1960) Tools and human evolution. *Scientific American* 203, 63-75.
White, L.A. (1947) Evolutionary stages, progress and the evaluation of culture. *Southwestern Journal of Anthropology* 3, 165-92.

White, L.A. (1949) *The Science of Culture: a Study of Man and Civilization.* New York, Farrar, Straus and Co.

White, L.A. (1959a) The concept of culture. *American Anthropologist* **61**, 227-51.

White, L.A. (1959b) *The Evolution of Culture.* New York, McGraw Hill.

Willey, G.R. and Phillips, P. (1962) *Method and Theory in American Archaeology.* University of Chicago Press, Phoenix Books.

Ugent, D. (1970) The potato. *Science* **170** (3963), 1161-6.

PHILIP BURNHAM

The explanatory value of the concept of adaptation in studies of culture change

The purpose of this short paper is to provoke discussion on the meaning and utility of the concept of 'adaptation' as it is employed in analyses of culture change. It will be argued that this concept is frequently used in untenable analogies with biological evolution that result in 'models' of culture change of dubious relevance to cultural phenomena. Recently, some anthropologists have sought to circumvent this problem by employing the adaptation concept in combination with general systems theory approaches. Such models of culture change, it is claimed, avoid many of the pitfalls of earlier functionalist explanations. The latter part of this paper is devoted to assessing the analytic utility of general systems approaches for studies of culture change.

In some anthropological circles, the view that culture is man's primary means of adapting to changing environmental and social circumstances is such an article of faith that there is seldom serious consideration of what is actually meant by the phrase 'cultural adaptation'. Quite commonly, Eskimo culture is cited as an apt, if somewhat extreme, example of how man's cultural capacity allows him to adapt to even the harshest circumstances. At such a gross level of analysis, such statements are unquestionably true, for it is apparent that culture does make the difference between life and death for the Eskimo as it most probably does for every other human living today.

It is only at a finer level of analysis that difficulties arise in discussing culture as man's adaptive dimension. Is all of culture positively adaptive or are there maladaptive traits? How would one assess and measure the adaptive advantages and disadvantages of a particular trait in a particular culture? What constitutes a single 'trait'? What is a culture? These are the types of questions that have arisen in the study of cultural adaptation, and their basis in a functionalist and evolutionary analogy between culture and biological organisms or species is not hard to recognize. Carneiro (1968:551-553) writes, for example:

> Culture, a uniquely human attribute, is something which man interposes between himself and his environment in order to ensure his security and survival. As such culture is adaptive . . . An evolutionary advance characteristically begins with an adaptive solution to an ecological problem and is followed by a series of readjustments whereby cultural elements successively further removed from the source of change are affected by the change and accommodate themselves to it . . . During the course of these kinds of readjustments within a culture, new traits appear which are alternative to, and therefore competitive with, existing ones. In this competition traits are subjected to the cultural equivalent of natural selection: the better adapted traits survive and expand, and the less fit decline and disappear.

Such functional explanations of culture change, as Carneiro notes (1968:554), have been popular at least since the time of Tylor (1958:1:62), yet to my knowledge, no one has yet managed to specify processes operative in culture that are realistic 'equivalent(s) of natural selection' or, for that matter, equivalents to any of the other key components of the biological evolutionary process. For the concept of cultural adaptation to stand in anything more than a metaphorical relation to biological adaptation, phenomena like natural selection, the genetic transmission of traits, and mutation must be shown to have operational parallels in culture process.

Reviewing the biological concept for a moment, it should be remembered that adaptation by animal and plant species to environmental variables is the result of greater numbers of offspring being born to those individuals among a breeding population who have the more favourable (adaptive) genetic makeup. This, of course, is the mechanism by which information about environmental potential is 'read' by a species. The more advantageous genes, in terms of the present environment, are thus transmitted in greater frequency to the next generation, changing the genetic composition of the population to a more adaptive mix. The ability of a population to adapt to an environment is, however, limited by the variety of genetic material available in the gene pool, and this in turn is eventually determined by the random phenomenon of mutation. There is no validity, therefore, in the abstract notion of maximum adaptation to an environment. There is only the relative notion of maximizing adaptation to a particular environment given the genetic material currently at hand. And it is even something of a moot point as to whether a population can normally be expected to be maximally adapted to its environment at any particular time, given the time lag factor in reproducing new generations and the fact of continual environmental change. In other words, even in biology it is dangerous to define maximum adaptation in terms of the present observed state of a particular population.

Despite such problems of method, biologists have clearly been successful in specifying the innately circular 'feedback' process by which natural organisms respond adaptively to environmental variables. Anthropologists have not yet been so fortunate. Since cultural traits are learned and not genetically transmitted, differential reproductive rates do not necessarily act as selective forces in the modification of culture. For cultural adaptation to be shown to be operative, a cultural substitute for natural selection must be isolated. Implicitly or explicitly, most discussion of cultural adaptation has centred around this problem, yet the solutions proposed so far do not seem adequate.

Many anthropologists have argued that man adapts culturally primarily by means of decision-making, in which the relevant environmental variables impinging on a particular cultural behaviour are recognized, weighed, and the most adaptive course chosen. Thus, for example, Yehudi Cohen (1968:47) describes the adaptive process as cumulative decision-making by a social group that increases the group's ability to make use of potential energy in the habitat. Cohen (1968:47) hedges, however, in describing the actual decision-making process when he states that adaptive decisions may be 'conscious or unconscious, deliberate or inadvertent'. The problem remains, therefore, of how adaptive decisions can be cumulative or directional in an evolutionary sense if they are made blindly, without reference to important environmental factors. The answer to this paradox seems to be that many anthropologists trust implicitly in human 'rationality' as assurance that decisions will be basically adaptive for the group involved.

At least since the time of Max Weber, however, it has been apparent that the concept of rationality is of questionable analytic significance. While it may be possible to set up *formal* criteria of rationality, as in Weber's discussion of bureaucracy, the concept is actually of little use in cross-cultural studies. The rationality of decisions must be judged by comparison to the values and knowledge of the particular society in question and not ethnocentrically against Western science or values.

If men make decisions on the basis of culturally defined scales of values which have no necessary relation to the adaptive significance of the trait from a biological point of view, one is thrown back on the dilemma of explaining how 'an adaptive solution to an ecological problem' (Carneiro 1968:553) is regularly reached. Elaborate game theory models or other mini-max analyses do nothing to answer this question either, since they merely serve to measure the success of particular behaviours, not to show how such decisions were arrived at. To use a word like 'solution', as Service notes (1971:25), is to employ, at best, a misleading figure of speech, and it reveals a continuing confidence in the 'rational' basis of the adaptive process.

This interest in rationality as an explanation of the adaptive process has culminated in repeated attempts to show the adaptive value of even the most 'irrational' cultural behaviour. The favourite subject for such studies has been ritual behaviour, which often has a tendency to appear 'irrational' to Western eyes. This might be termed the 'sacred cow syndrome' after the misguided but frequently-quoted article by Marvin Harris (1965) which attempts to demonstrate the adaptive advantages of Hindu behaviour regarding the sacred cow. (But see also Moore 1957, Rappaport 1968, or Piddocke 1969 for similar attempts.) The guidelines for the writing of such an article are to choose a behaviour which seems totally 'irrational' and then to search diligently for some unforeseen positive 'adaptive' function of the activity. Once found, the argument is advanced that the positive contributions of the behavioural trait to the society's survival exceed any negative effects it might 'naively' have been thought to possess and, hey presto, the dogma of culture's adaptive function is preserved. Such articles are immune to direct attack, since should some infidel attempt to tilt the balance against the trait in question, its defenders will search even more diligently for adaptive functions to compensate. Finally, if all else fails, it can be claimed that the trait in question must, at some earlier date, have had a positive function, but that the situation has been altered by modern social change. Here we come up against a direct parallel with the traditional and often-refuted functionalist technique of inventing 'needs' so that any trait can be shown to be functional or, at minimum, a survival of a former functional state. Such circularity is certainly no more acceptable when applied to the concept of adaptation.

Recently, however, in a more penetrating analysis of the adaptation concept, Alexander Alland (1970) has argued for a definition of cultural adaptation based on differential natality and mortality rates, i.e. a direct derivation from the biological concept of the coefficient of selection. Alland (1970:44) feels that the non-somatic transmission of culture traits does not rule out application of evolutionary concepts to human culture, since, as he argues, all that is required for evolution to be operative is the existence of mechanisms of variation, mechanisms of continuity, and environmental selection. It doesn't matter, he asserts (1970:46), that the mechanisms of variation and continuity are non-biological if they operate in biological systems. While the last sentence borders on doubletalk, we should not let it distract us from Alland's main idea that culture traits each have coefficients of selection which determine their adaptiveness and rate of retention or loss. This approach leads to great emphasis on the field of medical anthropology and a search for the cause-effect relations between cultural practices and disease transmission or other medical phenomena.

The problem with Alland's attempt to explicate the process of cultural adaptation is that it is more an explanation of demographic change than one of culture change. As Alland himself states (1970:47),

> In sum, it is the subject matter as well as the process of adaptation, and not the mechanisms of change, which should be seen as the same for somatic and cultural evolution. If one considers human populations as the subject matter for research rather than 'cultures', then these units may be treated equally well as behavioural or physical entities.

If we conceive, as Alland does, of each cultural trait having a coefficient of selection that determines cultural change, it seems highly probable that most traits will be found to have a coefficient of about zero (assuming that we have the methodology to determine such coefficients of selection in the first place). Thus, while food preparation techniques may have great relevance to mortality rates, pottery styles probably have none. Alland's concept of adaptation produces a theory of culture change which can only attempt to explain certain aspects of culture, the rest being relegated to the status of epiphenomena. In this respect, Alland's theory is reminiscent of Julian Steward's concept of the 'culture core' (1955:30), in which the presence of cultural features not closely related to subsistence and economy can only be explained by diffusion. Change in those cultural traits with zero coefficients of selection becomes unimportant to Alland's theory simply because the theory is inadequate to explain it. Indeed, if the concept of cultural evolution has any validity at all, it would seem to indicate that progressively smaller proportions of human behaviour have significant bearing on human natality or mortality.

In spite of these critiques of Alland's approach, I believe that it is one of the most serious attempts so far to devise a workable theory of cultural adaptation. The majority of the anthropologists employing the concept today ignore altogether their responsibility to isolate the 'adaptive mechanism' operative in cultural behaviour, and their use of the concept is consequently meaningless for analytical purposes. Some anthropologists, on the other hand, recognize the dilemma yet abdicate the responsibility. Elman Service, in his new book *Cultural Evolutionism: Theory in Practice* (1971:25, 26), does just this when he says:

> . . . down with prime-movers . . . the question of what is prime-mover in any case of specific evolutionary change is an empirical question, and the answer is not to be found in advance of research by commitment to a specific theory of prime-movers. Similarly, whether the adaptive solutions were produced by intellectual effort and choice from among alternatives, or whether they were functional adjustments unintended by anyone in the society is also a factual question, though usually impossible to answer for lack of evidence.

In short, while Service is not clear what produces adaptive changes in culture, he accepts the reality of the adaptive process as an article of faith. He has simply returned to the idea of 'specific' versus 'general' evolution advanced in Sahlins' and Service's *Evolution and Culture*

(1960). They believe that they can discern evolutionary trends in the general record of human culture, but when they look at specific instances, the trends dissolve into distressingly unconnected cases. Therefore, at the same time as they assert that evolution and adaptation are operative, we are told that we can't expect the data to bear out this contention. Such an approach hardly seems fruitful to those of us still interested in attempting to explain observed phenomena whether or not they fit into predetermined theoretical constructs.

Systems models and the cultural adaptation concept

In the last ten to fifteen years, models of culture change based on cybernetic or general systems theory concepts have come into vogue which make frequent use of the concept of adaptation. A great deal of jargon has been introduced into anthropology as a result, including terms like 'positive' and 'negative feedback', 'morphostasis', 'morphogenesis', and many others. We must not get bogged down in this terminology. The question of relevance to this paper is whether cybernetic or general systems theory models of culture change overcome the major problems that were not adequately solved by earlier functional explanations of change. It is all too easy to mask fundamental unsolved problems simply by rephrasing an analysis in unfamiliar terminology.

Many discussions of systems theory in anthropology begin with an attack on 'traditional functionalist theory', apparently to dissociate what is to follow from earlier critiques of functionalism. The reason for this is clear; 'general systems' are normally considered to have 'homeostatic' or 'goal-seeking' properties, and these concepts are just as teleological as traditional functionalist theory. The use of the term 'feedback' in itself does not explain away such problems of circularity. On the other hand, teleology in itself is not necessarily a negative quality in a model. As indicated previously, in the explanation of biological evolution, circularity is perfectly acceptable because the processes of natural selection and genetic transmission of traits have been shown to operate in such a manner. Many general systems theorists feel that they have avoided unacceptable teleology in explaining culture change if they follow the suggestions of Hempel (1959) and others and attempt to specify empirical ranges of tolerance limits within which cultural stability is maintained. (See for example, Rappaport 1968, Collins 1965, or Hill 1971.) Such an approach, of course, is equally possible in traditional functional analyses, yet it scarcely answers the problem of how man accurately recognizes such limits in order to adapt to them. In short, we have returned to the 'rationality' problem which is no better solved by sophisticated cybernetic analyses than it was by earlier functional studies. Man may have some fancy thermostat-like device for information control and decision-making which regulates culture change, but we have yet to discover it. As Hill blithely notes (1971:408),

> The most difficult variables to measure are those involving information (including communication), but it was agreed that in most cases we do not have to measure these; we can simply assume that responses to extra-systemic inputs require the transmission of information as well as decision-making process within the system.

In fact, upon careful examination, the concept of homeostasis and the derived ideas of tolerance ranges in cultural systems are easily recognized for what they are – definitional parts of a deductive model of culture. Thus, in terms of the strict rules recently proposed by Hill (1971:407) and his colleagues, a set of variables should not be considered a system unless their 'articulation . . . be regulated (maintained in steady-state) by homeostatic processes'. Once such axioms have been accepted, change can only be regarded as resulting from the influence of variables external to the system (Hill 1971:407). Certain authors are also at pains to distinguish between 'alterations in state' and 'systemic change' (Hill 1971:406), concepts which rest purely on the definitional qualities of idealized homeostatic systems. Arguments flare among systems theorists on points such as these but seldom on the subject of the behavioural correlates of the definitional components of the systems model. (Walter Buckley (1967:57) provides a refreshing change in this regard when he notes the interesting but imperfect analogy between trial-and-error learning and nutural selection.) And such an analytical approach becomes even more of a science fiction story in the hands of archaeologists whose cantankerous human subjects are safely dead (e.g. Hill 1971 or Clarke 1968).

One of the most telling critiques of homeostatic systems analyses has been written by one of the main sociological systems theorists, and I will quote him at length here (Buckley 1967:30, 31).

> In an organismic system we do have a relatively fixed structure that is normal for the species at a given time. This normal biological structure provides us with quite definite criteria against which to assess deviant or malfunctional structures and processes. As such tendencies toward deviance from the normal structure arise (due primarily to external causes such as disease, extremes of weather, and so forth), automatic homeostatic mechanisms of 'control' come into play to counteract them and conserve the normal structure. When these fail the organism disintegrates (dies) and fuses into the environment.
>
> A social system, however, does not have any such fixed, normal structure which, if changed beyond narrow limits, leads necessarily to the system's 'death'. In contrast to an organismic system, social systems are characterized primarily by their propensity to *change their structure*

> [author's emphasis] during their culturally continuous lifetime . . . Although there are certainly limits within which the features of a social system structure may vary and still remain compatible enough for system maintenance, we can argue that these limits, for a social system, may be relatively broad. And it is within these limits that most sociologically interesting questions are posed.

In short, it seems that the homeostatic assumption is still a throwback to the days of the organic analogy, and one must severely question whether models built on this assumption can hope to mimic cultural processes very convincingly. It is this lack of empirical behavioural correlates which has plagued the cultural adaptation concept from the start and which seems even more devastating to the successful application of this model of culture change than the methodological problem of measuring 'hopelessly broad' tolerance limits so frequently alluded to by the systems theorists themselves (Clarke 1968:55, but see also Hill 1971:407, 408, Rappaport 1968:230 or Buckley 1967:31). Once we agree to ignore observed data in testing the basic assumptions of our models in anthropology, or use these data selectively, we have entered the realm, as I have said, of science fiction.

A postscript

The argument presented in this paper thus far stands as written prior to the Sheffield conference. When I had an opportunity to read the preliminary drafts of the other papers before the conference, I was pleased to find that Wood and Matson had co-authored a paper arguing along many of the same lines as I. Particularly, we had both expressed similar critiques of the homeostatic systems model, as discussed by Hill (1971) and others, and had equated its basic assumptions with those of earlier functionalist approaches in anthropology. During the discussions at the Sheffield conference, this critique seemed to find quite general support among the participants, despite the dissenting view expressed by Bray in his paper.

The key problem that must be solved if we wish to develop a theory of sociocultural adaptation remains the one isolated in the body of this paper; we need realistic sociocultural analogues for the biological processes of natural selection and genetic transmission of traits. Wood and Matson are correct, in my opinion, to emphasize Walter Buckley's treatment of these problems in his book *Sociology and Modern Systems Theory*, although I am not as sanguine as they regarding the applicability of this model to archaeological studies of change.

The whole of Buckley's book can be seen as an explicit discussion of the adaptation concept in the light of various cybernetic and sociological theories. As Buckley (1967:66) persuasively argues, 'the new adaptive level we refer to as sociocultural . . . warrants scientific study in terms as distinct from a purely biological system as the analytical terms of the latter are from physical systems'. Significantly, Buckey's 'complex adaptive system model' moves away from homeostatic assumptions, and it also incorporates the important notion that sociocultural organization can be thought of as 'an organization of meanings' (1967:92-94). Such meanings arise in the process of social interaction, and Buckley emphasizes the work of symbolic interactionists such as G.H. Mead and exchange theorists such as Homans and Blau as having implications for his model.

The upshot of Buckley's model-building is to produce an ideal type of 'a sociocultural system with high adaptive potential' (1967:206), but to what extent actual societies exhibit or capitalise on such high adaptive potential remains problematic. The fact that, in Buckley's model, much of the organization of the system is internally generated, is another way of indicating that humans adjust their behaviour as much to psychological and cultural motivations as to environmental constraints. And even though these model components may be seen to be related in some complex and unspecified way, the outcomes of the interactions of these variables cannot be assumed to be environmentally adaptive or necessarily to perpetuate the system. As such, the adaptiveness of any sociocultural system cannot be asserted from first principles. It becomes a matter for empirical study, with particular attention being directed to the ability of the system in question to select and perpetuate successful behavioural strategies (Buckley 1967:206, 207).

The model of sociocultural adaptation that Buckley proposes, as he himself notes in his conclusion (1967:207), 'is complex, and it is not so comforting as an equilibrium or functionalist model'. Furthermore, many of the basic theoretical issues relating to the processes of sociocultural adaptation have not been solved. However, as a social anthropologist, I find Buckley's work impressive in its theoretical scope and its frequent attention to possible behavioural correlates of the various components of his model. His honest discussion of the daunting complexities surrounding the concept of sociocultural adaptation should serve as clear warning to anthropologists and prehistorians who might otherwise be seduced into simplistic applications of this concept whose empirical behavioural referents have yet to be adequately specified.

REFERENCES

Alland, A. (1970) *Adaptation in Cultural Evolution.* New York, Columbia University Press.

Buckley, W. (1967) *Sociology and Modern Systems Theory.* Englewood Cliffs, N.J., Prentice-Hall.

Carneiro, R. (1968) Cultural adaptation. *In* Sells, D. (ed.) *International Encyclopaedia of the Social Sciences* 3, 551-4.

Clarke, D. (1968) *Analytical Archaeology*. London, Methuen.

Cohen, Y. (1968) Culture as adaptation. *In* Cohen, Y. (ed.) *Man in Adaptation: The Cultural Present*. Chicago, Aldine.

Collins, P. (1965) Functional analysis in the Symposium Man, Culture, and Animals. *In* Leeds, A. and Vayda, A. (eds.) *Man, Culture, and Animals*. Washington, D.D., American Association for the Advancement of Science 78.

Harris, M. (1965) The myth of the sacred cow. *In* Leeds, A. and Vayda, A. (eds.) *Man, Culture, and Animals*. Washington, D.C., American Association for the Advancement of Science 78.

Hempel, C. (1959) The logic of functional analysis. *In* Gross, L. (ed.) *Symposium on Sociological Theory*. Evanston, Illinois, Row, Peterson.

Hill, J. (1971) Report on a seminar on the explanation of prehistoric organization change. *Current Anthropology* 12 (3), 406-8.

Moore, O.K. (1957) Divination – a new perspective. *American Anthropologist* 59, 64-74.

Piddocke, S. (1969) The potlatch system of the southern Kwakiutl. *In* Vayda, A. (ed.) *Environment and Cultural Behavior*. Garden City, N.Y., Natural History Press.

Rappaport, R. (1968) *Pigs for the Ancestors*. New Haven, Yale University Press.

Sahlins, M. and Service, E. (1960) *Evolution and Culture*. Ann Arbor, University of Michigan Press.

Service, E. (1971) *Cultural Evolutionism: Theory in Practice*. New York, Holt, Rinehart and Winston.

Steward, J. (1955) *Theory of Culture Change*. Urbana, University of Illinois.

Tylor, E.B. (1958) (1871) *Primitive Culture*. Gloucester, Massachusetts, Smith.

Section 2: Data processing and the measurement of variation

D.H. FRENCH

Theoretical and methodological aspects of data recovery

> Archaeologists must learn to ask the kinds of questions with which their data are equipped to deal. (Trigger 1971:332)

Sophistication of data-recovery techniques may lead to the possibility of 'high-grade' information: such a development would meet the demand for the adoption of sophisticated models and the positioning of the kinds of questions relevant to these models. There is, therefore, in developing archaeological techniques, the possibility of developing the problems that can be answered.

Any change in the questions asked must be met by a corresponding change in the standard of data-recovery with emphasis placed on techniques which are both definable and repeatable. Definitions of definable and repeatable standards might lead to the emergence of significant correlations and the possibility of testing them.

I am concerned here with excavation (more properly with excavation in the Near East) and with the problem of data-recovery in the field (i.e. from excavations) and I shall be discussing the implications of a single theme in two of its aspects: firstly, methodological theory and its application on excavations; secondly and conversely, the developments of recovery techniques and their impact on theorizing. What I am questioning is not the manipulation of data but the preparatory stages in their collection.

The principle underlying much of our work can be simply stated: that it is essential and (?) obligatory to define the problems before developing or choosing the means used to collect the data necessary to examine these problems and the hypotheses explicit in them. In other words, the questions asked dictate the methods of recovery; one selects the recovery technique to suit the problem in hand. There is, however, an additional aspect; since the techniques of recovering data are (at varying speeds, perhaps) becoming increasingly sophisticated, it is now possible that the questions asked should be of an order of sophistication equal to that of the available recovery-techniques.

This paper is devoted to illustrating these two aspects.

Data recovered on excavations can, in most instances, be divided into:

1. Macro-materials, i.e. gross or bulk materials;
2. Micro-materials, i.e. materials (of varying size and nature) which are not easily recovered, even by quite small tools, e.g. a pair of tweezers.

Macro-materials are such objects as can be easily recovered 'in the trench' by whatever means the excavator is using: pick, shovel, trowel, spoon, etc.; micro-materials are those whose recovery requires, or is facilitated by, a secondary process. This latter process is, on some excavations, a sieve, either wet or dry.

What is called into question, in excavating either macro- or micro-materials, is the nature of the sample, previously required and subsequently recovered. As I have, at the beginning, tried to state, the question itself presupposes the quality and quantity (in one sense, the 'bias') of the data to be recovered. Macro-materials, on this basis, may perhaps be used in treating 'macro-' (as it were) problems. It is imperative, however, in all cases, that the nature of the sample recovered be clearly and unequivocally defined. Thus:

1. Where was the material found, by what method and under what conditions?
2. How was the size and recovery method of the sample determined?

The ideal is to make clear the standard that has been adopted and the reasons for its adoption (see the account for the Deh Luran excavations in Hole, Flannery and Nealy 1969:23-28). It is perhaps less important to justify (and, as happens in some cases, to obscure the reasons for) the adoption of a large-sized sieve-mesh than to indicate what is the standard that has, in fact, been selected. To put the point another way, one might suggest that in outlining a programme of data-recovery there is a necessity to delineate the standard which may ignore the needs of others. 'Dutiful collection' of materials uninteresting to the collector is, on the ideal principle, less useful than the deliberate adoption of a coarse but mechanical recovery technique (*cf.* Higgs 1970:398).

The intention, therefore, is to determine the level or grade of information. In these terms, most published reports on e.g. chipped stone are useless for comparative studies which require to know the nature of the sample, i.e. quantity plus quality and comparability (see the commentary in Wright 1969; 47-52).

This last aspect – comparability – leads to a point made elsewhere: between excavated sites, what are the levels of possible comparability if there is no common standard of recovery?

For example: obsidian. The model of 'trade' has been suggested in treating this material, particularly after the completion of trace-analyses of individual specimens and groups. This aspect (trace-analysis) is not affected by problems of presence and absence, but the model as a whole can be seriously questioned when the factor of information-grade is introduced into a discussion, for instance, of weight-distance ratios; in such a case, there is an urgent necessity for a parallel treatment of the quality of the date (see, for example, the study in Renfrew 1969: 155-158). In other words, if there are no definitions of the samples collected there cannot be comparability or, therefore, any attempt to test significant correlations in the finding of obsidian at individual sites. The model of 'trade' is, thus, seriously hampered. At this level, a methodological standard becomes imperative.

One method (of data recovery) adopted on some excavations in the Near East is that of water-sieving. The technique is rather more than the washing or floating out of arbitrarily (i.e. not 'randomly', in the accepted sense of this word) chosen containers of soil. One method is now available for bulk water-sieving of large amounts of excavated soil efficiently and economically (French 1971).

The results of this water-sieving process are neither brilliant nor unexpected but the relevance to models adopted by archaeologists to explain culture-change, such as 'trade', is direct. The water-sieving method of data-recovery would, demonstrably, concern any analysis using weight-distance ratios in Anatolia. The recovery of marine-mollusca by this method on at least four sites (together with macro-materials from other excavated sites) has led to the formulation of a hypothesis concerning the multi-directional transportation (? exchange) of objects (? materials) in the Near East. I have attempted to illustrate the point by the use of a species of marine mollusc from the genus *Nassa* sp. The patterns of presumed directional movement are contrastable to those available for obsidian in, for example, the 7th and later millennia. The study of movement patterns ('trade', exchange, hunting, transhumance, and so on), based on excavated materials, may perhaps be greatly advanced by what is a mechanically simple process of data-recovery. From this instance as from others, one should perhaps conclude that models of explanation and interpretation are not sacrosanct; they are (? should be) always readily discardable.

If there is contrast to be revealed on such an elementary level, one wonders what might happen if definable methodological standards were more widely adopted. This question leads back to the starting-point: that recovery-techniques *must* keep pace with increasing sophistication in theorizing and, conversely, that theory cannot go beyond the limits of the recovery techniques. I would suggest that developments in these two aspects could be usefully harmonized.

A corollary to this last point is the aspect of efficiency and economy. In these days of financial restraints, the factor of efficiency in terms of time and money is not unimportant in planning archaeology strategy. The less that need be dug because the data is of an increasingly higher grade, the more rapid could (? should) become our publication programmes – for the immediate benefit of all concerned.

In conclusion I would present my apologies for re-iterating points which may seem obvious to some, but perhaps not all, excavators.

REFERENCES

French, D.H. (1971) An experiment in water-sieving, *Anatolian Studies* **21**.

Higgs, E.S. (1970) Review of Clarke, *Analytical Archaeology*, in *Proceedings of the Prehistoric Society* **36**, 396-9.

Hole, F., Flannery, K.V. and Neely, J.A. (1969) *Prehistory and Human Ecology of the Deh Luran Plain.* University of Michigan.

Renfrew, A.C. (1969) Trade and culture process in European prehistory. *Current Anthropology* **10**, 151-69.

Trigger, B. (1971) Archaeology and ecology. *World Archaeology* **2**, 321-36.

Wright, G.A. (1969) *Obsidian Analyses and Prehistoric Near Eastern Trade.* University of Michigan.

L. BOURELLY

The automatic processing of the results of an excavation at a prehistoric site – examination of occupation areas

In prehistoric studies, as in other disciplines such as, for instance, medicine or psychology, specialists now have at their disposition a considerable quantity of information revealed by observation, which they must order, sort out or reorganize so as to obtain the information they are looking for. If one considers – in order to simplify matters – that this mass of information is equal to the product of the number of objects multiplied by the average number of descriptive traits attributed to them, one notices that this increase of information results from the increase of both those terms. On the one hand the techniques of excavation are being perfected and allow more and more extensive digs to be undertaken, thus increasing the number of objects collected; on the other hand, the improvements of techniques of analysis coupled with greater specialization in research increases considerably the number of traits taken into account. Under these conditions it is becoming more and more difficult to examine everything, and therefore to understand everything by the traditional methods of investigation. The idea then occurs, quite naturally, of forging new tools, of envisaging new means and methods in order to master the information extracted with such difficulty and, if possible, to find new paths of research in domains so far inaccessible.

The development of large scale computers has created the possibility of controlling automatically vast collections of data, and computer-science today offers a possible solution to these problems. The conception, the execution, and research into the results of such an application constitute the three main lines of this study, undertaken in collaboration with M. de Lumley (Laboratory of Human Paleontology, Marseille), in order to bring to students of prehistory a practical aid in the control of their collections.

1. Organization of description and of documentation

The aim of this study, as we have just said, is to bring to the student of prehistory an aid in the study of a site by operating for him sortings, regroupings, counts, statistical operations or schemes that the computer will then execute in accordance with his needs. To this end the mass of documentation resulting from analysis had to be organized in such a way that it could be stored in binary form and exploited conveniently according to the demands of research.

Independently of the spatial distribution of the objects, which will be considered here as a characteristic (co-ordinates), the most natural categorization is based on the nature of the objects themselves (bones, tools, charcoal, sediments, pollen, etc.), each of these types of material giving birth to a particular field of documentary language. These fields are physically separated at the level of storage and will be consulted only in sequences.

Within a given field, the description of the objects is represented by a linear sequence of descriptive traits within the framework of faceted classification schemes (see Fig. 1, relation no. 1). This sequence includes both topographical elements and the characteristics of the object, thus permitting research on these characteristics (type of bone, nature of rock, type of splinter, etc.), relational terms (localisation, position, etc.), continuous arithmetical values (co-ordinates, dimensions . . .) or the specifications of the site under study (codification of stratigraphic layers, occupation levels, etc.). In the case of 'simple' objects, the necessary syntax for their description is part of the sequence of descriptive traits and can be the subject of a particular examination when the objects are 'complex' (composite tools). The description then includes sequences of terms, each of which gives a complete description of one aspect of the object without repetition of common parts. For these cases, a second type of syntactical relation is provided at the stage of interrogation in order to associate a group of terms with one aspect only of the object (see Fig. 1, relation No. 2).

Around this analytical organization, the facets and terms of the language are arranged in a hierarchic scheme order to introduce those notions of a semantic nature which have been considered useful for the study undertaken (Cros, Gardin and Levy 1968). These generic relations give birth to terms of a more and more general significance until the top of the hierarchy is reached which is the field under study (see Fig. 1, relation no. 3). In order to avoid ambiguity between the general terms which affect the regroupings implicitly contained in the questions and those terms which indicate simply a lack of precision in analysis, all the indeterminate cases are foreseen,

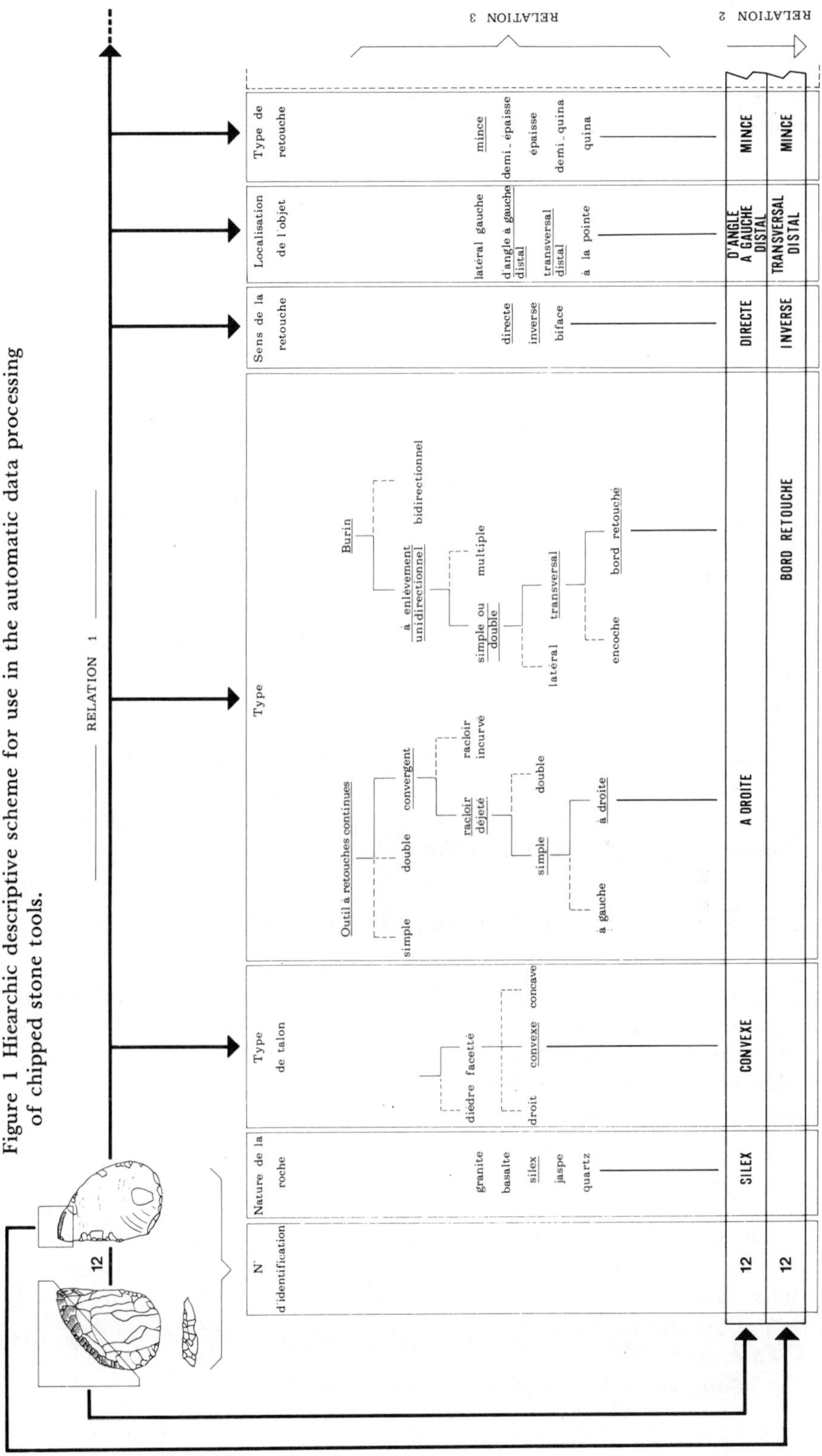

Figure 1 Hiearchic descriptive scheme for use in the automatic data processing of chipped stone tools.

thus imposing on all the terms of the analysis the status of terminal elements of the scheme. Among other things, this enables us to obtain perfect homogeneity of analysis. The regrouping of facts, although not necessitated by the form of interrogation, allows a global manipulation of the information when extracting the results (co-ordinates: x, y, z). The complete list of terms thus ordered forms the lexicon of the field under study (De Lumley and Bourrelly 1971). There are thus as many lexicons as fields studied.

2. *Interrogation*

The first function of this instrument is to execute rapidly all the possible regroupings of the objects that can be imagined by the student; such is the role of documentary research. The questions have then to be formulated in the documentary language and should be relevant to the content of analyses.

The co-ordinate operators which enable the student to enrich the interrogatory language are the Boolean operators AND, OR, NOT and, for the 'functions' which introduce arithmetical values (co-ordinates, dimensions . . .), the operator 'INCLUDES BETWEEN' (. . . ⩽ x ⩽ . . .). The use of these operators applying to all the terms of the lexicon permits all possible regroupings, however complex might be the question asked to the computer.

Examples of questions:

'List of *simple straight scrapers* obtained BY (AND) *fine retouching* OR *steep retouching* AND possessing *a natural back.*

'List of *tibias* OF (AND) *rabbits* presenting (AND) *notches* or *scratches* found IN (AND) *layer no. 5.'*

3. *Results and output of the system*

After the sortings affected by the questions asked of the machine, it is possible to extract all or part of the relevant analyses of objects. The selection of the criteria for extraction is done at the level of interrogation, using the terms of the upper part of the lexicon (facets and groups of facets).

Example: extract the horizontal co-ordinates (x,y) of the . . .
(*question*) fragments of diaphysis longer than 1,5 cm in the layer no. 5.

The second result obtainable on request is the counting of relevant objects. This count, coupled with the calculation of percentages, is the solution to a number of problems of a quantitative nature posed by prehistoric studies.

Example:

'Number of bones of carnivorous animals'

'Percentage of young rabbits in the layer no. 5.'

These two types of results, which are elementary in nature, can be considered either as definitive, in which case they are recorded by listing for immediate use, or as intermediary, in which case they are stored on magnetic tape in order to be used in a specific programme (calculations, tracing of maps, etc.).

The possibilities of conversational work with the computer, with projection of the results on a cathode-screen, should also be noted.

4. *Tracing of maps*

Among the great variety of particular programmes which may be added to this system of interrogation, one occupies a special position, exercising an important function in the study of a site: the tracing of maps. The problem is that of showing the spatial distribution of objects in the site by means of a cross-section and sectional elevation in order to examine the occupation levels of structures. This work, always extremely long when done by hand, should find in computer science an elegant and rapid solution in *digital graphic plotters* or even, more simply, in classical printing.

We have shown how it is possible to obtain the co-ordinates of certain categories of objects. These objects will therefore allow us to represent, at a given scale, their spatial distribution.

Sectional elevations are obtained by a division of the area into slices of varying depth (according to the site) within which the objects are projected into a plane, thus giving, in successive slices, a 'dynamic' image of the layers. The axis of these slices, also variable, permits the discovery of the line of greatest slope of the site, thus minimizing the errors due to the projection of objects within a given slice. From the clusters of points thus represented, the student may deduce the line of the layers or 'beds' which he is searching for and this result will then be re-introduced into the system as basic information and can be used for interrogation.

Within the layers of objects already discovered, it is possible, by the same procedure, to obtain cross-sections whose spacing and depth can vary, and which will give (if the density of objects is sufficient) a relief-map of the layer at different levels.

Finally, in a given occupation layer, it is possible to represent the distribution of objects by projection and thus to render clear certain particular features: focus-points (distribution of charcoal, etc.), enclosures (piling of stone), middens, etc.

5. *Consequences and extensions*

The examples given here are not exhaustive and the extension of this study will no doubt bring other results. In any case, the system thus initiated should permit the creation of a library of practicable programmes which could be studied later.

In addition, this system constitutes a data bank whose universatility will encourage comparative studies of several sites, putting at the disposal of each student basic information which he may study according to the demands of his own particular research. But, while the approach just described is relatively independent of the semantic content of the 'items' manipulated, its general application will demand, on the contrary, the creation of a precise and explicit terminology. This re-examination of basic information is both the price to pay for, and the first reward of mechanisation.

REFERENCES

Cros, R.C., Gardin, J.C. and Levy, F. (1968) *L'automatisation des recherches documentaires. Un modèle général LE SYNTOL*. Paris, Gauthier Villars.

De Lumley, H. and Bourrelly, L. (1971) Lexique des caractéristiques de l'industrie lithique. (Version no. 1) – C.A.D.A. mimeographed.

ROBERT WHALLON Jr.

Spatial analysis of palaeolithic occupation areas

The present problem and the 'functional argument'

One of the important current questions in European prehistory is that of the nature of variability among palaeolithic artifact assemblages. This question raises interesting methodological as well as theoretical problems. Theoretical considerations largely determine both the manner in which this variability is interpreted and the sort of explanations which are hypothesised for it. Building up a convincing explanation from an hypothesis, however, requires the drawing of new and untried implications from the hypothesis and their testing, developing appropriate methodological tools if necessary.

In putting forth his case for the 'functional argument', Binford (Binford and Binford 1966; Binford this volume) has drawn one major implication from his proposed explanation of the variability among middle palaeolithic assemblages and has applied to the analysis of these assemblages a statistical method specifically designed to test such implications. We would like to consider another implication which can be derived from the 'functional argument' and to point out to prehistorians concerned with this question some of the statistical methods which are available to them for testing it.

We refer to the implication that artifacts, classified into separate tool types, should be differentially distributed on prehistoric occupation floors as a result of their differential utilization in the various separate activities carried out by human groups at each location used or inhabited. These differential distributions, and the mutual co-variation of tool types in terms of their patterns of horizontal distribution, can be detected and defined by statistical techniques for spatial analysis. Spatial analysis is therefore discussed here in the suggestion that its application to the kind of palaeolithic materials studied by Binford would offer another and an independent test of his proposed 'functional' explanation.

The variation observed among these assemblages is the changing proportions of different tool types, and to a lesser extent of industrial waste. A necessary assumption for Binford's argument is that these tool types are defined by a typology which measures primarily 'function'. 'Function' is used here in the sense that such 'tools' represent categories of artifacts which differ from one another mainly in terms of the use to which they were put in mediating between man and his environment. It is not necessary that this typology exclusively reflects function, only that it primarily reflects function.

Given this kind of variability and the assumption just presented, it is easy to make the bridging argument that a human group exploiting an environment which, in terms of resources available for subsistence and maintenance, is geographically differentiated at any given time, seasonally differentiated throughout the year, and temporally differentiated by climatic change over a given span of time, will vary their activities, and thus also the kinds and proportions of the tools they use, in time and place in order best to exploit this environment for their survival. It follows that the variability in proportions of tool types from site to site will be a reflection of the differences in activities carried out at different times in these several places.

The many details of this argument have already been effectively exposed (Binford and Binford 1966; Binford this volume), and it is not our intention to repeat them. Binford's recent distinction between 'curating' and 'expedient' technologies (this volume), however, adds a significant new factor to the explanation of variability among palaeolithic assemblages which has to be taken into account. It does not substantially alter the theoretical bases of a 'functional' explanation, but can, by changing the prior assumptions on which they are based, considerably alter the nature of the bridging arguments and thus the specific test implications reached. It changes the implications and the methods relevant to spatial analysis only slightly, as we shall see.

Spatial analysis: theory

Proceeding from the same 'functional' hypothesis as Binford, one can draw another testable implication, making the same assumption that the typology used measures primarily function, or tool use. Instead of arguing then from the necessary differentiation of human activities within a geographical area, however, the bridging arguments are that at least some human activities will be spatially separated within most places of occupation and that the areal differentiation of activities will result in the differential distribution of tool types over an occupation area as a consequence of their different uses in the various activities carried out at that site.

These arguments can easily be supported by references to ethnographic analogies, but they also follow from the almost *a priori* impossibility of carrying out all the activities necessary for the subsistence and maintenance of a camp or settlement in the same place. This is particularly so in the case of activities which necessitate the use of differing amounts of space. Contrast, for example, the spatial requirements of hide stretching and of flint knapping. The former needs a large area, the latter a considerably smaller one, and the artifactual debris which one might expect from the first would be very sparse and dispersed over a relatively large area while that expectable from the second would be dense and concentrated in a relatively small area or areas. Separation is also necessary among activities which require fixed structures of different sorts. One cannot stretch and scrape hides in the place where one has built one's drying racks.

These examples are obvious, but are not necessarily trivial, since our arguments do not necessitate the constant spatial separation of all activities into mutually exclusive areas, only that some activities must, at least some of the time, be spatially distinct. From this it follows that, in areas of occupation where more than one activity was done, the potential exists for a spatial separation of activities, and that this potential increases in proportion to the size of the occupation and the number and diversity of activities carried out there.

We would therefore expect that the various tool types in palaeolithic sites will be differentially distributed over the area of occupation and that groups of tool types will be mutually correlated in terms of their patterns of distribution, particularly in the larger and richer sites. These groups should represent functionally associated tools, or 'tool kits', which were used in the same activity or activities. The distributions of these 'tool kits' should, in turn, often be associated with specific cultural features or with certain types or locations of sites.

Some correspondence between these spatially defined 'tool kits' and those defined through factor analysis of tool proportions (or counts) from different sites should exist. Disagreements between the two types of analysis should be interpretable. Some activities may regularly take place at the same location in an occupation, but in different relative frequencies from occupation to occupation. The tool kits pertaining to such activities would normally be separated by factor analysis but, of course, not by spatial analysis. Conversely, some activities which are regularly associated in the same camps may actually be consistently carried out in different areas within those camps. In this case, a spatial analysis would clearly separate tool kits which would be confounded in a factor analysis.

A lack of differential artifact distribution is likely to characterize sites at which a single activity took place. Overlapping of activity areas may partially cloud the picture of spatial separation of activities, but this is to be expected, and the available analytical techniques should be adequate to detect random overlapping of these areas as opposed to regular association. In terms of individual tool types, we may also anticipate some multiple associations with otherwise separate, spatially defined groups as a result of the multiplicity of function of many tools. These points are, however, primarily details to be handled by appropriate analysis and interpretation and are in no way modifications of the general arguments on which spatial analysis is based. It should be clear that the detection and definition through spatial analysis of differentially distributed tools kits within palaeolithic sites constitutes a powerful and independent test of the proposed 'functional' explanation of the observed variability of palaeolithic assemblages.

The test implication, drawn from the 'functional argument', of differential spatial distribution of tool types is fairly straightforward and easy to test and interpret if one can assume the simple situational production, use, and discarding of tools. The recognition of the differences between 'curated' and 'expedient' technologies (Binford this volume) and their relation to technological efficiency, however, introduces some new complexities into the problem.

These complexities are of more concern in the application of factor analysis than in spatial analysis. There is no clear control in factor analysis for the possibility of random disposal. Spurious correlations can be produced by random disposal of an unrelated series of tools at a relatively constant rate. Numbers and proportions of these tools will then be highly correlated as a consequence of varying lengths of occupation at different sites. The effect of 'curating' tools in a technology will probably be more evident and cause more analytical problems in factor analysis than in spatial analysis.

It is clear from Binford's exposition of the notions of curated vs. expedient technologies that there is no sharp dichotomy here between two essentially different kinds of technology. There is very likely no such thing as a purely curated or a purely expedient technology. One may more realistically conceive of a continuum of variation from virtually entirely expedient technologies to virtually entirely curated technologies. It is also unlikely that all tool types in any technology are curated or made and used expediently to the same degree. Expediently produced tools in any technology will be likely to exhibit strong patterns of spatial distribution, and spatial analysis is capable of detecting these patterns for single tool types, while factor analysis cannot.

It is also useful here to consider the most common manners in which tools will be discarded. Tools can simply be made, used, and left lying at the spot. This simplest of situations is definitionally the characteristic of a totally expedient technology. Elements of it are probably present in most, if not all, technologies. If curated carefully, tools will supposedly be discarded when broken or worn out. This will presumably be a more likely occurrance at the location of use than elsewhere. We can therefore expect a tendency for disposal at or near locations of intensive use, yet with a low density and with a number of activity locations which lack many of the most used tools entirely. Finally, accidental loss must always play a role, and in a highly curated technology we can expect this to be the most common form of disposal of certain kinds of tools.

Even in a highly curated technology, therefore, we can expect spatial distribution (and also distributions between sites) often to be patterned and systematic as well as random. Some tools will show concentrations at locations where they were discarded, broken or worn out, either at the place of use, or at the location of replacement where fresh tools take their place (e.g. the concentration of projectile point butts at the spot where new points are mounted on the shafts). Other tools will be randomly distributed (usually sparsely) as the result of loss. The random distribution within and among sites of a very common type of tool, however, would suggest its use as a highly multipurpose tool. Independent study of the distribution of broken or worn out artifacts in contrast to other artifacts may reveal something of the degree to which a technology curates its tools or makes and uses them expediently.

The test implication drawn from assuming that the typology of palaeolithic stone tools reflects primarily use or function is thus that at least some of these tool types will exhibit significant spatial patterning and mutual association with other tools on some occupation floors. This will be increasingly true as the size and richness of the occupation increases. Spatial patterning and mutual associations of tools in groups will be stronger, more common, be exhibited by more tool types, and represent the actual location of activities in which the tools were used to the degree that the technology is expedient as opposed to curating.

Once non-random distribution of 'function' tools is demonstrated, it must, in this frame of reasoning, be assumed to be the product of some regular pattern of human behaviour and as such both allows and demands explanation. Spatial clusters of tools do not necessarily have to represent items left in a place of use, as should be clear from the above paragraphs, but are the results, nonetheless, of regular human behaviour associated with the embeddedness of the technology in, or its articulation with, the rest of a total cultural system. They should therefore be perfectly susceptible of explanation by the prehistorian within the proper frame of reference.

Methods of spatial analysis

Analysis of patterns of spatial distribution of artifacts over occupation areas has been made several times. In all cases to date, however, the methods employed have involved simply the plotting of individual tool types, or other archaeological items, on a map of the occupation area. The distributions thus represented have been inspected by eye for 'significant' patterning, and the degree to which the patterns observed for two or more items are similar has likewise been decided by observation and subjective estimation (e.g. Leroi-Gourhan and Brézillon 1966; de Lumley *et al.* 1969). Even the most recently presented computer procedures for this sort of analysis (Bourrelly this volume) are only highly efficient techniques for the preparation of the various plots and maps which are subsequently to be examined by eye.

In view of the dependence of our interpretations upon the definition of significant spatial patterning and of distributional correlation among archaeological items, it would seem desirable to investigate the possibilities of applying objective, statistical methods to the analysis of spatial pattern in archaeological data. Such methods provide the double advantage of producing consistently reproducable results and of allowing a probabilistic test of the significance of patterning observed for each item. There are two statistical methods available for use in archaeology, dimensional analysis of variance and nearest neighbour analysis. They are applicable to very different kinds of data and under very different circumstances. A wide range of archaeological situations may thus be handled with these two methods.

Dimensional analysis of variance is a technique used in plant ecology for the detection of pattern in the distribution of individual plant species over an area. We call it here dimensional analysis of variance for convenience in reference. In the field of plant ecology it is most commonly referred to as the analysis of pattern using a grid of contiguous quadrats (Greig-Smith 1952, 1961; Thompson 1958; Kershaw 1957, 1964). Nearest neighbour analysis was also developed and applied in ecology (Clark and Evans 1954; Thompson 1956), but has also been adapted to problems in statistical geography (Dacey 1964).

Dimensional analysis of variance treats the occupation area as a series of sub-areas, proceeding from the smallest grid units through successive doublings of area. At each step, the variance in artifact count among areas is calculated. This is tantamount to testing for the degree of concentration of artifacts in one or more of the sub-areas to the relative exclusion of other areas. Peaks in variance at any size of area are evidence, therefore, of a tendency for artifact concentrations of approximately that size within the area considered.

Nearest neighbour analysis, on the other hand, proceeds from the density of artifacts per unit area to calculate the theoretically expected average distance from each artifact to its nearest neighbour, assuming random distribution of the artifacts. The actually observed mean distance to nearest neighbours is then compared with this expected value and tested to see if it is significantly different. If it is significantly smaller, this is of course clear indication of non-random spatial aggregations among the artifacts.

Dimensional analysis of variance uses counts per grid unit as its basic data. Nearest neighbour analysis requires two-dimensional co-ordinates for each item. There is thus an immediate and great difference in the archaeological data which they can handle. Nearest neighbour analysis, using finer and more precise data, is, as might be expected, in many ways more precise and gives finer results. Dimensional analysis of variance has, however, the great advantage that it can handle the large amount of archaeological data which has been gathered in grid squares. Nearest neighbour analysis can never be applied to such data. Excavated materials for which two-dimensional co-ordinates are available may be analysed by either method, the co-ordinates being simply used to assign items to their appropriate grid unit if necessary.

Dimensional analysis of variance is, in this sense, the more general method, but it has a number of severe restraints which limit its general applicability. In the first place, the total grid used in the analysis must be either square or rectangular. The number of grid units along any side must be some power of 2, i.e. 4, 8, 16, 32, etc. If the grid is rectangular, one side must be exactly twice as long as the other, e.g. 4 x 8, 32 x 64 etc. These are obviously quite limiting restrictions, particularly in light of the shapes of most excavation areas. It is often perfectly possible to construct such a grid by leaving aside a few irregular, peripheral squares of the original area or adding a few 'dummy' squares to fill out the necessary grid shape. Some excavation areas will be divisible into two or more appropriate grids which will fairly well cover the area. A number of excavations, however, will be of such a size and shape that it will in fact be impossible to construct a satisfactory grid which both covers the area reasonably well and is appropriate for a dimensional analysis of variance.

Nearest neighbour analysis fairly well eliminates these problems of size and shape of the area to be analysed. By dealing directly with the exact position of each object and the distances to nearest neighbours, it can handle virtually any size or shape of area. It has, however, problems with boundaries and the contiguity of excavated areas. If the area to be considered is so narrow that items are constantly or frequently nearer to walls of the excavation than to other items of the same type, the application of nearest neighbour analysis can be dangerously misleading. Lack of knowledge about the presence or absence of other items of the same type in unexcavated areas which lie closer to an item than its nearest known neighbour makes the calculation of nearest neighbour statistics unreliable. The area over which the items are distributed must consequently be continuous and unbroken. It is quite difficult to combine in the same analysis items from areas which are physically separated in any way.

Separate areas within the same site may rather easily be combined in the same analysis when using dimensional analysis of variance, however. The difference between the two methods here lies in the way in which correlation or covariation between types of items is determined after the fact of spatial concentration or aggregation has been established. In nearest neighbour analysis, the concentration is defined directly by linking those items which are significantly close to one another. Correlation or co-variation in spatial distribution must then be defined by the superposition of pairs of such directly defined concentrations and the derivation of some measure of the degree of their areal coincidence. Not only does this preclude or complicate the possibility of effectively combining data from separate areas in the same analysis, but it is also one of the weakest points of nearest neighbour analysis in general. Methods for comparing distributions, once they have been defined as significant spatial aggregations by nearest neighbour analysis, are so poorly developed as to be virtually non-existent, even though this step is of prime concern in archaeological analysis.

The procedure for defining spatial correlation when using dimensional analysis of variance is relatively simple, straightforward, and well known. The analysis of variance determines the presence or absence of spatial aggregation and defines the size of that aggregation in terms of units composed of 2, 4, 8, 16 etc. original grid units. The size of such a unit which most commonly represents the scale of spatial concentration of the items on the occupation floor is determined. The original data may then be converted to counts of items per unit area of this new size, representing the scale of observation which most directly and strongly reflects significant spatial patterning. These new counts then form the basis for the application of the standard techniques of correlation. Any manipulation of the correlation coefficients, from simple matrix ordering to factor analysis, may subsequently be applied for the definition of mutually covarying groups of items. Separate excavation areas can thus be analysed independently by dimensional analysis of variance, and the counts per new observation unit may eventually be combined into one set of data for the correlation analysis.

One might question here the whole idea of applying dimensional analysis of variance in this way as a preliminary to correlation analysis. Why not, for example, simply use the original counts by grid units as the basic data and apply a correlation analysis directly? The answer is that the size of grid unit used to observe a spatial distribution often, if not always, has a direct effect on the results of any analysis of concentration, correlation, or association in the data. It is quite easy to demonstrate that significant tendencies towards concentration or aggregation can be shown or made to disappear, and that highly positive correlations or associations can be turned into highly negative ones (and vice-versa) simply by varying the grid size in terms of which the data is expressed. Dimensional analysis of variance is therefore used to determine the grid size at which the tendencies to spatial patterning are best observed and expressed in the data. A correlational analysis based on data grouped in areal units of this scale may be expected to best reflect correlations and associations due to real similarities in spatial distribution.

It is possible, and in some cases even likely, of course, that more than one scale of spatial pattern is present in the data. Dimensional analysis of variance can easily detect such a situation. Simple nearest neighbour analysis cannot. In such cases, either where certain items exhibit more than one scale of concentration, or more commonly, where different groups of items exhibit different scales of pattern, it is highly advisable to carry out analysis of correlation on all scales of concentration. The effects of changing grid unit size may be expected to produce noticeable differences in the results of these separate analyses. In general, we would expect the archaeologically most meaningful results for any group of items to be obtained from an analysis carried out on data grouped to the size at which these items exhibit their strongest tendencies for spatial concentration.

In spite of its advantages for detection of multiple scales of pattern, there are some troublesome problems with the detection of spatial aggregations by dimensional analysis of variance. In the first place, the smallest scale of pattern which the method can in general reliably detect is in the order of twice the size of the original grid units (Kershaw 1957). Concentration in areas smaller than this, the size of the original grid units themselves, for example, will not reliably be revealed by this method. This is of particular concern in the case of excavations made in relatively large squares. When the original excavation units reach a size approximately equivalent to what we may expect to have been the size of most activity areas on a site, the presence or absence of these activity areas cannot be certainly demonstrated by dimensional analysis of variance.

Another problem with the definition of spatial concentrations by dimensional analysis of variance is that of shape. In the course of grouping the original grid units into blocks of 2, 4, 8, etc. units, the shape of the area covered by a block alternates between square and oblong. The range of shape of areas within which the concentration of artifacts may be detected is thus severely limited. Irregularly shaped, linear, or curved concentrations will be poorly or not at all defined by a method which operates on strictly regular, geometrically shaped areas.

Finally, as the size of the blocks into which the grid units are grouped is increased, the fineness or precision with which the scale or size of any concentration can be detected is greatly reduced. The area included in a block is doubled at each step in the analysis. The difference between the size of concentration revealed at any one block size and the next is not the same between any two points on the scale, but grows by a factor of several times as one proceeds to larger and larger block sizes. To say that a peak in concentration has been defined at block size 32 is only to say that an area of 32 original grid squares is the closest approximation provided by the analysis to the real size of the concentration, which must lie somewhere between block size 16 and 64 (Pielou 1969:105). As one proceeds to larger block sizes, the range of area within which the actual size of concentration may lie becomes very large.

Although it cannot detect multiple scales of pattern, nearest neighbour analysis is free of all these limitations of size, shape, and fineness of definition of areas of spatial concentration. Nearest neighbour analysis, by proceeding directly from the exact locations of the individual items in the sample, can detect clustering on the smallest scale at which it occurs and can precisely define the shape of the cluster.

It is clear that there is no 'ideal' choice between these two methods. Each is applicable under different circumstances and conditions, and each has its own peculiar range of advantages and problems. Which one should be chosen for the analysis of any particular set of data is a choice that must be weighed given the knowledge of the nature of the data, the problems at hand, and the above characteristics of these two methods. They are both applicable and available to test the implication drawn above from the 'functional argument' that palaeolithic tool types should often show significant spatial concentrations within sites, that certain groups of tools should be characterized by similar spatial distributions, that these distributions should often be relative to various cultural features, and that some correspondence should exist between the results of this kind of analysis and of factor analysis.

Examples

A full-scale application of spatial analysis to a palaeolithic occupation floor remains to be made. Examples of the application of dimensional analysis of variance and of nearest neighbour analysis may be useful, however, in illustrating their use in archaeology and the kind of results which may be expected from them.

Three early occupation floors in the tiny cave of Guila Naquitz, excavated by Kent Flannery in the Valley of Oaxaca, Mexico, have been fully analysed by dimensional analysis of variance. Eighteen types of items, including flints, faunal remains, and plant remains, were recovered and recorded in 1 metre grid squares. With slight modification, the original grid formed a square 8 x 8 metres in size. Table 1 gives the results of the dimensional analysis of variance for *Jatropha* or Susi nuts found on one of these floors. It is evident that there is a striking non-random spatial distribution of these nuts at all scales, from the original grid units to the largest grouping of 32 grid units, dividing the site into halves. At the same time, it is clear from the table that variance (mean square) rises neatly to a definite peak at block size 8 and declines rapidly thereafter. In this case, not only is non-randomness of distribution clearly demonstrated, but the scale of maximum concentration, an area of approximately 8 square metres, is definitely indicated.

Table 1: Dimensional analysis of variance for *Jatropha*, or Susi Nuts from Zone C, Guila Naquitz Cave, Oaxaca, Mexico.

Analysis of Variance:

Block Size	Degrees of Freedom	Mean Square	F. Ratio
1	32	7.6250	–
2	16	14.5000	1.90
4	8	13.5937	1.78
8	4	23.4062	3.07
16	2	6.9062	.91
32	1	7.5625	.99

Corrected Relative Variance (Variance/Mean Ratio):

Block Size	Relative Variance	Std. Error	Z Score
1	7.1765	.2500	24.71
2	13.6471	.3536	35.77
4	12.7941	.5000	23.59
8	22.0294	.7071	29.74
16	6.5000	1.0000	5.50
32	7.1176	1.4142	4.33

Dimensional analyses of variance for the other 17 items showed the same clear non-randomness of spatial distribution in every case. The majority of items also showed peaks of concentration at block size 8. The original data was prepared for a correlation analysis by regrouping into counts per block of 8 original grid units. The correlation matrix was calculated and ordered. Several groups of items could be defined from this ordered matrix. When the contents of these groups were examined, it was seen that each group represented either the products fruiting together within a single environmental zone or items exploited and/or processed by distinct work groups. Products from the upland forest were separate from products of the piedmont, and products of the hunt were distinct from collected vegetal foods.

Nearest neighbour analysis is being applied to the occupation floors from the upper palaeolithic rock shelter, the Abri Pataud, excavated by Hallam L. Movius, Jr., in Les Eyzies, Dordogne, France. The largest occupation area uncovered is Couche 3, the Proto-Magdalenian level. Lens 2 from this Couche represents the main occupation level. It has been excavated for a total length of 12 metres over which it is roughly 3-4 metres wide. The locations of several dozen different kinds of items over this occupation area have been recorded by three-dimensional co-ordinates. Many of these items have been subjected to nearest neighbour analysis. Analysis is continuing and will eventually be applied to all the occupation floors of this site.

Table 2. Nearest neighbour analysis of the distribution of sagaies in Couche 3, Lens 2, of the Abri Pataud, Dordogne, France.

```
 SAGAIE


NEAREST NEIGHBOR STATISTICS
            NUMBER OF                                     EXPECTED MEAN NEAREST
            OBSERVATIONS       AREA       DENSITY         NEIGHBOR DISTANCE

                 18          393249.9    .000046               73.90


                                                        STANDARD ERROR OF MEAN
MEAN NEAREST                                            NEAREST NEIGHBOR DISTANCE
NEIGHBOR DISTANCE      STANDARD VARIATE                 OF A RANDOM DISTRIBUTION

      53.28                   -2.265                          9.1054


A STANDARD VARIATE OF 1.96 (5% LEVEL OF SIGN.) USED TO DETERMINE
SIGNIFICANCE OF VARIABLE AGGREGATION


THE DIFFERENCE BETWEEN THE OBSERVED AND EXPECTED MEAN NEAREST
NEIGHBOR DISTANCE OF SAGAIE
IS SIGNIFICANT IN THE DIRECTION OF AGGREGATION.

ANALYSIS CONTINUES FOR  SAGAIE


HISTOGRAM OF NEAREST NEIGHBOR DISTANCES

   5      **
   4   ** **
   3   ** **
   2   ** **         **     **
   1 _**.**_**.**_**.**_**...**..___...___...___...___...___.**

    0.0  25.4  50.9  76.3 101.7 127.2 152.6 178.0 203.5 228.9 254.3
       12.7  38.2  63.6  89.0 114.5 139.9 165.3 190.8 216.2 241.6


FIVE PERCENT NORMAL CURVE CUTOFF POINT =129.8
```

As an example of our analysis, we present the results for sagaies in Table 2. Fig. 1 gives a computer graphic representation of the form of the distribution defined by the analysis. It is clear that there is a statistically significant tendency for sagaies to aggregate in this occupation area. The exact size and form of these aggregations have been determined by connecting all specimens closer together than the distance defined by the point on the distribution of nearest neighbour distances beyond which only 5% of the values would lie if the curve were truly normal. The areas bounded by these connecting lines are then filled in. The computer map of these spatial distributions is, of course, merely a representation, being a drastically scaled down version of a very large, accurate original used in the actual analysis.

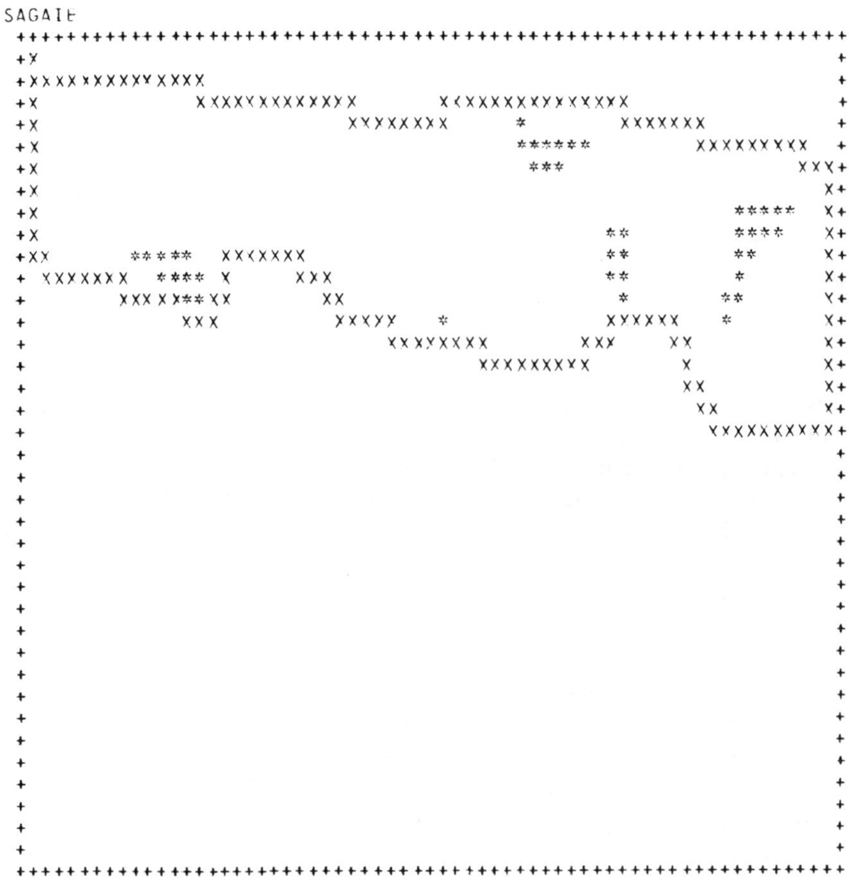

Figure 1 Computer graphic representation of the spatial aggregations of sagaies from Couche 3, Lens 2 of the Abri Pataud, based on the results of nearest neighbour analysis.

Such spatial concentrations of different items are then superimposed to determine the degree of resemblance between them.

Adequate and satisfactory methods for this step are still being sought. For the moment, the methods being used indicate that the distribution of sagaies on this floor shows some similarity with that of flake scrapers on the one hand and with that of segments of Gravette points on the other. Analysis is only partially complete, and these results are tentative. The results are adequate, however, to show the potential usefulness of the method and the possibility of using it to test the implications we have drawn above.

Conclusion

Explaining the nature of variability of palaeolithic artifact assemblages requires not only the formulating of explicit hypotheses, but also the rigorous testing of those hypotheses. We have outlined one approach to the testing of the hypothesis proposed by Binford, currently known as the 'functional argument', and we have discussed two statistical methods appropriate to this testing. It now remains to carry out this test on appropriate data. We are doing this for upper palaeolithic data from the Abri Pataud as illustrated above.

If clear differential spatial distribution of tool types, mutual co-variation of groups of tools in terms of their distributional patterns, and at least occasional association of such groups with cultural features or other non-artifactual items, as predicted from the 'functional argument', can be demonstrated by the method of spatial analysis, these results should lend considerable support to the 'argument'. The results of spatial analysis should give a good indication of whether or not the 'tool kit' interpretation of co-varying proportions of tools among assemblages is correct or at least partially so. If it is, we can expect the further results both of spatial analysis of individual occupation floors and of factor analysis of data from a series of occupations to give us a more complex and nuanced picture of human behaviour as organized by prehistoric cultural systems. In this picture, prehistoric cultural systems, like contemporary ones, will be seen to structure human behaviour differentially in space and time in response to the (natural and social) environmental context which a human group is exploiting or with which it is coping, as this environment varies geographically at any given time, seasonally throughout the year, and through time.

What are some of the further implications of the above discussion for future archaeological research? Practically, the demonstration of non-random spatial concentration of different artifact types on palaeolithic occupation floors should confirm a long-standing caution concerning archaeological sampling of these sites. This is that no single-area sample of a site will necessarily, or even probably, give an adequate representation of the range of materials or features present at that site or of their relative frequencies. This fact has been previously observed on quite different sorts of sites (e.g. Binford, Binford, Whallon and Hardin 1970:15).

But further, we must begin to take cognizance of the possibilities that different technologies, like different cultural systems, may be different not only in form, but in kind, behaving according to different principles. A given explanation, hypothesis, assumption, bridging argument, or method of analysis is not necessarily of general applicability simply because it appears to be useful or valid in one context. The possibly great difference between middle and upper palaeolithic technologies in terms of the degree to which they are expedient vs. curating technologies is a case in point. Our explanations will, therefore, as we understand more and more of the role of material items in cultural systems, have to take into account an increasing number of factors which enter into the behaviour of these systems.

It is in this connection, of understanding the various factors which may be involved in the articulation of material objects and physical remains with a total cultural system, that such 'ethno-archaeological' studies as that of Binford among the Nunamiut (Binford this volume) have tremendous potential value for archaeological studies. To make such studies worthwhile, however, our thinking must move away from simple formal similarities or analogies, even in the realm of process. We must begin to think of such studies as aids to the understanding of the nature of cultural systems and of the role of physical objects and locations in these systems. Armed then with this understanding, we may approach the archaeological record, not in an effort to find formal similarities or analogies with our ethnographic observations, but to compare and contrast the structure of variability in the archaeological record with that ethnographically known, attempting to define hypothetically the character of the cultural system or systems responsible for that record, even if we must hypothesize their very difference from what is observed ethnographically as in the case of the 'expedient' middle palaeolithic technologies contrasted to the Eskimos' careful 'curating' of their tools.

REFERENCES

Binford, L.R. and S.R. (1966) A preliminary analysis of functional variability in the Mousterian of Levallois facies. *In* Clark, J.D. and Howell, F.C. (eds.) *Recent studies in paleoanthropology. American Anthropologist* **68** (no. 2, pt. 2), 238-95.

Binford, L.R., Binford, S.R., Whallon, R. and Hardin, M.A. (1970) *Archaeology at Hatchery West.* Society for American Archaeology, Memoir 24.

Clark, P.J. and Evans, F.C. (1954) Distance to nearest neighbour as a measure of spatial relationships in populations. *Ecology* **35**, 445-53.

Dacey, M.F. (1964) Two dimensional random point patterns: a review and interpretation. *Papers of the proceedings of the regional science association* **13**, 41-58.

de Lumley, H. *et al.* (1969) *Une cabane Acheuléenne dans la Grotte du Lazaret (Nice).* Mémoires de la Société Préhistorique Française 7.

Greig-Smith, P. (1952) The use of random and contiguous quadrats in the study of the structure of plant communities. *Annals of Botany*, n.s. **16** (no. 62), 293-316.

Greig-Smith, P. (1961) Data on pattern within plant communities I. The analysis of pattern. *Journal of Ecology* **49**, 695-702.

Kershaw, K.A. (1957) The use of cover and frequency in the detection of pattern in plant communities. *Ecology* **38**, 291-9.

Kershaw, K.A. (1964) *Quantitative and dynamic ecology.* New York, American Elsevier Publishing Co.

Leroi-Gourhan, A. and Brézillon, M. (1966) L'habitation Magdalénienne no. 1 de Pincevent près Montereau (Seine-et-Marne). *Gallia Préhistoire* **9** (2), 263-385.

Pielou, E.C. (1969) *An Introduction to Mathematical Ecology.* New York, Wiley-Interscience.

Thompson, H.R. (1956) Distribution of distance to nth neighbour in a population of randomly distributed individuals. *Ecology* **37**, 391-4.

Thompson, H.R. (1958) The statistical study of plant distribution patterns using a grid of quadrats. *Australian Journal of Botany* **6**, 322-42.

Whallon, R., Jr. n.d. A new approach to pottery typology. *American Antiquity* (in press).

JENIFER KEIGHLEY

Some problems in the quantitative interpretation of ceramic data

This paper is an attempt to discuss the kinds of factors which inhibit the quantitative interpretation of culture change with special reference to the study of ceramic assemblages. In recent years, with the popularization of 'scientific archaeology' and the accompanying sophisticated techniques, there has developed an unawareness of some of the prerequisites for the *meaningful* study of culture change patterns; even the words 'culture change' themselves lead to a plethora of conflicting opinions. To explain and predict the properties of phenomena, archaeology, treated as a science, must include three elements – the facts observed, sets of abstract propositions made up into a small number of high order hypotheses and a larger number of lower order hypotheses, and ultimately, assuming the predictions of the hypotheses prove valid, generalizations. In order to quantify culture therefore, the collection of data involves a prior definition of the objects to be investigated, selection of relevant properties and measurement techniques, and the observation and measurement of these properties for each object or for a sample from the total population of objects.

In the application of even the most basic scientific method to archaeology, it would be a platitude (which *does* need reiterating) to remind oneself that any serious errors in the initial collection of data must inevitably give rise to serious distortions in the ensuing hypotheses and generalizations. Even the difficulties of a crucial stage like the observation of archaeological data should never be overlooked – it presupposes a language comprehensible to everyone; yet there is no common vocabulary in pottery analysis. In such conditions, we would do well to note Sir Karl Popper's (1963) comment that 'observation is always selective. It needs a chosen object, a definite task, an interest, a point of view, a problem. And its description presupposes a descriptive language . . . it presupposes interests, points of view and problems.' The painful point for us is simply this; some aspiring archaeologists have attempted to develop themes on 'culture', i.e. their 'generalization', in a manner which immediately casts doubts concerning the reliability of their data, and accordingly of the logic behind their own predictions. For archaeological aims, can we provide techniques which are good enough to control and estimate inaccuracies by regulating and standardizing observation, classification, speculation and testing?

Measuring culture change

While it is fairly easy to define various categories and processes of change it is much more difficult to try to analyse their functional and causal factors. How can we decide what the conditions of change are? Does change have to occur in a number of aspects of a culture, or only in one aspect of a culture, such as painted pottery decoration? How can these types of stability be compared with one another? Although one tries to limit the kinds of stability studied, it may eventually be impossible to compare these kinds collectively – for instance, with ceramic assemblages the change between shape and motif may be disproportionate; i.e. shape may change very much over a given period but motifs may stay the same. Further complications include questions as to whether the abandonment of one trait should count the same as the invention or adoption of a new one. You may have a retentive culture which is elaborating or constantly adding new features – is this stable relative to one which drops old features and adds few new ones? And equally important is the problem of *rate* of change and the fact that 'the total quantity of culture content probably does tend to increase but certainly at uneven rates in different periods and areas' (Kroeber, 1954:462). This is tantamount to Steward's (1963:12) idea that 'no culture has achieved so perfect an adjustment to its environment that it is static. Differences appearing in successive periods during the development of culture in any locality entail not only increasing complexity of qualitatively new patterns, but also quantitatively new patterns'.

The concept of pottery type and its limitations for quantitative analysis

The concept of artifact type is in itself a controversial subject. The validity of the type used depends on how well it serves its own purpose. Although we have to deal with vast groups of ceramic types, we must realize that the factors affecting change represent continuous variables; or, in other words, 'consistency in an assemblage of traits is found only over a short period of time and has a limited area, but as soon as the space-time framework is expanded, consistency vanishes in the course either of diffusion through space or of cultural change through time. Culture is a continuum in space and time and cannot be discretely packaged in periods and areas'. (Tugby, 1965:6).

Whatever its defects and potentialities, pottery type is not an adequate unit, and there are serious limitations to the application of the type concept for quantitative ceramic analysis. This springs partly from the fact that 'type' has diverse uses – for cross-dating, identifying intrusive elements, determining the influence of styles upon one another and so on. It also makes generalizations which, as Shepard (1965:317) points out, 'forces us to think in norms and forget the importance of divergent specimens'. If quantitative analysis is to be at all meaningful, then it needs enough data to show the co-variation of a series of things (traits, types or assemblages) and a set of criteria for judging the differences between units such as presence or absence of a certain feature, (Tugby 1965:4) or a count of a number of features such as a particular bowl or handle shape. This leads to the most pertinent question of all – how can we be sure that the frequencies of types in the sample will form the basis for an *objective* determination of a chronological sequence? However, as soon as we begin to analyse we become subjective because we have to select what we consider to be the differentiae of the culture we are investigating.

The nature of quantitative analysis means that we have to deal with sherds which are often difficult to analyse; this is primarily because many features have to be considered and their continuous variations, limits, associations and discontinuities must all be recognized. There are innumerable variations in features like burnish, fabric colour, slip colour etc. Moreover, it is impossible to apply types defined for one site to another site for comparative purposes, when these types are defined only in general terms, because all the important minor local variations must be considered when a chronological framework is to be established. Some factors 'vary continuously while others change discontinuously', and often different things have superficial resemblances. (Shepard 1965:343, 346.) In other cases, when the analyses of shape, fabric colour and design are extremely detailed and primarily the product of the particular sample the archaeologist is handling, further difficulties may arise as sufficient bodies of material are rarely available for comparative purposes. This is either because the standards of excavation would not merit detailed study anyway or because the material cannot be made available for study. These factors restrict attempts to make detailed analogies between cultures which 'look' alike, e.g. Vinca and Vesselinovo, where there are many vague similarities of shape and design.

Sampling problems

Inadequate sampling and faulty interpretation is responsible for much biased archaeological reconstruction. As Shepard says, 'no mathematical formula can rectify faulty analysis or confusion of cultural, individual or environmental factors . . . how often percentage frequencies of occurrence are reported from samples too small to give reliable results, even though it is very easy to determine the effect of the size of the sample and size of proportion of this universally used measure'. (Shepard, 1965:332). The ratio of certain things is more important than numbers listed on a chart; this absolute number is not important as it depends on the *size* of the area excavated. However, errors introduced by sampling and represented at only a few chosen sites must not be interpreted as concentrations. The main problem in uncovering sufficiently large areas is the necessity for the accompanying close stratigraphic control which will bring out small changes between sub-groups. Also, as Sherratt (personal communication) has pointed out, the development of sharp ceramic changes in certain parts of sites coinciding with changes in the type of occupation may simply represent changes in the distribution of occupied areas in the settlement. It cannot, however, be over-stressed that if a chronological sequence can be determined by a procedure which has no reference to the cultural interpretation of the data, then the causal relationships afterwards reconstructed may be supported by independent chronological evidence only where sound and meticulous excavation has taken place.

This brings the discussion to sieving. The size of samples will be affected by sieving operations, but the use of sieving must be relative to the particular problems in hand. The types of questions to be asked are how incomplete recovery gives a biased sample and what effect this bias has upon our overall conclusions about the site. Abrupt change in one feature may not be observed at all if over-shadowed by more prominent features, e.g. changes in the occurrence of a rare painted ware which will not be well represented on an unsieved site. The lack of adequate samples through bad excavation means that the sherds representing transition periods are small in number and more difficult to classify. The analysis of sieved versus unsieved pottery batches at the site of Sitagroi has shown that sieving increases especially the percentage of sherd numbers of the rarer painted wares, e.g. the fine painted 'Brown on Cream' and 'Brown on White' wares at that site, thus making the rarer wares more meaningful (Fig. 1). The Sitagroi analyses were determined, however, in terms of *weight* of sherds of the given fabric or type per kilogram of total pottery uncovered, the weight difference of the additional sieved fine wares made little difference to the overall results. But this was not the case for the heavier and darker Sitagroi

Grey Lustre ware, characteristic of the earliest phase at the site. Hand recovery was not efficient for this ware because it was not easily visible to the naked eye, and levels 58, 55 and 52 of the eleven metre sounding at the site yielded 21, 13 and 3 pieces respectively, compared with 288, 267 and 196 pieces for the corresponding sieved levels. (Fig. 1).

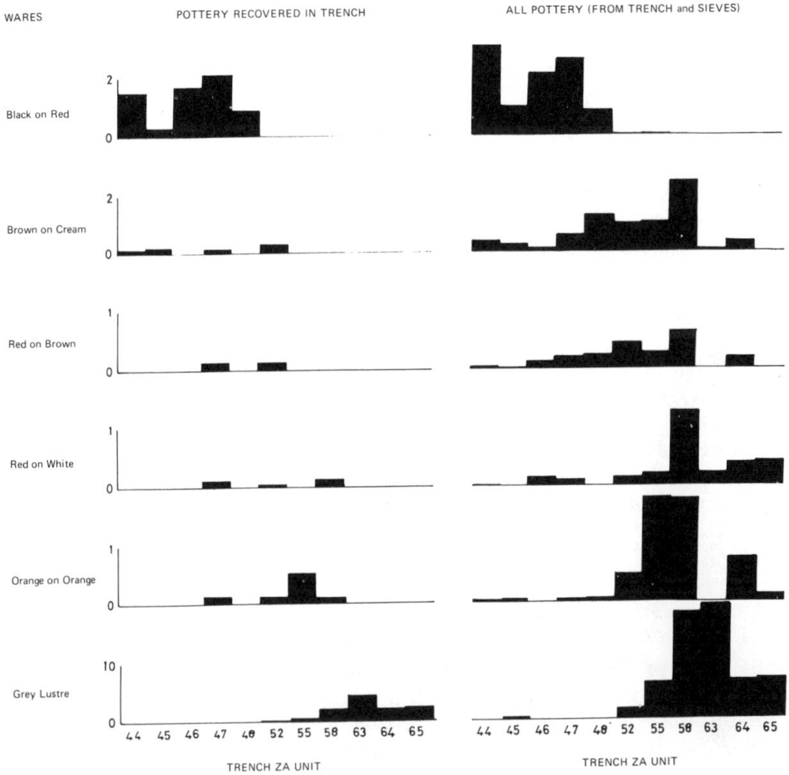

Figure 1 The frequency count feature sherds per kilogram of pottery of various wares in eleven test units from Trench ZA at Sitagroi, North Greece.

Although sieving is important in increasing sample size, there are drawbacks in the more detailed analysis of sieved sherds. These pertain to the recognition of shape – often sherds from the sieve are too small to be useful or diagnostic, and it becomes impossible to make the fine distinctions between bowls and jars and various handle types which one would wish to do. Similarly, painted motifs on small fragments are very often of little use in establishing overall patterns (e.g. minute fragments may have been part of larger painted sherds – this is especially true where the pattern is wide and sweeping, like the Sitagroi 'Black on Red' ware of the chalcolithic period; whole areas are unpainted and could therefore be classed as a completely different ware). These are only minor points concerned with interpretation; the problems will be different for other types of material. Sieving is necessary simply because it is impossible to trust normal methods of hand recovery, and because, for any quantitative work, an unbiased sample is vital. If problems of initial classification can be solved, the percentage distributions calculated from sieved ceramic data will show what was actually happening at the site in question, and not what is inferred to happen.

In conclusion, one can only reiterate an initial point which concerns the fact that in the application of quantitative, statistical ideas to archaeology, it is important to disregard standards and definitions drawn up without full regard for the practicability of their application to the problem in hand. We should not set up laws which cannot be put on effective trial, neither should we assume that highminded, esoteric theories will solve all our dilemmas. In a word, we need to take fresh stock of our analysis of tangible evidence.

REFERENCES

Binford, L.R. (1965) Archaeological systematics and the study of culture process. *American Antiquity* 31, 203-10.

Brainerd, G.W. (1951) The place of chronological ordering in archaeological analysis. *American Antiquity* 16, 301-13.

Braithwaite, R.B. (1953) *Scientific Explanation: a Study of the Function of Theory, Probability and Law in Science.* Cambridge, University Press.

Childe, V.G. (1963) *Social Evolution.* London, Watts.

Childe, V.G. (1957) *The Dawn of European Civilization.* London, Kegan Paul.

Flannery, K. V. (1965) Culture history versus culture process: a debate in American archaeology. Review in *Scientific American* 205, 119-22.

Heizer, R.F. and Cook, S.F. (1956) Some aspects of the quantitative approach in archaeology. *Southwestern Journal of Anthropology* 12, 229-48.

Kroeber, A.L. (1954) Review of culture; a critical review of concepts and definition. *American Anthropologist* 56, 461-8.

Kroeber, A.L. (1955) *Configurations of Culture Growth.* Berkeley University of California Press.

Moroney, M.J. (1967) *Facts from Figures.* Harmondsworth, Middlesex, Penguin.

Piggott, S. (1966) *Approach to Archaeology.* London, Black.

Popper, K.R. (1963) *Conjectures and Refutations.* London, Routledge.

Sahlins, M.D. and Service, E.R. (1960) *Laws of Evolutionary Potential.*

Shepard, A.O. (1965) *Ceramics for the Archaeologist.* Washington D.C. Carnegie Institute of Washington.

Steward, J.H. (1963) *Theory of Culture Change.* Urbana, University of Illinois Press.

Tugby, D.J. (1965) Archaeological objectives and statistical methods; a frontier in archaeology. *American Antiquity* 31, 1-15.

White, L.A. (1959) *The Evolution of Culture.* New York, McGraw Hill.

C. R. ORTON

The tactical use of models in archaeology – the SHERD project

For the purposes of this contribution, the term 'model' will be taken to mean 'mathematical model', in which a particular archaeological situation is represented by a set of mathematical statements. The statements do not constitute a hypothesis about the situation; rather, they provide a framework in which hypotheses can be formed and tested. The construction of the model precedes the application of mathematical techniques, which derive from the nature of the model itself.

Within this definition, it is useful to distinguish between what may be called 'strategic' and 'tactical' models. These terms refer to the use to which a model is put, rather than to any characteristic of the model. A strategic use is a study in which the outcome is of direct importance in itself, although it may also be a means to a larger end, while the results of a tactical model would be only a means to the larger end.

Most examples of the use of mathematics and statistics in archaeology in recent years consist of the application of a set technique (for example, principal component analysis, multi-dimensional scaling, cluster analysis – see Hodson 1969) to a particular problem. There is no explicit model to the situation – the techniques used are either borrowed from another discipline or developed in an empirical fashion. Such techniques are considered to be justified if they provide answers, but there is no real reply to the criticism that the methods are inappropriate because they do not transfer validly to an archaeological context. If satisfactory models could first be constructed, they could lead to techniques peculiarly suited to archaeological problems, possibly more suited to them than more general 'all purpose' techniques.

However, the task of constructing models, and developing techniques from them, is not likely to be easy, even in an apparently straightforward archaeological situation. Kendall's examination of the Flinders-Petrie sequence dating problem (Kendall 1963) is an example of the mathematical complexities that can develop from a simply-stated intuitive principle. In particular, the strategic problems, where most of the mathematical work has been concentrated, are likely to be the most difficult.

For this reason, it is suggested that, in order to gain experience and practice in the handling and behaviour of models, we should consider first the approach to some tactical problems. As a case-study of the use of mathematical models in a short-term exercise with limited objectives, the SHERD project is presented.

The project arose from the post-excavation work currently being undertaken on the waster material from a Romano-British kiln site in Highgate Wood, London. Brown and Sheldon have reported on the excavations (1969a, 1970) and on the post-excavation work in general (1969b), and the author has discussed the assumptions needed before statistical post-excavation work can be done (Orton 1970). The pottery from the site was very broken, few complete vessels being present, and the question was posed 'what was the production of the site?'. An essential stage in answering this question seemed to be the reconstruction of vessel forms from the sherds present. Post-excavation work (Sheldon *et al.* 1970) had shown that in general there were five categories of rim and three categories of base present, so that the reconstruction problem split into three sections:

1. To define vessel categories in terms of a rim category and a base category.
2. To establish the relationship between rim and base diameter in each vessel category.
3. To estimate the height and so to reconstruct the shapes of the vessels in each category.

It is the use of a model in stage 1 that will be described. The theory has already been covered in some detail (Orton 1971). The part of special interest here is that which relates the numbers of rim and base sherds found to the numbers of vessels represented. In the following, the suffix h refers to base categories, i refers to rim categories and j to lots. The number of vessels with base category h represented in lot j is Y_{jh}, and the number of base sherds found is y_{jh}. Similarly X_{ji} and x_{ji} refer to vessels with rim of category i, and to rim sherds of that category. The model adopted was

$$y_{jh} = g_h Y_{jh} + e_{jh}$$
$$\text{and } x_{ji} = f_i X_{ji} + d_{ji}$$

where the f_i and g_h represent the 'brokenness' of the different rim and base categories, and d_{ji} and e_{jh} are error terms, which are supposed to be Poisson type variables specified by

$$\text{var}(e_{jh}) = g_h Y_{jh}$$
$$\text{and var}(d_{ji}) = f_i X_{ji}$$

The number of base sherds of category h found in lot j is thus the realization of a Poisson variable with mean $g_h\ Y_{jh}$.

This model is constructed by supposing that the number of rim sherds in the lot which derive from any one vessel respresented is the realization of a Poisson variable with mean g_h. It is assumed that the numbers of rim sherds from different vessels are statistically independent, so that their sum is still Poisson, with a mean equal to $g_h\ Y_{jh}$. A similar argument can be applied to the base. It is, of course, possible for a vessel represented in a lot to have no rim sherds, or no base sherds, present in that lot.

In the SHERD project, this model has been used to establish the relationships between rim and base categories, and to provide a basis on which the reconstruction could proceed. It was possible to test that the model did in fact 'fit' the situation as observed.

The features of this model that are relevant to the discussion are:

1. It sets up a framework within which certain basic parameters are to be estimated.
2. It is not, in itself, a statement of interest to the archaeologist.
3. It can be tested to see whether it adequately describes the archaeological situation.
4. If accepted, it has implications for the units used in excavation and recording.

Models of this sort enable one to handle large quantities of data, by imposing a relatively simple algebraic and stochastic structure on the archaeological problem. They could also provide experience in the construction and use of mathematical models in situations where the archaeological problem can be simply stated, which would be of benefit in dealing mathematically with more complex archaeological problems.

REFERENCES

Brown, A.E. and Sheldon, H.L. (1969a and b) Excavations in Highgate Wood, 1966-8, parts 1 and 2. *The London Archaeologist* 1, 38-44, 60-5.

Brown, A.E. and Sheldon, H.L. (1970) Excavations in Highgate Wood, 1969. *The London Archaeologist* 2, 150-4.

Hodson, F.R. (1969) Searching for structure within multivariate archaeological data. *World Archaeology* 1, 91-105.

Kendall, D.G. (1963) A statistical approach to Flinders Petrie's sequence-dating. *Bulletin of the International Statistical Institute*, 34th Session, 657-80.

Orton, C.R. (1970) The production of pottery from a Romano-British kiln site: a statistical investigation. *World Archaeology* 1, 343-58.

Orton, C.R. (1971) On the statistical sorting and reconstruction of the pottery from a Romano-British kiln site. *In* Hodson, F.R., Kendall, D.G. and Tautu, P. (eds.) *Mathematics in the Archaeological and Historical Sciences*. Edinburgh, University Press.

Sheldon, H.L. *et al.* (1970) *A kiln and a pit group from Highgate Wood, excavated in 1968*. City Literary Institute, London.

J.VIRBEL

Methodological aspects of the segmentation and the characterization of textual data in archaeology: application to the mechanized processing of the Corpus of Latin Inscriptions

The mechanized utilization of the Corpus of Latin Inscriptions in many fields (general, economic, social, military history; archaeology; history of language and epigraphy) depends on the extremely variable nature of information contained in the inscriptions (date; location; social purpose; physical and stylistic nature; literary form etc.), on their present state of preservation, implying some work of restoration and interpretation, as well as on the constraints of explicitness and completeness made necessary by the use of computers. The methodological problems raised by the fundamental operations of segmentation (i.e. division of the data into 'segments' or elemental units) and characterization, specific to each analysis, are here defined.

Introduction

The methodological reflections presented here arose during the elaboration of a documentary system for the mechanization of both the editing and the use of volume VIII of the Corpus of Latin Inscriptions (CIL).* Here we intend to deal specially with the problem of the segmentation of the units of the corpus, first as a general outline of an analytical approach, then with reference to the particular units that the *texts* in fact are, i.e. the data of this corpus. We would like to underline the different constraints conditioning the operations of segmentation and particularly the very complex relations that this operation bears to the other stages of the analytical documentary approach.

* This experiment has been jointly conducted by technicians, scientists and professors of C.A.D.A. (CNRS), Marseille (MM. E. Chouraqui et J. Virbel), Institut d'Archéologie Méditerranéenne, C.N.R.S., Aix-en-Provence (M.M. Janon), and Faculté des Lettres et Sciences Humaines d'Aix-en-Provence (MM. M. Corbier et P.A. Fevrier).

The status of segmentation in documentary analysis

Very frequently in archaeological research, starting from hypotheses relating to the use and processing of the given material, one defines a set of characteristics, the presence or absence of which can be observed among the objects which are studied and which are regarded as relevant from the point of view of the planned study. The analysis sets out to define the corpus, then to retain and characterize the information. Its aim is a simple presentation of this information eventually, in a classified and tabulated form. To ensure the relevance of the documentary operations themselves, as well as to facilitate a possible mechanized processing, the analysis must be subject to a few constraints, especially regularity, exhaustiveness and reproducibility.

The diagram which follows shows the principal mutual links between the different stages of the documentary analysis as well as the multiple feedbacks called into play that a discursive, necessarily linear, presentation is generally bound to conceal.

The diagram opposite shows that these operations of segmentation and characterization of the initial data are closely dependent on a set of initial hypotheses about the use of the corpus as well as on the documentation products (form and content) that are to be obtained to make this use possible.

It is pertinent to observe that there often exists a 'natural' way of segmenting a given object, referring the example to perceptual habits or production techniques (in this case for example the different 'parts' of a vessel: ear, neck, spout, body, foot etc.; or of a tool: handle, blade, etc., but also for texts: words, morphemes, propositions, sentences, etc.). This particular segmentation soon loses its 'natural' aspect, and is seen both as arbitrary and irrelevant. Or it may harmonize with the segmentation designed for specific purposes and a particular corpus.

This we would like to illustrate now by considering the analysis texts.

The segmentation and characterization of the texts from CIL VIII

In the case of CIL VIII, several constraints were set either from the start or as the work developed: they can be summarized as follows:*

* We are only interested here in the *textual* aspect of the inscriptions, but they have many others: the nature of the material; decoration; geographical and historical locations; size; archaeological or architectural environment. Other problems of segmentation and characterization are raised here, dealing with each 'facet' of the description of the objects as well as with the articulation of these facets with one another.

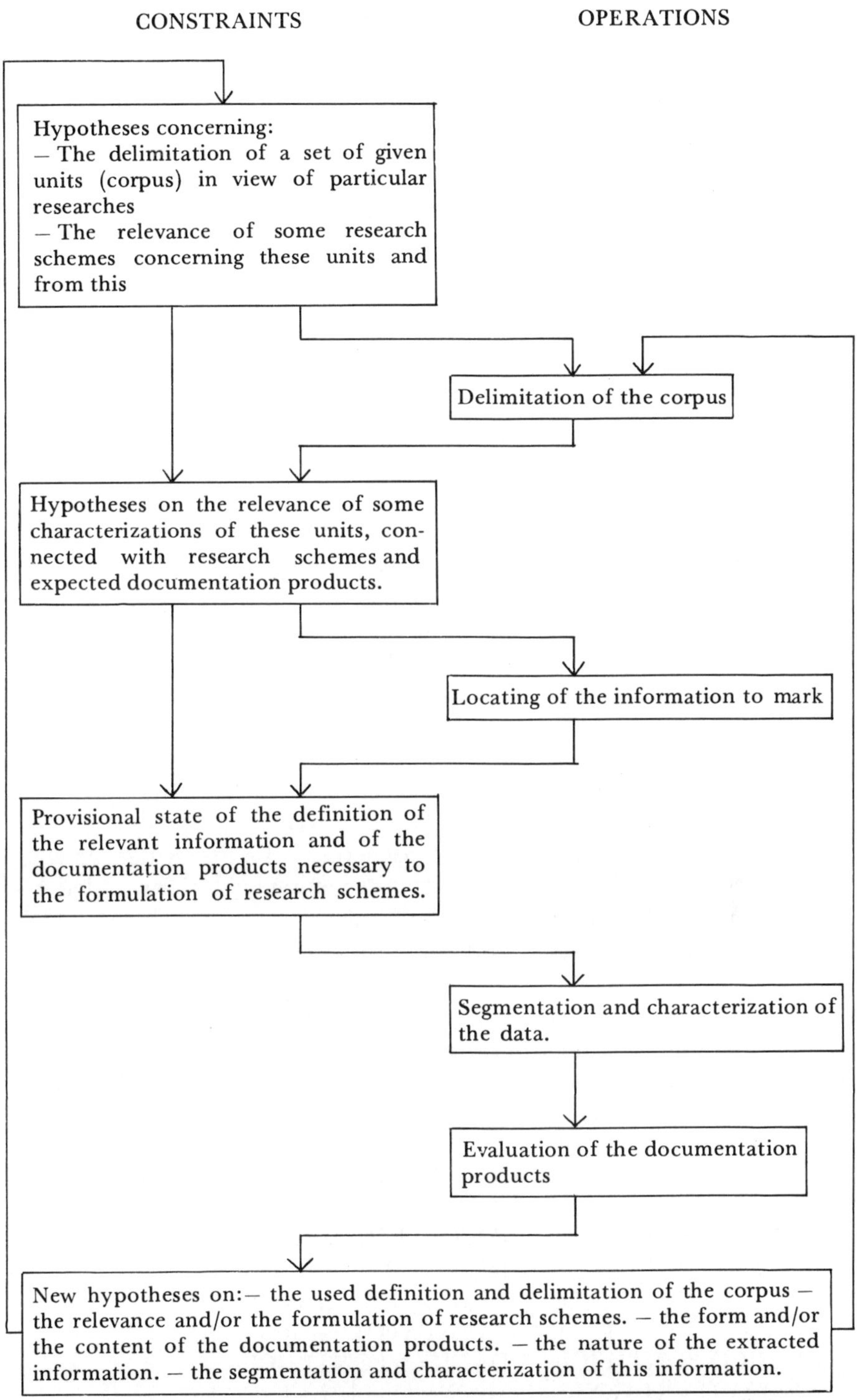
CONSTRAINTS
OPERATIONS
Hypotheses concerning: – The delimitation of a set of given units (corpus) in view of particular researches – The relevance of some research schemes concerning these units and from this
Delimitation of the corpus
Hypotheses on the relevance of some characterizations of these units, connected with research schemes and expected documentation products.
Locating of the information to mark
Provisional state of the definition of the relevant information and of the documentation products necessary to the formulation of research schemes.
Segmentation and characterization of the data.
Evaluation of the documentation products
New hypotheses on:– the used definition and delimitation of the corpus – the relevance and/or the formulation of research schemes. – the form and/or the content of the documentation products. – the nature of the extracted information. – the segmentation and characterization of this information.

1. A strict definition of the data of the corpus, regulating acceptance or rejection according to precise criteria, for example the nature of the material bearing the inscription.
2. The possibility of research on the initial data as well as on the characterizations of these data.
3. Consideration of the numerous fields for which Latin Inscriptions can be regarded as valuable data: general, military, economic, social history; human geography; genealogy; archaeology; literary, linguistic, epigraphy.
4. The necessity of interpreting and/or of restoring information in the numerous cases of shortenings, ligatures, siglas, errors or irregularities of language, mutilations, erasures, obliterations, etc. All these operations are conducted on the basis of a given state of historical knowledge.
5. The aim of a flexible access to the registered data to permit the use of a statistical or classifactory procedure on some of them.

These different constraints have resulted in the production of several documentation products, then to the definition of a general strategy of segmentation and characterization of data, allowing the constitution of these tools. These are of three types:

1. An edition of the text in three versions: a 'raw' version (as it is found on the inscription) an 'interpreted' version (containing several expansions and reconstructed parts), a 'canonical' version (bringing down lexical units to their canonical forms).
2. An automatic compilation of various tables and indexes (Emperors, Army corps, Trianomina, civil servants) together with two vocabulary indexes (actual and canonical forms).
3. A question-answering system concerning the literal data as well as the representations due to the characterizations added to them at the entry.

These different constraints being defined – those which concern the constitution and the manipulation of the corpus and those which consist of a sort of translation of the first ones through the definition of the required documentation products – we can show through an example how the problem of the segmentation and the characterization of the texts then clearly appears.

If we start with the text of column 1 (this is the raw version showing the punctuation marks, indicated by x, and the paragraphs).

1	2
IMPxCAESARI	IMP(ERATORI)CAESARI,
DIVI NERVAE Fx	DIVI NERVAE F (ILIO),
NERVAE TRAIANO	NERVAE TRAIANO,
AVGxGERMANICO	AVG(VSTO), GERMANICO
DACICO PONTIFICI	DACICO, PONTIFICI
MAXIMO TRIBVNICx	MAXIMO, TRIBVNIC(IA)
POTxVII IMPxIIII	POT(ESTATE) VII, IMP(ERATORI) IIII,
COSx PxP̂x	CO(N)S(VLE) V, P(ATRI) P(ATRIAE).

3

IMPERATOR CAESAR DIVVS NERVA FILIVS NERVA TRAIANVS AVGVSTVS GERMANICVS DACICVS PONTIFEX MAXIMVS TRIBVNICIA POTESTAS VII IMPERATOR IIII CONSVL V PATER PATRIA.

From this version, we want to generate version no. 2 the 'interpreted' one, and version 3, the 'canonical' one. The list of the segmentations necessary here for these three versions is apparently the following one:

1. A *lexical* segmentation delimitating words which are distinctive entries in the latin lexicon (in versions 2 and 3).
2. A *morphological* segmentation that makes possible the transition from DIVI to DIVVS, from PONTIFICI to PONTIFEX, etc. in state no. 3.
3. A *linear* segmentation preserving the page-setting in states 1 and 2.
4. A *semantic* segmentation for the insertion, if neccessary, of missing pieces of texts as it is the case between F and x NERVAE F(ILIO)xNERVAE.
5. A *syntactic* and *prosodic* segmentation which in state 2 simplifies reading and proves to be a help to interpretation by inserting punctuation marks.

In a parallel way, various characterizations must be associated with the information which according to its type must be retained, transformed, added or suppressed. For example, considering the different kinds of processing intended for the first word, IMP, this segment must be characterized from the beginning as:

IMP(ERATOR + I = Ø))ƀ.
 1 2 2 2 1

The first indication, 1, () characterizes a processing that will be ignored in state no. 1 and on the contrary performed in states no. 2 and 3; the second indication, 2, + = . . .) marks a morphological processing which is not done in state no. 1, which consists in taking into account the left part, included between + and = in state no. 2 and the right part, between = and), zero here, for state no. 3. (ƀ marks a blank, separating words). Thus we need five different segmentations to follow the editing constraints (the operations responsible for these segmentations need in fact about twenty variables that can be given different values according to the type of state).

For the constitution of other documentation products, a question-answering system or for the editing of tables, other rules of segmentation exist, some new, some corresponding to those above.

In fact this fragment of text deals with two emperors, Trajan and Nerva, and it is clear that any question put to the system concerning the inscriptions where Trajan, for example, is mentioned must entail the reference to this inscription. On the other hand, the mention of this emperor is here found in a particular phraseology that is different from many other inscriptions. The phraseological particulars occur at two levels. The *nature of the elements of nomenclature* (the fact that the name is preceded by the introductive elements IMP and CAESARI, which happens often but not invariably; the fact that there are two epithets GERMANICVS and DACICVS, that there is a kinship mark etc.) and the *particular phraseology of these elements,* (the fact that there is IMP and not IMPERATOR, GERMANICO and not GERM for example, etc.). Each of these data elements can be subject to a study independent of or combined with other types: thus one can be interested in all the inscriptions where Trajan is given the name of GERMANICVS or among these the ones in which the epithet is in full or only in a reduced form; one can also look for all the cases of emperors called GERMANICVS or DACICVS.

Thus we are led to the construction of a kind of general model for the naming of each Roman emperor and to express in the terms of this model the particular kinds of nomenclature found in the texts. Thus the model works on a new segmentation, a conceptual one; it includes the following elements:

A:	mention of IMPERATOR		Introductive Formula
B:	mention of CAESAR		
C:	mention of filiation		
D:	mention of name –	D1 – first name	
		D2 – second name	
		etc.	
E:	mention of AVGVSTVS		
F:	mention of epithets	F1: first epithet	
		F2: second epithet	
		etc.	
G:	mention of TRIBVNICIA POTESTATE		
H:	mention of CONSVL		Titles
I:	mention of IMPERATOR + number		
J:	mention of PONTIFEX		
K:	mention of PATER PATRIAE		
L:	mention of CENSOR		
M:	mention of DIVVS		

From this model, the text can be segmented and characterized (in state no. 1) as follows:

The problems of segmentation are here of two types. On one hand, starting from a segmentation into elements of designation we are led by degrees to the grouping of these elements into categories up to the reconstruction of the whole original text as a segmentation unit. This can eventually bring serious difficulties to the analysis (cf. Allard 1963, pp. 36-42).

IMPx	A	Introductive Formula	Reference to Trajan
CAESARI	B		
DIVI	M	Nomenclature of Nerva	
NERVAE	D1		
Fx	C		
NERVAE	D1	Names of Trajan	
TRAIANO	D2		
AVGx	E		
GERMANICO	F1	Epithets	
DACICO	F2		
PONTIFICI MAXIMO	J	Titles	
TRIBVNICxPOTxVII	G		
IMPxIIII	I		
COSxV	H		
PxPx	K		

On the other hand, this *conceptual segmentation* although it corresponds sometimes to the kinds of segmentation already mentioned, leads to the creation of new units which overlap with the first ones. Thus it will be noted that the characterization of concepts like PONTIFEX or TRIBVNICIA POTESTATE involves the presence of several words in the same segment and that moreover, here, this grouping leads to an overlap with linear segmentation. The conceptual segmentation of the CIL texts makes necessary the constitution of a lexicon of more than a thousand units, in some cases organized according to models comparable with that used for the nomenclature of emperors. It is not our intention here to deal with the questions raised by the formal expression of the results of this analysis. We only want to mention again that in the end the justification for the different segmentations imposed on the text and for the overlapping that they show is not so much a consequence of the methods dictated by the linguistic reality (although the segmentation that it involves is taken into account) as of the empirical need to make the results of the analysis compatible with the elaboration of the tolls which are needed. It is clear in the case of the conceptual aspect mentioned above that it is the refinement of the intended researches which forces to the separation of the elements A and B or H, I, J, K, L, and to the subdivision of categories D and F. Less precise documentary constraints would allow the model of nomenclature to be transformed by grouping A + B, H + I + J + K + L for example – which would naturally dictate a different conceptual segmentation of the text.

The specific nature of the material for this corpus bears very little on the general methodological reflections that we have brought forward at the beginning, which in several aspects are appropriate to the analytical study of material objects by the humane sciences in general.

It is hoped, therefore, that this problem in the manipulation of data and the perspective outlined for its solution will be found relevant more widely than in the field of Latin studies alone.

REFERENCES

The preceding comments refer to, and follow from, an analytical-critical approach in archaeology that has been recently called 'cartesian' (Borillo 1971) and about which more detailed developments will be found in the following bibliographical references, either general ones (Borillo 1971; Gardin 1963; 1968b), or more particularly oriented towards the subject of this paper (Allard 1963; Christophe 1958; Gardin 1961; 1968a).

Allard, M., Elzière, M. Gardin, G.C. and Hours, F. (1963) *Analyse conceptuelle du Coran, sur cartes perforées.* Paris-The Hague, Mouton.

Borillo, M. (1971) Formal procedures and the use of computers in archaeology: how they modify some aspects of the archaeological approach. *Norwegian Archaeological Review* 4, 2-27.

Christophe, J., Digard, F., Gardin, J.C. (1958) *Projet de Code pour l'Analyse des Textes Orientaux.* Centre d'Analyse Documentaire pour l'Archéologie, Centre National de la Recherche Scientifique, Code no. 6.

Gardin, J.C., Garelli, P. (1961) Etude par ordinateurs des établissements assyriens en Cappadoce. *Annales* **16** 1, 837-76.

Gardin, J.C. (1963) Problèmes d'analyse descriptive en archéologie. *In* Courbin, P. (ed.) *Etudes Archéologiques*, Paris, SEVPEN, 132-50.

Gardin, J.C. (1968a) Semantic analysis procedures in the sciences of man. *Informations sur les Sciences Sociales* **8**, 17-42.

Gardin, J.C. (1968b) Methods for the descriptive analysis of archaeological material. *American Antiquity* 32, 13-30.

JAMES DORAN

Explanation in archaeology: computer experiment

This note briefly describes a current experiment which focuses on the generation and evaluation by computer of complex explanatory hypotheses for archaeological data. By a complex explanatory hypothesis is here meant a small set of relatively general propositions, themselves tenable on *a priori* grounds, which, if true, maximally entail observations which have been made, and which are therefore adopted as true pending further observations. One of the objectives of the experiment is to give precise meaning to the concept of such an hypothesis in a specific archaeological context.

The computer science background

In recent years computer scientists have begun to explore ways in which computers can be programmed to formulate explanatory hypotheses for empirical data. Such computer programs are given a range of simple 'building blocks' out of which a wide variety of candidate hypotheses can be constructed. The most important work is that of Buchanan, Feigenbaum and Lederberg at Stanford University, with organic chemistry as the application area (see Buchanan and Lederberg, 1971; Buchanan, Feigenbaum and Lederberg, 1971; and many other papers). Progress towards a formal logic of induction is also relevant (for example, Meltzer 1970).

Such workers have typically seen three major components in the logical system needed to generate hypotheses. These are:

C1 – a set of primitive elements, together with a procedure by which a wide (possibly infinite) variety of potentially relevant hypotheses can be systematically constructed from them,

C2 – means of evaluating a particular candidate hypothesis, that is, of quantifying how good an explanation it is of the empirical data,

C3 – an effective way of combining C1 and C2 so that particular hypotheses are generated, considered, and modified or replaced, until one judged satisfactory is obtained.

If a computer program of this kind is to be written for a particular type of application, each of these components must be specified with total precision. Progress is made as we bring more and more of our intuitive ideas to this level of objective clarity.

The La Tène cemetery at Münsingen-Rain

I am exploring the prospects for automatic hypothesis generation and evaluation in archaelogy by reference to data drawn from the La Tène cemetery at Münsingen-Rain, near Bern, in Switzerland. This cemetery was excavated early in the present century, but has been published in full detail only recently (Hodson, 1968). It is of great importance, spanning as it does the early and middle La Tène, and providing an exceptionally rich and well-documented collection of metalwork.

In a little more detail, the main categories of evidence available from the excavation record are the following:

(a) the locations, orientations and depths of the 200 or so graves, almost all of which are inhumations,
(b) the estimated sex and age of many of the skeletons, and
(c) the grave good inventory for each grave (mainly weapons and jewellery in bronze) together with the position of each object relative to its skeleton.

With varying degress of success, relatively conventional studies of the cemetery (for example, Schaaff 1966; Hodson 1968) have sought to answer the following questions:

(a) what 'types' should be recognized among the grave goods, and how should they be used?
(b) what significant associations are there between particular types of artifact, or sets of artifacts, and particular categories (age/sex) of burial?
(c) to what extent is the cemetery spatially organized, for example by steady linear extension, or in family groups?
(d) what is the chronological sequence in which the graves were dug, and hence the sequence and duration of the various artifact types?

Of course, these questions are not considered without reference to our general knowledge of the La Tène. However this background knowledge is neither comprehensive nor very reliable, and it is arguable that as little reliance as possible should be placed upon it. A further point to be stressed is that these questions are not independent of one another, although it is natural to behave as if they were in the initial stages of a study. It is obvious enough that deciding, say, that a certain area of the cemetery has been reserved for female and child burials must have an effect upon our estimate of the cemetery's internal chronology.

A substantial amount of computer work has already been based upon the Münsingen material. This has concerned both automatic classification techniques (Hodson, Sneath and Doran 1966; Hodson 1970), and chronological seriation (for example, Kendall 1971). The present experiment can be seen as an attempt to extend this earlier work in a particularly promising direction (Doran 1971).

The computer program

An Algol 60 computer program, arbitrarily named SOLCEM, has been written which can seek an integrated interpretation of cemetery data such as those from Münsingen. The program relates conclusions drawn from different subsets of the data in much the way that an archaeologist might, and contains as subprograms classification and seriation procedures of the kind already applied to the Münsingen material.

SOLCEM processes the data in the following successive steps:

(a) the grave goods are classified by shape and decoration,
(b) a search is made for classes of object which are correlated with a specific age/sex group,
(c) using the conclusions of (b), if any, an attempt is made to decide the age/sex of graves not yet so classified,
(d) the spatial organisation of the cemetery is investigated seeking, for example, dispersion of the graves into age/sex groups,
(e) using the conclusions of (d), if any, a further attempt is made to assign age/sex to previously unclassified graves,
(f) the chronological sequence of the graves is sought, making the usual assumptions, and taking into account earlier conclusions, and
(g) finally the conclusions reached are expressed in terms of a probabilistic model of the formation of the cemetery.

Within each of these steps the program's capability is limited, sometimes very limited. In its present form the program is a tool for theoretical investigation, not a practical aid to archaeologists.

Experimentation

SOLCEM is being tested and developed using artificial data generated by a subsidiary Algol program, SIMCEM. This subsidiary program embodies a simulation of some of the processes by which cemeteries such as that at Münsingen come into being. The simulation, although complex, is primarily concerned only with objects and graves, and with their generation and deposition. There is no attempt to work with cultural, economic or environmental variables.

It is, of course, planned that when development of SOLCEM has proceeded sufficiently, it will be applied to the actual Münsingen excavation record. Accordingly these data are being thrown into machine usable form – a considerable task itself not without theoretical interest.

Theoretical issues

There is rather little direct connection between the present *ad hoc* organization of the SOLCEM program, based upon archaeological practice, and the developing theory of automatic hypothesis formation as sketched earlier. To attain a detailed understanding of the relationship between the two is the principal objective of the experiment. Key areas in which greater mathematical and practical insight is required are:

(i) the manner in which parallel consideration of alternative hypotheses is best organized,

(ii) the mathematical interrelationship between the different kinds of decision to be made, and the extent to which such considerations are usefully referred to an overall statistical estimation framework,

(iii) the most effective way of systematizing within SOLCEM the wide range of archaeological knowledge (for example, the various ways in which a cemetery might be spatially organized) upon which it must be able to call.

Archaeological benefits

Archaeologists may hope for two types of benefit if computer involvement in their subject can be expanded along the lines indicated here. These are:

(a) a much better understanding of just what it means to find and validate explanatory hypotheses in an archaeological context, and

(b) a new range of program tools, more specifically archaeological than those based on traditional multivariate statistics, to aid the interpretation of large amounts of detailed evidence.

The likelihood of the first of these benefits is hardly open to dispute. The ability of the computer to force elegant thoughts to come to terms with awkward facts is too well known. The second anticipated benefit is much less obviously realistic. Is it not the case that a computer program can, at most, reach just those conclusions about the Münsingen cemetery, say, which have already been reached by archaeologists? The answer is 'no'. There is no theoretical reason why a sufficiently elaborated version of the program discussed here should not make original and realistic suggestions for an archaeologist to consider both about the Münsingen cemetery and about other similar cemeteries. It is a matter of practical development.

Acknowledgments

I am grateful to Dr F.R. Hodson of the Institute of Archaeology, University of London, for much information about the Münsingen cemetery and its context, and to the UK Science Research Council for financial support.

REFERENCES

Buchanan, B.G., Feigenbaum, E.A., and Lederberg, J. (1971) A heuristic programming study of theory formation in science. *Second International Joint Conference on Artificial Intelligence, London, September 1971* (proceedings published by the British Computer Society).

Buchanan, B.G. and Lederberg, J. (1971) The Heuristic DENDRAL program for explaining empirical data. *I.F.I.P. Congress, Ljubljana, August 1971* (proceedings to be published).

Doran, J.E. (1971) Computer analysis of data from the La Tène cemetery at Münsingen-Rain. *In* Hodson, F.R., Kendall, D.G. and Tautu, P. (eds.) *Mathematics in the Archaeological and Historical Sciences* 422-31. Edinburgh, University Press.

Hodson, F.R. (1968) *The La Tène Cemetery at Münsingen-Rain*. Bern, Stämpfli.

Hodson, F.R. (1970) Cluster analysis and archaeology: some new developments and applications. *World Archaeology* 1 (3), 229-320.

Hodson, F.R., Sneath, P.H.A. and Doran, J.E. (1966) Some experiments in the numerical analysis of archaeological data. *Biometrika* 53, 311-24.

Kendall, D.G. (1971) Seriation from abundance matrices. *In* Hodson, F.R., Kendall, D.G. and Tautu, P. (eds.) *Mathematics in the Archaeological and Historical Sciences*, 215-52. Edinburgh, University Press.

Meltzer, B. (1970) The semantics of induction and the possibility of complete systems of inductive inference. *Artificial Intelligence* 1, 189-92.

Schaaff, U. (1966) Zur Belegung latènzeitlicher Friedhöfe der Schweiz. *Jahrbuch des Römisch-Germanischen Zentralmuseums Mainz* 13, 49-59.

PEDER MORTENSEN

On the reflection of cultural changes in artifact materials - with special regard to the study of innovation contrasted with type stability

In archaeology the explanations for cultural changes are widely dependant upon a reliable observation of the reflections of such changes in archaeological materials. Dealing for example with settlement patterns or artifact assemblages it is obviously important to describe and analyse in great detail the developments which can be traced within each group in time and space. But to be able to explain any change in the development it is also necessary to define and express as exactly as possible the nature and size of the change observed. One of the procedures involved in this process is the breakdown of artifact assemblages into smaller units (types and elements) that can be treated numerically. This allows for a quantitative comparison of traits from site to site and from layer to layer within the individual site. Consequently it also makes it possible to trace and express quantitatively the fluctuations and changes within a given material. In other words it seems possible through a statistical treatment of many small units, such as artifact types and type elements to measure the degree of change in comparison with the established tradition, i.e. to evaluate the degree of innovation contrasted with the type stability within a stratified collection of material. The implications of this principle can be demonstrated by an example chosen from Palestinian prehistory.

When Kathleen Kenyon excavated Jericho she found on top of a Lower Natufian structure a long sequence of proto-neolithic and so-called pre-pottery neolithic A layers, characterized by round, semi-subterranean houses and by a flint industry that could clearly be traced back to Natufian traditions. Around 8000 B.C. a defensive wall with an impressive tower was built around the PPNA-settlement. Nevertheless, Jericho was destroyed, and the destruction was followed by a considerable gap in time with apparently no habitation. About 7000 B.C. the site was reoccupied by people living in rectangular houses, and with a chipped stone industry which has been named the Tahunian or the pre-pottery neolithic B culture. The apparent cultural change that could be observed at Jericho led Kathleen Kenyon to the assumption that the PPNA-people had defended their settlement against the PPNB-people, and that these men of a 'different culture who seized possession of the valuable site of Jericho' were foreigners (Kenyon 1960:102). Stimulated by this interpretation and by the obvious similarity between Jericho's rectangular houses and the architecture at a couple of Syrian sites (Tell Ramad I and Ras Shamra V C) several authors accepted the idea that the PPNB-culture was brought to Palestine by an actual migration of people from the north (cf. eg. Mellaart 1965:39-40 and 46, and Kirkbride 1966: 59-60).

With this in mind it was interesting to find that Diana Kirkbride's excavations at Beidha, a stratified neolithic village in southern Palestine, seemed to confirm the general impression gained from Jericho. Here again round and curvilinear houses occupied the lower levels (VI–IV), followed in level III by a change in architecture. Most of the houses in levels III–II were rectangular, with small rooms arranged on each side of a central corridor. A second break in the architectural tradition was represented by the appearance of another type of rectangular house in level I (Kirkbride 1968:263-74). In this connection Diana Kirkbride pointed out the similarity between the round and semicircular houses from Beidha's early levels (VI-IV) and those found in the so-called pre-pottery neolithic A layers at Jericho. She also felt that the significant appearance in level III of the corridor buildings might 'represent an importation reflecting a new element in the population' (Kirkbride 1967:9 and 12-13).

Recently I had the opportunity to study the development of the chipped stone industry within the Beidha sequence (Mortensen 1970:1-54). Supposing that a migration of people, or a new element in the neolithic population, would be reflected in the stone inventory, one of my aims was to see if it would be possible within the flint tool tradition to show the presence of a change that could be linked with the transition from round to rectangular houses in the Palestinian sites.

The study was based on an examination of 44,248 pieces of stratified flint and 3 pieces of obsidian. Out of this bulk of material 3,885 pieces represented tools that could be divided into 15 type groups (such as arrowheads, scrapers, burins, sickle-blades etc.). The type groups were subsequently divided into 67 individual types.

A statistical treatment of the 67 types showed a strong type stability with minor fluctuations from the earliest to the latest level, a period of habitation covering about 400 years. The development seems to have been gradual, with a few types appearing and disappearing in the course of time. A similar impression is given by Fig. 1, which illustrates the relative proportions of the type groups throughout the sequence.

LEVELS	A	B	C	D	E	F	G	H	J	K	L	M	N	O	P	NUMBER OF PIECES
I	23	25	5	10	13	9	2	5	1	3	0.5	0.5	1	1	1	464
II	20	19	3	8	20	8	1	3	0.5	6	5	0.5	1	1	4	1113
III	28	20	4	7	14	9	0.5	3	1	3	5	0.5	1	1	3	506
IV	24	22	5	10	15	11	1	4	1	2	2	0	0.5	0.5	2	740
V	26	14	6	11	15	11	0.2	4	2	5	4	0	1	0.5	0.3	449
VI	29	15	3	11	15	12	0	4	1	3	6	0	0	0.5	0.5	613

ARTIFACT TYPE GROUPS

Figure 1 Beidha: seriation diagram showing for each level the relative distribution of artifact type groups, expressed in percentages.

The type stability, contrasted with innovation and the disappearance of old types, can also be studied in the graph, Fig. 2. The presence of a type in a certain level is here indicated by a horizontal bar. Since many of the houses at Beidha were dug down into lower levels it is not unlikely that some flint implements were brought up from the earlier habitations. For this reason we cannot draw too definite conclusions on the presence of a type in a late context, if it is represented by only one or two pieces. In contrast to this, we can put more weight on the appearance of new types through the sequence. It emerges that out of 67 types, 43 are represented in all levels, and that 4 types appear for the first time in level V, 8 types in level IV, 4 types in level III, and 2 types in level II. On the basis of Fig. 2 the quantitative analysis of type stability can be carried a little further:

The 49 types that survive from level VI to level V are in level V represented by 441 pieces, but only 8 pieces (i.e. 1.8% of the material in level V) represent the four new types. Thus we can say that the innovation in level V constitutes 1.8%, and that the type stability – expressed in percentages – is 98.2%. In the same way, the 8 new types in level IV (26 pieces) come to 3.5% of the total number of artifacts from this layer. The type stability in level IV is thus 96.5%, whereas the innovation represents 3.5%. Proceeding in this way it is possible to construct an *innovation curve* showing the level-by-level accumulation of new types expressed in percentages.

The diagram, Fig. 3, shows that the innovation curve rises most steeply from level V to level IV, although the greatest change in architecture comes with level III, – and that the change in architecture from level II to level I is not reflected in the chipped stone inventory. During a period of approximately 400 years the type stability at Beidha is so high (93.3%) that without any reservation we must assume that the chipped stone industry represents a strong traditional development from generation to generation within the same group of people. Consequently, we must conclude that the change from round to rectangular houses in Palestine was hardly caused by a migration proper from the north. Even the arrival of a new population element at Beidha would be reflected in the

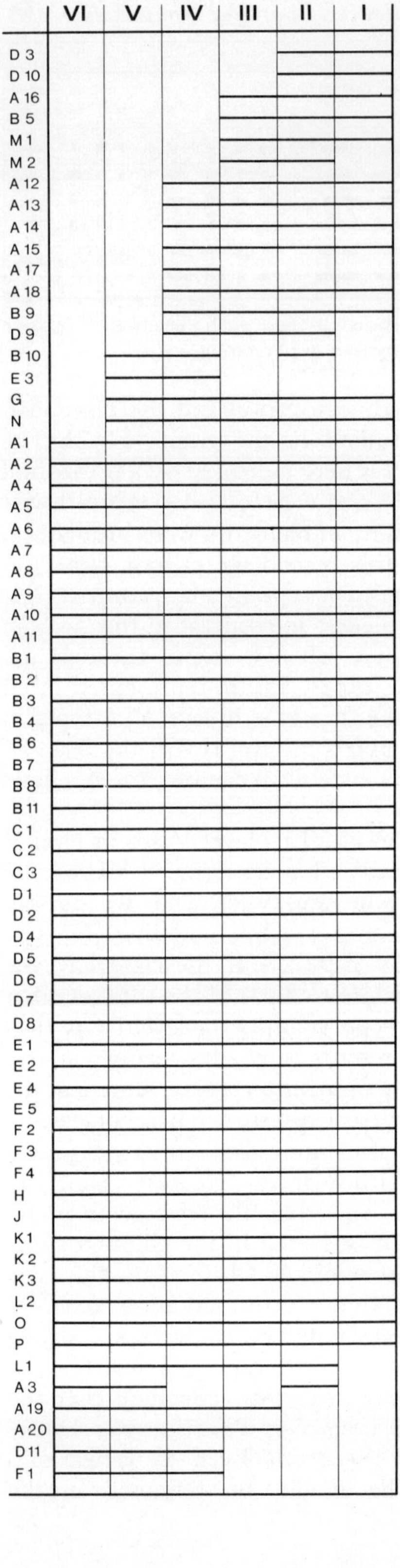

Figure 2 Beidha: diagram showing the distribution of artifact types through the sequence. Each type is indicated by a letter to denote the type group, followed by the number of the individual type.

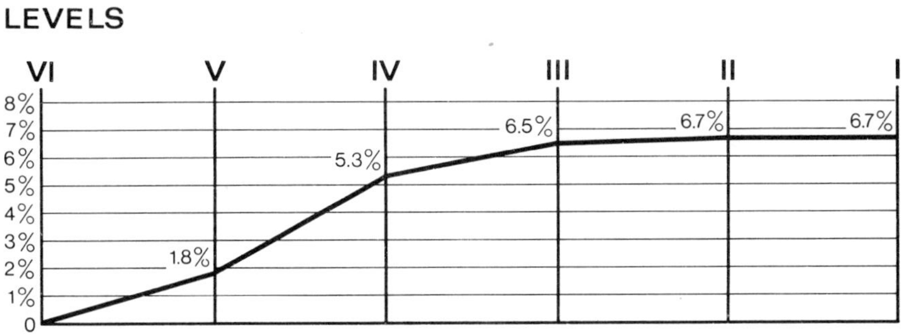

Figure 3 Beidha: diagram showing the degree of innovation as reflected by the chipped stone industry.

innovation curve, unless none of the new settlers occupied themselves with flint chipping, a very unlikely situation among a group of aceramic people in the early 7th millenium B.C.

On various levels the construction and interpretation of innovation diagrams are obviously beset with serious limitations. Essential for obtaining reliable and differentiated results are the character of the material and of its stratification as well as the sampling techniques used during the excavation. The typological framework on which the curves should be based is also of fundamental importance.

Given that these problems could be solved it might be possible to register most cultural changes within an area through a network of innovation diagrams. The interpretation of these, however, will in most cases be a subjective matter. The primary value of the innovation diagram for the archaeologist, therefore, seems to lie in its possible use as a sensitive reflector of changes of any kind in his material. In a future when innovation curves would be available for a series of sites related in time and space, they might prove helpful in the evaluation of the dynamics of cultural development within an area. In that case the quantitative information contained in the innovation curve would suggest an important step towards the qualitative analyses involved in producing explanations of cultural change.

REFERENCES

Kenyon, K.M. (1960) Excavations at Jericho, 1957-8. *Palestine Exploration Quarterly* **92**, 88-108.

Kirkbride, D. (1966) Five seasons at the pre-pottery neolithic village of Beidha in Jordan. *Palestine Exploration Quarterly* **98**, 8-72.

Kirkbride, D. (1967) Beidha 1965: An interim report. *Palestine Exploration Quarterly* **99**, 5-13.

Kirkbride, D. (1968) Beidha: early neolithic village life south of the Dead Sea. *Antiquity* **42**, 263-74.

Mellaart, J. (1965) *Earliest Civilizations of the Near East.* London, Thames and Hudson.

Mortensen, P. (1970) A preliminary study of the chipped stone industry from Beidha. *Acta Archaeologica* **41**, 1-54.

R. POLLNAC and A.J. AMMERMAN

A multivariate analysis of late palaeolithic assemblages in Italy

This study of late upper palaeolithic and epipalaeolithic flint assemblages in Italy is addressed to the level of interpretation that has been referred to as 'time-space systematics' (Sackett 1966). The aim of the analysis was to use the composition or structure of assemblages of retouched stone tools to try to arrive at regional or chronological groupings or a combination of the two. Structure in the assemblages was to be determined by the use of two multivariate statistical techniques which we have found to complement one another.

The analysis was performed on a group of 46 assemblages: 36 from Italy, 6 from Sicily and 5 from south-east France. The majority of the assemblages date to the period between about 12,000 B.C. and 6,000 B.C. In general, the Italian material, which is often referred to as Epigravettian, offers few opportunities for the identification of chronological horizons or regional groupings on the basis of individual diagnostic types. In previous attempts to analyse and interpret the Italian assemblages (Laplace 1964), little use has actually been made of data in primary type form. The data used in the analysis was drawn largely from the extensive work of Laplace (1966) on upper palaeolithic and epipalaeolithic assemblages in Italy. The data set included forty-six of the eighty-five primary types in the Laplace type-list. These accounted for 90% or more of the total number of retouched stone tools (not including fragments of backed blades) in each assemblage.

As a first step, a principal components analysis (Q-technique; see Table 1) was carried out on the data in standardized form. The resultant factor matrix was subsequently rotated to orthogonal simple structure (see Rummel 1970 for a description of how this can be done). The first six of the ten rotated factors are listed in Table 2; the first three rotated factors explained 52% of the total variance in the data set. In order to find out which tool types were most highly correlated with these factors, factor scores were calculated, using the regression estimate technique, for each of the forty-six primary tool types. The results of this part of the analysis are presented at the bottom of Table 2, where tool types are listed in descending order for each factor on the basis of their factor scores (using a cut-off value of 0.75).

The next step was to perform a cluster analysis on the same data set, which was again initially standardized. The clustering technique employed was the hierarchical grouping technique described by Veldman (1967). The results of this analysis are presented in Fig. 1. The factor matrix (from the first step) was then rearranged so that the order of appearance of assemblages in the matrix corresponded with the groupings produced by the cluster analysis. As can be seen in Table 2, there is considerable similarity between the results from the principal components factor analysis and the cluster analysis. The results obtained from the two different statistical techniques provide the analysis with a degree of convergent validity, as well as offering complementary information on the relationships between and structure of the assemblages.

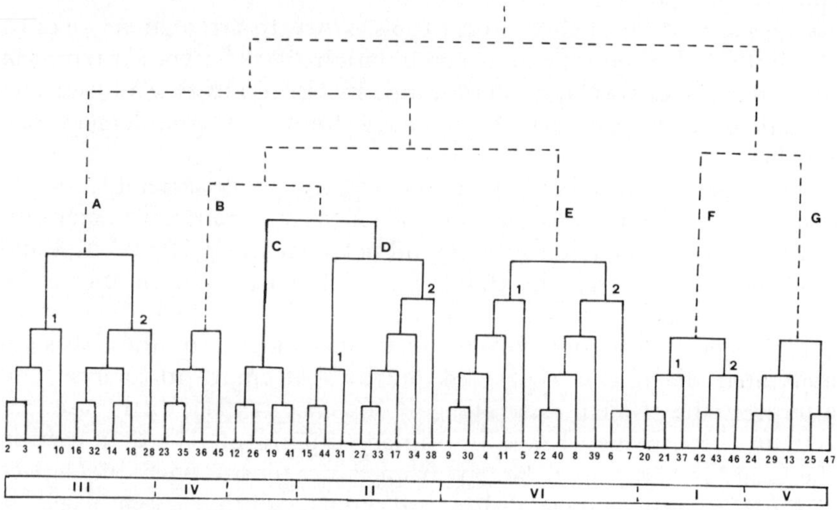

Figure 1 Cluster analysis of forty-seven assemblages; successive stages in the grouping process after the level of six groups are indicated by broken lines. The main Factor (see Table 2) associated with a group or cluster is indicated below the dendrogram.

We shall not attempt a detailed interpretation of the results here. Most of the Italian assemblages that are considered to be late Epigravettian are found in clusters A and E, which both show a certain amount of geographic diversity. The assemblages in A1 (see Fig. 1) come from southern Italy, while those in A2 are from central Italy. The assemblages in E2 represent both southern and northern Italy. This would seem to lend support to the view that marked regional differences or traditions are not easy to recognize, at least at the level of primary types, in the late Epigravettian assemblages of Italy (Ammerman 1971). It is interesting to note that the assemblages from Sicily and France do not appear in these two clusters: the 'foreign' assemblages make their appearance mainly in clusters B, C and D. These same clusters also happen to contain most of the 'early' Italian assemblages in the analysis. It is possible that these three clusters have taken up those assemblages that do not belong in clusters A, E, F and G. The latter, despite a few exceptions such as the presence of Cavallo D in cluster G, seem to represent much more unified groupings.

The three Montadian assemblages from south-east France (Escalon de Fonton 1967) are all found in F2. The other half of cluster F contains the three assemblages from the epipalaeolithic part of the deposit at Arene Candide in Liguria, which has yielded a radiocarbon date of about 8,300 B.C. The close chronological and geographic relationship here should be noted. The importance of the denticulates in the structure of certain Italian epipalaeolithic assemblages is also confirmed by the analysis. The two tool types most highly correlated with Factor I (the factor which explains the most variance within the data set) are both denticulates. Most of the assemblages that are known to be epipalaeolithic in date fall in clusters E2, F and G, which all have high or moderately high values on Factors I and V.

Table 1

1.	0.505	8.	0.897
2.	0.672	9.	0.916
3.	0.744	10.	0.931
4.	0.786	11.	0.943
5.	0.823	12.	0.952
6.	0.854	13.	0.959
7.	0.876	14.	0.966

Cumulative proportion of total variance for the first fourteen unrotated Factors.

Table 2: Rotated Factor Matrix (Varimax)

		Factors					
Assemblages		I	II	III	IV	V	VI
2	Romanelli A-B	.04	.03	–.86	–.08	–.03	–.07
3	Romanelli C	–.03	.22	–.89	.00	.02	–.12
1	Cipolliane 1	.07	.15	–.83	–.22	.08	–.36
10	Santa Croce	.30	.17	–.58	–.10	–.09	–.15
16	Ponte Lucano 2	–.02	.29	–.81	–.38	–.04	–.05
32	Ponte Lucano 5	–.06	.38	–.74	–.46	.01	–.01
14	Sezze Romano	–.05	.37	–.75	–.38	.08	–.19
18	Tana del Diavolo	.04	.55	–.59	–.41	.02	.06
28	Cipolliane 3	–.06	.59	–.63	–.04	.03	–.26
23	Riparo Mochi A	.00	.22	–.16	–.89	–.18	–.03
35	Castello	.00	.12	–.12	–.97	–.09	.00

36	Mangipane	−.05	.20	−.20	−.88	.03	−.10
45	Sablon	.22	.12	−.44	−.63	−.06	−.22
12	Cala delle Ossa	.03	.41	−.47	−.59	−.04	−.14
26	Corrugi	.35	.34	−.44	−.56	−.01	.05
19	Ponte di Pietra	.24	.17	−.04	−.49	−.63	.00
41	Calanca upper	.36	.57	−.16	−.41	−.38	−.17
15	Palidoro	.21	.66	−.20	−.55	−.22	−.17
44	Chinchon B	.27	.62	−.11	−.53	−.16	.10
31	Palidoro 5	.06	.65	−.34	−.38	−.18	−.20
27	San Teodoro A	.45	.73	−.25	−.25	−.12	−.26
33	San Teodoro B	.38	.73	−.33	−.21	−.13	−.22
17	Ortucchio A-D	.62	.59	−.28	−.25	−.19	−.16
34	San Teodoro C	.37	.62	−.28	−.45	−.26	−.10
38	A. Candide F1-F3	.29	.69	−.36	−.22	−.19	.06
9	Mura upper	.31	.43	−.34	−.12	−.05	−.72
30	Paglicci 9	.22	.73	−.37	−.11	−.07	−.43
4	Taurisano 1-5	.21	.22	−.31	−.09	−.21	−.74
11	Paglicci 4	.25	.24	−.46	−.15	−.25	−.35
5	Ugento P.Z.	.15	.35	−.22	−.03	.02	−.35
22	Stefanin IV	.43	.40	−.38	−.17	−.41	−.40
40	Stefanin V	.56	.39	−.41	−.37	−.24	−.28
8	Cavallo BIIb	.26	.53	−.30	−.24	−.33	−.44
39	Riparo Mochi C	.55	.49	−.08	−.07	−.25	−.52
6	Cavallo BI	.71	−.01	−.19	−.04	−.25	−.37
7	Cavallo BIIa	.47	.21	−.22	−.02	−.45	−.50
20	A. Candide I	.88	.15	−.32	−.12	−.13	−.08
21	A. Candide II	.82	.23	−.25	−.29	−.14	−.02
37	A. Candide III	.79	.42	−.08	−.07	−.06	−.17
42	Montade	.95	.16	.15	.00	−.03	−.13
43	Ventabren	.94	.05	.10	.01	−.06	.05
46	Cornille middle	.87	.20	.12	.03	−.26	−.10
24	Veia C IV-VI	.63	.23	.11	.02	−.67	−.13
29	Cavallo D	.74	.15	−.02	.03	−.50	−.11
13	Blanc upper	.74	.00	.13	.04	−.41	−.25
25	Pattaglia	.30	.23	−.14	−.15	−.73	−.36
47	Preta 6	.39	.12	.11	−.15	−.86	−.01
	Percentage of Total Variance on Factor	20.4	16.1	15.9	13.3	8.4	7.5

Variables (tool types in the Laplace type-list) are listed below in descending order on the basis of Factor Scores, using a cut-off value of 0.75 (in the same + or − direction as the Factor).

Factor
I: D2, D1, L1, R1
II: L2, L1, B2, LD2
III: L2, G3, G4, P2, G5, LD2
IV: PD4, G2
V: D1, T3, T1, A1, T2
VI: R2, L1, R1, G4, D8, G3, G2, LD1

REFERENCES

Ammerman, A.J. (1971) A computer analysis of epipalaeolithic assemblages in Italy. *In* Kendall, D.G. Hodson, F.R. and Tautu, P. (eds.) *Mathematics in the Archaeological and Historical Sciences.* Edinburgh, University Press.

Escalon de Fonton, M. (1967) Les séquences sédimento-climatiques du Midi méditerranéen du Wurm à l'Holocène. *Bulletin du Musée d'Anthropologie Préhistorique de Monaco* 14, 125-85.

Laplace, G. (1964) Les subdivisions du Leptolithique italien. Etude de typologie analytique. *Bullettino di Paletnologia Italiana* 73, 25-63.

Laplace, G. (1966) *Récherches sur l'origine et l'évolution des complexes Leptolithique.* Ecole française de Rome. Supplements 4.

Rummel, R.J. (1970) *Applied Factor Analysis.* Evanston, Northwestern University Press.

Sackett, J.R. (1966) Quantitative analysis of Upper Palaeolithic stone tools. *American Anthropologist* 66, 356-94.

Veldman, D.J. (1967) *Fortran Programming for the Behavioural Sciences.* New York, Holt, Rinehart and Winston.

L.M. GROUBE and J. CHAPPELL

Measuring the difference between archaeological assemblages

During a shared and volatile infancy in the 19th century, biology and archaeology adapted classification as a method of reducing the complexities of their rapidly expanding data. Classification offered not only a simple method for systematic description, but within the structure of the system, a measure of the degree of resemblance between various units and, particularly in biology, an explanation of the inter-relationships. With the burden of accumulating data and with new methods of detecting variation, classical taxonomy has becomes increasingly cumbersome and insensitive: new methods of establishing resemblances have been developed.

All such methods, including classical taxonomy, are concerned with establishing scales, or in more mundane terms, constructing measuring sticks by which the complex variation inherent in biology and archaeology can be more accurately and less subjectively 'measured'. The problems of establishing a scale were overcome in classical taxonomy by erecting a hierarchy of different scales by giving priorities to certain selected variables. This procedure avoided the mathematical complexities of establishing a single scale compiled from a multitude of variables each with their own range of variation and with an unknown degree of interdependence. The selection of the priority variables was largely determined by the utility of the final system; in fact the most powerful justification of classical taxonomy has always been that 'it works'.

The difficulties of establishing a more sensitive scale for measuring resemblances in biology, archaeology and the behavioural sciences come from the complexities of the detectable variation. Because, in many cases, the variation cannot be scored on interval or ratio scales, the powerful manipulations of arithmetic, upon which the precision of the physical sciences is based, cannot be applied. For this reason also many standard statistical tests are inapplicable and the establishment of standardized scales (such as are available to the physicist or chemist) is impossible. The number of attributes which can have detectable variation can be very large and with such multi-variation it is difficult to assess the importance of each type of scale or variation or to devise methods by which the discrete variations can be combined or summarized.

These problems are confronted in the approach which is usually called numerical taxonomy, and which has emerged in the non-physical sciences. The methods of numerical taxonomy, however, are not restricted to taxonomic problems, and a more appropriate description would be 'the systematics of resemblance', and it is fundamentally a method of establishing degrees of difference in terms of numerical scales. Its advocates claim for it a new objectivity. Similar methods had been developed in physical anthropology to measure racial variation (Pearson 1926; Mahalanobis 1930, 1936) and in archaeology by Kroeber (1940), Brainerd (1951), Robinson (1951) and Doran and Hodson (1966), although the community of these latter methods within the overall methodology of numerical taxonomy is not always understood. During recent years archaeologists have tended, as they did in the nineteenth century, to borrow the methods directly from biologists (e.g. Hodson, Sneath and Doran, 1966).

This paper is concerned with the usefulness of this new approach to the special problem of 'measuring' resemblance or difference between archaeological assemblages. It is necessary, however, to describe the methods and limitations of numerical taxonomy.

In its initial stages the methods of numerical taxonomy conform to standard practice in archaeology, viz: the observation of variation and isolation of relevant characters or attributes by which the individual or group can be distinguished. With archaeological data this selection is usually aided by the use of relevant tests of significance and interdependence. The next stage of coding the attributes is also familiar to archaeologists. Thereafter the special methods of numerical taxonomy which employ one of a number of indices of resemblance or difference, depart from standard archaeological methods and require a rather more detailed description.

Numerical taxonomy involves the pairwise comparison of each unit with every other in terms of a set of scaled attributes and this data is used to compile resemblance scores. The resultant matrix of resemblance score furnishes the basis of systematic classification of the units and to this end is subjected to some form of mathematical technique, usually involving systematic clustering and statistical discrimination.

The general procedure, omitting mathematical algorithms, is summarized in the following schema. Each of the stages shown here has its own technical problems and we shall deal with each in turn.

1. Observation of ensemble of units and selection of important attributes.
2. Setting up of attribute scales.
3. Measurement and organization of data into a matrix of the form:

Operational Taxonomic Units

Attributes		1	2	3
	1	S_{11}	S_{12}	S_{13}
	2	S_{21}	S_{22}	etc.
	3			

S_{ij} is the score of ith attribute for the jth unit

4. Calculation of resemblance coefficients (by use of an index of resemblance) and organization of this data into a matrix of the form:

Units

		1	2	3
	1	C_{11}	C_{12}	C_{13}
Units	2	C_{21}	C_{22}	etc.
	3			

C_{ij} is 'resemblance' between ith and jth units.

5. Systematic processing by chosen form of mathematical analysis.

Formalising the objects of study

Operational Taxonomic Units are the units of investigation being formal approximations of the real data and defined in terms of chosen attributes. In archaeology the OTUs vary from single artifacts through assemblages of artifacts to larger ensembles representing cultures. To avoid confusion with biologists' usage it is convenient to refer to *Operational Archaeological Units* (OAUs). Having formally identified the OAUs the next step towards discriminatory description is the setting up of scales for each of the defining attributes.

Scaling *(Siegel 1956; 21-30)*

Because the OAUs have culturally determined qualities of form as well as physical attributes such as specific gravity etc. there is a real problem in establishing scales for the systematic determination of all attributes. To indicate the problem we note that with stone artifacts, for example, such attributes as colour, hardness and length may vary over a range of many possible 'values', and thus can be referred to as *multistate* attributes. Other qualities of form such as decorative motifs, the significance of which can be merely in their presence or absence, may be regarded as *2-state* attributes. Upon examination the 3 examples of multi-state attributes given above are seen to differ qualitatively as follows:

(i) Colour. Our basic manipulation of this attribute is to divide it into a series of mutually exclusive classes such that the only relationship between coloured objects is one of equivalence/non-equivalence. This subdivision gives a *nominal* scale, the simplest case of which is our 2-state or present/absent attribute.

(ii) Hardness. In addition to the equivalence/non equivalence criterion, here we ask also the question 'more, or less hard?', and so achieve a *ranking* of mutually exclusive classes for our attribute scale. With such a ranked or *ordinal* scale there are, however, no normal arithmetic properties to the numbered levels in such a ranking because we make no attempt to evaluate the intervals between adjacent levels. e.g., the rank hardness difference between talc and calcite is 2 steps on Moh's scale, as is the difference between topaz and diamond, but the *absolute* difference within the latter pair is very many times that of the former.

(iii) Length, which is a standard physical attribute, is uniquely determined in terms of a number scale and thus scores can be arithmetically manipulated. Correct numerical scaling, either by integers or real (decimal fraction) numbers, gives *interval* scales.

The type of scale used for a given attribute may vary from one research worker to another according to perception of the diagnostic role of the attribute. For example, the attribute of colour is basically scaleable only at the nominal level (i.e. red/not red, etc.). However, colour can have ordinal signification (*more* red, etc.) when (a) it corresponds to a concealed attribute, such as the reflection of mineral concentration in soils by their colour (e.g., the well known Munsell soil colour scales), or (b) by direct ordination into scales for aesthetic or cultural reasons, as for example in the colour scales of Chevreul (Birren 1967).

The type of scale chosen for an attribute may thus be physically or culturally determined – things which from a physical point of view can be only readily scaled at ordinal level, say, may be placed into correspondence with a culture's monetary value system, and thus be manipulated at the interval scale level.

There is a compulsion to use interval scales for attributes, wherever possible, because the parametric statistical tests which can then be employed generally allow more powerful discrimination to be made than the non-parametric tests used with ordinal (or nominal) data.

Preparation of the data matrix

The data matrix, presenting a series of OAUs defined by scores along appropriate attribute scales, is usually organized with the OAUs as column scores and the attributes (or characters) as rows (Sokal and Sneath (1963). Pairwise comparison can proceed between either OAUs (columns: Q-analysis) or the attributes (row R-analysis) depending on the purpose of the analysis. Because, as will be seen in the next section, most indices of comparison involve amalgamation of differences calculated in various ways between individual column or row scores, care must be taken to ensure the *comparability* of the scores. The tactic adopted in the experiments described below, of scoring the disparate attributes of Oceanic adzes into frequency of occurrence scores, ensures that comparison is based on an array of different scores. It has the advantage of manoeuvring the nominal scaled adze date into scores with internal scale status, improving the definition of the final geometric model employed in the analysis.

Indices for comparison

Having collected data for an ensemble of OAUs under the heading of appropriately scaled attributes, the next decision is to do with choosing an index as basis for establishing resemblance. This is done in accordance with some centralizing intention, e.g. in the case of ontogenic succession the index should unambiguously reflect closeness of relationship.

The necessary question 'by how much do things differ?' entails logical compilation of pairwise comparisons of the attribute scores of OAUs. The compilation must comply firstly with the manipulative limits set by the scales, and secondly with the quality of the presumed differences. Let us clarify these points in turn.

(i) The formal difference between interval and ordinal scales requires that for the latter an index of comparison can be compiled only by non-parametric procedures, whereas for the former the more powerful manipulations of arithmetic are permissible. Interval scales themselves have an intrinsic limitation, viz. it is meaningful to compare ratios of *differences* between individual scores, but not meaningful to discuss the ratios of the scores themselves. The latter is possible only when the zero point for the scale is not arbitrary; satisfying this requirement gives the highest status scale, known as a *ratio* scale. A particular implication is that only when attributes are ratio scaled can we speak of 'degree of similarity'. Without ratio scaling we can only speak of degrees of difference.

(ii) The procedure for compiling a set of pairwise differences into a score for comparison of 2 OAUs differs according to whether one is concerned with gross differences or pattern differences. We may illustrate this distinction as follows:

Imagine 2 OAUs each being a collection of 100 axe blades. We measure some attribute e.g. length of each artifact and histogram the data (Fig. 1). Gross differences between the OAUs may be compiled by summing 100 individual pairwise differences. Pattern difference, however, refers in this case to the difference in shape of the histograms of the 2 OAUs and this is assessed by scaling one of the 2 sets of values to eliminate gross differences (dashed curve, Fig. 1) and then summing residual differences.

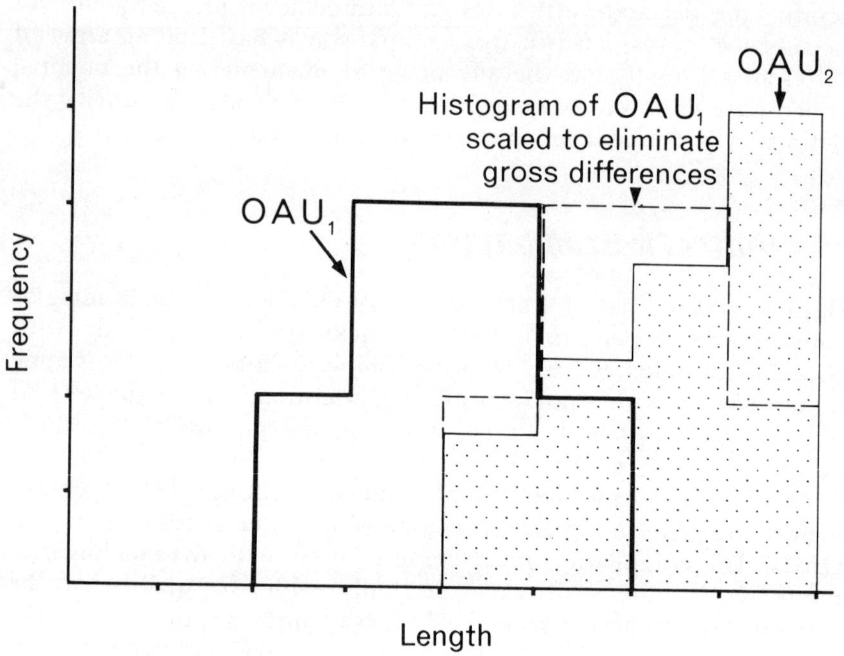

Figure 1 Histograms for 2 hypothetical OAUs, to illustrate gross differences vs. pattern differences.

These procedures are simple when the OAUs are defined in terms of only a single attribute, but in general a number of attributes are involved, which introduces an additional problem when we seek to attach meaning to a composite index. To illustrate the problem suppose a pair of OAUs with n interval scaled attributes. We have as data the attribute differences –

$$S_k = (X_{1k} - X_{2k})k = 1,.., n \quad (1)$$

where X_{1k}, X_{2k} are the scores for the kth attribute for the 1st and

2nd OAUs respectively.

We may seem to presume least if we compile a comparison index, I_{12}, by merely summing these scores e.g.

$$I_{12} = \sum_{k=1}^{n} S_k = \sum_{k=1}^{n} |X_{1k} - X_{2k}| \qquad (2)$$

(where the line brackets, |....|, indicate that all differences are taken as positive to eliminate ambiguities).

This simple summation is not strictly true to the intuition underlying the assessment of gross difference in terms of a single attribute, however, for in that case we make the assumption 'difference = distance apart of scores on the single attribute axis'. Translating this into the case of multiple attributes the assumption becomes 'difference = distance apart in the space defined by n attribute axes'. If these axes are independant then logical compilation of I_{12} is –

$$I_{12} = \sqrt{[\Sigma S_k^2]} = \sqrt{[\sum_{k=1}^{n} (X_{2k} - X_{2k})^2]} \qquad (3)$$

i.e. the Pythogorean distance measure.

The multiple attribute case involves also the problem of differences in diagnostic importances of the attributes. Treatment of this requires

(i) assignation by the research worker of weightings to each attribute proportional to their relative importances, and

(ii) adjusting the *range* of each attribute scale proportional to these weightings.

In the common case where lack of knowledge precludes assignation of weighting factors then in order to minimize bias in the analysis all scales must be *standardized* or given the same range.

Just as gross differences are assessed for the multi-attribute case in a manner analogous with the single attribute case, i.e. by compiling a distance measure such as equation (3), or a more sophisticated version such as Mahalanobis-D, so too are pattern differences assessed. The single attribute case is generally treated by a *correlation* measure e.g.

$$r_{12} = \sum_{i=1}^{m} (X_{1i} - \overline{X}_1)\ (X_{2i} - \overline{X}_2)/\sigma_1 \cdot \sigma_2 \qquad (4)$$

where X_{1i}, X_{2i} are the scores for the ith members of the 1st OAU and 2nd OAU, respectively, and $\overline{X}_1$, $\overline{X}_2$ are the means of the 2 OAUs. Scaling to eliminate gross differences (*v.* Fig. 1) is achieved by dividing by the standard deviations σ_1, σ_2. The multi-attribute case is treated in the same manner, and the resulting correlation coefficient r_{12} reflects the detailed correspondence of patterns. Statistical significance of r, and its non-parametric counterparts for ordinal and nominal-scaled data, is estimated when certain formal conditions, such as normal distribution of the data, are satisfied. We can now proceed, in the light of this sketch of scaling and index compilation, to practical analysis of an ensemble of OAUs.

Practical analysis of an ensemble of OAUs

Most OAUs are themselves assemblages of artifacts, with numbers ranging from a few tens of items to upwards of several hundred items. It is this fact that allows us to manoeuvre nominal scaled attributes to interval scale status in the form of frequency scores. Suppose that the presence/absence (two state nominal scale) of a feature is a matter of chance, then its frequency of occurrence amongst the artifacts making up the OAU can be taken as a probability, $P = n_i/N$, where n_i is the number of times the ith attribute occurs in an OAU containing N items. Similarly, the frequencies of class occurrence for a multistate nominal scale can be treated as probabilities of each class. To illustrate, consider the first attribute in Table 1 – this in a nominal scale with 9 states. The percentage frequencies of occurrence of each of these states for each of 22 OAUs is given in Table 2.

For purposes of classification we desire a distance measure for data of the following form:

1st Attribute:	State		OAU 1	OAU 2
	,,	1	X_{11}	X_{21}
	,,	2	X_{12}	X_{22}
	,,	3	.	.
	.	.	.	.
		k	X_{1k}	X_{2k}
	Totals		$\sum_k X_{1k} = 100\%$	$\sum_k X_{2k} = 100\%$

In accordance with the argument preceding equation (3), distances can be assessed on a Pythagorean basis, but to be consistent to the principle of least bias we must weight all differences equally. This is done by dividing each distance component (i.e. $(X_{1i} - X_{2i})^2$ for the ith state) by the mean value for that state. i.e., for n states –

$$d_{12} = \tfrac{1}{2}n \sum_{i=1}^{n} (X_{1i} - X_{2i})^2 / (X_{1i} + X_{2i}) \qquad (5)$$

When there is more than one multistate attribute this formulation still holds; if it is believed that attributes should be given equal weighting then frequencies of occurrence of each state can be converted to percentages within that attribute (as in table 2): if *states* themselves are reckoned to be equally important then the percentage scores should be biassed by scaling by the number of states within their parent attribute.

This formulation has been used as the basis for systematic classification of 22 assemblages (OAUs) of Oceanic adzes, defined according to table 1, and scores are given in table 2. Before proceeding to discuss this material we close this section by indicating formal properties of the distance statistic given by (5).

The standard hypothesis in statistical testing of the difference between 2 assemblages is the null hypothesis, i.e. that observed differences are only chance variations between 2 samples from 1 parent distribution. This null hypothesis may be tested by

$$X^2 = \sum_{i=1}^{n} \sum_{j=1}^{2} (0_{ij} - E_{ij})^2/(E_{ij}) \tag{6}$$

where Os are observed frequencies and Es are expected frequencies in table 3.

For a pair of OAUs, the expected frequencies are estimated by diving the observed frequencies by the means e.g.,

$$E_{11} = O_{11} / \tfrac{1}{2} (O_{11} + O_{12}).$$

Simple algebra shows that our distance measure, equation (5), is equivalent to (6) as long as the attribute states are brought to percentage frequencies in both OAUs, and thus d_{ij} is distributed as a χ^2 statistic, and standard significance tests can be applied.

Processing the coefficients of distance

The final stage of numerical taxonomy is directed at identifying systematic relationships between all OAUs in the light of their pairwise distance coefficients. The simplest of these techniques, familiar to archaeologists from the work of Robinson (1951), Clarke (1962), LeRoy Johnson (1968) and many others, is matrix sorting where the columns and rows of difference coefficient scores are sorted according to some principle, usually so that coefficients reflecting the smallest differences fall along the matrix diagonal. The order of OAUs along the axes of the sorted matrix offers a one-dimensional scale of relationship. In the earliest efforts of matrix sorting in archaeology the order of OAUs along the axes was taken as a chronological seriation, hence the claims of Brainerd (1951:311) to have devised a method for 'chronologically ordering archaeological deposits'. As LeRoy Johnson warns, however, the method (as with all seriation) is 'elementary similarity scaling', the order is simply a similarity or resemblance scale, and interpretation of this order as corresponding to chronological succession is an inference requiring independent validation (e.g. stratigraphic evidence) (LeRoy Johnson 1968:43).

This issue of relating the taxonomic relationships to reconstructions of prehistoric relationships is crucial. The problem of estimating *correspondence rules* entails assumptions concerning history of cultural exchange, diversification, and rates of cultural evolution of the groups represented by the OAUs. Thus the key to making an archaeologic interpretation of the systematic difference relationships always involves the use of a hypothesis, such as 'artifact evolution in two groups of common origin diverges monotonically from their point of separation'.

Regarding the matrix sorting method of identifying relationships between OAUs, it is important to note that perfect sorting is seldom attainable. Matrices exhibit what has come to be called 'strain' (△) (Kruskal 1964), where rows or columns in the matrix can take alternative positions without offending the sorting criteria. This is because the history of cultural diversification, for a region, is rarely likely to resemble a simple branching process, mainly because of reversals in cultural progressions, and cross-cultural exchanges of various sorts. More powerful multivariate sorting techniques significantly reduce strain, although the presence of this factor can generate misleading apparent grouping relationships (Jardine and Gibson 1968).

For more important reasons the systematic grouping of OAUs might in fact mislead the archaeologist. Firstly, the aura of formal precision, surrounding a modern multivariate grouping method, may camouflage the fact that such manipulation cannot generate correspondence rules. Secondly, much of the archaeologist's insight comes from perceiving serial relationships within an ensemble of OAUs, rather than from groupings. Thus it seems more fundamental to examine the geometric relationships between a set of OAUs, in the light of their pairwise distances. The criterion for a satisfactory number of dimensions should be based on the proportion of unexplained variance, which is indicative of strain. If a representation can be achieved in 2 or 3 dimensions then serial relationships can be seen almost as easily as in traditional one dimensional seriation. As we show below, a 3-dimensional model proves to be satisfactory for our test data, which is based on assemblages of Oceanic adzes.

Assemblage differences in Oceanic adzes

Assemblages of Oceanic stone adzes (housed in various New Zealand museums) were selected for an initial experiment aimed at testing the usefulness, as an aid to interpreting prehistory, of the principles of numerical taxonomy. The adze data offered two immediate advantages. The Oceanic situation, long accepted as a laboratory for problems of culture change, offered rigorous control over geographical separation, which is one of the important factors of archaeological variation. It could be anticipated that, despite the cross-movements and stray voyaging which did take place, isolation between the major island groups was effective enough to lead to the development of local variation. Thus, one of the organizing principles that might emerge from a study of Oceanic adzes would be spatial, corresponding to the geographic distance logistics of the Pacific Ocean. A second advantage was that Oceanic stone adzes had been successfully studied by classical taxonomic methods for over fifty years. Excavation in various parts of Polynesia had confirmed many of the hypotheses developed from these classifications, so that it could be fairly claimed that not only was it the most frequently surviving artifact in this area of the world but more was known about its development and dispersal than any other single artifact type.

The selected attributes and states and the data matrix of normalized frequency scores are given in tables 1 and 2. Although sample sizes (n) vary considerably they were considered adequate for the experiment. In one case (Niue) all the known adzes are recorded. Uniformity in some of the assemblages suggests that large samples would not have changed the percentage scores greatly.

The attribute list is relatively simple and is based on those features which have been shown to have diagnostic significance from earlier taxonomic work. The various attribute states cover most the more frequently occurring parameters of variation. All the attribute scales are, of course, *nominal* and as is frequently the case with such scales, decisions (particularly between some of the cross-section states) were sometimes arbitrary. Because of such uncertainties it was not anticipated that anything new would emerge from the exercise: the test was to ascertain whether despite these disadvantages, the methods of numerical taxonomy were sufficiently sensitive to yield plausible results.

Plausibility, of course, was based upon the authors' familiarity with adzes, personal involvement with some of the sites from which the assemblages were drawn as well as the rapidly expanding facts of Pacific prehistory. A more objective test of plausibility, of course, was the geographical constraints offered by the Oceanic situation.

The OAUs vary from island groups (e.g. Tuamotus) to single islands (Pitcairn) to individual sites or provinces (particularly in New Zealand). The assemblages were normalized into percentages of states within each attribute, but scores were not rescaled to adjust for variation in the number of states within the attributes.

The degree of variance explained was calculated for optimal arrangements of the OAUs in each of 1, 2 and 3 dimensions. Variance at each dimensional level was calculated by – (i) taking M+1 points to define an M–dimension grouping space. These points are initially a random selection from the ensemble of OAUs.

Co-ordinates from the remaining OAUs are calculated, and differences between observed and calculated pairwise distances are compiled to give the variance. Then (ii) the group of points chosen to define the space is varied until a minimum variance estimate is achieved. On this basis, the unexplained variance for the set of 22 Oceanic adze OAUs was found to be 40% for 1 dimension, 30% for 2 dimensions, and only 12% for 3 dimensions. Consequently, the distance data is easily represented almost without strain in 3 dimensions, and it was possible to construct an actual model scaled from the pairwise distance data. All the OAUs prove to be significantly different (χ^2 2-sample test; Siegel 1956:104), with probability of the null hypothesis < 0·1%, except for the Bougainville – New Guinea pair where it is 10%.

Not only do the overall relationships between OAUs emerge clearly in 3 dimensions, but also are serial trends of individual attributes clearly manifest (Fig. 2). The physical representation of the distance data in three dimensions, by the construction of an actual, tangible model analogous to those constructed by molecular biologists, is readily examinable. It serves as a convenient basis for comparison with postulates about the prehistory of Oceania.

Interpretation of the model

The final 3-dimensional model, as had been expected, had marked geographical axes both E/W and N/S, with islands in close proximity plausibly clustered with the model. The regions classically differentiated by ethnologists, such as Melanesia, Western Polynesia and Eastern Polynesia are clearly differentiated (Fig. 3a). Only the elongated cluster of sites from early and late sites in New Zealand fall out of the geographical pattern. The Tuamotian adze assemblage, in the actual sample remarkably like collections from early New Zealand sites, is also out of geographical position. Other organizational 'axes' are more difficult to detect: time is certainly not important in this model, as Fig. 3b demonstrates. The generally accepted chronological relationships dart about the model in various directions. The trend of the New Zealand sites, however, appears to be along a time axis, the earliest sites (Archaic) most like East Polynesian assemblages, the later sites predominating adzes closer to West Polynesian and Melanesian forms. The 'reversal' within the model is a reflection of the well-known but puzzling 'devolution' of the adze form in New Zealand when the varied and sophisticated East Polynesian adze kit brought by the earliest settlers was abandoned. If, as with the New Zealand data, a number of sites with known chronology had been available from each island group it is probable that the time axes would be as various as the islands themselves.

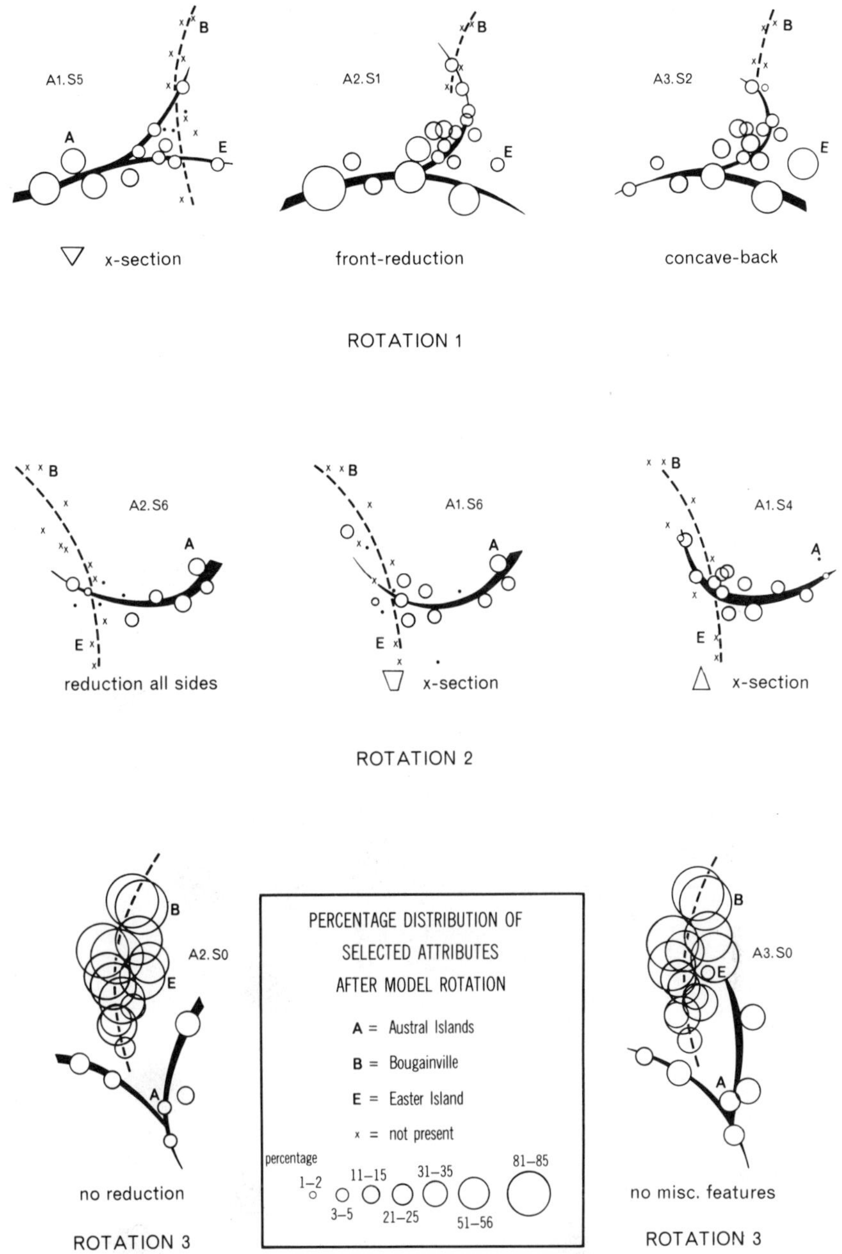

Figure 2 Systematic trends of selected attributes, across the 3-D framework of model of distance interrelationships of OAUs of Oceanic adzes.

The prehistoric lessons from the final model are not many. The attributes in the coding were the same as used in building the classical taxonomies of Oceanic adzes in use for over two decades. The importance of the attributes, however, has been confirmed. The

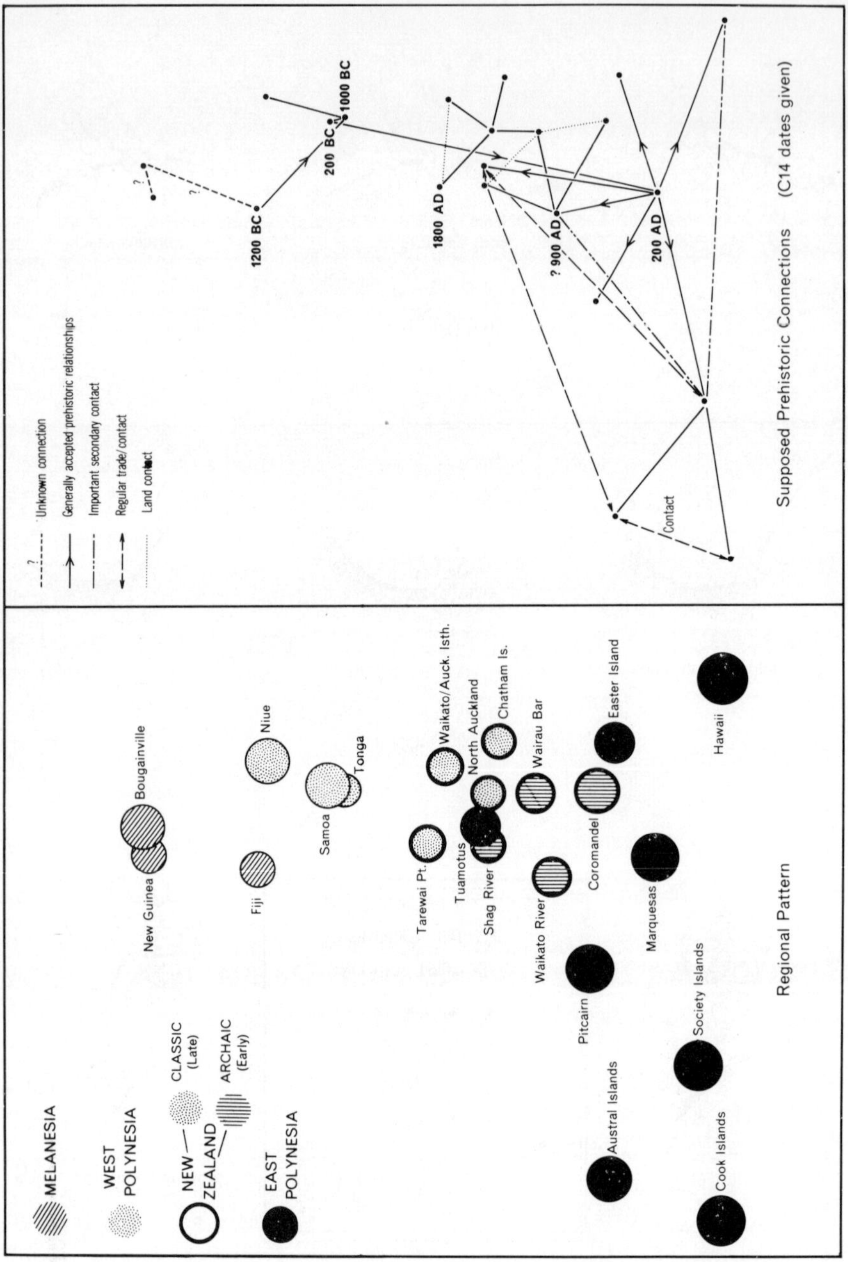

Figure 3 Two-dimensional projection of 3-D model.

new relationship between the Tuamotus and the earliest New Zealand sites is probably due to the inadequate sample of Tuamotuan adzes, but is not implausible. Many sub-groups within the major regional divisions are reinforced by the model: the Society

Islands, Cook Islands and Austral Islands form a separate triangular cluster, a reflection of the well-documented trade and political relationships between the groups. The slightly aberrant position of Easter Island is consistent with all other data. In most cases the relationships are as anticipated and substantiate the faith archaeologists have had in the diagnostic significance of stone adzes, particularly within Polynesia. Most of the relationships expressed in this model can be supported by other quite independent data including linguistic evidence and the results of excavations.

Table 1
Code for Describing Oceanic Adzes

Attribute:	*State:*
1. Cross-section at mid-point or shoulder of adze	
	0. Rectangular
	1. Back wider than front, rect.
	2. Front wider than back, rect.
	3. Sub-triangular, apex to front
	4. Triangular, apex to front
	5. Triangular, apex to back
	6. Subtriangular, apex to back
	7. Oval
	8. Lenticular
	9. Round
2. Grip (or tang)	
	0. No grip
	1. Front reduction only
	2. One side only
	3. Back reduction only
	4. Front and back
	5. Two sides
	6. All sides and front
	7. Front, sides and back
3. Miscellaneous features	
	1. No misc. features
	2. Concave back
	3. Lugs
	4. Ridge on shoulder
	5. Ridge on chin
	6. Hollow bevel

Table 2
Data Matrix for Oceanic Adzes

Operation Archaeological Units
Adze Assemblages from Oceania

Attributes		Wairau Bar (N.Z.)	Chatham Islands	Hawaii	Waitaki River (N.Z.)	Tonga	Waikato/Auck. Isthmus (N.Z.)	Tarewai Point (N.Z.)	Tuamotus	Society Islands	Shag River (N.Z.)	Samoa
1. X-section												
	0	40.1	37.8	60.7	38.6	38.9	43.7	75.0	18.9	7.3	36.7	18.9
	1	5.5	1.6	3.6	2.2	25.9	0.0	0.0	13.5	6.6	10.0	60.8
	2	14.2	39.1	35.7	25.1	24.2	31.2	11.1	18.9	14.7	28.3	4.1
	3	2.5	4.7	0.0	5.6	3.7	6.3	0.0	2.7	2.9	2.5	4.1
	4	14.6	0.0	0.0	14.2	1.8	6.3	0.0	18.9	5.9	3.3	3.4
	5	9.1	3.1	0.0	5.6	0.0	0.0	2.8	13.5	49.3	1.7	4.7
	6	0.4	1.6	0.0	4.1	0.0	6.3	0.0	13.6	9.6	3.3	1.3
	7	4.4	1.6	0.0	1.9	3.7	6.2	8.3	0.0	0.8	9.2	0.7
	8	7.7	3.1	0.0	1.5	1.8	0.0	2.8	0.0	2.9	4.2	2.0
	9	1.5	12.4	0.0	1.2	0.0	0.0	0.0	0.0	0.0	0.8	0.0
2. Grip												
	0	73.7	82.8	32.1	28.1	100.0	81.2	80.6	64.9	14.0	54.2	89.2
	1	15.3	15.6	67.9	52.1	0.0	12.5	5.5	27.0	37.5	22.6	8.1
	2	3.6	0.0	0.0	1.9	0.0	0.0	0.0	2.7	0.7	0.8	1.3
	3	0.0	0.0	0.0	0.0	0.0	0.0	0.0	0.0	2.9	0.8	0.7
	4	0.0	0.0	0.0	0.4	0.0	0.0	0.0	5.4	13.2	0.0	0.0
	5	5.8	0.0	0.0	15.7	0.0	0.0	13.9	0.0	1.5	20.8	0.7
	6	1.6	1.6	0.0	1.8	0.0	6.3	0.0	0.0	29.4	0.8	0.0
	7	0.0	0.0	0.0	0.0	0.0	0.0	0.0	0.0	0.8	0.0	0.0
3. Miscell.												
	1	55.1	79.7	35.7	54.7	88.9	81.2	91.7	75.7	43.4	81.7	94.6
	2	36.9	7.8	64.3	25.1	5.6	6.3	2.8	24.3	25.0	11.7	3.3
	3	0.7	1.6	0.0	1.9	0.0	0.0	5.5	0.0	12.5	0.8	0.7
	4	0.7	1.6	0.0	2.2	1.8	0.0	0.0	0.0	9.6	1.7	0.7
	5	0.7	3.1	0.0	4.1	0.0	0.0	0.0	0.0	2.9	0.8	0.0
	6	5.9	6.2	0.0	12.0	3.7	12.5	0.0	0.0	6.6	3.3	0.7
	n =	274	64	28	267	54	16	36	37	136	120	148

Table 2 (continued)
Data Matrix for Oceanic Adzes

Operational Archaeological Units
Adze Assemblages from Oceania

Attributes	Pitcairn	Nth. Auckland (N.Z.)	Niue	New Guinea	Marquesas	Fiji Islands	Easter Islands	Coromandel (N.Z.)	Cook Island	Bougainville	Austral Islands
1. X-section											
0	8.4	52.9	25.0	11.1	16.7	22.2	13.9	37.8	1.7	13.0	1.1
1	5.6	2.9	37.5	0.0	1.9	11.1	5.5	2.2	1.7	0.0	2.3
2	64.8	23.5	25.0	0.0	14.8	22.2	30.6	33.3	4.6	0.0	16.1
3	0.0	4.9	0.0	0.0	5.6	0.0	16.7	4.4	0.8	0.0	0.0
4	4.2	7.8	0.0	0.0	27.8	0.0	0.0	8.9	2.1	0.0	1.1
5	15.5	1.1	0.0	0.0	25.9	0.0	8.3	4.5	75.3	0.0	47.1
6	1.5	2.0	12.5	0.0	3.7	0.0	0.0	8.9	12.6	0.0	28.0
7	0.0	4.9	0.0	13.9	0.0	11.1	19.4	0.0	0.4	40.0	0.0
8	0.0	0.0	0.0	75.0	3.6	27.8	2.8	0.0	0.8	47.0	1.1
9	0.0	0.0	0.0	0.0	0.0	5.6	2.8	0.0	0.0	0.0	3.2
2. Grip											
0	46.5	79.4	100.0	97.2	29.6	88.9	86.1	71.1	9.0	100.0	24.0
1	5.6	11.8	0.0	0.0	61.1	5.6	11.1	17.8	80.0	0.0	29.0
2	11.3	0.0	0.0	0.0	1.8	0.0	0.0	0.0	0.0	0.0	0.0
3	4.2	1.0	0.0	0.0	1.9	5.5	2.8	4.4	0.0	0.0	0.0
4	0.0	1.0	0.0	0.0	0.0	0.0	0.0	2.2	0.0	0.0	0.0
5	21.1	4.8	0.0	2.8	1.9	0.0	0.0	4.5	6.6	0.0	7.0
6	11.3	2.0	0.0	0.0	3.7	0.0	0.0	0.0	4.0	0.0	38.0
7	0.0	0.0	0.0	0.0	0.0	0.0	0.0	0.0	0.4	0.0	2.0
3. Miscell.											
1	54.9	78.4	100.0	100.0	51.8	94.4	11.1	51.1	35.7	100.0	48.3
2	25.3	18.6	0.0	0.0	46.3	0.0	63.9	42.2	8.4	0.0	8.0
3	16.9	0.0	0.0	0.0	0.0	0.0	25.0	0.0	1.3	0.0	1.1
4	1.4	1.0	0.0	0.0	0.0	0.0	0.0	0.0	33.6	0.0	11.5
5	0.0	0.0	0.0	0.0	1.9	0.0	0.0	0.0	0.4	0.0	1.1
6	1.5	2.0	0.0	0.0	00	5.6	0.0	6.7	20.6	0.0	30.0
n =	71	102	8	36	54	18	36	45	238	15	87

Table 3

		OAUs			
$j \rightarrow$		1		2	
state:	1	0_{11}	E_{11}	0_{12}	E_{12}
	2	0_{21}	E_{21}	.	.
i	3	.	.	.	.
$\downarrow$	.	.	.	.	.
	.	.	.	.	.
	n	0_{n1}	E_{n1}	0_{n2}	E_{n2}
		——		——	
		$\sum_i 0_{i1} = 100$		$\sum_i 0_{i2} = 100$	

0_{i1} refers to the *observed* percentage frequency of the ith state for the 1st OAU, etc.

E_{i1} is the *expected* percentage frequency.

REFERENCES

Brainerd, G.W. (1961) The place of chronological ordering in archaeological deposits. *American Antiquity* **16**, 303-313.

Clarke, D.L. (1962) Matrix analysis and archaeology with special reference to British beaker pottery. *Proceedings of the Prehistoric Society* **28**, 371.

Doran, J.E. and Hodson, F.R. (1966) A digital computer analysis of Palaeolithic flint assemblages. *Nature* **210**, 688.

Hodson, F.R., Sneath, P.H.A. and Doran, J.E. (1966) Some experiments in numerical analysis of archaeological data. *Biometrika* **53**, 311.

Jardine, N. and Gibson, R. (1968) The construction of hierarchic and non-hierarchic classifications. *Computer Journal* **11**, 177.

Kroeber, A.L. (1940) Statistical classification. *American Antiquity* **6**, 29-44.

Kruskal, J.B. (1964) Nonmetric multidimensional scaling: a numerical method. *Psychometrika* **129**, 115-29.

LeRoy Johnson (1968) Item seriation as an aid for elementary scaling and cluster analysis. *Bulletin of the Museum of Natural History, University of Oregon* 15.

Mahalanobis, P.C. (1930) On tests and measures of group divergence. *Journal of the Asiatic Society Bengal* **26**, 541-88.

Mahalanobis, P.C. (1936) On the generalized distance in statistics. *Proceedings of the National Institute of Sciences India* **2**, 49-55.

Pearson, K. (1926) On the coefficient of racial likeness. *Biometrika* **18**, 105-117.

Robinson, W.S. (1951) A method of chronologically ordering archaeological deposits. *American Antiquity* **16**, 239-301.

Siegel, S. (1956) *Non-parametric Statistics for the Behavioural Sciences.* McGraw-Hill.

Sokal, R.R. and Sneath, P.H.A. (1963) *Principles of Numerical Taxonomy.* New York, Freeman.

JOHN ALEXANDER

The study of fibulae (safety pins)

The fibula or brooch of the archaeologist is the safety pin, although often elaborately ornamented, of everyday modern life. It is here defined as 'a fastener in which the point of the pin is held secure and is kept from harming the wearer by a catch and guard on the end of the bow' (Fig. 1). From its beginnings in Europe in the 15th-13th centuries B.C. (Alexander 1969) it has been adopted at different times and with varying enthusiasm all over the world. As an ingenious and useful minor invention with a single time and place of origin it is worthy of study, the more so since safety pins were rarely merely fasteners but objects of high fashion and indicators of status. The study of safety pins has so far been confined mainly to archaeologists who have been much concerned with their typology and chronology. There has been little concern of how and why they spread or how differing societies used them. Here a general model for their study is offered in the hope that the problems will also interest anthropologists, ethnographers and historians.

The General Model can be expressed as follows and each part of it will then be considered in turn.

KINDS OF EVIDENCE

Literary — Pictorial — Archaeological

LOCATION & OBJECT ANALYSIS

Materials, Construction Methods, Position, Distribution, Chronology

USES

Fasteners — Status Indicators

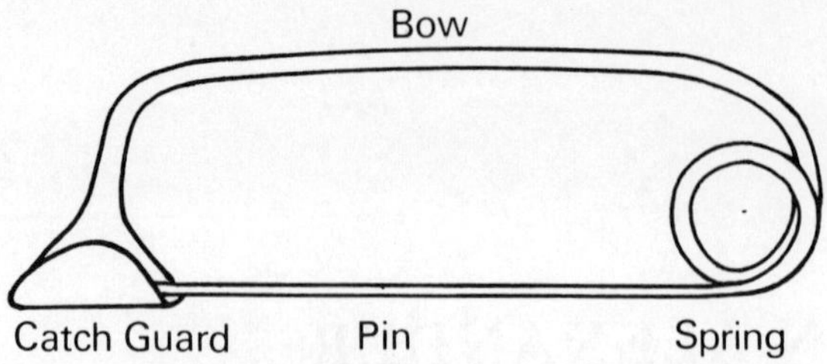

Figure 1 The fibula: principal features

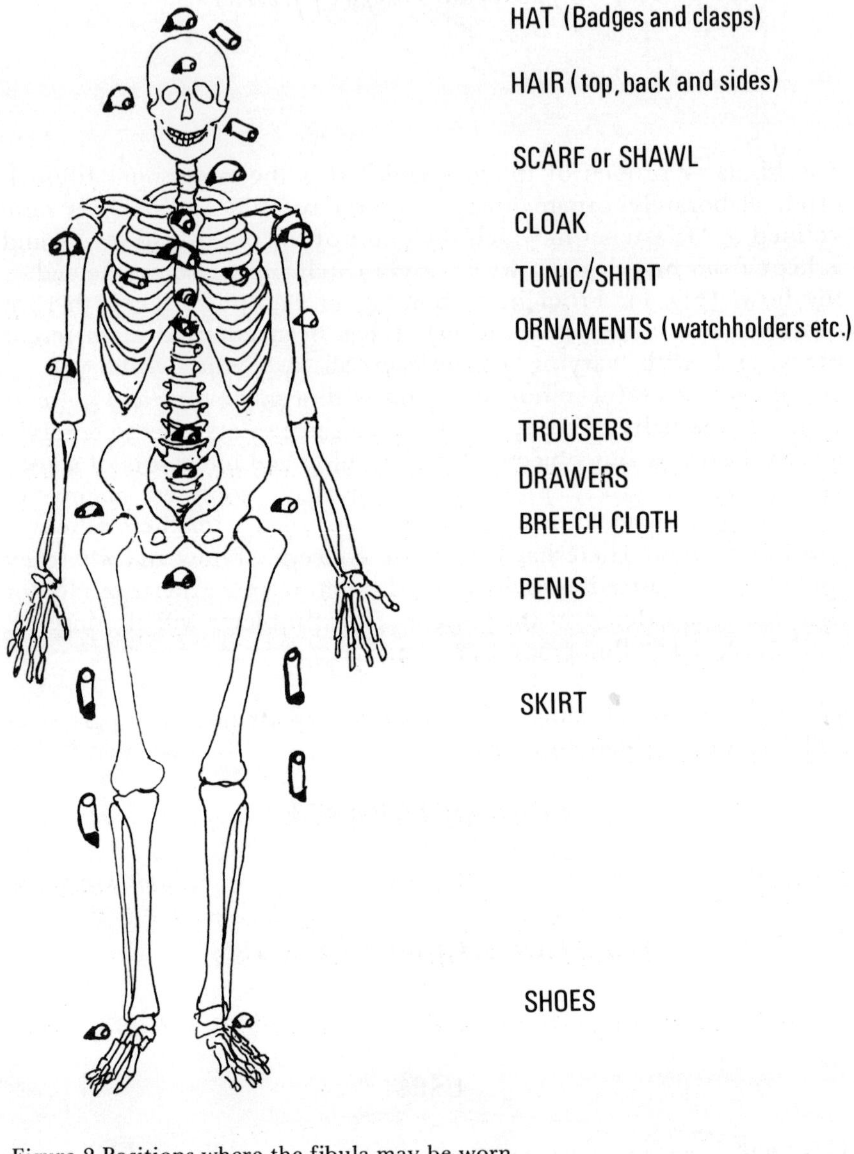

Figure 2 Positions where the fibula may be worn

Unless fibulae are studied in these three ways and using a wide variety of different kinds of evidence much of their significance is lost.

Kinds of evidence

Literary Since by the middle of the 2nd millennium B.C. literacy was already developing in the European mainland, the invention and later history of safety pins lies with the proto- and full historical period. The following kinds of literary evidence may be considered: epics (written or oral), travellers' descriptions, contemporary histories, ethnographic descriptions, linguistic evidence. They can be particularly useful in indicating the uses of fibulae. Lorimer's use of the Greek evidence (Lorimer 1950:370) is a good example of the use of literary evidence. Linguistic evidence, the names given to these fasteners in different languages and the relations between them, has been little studied. As an example of its possibilities the use of the term 'safety pin' after the taking out of a British Patent (no. 134) in 1857 in that name and its spread to other countries in the later nineteenth century is interesting (Klejn 1971). The term does not seem to have been used archaeologically until 1880.

Pictorial evidence may occur as follows:

- Three-Dimensional
  - Carved/Incised: Stone, Clay, Metal, Wood
  - Moulded/Cast: Clay, Metal
  - Modelled: Clay
- Two-Dimensional
  - Painted: Clay, Wood
  - Carved/incised: Clay, Wood, Stone, Metal
  - Moulded/Cast: Clay, Metal

Safety pins began to be represented in these ways from the 1st millennium B.C. onwards (e.g. Muscarella 1967:82) in Europe and Asia. They are of particular use in indicating how clothes were fastened (Lorimer 1950:355).

Archaeological evidence can be considered as follows:

- Excavated evidence
  - Clothed Inhumations
  - Other Burials
  - Hoards
  - Settlements
- Casual finds

Clothed inhumations are the most important kind of evidence here and much more study of the position of pins (see below) needs to be undertaken. For example a number of regional variations of usage and of status might well result in the 1st millennium B.C. Europe from such a study (Alexander 1961:7). Finds in other circumstances are less informative.

Location and object analysis

This second way of study has been attempted in incomplete and partial ways. Some factors, such as typology and chronology, have been much studied (e.g. Blinkenberg 1926, Hodson 1968) whilst others, like constructional methods and position, are neglected. The five main factors might be considered in the following way:

Materials

ONE PIECE (of metal)	TWO OR MORE PIECES	
	Metal and –	All Metal
		One or more of –
Bronze	Bone	Bronze
Iron	Ivory	Iron
Gold	Glass	Gold
Silver	Amber	Silver
Copper	Leather	Copper
	Coral	
	Stone	
	Fibre	

The variety in the combinations of material used may be stressed. The initial invention seems to have begun with experimenting in two or more piece forms of mixed metal and organic materials in the 15th-14th centuries B.C. (Lissauer 1911).

Constructional methods

May be further subdivided into (a) smithing technique and organization, and (b) typological analysis.

(a) The smiths have received little attention although a variety of ingenious local modifications to remove weaknesses in design or to accommodate local fashion exist (e.g. Sprockhoff's 'Spindlesfelden' type). Later organization is well documented from eighteenth-century Europe (Planché 1876:60). It might be studied as follows:

Techniques

Specialised by Technique (Bronze, Gold, Iron Silver smiths)

Forged Strip Bar Rivetted | Wire Strip Rivetted Soldered | Cast

Organisation

Specialised by Material (e.g. Goldsmith) | Specialised by Object (e.g. Brooch maker)

(b) Typological analysis has been much concentrated on in the last seventy years but the significance of many factors and their expression in quantitative terms remains unstudied. A list of 105 characteristics, exclusive of measurements, is offered for consideration in Fig. 3.

If one form of the earliest, and still most currently used, type (the violin bow, Fig. 1) is described under this system, sixteen major characteristics, excluding measurements, material and ornament, could be distinguished:

Violin Bow sub. type 'A':

Bow: Long in proportion to catch; flattened, thin, narrow, round cross-sections
Spring: Asymmetrical, one coil, round cross-section
Catch: Same plane as bow, semicircular, plain, symmetrical about bow terminal, small
Pin: Straight, part of bow
All from one piece Metal

Positional analysis

The position of the fibula in pictures, literary references or on excavated clothed inhumations is an underdeveloped study. Notable exceptions are Hägg 1968, Lorimer 1960 and Schlawbow 1961. In particular many thousands of excavated inhumations await attention of this kind; a scheme for this study is shown in Fig. 2.

Distributional analysis

Since fibulae are so numerous and so varied, many types, when plotted on maps, show definite regional concentrations. Some coincide with known tribes and confederations (Blinkenberg 1926, Benac and Ćović 1958). Since the early part of the century there has been little attempt at studying more than single traits or types and

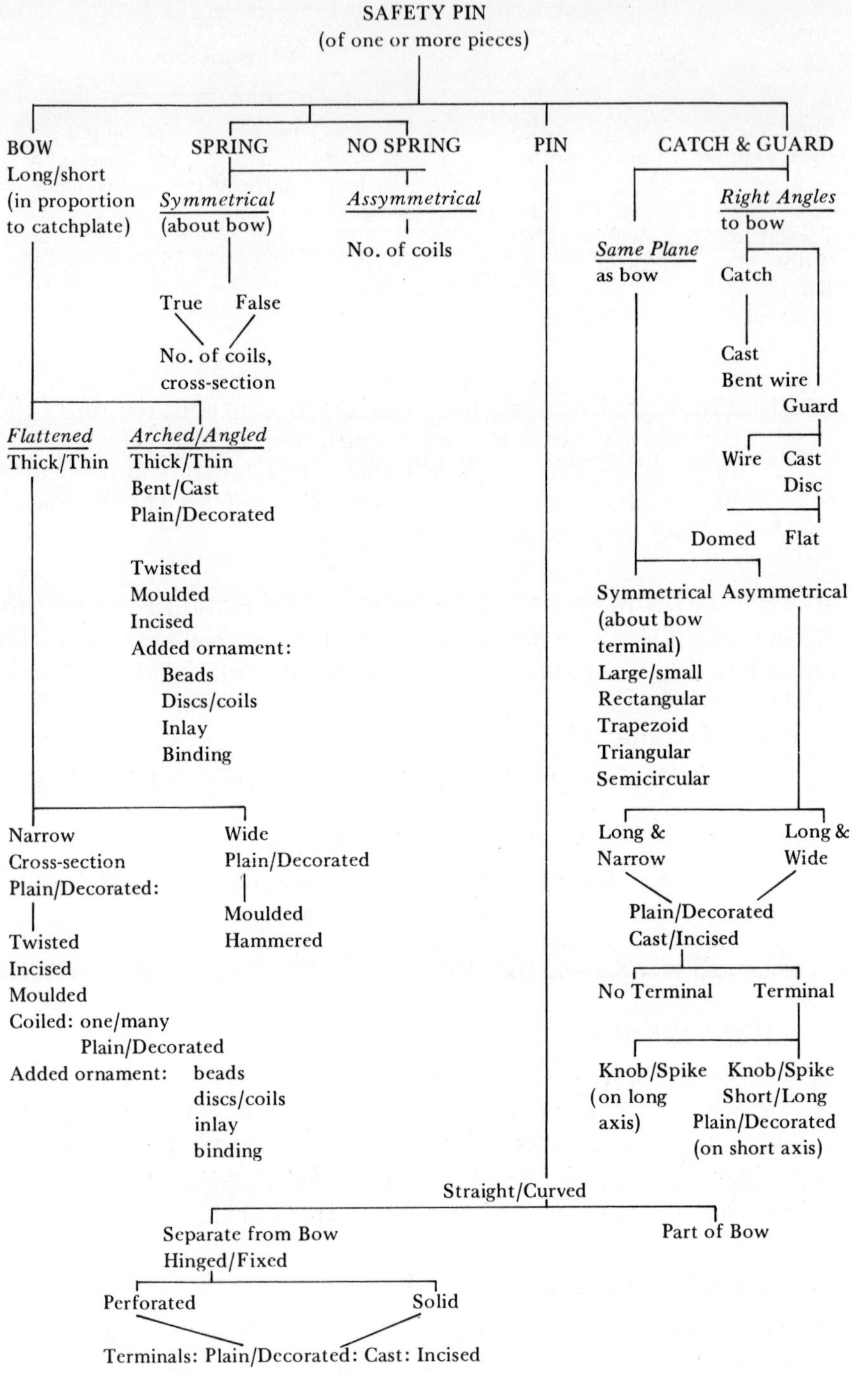

Figure 3 Typological characteristics of fibulae

much more might be done. Beltz (1913:659) attempted one of the last European syntheses, and outside Europe Stronach's (1959:181) work in Western Asia is outstanding. Localized studies in Iran (Girshman 1964:1) and the Levant (Birmingham 1963:80) should be noted.

Chronological analysis

Much work has been done here for fibulae have long been used as type fossils to help date other, less varied, classes of material (e.g. Sundwall 1943). Studies are mainly based on the following:

Vertical Stratigraphy	Horizontal Stratigraphy	Associations	Typological Variation

With application of more detailed methods, statistical techniques and seriation more detailed relative chronologies are being established (Doran 1971).

Uses

This phase in the study of fibulae might be considered the natural development from, and indeed the main reason for, most of the previous work, but so far little attention has been paid to it. The problem may be expressed as follows:

Safety Pins

- **Fasteners** (on the person)
  - Clothes
    - Male/Female
    - Hats/Scarves
    - Cloaks/Shawls
    - Tunics/Robes
    - Trousers/Drawers
    - Breach or loin cloths
    - Shoes
    - Can be shown by: Construction of pin Position
  - Hair
    - Male/Female
    - Top
    - Sides
    - Back
  - Penis
  - Watches Pendants Plumes, etc.
- **Ornaments** (non functional)
- **Fasteners** (of objects) Blankets, etc.
- **Status Indicators**
  - Can indicate:
    - Sex
    - Age
    - Social position
    - Wealth
    - Office
    - Political affiliations
    - Religious affiliations
    - Linguistic affiliations
  - Can be shown by:
    - Size
    - Shape
    - Material
    - Number
    - Where worn
- **Votive Offerings**

Whilst fastening is usually a factor in status indication, it is convenient to discuss the two separately.

(a) FASTENERS ON THE PERSON:

As can be seen from Fig. 2, there is no reason why an enthusiast should not use in excess of twenty safety pins at once. The positions shown can all be documented from historical evidence. When used merely as fasteners they may well be simple, undecorated, of the cheapest suitable material, and only the minimum number for safety or efficiency be used. Safety pins produced in Britain under the 1857 patent are good examples of this. They may also indicate local dress fashions (Hägg 1968:81). For example, the main north-east European prehistoric series had a guard at right angles to the bow and was so meant to stand off from the cloth, whilst the contemporary main Italian types hung flatly downwards. Many more local fashions remain to be worked out (e.g. Broholm and Hald 1935).

Ornaments

At some periods in the past, especially in eighteenth-century Europe, they appear to have been used merely as ornaments (Planché 1876:60) and were attached to any part of the person.

Contraceptives

Rarer uses as a male contraceptive are attested from Roman times (Ucko 1971:49) and even nineteenth-century France (Ucko 1971 quoting Dingwall 1925:55).

Fasteners of objects

Since 1857 A.D. safety pins have been widely used to fasten blankets and other objects. Their use in this way in earlier times is possible.

Votive objects

Fibulae were much used in religious dedications in the Aegean in the first millennium B.C. Unusable gold and silver copies were also made and offered (Hogarth 1908:151).

(b) STATUS INDICATORS:

Throughout their history it is as status indicators that fibulae have been widely used. Some of the main known uses from history and ethnography are shown in the model. In addition to position which may be non-functional, the use of rich materials and elaborate and decorated forms is usual.

This is perhaps the most important of fibula studies, for it may throw light on the structure of societies in a way only a few other things do. In the context of modern anthropologists' concern with structure it may help illuminate the interior of Dr Leach's 'black box'.

A short selection of well-documented examples is appended:

Age

Type worn by boys before admission to a gymnasium (first millennium B.C. Greece; Lorimer 1950:341).

Sex

Type worn by adult females in Danish late bronze age (Hägg 1968:85).

Social status

Gold and silver types forbidden to all English below the rank of Knight or clergy below bishops (Sumptuary Laws, Edward III-Henry VII).

Office

Stewards', technicians' and contributors' badges (Sheffield Seminar 1971).

Particular occasion

Going on active military service (first millennium B.C. Greece; Lorimer 1950:402).

Political or racial

Various types portrayed at Persepolis (Muscarella 1967:83).

Religious

Mediaeval European pilgrim's cap badges. Mortuary brooches, 19th century England.

Acknowledgments

I am grateful for the useful comments made at a Material Culture Seminar at University College, London at which my ideas were discussed, as also for comments in correspondence with Professor L.S. Klejn.

REFERENCES

Alexander, J. (1969) The dual origin of European fibulae. Paper read to the Prehistoric Society in 1969 (publication forthcoming).
Beltz, R. (1913) Die Bronze-und Hallstattzeitlichen Fibeln, *Zeitschrift für Ethnologie* **45**.
Benac, A. and Ćović, B. (1956-8) *Glasinac* I and II. Sarajevo.
Birmingham, J. (1963) Fibulae of the Levant, *Palestine Excavation Quarterly*.
Blinkenberg, C. (1926) *Fibules grecques et orientales*. Copenhagen.
Broholm, H. and Hald, M. (1935) *Dansk Bronzealders Dragter*. Copenhagen.
Dingwall, F.J. (1925) *Male Infibulation*. London.
Doran, J. (1971) Computer analysis of data from the La Tène cemetery at Münsingen-Rain. *In* Hodson, F.R., Kendall, D.G. and Tautu, P. (eds.) *Mathematics in the Archaeological and Historical Sciences*. Edinburgh, University Press.
Girshman, R. (1964) La fibule en Iran. *Iranica Antiqua* **4**, 2.
Hägg, I. (1968) Some notes on the origin of the peplos-type dress in Scandinavia, *Sarttyik ur Tor*. Uppsala.
Hald, M. (1962) *Jernalderns Dragt*. Copenhagen.
Hodson, F.R. (1968) *The La Tène Cemetery at Münsingen-Rain*. Bern.
Hodson, F.R. (1970) Cluster analysis and archaeology. *World Archaeology* **1**.
Hogarth, D.G. (1908) *Excavations at Ephesus*. London.
Klejn, L.S. (1971) Professor Klejn has pointed out in correspondence that the only word for safety pin in Russian is 'the English pin'. It was also a name used in France.
Lissauer, P. (1907 and 1911) *Zeitschrift für Ethnologie* **39** and **43**.
Lorimer, H. (1950) *Homer and the Monuments*. London.
Mansuelli, G. (1963) *Etruria and Early Rome*. London.
Muscarella, O.W. (1965) A fibula from Hasanlu. *American Journal of Archaeology* **69**, 3.
Muscarella, O.W. (1967) Fibulae represented on sculpture. *Journal of Near Eastern Studies* **26**, 2.
Planché, L. (1876) *Cyclopaedia of Costume*. London.
Schlawbow, K. (1961) *Trachten der Eisenzeit*. Neuminster.
Sprockhoff, E. (1938) *Marburger Studien*.
Stronach, D. (1959) The development of the fibula in the Near East. *Iraq* **21**, 2.
Sundwall, J. (1943) *Die älteren italischen Fibeln*. Berlin.
Ucko, P.J. (1971) Penis sheaths: a comparative study. *Journal of the Royal Anthropological Institute*.

BOHUMIL SOUDSKÝ

Higher level archaeological entities: models and reality

An ecosocial model of a neolithic microarea in central-eastern Bohemia is here presented analytically, and developed into a formal spatiotemporal model. The treatment is both vertical (referring to cultural changes in time among entities on levels inferior to that of 'culture', here called 'higher level entities') and horizontal (referring to cultural differences among entities in space, inferior to 'culture', also called 'higher level entities', namely areas → micro-regions → regions → (oikoumene of) subcultures).

Formal models for the neolithic technocomplex – being relatively simple because of the absence of trade, of craft specialization, of overproduction, and of social levels or classes – can, in view of this simplicity, serve as a starting point for the construction of models of more complicated technocomplexes.

Neolithic microareas as a good basis for the definition of higher level entities

As a basis for rethinking terms used daily in archaeology, I have chosen to deal with the neolithic technocomplex, and to refer to the site of Bylany with its sequence of phases, for the following reasons:

1. At Bylany, concrete and abstract entities have been distinguished by means of ranges in the relative frequency of relevant properties. The concrete entities (= phases) are defined analytically on the basis of established logical relations between features, and the higher level (abstract) ones, by synthesizing the definitions of phases. The higher level entities are not formed by sub-dividing or 'periodising' dubious entities called 'cultures', following a single stratigraphy or a doubtful typology, itself established *a priori.* Nor are they reached by comparisons in space and time, in reality polynomial but misunderstood as binomial, i.e. in time only.
2. The ecosocial model in the neolithic is simpler than in any other

subsequent technocomplex, and so is more easily conceived.

3. There are sufficient data, from Bylany and elsewhere, to permit the constitution of a formal model.
4. The primary neolithic is better known than the other primary technocomplexes. Spatially we know better where the primary neolithic (of the Old World) was located, namely in the Near East. So it is possible to separate, by comparison, the data of primary, of secondary and of tertiary cultural processes, a task not easy for later technocomplexes because interrelations become too complicated.
5. The neolithic model could thus become a basis for models for these later and complicated technocomplexes if enough data are, or will become, available.

Middle European middle neolithic ecosocial model

By considering logical relations between features, it has been possible at Bylany to formulate analytically properties which constitute, both qualitatively and quantitatively, criteria for habitation *phases* – criteria divided into taxa, subtaxa, half-taxa and non-taxa. The process has been described in some preceding papers (Soudský 1962-70) and will be treated in detail in volume I of the Bylany publication (Soudský, Zápotochá and Pavlů, in press) and probably in another more theoretical work. Here it is not the method which interests us, but its results and the theoretical principles deduced from them. So I will assume that the method is accepted and that the results are considered justified.

Both qualitative and quantitative analyses of the excavated material were necessary, and those properties specifically relevant to the chronological objective were considered in four main systems:

1. 'cl', Classes of pottery ware (ware is a preliminary assessment of technological properties),
2. 'm', Material of pottery (='clay'+'temper'+'surface treatment').
3. 'f', 'Forms' (=shapes of pottery).
4. 'o', 'Ornamentation' (=pottery decoration of the class 'LO').

The whole of the pottery of the Linear Pottery Culture (='LnK', card|LnK| = 'K')* is divided into four classes: 'LO'= with Linear incised Ornamentation, 'PO'= with Plastic Ornamentation, 'TO'= with 'Technical' Ornamentation (barbotine, finger and nail impressions, etc.), 'NO'= with No Ornamentation (including 'no perceived or no conserved decoration'). The last three classes were found to be irrelevant (or less relevant) to the chronological objective.

* Card |LnK| represents the quantity (cardinal number) of whole or fractional pots found in the given context.

The chronologically relevant properties have been established on the basis of pottery alone because, in the evolution of flint industry and polished stone industry one can distinguish only between 'early and middle neolithic' and 'late neolithic', i.e. only between different levels of technical complexity, here considered as higher level abstract entities. The same distinction has also been possible for ovens and probably for houses, where, however, another such entity has been established, called preliminarily 'latest neolithic' ('tardif'). Other kinds of finds do not furnish any chronological conclusions.

Closed finds are considered as *sets* and the archaeological features as *containers of sets* providing the sets with logical interrelations such as inclusions, exclusions, diachronisms, synchronisms and sequences. Only the sets composed of $\geqslant 50$ individuals of the class 'LO' ($O \geqslant 50$, card $|LO| = O$) can be analysed fully and classed in a phase. Thus, archaeologically, a phase is an assemblage, at a particular moment in time, of coexisting houses, pits and ovens, acting as containers of sets of finds. From the point of view of finds, this is the minimal period discerned or discernible in the life of a village. The analytical means should be chosen, by appropriate archaeological tactics, to permit this distinction. A result of this definition is that a phase, in the sense of 'habitation phase' is something concrete and explicit, quite different from the 'phases' of a culture or cultural group as used in other classificatory systems.

In reality a phase is conceived, at Bylany at least, as houses, pits, ovens, fields as well as a herd of animals belonging to about 24 families. (The pasture for the herd is included in the micro-environment, which together with the different sites and fields of the entire cycle constitutes the microarea, cf. *infra*). Including children this community numbered about 150 persons and remained in one location for about 14 years, as witnessed by a maximum of 14 year-levels in the grain silos. After these approximately 14 years, there was a transfer to another site for about another 14 years, and finally to a third, with a return to the original site after about 40 years, this lapse of time being witnessed by the average of 11 cms. on the diameter of oak stakes used for the construction of the houses of the next phase.

On a given site, this population needed about 63 ha. of agricultural soil: 3 ha. for the village, and twice 30 ha. as fields (f_1 and f_2), each exploited twice, probably as $f_1' \rightarrow f_2' \rightarrow f_1'' \rightarrow f_2''$, the f' being exploited for 4 years and f'' for three years. (Four years is the maximum for the available soil fertility and for emmer wheat cultivated with the slash-and-burn technique without ploughing, if exploited for the first time. Three years is the maximum if a field was exploited for the second time after a short fallow without a complete regeneration by forest vegetation (Soudský and Pavlů, 1972).) Therefore the economical model for Middle European middle neolithic agriculture,

as deduced from Bylany, is, for the three sites a/b*, c, and d/e:
[f_1'(a/b)→f_2'(a/b)→f_1''(a/b)→f_2''(a/b)→f_1'(d/e)→f_2'(d/e)→
f_1''(d/e)→f_2''(d/e)→f_1'(c)→f_2'(c)→f_1''(c)→f_2''(c)]
This regular change in sites is called a 'cycle', the agriculture 'cyclical', and the space where it took place the 'microarea', including the 'microenvironment', and defined as the minimum space where a community could live and lived *permanently*. The micro-environment comprised chiefly the nearer woods for pasture and forage, probably of a different type than the *Quercetum mixtum* wood cleared for fields. Pedologically, there is a difference between the chernozem on loess on a basis of gneiss without traces of illimerization (neolithic fields) and other types of soil (neolithic woods). The more distant woods were not a part of the micro-environment proper, in view of the virtual absence of hunting (game animals = 1.1–1.5% of the total of the bones). So, in the sequence of phases, a hiatus perceptible in the evolution of the discriminant properties will appear in every site location of the cycle. Thus, if we speak of uniting phases into a higher archaeological entity, it is implicitly understood that it is not only the uniting of phases on one site of the microarea, but of all the phases at all three sites of the microarea. A hiatus in the range of properties appears only in rare cases, and here if the ranges for other sites are also considered, the result is a partial overlap.

The real existence of the agricultural and settlement cycle can thus be demonstrated. In this terminology, we mean by 'sub-', a phenomenon of no general validity, by 'micro-', a phenomenon which cannot be subdivided – the minimum size, spatial or temporal, of a phenomenon. A sub-phase will therefore be a change, a reconstruction, a prolongation of a house or houses during a part of a phase, and sub-phases are in practice readily identifiable.

There are, at Bylany, in total 25 ± 2 phases in the a/b site, and (26 ± 2) x 3 phases (one being not attested on a/b) in the microarea, which therefore signifies chronologically (26 ± 2) x 3 x 14 years approximately for the total duration of the sub-early (LnK Ic) and middle neolithic (LnK II-IV) village.

Analysis: The definition of phases

The phases can be defined only by the most discriminant properties of the LO class of pottery, and only taximetrically, i.e. the taxa are expressed numerically by ranges of relative frequency and never by presence/absence of a taxon or of taxa. A phase viewed as a distribution of finds is then the unification of sets of finds in pits (f) included as subsets within the subsets of houses (m):

* a/b refers to adjacent settled locations which were not consecutively occupied.

$$p_i = [(m_j = (f_{j1} \cup f_{j2} \cup ..f_{jn})) \cup (m_k = (f_{k1} \cup f_{k2} \cup \dots f_{kn})) \cup \dots m_x \cup f_a \cup f_b \cup \dots f_y]$$

The sets of finds in isolated pits are included if they consist of $O \geqslant 50$.

Synthesis: the first level of vertical abstract entities: 'stages'

As long as there are only quantitative changes in the sequence of ranges of properties/attributes, the phases together constitute what is here called a 'stage'. Thus, a stage is a unification of sets of finds in phases, $st = (p_i \cup p_j \cup \dots p_n)$, where the taxa and sub-taxa remain qualitatively unchanged, showing only quantitative and consistent movements of intervals, generally in one direction: either rising, falling or staying unchanged. These changes are so far observed only in the 'technical' execution of the LO class ornamentation here designated o‴, and not in ornamental themes (here o″), not in variations (here o′), nor in any other properties like shape, ware, clay+temper+surface treatment.

We have defined an '-emic' system, whose attributes are included only when their relevance to the chronological aim has been demonstrated. These are called 'indices' and expressed in terms of relative frequency of ceramic attributes. They are designated by the Greek letters, $\alpha, \beta, \gamma, \delta, \epsilon, \zeta, \eta, \theta$.

In the purely descriptive '-etic' system also employed by us, which is more complete but less useful for the chronological objective, they represent categories of a subsystem labelled o‴, 'o' being the system of properties of ornamentation of the LO class (o″=motifs, o′=variations). Other subsystems of 'o' are also relevant but less discriminant, or so it seems: 'l' (width of the incised lines), 'lr' (*l*ignes sous *r*ebord, the number and the nature of the horizontal lines under rim). These attributes are also included in the '-emic' system and labelled (l=) $\lambda 1 - \lambda 4$, (lr=) $\rho 1 - \rho 5$. It is clear that λ represents a true independent variable, and the ρ index is a variable only partially independent. This is a source of some theoretical difficulties, reflected in calculation procedures (in the weighting of values). The same case arises for the special '-emic' index expressing the shape of the *Notenkopf* (π) in a Notenkopf ornamentation (ϵ): it is only partly independent.

At the beginning and at the end of a stage, the direction of movement, of the taxa (γ, α, ϵ_3, η, for the central-eastern Bohemian LnK-subculture) changes: the rising ones become constant or decline, the constant ones now rise or fall, as the proportional subtaxa do (δ / ϵ

"O"- system compared to other systems of attributes (Table 1)

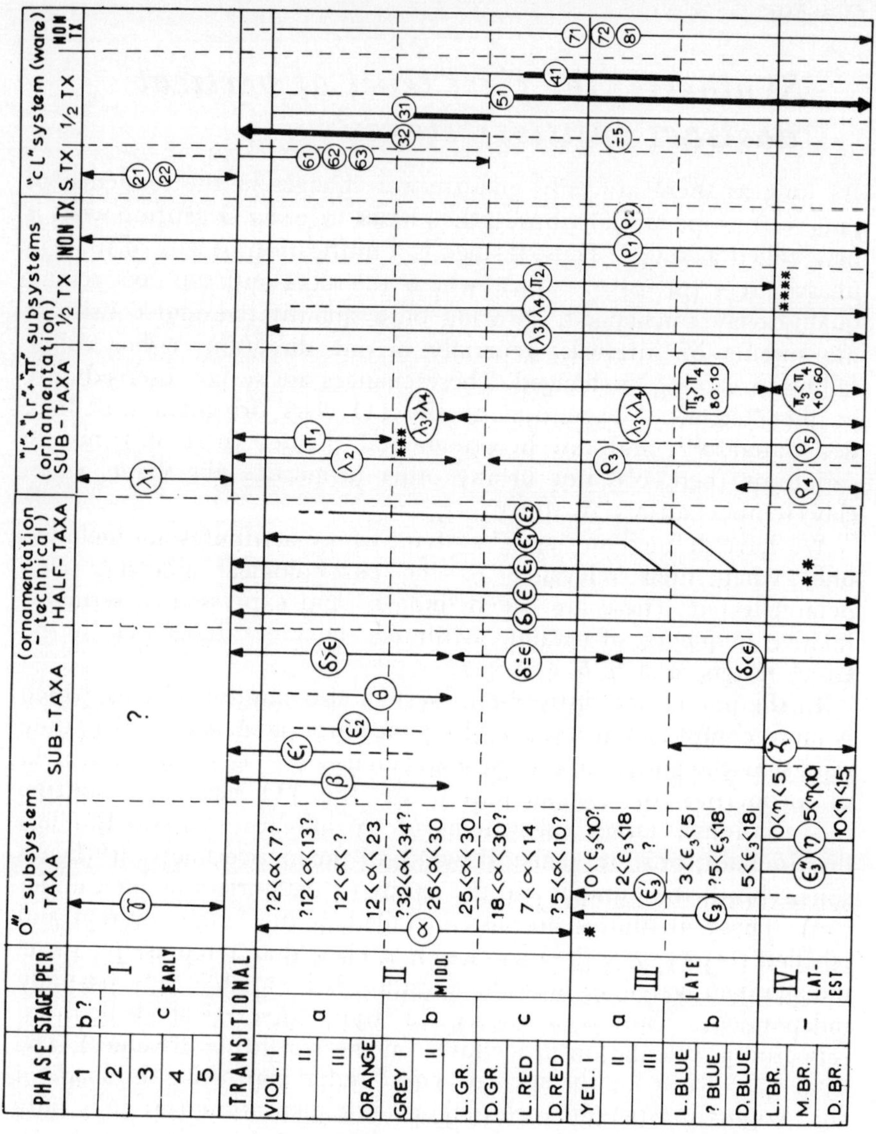

NOTES: * $\alpha < 5 \div 0$ ** $\epsilon_1 \equiv \epsilon_3$ partly conserved *** $\pi_1 < 4 \div 0$ **** $\pi_2 < 5 \div 0$
$\epsilon_2 \equiv \epsilon_3$ -I- -I-

Table 1a Table of the development of attributes through time in the pottery of Bylany and the definition of phases. The defining attributes of the different phases and periods are shown arranged in the various categories of the taxonomic system employed. The symbols in circles are names of attribute categories. In practice these are expressed as percentages of their relative occurence.

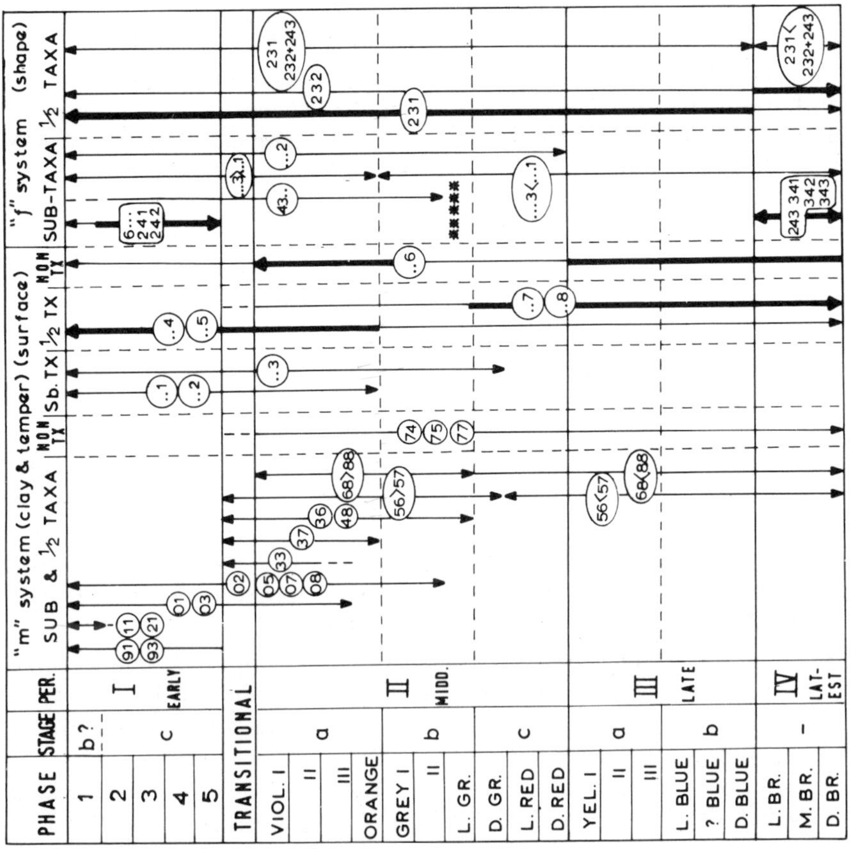

NOTE: ✱✱✱✱✱ f43.. <5 ∸ 0

Table 1b The development of attributes through time in the pottery of Bylany. See Table 1a.

etc.), and the other sub-taxa (β, θ, ζ) appear or disappear.*

Comment on Table 1

In the 'cl'-system (classes of ware) the early categories, both fine

* The difference between a taxon and a sub-taxon is that the latter is not necessarily present and that its intervals do not exactly express the chronological position of the phase. Generally, the medial values give a continuous curve, as Forde's ideal types do, but the frequencies do not. This optional presence of specific sub-taxa appears less clearly on the level of higher entities, but is clearly visible on the level of concrete subentities, such as 'house and its pits'. This is because a specific sub-taxon is in practice always seen somewhere in the pottery of each house, but not necessarily in every pit. The taxa are present in each subset with a nearly identical value, the range being relatively narrow. But subtaxa on the other hand are not only represented by large ranges and their ranges often begin with O. The half-taxa are attributes with no constant ranges developing through the whole culture (or sub-culture), or at least through a major part of a culture if there are changes on the level of technical complexity. In the LnK-culture, this change in technical complexity occurs between LnK I-early neolithic and LnK II-IV-middle neolithic. These half-taxa are, in o'''-subsystem, ϵ_1 ϵ_2 λ_3 λ_4 π_2 (but π_3 and π_4 are proportional relative sub-taxa, as δ and ϵ are, i.e. the absolute values are less important than the ratio between: δ/ϵ π_3/π_4), ρ_1-ρ_5, but ρ_3-ρ_5 are possibly sub-taxa.

and common, are sub-taxa. The fine ones (cl 21, 22) exist only in LnK I, the common ones (cl 61, 62, 63) in LnK I and IIa, b only. The standard categories seem to be half-taxa, which define the stages with their maximum frequency (category 32 the IIa stage, category 31 and IIb one, category 41 the end of IIc and the IIIa, IIIb and IV stages). The relative impoverishment of the late stages (IIIb, IV) of LnK is clearly seen. The later ware classes (cl 71, 72, 81) are non-taxa. So the end of LnK, period IV, can be defined by the presence of only one class of fine ware (cl 51, 'not-standard grey-brown') and by three classes of common ware (cl 71, 72, not-standard 'grey and black' and 'brown black-mottled', cl 81, 'standard red-and-black'), other classes being present in values near 0 (cl 32, 31, 41, all < 5), which is at least partially due to early intrusions.

In the 'm' system ('clay' – 'temper' – 'surface') the first two sub-systems constitute sub-taxa with LO (m 11) and PO-TO-NO (m 21) soft ware reserved to LnK Ib (perhaps not present at Bylany), with predominancy of 'muddy hard LO' (m 91) straw tempered, and not-LO categories (m 01) or light organic tempers LO (m 93) and not-LO classes (m 03) in the Ic stage. The m 01 and m 03 categories continue up to the middle of IIa stage, other tempers in undecorated pottery (m 02, 05, 07, 08) are attested to the middle of IIb (optimal) Linear Pottery stage. Categories of cleaned soft clay where the clay has been specially prepared with water before use (m 3 or m 4 – the odd numbers are for decorated ware, the even ones for undecorated) are sub-taxa of LnK IIa and IIb stages (light organic temper, m 33, of the beginning of LnK IIa, rough granulated, m 37, throughout LnK IIa, fine granulated, m 36, and sandy tempered, m 48, of LnK IIa and IIb stages). Cleaned hard clay categories (m 5 and m 6) are sub-taxa (m 53, light organic temper, LnK IIa and beginning of IIb) or half-taxa (m 56, fine granulated, m 57 rough granulated), but can be changed into proportional sub-taxa if one considers their ratio rather than absolute values: m 56 > m 57 in LnK IIa, IIb and at the beginning of IIc stages, m 56 < m 57 in the rest of Lnk IIc, in IIIa, IIIb and IV stages. The same phenomenon can be observed in common pottery, where cleaned hard sandy category (m 68) prevails upon the not-cleaned (m 88) one in LnK IIa, IIb stages, the ratio being reversed (m 68 < m 88) in LnK IIc, IIIa, IIIb, IV stages. The other not-cleaned clay categories (m 74, 75, 77) are not-taxa.

In the surface treatment subsystem the slip (m ..1,112) is a subtaxon of LnK I and IIa stages; red surface sub-taxon (m ..3) of LnK I, IIa, IIb and of the beginning of IIc stages; bad treatment ('wet hand', m ..4, 'half-polished', m ..5) half-taxon with high values in LnK I and IIa and a constant low value later. The polished surface is certainly not a taxon and seems not to be relevant to time. However, there are two different polishings, an early one and a late one: the curve has two maxima with a minimum in LnK IIc stage. The glossed surface is a half-taxon with high values in LnK IIc, IIIa, IIIb stages, and low values in LnK IIa, IIb and LnK IV stages.

In the 'f' system (shapes of pottery) only some categories of the three subsystems (rim-body-base) are sub-taxa or half-taxa, the main part being non-taxa (i.e. depending probably more on functional considerations than some esthetic creation relevant to time). The S-profiled rim (f 6...) is a sub-taxon of LnK I, its maximum being probably in LnK Ic. Sub-spherical bowls (f 231) have a high constant value in all periods but an abrupt decrease in LnK IV, being at this time replaced by the piriform (f 243) and the subpiriform (f 232) bowls. So these three categories, for LnK IV period, constitute a proportional half-taxon. $\frac{\text{f } 231}{(\text{f } 232 + \text{f } 243)}$. The open bowl (f 43..) is a sub- or half-taxon of Lnk IIa.

In the *sub-system 'base'*, the ratio between convex base without edge (f...1) and flat base without edge (f...3) is a proportional sub-taxon of LnK IIa (f...3> f...1) and a proportional half-taxon for the later periods and stages (where f...3< f...1). The flat base with edge (f...2) is an absolute sub-taxon of LnK 11a-c disappearing in LnK III and IV.

The second level of vertical abstract entities: the 'periods'

The period in a site is defined by the unification of stages, per = $(st_1 \cup st_2 \cup ... st_n)$, which have the same taxon-taxa. In practice a period has 2-3, maybe in some particular cases 4 stages. In o'''-subsystem these taxa are $\gamma, \alpha, \epsilon_3, \eta$.(The 3 taxon is probably not well chosen, and will be changed to express better the difference between $\epsilon_3{}'$ and $\epsilon_3{}''$). Thus, in the time dimension, a new period begins if the taxon or taxa change.

First level of horizontal abstract entities: the 'area'

We defined the microarea as the minimum space in which a human community could or did live *permanently*. The unification of several microareas gives an area. The area is thus a set of microareas which have the same quantitative differences in the taxa, i.e. the same definitions of phases. The comparison between areas is, therefore, possible on the level of phases. We have shown this by the comparison between the Bylany site and the Močovice site (14 kms.

to the east of Bylany). The differences between microareas exist in o″ and o′, o^c and o_2 subsystems of the pottery ornamentation. The other systems reveal total overlapping.

Second level of horizontal abstract entities: the 'region'

If we compare two or more neighbouring areas, the ranges of frequency in the various taxonomic categories are never comparable on the level of phases, but only on the level of stages, or not at all. The ranges of relative frequencies of taxa for stages are not however identical. The set defined by the unification of areas, whose ranges for the stages overlap in terms of the taxa, is called a region. The number of stages is the same in each region for every period, but we do not know if the number of phases is also the same in each region; probably not. We do not know if there is one level or more implied in the term 'region'. A subdivision has been proposed: 'subregion'. For the moment, however, there is nothing in the LnK material which would permit us to define any 'subregion'.

Third level of horizontal abstract entities: the 'subculture'

If we make a comparison between neighbouring regions, we observe that the range of attributes in the periods either do or do not overlap. If they do not overlap there is, or can be, a qualitative difference in the taxa and the sub-taxa. The set defined by the unification of regions whose intervals in the taxa overlap on the level of periods is called a *subculture*. We observe that the number of periods is the same. Between subcultures, there are qualitative differences in the taxa: the taxa change. Thus a chronological taxon (because our taxa have been chosen from the chronological standpoint) is valid only for one subculture. There are possibly not general chronological taxa valid for a whole culture except in the case where a culture has no subcultures.

A formal spatio-temporal model for neolithic culture (figs 1 and 2)

We saw that some changes in the chronological approach are comparable with analogous changes in the spatial approach. The taxa change between periods of the same subculture just as they change between subcultures in the same period. The tridimensional model or 'cube' of culture proposed by Klejn (1970), where space represents two dimensions and time the third dimension, can be reduced for the purpose of comparison to a square because one is working here in two dimensions: the spatial dimension (oikoumenê of a) 'subculture' and the temporal dimension 'period'. Analogous differences exist

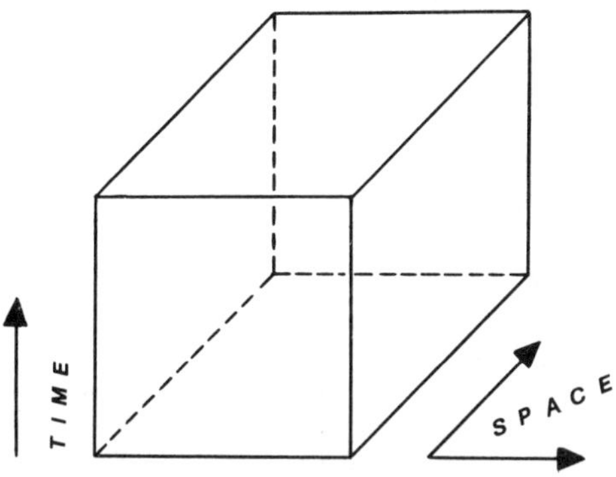

Figure 1 Klejn's formal model of a culture.

also between 'region' and 'stage', and hence the spatial (sub) dimension 'region' corresponds with the temporal (sub)dimension 'stage', and again, the spatial (undersub)dimension 'area' with the temporal (undersub)dimension 'phase'.

A neolithic culture is a set of archaeological entities hierarchically ranged in space and time. It may be represented by a cube-containing-cubes model. The highest horizontal level and the greatest vertical side of this cube are defined by *qualitative* changes in the chronologically relevant taxa; the immediately lower level and face by *qualitative* changes in the sub-taxa and by significant *quantitative* changes in the taxa. (Significant implying a change in the direction or alteration in the rate of change). The lowest level and then the smallest sides are defined by *quantitative* changes in the taxa. The half-taxa, and at least some sub-taxa – if not considered quantitatively – and possibly the non-taxa (i.e. attributes appearing as half-, sub- or not-taxa in the time-perspective which are possibly full taxa in other perspectives) assure, both vertically and horizontally, the unity of the culture. Those half-, sub- and not-taxa should be established for all kinds of material culture, for the economical basis of culture and for all social and ideological systems.

In terms of similarity, it should be noted that the similarity between subsets in every cube is greater than between subsets of different cubes. This implies that the only comparisons permitted and relevant are those between immediately neighbouring cubes. The comparison thus can only be vertical or horizontal, but never both – never oblique – nor should there be any cube between the compared cubes.

Practical application of this model reveals that the Linear Pottery

Culture is indeed a culture, divided into four periods with some 2 to 4 sub-cultures in the period LnK I, about 6 to 8 in the period LnK II, about 10 to 12 in LnK III, and 12 to 15 sub-cultures in LnK IV.

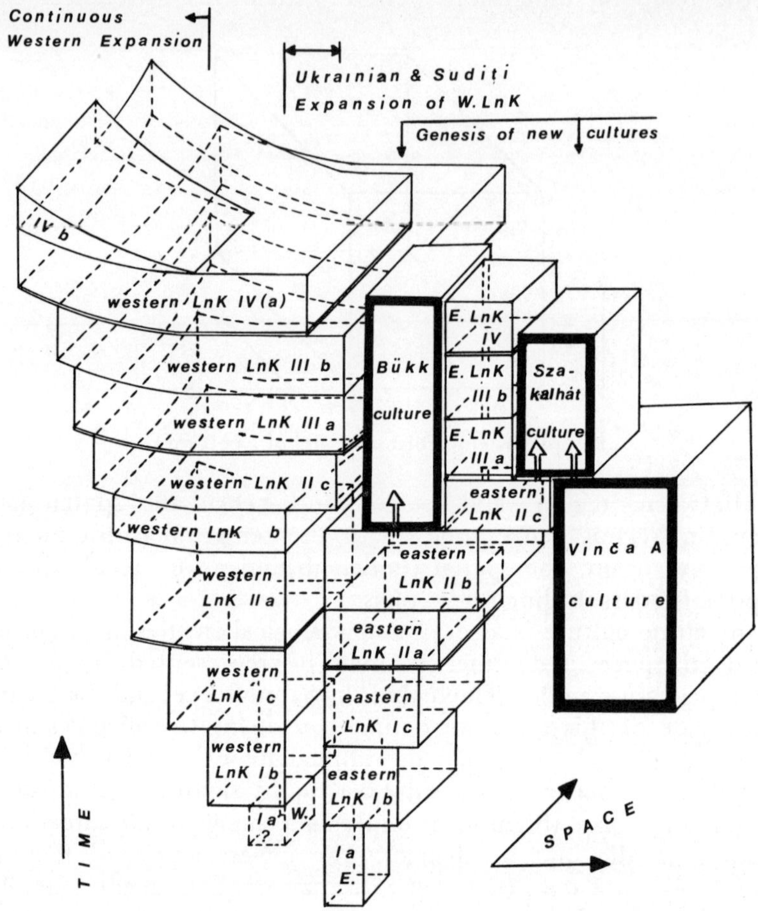

Figure 2 Formal model of the Linear Pottery culture. Only vertical higher level entities are distinguished; the horizontal ones are considered but not distinguished.

The Zeliezovce-group is then an eastern subculture of the western LnK culture, as are the Tiszadob- and the Gemer-groups. The Szatmar-group, however, is only a stage of period I (=Ib) of the LnK in one region and not a subculture. The Bükk-group ('group' is an entity not yet defined either in space or in time) is a culture, because of its different (chronological) half- and non-taxa. Possibly the number of periods in Bükk might not prove equal to the number of the synchronous periods of LnK: LnK IIc, III, IV (i.e. $2\frac{1}{3}$ periods) are contemporary with BK A, AB, B, C (i.e. 4 periods)). The Szilmeg group is not a subculture of the LnK-culture but probably an independent culture, because of its completely different (chronological) half- and non-taxa. The Szakalhat-Lebö-group is a southern subculture of the eastern LnK-culture or an independent culture unifying elements of LnK- and of the Vinca Culture. Its half- and non-taxa are not yet well known. In this sense the Maritsa-Gumelnitsa (Kodzadermen) complex can not be vertically two different cultures, but simply two periods of one culture, since Kodzadermen and Gumelnitsa are contemporary subcultures. The relation between the Maritsa and the Boian groups is, however, not yet clear. The situation of Boian is analogous to that of the Szakalhat-Lebö-group. The 'phases' of the Boian Culture are possibly not periods but merely stages. Their separation into periods has not yet been established. Nevertheless the differences between the 'Bolintineanu' and 'Giuleşti' stages of the Boian culture are greater than between the latter and the following 'Vidra' stage. Thus all the Balkan neolithic cultures require revision. It seems no longer possible to consider the Lengyl 'culture' as a unit either horizontally or vertically.

It is certainly impossible to transform the stratigraphy of one site into a relative chronology or a periodization of a whole culture. There is no reason, for instance, why the levels at Tangiru should define the phases of the Gumelnitsa 'culture' as a whole. The number of phases is comparable only in the same area, and only if the formal model is based on the Middle European ecosocial model. Nor are there reasons why the Let stratigraphy might define the periodization of the Cris Culture. It should be admitted, however, that there may be some restrictions in the application of the middle European middle neolithic formal model. Quite possibly it is not *the* middle neolithic model, but simply *one* of the several possible and valid middle neolithic models which might be formulated.

REFERENCES

Klejn, L.S. (1970) Problema opredelniya arkheologicheskoy kultury. *Sovyetskaya Arkheologiya* 1970 2, 37-51, 298-302.

Soudský, B. (1962) The neolithic site of Bylany. *Antiquity* 36, 198.

Soudský, B. (1965) Genèse, periodisation et économie du néolithique ancien en Europe centrale, *Atti del VI Congresso Internationale delle Scienze Preistoriche e Protoistoriche,* II, 278, Roma.

Soudský, B. (1966) *Bylany, osada nejstaršich zemědělcu z mladší doby kamenné.* Prague.

Soudský, B. (1967) *Principles of Automatic Data Treatment Applied on Neolithic Pottery.* Prague-Stockholm.

Soudský, B. (1968) Application de méthodes du calcul dans l'étude d'un site neolithique, in *Calcul et Formalisation dans les Sciences de l'Homme,* 131. Paris.

Soudský, B. (1970) Le problème des propriétés dans les ensembles archéologiques. In Gardin, J.C. (ed.) *Archéologie et Calculateurs,* 46. Paris. C.N.R.S.

Soudský, B. and Pavlů, I. (1971) The Linear Pottery Culture, settlement patterns of central Europe. In Ucko. P., Tringham, R. and Dimbleby, G. (eds.) *Man, Settlement and Urbanism.* London, Duckworth.

Soudský, B., Zapotocka, M. and Pavlů, I. In press. *Bylany I.*

RICHARD A. WATSON

Limitations on archaeological typologies and on models of social systems

Some archaeologists stress that there is no standard nor unique nor ideal nor perfect typology for any archaeological subject matter. Typologies are to be determined by the problems in hand, with explicit attention to the questions that are to be answered. This is surely true. What I want to comment on is the claim that 'typologies are *not* governed by the qualities inherent in the data, but rather by the *a priori* ideas of the investigator. Any assemblage of artifacts or set of assemblages can potentially be ordered into an infinite number of typological systems' (Evans and Hill 1970:27). I should like to make two points about this.

First, this formula is potentially misleading. It is quite valuable to indicate the artificial nature of typologies. We *do* make them up according to our needs, and we should use them rather than allowing them to use us. But although there is no *one* typology, as scientists we must assume that there is only *one* world. However many attributes the objects of this world may have, however many ways there are in which these objects can be described, we must assume that they are there with actual intrinsic characteristics observable by us all. If they were not there for objective, individual assessment for any observer, then we certainly could not check our observations and typings independently, and thus we would lose the public accessibility upon which the nature of objective scientific confirmation depends. That is, 'The attributes one chooses to work with should reflect one's problem, whereas the types defined by these attributes should reflect the real world' (Watson, LeBlanc, and Redman 1971:131).

There is no denying that there are philosophical problems about the nature and even the existence of the external material world (and about other minds). What I contend is that *as scientists*, archaeologists should not concern themselves with these metaphysical problems. As scientists, archaeologists begin with the assumption that there is only *one* world, describable in *many* ways.

My second comment is that while technically speaking there are an infinite number of possible typologies for any object (e.g., there are an infinite number of mathematical points on any artifact, so one could type the artifact with reference to any of the infinite number of combinations and permutations of sets of these points), practically speaking the number of possible typologies – while still very large – is strictly limited. Limitations are imposed in a variety of ways:

1. Typologies are limited first of all by the intrinsic physico-chemical and spatio-temporal characteristics of the object itself. If this were not true, *any* object would fit into any typology, and there would be no distinguishing anything in this world from anything else. However, the most distinctive feature of our world is that the things in it are similar to and different from one another in an immense variety of ways. Taxonomists long before Aristotle were classifying objects according to their similarities and differences. We must not let the fact that there are many *possible* typologies for the classification of any object distract us from the more basic fact that it is the sheer stubborn *objectivity* of the object that makes it possible to classify different objects as belonging to different types confidently at all.
2. Typologies are limited because many are translatable into others (even if only within tolerable limits). Different systems of measurement, such as by feet or by metres, are not logically different typologies because there are rules for translating one into the other. Point-by-point isomorphism is necessary if two typologies are to be said to be logically identical, but for practical purposes, the fact that two typologies that differ slightly pick out the same objects may be enough to make the choice between them so far irrelevant. (When two radically different typologies pick out the same objects, on the other hand, a possibly significant correlation is indicated.)
3. Typologies are limited, also, by our techniques of investigation, our instruments of observation, the spatial and temporal extent and the availability of the objects, and so on. This is obvious, and important, but I will not discuss it here as I have covered this point in detail elsewhere (Watson, R. 1966, 1969).
4. Related to this last, human abilities, interests, and desires also obviously limit typologies (*cf.* Bacon's idols). The objective method of science was developed in part to mitigate the human element in observation. But obviously scientists will still be influenced at least by their interests, which, if they cannot be dispensed with, can at least be taken into account.

This is enough to indicate my concern that we do not forget that the world is a dog that resists being collared by unfitting schemes. The 'real world' of physical objects may be challenged by philosophers, but except in extraordinary circumstances (with which cognitive anthropologists may be flirting), archaeologists necessarily assume the existence of this real world. .

Another question of importance here is about the relations of typologies to *meanings.* Attributes (characteristics, properties, qualities, features, etc.) are intrinsic in objects. Typologies are defined as sets of attributes, and even though typologies are arbitrary in the sense that men define them, typologies, particularly those derived from or designed for objects under investigation, are not completely arbitrary. That is, they are limited – as described above – by the actual attributes the objects have. In this sense, a large number of possible typologies can be said to be 'objectively' in objects, although our choice of this or that typology for use might be 'arbitrary'. Now just as men choose or design typologies for objects, they also give meanings to objects. But here the analogy stops. For where there are objective attributes of objects on which typologies are based (and on which typologies must be based if they are to be significant or useful), there is nothing at all in objects on which meanings necessarily must be based. We can (and someone probably has) take any object to mean anything. But the real world, solid and stubborn, does not *mean* anything in itself. It must be *interpreted*, and man puts the interpretation on it. We impose the typologies for our purposes, even though the intrinsic attributes or characteristics of objects determine whether an object is of this or that invented type. Thus, we might arbitrarily type or categorize objects according to several hundred of their physico-chemical and spatio-temporal attributes. This data might be stored in a computer, and all sorts of correlations might be derived. All of this information and the typology or typologies involved would still be without meaning or neutral in meaning (even though we decided what to measure) *until* we suggest some further, significant typology. In archaeology we might do this by calling the objects artifacts, and by hypothesizing some use that they had in the past. Then the objects – and the typologies – are given meaning, a meaning that is not in the objects in themselves. Thus, as archaeologists, when we cease to talk simply of external morphology, internal structure, and chemical or mineral constitution, and begin to talk of 'pots' or 'hand axes', then the objects begin to take on meaning (or better, are *given* meaning) as artifacts. Of course, many of the attributes we accept as being objective (and without specific meaning) in objects have been defined previously and given meaning by physicists, chemists, geologists, biologists, etc. for their purposes. The main point here is that archaeologists assume that the artifacts are at base physical objects with physico-chemical attributes, subject to basic physical laws, objects that are neutral in meaning so far as archaeological interests go. This is necessary if we are going to undertake the complex and difficult business of developing *archaeological* typologies.

Similar points can be made about anthropological and ethnological typologies. In particular, these comments apply to models of social systems (and pre-eminently to those developed by palaeoethnologists, i.e., archaeologists). One never begins studying a human community knowing absolutely nothing about it. One begins by knowing at least that the laws of physics operate among the physical objects – including the people – in the community. There is a large body of biological information that can also be taken for granted. People must eat and defecate. Males and females must have sexual intercourse (or at least males must provide sperm) if the people are to produce male and female children, the women have the babies (or at least provide ova), everyone in the society is mortal, etc. That there will be some elementary social structure is also known, based on the fact that human babies are born helpless and ignorant, so must be cared for and instructed. Although (as allowed for above) it is possible that all the babies in a society could be produced by artificially inseminating ova in bottles, one can usually assume that there will be a social structure involving the intercourse of males and females in a society. There will be social structures related to the production and distribution of food and other goods, and it seems clear that general models can be developed that allow very general predictions about the of communities given an estimate of the resource base, the level of technology, and the size and density of population (Watson and Watson 1969). The point here, again, is that although there is some overlap among the social sciences, the anthropologist or ethnologist can (and must) begin his study of any society taking as given not only much physical and biological information about human beings, but also a fair base of psychological and sociological information. Human beings are simply not capable of behaving just in *any* way at all. Human behaviour, like the behaviour of any other natural object, is explained by subsuming particular events under lawlike generalizations. Men are governed by natural laws, not in the sense that they do not have free choice to do many different things in most situations – because demonstrably similar men in similar circumstances do behave in many different ways – but in the sense that the ways men *can* behave are limited so that human behaviour can be described, explained, and predicted in terms of general regularities. As our knowledge increases, it is less and less likely that we will be surprised by the behaviour or social structure of human beings in any newly discovered society. Also, as we learn more about the relations of material culture to social structures, the more generally accurate will be our reconstructions of the cultures of ancient societies as based on archaeological evidence. (For a contrary view on this point, see Leach in this volume.) This is not because the variations on the theme of human culture are necessarily finite, but because in our systemic descriptions of human societies we have described and are beginning to understand most of the workable models as determined by the conjunction of the basic physical, biological, psychological, and social regularities that make up the foundation of natural laws on which all human societies must build.

REFERENCES

Evans, R.K. and Hill, N.J. (1970) The nature and significance of 'types' (abstract). *XXXV Annual Meeting, Society for American Archaeology, Book of Abstracts.* Museo Nacional de Antropologia, Mexico, D.F.

Watson, P.J., LeBlanc, S.A. and Redman, C.L. (1971) *Explanation in Archaeology: An Explicitly Scientific Approach.* New York, Columbia University Press.

Watson, R.A. (1966) Is geology different? a critical discussion of *The Fabric of Geology. Philosophy of Science* 33, 172-85.

Watson, R.A. (1969) Explanation and prediction in geology. *Journal of Geology* 77, 488-94.

Watson, R.A. and P.J. (1969) *Man and Nature: An Anthropological Essay in Human Ecology.* New York, Harcourt, Brace and World.

Section 3: The explanation of artifact variability in the palaeolithic

FRANÇOIS BORDES

On the chronology and contemporaneity of different palaeolithic cultures in France

In the last fifteen years, the Laboratory of Pleistocene Geology and Prehistory of the University of Bordeaux has undertaken the unglamourous task of establishing a sequence, as complete as possible, of the climatic and ecological variations during the Pleistocene, so as to get a relative chronology permitting the correlation, layer by layer when possible, of different shelters or open air sites in the southwest of France. We are still far from completion of our project, but already some important results have been achieved, which reach beyond mere chronology. This is the work of the whole laboratory, but I shall draw especially on the results of Miss M.M. Paquereau (Palynology), Mrs F. Delpech and M.F. Prat (Palaeontology), MM. H. Laville, Cl. Thibault, A. Debénath, J.P. Texier (Sedimentology) and Mrs D. de Sonneville-Bordes, MM. J.M. Bouvier and J.Ph. Rigaud (Prehistory). Some of these results are still unpublished.

The old scheme of evolution of prehistoric cultures was a very simple one: after the Abbevillian (or Chellean), then the oldest culture known, came the Acheulean, then the Mousterian. With the upper palaeolithic a drastic change occurred, and we had the Aurignacian, the Solutrean, and, at the end of the sequence, the Magdalenian. For a time this scheme was thought to be valid all over the world, and 'Magdalenian' was described from India, and 'Solutrean' in eastern Europe. Soon enough it became clear that this was not the case. However, the scheme of unilinear evolution was still applied to western Europe not so long ago.

The first indications that things were not that simple came when the Clactonian was recognized as a handaxeless culture, albeit contemporary with the Acheulean, at least in part. Then D. Peyrony introduced the idea of a Mousterian of Acheulean Tradition, different from the others, and interstratified with them in the Lower Shelter at Le Moustier. Up to this date the accepted sequence was, more or less, Mousterian of Acheulean tradition as the oldest, with Acheulean hangovers (handaxes), then Typical Mousterian, then 'evolved' Mousterian of La Quina type. In 1933, Peyrony went a step further in proposing his view of the parallel evolution of two different cultures, this time during the early upper palaeolithic: the Aurignacian and the Perigordian. Up to then, they had been lumped together under the single name of Aurignacian. This last point of view is still not accepted by some archaeologists, mainly in England, who prefer to see a replacement scheme of three different cultures, the Châtelperronian, the Aurignacian and the Gravettian, a position which becomes more and more difficult to hold.

As prehistory progressed, it became evident that the true picture was a complicated one, with regional differences in the evolution and the succession of palaeolithic cultures. And explaining these differences became an important problem. Let us have a look at some facts.

We have already alluded to the Clactonian. On this point, France does not bring much light, lacking at present any good Clactonian site. The Acheulean is a different matter: already, at the beginning of the century, V. Commont had pointed out the differences between the assemblages found at Saint-Acheul, in the same 'Red Sands', at Rue de Cagny on one hand, and Bultel-Tellier Pit on the other hand, some hundreds of metres apart. At Rue de Cagny, of about 300 handaxes found, 271 were of the 'limande-twisted' type (Commont 1908). In the other site this type was rare, and most of the handaxes were either lanceolate or cordiform in shape. Whatever the meaning of this, it remains that two contemporary (in a geological sense) assemblages were very much different.

For a long time, the exact meaning of 'contemporary' has been a stumbling block. Even today, with methods of absolute dating (C-14 for instance) the statistical error prevents knowing if two layers are really contemporary, in the sense of dating from exactly the same moment. Most of the time this does not matter too much, if it can be shown that they both belong to the same environment, that is that they were deposited under the same climatic conditions, with an identical fauna and flora. Then the environment can be taken into account: for instance, whether in a steppic period one of the two sites shows the presence, near by, of some trees, while in the other tree pollen is absent or very rare. However, the scattering of pollen in caves may not be purely random, and just now we are doing a detailed study of modern pollen deposition in caves, to ascertain the possible value of this variable.

We have already established for the two last great glacial periods, by pollen analysis as well as sedimentary analysis and palaeontology, a frame of climatic variations which seems in good accord from cave to cave. We can now date sequences and hope soon to be able to date even isolated layers. This framework was first established for two caves, Pech de l'Azé (Riss I, II, III, Würm I and II) and Combe-Grenal (Riss III, Würm I and II), but the same sequence occurs in part at other sites (Le Moustier, Würm I and II, Combe-Capelle, lower site, Würm I, etc.). Würm III has been studied at Roc de Combe, Laugerie-Haute, La Ferrassie, Le Flageolet, and Würm IV at Laugerie-Haute and Le Flageolet (La Madeleine is now under study) as well as in other less complex sites. The exact number of stadials and interstadials in the Würm is another question to be discussed elsewhere. It has not much importance for us now.

Würm I can be subdivided into the following sequence of climatic events: Phase I is cold and damp, then cold and drier. Phase II is much warmer, with up to 60% (at Combe-Grenal) of tree pollen, including a lot from deciduous trees. Phase III is cold and becomes drier and drier. Phase IV is again temperate, with up to 60% of tree pollen, and an almost post-glacial composition of the forest. Phase V is cold and steppic, Phase VI warmer again, but not so much, by far, as phase II or especially phase IV. Phase VII is very cold and steppic (Bordes, Laville and Paquereau, 1966).

At Combe-Grenal, most of the Würm I is occupied by Typical Mousterian, except layer 38, corresponding to phase VI, which contains a Denticulate Mousterian of Levallois facies. At Pech de l'Azé II, phase I is occupied by a Typical Mousterian of Levallois facies, but phase II sees the succession of Typical Mousterian, Denticulate Mousterian and Typical Mousterian again, all of them non-Levallois. Phase III is also Typical Mousterian, but of Levallois facies again. Phase IV and V are occupied by poor assemblages, belonging to the Quina-Ferrassie type. The succeeding layers are sterile. In the Lower Shelter at le Moustier, Phase I is not represented, phase II coincides with Typical Mousterian of Levallois facies, phases III and IV are almost sterile, and phases V, VI and VII correspond to Peyrony's layer G, i.e. Mousterian of Acheulean tradition with numerous handaxes. At Combe Capelle, the Mousterian of Acheulean tradition dates, from sedimentological studies, very probably from the same period, but pollen analyses are not yet made. There is little doubt, however, that it belongs to the end of Würm I, and so the layers situated below, with the Quina-Ferrassie type of Mousterian, are contemporary with the Typical Mousterian at Combe-Grenal. At La Micoque, over the Last Interglacial soil, is found a consolidated breccia, very much resembling in position and composition the first Würmian layer (phase I) at Pech de l'Azé II. This breccia was overlain by the Micoquian layer, which, from descriptions given at the time of its excavation, and by its fauna, could very easily correspond to Phase II of Würm I. A glance at Table I will show that different cultures flourished under the same environment, in sites not very far away one from the others.

Würm II has been divided at Combe-Grenal into 8 different phases, with fluctuations much less marked than in Würm I. Phase I is very cold and damp, Phase II cold and dry, steppic, Phase III a little less cold and damper, Phase IV very cold and steppic, Phase V a little less cold and damp, Phase VI colder and drier, Phase VII less cold, damper, Phase VIII very cold and dry. Just now we have less documentation about the contemporary cultures than in Würm I. However, in Phase I, we have at Combe-Grenal the succession Ferrassie Mousterian, then Typical, then Ferrassie again, then Quina. In Pech de l'Azé I, we have Mousterian of Acheulean tradition type A, with numerous handaxes. At Caminade shelter, we have Typical Mousterian. Phase II is occupied at Combe-Grenal by Quina Mousterian, while in Pech de l'Azé I we still have Mousterian of Acheulean tradition and in Caminade a poor assemblage which may be Typical Mousterian. Phase III sees the succession at Combe-Grenal of Quina, then Denticulate Mousterian. At Caminade it is Ferrassie Mousterian, while at Pech de l'Azé the sequence is not yet worked out for that level, but very probably this phase corresponds with at least part of the evolved Mousterian of Acheulean tradition (type B). Phase IV is occupied at Combe-Grenal by Quina Mousterian, then Denticulate Mousterian, while at Caminade it is Ferrassie Mousterian and in Pech de l'Azé probably the continuation of the Mousterian of Acheulean tradition. At Combe-Grenal, phase V corresponds to Denticulate Mousterian, while in Caminade this phase is sterile. Phase VI at the first site is Typical Mousterian, while in Caminade it is Ferrassie, then Quina Mousterian. We do not know the equivalent at Pech de l'Azé: it is probably part of the sterile top layers. Phase VII is occupied by Typical Mousterian at Combe-Grenal. This phase, if ever deposited, was eroded away at Caminade. And at Combe-Grenal the Mousterian of Acheulean tradition appears in a terminal position during Phase VIII. The Würm II sequence has not yet been worked out at le Moustier but it seems probable that Peyrony's very thick layer H, of Evolved Mousterian of Acheulean tradition, is contemporary with Phases I, II and perhaps III.

With Würm III comes the upper palaeolithic, even if, in Provence, some Mousterian may linger into the early part of this stage. The contemporaneity of the first stages of the Aurignacian and the Perigordian has been established on stratigraphical grounds at Roc de Combe and Le Piage in the Lot district but close to the Dordogne district border (Bordes and Labrot, 1967, Champagne and Espitalié, 1967). At Roc de Combe we find, from bottom to top: Mousterian, then erosion, Old Perigordian, Old Aurignacian, Old Perigordian, Aurignacian I, Aurignacian II, Aurignacian III or its equivalent, Perigordian with Gravette points, two layers of Perigordian with Noailles burins, then at the top Perigordian with numerous Gravette points, some Noailles, some Font-Robert points and some 'éléments tronqués'. At Le Piage, over the bedrock come three layers of Old Aurignacian, then Old Perigordian, then Aurignacian again. These interstratifications solve the problem of the contemporaneity of the oldest forms of Perigordian and Aurignacian.

But until recently, there was no definite proof of the contemporaneity of the Middle Aurignacian with the Middle Perigordian. Of course Aurignacian V at Laugerie Haute is situated over a very evolved Perigordian, but while this Aurignacian V is more Aurignacian-like than anything else, its roots in the older Aurignacian are not clearly known. But now sedimentary analysis has shown that the Perigordian with Gravettes at Roc de Combe (layer 4) is situated within the same climatic fluctuation as Aurignacian IV at La Ferrassie (Laville 1971). Some layers which can well be transitional between the Old Perigordian and the Middle Perigordian, as in Les Cottés (Pradel 1961) have not been dated yet, but would probably be contemporary with Aurignacian I of the Dordogne (Bordes 1968).

In D. Peyrony's scheme, the evolution of the Upper Perigordian, as established at La Ferrassie, was as follows: Perigordian 'V a', with Font-Robert points; Perigordian 'V b', with 'éléments tronqués', then Perigordian 'V c', with Noailles burins. This last is known now to have existed mainly during a warmer oscillation, cut in two parts by a short cold spell. But in Roc de Combe the Perigordian with Noailles burins begins in a cold period, contemporary with the Perigordian with Font-Robert points at La Ferrassie. So it seems that, rather than an evolution (Perigordian V a, b and c) we have a kind of trifurcation in culture variants, the elements of which may or may not be superposed in this order in different sites. At Roc de Combe as in Le Flageolet layer 6 (Rigaud 1969), we may find the three types (Noailles, Font-Roberts, 'éléments tronqués') all together.

All of that, of course, rather changes our outlook on the evolution of palaeolithic cultures, and instead of a linear evolution, we now have a mosaic of different cultures and different culture variants, more or less contemporary.

Coming back to the Acheulean, one of the results of the excavations at Pech de l'Azé II, Combe-Grenal (F. Bordes) or in open air sites near Bergerac (Guichard 1965, 1966) or in the Chalosse, one hundred miles south of Bordeaux (Thibault 1970), has been to put in evidence the existence of a southwest variant of the Acheulean, contemporary with the Rissian Acheulean of the north and centre of France. It differs, however, in the typology of its handaxes, and by the existence of flake-cleavers, and is related more to the Spanish Acheulean than to the 'classical' Acheulean of the Somme or Thames valleys. The boundary between this type of Acheulean and the classical one seems to lie more or less across the Dordogne district, and sporadic finds of 'Northern' Acheulean types of handaxes here and there south of the line point to some overlap. We have there a definite 'province' and some attention should be given to the significance of the existence of provinces, as opposed to the numerous interstratifications found in the Dordogne for many cultures (Bordes 1971).

The geographico-chronological study of the palaeolithic is in its infancy, but will be of tremendous importance for the understanding of the evolution of palaeolithic cultures and of their interaction. We have seen, for instance, that at Combe-Grenal the Würm I is almost entirely occupied by Typical Mousterian, while at Pech de l'Azé, distant about 6 miles as the crow flies, but on the other side of the Dordogne river, there are interstratifications. In the Charentes district, the Quina-Ferrassie type of Mousterian is very common, while the other types of Mousterian are very rare. In Provence (Lumley 1965) some valleys were occupied for a long time by one or other type of Mousterian, but the Mousterian of Acheulean tradition is completely unknown. As for the upper palaeolithic, it seems that when the Aurignacians arrived in the Dordogne, they swept the Perigordians out for some time, and we find inter-stratifications at the border (as in Roc de Combe) or evolved Old Perigordian in peripheral places, as in Les Cottés (Vienne) under *evolved* Aurignacian I. Then the Perigordians came back about the time of Middle Perigordian, and the Aurignacian sites (Aurignacian III and IV) became much rarer in the Dordogne. We have already discussed this point elsewhere (Bordes 1968). As for the Mousterian, we have demonstrated why we cannot accept Binford's interpretation of the different Mousterian types as only the reflection of different activities of basically the same cultural group (Bordes and Sonneville-Bordes 1970). Binford's point of view leads both to contradictions with facts, and to theoretical difficulties. On the other hand, these different Mousterian types are not an evolutionary sequence, as the interstratifications show, and they are not a consequence of a changing environment, since each of them existed under various different climatic conditions.

The only explanation which seems to fit the facts, at least at present, is the existence of different traditions, sometimes firmly settled in particular regions, and at other times moving to and fro. It is quite possible that the Mousterian of Acheulean tradition which, in the Dordogne, seems to belong to the end of Würm I and to Würm II, originated in the north of France, where it is known at the very early beginning of Würm I and maybe even at the end of the last Interglacial. It disappears from there, as do all the other types of Mousterian, when the loess deposits really began to be formed, and so may have moved south at that time. But it is again present in the North during the interstadials.

The Upper Magdalenian gives also some interesting information. For a long time it has been assumed that a Magdalenian without harpoons (where bone tools were preserved) was, by definition, Lower or at most Middle Magdalenian. When the Saiga antelope was found with it, this assumption was considered a certainty, since it was believed that there was a 'Saiga period', corresponding to Magdalenian I and II. However, more than ten years ago, D. de

Sonneville-Bordes, in her thesis (1960) pointed out that in some of these supposed Lower or Middle Magdalenian assemblages there were flint tools usually found only in the Upper or even Final Magdalenian, such for instance as the Azilian points. She emphasized this for the so-called Magdalenian III of La Chaire à Calvin, near Mouthiers (Charente), where Saiga was abundant (Sonneville-Bordes, 1963). This has now been corroborated by sedimentary analysis (Bouvier 1969). The same is probably true for Saint-Germain-la-Riviére (Gironde) and Cap-Blanc in the Dordogne.

Emergency excavations at Gare de Couze (Dordogne) in 1962 by Paul Fitte and myself have given us a perfectly typical Magdalenian VI with harpoons, but also with a relative abundance of microliths of geometric types: triangles, which are sporadically found in many Magdalenian sites, and are often numerous in Magdalenian II, and also trapezes, rectangles and semi-lunates, together with true microburins. But other sites, as carefully excavated, have given only a very few of these microliths, and it seems that at Gare de Couze we have a variant of Magdalenian VI, where there was considerable experimentation with types of microliths which were to become common and typical in the mesolithic (Bordes and Fitte, 1964). Other non-geometric microliths also foreshadow the mesolithic. But while Gare de Couze belongs without any question to Magdalenian VI, it is by no means a final Magdalenian, on the basis of the data of the sediments and the fauna. So numerous geometric microliths do not necessarily indicate either Magdalenian II or a very final Magdalenian, and the presence of Saiga does not necessarily indicate Lower Magdalenian.

Prehistory is now at a point where we have to accept the idea of contemporaneity not only of different culture variants, but also of different cultures, and this not only in different provinces, but also in interstratification in the same region. I do not think we have enough data now to try to solve this problem, except on a very general hypothetical level. One could try, for instance, to link the microliths of the Gare de Couze and the presence of numerous fishbones in its layers to the proximity of the Dordogne river. Or to explain the presence of these microliths and fishbones by the fact that all the excavated soil was water-sieved. But in the undoubtedly contemporary levels of Magdalenian VI at La Madeleine, where the soil in the recent excavations has also been water-sieved, there are very few geometric microliths and fishbones, although the site is just beside the Vezère river.

One interesting feature of the open sites excavated in the Dordogne (Acheulean, Mousterian, Perigordian, Aurignacian, Magdalenian) is that the tool kits do not seem, at a first approximation, to be very different from what it is seen in cave or shelter sites. Indeed, there is often a greater difference between the percentages of certain characteristic tools (handaxes, Gravette points) from two open-air sites than between them and those from the caves of shelters.

Tables I and II summarize the present results and show clearly the contemporaneity of different cultures of variants. It has often been said that a problem correctly stated is already half solved. I hope to have made some contribution to a clear statement of the problem.

Table 1
Contemporaneities during Würm I and II

Phase	Combe Grenal	Pech de l'Azé II	Pech de l'Azé I	Moustier	Micoque	Combe-Capelle
VIII	M. Ach. Trad.					
VII	Typical M.					
VI	Typical M.			← ?		
V	Denticulate M.		?			
IV	Denticulate M. Quina M.		←M. Ach. Trad.	Typical		
III	Denticulate M. Quina M.			→ ?		
II	Quina M.		M. Ach. Tr.	← ?		
I	Quina M. Ferrassie M. Typical M. Ferrassie M		M. Ach. Tr.	M. Ach. Tr.		
Interstadial	Weathering		Erosion	Weathering		
VII	Typical M.	Sterile		M. Ach. Tr.		←→ ?
VI	Denticulate M.	Sterile		M. Ach. Tr.		M. Ach. Tr.
V	Typical M.	Quina-Ferrassie M.		M. Ach. Tr.		Quina-Ferrassie ←→ ?
IV	Typical M.	Quina-Ferrassie M.		Sterile		
III	Typical M.	Typical M.		Sterile	Sterile	
II	Typical M.	Typical M. Denticulate M. Typical M.		Typical M.	Micoquian	
I	Typical M.	Typical M.			Sterile	

Table II

Contemporaneities at Roc de Combe and La Ferrassie

Climate	Roc de Combe		La Ferrassie	
	1	Evolved Perigordian with Noailles, Font-Roberts "éléments tronqués". Numerous Gravette points.		
Temperate damp	2	Perigordian with Noailles burins	L :	Perigordian with Noailles burins
Cold, dry	3	Perigordian with Noailles burins	J :	Perigordian with Font-Robert points
Temperate damp	4	Perigordian with Gravettes	H'':	Aurignacian IV
Cold, dry	5	Evolved Aurignacian	H' :	Aurignacian III
Temperate damp	6	Aurignacian II	H :	Aurignacian II
Cold, dry	7	Aurignacian I	F :	Aurignacian I
Unstable climate	8	Old Perigordian	E' :	Old Aurignacian
	9	Old Aurignacian	E :	Old Perigordian
	10	Old Perigordian		

Mousterian in both sites

REFERENCES

Binford, L.R. and S.R. (1966) A preliminary analysis of functional variability in the Mousterian of Levallois facies. *American Anthropologist* **68**, 2 (Part 2), 238-95.

Binford, L.R. and S.R. (1968) Stone tools and human behaviour. *Scientific American* **220**, no. 4, 70-84.

Bordes, F. (1968) La Question périgordienne. *In La Préhistoire, problèmes et tendances.* Editions du Centre National de la Recherche scientifique. 59-70. Paris.

Bordes, F. (1971) Observations sur l'Acheuléen des grottes en Dordogne. *Munibe* **XXIII** 1, 5-24.

Bordes, F. and Fitte, P. (1964) Microlithes du Magdalénien supérieur de la Gare de Couze. *Miscelanea en Homenaje al Abate Henri Breuil,* Diputation Provinciale de Barcelona, Instituto de Prehistoria y Arquelogia, 259-67.

Bordes, F. and Labrot, J. (1967) Stratigraphie de la grotte de Roc de Combe. *Bulletin de la Société préhistorique française*, 15-28.

Bordes, F., Laville, H. and Paquereau, M.M. (1966) Observations sur le Pléistocène supérieur de Combe-Grenal. *Actes de la Société linnéenne de Bordeaux* **103**, serie B, no. 10.

Bordes, F. and Sonneville-Bordes, D. de (1970) The significance of variability in Palaeolithic assemblages. *World Archaeology* **2**, 61-73.

Bouvier, J.-M. (1969) Existence de Magdalénian supérieur sans harpons: preuves stratigraphiques. *Comptes rendus de l'Académie des Sciences de Paris* **268**, 2865-6.

Champagne, F. and Espitalie, R. (1967) La stratigraphie du Piage. *Bulletin de la Société préhistorique française*, 29-34.

Commont, V. (1908) Les industries de l'ancien Saint-Acheul. *L'Anthropologie* **XIX**, 527-72.

Guichard, J. (1965) Un faciès original de l'Acheuléen: Cantalouette (Dordogne). *L'Anthropologie* **69**, 413-64.

Guichard, J. and Guichard, G. (1966) A propos d'un site acheuléen du Bergeracois (Les Pendus, Commune de Creysse). Bifaces-Hachereaux et hachereaux sur éclat. *Actes de la Société linnéenne de Bordeaux* **103**, série B, no. 5.

Laville, H. (1971) Sur la contemporanéité du Périgordien et de l'Aurignacien: la contribution du géologue. *Bulletin de la Société préhistorique française* (in press).

Lumley, H. de (1965) La grande révolution raciale et culturelle de l'Interwürmien II-III. *Cahiers Ligures de Préhistoire et d'Archéologie* **14**, II.

Peyrony, D. (1933) Les industries aurignaciennes dans le bassin de la Vezère. Aurignacien et Périgordien. *Bulletin de la Societe préhistorique française*, 543-59.

Pradel, L. (1961) La grotte des Cottés. *L'Anthropologie* **65**, 229-70.

Rigaud, J.Ph. (1969) Note préliminaire sur la stratigraphie du gisement du Flageolet I. *Compte Rendu des Séances mensuelles de la Société préhistorique française*, no. 3, 73-5.

Sonneville-Bordes, D. de (1960) *Le Paléolithique supérieur en Périgord.* Bordeaux. Delmas.

Sonneville-Bordes, D. de (1963) Etude de la frise sculptée de la Chaire-à-Calvin, commune de Mouthiers (Charente). *Annales de Paléontologie* **XLIX**, 181-93.

Thibault Cl. (1970) Recherches sur les terrains quaternaires du Bassin de l'Adour. PhD dissertation, MS, Laboratoire de Géologie quaternaire et Préhistoire, Bordeaux.

LEWIS R. BINFORD

Interassemblage variability - the Mousterian and the 'functional' argument

Since the initial publication of my preliminary results (Binford and Binford 1966 and 1969), designed to explore the character of inter-assemblage variability in the Mousterian, a number of objections have been raised to the view expressed and the results obtained. I will attempt to clarify several points which I think have served to confuse the issue and attempt to answer a number of the objections which have been raised to the arguments thus far set forth.

Central to the issues are what I consider to be rather limited notions about culture itself and the manner in which it serves man as a clearly successful adaptive basis for the organization of behaviour. Possibly the best way to make my point is to contrast what I might refer to as an archaeologist's and an ethnologist's perspective of culture. Let us imagine ourselves as ethnologists placed in the situation of evaluating the degree that two neighbouring communities are culturally alike or culturally different. From a traditional point of view they are culturally alike if they have similar cultural repertoires regarding the behaviours appropriate to similar sets of recognized situational stimuli. As ethnologists we may investigate this problem by attempting to observe the behaviour of the members of each group in the contexts of similar stimulus situations. If members of both groups respond to these control stimuli with identical or similar ranges of behaviour, then we have to conclude that both brought to the situation similar repertoires of culture, both in terms of the cognitive structure for the analysis of the stimuli and a learned pattern of appropriate response. For the purposes of ethnographic investigation we may not be concerned with whether or not one group exhibits behaviours in response to uncontrolled stimuli that distinguish it from the other. Clearly these behavioural differences refer to the differential distribution of stimuli and their relative frequencies of occurrence in the environments of the two groups. We might then say that behaviour variation is the byproduct of the interaction between the kinds and frequencies of environmental stimulus and the kinds of cultural repertoire which persons bring to these stimulus situations.

The archaeologist is in the position of being limited to the observation of the byproducts of behaviour itself. When we observe varying frequencies in the association of conventionally recognized forms of tool or forms of modification in the environment, we are directly seeing the results of behaviour. I have pointed out that behavioural variability is the result of the interaction between stimuli and the learned and traditional responses considered appropriate to the stimuli. We are therefore inevitably faced with the problem of determining whether the behavioural differences result from differences in the response repertoire of the actors or to the differences in the character and distribution of stimuli presented differentially to varying segments of a culturally homogeneous population.

My original research was directed towards the solution of this problem. It was argued that if similar or identical patterns of co-variation among similar tool classes could be shown to cross-cut recognizably different assemblage 'types', then the probability would be high that the assemblage types derive their consistent associational patterning from the organized distribution of stimuli, and not from the differential distribution of distinct cultural repertoires among population segments. I was successful in the original preliminary work and have been more successful since in the demonstration that there are consistent organizational properties which cross-cut consistent patterns of association (assemblage types). The organizational properties to which I refer are consistent patterns of mutual co-variation between sets of tools, regardless of whether they occur in assemblages which are considered similar or different in terms of associational patterning – e.g. Quina versus Typical Mousterian.

The debate which has followed the presentation of these ideas is largely reducible to a number of misunderstandings, irrelevant arguments, and points about which there is no contention. I will treat the arguments offered by the three authors of major critical works.

Arguments of Desmond Collins

In a paper treating the problem of Clactonian and Acheulian assemblage variability (1969), Collins presents an interesting distortion of my ideas and an irrelevant argument against them. He argues that, 'it is a mistake to contrast cultural and functional explanations of an artifact form' (1969: 268), justifying this position by pointing out that 'every illustrated ethnographic book is a corpus of refutations of the notion that knives, spearheads, and scrapers take the same form everywhere so long as they are used for the same purpose' (1969: 268). In these points I concur, but I see no possible relationship between them and the views which I have expressed. In the first place I never addressed myself to the problem of explaining differences between different forms of tools. My concern was with differences in proportional frequencies of typologically identical forms of tools as they occur in distinctive assemblage forms.

In a more recent article (1970), Collins continues to argue against a straw man; the 'functional hypothesis' presumably refers to my work though he does not cite it. He states:

> Functional hypotheses conflict with cultural hypotheses only when they insist that the close similarities which recur between assemblages are caused or determined by function, and they will recur without the factor of culture tradition. Such 'pure' functional hypotheses are both more recent and less carefully developed than the culture view of Childe and Warren. In particular they offer no explanation of how function can determine the similarities, and accordingly they can be tested only in a partial and unsatisfactory way, as the two examples below show. (Collins 1970:18)

Collins proceeds to offer his devastating evidence, pointing out that if two different assemblages were to be found in such similar contexts as kill sites, such evidence would disprove the 'functional' argument. I fail to see how this argument relates in any way to those which I have set forth. I have made no arguments against the existence of culture; I have never suggested that culture is not manifest in the archaeological record or that observable differences in the archaeological record might not have cultural significance. What I have suggested, however, is that behaviour is the byproduct of the interaction of a cultural repertoire with the environment. The archaeological record is the direct result of behaviour. Variations in the frequency with which certain culturally patterned behaviours will be executed is referable to the character of the environmental and adaptive situations in which cultural man finds himself at different points in time and space. To equate the archaeological record directly with the cultural repertoire of culture bearers is to ignore the reality of their adaptive behaviour and the advantages which a culturally based form of adaptation offers.

Collins has offered yet another argument against, as he phrases it, 'the functional explanation of assemblage types' (1970:17). He points out that there are ethnographic and behavioural precedents for recognizing the differential distributions of behaviour both temporally and spatially for members of a 'single community'. However, he argues that this should not be manifest in the archaeological record because 'each type (assemblage with reference to differentiated behaviour) would have been left somewhere within the confines of their territory over a similar period of time. But as time passed one would expect that the assemblage types would often come to be left at the same site. The overall distributions of the assemblage types would inevitably remain similar' (Collins 1969:268). This argument makes a number of unwarranted assumptions. First, it assumes that environment for adaptive purposes is homogeneous and that human groups randomly distribute in the environment; this implies that, given a sufficient sample of events and sufficient passage of time, all behaviours are equally likely to occur at any location. This is demonstrably not the case. The environment is a complex ecological organization in which the energy and materials needed to maintain a human group are differentially distributed; it follows that all the activities necessary to the group's successful survival will not be performed at any one location. This differential distribution of matter and energy in the habitat insures that during a stable environmental episode the probabilities of different activities clustering at different locations is quite high. In the context of unstable environmental conditions it insures that a single location may offer very different advantages to a group in direct relation to the degree and character of environment change. In regard to the differential distribution of assemblage types over broad geographical provinces, such differential clustering may well be expected since the environment may be expected to vary across such regions. It is a matter for investigation to what degree there is a correspondence between behavioural variation across environmental zones and differences in the cultural repertoires of the persons so distributed; the simplistic equation of behaviour with culture is not an answer.

Arguments of Paul Mellars

The criticisms of Paul Mellars have been very different in character. His work has been concerned with a refinement in the recognition of patterning in the archaeological record and a demand that this patterning be explained. He has further investigated some of the apparent lack of correlation between the patterns of assemblage variation and the variation exhibited by environmental indicators as published. I will try to consider Mellars' scepticism in a very different manner since it is obviously presented in a sincere attempt to increase our understanding of the past.

> By far the strongest argument against a purely functional interpretation of Mousterian industries in Southwest France is provided by evidence from the relative chronology of three of the major industrial variants – the Ferrassie, Quina and M.A.T. groupings of Bordes' Taxonomy. The evidence suggests that in the area under consideration industries belonging to each of these groupings may well be confined to a single, relatively brief span of time, and that contrary to earlier beliefs, the time ranges occupied by these variants may not have overlapped to any appreciable degree. (Mellars 1970:76)

Mellars, then, has pointed out that the variants of the Mousterian are not randomly distributed temporally; and Bordes has shown that they are not randomly distributed spatially (1970:73). These demonstrations mark the beginning of the recognition of some patterning in the bewildering array of Mousterian variability. My impression is that a clustering of cases of Typical Mousterian is demonstrable for much of Würm I in the French sequence. Mellars may be correct in suggesting that, at least on the basis of the sample available, a clustering of Ferrassie followed by Quina variants is demonstrable for the first half of the Würm II oscillation. Of all the variants, Denticulate seems to exhibit the least tendency of cluster temporally. Bordes has long recognized some temporal significance in variations in the M.A.T. (Mousterian of Acheulean Tradition), and further noted its clustering at the beginning and the end of Würm I, II sequence. The statistical clustering of assemblage types against a temporal reference dimension does not, however, necessitate an evolutionary argument that one form of assemblage was the 'ancestor' of another. Similarly, it does not necessarily affect my arguments to any appreciable extent. I anticipate some patterning in the assemblage variability, although I do not anticipate the same patterns to be demonstrable from different regions, and I do not anticipate an exclusive sequential arrangement of all the variability. The clustering of Charentian – like Mousterian – in the early phases of the Near Eastern sequence as opposed to its generalized placement in the Southwestern French sequence is a case in point. The lack of apparent temporal patterning currently demonstrable in the Denticulate variant is another relevant case in point. Why do I anticipate some temporal patterning? Because there was a rather significant amount of environmental change occurring during the course of time represented by the Mousterian assemblages in question. I would clearly anticipate some behavioural accommodations. To what degree behavioural change is to be equated with cultural change is as I have pointed out previously something to be investigated not simply assumed.

The second major point of argument made by Mellars is stated as follows:

> By analogy with the behaviour of recent hunting and gathering societies one might expect that the specialized activities which led to the production of contrasting forms of assemblage would be undertaken at distinct types of settlement location, suited to the exploitation of differing environmental resources . . . In fact, the existing data from Southwest France provide very little evidence for patterning of this kind; not only are the overall geographical distributions of the different Mousterian variants broadly similar, but horizons representing two or more of these variants have frequently been encountered on precisely the same sites . . . The outstanding example of this is provided by the sequence at Combe-Grenal in which all five of the major Mousterian groupings . . . occur within a single stratigraphic column. (Mellars 1970:77)

There are seemingly two points to be discussed in answer to this argument. First, Mellars is incorrect in asserting that the overall distribution of Mousterian assemblage types as recognized by Bordes exhibit the same 'overall geographical distributions'. My own experience contradicts this point and certainly Bordes has amassed data which are directly contrary to this position.

> Some territories seem to have been occupied for very long times by the same type of Mousterian. In Charente, the M.A.T. is not quite unknown, but rare, while the Charentian seems to be almost the absolute master. The Combe-Grenal region seems to have been occupied throughout Würm I by Typical Mousterian, with the exception of a very brief incursion of Denticulate Mousterian . . . In Provence . . . territorial continuities seem very strong, and the M.A.T. is unknown. (Bordes and Bordes 1970:73)

I might add that on the Paris plain, Typical, Denticulate and Ferrassie are most abundant with Quina all but absent. Other cases of the differential distribution of the recognized types could be cited which are contrary to Mellars' assertion. Secondly, Mellars appears to ignore the evidence of environmental changes when asserting that single sites yield stratigraphically arranged examples of the different variants. By citing Combe-Grenal Mellars leaves himself open; my analysis of that stratigraphic sequence will show a remarkable association between marked changes in the environment and changes in the composition of assemblages. In general there is a good correspondence between the stability of the environment and the stability of the assemblage form. I do not wish to imply that there is a causal relationship between the form of the environment and the form of the assemblage, only that the utility of a given location for particular forms of human use is modified with changes in the environment. During periods of roughly similar environments, a given location is utilized in roughly similar ways, although other contemporary locations in the same area may be utilized in different ways depending upon the particular characteristics of the location in the context of the economic geography of the groups represented.

I conclude that Mellars' second set of arguments is undermined by misinformation about the character of geographical variation in the frequency of occurrence of recognized Mousterian variants, and by his failure to consider the dynamics of environment as a conditioning factor in the occurrence of different Mousterian variants.

The third argument presented by Mellars against a 'functional' view of assemblage variability has to do with the flaking techniques used in the manufacture of tools. Mellars argues that there is a correspondence between the forms of the assemblage and the techniques used in production, suggesting that such a correspondence is 'more suggestive of stylistic than functional patterning within the material' (1970:80). I question whether this type of correspondence can be demonstrated.

Bordes long ago pointed out that the Denticulate variant was known in four different forms with regard to the index of Levallois debitage, index of faceting, and variations between real and essential indexes. At that time Bordes recognized a Denticulate Mousterian of Levalloisian facies and with Levallois debitage; one of non-Levalloisian facies but with Levallois debitage; one with non-Levallois debitage but with a high index of faceted platforms; and a non-Levallois, non-faceted variant (Bordes 1963:45-6). Such variability clearly indicates that at least for the Denticulate Mousterian there is no necessary correspondence between the type of Mousterian as described by the content of the assemblage and the degree of faceting on the butt of flakes or the degree that Levallois technique was being used.

Bordes further contradicts Mellars' arguments directly:

> It is interesting to note that some assemblages, Quina by their Quina index, are assigned to Ferrassie because of their debitage (very Levallois) and conversely some assemblages, Quina by their debitage, have a Quina index which puts them in the Ferrassie type. (1970:71)

Thus I must conclude that Mellars' third argument is presented on the basis of a poor understanding of the character of variability exhibited by Mousterian materials. In way of further comment I must point out that my original work and the work currently under way (which attempts to test the degree that properties can be anticipated to exist if some behavioural model of the past is employed) are in no way directed toward the explanation of variation in technique. I have been working almost exclusively with the content of assemblages as measured by Bordes' type list; my attention has not been directed toward understanding the patterns of variation in technique which clearly cross-cut the recognized Mousterian variants as opposed to corresponding with them as Mellars has argued.

The fourth major point presented as evidence against the utility of my approaches is a very fascinating one and one to which I will return with some additional comments later.

Mellars points out that

> It is important to remember that an exclusively functional interpretation of Southwest French Mousterian industries would carry with it the implication that the behaviour of the Middle Palaeolithic communities who occupied this region was substantially different from that of the succeeding Upper Palaeolithic populations in the same area. (1970:80)

This argument is documented by asserting that research has failed to reveal 'any appreciable variations with the Upper Palaeolithic assemblages of this region which demonstrably reflect functional variability of the "interlocational" form' (ibid.:80). He goes on to suggest that all recognized variability is 'unquestionably of chronological and/or "cultural" significance'.

I don't know exactly how to answer this point since I find it self-contradictory. For instance, alterations between Aurignacian and Lower Perigordian are now clearly documented in the Dordogne. If Mellars is referring to the properties of industrial alternation seen in the Mousterian as the criteria for recognizing 'functional variability of the "inter-locational" form', then he is clearly in error. Similarly I might point out that the once supposedly clear chronological succession of Perigordian Va, b and c has been challenged by well-documented excavations at Flageolet (Rigaud 1971). I do not wish necessarily to suggest that such variability may ultimately be referable to 'functional variation' although it is a possibility. I only wish to point out that Mellars' generalizations regarding the character of variability in the upper palaeolithic may be questioned on empirical grounds.

Now to the more important question and the one to which I feel Mellars is referring. I would agree that there is a much greater degree of temporal patterning demonstrable in the upper palaeolithic than is currently demonstrable for the Mousterian, in spite of Mellars' arguments to the contrary. Secondly, I am of the opinion that this contrast does point to major organizational differences between middle and upper palaeolithic cultural systems. At present I am confident that at least part of the contrast derives from the character of the typologies utilized for evaluating variability in the two periods. Bordes' tool typology for the middle palaeolithic is demonstrably of wide applicability. It is equally useful for summarizing materials from North Africa, the Near East, Central Europe, and even China as Bordes has demonstrated. By way of contrast, when the standard 'type list' used for upper palaeolithic materials in the southwest of France is applied to materials from areas distant from the region itself, substantial modifications are necessary to accommodate its typological features to areas outside of southwestern France. One might conclude from this that (a) the middle and upper palaeolithic typologies are measuring substantially different kinds of variability, or (b) there is a contrast in the character of variability between the middle and upper palaeolithic. Regardless of the position taken, the upper palaeolithic and the middle palaeolithic are clearly different as they are currently known through typological valuations. Thus, this difference is in no way an argument against explanatory attempts which demand that a difference be recognized. At best it is an excellent argument against an attempt to argue that variability in both is to be understood in the same terms (the position of those favouring a 'cultural' interpretation of the variability in both).

It is my personal opinion that the upper palaeolithic typology is a compound instrument for measurement which incorporates as equal units characteristics reflecting stylistic as well as functional features. Since taxonomic priority is generally given to features believed to be most discriminating temporally, as in the case of the old Perigordian V sequence, we more often see a temporal patterning in the taxonomic variants. In the middle palaeolithic such monitors of temporal variation are difficult to identify and priority for taxonomic purposes is given to numerical superiority as in the distinction between Denticulate vs. Charentian, etc. I suggest that the middle palaeolithic typology incorporates few if any stylistically significant characteristics and is therefore a better instrument for monitoring pure behavioural variation; whereas the upper palaeolithic typology incorporates both and therefore monitors simultaneously behavioural and organizational variation at the ethnic level. This position leads us back to the original question: does our difficulty in identifying characteristics which exhibit clear temporal clustering for the middle palaeolithic reflect major differences between the middle palaeolithic and the upper palaeolithic? My opinion is that it does and thus far I have been unconvinced that patterned 'stylistic' variability has been demonstrated in the archaeological record prior to the upper palaeolithic. This is not to say that variability does not exist in the particular characteristics of shape, size and management procedure, which we have learned are frequently of stylistic significance; nevertheless, the demonstration that this variability exhibits any directional patterning is thus far lacking to my satisfaction.

I would argue contrary to Mellars and suggest that there are major differences between the middle and upper palaeolithic as currently known and that these differences demand explanation.

The final argument which Mellars offers has to do with the recognition that marked environmental changes occurred during the course of Mousterian occupation of southwestern France. He further suggests that because of this, one would expect on purely *a priori* grounds that some chronological patterning might be demonstrable. This is exactly the point which I made in answer to his second argument. Here we agree, but to what degree this expectation is an argument against a 'functional' interpretation of interassemblage variability is quite unclear to me.

After Mellars discusses the problem of Mousterian variability in southwest France, he more specifically addresses himself to the published results of my students and myself on the problem of interassemblage variability in the Near East and Spain. Mellars' criticisms of these published works will be taken up point by point.

> *1. In the first place one may challenge the initial assumption that the groupings of total types which constitute the different factors represent functional 'tool kits'* (Mellars 1970:83)

Mellars goes on to argue that an alternative interpretation might be that they represent 'associated [tools] for cultural rather than functional reasons'. He then proceeds to suggest that if a factor analysis were done of upper palaeolithic assemblages the results would be factors which grouped the tools most diagnostic of each recognized phase of cultural systematics in the region. He concludes that to interpret such 'factors' as tool kits would not accord with our understanding of the assemblages in question. With this I totally agree. The point at issue is whether or not this is a relevant argument. I would say that it is not. Clearly if one were to perform a factor analysis and the factor scores for a given factor were to exhibit substantial temporal clustering, one might reasonably investigate the proposition that the factor isolated was of cultural chronological significance. However, the actual results of the Near Eastern analysis, Spanish analysis, and my unpublished analysis of the Combe-Grenal materials from southwestern France *do not* demonstrate any discrete temporal clustering for the factors isolated. On the other hand, there is some statistical clustering of factors corresponding nicely with directional changes in the environment, particularly in the southwest data. To account for the factor groupings in cultural terms would demand (1) equating each factor with an independent cultural tradition of which there are fourteen represented in the materials from Combe-Grenal, and (2) visualizing a situation in which these cultural traditions blended and hybridized in a manner unrelated directly to the time sequence or the demonstrated changes in the environment. In short, the temporal patterning envisioned for the hypothetical upper palaeolithic factors is clearly not demonstrable in the analysed cases of the Mousterian, nor is it demonstrable for the correspondence between their presence and the currently recognized types of Mousterian. I fail then to find any support of Mellars' position.

> *2. If one accepts . . . that the factors do represent tool-kits . . . the essential problem here is to decide how far the separate factors represent different, and how far similar activities*

This problem, that of imparting significance to observations made on the archaeological record, is the essential problem of archaeology and is not unique to the use of any given technique. Pointing it out as a problem is in no way a criticism of any given technique used for looking at the archaeological record. I can only paraphrase Mellars' conclusions as follows: until more reliable evidence is available concerning the particular functions for which Mousterian tools were intended, the problem of deciding how far the different 'tool-kits' represent similar and how far dissimilar *cultures* will remain without any satisfactory solution.

The final point of Mellars' arguments to which I will address myself is a curious one in which he makes the major point of my argument and then tries to use it against me! He argues:

> If it could be demonstrated by factor analysis or other means that all of the variability displayed by assemblages can be accounted for entirely by variations in the activites undertaken in the different horizons, it is difficult to see why this should rule out the possibility that the different types of assemblage were manufactured by distinct ethnic groups. All that one could logically infer would be that this particular line of inquiry had failed to reveal evidence for such ethnic differentiation . . . To infer that because two assemblages appear to reflect rather different economic activities they must have been produced by the same human group would seem a curious non-sequitur. (1970:84)

With which argument I concur. I defy Mellars or anyone else to produce a reference documenting any opinion offered by me as to the nature or the ethnic organization of human groups responsible for the variability in the Mousterian. I have only asserted that the typology, an instrument for measurement, was monitoring primarily activity variation and not stylistic variability. In the absence of any instrument for measuring ethnic affinity, there is no way of evaluating the ethnic character of the groups responsible for the behavioural variability documented. On the other hand, the ability to demonstrate a strong identity in the patterns of covariation between identical sets of tools among diverse sets of assemblage types seems to me to be strong evidence that the patterns of use for the mutually covariant tool forms were similar in a variety of associated contexts. That does appear to me to be clear evidence that at least in this aspect of culture the units represented were very similar. The degree that they thought of themselves as members of a consciously recognized community is something which I cannot see any evidence for or against at the present time. In short, the variability documented in the archaeological record prior to the upper palaeolithic appears to lack any significance whatsoever with regard to the ethnic composition of groups. Could it be that ethnicity as we think of it was not yet a part of the cultural environment of man?

Arguments of François Bordes

In attempting to answer the criticisms of Bordes I am dealing with a very different kind of opponent. If Desmond Collins argues from a position of ignorance as to the character of my arguments and Mellars argues from a position lacking a clear understanding of the character of variability in the Mousterian itself, François Bordes argues from a position of strength. He has an unquestionable knowledge of the Mousterian and a well-informed understanding of my argument. Disagreements may then take us into very different and more profitable fields of discussion.

I will try to clarify some of the differences between Bordes and myself. I once stated that:

> in view of the demonstrated alternation of industries, one must envision a perpetual movement of culturally distinct peoples, never reacting to or coping with their neighbours. Nor do they exhibit the typically human characteristics of mutual influence and borrowing. Such a situation is totally foreign, in terms of our knowledge of *sapiens* behaviour. (Binford and Binford 1966:240)

Bordes answers this point by referring to demonstrated 'traditions' defined currently as having great integrity over long periods of time. If one accepts the demonstrated differences between assemblages as of ethnic significance, then he is correct in pointing out that contemporary assemblages of different form are documented. The crucial point not faced by Bordes is whether documented stability and/or contemporaneous variability refer to ethnic distinctions. In his answers, Bordes clearly assumes that they do. I make no such assumption. Our difference then is over the *assumed* significance of variability, a point to which I will return.

In further arguing against the proposition I have set forth, Bordes makes an impressive case against one of my assumptions as to the character of life during middle palaeolithic times. Crucial to my model of the past is the proposition that man relied strongly on mobility as a major strategy in his subsistence practices. This mobility would have insured that activities were differentially performed not only in space, but through a seasonal cycle in varying combinations. This differential performance would insure that a complicated set of associations of tools related to the spatially and temporally differentiated activities performed would remain. Bordes points out that Bouchud's (1966) study of reindeer teeth and antlers from a number of Mousterian locations leads him to conclude that the sites were occupied in many cases on a year-round basis. If this finding were upheld my position would clearly be damaged. On the basis of the data available to him, Bordes is clearly justified in rejecting my position. At this point I must either accept defeat or offer very powerful evidence that the conclusions of Bouchud might be reasonably doubted.

I would like first to point out that for purposes of evaluating the season of death for the reindeer studied, Bouchud relied exclusively on the data from teeth. Antlers were not systematically considered. Bouchud makes use of two kinds of information for purposes of determining month of death of the reindeer represented in the Mousterian levels which he studied. First, Bouchud found from his study of a large sample of archaeologically recovered mandibles that the overall configuration in the increasing evidence of wear on teeth was amenable to arrangement into a continuum. He was able to correlate certain patterns of increasing attrition on teeth with the sequence of permanent tooth eruption. In order to convert these demonstrable properties of teeth into a usable scale for evaluating the month of death several facts are necessary and one very important assumption.

First it is necessary to know whether all reindeer are born at the same time, and second when birth is likely to occur. On the basis of available data drawn from studies of Siberian animals, one can clearly state that these animals exhibit a definite birth cycle, such that the vast majority of the births occur about the same time and this is generally during the latter part of May and the early part of June. Already we have introduced a problem of population statistics. All births are not simultaneous, and there is variability from year to year in the exact period of birth. Bouchud assumes for purposes of his analysis that *all* births are simultaneous, and regular from year to year. The next crucial point in Bouchud's analysis is the maturational dating of the period of permanent tooth eruption. For instance, Bouchud adopts an estimate of 27 months as the elapsed maturational time for the completed eruption of the premolars. Recent studies of Alaskan Caribou show that complete eruption may occur as early as 22 months after birth, and as late as 26 months with an average completed eruption time of 24 months. (Skoog 1968, 74). Two points are of significance: (1) actual field sampling revealed a span of four months over which eruption might occur, and Bouchud assumed that it was simultaneous for all individuals; (2) Bouchud was off three months in his estimate of mean eruption time ensuring that teeth from the same animal killed on the same date would be tabulated in two different months since his estimates of eruption time for the second molar were accurate. Further compounding the problem are his estimates for the first and third molar. He estimated three months for the first molar where current data shows that four months is the best mean estimate with a range of two months. The third molar has a mean completed eruption age of twenty-five months from birth with a range of six months. Bouchud again estimated 24 months and assumed a simultaneous eruption date for all individuals. These errors insure that a single animal (two and a half years old) killed in November would be tabulated on Bouchud's scales as evidence for animals killed by premolars in September, third molar in October, second molar in November, and first molar in December. Since Bouchud was tabulating isolated teeth, in the main, and not mandibles, quite clearly his errors in eruption time for the different teeth insure that 'evidence' for continuous occupation will be accumulated. Each diagnostic tooth group from a single individual will yield a different estimate of the month of death spanning the three months before and one month after the actual death. Add to the above error the error arising from the fact of demonstrable individual variability in eruption time and we are further assured of a continuous distribution.

To complicate the picture further, Bouchud made the assumption, since he could demonstrate a continuous sequence of attrition on teeth, that attrition proceeded at a constant rate. It was this assumption which made it possible for him to assign a month of death to fully erupted permanent teeth. Two facts are of importance here: (1) current research shows that rates of attrition are not constant throughout the year, varying particularly with the character of the diet. Most attrition occurs when sedges are a major component of the diet, which among the animals currently under study is during the late summer and fall. Attrition seems to be all but absent during the winter months as does growth in teeth. (Skoog 1968, p. 70). Although attrition may appear as a morphological continuum, the assumption that it proceeds at a continuous and constant rate is not justified. This unjustified assumption stands behind Bouchud's ageing scale for tooth wear. Thus, we may anticipate that these age estimates for month of death based on that scale are certain to be inaccurate. This would be particularly true for animals dated to the winter months since both degree of tooth development and the character of attrition is arrested during the winter. Animals in early March appear very much as they did in late October. The compounding of all this error, and its differential distribution, ensured by the fact Bouchud was independently estimating the month of death from premolars, 1st, 2nd and 3rd molars as well as the attrition on premolar milk teeth, with all five scales then being summed and a mean presented, ensures that the data will be continuously distributed around the year except in cases where near identical individuals make up a very small sample.

Thus I feel quite confident in dismissing Bouchud's analysis as conclusive that the Mousterian sites studied were occupied on a year-round basis. In fact I am confident that a re-analysis, making use of populational approaches and the refined data now available on periods of tooth eruption and the character of the attrition process, would demonstrate conclusively that they were indeed occupied exclusively on a short term basis.

Bordes likes to point out that many of the layers are thick and frequently appear to have accumulated over a long period of time. He argues: 'We should then presuppose a kind of covenant between Mousterian tribes, reserving such and such a cave for summer activities and some other one for winter activities' (1970:66). This is an old idea between Bordes and me and was expressed in jest in the cartoon on p.xi, presented to me in good humour in 1968. The difficulty is that I have never argued that each of the four types of Mousterian as known in Bordes' assemblage typology was either a single activity or a single and consistent combination of activities. I anticipate some differentiation in behaviour and hence in assemblage forms which should show seasonal correlates, yet I am not at all convinced that such correlations would be with the most frequent forms such as scrapers and denticulates, which currently tend to serve for discriminating between the different types of Mousterian assemblage. Secondly, the consistent utilization of a single location over a long period of time for essentially the same purposes does not seem to me to require 'covenant', since unlike Bordes I do not picture the territory filled by ethnically different peoples. I envision a territory utilized differentially to the advantage of the occupants. That there should be a consistency in the way it is utilized sometimes spanning a long period of time does not appear surprising, and I would expect such consistency to be disrupted only in the face of environmental change which would tend to modify the utility of locations for particular use.

Bordes has pointed out, and quite justifiably, that many of the kinds of location among which we might expect some differentiation in activities on strictly *a priori* grounds are rare or unknown in southwestern France for the Mousterian. He has further pointed out that there are documented cases where very similar assemblage forms are known from open as well as cave locations (1970:68). He argues that 'the difference of type of site, and therefore, theoretically at least, of activities, does not transform one type of Mousterian into another'. This is very true; however, I have no way of knowing at this time what the determinants of different activities were during the Mousterian and therefore no way of evaluating the degree that the difference between cave and open locations might be correlated in a consistent manner with activity differentiation. If this is true for the same general geographic area, it is certainly true for locations as topographically and ecologically different as the areas around Sarlat and Bergerac.

Bordes has warned against the dangers of ethnographic comparisons pointing out that the Mousterian peoples of southwestern France were not Eskimos or Australian Aborigines. This is a point worthy of comment and one in the context of which Bordes himself has offered some interesting arguments. I have recently been studying the hunting strategies of the Nunamiut Eskimos* as a means of learning something about what it is like to live in a tundra environment – the degree that different problems present themselves for solution as a function of seasonal changes and the particular strategies followed in hunting caribou. My motives for undertaking this research were directly related to my work on the Mousterian, particularly that of the climax of the Würm II cold period as recorded in the pollen profiles from Combe-Grenal. These Eskimos are currently sedentary, a condition postulated by Bordes to have characterized the Mousterian peoples.

Without going into all the fascinating details of this research, I would like to point out some interesting facts. I have accompanied the Nunamiut hunters on practically all of their different kinds of

*Research supported by the Wenner-Gren Foundation for Anthropological Research and the National Science Foundation.

hunting and subsistence activities. I have noted what they in fact do on these locations and in turn what debris remains for the archaeologist. The most striking fact to emerge from this research is that with regard to artifacts *per se* there is little correlation between what is done and the artifacts remaining. Their technology is what I will call an almost exclusively *curated* technology, in which a tool once produced or purchased is carefully curated and transported to and from locations in direct relationship to the anticipated performance of different activities. Under such an efficient system of technoeconomy the archaeological record is more properly considered a record of the organization of entropy as opposed to the organization of the ongoing activity structure of the group. Almost any item has a different life expectancy and will be discarded more in terms of its estimated utility for future use than as any direct reflection of its context of use or importance in the ongoing technology. Over time there is an accumulation of archaeologically relevant debris on sites which are clearly different in terms of observed activities. Nevertheless, taking a strict archaeological perspective the contents of these sites are grossly similar in that the most common items on all are generally similar and are those items most expendable, of least importance in the ongoing technological system. Plotting these assemblages by means of cumulative graphs shows that they exhibit, in general, less variability in content than might be currently demonstrable between many different assemblages from the upper palaeolithic assignable to a given 'cultural phase'. Locations which are demonstrably very different from the behavioural standpoint are only differentiated archaeologically by items which are rare and almost always broken and modified heavily through use. The other context of differentiation is the erratic occurrence of rare items in mint condition which were cached in anticipation of future use and as a result of unanticipated events were never recovered. These generalizations apply to the fabricated tools; however, they do not apply to the immediate byproducts of the activities performed, such as parts of animals differentially discarded, or consumed as a function of the logistics of hunting. The differences in the sites are clearly reflected and very marked in the differential remains of consumption and of processing of animals in the context of the logistics of getting the animal from its location of kill to its location of consumption.

Returning to the patterns of variation in tools for a moment, it is clear that the character of the archaeological record and the degree that it is a direct reflection of the activities performed at any given location will vary inversely with the degree that there is an efficient economizing techno-logistics system in operation. The more that tools are curated, transported, and preserved for future use, the less correspondence there will be between the behavioural context of their use and their associated occurrence in the archaeological record.

Similarly, there will be an inverse relationship between their importance in the ongoing behavioural system and their frequency in the archaeological record. Differential frequencies between archaeologically observable classes of artifacts, all of which are curated and maintained as a continuous part of the technological tool kit of individuals or groups, will reflect directly the different replacement rates between the various tool classes and not their importance in the ongoing behavioural system. There may be some correlation between replacement rates and the frequency with which things are used; however, this would be greatly modified by the degree that different raw materials with different stress properties were employed in their manufacture.

Another observation made among the Nunamiut which may be of some significance is that the degree that conscious stylistic variation occurs in the products of craft production appears to vary inversely with the degree that the item produced is considered expendable. Items produced expediently and discarded in the immediate context of use exhibit less investment from the individual standpoint and hence have less of the identity of the manufacturer expressed through individualized and group conscious 'stylistic' characteristics. On the other hand, items which are produced with the clear anticipation of long-term use and long-term association between the manufacturer or others for whom he is serving as the producer, exhibit a greater tendency to range in patterned stylistic expression and formal diversity. Thus I would anticipate that the best material markers of ethnic identity might well be found in items curated and preserved for relatively long periods of utilitarian life within the technological system. These of course would be items which were relatively rare in assemblages for the reasons outlined above.

Bordes has pointed out that the analysis by Carmel White and Nicholas Peterson (1969) of materials from Australia has revealed a dichotomy between sites linked to seasonal occupation of the plateau and coastal plain. Bordes correctly points out their findings as follows:

> The main tool types present at Tyimede are similar to the range found in the plain sites, including points, small scraper-adzes, utilized flakes and edge ground axes, but the Tyimede assemblages differ in one major way from their plain counterparts, for many of the stone tools here seem to have been manufactured in situ; the overall ratio of tools to waste flakes is 1 to 25 (in the plain sites, the ratio is 1 to 5). (Bordes 1970: 72, quoting from White and Peterson 1969)

Bordes continues to argue as follows:

> Roughly speaking, we have to do with two sites belonging to the same culture, one in which tools were frequently made on the spot, and in the other less so. In our graphs, where we do not count flakes, even utilized, with the 'true' tool, the two sites, following what the authors say, would

> very probably yield comparable diagrams, and we would never interpret them as different industries. Completely different is the case of the Mousterian facies, where, in the first place, we have to do with semi-sedentary people present all the year round at the site, and, in the second place, we are concerned with differences in the tool types and their proportions, which are sometimes very strong. (1970:72)

In this argument I fear Bordes has violated his own warning against the use of ethnographic comparisons. He has cited the Australian data and the apparent lack of differentiation in the archaeological record among differentiated locations as evidence that the differentiation noted in the Mousterian could not refer to differentiated activities. Any student of Australian technology will readily characterize their technology as a highly efficient system in which tools are curated, transported, and preserved. As White and Paterson found, the only items directly to reflect differentiated activities are the immediate byproducts of those activities – manufacturing debris – not the tools used. This is of course what we observed among the Nunamiut. Bordes in another argument points out a most important point offering strong support for my contentions. He states: 'In the caves or shelters, as well as on the open-air sites, one usually finds not only the tools, but also the cores, flakes, chips, etc., which indicate that fabrication and *utilization* of the tools took place in the same area.' In short, Bordes argues that the Mousterian tools were in the main expediently manufactured and used. This is clearly not the case among the Australians or the Nunamiut where their tools are curated, preserved and transported. Clearly then, under conditions of expedient tool production and use, we would expect the variations in tools more directly to reflect differences in the activities performed. Bordes in his citation of the Australian data has failed to consider the big differences between the Australian Aborigines and the Mousterian.

Conclusions and a summary of the 'funtional argument'

In the discussion of Mellars' criticisms, I introduced the idea that ethnicity may not have always been a component of the cultural environment of man. This suggestion is in need of further clarification since it bears directly on one of the assumptions which served operationally in the context of the original statement of the 'Functional Argument'. In the context of the history of the development of the approaches and arguments being discussed under the rubric of the Fuctional Argument the initial question which I asked myself was, what is Bordes' taxonomy measuring? It is quite easy to defend the position, since any taxonomy is an instrument for measurement, that the answer to the question, what does a given taxonomy measure is central to prehistory. Bordes in personal conversation and in a discussion of the principles employed in the development of his middle palaeolithic 'type list' refers to (a) variations in the orientation, and (b) variations in the form of the working edge, as being the two major dimensions along which variants are grouped into tool types. It seems reasonable to proceed as if such variation may bear some relationship to the way tools were used and the particular technical acts which they enhanced. In short the middle palaeolithic typology was designed to differentiate fabricated stone forms into taxa on the basis of properties potentially related directly to their differential design as implements employed to enhance the transfer of energy from a source – a human – to some other object upon which work was being performed. A reasonable suggestion as to what Bordes' taxonomy is measuring is the character of differentiation in the design of tools as such. If true then one might reasonably expect that variations in their frequency and patterns of association might be referable to the character of the work being performed and hence the context of the activities in the course of which they were used. Archaeologists and the layman alike have long been aware that the character of the morphology and the distribution of material items among contemporary peoples varied also in terms of social variables. It has been this observation that has led archaeologists to make use of variability in material items as a clue to the social arrangements of persons in the past. I was led to reject the relevance of this observation to the tools of the middle palaeolithic for a number of reasons. First the character of variability as documented for the Mousterian was manifest in different proportional frequencies between similar tool forms in different locational contexts. Among contemporary peoples ethnicity is more frequently directly demonstrable through morphological variations between different localized groups with respect to roughly analogous functional classes of tools. It is difficult to see how a denticulate is a functional equivalent of a Quina scraper.

More important however is the recognition that for variability in tools and other material items to be of direct cultural significance in the sense of having recognized symbolic significance, this variability must be cognitively recognizable. If an item is to serve to express conscious ethnic, or individual identity, it must be something which is immediately and directly perceived. I find it difficult to imagine that something as remote from reality as a scraper index could have direct ethnic or social symbolic significance.

The argument, as generally presented, in which variability in the Mousterian is viewed as 'cultural', and hence indicative of different traditions, must make an interesting assumption, namely that the cultural background and hence tradition which refers to the design of tools is essentially identical for all recognized 'cultural traditions'. This is necessary in that the morphological variants of tools, the types, are for purposes of the taxonomy identical in the different traditions. It is variability in the proportional frequencies of these similar morphological forms which is said to distinguish the traditions. One must envision a pattern of behaviour culturally transmitted which ensures that once a site is occupied the occupants busy themselves with producing and discarding a wide variety of tool forms in a set and traditional pattern of proportional frequencies. Such an expectation must either deny any relationship between these items and the character and magnitude of work performed in the context of which they would be used – or a lack of variability in the work performed by members of a similar tradition. The latter proposition, when pushed, seems to be that preferred by traditional archaeologists. They argue that tradition A preferred to do one thing or tradition B preferred to do something else if some demonstration of a relationship seems forthcoming between frequencies of tools and the character of work performed. The specificity of the ecological niche which one would have to imagine if the tools were in fact tools and yet there was no variation in the character of work performed by persons representative of the different traditions would directly militate against these traditions exhibiting any long duration in the face of environmental change or any common distribution across a variety of environmental zones viewed geographically. Of course we know that just the reverse is demonstrable. Since we have already shown that we would have to postulate similar cultural traditions for the context of tool design but different ones for the context of tool association, it seems more reasonable to recognize that social and ethnic considerations do not seem to be operative at the level of tool design, since typologically identical forms are demonstrably distributed over half the inhabited world during the middle palaeolithic. To demand that they are being expressed in a form which is not cognitively apparent, e.g. proportional frequencies varying between locations in identical tool forms, clearly goes beyond any understanding of the functions of culture and its dependence upon cognitively recognizable expediently assigned meanings to form – i.e. symbols.

Thus I made the operational assumption that Bordes' typology was discriminating fabricated forms with respect to their properties as tools, and that explanations as to their variations in frequency must be referable to differences in the character of work performed with their aid. Insofar as I may be successful in demonstrating this, I will have demonstrated that ethnicity and other social considerations are not being monitored at all by our current instruments for measurement, our taxonomies of the middle palaeolithic.

The objection may be raised – There are differences in the morphology of tools, in their shape as among handaxes, or their metrical properties, etc. How can you say there is no stylistic variability of social significance? I am not saying that there is no variability or that there is no variability which from a modern perspective we might expect to have social significance. I am saying that the variability demonstrable for the earlier time ranges has not been demonstrated to pattern in such a way as to be suggestive of its having social significance. Even if spatial clustering at a contemporary time period in these morphological properties, or even some limited directionality through time in patterns of morphological variability were recognizable, patterning may well be referable directly to the operation of stochastic processes such as 'drift' (Binford 1964), or others not thus far explored. Such patterning may well inform us about the degrees of isolation between population segments but in no way inform us as to their being partitioned into consciously recognized ethnic units or culturally bounded social units. My original hypothesis was then offered regarding the character of the middle palaeolithic typology. It was proposed that it was measuring formal variability that reflected exclusively tool design. In order to test this proposition a number of test implications had to be deduced and a series of bridging arguments offered. These were developed as follows:

If Bordes' typology is measuring varying degrees of functional differentiation among tools, then assemblages defined in terms of summary tool frequencies must be compounds resulting from the various differentiated work units – activities – in the context of which the functionally differentiated tools were used.

If this is true, then we should be able to identify organized units-clusters of mutually co-variant tools, which maintain the same pattern of organization across a variety of assemblage types.

This was essentially as far as my basic reasoning had gone at the time of the analysis of the Mousterian material from the Near East (Binford and Binford 1966).

The results of these preliminary studies were rewarding in that in experimenting with techniques which would allow us to isolate units of organization within and among assemblages, multivariate analytical techniques seemed to provide the appropriate tools. The application of these techniques did in fact result in the recognition of mutually co-variant groups of tools which maintained their organizational integrity across the recognized types of Mousterian assemblage as defined by Bordes. Two important points were established in these preliminary studies. The first has been demonstrated in print and I am prepared to demonstrate even more forcefully in a forthcoming publication, that the assemblage types as defined currently for the Mousterian are *not* homogeneous units when analysed into components of mutually covariant sets of tools. I quote from my original results:

> Do the types of the Mousterian assemblages isolated by Bordes always correspond to the same combinations of factors? Our response here is

> negative. The total assemblage from Shubbabiq was classified by Bordes' techniques as Typical Mousterian and was found to have strong resemblances to Level 7 of Jabrud. However, when the two assemblages are analyzed in terms of factor content, they are seen to be quite distinct. The material from Shubbabiq is dominated by Factor I, with Factors II and III as minor contributors, while Level 7 from Jabrud was primarily controlled by Factor V, with minor contributions from Factors I and IV. (Binford and Binford 1966:287)

It is this failure of correspondence between the assemblage taxonomy when total assemblages are compared, using discriminatory criteria weighted in favour of commonly occurring forms such as denticulates, scrapers, etc., versus discrimination based on the common presence of tool classes demonstrably related to one another in co-variant fashion, which has, I feel, contributed to the failure of researchers to uncover any strong correlations between assemblage types as defined by Bordes and environmental characteristics such as seasonal variation, character of the fauna studied etc. Thus 'tests' of my arguments which are alleged to demonstrate an absence of expected relationships between assemblage variability and the environment conducted with the current taxonomy of assemblages are clearly irrelevant to my arguments. I have never said that I had such expectations, only that those sets of tools exhibiting strong patterns of mutual co-variation *across* assemblage variants should be related to consistent features of the environment playing conditioning roles in human behaviour.

The second major point and one to which none of the critics have addressed themselves, is simply that consistent patterns of mutual co-variation as demonstrable between tool classes, cross cut the recognized forms of assemblage variation. This is a fact and not an inference or an interpretation. It is clearly as much a fact as are the summary proportional frequencies of the various tool classes. No critic, other than Bordes, has even acknowledged this fact. Any criticism of the approaches I have taken must seek to destroy the factual character of this observation, and/or offer an alternative explanatory argument with clear test implications. No critic has yet done either, and most have ignored the factual character of my findings.

These factual findings provided me with the confidence to pursue as potentially productive further research aimed at specifying in behavioural terms the contexts in which the observed patterns of mutual co-variation were generated. The obvious place to start was with further study of the Mousterian. With the aid of a grant from the National Science Foundation and the hospitality of François Bordes, I began to study and organize the data from Bordes' excavations at Combe-Grenal with particular emphasis on the fauna, the character of the raw materials used in tool production, the character of the debris, and the data on features such as hearths, etc.

These were studied with an eye to the possibility of demonstrating correlations between the components of assemblages shown to vary independently of one another and to cross-cut the recognized assemblage types, and indicators of behaviour and the activities related to the subsistence and maintenance of human groups. Quite early in this research it became clear that there was tremendous variability in the nature of the faunal remains present as viewed in terms of anatomical parts as well as in the species present. It was with the aim of gaining some insight into the behavioural contexts within which differential associations of anatomical parts are produced at different locations that I began my research among the Nunamiut Eskimos. Simultaneously a number of critics began to bombard me with arguments drawn largely from upper palaeolithic data or modern ethnographically documented cases. I was uneasy with such arguments, having clearly the intuitive impression that the upper palaeolithic was different in a very relevant manner. I asked myself to what degree is the upper palaeolithic typology apt to be measuring the same thing as the middle palaeolithic typology? My conclusions were that the probability was slight and that stylistic features of cultural significance were being monitored at least in part by the upper palaeolithic typology. However, this answer was not completely satisfying since there were other differences, particularly in the degree that marked variations among assemblages could be demonstrated even if one eliminated from consideration those tool types which apparently were more informative of stylistic or social differences as opposed to those having more direct functional reference. The solution to this problem presented itself in the data obtained from the Nunamiut. A clear relationship exists between the efficiency of the technology (as measured in terms of the utility derived from a tool expressed in terms of the energy expended in its production) and the degree that archaeological remains will reflect the organized entropy of the system versus the organized activities executed in the context of ongoing behaviour. Clearly we can reasonably expect the efficiency of the technology as defined above to exhibit marked variation among different cultural systems and exhibit changes through time, in the direction of increasing efficiency. We can well expect that the very early use of technological means was relatively inefficient and probably characterized by the total expedient manufacture and use of tools. Under such conditions we would expect great variety in assemblage composition which would be directly referable to the activity variation performed at different locations. Systems of the modern era are generally characterized by rather efficient techno-systems such as those of the Nunamiut and the Australian Aborigines. The recognition that technological efficiency as conceived above was a variable phenomenon which might well be expected to exhibit some directional trends in the history of cultural evolution, and that differences in such efficiency might well have profound effects on the character of the archaeological record itself, was a very exciting idea. Taking the implications further, we can deduce a series of consequences for the character of the archaeological record. If technological efficiency is increasing then there should be a concomitant decrease through time in the magnitude of intersite variability at the regional level. Conversely, as technologies become more efficient there should be an increase in inter-regional diversification as manifest in items relatively rare in the total assemblage. These expectations seem to be strikingly realized in the overall character of the palaeolithic.

Almost every time we get new data on living floors of the very early time ranges, we find that they are relatively distinctive and that the growing body of interassemblage comparisons requires more and more complicated forms of systematics to accommodate the variability (for instance, see Mary Leakey, 1967) when summarized in terms of proportional frequencies of tools. Similarly, we find that frequently analagous comparisons take us to locations rarely located in contiguous geographic zones. As we approach more closely the contemporary era, we find more correlation between particular regions and the frequency with which similar tool forms are manifest in assemblage types. Yet consistent associational groupings are seen among areas widely separated geographically where the same forms of tools are being manufactured and used. A good example might be the Mousterian of North Africa versus the Mousterian of southwestern France or Central Europe. Not until the upper palaeolithic, and then probably the later phases of it, do we find a reduction in intersite variability within a region as measured by proportional frequencies of tools, and increasing regional differentiation as marked by unique tool forms and stylistic variants of analagous tools. The situation of the palaeolithic is well reflected in the character of the archaeologist's systematics. For the early time ranges, more and more argumentation requiring the postulation of 'parallel phyla', and complicated arguments of cultural blending accounting for the variability documented regionally and in broadly contemporary time periods, is the order of the day. My guess is that as more work is done in the Rissian levels and the Acheulean proper, more and more facies will be recognized and more and more parallel phyla will be postulated. On the other hand the systematics of the upper palaeolithic have a very different character. Variability as summarized by proportional frequencies tends to exhibit both temporal and spatial clustering. We must learn numerous regional sequences as we find the systematics of one region rarely applicable to that of another without substantial modification. This same contrast is becoming evident in New World studies as we push back further in time. It has recently been proposed that in South America at the threshold of a knowledge of human occupancy there were seven major traditions, the Edge-Retouched tradition, Burin tradition,

Biface tradition, Side Scraper tradition, Fluted Point tradition, Blade tradition and Bi-Point tradition (Lanning 1970). These traditions are recognizable by comparisons in the proportional frequencies of tools between locations and frequently from the same general regions. Needless to say there are many cases of hybrid cultures.

These contrasts seem to cry out for explanation, and at present the only attempts are in the direction of postulating much greater migration and movement of isolated peoples for the earlier time ranges. I suggest that much of this contrast derives from differences in the degree that tools were expediently manufactured or alternatively curated and preserved in anticipation of future use. A corollary of this is the suggestion that the degree of stylistic and artisan investment manifest in products varies directly with the degree that tools are curated and are considered constant parts of a person's equipment for carrying out his roles.

What started out as an unrecognized necessary assumption – namely that the Mousterian tools were expediently used and manufactured, the assertion that organized relationships between tools were directly referable to the ongoing activity structure of the social system represented – turns out with greater understanding to be a variable phenomenon. It is in need of explication before reliable assertions can be made regarding the significance to be attached to variations in inter-locational associational patterns.

Returning then to the specifics of my progress on the 'Mousterian' problem, I am currently working up my data from the Nunamiut on the logistics of hunting and the behavioural contexts in which anatomical parts of animals are directly disposed of at different junctures of the logistics process, from procurement to the final steps of consumption. Since this is a direct disposal process not modified by curating except in a minor way relating to the effectiveness of food preservation techniques, my results should have some direct applicability to the past. I am sufficiently aware of the patterns of variation in the Combe-Grenal data and similar patterns in the Nunamiut data to anticipate (a) that I will be largely successful in specifying with some reliability the behavioural context responsible for the differential frequencies of anatomical parts in the Combe-Grenal assemblages, and (b) that many of the sets of co-variantly related tools will be shown to vary directly with variations in anatomical parts understood from a behavioural perspective. I clearly anticipate the demonstration of tool frequency variation in correlation with other variable referable to the environment as conditioners of behaviour.

To what degree these demonstrations once available for evaluation and criticism will convince my colleagues of the value inherent in the 'functional approach' I cannot predict. Nevertheless, I would like to offer a few general comments on the nature of our science. My arguments have already touched off what I consider to be a healthy and in many ways colourful discussion which goes directly to the basic issues of archaeological science. The current discussion revolves around the problem of *what significance can we as prehistorians justifiably attach to our contemporary observations on the archaeological record.* All our observations are contemporary, only by attaching significance to certain observations can we succeed in referring these observations reliably to the past. If successful at this stage we go on to offer certain propositions about the character of the past by attributing significance to our archaeological observations. The traditional archaeologist made this attribution of significance in terms of conventions which equated measurable differences in the properties of the archaeological record with ethnic differences between peoples in the past. If this were justified then any taxonomy, which consistently employed whatever criteria, should yield comparable results varying only in the possible levels of discrimination. Clearly, on this view, the use of different taxonomic devices should never yield incompatible results, since they are all presumably measuring the same thing, possibly varying only in their discriminatory powers. I can clearly demonstrate, however, that a taxonomy generated on the basis of grouping assemblages as alike in terms of their similar organizational properties as measured by demonstrably different sets of co-variantly related tools will be *incompatible* with the taxonomy which groups assemblages on the basis of gross similarities in the proportional frequencies of tools with priority given to frequently occurring forms. Which taxonomy is correct? That is the wrong question to ask, we should concern ourselves with the question of what each is measuring. Both are valid; clearly the differences derive from the different properties of the archaeological record being systematically monitored and hence measured. The demonstration of the valid derivation of incompatible taxonomic evaluations of the archaeological record should make obsolete the glib assumption that we know what significance to attach to taxonomically recognized properties of the archaeological record.

How then do we go about the task of reliably attributing significance to our observations on the archaeological record? The scientific basis for the confident assignation of significance to observations made is the degree that we can refer to law-like propositions for justification. Thus the use of C-14 tests, principles of stratigraphy, etc., are all justifiable by reference to law-like statements in which we may confidently assume the principle of uniformitarianism – the laws operative in the past were the same as those operative at the present. Only when archaeologists address themselves to the difficult task of formulating and testing laws will we be able confidently to ascribe significance to our observations on the archaeological record. I have in this paper offered for testing such a hypothesis of law-like potential regarding the economizing character of the technology and the character of variability in the archaeological record. Operationalizing and verifying this hypothesis would make possible the simultaneous explanation of certain properties of the 'living archaeology' of the Nunamiut and the Australian Aborigines as well as the Mousterian peoples of south-western France. In addition it would make possible a much greater understanding of the demonstrable contrasts in the lifeways as recorded archaeologically for the peoples of the lower-middle and upper palaeolithic and provide us with explanatory understanding of some of the directional trends demonstrable through this vast span of time.

I would like to suggest that what has been summarized by my critics as the 'functional argument' is really an appeal to archaeologists to explain their observations. This means addressing themselves to the difficult task of determining what our taxonomies are measuring and what demonstrated patterning refers to in the organization of past human systems of adaptation out of which these patterns derived. I never opposed a 'functional' interpretation against a 'cultural' interpretation. I have been attempting to develop and oppose an explanatory against an *interpretation* strategy as to the significance of variability observed in the archaeological record.

REFERENCES

Binford, L.R. (1963) Red ocher caches from the Michigan area; a possible case of cultural drift. *Southwestern Journal of Anthropology* **19**, no. 1, 89-107.

Binford, L.R. and S.R. (1966) A preliminary analysis of functional variability in the Mousterian of Levallois facies. *In* Clark, J.D. and Howell, F.C. (eds.) *Recent Studies in Palaeoanthropology*. American Anthropologist **68**, no. 2 part 2, 238-95.

Binford, L.R. and S.R. (1969) Stone tools and human behaviour. *Scientific American* **220**, no. 4, 70-84.

Bordes, F. (1963) Le Mousterian à denticulés. *Acta Archeologica* **13-14**, 43-9.

Bordes, F. and de Sonneville-Bordes, D. (1970) The significance of variability in Palaeolithic assemblages. *World Archaeology* **2**, no. 1, 61-73.

Bouchud, J. (1966) *Essai Sur le Renne et la Climatologie du Paléolithique Moyen et Supérieur.* Imprimerie Magne, Périgueux.

Collins, D. (1969) Culture traditions and environment of early man. *Current Anthropology* **10**, no. 4, 267-316.

Collins, D. (1970) Stone artifact analysis and the recognition of culture traditions. *World Archaeology* **2**, no. 1, 17-27.

Lanning, E. (1970) Pleistocene man in South America. *World Archaeology* **2**, no. 1, 90-111.

Leakey, M.D.L. (1967) Preliminary survey of the cultural material from Beds I and II, Olduvai Gorge, Tanzania. *In* Bishop, W.W. and Clark, J.D. (eds.) *Background to Evolution in Africa*, 417-46. Chicago, University Press.

Mellars, P.A. (1965) Sequence and development of Mousterian traditions in South Western France. *Nature* **205**, 626-7.

Mellars, P.A. (1970) Some comments on the notion of 'functional variability' in stone-tool assemblages. *World Archaeology* **2**, no. 1, 74-89.

Rigaud, J-P. (1971) Personal communication.

Skoog, R.O. (1968) *Ecology of the Caribou in Alaska.* Doctoral dissertation,

University of California, Berkeley, University Microfilms, Inc., Ann Arbor, Michigan.

White, C. and Peterson, N. (1969) Ethnographic interpretation of the prehistory of Western Arnhem Land. *Southwestern Journal of Anthropology* 25, no. 1, 45-67.

P.A. MELLARS

The character of the middle - upper palaeolithic transition in south - west France

The transition from the middle to the upper palaeolithic stages is arguably one of the most important developments in human history. Events which are customarily linked with this development include the evolutionary replacement of 'archaic' by 'modern' forms of Man, and the appearance of a range of striking cultural innovations – including the first systematic use of bone, antler and ivory for tool manufacture, the adaptation of animal teeth, marine shells etc. as personal ornaments, and the emergence of a sophisticated naturalistic tradition of art.

In view of the universally acknowledged importance of these developments it is perhaps surprising that so few attempts have been made to document the character of the middle-upper transition in detail. Most of the discussions of this topic which have appeared in the literature have been conducted at a very generalized, superficial level, and very few attempts have been made to analyse the factual data on which the generalizations are based. The primary aim of the present paper is therefore an empirical one: to examine closely the evidence from one particular area in an attempt to define what the true pattern of cultural innovations at the time of the middle-upper palaeolithic transition was. Owing to limitations of space, treatment of this topic has had to be selective. Attention has been paid to those aspects which appear to the writer most significant, and for which sufficient evidence exists to enable discussions to rise above a purely speculative level.

A few comments on the scope of the paper are necessary. Geographically, the scope is restricted to southwestern France, and most of the observations will be confined to sites in what is generally known as the 'Perigord' area. In fact, the term Perigord will be employed here with rather expanded connotations to refer to the whole of the area covered by the present-day Departments of Dordogne, Charente, Lot and Vienne. The reasons for choosing this area are two-fold: first because this is the area of which the writer has the best first-hand knowledge; and second, because the evidence relating to the upper and middle palaeolithic periods in this region is richer than that for any other area of comparable size which has so far been investigated.

Chronologically, discussions will be restricted to sites occupied during the last glacial period. Thus, for the purposes of the present paper the terms 'middle palaeolithic' and 'Mousterian' should be understood as applying only to sites dating from the first half of the 'Würm' glaciation.

Owing to the vastness of the bibliography relating to middle and upper palaeolithic sites in southwest France, no attempt has been made to provide full references for all of the sites discussed. Much fuller referencing for these sites will be found in Madame de Sonneville-Bordes' *Le Paléolithique Supérieur en Périgord* (1960) and M. Bourgon's *Les industries Moustériennes et Pré-moustériennes du Périgord* (1957). For further detailed references to middle palaeolithic sites see Mellars (1969) and for Solutrean sites, Smith (1966).

Stone tool technology

The text-book generalization that middle palaeolithic implements are manufactured from flakes whereas upper palaeolithic tools are made on blades appears, on close inspection to be a rather misleading oversimplification. As Bordes and others have pointed out (Bordes 1961a:810; 1968:27; Sonneville-Bordes 1963:348), elongated, regular blades can be found in most middle palaeolithic assemblages and in most cases there can be no doubt that these pieces were struck from specially prepared blade cores (cf. Bordes 1954a: fig. 37, no. 1). It is true that in most middle palaeolithic industries frequencies of such pieces are comparatively low (generally less than 10% of the total assemblage) but in a number of well documented instances overall blade frequencies of between 15 and 30% have been recorded (Bourgon 1957:135-6; Bordes 1954b:447).

Clearly, then, the idea of deliberately preparing cores for the production of elongated, parallel-sided flakes was in no sense an invention of upper palaeolithic man. The question of how these blades were removed from the core is more problematic. Few people would deny that the 'indirect percussion' or 'punch' technique of blade production was employed throughout the greater part of the upper palaeolithic period, and there are grounds for thinking that in southwest France this technique was in use at least as early as the initial Aurignacian stage. On the other hand, experiments have shown that quite sophisticated-looking blades can be produced by skilful application of the direct percussion technique, and Bordes (1971:4) has recently stressed the difficulties of telling whether individual pieces were produced by one technique or the other. As things stand at present, therefore, it would seem impossible to draw any firm conclusion as to the precise point at which the punch technique of blade production was introduced.

Moving from methods of primary flake production to techniques of retouching it would appear that in this sphere again there are few developments which serve to separate the upper from the middle palaeolithic. Most of the basic methods of retouching employed in upper palaeolithic industries – sharpening of an edge by means of 'invasive' retouch, blunting of an edge by 'backing', even the distinctive 'fluted' retouch found on certain Aurignacian tools – are clearly foreshadowed in middle palaeolithic industries (Bordes 1961b). The only form of retouching which appears to be entirely confined to the upper palaeolithic is that of 'pressure-flaking', but this technique does not appear in southwest France until a relatively advanced stage of the upper palaeolithic sequence (Bordes 1968:24).

The most original feature of upper palaeolithic stone-tool technology therefore lies in the shapes of the finished tools rather than in the techniques of manufacture. The progression from the middle to the upper palaeolithic periods in all parts of the Old World appears to have been accompanied by a comparatively rapid development of entirely new *forms* of stone implements. In western France the first clear impact of this florescence can be seen in the Aurignacian industries. Even if one accepts that crude prototypes of nosed and carinated end-scrapers can be identified in certain Mousterian assemblages, at least four distinctive tool-types which appear with the Aurignacian industries (Dufour bladelets, Font-Yves points, *busqué* burins and strangulated blades) are totally without parallel in middle palaeolithic contexts. The ensuing Upper Perigordian phase was marked by a further influx of at least five new types, including Gravette points, *fléchettes*, Noailles burins, Font-Robert points and truncated elements. The Solutrean episode appears to be characterized by only two new tool forms – pressure-flaked leaf-points and single-shouldered points – but during the Magdalenian phase a further impressive array of new types can be identified (multiple, star-shaped borers, denticulated bladelets, parrot-beak burins, 'Laugerie Basse' points, and a wide range of geometric microlithic forms) (Sonneville-Bordes 1960, 1963).

The point which clearly emerges is the immense originality of upper palaeolithic societies in devising new forms and varieties of stone tools – an originality which is not confined to a single point in the succession but which manifests itself repeatedly throughout the whole of the 20-25,000 year development. The contrast with the middle palaeolithic could hardly be more pronounced. It is in fact difficult to think of a single well-characterized tool-form found in middle palaeolithic industries which does not have an ancestry extending back at least to the penultimate ('Riss') glaciation; this applies not only to such basic forms as hand-axes and *racloirs*, but to more idiosyncratic types such as *limaces*, blunted-back knives and denticulates (Bordes 1961b). This is not to suggest that middle palaeolithic industries were static in a *quantitative* sense (i.e. with respect to the relative frequencies and dimensions of different implements) but the capacity for devising qualitatively *new* varieties of tools appear to be much more characteristic of the upper palaeolithic stage.

Bone - working technology

Differences between the middle and upper palaeolithic periods in the use of bone, antler and ivory for tool manufacture are perhaps even more striking and fundamental than those in stone-tool technology. It has of course been recognized for a long time that middle palaeolithic societies were in the habit of *utilizing* fragments of bone and antler for a variety of purposes; but the crucial point is that these groups rarely made any attempt to *shape* these materials to any appreciable degree. Thus the so-called *compresseurs* found in abundance in certain Mousterian levels (especially those belonging to the 'Charentian' variant) are simply dense fragments of bone which were used (apparently) as anvils in some industrial activity (Henri-Martin 1907-10). The *poinçons* recovered from such sites as the Abri Chadourne, L'Ermitage and Pech de l'Azé are essentially naturally-pointed fragments of bone the tips of which have been improved to some extent by grinding (Bordes *et al.* 1954; Pradel and Pradel 1954; Bordes 1954-55: for a more carefully worked example see Henri-Martin 1932:681). The most ambitious attempts at bone working so far reported from middle palaeolithic contexts in southwest France would appear to be the three fragments of reindeer antler, each bearing a circular perforation, found by Favraud (1908:64) in the Quina-Mousterian deposits at Petit-Puymoyen in the Charente; to the best of the writer's knowledge the latter pieces are without parallel from other Mousterian sites in this region.

The essential originality of upper palaeolithic groups therefore lay in their ability to shape bone, antler and ivory into a variety of relatively complex and carefully controlled forms. As early as the initial Aurignacian phase in the Perigord at least five or six clearly differentiated forms of bone artifacts were in use (Sonneville-Bordes 1960: 41-140). Several of these tools (for example, the split-base point) must have gone through several stages of manufacture, including cutting or sawing to obtain the basic outline followed by extensive grinding to regularize the surface. The distinctive 'groove and splinter' technique for dividing up large pieces of bone and antler was certainly in use by the end of the Aurignacian phase in the Perigord and has been reported from still earlier (Châtelperronian) contexts in central France (Sonneville-Bordes 1960:22; Leroi-Gourhan 1965:38, 62).

As in the case of stone artifacts, a variety of new forms of bone and antler implements were introduced at different points during the upper palaeolithic succession. Bevel-base lance heads, *sagaies d'Isturitz* and the enigmatic *bouchons d'outre* were introduced during the Upper Perigordian stage; eyed sewing needles and (apparently) spear-throwers came into use during the Solutrean; while the Magdalenian saw the introduction of a whole range of new types including fork-base points, 'snow-knives', trident spear-heads, and both unilateral and bilaterally barbed 'harpoons'. Clearly, successive populations throughout the upper palaeolithic were no less inventive in the working of bone and antler than in their approach to stone-tool manufacture.

Personal ornaments

Small objects for which no obvious functional explanation can be found and which are plausibly interpreted as items of personal adornment are among the most frequent objects found on upper palaeolithic sites. Among the earliest of such objects must be the series of grooved and perforated animal teeth recovered from the Châtelperronian horizons at Arcy-sur-Cure in central France (Leroi-Gourhan 1965:40). In southwestern France perforated animal teeth make their first appearance in the earliest Aurignacian levels and subsequently occur in abundance during all the later stages of the upper palaeolithic. Perforated marine shells, belonging to a variety of species, show a similar chronological distribution extending from the Aurignacian (at least eight recorded sites) to the end of the Magdalenian. Even more enterprising products are the small beads and pendants deliberately manufactured out of bone, antler and ivory; these pieces again seem to span the entire time-range from the early Aurignacian to the late Magdalenian (Sonneville-Bordes 1960).

As Clark and Piggott have recently stressed (1965:61), personal ornaments of this nature are virtually if not entirely lacking from earlier palaeolithic contexts in Europe. The only example so far reported from a middle palaeolithic level in southwest France is a single perforated fox tooth found by H. Henri-Martin (1907-10: pl. 28) at the site of La Quina; in the absence of supporting evidence from other sites it would clearly be unwise to attach too much significance to this discovery. A better case can perhaps be made out for the practice of body painting in the middle palaeolithic (Bordes 1961a; 809; 1968:145). Fragments of colouring matter (red ochre and black manganese dioxide) occur abundantly in many Mousterian levels in the Perigord, and the appearance of certain of these pieces has been taken to suggest that they were applied directly to a soft, smooth surface (Bordes 1954-5:425); but whether the surface in question was human skin, animal hide or some other material can hardly be ascertained from the surviving evidence.

Subsistence activities

It is probably safe to assume that throughout the greater part of the last glaciation the bulk of the food supply of all human groups living in the middle latitudes of Europe was provided by the hunting of large herbivorous mammals. This is suggested not only by the sheer abundance in which bones of these species occur in middle and upper palaeolithic occupation levels, but also by ethnographic data on recent hunter-gatherer societies living under analogous environment conditions (Lee and De Vore 1968:7, 41-3). The points which I wish to examine here are: (1) the extent to which hunting was focussed on a *single* species of animal at different stages of the middle-upper palaeolithic succession; and (2) the extent to which the food supply produced by hunting was supplemented from other sources – notably from fishing and fowling activities.

From the data set out in Table 1 it will be seen that the greater part of the meat supply in the overwhelming majority of middle and upper palaeolithic settlements in southwest France was provided by the hunting of one or more or four principal species – reindeer, horse, bovids, and red deer. The clear priority of reindeer over the other species in this regard also emerges clearly from these data – a priority which is especially marked during the later (Solutrean and Magdalenian) stages of the upper palaeolithic.

PERIOD	DOMINANT SPECIES			
	Reindeer	*Horse*	*Bovids*	*Red Deer*
Mousterian	28	8	17	15
Châtelperronian	2	1	1	–
Aurignacian	23	3	3	–
Upper Perigordian	18	3	2	–
Solutrian	22	–	–	–
Magdalenian	21	–	–	1

Table 1 Principal faunal species encountered in Mousterian and upper palaeolithic horizons in the Perigord area. The figures indicate the total numbers of occupation levels belonging to each period in which remains of the species indicated are clearly predominant.

It has been suggested by certain authors that the intensive hunting of a single species of animal may be symptomatic of a particular level of cultural development among hunter-gatherer societies (Binford 1968a:56; Binford and Binford 1966). Reliable quantitative data bearing on this issue are difficult to obtain from the existing literature, but such information as can be assembled is set out in Table 2. The information presented in this table certainly appears to bear out the idea that the highly specialized hunting of one species of animal was particularly characteristic of the upper palaeolithic period. In every recorded instance this intensive hunting focusses on the reindeer; in appreciably more than half of the upper palaeolithic levels for which quantitative information is available the overall frequency of reindeer is greater than 90%, and in certain levels (notably some of the Solutrean horizons at Laugerie Haute West) frequencies of up to 99% have been recorded (Smith 1966:65-106). Frequencies of this order have not so far been recorded in *any* Mousterian levels in southwest France; the highest definitely recorded frequency is that of 87% of reindeer reported by Van Campo and Bouchud (1962) for a Typical Mousterian horizon at the Roc de Marsal. The highest faunal percentage recorded throughout the long Mousterian succession at Combe-Grenal is circa 84% (layer 50: also Typical Mousterian) which in this case relates to red deer instead of reindeer (Bordes and Prat 1965).

After contemplating these figures it is rather surprizing to examine the faunal percentages recorded for two of the lowermost occupation horizons at Combe-Grenal (layers 59 and 60). These levels are attributed on geological grounds to the end of the Riss glaciation, and contain fairly rich Acheulian industries. The overall frequencies of reindeer bones in these deposits (based on faunal assemblages of 611 and 63 identifiable remains) have been calculated respectively as 97 and 93% (Bordes and Prat 1965).

The foregoing data force one to consider whether the observed variations in the composition of faunal assemblages from middle and upper palaeolithic levels should be attributed more to climatic than to cultural factors. This is a question to which a conclusive answer can hardly be given at the present time. On the basis of micro-faunal and other studies Bouchud (1966:244) has asserted that the extremely high percentages of reindeer encountered in the Upper Perigordian levels at the Abri Pataud *cannot* be explained solely in climatic terms. The consistency of similarly high reindeer frequencies throughout the entire Solutrean succession at Laugerie Haute may argue in the same direction, as there are grounds for thinking that part of these deposits accumulated during a relatively mild climatic phase (Laville 1964; Delporte 1968). However, until the true pattern of climatic events during the last glaciation has been more securely documented it would be unwise to draw any firm conclusions with regard to the climatic versus cultural factors responsible for the composition of the faunal assemblages under review.

In addition to bones of the four major herbivorous species referred to above, almost all middle and upper palaeolithic sites in southwest France have yielded remains of a wide range of additional mammalian species – ibex, chamois, roe deer, fallow deer, wild pig,

SITE		DOMINANT SPECIES	%
Mousterian			
C. Grenal	54	Red deer	74 (B)
	52	Red deer	70 (B)
	51	Red deer	69 (B)
	50	Red deer	84 (B)
	50A	Red deer	75 (B)
	46-9	Red deer	56 (B)
	42-5	Red deer	73 (B)
	41	Red deer	57 (B)
	40	Red deer	65 (B)
	37-9	Red deer	49 (B)
	36	Red deer	46 (B)
	35	Red deer	50 (B)
	32-4	Bovids	41 (B)
	29-30	Reindeer	36 (B)
	28	Reindeer	59 (B)
	27	Reindeer	57 (B)
	25	Reindeer	60 (B)
	24	Reindeer	70 (B)
	23	Reindeer	70 (B)
	22	Reindeer	63 (B)
	21	Reindeer	47 (B)
	20	Reindeer	52 (B)
	18-19	Reindeer	62 (B)
	17	Reindeer	46 (B)
	15	Horse	55 (B)
	14	Horse	67 (B)
	13	Horse	55 (B)
	11-12	Bovids	43 (B)
	8-10	Red deer	38 (B)
	4-7	Reindeer	40 (B)
La Chapelle		Reindeer	55 (A)
Roc de Marsal		Reindeer	87 (B)
Hauteroche		Reindeer	79 (A)
Mas-Viel		Horse	56 (B)
C. Capelle Ht.		Bovids	60 (B?)
Le Moustier G		Bovids	82 (B?)
Le Moustier H		Bovids	75 (B?)
Les Cottés		Bovids	58 (A)

SITE		DOMINANT SPECIES	%
Aurignacian			
La Chèvre AI		Reindeer	79 (B)
La Chèvre AII		Bovids	49 (B)
Les Rois AI		Reindeer	80 (A)
Les Rois AII		Reindeer	57 (A)
A. Pataud	13/14	Reindeer	99 (B)
	12	Reindeer	72 (B)
	11	Reindeer	62 (B)
	7	Reindeer	70 (B)
Upper Perigordian			
La Chèvre		Reindeer	78 (B)
Roc de Gavaudun		Reindeer	47 (B)
La Gravette		Reindeer	97 (B)
A. du Facteur		Reindeer	95 (B)
Laugerie Ht. PVI		Reindeer	97 (B)
A. Pataud	PIV	Reindeer	90 (B)
	PV	Reindeer	87-98 (B)
	PVI	Reindeer	93 (B)
	'Proto-Magd'	Reindeer	80 (B)
Solutrean			
Laugerie Ht.	12d	Reindeer	96 (B)
	12c	Reindeer	97 (B)
	12b	Reindeer	97 (B)
	12a	Reindeer	97 (B)
	11a	Reindeer	93 (B)
	10	Reindeer	89 (B)
	8	Reindeer	98 (B)
	7	Reindeer	99 (B)
	6	Reindeer	99 (B)
	5	Reindeer	97 (B)
	4	Reindeer	98 (B)
	3	Reindeer	97 (B)
	1	Reindeer	94 (B)
A. Lachaud		Reindeer	89 (B)
Magdalenian			
La Madeleine MVI		Reindeer	97 (B)
G. de Couze lower		Reindeer	95 (B)
G. de Couze upper		Reindeer	96 (B)
Flageolet		Reindeer	95 (B)
Combe-Cullier lower		Reindeer	89 (B)
Combe-Cullier upper		Reindeer	91 (B)

Table 2 Recorded frequencies of the dominant faunal species in various middle and upper palaeolithic occupation levels in the Perigord area. Insofar as the published data permit the percentages are based on the total faunal remains with the exception of micro-fauna and birds. The figures relate either to the numbers of bones (B) or numbers of individual animals (A) represented. Information from Arambourou and Jude 1964; Bouyssonie *et al.* 1913; Bordes and Prat 1965, Bouchud 1966, Delpech 1970; Delporte 1968; Momméjean *et al.* 1964; Mouton and Joffroy 1958; Niederlender *et al.* 1956; Peyrony 1925, 1930; Pradel 1957, 1961; Van Campo and Bouchud 1962; Unpublished information on faunal assemblages from the Abri Pataud kindly provided by Prof. H.L. Movius Jr.

common fox, arctic fox, woolly rhinoceros, mammoth etc. The remains of these species invariably occur in small proportions and presumably represent animals which were caught either to relieve the monotony of the meat supply or to provide some useful raw material. The presence or absence of the different species during various stages of the middle and upper palaeolithic show no obvious cultural patterning, and the occurrence of several species (e.g. roe deer, wild pig, arctic fox) almost certainly owes more to climatic than to cultural factors.

The presence of bird bones in the southwest French sites is of debatable economic significance. As Clark (1952:26) has pointed out, many of these remains may have been introduced into the caves and rock shelters by foxes and other predators. It is only towards the end of the upper palaeolithic that bird bones occur in sufficiently large numbers to suggest purposeful fowling activities. (Milne Edwards 1865-75). Remains of various species of grouse (*Lagopus albus, L. mutus, L. scotticus*) are particularly numerous in certain late Magdalenian levels, occurring abundantly at such sites as Limeuil (Magdalenian VI), Grotte des Eyzies (Magdalenian VI), Fontales (Magdalenian V) and La Madeleine itself (Magdalenian IV, V and VI). In these sites, as in the contemporary sites of south Germany, there seems little doubt that fowling was undertaken as a deliberate activity, and was presumably of some economic importance.

The recovery of evidence for fishing activities on prehistoric sites depends to a large extent on conditions of preservation and, above all, on the diligence of the excavator: there are grounds for thinking that only a fraction of the fish bones which actually survive in archaeological deposits will be detected by normal excavation procedures (Mellars and Payne 1971). Nevertheless, it seems significant that the only discoveries of fish bones which have so far been reported from southwest French sites derive exclusively from upper palaeolithic levels. Of the 14 sites definitely known to have produced such remains, three belong to the Upper Perigordian phase (La Gravette, Abri Pataud, Laugerie Haute), four to the Solutrean (Badegoule, Pech de la Boissière, Fourneau du Diable, Liveyre), and at least six to the Magdalenian (La Madeleine, Laugerie Basse, Limeuil, Abri Villepin, Abri Lachaud, Gare de Couze). The great majority of the fish bones which have been specifically identified appear to belong to salmon, although a variety of additional species (trout, carp, pike, bream, dace, chub) have also been recognized (Sauvage 1865-75).

Precisely what significance should be attached to the representation of fishes in palaeolithic art is plainly debateable. Even so, one can hardly fail to be struck by the frequency with which engravings and sculptures of fish have been encountered on mobiliary art objects from southwest French sites. From south-western France as a whole, over 70 separate representations of fishes have been reported from at least 24 different sites. According to the data assembled by Breuil and Saint-Périer (1927) it would appear that the great majority if not all of these representations derive from Magdalenian levels. Unfortunately, many of the representations are either too schematic or too incomplete for the species of fish to be recognized, but from the forms identified with some certainty by Breuil and Saint-Périer the following figures can be compiled: salmon – eight examples; trout – seven examples; 'salmonids' (either salmon or trout) – 13 examples; pike – eight examples; eel – two examples.

On the basis of the above data a case could be made out for thinking that fishing became a particularly important economic activity towards the end of the upper palaeolithic period. A final observation which possibly adds some weight to this conclusion is the tendency for Magdalenian settlements (especially those belonging to the late Magdalenian) to be situated at very low elevations, frequently in close proximity to river banks. In fact some of these sites (e.g. La Madeleine itself and the nearby 'Bout-du-Monde' rock-shelter) are located so close to river level that they are occasionally inundated at times of flooding (Sonneville-Bordes 1960:329). One might perhaps see in this choice of settlement location evidence of an increasing awareness of the economic potential offered by river resources.

Dimensions of settlements

Accurate quantitative information on the dimensions of middle and upper palaeolithic settlements in southwest France is even more difficult to obtain than that relating to subsistence activities. It is only during the past ten years or so that the interest of excavators has extended to the horizontal, as opposed to vertical, aspects of cave and rock-shelter deposits, and in many cases the length and complexity of these sequences make it impracticable to excavate more than a limited area of any site.

Nevertheless, a careful and critical search through the literature reveals some interesting data on the relative dimensions of middle and upper palaeolithic settlements. The most significant fact which emerges is the very large dimensions attained by many (though by no means all) of the upper palaeolithic settlements. In the case of cave and rock-shelter sites the most sensitive dimension is the lateral extent of the occupation debris measured along the cliff face. From the data summarized in Table 3 it will be seen that in at least seven or eight cases upper palaeolithic horizons have been found to continue for overall lengths of between 40 and 100 metres and in one instance – the celebrated Laugerie Haute rock shelter near Les Eyzies – several occupation horizons appear to extend continuously over a distance of some 180 metres (Peyrony and Peyrony 1938).

Even larger occupation areas have been recorded in some of the upper palaeolithic open air sites which have recently been excavated in the Perigord area; in particular, the Magdalenian settlement of Solvieux in the Isle valley has been estimated to cover an area of approximately 10,000 square metres (Bordes 1959:157).

PERIOD	TYPE OF SITE	DIMENSIONS (in metres)
Aurignacian		
La Quina	Rock shelter	52 x 10
Laussel	Rock shelter	50 x 12
Abri Pataud	Rock shelter	50 x 10 (?)
Upper Perigordian		
Laussel	Rock shelter	72 x 10
Abri Pataud	Rock shelter	50 x 10 (?)
Les Vachons	Rock shelter	50 x 5
Laugerie Haute	Rock shelter	180 x 35
Solutrean		
Laugerie Haute (Lower Sol.)	Rock shelter	180 x 35
Laugerie Haute (Middle Sol.)	Rock shelter	180 x 35
Badegoule	Rock shelter/open site	45 x 25
Magdalenian		
Laugerie Haute	Rock shelter	180 x 35
La Madeleine	Rock shelter	5,000 sq. metres
Solvieux	Open site	10,000 sq. metres

Table 3 Dimensions of some upper palaeolithic settlements in southwest France. (N.B. These figures should be regarded as approximate only; the dimensions quoted refer to the *observed* extent of occupation deposits and in some cases the true dimensions of the settlements may be appreciably larger than the figures shown.) Information from Bordes 1959, 1970; Bouyssonie & Sonneville-Bordes 1956; Couchard 1966; Henri-Martin 1931; Lalanne and Bouyssonie 1946; Peyrony and Peyrony 1938.

Any attempt to proceed from these occupation areas to an estimate of the sizes of the human groups who inhabited the sites would encounter difficulties from several points of view. The most obvious problem stems from the impossibility of demonstrating that the whole of an area over which occupation material is distributed was occupied at one and the same time. On a purely empirical level, however, it is worth observing that occupation areas comparable with those recorded in the larger upper palaeolithic settlements have very rarely, if ever, been encountered in middle palaeolithic sites. Most Mousterian sites in southwest France consist of fairly small caves and rock shelters, rarely exceeding 20-25 metres in any dimension. A possible exception to this generalization is provided by the site of La Quina in the Charente, but even here it remains to be demonstrated that the Mousterian levels continue for more than 30-35 metres along the rock face (Henri-Martin 1923).

Perhaps the most instructive comparison between middle and upper palaeolithic settlement dimensions was recorded in the excavations of Lalanne at the large rock shelter of Laussel. According to the longitudinal section reproduced by Lalanne and Bouyssonie (1946) two superimposed Mousterian levels at the base of this succession show overall lengths of 18 and 37 metres respectively. Overlying deposits containing Aurignacian and Upper Perigordian industries, on the other hand, were found to extend continuously for distances of at least 50 and 72 metres. In this particular case there would seem to be a strong suggestion that the upper palaeolithic communities who inhabited the rock shelter were appreciably larger than the middle palaeolithic groups who occupied the same site.

Evidence for seasonal occupation

The principal data bearing on the seasonal occupation of middle and upper palaeolithic sites in southwest France has been set out in a number of papers by J. Bouchud (1954, 1966 etc.). At present, substantial quantities of information on this topic are available for six Mousterian levels, five Aurignacian levels, four Perigordian levels, seven Solutrean levels, and eight Magdalenian levels. According to Bouchud (e.g. 1966:239-40) the great majority of these horizons provide evidence for occupation during all seasons of the year, although in a few cases a concentration of occupation (or hunting activities) during one particular season is apparent. The principal limitation of the Mousterian data arises from the fact that the only levels for which substantial quantities of seasonal information are available belong to the 'Charentian' variant; much more information on the other types of Mousterian – Typical, Denticulate, Mousterian of Acheulian tradition – is clearly required. Nevertheless, as the evidence stands at present there are no positive grounds for thinking that markedly different patterns of seasonal movement were practised in southwest France during the middle and upper palaeolithic periods.

In connection with this question, however, it is perhaps relevant to point out that upper palaeolithic communities appear to have gone to greater lengths to modify or 'improve' the accommodation in the rock shelter settlements than did their Mousterian predecessors. In several sites (Abri Cellier, Abri Pataud, Fourneau du Diable, Le Placard, Abri Villepin) there is evidence that upper palaeolithic occupants dug out pre-existing deposits from the floors of rock shelters so as to produce more roomy or more regular living areas. In other cases (Font Robert, Laugerie Haute, Abri Laraux, Puy de Lacan, Abri Lachaud) it would seem that limited areas of the floors of rock shelters were carefully paved with pebbles from nearby rivers. And in at least four cases (Les Rois, Laugerie Haute, Pech de la Boissière, Fourneau du Diable) artificial stone walls appear to have been constructed around the edges of living areas, supposedly with the intention of supporting superstructures made of branches and animal skins (Sonneville-Bordes 1960; Breuil and Lantier 1965).

Evidence from similar attempts at improving the accommodation in caves and rock shelters has only rarely been recorded in middle palaeolithic sites. The only two examples known to the writer are the possible traces of limestone paving noted by Peyrony (1934) in the Mousterian levels at La Ferrassie, and a short length of dry-stone walling encountered in shelter I at Pech de l'Azé (Bordes 1954-55). These observations might conceivably be taken to indicate that upper palaeolithic societies regarded the cave and rock shelter sites as more permanent 'home-bases' than did the middle palaeolithic groups who preceded them.

Long - distance contacts

It has been recognized for almost a century that upper palaeolithic groups living in the Perigord area maintained some form of contact – either as a result of extensive seasonal migrations or through the operation of some kind of trade – with coastal areas. Lartet and Christy (1865-75) recorded the presence of several species of marine shells in at least two of their Perigord excavations (Laugerie Basse and Cro-Magnon) and the same observation has since been repeated at a large number of other sites (Abri Castanet, Abri Cellier, La Combe, La Ferrassie, Fourneau du Diable, La Gravette, Abri Jolivet, Abri Laraux, Laugerie Haute, Abri Pataud, Pech de la Boissière, Abri du Poisson, Roc de Gavaudun, Les Vachons etc.). While many of the shells found in these sites are of species which at present inhabit both Atlantic and Mediterranean waters, certain other forms (e.g. *Purpura lapillus, Littorina obtusatus, Nassa mutabilis, Cyprea lurida*) are claimed to be confined to one or other of these sources. Shells deriving from both areas have been found in occupation levels going back to the earliest Aurignacian stage (e.g. Peyrony 1935:437). The main problem here would seem to be an ecological one; granted that the species in question are currently restricted to one or other of the Atlantic/Mediterranean sources, how far can it be assumed that the same distributions would hold good under the reduced temperature and sea-level conditions of the late Pleistocene? Whatever the true source of the shells, however, the fact remains that many upper palaeolithic groups in the Perigord area had access to material resources over distances of at least 150-200 kilometres.

To the best of the writer's knowledge the only analogous evidence from middle palaeolithic sites consists of a single fragmentary *Pecten* shell said to derive from the Quina Mousterian levels at Petit-

Puymoyen (Favraud 1908:50). However, in view of the shallowness of the deposits which overlie the Mousterian horizons at this site, it seems questionable how much reliance should be placed on this discovery. Of course, the whole negative aspect of the evidence from middle palaeolithic sites is of debatable significance; since the prime motive of upper palaeolithic groups for collecting shells seems to have been the desire for personal ornaments, it is arguable that the absence of such objects from earlier contexts simply reflects a lack of interest in this form of cultural expression. More reliable evidence on the question of long distance contacts during the palaeolithic is likely to come from studies of the sources of flint used in tool manufacture. Unfortunately, the only work so far published along these lines would appear to be that undertaken by Valensi (1959) on material from the upper palaeolithic horizons at the Abri Pataud. On the basis of microscopic analyses Valensi was able to show that a small proportion of the flint used in the Proto-Magdalenian level at this site was obtained from sources in the Isle valley approximately 50 kilometres to the northwest. When studies of this kind are applied on a wider scale we shall be in a much better position to make statements on the extent to which different palaeolithic communities maintained trading or other contacts over long distances.

Population densities

PERIOD	NUMBER OF SITES
Mousterian	32
Châtelperronian	12
Aurignacian	44
Upper Perigordian	42
Solutrean	38
Magdalenian	75
Total number of Upper Palaeolithic sites	168

Table 4 Total numbers of cave and rock shelter sites in the Perigord area in which levels belonging to different stages of the middle and upper palaeolithic are represented. Data from Peyrony 1949:9, 49-51.

The data reproduced in Table 4 are taken from a comparatively little-known paper by Denis Peyrony (*Le Périgord Préhistorique: essai de géographie humaine*) published in 1949. The figures relate to the total numbers of cave and rock shelter sites in the Perigord area in which levels representing different stages of the middle and upper palaeolithic have been identified. Although it is over two decades since these figures were compiled it would seem that the number of entirely new sites which have come to light during this period is very small (Sonneville-Bordes 1960). In order to ensure strict comparability of data therefore, it is perhaps best to take Peyrony's statistics as they stand.

The most striking aspect of the figures from the present view point is the great disparity between the total numbers of middle and upper palaeolithic sites recorded. The figures in question – 32 sites for the Mousterian as compared with 168 for the upper palaeolithic – differ by a factor of approximately x5. It is important to remember that these statistics relate to very similar spans of time; on the basis of current radiocarbon estimates the Mousterian industries of the Perigord must span a period of at least 25-30,000 years, which is at least as long as that occupied by the whole of the upper palaeolithic sùccession. What is perhaps even more significant is that the total number of Mousterian sites is somewhat less than that recorded for *any one* of the four principal stages of the upper palaeolithic sequence (ranging from 38 sites for the Solutrean to 75 for the Magdalenian); in this case one is comparing a total time span of 25-30,000 years with individual periods of around 4-6,000 years.

The uncertainties involved in attempting to proceed from these statistics to an estimation of relative population densities during the middle and upper palaeolithic periods are too obvious to require emphasis. In the first place it will be noted that the figures apply only to cave and rock shelter sites. It is now known that open air sites in the Perigord region were occupied during all stages of the middle and upper palaeolithic, and in the present state of evidence it seems impossible to make any reliable assessment of even the relative numbers of these occurrences. All that one can suggest in this context is the possibility that hunter-gatherer communities living under closely similar environmental conditions might be expected to show similar patterns in their occupation of cave and open-air locations.

A second obvious problem concerns the extent to which deposits in cave and rock shelter sites may be progressively destroyed – or in some other way 'lost' – through the passage of time. In this connection it will be recalled that the average age of the Mousterian deposits under review is likely to be approximately twice that of the upper palaeolithic levels. There is no doubt that if one were to envisage a sufficiently rapid rate of site destruction (say an exponential rate in which 75-80% of existing sites were lost over a 25,000 year period) this could account for the observed difference in the numbers of surviving middle and upper palaeolithic settlements. Viewed as a whole, however, the total pattern of site frequencies recorded by Peyrony does not suggest a very fast rate of site destruction. A particularly interesting observation in this connection is the marked stability in the numbers of sites recorded for the Aurignacian, Upper Perigordian and Solutrean phases of the upper palaeolithic (44, 42 and 38 sites respectively). To account for these figures on the assumption of a very rapid rate of site loss it would be necessary to postulate that the original number of sites occupied during these periods *decreased* sharply from the Aurignacian to the Solutrean phase. Clearly, no firm solution to this and other problems can be offered in the present state of evidence, but the data seem sufficient at least to hint at the idea that the transition from the middle to the upper palaeolithic was accompanied by an appreciable increase in population densities in southwest France.

One further conspicuous feature which emerges from Table 4 is the sharp increase in the number of sites occupied during the Magdalenian period, as compared with the stability of site frequencies during the three preceding stages of the upper palaeolithic. The increase in this case is by a factor of almost x2. That this phenomenon reflects a further substantial increase in population numbers during the terminal stages of the upper palaeolithic has already been suggested by Bordes (1968:238), Sonneville-Bordes (1960:498; 1965:109) and others.

Conclusions

Perhaps the most striking feature which emerges from this survey of cultural developments around the time of the middle-upper palaeolithic transition is the range of different aspects of behaviour which appear to have been affected. With the data from south-western France primarily in mind, these may conveniently be summarized under three headings:

1. *Material technology*

The most important contrast between middle and upper palaeolithic stone-tool technology lies in the much wider range and complexity of tool-forms encountered in upper palaeolithic industries, and in the rapidity with which these forms changed through the course of time; the ingenuity displayed by successive upper palaeolithic populations in devising qualitatively new varieties of stone implements contrasts with the marked stability of tool forms apparent throughout the whole of the middle palaeolithic phase. Technically, the introduction of the punch technique of blade production must be seen as an important development, but there is still some uncertainty as to the precise point at which this innovation appeared.

With regard to the working of bone, antler and ivory, it would appear that the treatment of these resources as plastic materials which could be shaped into various complex and carefully controlled forms was effectively restricted to the upper palaeolithic stage; whilst middle palaeolithic communities undoubtedly *utilized* fragments of bone and antler for a variety of purposes, they rarely made any attempt to modify the shapes of these materials to any appreciable degree. Once again, the rapidity with which new forms of bone implements were introduced as the upper palaeolithic progressed is impressive.

2. *Subsistence activities*

The upper palaeolithic appears to have been characterized by at least two important developments in this sphere: (1) by a much greater emphasis on a *single* species of animal as the major food resource; and (2) by a broadening of the subsistence base to include both fish and (less certainly) birds as regular elements in the food supply.

Methods of hunting are clearly much more difficult to infer from the archaeological record, but the extremely high frequencies of reindeer remains encountered in many upper palaeolithic levels are surely suggestive of the kind of large-scale co-operative hunting strategies employed by recent arctic-living groups such as the Eskimo and Yukaghir. As in the societies just mentioned it may well be that the efficiency of the hunters was increased by the use of bows and arrows throughout the greater part of the upper palaeolithic phase. It is equally tempting to suggest that upper palaeolithic groups may have possessed improved techniques for preserving and storing food, so as to ensure more even and dependable food supplies throughout the year-round cycle. Unfortunately, neither of these suggestions can at present be adequately tested against the archaeological data.

3. *Demography and social organization*

Social developments at the time of the middle-upper palaeolithic transition appear to have been characterized on the one hand by a substantial increase in overall population densities, and on the other hand by an increase in the maximum size of co-residential social groups. Evidence for the former is provided by statistics on the total numbers of cave and rock shelter sites occupied during various stages of the middle-upper palaeolithic sequence. Although strictly outside the scope of the present discussion, it is interesting to observe that evidence for a further expansion in population is apparent during the final (Magdalenian) stage of the upper palaeolithic.

Sizes of co-residential social groups must be inferred from dimensions of settlements as defined by the distribution of occupation debris. While estimates of the actual group sizes involved are particularly difficult, estimates in the region of 100-500 people do not seem unreasonable for some of the larger upper palaeolithic settlements (e.g. Laugerie Haute, La Madeleine, Solvieux). An obvious function of such large social aggregates would be to engage in the large-scale co-operative hunting of reindeer and other migratory herd animals at favourable times of the year. It is precisely this kind of social grouping which David (this volume) has postulated for his 'regional band villages' occupied by 'Noaillian' communities during the Upper Perigordian phase. Whilst the possibility of similar aggregations during the middle palaeolithic stage should certainly not be ruled out, it would seem that clear evidence of such groupings as yet remains to be found.

It is worth recalling here that similar suggestions with regard to the social organization of middle and upper palaeolithic communities have been made recently by Sally R. Binford (1968b:148) on the basis of burial customs. To use her own words: 'The structural similarities in burial practices observed for the near eastern Mousterian and the upper palaeolithic may indicate that one element in the complex of changes leading to the appearance of fully modern man might well have been a new form of social organization, one in which greater corporate awareness . . . played a role.' Her further suggestion (p. 147) that the appearance of personal ornaments in the upper palaeolithic might indicate 'an increased means of symbolizing the status of individuals' is interesting, but is more difficult to test against the archaeological evidence.

As pointed out in the Introduction, the primary aim of this paper has been to present factual evidence for cultural differences between the middle and upper palaeolithic stages rather than to offer an explanation for these differences. In conclusion, however, it is perhaps worth commenting briefly on what may be termed (for want of a better expression) the 'ethnic' aspect of the middle-upper palaeolithic transition. Does this phenomenon reflect an 'invasion' of new human groups into southwest France, or does it represent simply a rapid accumulation of cultural changes occurring *within* the indigenous populations?

As several authors have recently emphasized (e.g. Bordes 1968:147; Leroi-Gourhan 1965:36; Movius 1969:112) the earliest clear manifestations of upper palaeolithic technology in western and central France are embodied in the 'Perigordian I' or 'Châtelperronian' assemblages. These occurrences contrast with the preceding Mousterian assemblages in at least three major respects (Leroi-Gourhan 1965; Arambourou and Jude 1964; Movius 1969): (1) they contain relatively numerous and well made specimens of both end scrapers and burins; examples of these types which have been encountered in middle palaeolithic assemblages are both infrequent and for the most part 'atypical' in form (cf. Bordes 1961a:804); (2) they contain more extensively worked examples of bone and ivory implements than any which have so far been reported from middle palaeolithic contexts; and (3) they show clear evidence for the use of animal teeth and other objects as personal ornaments. Unfortunately, the available data from Châtelperronian sites are too limited to allow reliable observation to be made on other aspects of behaviour (subsistence activities, sizes of settlements etc.) but from the point of view of material technology there seems little room for doubt that the Châtelperronian assemblages provide the earliest unambiguous evidence for the impact of specifically upper palaeolithic ideas in western France.

In the writer's opinion the arguments in favour of ethnic and cultural continuity between the Châtelperronian and latest Mousterian populations in southwest France are virtually conclusive. As Bordes has repeatedly stressed (e.g. 1961a:808; 1968:105) connections are particularly apparent between the Châtelperronian and the 'Acheulian tradition' variant of the Mousterian. Very briefly, the case may be summarized as follows: (1) Typologically, one may refer to the obvious similarities between the type-fossil of the Châtelperronian – the Châtelperron point – and the Mousterian backed knife. In fact, the Châtelperron point can be seen as nothing more than a Mousterian backed knife translated into a blade technology (Bordes 1961a:804); (2) Geographically, a close correspondence can be observed between the overall distributions of the Mousterian of Acheulian tradition and Châtelperronian industries; neither variant is found to the east of the Rhône valley in France, while both forms show an extension into northern Spain (Bordes 1961a:804); 170; Freeman and Echegaray 1970); (3) Lastly there is the interesting chronological coincidence that the Mousterian of Acheulian tradition variant appears, on the basis of a large body of stratigraphic observations (Mellars 1969), to be the most recent of the major Mousterian variants in southwest France. This point has not generally been recognized in the literature hitherto but clearly provides strong support for the notion of Mousterian of Acheulian tradition-Châtelperronian continuity.

The implications of the foregoing evidence with regard to the human physical types responsible for the Mousterian of Acheulian tradition and Châtelperronian industries remain to be worked out (cf. Bordes 1968:105). But from the view-point of the archaeological evidence there seems little doubt that the first exponents of upper palaeolithic technology in southwestern France were of essentially local, as opposed to exotic, origin.

Acknowledgments

I am grateful to Professor F. Bordes and Professor H.L. Movius Jr. for reading this paper and making valuable suggestions. I am particularly indebted to Professor Movius for allowing me to incorporate unpublished information on his recent excavations at the Abri Pataud.

REFERENCES

Arambourou, R. and Jude, P.E. (1964) *Le gisement de La Chèvre à Bourdeilles (Dordogne).* Périgueux, Magne.

Binford, L.R. and S.R. (1966) The predatory revolution: a consideration of the evidence for a new subsistence level. *American Anthropologist* **68**, 508-12.

Binford, S.R. (1968a) Variability and change in the Near Eastern Mousterian of Levallois facies. *In* Binford, S.R. and L.R. (eds.) *New Perspectives in Archaeology*. Chicago, Aldine.

Binford, S.R. (1968b) A structural comparison of disposal of the dead in the Mousterian and the Upper Palaeolithic. *Southwestern Journal of Anthropology* **24**, 139-54.

Bordes, F. (1954a) Les limons Quaternaires du bassin de la Seine. *Archives de l'Institut de Paléontologie Humaine*, Mémoire 26.

Bordes, F. (1954b) Le Moustérien de l'Ermitage (fouilles L. Pradel): comparaisons statistiques. *L'Anthropologie* **58**, 444-9.

Bordes, F. (1954-55) Les gisements du Pech de l'Azé (Dordogne): le Moustérien de tradition Acheuléene. *L'Anthropologie* **58**, 401-32, and **59**, 1-38.

Bordes, F. (1959) Informations archéologiques: circonscription de Bordeaux. *Gallia-Préhistoire* **2**, 156-67.

Bordes, F. (1961a) Mousterian cultures in France. *Science* **134**, 803-10.

Bordes, F. (1961b) *Typologie du Paléolithique Ancien et Moyen.* Bordeaux, Delmas.

Bordes, F. (1968) *The Old Stone Age.* London, Weidenfeld and Nicolson.

Bordes, F. (1970) Informations archéologiques: circonscription d'Aquitaine. *Gallia-Préhistoire* **13**, 485-511.

Bordes, F. (1971) Physical evolution and technological evolution in man: a parallelism. *World Archaeology* 3(1), 1-5.

Bordes, F., Fitte, P. and Blanc, S. (1954) L'Abri Armand Chadourne. *Bulletin de la Société Préhistorique Française* **51**, 229-54.

Bordes, F. and Prat, F. (1965) Observations sur les faunes du Riss et du Würm I en Dordogne. *L'Anthropologie* **69**, 31-45.

Bouchud, J. (1954) Le renne et le problème des migrations. *L'Anthropologie* **58**, 79-85.

Bouchud, J. (1966) *Essai sur le renne et la climatologie du Paléolithique Moyen et Supérieur.* Périgueux, Magne.

Bourgon, M. (1957) Les industries Moustériennes et Prémoustériennes du Périgord. *Archives de l'Institut de Paléontologie Humaine,* Mémoire 27.

Bouyssonie, A. and J. and Bardon, L. (1913) La station Moustérienne de la "Bouffia" Bonneval à La Chapelle-aux-Saints. *L'Anthropologie* **24**, 609-34.

Bouyssonie, J. and Sonneville-Bordes, D. de (1956) L'Abri no. 2 des Vachons. Fouilles J. Coiffard. *Congrès Préhistorique de France* **15**, 271-309.

Breuil, H. and Lantier, R. (1965) *The Men of the Old Stone Age.* London, Harrap.

Breuil, H. and Saint-Périer, R. de (1927) Les poissons, les batraciens et les reptiles dans l'art Quaternaire. *Archives de l'Institut de Paléontologie Humaine,* Mémoire 2.

Clark, J.G.D. (1952) *Prehistoric Europe: the economic basis.* London, Methuen.

Clark, J.G.D. and Piggott, S. (1965) *Prehistoric Societies.* London, Hutchinson.

Couchard, J. (1966) La stratigraphie du gisement de Badegoule-ouest, commune de Lardin (Dordogne). *L'Anthropologie* **70**, 17-28.

Delpech, F. (1970) L'abri Magdalénien du Flageolet II – paléontologie *Bulletin de la Société Préhistorique Française* **67**, 494-9.

Delporte, H. (1968) L'abri du Facteur à Tursac (Dordogne). *Gallia-Préhistoire* **11**, 1-145.

Favraud, A. (1908) La station Moustérienne du Petit-Puymoyen, commune de Puymoyen (Charente). *Revue de l'école d'anthropologie* **18**, 46-66.

Freeman, L.G. and Echegaray, J.G. (1970) Aurignacian structural features and burials at Cueva Morin (Santander, Spain). *Nature* **226**, 722-6.

Henri-Martin, H. (1907-10) *Recherches sur l'évolution du Moustérien dans le gisement de la Quina (Charente): Vol. I – Industrie osseuse.* Paris, Schleicher.

Henri-Martin, H. (1923) *Recherches sur l'évolution du Moustérien dans le gisement de la Quina (Charente): Vol. II – Industrie lithique.* Angoulême, Ouvrière.

Henri-Martin, H. (1931) *La station Aurignacienne de la Quina.* Angoulême.

Henri-Martin, H. (1932) Sur un épieu en os de l'époque Moustérienne trouvé à la Quina. *L'Anthropologie* **42**, 681-2.

Lalanne, J.G. and Bouyssonie, J. (1946) Le gisement Paléolithique de Laussel. Fouilles du Docteur Lalanne. *L'Anthropologie* **50**, 1-163.

Lartet, E. and Christy, H. (1865-75) *Reliquiae Aquitanicae, being contributions to the archaeology and palaeontology of Périgord and the adjoining provinces of southern France.* London, Baillière.

Laville, H. (1964) Recherches sédimentologiques sur la paléoclimatologie du Wurmien recent en Périgord. *L'Anthropologie* **68**, 1-48, 219-52.

Lee, R.B. and De Vore, I. (1968) *Man the hunter.* Chicago, Aldine.

Leroi-Gourhan, André and Leroi-Gourhan, Arlette. (1965) Chronologie des grottes d'Arcy-sur-Cure (Yonne). *Gallia-Préhistoire* **7**, 1-64.

Mellars, P.A. (1969) The chronology of Mousterian industries in the Périgord region of southwest France. *Proceedings of the Prehistoric Society* **35**, 134-71.

Mellars, P.A. and Payne, S. (1971) Excavation of two Mesolithic shell middens on the island of Oronsay (Inner Hebrides). *Nature* **231**, 397-8.

Milne-Edwards, A. (1865-75) Observations on the birds whose bones have been found in the caves of southwest France. *In* Lartet and Christy (1865-75), 226-47.

Momméjean, E., Bordes, F. and Sonneville-Bordes, D. de (1964) Le Périgordien supérieur à burins de Noailles du Roc-de-Gavaudun (Lot-et-Garonne). *L'Anthropologie* **68**, 253-316.

Mouton, and Joffroy, R. (1958) Le gisement Aurignacien des Rois à Mouthiers (Charente). *Gallia Supplement* no. 9.

Movius, H.L. Jr. (1969) The Châtelperronian in French archaeology: the evidence of Arcy-sur-Cure. *Antiquity* **43**, 111-23.

Niederlender, A., Lacam, R., Cadiergues, and Bordes, F. (1956) Le gisement Moustérien du Mas-Viel (Lot). *L'Anthropologie* **60**, 209-35.

Peyrony, D. (1925) Le gisement préhistorique du Haut de Combe-Capelle: Moustérien de tradition Acheuléenne. *Association Francaise pour l'Avancement des Sciences* **49**, 484-9.

Peyrony, D. (1930) Le Moustier: ses gisements, ses industries, ses couches géologiques. *Revue Anthropologique* **40**, 48-76, 155-76.

Peyrony, D. (1934) La Ferrassie. Moustérien-Périgordien-Aurignacien. *Préhistoire* **3**, 1-92.

Peyrony, D. (1935) Le gisement Castanet, vallon de Castelmerle, commune de Sergeac (Dordogne). *Bulletin de la Société Préhistorique Française* **32**, 418-43.

Peyrony, D. (1949) *Le Périgord Préhistorique: essai de géographie humaine.* Périgueux, Société historique et archéologique du Périgord.

Peyrony, D. and Peyrony, E. (1938) Laugerie Haute. *Archives de l'Institut de Paléontologie Humaine,* Mémoire 17.

Pradel, L. (1957) Le Moustérien de l'abri de la Grotte à Melon à Hauteroche. *L'Anthropologie* **61**, 420-35.

Pradel, L. (1961) La Grotte des Cottés, commune de Saint-Pierre-de-Maillé (Vienne). *L'Anthropologie* **65**, 29-70.

Pradel, L. and Pradel, J.H. (1954) Le Moustérien évolué de l'Ermitage. *L'Anthropologie* **58**, 433-43.

Pradel, L. and Pradel, J.H. (1966) La station Paléolithique du Raysse, commune de Brive (Corrèze). *L'Anthropologie* **70**, 225-54.

Sauvage, H.E. (1865-75) On fishing during the reindeer period. *In* Lartet and Christy (1865-75), 219-25.

Smith, P.E.L. (1966) *Le Solutréen en France.* Bordeaux, Delmas.

Sonneville-Bordes, D. de (1960) *Le Paléolithique Supérieur en Périgord.* Bordeaux, Delmas.

Sonneville-Bordes, D. de (1963) Upper Palaeolithic cultures in Western Europe. *Science* **142**, 347-55.

Sonneville-Bordes, D. de (1965) *L'Age de la Pierre.* Paris, Presses Universitaires de France.

Van Campo, M. and Bouchud, J. (1962) Flore accompagnant le squelette d'enfant Moustérien découvert au Roc de Marsal, commune du Bugue (Dordogne) et première étude de la faune du gisement. *Comptes Rendus Hebdomadaires de l'académie des Sciences* **254**, 897-9.

Valensi, L. (1959) De l'origine des silex Protomagdaleniens de l'Abri Pataud, les Eyzies. *Bulletin de la Société Préhistorique Française* **56**, 80-4.

NICHOLAS DAVID

On upper palaeolithic society, ecology, and technological change: the Noaillian case

The upper palaeolithic cultures of southwestern France are variations on a theme. From Aurignacian to middle Magdalenian there are no major technological developments, in White's terms no significant increases in man's capacity to generate energy (White 1949:367 ff.). The sequence of cultures demonstrates a series of slightly differing approaches to the major economic end, the killing of reindeer and, less often, other animals. Shifting preferences for armatures of bone and stone suggest that there can have been little to choose between hunting technologies.

Three kinds of culture change have repeatedly been recognized in the upper palaeolithic sequence. There is the more or less gradual replacement of types by substitute forms, as for example of harpoon types in the Magdalenian. Such change, the product of minimal innovations, of fashion or of cultural drift, is common to all cultures and to many aspects of culture. It will not be considered here for the elucidation of any single instance requires an historical and particularist approach that cannot be applied. The second sort of change includes sudden shifts in technology and typology occuring within a culture period; archaeologists often use discontinuities of this nature for the definition of phases, within which there may be a high degree of assemblage stability or minor serial replacement and development of types. In the third kind of change the contrast between succeeding assemblages is such that the prehistorian is led to speak of the replacement of one culture by another. Only the second and third kinds of culture change will be considered below, and only in their structural, not their historical or cultural, aspects. It can never be known why Solutrean culture changed into, or was replaced by, that which we term Magdalenian, but it may be possible to identify factors operating in the upper palaeolithic that, on the one hand, encouraged the maintenance of tool-making traditions for periods of centuries, and, on the other, produced abrupt changes within archaeological cultures and from one culture to another.

The dynamics of upper palaeolithic culture change are as yet little understood and even little discussed. Flint tools do not evolve under the pressures of natural selection, and while man, in common with other organisms, interacts with his environment in a continuing process of adaptation, this is no explanation of culture change but merely a framework within which the problem may be approached. Emphasis has often been placed upon migration as an agent of change (Breuil 1912; Garrod 1938; Clark and Piggott 1967:70-1; Sherratt this volume). The Aurignacian may have arrived from the east and the Noaillian is perhaps an intruder from Mediterranean Italy into southwest France (David 1966:605-6), but as the archaeology of the Mediterranean basis becomes better known there are fewer and fewer chances of finding exotic ancestors for the Upper Perigordian/Gravettian, the Solutrean or the Magdalenian. On the other hand the differences between these cultures are too great to be explained by differential use of the various sites at different times by the same or similar culture groups (Binford and Binford 1966; Binford this volume). Neither can diffusion provide a dynamic, for both migration and diffusion are merely descriptions of processes of which the efficient causes remain unknown. There remains the possibility that many of the cultural developments in southwestern France are the products of the reformulation and recombination of culture traits either already present in the region or developed in response to exceptional stimuli.

The premise of the present case study is that neither culture change nor stability can be understood without some prior understanding of the environment within which the events took place, of the numbers of people involved, of their technology and economy, and of the mechanisms whereby ideas were transmitted from person to person and from generation to generation, that is to say, of their social organization. There is direct evidence only on the environment, technology and economy; estimation of population densities and gross features of social organization must depend upon ethnographic analogy controlled by reference to excavated data.

In the following sections I outline the archaeology of the Noaillian culture and discuss its environment and economy and attempt estimates of population and social organization. Finally I suggest an environmental factor that might have stimulated irregular developments in technology such as characterize this and other upper palaeolithic cultures.*

* Statements made below about Noaillian archaeology, including its identity as a culture separate from the Upper Perigordian/Gravettian, are documented at tedious length in David 1966.

Noaillian archaeology

The absolute dating of the Noaillian is uncertain. A date from the Abri Pataud (Movius 1966; Radiocarbon 9(1967):114-5) of 27,060±370 B.P. (GrN-4280) for the middle portion of the occupation level conflicts with another from the nearby Abri du Facteur of 23,180±1,500 B.P. (Gsy-69) (Delporte 1968:91), associated with a series that on typological grounds, should be considered earlier. The Noaillian occupation of the Abri Pataud follows the Perigordian IV which is dated to 26,600±200 B.P. (GrN-4477) and 28,150±225 (GrN-4634), and precedes by a considerable period the Perigordian VI, with dates of 22,780±140 B.P. (GrN-4506) and 23,010±170 B.P. (GrN-4721). The combination of these dates suggests that the culture was present in the Perigord for a period of at least 2,000 years from, say, 27,000 to 25,000 B.P. or rather later.

The Perigordian IV – Noaillian sequence falls between two cold, dry episodes of the Würm III stadial, the first contemporary with the Aurignacian II, the second preceding and continuing into the Perigordian VI and Proto-Magdalenian. Laville (1969:79), basing his interpretation upon a considerable body of palaeoclimatic data, states that the early Perigordian IV appears during a period of climatic amelioration during which 'les groupements forestiers se développent et comprennent de nombreux feuilles thermophiles'. The amelioration is interrupted by a brief colder episode, contemporary with the late Perigordian IV, and then continues into the Noaillian, which is characterized by 'conditions relativement douces et humides' (Laville and Thibault 1967:2366). From the most complete sequence, that of the Abri Pataud, it would appear that the Noaillian ends shortly before the maximum of this milder episode, the Würm IIIa/IIIb or, as Arlette Leroi-Gourhan (1968) terms it, Tursac Oscillation.

The centre of Noaillian distribution lies in Aquitaine (used here as a synonym for 'le Sud-Ouest'). The culture occurs in three regional facies, one in the Mesozoic plateaus and plains to the west of the Massif Central (a region henceforth described as the Greater Perigord), another along the northern slopes of the Pyrenees, and a third in northeastern France represented only by series from the Grottes du Renne and du Trilobite at Arcy-sur-Cure (Leroi-Gourhan, A. 1961; Leroi-Gourhan, A. and A. 1965; Bailloud 1953; Parat 1903; Breuil 1918). The Greater Perigord facies is divisible into two phases, the first characterized by very high percentages of Noailles burins, the second by improved blade production, the replacement of Noailles burins by the Raysse type (Movius and David 1970), and many other less striking typological developments. Sites of the early phase are widely distributed in and around the Perigord, while the later phase is largely restricted to the Vézère valley between Brive and Les Eyzies. The Noaillian of the Pyrenees is best known from the de Saint Périers' excavations at Isturitz, where levels IV and III are Noaillian and IIIa a mixture of Noaillian and Solutrean (Saint-Périer 1952). The facies is well differentiated from that of the Greater Perigord by many typological and quantitative features, including the presence of retouched points or knives, the virtual absence of Raysse burins, and a greater variety of tools and weapons of bone and antler. Little development takes place in the flint tool kit, while definite changes occur in the bone and antler component. There is some evidence that the Pyrenean facies may have persisted long after the disappearance of the Noaillian in the regions to the north (David 1966:527-32; McCollough 1971:330-1). The Arcy facies appears to be a late and isolated offshoot from the Greater Perigord. Noailles burins are virtually absent and the most characteristic tool is the burin-point (Movius and David *op. cit.*).

Noaillian environment

The last Glacial environment of Aquitaine is nowhere duplicated today. According to Butzer (1964:136-9, 374), Pleistocene low latitude tundras and forest tundras probably carried a greater biomass than modern tundras in the high latitudes, and the warmer summers would have favoured plant growth. The distribution of Noaillian sites, with the exception of the Arcy vicinity, is almost certainly south of the permafrost zone, although sporadic permafrost is possible (Butzer 1964:269 (Fig. 51), 273), although very unlikely during the Perigordian IV-Noaillian period. It is clear from the work of Laville and Thibault, Bouchud, and Arlette Leroi-Gourhan that the classic view that a tundra/taiga environment existed in Würmian Aquitaine is no longer tenable. The most precise data yet available come from the Abri du Facteur; here arboreal pollen increases from less than 1% to almost 7% in the Noaillian levels and a steppic environment is suggested (A. Leroi-Gourhan 1968:130). Laville emphasises the humidity indicated by the nature of deposits (Laville 1968:144). Bouchud considers the fauna – with 95% reindeer – as evidence of 'steppe sous climat modérément froid, assez humide, aux étés frais' (Bouchud 1968:120). Open forest, he believes, was not far away. It is important to realize that these conclusions are applicable only to the earlier Noaillian phase and that, on the evidence of the Abri Pataud deposits, the climate continued to ameliorate into and even after the late Noaillian. Leroi-Gourhan also cites preliminary work by Couteaux on the pollen from the site of Les Jambes, likely to date from near the maximum of the Tursac Oscillation (Célérier *et al.* 1967), which indicates a 'flore assez tempérée'. The reports, as yet unpublished, of the Abri Pataud team of specialists are expected to confirm and amplify these conclusions.

Perhaps most important to the creation of an environment

attractive to man was the variety of habitats and thus of resources. Bouchud (*op. cit:* 120), speaking of the reindeer, says that, 'Dans le Sud-Ouest de la France, région de faible étendue, mais aux paysages diverses, *des déplacements de faible importance* permettaient à ses ancêtres pléistocènes de retrouver le biotype de leur choix, soit en altitude, soit au voisinage de la mer'. Nevertheless the Perigordian and Noaillian occupants of the Greater Perigord appear to have made relatively little use of this variety. As at other times in the upper palaeolithic, reindeer are always an important element in the fauna (see Mellars this volume: 262, Table 2) and account for 90% or more of animal remains in the majority of upper palaeolithic series for which quantitative data are available. The reindeer, not in themselves evidence of rigorous climatic conditions, are often associated with cattle, horse, red deer, roe deer, chamois, ibex and other animals including wild boar. Only at Arcy, where mammoth is also important (Bailloud 1953:344) and in the Pyrenees (as for example at Isturitz where horse was the preferred prey together with reindeer and red deer) is there convincing evidence of a more balanced hunting pattern.

The extraordinarily high frequencies of reindeer in Noaillian faunas are proof of specialization and *prima facie* evidence of an over-specialization potentially or actually deleterious to the maintenance of Noaillian society.

Estimates of Noaillian economy and population

Living caribou and reindeer exhibit marked seasonal behaviour patterns that in turn impose certain kinds of response on those who would exploit them. For this reason and on account of the documented Noaillian specialization on reindeer as *the* game animal, I will rely upon caribou hunters for ethnographic analogies rather than upon peoples living in climes perhaps more similar to that inferred for Pleistocene Aquitaine but hunting animals that behave in quite different ways.

Among the documented tribes of the North American arctic there are many that make very significant use of caribou, but only three that primarily depend upon this resource. These are the Nunamiut Eskimo (Gubser 1965; Campbell 1968), the Nabesna (Upper Tanana) Athapaskans (McKennan 1959), and the northern bands of the (Montagnais-) Naskapi (Turner 1894; Speck 1935; Speck and Eiseley 1939).

Gathering, for which we have no direct evidence, is likely to have been at least as important to Noaillians as to recent hunters of the North American arctic and the northern plains Amongst land mammal hunters in these areas dependence upon the gathering of wild plants and small land fauna is in the range of 6-25%, and tends to increase from north to south.* A figure in the upper part of this range is likely for the Noaillians. Fishing may also have been important in contributing to the diet; even among interior tribes of northern North America dependence may reach 36-55%. On the other hand fish bones are not reported from many Noaillian sites and although quite well preserved were rare at the Abri Pataud. Neither at this nor at any other time are fish commonly represented in upper palaeolithic art. We would estimate Noaillian dependence upon fish (the Ethnographic Atlas category includes sea mammals) to be of the order of 6-15%. The highest degree of dependence upon the hunting of land animals and birds recorded for tribes of the arctic is 66-75% among the Nunamiut and northern bands of the Naskapi.†

On the northern Great Plains hunting and fowling commonly provided 76-85% of the diet. Given the faunal evidence, so high a level of dependence upon the product of the hunt does not seem unlikely for the Noaillians.

In Table 1, a range of likely Noaillian subsistence patterns is set out, together with the names of the North American tribes that exhibit similar economics.

Percentage of subsistence obtained by:

Gathering of wild plants & small land fauna	Hunting Trapping	Fishing Shellfish Sea mammals	Comparable North American Tribes
6-15%	66-75%	16-25%	Nunamiut, Naskapi
6-15%	76-85%	6-15%	—
16-25%	56-65%	16-25%	Nabesna, Montagnais (especially Lake St John), Plains Cree
16-25%	66-75%	6-15%	Assiniboin

Table 1 Possible Noaillian subsistence economies and comparable North American tribes. Source: *Ethnographic Atlas.*

The Nunamiut are retained in spite of the disagreement between Campbell and the Ethnographic Atlas over their subsistence economy since the figures given by Campbell are possible for the Noaillians and, in many other respects, the Nunamiut offer good parallels for

* Unless otherwise noted the statistics on subsistence given here are taken from the *Ethnographic Atlas,* published in instalments in the journal *Ethnology.* See Murdock (1967) for a summary.

† Campbell (1968) gives different and probably more accurate figures for the Nunamiut:

Gathering	—	considerably less than 5%
Fishing	—	in most years less than 15%
Fowling	—	less than 5%
Hunting	—	the remainder i.e. approximately 80-85%.

several features of Noaillian life. If it is accepted that economy and environment are important factors in determining population, then it is the Nunamiut, Naskapi, and the Nabesna that offer the best analogies for the Noaillians. Since the Pleistocene environment probably had a greater carrying capacity than the tundra and forest tundra of today, the Plains Cree and the Assiniboin, who had adopted full horse culture and firearms, are included to attach a likely upper limit to the population estimates (Table 2).

Area and Tribe	Popul-ation	Territory (100 sq. km.)	Density per 100 sq.km.	Population Estimate for Noaillian Aquitaine (c.90,000 sq.km.)	Authority
ARCTIC					
Montagnais-Naskapi and Tete de Boule	5,500	12,550	0.44	400	Kroeber, 1939
Nabesna	152	250	0.61	550	McKennan, 1959
Nunamiut	1,400	1,709	0.82	740	Campbell, 1968
NORTHERN PLAINS AND PRAIRIES					
Plains Cree	3,000	1,567	1.91	1,720	Kroeber, 1939
Assiniboin	10,000	1,714	5.83	5,250	Kroeber, 1939

Table 2 Noaillian population estimates.

Two points stand out immediately from these statistics. The estimated population figures are minute – far smaller than those suggested on unclear or at least inadequately documented grounds by Nougier (1954). Second, the range of the estimates is wide, the uppermost being over fifteen times as large as the smallest. The Montagnais-Naskapi figure is unreliable, but may be considered a minimum. The Indians say that Nabesna population has declined greatly, perhaps after exposure to white man's diseases (McKennan 1959:19), Gubser (1965: Appendix A) also implies that Nunamiut population fluctuated very considerably even before the impact of white contacts. An aboriginal figure for average population twice or three times that of 1930 is not unreasonable for the Nabesna and would put them at roughly the same density as the Plains Cree. From these statistics we may infer a Noaillian population that might at times have reached 2,000 or more, averaging something of the order of 750-1,250 individuals.

The economic and social organization of caribou hunters

Birdsell has termed the largest social group to be found among hunters and gatherers the 'dialect tribe'. It 'lacks all aspects of political authority, and simply consists of an aggregation of local groups in spatial proximity . . . the size of the dialectical tribal unit is insensitive to regional variations in both climatic and biotic factors. Its primary determinants are competence in speech and mobility on foot' (Birdsell 1968:232). For the Nunamiut, mobility, not on foot, but by dogsled is the crucial variable, allowing a tribal population more than double Birdsell's estimate of 500 for Pleistocene populations. The nature of the largest social group among the Montagnais-Naskapi is unclear, but the Nunamiut tribe, and it would seem the Nabesna also, is distinguished from its neighbours by economic and linguistic differences, and by a strong tendency for marriage to take place within the tribe (Campbell 1968:1). This is in accordance with Helm's (1968:118) suggestion that 'the tribe may be defined as the greatest extension of population throughout which there is sufficient intermarriage to maintain many-sided social communication'. The Nunamiut are both conscious and proud of their tribal identity.

The size of the local group is primarily dependent upon the distribution of food resources. 'Where plant and animal resources are largely raised locally and comprise a wide variety of forms, the size of exploitative groups will be small, and figures tend to oscillate around an equilibrium value of 25 persons . . . Where food resources become more concentrated, the dietary becomes more specialized and local group structure frequently changes . . . the average size of local groups may range between 500 and 100 individuals, and may in some exceptional cases reach several hundred persons' (Birdsell 1968:234). Birdsell's generalization is amply borne out by data from the arctic. The caribou are at certain times of year a concentrated resource, at others widely dispersed over the tundra and in the forest. Nunamiut band organization of the late 19th century can best be understood as a function of the ever-changing relationship between the animal and human populations within Nunamiut territory. At that time the tribe was divided into four major named groups, each of which might consist of one or more regional bands (Gubser 1965: Appendix A). (The term 'regional band' is taken from Helm (1968:118).)

The larger groups, which we may for convenience term the *sub-tribe*, did not function as an organized unit (unless it was coincident with the regional band) even for warfare against neighbouring Indians. When bands met for trade and socializing, as would happen at the end of the winter before the ice broke up, there seems to have been no specific desire to bring the sub-tribe together, although by the mere fact of proximity it is likely that there was more intra- than inter-sub-tribe contact. In contrast to the sub-tribe, which rarely assembled at one place and at one time, the regional band (also named) had a permanent home base, a village occupied from about the middle of September to mid-October and in April and May. Within the village was a ceremonial house that may be said to symbolize the existence and unity of the band. The regional band would also assemble either at the village or at special hunting camps for the spring and autumn caribou drives. According to Gubser the band might number between 50 and 150 individuals and might attain as many as 400 for a year or two. Campbell, writing of the Nunamiut as they were in about 1875, suggests regional bands averaging 70 persons or more with a range of from 25 to 100.

The number of Nunamiut bands was variable. Band continuity rested upon the maintenance of equilibrium between man and caribou within a territory, and the balance was fragile, intrinsically unstable as a consequence of the striking fluctuations in the numbers of caribou and other arctic fur-bearing animals (Elton 1930:18-21; 1942; Chapter 18). Another consequence of cycles in the abundance of game is that bands must be fluid in their composition, gaining or losing personnel as current resources require. The primary basis for band organization among the Nunamiut, Montagnais-Naskapi and Nabesna is kinship, but there is no evidence that bands of caribou hunters tend or tended to be organized along patrilineal – or matrilineal – lines. Consanguinity was emphasized over affinality, in part because consanguineal relatives acted together in time of feud. Lee and DeVore (1968:8) express the consensus of opinion among 'Man the Hunter' symposiasts in their statement that 'the fluid organization of recent hunters has certain adaptive advantages, including the adjustment of group size to resources, the levelling out of demographic variance, and the resolution of conflict by fission'. The greater the need continually to adjust group size, the more advantageous the kinship system that creates the largest number of links that can be called into play in the forming of residential associations (Gubser 1965:134, 136). Certainly in the Noaillian context there is no reason to suggest that patrilineality or patrilocality was the only or main principle operative in group formation.

The subdivision of the regional band is the household cluster, an exploitative unit consisting of a very few families, which formed after the breaking of the herds when the Nunamiut dispersed to hunt and trap. The household cluster, unlike the regional band, endured only for a few seasons and was not identified with a territory unless from year to year.

The larger the social unit and its territory, the less it is affected by local variation in the abundance of game or changes in the human population. The tribe is more lasting a unit than the sub-tribe, and the sub-tribe than the regional band. In times of population increase a regional band might leave the territory of the sub-tribe and, remaining separate for many years, lose its identification with the larger group, becoming a sub-tribe itself, at first consisting of a single regional band. If population again decreased, the surviving members might rejoin the original unit. For there are absolute limits at both extremes of the wide range of possible band sizes – if the group became too small it could no longer manage a successful caribou drive, if it became too large population outran resources. A combination of Gubser's and Campbell's figures gives a range of 25 to 400 persons, but bands at the upper and lower ends of the range were chronically unstable (Gubser 1965:167). Seen over long periods of time sub-tribes and regional bands underwent a continuing process of fission and fusion.

Amongst the Montagnais-Naskapi of the early 1900s, there is a clear distinction between the migratory regional bands of the taiga/tundra north of 52 degrees N. Latitude, and the smaller, more sedentary, groups in the forests to the south (Speck and Eiseley 1942). The former depended heavily upon caribou and to a lesser extent on fish. In both these main economic pursuits the regional band functioned as a unit, subdividing into groups of a family or two in times of food shortage. Regional bands in the south, more heavily involved in the fur trade, congregated in the summer around lakes or rivers or on the shore of the gulf of the St Lawrence, but were split into very small groups, sometimes of only one family, during the winter when they occupied recognized hunting and trapping territories. These differences in band organization are attributable primarily to the concentration of the barren-ground caribou herds for at least part of the year in the northern zone, while, to the south, 'game is more diversified and more abundant though smaller in size, and scattered through the forests' (ibid.: 220). In both zones the bands appear to have been relatively fluid in composition and to have split or united in response to changes in resources and in the demand for furs.

The southern part of Nabesna territory is a land of mountain ranges and intermontane basins, home of the mountain sheep. To the north, thick spruce forests grow in the broad, flat valley of the upper Tanana river, and there are many ponds and lakes. Caribou migrate through the region twice a year and are the staple game, but a variety of other animals are taken, moose, bear, rabbits, and muskrat, besides species that increased in importance with the fur trade. At the time of McKennan's study in 1929-30 the Nabesna hunted with rifles and lived in five local bands, numbering between 16 and 59 individuals, each with a home village. Sub-tribes and regional bands did not exist unless they be considered coincident with the tribe. There is no evidence of Nabesna band organization prior to the acquiring of firearms and their participation in the fur trade.

Regional bands might have existed or local bands have co-operated for the caribou drives, but it seems likely that, as among the southern Montagnais, the more dispersed resources of the forest would have encouraged the formation of groups smaller than those found among the Nunamiut for at least the greater part of the year.

Whether in the tundra or in the forest, firearms are an important factor in determining the size of the exploitative group. The smallest Nabesna band numbered only five adult males. Even during the caribou migrations Nunamiut hunters can now act more or less independently or in small groups (Gubser 1965: 325-6). A shift from a subsistence economy towards participation in the fur trade, because it implies the hunting of animals that are widely scattered in the forest, is also associated with a decrease in group size. Variation in the size of the exploitative unit in the forest is a function of development towards a monetary economy, in particular the proportion of subsistence requirements obtained through purchase. The process leads to the development of family hunting territories (Leacock 1954).

Noaillian social organization

The following attempt at reconstruction applies only to the Noaillian facies of the Greater Perigord. The Noaillian of the French Pyrenees and Spanish Basque provinces will be separately treated in a later paper by Major McCollough and myself.

Our examples of recent caribou hunters have been taken from three language families, Eskimo, Algonkin and Athapaskan, but in spite of the implied culture-historical differentiation there is a strong suggestion that their band organizations were a function of three fundamental synchronic variables, environment, technology (especially hunting technology) and economy. In tundra or forest tundra with seasonally migrating caribou herds a primary resource, the regional band is an important exploitative and social unit. When the herds break up, humans follow suit. Game in the forest is dispersed throughout the year and is there absolutely more abundant. The corresponding human group is the local band, while the regional band, if it exists at all, has little or no political or exploitative function, but is the group within which most interaction takes place, congregating mainly in order to engage in trade and many-sided social activities.

The Noaillians were neither equipped with firearms nor were they participants in a Fur Trade. Regional bands would seem imperative in the Greater Perigord for the efficient slaughter of the reindeer during their spring and autumn migrations to and from the slopes of the Massif Central, but, with both the tundra and forest varieties and other ungulates present in the region, the band may have split up into smaller groups for the larger part of the year. Some would have remained in the outer apron of the Massif while others followed the reindeer upland in the summer or down to the riverine plains in winter.

Members of Nunamiut bands 'identified themselves as inhabitants of a region – usually a large valley or an area dominated by a lake or a major river junction' (Gubser 1965:165). An average band territory of 8,500 sq.km. (much of it unoccupied or scarcely exploited) can be calculated from Campbell's data. For two reasons Noaillian band territories are likely to have been smaller. They possessed neither boats nor dog-sleds, and the lack of the latter, especially, must greatly have restricted the mobility of huntsmen and the range over which contacts could be maintained.

On the other hand the supposed greater biomass and variety of resources, including vegetable, in Pleistocene Aquitaine, may have required less movement in the food quest. More even distribution of game may also have permitted more stability in membership and territory of regional bands and local bands or household clusters. Band size, with higher biomass compensated by decreased mobility probably fell within the same wide range as among the Nunamiut.

Any attempt to control such inferences by reference to the archaeological data faces the problem of sampling. We have no alternative, for example, but to exclude the presently submerged Pleistocene coastline of Aquitania from consideration even though the sea coast might have been regularly visited. Virtually no sites are known from outside the limestone regions. Even within the classic area whole classes of sites, fishing camps for example, may have been destroyed by natural causes, and there are only two known open sites, Plateau Baillart (de Sonneville-Bordes 1953) and Les Jambes (Célérier 1967). Nor can we know how many sites were actually in use at the same time. There can, it seems, be no hope of controlling ethnographic inference by reference to the archaeology, but only of checking for conflicts between them.

One way in which this might be done is by studying different types of settlement. Campbell (1968:15-17) classifies the settlements of the Tulaqmiut band of the Nunamiut as follows:

Type 1	The villages of regional bands.
Type 2	Settlements of household clusters.
Type 3	Hunting or fishing camps 'occupied by one to five males for periods of from two to five days'.
Type 4	Collecting (rather than hunting) camps 'occupied by one to eight individuals, usually males, from typically one to four days'.
Type 5	Camps for trading and visiting where the Tulaqmiut met members of other bands and of other Eskimo tribes and which were 'abandoned by all

or nearly all occupants at the close of the trade rendezvous'.

Type 6 Overnight camps for travellers.

To this listing we should add camps for the band caribou drive, which among the Tulaqmiut coincided with the band village.

Type 1 settlements should be recognizable archaeologically by their large area and rich series of artifacts covering the whole typological range. As they were occupied at various times of the year by the whole band and by some members throughout the year, there should be little evidence of seasonality of occupation. Type 2 settlements should be smaller, but still with a complete tool kit, and may show signs of seasonality. Type 3 settlements, even if recurrently occupied, may be expected to leave less archaeological remains, but might be recognizable by a specialized tool inventory and by seasonality. Settlements of types 4 and 6 are unlikely to be recognizable, and the same is true of Type 5 unless, as was sometimes the case in the arctic, they coincide with settlements of other types. Camps for reindeer drives might be recognizable by the huge predominance of the bones of these animals, by a high proportion of weapons and butchery tools, and by marked, possibly bimodal, seasonality.

The kinds of information required for the identification of settlement type can be summarized: the area of occupation, the size of the assemblage and the frequencies of artifact types, and data on seasonality. These are minimal requirements but even so are not met in the large majority of cases. The term 'Perigordian Vc' is indicative of failures to separate many Perigordian and Noaillian levels. Many assemblages that are now irretrievably dispersed were not adequately typed at the time of their, often summary, publication. Although Bouchud (1966; 1968) has done valuable work on seasonality (but cf. Binford this volume: 238), there is information on only a few sites. The identification of the settlement types represented by Noaillian sites must for these reasons be considered highly speculative (Table 3), cf. de Sonneville Bordes (1960) and David (1966) and references there cited for relevant evidence.

The Abri Pataud and the Abri du Roc de Gavaudun are likely band villages of the early phase. In the same period the Abri Labattut, a large but much mistreated site, is conceivably a candidate for the same status, but is more probably of Type 2. In the Brantôme locality (locality is used here as defined by Willey and Phillips (1958:18)) the twin Abris du Bonhomme and Durand-Ruel might also represent a band village. The Abri Pataud remains a centre in the late phase of the Greater Perigord facies, and the Brive locality is more intensively occupied than in the early phase. The Grottes Lacoste and Pré-Aubert, next to each other in the little Planchetorte valley, might represent a band headquarters that was occupied and

Table 3

Noaillian sites of the Greater Perigord by phase, locality and suggested settlement type

Phase	*Locality*	*Suggested settlement type* *Type 1*	*Type 1 or 2*	*Type 2*	*Type 2 or 3*	*Undeterminable or Other*
EARLY	LES EYZIES	Abri Pataud 4	A. Labattut	A. du Facteur B	Grotte d'Oreille d'Enfer A. Pagès D A. du Poisson D A. du Masnègre B	A. des Merveilles Ferrassie L and Grotte A. de Fongal
	DORDOGNE VALLEY				Combe-Capelle G	Roc de Combe 2-3? G. de Péchialet A. de Cantelouve Termo-Pialat
	BRIVE				G. de Noailles 4	G. de la Font-Robert Bos-del-Ser
	BRANTÔME		A. du Bonhomme with A. Durand-Ruel			Fourneau du Diable
	VILHONNEUR			A. André-Ragout E, F		A. du Chasseur
	GAVAUDUN	A. du Roc de Gavaudun 2				A. Peyrony Plateau Baillart
	Other				A. Lespaux 2-4 A. de Laraux 3	A. du Roc de Cavart 4 A. des Battuts G. de Rouset, Les Vachons

Table 3 (cont.)

Noaillian sites of the Greater Perigord by phase, locality and suggested settlement type

Phase	*Locality*	*Suggested settlement type*				
		Type 1	*Type 1 or 2*	*Type 2*	*Type 2 or 3*	*Undeterminable or Other*
LATE	LES EYZIES	A. Pataud 4	A. de Laussel		A. de la Roque-St.-Christophe A La Rochette 1	
	BRIVE	G. Lacoste 1-3	G. Lacoste 1-3 with G. de Pré-Aubert I-III	A. du Raysse 4	G. de Bassaler-Nord 4	G. de Champ* G. Thevenard*
	PERIGUEUX				Les Jambes 2,3	A. du Petit-Puy-Rousseau*
	BRANTÔME				La Chèvre	

* Phase attribution uncertain

reoccupied several times during the phase. The Abri du Raysse 500 m upstream might have formed part of the same settlement. The Abri de Laussel, plundered rather than excavated, is a weak candidate for Type 1 status. It is poorly located on a side valley of the Vézère and is only 8 km. distant from the Abri Pataud.

The Noaillian preference for bone and antler armatures, not preserved under certain soil conditions, may be the explanation why no sites can be classified in Type 3 (hunting camps). Alternatively, such sites may have been destroyed or have gone unrecognised, or, possibly, were never required on account of the more even dispersal of game throughout the region and the limitation to travel on foot. Whole household clusters may have moved from site to site, while hunters erected temporary shelters that have not survived in the archaeological record. Sites identified as Type 2 or 3 are classed as such rather because there is insufficient evidence to place them in Type 2 than for any positive indication that they are hunting camps.

Obviously, given the data to hand, there is little to be concluded from this attempt at analysis. Nothing however conflicts with the view that Noaillian social organization as it is expressed in types of settlement may not differ significantly from that of recent caribou hunters. Neither do the data conflict with our estimates of population. There is evidence from the Greater Perigord for a maximum of four regional bands in the early and three in the later phase. For what they are worth these figures suggest a Noaillian population in the lower part of the range suggested above.

The expression of social organization in material culture

No detailed studies of Nunamiut, Naskapi, or Nabesna material culture exist, nor is there any study of inter-band variation in material culture among hunter-gatherers, nevertheless some useful inferences may be drawn, in particular from Gubser's data. Band composition among the Nunamiut varied in response to the available resources, because of feuding and visiting, and because, due to the small band size, it was often necessary to seek a wife elsewhere. Besides informal visiting there were periodic meetings that brought together members of different sub-tribes and tribes, for inter-Eskimo relations were generally friendly and members of a different tribe would even occasionally attach themselves to a Nunamiut band (Gubser 1965:341). 'The Nunamiut feel that they are one people distinct from the coastal Eskimos of Alaska and the Mackenzie River Eskimos to the east, and the Eskimo living in the timbered regions of the Kobuk and other nearby rivers . . .' (ibid:44). This tribal consciousness (also reported by Campbell (1968:3)) is an expression of economic, social, and linguistic differentiation. It seems probable that it would also have been expressed in material culture and that, unless there were major differences in environment or economy from one part of the tribal territory to another, such a network of contacts would result in a basic similarity in technology throughout the territory, perhaps with clines of styles and techniques between distant points as new ideas and practices were rapidly diffused.

The pattern of distribution of Noaillian material culture corresponds, I believe, rather precisely with that inferred for recent caribou hunters. Within each regional facies there are, with few exceptions, no demonstrable variations in artifact typology or frequencies that cannot be attributed to temporal, i.e. phase, differences, or to differential availability of raw materials, or, more depressingly, to failure by the archaeologist to distinguish between Noaillian and Perigordian levels. Series from Brive in the Corrèze, where flint is harder to find and nodules are smaller than in the Dordogne, are not differentiated by style or technique from those in the Les Eyzies or neighbouring localities, but only by absolute artifact size (David 1966: Appendix A). Within the two major facies, the Pyrenean and the Greater Perigordian, it would be possible to insert artifacts from one site into another assemblage of the same phase without fear of detection.

I would conclude that, with exceptions to be considered below, the Noaillian industry of France represents three related tribes, one living in the northern foothills of the Pyrenees, another in the Greater Perigord, and a third in the region of Arcy-sur-Cure.

There remain a small number of assemblages that cannot be interpreted in these terms. They include series from the Abri Lespaux (levels 2, 3, and 4), 23 km. east of Bordeaux (Cousté and Krtolitza 1965), materials from the Grotte de Noailles itself (Bardon and Bouyssonie, J. and A. 1905; Andrieu and Dubois 1966), from level 3 at the Abri de Laraux in Vienne (Pradel and Chollet 1950), all of which are datable to the early phase by the typology of the diagnostically Noaillian types represented. In spite of the recent control excavations by Andrieu and Dubois at the Grotte de Noailles, I remain unconvinced that their 'unmixed' series represents a true assemblage (David 1966:415-422). In the late phase, series from Les Jambes near Périgeux (Célérier 1967) and from thin horizons in the weathered eboulis that separates the main Noaillian occupation from the Perigordian VI at the Abri Pataud are equally problematic.

Acculturation

The Noaillian is believed intrusive into Aquitaine and, at the Abri Pataud, is intercalated between the Perigordian IV and VI. At La Ferrassie and elsewhere it appears after the Perigordian Va and Vb phases, although, as Bordes (this volume) and his team have shown, within the same climatic phase. If, as is generally accepted, the Perigordian VI is related to earlier Perigordian manifestations, then it follows that either in Aquitaine or in neighbouring areas there must have been Perigordians who were contemporary with Noaillians. I have argued (David, 1966:459-68) that the best archaeological evidence of them is assemblages from Level 4 in Abris 1 and 2 at Les Vachons, where a few Noailles burins and other diagnostically Noaillian types occur in an otherwise Perigordian assemblage that might well be redesignated a true Perigordian Vc. It is tempting to consider the two main culture groups in Aquitaine at this time as different from each other as the Indians and Eskimo of the North American arctic.

Although Indians and Eskimo may commonly have lived in a state of endemic enmity, diffusion of culture traits occurred up and down the northwest coast (Drucker 1955), while for the inland regions, Gubser again provides pertinent information. Fighting, usually over territorial infringements, was common, but there were still opportunities for peaceful interaction. 'According to the Nunamiut, the Indians learned many things from the Eskimo about building moss houses, trapping, hunting and *making implements*' (my emphasis). And again, 'After the fighting . . . Indians and Nunamiut lived together peaceably for many years, perhaps just less than a generation . . . Indians learned to use the corral for taking caribou during a migration' (Gubser 1965:45). There is no reason to suppose that such relationships were peculiar to the American arctic.

The Noaillian sites at which acculturation is suspected have in common that they were excavated with sufficient controls to make the mixture of Noaillian and Perigordian horizons unlikely, but yet show frequencies of backed blades and points that are atypically high for Noaillian assemblages with correspondingly lower percentages of Noailles burin types. Furthermore three of the sites, Lespaux, Laraux, and Noailles, are located away from the main Noaillian concentration, while the Abri Pataud samples are very late, coming from the lower portion of the eboulis that separates the Noaillian from the Perigordian VI and which represents the maximum of the Tursac oscillation. There is reason to believe that the Les Jambes materials may be more or less contemporary and also postdate other Noaillian series of the late phase (Célérier *et al.* 1967; David n.d.).

Acculturation is most likely to occur at sites that are marginal, whether in space or in time. The archaeological evidence, typological, distributional, and chronological, is suggestive of acculturation between Noaillian and Perigordian groups, but, even while demonstrating the fact of acculturation as a mechanism of upper palaeolithic culture change, the archaeology cannot explain why acculturation should take place.

A suggested dynamic for culture change

The richness of the archaeological record is sufficient testimony that southwestern France, with its caves and shelters, valleys and plateaus, its sources of flint and, above all, abundant game, offered an especially favourable habitat for upper palaeolithic man. But we should beware of considering Aquitaine as a glacial Eden, for there were two ever-present threats to the continuing well-being of the human population, their very small numbers and their specialization on reindeer as a game animal.

Under laboratory conditions extreme cases of specialization can be duplicated. Numerous experiments have shown that where prey and predator live in a confined space under conditions equally suitable to both, the predators will first kill off their prey and then succumb themselves to starvation (Andrewartha and Birch 1954:438 ff.). The balance of nature does not exist. Under natural conditions neither prey nor predator is so confined, the environment changes about them and animals may modify their behaviour. As a result, 'Any animal community that is watched for a number of years presents a restless picture of unending changes in numbers, which are more often than not accompanied by striking changes in their habits of life' (Elton 1942:23). Such fluctuations may be of very great magnitude and are perhaps nowhere so marked as in the arctic. The numbers of many birds and mammals from mice to moose show periods of increase and decrease that are experienced also, directly and indirectly, by the human population.

Caribou are no exception; their range and numbers are at present decreasing in North America as a result of the destruction of mature forests, in which they find their lichens, by forest fires and logging. Predators take their toll and other causes, disease and perhaps increased uptake of radioactive materials, are contributory factors. In the words of a game biologist, 'the prediction for caribou conservation in North America must be a gloomy one if present trends are not reversed' (Taber 1965:219). On a more limited scale Elton has given us a well-documented account of variations in the abundance of caribou in the Labrador Peninsula from the latter half of the 19th century until recent times, and of their catastrophic effects on the Naskapi Indians (Elton 1942; part IV). The Indians in this area used to rely upon three great herds of caribou; the western herd began to fail in the 1880s and 90s, the central herd from the late 1890s onward, and the eastern herd after the introduction of rifles in 1903-4. The extent of the decrease can be seen in the figures for caribou hides traded into Moravian missions in the eastern part of the area. From a high of 13,567 hides traded over the period 1894-1903, the number fell to zero between 1914 and 1923. The decline was no less marked in the central and western regions. Only in recent years have the herds again begun to increase. Elton attributes the decline to a variety of causes including forest fires, glaze storms that covered the lichens with sheets of ice, the increased frequency of milder winters over a twenty year period, disease, the difficulty of recreating herd traditions once smashed, predators other than man, and native slaughtering, particularly effective after the introduction of rifles. All but the last of these factors might have operated in the upper palaeolithic.

The overall drop in numbers and local failures brought about by variation in migration patterns had appalling consequences among the Naskapi. In the winter of 1892-3, between one hundred and fifty and two hundred of the three hundred and fifty Indians trading into Fort Chimo starved to death (Elton 1942:359), and from among numerous records of privation, misery and death, Elton (1942:381) cites this passage in a letter given in evidence to the committee of the Hudson's Bay Company in 1851 – that is *before* the main decline – 'Starvation has, I learn, committed great havoc among our old friends the Nascopies, numbers of whom met their death from want last winter; whole camps of them were found dead, without one survivor to tell the tale of their sufferings'. Elton concludes, 'For hundreds of years the Indian population must have starved at intervals, giving the deer opportunity to increase, then killing deer heavily until another failure to cross their erratic tracks caused more Indians to starve' (1942:385).

Thus on grounds both theoretical and of the Canadian experience, it is to be expected that upper palaeolithic populations of reindeer, the preferred prey, and of men their predators would have fluctuated widely *even without broad scale climatic or environment change.* What would have been the effects of such fluctuations upon a population so small as that estimated for Pleistocene Aquitaine? Animal populations have an innate tendency to increase, but in natural populations the *actual* rate of increase 'associated with increasing sparseness of the population may be carried so far that (it) becomes negative and the population proceeds to dwindle to extinction' (Andrewartha and Birch 1954:335). This threshold has been estimated for reindeer herds in the Eurasian tundra as between 300 and 400 individuals (Allee *et al.* 1940:401). In the case of man the calculation is subject to the caution that human populations are affected by economic and social factors besides the biological. Sauvy (1969:30) suggests that in a case of almost complete genetic isolation – such as may be inferred for many upper palaeolithic populations – a population minimum of 400-500 may obtain for purely demographic reasons, although polygamy or seasonal sexual promiscuity might reduce this figure to 300-400. He continues: 'A smaller population grows fairly quickly to the minimum size, or shrinks, but does not remain stable near its initial state.' If the estimated figures for Noaillian tribal populations approximate reality, then there is reason to suppose that, even in the unlikely event that the numbers of game remained constant, the human population might, for independent biological reasons, be chronically unstable. *It follows that the combination of effects of natural fluctuations in both prey and predator populations might, at long intervals, be so great as to disrupt the society of the predators, causing the collapse of the band organization and a breakdown in the system of transmission of culture from generation to generation and from place to place.*

Further consequences can be suggested. Following a major downward fluctuation the greatly reduced population would be likely to differ from its parent population by the Sewall Wright or 'founder' effect (Harrison *et al.* 1964: 174-5). With the deaths of many members of the society, and perhaps disproportionately of its oldest and youngest members, analogous processes would act upon their culture. This is *not* to say that natural selection operates on tool types, but that the less organized a system, the less predictable its behaviour. Unless we believe that palaeolithic man mechanically turned out the 'correct' proportions of end-scrapers and other tools, we should expect changes in the frequencies of types. Innovations, even if they did not occur more often under conditions of stress, might spread more readily in a small population and thus become conspicuous in the archaeological records. With the collapse of the mechanisms that ensured culture contacts over wide areas, a variety of local facies could develop. Finally, in an effort to recreate viable exploitative groups, surviving members of different tribes might join forces and produce new industrial facies by acculturation.

Fluctuations in the availability of game may be continual but only very exceptionally catastrophic. Cultural stability is far more striking a feature of the upper palaeolithic than is drastic change. The same set of social and ecological factors helps to provide an explanation. First, the para-archaeological evidence leaves little doubt that the environment was more favourable than that of any of the arctic peoples we have used in analogy and, being more varied and diverse, offered a wider choice of subsistence strategies. Second, the band organization of recent caribou hunters has been worked out and maintained over long periods precisely because of its efficiency in coping with the fluctuating and exacting conditions of arctic life.

Perhaps the most important factor in achieving adaptability is lack of rigidity in the recruitment of exploitative groups, giving the system the potential to maintain itself while allowing fusion and fission of its component elements. In times of abundance new bands bud off from their parent group, and since population density is kept at a low level by recurrent periods of shortage, over-crowding and pressure on these resources – which might result in major innovations – never, or only very exceptionally, become a problem over the long term. Unless a band moves far enough away to cut itself off from contacts with other groups, periodic meetings, intermarriage and visiting suffice to keep alive the contacts necessary for the preservation of a unified culture. Conversely, local bands may be snuffed out in the course of a hard winter, but those groups that manage to survive can, if necessary, band together. The system is able to cope with all but the most intense fluctuations and the culture is preserved.

Let us now confront this scaffolding of speculation against archaeological data. The early phase of the Noaillian may be supposed to have persisted virtually without change for a period, if not of a thousand, then at least several hundred years. It is distributed in two regional facies over a large portion of Aquitaine. Then, at the Abri Pataud, there is a marked decrease in the intensity of occupation and in the succeeding subdivision of the level is found an assemblage that, while still clearly Noaillian, shows technological and typological differences of some magnitude. The changes appear suddenly; none of the many Noaillian sites have produced series intermediate between those of the early and late phases, and it is at this moment in time that the distribution of the Noaillian in the Perigord becomes effectively reduced to the valley of the Vézère and its tributaries with only minor evidences of occupation to the north and south. Unless archaeological sampling is thoroughly misleading, the Noaillians have suffered a considerable population reverse. Most significantly it would appear that the environment remained constant at this time; Pyrenean assemblages that are presumed contemporary show no indication of sudden change.

At some time during the early phase there may have been acculturation of Noaillians and Perigordians at marginal sites. Whether this occured simultaneously with depopulation in the centre of the territory cannot be determined on present evidence.

Following the establishment of the late phase in the Les Eyzies, Brive and nearby localities, the phase continues with little or no typological change, and then stops before the maximum of the Tursac oscillation. The region appears once more to have been depopulated. The only evidences of occupation are the thin horizons with eboulis at the Abri Pataud and perhaps also the Les Jambes series from near Périgueux (Célérier 1967; Célérier et al. 1967). There is again the suggestion in these assemblages that acculturation was taking place. It is also worthy of note that the next occupation known in the Les Eyzies locality, to which it is restricted, is the Perigordian VI. This phase diverges from all other Perigordian manifestations in the abundance of its bone and antler component and in its much higher frequencies of truncation burins. Both characteristics might be expected from a meeting of Noaillian and Perigordian minds.

As far as can be told the Noaillian occupation of the Pyrenean Piedmont continued well after that of the Perigord, indeed until the appearance of Solutrean in the area. Why this should be is not altogether clear, though, on the basis of the evidence from Isturitz, it may be suggested that the Noaillians there were far less dependent upon a single game animal and, besides reindeer, killed large numbers of horses, red deer and bovids.

Summary and conclusions

Technological change can only be understood in the context of the habitat, economy, and society of the culture concerned. I have attempted, by a process of inference based upon ethnographic analogy, to estimate Noaillian population and to reconstruct gross features of their social organization. The band organisation inferred is highly adaptive to an environment in which the numbers of animals are subject to wide, short term fluctuations. The continuance of the culture is assured by the reduplication of social groups when game is abundant, and, in hard times, by their recombination and absorption. Long periods of technological uniformity in the upper palaeolithic are explicable in these terms. Population density was generally low and there was space for the accommodation of temporary population increases even without, or with very rare, migration. As a result overcrowding appears never to have provided a stimulus for revolutionary technological innovations, for example, the domestication of reindeer, while minor innovations, in competition with established types, were disseminated throughout the culture and show up archaeologically in a coherent and recognizable matrix.

At long intervals, failure of the game may have had catastrophic effects on the sparse upper palaeolithic population, overloading capacity for social adaptation with consequent disruption of the mechanisms for the transmission of culture. When social organization collapsed culture traits would be subject to processes of selection comparable, but not identical to those acting on gene frequencies in small populations. Percentages of types might undergo rapid changes and some innovations be more readily accepted, with the result that, when the population again built up to archaeological visibility, it would appear to the prehistorian as if a cultural replacement rather than a resynthesis had taken place. It should be emphasized that, in the arctic and elsewhere, drastic declines in the numbers of game animals are not necessarily induced by or correlated with environmental shifts on a scale likely to be identifiable in the Pleistocene record. *The motive force for cultural developments need not be supplied by climatic change; the tensions present within a 'stable' ecosystem are themselves a sufficient dynamic.* By the same token there is no need to call on other factors that might, *ex machina*, have brought about depopulation, but which, like epidemics, infanticide, or internecine warfare, are either less probable, or only with more difficulty demonstrable, or, above all, less parsimonious as explanations.

The archaeological data are inadequate to allow proper testing of my hypotheses, but the Noaillian case would seem to conform to the predictions. Sudden technological changes, seemingly associated with depopulation, occur at a time of stable environmental conditions. After the late phase, which ends before the maximum of a warmer, wetter interval, there are few traces of occupation in the Greater Perigord. What little evidence there is suggests that Noaillian-Perigordian acculturation may have been taking place. If so, then this process may ultimately be responsible for the anomalous characteristics of the succeeding industry, the Perigordian VI. Emigration, another possible response to changing circumstances, may be indicated by the appearance at Arcy-sur-Cure of an atypical Noaillian industry related to the late phase of the Perigord. In the Pyrenean piedmont, more diversified hunting practices may have contributed to the persistence of the Noaillian into Solutrean times.

The dynamic proposed has saddening implications for upper palaeolithic archaeology. If change can occur as the product of severe environmental stress acting on a greatly reduced population, the process will be correspondingly difficult to document. The poorest occupation horizon in nearly sterile eboulis must be as painstakingly excavated as the richest hearth. Testing of the hypothesis will require exceptionally thorough and refined analyses of the faunal remains to determine whether over-hunting is indicated by changes in the age structure of the prey sample, or over-grazing by a decrease in their average bone density. Even so the phenomena may be often of such short term that they do not show up in the archaeological record – unless some serendipitous prehistorian should one day stumble on a site littered with skeletons in attitudes suggesting death by starvation, a gruesome picture but one not unknown in the arctic (L.R. Binford, oral communication).

There are many aspects of upper palaeolithic life, for example the influence of magic and religion upon technology, that have not been discussed above but which may be of significance for the understanding of cultural development. My reading of the dynamic will undoubtedly prove inadequate to explain many instances of technological change, although it might be profitable to look from this viewpoint at the Proto-Magdalenian and the Aurignacian V, precursors of the Solutrean, and at the puzzling early phases of the Magdalenian. Of one thing I am sure, that typological methods have progressed far enough for our attention to be profitably turned away from the tools to the ethnography that they embody.

Acknowledgments

I would like to express my thanks to Hallam L. Movius, Jr., who directed my studies and allowed me to make use of the Abri Pataud materials in my research, and to the Wenner-Gren Foundation for their award of a Pre-Doctoral Fellowship without which I would have been unable to complete the work. My sincere thanks are also due to my many French and Italian friends and colleagues who showed me their collections and talked them over with me, and especially to Harvey M. Bricker, for his as yet unpublished clarification of the Perigordian side of the question and for the many ideas which I owe to our discussions over a period of years.

REFERENCES

Allee, W.C., Park, O., Emerson, A.E., Park, T. and Schmidt, K.P. (1949) *Principles of Animal Ecology*. Philadelphia and London, W.B. Saunders.

Andrewartha, H.G. and Birch, L.C. (1954) *The Distribution and Abundance of Animals*. Chicago, University Press.

Andrieu, P. and Dubois, J. (1966) Travaux récents à la grotte éponyme de Noailles. *Bulletin de la Société Préhistorique Française* 63, C.R. des Séances Mensuelles 5, CLXVII-CLXXX.

Bailloud, G. (1953) Note préliminaire sur l'industrie des niveaux supérieurs de la Grotte du Renne. *Bulletin de la Société Préhistorique Française* **50** (5-6), 338-45.

Bardon, L. and Bouyssonie, J. and A. (1904) Monographie de la Grotte de Noailles (Corrèze). *Bulletin de la Société Scientifique, Historique et Archéologique de la Corrèze* 27, 65-84.

Binford, L.R. and S.R. (1966) A preliminary analysis of functional variability in the Mousterian of Levallois facies. *American Anthropologist* **68** (2), pt. 2, 238-95.

Birdsell, J.B. (1968) Some predictions for the Pleistocene based upon equilibrium systems among recent hunter-gatherers. In Lee and Devore 1968, 229-40.

Bouchud, J. (1966) *Essai sur le Renne et la Climatologie du Paléolithique moyen et supérieur*. Périgueux, Imprimerie Magne.

Bouchud, J. (1968) L'Abri du Facteur à Tursac (Dordogne) II. La Faune et sa signification climatique. *Gallia Préhistoire* **11** (1), 113-21.

Breuil, Abbé H. (1912) Les subdivisions du Paléolithique supérieur et leur signification. *XIV Congrès Internationale d'Anthropologie et d'Archéologie Préhistorique*, (Genève), 165-238.

Breuil, Abbé H. (1918) Etudes de morphologie paléolithique III. Les niveaux présolutréens de Trilobite. *Revue Anthropologique* **28**, 309-333.

Butzer, K.W. (1964) *Environment and Archaeology*. Chicago, Aldine.

Campbell, J.M. (1968) Territoriality among ancient hunters: interpretations from ethnography and nature. *In* Meggers, B.J. (ed.) *Anthropological Archaeology in the Americas*, 1-21. Anthropological Society of Washington.

Célérier, G. (1967) Le gisement périgordien des Jambes, à Périgueux (Dordogne). *Bulletin de la Société Préhistorique Française* **64**. Etudes et Travaux 1, 53-68.

Célérier, G., Laville, H. and Thilbault, C. (1967) Etude sédimentologique du gisement préhistorique des Jambes, à Périgueux. *Bulletin de la Société*

Préhistorique Française **64**, Etudes et Travaux 1, 69-82.

Clark, G. and Piggott, S. (1967) *Prehistoric Societies.* New York, Knopf.

Cousté, R. and Krtolitza, Y. (1965) L'abri Lespaux et la question du Périgordien en Gironde. *Revue Historique et Archéologique du Libournais* **33**, 47-54.

David, N.C. (1966) *The Périgordian Vc: an Upper Palaeolithic Culture in Western Europe.* Ph.D. Thesis, Harvard University.

David, N.C. n.d. Revised edition of David, 1966.

Delporte, H. (1968) L'Abri du Facteur à Tursac (Dordogne) I. Etude générale. *Gallia Préhistoire* **11** (1), 1-112.

Drucker, P. (1955) *Indians of the Northwest Coast.* New York.

Elton, C. (1930) *Animal Ecology and Evolution.* Oxford, Clarendon Press.

Elton, C. (1942) *Voles, Mice and Lemmings: Problems in Population Dynamics.* Oxford, Clarendon Press.

Garrod, D.A.E. (1938) The upper palaeolithic in the light of recent discovery. *Proceedings of the Prehistoric Society.* n.s. **4** 1-26.

Gubser, N.J. (1965) *The Nunamiut Eskimos: Hunters of Caribou.* New Haven and London, Yale University Press.

Harrison, G.A., Weiner, J.S., Tanner, J.M. and Barnicot, N.A. (1964) *Human Biology: An Introduction to Human Evolution, Variation and Growth.* Oxford, Clarendon Press.

Helm, J. (1968) The nature of Dogrib socioterritorial groups. *In* Lee and Devore 1968, 118-25.

Kroeber, A.L. (1939) *Cultural and Natural Areas of Native North America* University of California Publication in American Archaeology and Ethnology (Berkeley) 38.

Laville, H. (1968) L'Abri du Facteur à Tursac (Dordogne), IV. Etude sédimentologique du remplissage. *Gallia Préhistoire* **11** (1), 133-45.

Laville, H. (1969) Le remplissage des grottes et abris du sud-ouest de la France. In *Etudes Françaises sur le Quaternaire,* supplement to *Association Française pour l'Etude du Quaternaire,* Bulletin, 77-80.

Laville, H. and Thibault, C. (1967) L'oscillation contemporaine du Périgordien supérieur à burins de Noailles, dans le Sud-ouest de la France. Comtes Rendus de l'Académie de Sciences **264**, 2364-6. Série D. Paris.

Leacock (1954) *The Montagnais 'Hunting Territory' and the Fur Trade.* American Anthropological Society. Memoir 78.

Lee, R.B. and Devore, I. (eds.) (1968) *Man the Hunter.* Chicago, Aldine.

Lee, R.B. and Devore, I. (1968) Problems in the study of hunters and gatherers. *In* Lee and Devore 1968, 3-12.

Leroi-Gourhan, André (1961) Les fouilles d'Arcy-sur-Cure. *Gallia Préhistoire* **4**, 3-16.

Leroi-Gourhan, Arlette. (1968) L'Abri du Facteur à Tursac (Dordogne) III. Analyse pollinique. *Gallia Préhistoire* **11** (1) 123-32.

Leroi-Gourhan, Arlette and André (1965) Chronologie des grottes d'Arcy-sur-Cure. *Gallia Préhistoire* **7**, 1-64.

McCollough, M.C.R. (1971) *Perigordian Facies in the Upper Palaeolithic of Cantabria.* Ph.D. Thesis, University of Pennsylvania.

McKennan, R.A. (1959) *The Upper Tanana Indians.* Yale University Publication in Anthropology. 55.

Movius, H.L. Jr. (1966) The hearths of the Upper Perigordian and Aurignacian horizons at the Abri Pataud, Les Eyzies (Dordogne), and their possible significance. *American Anthropology* **68** (2), pt. 2,296-325.

Movius, H.L. Jr. and David, N.C. (1970) Burins avec modification tertiaire du biseau, burins-pointe et burins du Raysse à l'Abri Pataud, Les Eyzies (Dordogne). *Bulletin de la Société Préhistorique Française* **67**, Etudes et Travaux 2, 445-55.

Murdock, G.P. (1967) The Ethnographic Atlas: a summary. *Ethnology* **6** (2).

Nougier, L.R. (1954) Essai sur le peuplement préhistorique de la France. *Population* 9 (2), 241-74.

Parat, A. (1903) Les grottes de la Cure XXI. La Grotte du Trilobite. *Bulletin de la Société des Sciences Historiques et Naturelles de l'Yonne,* Auxerre, 56 (1902), part 2, 49-88.

Pradel, L. and Chollet, A. (1950) L'abri périgordien de Laraux, commune de Lussac-les-Châteaux (Vienne). *L'Anthropologie* 54, 214-27.

Saint-Périer, R. and S. de (1953) *La Grotte d'Isturitz III. Les Solutréens, les Aurignaciens et les Moustériens.* Archives de l'Institut de Paléontologie Humaine 25.

Sauvy, A. (1969) *General Theory of Population.* London, Weidenfeld and Nicolson. (Original publication in French 1966, Presses Universitaires de France).

Sonneville-Bordes, D. de (1953) Le Paléolithique supérieur du plateau Baillard à Gavaudun (Lot-et-Garonne). *Bulletin de la Société Préhistoire Française.*

Sonneville-Bordes, D. de (1960) *Le Paléolithique Supérieur en Périgord.* 2 vols. Bordeaux, Delmas.

Speck, F.G. (1935) *Naskapi.* Oklahoma, Norman.

Speck, F.G. and Eiseley, L.C. (1942) Montagnais-Naskapi bands and family hunting territories of the central and southeaster Labrador peninsula. *Proceedings of the American Philosophical Society* 85 (2), 215-42.

Taber, R.D. (1965) Land use and native cervid populations in America north of Mexico. *Transactions of the VIth Congress of the International Union of Game Biologists* (Bournemouth 1963), 201-25.

Turner, L.M. (1894) Ethnology of the Ungava district, Hudson Bay Territory. *Smithsonian Institution, Bureau of American Ethnology,* 11th Annual Report (1889-90), 167-349.

White, L.A. (1949) *The Science of Culture.* New York, Grove and London, Evergreen.

Willey, G.R. and Phillips, P. (1958) *Method and Theory in American Archaeology*. Chicago, University Press.

C. B. M. McBURNEY

Measurable long term variations in some old stone age sequences

The following is a preliminary discussion of a series of statistical experiments carried out on some stratified sites of Pleistocene and Epi-Pleistocene age. All yield remains which can reasonably be assigned to communities living by hunting and gathering, repeatedly visiting the same caves and rock shelters.

The sites chosen are multi-level sites and with one exception afford direct evidence of time calibration on the basis of multiple C-14 readings. An additional check on the time calibrations was made by a systematic study of the relation between depth and age. As a result there is reason to believe in each case that the accumulation of deposits is the result of a purely natural geological process virtually unaffected by the presence or absence of human occupation. This does not of itself rule out the possibility of changes or even discontinuities in sedimentation rate due to other (non-anthropogenic) causes, but the correlation coefficients calculated between age and depth in each case, and study of the regression equations of age on depth based on them showed no significant signs of departure from linearity or break in continuity. The coefficients themselves were high – in one case as high as .98 and thus significant to a high level of probability. There is furthermore little reason to suspect significant distortions of the time estimates such as appear to have seriously affected conclusions at a later period (Renfrew 1970:119). Although some irregularities in the radio-carbon flux are of course to be expected, in the time intervals at issue they were either of small absolute amplitude or too small in relation to the total intervals discussed to be relevant to the numerical deductions here offered.

This preamble is deemed necessary owing to the relative lack of systematic deductions from physical time-measurement in this branch of prehistory. Although individual observations have multiplied it seems to the writer that an important field of enquiry here has been largely neglected.

This concerns the *rate of change* in elements of the material culture of various societies over prolonged periods. It is clear for instance that 'patterns of change' assume quite different forms when related to even approximate time-scales as compared to those which may be guessed at from a mere succession. The supposed 'sudden change' may turn out to be nothing more than part of a long-sustained trend while on the other hand suggested 'seriations' may turn out to have significant kinks which demand specific explanation.

Attention must now be called to a further requirement if this line of argument is to be pursued. If we are concerned with rates of change then amplitude as well as period comes equally into question. To put it differently the elements whose change we are studying require to be as reliably quantified or measured as they are dated.

Furthermore, the entities with which the stone age specialist is concerned differ in a number of respects from those which form the material of later periods of study. The stone age specialist of today, as Professor F. Bordes and others like him have been at pains to stress, is concerned more with the characteristics of *assemblages* than with *individual objects*. Thus the proto-historian working on later periods may well concentrate on a single relatively complex object such as a carefully contrived sword, brooch, decorated pot or the like, the subject of a considerable degree of individual initiative in its original maker. The early prehistorian on the other hand, working on an assemblage produced by a group of individuals over a period of hours or weeks, is virtually dealing with a pattern of preferred behaviour liable to be repeated in nearly identical form by the same group on numerous occasions. Of course the difference is ultimately one of degree rather than kind in that both situations contain elements due to tradition as well as immediate functional requirement and occasional traces of individual idiosyncracy. In both it may be said that the ultimate objective of study is to distinguish the traditional element handed on from one generation and group to the next, from the 'norm' of individual variation and the vagaries of the immediate functional necessity.

Again, it is important to realize that a tradition, whether a method of skinning a buck or depicting a religious scene, is subject to growth, mutation, atrophy, and even disappearance. The one thing it is not (though this often seems to be forgotten) is a *static* entity like say the 'classic' version of a language postulated by old fashioned grammarians. To put it rather elaborately I would say that the ideal approach should aim at being a calculus of infinite variation rather than an arithmetic of discrete numbers.

This raises of course by implication the age-old issue, as old perhaps as the study of anthropology itself, of the relative importance in culture change of sudden 'stochastic' changes by mutation or invention rather than large numbers of small changes combining to form a sustained trend. The two explanatory conceptions have been stressed to very varying degrees by different workers of differing outlook. Thus in the extreme some enthusiastic functionalists end by virtually denying the existence of long term trends of any kind. For them, any modification of behaviour is the direct result of response to immediate necessity or stimulus, and there is no such thing as time-lag in response or a pattern of socially sustained accretion which we might call tradition.

A further corollary of such a position in some minds would be that the same circumstances always lead to the same optimum response. Such a conclusion of course ignores the whole body of ethnographic data which indeed rendered it untenable long ago by showing in the clearest fashion that closely similar circumstances often evoke widely varying responses subsequently perpetuated in highly idiosyncratic lines of development.

To say this is not of course to deny the importance of direct functional response which must frequently occur, but simply to emphasise that the functioning of an economic, industrial or artistic culture, as studied by the ethnographer at a point in time or by the archaeologist over a prolonged period, must be the product of many diverse factors.

Granted then that it is the particular task of the archaeologist to disentangle these factors, how best can he set about it with the materials at his disposal? From the way in which I have just presented the different prevailing points of view it will be clear that I view this problem as basically statistical. Our objective is to study the nature of the responses of a community to its environmental stimuli so that we may isolate as far as possible the element of standardised or traditional responses developed over a prolonged period. This amounts in statistical terms to a systematic comparison between quantified stimuli in the environment and similarly quantified elements in the surviving traces of the material culture. The record of neither will of course be complete and both must be subject to the ordinary limitations of sampled statistical data.

Over the past few years we have been spending time and effort in Cambridge to devise suitable methods to this end and apply them to appropriate cases. The development of this approach owes a great deal to the advent of computer facilities since although there is little new in several of the key statistical devices, their application on the scale required would otherwise be quite impracticable.

The basic analytic tool is simply that of the coefficient of correlation. For the benefit of those possibly unfamiliar with statistical methods this is a device for measuring the degree to which two variables resemble one another. This *may*, but does not necessarily, mean that there is a direct causal relation between the two. In order to understand the type of analysis we have been undertaking it is necessary to pursue this point a little further.

One can imagine for example an archaeological situation in which in a sequence of layers there were quantifiable traces of umbrellas and melon cultivation, such that every time there was an increase in melons there was a corresponding increase in umbrellas. This could, but would not necessarily, mean that melon cultivation required umbrellas; an alternative would be that both resulted from periodic or systematic increases in rainfall. The situation would be clarified if the layers contained in addition to umbrella ribs and melon seeds some direct indication of rainfall. Thus if we calculated (as opposed to guessing) and compared the three correlations Melons to Rainfall, Umbrellas to Rainfall, Melons to Umbrellas, we might find that the third coefficient was substantially less than the other two. The same result can of course be made still clearer by more extended devices that penetrate the situation more deeply.

In general, however, the first step is to calculate a matrix of correlation coefficients of all variables against all. This means $\frac{N(N-1)}{2}$ coefficients where N is the total number of variables.

This is of course a rapidly accruing figure so that the practical value of a computer needs little stressing. In a recent experiment there were over 350 coefficients each one of which would have taken 2-3 hours to calculate and check, amounting to say the impossible figure of 1,000 hours with a desk calculator. Using a computer (apart from time of input) the whole operation was complete in seconds.

It will be noticed, however, that even systematic comparison of 350 coefficients for explanatory purposes, raises further problems of time and labour. These can be saved substantially by using the computer to do the sorting, as with a suitable program which produces a diagram from which the main pattern of inter-relations can be read at a glance.

It must be realized, however, that any such re-ordering of the primary correlation matrix does not in fact remove its basic ambiguities. In a large number of cases it will still be unclear whether A is correlated primarily to B, or secondarily where both are related to C, and so on through a network of causation.

Moreover, since all archaeological situations however careful the field collection are necessarily incomplete, that is to say that they never in practice contain a record of all relevant variables (nor would it be practicable to study these if they did), it might appear at first that the whole operation is foredoomed. In fact however in this as in other field studies common sense plays an important part in interpretation. We need scarcely ask ourselves whether umbrellas give rise to melon cultivation, or for instance whether an increase in end-scrapers is the primary cause of an increase in gazelles. Incomplete though the record may be it is still susceptible to considerations of a practical kind often usefully based on observed ethnographic data. Thus it is worthwhile to pursue systematic collection of data and subject them to equally systematic and structured analysis within those limits.

Modern statistics obtained by automatic calculation afford indeed a whole range of insights into a complex network of data of which the raw correlation matrix is merely the first stage. A relatively simple device which deserves to be better known among archaeologists than it appears to be is Partial Correlation. Using this and starting from the raw matrix one can in effect see what would have happened to umbrellas if we had varied the melons but held the rainfall constant and vice versa. For instance we might have found that the correlation melons/umbrellas without the factor of rainfall was nil or again that, let us say, it was really dependent on a fourth factor concerned with economic prosperity.

Thus Partial Correlation affords us an insight which we could not possibly obtain from the original matrix as it stood, or simply from its rearrangement in a linkage pattern. More sophisticated devices which take us still further into the implications of the data and can readily be applied by computer are, for instance, Principal Components and various forms of factor analysis, although the extent to which these can be usefully applied and valid deductions drawn from them is of course always dependent on the initial validity and quantity of the primary data. In a sense also the more involved and elaborate the processing the more difficult realistic and practical conclusions become.

In the final section of this paper I shall describe briefly the results of applying the first mentioned methods of analysis to four different and contrasted situations in order to display the patterning of various elements in the culture and their relation to environmental factors.

The most complete situation is that of Ali Tappeh (McBurney 1968:385) on the Caspian, whence I published the correlation matrix of the primary data and an informal interpretation some years ago (McBurney 1968). Briefly the site offered 23 layers spread over no more than about 1800 years – an exceptional situation allowing variation in tool frequencies to be studied in unusual detail. Eight tool classes were in fact calibrated, related to 10 species of mammals of economic significance and 10 species of small snail (too small for food) affording indirect indication of changes in the total ecology. By coincidence the site was found to span a period of exceptionally marked ecological change during the closing phases of the Pleistocene ice age, contemporary with the Bølling, Middle Dryas, Allerød and Younger Dryas phases further west. An inspection of the relative importance of different species layer by layer showed considerable differences in patterning through time. Some, notably Gazelle, which formed a dominant element in the diet, were subject to long-term trends in addition to shorter period oscillations. Treating time as a variable and assuming that the faunal variations were the independent variables and tool frequencies the dependent variables, it became possible to isolate and examine the role of each separately either with or without the time component. As a result it appeared that some tools were highly correlated to time and only influenced

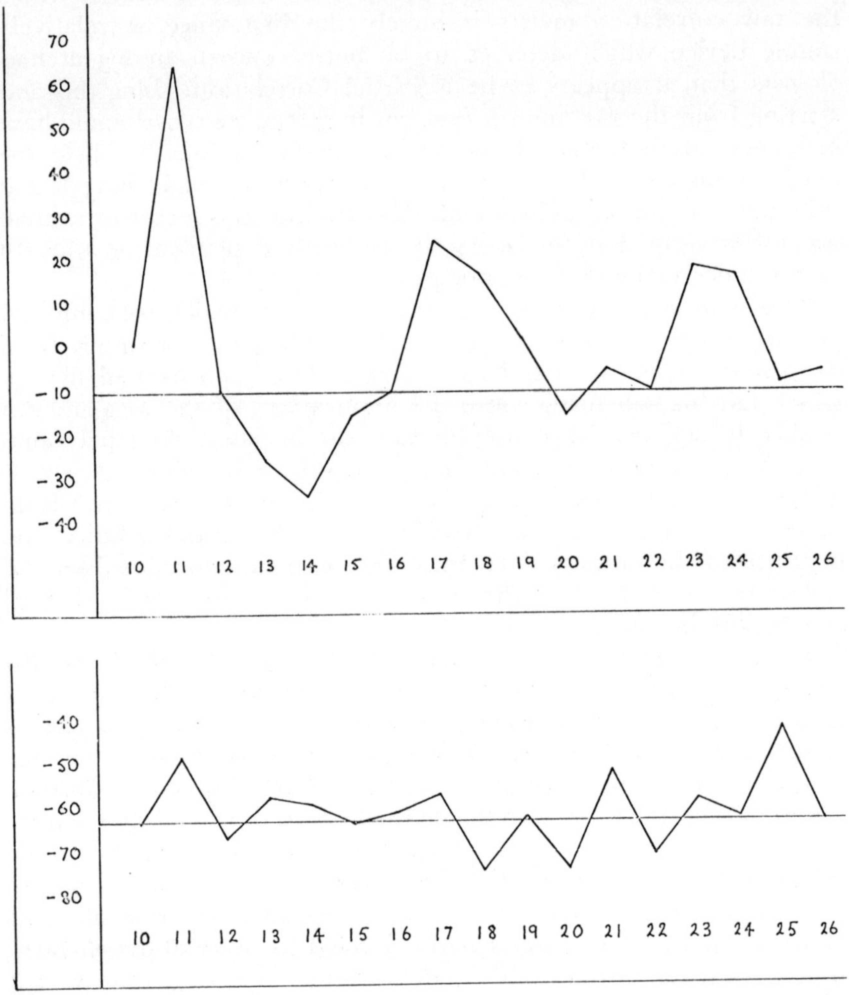

Figure 1 Partial Correlations at Ali Tappeh between Truncated Blades (Upper) and Crescents (lower) with time, as modified by holding successively variables 10 (Phoca), 11 (Gazella), 12 (Caprines), 13 (Equus), 14 (Sus), 15 (Bos), 16 (Cervus), 17 (Canis), 18 (Micromammalia), 19 (Subzebrinus), 20 (Jaminia), 21 (Pomatias), 22 (Succinea), 23 (Helicopsis crenimago), 24 (Euomphalia), 25 (Neritina), 26 (Parmacella). Note that Crescents have a significantly negative association with time (ie. grow rarer through time) and that this tendency is not cancelled by removing the effect of any one animal or molluscan association; as far as these are concerned they offer no explanation and the tendency appears to be a genuine chronological trend. Alternatively in the case of Truncated Blades an insignificant negative correlation is cancelled by factors 17, 18, 23 and 24, and actually rendered significantly positive by holding 11 (Gazella); the use of this tool for purposes other than Gazelle hunting was actually increasing and not decreasing. Data as for Table 1.

to a minor degree by either mammals or general ecology (as reflected by the snails). Variation in the frequencies of other tools on the contrary was almost wholly explained by concomitent variations in one or more animal species. This diversity of inter-dependence was a marked and unexpected pattern. Conversely particular species taken separately could be seen to evoke special classes of tools to the exclusion of others (see Table 1).

Species	**Tools**							
	Hunting						Processing	
	BONE POINTS	BACKED BLADES	TRUNCATED BLADES	MICRO-TRIANGLES	LUNATES	NOTCHES ETC.	EYED NEEDLES	END SCRAPERS
GAZELLA	.12	**.58**	**.55**	–	–	–	.41	.08
SUS	–	.30	**.57**	.19	–	–	.79	.24
MICRO-FAUNA	–	.13	.44	–	–	–	.46	.28
EQUUS	–	**.67**	**.56**	**.60**	.21	–	**.59**	–
CERVUS	.18	.43	.15	**.72**	.23	–	.12	–
BOS	**.73**	.34	.31	–	.02	.06	.25	–
CAPRA/OVIS	.25	–	–	–	.14	**.46**	–	–
CANIDAE	–	–	–	–	.04	**.44**	–	.18
PHOCA	–	–	–	–	–	.39	–	.23

Table 1. Ali Tappeh

Sorted matrix of Partial Correlations between separate Tool classes and mammalian species. Note significant affinity of Gazella, Sus, Equus (and possibly Micro-fauna) with Truncated Blades and Eyed Needles; Gazella, Equus (and possibly Cervus) with Backed Blades; Equus and Cervus with Micro-triangles; and Bos alone with Bone Points. A connection is possible between Notched blades (apparently for wood-working on shafts) and three small mammals, Capra, Canidae and Phoca. There is no specific affinity with End-scrapers, believed to have been used for general wood-working on the evidence of Micro-wear.

The *prima facie* implication of this situation certainly appears to be that both the data and the method of analysis are capable of isolating long term trends in the reactions of a society to its environmental needs. Clearly the former will for instance have greater diagnostic value for the identification in time and space of a particular on-going community, through characterization of the more stable features of its material culture.

In order to test this conclusion two other similar analyses were carried out on contrasting situations. The first was drawn from material from the Haua Fteah (see Table 2), since this was available for detailed study in our own collections. The complex chosen was that which I have termed Eastern Oranian (McBurney 1967:185). It lasted about 6,000 years and comes from a Mediterranean type environment as opposed to the near tropical jungle and plain of Ali Tappeh, although overlapping in time. Over this longer period also analysis of the correlation matrix between individual tools and animal species suggests that some are specifically associated to time, but others, the majority, show a close relation to individual animal species of economic significance.

Species	Hunting Tools						Other		Processing Tools					
	BACKED BLADES SMALL	TRUNCATED BLADES	TRIMMED BLADES	BACKED BLADES LARGE	REVERSED BACKED BLADES	MICRO-BURINS	RETOUCH WASTE	UNCLASSIFIED TOOLS	CORES	BURIN SPALLS	BURINS	END-SCRAPERS	FLAKE SCRAPERS	AWLS
ALCELAPHUS	.33	.12	.82	–	.28	–	.06	.52	.31	.33	.50	.51	.23	.50
BOS	.55	–	.28	–	.58	–	–	.39	.51	–	.43	.51	.51	.03
GAZELLA	–	.43	–	.62	–	.70	.73	–	–	.22	–	.07	–	–
AMMOTRAGUS	–	–	–	.65	–	.20	.15	–	–	.28	–	–	–	–
CAPRINES	–	.41	–	.75	–	.82	.79	–	–	.38	–	–	–	–
CANIS	.22	–	.06	.16	–	–	–	.26	–	.40	–	.54	–	–

Table 2. Haua Fteah (Oranian Layers only). Table of Partial Correlations between Mammalian fauna and artifact classes holding Time. Note similar associations between Gazella and Caprines and to some extent Ammotragus, while individually different associations occur with Alcelaphus, and Canis respectively. Data from McBurney, 1967.

A substantially longer sequence is offered by the admirably detailed data published by O.P. Chernysh from Molodova V in the Ukraine (Table 3, cf. Chernysh 1961; Ivanova and Chernysh 1965:197). Here once again the same pattern prevails, this time over a duration in the order of 20,000 years. Both Partial Correlation and Linkage methods (to be described in greater detail in a forthcoming paper in the *Proceedings of the Prehistoric Society*) reveal the diversity and specificity of the relations between different tools classes and differing economic resources.

Partial correlation matrices have also been produced for a fourth situation: that of the early Mousterian site of Cotte St. Brelade in Jersey in the Channel Islands (McBurney 1971). Here a sequence of 12 occupation layers occur in the loess infilling of a large coastal rock shelter. They were formed apparently by wind action during the rise in sea-level to the 8 m. Eemian strand line following the Rissian low level. Fauna is poorly preserved and only an approximate and indirect indication of elapsed time is available – in the order of 10,000 years. Nevertheless the consistent nature of the deposit is suggestive of a continuous and relatively unvarying rate of deposition, so that depth alone gives a first approximation of the relative age of the various horizons. On this basis we can reasonably relate the industrial changes to elapsed time on the one hand, and to variations in raw materials on the other. Virtually no flint or chert are available on the island at the present level of the sea.

Since there is independent reason to believe that the sea was rising relative to the land and thus submerging the sources of raw material during the period of occupation, we have the unusual circumstance of being able to study the reactions of a group responding to imposed changes in raw material.

The tool attributes compared to the four variables – % flint, quartz, greenstone and time – were deliberately chosen to be of a generalized nature for the initial experiment before embarking on the quantification of more detailed typological criteria. The selected mean dimensions of the various components were percentages and dimensions of cores, flakes, retouched tools, bifaces, etc. (It is planned to use Bordes' sub-groups at a later stage in the same fashion). What has emerged so far is that out of the 13 attributes studied most show significant and close affinity (positive or negative) for greenstone; a few are significantly related to quartz, but only one or two show any specific relation to time (negative or positive). This is in interesting contrast to the upper palaeolithic industries just referred to. Whereas in all of the latter there are clear signs of some features showing well defined and specific relation to time (or to put it differently a long term developmental trend), the Mousterian-like complex at St Brelade shows such tendencies to a far less marked degree. Indeed it is perfectly possible that such traces of trend as do appear at St Brelade may ultimately turn out to be largely or wholly

Species	Hunting Tools					Other	Processing Tools				
	BACKED BLADES	TRUNCATED BLADES	POINTS MISC.	NOTCHES ETC.	MICRO-GRAVETTES	RETOUCHED BLADES	BURINS	END-SCRAPERS	COMPOSITES	AWLS	CORE-SCRAPERS
MAMMOTH	—	—	—	—	.03	—	**.78**	—	.27	—	—
ELK	—	—	—	—	—	—	**.62**	—	—	.02	.23
REINDEER	—	—	—	—	—	.14	**.71**	—	.25	—	**.50**
RHINOCEROS	.47	**.62**	**.58**	**.77**	—	—	—	—	—	.24	—
BISON	.29	.30	.42	**.50**	—	—	—	—	.26	—	—
WILD OX	.47	.23	.01	.15	—	—	—	.09	—	—	—
HORSE	**.66**	**.61**	**.50**	**.57**	.15	.07	—	**.68**	—	.22	—
DEER	.35	.23	.08	.25	.25	—	—	.19	—	**.73**	—
WOLF	.02	.15	—	—	.35	—	.19	—	.09	**.65**	—
HARE	—	—	—	—	.39	—	.24	—	.31	.23	.03
BIRD	.38	—	—	—	**.86**	—	.09	.20	—	**.54**	—
FOX	.25	—	—	—	**.76**	—	—	**.60**	.05	—	—
UNIDENTIFIED (A)	.45	—	—	—	**.93**	—	—	**.52**	—	.10	—

Table 3. Molodova V (Ukraine)
Sorted matrix of Partial Correlation coefficients relating animal species to tools holding time. Extensive use of ivory and antler at this site may be compared to high coefficient between burins and Mammoth, Elk and Reindeer, and absence of correlation with remaining large mammalia. Note a similar degree of specificity in Hunting Equipment for the latter (mainly non-herding) species. Small species are characterised by notably higher affinity for micro-gravettes. Data from O.P. Chernysh (1961).

related to immediate hunting or other exigencies rather than time.

Whether this proves to be so or not it is certainly an interesting field for enquiry to investigate different types of what one might call 'cultural growth-potential' as opposed to *ad hoc* reactions at these two very different stages in human development.

In conclusion, what I would like to claim for our current programme at Cambridge is briefly this. It is based on a dynamic rather than a static concept of culture itself, and hence of the material output of culture with which the archaeologist has to deal. The difference in behaviour between independent societies whether conceived in theory or studied empirically from their products, is not the difference between random oscillations about a static target or template but rather between harmonic systems operating in response to differing principles. It is these characteristic patterns of response, rather than fixed averages as heretofore, which should form the basis of comparison.

One practical point already seems to emerge and affects in particular deductions drawn from so-called 'seriation patterns'. It has been widely claimed in the last few years that these afford a basis for re-assembling a series of otherwise undated artifacts (or groups of artifacts) in their original time sequence. It has also been suggested that for the purposes of seriation *all* characteristics are of equal value. As far as palaeolithic and mesolithic assemblages are concerned, the results just described suggest that this can be a seriously misleading assumption. As far as I know ours is the first attempt to submit it to direct experimental test.

Nevertheless it should be pointed out to enthusiastic functionalists that although time trends are rarer than has sometimes been supposed, there *is* positive evidence of their existence and that of a kind that cannot easily be ignored.

While I would not wish to claim too much for our initial results, I should nonetheless like to conclude this brief exposition with a plea for more, and more carefully structured analyses of actual data, and fewer purely polemical discussions such as have been appearing recently in some of our scholarly journals.

REFERENCES

Chernysh, A.P. (1961) *The Palaeolithic site of Molodova V* (in Ukrainian). Kiev.

Ivanova, I.K. and Chernysh, A.P. (1965) The palaeolithic site of Molodova V on the Middle Dnestr. *Quaternaria* 7.

McBurney, C.B.M. (1967) *The Haua Fteah (Cyrenaica) and the Stone Age of the S.E. Mediterranean.* Cambridge, University Press.

McBurney, C.B.M. (1968) The cave of Ali Tappeh and the Epi-Palaeolithic of Iran. *Proceedings of the Prehistoric Society* 23.

McBurney, C.B.M. (1971) Preliminary report on the excavations at the Cave of Cotte de St Brelade, Jersey. *Proceedings of the Prehistoric Society* (in press).

Renfrew, C. (1970) New configurations in Old World archaeology. *World Archaeology* 2, 2.

JAMES R. SACKETT

Style, function and artifact variability in palaeolithic assemblages

The debate being conducted by palaeolithic archaeologists today over the relative roles of tradition and activity in assemblage variability parallels in many respects the classic nature-nurture debate among biologists concerning human variability. Like the early literature of this more famous controversy, our present efforts may in future perspective seem hasty, overschematic, and indeed naive. This is probably inevitable, since the question of where our current taxonomies reflect differences of historical tradition and where they do not is itself a crude one in comparison to the variety of subtler problems that must one day be raised if we are to comprehend the cultural reality which lies behind our assemblages. Nonetheless, it is precisely this kind of amphibian question that is needed to help conduct palaeolithic research over the transition from one paradigm to the next. For it allows us to shift our concern from the traditional problem of ordering variability to the more novel one of interpreting it, without simultaneously having to give up either the empirical emphases of current research or, at least for the time being, the established taxonomies with which we are familiar.

Currently the debate focuses upon the middle palaeolithic or Mousterian complex as it is defined by François Bordes. The argument is in essence whether the four assemblage types making up this complex represent four historically distinct cultural traditions or whether, regardless of what temporal or geographic clustering may also be involved, they instead represent recurring activity-sensitive expressions taken by a single tradition. It is hard to conceive of a more ideally clear-cut problem.

Nevertheless, without attempting to downgrade either the intrinsic importance of this debate or the value of the contributions made by its protagonists, it should be pointed out that this controversy makes up only a small part of the general question. Presumably the basic issues are the same whenever the similarities and differences of *any* two or more artifact assemblages are compared, and there is consequently as much profit in exploring variability in the areas where agreement reigns as in those where we disagree. Why, in other words, though they differ over the Mousterian, do the bulk of our colleagues agree that Magdalenian and Solutrean assemblages in the Perigord belong to distinct regional traditions, that there is historic continuity between the African Acheulian and the Fauresmith, and that the relationship between the European Acheulian and the Clactonian remains problematic? It is only by viewing the question in this broader perspective that it will become possible to distinguish between the assemblage variability issues that are peculiar to specific blocks of data and specific research strategies and those that are truly basic to all palaeolithic data and to archaeological method and theory in general.

There exists at present no general model or conceptual framework which allows us to see the question with such clarity, naked and unencumbered with the trappings of any specific culture-historical problem. In part the absence of a model applicable to the general case is simply an indication that we have been too occupied with our own parochial affairs to undertake the monumental synthesis this would require. Upon reflection, however, most of us would probably admit that we also hesitate because the conceptual tools available to us are themselves inadequate to the job. The traditional notions used in defining and comparing assemblages often seem too imprecise or (at least as they are currently understood) too ambiguous to meet the special issues raised by the variability question. At the same time, the new notions which have been introduced in debating variability in specific archaeological cases are as often not easily translated to the level of abstraction the general case requires. In fact, the task involved in simultaneously sharpening up traditional notions and generalizing new ones is in its totality so great that it will probably be wisest to explore in piecemeal fashion several of the manifold components that will ultimately combine to make up our general model before attempting to construct the model itself.

Now, the most basic component of all comprises archaeological systematics and taxonomy, particularly as these find expression in artifact typology. The fundamental importance of this component stems from the fact that it furnishes the systems of measurement by means of which variability is translated into standardized units and thereby made amenable to systematic description and analysis. It is then artifact typology which mediates between the prehistorian and the archaeological record, choosing those aspects of its variability that are to be realized for purposes of scientific enquiry from the seemingly infinite array of those which actually exist in it.

Consideration of this component logically calls for examination of three distinct questions: (1) what do the notions of tradition and activity really mean when applied to artifact typology; (2) how do we determine if a given typology is making activity-sensitive or tradition-sensitive discriminations in variability; and (3) what new concepts and analytic procedures might aid the design of more refined and more informative classifications than those now available in making such discriminations? As a tentative beginning to a subsequent more detailed examination of artifact typology along these lines, the remainder of these pages will be devoted to observations concerning the first of these questions.

The argument to follow entails a rather specific conception of the two units archaeological taxonomists universally employ in ordering variability, the *artifact* and the *assemblage.* While the notion of artifact logically embraces any concrete manifestation of human behaviour, including 'features' like hearths or structures and 'palaeo-ecological' data like butchered animal bones, it will lend focus to the discussion to restrict the term to its conventional meaning of portable objects, in particular, stone and bone tools. A broad spectrum of culturally conditioned activities presumably invested the conception, manufacture, and use of any given artifact, and artifacts are of course studied precisely because the patterns of formal attributes they exhibit are believed to reflect these activities. An assemblage, on the other hand, is a sample of artifacts drawn from a specific space-time locus that is believed to delimit a meaningful complex of such activities. This logically might range in scope from a single locality within a site, such as the boundaries of a house or butchering area, to a major block of space and time (e.g., the stone age of Australia). However, here it will prove convenient to limit the notion of assemblage to its most conventional form, that is, an artifact sample drawn from a unique site unit (most often a stratum) which presumably refers to the occupation of a specific prehistoric social group.

Archaeological systematics is founded upon the perfect complimentariness of these two units: artifacts provide the formal content of assemblages, while assemblages in turn furnish the space-time contexts without which artifacts could not be viewed in culturally meaningful terms. It follows that all questions of prehistoric taxonomy may be referred to but two provinces, the classification of artifacts and the classification of assemblages. Since the first exclusively entails grouping artifacts by one means or another into classes, it is called *artifact typology.* The second, on the other hand, involves the two quite different operations of handling assemblages as discrete entities (as in regional sequences and space-time grids) and of grouping them into typological classes (e.g. 'Magdalenian V', 'hunting camp', etc.). As a consequence, this province deserves the more general name of *assemblage ordering.*

Armed with these definitions, we are now ready to attempt to define in explicit terms how we as journeyman archaeologists intuitively employ the notions of tradition and activity in artifact typology. Any artifact can be regarded from two contrasting, but fully complementary, points of view. First, we can regard it in terms of its role and meaning in the immediate cultural setting in which we find it. Here then our interest concerns 'what was going on', that is, the artifact itself as it was manufactured and in turn used among a given group of people. Second, we can view the artifact not for its own sake but rather as an indicator of the historic or 'genetic' framework of its cultural setting, in other words the network of relations which allied our given group of people with other such groups and over which the culturally conditioned ideas and practices it shared with them were transmitted. When conceptualized as a distinctive block of traits occupying a definable segment of space and time this framework is called a *cultural tradition* (although alternate terms ranging from 'phylum' or 'culture' to 'sub-tradition' and 'facies' are often substituted according to the relative temporal and geographic magnitude involved and the degree of historical independence it bears in relation to other recognized traditions). It should be noted that the term tradition may also be used in the generic sense in referring to any historico-genetic context; thus, to say that parrot-beaked burins are diagnostic of Final Magdalenian times in the Perigord is to make a statement about tradition.

It is logically convenient to view these two contrasting perspectives, artifact in operation vs. artifact as indicator of cultural tradition, as properties or dimensions of our phenomena themselves. Henceforth, I shall refer to the first as the *functional mode* of an artifact, and the second as its *stylistic mode*. These modes logically extend to artifact variability as well and it is therefore quite valid to refer to the 'functional' or 'stylistic' modes of individual formal attributes of artifacts.

Care must be taken not to let narrower, if more familiar, meanings of these terms encroach upon the very broad sense I give them here. Thus, aside from the fact that it concerns what was going on *per se* in a specific archaeological context, rather than the historico-genetic significance of what was going on, my use of the term function implies no necessary similarity in outlook or approach to any specific 'functional' school of interpretation in anthropology or archaeology. Equally important, it does not solely imply the realm of techno-economics. It is true that, due both to the ecological orientation of current thinking and the fact that most empirical data from the palaeolithic more or less directly reflects utilitarian tasks, our considerations tend to emphasize this realm. However, not all artifacts were designed primarily to meet techno-economic ends, nor, as Ralph Linton and Lauriston Sharp remind us, are social and ideological factors likely to have failed to leave their imprint upon any manufactured thing. In short, any statement about how an artifact was made, the various ways in which it was used, the meaning it may have had to its owners, and the manner in which it indirectly reflects any other activities belonging to the on-going cultural situation in which it served, is here considered to be a functional statement.

The concept of style has proved to be particularly elusive to archaeologists. The term has been applied variously to patterns of artifact variation which (1) are real but which are simultaneously so subtle in expression and so subjective in comprehension as to defy objective and systematic definition; (2) which constitute the residue of patterning that is left over once techno-economically determined patterns have been accounted for; and/or (3) which, consciously or not, are believed to have symbolized social distinctions between and within prehistoric human groups. The recognition of style analytically may in practice entail consideration of all of these partially overlapping notions. Again, however, our meaning here is much more comprehensive, as style is viewed as an aspect of every pattern visible in any archaeological situation. It is based upon the notion that there are usually alternative means of achieving the same end, that the specific expression any given artifact assumes results in a sense from a choice made among several equally valid and feasible options, and that the choice made in any given cultural situation is determined by its historico-genetic setting. It is the overall coherence and congruence to such choices among historically related groups which allows us to distinguish and define traditions, even when no significant functional differences may be apparent between them. Thus any statement which concerns the manner in which artifact variability is symptomatic of tradition is by definition a stylistic statement.

The preceding may be clarified by reference to Fig. 1. This depicts the claw hammer with which my youngest son has been trying to dismantle a bicycle just outside the room where I am attempting to concentrate. Viewed in the functional mode, the most obvious property of this item of equipment is its suitability for serving the utilitarian ends of driving and drawing nails and, in a broader sense, for hammering in general. But it also functionally reflects in a secondary manner a variety of other activities typical of the cultural milieu in which it was made and used, ranging from the techno-economic (iron smelting and forging), through the social (the craft specialization which necessarily accompanies industrialized metallurgy), to the ideological (the aesthetic and tactile qualities it holds for us, and, especially important to my son, the manly roles attached to it). It takes considerable knowledge of our culture and the specific contexts in which hammerstones are found to infer many such activities, but they are there nevertheless. At the same time, its stylistic mode is equally prominent and richly endowed. In fact, depending upon the degree of detail with which it is regarded, this hammer gives evidences of being a product of any number of historico-genetic contexts along a progressively narrowing scale of space-time loci extending from Western Civilization during the past century to the Estwing Manufacturing Company of Rockford,

Illinois, during the past decade.

Implicit in the above are two additional points that deserve mention. First, the individual formal attributes used to describe and define artifactual variability are themselves significant in both the functional and stylistic modes. The distinctive handle of the Fig. 1 hammer, for instance, is covered by a rubber sleeve whose texture and punctated surface provide a firm grip for the implement. Viewed in this sense its attributes clearly have functional significance. However, reference to a broad array of hammers such as that sample in Fig. 2 reveals that this functional role can be satisfied as well by a handle of similar form whose exterior is made of laminated leather (b); by a fibreglass, metal, or wooden handle bearing fluting (e), knobs, or corrugations; or, as is most common, simply by a plain wooden handle whose profile, cross-section, and surface finish fall within certain broadly prescribed limits (c and d). In the sense that they constitute more or less equally valid ways of meeting the same functional end these are to be considered stylistic differences. And, when viewed in this context, the attributes of the handle of our first hammer (a) constitute but one of these functionally isomorphic options and hence are also to be considered stylistically significant. Consideration of Fig. 2 will reveal that stylistic and functional dualism is equally apparent among attributes of hammer heads.

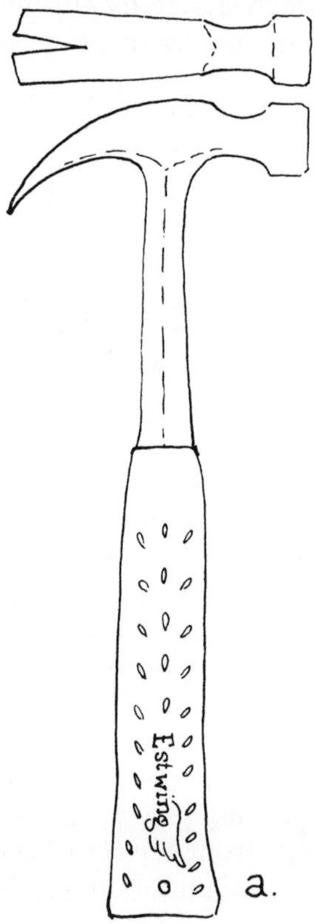

Figure 1

a.

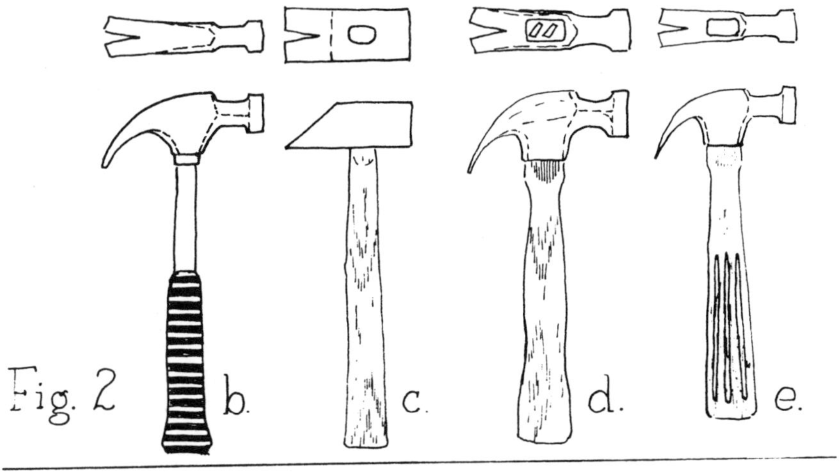

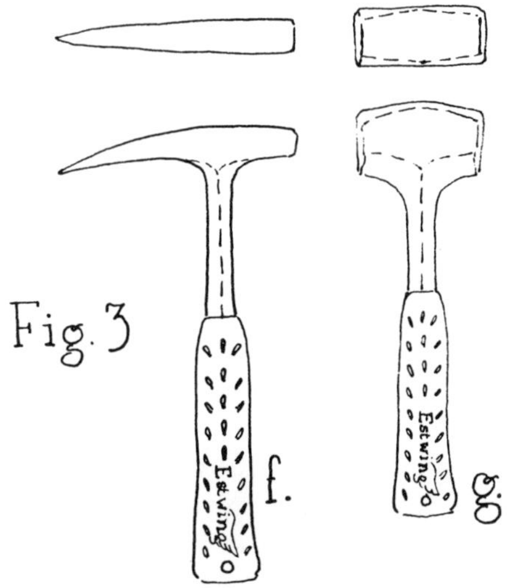

Figures 1 to 3 Variability in hammers of the 20th century A.D. a. Estwing; b. True Temper; c. Manufrance; d. American Special; e. Plumb; f. Estwing (geologist's pick); g. Estwing (sledge).

This last comment raises the second point, which is that any culturally meaningful patterns that appear in artifact variability can usually be seen redundantly expressed by several different attributes. Often this means no more than that there are alternate ways of giving attributal definition to any pattern. Thus the features 'buskoid' and 'polyhedric asymmetric dihedral' might easily refer to the same burin, and one man's 'fan-shaped scraper' could be another's 'endscraper on a blank with converging profile'. But often the redundancy does involve what clearly must be regarded as distinct formal expressions. These for obvious reasons most frequently occur in the stylistic mode. For example, the historico-genetic distinctiveness of the Fig. 1 hammer is expressed in such disparate ways as the shape of its head, its ridged shank, and the pattern in which the rubber grip is punctated, while not only the head form but also the contour of the handle and the fact that the head is painted green distinguish the French hammer (c) from the rest illustrated in Fig. 2.

Now let us explore briefly how these notions apply to artifact typology and whether they help explain some of the patterns and problems that arise in making inter-assemblage comparisons of artifact variability. An artifact type may be defined by considering a group of artifacts which is considered in some sense culturally meaningful and whose members share in common a distinctive cluster of formal attributes. Any given type, like any individual formal attribute, is inherently dualistic and, depending upon how it is viewed, can present either a functional or a stylistic aspect. For example, a split-base bone point can be viewed on the one hand as a functioning part of a missile system or, on the other, as a diagnostic of Stage I of the Aurignacian cultural tradition. In the same manner, cordiform hand-axes and Noailles burins may be regarded as either utilitarian implements or as symptomatic *fossiles* of cultural tradition (respectively, Mousterian of Acheulian Tradition and Perigordian Vc). There is logically a functional aspect to even the least utilitarian artifact types; the heavily engraved *baton de commandement*, for example, may have served symbolically as a badge of status or as an item of ritual equipment. And, by the same token even the most broadly defined utilitarian category may still be viewed in the stylistic mode. To take an extreme example, the artifact class 'stone hunting equipment' is historico-genetically restricted to pre-industrialized societies.

However, when actually employed in inter-assemblage comparisons of artifactual variability, a given tool type can assume the significance of only one of its modes at a given time. As in the case of the attribute, which of the two modes is expressed depends upon the context in which the type is regarded. Context here of course occupies the realm of assemblage ordering and is defined by the nature of the taxonomic relations which exist among the assemblages whose collective variability is being analyzed. This is easily illustrated by reference to the split-base bone point noted above. When the context in which it is viewed consists uniquely of Aurignacian I assemblages, this tool type is usually considered to mark a functionally significant segment of artifactual variation. On the other hand, its mode usually shifts when the context expands to include additional assemblages drawn from the different temporal stages of the Aurignacian development. This is because the collective variability now under consideration incorporates other bone point types, such as lozenge-shaped forms with flattened and oval sections (diagnostic of Aurignacian IV). These are known stratigraphically to have been successive temporal replacements for the split-base form and they are consequently regarded as functionally isomorphic variations of the single typological theme 'bone projectile point'. When viewed against the background of variation described by these other types the split-base form must therefore assume the stylistic mode.

There remains the question of why a type can assume but one mode at a time. The answer presumably lies in the fact that the attributes used to define it can themselves assume but one mode at a time and that, in order to form a meaningful type cluster, they must all agree in the mode they adopt in any given context. This last requirement is not as difficult to achieve as it may seem, since only a very small number of the potentially significant attributes possessed by artifacts ever enter into a single type cluster. Inherent in this fact, by the way, is the solution to the problem of how both modes of a given artifact may be employed in the same context when any single type to which it is assigned can by definition express only one. It simply entails constructing a second type based upon a cluster chosen from those of the remaining attributes which assume the contrary mode in that context. In *manifold typology* of this sort the two types to which a given artifact is assigned will necessarily be cross-cutting categories whose membership will tend to differ markedly. For example, were the hammer illustrated in Fig. 1 grouped with those in Fig. 2 to make a functionally significant type, it would in turn be logical to group it with the items shown in Fig. 3 to form a type stylistically significant in the same context. The fact that these items consist of a geologist's pick and a hand sledge is here irrelevant, since our interest in this case lies solely in the manner in which attributes indicate historico-genetic relations.

It is of course one thing to talk of modern hammers or even of bone Aurignacian points and quite another to explain the problems that are generated by the application of a specific artifact typology to a specific field of inter-assemblage variability. The functional and stylistic aspects of patterning remain unclear in most areas of formal variation codified in the established typologies. And it is highly unlikely that any of them in the ensemble consistently makes stylistic or functional discriminations in any given context. Moreover, because they are unlikely to have been defined in terms of a single taxonomic frame of reference, the artifact categories of the same typology whose modes do happen to agree in one context may still disagree in another. But in any case, it seems obvious that debates over assemblage variability can be viewed as disagreements about the modal significance of typological variation. I hope the preceding discussion suggests that, when redefined in such terms, they may at least be given more clear-cut theoretical formulation than they currently enjoy.

Section 4: Change in population density, subsistence and land use

PAUL M. DOLUKHANOV

The neolithization of Europe: a chronological and ecological approach

Numerous palaeogeographical data secured during the last decades enable us now to carry out reliable reconstructions of the natural environment of prehistoric settlements. At the same time the accumulation of radiocarbon dates (with deviations in C-14 content taken into account) makes questions of time relationships much clearer than ever before.

As a theoretical basis for a complex ecological approach toward prehistoric studies the principles of General Systems theory (L. von Bertalanffy 1956; Ross Ashby 1955; Blauberg *et al.* 1970) may be successfully used.

In the Soviet Union the principles of systems theory are being successfully applied to the study of landscapes and biocoenoses (Grigor'ev 1954; Sukačev 1964; Aleksandrova 1966; Kurkin 1970). In recent years systems theory has been successfully used in the social sciences also (Anabeghian *et al.* 1970).

In prehistoric studies attempts to interpret economic processes in terms of ecosystems were initiated by J.G.D. Clark (1952). The notion of ecosystem deprived of its original deterministic character proved to be highly fruitful in human geography and in biology (Stoddart 1967).

In terms of systems theory, the landscape sphere and human society may be regarded as a complex dynamic system ('eco-sociosystem') elements of which are being subjected to feedback regulation. The existence of 'an intercommunicating network of attributes or entities forming a complex whole' (Clarke 1968:43) is one of the principal features of a system. Inside the ecosystem such entities as climate, vegetation and fauna are of vital importance. Inside the sociosphere, the 'intercommunicating network' is constituted by such entities as economic structure and by productive forces, including material culture and demographic structure.

A close study of ecological and archaeological data supported by a solid chronology makes it possible to build up a number of eco-social models and to follow up their evolution in time and space.

The first state of the eco-social system considered here corresponds to the upper palaeolithic, which in geological terms is equivalent to the last major Upper Pleistocene glaciation. According to the most reliable reconstructions, the vegetational cover during the maximum phase of the last glaciation 'had no direct analogies in the present day vegetation' (Gričuk, 1965). In the east European plain the following vegetational zones may be distinguished from north to south: zone of periglacial vegetation; light birch and larch forests; periglacial open woodland; periglacial steppes (Gričuk 1969). During the same period, periglacial vegetation of more oceanic character prevailed in western Europe.

The periglacial landscapes contained a distinctive fauna which included large herd animals (the so-called mammoth complex). The economy of the upper palaeolithic tribes dispersed in the periglacial area was based on 'the special hunting of migratory herd animals' (S.R. Binford 1970). A comparatively high biomass at the disposal of the upper palaeolithic tribesmen caused a markedly high population density and the elaboration of an advanced blade technique. Inside the periglacial area it is possible to distinguish several sub-zones characterized by the different orientations of specialized hunting.

The above-described state of the eco-social system underwent a change, due to the profound shift in the landscape sphere, at about 10,000 years B.P. This shift, caused by the last maximum of solar radiation reaching the earth's surface (Milankovitch 1938; van Woerkom 1953), is being established throughout the world (Khotinsky 1971; Dansgaard *et al.* 1970; Fig. 1).

Inside the ecological system the most important changes manifested themselves in 1) displacement of the periglacial vegetation by the post-glacial forests and steppes and 2) extinction or disintegration of the periglacial mammoth complex and formation of the Holocene fauna, consisting of forest and steppe non-herd animals of much smaller size.

The economy of the mesolithic tribes, spread in forests and steppes of early post-glacial Europe, was based on the hunting of comparatively small Holocene game and on exploitation of aquatic resources. S.N. Bibikov (1950) characterizes this economic structure as 'a crisis of hunting economy'. Deficiency in the biomass as compared to the upper palaeolithic period provoked dynamic responses in the demographic structure: a demographic recession on the one hand, together with the spread of mesolithic hunters and fishers into the ice-freed areas of the extreme north. Changes inside the ecological system and in the economic structure caused corresponding changes in the material culture: in the first place in the forms of tools. Two main provinces may be distinguished inside mesolithic Europe: microlithic (both non-geometric and geometric) zones and axe-zones (these zones partly overlap). These provinces are closely connected with landscape features and structures of eco-

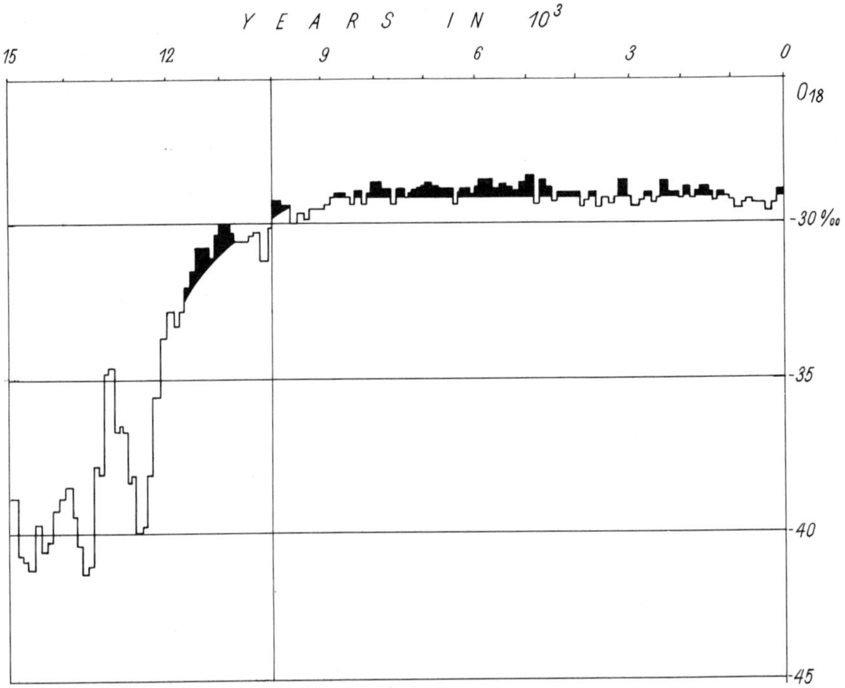

Figure 1 Palaeoclimatic record, Camp Century, Greenland. Oxygen isotope ratios versus calculated age. (*After* Dansgaard *et al.* 1970).

nomic pattern. Thus the axe-zone of northern and eastern Europe nearly coincides with the pine and birch forests area and the distribution of elk in the Pre-Boreal and Boreal periods.

The change in the ecosystem in the specific conditions prevailing in the Near East led to the appearance of a food-producing economy. In words of V.M. Masson (1971:133): 'the appearance of food-production was caused both by environmental conditions and by the factors within human society.' With the latter set of factors one should classify change in demographic structure as postulated by L.R. Binford (1968:334): incipient cultivation in 'tension zones where less sedentary populations are being moved in on by daughter groups from more sedentary populations'. The piedmont of the Zagros-Taurus mountain belt played the role of the 'tension zone' in the Near East. The ecological shift now firmly confirmed for the Zagros piedmont (a change from the periglacial vegetation to an oak-pistachio savanna after 11,000 years B.P.; Wright 1968), and the variety of domesticable cereals and animals, were among environmental factors which caused incipient food-production in this area as early as 10,000-9,000 years ago.

Demographic processes which take place when new economic structures are being introduced (in our case food-producing) may be regarded as processes of populating previously unoccupied ecological niches. As Birdsell (1957) has shown, the growth curve reflecting the intrinsic rate of the population in such cases is logistic in general form (Fig. 2). Birdsell has equally shown that when any

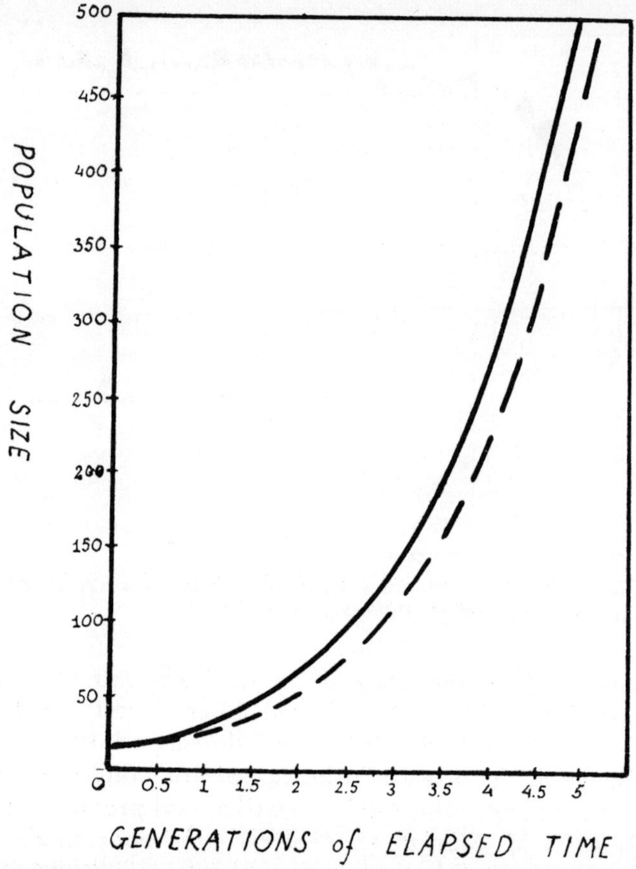

Figure 2 Intrinsic rate of population increase for Pitcairn and Bass Strait Islanders. (*After* Birdsell 1957).

given habitat is saturated to its carrying capacity the process of budding-off prevails. As follows from palaeogeographical investigations, the budding-off of the surplus population always proceeds into ecological niches closest (but not identical) in their ecological characteristic to the initial habitat. Probably this process was at least partly responsible for the spread of the farming economy across the plain of the Near East from 9,000 to 7,000 years B.P. At the same time the set of ecological factors (abundance of hunting resources) can explain the long survival of 'islands' of hunting economy (Tell Mureybit).

Numerous radiocarbon dates and palaeogeographical data make it possible to follow up the process of neolithisation in Europe in detail.

The spread of the farming economy in south-east Europe took place between 9,000 and 7,000 B.P., which corresponds to the first wave of the Holocene climatic optimum established in Eurasia (Khotinsky 1971). The vast territories of southeast Europe were covered by that time with light broad-leaved forests similar enough in their ecological characteristics to those of the Near Eastern plains (Higgs *et al.* 1967; Pop 1961; Boscaiu 1971) (Fig. 3).

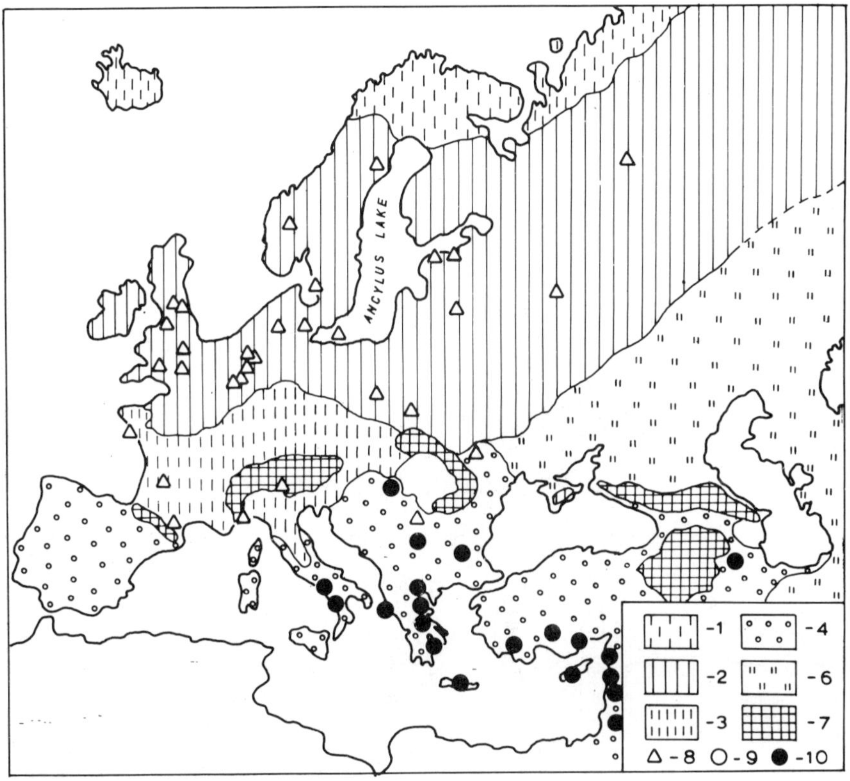

Figure 3 Europe 8000-7000 B.P. showing radiocarbon dated sites within this period.
1, tundra; 2, pine and birch forest; 3, mixed oak-pine-birch forest; 4, broad-leaved forest; 6, steppe and desert; 7, mountain vegetation; 8, mesolithic sites; 9, sites of 'forest' neolithic (hunting and fishing economy); 10, sites of neolithic with farming economy.

The oldest neolithic area in Europe includes most of the Balkan peninsula, the lower Danube and the northwestern Pontic area. This zone played a decisive role in the process of European neolithisation. The essence of this process lies in the evolution of economic and demographic structures in the eco-social system: overpopulation of the initial neolithic zone following the introduction of new economic structure.

The global warming of climate, the Altithermal, corresponding to the Atlantic period in the Blytte-Sernander scheme, was of vital importance for the neolithization process. In the initial phase of the Atlantic period there took place the comparatively rapid spread of the Linienbandkeramik settlements in the loess plain of Europe, and those of impresso pottery in the western Mediterranean (7,000-6,000 B.P.). Both these neolithic waves were genetically connected either with the early Balkan neolithic or with the neolithic of the eastern Mediterranean (Quitta 1962; 1964; 1971) (Fig. 4).

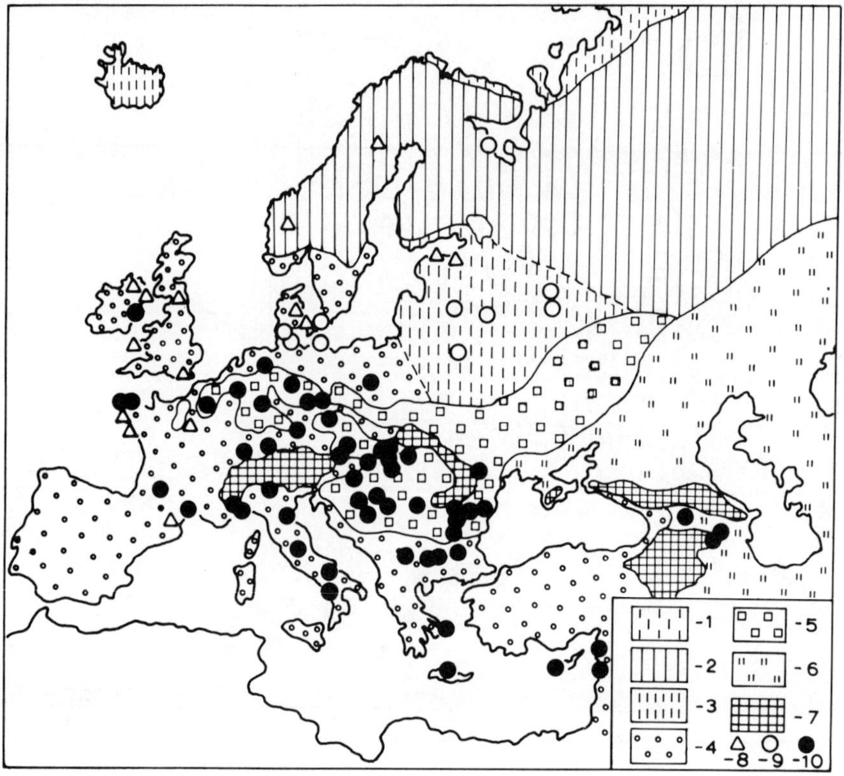

Figure 4 Europe 6000-5500 B.P., showing radiocarbon dated sites within this period.
1, tundra; 2, pine and birch forest; 3, mixed oak-pine-birch forest; 4, broad-leaved forest; 5, open woodland on loess soils; 6, steppe and desert; 7, mountain vegetation; 8, mesolithic sites; 9, sites of 'forest' neolithic (hunting and fishing economy); 10, sites of neolithic with farming economy.

As follows from the observations made by R. Tringham (1968) and B. Gramsch (1971) mesolithic hunters/fishers and neolithic farmers had a quite different settlement pattern. Mesolithic camp sites were situated in most cases on sand dunes or on light soils (leichte Böden) whereas early neolithic settlements were established on fertile loessic soils or in morainic areas. The first areas were covered in the Atlantic period with pine forests; open mixed oak forests prevailed in the areas of neolithic settlement (Gramsch 1971). This means that the neolithization process in central and western Europe may be interpreted as the population of an unoccupied ecological niche.

The genesis of 'forest neolithic' or 'subneolithic' cultures in eastern Europe may be also linked up with the Balkan early neolithic. The vast territories of eastern Europe were covered in the Atlantic period with pine and birch forests, with an admixture of broad-leaved species in the north, and with pine or broad-leaved forest-steppe vegetation in the south (Neustadt 1957; Artyusenko 1970). These ecotopes contained large quantities of comparatively large animals: elk (in the first place), red deer, bear, wild boar etc. (Fig. 5). This ecological niche throughout the Atlantic and Sub-Boreal

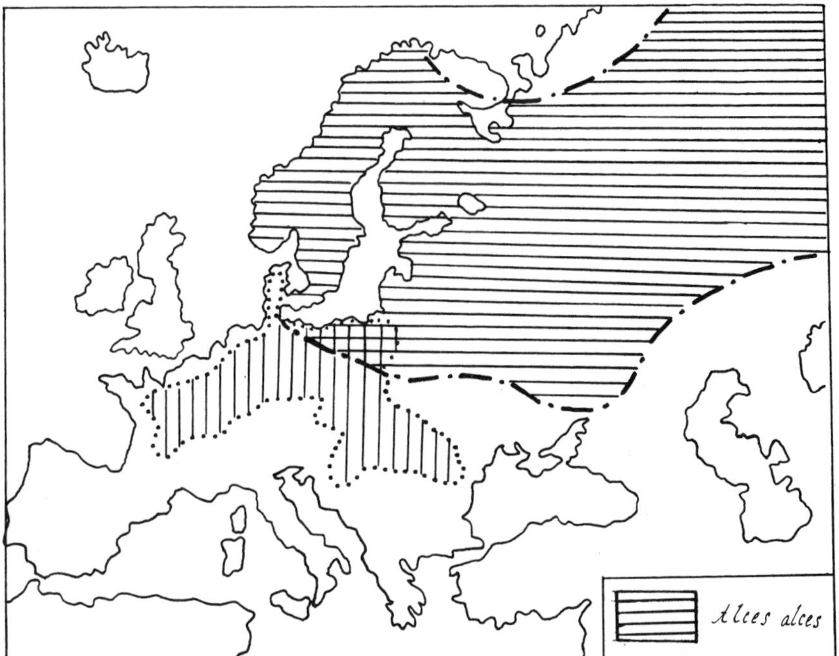

Figure 5 The distribution of Elk (*Alces*) and Red Deer in the Holocene.

period was rich enough in natural resources to provide a substantial basis for mesolithic forms of economy (hunting, fishing, food-gathering). It seems logical to suggest that a part of the surplus population was budding off from the initial neolithic zones into these ecological niches, rich in natural resources. This population was gradually losing its agricultural habits and was acquiring a mesolithic way of life as the one most adapted to the local ecological conditions. Thus hunting provided the bulk of food to the Bug-Dnestr culture settlers, who were genetically connected with the Balkan neolithic (Danilenko 1969). Hunting was the basis of the economy of the Dnepr-Donets culture in the Ukraine (Telegin 1968). At the same time a vast area of stock-breeding cultures was forming in the east Pontic steppes.

An intensive outflow of surplus population from the neolithised zones into the areas which were productive in terms of a hunting/fishing economy took place in the 4th millennium B.C. An outflow of the surplus population from the Linienbandkeramik area northwards may explain the appearance of Ertebölle-Litzow culture settlements on the south Baltic shores. B. Gramsch (1971) writes: 'die Keramikfertigung in der Ertebölle-Ellerbekkultur . . . konnte auf den Kontakten zu donauländischen Gruppen Mitteleuropas beruhen'.

Basically similar processes can be reconstructed for the territories of eastern Europe. In the course of the 4th millennium B.C. a more or less homogenous ethnic group, which used conical vessels covered with rows of comb impressions, spread over vast territories of the western part of the East European plain. This type of pottery may be genetically connected with the Bug-Dnestr ware (Danilenko 1969). Two camp-sites belonging to this oldest phase of the east European 'forest neolithic' are now dated by C-14, namely, Osa in the Eastern Latvia (Zagorskis 1967) with three dates between 6040 and 5630 B.P., and Zacen'e in Central Byelorussia (Černyavski 1971): 5450 ± 70 B.P. On the basis of these data the initial spread of the 'forest neolithic' comb decorated pottery may be dated to the first half of the 4th millennium B.C.

Simultaneously, in the central districts of the U.S.S.R., there appear the earliest camp-sites of the pit-and-comb pottery culture. Two C-14 dates not at our disposal make this suggestion valid: that of the Ivanovskoye III camp-site in the Yaroslavl' oblast' 5730 ± 120 B.P. (Neustadt *et al.* 1969) – and that of Zarečʼye in the Moscow oblast' (excavations by V.A. Raušenbach, unpublished) – 5670 ± 50 B.P.(Fig. 6, 7).

The economy of the early 'forest' neolithic was largely the same as in the mesolithic, with hunting of the Holocene fauna (elk, red deer, bear, wild boar) (Fig. 8), and of sea animals, and intensive fishing and food collecting. The settlement pattern is nearly always the same as that of the mesolithic settlements. The similarity of the ecological factors and economic pattern leads to the similarity in the material culture: the tool kit of the early 'forest' neolithic is nearly the same as that of the local mesolithic. This similarity is often quoted as 'a proof' of the local origin of the 'forest' neolithic.

Modern population genetics may provide a necessary basis for a clearer understanding of such processes as the formation of cultural units. As we have tried to show, the spread of bearers of the new economic structure may be interpreted as resulting in the population

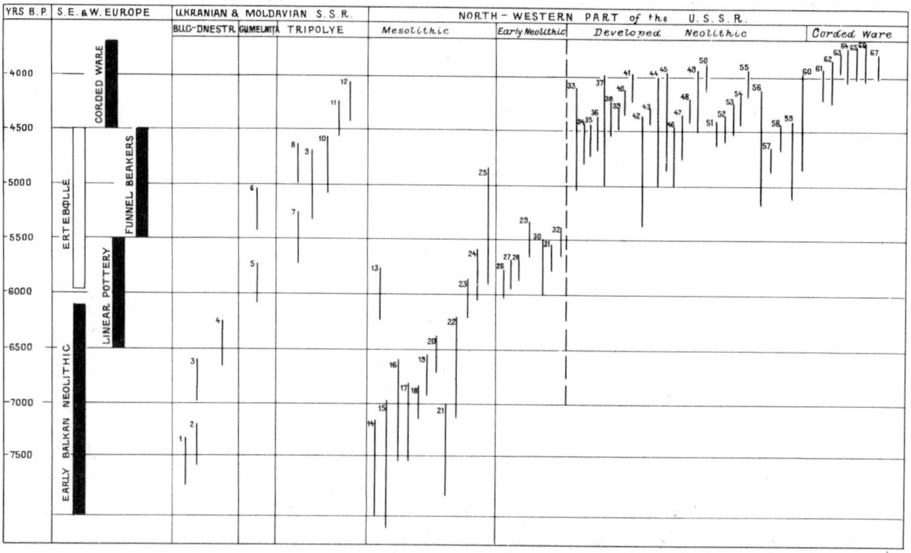

Figure 6 Radiocarbon chronology of the mesolithic and neolithic of European U.S.S.R. in the framework of south-eastern and western Europe.

I – Soroki 2, layer 3 (aceramic), Bln-588; 2 – Soroki 2, layer 2 (aceramic), Bln-587; 3 – Soroki 2, layer I, Bin-586; 4 – Soroki 5, Bin-589; 5 – Vulkaneşti, Mo-417; **6** – Vulkaneşti, LE-640; **7** – Novye Ruseşti, Bln-590; **8** – Chapayevka, Bln-63I; **9** – Soroki 2, BM-494; **10** Soroki 2, BM-495; **II** – Mayaki, Bln-629; **12** – Mayaki LE-629; **13** – Kunda, TA-16; **14** – Osa, Bln-770; **15** – Osa, LE-811; **16** – Osa, LE-812; **17** – Osa, LE-810; **18** – Narva, layer 3, TA-53; **19** – Narva, layer 3, TA-25; **20** – Narva, layer 3, TA-41; **21** – Narva, layer 2, TA-52; **22** – Narva, layer 2, TA-40; **23** – Narva, layer 2, TA-17; **24** – Narva, layer 2, TA-33; **25** – Narva, layer I, TA-7; **26** – Osa (early neolithic) LE-961; **27** – Osa (early neolithic) LE-962;**28** – Osa (early neolithic), LE-850; **29** – Zacen'e, LE-960; **30** – Berendeyevo, GIN-112; **31** Zareč'ye, LE-969; **32** – Besovy Sledki, GIN-129; **33** – Sarnate, TA-26; **34** – Sarnate, Bln-769 **35** – Sarnate, TA-265; **36** – Sarnate, LE-814; **37** – Sarnate, TA-24;**38** – Šventoji (lower layer) TA-247; **39** – Šventoji (lower layer) Bs-23; **40** – Šventoji (lower layer) LE-904; **41** – sventoji (lower layer) LE-833; **42** Kääpa (Narva type pottery) TA-5; **42** – Zedmar D, LE-848;**44** – Kääpa (pit-and-comb pottery) TA-6; **45** – Kääpa (pit and comb pottery) TA-4; **46** – Piestina, LE-750; **47** – Piestina, LE-748; **48** – Piestina, LE-867; **49** – Nainiekste, LE-648; **50** – Zalavruga I, GIN-130; **51** – Usvyaty IV B, TA-105; **52** – Usvyaty IV B, TA-244; **53** – Usvyaty IV B, TA-243; **54** – Usvyaty IVB, TA-202; **55** – Usvyaty IV B, TA-203; **56** – Ivanovskoye III, GIN-241; **57** – Pleščeyevo IV, GIN-115; **58** – Pleščeyevo IV, LE-970; **59** – Strelka, MO-1; **60** – Gorbunovo, Mo-2; **61** – Šventoji (upper layer) TA-242; **62** – Šventoji (upper layer) Vs-22; **63** – Šventoji (upper layer) LE-855; **64** – Abora, LE-671; **65** – Abora, LE-749, **66** – Krivina, LE-757; **67** – Osovec, LE-936

Note. All dates shown are based on the Libby value (5570 ± 30) with two standard errors, without dendrochronological calibration.

leaving its original habitat. In doing so '. . . the migrant will bring not the entire gene pool of the original population but only a small slice of it' (Dobzhansky 1968). This implies that the bud-off population is

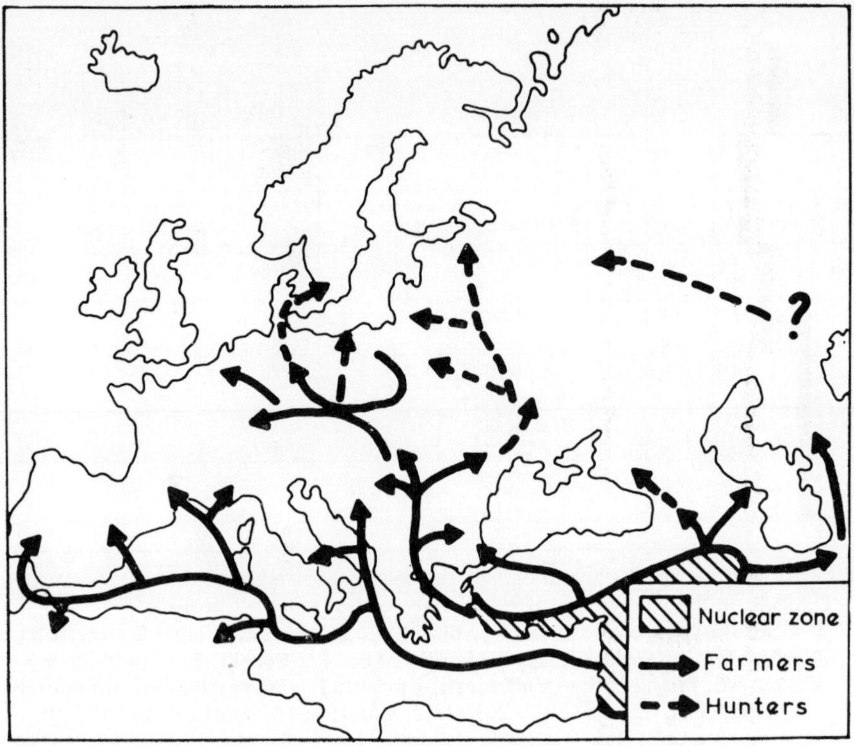

Figure 7 The neolithization of Europe, 8000 – 5000 B.P.

never identical (either genetically or culturally) with the original one.

A population spread over a vast area is necessarily split into a number of genetic isolates by virtue of geographical and social factors. Random genetic drift will always lead to the accumulation of different genetic mutations in different isolates (Efraimson 1970).

A disintegration of a homogenous population into a number of isolates may be illustrated by numerous archaeological examples. The best is the Linienbandkeramik culture, which splits in its later phases into a number of local groups. Analogous processes can be followed up in the evolution of the 'forest' neolithic.

In the course of the 3rd millennium B.C. there took place the spread of the agricultural population north- and westwards from the initial settlement area in central and western Europe. Simultaneously, the early neolithic substratum in eastern Europe split into a number of 'forest' neolithic cultures: Dnepr-Donetz in the Ukraine (middle and late phases): Neman and Narva cultures in Byelorussia; Usvyaty, Piestina, Narva, Sarnate, Narva-Nieman cultures in the eastern Baltic area. (Fig. 9).

At the same time, later derivatives of the pit-and-comb pottery culture spread to the north, west and south, reaching the eastern Baltic area, Byelorussia and the Ukraine.

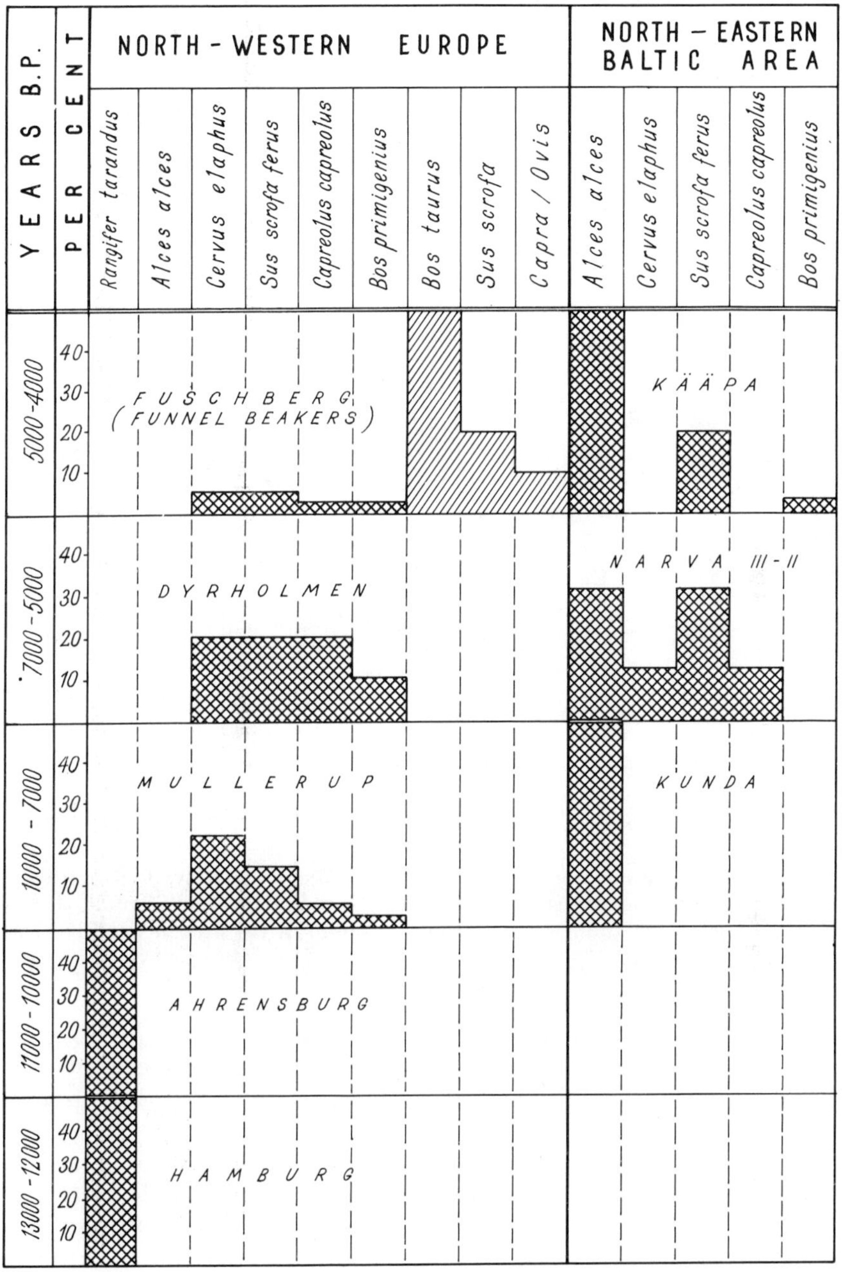

Figure 8 Faunal remains from mesolithic and neolithic sites in north-west and north-east Europe.

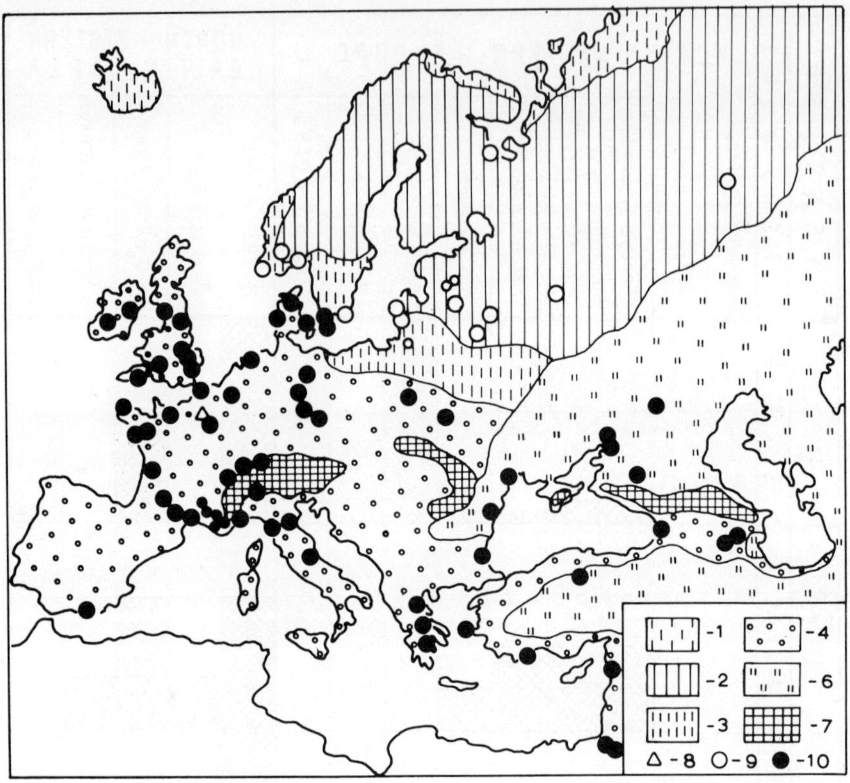

Figure 9 Europe 4500–4000 B.P., showing radiocarbon dated sites within this period.

1, tundra; 2, pine and birch forest; 3, mixed oak-pine-birch forest; 4, broad-leaved forest; 6, steppe and desert; 7, mountain vegetation; 9, sites of 'forest' neolithic (hunting and fishing economy); 10, sites of neolithic with farming economy.

The settlement pattern of late 'forest' neolithic cultures does not change as compared to the early phases: although a more intensive occupation of river valleys, of lake basins and of peat bogs took place.

These are the main tendencies in the evolution of eco-social systems during the Late Pleistocene – Early and Middle Holocene. Further studies must concentrate on the quantitative evaluation of concrete ecotopes and of their carrying capacities; on quantitative and functional analysis of material culture; and on detailed analysis of the economical and demographical structures of prehistoric settlements. On the basis of such data it would be possible to build up reliable dynamic models for this crucial period of human prehistory.

REFERENCES

Aleksandrova, V.D. (1963) Opyt analiza yavleniy samoregulyacii v fitocenoze s točki zreniya nekotoryh idei kibernetiki. *Primenenie Matematiceskih Metodov v Biologii.* Leningrad.

Anabeghian, N.G. *et al.* (eds.) (1971) *Modelirovanie Social'nyh Processov.* Moskva, Nauka.

Bertalanffy, L. von (1956) General Systems theory. *General Systems* vol. I.

Boscaiu, N. (1971) L'évolution postglaciaire de la végétation du défile de la Danube. *Abstracts and Reports of the Third International Palynological Conference.* Novosibirsk.

Bibikov, S.N. (1950) Pozdneišii paleolit Kryma. *Materialy po Červerticnomu Periodu SSSR* 2, 122-3, Moskva-Leningrad.

Binford, L.R. (1968) Post Pleistocene adaptation. *In* Binford, S.R. and L.R. (eds.) *New Perspectives in Archaeology*, 313-42. Chicago, Aldine.

Binford, S.R. (1970) Late Middle Pleistocene adaptations and their possible consequences. *Bioscience* 20, no. 5, 280-3.

Birdsell, J. (1957) Some population problems involving Pleistocene Man. *Cold Spring Harbor Symposia on Quantative Biology* 22, 47-69.

Blauberg, I.V., Sadovski, V.N. and Yudin, E.G. (eds.) (1970) *Problemy Metodologii Sistemnogo Issledovaniya.* Moskva.

Clark, J.G.D. (1952) *Prehistoric Europe – The Economic Basis.* London.

Clarke, D.L. (1968) *Analytical Archaeology.* London.

Čierniavski, M.M. (1971) *Neolit Severo-zapadnoi Belorussi.* Avtoreferat kandidatskoi dissertacii. Minsk.

Dansgaard, W., Johnsen, S.J., Clausen, H.B. and Langway, C.C. Jr. (1970) Ice cores and palaeoclimatology. *In* Olsson I.U. (ed.) *Nobel Symposium 12. Radiocarbon Variations and Absolute Chronology*, 337-51. Stockholm.

Danilenko, V.N. (1969) *Neolit Ukrainy.* Kiev.

Dobzhansky, Th. (1968) Genetic drift and selection of gene systems. *In* Cohen, Y.A. (ed.) *Man in Adaptation.* Chicago.

Efraimson, V.P. (1970) Problemy populacionnoy genetiki čeloveka. *Problemy Medicinskoy Genetiki*, 154-71. Moskva.

Gramsch, B. (1971) Zum Problem des Uebergangs vom Mesolithikum zum Neolithikum im Flachland zwischen Elbe und Oder. *In* Schlette, F. (ed.) *Evolution und Revolution im Alten Orient und in Europa.* Berlin.

Gričuk, V.P. Palaeogeografiya Severnoy Evrophy. v pozdnem pleystocene. *In* Gerassimov, I.P. (ed.) *Posledniy Evropeyskiy Lednikovyi Pokrov*, 198-9. Moskva.

Gričuk, V.P. (1969) Rastitel'nost' na Russkoi ravnine v pozdnem paleolite. *In* Gerassimov, I.P. (ed.) *Priroda i Razvitie Pervobytnogo Obščestva.* Moskva.

Grigor'ev, A.A. Geograficeskaya zonal'nost' i nekotorye eyë zakonomernosti. *Izvestiya Akademii Nauk SSR, ser geograf.*, no. 5, 6.

Higgs, E.S., Vita-Finzi, C., Harris, D.A. and Fagg, A.E. (1967) The climate, environment and industries of Stone Age Greece, part III. *Proceedings of the Prehistoric Society* 33, 1-30.

Khotinsky, N.A. (1971) Transeuroasiatic correlation of the events in the Holocene history of vegetation and climate of the boreal area of Eurasia. *Report of the Third International Palynological Conference,* Novosibirsk.

Kurkin, K.A. (1970) Nekotorye metodologičeskie problemy issledovaniya biocenosov i landšaftov. *In* Blauberg, I.V. *et al.* (eds.) *Problemy Metodologii Sistemnogo Issledovaniya*, 268-88. Moskva.

Masson, V.M. (1971) Poselenie Džeytun. *Materially i Issledovaniya po Archeologii SSSR.* Leningrad.

Milankovitch, M. (1938) Astronomische Mittel der erdgeschichtlichen Klimate. *Handbuch der Geophysick* Bd. 9, 593-698. Berlin.

Neustadt, M.I. (1957) *Istoriya Lesov i Paleogeografiya SSSR v Golocene.* Moskva.

Neustadt, M.I., Zavel'ski, F.S., Miklyaev, A.M. and Khotinsky, N.A. (1969) Kompleksi stoyanok mezolita i neolita na bolotah Berendeevo i Ivanovskoe. *In* Neustadt, M.I. (ed.) *Golocen.* 129-38, Moskva.

Pop, E. *Mlaştinile de Turbă din Republica Populară Romînă.* Bucureşti.

Quitta, H. (1962) Zur ältesten Bandkeramik in Mitteleuropa. *Aus Ur- und Frühgeschichte.* Berlin.

Quitta, H. (1964) Zur Herkunft des frühen Neolithikums in Mitteleuropa. *Varia Archaeologica.* Berlin.

Quitta, H. (1971) Der Balkan als Mittler zwischen Vorderem Orient und Europa. *In* Schlette, F. (ed.) *Evolution und Revolution im Alten Orient und in Europa,* 38-63. Berlin.

Ross Ashby, W. (1965) *An Introduction to Cybernetics.* London.

Stoddart, D.R. (1967) Organism and ecosystem as geographical models. *In* Chorley, R. and Hagget, P. (eds.) *Models in Geography,* 511-48. London 1967.

Sukačev, V.N. (1964) *Osnovy Lesnoy Biocenoligii.* Moskva.

Telegin, D. Ya. (1968) *Dnepro-Doneckaya Kul'tura.* Kiev.

Tringham, R.A. Preliminary study of the early neolithic and latest mesolithic blade industries in Southeast and Central Europe. *In* Coles, J. and Simpson, D.D.A. (eds.) *Studies in Ancient Europe.* Leicester University Press.

Woerkom, A.J.J. van (1953) The astronomical theory of climatic changes. *In* Shapley, H. (ed.) *Climatic Change,* 147-57. Cambridge, Mass., Harvard University Press.

Wright, H.E. Jr. (1968) Natural environment of early food production North of Mesopotamia. *Science* **161**, 334-9.

Zagorskis, F.A. (1967) *Rannii i Srednii Neolit Vostocnoi Latvii.* Avtoreferat kandidatskoi dissertacii. Riga.

A.J. AMMERMAN and
L.L. CAVALLI - SFORZA

A population model for the diffusion of early farming in Europe

The spread of early farming in Europe is a subject of interest to a number of disciplines ranging from prehistory and palaeoecology to genetics. The generally held view sees early farming of the type practised in Europe as having emerged in the Near East (Ucko and Dimbleby 1969). From there, it appears to have spread first to Greece and the Balkans and subsequently over the rest of Europe (Clark 1965; Neustupný 1968). In this paper,[1] we shall present a model that may describe how the diffusion of early farming took place. In a previous paper (Ammerman and Cavalli-Sforza 1971), we have shown that the 'wave of advance' model is compatible with the observed rate of spread of early farming in Europe. Here we would like to discuss various aspects of the model in more detail and at the same time indicate ways in which the model may be related to different lines of archaeological and genetic evidence.

Cultural versus demic diffusion

The spread of early farming can be viewed as a process of diffusion which can be explained in two essentially different ways. These need not be mutually exclusive but merit being clearly distinguished at the conceptual level. According to the cultural or stimulus diffusion mode of explanation, domesticated strains and 'technological' know-how related to early farming would be passed on from one group to another independently of significant geographic displacements of the groups. A model of this type was suggested for instance by Edmonson (1961). This mode of explanation is one that prehistorians have come increasingly to rely upon as their discipline has developed during the course of the present century. The extent of the acceptance of this mode is reflected, to take an example

[1] The research reported in this paper was supported in part by a grant from the U.S.A.E.C., contract number AT(04-3)-326.

immediately at hand, in the comments by various authors following Edmonson's article on 'Neolithic diffusion rates'. While those offering comments are critical of many aspects of the paper, there appears to be little resistance to the basic assumption that what is being measured, if one attempts such a measurement, is a rate of stimulus diffusion.

Alternately, the spread can be seen as diffusion due to population growth and displacement. We shall refer to this type of process in general as *demic* diffusion. By this concept taken in a strict sense, we mean that people carry with them their own culture, and that if they for some reason expand geographically, so does their culture. The demic mode of diffusion will be most relevant in situations where marked changes in demographic pressure are concerned. In the case of the spread of early farming, there are reasons for thinking that early farming permitted population growth based upon augmented food production, even though few specific estimates of the population density of prehistoric groups living under different economic conditions have been hazarded to date (Braidwood and Reed 1957). A decrease in death rate or an increase in birth rate can lead to a demographic expansion. Farming, as a component of a subsistence economy, can be expected to offer greater potential (in the form of the storage of wheat and barley) for the redistribution of food resources during the year. It may thus have mitigated seasonal food shortages which, in a temperate zone such as Europe, were probably an important cause of mortality, direct and indirect, among groups of hunter-gatherers. In addition, the pattern of reproductive behaviour may have changed, so that women during their lifetime had an increased number of offspring. The possession of domesticated cereals and stock thus may have led to an increased net reproductive rate, lasting for some generations, until a new plateau of population density was reached.

It has been shown mathematically (Skellam 1951; Kendall 1965) that if such a phenomenon of increase in population numbers coincides with a modest local migratory activity, random in direction, a wave of population expansion will set in and progress at a constant radial rate. This model will be referred to as that of the diffusional population wave of advance or simply 'wave of advance'. This mode of demic diffusion may be distinguished from 'colonization', which in its conventional meaning is the intentional settlement by a coherent group of people, usually in a distant land. A familiar example of colonization is that which is recorded in classical Greek history. By contrast, the 'wave of advance' model would be one involving slow, continuous expansion with movements usually being over short distances. Both this and colonization can be considered as different extreme models, belonging to the general class of the demic mode of diffusion.

In order to examine the validity of the wave of advance model, the advance of the wave front with time should be investigated. One study along related lines concerned the spread of the muskrat, *Ondathra zibetica*, in Central Europe since its introduction in 1905. It was shown (Skellam 1951) that the square root of the area occupied at successive times increased linearly with the year, exactly as expected under the model of the diffusional population wave of advance.

The regular advance of the wave front

In our case, data are not yet numerous enough to allow us to build contours at various time intervals for the whole area of diffusion. Another approach to measuring the rate of advance involves taking the distances between points on the wave front and the centre of diffusion, which can be taken as estimates of the radius of the wave front at various times, and plotting these distances against time itself. Under the model of the wave of advance, the radius of the wave front should vary linearly with time.

In a previous paper (Ammerman and Cavalli-Sforza 1971), the measurement of the rate of spread of early farming in Europe was considered in detail. Here we shall only attempt to summarize briefly the results of the analysis. The spread of early farming was viewed in terms of the diffusion of domesticated cereals (wheat and barley) in Europe. The rate measurement was taken for several different possible centres of diffusion in the Near East which have produced evidence for the domesticated cereals at early dates. It is perhaps worth mentioning here that there is little evidence or reason for suspecting the local domestication of emmer and barley in Europe. One is not faced with the possible problem of independent centres of domestication and subsequent diffusion within Europe. The method used for the rate measurement involved plotting the dates of various early neolithic sites, taken as estimates of the arrival time of the cereals in different parts of Europe, against the distances of the respective sites from a given centre of diffusion (see Fig. 1). These 'plots' were then tested for a linear relationship, the expected pattern for a constant radial rate, by the linear correlation coefficient. The European data gave correlation coefficients ranging from 0.89 (±0.03) when Jericho was used as the centre of diffusion to 0.85 for Jarmo and being respectively 0.83 for Cayönü and 0.84 for Ali Kosh. These correlations are all very high, and as the figure also shows, the fit of a straight line to the data is remarkably good. The overall rate of diffusion is given by the slope of the solid line in Fig. 1. This turns out to be very nearly 1 km per year, varying slightly depending upon the centre of diffusion chosen.

The good fit of the data to a straight line, representing the advance of the wave front with time, is thus in agreement with the wave of

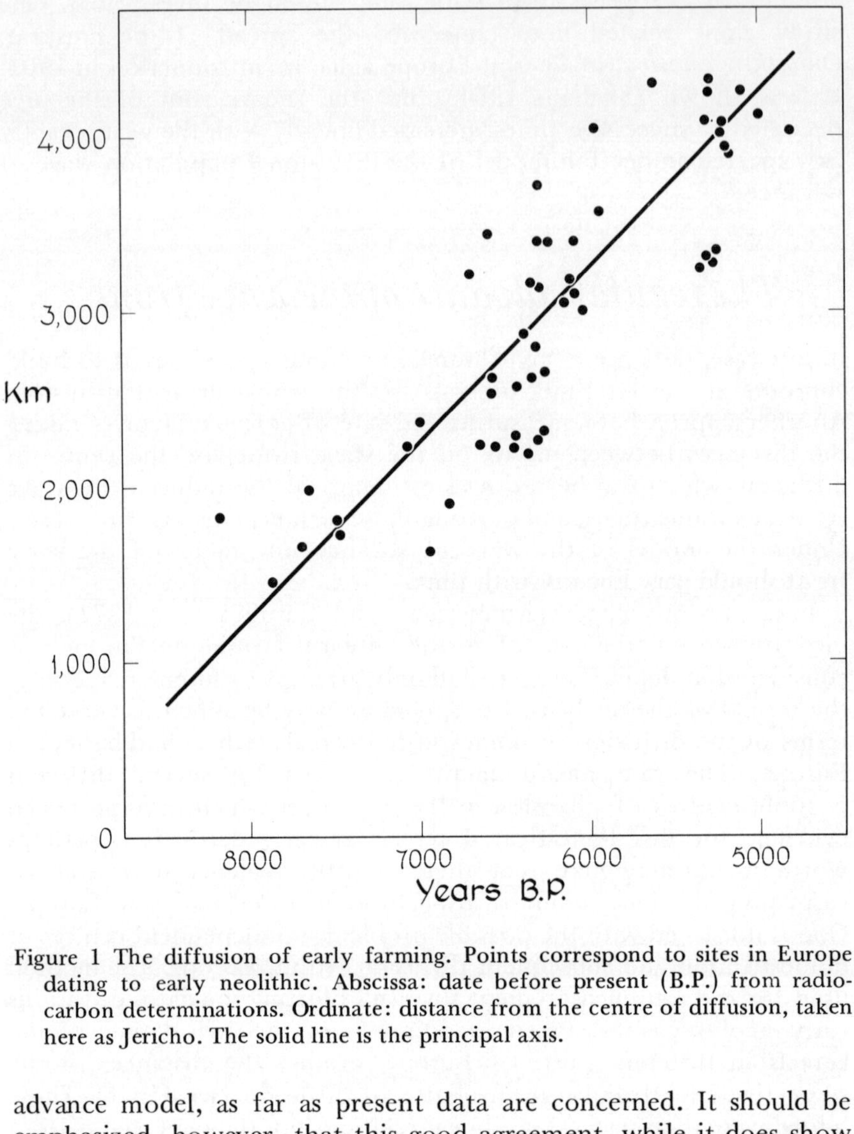

Figure 1 The diffusion of early farming. Points correspond to sites in Europe dating to early neolithic. Abscissa: date before present (B.P.) from radiocarbon determinations. Ordinate: distance from the centre of diffusion, taken here as Jericho. The solid line is the principal axis.

advance model, as far as present data are concerned. It should be emphasized, however, that this good agreement, while it does show that the observed rate and the model are compatible, does not in itself lead to a straightforward acceptance of the model. Models based on purely cultural diffusion could be constructed to yield the same formal picture, namely one of proportionality of the wave front radius with respect to time. This agreement is not sufficient in itself to discriminate among the various possible modes of diffusion and a validation of the model requires investigation of other possible sources of evidence.

The model

The model which we are calling 'wave of advance' originated with Fisher (1937), who actually described the wave of advance of an *advantageous gene.* Fisher gave a solution for the stationary form of the wave, describing the spread of an advantageous gene in a one-dimensional habitat. D.G. Kendall (1948) gave, by another mathematical approach, a model of the spread of a population growing exponentially (that is, whose number N increases with time t according to the equation $dN/dt = \alpha t$ where α is the growth rate and diffusing in a two-dimensional space. Skellam (1951) extended this work in various ways and in particular to a population growing according to a logistic curve that is, with $dN/dt = \alpha N(1 - N/N_{max})$, where N_{max} is the maximum population number). In the formulation of the model (see the Appendix), there are two terms – a growth component and a migration component – which determine the rate of advance of the wave front. The rate of advance, the constant ρ, is approximately $\rho = \sigma\sqrt{(2\alpha)}$, where σ is the standard deviation of the 'migration' and α the growth rate in the exponential or the initial growth rate in the logistic mode of population increase.

We have already discussed several reasons for thinking that the spread of early farming in Europe was associated with increases in population density. It may be useful here to expand on what is meant by logistic growth. The difference between exponential growth, where the same rate of growth continues indefinitely through time, and logistic growth, where the growth rate is high at the beginning but slows down in time and eventually stops as an upper limit of population density is approached, is shown in Fig. 2. Logistic or more generally sigmoid growth is 'realistic' in allowing the growth rate to be responsive to the carrying capacity of the environment or land. Instead of setting a permanent upper limit or saturation level for population density, it may be preferable to think in terms of a gradual increase in density through time, related to subsequent advances in technology, for those areas well behind the wave of advance. A mathematical refinement that is possible here would be to have population growth follow essentially a logistic form but with allowance made for the asymptote, the saturation level, to increase slowly with time. Such a treatment would tend to make the growth component of the model more 'realistic'. But in terms of the actual rate of advance of the wave front, this refinement would lead to only minor differences in comparison with the use of the standard form of logistic growth, so that the latter provides a good approximation for our present purposes.

It should be emphasized that under a basically logistic mode of population increase the growth rate that really matters is not that of

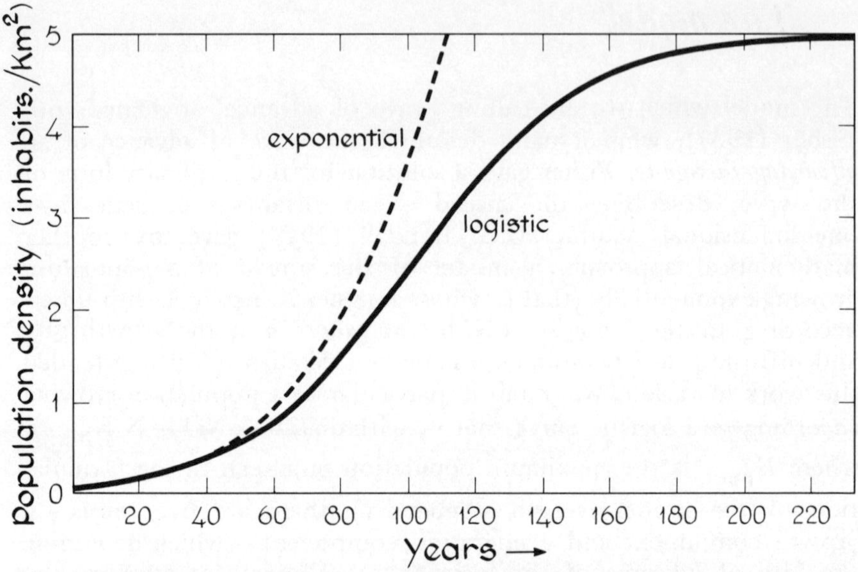

Figure 2 Population growth curves. Under logistic growth, a population starting at a density of 0.1 inhabitants/km^2 multiplies at an initial rate of 3.9 per cent per year ($\alpha = .039$), which determines a doubling in about eighteen years. The growth rate slows down continuously until it reaches zero when saturation occurs at 5 inhabitants/km^2. If growth continued indefinitely at the initial rate the dotted curve of exponential growth would result.

the early farming population as a whole but rather that occurring in the 'growing fringe' at the periphery of the spread. It is in this area that dynamic changes in population density are taking place. The concept of the 'growing fringe' is in many ways comparable to that of the 'frontier', as used by geographers concerned with describing the westward expansion across the United States and Canada during the nineteenth century. In one study (Wishart, Warren and Stoddard 1969) of the spread across America, which incidentally differs in a number of significant ways from the spread of early farming in Europe, a wave model and dynamic changes in population density have been profitably used in defining the 'frontier'.

Estimates of the doubling times of populations which have settled an 'empty' space and can multiply freely for a few generations are limited to very few cases. Two were analysed by Birdsell (1957) for use in his model of the settlement of Australia by aborigines. In both cases the doubling time was approximately 20 years. In Fig. 3, several curves for logistic growth are given based upon different doubling times. The population density at saturation used in computing these curves was 5 inhabitants per km^2, while the density taken as a base line prior to the appearance of early farming was 0.1 inhabitants per km^2. It is worth mentioning that the order of increase in population density adopted here is perhaps on the conservative side, being about one-tenth of that suggested by Braidwood and

Reed (1957) in their attempt to estimate 'terminal food-gathering' and 'primary village-farming' densities. In future work, it will be interesting to see if these density values, which were selected with reference to modern demographic data, can be replaced with direct or indirect estimates of the order of increase in population density permitted by early farming in various parts of Europe. Ideally, one would like to compare the density of 'late' mesolithic groups in an area with that of the early farming population living some centuries after the onset of early farming in the area.

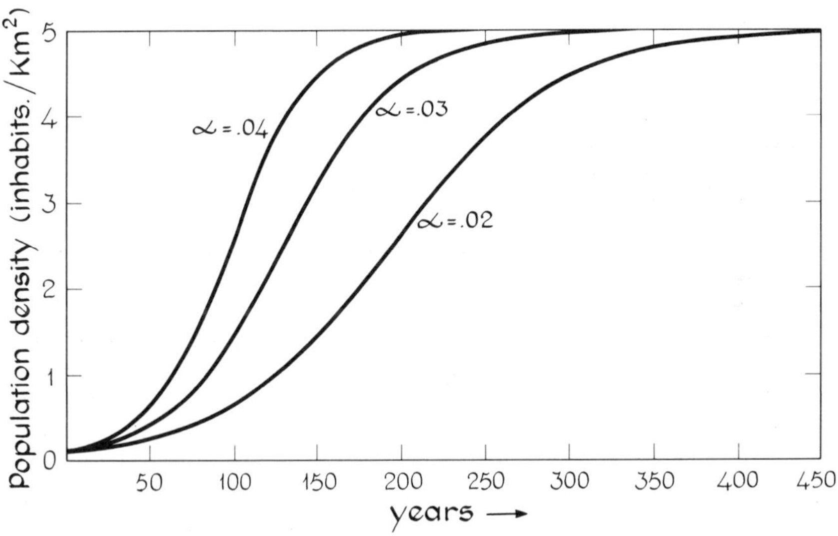

Figure 3 Logistic growth curves with respective initial growth rates of 2, 3 and 4 per cent per year.

We should also examine the migration component in more detail. In the case of random diffusion or random migration, which is mathematically the simplest case to consider, the distribution for migration in two dimensions is represented by Fig. 4a, where the values of the z-axis, generating the bi-dimensional 'normal' or Gaussian surface, give the probability that an individual located at the beginning at point 0 will be at a point of coordinates $(x_1\ y_1)$ after a given time. It is usually more convenient for this distribution surface to be transformed into a distribution curve with the distances plotted along one axis as is shown in Fig. 4b. Here the distance of an individual from the starting point is given by $d_1 = \sqrt{(x_1^2 + y_1^2)}$. The 'flatness' or 'peakedness' of the bi-dimensional Gaussian surface (Fig. 4a) and of the distribution of the distances (Fig. 4b) are both determined by σ, the standard deviation of the 'migration'.

In the case of genetic studies based upon living populations or historical demographic data, it is possible to produce migration distributions directly from observations (Cavalli-Sforza 1962). This

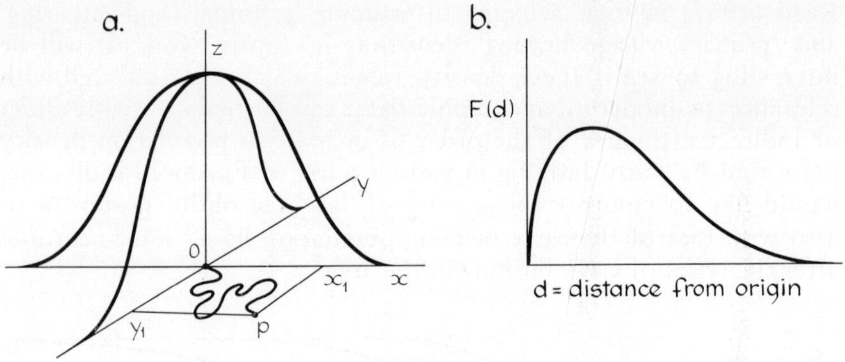

Figure 4 (a) Distribution of migration distances, assuming that migration is random in direction, in two dimensions, x and y. For example, an individual starts his migration at the origin (x = 0, y = 0), and after following an irregular path, arrives at point P (x_1, y_1) at a given time. The value $z = f(x, y)$ gives the frequency of individuals expected to be at point (x, y) at a given time, t. (b) The distribution surface on the left hand has been transformed into a distribution curve (in one dimension), where distances from the origin are given by $d = \sqrt{(x^2 + y^2)}$.

type of study often involves a comparison of the residence of parents and offspring considered in terms of a time unit of one generation. Such observed distributions can in turn be analysed and compared with the theoretical curve for normal or random migration. In our case, it is evident that we are not in a position at the present time to arrive at migration distributions from direct observations. We shall assume here, as a first approximation, that the migration distribution does conform to the normal case. The important quantity that we need to know then is σ, the standard deviation of the 'migration'. While it may be possible to estimate σ directly from archaeological evidence in the future, we can at present only estimate it indirectly from the observed ρ, the rate of advance of the wave front, and various rates of population growth. If one takes a doubling time in population size of 18 years ($\alpha = .039$), for example, as an appropriate value for population growth – at least for the initial rate in the logistic growth curve – one can then compute from it and the observed ρ (1 km per year) the value of the migration constant σ expected to hold on the basis of the wave of advance model (see Appendix). This turns out to be 18 km per generation of 25 years.

The following additional comment may be useful in evaluating the results of indirect estimates of σ. Even if the population growth rate were considerably different from the one used above, the value of σ would not change much, since it varies proportionately to its square root. Thus, if the population in the 'growing fringe' doubled at half of the rate taken before (every 35 years, or $\alpha = .02$), the value of σ would change from 18 to 25 km per generation. It may be noted that in studies of the migration distributions of modern primitive populations and peasant populations in Europe during recent historical times estimated values of σ tend to range between 10 and 20 km per generation (Cavalli-Sforza and Bodmer 1971).

It is worth considering briefly the meaning of σ in its archaeological context of the pattern of settlement formation and relocation in the 'growing fringe'. As is often the case, the mathematical representation simplifies the diffusion process making it continuous in time and space. Although in reality the process is discontinuous, as individuals and more often families or small groups will settle at a distance from a previous settlement, it does operate over short intervals of space and time and so the theory provides a useful approximation. The frequency with which a new settlement is formed, expressed as a function of the distance at which it takes place, defines the migration distribution subsumed in the model and determined quantitatively by σ. There may be areas in Europe where sufficient knowledge of patterns of settlement formation is available, so that σ can be estimated directly from archaeological evidence and compared with the indirect estimates put forward here.

Computer simulation of the wave of advance

Having discussed the growth and migration components more or less separately, we can now consider what happens when the two are brought together. A concrete way of examining their integration in the model is provided by the computer simulation shown in Fig. 5. Previous simulation studies have demonstrated that, given the conditions required by the model, a wave front with a constant radial rate of advance will be established (Cavalli-Sforza and Bodmer 1971:487). This holds for simulations done in both one and two dimensions. It is worth mentioning that computer simulations can be carried out at varying levels of complexity. The simulation presented in Fig. 5 should be regarded as an initial one, carried out along the essential lines of the model. In future work, more elaborate simulations can be attempted, once estimates are available for certain parameters, such as distributions of settlement sizes, that one may want to incorporate in the simulation.

In the simulation program, time and space are treated discontinuously, which probably gives a better approximation to archaeological reality, and the correspondence with Fisher's analytical model, in which both vary continuously, is only approximate. Under a continuous treatment of time, the migration rate necessary to give the same rate of advance would be somewhat smaller than in the computer simulation. For convenience, the simulation was carried out in a one-dimensional space; a simulation in a two-dimensional space and using the same numerical values would yield essentially the

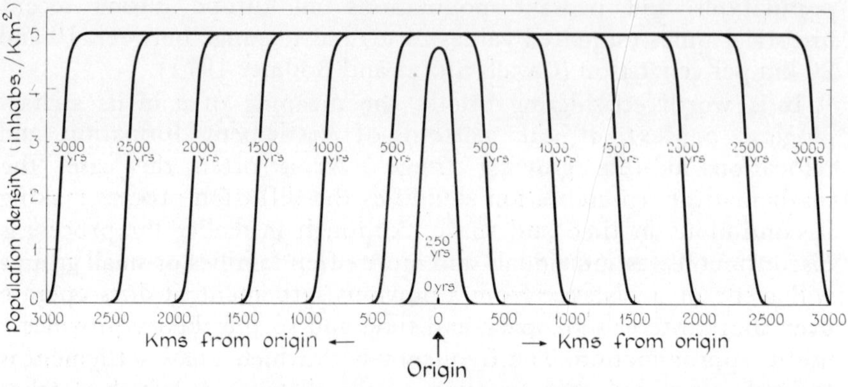

Figure 5 Computer simulation of the wave of advance. The curves give the population densities observed at various times from the beginning and distances from the origin of the simulated spread of early farming in Europe.

same pattern as Fig. 5. The population starts at a density of 0.1 inhabitants/km^2 at the origin in time and space. Population growth follows the logistic mode with an initial growth rate of 3.9% per year (i.e., a doubling time of eighteen years) and reaches a density at saturation of 5 inhabitants/km^2. Migration concomitantly takes place at the rate derived indirectly above (i.e., $\sigma = 18$ km per generation) in order to have a rate of advance of 1 km/year. Of the many ways to arrive at this migration distribution, one fairly straightforward approach is to have each year 13.2% of those living in the 'growing fringe' move (at random in direction) 10 km apart. Here the proportion of the population migrating per unit time (i.e., 0.132) is equal to σ^2, the variance of the distribution per unit time. After t time units the variance is $t\sigma^2$, and therefore, in a generation of 25 years, the variance is 25 x 0.132 = 3.3, and the standard deviation of the migration is $\sigma = \sqrt{3.3} = 1.8$. In the space unit employed in the simulation program (i.e. 10 km), the standard deviation is then 18 km per generation. The curves in Fig. 5 give the population densities observed at various distances from the origin (given on the abscissa) and times from the beginning (given on each curve) of the simulated spread. As the figure shows, the simulation does give rise to a wave front that advances at the expected rate of about 1 km/year.

Discussion

From the viewpoint of the validation of the model, it should be apparent that the question of increases in population density is of leading importance. This is the main assumption or condition required by the wave of advance model. With respect to local migration, there is really no question of whether it is present or not, especially where shifting forms of agriculture are concerned. The question here is that of trying to get a measure of actual migration distributions. If the order of increase in population density can be estimated and the estimates show significant demographic changes, this will provide clear support for the model. If this can be shown, it seems almost unavoidable that a model of demic diffusion such as the one described here must account at least for part of the observed rate of diffusion of early farming. The analysis of archaeological evidence may indicate that cultural diffusion also played a role and even suggest its relative importance. Direct assessment of g (where $g = \sqrt{2\alpha}$; see Appendix) and σ values from archaeological evidence, if these become possible in the future, could help in elucidating whether or not all the observed rate of advance of the wave front, ρ, is due to demic diffusion, since in this case $\rho = \sigma g$. If cultural or stimulus diffusion also played a role, then $\rho > \sigma g$. Those parts of Europe where extensive fieldwork shows 'late' mesolithic groups to be legitimately absent or very sparsely represented will provide good opportunities for the study of demic diffusion in a 'pure', as opposed to a potentially mixed, state.

In those areas where 'late' mesolithic groups are definitely known it will be useful to examine the interaction or relation between the arriving early farming and the resident mesolithic populations. This would involve a close study of the archaeological evidence connected with the late mesolithic and early neolithic cultures in an area. One would want to know, for example, whether a mesolithic population was (a) absorbed by or (b) forced out or exterminated by expanding neolithic populations; (c) whether the mesolithic groups adopted certain elements common to the neolithic and yet maintained the identity of part of their material culture; or (d) whether mesolithic and neolithic populations existed side by side in the same area for a period of time with little or no cultural exchange taking place. This list could, of course, be expanded. It must also be admitted that these kinds of interpretation are not particularly easy ones for the prehistorian to make. On the other hand, it is likely that, in specific case studies where a reasonable amount of information is available, the options can be reduced to a limited set of alternate hypotheses. A set of this sort may in itself be of use in making it possible to discriminate between the two modes of diffusion.

A further corollary of demic diffusion should be considered. The population wave of advance accompanying the spread of early farming has a high probability of being reflected in the genetic composition of the resulting populations. If the early farmers or 'neolithics' forced out or exterminated all the 'mesolithics' in an area, the genetic type after diffusion would be pure neolithic. If the neolithics increased in numbers, migrated to new areas, mixed freely or almost so with mesolithics there, and again restarted the cycle by expanding in numbers, then one would expect to see a gradual progressive dilution of the original neolithic type. The final result would then be pure neolithic at the centre of diffusion, and almost pure mesolithic at the periphery, with an approximately exponential gradient, whose initial slope would be a simple function of the density increase permitted by the early farming economy. Naturally, conditions for observing this gradient require that there is, at the beginning, a sufficiently clear-cut genetic difference between 'neolithics' and 'mesolithics', and that later migrations or other causes of evolution did not cancel or substantially alter this gradient. Unfortunately, it seems possible that the genetic difference between the early farmers of the Near East and European mesolithics was not particularly marked.

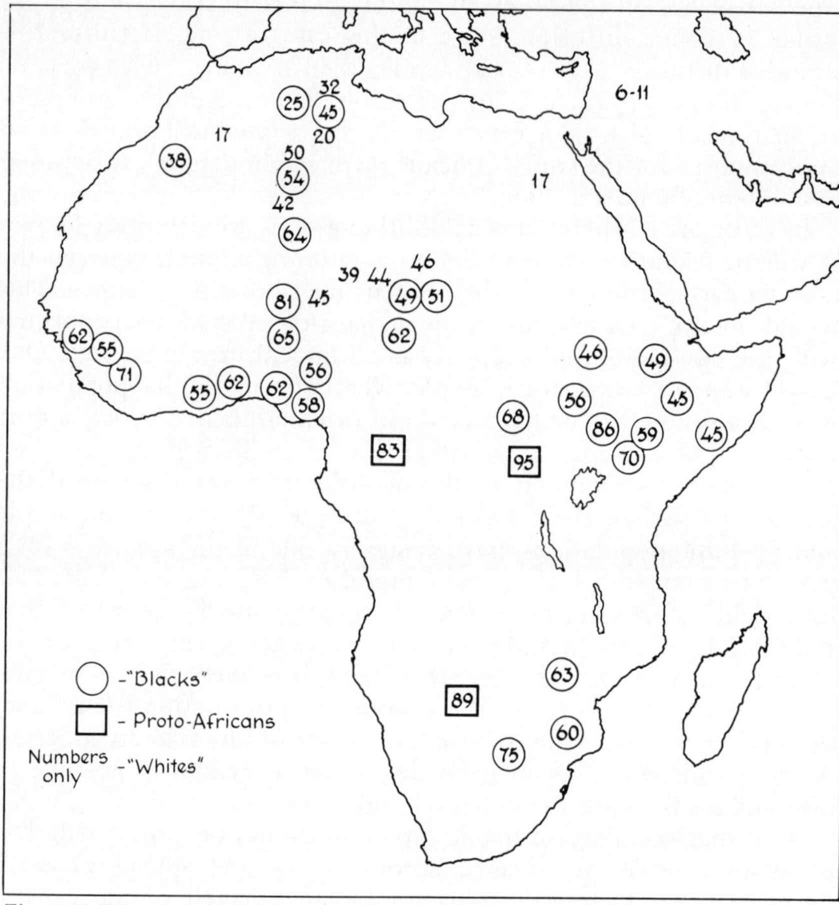

Figure 6 Percentage frequencies of the Rh_0 gene and the approximate locations in Africa of the groups to which they refer.

In Africa, the situation may be more favourable for observing a gradient of this type, since there were no doubt much clearer genetic differences at the start. The high frequency of the Rh_0 allele among

Africans versus a low frequency in Asia and Europe was the first known example, but no longer the only one. In the Sahara and Ethiopia, Rh_O gene frequencies (as well as those of other African genes) tend to be intermediate between those of Eurasia and those of Central and South Africa (Mourant 1954). Among Western Africans and descendents of the Bantu invasion of Central and South Africa, they tend to be smaller than among proto-africans (Cavalli-Sforza *et al.* 1969). In Fig. 6, Rh_O gene frequencies for various groups in Africa have been plotted, showing a notably consistent increase with distance from the Near East. In most cases, the exceptions to this general trend can be explained by later invasions and migrations that are known historically. For instance, the very low values in northwest Africa are for Berber tribes. The intermediate value in the extreme south are Bantus who probably originated in Nigeria. The highest values are for Bushmen and Pygmies, proto-africans, who are still essentially hunter-gatherers. The above example of a genetic gradient should be taken as strictly preliminary, since a proper evaluation should take into account not a single gene but consider synthetically all of the potentially available genetic evidence.

Appendix

We will follow here Skellam's formulation, according to which, calling Ψ the population density, t the time:

$$\frac{\delta \Psi}{\delta t} = \alpha f(\Psi) + \beta \nabla^2 \Psi \qquad (1)$$

where the first term of the sum indicates the growth component, α is the growth rate, $f(\Psi)$ is the growth function, being $f(\Psi) = \Psi$ for the exponential, and $f(\Psi) = (1 - \Psi)$ for logistic growth. The second term of the sum refers to the diffusion component. β is the diffusion coefficient and is equal to half the mean square distance travelled per unit time, σ^2. The operator ∇^2 is $\nabla^2 = \frac{\delta^2}{\delta x^2} + \frac{\delta^2}{\delta y^2}$ if referred to the two space coordinates x, y, or $\nabla^2 = \frac{\delta^2}{\delta r^2} + \frac{1\delta}{r\delta r}$ if referred to the distance $r = \sqrt{(x^2 + y^2)}$.

The rate of advance of the wave front ρ, to which we refer as the overall diffusion rate, is approximately $\rho = \sigma\sqrt{2\alpha}$. More exactly, it would depend upon the particular density value chosen to identify the wave front. The advancing wave will have a population density falling off towards its periphery. Calling $g = \sqrt{2\alpha}$, from it and $2 = e^{\alpha\tau}$

where τ is the doubling time in years, $g = 1.177/\sqrt{\tau}$. If one wants to estimate σ from ρ and g, then $\sigma = .85\rho\sqrt{\tau}$ with ρ in km per year, σ expressed in time units of one year.

The indirect estimate of σ mentioned earlier was computed from the formula $\rho = \sigma\sqrt{2\alpha}$ as follows. Using values of ρ = 1 km/year and α = 3.9%, we have $1 = \sigma\sqrt{2 \times .039}$. Solving for σ, we get σ = 3.58 km per year. Here the mean square distance travelled per year is given by $\sigma^2 = 12.8$. To obtain the standard deviation (σ_g) in terms of a time unit of one generation (25 years), we have $\sigma_g^2 = \sigma^2 \times 25 = 320$; and σ_g = 17.9 km per generation.

There are as yet unsolved mathematical problems concerning the stability of the wave front, especially in the two-dimensional case. This is true of functions such as (1) which are continuous in time and space and where a complete analytical solution is not yet available. Numerical solutions are therefore necessary. This usually involves a discontinuous treatment of time and space as in the computer simulation shown in Fig. 5. Since human populations tend to space themselves as discontinuous aggregates, the treatment of space in the simulation may supply us with a better approximation to the real situation.

REFERENCES

Ammerman, A.J. and Cavalli-Sforza, L.L. (1972) Measuring the rate of spread of early farming in Europe. *Man.* 6: 674-88.

Birdsell, J.B. (1957) Some population problems involving Pleistocene man. *Cold Spring Harbor Symposium in Quantitative Biology* 22, 47-69.

Braidwood, R.J. and Reed, C.A. (1957) The achievement and early consequences of food-production: a consideration of the archaeological and natural-historical evidence. *Cold Spring Harbour Symposium in Quantitative Biology* 22, 19-31.

Cavalli-Sforza, L.L. (1962) The distribution of migration distances: models and applications to genetics. In *Human Displacement* (Entretiens de Monaco en sciences humaines, Première session) 139-58.

Cavalli-Sforza, L.L. *et al.* (1969) Studies on African Pygmies, I. A pilot investigation of Babinga Pygmies in the Central African Republic (with an analysis of genetic distances). *American Journal of Human Genetics* 21, 252-74.

Cavalli-Sforza, L.L. and Bodmer, W. (1971) *The Genetics of Human Populations.* San Francisco, W.H. Freeman Co.

Clark, J.G.D. (1965) Radiocarbon dating and the expansion of farming culture from the Near East over Europe. *Proceedings of the Prehistoric Society* 31, 58-73.

Fisher, R.A. (1937) The wave of advance of advantageous genes. *Annals of Eugenics, London,* 7 355-69.

Edmonson, M.S. (1961) Neolithic diffusion rates. *Current Anthropology* 2, 71-102.

Kendall, D.G. (1948) A form of wave propagation associated with the equation of heat conduction. *Proceedings of the Cambridge Philological Society* 44, 591.

Kendall, D.G. (1965) Mathematical models of the spread of infection. In *Mathematics and Computer Science in Biology and Medicine.* 213-25.

Mourant, A.E. (1954) *The Distribution of the Human Blood Groups.* Oxford. Blackwell.

Neustupný, E. (1968) Absolute chronology of the Neolithic and Aeneolithic periods. *Slovenska Archaeologia* **16**, 19-56.

Skellam, J.G. (1951) Random dispersal in theoretical populations. *Biometrika* **38**, 196-218.

Ucko, P.J. and Dimbleby, G.W. (eds.) (1969) *The Domestication and Exploitation of Plants and Animals.* London, Duckworth.

Wishart, D.J., Warren, A. and Stoddard, R.H. (1969) An attempted definition of a frontier using a wave analogy. *The Rocky Mountain Social Science Journal* **6**, 73-81.

G.W.W. BARKER

Cultural and economic change in the prehistory of central Italy

This paper puts forward some hypotheses on the nature and significance of prehistoric culture change in the archaeological record of central Italy. Necessarily it is a summary account, but I have tried to select a few apposite topics to illustrate my general thesis. This stems from two years' research and fieldwork in central Italy, based on the British School at Rome, where I have been collating and interpreting the existing evidence for prehistoric economies in the area. Full discussion of the data from which these hypotheses were formulated, will be set out in a Ph.D. thesis at the University of Cambridge; a more detailed account of part of this research, however, is contained in a forthcoming article on the bronze age of central Italy (Barker 1972).

Little or no attempt has been made in the past to integrate the prehistory of central Italy with the environment or general ecology of the peninsula. An accurate if rather bald summary of the accepted sequence of prehistoric culture change here would be as follows:

> Palaeolithic and mesolithic peoples led a 'catch-as-catch-can' existence as nomadic hunter-fisher-gatherers. In about 5000/4500 B.C. neolithic settlers arrived on the shores of Italy, bringing agriculture and other new techniques such as the ability to make pottery and tools of polished stone; these settlers introduced a new economy of stock-keeping and cereal agriculture. This situation was destroyed by the advent of eneolithic or copper age peoples *c.*2500 B.C., who brought social upheaval and nomadic pastoralism in their wake: as a result, the following 'Apennine bronze age' was characterized by large-scale transhumance between winter coastal and summer upland pastures. Towards the end of the bronze age, however, this pastoralist society reverted to settled agriculture.

The prehistory of central Italy conventionally has been thought to be a series of neat cultural phases, each with its economic label, developing with regional variations one after the other. All the arguments so far used to explain changes in culture and economy have drawn on two simple factors – population invasion or human whim: culture change, with its concomitant economic change, was according to the current explicit or implicit model sudden and total across central Italy and is assumed to have taken place free from even the most general or long-term constraints imposed by the prehistoric environment.

My own attempts to build alternative models of cultural and economic change have drawn from three sources of data: the material assemblages, particularly from recent stratified excavations (for the current framework was largely constructed without their help); palaeolithic, neolithic and bronze age faunal samples; and the evidence of the location of the sites themselves. This last was built up by the analysis of the territories or 'site catchments' (Vita-Finzi and Higgs 1970) of a large number of sites of each period, repeated at some sites several times in each season during the two years of fieldwork. My main thesis is that, to a greater or lesser degree, mobile economies can be detected in the archaeological record of central Italy from the palaeolithic onwards and were often the dominant component of prehistoric economy in some areas until the latter part of the bronze age.

The most obvious feature of central Italian climate is the hot dry summer, which is particularly fierce on the western and eastern lowlands. The summer drought is a severe limiting factor and its effect is concentrated on the lowlands by the drastic changes in topography in comparatively short distances. Stock economy therefore has to adapt in some way to seasonal pasture. The traditional response to the constraints of climate and topography in central Italy has been stock transhumance: this is documented from the Roman period (White 1970:306-16) through the Middle Ages (di Cicio 1966; Faraglia 1903) until the last century (Craven 1838:259-63) and survives today despite modern land hunger for the lowland pastures (Barbieri 1955; Ortolani 1941). Evidence for mobile economies appears throughout the prehistoric record in central Italy. Furthermore, without simply seeking gross deterministic hypotheses, I believe that we cannot afford to ignore the implications of mobile economies when we turn to explanations of 'regional' change and/or insularity detected in the culture sequence in the area.

Professors Palma di Cesnola and Radmilli and Dottoressa Vigliardi were kind enough to allow me to work in the faunal samples from their palaeolithic excavations. One point to emerge from this study has been the evidence, albeit fragmentary, for changes in the predator-prey relationship between palaeolithic man and the game he exploited. On the western side of central Italy, for example, middle palaeolithic sites are confined to the lowlands and lower valleys of Lazio (Fig. 1) and their food debris demonstrates the exploitation of

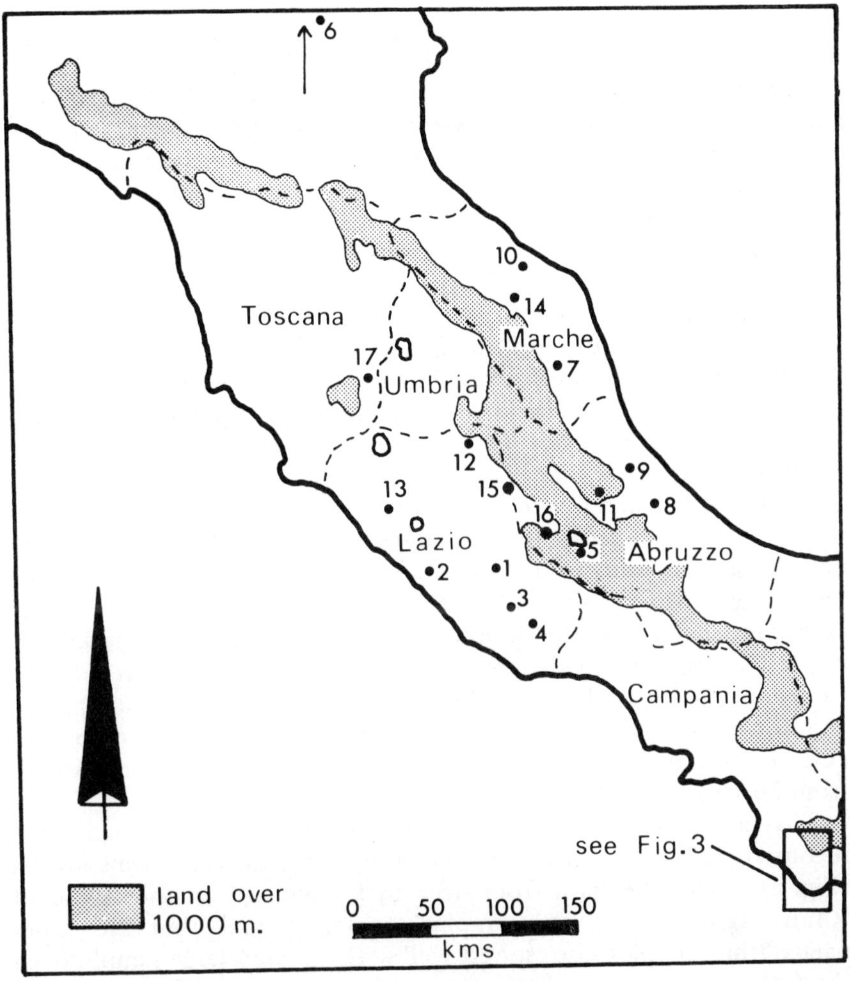

Figure 1 Central Italy: sites mentioned in the text.
1. Grotta Polesini; 2. Palidoro; 3. Cisterna; 4. Grotta Jolanda; 5. Fucine Lake sites; 6. Molino Casarotto (north of the map near Vicenza); 7. Maddalena di Muccia; 8. Grotta dei Piccioni; 9. Villaggio Leopardi a Penne; 10. Ripabianca di Monterado; 11. Capo d'Acqua; 12. Valle Ottara (or Petescia); 13. Tre Erici; 14. Conelle; 15. Val di Varri; 16. Grotte Cole I e II, Petrella; 17. Grotta dell'Orso.

a broad spectrum of game, such as *Palaeoloxedon antiquus, Dicerorhinus merckii, Cervus elaphus, Bos primigenius, Equus caballus* and occasionally *Hippopotamus amphibius* (on the low-lands) and *Capra ibex* (inland). As cold and aridity increased during the latter part of the last glaciation (Bonatti 1970; Frank 1969), conditions increasingly favoured the large herbivores, especially red deer (*Cervus elaphus*) and 'steppe' horse (*Equus hydruntinus*), with their ability to move overland between the seasonal pastures. At the same time, the archaeological record shows that the upper palaeolithic bands probably followed the game from western lowland camps such as the Grotta Polesini (Radmilli 1953; Fig. 1, site 1), Palidoro (Blanc 1955; Chiappella 1956; Fig. 1, site 2), Cisterna (Segre 1956; Fig. 1, site 3) and the Grotta Jolanda (Zei 1953; Fig. 1, site 4) into the Apennines, particularly to the summer pastures around the Fucine Lake, where a number of contemporary deposits have been excavated in caves on the edge of the lake basin (Cremonesi 1968; Grifoni and Radmilli 1964; Radmilli 1956 and 1963; Fig. 1, site 5). Comparable developments have been demonstrated in Epirus in Greece (Higgs, Vita-Finzi, Harris and Fagg 1967). In neither area do middle palaeolithic economies seem to have entailed the exploitation of the uplands or a heavy reliance on one or two species; in both areas a much closer relationship developed with one or two animals in the latter part of the last glaciation, involving movement with the game to the high pastures during the summer months.

On the other hand, a recent analysis carried out by the writer of middle and upper palaeolithic faunal samples from four coastal caves near Marina di Camerota in southern Campania (Palma di Cesnola 1967, 1969, 1969a; Vigliardi 1968, 1968a) showed that one animal alone, red deer, was the dominant meat source in both middle and upper palaeolithic sites. Climatic change in this period was inferred from microfaunal changes (Bartolomei, personal communication) and the period almost certainly encompassed some sea regression (Fig. 3), but red deer levels were unaffected throughout and varied from 70% to over 90%.

The mortality ages of the deer at three of the caves were reconstructed from stages of tooth eruption and wear in mandibles (Fig. 2), using the data from deer of known age on the Island of Rhum (Lowe 1967); the samples are fairly small, but the upper palaeolithic samples correspond well with the very large sample from the Grotta Polesini. At the Grotta del Poggio, the middle palaeolithic band culled mature animals, on modern data between 3 and 8 years old. At the Grotta Cala, however, and at the contempary shelter on the other side of the gorge called the Grotta Calanca (Fig.3), the upper palaeolithic bands still killed the deer between these ages, but also quite clearly selected young deer in their first year of life. Calving probably took place in June and July and on tooth eruption data the first year deaths at the upper palaeolithic caves occurred in the second rather than the first six months of life. Therefore one feature of upper palaeolithic economy at Camerota seems to have been the systematic culling of young deer during the winter months. These layers at the Grotta della Cala have been dated by C-14 to *c.* 27,000 and 25,000 B.P. (Palma di Cesnola, 1971). Data on modern deer behaviour suggest that the deer would have moved up the Mingardo river each spring to the pastures 30-40 km to the north (Fig. 3) and returned for the rut in the autumn to the coast and

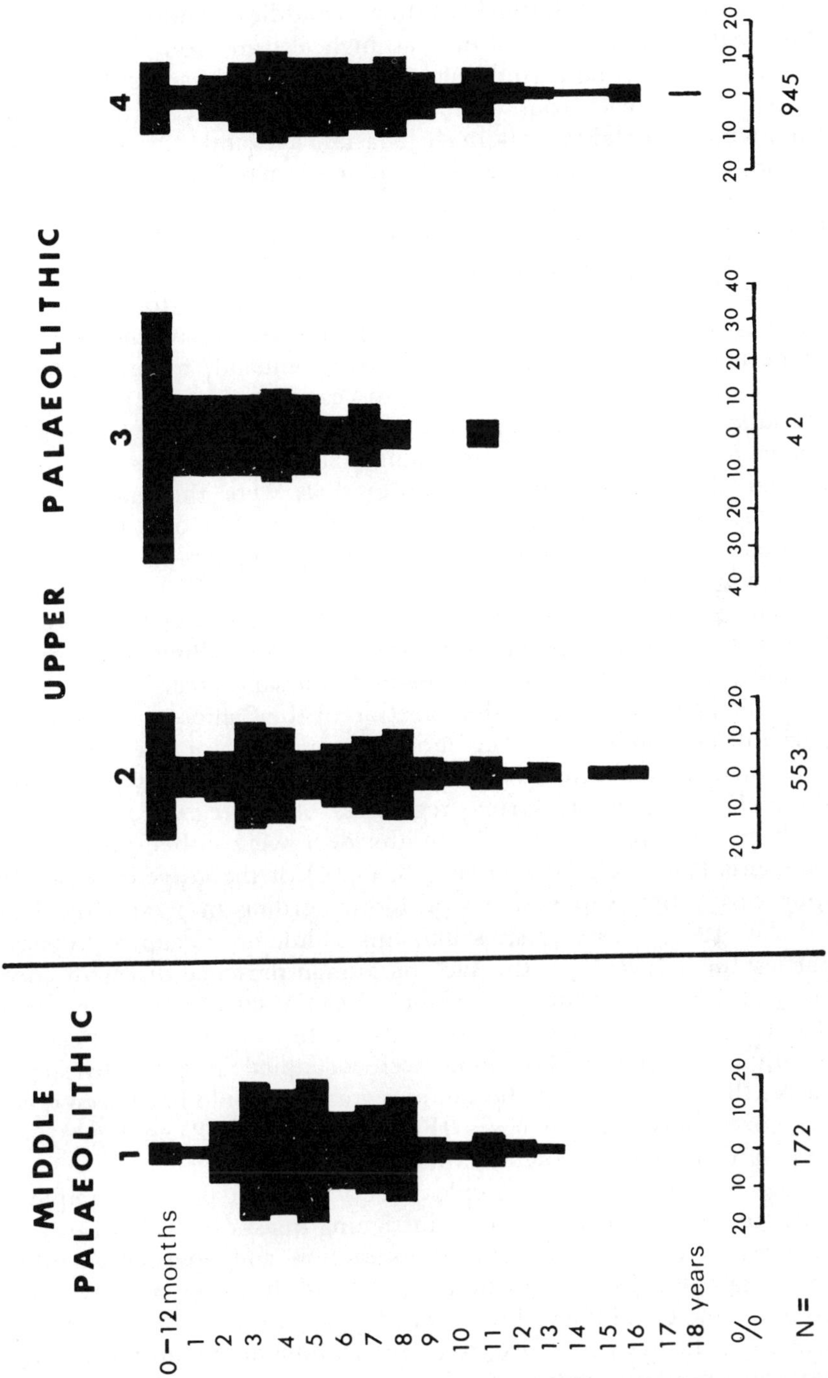

Figure 2 Mortality ages of red deer (*Cervus elaphus*) constructed from mandibular tooth eruption and wear, after Lowe (1967).
1. Grotta del Poggio; 2, Grotta della Cala; 3. Grotta Calanca; 4. Grotta Polesini.

lowlands (Darling 1937:96-112). Inland middle and upper palaeolithic flint scatters have been found at high altitudes on these summer pastures (Stradi and Andreolotti 1964), which are still used by transhumant flocks from the coast (Fig. 3). In the face of this evidence for a winter mortality peak in the coastal caves and for summer camps inland, together with what we know of modern red deer behaviour, it is likely that both middle and upper palaeolithic bands occupied the Camerota caves during the winter months, but moved inland to the head of the Mingardo river during the summer.

It is probably impossible to extract much more information from the Camerota samples, particularly on the nature of the cull. In a modern reindeer economy in western Greenland, for example, the nature of the cull varies from year to year (Sturdy 1972): more does are killed in a good calving year, while in a bad year the Lapps select barren does, older animals and young males. Nevertheless, despite the annual fluctuations, Sturdy reports that, were the main autumn camp to be excavated in a few thousand years, 'the only major trend to emerge from the bones about killing proportions might be a tendency to select young males' (Sturdy 1972: 187-8). Whatever the makeup of the kill, however, Fig. 2 suggests that the upper palaeolithic bands systematically practised a more intensive culling policy on the deer than the middle palaeolithic bands in the same area.

In the light of this data, the selection of the Camerota caves by the palaeolithic bands is all the more remarkable, for the 'two hour' catchment area is effectively walled in on three sides by precipitous slopes (Fig. 3). In the spring, regardless of sea regression, the only exits to the inland pastures for the deer were either through the Bulgheria-Penniniello saddle (Fig. 3, no. 4) or the gorge between the four caves. In Lapp systems of loose herding in west Greenland (Sturdy 1972) strategic sites like this saddle are occupied by small parties for a few days; the fact of human presence drives the deer away and by the occupation of such sites the seasonal movements of the deer are manipulated by the herders to suit their own needs. If the Bulgheria-Penniniello saddle were occupied in spring by such a party, the only route to the summer grazings would have been down the gorge between the caves (Between (1) and (2) in Fig. 3) and westwards to what is now the Mingardo estuary.

The Camerota faunal sample is very much a pioneer sample in Italy; at the very least, it poses intriguing questions which can only be tested by far more rigorous extraction and analysis of other, larger, samples. Even with the data at hand, however, we have some insight, albeit shadowy, into economy in one area during the last glaciation. In the first place, red deer was the dominant meat source over an enormous period of time at Camerota; the deer probably moved between winter and summer pastures, in turn followed by the palaeolithic bands; in some way the manner of exploitation changed in the upper palaeolithic, though the details of this are necessarily

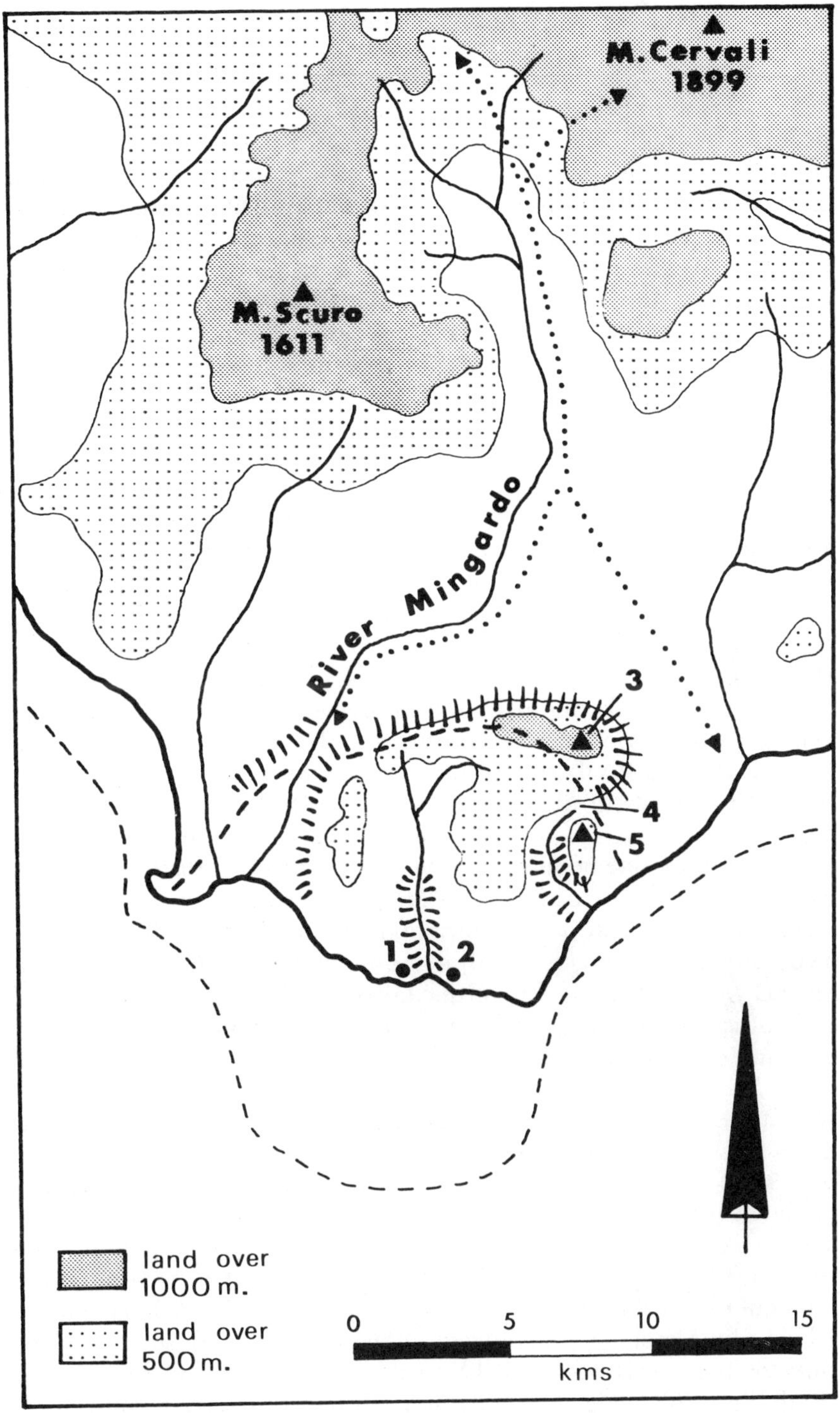

Figure 3 Hypothetical exploitation of the Camerota caves.
Dotted lines indicate modern transhumant routes; light dashed line shows sea regression to -100 metres, heavy dashed line shows the extent of the (two hour) 'territory' or 'site catchment' from the caves. 1. Grotta Calanca and Grotta Taddeo; 2. Grotta della Cala and Grotta del Poggio; 3. Monte Bulgheria (1224m.); 4. saddle; 5. Penniniello (660m).

blurred; finally, the faunal and 'territorial' data appear to correlate in some ways with Sturdy's example of a Lapp system of herd following or loose herding, which involves a degree of manipulation at certain times of the year, particularly in the autumn and spring. It remains an hypothesis, but an hypothesis which is testable in the future. To my mind the Lapp analogy fits the evidence of the cull and the location of the sites at least as well as those of other systems of animal predation employed by modern hunter-gatherers. The fact that it fits in even the grossest sense at Camerota should entail its inclusion in the list of 'ethnographic possibles' used in the interpretation of palaeolithic faunal samples.

In Marche and Abruzzo the fertile lowlands bear some of the highest cereal yields today in the peninsula – often over 50 quintals per hectare, (compared with some 30-40 on the Apulian Tavoliere, for example). Furthermore, the summer pastures for stock are but one or two days' march away, to the west. Here on the lowlands the first dated sites with pottery, cereals and caprines appear, according to C-14, *c.*4,500 B.C. or slightly earlier. As in southern Italy (Whitehouse 1968), early painted wares appear sporadically on most sites, together with the plain and impressed coarse wares. The cereal evidence consists of identifications of carbonised remains in pottery filler (Evett and Renfrew 1971) and as yet we have no idea of the role played by cereals in the economy of the Marche and Abruzzo sites. Unfortunately their economic significance has as yet been demonstrated at only one neolithic site in Italy, far to the north (Fig. 2, site 6) at Molino Casarotto in the Berici Hills on the northern edge of the Po valley. Here excavations by Birmingham and Ferrara Universities in 1969 and 1970 (Broglio 1970) demonstrated both the appearance of cereals *c.*4,500 B.C. at a neolithic lakeside village and their complete insignificance compared with the enormous exploitation of water-chestnut gathered from the lake (Jarman 1971).

At Maddalena di Muccia in Marche, (Lollini 1965; Fig. 1, site 7), so far our earliest site in central Italy, dated by C-14 to 4630 B.C. ± 75 (R-643), the faunal percentages were dominated by pig (50%) and red deer (*c.*25%) and caprines played only a small part in the economy (15%). In northern Italy the analysis of neolithic and bronze age faunal samples indicated that caprines, which appeared sporadically at about this time at Molino Casarotto, were not fully integrated into the economy until perhaps a millennium later (Jarman 1971). In Marche and Abruzzo, however, caprines seem to have thrived and levels rise swiftly to 40% at the Grotta dei Piccioni (Radmilli 1963a; Fig. 1, site 8) in levels dates to 4297 ± 130 (Pi-46), 44% at the Villaggio Leopardi, an open site near Penne (Cremonesi 1966; Fig. 1, site 9) dated to 4228 B.C. ± 135 (Pi-101) and 64% at Ripabianca di Monterado in Marche (Lollini 1965; Fig. 1, site 10), a site with dates from 4310 B.C. ± 85 (R-599a) to 4190 B.C. ± 70 (R-598a).

It is doubtful how much of this was attributable to the wholesale arrival of a 'neolithic people' on the eastern lowlands. At Capo d'Acqua, for example, inland from the Grotta dei Piccioni, (Bonuccelli and Faedo 1968; Tozzi 1966; Fig. 1, site 11), a mesolithic camp by a small lake with bones of red deer, pig and cattle was succeeded by a site with identical flintwork (identical too to the industry at the Grotta dei Piccioni), a wild fauna and a few caprines, a few sherds of plain and impressed ware, *figulina* (a local finer ware on the eastern sites) and one painted sherd (Bonuccelli and Faedo 1968). Indeed a similar lithic continuity has been noticed in many parts of central Italy, particularly west of the Apennine watershed (Acanfora 1962-3; Calzoni 1939; Östenberg 1967: 159-169; Radmilli 1951-2; Rellini 1920). Perhaps of greater interest and signifance, therefore, are the processes at work, the rates at which we can detect the integration of different facets of the 'neolithic economy' into different parts of central Italy.

West of the Apennines, for example, the three C-14 dates available suggest that pottery came into use at roughly the same time as on the Adriatic side of central Italy. Sasso pottery has been dated to 4130 B.C.± 200 (R-676) at the Grotta dell'Orso in Toscana (Grifoni 1967; Fig. 1, site 17), and still appears at Tre Erici (Östenberg 1967: 159-169; Fig. 1, site 13) in a level dated to 3445 B.C. ± 80 (St-1344), contemporary with the use of *figulina* at Valle Ottara (Acanfora 1962-3; Fig. 1, site 12), an inland site dated to 3450 B.C. ± 145 (Pi-28). On the other hand, economic change was disparate: caprines and swine were the most important animals killed at the Grotta dell'Orso (Grifoni 1967: 108), yet deer dominated the faunal sample at Valle Ottara (Acanfora 1962-3: 115). Caprines were the only significant stock animal here (23%) and, as in northern Italy (Jarman 1971) deer seem to have been replaced by caprines only in the late neolithic in some areas of central Italy.

Between *c*.4500 and *c*.1000 B.C. we can discern several 'economic units', each of lowland and contiguous upland areas, in which the developments and changes in material assemblages often appear remarkably discrete. In the late glacial we suggested that palaeolithic bands probably moved up with the deer each summer to the Fucine Lake from the western lowlands. Fishing settlements ringed the lake as it began to dry up during the postglacial. Flocks were an important component of the economy of the neolithic and eneolithic sites here; unless they were stalled each winter as they are today, in the absence of fodder crops it seems likely that they were taken to lowland pastures each autumn. The development of the assemblages in the caves on the southern edge of the lake from the neolithic to the late bronze age (Cremonesi 1968; Grifoni and Radmilli 1964) is remarkably similar to the sequence at the Grotta dei Piccioni to the east on the lowlands. Of course we cannot link sites in direct social terms, but the undoubted ties between these sites probably express the kind of economic as well as cultural relationship which developed between the Fucine Lake and the eastern lowlands. I have argued elsewhere that the Conelle (Fig. 1, site 14) – Ortucchio (Fig. 1, site 5) 'eneolithic' ceramic assemblage probably persisted in these areas east of the watershed at a time when the 'Apennine bronze age' culture was developing to the west (Barker 1972). Settlement of the Fucine basin and eastern lowlands developed with remarkably little influence in the material assemblage from the Apennine bronze age sites to the west for much of the bronze age, although shepherds from the western plains probably camped in the hills to the north and west of the lake each summer, at Val di Varri, for example (Güller and Segre 1948; Fig. 1, site 15) and the Grotta Cola II (Radmilli 1957; Fig. 1 site 16).

The evidence for bronze age economies is much fuller in the west and has been examined in some detail (Barker 1972). Mobility, as has often been suggested, *is* important in the 'Apennine bronze age', but no more so, I suggest, than in the neolithic in the same area, and indeed in the upper palaeolithic besides. The full 'neolithic' economy, in the sense of cereal agriculture and stock-keeping on a large scale, only appears to have developed here in the latter part of the bronze age towards the end of the second millennium B.C. During this period we can detect the growth of upland villages related archaeologically to camps on the western plains, the latter unrelated to nearby lowland settlements practising mixed cereal and stock economies. These developments coincide with the first major pottery scatters and the rapid growth of settlement evidence on the western lowlands, recovered for example by the Etrurian survey of the British School at Rome (Ward-Perkins *et al.* 1968, compare his Fig. 2 with Figs. 27-33). This evidence would tend to support the hypothesis that in this area at least population pressure was the principal factor which brought about the development of the social and economic dichotomy between lowland settlements on the one hand, and, on the other, permanent highland villages whose shepherds took the flocks from the highest summer pastures down to the western plains each winter. If this is correct, then the broad pattern of exploitation found from Roman to modern times had probably developed by the end of the bronze age in Etruria by *c.* 1,000 B.C.

These are some of the economic patterns which are emerging in central Italy. Despite the deficiencies of economic data in this area, manifold both in their quality and quantity, there is enough to prompt us to formulate several testable hypotheses on the processes of economic change. The differing rates of economic change and adaptation ought to be as illuminating as rates of change seen in the culture sequence in the prehistory of central Italy and what little we see even now appears to be fundamental to our understanding of both.

REFERENCES

Acanfora, M.O. (1962-3) Gli scavi di Valle Ottara presso Cittaducale. *Bullettino Paletnologia Italiana* **14**, 73-154.

Barbieri, G. (1955) Osservazioni geografico-statistiche sulla transumanza in Italia. *Rivista Geografica Italiana* **62**, 15-30.

Barker, G.W.W. (1972) Rates of cultural and economic growth in the Bronze Age of central Italy, *Proceedings of the Prehistoric Society* **38** (in press).

Blanc, A.C. (1955) Giacimento del palaeolitico superiore ad *Equus hydruntinus* e sovrapposti livelli con ceramica neolitica e dell' età del bronzo, nella cava di travertino di Palidoro (Roma). *Quaternaria* **2**, 308-9.

Bonatti, E. (1970) Pollen sequence in the Lake Sediments. *In* G.E. Hutchinson (ed.) *Ianula – an account of the history and development of the Lago di Monterosi, Latium, Italy* (Transactions of the American Philosophical Society **60**, part 4) 26-31.

Bonuccelli, G. and Faedo, L. (1968) Il villaggio a ceramica impressa di Capo d'Acqua. *Atti della Società toscana di Scienze naturali* Serie A, **75**, 87-101.

Broglio, A. (1970) Risultati delle recenti richerche sui Neolitico e sull' Eneolitico del Veneto, del Trentino e del Friuli. *Odeo Olimpico* **8**, 65-79.

Calzoni, U. (1939) Un fondi di capanna scoperto presso Norcia (Umbria). *Bullettino di Paletnologia Italiana* **3**, 37-50.

Chiappella, G.V. (1956) Scavo nel giacimento superiore di Palidoro, Roma, *Quaternaria*, **3**, 263-4.

di Cicio, P. (1966) Il problema della Dogana delle Pecore nella seconda metà del XVIII secolo. *La Capitanata* **4**, 63-72.

Craven, K. (1838) *Excursions in the Abruzzi*, vol. 1. London, Bentley.

Cremonesi, G. (1966) Il villaggio Leopardi presso Penne in Abruzzo. *Bullettino di Paletnologia Italiana* **17**, 27-49.

Cremonesi, G. (1968) Contributo alla conoscenza della preistoria del Fucino: la Grotta di Ortucchio e la Grotta la Punta. *Rivista di Scienze Preistoriche* **23**, 145-204.

Darling, F.F. (1937) *A Herd of Red Deer: a Study in Animal Behaviour.* London, Oxford University Press.

Evett, D. and Renfrew, J. (1971) L'agricoltura neolitica italiana: una nota sui cereali. *Rivista di Scienze Preistoriche* **26**, 403-9.

Faraglia, N.F. (1903) *Intorno all' archivio della Dogana delle Pecore di Puglia.* Naples, A. Tessitore e Figlio (Stab. tib. dell'Università).

Frank, A.H.E. (1969) Pollen stratigraphy of the Lake of Vico (Central Italy) *Palaeogeography, Palaeoclimatology, Palaeoecology* **6**, 67-85.

Grifoni, R. (1967) La Grotta dell'Orso di Sarteano – il Neolitico. *Origini* **1**, 53-115.

Grifoni, R. and Radmilli, A.M. (1964) La Grotta Maritza e il Fucino primo dell'età romana. *Rivista di Scienze Preistoriche* **19**, 53-127.

Güller, A. and Segre, A.G. (1948) La stazione énea del grottone di Val di Varri nell'Appennine abruzzese. *Rivista di Antropologia* **36**, 269-81.

Higgs, E.S., Vita-Finzi, C., Harris, D.R. and Fagg, A.E. (1967) The Climate, Environment and Industries of Stone Age Greece: part III. *Proceedings of the Prehistoric Society* **33**, 1-29.

Jarman, M.R. (1971) Culture and economy in the north Italian Neolithic. *World Archaeology* **2**, no. 3, 255-65.

Lollini, D.G. (1965) Il Neolitico nelle Marche alla luce delle recenti scoperte. *Atti VI Congresso delle Scienze Preistoriche e Protostoriche*, 209-15.

Lowe, V.P.W. (1967) Teeth as indicators of age with special reference to red deer *(Cervus elaphus)* of known age from Rhum. *Journal of the Zoological Society of London* **152**, 137-153.

Östenberg, C.E. (1967) Luni sul Mignone e problemi della preistoria d'Italia. *Acta Instituti Romani Regni Sueciae* Series 4, 25, 1-306.

Ortolani, M. (1941) Pastorizia transumante e bonifica integrale. *Geopolitica* 3, 276-80.

Palma di Cesnola, A. (1967) Gli scavi nelle grotte di Marina di Camerota (Salerno) durante gli anni 1965-1967. *Atti della XI e XII Riunione Scientifica dell'Istituto Italiano di Preistoria e Protostoria*, 199-217.

Palma di Cesnola, A. (1969) Il Musteriano della Grotta del Poggio a Marina di Camerota (Salerno). *Scritti sul Quaternario in onore di Angelo Pasa.* Museo Civico di Storia Naturale, Verona, 93-135.

Palma di Cesnola, A. (1969a) Le ricerche e gli scavi a Marina di Camerota (Salerno) durante il biennio 1968-1969. *Rivista di Scienze Preistoriche* **24**, 195-217.

Palma di Cesnola, A. (1971) II Gravettiano evoluto della Grotta della Cala a Marina di Camerota (Salerno). *Rivista di Scienze Preistoriche* **26**, 259-324.

Radmilli, A.M. (1951-2) Notizie preliminari sulla grotta sepolcrale 'Patrizi' di Sasso-Furbara. *Bullettino di Paletnologia Italiana* **8**, parte 4, 100-4.

Radmilli, A.M. (1953) Gli scavi della Grotta Polesini. *Bullettino di Paletnologia Italiana* **8**, Parte 5, 23-31.

Radmilli, A.M. (1956) Il paleolitico superiore nella Grotta Clemente Tronci a Venere dei Marsi, territorio del Fucino. *Bullettino della Società Geologica Italiana* **85**, 94-116.

Radmilli, A.M. (1957) Insediamento neolitico nella Grotta Cola II a Petrella di Cappadocia. *Atti della Società toscana di Scienze naturali* Serie A, **64**, 40-8.

Radmilli, A.M. (1963) Il paleolitico superiore nel Riparo Maurizio. *Atti della Società toscana di Scienze naturali* Serie A, **70**, 220-43.

Radmilli, A.M. (1963a) *La preistoria d'Italia alla luce delle ultime scoperte.* Florence, Istituto Geografico Militare.

Rellini, U. (1920) Cavernette e ripari preistorici nell'Agro Falisco. *Monumenti Antichi Lincei* **24**, 8-181.

Segre, A.G. (1956) Scoperte di Paleolitico e del Bronzo nei travertini di Cisterna (Latina). *Rivista di Antropologia* **43**, 367-82.

Stradi, F. and Andreolotti, S. (1964) Secondo rinvenimento in superficie di industrie del paleolitico superiore e medio sul Monte Alburno (Salerno). *Atti della VIII e IX Riunione Scientifica dell'Istituto Italiano di Preistoria e Protostoria* 291-301.

Sturdy, D. (1972) Exploitation patterns of a modern reindeer economy in West Greenland, in Higgs, E.S. (ed.) *Papers in Economic Prehistory*, London, Cambridge University Press 181-90.

Tozzi, C. (1966) Il giacimento mesolitico di Capo d'Acqua (L'Aquila). *Bullettino di Paletnologia Italiana* **17**, 13-25.

Vigliardi, A. (1968) Il Musteriano della Grotta Taddeo (Marina di Camerota, Salerno). *Rivista di Scienze Preistoriche* **23**, 245-59.

Vigliardi, A. (1968a) Prima campagna di scavi nel deposito paleolitico superiore di Grotta Calanca (Marina di Camerota, Salerno). *Rivista di Scienze Preistoriche* **23**, 271-314.

Vita-Finzi, C. and Higgs, E.S. (1970) Prehistoric Economy in the Mount Carmel Area of Palestine. Site Catchment Analysis. *Proceedings of the Prehistoric Society* **36**, 1-37.

Ward-Perkins, J.B. (1968) with Kahane, A. and Murray Threipland, L. The Ager Veientanus, north and east of Veii. *Papers of the British School at Rome* **36**, 1-218.

White, K.D. (1970) *Roman Farming.* London, Thames and Hudson.

Whitehouse, R.D. (1968) Settlement and economy in Southern Italy in the Neothermal Period. *Proceedings of the Prehistoric Society* **34**, 332-67.

Zei, M. (1953) Esplorazione di grotte nei pressi di Sezze-Romano. *Bullettino di Paletnologia Italiana* **8**, parte 5, 102-7.

C.M. NELSON

Prehistoric culture change in the intermontane plateau of western north America

Introduction

There are two fundamental approaches to the explanation of prehistoric culture change. The most widely applied is ethnographic analogy, the explanation of prehistoric events through the use of ethnographically identified patterns and processes which have no direct historic link with the changes they are used to explain. Though this is the only method available in the analysis of remote prehistoric periods, it is also possible to deal with prehistoric culture change as an historical problem wherever ethnographic data is sufficiently detailed. The foundations of this approach were laid decades ago (e.g. Sapir 1916) and numerous archaeologists have implicitly utilized it in dealing with the recent prehistoric remains which they have encountered.

This paper explores the possibility of operating more directly from the ethnographic record by identifying those aspects of economic organization which leave tangible archaeological remains, tracing the origins of these in the prehistoric record, and using the information so acquired to generate an explanatory hypothesis. The case study presented is drawn from a portion of the Intermontane Plateau of western North America (Freeman, Forester, and Luphur 1945) which corresponds roughly to Kroeber's (1939: Map 6, Table 18) Columbia-Fraser culture area (Fig. 1). This area has been occupied throughout prehistory by hunters and gatherers and at contact contained societies with band and simple tribal social organizations. Since similar degrees of social and economic integration characterize much of the world's prehistory, this study is also an example of the detail in which events can be reconstructed from palaeolithic remains given a sufficient amount of information.

Physiographic and climatic patterning of culture in the Intermontane Plateau

Topography, climate, and drainage have always profoundly effected the demography and economy of human populations in the Intermontane Plateau. The heart of this physiographic province is composed of a broad ramp of Miocene basalt which slopes gently westward from the foothills of the Rocky mountains to the deeply incised valley of the Columbia River. Much of this area, usually referred to as the Columbia Plateau, receives less than 10 in. of rain per year and in consequence has a seasonally and geographically restricted supply of surface water. The Columbia Plateau is ringed with hills and mountains which are bordered by and contain numerous permanently flowing streams and rivers. Temperatures decline and precipitation increases markedly with altitude. This produces marked zonation of the plant communities and in some areas it is possible to travel from a semiarid biotic community subsisting on less than 10 in. of precipitation a year to forests of pine and fir subsisting on more than 30 in. of rain per year over a distance of 10 miles or less (Fig. 1). It is this area of transitional biotic communities, which commonly ranges from 10 to 50 miles in breadth, which supports the densest populations of game animals such as deer, elk, mountain sheep, and pronghorn antelope.

Low temperatures and snow severely limit the distribution of human population during the winter months from October to March. Though the bulk of the Columbia Plateau lies only between 1000 and 1500 feet above the sea level, winters are nonetheless severe. Temperatures frequently drop between 10 and 40°F. below freezing in all but the most sheltered areas. As a result, the human population is concentrated in the narrow, sheltered valleys of the major rivers at the fringes of the Columbia Plateau. Many of the ungulates are driven into the same areas as snow buries their forage at higher elevations. Palynological evidence (Hansen 1944; 1947; 1955; Heusser 1960) suggests winter temperatures severe enough to effect human populations in this fashion throughout the prehistoric record.

The distribution of important edible plants, such as the tubers of kouse and camas, is also effected by climate and topography. Maturation of these plants is linked with altitude and temperature. Although they mature enough to be eaten early in the spring in the warmest, most sheltered portions of the Columbia Plateau, they can still be gathered late in the fall in the surrounding mountains. Archaeological evidence suggests that successive, geographically patterned root harvests must have been an important aspect of the yearly economic round for the last 6,000 years of prehistory.

The most stable source of protein for Plateau peoples comes in the form of salmon whose spawning migrations follow a highly predic-

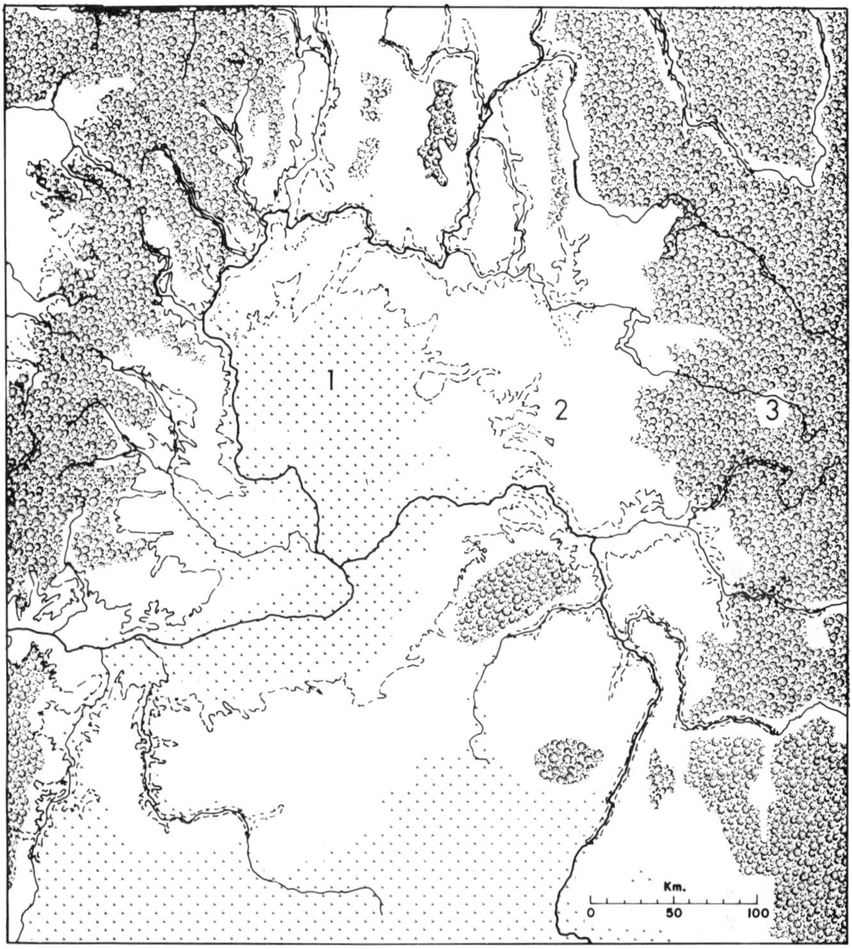

Figure 1 Biotic zones and exploitation areas in the Columbia Plateau (modified from Piper 1906, St. John 1937 and the U.S. National Atlas 1971).
1, semi-arid desert. 2, semi-arid to well-watered grasslands and open forests of yellow pine. 3, dense forest of fire and white pine, and alpine vegetation at higher altitudes. Zone 2 contained the greatest biomass usable by hunters and gatherers.

table four year cycle. Migratory salmon are typically in the trunk streams and their stable tributaries from late in the spring to the end of autumn. Due to the absence of streams in the central portion of the Columbia Plateau, nearly all the salmon are funnelled into the surrounding hills and mountains, a pattern which is apt to have been stable since the end of the Anathermal some 8,000 years ago.

Ethnographic economic patterns

Ethnographic economic patterns in the Columbia-Fraser culture area are reasonably well known through the work of Ray (1932; 1936; 1939; 1942), Anastasio (1955), Schwede (1966; 1969), Spinden (1908), Teit (1900; 1906; 1909; 1928; 1930), and others. The following description, drawn primarily from these authors, is a generalized summary of features commonly held by groups whose territories adjoin the arid heartland of the Columbia Plateau.

Two kinds of data are apt to be useful when attempting to reconstruct the archaeological parameters of an ethnographically reported economic pattern: the functional associations of durable tools and the economic associations of demographic patterns reflected in the remains of archaeological sites. Much is known of numerous tool categories common throughout the Plateau (e.g. Ray 1942). The majority are perishable or possess a broad spectrum of potential uses so that they are of little use in reconstructing economic activities. Implements useful in such a task are limited to hopper mortars, pestles, and hammerstones used in the preparation of kouse and camas, stone and bone handles for digging sticks, composite harpoon valves, leister prongs, and the barbs of salmon spears used in fishing, gages and shuttles used in the manufacture of nets, and flaked stone and ground bone points used in hunting large game animals. These tools enter the archaeological record and undergo stylistic modifications in a piece-meal fashion, giving the prehistory of the area an apparent stability. This has been interpreted by many in terms of gradual change through the accretion of new artifact types and processes (Daugherty 1962; Butler 1966). A greater reliance on demographic data can be used to generate a more detailed and dynamic view of prehistoric culture change, as will be shown hereafter.

Defining the archaeological parameters of an economic organization through the use of demographic data is more complex, however, for it requires a careful consideration of the effects which the economic organization imposes on archaeologically identifiable settlements and their contents. For this purpose, the yearly economic round can be divided into two major segments: (1) the winter concentration of families into villages, and (2) the dispersal of the village band to a succession of temporary camps during the spring, summer, and fall. These camps were maintained while obtaining the surpluses of fish and edible roots necessary to support villages during the winter months. These activities were organized as follows throughout most of the Columbia Plateau.

Winter villages were occupied for about five months and abandoned as early in the spring as weather permitted. The cramped, unhygenic conditions in winter houses are frequently cited as the reason for this exodus to nearby camps, but the stress which most ethnographers place on winter hardships and hunger also makes it clear that the consumption of available food supplies was often as important a factor. The first spring camps were located near the winter villages in areas where the earliest edible plants appeared and where pocket gophers, ground squirrels, rabbits, birds, and other small animals were plentiful. These camps were left after a few weeks. With the exception of the infirm and a few able individuals left behind to care for them, village bands split into families and moved to the spring root gathering areas in the arid heartland of the Columbia Plateau or in the warmer areas flanking the Blue Mountains. During this period women gathered and prepared roots while men hunted antelope, rabbits, and other small animals. Though the products of the hunt were consumed on the spot, the bulk of the roots were dried, pulverized and ground into a coarse flour, and moulded into cakes so they could be carried with ease.

Late in April or early in May the root gathering camps were abandoned and families moved to summer fishing sites. Throughout much of the Columbia Plateau this meant moving outward from the semiarid interior to the surrounding hills and mountains. During this move, the dried rootmeal was stored at or near the winter village.

The summer fishing camps were occupied for nearly four months. During this period weirs or traps were built or repaired and as many as six successive salmon runs exploited along the small rivers and streams which spread in a wide arc along the margin of the Columbia Basin. The size of these camps depended on the importance of the local runs, the convenience of the location and the amount of labour required to maintain the weirs and process the salmon. When caught, fish were filleted, dried on racks and frequently ground into meal.

Summer fishing camps were abandoned at the end of August. Some families returned to the major trunk streams where they put the prepared fish in storage and continued to fish with seins, dip nets, and spears. Though these methods are not as effective as the use of weirs, spawning salmon deteriorate too rapidly after the beginning of September to be of much use if left to enter the smaller rivers and streams in which they will soon die. Moreover, salmon which spawn in the spring after wintering in the Snake and Columbia rivers become available in September.

When the summer fishing camps dispersed, other families moved higher in the surrounding mountains in order to collect late maturing roots, gather berries, and hunt, sometimes from a succession of small camps. These people returned to the winter villages in October as the autumn weather failed. Houses were cleaned and repaired, food stores secured, and the deepening of winter awaited.

Winter villages were explicitly located and, with the exception of a few natural fisheries, controlled all rights to local resources. Precise figures for the number of families or individuals commonly sheltered by a single village are not available, but ethnographic reports and archaeological evidence both suggest they commonly contained three to ten houses each of which might have contained one to three families, or a grand total of 20 to 100 individuals. The traditional dwelling was a semi-subterranean pit house between five and ten meters in diameter. It was usually excavated to a depth of one or two meters and in some areas might be lined with wooden planks or stone slabs. House roofs were covered with earth and therefore required substantial structural members. In the semiarid areas of the western and southern Columbia Plateau beams and uprights had to be salvaged from abandoned houses or transported from the nearest stand of suitable timber, often over a considerable distance.

The labour required to erect and maintain pit houses, the recognized control of local resources, and the need for specially prepared storage facilities all tended to stabilize the location of winter villages. In its turn this stability produced a host of subsidiary phenomena which are easily identified during archaeological surveying.

1. Storage facilities are frequently in the form of pits within the village or in nearby rock shelters.
2. With the exception of some individuals who die under ritually unfavourable circumstances, all people are interred in formally identified burial areas adjacent to village sites. The hardships of life during the closing months of winter and the custom of leaving the infirm in the vicinity of the winter village throughout the year insure the growth and maintenance of burial yards in the vicinity of any stable village.
3. A complex cycle of religious rituals had its focal point in the winter village and often produces tangible remains such as pictographs, petroglyphs, rock alignments, and sweat houses.
4. The winter village often acquires a series of satellite camp sites by virtue of the fact that these had to be located near early spring root gathering locations, fall fishing stations, and winter hunting camps.
5. Stored supplies of salmon, kouse, and camas were never accumulated in sufficient quantities to maintain a winter village against the threat of an unduly severe winter. As a result deer, elk, mountain sheep and antelope were hunted most extensively during the winter months. Carcasses were returned to the village virtually intact and in this way large quantities of bone were introduced into household refuse. Though dogs were kept only a very small proportion of the discarded bone shows any signs of gnawing.
6. Fresh water mussels were commonly gathered to supplement winter food supplies. Their shells frequently occur in localized middens within the winter village site.
7. The manufacture and repair of a wide variety of implements normally was undertaken in the winter during forced periods of inactivity. Coupled with the activities of the winter village, this custom tended to concentrate the widest possible variety of material objects in the site complex utilized by the village.

8. By virtue of the crucial geographic position and economic functions of the winter village, it will be substantially larger than the camps which its members exploited in root gathering and fishing. Such camps tend in the main to be small, lack structural remains, and contain faunal remains and artifacts appropriate to their economic functions.

These features characterize at least a part of the archaeological record throughout the Columbia Plateau. Their history in that record should document the emergence of ethnographic patterns since any alteration affecting the accumulation and storage of quantities of salmon, kouse, and camas, or the efficiency of winter hunting will be reflected in the settlement pattern.

The archaeological parameters of the winter village pattern

Sites which display the characteristics of winter villages are abundant in the Columbia Plateau. Though our knowledge of the distribution of ethnographically reported winter villages and archaeological sites is far from complete, there is enough information to produce obviously related patterns (Figs. 2 and 3). Winter villages, pit houses, and the archaeological site complexes which document the former location of winter villages cluster around the semiarid heartland of the Columbia Plateau and extend into the protected valleys and lake basins of the northern Columbia basin.

The exact relationships between specific site complexes and ethnographically reported villages is, however, more difficult to assess. In most areas we lack sufficiently detailed ethnographies and exhaustive archaeological surveys to do more than identify the most obvious specific relationships. The most detailed comparison available is provided by Nelson and Rice (1969) who, in co-operation with Schwede (1966), have documented the relationships between Nez Perce settlement patterns and the archaeological distribution of sites along a portion of the Snake River on the south-eastern periphery of the Columbia Plateau.

Schwede's analysis indicates that Nez Perce villages functioned at three territorial levels. The central concept is that of the village area, the geographic space in which the village controlled the utilization of all resources. The village locus, or site, theoretically might be located anywhere within the village area, but in practice there never seems to have been more than three separate sites which were occupied in a sporadic rotation. Finally, a zone of economic exploitation extended outward from the village area. This zone overlapped with the zones of other villages and the resources which it contained were held in common by all Nez Perce. Temporary use of a specific resource was

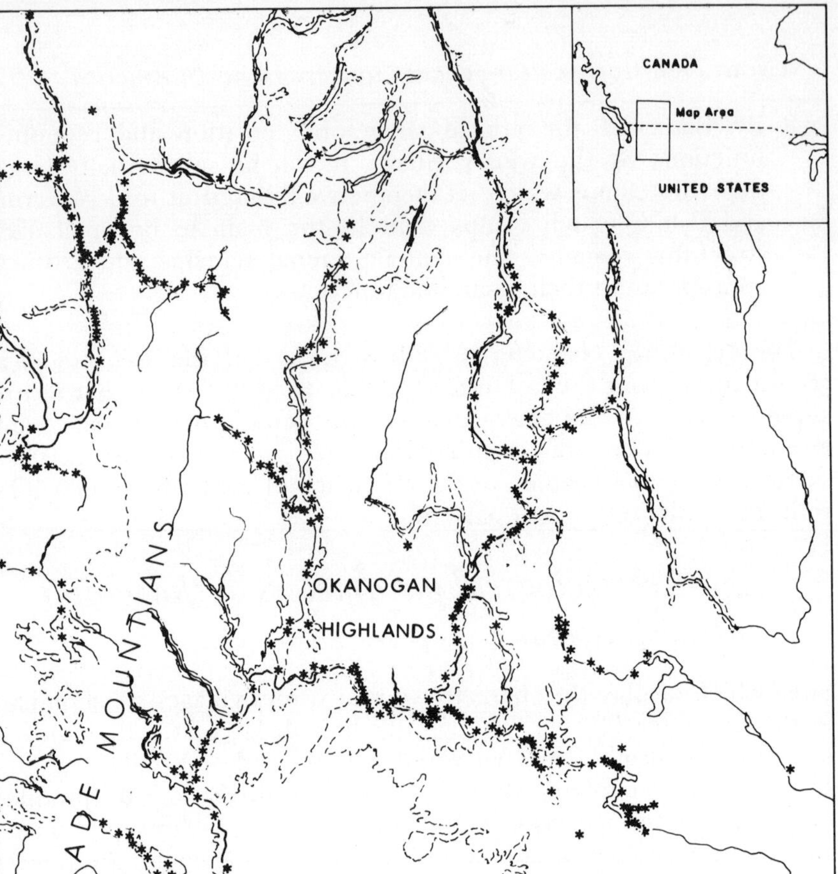

Figure 2 Ethnographically reported winter villages in and around the Columbia Plateau (summarized In Ray 1932, 1936; Schwede 1966; M. Smith 1950; Swanton 1952; and Teit 1900, 1906, 1909). Villages are represented by stars superimposed on the river system. The 2,000 foot contour is shown by a broken line.

(Data for Fig. 3 in part from Borden 1956; Butler 1966; Caldwell 1954; Caldwell and Mallory 1967; Chance 1968; Coale 1956; Collier, Hudson and Ford 1942; Cressman 1960; Daugherty 1952; Daugherty, Purdy and Fryxell 1967; Drucker 1948; Grabert 1966, 1968; Gunkel 1961; Kenaston 1966;

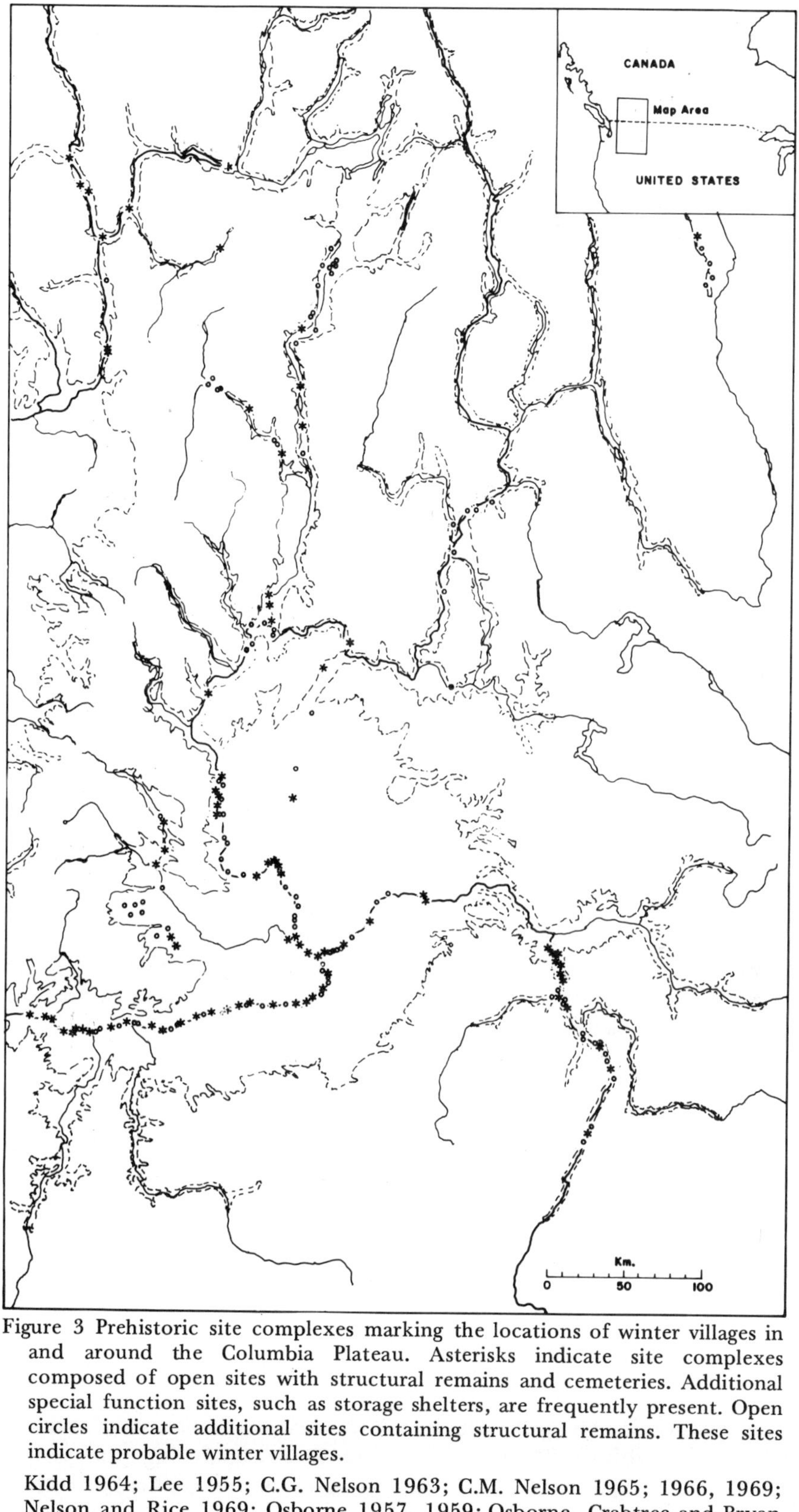

Figure 3 Prehistoric site complexes marking the locations of winter villages in and around the Columbia Plateau. Asterisks indicate site complexes composed of open sites with structural remains and cemeteries. Additional special function sites, such as storage shelters, are frequently present. Open circles indicate additional sites containing structural remains. These sites indicate probable winter villages.

Kidd 1964; Lee 1955; C.G. Nelson 1963; C.M. Nelson 1965; 1966, 1969; Nelson and Rice 1969; Osborne 1957, 1959; Osborne, Crabtree and Bryan 1952; Pavesic, Lynch and Warren 1964; Rice 1968a; Smith 1900, 1910, 1913; Warren 1959, Warren, Sims and Pavesic 1968; Weeks 1962).

obtained simply by occupying the camp site with which it was associated.

The archaeological confirmation of winter villages reported by Schwede was found to be excellent. All ethnographically reported areas contain large stratified sites and burial yards. The vast majority contain clear surface indications of structural remains and geographically differentiated site complexes. Most also contain storage shelters or other special features, such as petroglyphs. In some cases, however, well differentiated site complexes are divided between two adjoining villages. This may reflect informant error, overlapping village areas, or possibly even the budding of villages in protohistoric times.

Archaeological history of the winter village pattern

Identifying the relationships between ethnographic economic patterns and the archaeological phenomena to which they are related historically is only the first step in explaining their origin. In this case it should be possible to document the origins of the ethnographic economic pattern by considering the prehistory of the winter village pattern. This pattern emerges throughout the Columbia Plateau in the 500 years preceding 2000 B.P. In any given area the appearance of winter villages is sudden but there is a time vector operating from the northern portion of the Columbia River basin southward along the western flank of the Columbia Plateau and thence eastward along its southern margin (Nelson 1969: 47-8). The appearance of winter villages on the floodplains of rivers at this time was first noted by Swanson (1956: 1962) who thought it represented a shift in village or settlement location. In fact, it recorded the first appearance of semipermanent villages.

The introduction of winter villages is coupled with an increase in the average density and size of sites (Nelson 1969: 42-5). In as much as winter populations were always restricted to the areas in which winter villages came to be established, a significant increase in population must have occured during or shortly after the introduction of site complexes. This, in turn, suggests that the emergence of the winter village pattern must have brought with it substantial changes in the economic organization of Plateau peoples.

The economic basis for change

The economic changes which made the maintenance of winter villages possible can only be inferred by analysing the major economic components of the ethnographic pattern. There are three majour resources essential to the maintenance of winter villages: (1) stored surpluses of kouse and camas, (2) stored surpluses of salmon, and (3) the successful winter hunting of ungulates. Although the efficient combination of all these resources is indirectly indicated by the presence of site complexes, the most direct evidence for each taken individually lies in functionally associated implements and the frequency of faunal remains in wintering sites.

Winter hunting is reflected by the presence of projectile points and the faunal remains of deer, elk, mountain sheep, and antelope. These, together with edge-worn skin working tools, are abundant at wintering sites throughout Plateau prehistory. Though quantative figures are not available, no observable qualitative change occurs in the ratio between debris from the manufacture of stone tools and the remains of large game animals when site complexes are introduced. It is therefore unlikely that changes in hunting techniques were responsible for the emergence of winter villages.

The preparation of kouse and camas for eating and storage is closely linked to the hopper mortar, shaped pestle, and unshaped hammerstone with the appropriate type of pecked platforms. The hopper mortar and pestle were widely adopted in the Plateau sometime prior to 4000 B.P., some two millennia prior to the introduction of the winter village pattern. Root gathering stations are also known from an early date (Daugherty 1952:45GR27, Feature 1; Nelson 1969:55). Thus, there is no concrete evidence to suggest that major innovations were made in the exploitation of camas and kouse at the time the winter village pattern emerged in the Plateau.

The utilization of salmon is the most difficult of the three resources to assess. Ethnographic records document the systematic ritual destruction of salmon bones by many groups (e.g. Ray 1932; 1942). Most salmon were taken on tributary streams with weirs and traps. Butchery practices normally involved removing the head and filleting the meat from the backbone and ribs. The gut sack and enclosing boney structure were discarded, usually on the beach as salmon fishing took place at low water. Butchered fish were hung on racks to dry and afterwards might be ground into meal together with any bones they might still contain. The remains were then transported back to the winter village. Thus in the winter village the frequency of salmon remains will not directly reflect the dietary importance of salmon, while at fishing camps the abundant preservation of fish remains will only occur under the most favourable of circumstances (e.g. Cressman 1960).

The interpretive difficulties which this presents are compounded by a lack of firm archaeological data on the frequency of various types of faunal remains. Nevertheless, some trends do appear to be emerging (Nelson 1969: 56-7). Prior to the introduction of the winter village pattern fish bones of all types are generally rare, constituting from 0-3% of all bones by number. Of these approximately half come from cyprinids which may be obtained throughout the year or which spawn in the rivers early in the spring. The remainder are also salmonid. After the introduction of the winter village pattern, the remains of fish increase to an average of *c*.8-10% by number, while the ratio of salmonid to cyprinid remains seems to increase at least fractionally. These conclusions must be regarded tentatively until a good deal more quantative data is available, but they do provide a *prima facie* case for a change in fishing practices at the time winter villages were introduced.

Fishing implements, portions of which might survive in the archaeological record, include leisters, composite harpoons, the three-pronged salmon spear, and notched stone weights. Net weights and leister barbs are occasionally found in contexts which may antedate the emergence of winter villages, but composite harpoon heads and the barbs from three-prong salmon spears are strictly associated with the winter village pattern. These implements are closely associated with the use of weirs. Their appearance seems to herald the introduction of a new and more efficient fishing technology capable of producing significant surpluses of high protein food (Nelson 1969:56-57).

If this interpretation is correct, the emergence of the winter village pattern and the ethnographically associated economic organization was linked directly with the introduction of more sophisticated fishing techniques which included the construction of weirs designed to pool large numbers of spawning fish. Ethnographic reports suggest that this was the most efficient way of taking salmon in large quantities. Without the use of weirs it is quite possible that winter villages could not be supported in many areas of the Plateau. The introduction of weirs and related paraphernalia may be viewed as the impetus which led to the emergence of the winter village pattern. The question is how.

The origin of economic change

If it is assumed that the crucial economic factor in the emergence of the winter village pattern was the introduction of new and superior fishing techniques, then it becomes necessary to identify the source of that introduction. A wide variety of fishing spears and harpoons were in use along the coast of Washington and British Columbia and in the western Canadian Plateau well before the emergence of the winter village pattern in the adjoining Columbia Plateau. It is also likely that weirs were being employed, though only the most indirect archaeological evidence has yet been found (Nordquist 1961).

C-14 dates on the appearance of winter villages in the Columbia Plateau (Nelson 1969:47-8), the spread of a specific house type known earliest in the Thompson River basin of British Columbia, the apparent realignment of trading patterns (Nelson 1969:45-6), and linguistic evidence all support the hypothesis that the new fishing techniques were introduced from the western Cascades of southern British Columbia.

C-14 dates indicate that winter villages were first introduced along the northwestern periphery of the Columbia Plateau in the vicinity of the Okanogan Highlands between 600 and 900 B.C. By 50 or 100 B.C. the construction of winter villages had spread southward along the Columbia River past Walulah Gap and eastward along the Snake River and into the adjoining portions of western Idaho. During this process, the western and southern margins of the Columbia Plateau were host to the circumperipheral diffusion of stylistic elements, particularly the shape of projectile points. Point types developed along the eastern foothills of the Cascade Mountains were diffused southward along the Columbia River, types prevalent along the Columbia River were in turn diffused up the Snake River, and point types along the lower Snake River spread into western Idaho (Nelson 1969:61). Introduced varieties never completely replaced indigenous types. The balance of new and traditional forms is highly variable from area to area and traditional forms frequently undergo stylistic changes inspired by newly introduced forms. The widespread introduction of certain decorative motifs applied to bone tools and ornaments, the stylistic shift in petroglyph motifs in the southeastern Columbia Plateau, and changes in site demography in the western foothills of the Cascade Mountains may also date from this period (Nelson 1969; Rice in Swanson *et al.* 1970:123).

The direction of diffusion along the periphery of the Columbia Plateau together with the temporally vectored introduction of winter villages strongly suggests a source area somewhere in southern British Columbia. This interpretation is further supported by the introduction of a complex type of semi-subterranean house along the northwestern periphery of the plateau at the time the winter village pattern was introduced. This pit house type was excavated to as much as two meters below ground level and contained an unbroken internal bench, possibly for sleeping or storage. This variety of house was subsequently diffused as far southward as the Klamath Basin in Oregon (Cressman 1956), but occurs as early as the middle of the second millennium B.C. in the Thompson River basin of British Columbia (Sanger 1963:1966). Thus the diffusion of this house type has accompanied the spread of the winter village pattern itself.

The spread of the winter village pattern also seems to have affected the traditional patterns of trade between the Columbia Plateau and adjacent regions. Prior to the introduction of winter villages, identifiable trade goods are limited primarily to *Olivella* shells from the coast of Washington or Oregon and obsidian from the northern periphery of the Great Basin. These goods were heavily concentrated in the southern portion of the Columbia Plateau and must have been traded in from the south, west, and east. With the advent of the winter village pattern *Dentalium* shells, jade adzes, and mussel shell adzes are introduced from the Canadian Plateau and the coast of northern Washington and British Columbia. The addition of this northerly trading pattern does not noticeably alter trading relations in the southern part of the Plateau (Nelson 1969:45-6).

The final piece of corroborative evidence is linguistic. The type case for Swadesh's application of glottochronology to a non-literate language family was Salish which is spoken on the coast of Washington and British Columbia, through much of the Thompson-Fraser river basin, and throughout the northern two-thirds of the Columbia River basin. A variety of linguistic analyses (Swadesh 1950; 1952; Suttles and Elmendorf 1962; Elmendorf 1965) show that Salishan communities were first established on the western side of the Cascade Mountains and that they subsequently spread across the divide somewhere in southern British Columbia or northernmost Washington, spreading south and east along the western and northern margins of the Columbia Plateau. Elmendorf (1965) estimates that the initial spread into the Okanogan Highlands may have been complete by *c.* 1000 B.C., with subsequent spread to the south and east continuing as late as A.D. 1000. The archaeological evidence as interpreted here would suggest a more limited time span for the final spread of Salishan, beginning around 600 B.C. and terminating not later than *c.* A.D. 100. All in all this is an extraordinarily good fit considering the statistical limitation of glottochronology.

The dynamics of change

It has been suggested that the winter village pattern, hallmark of ethnographic economic organization, was introduced into the Columbia Plateau together with an improved fishing technology and the Salish language from an adjacent portion of British Columbia. What model of change can be used to explain this phenomenon most adequately? A simple migration model is ruled out by the remarkable stability of tool types and techniques of tool manufacture during a time of profound economic and linguistic change, the limited local diffusion of projectile point styles, the failure of diffused styles to supplant local counterparts, and the failure of the material culture of the region of origin to move *en masse* into and throughout the Columbia Plateau. Classically defined diffusion, on the other hand, is hard pressed to explain the spread of Salishan or so complete an adoption of a foreign economic organization which must also have entailed at least some re-orientation of band structure and religious practices. The following hypothesis combines some aspects of each of these classic devices and so might be called 'migrafusion' or 'progressive local immigration' for those whose passion it is to classify explanations.

By approximately 1000 B.C. the Thompson-Fraser river basin contained a highly differentiated series of societies heavily adapted to a highly restricted set of riverine resources of which salmon was the most important. To date archaeological work in this area has produced an astounding variety of well differentiated industries which are short-lived and confined to small geographic areas. If material culture were being used to differentiate groups which were competing for the resources, this archaeological diversity could be interpreted as an indirect reflection of population pressure. If this pressure were severe enough in downstream sections of the basin, chronic shortages of fish might occur upstream, especially every fourth year when the salmon runs are minimal in size. Whatever the cause might have been, Salishan communities occupying the eastern margin of the Thompson-Fraser basin must have expanded over the divide into the Columbia basin at a point where the headwaters of local streams provided a source of spawning salmon. Bands speaking Athabaskan or Sahaptin may have traditionally utilized these areas, but if they did not possess weirs their use of the salmon would be inefficient. Salishan communities could easily set up their weirs in unused sections of streams with little initial impact on their neighbours ability to obtain their usual quota of fish and with little or no interference with their traditional economic prerogatives.

The act of establishing permanent fishing stations in border areas with non-Salishan bands would soon lead to contact and potential acculturation. In order for the Salishan community to continue its expansion into the adjacent territory of another band, however, a situation would have to exist in which the rights to economic resources diffused more rapidly into the Salishan community than the ability to construct and man fishing sites diffused outward into the surrounding territory. Such factors might have included a reluctance to accept economic innovations, a reluctance on the part of the Salish to impart details of the construction of weirs, traps, and harpoons, the inability of the non-Salishan bands to muster the man power necessary to construct and maintain weirs, or a social system ill-adapted to the co-operative accumulation, storage, and redistribution of large food surpluses.

Whatever the specific combination of factors, the non-Salishan bands failed to adopt the more efficient fishing techniques of their neighbours with sufficient dispatch. The diffusion of economic rights through intermarriage overtook them all too soon. This intermarriage may have come about when the more efficient utilization of salmon produced situations in which Salishan villages were substantially better off than the neighbouring bands during periods of winter hardship. On the other hand, marriage into adjacent villages may have come about in an effort to clarify territorial relationships or simply because individuals sought to extend their kin base as far as possible as insurance against economic hardships. Whatever reasons non-Salishan families had for marrying into nearby villages, the Salish would logically welcome intermarriage as a way of cementing their rights to the newly acquired economic resources and as a means of extending their fishing stations into new areas.

Extensive intermarriage would lead to the establishment of winter villages in non-Salishan territory. If such villages were dominated by Salishan speakers, the primary language might well be Salish. Thus, as intermarriage proceeded, as rights diffused and winter villages budded into the territory of adjoining bands, Salish would slowly advance behind a frontier of bilingual communities. This process would be halted by any of three sets of factors: (1) the distribution of salmon, (2) social or economic factors which favour the diffusion of fishing technology more rapidly than the diffusion of rights in fishing resources, and (3) social or linguistic factors which inhibited the spread of the Salish language.

In the Columbia River basin north of the semi-arid heartland of the Columbia Plateau, east of the Cascade Mountains, and west of the Rocky Mountains, the distribution of salmon effectively controlled the spread of Salishan communities. On the western margin of the Columbia Plateau, however, Salish failed to spread southward though the winter village pattern continued to spread around the southern margin of the Plateau along the Snake River into Idaho. The reasons for this are unknown and might easily involve factors which cannot be assessed archaeologically. Nonetheless, the modern boundary of Salish along the western edge of the Columbia Plateau coincides well with two other phenomena. First it occurs in an area where fishing streams are limited to a narrow corridor, a geographic factor which may have inhibited the budding of Salishan villages. Second, it corresponds to the boundary between two archaeologically defined areas which split the Columbia Plateau in two. The southern portion of this area is characterized by the use of flaked cobble implements. This tradition is well defined by 8000 B.P. and usually accounts for between 40 and 80% of all stone tools in any archaeological occurrence. Tool forms and patterns of edge damage are remarkably stable and survive numerous changes in projectile point styles and even the introduction of the winter village pattern itself. By 4000 B.P., and possibly much earlier, the northern half of the Columbia Plateau is characterized by assemblages which contain only a very few cobble implements of narrowly restricted form. These are stylistically different from their counterparts in the south and form less than 3% of most assemblages. Instead, a wide variety of flake implements take the place of the cobble tools so abundant in the south, a substitution which is both functional and stylistic.

If these very conservative tool kits somehow reflect long established differences in the distribution of languages or social structures, they may help to explain the failure of Salish to spread into the southern Columbia Plateau.

Protohistoric changes in the winter village pattern

The horse was introduced into the Columbia Plateau in approximately A.D. 1750 and instantly revolutionized the transportation system. This in turn rapidly affected the religious, social, and economic aspects of Plateau cultures. Ray (1939) has extensively discussed some of the social and religious effects which the horse made possible. The impact of the horse is also clearly evident in three aspects of the archaeological record.

1. Travel by horse greatly increased the frequency of contact among groups and encouraged the exchange of goods and ideas. Thus the plateau became an exchange point along a vastly extended and very active trading network which drew goods from as far away as the Great Plains, the Pueblo areas of the southwest, the coast of California, and Alaska. This is evident in the sudden appearance of large quantities of grave goods almost all of which are trade items. It is also reflected in the diffusion of projectile point types, stylistic motifs, and the like. Prior to the introduction of the horse there were a number of regions within the Columbia Plateau, each characterized by a distinctive assemblage of projectile point types, gambling bones, bone points, and the like. With the introduction of the horse the extensive diffusion of these local types produces a convergence towards a pan-Plateau material culture.
2. Settlement patterns are drastically effected. The horse can be used to transport food surpluses over much greater distances. As a result, villages become fewer and much larger, being located only in the most favourable wintering areas including some in the central part of the Columbia Plateau which could not be occupied with ease before.
3. The nature of the settlements, themselves, changes. The transportation of structural members and fuel is of little consequence. Pit houses therefore become larger, reaching diameters greater than 20 metres, and are finally altogether replaced by portable mat lodges which can be moved and reassembled with comparative ease.

Acknowledgments

The author gratefully acknowledges the Washington Archaeological Society and the Grant County Public Utility District for supporting much of the research which has led to this synthesis. Thanks are also extended to the many individuals who helped in this work, and especially to David G. Rice and Deward E. Walker whose critical appraisals of earlier drafts have been invaluable.

REFERENCES

Anastasio, A. (1955) *Intergroup Relations in the Southern Plateau.* Ph.D. Dissertation, University of Chicago.

Borden, C.E. (1956) Two surveys in the East Kooteney region. *Research Studies of the State College of Washington* 24, 73-111.

Butler, B.R.B. (1966) *A Guide to Understanding Idaho Archaeology.* Pocatello. Special Publication of the Idaho State University Museum.

Caldwell, W.W. (1954) An archaeological survey of the Okanogan and Similkameen valleys of British Columbia. *Anthropology in British Columbia* 4, 10-25.

Caldwell, W.W. and Mallory, O.L. (1967) Hells Canyon archaeology. Smithsonian Institution, River Basin Surveys, *Publications in Salvage Archaeology* no. 6.

Chance, D.H. (1968) Archaeological survey of Coulee Dam National Recreation Area. Part 2: Spring Drawn-Down of 1967. *Report of Investigations,* no. 42. Laboratory of Anthropology, Washington State University, Pullman.

Coale, G.L. (1956) Archaeological survey of Mt. Sheep and Pleasant Valley Reservoirs. *Davidson Journal of Anthropology* 2, 1, 11-30.

Collier, D., Hudson, A.E. and Ford, A. (1942) Archaeology of the Upper Columbia Region. *University of Washington Publications in Anthropology* 9, 1-178.

Cressman, S. (1956) Elamath prehistory: the prehistory of the culture of the Klamath Lake area, Oregon. *Transactions of the American Philosophical Society* 46, part 4.

Cressman, S. (1960) Cultural sequences at the Dalles, Oregon: a contribution to Pacific Northwest prehistory. *Transactions of the American Philosophical Society* 50, part 10.

Daugherty, R.D. (1962) The intermontane Western tradition. *American Antiquity* 28, 144-50.

Daugherty, R.D., Purdy, B.A. and Fryxell, R. (1967) The descriptive archaeology and geochronology of the Three Springs Bar archaeological site, Washington. *Reports of Investigations,* no. 40. Laboratory of Anthropology, Washington State University, Pullman.

Drucker, P. (1948) *Appraisal of the Archaeological Resources of Long Lake and Potholes Reservoirs in East Central Washington.* Smithsonian Institution, River Basin Surveys, Columbia Basin Project. Mimeographed report. Eugene.

Elmendorf, W.E. (1965) Linguistic and geographic relations in the northern plateau area. *Southwestern Journal of Anthropology* 21, 63-77.

Freeman, O.W., Forester, J.D. and Luphur, R.L. (1945) Physiographic Divisions of the Columbia Intermontane Province. *Annals of the Association of American Geographers* 35, 53-75.

Grabert, G.F. (1966) *Archaeology in the Wells Reservoir, 1965.* Mimeographed. University of Washington, Seattle.

Grabert, G F. (1968) North-central Washington prehistory. *Reports in Archaeology,* no. 1. University of Washington, Seattle.

Gunkel, A. (1961) A comparative cultural analysis of four archaeological sites in the Rocky Reach Reservoir region, Washington. *Theses in Anthropology,* no. 1. Washington State University, Pullman.

Hansen, H.P. (1944) Postglacial vegetation of eastern Washington. *Northwest Science* 18, 79-86.

Hansen, H.P. (1947) Postglacial forest succession, climate and chronology in the Pacific northwest. *Transactions of the American Philosophical Society* 37, part 1.

Hansen, H.P. (1955) Postglacial forests in south central British Columbia. *American Journal of Science* 253, 640-58.

Heusser, C.J. (1960) Late Pleistocene environments of north Pacific North America. *American Geographical Society Special Publication*, no. 35.

Kenaston, M.R. (1966) The archaeology of the Harder site, Franklin County, Washington. *Reports of Investigations*, no. 35. Laboratory of Anthropology, Washington State University, Pullman.

Kidd, R.S. (1964) Ginkgo petrified forests archaeological project: report on survey and excavation conducted in 1961. Mimeographed report, University of Washington, Seattle.

Kroeber, A.L. (1939) *Cultural and Natural Areas of Native North America.* Berkeley, University of California Press.

Lee, W.T. (1955) An archaeological survey of the Columbia Basin project in Grant County, Washington. *Davidson Journal of Anthropology* 1, 2, 141-53.

Nelson, C.G. (1963) The Symons examination of the upper Columbia River. *Washington Archaeologist* 7, 2, 1-41.

Nelson, C.M. (1965) Archaeological reconnaissance in the Lower Monumental and Little Goose Dam Reservoir areas, 1964. *Reports of Investigations*, no. 34. Laboratory of Anthropology, Washington State University, Pullman.

Nelson, C.M. (1966) A preliminary report on 45C01, a stratified open site in the southern Columbia plateau. *Reports of Investigations*, no. 39. Laboratory of Anthropology, Washington State University, Pullman.

Nelson, C.M. (1969) The Sunset Creek site (45-KT-28) and its place in plateau prehistory. *Reports of Investigations*, no. 47. Laboratory of Anthropology, Washington State University, Pullman.

Nelson, C.M. and Rice, D.G. (1969) Archaeological survey and test in the Asotin Dam reservoir area, southeastern Washington. *Reports of Investigations*, no. 46. Laboratory of Anthropology, Washington State University, Pullman.

Nordquist, D. (1961) A fish weir fragment from 45SN100. *Washington Archaeologist*, vol. 5, nos. 8-9, 6-9.

Ray, V F. (1932) The Sanpoil and Nespelem, Salishan peoples of northeastern Washington. *University of Washington Publications in Anthropology*, 5.

Ray, V.F. (1936) Native villages and groupings of the Columbia basin. *The Pacific Northwest Quarterly* 27, 99-152.

Ray, V.F. (1939) Cultural relations in the plateau of north-western America. *Publications of the Frederick Webb Hodge Anniversary Publication Fund* 3, 1-154. Los Angeles.

Ray, V.F. (1942) Culture element distributions: XXII, plateau. *University of California Anthropology Records* 8, no. 2.

Rice, D.G. (1968a) Archaeological investigations in the Coulee Dam National Recreation area, Spring 1968. *Reports of Investigations*, no. 45. Laboratory of Anthropology, Washington State University, Pullman.

Rice, D.G. (1968b) *Archaeological reconnaissance: Ben Franklin Reservoir Area, 1968.* Washington State University, Laboratory of Anthropology.

Rice, D.G. (1968c) Archaeological activities of the Mid-Columbia archaeological society, 1968. *Annual Report.* Mid-Columbia Archaeological Society. 7-17.

Rice, D.G. (1968d) *Archaeological Reconnaissance: Handford Atomic Works.* Washington State University.

Rice, D.G. (1969) Archaeological reconnaissance: south-central cascades. *Occasional Paper*, no. 2. Washington Archaeological Society.

St. John, H. (1937) *Flora of Southeastern Washington and of Adjacent Idaho.* Students Book Co., Washington State University, Pullman.

Sanger, D. (1963) Excavations at Nesikep Creek (EdRk:4), a stratified site near Lillooet, British Columbia: preliminary report. *National Museum of Canada Bulletin* 193, 130-61.

Sanger, D. (1966) Excavations in the Lochnore-Nesikep Creek locality, British Columbia: interim report. *Anthropology Papers*, no. 12 (Ottawa).

Sapir, E. (1916) The time perspective in aboriginal American culture: a study in method. *Geological Survey Memoir*, no. 90. (Canada. Department of Mines. Ottawa.)

Schwede, M.L. (1966) *An Ecological Study of Nez Perce Settlement Patterns.* M.A. Dissertation, Washington State University, Pullman.

Shiner, J.L. (1961) The McNary reservoir: a study in plateau archaeology. *Bureau of American Ethnology*, Bull. 179, 149-260.

Smith, H.I. Archaeology of Lytton, British Columbia. *Memoirs of the American Museum of Natural History*, vol. 2, part 3 (1899).

Smith, H.I. Archaeology of the Thompson river region, British Columbia. *Memoirs of the American Museum of Natural History*, vol. 2, part 6 (1900).

Smith, H.I. (1910) The archaeology of the Yakima valley. *American Museum of Natural History, Anthropological Papers*, vol. 6, part 1.

Smith, H.I. (1913) The archaeological collection from the southern interior of British Columbia. *National Museum of Canada Geological Survey*, Bull. 1290.

Smith, M.W. (1950) The Nooksack, the Chilliwack, and the Middle Fraser. *Pacific Northwest Quarterly* 41, 330-41.

Spinden, H.J. (1908) The Nez Perce Indians. *Memoirs of the American Anthropological Association* 2, 165-274.

Suttles, W. and Elmendorf, W.W. (1962) Linguistic evidence for Salish prehistory. *Symposium on Language and Culture: Precedings of the 1962 Annual Spring Meeting of the American Ethnological Society*, 41-52.

Swadesh, M. (1950) Salish internal relationships. *International journal of American Linguistics* 16, 157-67.

Swadesh, M. (1952) Salish phonologic geography. *Language* 28, 237-48.

Swanson, E.H. (1956) *Archaeological Studies in the Vantage Region of the Columbia Plateau, Northwestern America.* Ph.D. Dissertation. University of Washington, Seattle.

Swanson, E.H. (1962) The emergence of plateau culture. *Occasional Papers of the Idaho State College Museum*, no. 8.

Swanson, E.H., Aikens, C.M., Rice, D.G. and Mitchell, D.H. (1970) Cultural relations between the plateau and Great Basin. *Northwest Anthropological Research Notes* 4, 65-125.

Swanton, J.R. (1952) The Indian tribes of north America. *Bureau of American Ethnology*, Bull. 145.

Teit, J.A. (1900) The Thompson Indians of British Columbia. *Memoirs of the American Museum of Natural History* 2, part 4.

Teit, J.A. (1906) The Lilloet Indians. *Memoirs of the American Museum of Natural History* 4, part 5.

Teit, J.A. (1909) The Shuswap. *Memoirs of the American Museum of Natural History* 4, part 7.

Teit, J.A. (1930) The Salishan Tribes of the Western Plateau. *Annual Report of the Bureau of American Ethnology* 45, 23-396.

Warren, C.N. (1959) *Wenas Creek: A Stratified Site on the Yakima River, Its Significance for Plateau Chronology and Cultural Relationships.* M.A. Dissertation, University of Washington, Seattle.

Warren, C.N., Sims, C. and Pavesic, M.G. (1968) Cultural chronology in Hells Canyon. *Tebiwa* 11, 1-37.

Weeks, Kent R. (1962) *Fort Simco Archaeological Survey: Report of the 1961 Season.* Mimeographed report. University of Washington, Seattle.

DAVID R. HARRIS

The prehistory of tropical agriculture: an ethnoecological model

In the broadest perspective of cultural change, which surveys the whole of man's development from his hominoid beginnings to the present, the transition from dependence on wild foods to controlled food production appears pre-eminently important. Many attempts have been made to 'explain' this crucial transition, chiefly with reference to particular places and periods such as 'neolithic' Southwest Asia and Mesoamerica, and there has been much vigorous argument over the relative importance of diffusion and independent innovation in the early development of agriculture. But running through these debates there has been persistent confusion as to whether the primary objective is explanation of particular sequences of events in their unique spatial and temporal contexts or the formulation of explanatory hypotheses of more general application.

To scholars reared in the culture-historical tradition that flourished in Germany and America in the earlier decades of the 20th century the major objective was the explanation of particular cultural phenomena in specific spatial and temporal contexts, whereas in recent decades more emphasis has been placed on the search for cross-cultural regularities and the formulation of law-like generalizations. The earlier concern with historical particularization developed largely as a reaction to the broad generalizations of late 19th century theorists of cultural evolution, such as Lewis Morgan and Herbert Spencer, and it has in its turn been succeeded by a revival of interest in an evolutionary approach to the explanation of culture change. This has been most conspicuous among American anthropologists, particularly those who have adopted and elaborated the ideas of Leslie A. White, but it was also vigorously championed in Britain by V. Gordon Childe.

While this shift in objectives and modes of explanation has occurred among cultural anthropologists (Watson and Watson 1969; Sahlins and Service 1960), and to a lesser extent among archaeologists (Trigger 1971, 1970; Clarke 1968; Binford and Binford 1968), a similar paradigm-shift has been taking place in related social sciences. This is especially true of human geography where the change from a dominantly ideographic to a nomothetic methodology has made rapid headway in recent years (Harvey 1969; Chorley and Haggett 1967). And in both anthropology-archaeology and human geography this shift has been accompanied by an increasing commitment to the use of quantitative techniques in the processing and interpretation of data (Isaac 1971; Harvey 1969: 179-386).

Explanation of the transition from food-collecting to plant and animal domestication and agriculture can thus be approached with two different but complementary objectives in view: first, to seek to understand it as the transformation from one major level to another in man's overall cultural progress, which implies a generalizing cultural-evolutionary approach, and second, to reconstruct the actual sequence of events that took place in specific locations at known times, which is the aim of the particularizing culture-historical approach. In other words, adopting the terminology clarified by Sahlins and Service (1960:12-44), the two methodological approaches are those respectively of general and specific cultural evolution. While it may be agreed that it is the detailed study of specific cultural sequences that yields the 'hard facts' on which interpretation and validation depend, it may equally be argued that in the absence of cross-cultural generalizations the significance of local data cannot be fully evaluated. Furthermore the general evolutionary approach affords the possibility of prediction, of formulating law-like generalizations that may be tested against the specific bodies of data that they seek to explain. In this way the two approaches of specific and general evolution – the one ideographic and particularizing, the other nomothetic and generalizing – can be regarded as complementary, although their objectives and methods remain distinct. Both are called for in attempts to explain processes of culture change, not least that of mankind's transition from a hunting and gathering to an agricultural way of life.

The aim of this paper is to approach the problem of the origins and early development of agriculture in the tropics primarily from a nomothetic point of view, with the hope of formulating predictive generalizations that may subsequently be tested as relevant data accumulates. The case for adopting this approach rests partly on its intrinsic merit and partly on the fact that at present archaeological data relevant to the prehistory of tropical agriculture is too meagre to allow the culture-historical reconstruction of more than one or two isolated sequences. This paper is therefore largely speculative. It is presented as a hypothetical model which invites rejection, confirmation, or modification, rather than as a well established theory.

In the absence of adequate archaeological data, understanding of the prehistory of tropical agriculture may be advanced by the construction of a model based on data drawn not from prehistoric archaeology itself but from the related domains of ecology and ethnology. In the main part of this paper a series of ecological-ethnological inferences as to the origins and early development of agriculture in the tropics will be put forward and in the conclusion these predictive generalizations will be tested against some of the available archaeological evidence.

The ethnoecological model

As has been argued elsewhere (Harris 1969), the analysis of natural ecosystems according to the criterion of species diversity also provides a valuable method of analysing agricultural systems. The distinction between modern (neotechnic) and traditional (palaeotechnic) agriculture rests not only on the dominant type of energy that man applies to each system – power from combustible fuels or human and animal labour (Wolf 1966) – but also on their ecological complexity. Neotechnic agricultural systems of the modern world are characterized by low species diversity and production concentrates upon raising maximum numbers of optimum sized crops and domestic animals of one or two preferred species. On the other hand palaeotechnic agricultural systems of the traditional world exhibit greater ecological diversity and raise more complex assemblages of plant and animal species each of which is represented by relatively fewer individuals.

The contrast between biotically complex and simple ecosystems is accentuated by the fact that the more complex systems are also structurally and functionally more diverse and inherently more stable (i.e. less liable to major temporal and spatial fluctuations in their populations) than simpler systems (Woodwell and Smith 1969): in the former a greater variety of ecological niches is available for species at all trophic levels, and because alternative paths for energy flow and greater genetic diversity exist within the system homeostasis is more readily maintained when environmental changes, such as the reduction, removal, or introduction of organisms by man, take place. This generalization may be applied to agricultural systems as well as to natural ecosystems. For example, the contrast in ecological stability that exists between the highly complex and stable tropical rain forest and the much simpler and less stable boreal forest may be paralleled on a smaller scale by the contrast between the complexity and stability of a polycultural swidden plot in which many different species of crops are grown in structural and functional interdependence (Harris 1971; Rappaport 1971) and the simple, unstable plant community of a monocultural plantation which is characteristically subject to devastating attacks by species-specific pathogens.

The comparison of ecologically complex and simple agricultural systems suggests a basic contrast in the ways in which cultivation changes natural ecosystems: at one extreme cultivation involves the large-scale replacement of the wild biota by domesticated and semi-domesticated organisms, or, in other words, the transformation of a natural into a largely artificial ecosystem created and maintained by man; while at the other extreme cultivation proceeds by the substitution of selected domesticates for wild species in equivalent ecological niches, or the manipulation of the natural ecosystem rather than its replacement. Thus when cultivation is based on ecosystem-manipulation, as in polycultural swidden plots in tropical forests, it achieves the objective of channeling energy to man through cultivated plants by substituting for wild species in equivalent spatial and functional niches a mixed assemblage of cultivated trees, shrubs, climbers, herbs, and root crops, thus simulating the structure and dynamics of the natural ecosystem without wholly replacing it. On the other hand, agriculture based on ecosystem-transformation, as in tropical wet-padi farming, involves the almost total destruction of the pre-existing natural ecosystem and its replacement by an artificial system with quite different structural properties and energy transfers: as Geertz has succinctly expressed it, wet-padi as opposed to swidden cultivation involves not 'the imitation of a tropical forest, but the fabrication of an aquarium' (Geertz 1963:31).

The dichotomy between cultivation by ecosystem-manipulation and by ecosystem-transformation can be seen not only as representing two extremes in the degree of ecological change induced by cultivation, but also as a temporal progression from earlier to later forms of agriculture. The development of the ecologically simpler and more specialized agricultural systems that are associated with ecosystem-transformation implies protracted time for the domestication and selective breeding of the relatively few highly productive crops and domestic animals on which such systems depend, as well as for the elaboration of complex societies adapted to their maintenance: the replacement of tropical forest by plantations or wet-padi pond-fields, of temperate woodlands or grasslands by wheat farms or cattle ranches, or of desert shrublands by irrigated oases, represents the ultimate expression of secular processes of ecological, genetic, and cultural experimentation and adjustment that have their origins far back in prehistory. Prior to the emergence of such specialized agricultural systems cultivation by ecosystem-manipulation would have been the dominant mode of agriculture, involving, for example, the substitution of fruit-bearing tree crops for wild tree species in the tropical forests of Southeast Asia, Africa, or the Americas, of small-grained cereal crops for wild grasses in the woodlands and grasslands of prehistoric Southwest Asia, or of free-ranging pigs and cattle for wild scavengers and browsers in the forests of prehistoric Europe.

A long phase of cultivation by ecosystem-manipulation may therefore be postulated, extending from man's earliest experiments in plant and animal domestication up to the emergence of specialized agricultural systems in various parts of the world. In terms of general evolution this phase represents a level preliminary to that of agriculture in the strict sense – here taken to imply the prolonged cultivation of fixed fields – and it may be equated with the stage of 'incipient agriculture' formulated by archaeologists for the Near East, Mexico, and elsewhere. But rather than use this latter term, which has deterministic overtones, the fundamental contrast between early cultivation by ecosystem-manipulation and later agricultural transformations may be better expressed by distinguishing an initial level of 'proto-cultivation' from the later development of 'specialized agriculture' in its various forms. To postulate that these levels of development have general evolutionary significance is not to imply that the first everywhere preceded the second – specific evolutionary case-histories show clearly that specialized agricultural systems have frequently been introduced into areas previously without any form of cultivation – but it does help to focus attention on the long period during which human groups, both within and beyond the tropics, experimented with cultivation and domestication prior to the emergence of societies adapted to and largely dependent on the techniques and products of specialized agriculture.

What then can ecological-ethnological inference tell us about the types of habitat and human group among which proto-cultivation is most likely to have arisen? I have previously argued (Harris 1969:7-9) that cultivation probably originated with the manipulation of relatively complex ecosystems in which a wide variety of wild plants and animals were used for subsistence by forager bands localized within circumscribed territories. Such bands of gatherers, fishermen, and hunters of small and slow game characteristically develop an intimate knowledge of the plants and animals in the limited area they inhabit and it is suggested that close involvement with certain of these, as items in a seasonally scheduled pattern of wild food procurement (Flannery 1968), or as organisms of utilitarian or ritual significance, led gradually to their domestication and incorporation into a system of proto-cultivation.

The more complex ecosystems occupied by such forager bands would mainly have been forested and wooded areas, particularly within the tropics, and forest-edge habitats and other ecotone situations where biological productivity is high and seasonal variation in plant and animal resources at a maximum are likely to have been preferentially selected for occupation. There foraging populations could more readily obtain an assured supply of plant and animal foods which would have reinforced tendencies towards sedentism and thus facilitated the selection of advantageous mutations through many generations of wild and semi-domesticated plants. In this way the transition may have taken place first from the broad-spectrum gathering of wild species to the repeated harvesting of familiar and favoured plants, and later from deliberate planting to full domestication and regular cultivation. And, as Hawkes has pointed out, the disturbed, open habitats created by man around permanent or semi-permanent living sites would have been exceptionally well suited to colonization by the weedy ancestors of later cultigens (Hawkes 1969:18-20).

If account is taken of the ecological requirements of some of the principal cultigens themselves, and by extension of their presumed wild ancestors, it is apparent that they share a common adaptation to pronounced seasonality of climate. In so far as they provide concentrated food resources in the form of seeds, fruits, or enlarged roots and stems, man is in effect exploiting a range of adaptations which enable the plants to survive periods during which growth is curtailed by drought or cold. Within the tropics, except at high altitudes where cold becomes a significant limiting factor, the adaptation is principally to dry seasons of varying length and intensity. Survival through dormant periods, when growth is checked by lack of moisture, is achieved by means of both seed reproduction and specialized storage organs such as tubers, corms, and rhizomes, which allow growth to resume rapidly once drought ends and the rains return. These two natural survival strategies underly the contrast between traditions of cultivation based on seed-reproduced plants (seed-culture) and those based on the reproduction of crops by vegetative propagation (vegeculture) and both point to the broad zone of intermediate tropical climate, where the dry season lasts from 2½ to 7½ months in the year (Troll and Paffen 1963), as that in which the cultivation of tropical food crops is most likely to have originated. There, between the equatorial evergreen rain forests and the perennial deserts, lie the probable homelands of the great majority of tropical cultigens.

Within this vast area of the tropics there are of course further zonal contrasts of climate and vegetation of differential significance to the origins of plant domestication. If the intermediate zone is subdivided into areas of longer and shorter dry season (7½-5 and 5-2½ dry months respectively) it may be inferred that the former, with a dominant vegetation cover of semi-evergreen and deciduous forest, is the probable native habitat of those cultigens that are adapted to growth under a light tree canopy, such as yams, common bean, and other climbers; whereas the latter, with a dominant cover of deciduous woodland, savanna, and xerophytic shrubs, is the homeland of more drought-tolerant, open-canopy, upright-stemmed cultigens, including certain root crops such as manioc, and tropical cereals such as maize, sorghum, and various millets. In the absence of precise, empirical data on the origins of a wide range of tropical crops these generalizations cannot be tested and further refined, but where some up-to-date evidence does exist, as for example for yams (Alexander and Coursey 1969), common bean (Gentry 1969), manioc (Renvoize 1972), and sorghum (De Wet and Harlan 1971; Harlan 1971:471), it tends to confirm ecological expectation.

The distinction between areas of longer and shorter dry season may also be significant for the origins of tropical cultivation systems themselves. Judging from ethnological evidence of traditional agricultural practices in the tropics, the contrast between systems based primarily on seed crops and on vegetatively reproduced crops is fundamental and long established. Vegeculture based mainly on root, stem, and fruit crops is most characteristic of the tropical lowlands of South America and Southeast Asia where its indigenous status is suggested by major aboriginal dependence on cultigens of local origin, such as manioc and sweet potatoes in South America, and yams, taro, and banana in Southeast Asia. In tropical lowland Africa vegeculture appears well established – or persistent – as an indigenous mode of cultivation only in the 'yam zone' of West Africa where the native Guinea yams (*Dioscorea cayenensis and D. rotundata*) are of prime importance (Coursey 1967:22-5 and 197-203); while elsewhere in the tropical lowlands of the continent traditional vegeculture is dependent more on crops, for example the banana (McMaster 1962), introduced in pre-European times from Southeast Asia. Although markedly drought-tolerant varieties of root crops exist, such as manoic and certain yams, the overall adaptation of the lowland vegecultural crop complex appears to be to the lightly forested habitats of shorter dry season rather than to the more arid areas. Vegeculture is also adapted to more humid tropical conditions and today systems of cultivation largely dependent on vegetatively reproduced crops can best be observed deep in the equatorial evergreen rain forest, as for example in the upper Orinoco area of southern Venezuela (Harris 1971); but, as is suggested later in this paper, this humid forest adaptation probably represents the end result of a process of retreat in the face of competition from seed-cultural systems.

If lowland vegeculture is best adapted to areas of shorter dry season, seed-culture, which is based primarily on cereals and other relatively short-lived annuals and perennials which concentrate nutrients in their seeds, appears best adapted to semi-arid areas of longer dry season. The dominant indigenous crops of tropical seed-culture, such as maize, beans, and cucurbits in America, rice and millets (principally *Setaria italica* and *Panicum miliaceum*) in south and east Asia, and sorghum and millets (principally *Pennisetum typhoideum* = *P. americanum* and *Eleusine coracana*) in Africa, are essentially heliophilous plants of open-canopy woodlands, shrublands, and savannas, and it is in such semi-arid, ecologically complex environments that seed-culture probably originated.

Both vegeculture and seed-culture occur as traditional systems of cultivation in highland as well as lowland situations within the latitudinal tropics, but as altitude increases so they exhibit progressively closer adaptation to low temperatures than to lack of moisture. Climatically speaking the highland forms of vegeculture and seed-culture are extra-tropical, but in terms of cultivation techniques and to a considerable extent in terms of the crops themselves they show continuity with lowland forms. Highland forms of seed-culture exist in all three tropical continental areas where they are based principally on more cold-tolerant varieties of crops that are well established in the lowlands, but in certain uplands seed crops of local origin are dominant in the highest areas of cultivation, for example quínoa and cañihua (*Chenopodium quinoa* and *C. pallidicaule*) in the central Andes (Gade 1970; Simmonds 1965) and tef (*Eragrostis tef*) in northern Ethiopia (Simoons 1960: 99-104). Highland vege-culture is most elaborately developed in the Andes where it is based on locally domesticated root crops, principally the white potato, together with the minor tuberous cultigens known as ulluco (*Ullucus tuberosus*), oca (*Oxalis tuberosa*), and añu (*Tropaeolum tuberosum*). It exists elsewhere on a smaller scale, as in the southern part of the Ethiopian massif where the ensete or 'false banana' (*Ensete edule* = *Musa ensete*), a vegetatively reproduced plant the false stem and young shoots of which are eaten, is a staple crop (Simoons 1960:89-99; Smeds 1955), and in the central highlands of New Guinea where a form of vegeculture is practised which is based on taro, yam, the introduced sweet potato, and a minor root crop, *Pueraria lobata* (Strathern 1969; Watson 1968, 1964).

Ecological inference thus leads us to hypothesize that it was in the intermediate tropical zone that systems of proto-cultivation arose and that a differential emphasis developed on vegecultural crops in the sub-humid areas of shorter dry season and on seed crops in the semi-arid areas of longer dry season. However such inference tells us nothing directly about the techniques involved in cultivation. To add a technological component to the model we need to turn to ethnology and human geography.

Examination of traditional agriculture within the tropics suggests that among primitive cultivators two contrasted systems of cultiva-tion are widespread and frequently co-exist within the same community: namely shifting or swidden cultivation, which is a long-term fallowing system involving the cultivation of temporary plots for shorter periods than they are fallowed, and fixed-plot horticulture or 'garden culture' which involves the long-term cultiva-tion of small areas in the immediate vicinity of the cultivators' settlement. Either system may incorporate seed-reproduced and/or vegetatively reproduced crops but there is a tendency for the cereals and other seed-reproduced annuals to be concentrated in swidden plots while vegetatively reproduced perennials may be important components of either swidden or fixed plots. Both systems are small-scale and depend on ecosystem-manipulation rather than the creation of artificial ecosystems by large-scale transformations, although prolonged small-scale disturbance may lead to pronounced modification of the environment. The techniques employed for clearance, cultivation, and harvesting are rudimentary, normally being limited to human labour using simple tools such as axes, knives, planting-sticks and hoes. For most agricultural tasks the unit of labour is the family, and neither system implies a level of social organization more complex than that of the simple segmentary tribe; communities are characteristically decentralised, autonomous, largely self-sufficient groups living in small dispersed hamlets or villages (Harris 1972; Sahlins 1968:31-2).

In contrast to swidden cultivation and fixed-plot horticulture most other systems of traditional agriculture in the tropics involve ecological transformation. They lead to the large-scale and more permanent replacement of the natural ecosystem by an artificial agricultural system which tends to be ecologically simpler but technologically more complex than systems of shifting cultivation and fixed-plot horticulture. This is particularly evident in systems of hydraulic agriculture, such as wet-padi and dry-land irrigation farming, in which maintenance of fertility and continuity of production is made possible by the control of water supplies. In these specialized systems the productive process is focused upon a relatively small number of preferred crops but the technology that services the system is more complex, often involving the use of animal as well as human labour and demanding considerable constructional and engineering skill for the creation and maintenance of hydraulic works. In these and other specialized systems many agricultural tasks require units of labour greater than the family and social organization is at a level more complex than that of simple segmentary tribes; greater social integration is achieved through the medium of ranked chiefdoms or socially stratified states with a dependent peasantry who are capable of providing the large labour force necessary for major agricultural tasks (Sahlins 1968:24-7 and 42-4; Wolf 1966:25-30).

On the basis of this normative characterization of traditional systems of tropical agriculture it is possible to elaborate the postulated general evolutionary sequence from proto-cultivation to specialized agriculture. This necessitates consideration of the evolutionary relationships between fixed-plot horticulture and swidden cultivation on the one hand and between these two systems and types of specialized agriculture on the other.

It is often tacitly assumed and sometimes explicitly postulated (for example by Boserup 1965:16-18) that shifting cultivation preceded other systems of cultivation in the world-wide development of agriculture. This view is based mainly on the customarily simple technology of surviving swidden cultivators in the tropics, but it overlooks the still simpler cultivation techniques involved in most tropical fixed-plot horticulture. The existence of small domestic plots or gardens adjacent to the homes of primitive cultivators is such a widespread but inconspicuous phenomenon in the tropics that it tends to be ignored. Yet such plots are often highly productive and contribute essential plant products to the domestic economy (Kimber 1966; Simoons 1965; Anderson 1952:136-42, 1950). Ecologically they tend to be complex, with many plants of different life form growing in structural and functional inter-dependence; but the plots require relatively little effort to plant, harvest, and fertilize with domestic refuse. By comparison, swidden cultivation demands more expenditure of time and energy in clearing and tending plots as well as travelling to and from them. Domestic plots also afford easier opportunity to tend and harvest individual plants at optimum times and to ward off animal and human predators. On these grounds alone one might postulate that fixed-plot horticulture preceded swidden cultivation in the evolution of tropical agriculture, but this presumption is further strengthened if the probable role of domestic plots in the process of plant domestication is considered.

As Anderson (1952:149-50) and others have suggested, nitrogen-rich refuse heaps in the vicinity of settlements would have provided ideal sites for colonization by potential cultigens and for experiments in cultivation. The fact that a large proportion of crop plants are notably nitrogen-demanding lends support to this idea, but a still more significant factor may be that cultivation close to dwellings implies the probable transfer – intentionally or accidentally – of the potential cultigen from its natural habitat to the man-modified habitat of the settlement area. Such transfer may have had great significance in the earliest stages of domestication for it would have facilitated isolation between the potential cultigen and its parent population. This would have resulted in a reduction of natural selective pressures and a consequent increase in the survival of less well adapted mutants, such as those with imperfect seed-dispersal mechanisms, which would then become available for conscious or unconscious selection by man.

More significantly still, as Heiser has recently stressed, isolation would reduce opportunities for free inter-crossing between the potential cultigen and its wild relatives – assuming that, like most original cultigens, it was a cross-fertilizing species – thus allowing the more rapid fixation of characteristics valuable to man; and at the same time transfer to a new habitat might bring the plant within range of other varieties or species with which hybridization could occur and so increase the chances of genetic recombination producing new potential cultigens (Heiser 1969:229). Such a mixture of isolation and occasional hybridization would provide a genetic environment ideally suited to the emergence of domesticated variants through the selection and fixation of desirable characteristics; and the transfer of plants to the immediate neighbourhood of settlements may have been the chief way in which early man created this genetic situation. The temporary clearings of swidden plots located at some distance from the settlement in less modified habitats would not have isolated potential cultigens so effectively from their wild relatives; nor of course are such plots likely to have been deliberately cleared, planted, and harvested until the concept of cultivation was itself established and some cultigens of evidently superior value to wild plants were available. It seems therefore distinctly improbable that swidden represents the first system of cultivation practised by man. It is more convincing to postulate fixed-plot horticulture, probably in the form of small domestic 'gardens' close to dwellings, as a model for man's earliest system of proto-cultivation.

It has sometimes been suggested, notably by Sauer (1952), that man learned to propagate plants vegetatively before growing them from seed. It is true that tropical agriculture is remarkably rich in asexually reproduced cultigens, the domestication of which may have required longer periods of time than that of annual seed crops because, once a vegetatively reproducing population was established, there would have been fewer opportunities for genetic recombination and hence for rapid evolutionary change. It is quite probable that in many parts of the tropics, particularly the sub-humid areas to which many vegecultural crops appear ecologically best adapted, the domestication and cultivation of asexually reproduced cultigens preceded that of annual seed crops and if so domestic plots near dwellings would have provided ideal sites for the close and continuing attention to individual plants and clones that the domestication and persistence of such cultigens presupposes. But domestic plots could equally well have provided appropriate sites for experimentation with seed crops which provide multiple fruit from each plant and are capable of perennial growth, particularly trees, shrubs, and climbing herbs, such as avocados and perennial chili peppers and cucurbits. Such plots would have been less well suited to the annual cultivation of cereals and other crops of which many individual plants are required to make up a worthwhile harvest and which could be more appropriately cultivated in larger plots specially cleared for the purpose.

These speculations help to clarify the question of the evolutionary relationship between fixed-plot horticulture and shifting cultivation and suggest that, if the former did precede the latter in the tropics, one reason for the development of swidden plots may have been the desire to cultivate larger sites better suited to the requirements of annually planted cereals and other cultigens which were gradually becoming established as staple crops. In selecting such sites preference would probably have been given to less heavily vegetated areas where natural or human agency prevented the development of closed-canopy plant communities, as along unstable stream courses or in areas disturbed by frequent hunting and gathering. There less clearance by cutting and burning would have been necessary and, in the case of riparian sites, the existence of relatively moist and fertile alluvial soils would sometimes have conferred an added advantage.

A shift or expansion of proto-cultivation from domestic to swidden plots may also have resulted from, or been accentuated by, population increase. Expansion to larger, more open and fertile alluvial sites following intensification in the agricultural use of village plots as a result of population increase has been reported from Panama (Covich and Nickerson 1966); and this process may have occurred widely in the remote past when the development of both sedentism and plant domestication led to increases in population and in dependence on cultivated foods. That a shift from a mobile to a mainly sedentary life can trigger off large and rapid increases in population by decreasing intervals between pregnancies and reducing such checks on the birth rate as miscarriage and infanticide has recently been shown by Binford's work among the Eskimo and Lee's among the Bushmen (Binford 1971: personal communication). If such changes followed the establishment of sedentary settlements in the past, it is possible that under the resulting unaccustomed pressure of population attempts would have been made to increase and regularize the contribution of cultivated products to the domestic economy by such means as swidden cultivation. A further factor that may have stimulated an expansion of proto-cultivation to swidden plots is inter-group warfare, a behaviour pattern which today drives certain south American swidden cultivators to locate clearings far from their villages (Chagnon 1967:118-9) and which may have had a similar effect in the past.

Once swidden cultivation became an established system of production, and dependence on cultivated foods came to exceed dependence on wild foods, a new phase in the evolution of agriculture in the tropics was inaugurated. The opportunities for swidden cultivators, equipped with a variety of domesticated cultigens and practising a shifting-field system, to occupy new areas were now greater than when fixed-plot horticulture was practised as the main or only form of cultivation. It is not suggested that mobility of settlement is a necessary or even a usual concomitant of swidden cultivation (Harris 1972), but only that dependence on swidden implies a greater possibility or likelihood of group migration and the diffusion of agriculture to new areas. Adoption of swidden cultivation by forager populations may be one of the principal ways in which agriculture spread within and beyond the tropics, although the failure of many hunter-gatherer groups to adopt agriculture is historically well documented and such spread may have resulted more from population increase and expansion by already established cultivators.

The potential for mobility of different systems of swidden cultivation also demands consideration because it has far-reaching implications for the prehistory of agriculture in the tropics. The most significant contrast is between those systems in which seed crops and vegetatively reproduced crops respectively predominate. In vegecultural swidden plots plant diversity tends to be greater, plant stratification more intricate, and the canopy of vegetation more completely closed than in seed-cultural plots. Vegecultural plots thus represent more complex ecosystems with greater ecological stability, and this tendency is accentuated by the fact that opportunities for soil erosion are reduced because the soil is more completely and continuously shielded by plant cover.

The two systems also make contrasted demands on soil fertility. Whereas under vegeculture productivity focuses upon starch-rich root and tree crops which make relatively small demands on plant nutrients, under seed-culture the staple crops yield considerable amounts of protein as well as starch and tend to make heavier demands on soil nutrients. When the seed cultivator harvests his crop of cereals he removes for consumption a greater fraction of fertility than when the vegeculturalist digs up his tubers, corms, or rhizomes. Other factors being equal, declining yields become apparent sooner in seed-cultural plots; for this reason, and because their open-canopy structure renders them more liable to weed invasion and soil erosion, they tend to be cultivated for shorter periods than vegecultural plots. On ecological grounds therefore we should expect seed-cultural swidden systems to exhibit a greater tendency than vegecultural systems to expand into new areas.

This inference is strengthened if the dietary effectiveness of the two systems is also compared. Because of the low protein content of most root crops, vegeculturalists who lack staple seed crops are dependent on alternative sources of protein to obtain a balanced diet. In the tropics wild terrestrial and aquatic animals and fish commonly satisfy this need, together with limited amounts of protein from wild and cultivated plants, and, in some areas, from domestic livestock as well. A large measure of dependence on wild animal protein ensures the persistence of hunting and fishing as important subsistence activities among tropical vegeculturalists, thus enhancing the inherent ecological stability of the system by limiting it to areas with assured supplies of animal protein, such as riparian, coastal, swamp- and savanna-edge habitats. Seed-culture on the other hand provides a more adequate and better balanced vegetable diet and thus frees communities from major dependence on hunting and fishing and allows expansion into new habitats where animal protein is less readily available.

On the basis of these ecological and dietary contrasts between the two systems an evolutionary development may be predicted whereby seed-cultural swidden should gradually gain spatial ascendancy over vegecultural swidden by a process of territorial expansion. Assuming that the homelands of seed-culture lie in the woodlands, shrublands, and savannas of the semi-arid tropics we should expect the systems of seed-crop swidden that have evolved in these areas, such as those based on maize in America, sorghum and millets in Africa, and upland rice and millets in Asia, to be less stable and more liable to progressive migration than the inherently more stable vegecultural swidden systems of the sub-humid tropical forests.

The last question to consider in this hypothetical model of the prehistory of tropical agriculture is how specialized types of traditional agriculture may have evolved from systems of proto-cultivation. As was suggested earlier, specialized agricultural systems are characterized by relative ecological simplicity which arises from concentration on a small range of domestic plants and animals. This contrasts with a relatively high level of technological complexity which in traditional agriculture is associated with both higher demands for labour and a greater capacity to support population per unit area of cultivated land. By comparison with swidden cultivation, specialized agricultural systems are characterized by more continuous and intensive land use which depends on the maintenance of soil fertility either by direct soil enrichment or by the control of water supplies. In the tropics most palaeotechnic specialized agricultural systems achieve this continuity and intensification of production by methods of hydraulic cultivation, such as wet-padi farming, dry-land irrigation in its various manifestations, and forms of drained-field agriculture (Armillas 1971; Denevan 1970; Wilken 1969); although in parts of the tropics intensive, continuous cultivation, particularly of tree crops, is based on soil enrichment through the use of plant and animal fertilizers.

Space does not permit lengthy speculation about the evolutionary relationships of these various types of specialized agriculture to swidden cultivation and fixed-plot horticulture, but a few factors of possible significance may be mentioned. In so far as intensification of output per unit of cultivated land is a common denominator of specialized agriculture it may be argued that it generally resulted from population increase. This is the point of view of Boserup (1965) and others (Harner 1970; Smith and Young 1970), but it cannot be assumed to have general applicability and it leaves unanswered the question of what changes in demographic factors precipitated the presumed population increases. Perhaps, as has already been suggested, the progressive development of sedentary life triggered off large-scale increases in population, although these need not necessarily have led to agricultural intensification. Other factors that may have operated widely to forge more intensive and permanent systems of agriculture are demands for tribute emanating from ceremonial and political centres, warfare, and, as Carneiro (1970) has recently suggested, 'environmental circumscription'. The relative merits of these ideas cannot be debated here, but it is unlikely that any one factor had over-riding significance in the limited areas of the tropics where specialized agriculture developed:

the emergence of intensive systems such as wet-padi, dry-land irrigation, drained-field agriculture, and specialized tree cropping, probably involved a variety of evolutionary developments from pre-existing systems of proto-cultivation.

In the light of the preceding discussion the general ethnoecological model may be recapitulated as follows. Palaeotechnic agricultural systems of the traditional world are ecologically more complex and stable than modern neotechnic systems, and those palaeotechnic systems, such as fixed-plot horticulture and polycultural swidden cultivation, that depend on ecosystem-manipulation are more ancient than those specialized systems that involve ecosystem-transformation, such as wet-padi farming, dry-land irrigation, drained-field agriculture, and specialized tree cropping. A long phase of proto-cultivation based on ecosystem-manipulation preceded the emergence of specialized agriculture, and proto-cultivation itself probably arose among forager bands who exploited a broad spectrum of wild plants and animals in territorially restricted, ecologically diverse habitats, particularly in ecotone situations.

Forested and wooded areas within the seasonally dry, intermediate tropical zone are the homelands of most tropical cultigens, and lowland seed-crop and vegecultural crop complexes are respectively best adapted to semi-arid and sub-humid areas of longer and shorter dry season. Different systems of proto-cultivation developed in this broad zone and fixed-plot horticulture probably preceded swidden cultivation because small domestic plots adjacent to dwellings afforded optimal sites for the care of individual plants and because the transfer of potential cultigens from their wild habitats to such plots provided a genetic environment ideally suited to the emergence of domesticated variants through the selection and fixation of desirable characteristics.

Thus the tending of small domestic 'gardens' close to dwellings probably represents man's earliest system of proto-cultivation in the tropics. It would have been best suited to the cultivation and domestication of vegetatively reproduced plants and seed-reproduced perennial climbers, shrubs, and trees, whereas cereals and other herbaceous crops would have been more effectively cultivated in larger plots cleared specifically for the purpose. Shifting cultivation provided a means of cultivating these and other staple crops on a larger scale, and a shift or expansion of proto-cultivation from domestic to swidden plots may have resulted from population increase and/or inter-group warfare.

As swidden cultivation became established the migration of cultivators and the diffusion of agriculture to new areas became more probable. Seed-crop swidden systems, which are ecologically less stable and dietetically more self-sufficient than vegecultural systems, are likely to have expanded territorially and gradually gained spatial ascendancy over vegeculture. Finally, in limited areas of the tropics, specialized palaeotechnic agricultural systems developed in diverse evolutionary directions and probably as a response to a variety of factors including population increase and politico-ceremonial demands for tribute.

Having outlined a hypothetical model of agricultural prehistory in the tropics, its assumptions and predictions should next be tested against available evidence. This can only be done here in a limited way, but an attempt will be made in the last part of this paper to examine some of the hypothetical constructs in the light of archaeological evidence from the tropics of America, Southeast Asia, and Africa.

The archaeological evidence

In the American tropics the most complete and detailed data on the origins and development of prehistoric subsistence systems come from the findings of MacNeish, Flannery, and their co-workers in Mexico, particularly from the sequences studied in the Tehuacan and Oaxaca valleys (Byers 1967; Flannery *et al.* 1967). These investigations were carried out in semi-arid upland environments with over five dry months in the year and the sites excavated lie in zones of marked ecological complexity. The data obtained indicate the development of a distinctive seed-cultural tradition from as early as the 7th millennium B.C. and the inferred pattern of subsistence activities prior to the beginnings of food production suggests broad-spectrum foraging rather than a pronounced dependence on a limited number of wild foods. Both these findings confirm ethnoecological expectation, but still more interesting is the sequence of different types of agriculture that MacNeish has reconstructed for Tehuacan (Byers 1967:304-7). He suggests that there the two earliest types of agriculture were 'barranca horticulture', which involved 'the planting of individual hardy cultivars in the barrancas near the cave sites', and 'hydro-horticulture' which 'means that individual domesticates – avocado trees and chili plants – were planted beside springs or along the flanks of the Rio Salado'; later 'barranca agriculture' developed which depended on 'the planting of such grains as corn and amaranth in fields (albeit in this phase very small), in the arroyo bottoms, or on low terraces next to arroyos or barrancas', and still later the irrigation agriculture of maize and the cultivation of fruit trees in well-watered orchards became major subsistence activities (Byers 1967:306).

This tentative sequence is at present the most complete reconstruction of early agricultural evolution available from any part of the tropics and it accords remarkably well with the hypothetical model presented here. The initial planting of individual multi-fruiting perennials close to settlement sites suggests proto-cultivation in the form of small-scale fixed-plot horticulture, even though, as MacNeish remarks (Byers 1967:306), 'whether the plants grew in actual gardens or not is open to question'; and the later development of maize and amaranth cultivation in small fields prepared for the purpose is in line with the postulated beginnings of specialization – in areas of seed-culture – on cereals and other herbaceous plants as staple crops. The still later development of hydraulic cultivation in the form of irrigated maize fields and fruit orchards likewise fits theoretical expectation by heralding the establishment of fully specialized agriculture. The role of swidden cultivation in the sequence presents the main problem of interpretation. MacNeish (Byers 1967:306) confesses that 'whether this method began prehistorically is difficult to tell' and guesses that it was practised if at all only marginally along the valley sides late in the prehistoric period. If this surmise is correct the failure of swidden to attain local importance may be due to early concentration in a markedly semi-arid environment on hydraulic methods of cultivation which facilitated the transition from proto-cultivation to specialized irrigation agriculture.

Nowhere else in the American tropics is evidence of early agriculture available on the scale and continuity of the findings from Tehuacan and Oaxaca, but MacNeish has now begun to probe the origins of food production in the high-altitude environment of the Peruvian Andes where he has recovered some evidence suggesting that seed-reproduced plants such as gourd (*Lagenaria* sp.), maize, squash, and possibly beans were being cultivated by 2500 B.C. if not earlier (Pickersgill 1971: personal communication; MacNeish *et al.* 1970; MacNeish 1969). This rather meagre evidence goes some way to confirm the expected early importance of seed crops in this high-altitude environment; but as yet there is no evidence to throw light on the origins of the highland vegecultural tradition, apart from the presence late in the preceramic sequence of artifacts resembling hoe blades which may possibly indicate root-crop cultivation (MacNeish *et al.* 1970:39).

In northern South America on the other hand there is some evidence to suggest that vegeculture may have preceded seed-culture in the tropical lowland environment. At Momíl in northern Colombia and Rancho Peludo in northwestern Venezuela grinding stones, which probably imply the preparation of flour from seed crops such as maize, occur stratigraphically above pottery griddles, which are associated with the baking of cassava bread from bitter manioc. This evidence – exiguous though it is in the absence of remains of the plants themselves – suggests an intrustion of seed-culture into an area in which vegeculture was already established, and direct and indirect dating of these sites indicates that vegeculture may have given way to seed-culture in this area during the millennium 500 B.C. to A.D. 500 (Bischof 1969; Rouse and Cruxent 1963: 5-6 and 53-4; Reichel-Dolmatoff 1957).

This possibility needs to be substantiated by further investigation, but it goes some way to confirm the ecological prediction that vegeculture based on manioc and other low-protein cultigens would tend to give way before an intrusive, more protein-rich seed-crop complex. It is quite probable that maize-dominated seed-culture gradually spread into lowland South America from the west and north during prehistoric times, modifying or replacing vegecultural traditions of cultivation as it did so. However the superior ecological adaptation of vegeculture to the more humid tropical environment, which is clearly evident today in the upper Orinoco area (Harris 1971), may have limited and delayed the penetration of maize and other seed crops into the evergreen rain forests of the Orinoco and Amazon basins and eastern uplands during prehistoric and historic times.

A strong case for the development of manioc-based vegeculture in the northern interior of tropical lowland South America has also been presented recently by Lathrap (1970). He suggests that various forager populations subsisting by hunting, fishing, and gathering in the interior forests of the Amazon and Orinoco basins began experimenting with the domestication of manioc and other useful plants prior to 5000 B.C. and that the Tropical Forest Culture based on root-crop cultivation was well established by 3000 B.C. (Lathrap 1970:45-67). These speculations are well founded ecologically but their confirmation awaits the accumulation of more definite evidence.

Another recent and significant contribution to knowledge of pre-European agricultural evolution in tropical America has come from the discovery of extensive relict systems of raised or ridged fields (Denevan 1970, 1966; Parsons 1969; Smith, Denevan and Hamilton 1968; Broadbent 1968; Parsons and Denevan 1967; Parsons and Bowen 1966). They occur mainly in seasonally flooded or permanently moist plains, principally in lowland savannas from northern Colombia to northwestern Argentina but also in the highland basins of Titicaca and Bogotá. Little is known about the cultivation practices associated with these ridges, ditches, mounds, and platforms, for there are virtually no references to their use in the documentary record of the colonial period. None has yet been directly dated archaeologically, but they are certainly aboriginal and they appear to have made possible the relatively intensive cultivation of otherwise agriculturally unusable terrain, chiefly in seasonally flooded or permanently moist areas. It is not known what the dominant crops grown by this technique were, but analogy with other types of drained-field agriculture in the Americas and with contemporary ridged-field cultivation in New Guinea suggests that root crops were probably more important than seed crops. It has also been suggested that certain of the ridge patterns may represent former fish ponds (Broadbent 1968:142; Parsons and Denevan

1967:98); if so then they could have contributed valuable protein to any agricultural system based upon starch-rich root crops.

In view of the occurrence of these relict field systems through much of northern and western South America – and their presence in middle America has now been demonstrated by finds along the Candelaria and Usumacinta rivers in southeastern Mexico (Siemens and Puleston 1971; Puleston 1971: 334) – it appears that systems of hydraulic cultivation were more varied and widespread in the aboriginal New World than has hitherto been realized. Not only did intensification of agricultural land use – whether as a response to population increase or for varied reasons – lead to specialized types of dry-land irrigation agriculture and to related forms of specialization such as terracing (Donkin 1971), but techniques for the intensive cultivation of wetlands were also evolved in the American tropics, perhaps as an extension of the proto-cultivation of manioc and other root crops in alluvial soils along the rivers.

Evidence for the origins and early development of agriculture in the Old World tropics is at present much more meagre than for the tropical New World. Major archaeological investigations into the beginnings of food production in the Old World have so far focused upon the dry lands of Southwest Asia and only recently has there been an awakening of archaeological interest in the origins of agriculture in tropical Africa and Southeast Asia (for example for Africa Clark 1970; 1967: 187-223; Posnansky 1969; Shaw 1969; Davies 1968, 1967; and for Southeast Asia Higham 1972; Golson 1971; Gorman 1971, 1969; Solheim 1971, 1969; Chang 1970; Yen 1970).

It has long been known that Southeast Asia is the homeland of a wide variety of cultivated plants (Li 1970), many of which now have a pan-tropical distribution as economically important crops, but with the notable exception of Sauer's speculative work on the origins of agriculture, in which Southeast Asia was accorded a primary role (Sauer 1952:24-34), the region has attracted little attention. Now however archaeologists have started to investigate the beginnings of food production both in mainland Southeast Asia and in the Indonesian and Melanesian islands.

So far the most explicit data from the mainland come from Gorman's work at Spirit Cave in northwest Thailand (Gorman 1971), 1969). This site lies in a zone of sub-humid climate and high ecological diversity and excavation has yielded remains of twelve genera of exploited, mainly seed-reproduced plants (*Aleurites, Areca, Canarium, Cucumis, Lagenaria, Madhuca, Piper, Prunus, Pisum* or *Raphia, Terminalia, Trapa, Vicia* or *Phaseolus*) which have been radiocarbon dated to between 6000 and 8000 B.C. Some of these plants may represent actual cultigens, but the plant assemblage as a whole suggests the exploitation of a group of wild or semi-domesticated species which provided food, condiments and stimulants, oil, and domestic utensils. Indeed it seems probable that the Spirit Cave finds represent a very early phase in the evolution of plant domestication equivalent to the postulated transition from broad-spectrum gathering to the repeated harvesting of familiar and favoured plants. Whether they also indicate a form of proto-cultivation cannot be determined, although detailed study of the plant remains may throw light on the question. If cultivation was practised then it is likely – in view of the mixed assemblage of trees, shrubs, climbing and ground plants present, as well as the absence of cereals – that the plants were raised in small domestic plots rather than in temporary swidden clearings or more permanent fields. A similar but more limited assemblage of plant remains has recently been recovered from four prehistoric cave sites in Timor (Glover 1970) where finds of *Aleurites, Areca, Celtis, Lagenaria,* and *Piper*, as well as of the American cultigen *Arachis,* have been identified with varying degrees of confidence by Yen (Glover 1970: App. 10: 46-50). As a Spirit Cave, this assemblage suggests the harvesting of domestically useful wild or semi-domesticated species rather than their systematic cultivation.

The discoveries at Spirit Cave also provide evidence of a later phase in the evolution of agriculture in Southeast Asia. An introduced complex of stone tools and pottery dated to about 6000 B.C. includes ground stone knives which, by comparison with Indonesian examples, are interpreted as rice-harvesting knives (Gorman 1971:314). It is suggested that they indicate the introduction of rice, which is itself associated with a shift in settlement from upland sites to lowland plains where early agricultural villages such as Non Nok Tha which has yielded indirect evident of rice (Higham 1972; Bayard 1971; Solheim 1971) and Ban Kao (Sørensen and Hatting 1967) developed. This settlement shift could be interpreted as evidence for local evolution from upland proto-cultivation to the more specialized lowland cultivation of rice, probably by swidden rather than by more intensive wet-padi methods; but it also lends support to the idea of a general southward diffusion from China of cereal-based seed-culture.

The idea that in Southeast Asia seed-culture based on millet and rice progressively replaced indigenous systems of vegeculture based on taro, yams and other vegetatively reproduced cultigens is implicit in the work of Burkill (1951) and Barrau (1965a and b), both of whom have stressed the formerly greater importance and wider distribution of root crops in Southeast Asian subsistence economies. It is also supported by Spencer (1966:111-4) who has shown the historical retreat of taros and yams eastward through the Indonesian archipelago.

Such a process of replacement is consistent with the ecological postulate that vegeculture would tend to give way before intrusive seed-cultural systems, and it receives further support from the recent suggestion by Chang (1970:183-4) that the 'neolithic' Lungshanoid expansion through northern, eastern, and southeastern China was associated with the southward diffusion of seed-crop cultivation based on foxtail millet (*Setaria italica*), broomcorn millet (*Panicum miliaceum*), and rice. If, as is probable, millets were cultivated by swidden methods in the earliest 'neolithic' Yang-shao culture of north China (Wheatley 1971:23-6; Ho 1969:15-8; Chang 1968:85-92) then we can envisage a gradual southward diffusion of an ecologically unstable seed-crop swidden system, to which upland rice was added at some as yet unknown time. This system would ultimately have replaced ecologically more stable, predominantly vegecultural systems over most of mainland southeast Asia and Indonesia, in parts of which intensive wet-padi cultivation subsequently developed. The general replacement of vegecultural systems did not occur historically east of Indonesia and they persist today, in varied adaptations to insular conditions, in New Guinea (White 1970; Brookfield and White 1968; Golson *et al.* 1967; Clarke 1966; Watson 1965) and the rest of the Pacific world (Golson 1972, 1972; Yen 1970; Green and Kelly 1970; Yawata and Sinoto 1968; Highland *et al.* 1967).

Even less archaeological evidence is available on the origins and early development of agriculture in tropical Africa than in Southeast Asia. Most archaeologists working in Africa are primarily concerned with the palaeolithic, although Clark (1971, 1970:187-223, 1967, 1962), Shaw (1969), Davies (1968, 1967:147-234, 1960), and others have made notable contributions to understanding of the African 'neolithic'. Most of the limited evidence at present available relates to western tropical Africa and comment will be restricted to that part of the continent.

The existence of an ancient centre of vegeculture in tropical West Africa, which is suggested mainly by the local importance of the indigenous Guinea yams, is supported by indirect evidence only. No archaeologically preserved remains of root crops have so far been recovered and the conjecture that vegeculture is of considerable antiquity there rests mainly on the fact that vegecultural techniques are deeply embedded in the agricultural and ceremonial traditions of peoples living in the 'yam zone' (Coursey 1967:22-5, 75-88 and 197-203). It is possible that some of the stone artifacts found in 'mesolithic' contexts in western and central Africa represent the blades of vegecultural planting-sticks or hoes rather than woodworking tools or the points of digging-sticks used for collecting wild vegetable foods. Davies (1968:479-81, 1967:205-16) has used such evidence to argue for a 'protoagricultural' stage in West Africa based on the collection and planting of tubers. Botanical, linguistic, and ethnological evidence has also been adduced in support of the early domestication of root crops in West Africa, particularly by Coursey (1967:7-13) who argues strongly for the ancient cultivation of indigenous yams and suggests that the existence of prohibitions on the use of iron tools for digging yams which are to be used in 'new yam' festivals implies that yam cultivation predates the beginning of the West African 'iron age' (Coursey and Coursey 1971:478). If these speculations are correct – and Posnansky (1969) has suggested that yam cultivation may have begun in West Africa between 2500 and 1500 B.C. – then it appears that vegecultural systems of proto-cultivation may have developed early in the sub-humid areas of western tropical Africa. This idea accords well with ecological expectation and parallels the probable antiquity of vegeculture in the sub-humid tropics of South America and Southeast Asia.

The evidence for early seed-culture in western tropical Africa is only slightly less exiguous than that for vegeculture. In the long dry-season 'Sudanic' zone of West Africa a traditional seed-crop complex exists which includes certain cereals, such as sorghum (*Sorghum bicolor*) and bullrush or pearl millet (*Pennisetum typhoideum* = *P. americanum*), which probably originated within the 'Sudanic' zone north of the Congo basin, and others, such as fonio and black fonio (*Digitaria exilis* and *D. iburua*), the millet *Brachiaria deflexa*, and African rice (*Oryza glaberrima*), which are more definitely thought to be of local West Africa origin (Harlan 1971:470-1; De Wet and Harlan 1971; Baker 1962; Portères 1962). Direct evidence of seed plants, usually in the form of pottery impressions, has so far been recovered archaeologically at only a few West African sites: for example, impressions of pearl millet and *Brachiaria deflexa* at Tichitt-Walata in southern Mauritania dated to about 1100 B.C. (Munson 1970, 1968:11) and possibly of pearl millet at Ntereso in northern Ghana dated to the 2nd millennium B.C. (Davies 1968:481), although at the latter site both the identification and the dating is uncertain. Also in Ghana, at the K6 site of the 2nd millennium B.C. Kintampo culture, remains of cowpea (*Vigna unguiculata*) have been recovered (Flight 1970 and personal communication 1972). Such finds suggest that seed-culture was being practised in West Africa at least by 1000 B.C., and perhaps considerably earlier in view of the 4th millennium dates attributed to several 'neolithic' sites in the western Sahara (Clark 1967:11-3).

Leaving aside the question of whether knowledge of seed-culture was initially diffused across the Sahara from the north, both ecological inference and the limited direct evidence available suggest that in western tropical Africa seed-culture became established first in the drier savannas and deciduous forests of 'Sudanic' West Africa and that seed cultivators, probably practising swidden methods, later expanded southward into parts of the more humid evergreen forest zone. For example, African rice, which probably originated in the area of the 'inland delta' of the Niger, appears to have moved gradually south, eventually reaching the rain-forest zone in present-day Ivory Coast (Portères 1962:197-201, 1955, 1950); there is also evidence to suggest that it was being cultivated in the Casamance valley of southern Senegal by the beginning of the Christian era (Linares de Sapir 1971:41-3). Although detailed information on other crop movements is lacking, there is little doubt that the penetration of vegecultural systems by other seed crops in West Africa has continued through historic times and up to the present (Vermeer 1970; Coursey 1967:142). Thus, despite the inadequacy of the data, it appears that a pattern of seed-culture expanding into areas of vegeculture can be discerned in West Africa, just as it can in the Asian and American tropics.

It is clear from this summary review of evidence on the origins and early development of agriculture in the tropics that knowledge of the spatial and temporal processes involved is still very limited. But progress in our understanding of the crucial transition from foraging to agriculture depends both on the acquisition of factual evidence and on the formulation of hypotheses to integrate data and prompt future investigations. The purpose of the general evolutionary model outlined here is to increase understanding of the prehistory of tropical agriculture in a cross-cultural context and on a pan-tropical scale, but it is offered as a speculative invitation to further enquiry rather than as a firmly established theory.

REFERENCES

Alexander, J. and Coursey, D.G. (1969) The origins of yam cultivation. *In* Ucko, P.J. and Dimbleby, G.W. (eds.) *The Domestication and Exploitation of Plants and Animals*, 405-25. London, Duckworth.

Anderson, E. (1952) *Plants, Man and Life*. Boston, Little, Brown.

Anderson, E. (1950) An Indian garden at Santa Lucia, Guatemala. *Ceiba* **1**, 97-103.

Armillas, P. (1971) Gardens on swamps. *Science* **174**, 653-61.

Baker, H.G. (1962) Comments on the thesis that there was a major centre of plant domestication near the headwaters of the River Niger. *Journal of African History* 3, 229-33.

Barrau, J. (1965a) L'humide et le sec. An essay on ethnobiological adaptation to contrastive environments in the Indo-Pacific area. *Journal of the Polynesian Society* 74, 329-46.

Barrau, J. (1965b) Histoire et préhistoire horticoles de l'Oceanie tropicale. *Journal de la Société des Océanistes* 21, 55-78.

Bayard, D.T. (1971) Excavations at Non Nok Tha, Northeastern Thailand: an interim report. *Asian Perspectives* 13, in press.

Binford, L.R. (1971) Personal communication.

Binford, S.R. and L.R. (eds.) (1968) *New Perspectives in Archaeology*. Chicago, Aldine.

Bischof, H. (1969) Contribuciones a la cronologia de la Cultura Tairona. La Cultura Tairona en el Area Intermedio. *Verhandlungen des XXXVIII Internationalen Amerikanistenkongresses Stuttgart-München* Munich, Band 1, 259-80.

Boserup, E. (1965) *The Conditions of Agricultural Growth*. London, Allen and Unwin.

Brookfield, H.C. and White, J.P. (1968) Revolution or evolution in the prehistory of the New Guinea Highlands: a seminar report. *Ethnology* 7, 43-52.

Broadbent, S.M. (1968) A prehistoric field system in Chibcha territory, Colombia. *Nawpa Pacha* 6, 138-47.

Burkill, I.H. (1951) The rise and decline of the greater yam in the service of man. *Advancement of Science* 7, 443-8.

Byers, D.S. (ed.) (1967) *The Prehistory of the Tehuacan Valley. Vol. 1. Environment and Subsistence.* Austin and London, University of Texas Press.

Carneiro, R.L. (1970) A theory of the origin of the state. *Science* 169, 733-8.

Chagnon, N.A. (1967) Yanomamö social organization and warfare. *In* Fried, M., Harris, M. and Murphy, R. (eds.) *War: the Anthropology of Armed Conflict and Aggression*, 109-59. New York, Natural History Press.

Chang, K. (1970) The beginnings of agriculture in the Far East. *Antiquity* 44, 175-85.

Chang, K. (1968) *The Archaeology of Ancient China.* 2nd ed. New Haven and London, Yale University Press.

Chorley, R.J. and Haggett, P. (eds.) (1967) *Models in Geography.* London, Methuen.

Clark, J.D. (1962) The spread of food production in Sub-Saharan Africa. *Journal of African History* 3, 211-28.

Clark, J.D. (1967) A record of early agriculture and metallurgy in Africa from archaeological sources. *In* Creighton, G. and Bennett, N.R. (eds.) *Reconstructing African Culture History*, 3-24. Boston. Boston University Press.

Clark, J.D. (1970) *The Prehistory of Africa.* London, Thames and Hudson.

Clark, J.D. (1971) A re-examination of the evidence for agricultural origins in the Nile Valley. *Proceedings of the Prehistoric Society* 37 34-79.

Clarke, D.L. (1968) *Analytical Archaeology*. London, Methuen.

Clarke, W.C. (1966) From extensive to intensive shifting cultivation: a succession from New Guinea. *Ethnology* 5, 347-59.

Coursey, D.G. (1967) *Yams.* London, Longmans, Green.

Coursey, D.G. and C.K. (1971) The new yam festivals of West Africa. *Anthropos* 66, 444-84.

Covich, A.P. and Nickerson, N.H. (1966) Studies of cultivated plants in Choco dwelling clearings, Darien, Panama. *Economic Botany* 20, 285-301.

Davies, O. (1968) The origins of agriculture in West Africa. *Current Anthropology* 9, 479-82.

Davies, O. (1967) *West Africa before the Europeans: archaeology and prehistory.* London, Methuen.

Davies, O. (1960) The neolithic revolution in tropical Africa. *Transactions of the Historical Society of Ghana* 4, 14-20.

Denevan, W.M. (1970) Aboriginal drained-field cultivation in the Americas. *Science* 169, 647-54.

De Wet, J.M.J. and Harlan, J.R. (1971) The origin and domestication of *Sorghum bicolor. Economic Botany* 25, 128-35.

Donkin, R.A. (1971) Agricultural terracing in the aboriginal New World. Paper read at the Annual Conference of the Institute of British Geographers. University of Sussex. Mimeo, 18 pages.

Flannery, K.V. (1968) Archaeological systems theory and early Mesoamerica. *In* Meggers, B.J. (ed.) *Anthropological Archaeology in the Americas*, 67-87. Washington, D.C., Anthropological Society of Washington.

Flannery, K.V. *et al.* (1967) Farming systems and political growth in ancient Oaxaca. *Science* 158, 445-54.

Flight, C. (1970) Excavations at Kintampo. *West African Archaeological Newsletter* 12, 71-2.

Gade, D.W. (1970) Ethnobotany of Canihua (*Chenopodium pallidicaule*), rustic seed crop of the Altiplano. *Economic Botany* 24, 55-61.

Geertz, C. (1963) *Agricultural Involution. The Process of Ecological Change in*

Indonesia. Berkeley and Los Angeles, University of California Press.
Gentry, H.S. (1969) Origin of the common bean, *Phaseolus vulgaris. Economic Botany* 23, 55-69.
Glover, I.C. (1970) *Excavations in Timor.* Unpublished thesis submitted for the degree of Ph.D. in the Australian National University, Canberra.
Golson, J. (1972) The Pacific Islands and their prehistoric inhabitants. *In* Ward, R.D. (ed.) *Man in the Pacific Islands.* Oxford, Clarendon. In press.
Golson, J. (1971) Both sides of the Wallace Line: Australia, New Guinea, and Asian prehistory. *Archaeology and Physical Anthropology in Oceania* 6, 124-44.
Golson, J. *et al.* (1967) A note on carbon dates for horticulture in the New Guinea Highlands. *Journal of the Polynesian Society* 76, 369-71.
Gorman, C.F. (1971) The Hoabinhian and after: subsistence patterns in Southeast Asia during the late Pleistocene and early Recent periods. *World Archaeology* 2, 300-20.
Gorman, C.F. (1969) Hoabinhian: a pebble-tool complex with early plant associations in Southeast Asia. *Science* 163, 671-3.
Green, R.C. and Kelly, M. (eds.) (1970) *Studies in Oceanic Culture History.* Honolulu, Bishop Museum, Pacific Anthropology Records.
Harner, M.J. (1970) Population pressure and the social evolution of agriculturalists. *Southwestern Journal of Anthropology* 26, 67-86.
Harlan, J.R. (1971) Agricultural origins: centers and noncenters. *Science* 174, 468-74.
Harris, D.R. (1972) Swidden systems and settlement. *In* Ucko, P.J., Tringham, R. and Dimbleby, G.W. (eds.) *Man, Settlement and Urbanism*, 245-62. London, Duckworth.
Harris, D.R. (1971) The ecology of swidden cultivation in the upper Orinoco rain forest, Venezuela. *Geographical Review* 61, 475-95.
Harris, D.R. (1969) Agricultural systems, ecosystems and the origins of agriculture. *In* Ucko, P.J. and Dimbleby, G.W. (eds.) *The Domestication and Exploitation of Plants and Animals*, 3-15. London, Duckworth.
Harvey, D. (1969) *Explanation in Geography.* London, Edward Arnold.
Hawkes, J.G. (1969) The ecological background of plant domestication. *In* Ucko, P.J. and Dimbleby, G.W. (eds.) *The Domestication and Exploitation of Plants and Animals*, 17-29. London, Duckworth.
Heiser, C.B. Jr. (1969) Some considerations of early plant domestications. *Bio Science* 19, 228-31.
Higham, C.F.W. (1972) Initial model formulation *in Terra Incognita. In* Clarke, D.L. (ed.) *Models in Archaeology*. London, Methuen. In press.
Highland, G.A. *et al.* (1967) *Polynesian Culture History: Essays in Honor of K.P. Emory.* Honolulu. Bishop Museum Special Publication 56.
Ho, P. (1969) The loess and the origin of Chinese agriculture. *American Historical Review* 75, 1-36.
Isaac, G.L. (1971) Whither archaeology? *Antiquity* 45, 123-9.
Kimber, C. (1966) Dooryard gardens of Martinique. *Yearbook of the Association of Pacific Coast Geographers* 28, 97-118.
Lathrap, D.W. (1970) *The Upper Amazon.* London, Thames and Hudson.
Li, H. (1970) The origin of cultivated plants in Southeast Asia. *Economic Botany* 24, 3-19.
Linares de Sapir, O. (1971) Shell middens of the Lower Casamance and problems of Diola protohistory. *West African Journal of Archaeology* 1, 23-54.
MacNeish, R.S. (1969) *First Annual Report of the Ayacucho Archaeological-Botanical Project.* Andover, Massachussetts. R.S. Peabody Foundation.
MacNeish, R.S. *et al.* (1970) *Second Annual Report of the Ayacucho Archaeological-Botanical Project.* Andover, Massachussetts. R.S. Peabody Foundation.

McMaster, D.N. (1962) Speculations on the coming of the banana to Uganda. *Journal of Tropical Geography* **16**, 57-69.
Munson, P.J. (1970) Corrections and additional comments concerning the 'Tichitt Tradition'. *West African Archaeological Newsletter* **12**, 47-8.
Munson, P.J. (1968) Recent archaeological research in the Dhar Tichitt region of south-central Mauritania. *West African Archaeological Newsletter* **10**, 6-13.
Parsons, J.J. (1969) Ridged fields in the Rio Guayas valley, Ecuador. *American Antiquity* **34**, 76-80.
Parsons, J.J. and Bowen, W.A. 1966. Ancient ridged fields of the San Jorge river floodplain, Colombia. *Geographical Review* **56**, 317-43.
Parsons, J.J. and Denevan, W.M. (1967) Pre-Columbian ridged fields. *Scientific American* **217**, 93-100.
Pickersgill, B. (1971) Personal communication.
Portères, R. (1950) Vieilles agricultures de l'Afrique intertropical. *L'Agronomie Tropicale* **5**, 489-507
Portères, R. (1955) Historique sur les premiers échantillons d'*Oryza glaberrima* St. recueillis en Afrique. *Journal d'Agriculture Tropicale et de Botanique Appliquée* **2**, 535-7.
Portères, R. (1962) Berceaux agricoles primaires sur le continent africain. *Journal of African History* **3**, 195-210.
Posnansky, M. (1969) Yams and the origins of West African agriculture. *Odu* **1**, 101-7.
Puleston, D.E. (1971) An ecological approach to the origins of Maya civilization. *Archaeology* **24**, 330-7.
Rappaport, R.A. (1971) The flow of energy in an agricultural society. *Scientific American* **224**, 116-32.
Reichel-Dolmatoff, G. (1957) Momil: a Formative sequence from the Sinú Valley, Colombia. *American Antiquity* **22**, 226-34.
Renvoize, B.S. (1972) The area of origin of manioc (*Manihot esculenta* Crantz) as a tropical American crop plant – a review of the evidence. *Economic Botany*. In press.
Rouse, I. and Cruxent, J.M. (1963) *Venezuelan Archaeology*. New Haven and London, Yale University Press.
Sahlins, M.D. and Service, E.R. (eds.) (1960) *Evolution and Culture*. Ann Arbor, University of Michigan Press.
Sauer, C.O. (1952) *Agricultural Origins and Dispersals*. New York, American Geographical Society.
Siemens, A.H. and Puleston, D.E. (1972) Ridged fields and associated features in Southern Campeche: new perspectives on the Lowland Maya. *American Antiquity* **37** 228-39.
Simmonds, N.W. (1965) The grain chenopods of the tropical American highlands. *Economic Botany* **19**, 223-35.
Simoons, F.J. (1965) Two Ethiopian gardens. *Landscape* **14**, 15-20.
Simoons, F.J. (1960) *Northwest Ethiopia. Peoples and Economy*. Madison, University of Wisconsin Press.
Smeds, H. (1955) The ensete planting culture of Eastern Sidamo, Ethiopia. *Acta Geographica* **13**, 1-39.
Smith, C.T., Denevan, W.M. and Hamilton, P. (1968) Ancient ridged fields in the region of Lake Titicaca. *Geographical Journal* **134**, 353-67.
Smith, P.E.L. and Young, T.C., Jr. (1972) The evolution of early agriculture and culture in Greater Mesopotamia: a trial model. *In* Spooner, B. (ed.) *Population Growth: Anthropological Implications*. Boston, M.I.T. Press. In Press.
Solheim, W.G. (1971) Northern Thailand, Southeast Asia, and world prehistory. *Asian Perspectives*. In press.
Solheim, W.G. (1969) Reworking Southeast Asian prehistory. *Paideuma* **15**, 125-39.

Sorensen, P. and Hatting, T. (1967) *Archaeological excavations in Thailand. Vol. II: Ban Kao*. Copenhagen, Munksgaard.

Spencer, J.E. (1966) *Shifting cultivation in Southeastern Asia. University of California Publications in Geography* **19**. Berkeley and Los Angeles, University of California Press.

Strathern, M. (1969) Why is the Pueraria a sweet potato? *Ethnology* **8**, 189-98.

Trigger, B.G. (1970) Aims in prehistoric archaeology. *Antiquity* **44**, 26-37.

Trigger, B.G. (1971) Archaeology and ecology. *World Archaeology* **2**, 321-36.

Troll, C. and Paffen, K.H. (1963) Map 5. Seasonal climates of the earth. *In* Landsberg, H.E. *et al., Weltkarten zur Klimakunde*. Berlin, Heidelberg, New York, Springer-Verlag.

Vermeer, D.E. (1970) Population pressure and crop rotational changes among the Tiv of Nigeria. *Annals of the Association of American Geographers* **60**, 299-314.

Watson, J.B. (1968) Pueraria: names and traditions of a lesser crop of the Central Highlands, New Guinea. *Ethnology* **7**, 268-79.

Watson, J.B. (1965) From hunting to horticulture in the New Guinea Highlands. *Ethnology* **4**, 295-309.

Watson, J.B. (1964) A previously unreported root crop from the New Guinea highlands. *Ethnology* **3**, 1-5.

Watson, R.A. and Watson, P.J. (1969) *Man and Nature. An Anthropological Essay in Human Ecology*. New York, Harcourt, Brace and World.

Wheatley, P. (1971) *The Pivot of the Four Quarters. A Preliminary Enquiry into the Origins and Character of the Ancient Chinese City*. Edinburgh, University Press.

White, J.P. (1970) New Guinea: the first phase in Oceanic settlement. *In* Green, R.C. and Kelly, M. (eds.) *Studies in Oceanic Culture History*. Honolulu. Bishop Museum, Pacific Anthropology Records.

Wilken, G.C. (1969) Drained-field agriculture: an intensive farming system in Tlaxcala, Mexico. *Geographical Review* **59**, 215-41.

Wolf, E.R. (1966) *Peasants*. Englewood Cliffs, N.J., Prentice-Hall.

Woodwell, G.M. and Smith, H.H. (eds.) (1969) *Diversity and Stability in Ecological Systems. Brookhaven Symposia in Biology* **22**. Brookhaven. National Laboratory, Biology Department.

Yawata, I. and Sinoto, Y.H. (eds.) (1968) *Prehistoric Culture in Oceania. A Symposium*. Honolulu, Bishop Museum Press.

Yen, D.E. (1970) The development of agriculture in Oceania. *In* Green, R.C. and Kelly, M. (eds.) *Studies in Oceanic Culture History*. Honolulu. Bishop Museum, Pacific Anthropology Records.

A.G. SHERRATT

The interpretation of change in European prehistory

Introduction

Although the speculations of social philosophers and anthropologists on the early history of man played an important part in the genesis of a systematic study of the past, and have continued to do so in Marxist explanations of prehistory, European archaeology in general has been curiously isolated from the development of anthropological theory. While in part a healthy reaction to generalized theories which provided little help in explaining specific features of the archaeological record, this attitude has produced a striking lack of theoretical discussion which might suggest new models for testing.

For most of the present century, archaeological research in Europe has been concerned largely with providing a chronological and cultural framework, in order to make it possible to place assemblages and stray finds in an ordered context. For these kinds of problem, a relatively crude set of ideas about the workings of prehistoric societies was adequate. The main need was for a set of units to define similarities in material culture in a way useful for this kind of comparison. With only a small number of excavated sites, the assumption that similarities in material culture between different regions were the result of contact between contemporary groups allowed a 'chest of drawers' chronology to be built up, which served to isolate the main gaps in regional sequences. The reasons why such similarities should exist were irrelevant to the problem of providing a framework.

In order to explain the changes which were evident from this reconstructed series of cultures, some mechanism had to be invoked. One answer was found in the idea of diffusion, another in the idea of migration: these two concepts provided the main explanatory models in every day use.

Diffusion theory was an extension into prehistory of the kinds of explanation used, for example, in the history of art, where styles in sculpture and painting can legitimately be illuminated by tracing the spread of the influence of particular schools. What was not commented on was that such phenomena had been studied mainly in urban societies whose social structure and communication networks were very different from those of prehistory. A proliferation of technical terms (Typenfront, Kulturübertragung) merely gave archaeological literature an esoteric flavour without providing analytical depth.

Migration theory was largely influenced by ideas current in comparative philology, particularly reconstructions of Indo-European origins. The models suggested by this assumed a small number of expanding cores which gradually differentiated into separate but related units. In this reconstruction 'cultural achievement' expressed the inherent genius of particular peoples. The explanation of periods of cultural florescence could then be reduced to a problem of tracing the origin of the ethnic group concerned. This model was applied not only to stylistic features, but was also used to explain differences in economy, settlement pattern and technology: but it was religion, as evidenced for example by burial-rite, which was considered as the most conservative element, and therefore the most diagnostic in tracing cultural origins.

As there were few explicit criteria for distinguishing between the two phenomena of diffusion and invasion, endless controversy resulted over their relative importance. Both, however, tended to be used as labels rather than explanations, as the reasons for movements of peoples and cultural influences remained unclear.

One of the few attempts to complete this theoretical framework by providing an answer to these problems was made by V.G. Childe (1958). His explanation for the supposed predominance of the Near East was based on the idea that an agricultural surplus in the special conditions of Egypt and Mesopotamia set in motion a process of urbanisation and colonial expansion whose effects reached ultimately as far as the British Isles. The advent of radiocarbon dating, which has fundamentally altered the reconstructed relationship between the European and Near Eastern sequences, and critical examination of Childe's theory of urbanisation, have rendered this model untenable (Renfrew 1971).

The reasons for large scale migrations have usually been sought in the idea of a 'reservoir' of nomadic peoples on the eastern frontiers of Europe. This view rests largely on a confusion between the specialized animal-based economies of Central Asia and the kinds of mixed farming practised on the fertile chernozems of the Ukraine. The actual archaeological basis for the idea, however, is slender and its vitality has rested largely on the speculative philological reconstruction of an 'Indo-European homeland'.

For the kinds of question which could be raised with the relatively small number of well-excavated sites available until recently, such a limited theoretical basis was adequate. With an increasing body of material evidence and the solution of the major chronological problems, the lack of a more than rudimentary body of theory has become increasingly apparent. While new ideas (particularly from New World archaeology) are producing an invigorating effect, it remains true that much discussion of concrete problems in European archaeology is still conducted within the framework and language of a previous generation of research – even where cast in a quantitative or pseudo-quantitative form.

One of the effects of the continuing dominance of diffusion and migration theory has been to divert attention from aspects of prehistory which could form the basis of alternative interpretations. The search for 'cultural origins' using typological parallels for artifacts and monuments has taken precedence over the analysis of function: the attribution of any change to new sorts of people has inhibited the development of a theory of economic growth and obscured possible causal relationships between successive patterns of settlement.

Changes in land use in neolithic and later Europe

One of the features of Childe's model of European development which led him to stress the importance of contact with the Mediterranean and the Near East was the idea that neolithic economies were handicapped by a surplus too small to guard against natural disasters. The introduction of metal-working, requiring a surplus for exchange, was seen as a critical stimulus to specialization and more effective techniques of production (Childe 1954). The effect of this was to provide an alternative to the 'wasteful' method of economic expansion by enlarging the area of the settlement.

There is now however sufficient information on the distribution and character of neolithic and later settlement in Europe to test this idea and its implications for models of economic development. A point which has not been sufficiently stressed is the limited range of soil types on which neolithic agricultural settlement was concentrated. Although this has often been noted in connection with the loess areas of Central Europe (Clark 1952:96), it can be seen as a fundamental characteristic of this phase of settlement: in southeast Europe, as in Iran and Turkey (Flannery 1969:8; Cohen 1970), soil moisture was a critical factor determining choice of location (Sherratt 1972). The relatively small neolithic population could in fact select soils such as fertile alluvial areas whose potential yield was many times greater than that of areas later taken into cultivation (Allan 1972). The idea of neolithic agriculture as a risky affair with no possibility of surplus production and an inherently limited capacity for expansion is not merely untrue, but the exact opposite seems likely.

The point is well illustrated by the development of settlement in south central Anatolia, as illustrated by Dr D.H. French's survey of

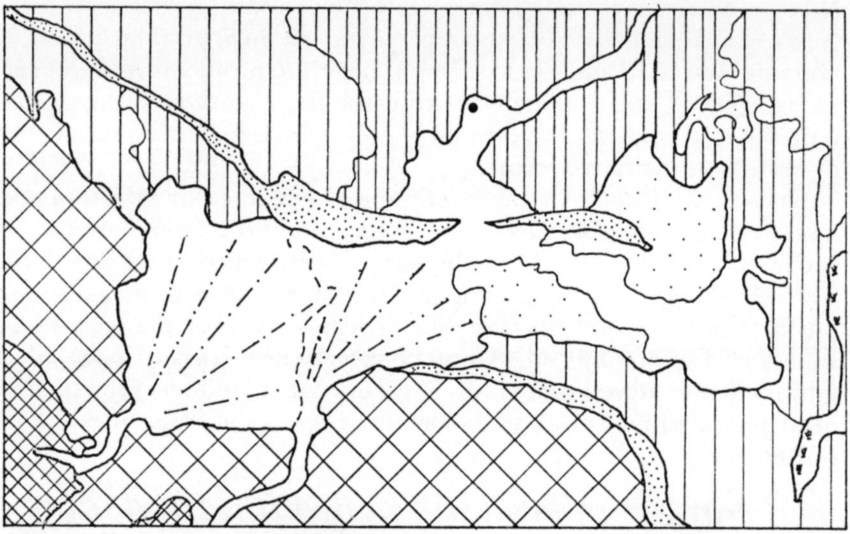

Scale: 0 km. 10 km.

Figure 1 Distribution of known sites in the Çumra area of the Konya Plain, Turkey. (Data for figures 1-4 taken from French 1970.) Sixth millennium.

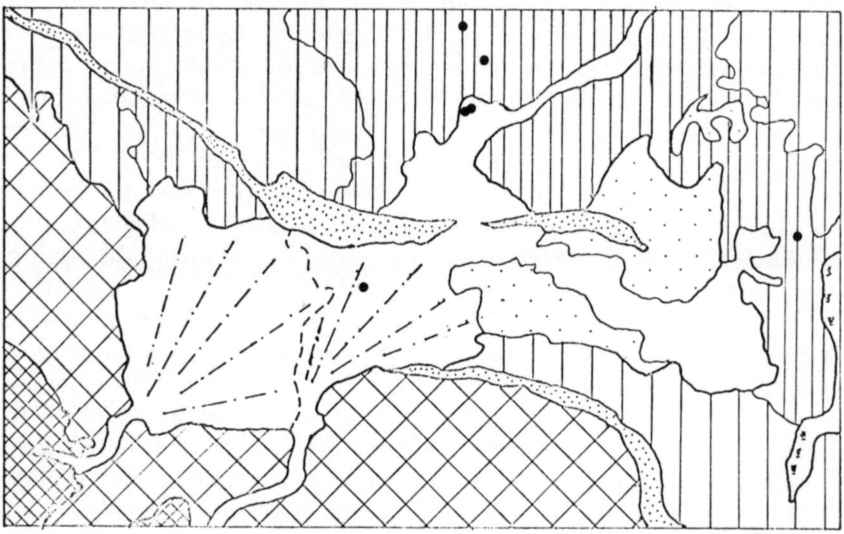

Scale: 0 km. 10 km.

Figure 2 Distribution of known sites in the Çumra area: fifth millennium.

the Çumra region (French 1970). This is one of the better-watered areas of the Konya Plain where rivers draining from the Pisidian lake district enter the plain from the west. These rivers have built up alluvial fans with an area of backswamp at their edge, surrounded by marls and sands representing old lake bottom deposits and shorelines.

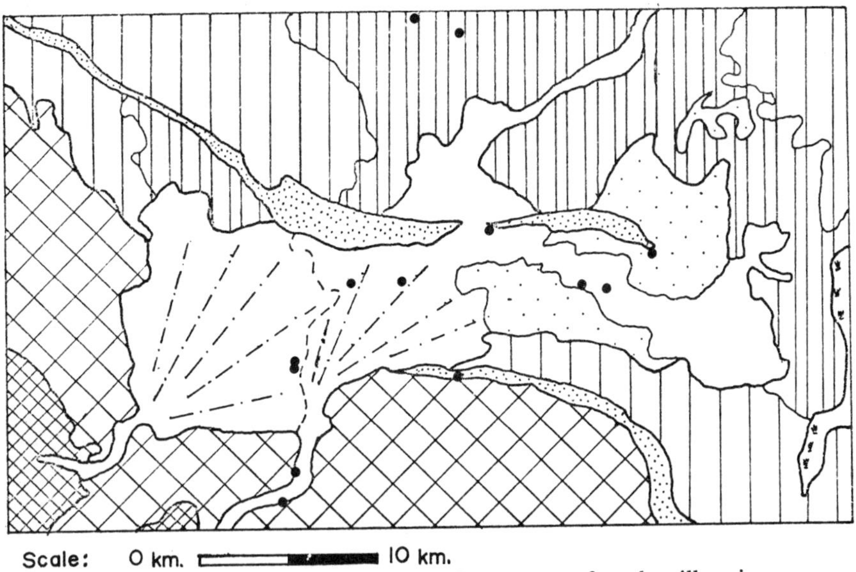

Figure 3 Distribution of known sites in the Çumra area: fourth millennium.

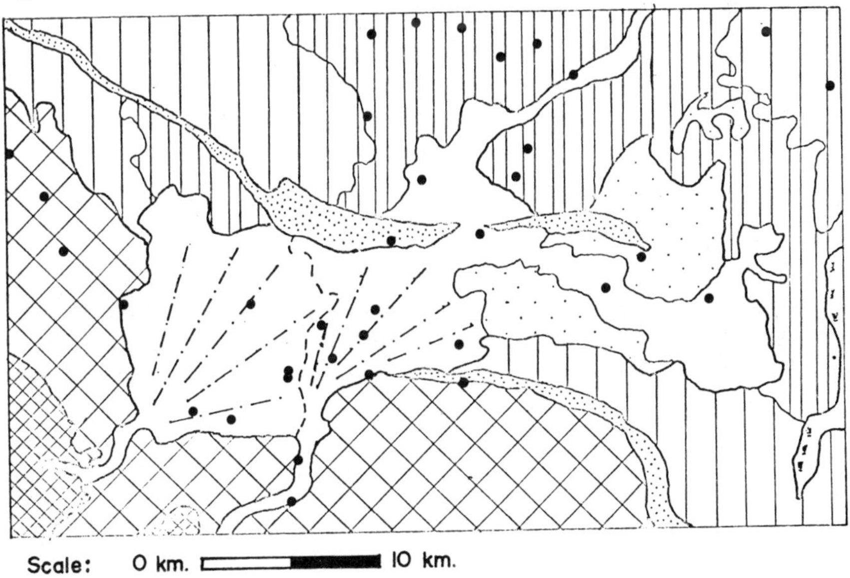

Figure 4 Distribution of known sites in the Çumra area; third millennium.

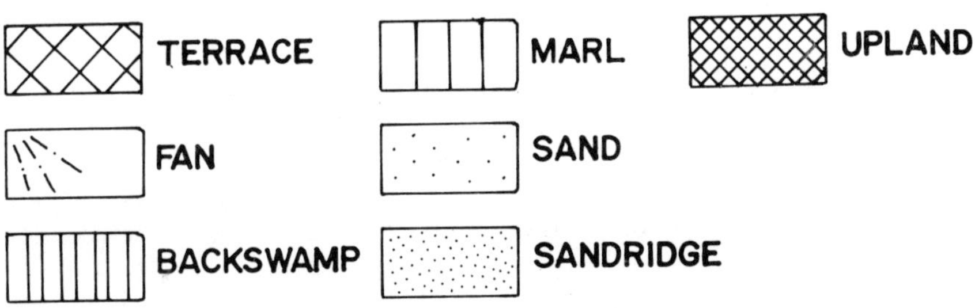

Sixth and 5th millenium sites (Figs. 1, 2), including the major site of Catal Hüyük, show a strong concentration on the backswamp soils in a way comparable to the concentration in 'intermontane plains with a high sub-surface water-table and frequent marshy areas' in the Zagros (Flannery 1969:81). Fourth millenium sites (Fig. 3) are found higher up the rivers on the fan itself, while the most radical expansion occurs in the 3rd millenium (Fig. 4) when sites occur in a wide variety of situations not previously occupied, for instance on the terraces.

The long period of initial concentration adjacent to areas of high water-table is significant for the interpretation of early neolithic settlement in general, and for the models of change considered at the end of this paper. For the spread of early agricultural settlement in Europe, for instance, it suggests that the pattern of dispersal might be strongly influenced by the distribution of a sharply-defined series of suitable environments for cereal-growing. Such constraints would explain the lack of early neolithic sites in the Cyclades, for instance, and the restricted occurrence of cereal-based economies in the neolithic of peninsular Italy (Barker, this volume).

It is also important in explaining the pattern of long-occupied tell sites that are common in the neolithic and copper ages of the Balkans, and their rareness elsewhere. The area of highly-productive land accessible from an individual settlement which is not using intensive agricultural techniques such as irrigation is critical for the length of time for which such a location can be occupied. Allan (1972) has noted that 'semi-permanent cultivation soils' such as river alluvium require a crop/fallow ratio of approximately 1:1, and that on permanently moist soils continuous cropping is sometimes possible. Tell sites are characteristically found in alluvial basins such as the Marica valley, the Plain of Thessaly, or the floodplain areas of the Lower Danube, with wide areas of these soils available to them. Away from the major basins, neolithic sites in the Balkans are also found where smaller areas of soil with a high water-table occur, by springs or rivers. In these situations, continuous settlement is not possible and tells are not found.

If this picture of a restricted area of early neolithic settlement in Europe is accepted, then the expansion of settlement and the adaptations required to support it provides a basic process of change operating in subsequent periods. Flannery (1969) has drawn attention to the sociological implications of changing land-use in Iran, in which highly-productive land formed a decreasing proportion of the area occupied. While less marked, a comparable process can be inferred for the situation described here. The spread of settlement to areas where yields were more vulnerable to fluctuations in rainfall, for instance, would have increased the need for redistributive mechanisms which would allow local surpluses to be fully used. As metal ores occur for the most part in upland areas probably seasonally exploited by peripheral groups, the circulation of metal objects may have had an important role in such exchange-cycles.

In northern Europe, the later phases of the neolithic have often been associated with the arrival of Indo-European groups from eastern Europe with a new economic emphasis. Settlements of the Corded Ware culture group do in fact demonstrate an increased use of less fertile sandy soils. However, the present podsolized soils and heathland character of these areas are not an original feature, but have been demonstrated to be an indirect result of human activity (Waterbolk 1956, 1964). A similar pattern appears in the bronze age in England in marginal upland areas such as the North York moors (Fleming 1971) where clearing for arable resulted in the spread of *Calluna* heathland. In Holland, the increasing podsolization and soil erosion during the bronze age made inland areas increasingly uninhabitable, and both here and in Zealand (Mathiassen 1957) a shift of settlement to the coastal zone is evidenced (Waterbolk 1962).

During the iron age in northern and central Europe evidence from areas such as England (Ellison and Harriss 1972), Denmark (Mathiassen 1948) and Switzerland suggests that remaining heavier soils, especially clay, were increasingly occupied for arable cultivation, and this process continued into the Middle Ages (Smith 1967). In Bulgaria and Romania too, late bronze age and iron age tumuli cover wide areas of the thinner of dryer lowland soils, for instance on the Tertiary limestones around the Marica valley (Tsonchev 1963) or the higher loess terraces of the Lower Danube.

In Mediterranean Europe a somewhat different pattern of economic expansion took place. Whereas in northern Europe arable and pastoral elements are closely interdependent through the use of stubble grazing and the recycling of manure, in Mediterranean husbandry different elements such as the intensive cultivation of fruits or irrigated crops and extensive transhumant pastoralism can be developed independently. There are also differences in the character and amounts of soils suitable for arable cultivation: the glacial clays of northern Europe allowed a further local expansion of local cereal cultivation at a time when the lowland basins of peninsular Greece could increase production only by highly intensive methods. In consequence there is a much more marked pattern of local specialization and a need for centres of exchange.

Lowland agriculture seems to have made increasing use of crops such as vines and olives in the bronze age (Renfrew, 1972). The high labour requirements of these (Chisholm 1968) and the evidence for drainage in Mycenaean times (Hope Simpson 1965) indicate the intensive forms of cultivation which had come into use. These were complemented by the extensive use of upland areas for sheep grazing. The more extensive forms of transhumance in historical times in the Balkans (Roglić 1961) were closely associated with urban exchange-centres where animal products and metals were traded for grain and salt. These economic contrasts between adjacent zones would be a major factor favouring political integration, and the development of the Mycenaean states.

Discussion

The patterns of economic change in neolithic and later Europe are clearly related to the potential of cereal-based economies to overcome constraints on production in environments where a wide range of soils is suitable for arable cultivation. But while the adaptability of cereal cultivation to a wide range of habitats explains the *potential* for expansion, it does not explain why it actually occurred.

The kinds of change involved in increasing the productivity of subsistence farming have been discussed by Ester Boserup (1965). She points out that an increased frequency of cropping in order to raise output from a given area necessarily involves increased labour input. Similar factors apply in expanding cultivation to poorer soils: a comparable yield can only be achieved from cultivating a larger area or by manuring and irrigation. For these reasons she suggests that changes to more intensive systems of agriculture only occur when they are made necessary by pressure of population. Adaptation is seen as an automatic response to the growth of population above a critical threshold.

Such changes are essentially different from the process which economists label 'growth', which is characterized by a general increase in real income per head. In preindustrial economies, increases in population may as often lead to a reduction in standard of living for the bulk of the population. The recognition that family limitation practices may be sensitive to changes in the standard of living (Carr Saunders 1922; Stott 1962; Wrigley 1969) implies that stabilization of population levels may be as likely an outcome as changes in technique when such critical thresholds are reached. Although stabilization of population has been discussed largely in the context of mobile populations under strong environmental constraints (e.g. Birdsell 1968), where direct limitation by infanticide is often found, the range of techniques for limiting population found even in agricultural societies (Carr Saunders 1922) and the effectiveness of indirect social mechanisms such as deferment of marriage (Laslett 1965) suggest that even sedentary groups are not incapable of limiting their populations. The contraints on community size produced by patterns of co-operation, for instance in seasonal work-load peaks, define optimal limits which may be rigidly enforced by social convention.

Such factors favouring stabilization must be taken into account in modelling the relationship between population growth and advances in technique. As Binford (1968) has pointed out in another context, due account must be given to factors leading to a *loss* of stability. As cereal agriculture involves alterations in the structure of local ecosystems, such factors are often inherent in this form of exploitation. By removing forest-cover and replacing local species by plants and animals formerly restricted to marginal habitats of low complexity, checks on irreversible processes of soil degeneration may be removed. Equally important however are environmental changes when these affect critical aspects of local farming systems. In the case of neolithic settlement in southeast Europe discussed above, the concentration on areas with a high water-table would mean that changes in hydrology could affect a large proportion of the population. This is especially so in areas such as neolithic Switzerland, and extensive changes in lake levels in the postglacial have been documented from stratigraphic work both here and in Denmark (Guyan 1958; Jorgensen 1963).

Loss of stability does not of course inevitably lead to progressive adaptation of technique. Nevertheless as a means of bringing about local pressure of population through a lowering of the ceiling it is an important factor in provoking change, partly through positive selective pressure and partly by altering the structure of local systems – Postan, for instance, has pointed out (1962) the better balance between livestock and arable following the Black Death in 14th-century England. Looked at in this way, there is no need to invoke a simple causal role for population growth, constantly forcing economic progress by an inexorable growth in numbers. As there are few intrinsic advantages to raising population levels in preindustrial situations, it is possible that such changes came about largely as consequences of attempts to preserve existing population levels in declining environment.

Conclusion

As evidence on prehistoric economies accumulates from analyses of food remains, artifactual studies and inferences from site locations, it is becoming increasingly possible to treat the development of cultural systems as functional units. Emphasis has shifted from attention to the origins of specific features to their role in the system as a whole. At the same time recognition that the use of 'chest of drawers' models has often exaggerated the contrast between successive assemblages to produce artificial discontinuities has led to a decline in theories involving outside influence. Both of these factors have brought about the mechanisms of change which can be tested against the growing body of environmental and cultural data. Although at present much of such thinking is still in the realm of speculation, ideas of this kind are essential components of a full explanation of prehistoric developments.

REFERENCES

Allan, W. (1972) Ecology, techniques and settlement patterns. *In* Ucko, P.J., Tringham, R. and Dimbleby, G.W. (eds.) *Man, Settlement and Urbanism.* London, Duckworth.

Binford, L.R. (1968) Post-Pleistocene adaptation. *In* Binford, S.R. and L.R. (eds.) *New Perspectives in Archaeology*, 313-41. Chicago.

Birdsell, J.B. (1968) Some predictions for the Pleistocene based on equilibrium systems among recent hunter-gatherers. *In* Lee, R.B. and Devore, I. (eds.) *Man the Hunter*, 229-40. Chicago.

Boserup, E. (1965) *The Conditions of Agricultural Growth.* London.

Carr-Saunders, A. (1922) *The Population Problem.* Oxford.

Childe, V.G. (1954) *What Happened in History.* London.

Childe, V.G. (1958) *The Prehistory of European Society.* London.

Chisholm, M. (1968) *Rural Settlement and Land Use.* London.

Clark, J.G.D. (1952) *Prehistoric Europe; the Economic Basis.* London.

Cohen, H.R. (1970) The palaeoecology of south central Anatolia at the end of the Pleistocene and the beginning of the Holocene. *Anatolian Studies* **20**, 119-38.

Ellison, A. and Harriss, J. (1972) Settlement and land use in the prehistory and early history of southern England. *In* Clarke, D.L. (ed.) *Models in Archaeology.* London.

Flannery, K.V. (1969) Origins and ecological effects of early domestication in Iran and the Near East. *In* Ucko, P.J. and Dimbleby, G.W. (eds.) *The Domestication and Exploitation of Plants and Animals*, 73-100. London, Duckworth.

Fleming, A. (1971). Bronze age agriculture on the marginal lands of north-east Yorkshire. *Agricultural History Review* **19**, 1-24.

Guyan, W.U. (1955) *Das Pfahlbauproblem.* Basel.

Hope Simpson, R., (1965) *A Gazeteer and Atlas of Mycenaean Sites*, London.

Jorgensen, S. (1963) *Early Postglacial in Aamosen.* Geological Survey of Denmark. Copenhagen.

Laslett, P. (1965) *The World We Have Lost.* London.

Mathiassen, T. (1959) *Nordvestsjaellands Oldtidsbebyggelse.* Copenhagen.

Postan, M.M. (1962) Village livestock in the thirteenth century. *Economic History Review*, 2nd series, **15**, 219-49.

Renfrew, A.C. (1969) The autonomy of the southeast European copper age. *Proceedings of the Prehistoric Society* **35**, 12-47.

Renfrew, A.C. (1972) *The Emergence of Civilization: the Cyclades and the Aegean in the Third Millennium B.C.* London, Methuen.

Roglić, J. (1961) The geographical setting of medieval Dubrovnik. *In* Pounds, N. (ed.) *Geographical Essays on Eastern Europe.* Indiana.

Smith, C.T. (1967) *An Historical Geography of Western Europe.* London.

Sherratt, A.G. (1972) Socio-economic and demographic models for the neolithic and bronze ages of Europe. *In* Clarke, D.L. (ed.) *Models in Archaeology.* London.

Tsonchev, D. (1963) *Archeologicheski Pametnitsi po Iuzhnite Sklonove na Penagiurska Sredna Gora.* Sofia.

Waterbolk, H.T. (1956) Pollen spectra from grave mounds in the Netherlands. *Palaeohistoria* **5**, 1-13.

Waterbolk, H.T. (1962) The lower Rhine basin. *In* Braidwood, R.J. and Willey, G.R. (eds.) *Courses toward Urban Life*, 227-53. Edinburgh.

Waterbolk, H.T. (1964) Podsolierungserscheinung bei Grabhügeln. *Palaeohistoria* **10**.

MAURIZIO TOSI

Early urban evolution and settlement patterns in the Indo-Iranian borderland

The city, taken as the nucleus of demographic and economic concentration is necessarily the direct expression of a productive economy. As such, it can hardly be defined as a cultural model or type in itself, since it has no alternatives worthy of consideration. Any discussion must therefore concentrate on the various *types* of cities exploiting the ecological environment and, even more, on the predominant economic system. The different stages of evolution of human communities – agricultural-pastoral, mercantile and industrial – have created different formulas; nevertheless, the city remains a point of confluence in its initial phase, and its growth is closely linked to possibilities of concentration and cohabitation, as well as to its capacity for attracting external groups.

If we consider the city as a single cultural model or type, we pose the problem falsely; and the discussion that results can only be circular. The question must be looked at in terms of origins, as we examine the steps in the process of formation that preceded and prepared the city's full development. The analysis is applied to a specific geographical sector in which my competence comes from direct experience: Iran and the adjoining regions to the east, the theatre of a process of urbanization that was certainly related to the beginning of the great proto-Indian metropoleis of Mohenjo Daro and Harappa. I shall also try to establish in the light of the available data, whether, or not the phenomenon of urbanization took on certain characteristics in these regions that might distinguish it from the Mesopotamian model, exemplified by the late 4th millennium cities of Sumer.

Early agricultural developments in Turkmenia

In the dynamics of primitive urban development, one must differentiate the *areas of early agricultural development* from the *areas of productive increase.* Even though an eventual superimposition of the two areas cannot be excluded *a priori*, they usually remained separate in southwest Asia.

Flood cultivation, the only kind that in semi-arid alluvial plains allows intensive exploitation of the soil, can only be extended over large areas through the massive use of canal systems, necessarily integrated into a unified system under organic political control. It may be supposed that the colonization of the great flood valleys took place by degrees, but it would have been possible only for communities with several hundred workers, already possessing adequate technical means and, even more important, a well-developed social and economic system. As R. Braidwood clearly pointed out, the demographic and technological potential of the proto-agricultural tribes in the regions of the plateau above the 3,000 ft. level (Kurdistan), in the oases rich in springs (Kashan) or in the *fans* at the foot of mountains (southern Turkmenia), gradually increased. The crucial phase in the process of urbanization is the transition from the area of *early agricultural development* to the *area of productive increases.* This definitely marks the end of the so-called 'neolithic economy' based on minimum accumulation and a slow rate of demographic increase. The change in this case is a consequence of major increase in the rate of growth of wealth and population.

The first agricultural communities of southwest Asia are generally characterized by certain common elements: densely populated villages with residential units of a one-room type so tightly packed together as almost to form a single structure (Fig. 1); painted ceramics of excellent workmanship; small structures of family use for preserving cereals; widespread employment of stone products stemming from the mesolithic tradition; fertility cults expressed through anthropomorphic, broad-buttocked figures; and the limited importance of animal breeding, as can be seen in the large number of wild animal remains. We also find these characteristics in the regions of northern Iran first involved with a productive economy: from the Kashan valley, from sites along the Elburz range and from the Gorgan plain, as far as southern Turkmenia (Mellaart 1970: 290-303). In the 5th millennium, however, the most unified complex appears at Dzejtun near Ashkhabad, where the local mesolithic tradition is still alive (Masson, 1971:9-25). At this point it should be stressed that the neolithic economy does not appear in any early Iranian context as a split with preceding traditions, but rather as a grafting of new techniques, whose logical result was the setting-up of a new social order. An analysis of the lithic production can lead to a partial understanding of the phenomenon, but it is not easy to extend to the semi-arid regions of Iran the dynamics of economic groups and systems that Piggott postulated for the neolithic in the British Isles and Scandinavia. The fact is that in these semi-arid regions the mesolithic economy lived in a permanent state of crisis. It seems extremely unlikely that it could have opened a path for itself

Figure 1 Dzejtun (near Ashkabad, Turkmenia). Plan of the neolithic settlement during its maximum expansion. Note the agglomeration of single-room dwellings. (after V.M. Masson).

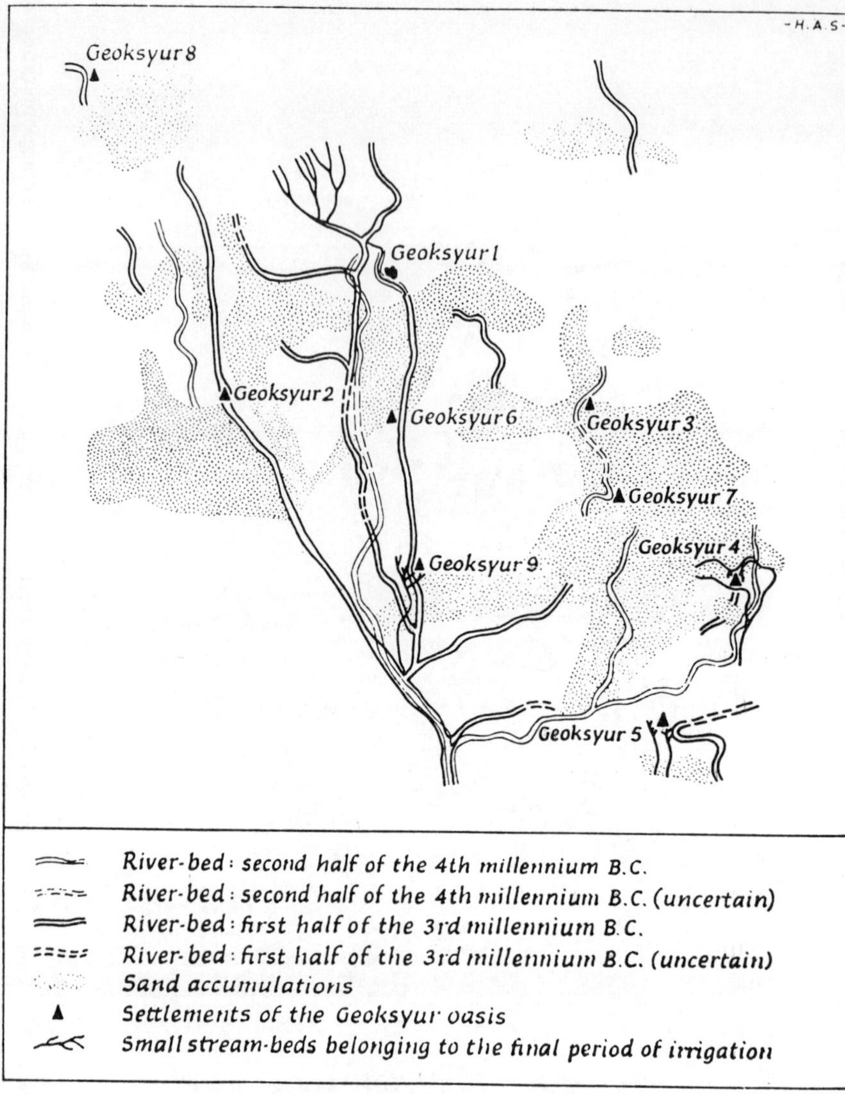

Figure 2 Human settlement on the Tedzen Delta in fourth millennium B.C. Even considering the chronological variations among the different sites, the regular land division pattern is quite evident. (after G.N. Lisicyna).

to the new system of production.

The first agricultural settlements were not logically structured on the basis of a division of the land, and it would be useless to seek a coherent settlement pattern in the way they were distributed. They arose in the most favourable areas, forming themselves almost naturally where geographical and economic conditions really met the needs of such primitive proto-agricultural communities. Since an actual sub-division of the territory did not take place, human

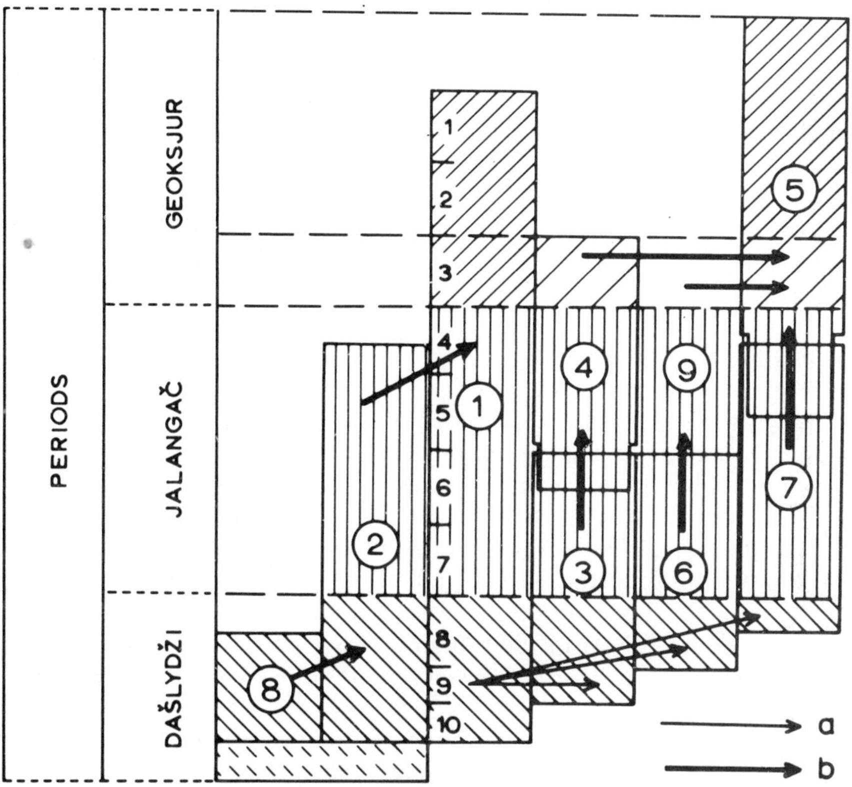

Figure 3 Scheme of internal migrations in the Tedzen Delta during fourth millennium B.C. a = early migration: b = later migration.

settlement was sporadic. The rather few settlements of the Dzejtun culture were set quite a way from one another, near small *fans* at the foot of hills, in southern Turkmenia. This represents a model region because of the continuity of the documentation that has come down to us.

In early chalcolithic times, about 4000 B.C., a group of settlements was created about 200 km. further east of the Tedzen delta – a well-watered zone of about 400,000 square metres – by migrants from the Dzejtun area (Hlopin 1972). Here the relationship between water and settlement is emphasized, for even though there is evidence for the ability of the farmers of the zone in digging complex canal systems (Lisicyna, 1969: 280-2), they were forced at least twice to move their villages to keep up with the shifting course of the water (Fig. 3) till finally the situation became impossible, and the entire region was abandoned at the end of the 3rd millennium The exploitation of the Tedzen delta, at the time of its greatest prosperity (3600-3300 B.C.), is documented by seven regularly-spaced settlements, of about 2-4 acres each (Fig. 2). Identical plots of land were cultivated in all, and, to judge by the size and quality of the finds, no settlement stands out as being more important than the rest.

In the second half of the 4th millennium, the Tedzen delta became progressively silted up and all the chalcolithic settlements were abandoned. The inhabitants moved west to the fertile strip at the foothills near the eastern Kopet Dagh, starting the new site of Hapuz Tepe (Sarianidi 1969:117). In this specific case the move was casual, but the settlement pattern was not maintained, since economic accumulation and demographic increase had progressed in the meantime. Here, as elsewhere, the third and last stage is marked by huge urban agglomerations, some like Altyn Tepe, Namazga Tepe, extending over 200 acres (Fig. 5). They were surrounded by modest villages of 2-4 acres, scattered randomly around the urban centres for a range of about 30 km. The absence of intermediate centres and the urban concentration itself may be direct results of an almost total political and economic centralization.

The first two stages of urban development in southern Turkmenia – Dzejtun and Geoksjur – thus proceed parallel to that in Mesopotamia (Hassuna, Halaf and, in part, Al'Ubaid periods), while it differs from the latter in its more advanced phase. In Mesopotamia, in fact, from the Uruk and Jemdet Nasr periods, a few centuries earlier than the full urban development in Turkmenia (Namazga V period), the central nuclear city, covering an area of more than 200 acres, was surrounded by a circle of medium-sized cities, each in turn surrounded by small villages (Adams 1958). The territory was thus progressively covered by an uninterrupted series of radial centres, from the urban centre to the furthest farm. This settlement pattern can evidently be equated with a political class structure of pyramidal form, each group of which corresponded to clearly-defined centres of power on each level (Udy 1959). It is clear that this anticipates, in a certain sense, the European city model.

In southern Turkmenia during most of the 4th millennium, the absence of intermediate centres is not casual; it probably reflects specific economic and social conditions. Nevertheless, central Asia's oldest urban civilization is identifiable here and seemingly without direct influence from the Mesopotamian world, and we wish above all to see whether this settlement pattern represents an isolated fact or if it may not be an actual model. The dialectic between large urban conglomerations and territory covered with small villages forms the typical elements of the so-called Asian method of production in India and China, which today can be traced back to the first urban experiments.

Can we, then, as early as the 3rd millennium B.C., distinguish a *European model*, as reflected in the Mesopotamian cities, from an *Asian model* visible already in the cities of southern Turkmenia? Hardly, for this would be too simplified a theory, poorly adapted to such a complex phenomenology, one so spread out in both time and space.

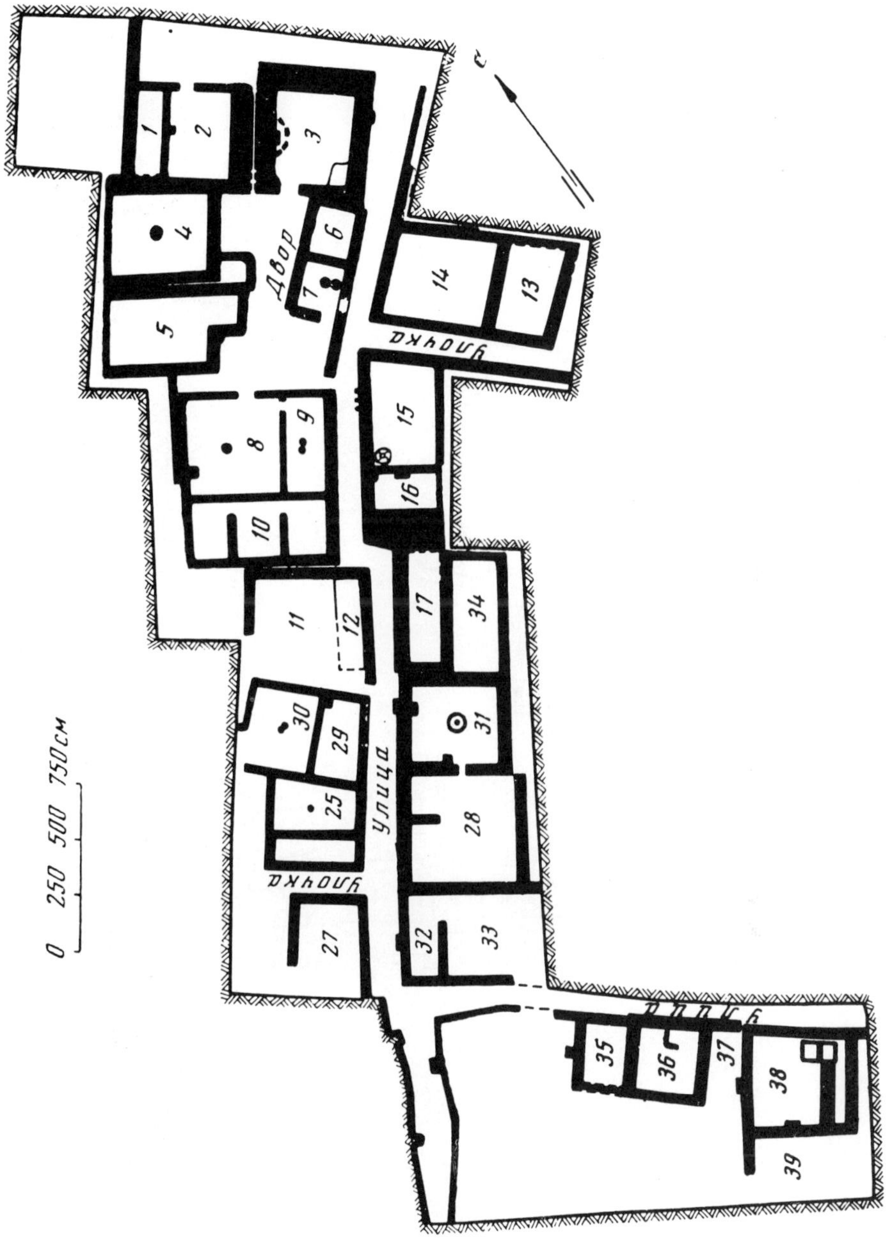

Figure 4 Geoksjur I. The regular plan of the late forth millennium settlement with multiple-room dwellings concentrated in small blocks, divided by narrow lanes. (after V.I. Sarianidi).

But it does nonetheless possess a certain validity when seen in the framework of its precise historical context. We shall see how the particular subdivision of the territory and its consequent use

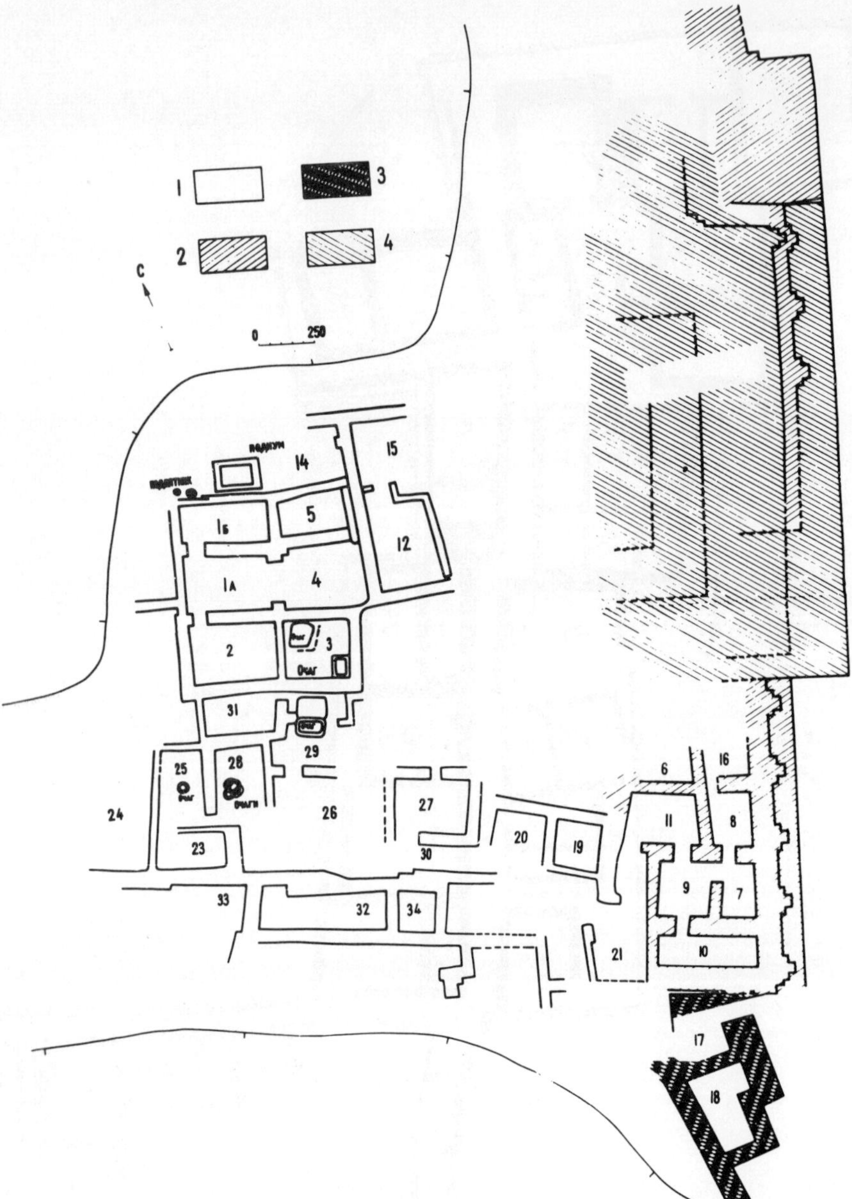

Figure 5 Altyn Tepe. The final stage of proto-urban development as evidenced by the town plan on the eastern flank of the hill. Compounds of large houses and monumental architecture demonstrate class division and accumulation of wealth. (after W.M. Masson). (Scale in cms.)

mentioned above in regard to the cities of southern Turkmenia, were not an isolated phenomenon in the proto-urban civilization of 3rd millennium Asia.

Urban developments in Sistan

As we have seen, southern Turkmenia was an area of primary agricultural development. From the second half of the 4th millennium with the slow but constant increase in the homogeneity of its cultural complex, both economic growth and demographic increase were such as to foreshadow the more mature stages of the process of urbanization.

The inadequate water supply of the foothill streams could no longer meet the increased needs of the community with the result that the new human concentration forms on the delta of the Tedzen River. This is a natural network of canals, branching off in a north-south direction and finally dwindling away in the sandy dunes of the Karakorum. The remains of nine settlements have been located along the arms of the delta (Fig. 2). The population was distributed into small clusters of houses, with each nucleus controlling an almost identical area of land (Fig. 4). This decentralization of the inhabitants was naturally accompanied by a limited production and an economy with very limited possibilities for expansion. It is interesting to note, though, that a basically homogenous material culture in which the inter-regional differences of the earlier periods are no longer seen, corresponds to the social differentation of the groups.

Pottery of the Geoksjur type had already been noted by Piggott in the Quetta valley (Piggott 1947:131-133). These ceramics, seen to be wholly original, were called 'Quetta ware' and provisionally dated to the first half of the 3rd millennium. Later research, carried out by W.A. Fairservis Jr., helped to reconstruct a good regional sequence, subdivided into seven periods, in which the Quetta ceramics appeared in the last two, breaking a local tradition that can be seen in the so-called Kechi Beg ware.

The appearance of Quetta ware coincides with the arrival of a more complex material culture, with mould-seals, figurines, alabaster vases and more structurally advanced architecture. The number of settlements located in this narrow Pakistani valley at this time is far greater than that of earlier periods, a sign of consistent demographic increase.

The Quetta ware was later recognized in the proto-urban layers of Mundigak, a large settlement located and excavated by J.M. Casal, in a narrow valley adjoining the course of the Arghandab near Qandahar, 40 km above the point where the river joins the Hilmand. The Mundigak excavations have brought to light the very rich remains of a culture, on the verge of urbanization. It is characterized by this 'Quetta ware' (Period IV, 1), accompanied here by monumental buildings, a better urban road system and more comfortable housing.

This extraordinary development remained isolated in the general

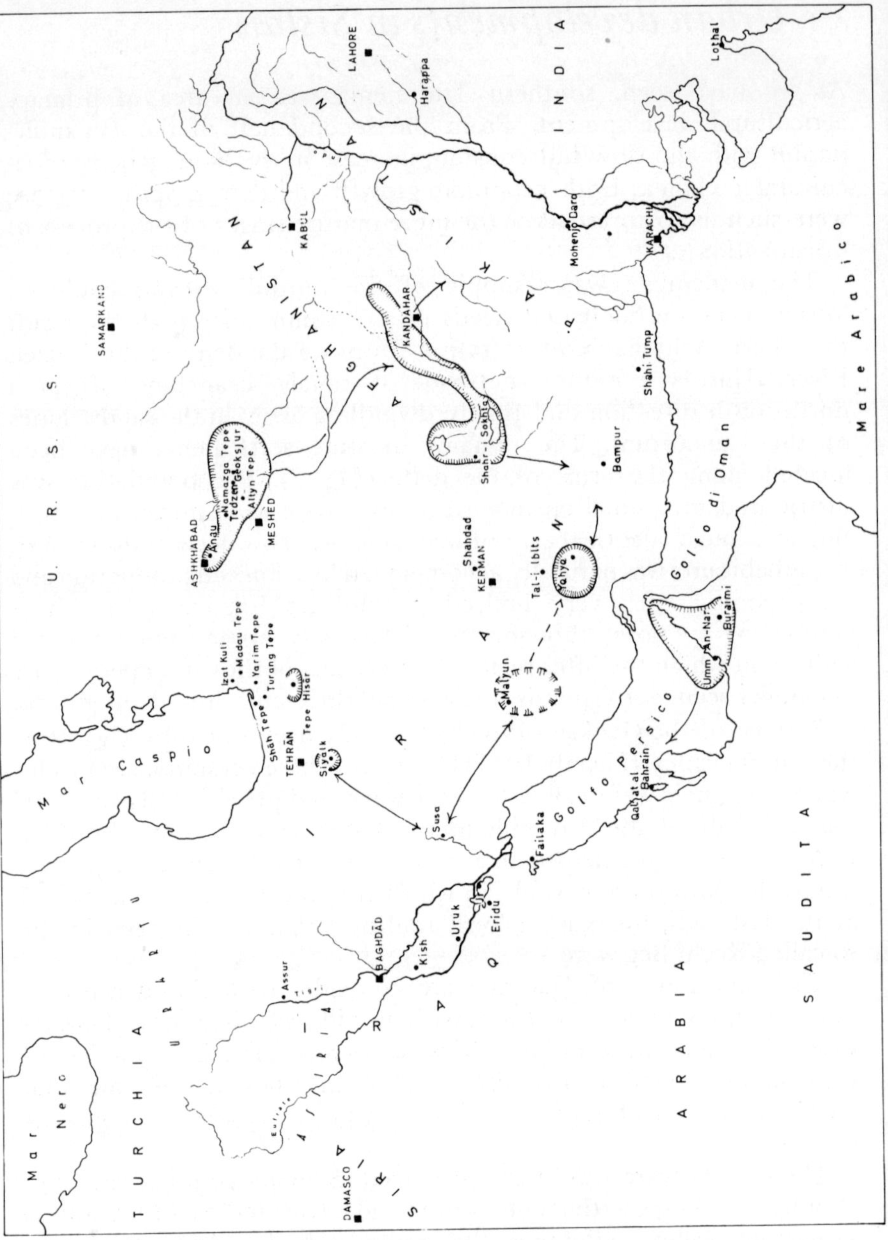

Figure 6 Foci of early urbanization in the Iranian Plateau during the fourth and third millennia B.C. Arrows show the major inter-connecting routes and directions of expansion. The shaded boundaries indicate areas with proto-urban sites at the end of the fourth millennium B.C.

geographical context. Casal, who tried to face the problem, never thought of a possible link between Mundigak and the course of the Hilmand, the most important river between Mesopotamia and the Indus. It now seems obvious, in fact, that such a large waterway must have favoured human settlement and increased – especially in the areas capable of being irrigated – the potential for economic growth. And we can see that a phenomenon of the Mundigak type is fully understandable in the broader terms of a proto-urban civilization that had its catalyzing element in the Hilmand.

The meaning of the Geoksjur phenomenon became much clearer with the results of the research carried out in Persian Sistan (Tosi 1969:380-6).

Sistan consists of a huge depression in which the course of the Hilmand is dispersed through a network of canals that finally flow together to form Lake Hamun-i Hilmand. At least thirty 3rd millennium settlements have been found in the southern part of the region, over an area of about 16,000 square kilometres; the northernmost and most extensive of these settlements is Shahr-i Sokhta, which spreads over about 200 acres (Fig. 8). The other settlements which crowd the dried-out branches of the delta are never larger than 4 acres. We thus have here a settlement pattern similar to that of southern Turkmenia in the 3rd millennium B.C. (Fig. 7).

The cultural sequence of Shahr-i Sokhta can be divided into four main periods (I-IV). Here too the most ancient horizon is marked by the Geoksjur ware, identical to the products of Mundigak III and the Quetta ceramics. This tie with Mundigak is maintained in all the later periods of Shahr-i Sokhta's history, so that we are able to recognize the corresponding piece for ever single object or potsherd, up or down the Hilmand. Indeed Sistan's extraordinary urban development would not have been possible if upriver, where the flow was easily directed or interrupted (since the Arghandab is the last tributary the Hilmand receives before it crosses the almost 300 km of the Registan desert), a friendly and culturally similar people had not been established. The cultural material of the two prehistoric cities confirms in its similarity a need that was often felt in the later history of the region. Some hundreds of thousands of ceramic fragments, especially from the strata of periods II and III at Shahr-i Sokhta, add further proof of the cultural ties with Mundigak IV, 1-2, as do the lithic production, metallurgical techniques, building structures and standard brick sizes. By now one can speak without exaggeration of a *Hilmand civilization* developing during the 3rd millennium on a common basis: the diffusion of the Geoksjur culture (Fig. 9).

This exceptional diffusion of cultural models can be justified when one considers in detail the meaning of 'Urban Revolution'; noting the radical overthrow of values that such a phenomenon caused when

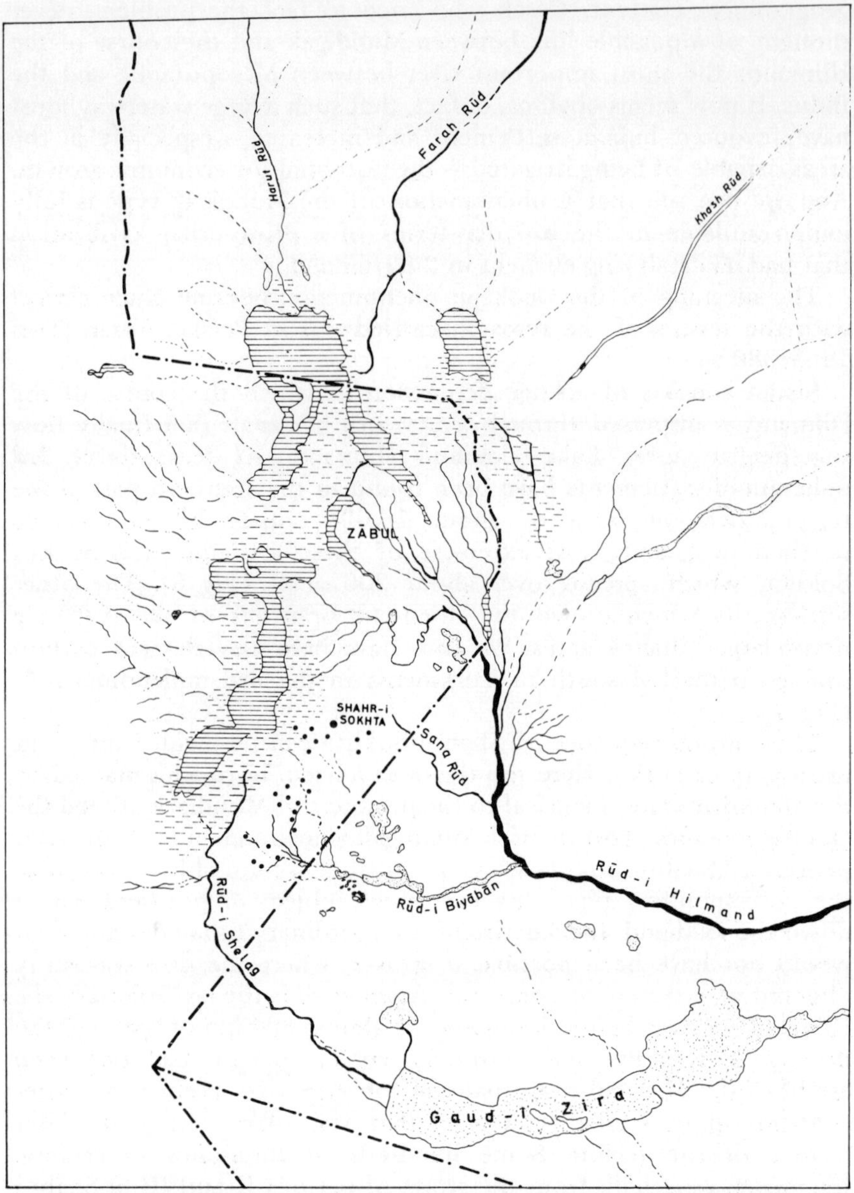

Figure 7 Settlement pattern in Iranian Seistan at the latest stage of early urbanization (period Shahr-i Sokhta III). Note the dissemination of small sites south of the city along the banks of the dried delta of the Hilmand. Small dots indicate sites of 1-2 ha; Shahr-i-Sokhta is over 100 ha. in area.

modest farm villages were transformed into the first cities with a differentiated social structure (Childe 1950). On the other hand, the term 'Revolution' is seen as an over-simplification when one considers the slow rate of economic growth of the neolithic communities. Urban development was certainly dependent on a large human potential, by means of which it imposed itself on the surrounding regions with a pressure all the greater the closer that development draws to its final phase. When it reached the stage of maturity this slow formative process, always open to the outside world thanks to lively cultural exchanges, exploded into the actual revolutionary climax; and the communities that were its direct protagonists diffused their material culture along with their ideas. In this way their technological and social achievements together with their cultural patterns, were absorbed by peoples geographically distant, who progressively adapted them to different tastes, customs and needs.

So at the end of the 5th millennium, the chalcolithic models elaborated in northern Mesopotamia were present in a good part of southwest Asia and were most easily adapted by those communities – and we presume such was the case of Turkmenia in the Kara Tepe period – whose degree of maturity was closest to the centre of origin. This intense cultural dialectic, which saw concepts often used antithetically fused into a unified mechanism (like diffusion and polycentric growth), determined during the 3rd millennium a kind of chain reaction that involved the entire Indo-Iranian frontier and perhaps even pushed along the plains of the Murghab, the Amu Darya and the Syr Darya towards central Asia.

It is most interesting to note the direct correspondence between the beginning of settlement in the Sistan area (Shahr-i Sokhta I) and the abandonment of the Tedzen delta sites at the end of the 4th millennium (Geoksjur period). In fact, the ceramic types from the highest levels of Geoksjur I have direct parallels with those of Mundigak IV, 1, Damb Sadaat II and Shahr-i Sokhta I.

The Geoksjur culture repeats the Halaf phenomenon in different forms: its cultural models, the handsome two-colour ceramics and perhaps part of the very population of Turkmenia spread over a territory ten times greater than that occupied by the preceding farming cultures of Dzejtun and Kara Tepe.

In southern Turkmenia, at Mundigak and Quetta, as well as in Sistan, the Geoksjur ware accompanies the process of urbanization which takes shape in different forms. While in Turkmenia it is derived from the chalcolithic types of the Kara Tepe horizon, at Mundigak and Quetta its appearance heralds a complete break with earlier tradition, and is therefore an intrusive element. Finally, at Shahr-i Sokhta, this pottery represents the product of the first groups to settle in the region, who were already able to control the productive but dangerous floods of the Hilmand.

In these three adjacent regions, the 'urban revolution' took three different courses: in southern Turkmenia with an orderly growth of the neolithic economy; at Mundigak and Quetta with a violent break in local traditions possibly due to the infiltration of extraneous

Figure 8 Shahr-i Sokta. Residential area with large houses. Period II (2,700-2,400 B.C.).

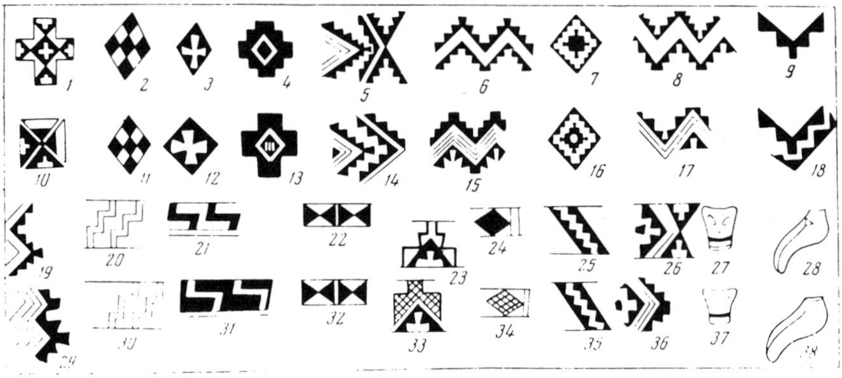

Figure 9 Evidence of connections between painted patterns on pottery from Geoksjur (nos. 1 to 9 and 19 to 28) and Quetta valley (nos. 10 to 13 and 29 to 36) sites. (after V.M. Masson).

elements; and in Sistan as initial colonization. In any case the break corresponds to the rapid decrease of population in the Tedzen delta.

The main point here is that on the basis of recent results, the transition from one type of society to another is always documented in the same way by archaeological evidence. In other words, the spread of the cultural elements of the Geoksjur culture – pottery, architecture, figurines – was homogeneous, despite the diversity of the geographical and ethnological situations encountered.

Yet despite the similarities in the finds, the various groups nevertheless show distinctive features which lead us to reject any purely invasionist hypothesis. Even if one cannot deny that the Turkmenian farmers settled down in the new regions, it is still true that their ties to the mother country must have gradually become weaker. In the course of the 4th millennium, southern Turkmenia and the Hilmand valley developed along parallel (even if basically different) lines in each sector of material culture. To the almost total similarity we find in the material:

Namazga III = Mundigak III-IV, 1 = Shahr-i Sokhta I

there only corresponds, in the following Namazga IV-V periods, a vague resemblance to be found in material from Mundigak IV 2-3 and Shahr II-IV.

The picture therefore seems fairly complete: two main areas of productive increase, Mesopotamia and southern Turkmenia, border on the vast Iranian plateau which is open to the influence of both, but nonetheless endowed with its own personal and specific cultural elements. In the first half of the 3rd millennium, urban life is present not only in Khuzistan, exposed to the Mesopotamian world, but also in Fars, Kerman, Siyalk, Gorgan and Sistan. The great flood plains such as those of Mesopotamia and the Indus valley show a linear development tending towards cultural centralization, as opposed to the Iranian plateau, which has an irregular, decentralized and discontinuous evolution, even if there was a considerable concentration of men and goods everywhere.

<table>
<tr><th>Turkmenia
(Namazga)</th><th>Afghanistan
(Mundigak)</th><th>Quetta
(Damb Sadaat)</th><th>Sistan
(Shahr-i Sokhta)</th></tr>
<tr><td rowspan="2">V</td><td>IV,3</td><td rowspan="4"></td><td>IV</td></tr>
<tr><td rowspan="2">IV,2</td><td rowspan="2">III</td></tr>
<tr><td rowspan="2">IV</td></tr>
<tr><td rowspan="2">IV,1</td><td rowspan="2">II</td></tr>
<tr><td>Tedzen Delta abandoned</td><td>III</td></tr>
<tr><td rowspan="3">III</td><td>III</td><td>II</td><td>I</td></tr>
<tr><td>II</td><td rowspan="3">I</td><td rowspan="3"></td></tr>
<tr><td rowspan="2">I</td></tr>
<tr><td>II</td></tr>
</table>

▬▬▬ = limit of introduction of the Geoksjur ceramics.

The rise of the Indus civilisation

In the middle of the 3rd millennium, urban society developed along similar lines on a scale that varied with the availability of local resources, in those regions of Iran which had adequate water supplies or were crossed by the currents of mercantile commerce. However, for all these communities, hemmed in between deserts and mountains, there were always problems of space limiting any absolute and unconditioned urban growth. In fact, they were already in full crisis about the end of the 3rd millennium. Their final collapse, which can be assigned to the first centuries of the 2nd millennium, may have been hastened by internal social tensions and population movements from the north (Hlopina 1972).

But just as the Iranian cultures reached the peak of their development and immediately began to decline, in the middle of the 3rd millennium, a new and great urban civilization was born to the east of Iran; the Indus civilization.

In the present state of our knowledge, it is hard to say what influence the proto-urban cultures of eastern Iran and Turkmenia may have had on the formation of the Indus civilization. It arose and developed over an enormous territory which is without limitations of any kind. Here expansion and centralization, the essential elements for urban growth, reached their highest values, so that the Indus civilization can with good reason be considered one of the most interesting of protohistoric antiquity.

The first farming cultures recognized in the flood plain of this great river already show their own individual characteristics. They furnish in the different sectors of material culture prototypes for the Indus civilization which clearly descended from them (Wheeler 1966:9-13). If the local cultures of pre-defence Harappa, Kot Diji, Amri and Kalibangan are included, the start of this civilization can be dated to 2600-2500 B.C., some 500 years after the Geoksjur culture and its Iranian derivatives. It is likely, therefore, that the nearby Turkmenian centre of regional development contributed in some degree to the formation of the first agricultural communities founded in the Indus valley.

The technical skills there – canalization, metal-working, pottery kilns, etc. – were those elaborated in the diffusion area of the Geoksjur culture. Elements of this culture have not been found – at least up to now – south of Kalat, in northern Baluchistan. Nor do the products of Amri or of Kot Diji show any serious point of contact. Very recent excavations made in Pakistani territory – at Jalilpur in Punjab, and at Gumla in the Gomel valley – have brought to light ceramic material typologically similar to that of Namazga III and Shahr-i Sokhta I. According to G.H. Dales, period II at Jalilpur could represent a good link between Shahr-i Sokhta I and period IA at Amri. It is still too early to interpret this new data. The fact remains, though, that little is yet known about the prehistory of Sindh and Baluchistan, and the future may well hold new and interesting discoveries.

In the later Indus civilization, which represents the summit of the whole slow cultural growth of the Indo-Iranian area, the settlement pattern characteristic of the Geoksjur culture and its derivatives is again seen. For example the region of Lake Machhar on the lower course of the Indus, had a large urban nucleus, Mohenjo Daro, surrounded by a series of minor sites – Chanhu Daro, Kot Diji, Lohumjo Daro, etc. The zone is formed by a depression bounded on the west by the Kirtar mountains and on the east by the course of the Indus itself. There has been a great deal of silting of the clay which may have caused the disappearance of the minor settlements.

At any rate, the remaining sites allow recognition of the structure of the original settlement pattern. Mohenjo Daro extends today for almost 300 acres, but one can reasonably assume that it was once much larger, and that during the centuries part of it was washed away by the floods of the Indus. None of the other centres, for a range of about 50 km, covers more than 20 acres each, including Kot Diji and Chanhu Daro.

This very strong centralization seems to be partly repeated on the Cutch peninsula in Gujarat, where a mature expansion of the Indus civilization took place. Lothal, with its port, its high concentration of craftsmen and its evolved urban structure, was the nucleus of the region. The numerous centres flanking it on the peninsula reveal in their size and rather unsophisticated material culture that they are basically just farm villages.

More thorough studies of this interesting question are being made. They may reveal to us whether this was a local phenomenon, or whether it may not rather be a social structure which in effect conditioned the birth of the method of Asian production, with its capillary distribution of villages and the concentration of goods and specialized labour in large cities.

The cities of eastern Iran and the Indus thus offer, at an early date, an urban model which appears again at the end of the 2nd millennium B.C., in the great plain of the Yellow River, with the palace-cities of its Shang rulers.

REFERENCES

Adams, R.McC. (1958) A survey of ancient water-courses and settlements in central Iraq. *Sumer* 14, 101-3.

Childe, V.G. (1950) The Urban Revolution. *Town Planning Review*, 3-17.

Hlopin, I.N. (1972) Ancient farmers in the Tedzen delta. *East and West* 22.

Hlopina, L.I. (1972) Southern Turkmenia in the late bronze age. *East and West* 22.

Lisicyna, G.N. (1969) The earliest irrigation in Turkmenia. *Antiquity* 43, 279-88.

Masson, V.M. (1971) *Poselenie Džejtun*. Leningrad, Nauka.

Mellaart, J. (1970) The earliest settlements in western Asia from the ninth to the end of the fifth millennium B.C. *Cambridge Ancient History* part I, 248-303.

Piggott, S. (1947) The chronology of prehistoric north-west India. *Ancient India* I, 131-42.

Sarianidi, V.I. (1969) Novie Raskopki na Hapuz-depe, *Kratkie Soobsenija Istituta Archeologii* 115, 116-23.

Tosi, M. (1969) Excavations at Shahr-i Sokhta, preliminary report on the second campaign. *East and West* 19, 283-386.

Udy, S.H. (1959) The structure of authority in non-industrial production, *American Journal of Sociology* 64, 6.

Wheeler, R.E.M (1966) *Civilisations of the Indus Valley and Beyond.* London, Thames and Hudson.

McGUIRE GIBSON

Population shift and the rise of Mesopotamian civilisation

The past few years have witnessed a surge of interest in the origins of civilization, a field once studied by a mere handful of scholars. From grand, but rather simplistic, explanatory models built on prime causes (technical innovation, irrigation) we have come to more involved theories that additionally include attention to environment, microenvironments, and population (Adams 1955, 1966, 1970; Coe and Flannery 1964; Sanders 1968; Carneiro 1970; Young 1970). The focus of such studies has shifted from considerations of 'the city' or 'stages' in cultural development to the processes that brought about such results. Spurred by locational analysis, investigations tend to look at the city as part of a region, in relation to other cities and other types of settlement (Adams 1969, 1970; Johnson, 1970). No one has, as yet, proposed a truly unified model, taking into account as closely interdependent variables the natural and other forces that resulted in civilization. The tendency has been to work with one major factor, or a few, and to reject previous attempts based on some other prime mover. Thus, Childe and Wittfogel had a vogue, which spawned research (e.g. Steward *et al.* 1955) that slowly turned away from irrigation as a first cause. The work of Robert McC. Adams, the leading scholar on the problem, had undergone a development wherein an initial assessment (1955) included population increase or shift, technological improvements, an evolution of social stratification and militarism viewed in terms of stages with irrigation as a stimulus. Thereafter, irrigation was de-emphasized (1960), and social organization and population highlighted (1957, 1958, 1962). However, it was concluded that 'appreciable population increases followed, rather than preceded, the core processes of the Urban Revolution . . . [with] simply no evidence for gradual population increases that might have helped to precipitate the Urban Revolution' (Adams 1966:44-45; cf. 1965:42). Adams' more recent work (1969, 1970) has had an ecological and demographic cast, presented in a more systemic manner, rather than in terms of one major factor considered against a more or less static background of other major variables.

The newest general explanatory model for the rise of civilizations (Carneiro 1970) depends heavily upon population shift, or growth, within a circumscribed area, i.e. a relatively restricted region of fertile land bounded by poor or unattainable land. The theory seems, at this time, very tenable, based as it is on explicit or implicit consideration of societal, resource, demographic, and environmental factors. However, it would be difficult to test a model built on so grand a scale.

Cuyler Young (1970), dealing with only one geographical area, has proposed a very intriguing scheme, based on population pressure, for the growth of civilization in Mesopotamia. The design is derived from the work of E. Boserup (1965), who holds that population increase is an independent variable that brings about agricultural intensification, technological, economic and social changes. A decrease in population pressure will result in a decrease in intensification, etc.

Stated briefly, Young's thesis rests on migration into the alluvium from the fringes, the uplands of Mesopotamia, coupled with increased natural population growth resulting in colonization of broader stretches of territory, reaching to marginal land. The marginal zones are supposed to have been more susceptible to salination, of lower fertility and more difficult to supply with water. This complex of factors is seen to have produced 'a collapse inward of the environment available for agriculture exploitation, with those areas colonised last being the first to experience declining production and eventually enforced abandonment' (1970:6). This deterioration and forced movement into smaller areas is seen to have stimulated intensification of agricultural, irrigation and organizational systems, resulting in civilization.

Young's basic data are the patterns of settlement in 'Greater Mesopotamia' from the 7th millennium onward. From a gradual increase in small, dry-farming, upland sites, he sees an enormous increase in settlements (= population) that includes a spread to the lowlands and occupation of the Khuzistan plain, 'Finally, pressures to migrate were . . . sufficiently strong that we find occupations reported from southern Mesopotamia proper' (1970:3). Irrigation was introduced at about this time (6th millennium), and from 6000 to 4500 B.C., population is estimated by Young to have increased in Greater Mesopotamia '13-fold'. In the ensuing late Ubaid period, the border area of Khuzistan was very heavily settled, while the alluvial core had a rise in the number of settlements, though still few and scattered.

A slightly larger number of sites in the Ur/Eridu area is seen as an indication of primary settlement in the south (from Khuzistan, if I read the section correctly), with a secondary spread northward. One must connect with this proposal Adams' suggestion of a possibility of considerable migration of peoples into the Mesopotamian plain from the eastern part of Arabia, where there are numerous abandoned

Ubaid sites. A concurrent spread of settlement took place all over Greater Mesopotamia, and westward toward the Mediterranean. There seems to have been some contraction in the uplands in the Protoliterate, and by Early Dynastic I, there was a marked decline in that region which Young correlates with a marked increase in population in southern Mesopotamia that 'might be attributed in part to immigration from the other zones of Greater Mesopotamia' (1970:4; cf. Adams 1955:10).

At this point, it would be best to turn to Adams' outline of developments in the alluvium, dealing with the various subareas in turn.

> Uruk was a substantial ceremonial center, probably approaching urban proportions . . . by the mid-fourth millennium B.C., and perhaps earlier. Around it lay a very large number of small towns and villages, unimodally distributed in size rather than forming a differentiated, tiered hierarchy suggestive of an economically or administratively differentiated network centered on Uruk. (Adams 1970:3)

It is important to note Adams' additional conclusion from the irregular, non-linear spacing of Uruk Period settlements that villages depended on natural streams utilized for small-scale, non-intensive irrigation (1968:115). Also, some of the settlements appeared to form small clusters around slightly larger centres which Adams likens to Ottoman period sheikh's *qala*'s.

In the Jemdet Nasr period (late 4th millennium), the settlement pattern gradually changed, with the rise of towns intermediate in rank between the villages and Uruk. At the same time, elongated, linear clusters began to form, indicating a shift to artificial canals. Meanwhile, to the northeast, the area around Umma, previously unoccupied, was settled in linear clusters of large towns.

The next step in the process at Uruk is described as follows:

> At around the beginning of the third millennium the city seems to have expanded by a full order of magnitude, perhaps housing as many as forty or fifty thousand inhabitants on the 400 hectares within its newly constructed defensive wall. The evidence of simultaneous, widespread abandonment of small settlements in its hinterlands leaves little doubt that this extraordinary growth was essentially an implosive process, transferring rural population into a new, urban setting in response to some combination of internal tendencies toward the consolidation of political leadership and external military threats. (Adams 1970:3)

In the area of Ur, the pattern is, in general, similar, but there are marked differences in detail. 'Initial agricultural settlement . . . may have been earlier and denser than around Uruk' (Adams 1970:3), i.e. earlier in the Ubaid period, but the city of Ur never reached the size of Uruk and became a city only in Early Dynastic III. From the Uruk period, most of the population in the area was concentrated in either Ur or Eridu, there being few small rural settlements. It is my assumption that the Ur pattern was much affected by its location on the margin of the true desert while agricultural resources would have been scarcer.

The Diyala area material presents another divergent pattern. (Adams 1970:4). This area dependent not on the Euphrates, but on another river system, witnessed an increase in Uruk and Jemdet Nasr settlements, after an initial sparse Ubaid occupation, and the growth tends to appear in clusters. However, city formation did not result in Early Dynastic times. Instead, the population spread into formerly unoccupied, marginal areas (Adams 1965, Young 1970:5). Cities came into being in this area centuries later.

The process of urbanization around Nippur has been likened by Adams to that which occurred around Uruk (1970:4). However, the abandonment of the countryside, and the (inferred) growth of the city of Nippur is said to have taken place somewhat earlier than at Uruk. In a survey of the region east and north of Nippur, Adams noted the complete absence of Jemdet Nasr sites following upon a significant spread of Uruk settlements. This abandonment has been linked to the fact that 'a formerly important channel of the Euphrates in the vicinity fell permanently into disuse at about this time' (Adams 1970:4).

The change in this easternmost branch of the ancient Euphrates must be taken into account in viewing the Akkad region, farther upstream. As published (Adams 1957, 1958), Adams' maps of the Akkad Survey combine the settlement patterns of several early periods, and thus tend to give a distorted view of the extensiveness of settlement, especially for the Ubaid. Taking only those sites that yielded Ubaid pottery, Adams has recently shown (*in* Gibson, in press) that there were in Akkad only about a dozen widely-spaced Ubaid sites, two of which lay along the easternmost channel. It is to be noted that one of the Ubaid sites, Tell Uqair, was of such a size that Adams termed it a town. Kish, which was to become the paramount city in Akkad, was, in the Ubaid Period, only two villages more than a kilometer apart on a western branch of the river.

For the Uruk and Jemdet Nasr periods in Akkad, Adams (*in* Gibson, in press) notes a greatly increased number of settlements (more than 44) spread over a large area. Settlements along the easternmost channel increased to eight sometime during these periods and it and the Jemdet Nasr branch together carried more than two-thirds of the sites recorded.

It is unfortunate that in Adams' Akkad Survey and in my Kish Survey of 1967 (Fig. 1), the Uruk and Jemdet Nasr periods were combined as Protoliterate. We are, thus, deprived of the sharp temporal separation needed to show the date of the shift in the river channel. Adams' reconstructions of the settlement pattern (Figs. 1-2) thus seem to indicate that the easternmost line was abandoned *after* the Jemdet Nasr period, whereas we have seen above that the

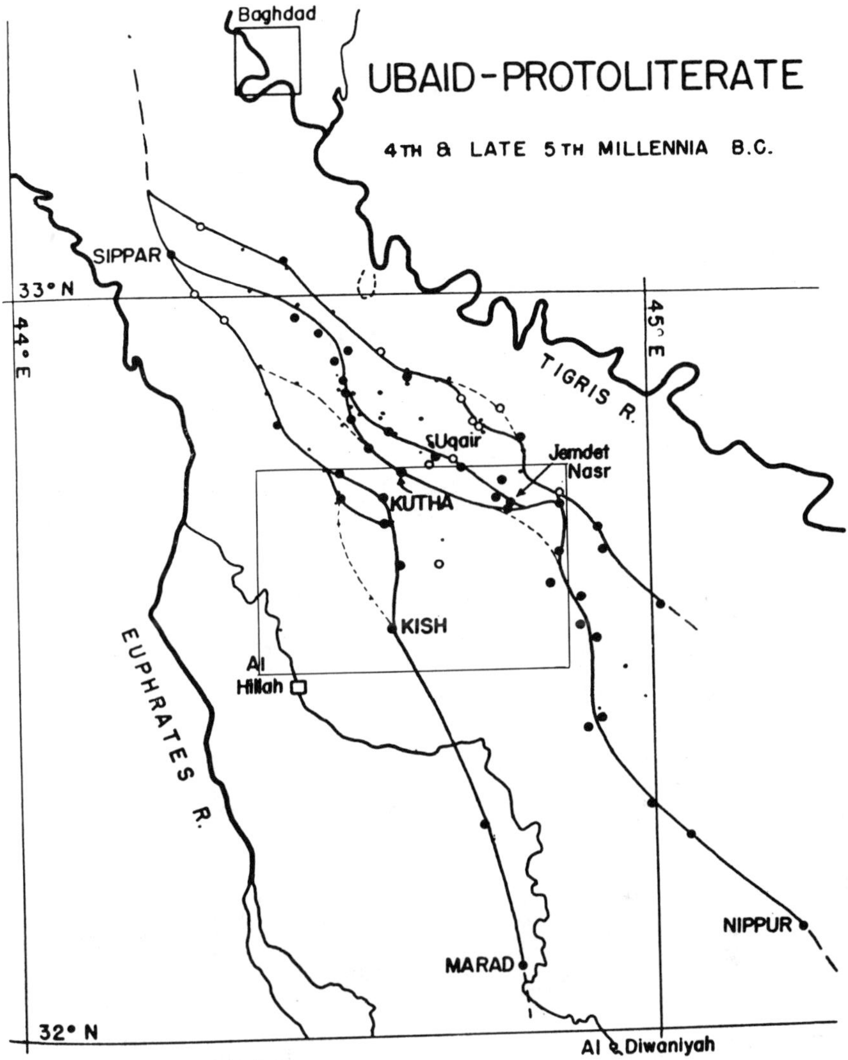

Figure 1 Adams' Akkad Survey with Gibson Kish Survey area superimposed (box), from *Sumer* 14 (1958).

abandonment occurred *before* the Jemdet Nasr period.

Although my Kish survey touched in its northeast corner only a small part of the easternmost line, and although we cannot show directly the abandonment of the branch, we can tentatively indicate some effects of it.

In carrying out my survey (Fig. 3), and in reviewing the sites listed by Adams as Protoliterate, it became clear that not only did most settlements tend to lie on the easternmost and Jemdet Nasr channels, but that the sites there were generally larger than in western portion of the survey area. Further, in reviewing my field notes, it appears

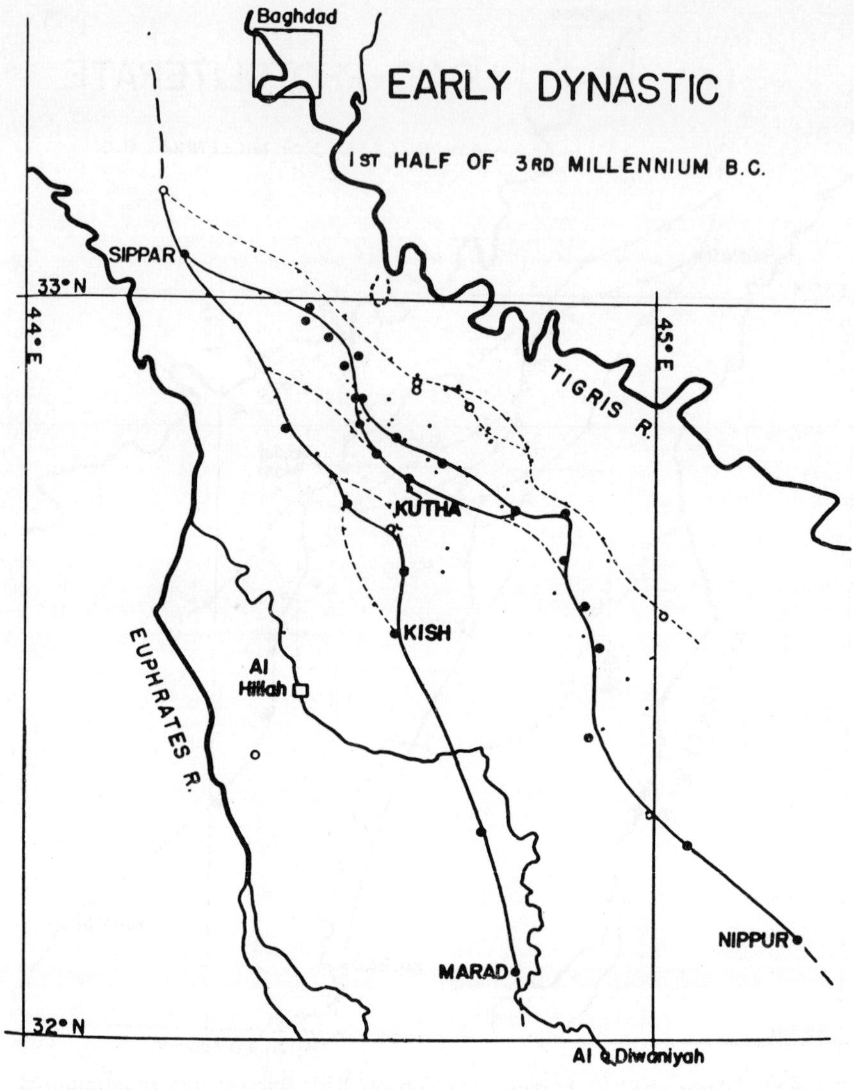

Figure 2 Adams' Akkad Survey, Early Dynastic period, from *Sumer* 14 (1958).

that Uruk period sherds, which were much less frequently found than Jemdet Nasr material, came mostly from sites in the eastern part of the survey. Jemdet Nasr sherds were found on all Protoliterate sites. The pattern thus displayed, a heavier concentration of settlement (= population) in the east throughout the Protoliterate, but with a wider spread westward in the latter half, may suggest a geographical adjustment as population shifted from the abandoned channel into the Kish area in Jemdet Nasr times.

The phenomenal burst of growth that changed two Jemdet Nasr villages into the Early Dynastic twin-city of Kish (Fig. 4) is

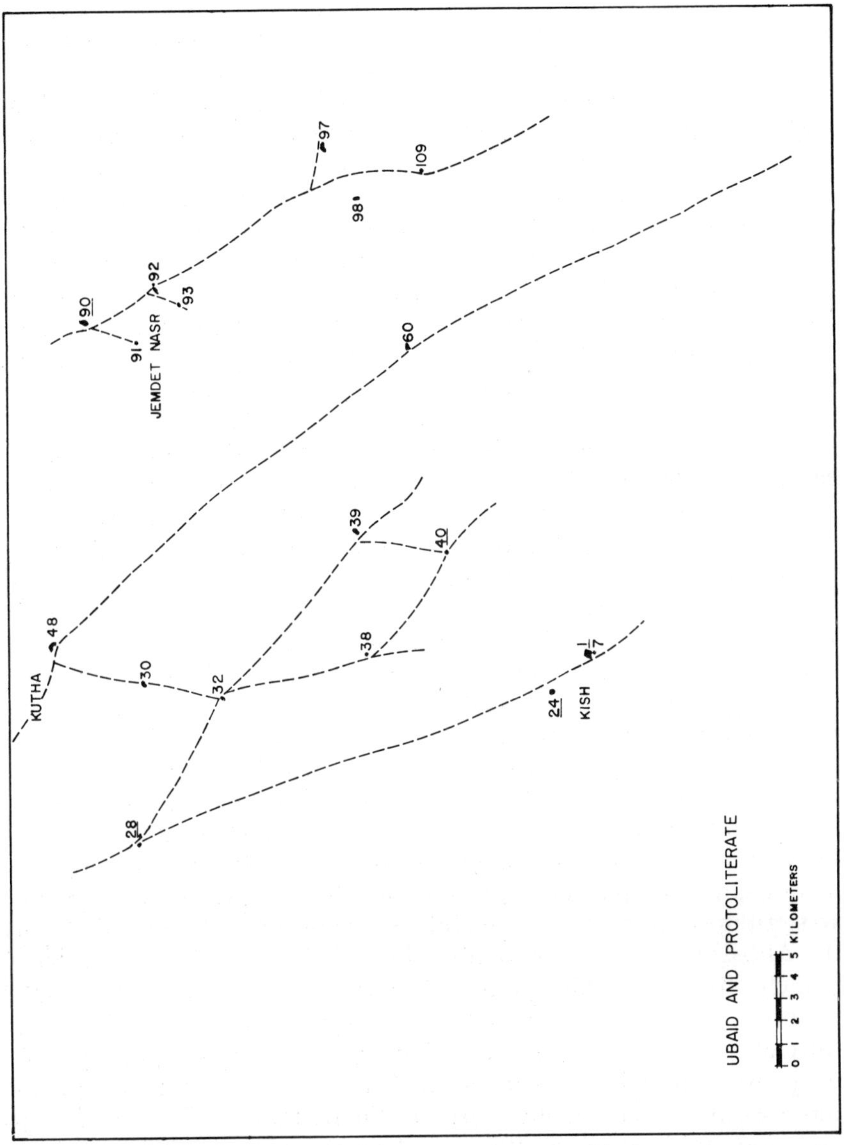

Figure 3 Kish Area. Ubaid and Protoliterate periods. Ubaid sites underlined.

comparable to that which took place at Uruk during the same time. Although only a fraction the size of Uruk, Kish's fifty or so hectares must be reckoned as 'urban' in its time and place. The absorption of smaller settlements that characterized Uruk's growth did not occur with such totality at Kish, but there was a marked reduction in the number of settlements in the region. Most of these settlements were considerably larger than earlier sites, and there is little evidence of survival of small villages.

Before going further, it would be well to summarize the foregoing information from settlement pattern. The accompanying table (Table 1) makes clear that though there were regional variations, there does seem to be a pattern shared most strikingly by Uruk, Nippur and the Kish area. Relatively few, small, settlements were succeeded by a greater number of settlements of unequal size over a wider area. After a period of maximum spread to the limits of an area, and dispersal into small settlements, accompanied in one instance by occupation of unoccupied territory (marginal areas), a city formed with startling rapidity. The regions that do not seem to conform, the Diyala, Ur/Eridu, and Umma are marginal in terms either of river system, resources (Ur/Eridu), or demography (Umma, a spin-off from Uruk). Clearly the main areas for the construction of our model are the first three, along what was considered historically the main bed of the Euphrates. It is also evident that the abandonment of the easternmost branch of the river and a subsequent shift of most of the population westward (leaving some to go over to nomadism or to another geographical location) must be considered crucial in the process of urbanization in Mesopotamia.

There is historically documented evidence for massive shifts in Euphrates channels and the effects on broad areas. In general, the river seems to have a tendency to move towards the west. We have seen that in the earliest periods of settlement, the major line of the river appears to have run in the region of Jemdet Nasr. However, for most of Babylonian history, a bed through Kish, Nippur, Shuruppak and Uruk was called the Euphrates, though the Jemdet Nasr line and others still flourished (see Gibson, in press). With the Neo-Babylonian period, the channel through Babylon was clearly the main channel of the river. By the Early Islamic period, however, the westernmost channel through Kufa was considered dominant. During the Abbasid period, the Babylon (Hilla) line was restored as the main branch. By the middle of the 19th Century, according to various European travellers, the Babylon (Hilla) line was experiencing grave difficulties. Attempts to keep adequate water flowing in that bed were only sporadically successful. The river tended to prefer the more western channel, due in part to the buildup of silt in the mouth and along the bed of the Babylon (Hilla) branch. Finally, after years of ineffectual repairs, and the dwindling of water in the Babylon (Hilla) line that resulted in the abandonment of progressively larger areas of land, the controlling dam at Hindiyah gave way and was not repaired for more than a decade. When H.W. Cadoux (1906) saw the affected area shortly after the break, broad stretches of cultivation were deserted. Only a few sheikh's forts were still occupied on the river, where wells, dug in the middle of the bed, furnished enough water to support a few persons. Unfortunately, we do not have at hand specific records of movements of the displaced farmers, villagers, etc., onto the western branch. The social, political, and

Table 1. The rise of cities in Mesopotamia

Periods →	Ubaid	Uruk	Jemdet Nasr	ED I
Uruk	Small, few, dispersed, non-linear.	Uruk=town+; ceremonial centre. Numerous new settlements, wide-spread, non-linear. Clusters	Hierarchy of settlement, clusters, linear, spread to margins, *Maximum dispersal.*	City. A few large towns. Country-side abandoned Linear.
Nippur	Small. few dispersed. Ňippur=ceremonial center.	Numerous new settlements, wide-spread, linear.	Nippur (city?), few towns. Countryside abandoned.	City.
Kish	Few, dispersed. Large and small. Linear.	Increase in number of settlements, esp. eastern area. Larger, more numerous in JN. Linear *Maximum dispersal.*		City. Fewer sites, most larger than previously.
Umma			Dense clusters of large towns. Linear.	Not a city.
Ur/Eridu	Earlier, more numerous than at Uruk. Ur, Eridu= towns, ceremonial centers. Linear.	Eridu grows; Ur declines. Few villages.	Ur grows; Eridu± abandoned. Few other sites.	Not a city.
Diyala	Small, few, dispersed. Linear.	Numerous new settlements, move to marginal land. Clusters. Linear.		Hierarchy of settlement. No cities.

economic adjustments due to the influx into an area already occupied should be reflected vividly in local Ottoman records. Such data would be invaluable as a source for information on sudden population shifts.

Changes in the river's flow can come about more abruptly than happened in the case just described. The river can change drastically in response to high flood. Late in the Sassanian period, floods destroyed hundreds of settlements in the alluvial plain and caused the shift of water from a line through Kutha into other lines. Whole

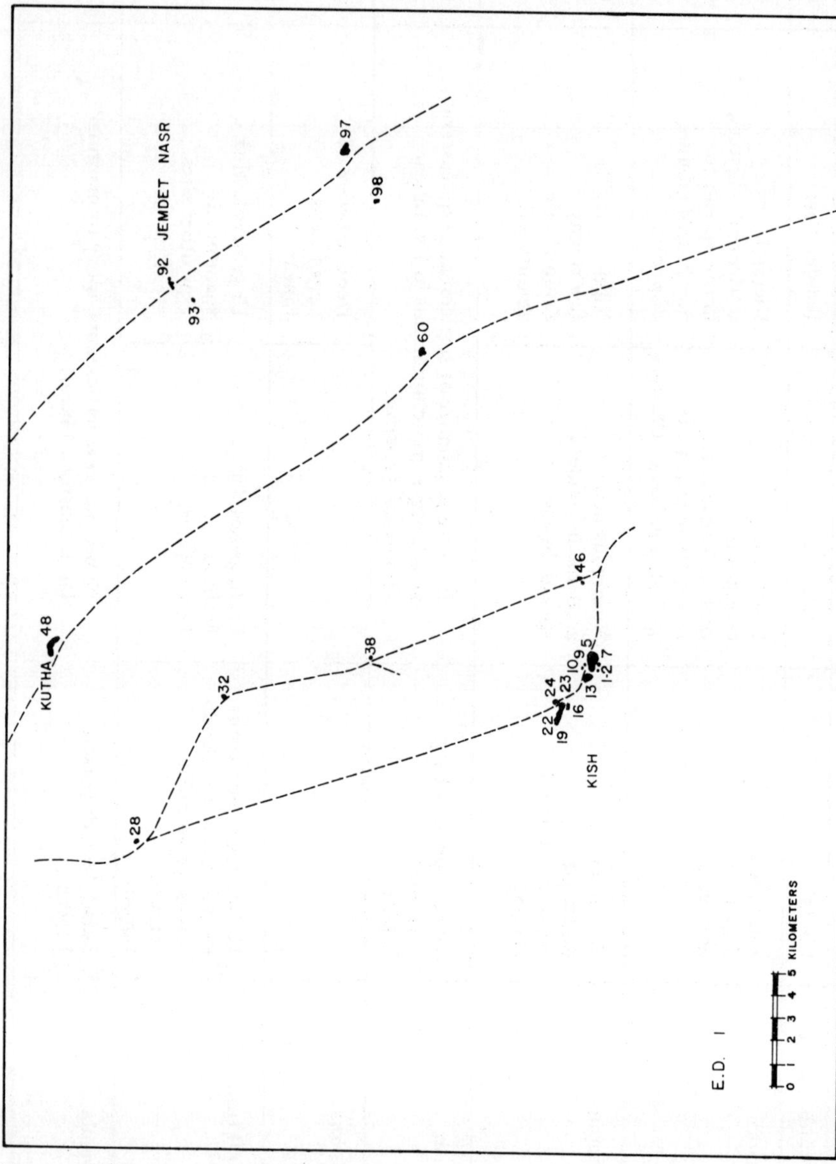

Figure 4 Kish Area. Early Dynastic I.

tracts of the central alluvium were left uninhabitable and canals were not re-established there on the same scale until the Abbasid period (Gibson, in press).

In order to illustrate adjustments made by man in response to population growth or shift, I would like to introduce at this point a scheme proposed by Robert Netting (1969) for an ethnographic situation. In an agricultural area of Nigeria, Netting has suggested, rainfall, soil, terrain, techniques of intensive agriculture and certain features of demography, settlement pattern, work group organization and land-tenure are functionally interdependent. In the case of the Kofyar, Netting describes an initial condition in which population density was very high. Defensible, upland villages consisted of dispersed homesteads with small households (5.3 persons) composed almost entirely of nuclear families. Land was held and inherited by individuals. The subsistence base was one of high intensity, utilizing terracing, planting of several types of crops, and raising livestock. During the past thirty years, since warfare has been halted in the area, some of the Kofyar have moved onto lowlands which are easily worked and have high initial fertility. Farming is of low intensity, shifting when yield begins to drop. Individual farmsteads are larger and widely spaced, population density is much lower than in the older upland villages, but the individual households are larger, with a greater frequency of extended families. Land is held on usufruct, not owned.

Netting compares the Kofyar example to another case among the Igbo (1969:104 ff). Here, originally, villages of extended family households, doing shifting cultivation on land assigned for usufruct, radiated from a central meeting place. Recently, the individual villages have begun to break up and disperse over the landscape due to population pressure. Extended family households have disintegrated into nuclear family units, living in individual homesteads, directly owning and working small plots of permanent garden and orchard land. In these areas of dispersed settlement, population density is very high.

Clearly, in these two cases, high population density, intensive agricultural practices, nuclear family units, and individual land tenure co-occur. Taking the information given, one can propose that we are seeing a sequence of steps in one process. One can take the move of the Kofyar into the lowlands as an example of initial occupation of a region. There then appears to be a sequential gap in which the lowland settlements would grow, go through the process of budding off themselves, and reach a point at which there would occur ranked clusters of sizeable settlements, such as occur in the initial Igbo situation. The next step is the disintegration of large settlements into small units spread over the landscape. Given the fact that the small settlements are a reflection of the most intensive agriculture, any rise in density would soon bring the law of diminishing returns into operation. Competition for land should be intense and warfare and concentration for defense result, if allowed. Modern conditions tend to make tribal warfare impossible, so the excess population is drawn to already existing major cities for work.

Taking the notions thus far discussed, it is now proposed to construct a model for the rise of civilization in Mesopotamia. Major variables in this model are:

1. Geography	Alluvial plain, with specialized niches (irrigated land, steppe, swamp, etc.).
2. Climate	No drastic alterations since the end of the Pleistocene, but some minor variations.
3. Resources	Land, water, local fauna and flora. Absence of stone, ores, etc.
4. Population	Growth and/or shift.
5. Social Organization	Must be derived by inference from archaeology and extrapolation back from written records.
6. Technology	Irrigation, agricultural intensification, innovation. Crafts for work in local or imported materials.
7. Trade	Necessary to obtain basic and exotic goods.

The model (Fig. 5) attempts to utilize these variables, keeping the three major areas (Uruk, Nippur, and Kish) as the focus. The processes occurring in the other three areas (Ur/Eridu, Umma, and the Diyala) will be seen to fit into only certain parts of the model.

An initial population coming into an area of unrestricted land spreads out (Step 1) and begins low-level irrigation farming, while setting up some sort of trade network for the acquisition of basic and exotic resources. The fertility of the land, worked with even low-level irrigation, results in a growth of population, while additional numbers may be entering from outside the area. Resources are strained, and the result is a budding off of settlement (Step 2), and occupation of more land. There is a concurrent intensification of social organization and expansion of the trade network to serve the broader area, and a likely development in specialization for manufacture of certain trade and luxury items. Population growth through reproduction or addition from outside occurs, straining resources and resulting in further budding off. This time (Step 3), settlements tend to appear in clusters and older settlements continue to grow. The trade network is expanded and full-time craftsmen work the imported materials and prepare goods for export. Population increases. At this point, the main part of the alluvium is affected by the abandonment of a river channel and a population shift. In this one occurrence we have the effect of a tremendous population growth, since there is a diminution of available agricultural land.

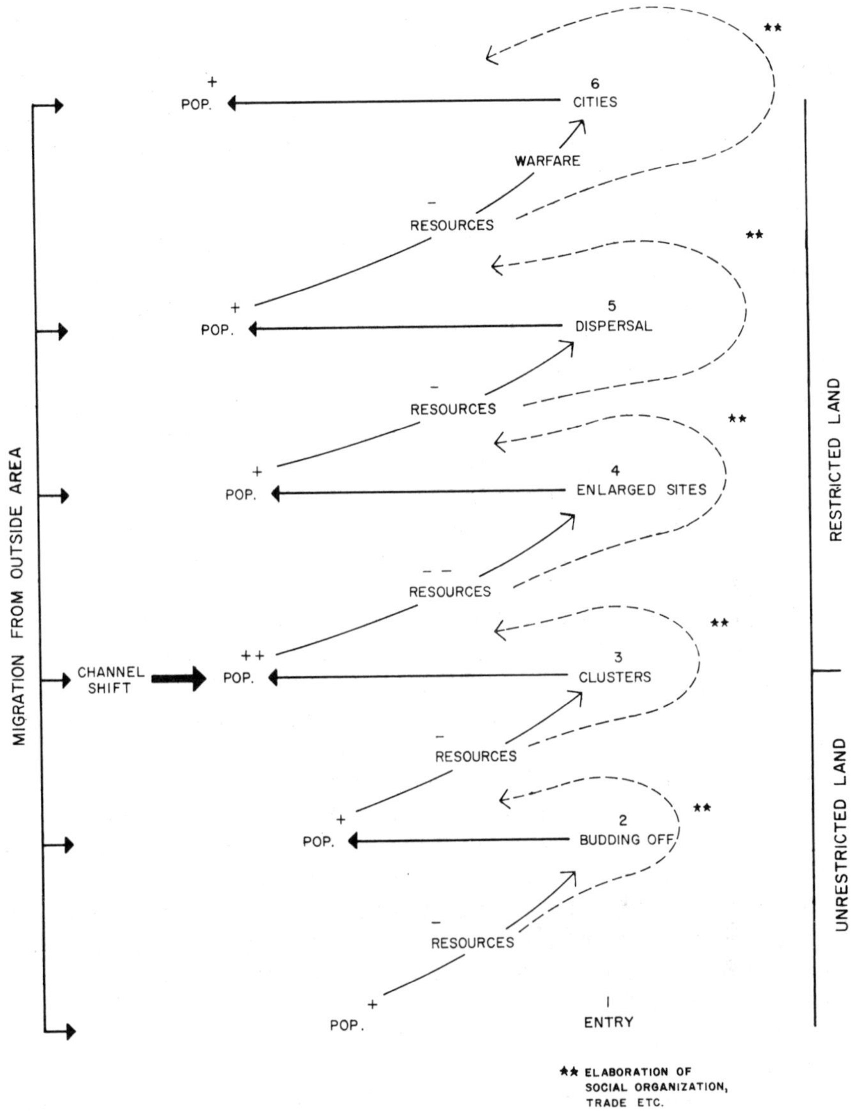

Figure 5 Model for the rise of civilization in Mesopotamia.

There are restrictions against moving farther out, since most of the agricultural land available through techniques of low-level irrigation is already occupied. Likewise, at this stage the level of organization is not sufficient to mobilize the manpower needed to exploit some marginal areas, since 'social units [are] prevailingly small and highly localized' (Adams 1970:5). Faced with a greatly increased population density and consequent strain on resources, the response is to intensify agriculture, irrigation, social organization, and the economic network. There occurs a short-term enlargement of already-existing settlements (Step 4) to a point where work in large units no longer produces a commensurate yield. There then occurs a disintegration of most larger settlements and a dispersal over the landscape in small settlements (Step 5), probably involving basic family units working small plots of ground with very intensive methods. This intensification, plus the yield from increased external trade and more complex social organizations, allows population to increase. Social organization, trade and craft specialization intensify further. Variations in status, based on individual holding of more advantageous land, plus individually accumulated capital, are seen as effecting vast changes in social systems. Competition for goods, especially for land, is now so intense that warfare becomes common and is increasingly better organized. Population centres, by now highly organized and fed by trade and warfare, require manpower and the excess rural population moves to take advantage of the need. Life in dispersed settlements becomes less desirable due to the obvious disparity in wealth between the countryside and the growing towns, as well as impossible due to warfare. Implosion occurs, resulting in cities (Step 6).

Except for the Uruk region, one cannot fully assess how closely the model fits the data outlined for Mesopotamia, since most of the other surveys lacked fine enough temporal distinctions. In the Uruk area, Steps 1-3 are in evidence in the Ubaid and Uruk periods. Adams' evidence of hierarchy of settlement and dispersal in the Jemdet Nasr period, plus the movement into the marginal Umma region, are taken as evidence of Steps 4-5. The Umma area is to be seen not merely as a spin-off from the Uruk development, but as entering the model at Step 4 and carrying on from there.

Nippur has Steps 1-3 in the Ubaid and Uruk periods, but the survey, being concentrated on the eastern side of the city, has evidence only of the abandonment of the easternmost channel of the river, not the effect on the area west of it. To obtain the whole sequence, one needs better information on settlement west of Nippur.

The Kish area has Steps 1-3, but the combination of Uruk and Jemdet Nasr material into Protoliterate allows no sharp discrimination of further steps.

The Diyala region shows clearly an unrestricted situation, building up to clustering of settlement (Steps 1-3) by late Protoliterate. However, being unaffected by the shift in the river and the consequent diminution of land, population growth is expressed in further budding off and formation of a hierarchy of settlement, rather than in dispersal and city formation.

The Ur/Eridu region seems to have experienced Steps 1-2, by the end of the Ubaid period, but the rest of its pattern seems not to conform with the model. The growth of the town in Jemdet Nasr times, and the lack of rural sites, may indicate some reaction to the demographic pressures farther north, but the nonformation of a city in Early Dynastic I clearly indicates that other factors were in operation in this area. It has been suggested above that Ur was in a marginal region, and its particular ecological limitations should be investigated and incorporated more systematically into the model. Such should be the case for all the areas. However, detailed ecological studies have not been done for Mesopotamia. Likewise, not enough detailed information is available for climatic fluctuations in the region in the periods involved. Minor variations could have had severe effects on animal, plant and human life, necessitating movements into the alluvium. For this model, climate and geography have, of necessity, been considered more or less as constants. At least for the three principal areas, Kish, Nippur and Uruk, conditions seem to have been similar enough geographically to justify that action.

The model obviously derives much from Boserup (1965), assuming a continued population growth. However, intensification of social organization and trade to relieve pressure on resources is introduced to allow the increase in population. The intensification in social organization, agricultural techniques, trade, etc., would not only allow but encourage population growth, as manpower requirements became increasingly greater. Nonetheless, a drop in population could occur, and a shift would be expected back to a less intensive level of organization, agriculture, etc. In this model, such an occurrence should be merely a reverse of the process. The steps should still hold. At a later date, with a rise in population, or a strain on resources, the process should resume in intensification.

The role of trade in the development of early civilizations has been elaborated by several scholars, but most systematically by William L. Rathje (1970, 1971), who read a draft of this paper and made many valuable suggestions. Trade and the accumulation of capital are factors that allow resources to balance population. However, the ability to move into unoccupied land or, alternately, to intensify agricultural practices are equally important. It is at the point where, with given technology, no further spread is possible that trade and the accumulation of capital, plus concomitant intensification of social organization, become the predominant forces allowing and encouraging population growth.

As population rises, competition should bring about more complex organization at an increasingly accelerated rate. Thus, in Mesopotamia, it required about three millennia to reach Step 3 (*c.* 3200 B.C.), but less than three centuries to go through Steps 4-6. However, the quickening of the pace cannot be accounted for merely by natural population growth. The trigger for the acceleration is seen in the abandonment of the eastern-most channel of the Euphrates at the end of the Uruk period, resulting in marked demographic and organizational readjustments. Cities might have come into being in Mesopotamia without this crisis, after a much longer period of population growth, but such seems not to have been the case. The secondary cities, such as Umma, Babylon, Eshnunna, etc., I would suggest, formed in reaction to the older cities. As the primal cities grew stronger and more aggressive both in trade and warfare, the populations in other areas were forced to aggregate to meet the threat. The trigger for the formation of secondary cities would then have been not population shift due to a natural disaster, but the rise of complex social organizations in a few areas that so upset the resource equilibrium that the only workable adjustment was the elaboration of similar complex organizations. Thus, the application of the model to other areas in Mesopotamia might show basic similarities in development, but with one or more steps omitted. The aggregation into cities by royal decree cannot be ruled out, since, in the secondary cities, it is assumed that social factors were the predominant forces triggering change.

The model can, I think, be tested. More intensive surface survey and a better discrimination of subperiods are obviously needed. Some part of the model might have relevance for areas outside Mesopotamia, but such wide application is not the object of this paper. The model has been constructed for the rise in civilization in Mesopotamia, and on that basis alone, seems useful.

REFERENCES

Adams, Robert McC. (1955) Developmental stages in ancient Mesopotamia. *In* Steward, J. *et al. Irrigation civilizations: A Comparative Study*, 6-18. Washington, D.C., Pan American Union.

Adams, Robert McC. (1957) Settlements in ancient Akkad. *Archaeology* **10**, 270-3.

Adams, Robert McC. (1958) Survey of ancient water courses and settlements in central Iraq. *Sumer* **14**, 101-3.

Adams, Robert McC. (1960) The evolutionary process in early civilizations. *In* Tax, S. (ed.) *Evolution after Darwin*, Vol. II, 153-167. Chicago, University Press.

Adams, Robert McC. (1962) Agriculture and urban life in early southwestern Iran. *Science* **136**, 109-22.

Adams, Robert McC. (1965) *Land Behind Baghdad: a History of Settlement on the Diyala Plains.* Chicago, University Press.

Adams, Robert McC. (1966) *The Evolution of Urban Society.* Chicago, Aldine.

Adams, Robert McC. (1969) The study of ancient Mesopotamian settlement patterns and the problem of urban origins. *Sumer* **25**, 111-24.

Adams, Robert McC. (1972) Patterns of urbanisation in early southern Mesopotamia. *In* Ucko, P.J., Tringham, R. and Dimbleby, G.W. (eds.) *Man, Settlement and Urbanism.* London, Duckworth.

Boserup, E. (1965) *The Conditions of Agricultural Growth: The Economics of Agrarian Change under Population Pressure.* Chicago, Aldine.

Cadoux, H.W. (1906) Recent changes in the course of the lower Euphrates. *The Geographical Journal* **28**, 266-76.

Carneiro, R. (1970) A theory of the origin of the state. *Science* **169**, 733-8.

Coe, M.D. and Flannery, K.V. (1964) Microenvironments and Mesoamerican prehistory. *Science* 143, 650-4.

Gibson, McG. (In press) *The City and Area of Kish.* Miami, Florida, Field Research Enterprises.

Johnson, G. (1972) Some mathematical analyses of urban settlement in lowland Mesopotamia. *In* Ucko, P.J., Tringham, R. and Dimbleby, G.W. (eds.) *Man, Settlement and Urbanism.* London, Duckworth.

Netting, R. McC. (1969) Ecosystems in process: a comparative study of change in two west African societies. *In* Damas, D. (ed.) *Ecological Essays*, 102-12. Ottawa: National Museum of Canada, Bulletin No. 230.

Rathje, W.L. (1970) Socio-political implications of Lowland Maya burials: methodology and tentative hypotheses. *World Archaeology* **1**, 359-74.

Rathje, W.L. (1971) The origin and development of Lowland Classic Maya civilization. *American Antiquity* **36**, 275-85.

Sanders, W.T. (1968) Hydraulic agriculture, economic symbiosis and the evolution of states in central Mexico. *In* Meggers, B.F. (ed.) *Anthropological Archaeology in the Americas*, 88-107. Washington, D.C., Anthropological Society of Washington.

Steward, J. *et al.* (1955) *Irrigation Civilizations: A Comparative Study.* Washington, D.C., Pan American Union.

Young, T. (1972) Population densities and early Mesopotamian origins. *In* Ucko, P.J., Tringham, R. and Dimbleby, G.W. (eds.) *Man, Settlement and Urbanism.* London, Duckworth.

Section 5: The investigation of social change

VERNON REYNOLDS

Ethology of social change

All primate social systems are adaptable according to environmental conditions, but only the human primate acts to change the system. Chimpanzees in captivity develop leaders with a definable role, and the group becomes cohesive, whereas in the forest they are scattered nomads; but their adaptability has limits: captive chimpanzees do not co-operate in a plan of escape. Vervet troops densely packed on an over-populated island in Lake Victoria become territorial and aggressive, whereas on the open spaces of the savannahs they have peaceful relationships with neighbouring troops when they meet, but no troop on the island has ever tried to take over the island and make the others into slaves. The baboons marooned on an island in Lake Kariba split up to maximize their foraging chances but they didn't and couldn't decide to turn to fishing for subsistence. Primates in zoos have suffered for over a century from lack of space, companionship, materials, activity, and while they adapt as well as they can, we have still to see the first monkey colony go on hunger strike, or start a revolution.

Whimsical though these examples seem, they illustrate an important distinction between *adaptability* or *variability* in a system, and actual *social change.* Only a comparative look at the human species, among other primate species, can isolate just what are the behavioural responses we show because we are primates, and what are unique to us as the human species. Thanks to a recent very clear analysis of the wild primate data by Kummer (1971), we can state fairly confidently that certain traits, or parameters of adaptability, are characteristic of primate species: that in conditions of over-population and lack of space primate groups tend to respond by setting up exclusive territories, or by increasing the intolerance and aggression between groups; that according to habitat and food distribution, primate groups are able to adapt the size of the troop or community and the degree of dispersal or cohesion of social units. Furthermore studies of primate groups in captivity have demonstrated that in confined spaces and bereft of responsibility for their own foraging, the structural relationships of the group become intensified. Antagonisms are increased and the dominance hierarchy is tightened up; roles which appear only in a functional context in the wild become defined and fixed in captivity, for example the leader chimpanzee (Reynolds and Luscombe 1968), the despot and the omega monkey, and in the rhesus colony I studied (Reynolds 1970) even the temporary sexual consort typical of this species had been transformed into a permanent partner for the dominant male; she groomed him, sat with him, and dominated all the other females. When she died, another female took over the complete role.

What has been found to be most resistant to modification in primates is the species-specific pattern of relationships which determines the structural form of groups. Primates have broadly two main types of social system. First there is the type that is based on the family as the basic social unit within a wider population, such as the one-male harems of the hamadryas, gelada or patas, or the pair and off-spring of the gibbon or *callicebus.* This type of system depends on strong and permanent bonding between mates, and antagonism between adult males expressed by mutual avoidance, or aggressive defence by the male of his family or territory against intruders. The second type of system is the troop or community organization found in common baboons, chimpanzees, macaques and some other monkey species. This system depends on strong maternal and sibling bonding which extends into adult life and results in the association of uterine kin. Females develop matrilineages which form the stable core of the troop; males maintain a special relationship with their matrilineage through life (Kawai 1965, Kawamura 1965). Sexual liaisons are temporary and promiscuous. Male antagonism may be expressed in competition over status, but once dominance is settled, males of similar rank often become strongly bonded. These two structural types, built upon different kinds of bonds and antagonisms, are determined according to species (Nagel in press).

The social group is the essential environment for the expression of the species-typical patterns of interaction and relationships, and each species has a range of population size beyond which the troop splits into two similarly structured entities. For macaques the maximum observed has been over 500 monkeys but this was in conditions of artificial feeding. Most troops split when populations of 1-200 are reached (Koford 1963, Sugyama 1960). When numbers of primates are released into captive or semi-captive situations, groups form based on the species-specific patterns of bonding. For example hamadryas males immediately start to herd females into harems (Kummer 1971:101), but rhesus monkeys form stable groups of females, to which bands of males become attached later (Vandenbergh 1967).

Thus a fair generalization on the primate potential for adaptability would be to say that the primate group itself, with a species-typical structural form of inter-individual relationships based on bonding and antagonism, is resistant to change; if the group structure is destroyed new groups with the same pattern will emerge: the effect of some environmental pressures is to intensify the bonds and antagonisms making necessary stricter control by dominance and greater definition of roles. Especially in two areas of life, the *relationship of the group to its habitat*, and the *relationship between group and group*, primate social systems show predictable responses of adaptation according to environmental pressures.

Man and the intervening variable

If we now leave the rest of the primate world and consider the human species, we can begin to investigate whether humans may perhaps remain limited by their inheritance of primate behaviour, and what potentials they have built upon and developed into unique human characteristics.

Typically, human social systems combine the structural relationships of both the main types of primate system described above. Humans combine the pattern of one-male family units with kinship bonds maintained by each partner separately in the wider community. Antagonism between male heads of family units may be directed into competition over status in the wider community, and yet it often co-exists with strong male bonding mechanisms in the dominance structure of the whole group. Socially it is more complicated to be a human than any other primate, as there are a number of competing bonds to be considered. However, human group structures do appear to share a common species-characteristic basis, and a resistance to change such as is found among other primates, in that the emotional and motivational commitments of most humans, wherever they are, go into personal, sexual, or kinship ties, or into achieving status in the group. We can identify this bio-social structure of the group therefore as a conservative force, a force that is resistant to change.

If we now consider the two areas in which other primates in fact show most adaptability, we see it is in just these areas that humans have instituted most social changes both in the past and now: in the relationship of group to habitat or physical environment, and in the relationship of group to other groups or social environment.

However, no other primate species, whatever the environmental pressure, has been known to change its means of subsistence (except by a long evolutionary process of modification and selection), nor has any group of primates attempted to subjugate or coerce a group of conspecifics. This type of change is characteristic of humans, and cannot be explained in terms of adaptation, or any *direct* relationship between environmental conditions and behaviour. We have to recognize that man has evolved certain unique capacities which to some extent change the relationship between the perceived environment and his own behaviour. Along with the progressive increase in complexity of the human brain during the last 2 million years or so, man has been receiving and assessing more information than any other species, he has developed means of communicating and discussing it, and he organises it into conceptual models of reality; successive generations try to fit all the subsequent incoming information into the prevailing working model of reality (only rejecting the model when the discrepancy becomes too great), and they have striven to anticipate symbolically how certain human actions might be effective in pushing the model of reality closer to some idealized model.

There are several qualitatively new behavioural phenomena in this compared with other primate species: there is the *active* impetus of the perceiving and organizing organ, the tendency to acquire more information and to fit incoming data into the working schema; there is the ability to *symbolize* aspects of the environment, relationships between human and environment, social relationships, actions and effects of actions, and moreover to communicate and discuss these symbols with others by means of language; and there is the whole concept of the ideal, the *perfect model*, which can be symbolized, aimed at, yet need never have been experienced.

The energy impelling the brain's quest for information and organization of models of reality merits putting it on a level with other major motivational patterns in man such as parental, sexual or dominance behaviour, and it cannot be ignored in any discussion of human behaviour.

Thus in the case of the human species, interaction between group and environment and between group and group became mediated by the *interpretation of the total situation* including remembered past, current motivations and future possibilities. This does not mean that the normal primate patterns of adaptation and direct response by the social system to the physical and social environment ceased to operate, but that with conscious human effort they could sometimes be over-ruled or postponed in pursuit of more long-term benefits envisaged.

But only by group agreement can this happen. And thus it is obvious that the interpretation of the total situation, or the hypothesis of reality held at any point in time by a particular group, is itself limited by other variables – not merely by the availability of information, but also by the social system in operation, and the values resulting from cultural adaptations to that system.

So, for example, in a simple social system based on the group in ecological equilibrium with its environment, within which the bonds are based on kinship and inter-individual friendship and shared subsistence, and the dominance structure is the result of age and the interaction of personalities, no plan of action for change is going to get far unless the leading males think of it themselves or can be persuaded by argument.

And again, if the cultural adaptations to the system and method of subsistence have produced a fatalistic set of beliefs about the world, and value is put on stolid endurance, the leaders are less likely to be persuaded by arguments for active change, than if they have a past in which opportunism has been rewarded, and have a set of beliefs that the gods help those who help themselves. In either situation, natural disasters, population increases, encroachment of other groups, are going to be factors in the total assessment, but no more.

Some actions for change are exploratory, such as those which must have preceded experiments in different methods of subsistence, technology, colonization of new lands; other actions for change are responsive such as the Hebrews' decision to unite the tribes under the military leadership of Saul against the Philistines. But whether exploratory or responsive, actions for change bear no direct correlation with social or physical environmental conditions, because they are based on the variable intervening factor of the group's interpretation of its own relationship to others and to the environment. And the values and judgments which bear on this interpretation are themselves influenced by the existing social system and by cultural adaptations to the system.

But it is this human characteristic of organizing the data of life into a meaningful conceptual framework, a hypothesis of reality, and the capacity to imagine better or ideal models without experiencing them, which must be seen as the main instrumental factor in initiating purposeful changes in subsistence methods or in social systems; and it is also the main factor of variability in the different behaviours of different groups and different populations, even when facing similar sets of circumstances. Others who have put forward similar theories recently include Forde (1970) and Gregory (1971).

But although all things can be imagined, and some can be put into practice, not all have lasting success and viability, perhaps in part because of the limits of primate, even human, adaptability. We can investigate the problem of how action and change are followed by periods of adjustment and to what extent adjustment can be seen in terms of the resurgence of species-characteristic patterns of behaviour.

Model applied to case histories

An ethological model of social change might then be: hypothesis followed by action followed by change in the system followed by adaptation and resurgence of species-typical patterns and responses, followed by a new assessment and new hypotheses which may in turn lead to new actions.

I want now to consider a few simplified cases of known social change and apply the model to them.

First, the process of change from nomadic non-territorial hunting bands with flexible and changing composition, into fixed lineage groups holding stock or land. The entire human species could still be living happily in nomadic hunting bands all over the world in 1971 (a lot more contented socially and with an infinite future in terms of resources) if it had not been for the fact that some groups produced occasional men of vision who were not content to play dice and sharpen spears on their lazy days. Once the hypothesis of the relationship between seeds and crops of wild wheat and other plants, or the seasonal pattern in the migration of ungulates was understood, some groups, where a thinker combined his cleverness with an effective personality and was able to overcome the reactionary elements in the group, were persuaded to invest a little more time in purposeful cultivation, or to follow the herds one year. In many groups a rigid structure of dominance relationships or a conservative set of cultural values incompatible with change, must have precluded action.

However, once a band had taken the decisive step and become dependent on a particular kind of resource, the social situation changed and predictable social processes took over. Human groups owning 'property' on which their survival depended became 'captive', and like captive chimps which can no longer disperse and avoid personal clashes, no longer renew hope and friendliness by continual movement, instead tightened their dominance hierarchies in response to increased antagonism within the group, and defined specialist roles necessary for group co-operation and cohesion; also when localized resources became all-important they had to be defended, and groups became more territorial, more exclusive, and more antagonistic to others in the neighbourhood, as do vervet monkeys or langurs in areas where resources are limited. The clarification of the lineage connections is probably another result of increasing dependence on fixed resources or property, a trend also seen in Japanese monkeys.

And so the early nomadic hunting bands, once their method of subsistence was changed, became quite inexorably transformed over the generations into fatalistic propitiating hierarchically organized agricultural peoples, or cohesive and aggressive pastoral tribesmen, or territorial fishermen. But the bonds and antagonisms within groups remained essentially the same. Antagonisms now were expressed by aggression rather than avoidance, or repressed altogether; while much greater social control was necessary over pairings and residence because of the inheritance of property and rights. But communities were nevertheless economically self-determining groups in that they acted directly on their own environment, and were socially and politically equal to other surrounding ones; within them species-typical behaviour could still be fully expressed.

The most significant social revolution changed forever the relationship between group and group: the change from small self-determining agricultural or pastoral communities to large populations of many thousands of people whose economic, social and political centre was the city. This happened first so far as we know three or four thousand years B.C. on the alluvial deltas of Egypt, Mesopotamia and Northern India and a little later round the Mediterranean coasts; it happened according to the same pattern in another alluvial river valley in Mexico about 180 B.C. (MacNeish 1968); cities came to Britain and Europe with the Romans, and the process accelerated with the Normans; it happened in parts of West, South and Central Africa a thousand years ago, and has spread more widely over the last 100 years.

There are those who see the development of city organization as the inevitable culmination of a sustained process of greater and more efficient mastery of the environment; technological innovation leads to surplus produce (Allan 1972), population growth leads to intensified agricultural methods (Cuyler Young 1972), intensified agricultural methods and water-control lead to population growth which leads to changes in the social system (MacNeish 1972) or the intensified agricultural methods and water-control lead to a surplus of produce which results in trading centres (Russell 1967, Blouet 1972), or the merchant as entrepreneur stimulated desire for trade (Vance 1970). Like the earlier Central Place Theory, these schemes implicitly assume that humans have an inbuilt and consuming drive for more material goods and greater economic complexity, when in fact this is a drive engendered only by a particular form of social system. These theories miss the point that human groups respond to and act on the environment through the intervening variable of their own collection of ideas and values; that it is the type of social system that attributes values to functional roles and material things, and that changes in the social system and correlated ideas must *precede* the transition to an urban economy. Population growth in present day simple agricultural communities is followed by splitting up (Carneiro 1961, Forge 1970), just as it is in monkeys, and others have pointed to the social rather than the ecological limiting factors on community size (Flannery 1970, Harris 1970, Reynolds 1970). The changes associated all over the world and at all periods with the development of cities tell a consistent story about human action and human adaptation and response. Simple communities begin to increase in number and size, then a relatively sudden and large increase in population is correlated with all the signs of a stratified political structure with big central buildings, and a reorganized economy based on new technology or hydraulic systems, and labour drawn away from the land to operate it; fortifications spring up; trade, especially the importing of luxury goods or building materials increases. Mines are opened, crafts and specialized skills spring up.

The pattern is the same though the scale differs, whether it is Mesopotamia, Mexico, Roman Britain, South Africa, or British India. In terms of human behaviour and the observable and documented responses of social groups, the change from living in small autonomous personalized communities bound in direct relationship to their environment, to the stratified city with a powerful elite class, and organized slave labour, is an enormous and distinct step in human social organization.

It could only have been imposed by conquest (as Plato said over 2,000 years ago), by a group with a powerful purpose derived from their own hypothesis of reality, and model of possibility. In the case of Mesopotamia, we know that the population of the hill settlements had increased greatly during the 4th millennium, and the increasing density may well have sparked off territorial disputes and conflicts just as it does in the monkey examples given earlier; especially if some of the tribes were herders, tightly knit, organized hierarchically, mobile and aggressive, exploration and the search for new lands would be likely to occur. A first wave of immigrants tried out the area. Then some groups conceived the plan of taking over the simple riverine settlements and using the inhabitants to work for them. They did this easily because they were aggressive and mobile and used to fighting, and probably thought of themselves as different from those they conquered.

Thus, one group took power over others, and maintained it in the first place by force of arms, and began to control the other groups as if they were part of the material environment. This step was not itself an inevitable response to circumstances, but it set in motion inevitable processes of primate adaptation. The enslaved labourers must have had little chance of doing anything at first, but after a while those that could began regrouping into social and economic territories, restructuring themselves into communities who shared a craft or skill and a section of the city, instead of land or stock.

In this way some sort of natural groupings were restored in which some sections at least of the enslaved population could structure the species-specific bonds and antagonisms which give meaning and form to human life. But because the new groups (conquerors and conquered alike) were all captive, being bound up together now in the new form of economic organization, with no space to expand, no freedom to move away, responses similar to those of captive primates began to show in the antagonisms between groups, eruption of violence in social interaction, in particular the increasing differentiation of roles within rigid hierarchies of authority. Thus we can suggest that in these examples the social system of the conquered peoples was forcibly changed, and then they adapted to the changed situation, on the basis of typical primate responses.

The adaptation of the elite group, who for survival now had to maintain political dominance, superior class status, and for the progress of the economy use the slaves as tools operating on the physical environment, was even more interesting. Their response to their intrinsically unstable situation (for no longer were they subsisting directly in relationship with their environment, but through the intermediary manipulation of an alien population) was to magnify the difference between themselves and the labouring masses, to exaggerate everything in the life style, to attempt to become larger than life. Thus no longer were they content with simple dwellings made of reeds or mud, hide tents, or even stone huts, but they must have huge buildings made with enormous slabs; no longer did they wear a shiny stone or bangle to attract the eye of a sexual partner but they must be bedecked with glitter and colours; no longer clothing to protect them from the sun or hold warmth at night, but the finest most bedazzling material that could be got; everything that assailed the senses had to be intensified; the entire elite group took up this grandiose life style, not because of any instinctive love built into the human species for these material objects in themselves, but because their adaptation to the new class system necessitated their appearing awesome and of a supernormal type. Hence the subsequent importing of quantities of stone from the hills, the enormous buildings and waterworks, the trade in metals, cloths and spices. The instability inherent in the dominance of a military elite over a submissive population threw up the phenomenon of the class system many times over in the history of the world, and always gave rise to this curious display of an exaggerated and unrealistic scale of life among the dominant. When the autonomy and equality of human groups was lost, the natural balance contained in the structural relationships within the group, and the kinship ties and respect for the integrity of other groups was lost too, and the desperate race for status, as separate from functional role, was on.

The basic instability of the superior elite subsisting only by means of the lower orders, and not by their own labour, also meant that all their energies went into the social and political aspects of life, in particular as we have seen maintenance of grandeur compared to the workers of their own society, but also competition with other neighbouring elites. The rise and fall of empires, the fighting over control of trading routes and gold and copper mines, the excesses of expansionism, all derive, in behavioural terms, from the striving of one military elite after another to display greater and greater material wealth to maintain or increase its superior status in relation to its own people and to other competing elites. The resulting cultural values of this class-based social system encouraged expansionism and power-seeking.

Other examples must be even briefer. Attempts to change the relationships between groups include not only the conquest by one group of others, but attempts in the opposite direction aimed at reinstating a greater degree of equality between groups. The Greek moves in the 6th and 5th centuries B.C. towards a measure of democracy is an example of this type of social change. The fact that it was the Greeks who initiated this move, and none of the other populations in the same bondage to the aristocracy in other places, resulted from the philosophical developments of the previous 200 years, and the belief in opportunistic and individualistic rather than fatalistic gods; the hypotheses of reality and the models of possibility developed in Greece made action conceivable, and once this was taken up by personalities who saw means of enhancing their own status within their own groups in this way, action for change began.

Resistant structure of human groups

What is the basic structure of the human group? Theoretical predictions based on the study of equilibrium systems ecologically adapted to primitive hunting and gathering (Birdsell 1968) agree with actual modes found among existing hunter-gatherers, that the evolutionary adaptation of man is geared to communities around 500 persons sharing a regional identity, and consisting within that of bands or households, of around 25 persons, linked by a kinship nexus. And strangely enough however populations are uprooted and resettled in shapeless masses, however complex and enormous our political and economic organization becomes, human grouping and regrouping into something resembling this fundamental pattern cannot be stopped. When kinship no longer provides the bonds, we use friendship, or pastime, or profession, or ideology, or neighbourhood to provide the binding force of the group; when we can no longer live, work, play, love, mate, rear children and die in the *same* coresidential group, we form or join different groups for different activities. But we must bond, first within the family, and secondly within a wider group, with whose activities and aims we can identify, for human life to have form and meaning. The other side of the coin is the antagonism of group for group, which is intensified when they are forced to share the same economic territory, and this seems to be something we cannot work out satisfactorily by adaptation. If we cannot return to the self-sufficiency of the group, then the relationship of group to group has to be purposefully ordered in one way or another; the class system is one way, the Communist experiments in China and Cuba are another; the uncontrolled antagonistic jostling of groups in big American cities is a sign of social strain which may lead to a new assessment and a new hypothesis for change.

Ways of ordering these relationships between group and group in a large and complex political and economic organization vary according to the working hypotheses of reality operating. These very hypotheses are changing all the time in most of the world due to the fantastic seeking for and communication of information going on at present.

One behavioural experiment in line with basic human group structure is the Chinese commune, which is divided into competitive brigades, within which teams of about twenty families share and work the land together (Riboud 1966, Myrdal 1969). In these communes, the brigades, which are about the size of the regional communities of the hunters, have regained control over their own shared economy, and have some degree of social and political determination of their own. Bonds of kinship, living together and working towards a common aim, bind the group as does the competition with other teams, brigades and communes, who stand in a relationship of political equality one to another.

Another experiment is the kibbutz of Israel, (Spiro 1966), where a hypothesis led to the setting up of communal farms, with total communal rearing of children, and equality of the sexes. Whether by accident or design or sheer practicality, the kibbutz system coincided with one of the fundamental human patterns – the community of a few hundred persons with a shared economy and political self-determination. The sense of belonging and purpose engendered in the kibbutzim is testified by all. The children were reared communally, and there was no economic foundation to family life. This looks on the face of it like an attempt to destroy the family, and was so intended. But in fact people continued to love and play with their own children especially at bedtime, and family life became a shared emotional intimacy, part of the relaxation of leisure hours, and ensured the continuity of the bonds. It seems, however, that now the dedicated kibbutzim are on the way out, replaced by the co-operatives, where each family unit lives separately but as part of the community. Another attempt to abolish the family that failed occurred in post-revolutionary U.S.S.R. (Geiger 1968).

Occasionally, consideration of the inequalities and suffocation of living in a class-based unjust society, leads groups of people to take up the hypothesis that *all* structuring within groups and between groups is wrong; they come up with the idea that individuals must not have defined roles and relationships but are or should be permanently and totally free and equal. The early Christians argued thus, if need be scorning their personal family responsibilities, in order the better to declare infinite brotherly love for the world in general. Finally, when given establishment backing by the whim of an emperor, they developed into an unequal, rigidly structured system, in order to maintain their political territory. The model: hypothesis, action for change, then a long period of adaptation and resurgence of species-characteristic patterns, is exemplified once again. The most recent attempts to deny the fundamental need for humans to live in structured groups come from the hippie communes in America. A recent sympathetic survey of about a dozen communes (Hedgepath and Stock 1970), showed that those that insisted on open membership, individual responsibility rather than a defined hierarchy of authority, and sexual freedom, tended to last only a few months before people drifted away due to personal antagonisms, sexual jealousies, or diseases caused by lack of hygiene in the food preparation and sanitary arrangements. The two most successful of all are definite economic co-operative ventures, farming the land in one case and running a vegetarian restaurant in the other. Both of these have recognized couples, although the children are brought up communally, while knowing they belong to their own parents. Both of these communes have defined roles and rotas of work, and are built round a founding male figure. Both have explicit rules concerning hygiene and drug-taking. And thus the bonds are established, the antagonisms controlled, but alas, out goes infinite brotherly love for, as the two investigators in the above survey found, one deranged hippie was found wandering from commune to commune, thrown out after a few days at each, because he would not play his role, do his work, conform to the structure, which made the group a viable human system.

Summary

A model of social change is suggested, based on historical case-histories, and patterns of human behaviour, and which assumes that man shares with other primate species common patterns of response and adaptability to external circumstances.

The evolution of the uniquely large and complex human brain, however, with its impelling drive to categorise and communicate information to create working hypotheses of the social and physical world, and to symbolize and anticipate alternative actions, transformed completely the relationship between environmental forces and the response of the human group. An unpredictable relationship exists between environmental circumstances and the action of human groups, because of the intervening variable of discussion of alternative ideas limited by the prevailing model of reality and the social structure of the group.

And out of this process of discussion and decision, purposeful action sometimes results. Action accounts for major changes in the past and present; changes in the dominance relationships between groups, changes imposed on the size and constitution of the group, changes in the group's means of subsistence and economic organization; and attempts to change the fundamental structure of bonds and antagonisms with a group.

Action is however followed by a period during which the species-characteristic patterns of behaviour reassert themselves in the new circumstances, new groups and new bonds form to replace the old shattered ones, and the system adapts within the limits of tolerance. There seem to be two main forms of social organization of large and complex economic systems which are viable. One is a class-system based on power and display of grandeur by a superior elite, bolstered up by a strong fatalistic belief system. The other involves small groups of people living together, operating their own economy, and sorting out their own dominance hierarchy, allowing antagonism expression in competition with other groups, and integrating the groups by means of representation into the larger economic and political organization. Laissez-faire systems tend to be unstable because the natural antagonism between groups is not controlled, and because groups themselves are unstable, not being in functional relationship with the environment; however, such systems are fertile ground for new hypotheses for change.

REFERENCES

Allan, W. (1972) Ecology, techniques and settlement patterns. *In* Ucko, P., Tringham, R. and Dimbleby, G.W. (eds.) *Man, Settlement and Urbanism.* London, Duckworth.

Birdsell, J.B. (1968) Some predictions for the Pleistocene based on equilibrium systems among recent hunter-gatherers. *In* Lee, R.B. and De Vore, I. (eds.) *Man the Hunter.* Chicago, Aldine.

Blouet, B.W. (1972) The evolution of settlement patterns. *In* Ucko, P., Tringham, R. and Dimbleby, G.W. (eds.) *Man, Settlement and Urbanism.* London, Duckworth.

Carneiro, R.L. (1961) Slash-and-burn cultivation among the Kuikuru and its implications for cultural development in the Amazon Basin. *In* Wilbert (ed.) *The Evolution of Horticultural Systems in Native South America.* Anthropologica supp. no. 2.

Cuyler Young, T. (1972) Population densities and early Mesopotamian urbanism. *In* Ucko, P., Tringham, R. and Dimbleby, G.W. (eds.) *Man, Settlement and Urbanism.* London, Duckworth.

Flannery, K.V. (1972) The origins of the village as a settlement type in Mesoamerica and the Near East: a comparative study. *In* Ucko, P., Tringham, R. and Dimbleby, G.W. (eds.) *Man, Settlement and Urbanism.* London, Duckworth.

Forde, D. (1970) Ecology and social structure. *Proceedings of the Royal Anthropological Institute.*

Forge, A. (1972) Normative factors in the settlement size of neolithic cultivators (New Guinea). *In* Ucko, P., Tringham, R. and Dimbleby, G.W. (eds.) *Man, Settlement and Urbanism.* London, Duckworth.

Geiger, H.K. (1968) *The Family in Soviet Russia.* Harvard University Press.

Gregory, R. (1971) Views. *The Listener* no. 2216 vol. 86. Sept. 16th.

Harris, D.R. (1972) Swidden systems and settlement. *In* Ucko, P., Tringham, R. and Dimbleby, G.W. (eds.) *Man, Settlement and Urbanism.* London, Duckworth.

Hedgepath, W. and Stock, D. (1970) *The Alternative: Communal Life in New America.* London, Collier-Macmillan.

Kawai, M. (1965) *On the system of social ranks in a natural troop of Japanese monkeys.*

Kawamura, S. (1965) *Matriarchal social ranks in the Minoo B group: a study of the rank system of Japanese monkeys. In* Altmann (ed.) *Japanese*

Monkeys. A collection of translations. Yerkes Regional Primate Centre.

Koford, C.B. (1963) Group relations in an island colony of Rhesus monkeys. *In* Southwick (ed.) *Primate Social Behaviour.* Van Nostrand Insight series. New York.

Kummer, H. (1971) *Primate Societies; Group Techniques of Ecological Adaptation.* Chicago, Aldine.

MacNeish, R.S. (1968) Social implications of changes in population and settlement pattern of the 12,000 years of pre-history in the Tehuacan valley of Mexico. *Proceedings of the IVth Congress of the International Economic History Association.* University of Manitoba Press.

MacNeish, R.S. (1972) The evolution of community patterns in the Tehuacan valley of Mexico and speculation about the cultural processes. *In* Ucko, P., Tringham, R. and Dimbleby, G.W. (eds.) *Man, Settlement and Urbanism.* London, Duckworth.

Mydral, J. (1969) *Report from a Chinese village.* Harmondsworth, Penguin.

Nagel, U. Social organization in a baboon hybrid zone. In *Proceedings of the 3rd International Congress of Primatology.* In press.

Reynolds, V. (1970) Roles and role change in monkey society: the consort relationship of Rhesus monkeys. *Man* 5, no. 3.

Reynolds, V. (1972) Ethology of urban life. *In* Ucko, P. Tringham, R. and Dimbleby, G.W. (eds.) *Man, Settlement and Urbanism.* London, Duckworth.

Reynolds, V. and Luscombe, G. (1968) Chimpanzee rank orders and the function of displays. *In* Proceedings of the IInd International Congress of Primatology. Karger Basle.

Riboud, M. (1966) *The Three Banners of China.* London, Collier-MacMillan.

Russell, W.M.S. (1967) *Man, Nature and History.* Aldus Books.

Spiro, M.E. (1966) *Children of the Kibbutz.* Cambridge, Harvard University Press.

Sugyama, Y. (1960) On the division of a natural troop of Japanese Monkeys at Takasakyama. *Primates* 2, 10-144.

Vance, J. (1970) *The Merchant's World: The Geography of Wholesaling.* Englewood Cliffs, N.J., Prentice-Hall.

Vandenbergh, J.G. (1967) The development of social structure in free-ranging Rhesus monkeys. *Behaviour* 29, 179-94.

BRYONY ORME

Archaeology and ethnography

The use of ethnography in archaeological interpretation has frequently been discussed, and it has been either condemned or found essential to valid interpretation time and again. Yet these theoretical considerations have had little impact on the various ways in which ethnography is used – even by those who have contributed to the theoretical discussion. In general terms, the archaeologist's use of ethnography has not changed for several centuries, and it does not seem likely that it will alter radically in the near future.

Current opinion ranges from Freeman's emphatic rejection of ethnographic analogy (Freeman 1968), to Ucko's rejection of archaeology as an independent discipline. Freeman argues from the position that 'the most serious failings in present models for interpreting archaeological evidence are directly related to the fact that they incorporate numerous analogies with modern groups' (ibid.:262); he claims that prehistory is being prevented from independent development: 'The use of analogy has demanded that prehistorians adopt the frames of reference of anthropologists who study modern populations and attempt to force their data into those frames, a process which will eventually cause serious errors, if it has not done so already' (ibid.:262). An important factor in his argument is the biological difference between prehistoric and modern man, which implies a different range of behaviour patterns, hence to use the one for the interpretation of the other is limiting and 'deleterious to research since it prevents the discovery that the postulated similarities do not exist' (ibid.: 265). Freeman cannot, and does not, entirely dismiss the use of ethnography, but he does set up a 'model minimising analogy'.

Freeman's position is not dissimilar to that taken by Binford at times. In 'Archaeological perspectives' (Binford 1968a), he writes: 'Fitting archaeological remains into ethnographically known patterns of life adds nothing to our knowledge of the past. In fact, such a procedure denies to archaeology the possibility of dealing with forms of cultural adaptation outside the range of variation known ethnographically' (ibid.:13). However, in the same paper he enlarges and modifies this statement: he acknowledges the 'role of ethnographic training for archaeologists, the use of analogy, and the use of imagination and conjecture' (ibid.:17), and suggests that it is not so much the use of analogy which is at fault, as the lack of adequate testing of the hypotheses derived from such analogies. This last point is discussed at length in 'Smudge pits and hide smoking' (Binford 1967), a paper in which he sets out an extensive example of the use of ethnohistorical evidence for the interpretation of an archaeological feature.

From this, and from his contributions to *Man the Hunter* (Binford 1968c), one might assume that his use of analogy would be limited, both to the more tangible aspects of interpretation, and in the frequency that he had recourse to it. But in 'Post-Pleistocene adaptations' (Binford 1968b), he makes considerable use of both ethnographic data and theory – enough for the article to be used as an example of an ethnographic model, in contrast to the ecological approach of Higgs and Jarman, in a recent paper by J.C. Harriss (1971). Though both positions are somewhat exaggerated by Harriss for the sake of contrast, he does bring out the considerable reliance which Binford places on data from modern primitive peoples to suggest post-Pleistocene situations and conditions.

In general, American archaeologists approach the problem in a rather different way from the Europeans. This may be partly due to the different academic set-up, with archaeology being a sub-discipline of anthropology, but also, I suspect, to the historical situation. By this, I mean the fact that the Americans have always been able to make use of, and have relied heavily on, ethnohistory. For them, there can often be documented continuity between prehistory and history to the present day – as is evident in many American archaeology publications, and in much of the work being done in Latin America. I would suggest that the easy availability of such evidence has had two results: the one being the development of 'action archaeology', or the study of the archaeology of living groups, the other being a distrust of general ethnographic parallels (as opposed to specific ones), because their validity cannot be checked in the way that it can be for the ethnohistorical evidence. But this is to confound two different approaches: the use of ethnohistory is a distinct technique, and its philosophy is not that of ethnographic analogy.

Ethnohistory has had less impact on recent European archaeology, and it is generally considered that there is a relative scarcity of raw materials. Nevertheless, it has its equivalents in the relatively undeveloped field of folklore, which few prehistorians apart from J.G.D. Clark (1951) have considered in any detail; on the whole it is the province of the post-Romanists. More recently, David Clarke (1970:ch. 9) has outlined a way in which such material could be used in writing European prehistory, but in general such methods have received little support, at least among English prehistorians.

However, there is one aspect that should not be ignored, and that is the enormous importance of Roman literary sources, which are none the less ethnohistorial for being Classical. In the earlier stages of the development of prehistory, these were used extensively, at times even providing the whole framework for prehistory, and they were always essential to iron age studies. In fact, these sources became so thoroughly incorporated in the conception of later European prehistory that they ceased to be acknowledged. But Caesar and Tacitus have contributed as much to European prehistory as Raleigh and Sahagun have to that of Middle America.

Having claimed that ethnohistory is thought to be relatively unimportant in modern European prehistory, it is satisfactory to note that few of the papers presented to the 1970 Research Seminar on Settlement and Urbanization make use of such data to this end (e.g. Simonsen 1972), whereas a fair number of those dealing with extra-European regions do use this type of evidence (e.g. Bray, Gathercole, MacNeish). These papers also show clearly the difference in the use of ethnohistory, which is neither more nor less than the history of the region applied in a very specific fashion to archaeological problems, e.g. the identification of recorded sites, and the use of ethnography, where the principle that one is working on must be one of comparison.

It is interesting to see that the majority of the contributors to the 1970 Seminar do make use of ethnography, some almost without realizing it, some in a very explicit fashion, as Desmond Clark in 'Mobility and Settlement Patterns in sub-Saharan Africa'. Like Binford and Ucko, Clark stresses the need to re-examine the archaeology in the light of the ethnographic example: 'Ethnography can, however, provide at best only approximations that need to be tested against the specific archaeological data'. He dismisses any need for temporal or cultural continuity, but does hold that the 'lengthy adaptation of broadly comparable economies within habitats, changed to some extent certainly, but still closely similar to those of prehistoric times' yields the most satisfactory parallels. This is to admit to a degree of economic determinism that is held by many other prehistorians, though not all have formulated their views as clearly. A similar deliberate use of parallels, though not necessarily with the economic overtones, may be seen in contributions from Flannery, Harris, Isaac and Tringham, among others.

A rather different use of ethnography appears in several papers, notably those of Brothwell, Harlan and Hodges. The subjects tend to be 'specialist', in that they lie outside the competence of most general archaeologists, and they draw on equally specialized ethnographic data. For example, Hodges discusses the range of uses to which mud-brick can be put, and its structural possibilities, taking a wide variety of examples from modern societies that build in this material – obviously a more realistic and more rewarding approach than London-based speculation and experiment. Harlan's botanical and Brothwell's medical data must be virtually impossible to obtain without recourse to living, non-westernised societies. So, whilst remembering that one is only increasing the possibilities rather than providing an exhaustive catalogue, the value of such studies to prehistorians must surely be appreciated.

The Seminar also provides several examples of an approach to culture change which is neither simple archaeology nor pure anthropology. I am referring to those authors who have taken a specific problem of social existence, and discussed it from an anthropological angle, but at the same time are aware of the implications for archaeology of their suggestions and conclusions, and make a positive attempt to link the two areas. Forge and Lee tackle the problem of group size – not in an identical fashion, nor do their conclusions entirely agree – but both are trying to find the factors behind certain observed regularities in their data, and considering the relevance of this for prehistory. Rowlands deals with the rather different subject of defence in a similar fashion.

These examples, as much as the more theoretical arguments discussed earlier, should give some idea of the current use of ethnography in archaeological interpretation.

If one considers articles such as 'Ethnography and archaeological interpretation of funerary remains' (Ucko 1969a), it is apparent that Ucko's attitude to the use of ethnography is closest to the last group mentioned above. He takes an attitude which is diametrically opposed to Freeman, in saying that archaeology cannot exist without anthropology, that it should not attempt to do so, and that, far from being very restrictive in one's choice of ethnographic material, it is possible to draw information from a very wide range of societies, provided that one then tests the possible models rigorously against the archaeological data. In view of this, factors such as economic or technological similarity, and geographic or temporal continuity, to which several people have devoted a lot of space, are not held to be necessarily relevant, nor does the presence of a literate population necessarily preclude the use of information from a particular society – 'funerary practices' includes an example from a Buckinghamshire graveyard.

Ucko has discussed the use of parallels in a variety of contexts. Perhaps the most detailed discussion is to be found in *Palaeolithic Cave Art*, from which the following passages are quoted, as being representative of his views and a fitting end to this theoretical survey: 'The more varied and the more numerous the analogies that can be adduced, the more likely one is to find a convincing interpretation for an archaeological fact. The more numerous and the more detailed the parallels, the more likely one is to be able to assess the likelihood of a particular parallel being a significant one, and the greater the possibility of checking against the content and the context of the archaeological material' (Ucko and Rosenfeld 1967:157). 'The many occasions when the systematic use of ethnographic parallels has in fact added a deeper understanding to the bare archaeological facts or offered the archaeologist a possible means of interpreting his material are, perhaps, more convincing than any of the theoretical justifications'. (ibid.:158).

Turning now to the earlier part of this century, one can see that the uses made of ethnography, and the arguments on this topic, were very similar to those of the present day. I feel it is not entirely coincidence that the first issue of *Antiquity* (1929) has an article by Firth on Maori hillforts, intended for the edification of archaeologists, with an editorial comment from Crawford that 'we learn, by comparison, to understand the dumb language of prehistoric earthworks', and the *Proceedings of the Prehistoric Society* 1971 has an article on New Zealand fortifications by Bellwood, who writes: 'To readers engaged in the study of European hillforts it is hoped that this paper has presented information which is at least of interest, if not of direct interpretive value.' (Bellwood 1971:92). The intention is Crawford's, if not the language and the assurance. Moreover, in the same volume, Ellison and Drewett make extensive use of Maori data to interpret British hillforts, including data from Firth (1929).

Many of the suggestions and the qualifications discussed in the first part may be found in earlier work, as in Tallgren's 'The method of prehistoric archaeology' (1937). Consider the following with Rouse ('The place of peoples in prehistoric research') in mind: 'In short, forms and types, that is, products, have been regarded as more real and alive than the society which created them and whose needs determined these manifestations of life.' (ibid.:155). And Binford would probably agree with this: 'An undeniable weakness of prehistoric archaeology . . . is the stereotyped attitude adopted towards historical and cultural phenomena. No state of culture, no evolutionary stage, is or ever has been uniform . . . The reconstruction of a given culture-period is a purely theoretical affair.' (ibid.:155).

Tallgren next discusses a problem which has cropped up again and again in European prehistory, and which is familiar to us through the works of Childe, Hawkes, Piggott, etc. I will quote his remarks at some length, to show that the resemblance to the post-war material is not merely due to the judicious selection of ambiguous phrases:

> Another obvious weakness of prehistoric archaeology is the tendency to see, first, a uniform population or ethnic group behind cultural phenomena, that is, behind the forms of material culture; we have also been too apt to see, in cultural connections and particularly in cultural transmissions, the movements and migrations of *peoples* instead rather of the products of different social classes and of commerce . . . Material culture often cannot be equated with a people . . . Even when the

economic structure and geographical environment are identical and are associated with the same mode of living, it is evident in the case of a well-studied living material culture, that 'nationality', 'people', 'ethnic group', does not always impress its mark on the products of material culture, and hardly even those of intellectual culture.

There were undoubtedly ethnographic provinces in prehistoric Europe. It is easiest to distinguish the latest, protohistoric ones, with the help of facts and documents of a historical and philological nature or by means of the study of place-names. One can do this, for example, for the Celtic and Germanic groupings at the beginning of the Roman period. The remarks set down here apply above all to the preceeding prehistoric periods, when it is impossible to throw any light on the nationality of the period by means of the relics of their material culture. (ibid.: 156-8)

I hope that this shows the essential similarity of the problems, over a far greater range than simply the use of ethnography. Though the data and the jargon may have altered as a result of our own cultural development, the subject matter is much the same, as the following examples should indicate.

In 1938, Steward and Setzler wrote an article on 'Function and configuration in archaeology'. In this they set out a hierarchy of archaeological considerations which foreshadows Willey's 'What archaeologists want' (1953) and Hawkes' 'Archaeological theory and method' (1954). Or, to look in the other direction, their call for the classification of artifacts in categories such as horticulture, hunting and dress, rather than stone, bone, wood, etc., is very close to Harlan Smith's 'The ethnological arrangement of archaeological material' (1899).

In 1939, Donald Thompson's 'The seasonal factor in human culture' appeared in the *Proceedings of the Prehistoric Society*. His aim is stated in the opening paragraph: 'In the interpretation of the evidence provided by archaeological investigation it is important to realize its limitations, and to appreciate the complexity of the factors involved. From this point of view it is hoped that a demonstration of the influence of the seasonal factor in the life of a contemporary nomadic hunting group, living under 'stone-age' conditions in Northern Australia, may be of interest. An onlooker, seeing these people at different seasons of the year, would find them engaged in occupations so diverse, and with weapons and utensils differing so much in character, that if he were unaware of the seasonal influence on food supply, and consequently upon occupation, he would be led to conclude that they were different groups.

'Although there is a relatively rich material culture, it can be shown that little would remain to suggest to an archaeologist of the future, the extent and the complexity of the culture.' (Thompson 1939:209).

I would compare the intentions of this article, which is a type of 'object-lesson' for archaeologists taken from ethnography, with recent work such as Ucko's 'Funerary remains', and particular points, such as the inventories of material culture, with Ascher's work on the Seri Indians (1962) or Longacre and Ayres' 'Archaeological lessons from an Apache Wickiup' (1966).

My purpose in citing these three examples from the late thirties is to show that the present range of opinion and diversity of method with regard to the use of ethnography by archaeologists, is in no significant way different from that of earlier prehistorians. The same problems are recognized, the same possibilities and similar pitfalls. No major theoretical advance has been made in the use of ethnography in recent years. The reasons for this, will, I hope, become apparent later, but it should be emphasized here that no advance may be necessary or possible within the present framework of prehistory.

I would even claim that, allowing for cultural differences, the use made of ethnography has not changed since the early modern period, let alone since the heyday of the 19th century. The men who are generally regarded as the founders of modern archaeology had frequent recourse to ethnographic material – and *not* on the lines of Sollas's 'Mousteroids of the Antipodes'. Wilson (1851), Evans (1860), Christy and Lartet (1875) are perhaps best known for the recognition and identification of artifacts, largely by means of comparison with the material culture of primitive groups; Lubbock (1865), Morgan (1877) and Tylor (1865) created a more sweeping outline of prehistoric social development, which relied just as heavily on ethnography – indeed, it is often hard to distinguish the anthropological from the archaeological in their works, just as Huxley (1863) used physical anthropology and Lyell (1863) used geology in an inextricable combination with material which we would now classify as 'prehistory'.

However, the 19th century is comparatively well-known, whereas the earlier period (the later 16th and the 17th century) is not, but deserves to be. In reviewing the overall development of prehistory, it appears that the ethnographic model played an essential part in the emergence of the discipline, and there was no prehistory as we know it until ethnography was incorporated in the discipline.

The first signs of prehistory, as opposed to myth and legend, may be seen in England in the late 16th and 17th centuries, and they are closely connected to the reports of the Elizabethan seamen. The first representation of Ancient Britons as other than Tudors, Romans or mythical heroes is to be found in de Bry's 1590 edition of Harriot's 'Brief and True Report of the new found land of Virginia', to which he added John White's excellent watercolours of the Indians, (White and Harriot both spent some time with the Virginians), and at the very end of the book, five plates entitled:

som picture
OF THE PICTES
which in the olde
tyme dyd habite one part of the
great Bretainne

Below this, de Bry wrote: 'The painter of whow I have had the first of the Inhabitans of Virginia, give me allso thees 5 Figures fallowinge, fownde as hy did assured my in a oolld English cronicle, the which I wold well sett to the ende of thees first Figures, for to showe how that the Inhabitants of the great Bretannie have been in times past as sauuage as those of Virginia.'

Not only does de Bry draw an explicit parallel, but a glance at the plates suggests that the 'oolld cronicle' was brought in merely to provide a little spurious authenticity: the Pictes and their Neighboures are very like the Virginians, and the unpublished set of originals in the British Museum shows even closer kinship to the Chieff Lorde of Roanoac.

The important point here is, that until ethnography was used to provide a model, in a rather literal sense, the Ancient Britons were lordly ancestors of the Tudors, heroic Trojans, or more saintly followers of Joseph of Arimathea. But in the late Elizabethan era, the naked savage became acceptable as a forebear, thanks largely to the high quality of the explorers' reports, which gave a picture of primitive life that could be transposed without any disgrace, even with a certain dignity of independence, to the Originall Inhabitants.

The Virginian analogy was soon taken up by other authors – for example, by John Speed in 1611, by Samuel Daniel in 1612. The material was used to suggest actual physical appearance, to provide a model for social organization, to interpret artifacts, to suggest ways of making and using them, and to explain customs that seemed incomprehensible to the Elizabethans and Jacobeans. Speed, for example, supports the notion that the Ancient Britons went naked – a practice which no civilized man of the 17th century would follow in the British climate – by referring to the Virginians (Speed 1611:179b).

By the end of the century, it was common practice for ethnography to be used as an aid in writing prehistory; and Dugdale, Aubrey and Plot are not that far in their approach from Wilson, Lubbock and John Evans, or even from the 20th century. Ethnography has enlarged on contemporary experience from the time Speed used it to justify the nakedness of his ancestors, to Pownall's musings on the relations of Woodlandmen to Landworkers (1773:241ff), to Ucko's survey of burial customs. It has been used to recognize artifacts and to suggest how they were made and used, from the early days of the Ashmolean, when Dr Robert Plot and his father-in-law Dugdale and his assistant Lhwyd put an end to thunderbolts and elf-arrows (Plot 1686:392-7; Dugdale 1656:778;

Lhwyd 1713:93ff), to Nilsson's classic 'The Primitive Inhabitants of Scandinavia' of 1843, to Binford's Smudge Pits. And it had been in constant use to provide a model of 'uncivilized' existence in the widest sense, so much so that a reversal of the analogy is almost taken for granted: neolithic New Guinea and iron age Africa are not terms that everyone would accept, but they will doubtless not be abandoned.

It was suggested above that the reason why there has been no change in the way that ethnographic parallels are used, nor any development in theoretical approach, is that it is neither possible nor necessary, given the present philosophy of prehistory. It is based on an evolutionary model, which was taken up to the exclusion of virtually all other approaches in the 19th century, before Darwin published *The Origin of Species*, and which was apparent long before this, whether explicitly as in Pownall's New Grange article, or Aubrey's comments on prehistoric Wiltshire (1670:24-6), or implicitly in any of the early authors I have mentioned. It does not seem to me that developments such as environmental archaeology, or the more refined mathematical approaches, fall outside the evolutionary model: they are, fundamentally, variations on technique within the existing framework.

For archaeologists, ethnography has always been viewed, maybe unconsciously, from this standpoint of an evolutionary prehistory – an attitude which can be traced back to the Romans, and which became embedded in the western mind thanks to the classic works of Lubbock, Tylor and Morgan, and the controversy that followed Darwin's publication of *The Origin of Species.*

Over the last 150 years (and before that in more general terms), ethnographic and archaeological societies have been described by reference to similar models – whether technological, economic, social, etc., they are all evolutionary; having this common referent, comparison has been frequent and easy, possibly too easy. This may be one reason why there has been so much argument along the lines of valid 'levels' of analogy and interpretation, which, if one recognizes the influence of the evolutionary model, becomes largely irrelevant. If one can strip off the terminology of 'stages of development', each with its particular set of attributes, both sides of an analogy can be approached in a far less rigid fashion, with fewer constraints. For ethnography, there would be less typecasting of the enormously varied range of material; for archaeology, problems such as the proper definition of the term 'neolithic' would not arise, but for the generally unrecognised boundaries, and the failings, of the evolutionary model.

Prehistory cannot avoid being developmental – no environment is in equilibrium in the long run, and change is a basic factor of all human culture. The problem of culture change must therefore form an integral part of any enquiry. Moreover, the evolutionary model works in a consistent and satisfactory manner, which is normally considered justification enough for its use. One cannot deny that human society has changed and diversified and become increasingly complex. But one can recognize that prehistory is not only reindeer caves, kitchen middens and lake villages, nor a matter of palaeolithic to iron age, nor even 'Man the hunter', 'Domestication and exploitation' and 'Settlement and urbanization'. Certainly, all these approaches are valid, but one does not have to view all the evidence within the same framework.

It is equally important not to force this pattern on the ethnographic material. For present-day primitive societies are *not* a recapitulation – they are not a colour supplement 3D reconstruction of the development of the embryo that became western civilization.

One of the arguments of this paper has been that the preoccupations of archaeologists have changed little over the centuries. Before any disbelieving New Archaeologists of the 1970s dismiss this claim out of hand, I would ask them if the following quotation was not reminiscent of the more progressive, theoretical discussion of this seminar:

> To be serious, I am really of the opinion that if the study of antiquities, in these parts respecting the origin and first ages of nations, be pursued in this line of experimental inductive theorems, which do not pretend to have found out truth, but are only searching their way to it; learning would become more productive of real knowledge.

This was written in 1795, by Thomas Pownall, in the preface to 'An Antiquarian Romance' (p.xiii).

In summary, I would reiterate the point that prehistory has never existed without ethnography, and that archaeologists have relied on models taken from non-western societies to a greater degree than is generally recognized – and it could be said that those who have not are among the less competent prehistorians. Furthermore, I would suggest that, whilst specific parallels, such as ways of working wood or making pottery or clearing forest, will continue to be useful, prehistory will develop most through the more general investigations into the regularities of human behaviour – or lack of them.

REFERENCES

Ascher, R. (1962) Ethnography for archaeology: a case from the Seri Indians. *Ethnology* 1:360.

Aubrey, J. (1670) *An Introduction to the Natural History of the Northern Division of Wiltshire.* London 1714.

Bellwood, P. (1971) Fortification and economy in prehistoric New Zealand. *Proceedings of the Prehistoric Society* 37 (1): 56-95.

Binford, L.R. (1967) Smudge pits and hide smoking: the use of analogy in archaeological reasoning. *American Antiquity* 1, 1-12.

Binford, L.R. (1968a) Archaeological perspectives. *In* Binford, L.R. and S.R. (eds.) *New Perspectives in Archaeology*, 5-32. Chicago, Aldine.

Binford, L.R. (1968b) Post-Pleistocene adaptation. *In* Binford, L.R. and S.R. (eds.) *New Perspectives in Archaeology*, 313-41. Chicago, Aldine.
Binford, L.R. (1968c) Methodological considerations of the archaeological use ethnographic data. *In* Lee, R.B., and Devore, I. (eds.) *Man the Hunter*, 268-73. Chicago, Aldine.
Bray, W. (1972) Land use, settlement pattern and politics in Prehispanic Middle America. *In* Ucko, P.J., Tringham, R. and Dimbleby, G.W. (eds.) *Man, Settlement and Urbanism.* London, Duckworth.
Brothwell, D. (1972) Community health as a factor in urban cultural evolution. *In* Ucko, P.J., Tringham, R. and Dimbleby, G.W. (eds.) *Man, Settlement and Urbanism.* London, Duckworth.
De Bry, T. (1590) *America*, part 1. Frankfort.
Christy, H. and Lartet, E. (1875) *Reliquae Aquitanica.*
Clark, Desmond (1972) Mobility and Settlement patterns in sub-Saharan Africa. *In* Ucko, P.J., Tringham, R. and Dimbleby, G.W. (eds.) *Man, Settlement and Urbanism.* London, Duckworth.
Clark, J.G.D. (1951) Folk culture and the study of European Prehistory. *In* Grimes, W.F. (ed.) *Aspects of Archaeology.*
Clarke, David (1968) *Analytical Archaeology.* London, Methuen.
Crawford, O.G.S. (1927) *Antiquity* 1.
Daniel, S. (1612) *The First Part of the History of England.*
Dugdale, W. (1656) *The Antiquities of Warwickshire Illustrated.*
Ellison, A. and Drewett, P. (1971) Pits and Post-holes in the British Early Iron Age. *Proceedings of the Prehistoric Society* 33 (1), 183-94.
Evans, J. (1860) Reigate Flints. *Proceedings of the Society of Antiquities.* January 1860.
Flannery, K. (1972) The origins of the village as a settlement type. *In* Ucko, P.J., Tringham, R. and Dimbleby, G.W. (eds.) *Man, Settlement and Urbanism.* London, Duckworth.
Freeman, L. (1968) A theoretical framework for interpreting archaeological materials. *In* Lee, R.B. and Devore, I. (eds.) *Man the Hunter.* 262-67.
Forge, A. (1972) Normative factors in the settlement size of neolithic cultivators (New Guinea). *In* Ucko, P.J., Tringham, R. and Dimbleby, G.W. (eds.) *Man, Settlement and Urbanism.* London, Duckworth.
Gathercole, P. (1972) The study of settlement patterns in Polynesia. *In* Ucko, P.J., Tringham, R. and Dimbleby, G.W. (eds.) *Man, Settlement and Urbanism.* London, Duckworth.
Harlan, J. (1972) Crops that extend the range of agricultural settlement. *In* Ucko, P.J., Tringham, R. and Dimbleby, G.W. (eds.) *Man, Settlement and Urbanism.* London, Duckworth.
Harris, D. (1972) Swidden systems and settlement. *In* Ucko, P.J., Tringham, R. and Dimbleby, G.W. (eds.) *Man, Settlement and Urbanism.* London, Duckworth.
Harriss, J. (1971) Explanations in prehistory. *Proceedings of the Prehistoric Society* 37 (1) 38-55.
Hodges, H. (1972) Domestic building material and ancient settlements. *In* Ucko, P.J., Tringham, R. and Dimbleby, G.W. (eds.) *Man, Settlement and Urbanism.* London, Duckworth.
Huxley, T. (1863) *Man's Place in Nature.*
Isaac, G. (1972) Comparative studies of pleistocene site location in East Africa. *In* Ucko, P.J., Tringham, R. and Dimbleby, G.W. (eds.) *Man, Settlement and Urbanism.* London, Duckworth.
Lee, R. (1972) Work effect, group structure and land use in contemporary hunter-gatherers. *In* Ucko, P.J., Tringham, R. and Dimbleby, G.W. (eds.) *Man, Settlement and Urbanism.* London, Duckworth.
Lhwyd, E. (1713) Letters published in *Philosophical Transactions of the Royal Society* 1713:93ff.

Longacre, W.A. and Ayres, J.E. (1966) Archaeological lessons from an Apache Wickiup. *New Perspectives in Archaeology*. 151-60.

Lubbock, Sir John (1865) *Prehistoric Times.*

Lyell, Sir Charles (1863) *The Geological Evidences of the Antiquity of Man.*

MacNeish, R. (1972) The evolution of community patterns. *In* Ucko, P.J., Tringham, R. and Dimbleby, G.W. (eds.) *Man, Settlement and Urbanism.* London, Duckworth.

Morgan, L. (1877) *Ancient Society.*

Nilsson, S. (1863) *The Primitive Inhabitants of the Scandinavian North.* (English edition, ed. Lubbock.)

Plot, R. (1686) *The Natural History of Staffordshire.* Oxford, printed at the Theater.

Pownall, T. (1770) A description of the sepulchral monument at New Grange. *Archaeologia* II:236-75.

Pownall, T. (1795) *An Antiquarian Romance.*

Rowlands, M. (1972) Defence: a factor in the organization of settlements. *In* Ucko, P.J., Tringham, R. and Dimbleby, G.W. (eds.) *Man, Settlement and Urbanism.* London, Duckworth.

Simonsen, P. (1972) The transition from food gathering to pastoralism in N. Scandinavia. *In* Ucko, P.J., Tringham, R. and Dimbleby, G.W. (eds.) *Man, Settlement and Urbanism.* London, Duckworth.

Speed, J. (1611) *The History of Great Britaine.*

Steward, J.H. and Setzler, F.M. (1938) Function and configuration in archaeology. *American Antiquity* 4, 4-10.

Tallgren, A. (1937) The Method of prehistoric Archaeology. *Antiquity* 11, 152-61.

Tringham, R. (1972) Territorial demarcation of prehistoric settlements. *In* Ucko, P.J., Tringham, R. and Dimbleby, G.W. (eds.) *Man, Settlement and Urbanism.* London, Duckworth.

Tylor, E. (1865) *Researches into the Early History of Mankind.*

Ucko, P.J. (1969) Ethnography and archaeological interpretation of funerary remains. *World Archaeology* 1, 262-77.

Ucko, P.J. and Rosenfeld, A. (1967) *Paleolithic Cave Art.* London.

Wilson, D. (1851) *Archaeology and the Prehistoric Annals of Scotland.* Edinburgh.

D.H. MELLOR

On some methodological misconceptions

In the last twenty years an account of method in natural science well summarized in Hempel (1966) has become accepted almost to the point of orthodoxy. For convenience I refer to it hereafter as the 'HD' (hypothetico-deductive) account, though it has many other features and can accommodate statistical and inductive, as well as deductive, inference. That it applies also to social sciences has always been more disputed (e.g. Winch 1958), and the HD account has recently been challenged even on its home ground (e.g. Feyerabend 1962). These disputes have come to concern archaeologists because the HD account has been explicitly adopted by the so-called 'new archaeology' (e.g. Binford 1968; Clarke 1968). In particular the HD account of explanation by deduction from (initial conditions and) independently confirmed theories or covering laws has appealed to the new archaeologists. They have seen in it a rationale for constructing theories of prehistoric societies that shall explain the archaeological record and yet be independently testable, e.g. by observing similar societies of the present day.

That the HD account provides any such rationale for archaeological theorizing has been disputed (e.g. by Leach, this volume, 761-71) on grounds partly general and partly specific to archaeology, Many of the objections, however, credit scientific method with implausible features which the HD account does not entail. These features, if they existed, would certainly prevent any available evidence from confirming theories of prehistoric social structure; they would equally have prevented the confirmation of almost every accepted theory in natural science. Meeting the objections will not of course show that attempts to confirm archaeological theories will be successful, merely that the subject matter does not so guarantee failure as to make the new archaeology a futile enterprise.

1. *Paradigms*

One argument appeals to the fashionable notion of a 'paradigm' (Kuhn 1962). It adopts the premise that introducing the HD account into archaeology amounts to adopting a new paradigm (Sterud, this volume, 3-17). This paradigm is then identified with that of functionalism, which it is said social anthropology is now abandoning in favour of structuralism. It is thence inferred that in due course archaeology will follow suit (Leach, this volume, 762).

If these fraternal anecdotes are to be pertinent to archaeologists at all, they must be supposed to provide reason for archaeology to decline the HD account now and skip straight to the next paradigm, thus catching up with the social anthropologists. In fact the anecdotes clearly provide no such reason. If 'paradigms in this Kuhnian sense are neither good nor bad' (Leach 762) then there is no more reason for archaeology to change to structuralism than for social anthropology to revert to functionalism. Nor does one science having adopted such a paradigm provide any basis in general for the historical prediction that another will follow suit in *N* years, or for belief that it should do so.

In any case the HD account is not a paradigm in Kuhn's sense. Its criteria of explanation apply as well, if at all, to any Kuhnian paradigm. For example, the change from Newtonian to relativistic mechanics was an archetypal paradigm shift. It changed radically what statements of motion needed, and what could provide, mechanical explanation. But none of this bears on the question whether, in both Newtonian and relativistic mechanics, successful explanation needs *inter alia* to be, or to approach, deductive explanation. The arguments for and against the HD account are quite independent of the subject matter of particular sciences and hence quite unaffected by changes in their paradigms.

There is an arguable exception to the HD account's indifference to subject matter, namely that it cannot fit the human sciences. The argument here is that people's actions, being intentional, cannot fall under the covering laws which HD explanation requires. To this argument I return later (497-8). Here I note only that it needs the premise that people *do* indulge in such inherently unpredictable behaviour, not merely that an (e.g. structuralist) assumption to that effect has been made paradigmatic in some other social science.

Lastly, it is essential to realize that HD explanation does *not* entail functionalism (Leach, 762, 768), behaviourism (762-8), or restriction to simple (770), cause-effect (768-9) or economic (768-9) explanation, or any such other specific doctrine about the form or content of admissible laws and theories. Since the archetypal natural sciences plainly do not so restrict themselves in their explanations, the HD account would long ago have been rejected had it attempted to impose such constraints.

Nor does the HD account entail any kind of 'black box' doctrine of an instrumentalist or positivist kind (see e.g. Nagel 1961: ch. 6) restricting the knowable content of scientific theories to what can be checked by more or less direct observation. I turn now to a second argument against the new archaeology which in effect saddles it unjustly with just such a 'black box' doctrine (Leach, this volume, 765-8).

2. *Black boxes*

Logical positivists wished to show how the content of scientific theories could be reduced (i.e. shown logically equivalent) to what can be observed (e.g. Russell 1914). Their premises were that established scientific theory provides empirical knowledge and that observation is the only source of such knowledge. Assertions about unobservable things and events cannot therefore be known, so that knowable theories apparently about unobservables must in fact be reducible to statements about observables. The reductionist programme failed, and the too stringent standards for both knowledge and observation which led to it have long since been relaxed by empiricist philosophers who still maintain an HD account of explanation (e.g., besides Hempel, Braithwaite 1953, Carnap 1966, Nagel 1961). On the HD account explanatory theories must indeed have as consequences the observable matters they purport to explain. But for the theories to be independently knowable these consequences need by no means exhaust their factual content.

Now consider the 'black box' picture of HD explanation in science generally and archaeology in particular (Leach, 765-8). The assumption is that only the output (the archaeological remains) *y* and perhaps the input (the prehistoric environment) *x* are observable. (We may waive the problems of observing the input: the essential objection is not to making inferences to such nonhuman features of the past as the presence of rocks and rivers, climatic changes etc. If we can meet the much stronger objections to inferring the contents of the black box, the input will pose no great problems.) A functional relation *F* may then be establishable between the input and output, but nothing, it is claimed, will follow from this about the contents of the box (in the case of archaeology, the structure of the prehistoric society). Hence any HD theory about the society which is *not* reducible to terms of this functional relation must remain forever unknowable, the merest speculation. In particular, the objection runs, it is vain to hope that the collection of present data could ever confirm such a theory. Such data can at best tell us merely about the input and output of the society; all they can confirm are hypotheses about the value of *F*.

This objection itself rests on positivist premises which no HD account need incorporate and which would rule out theorizing in the most hard core physical sciences, never mind in archaeology (see e.g. Hempel 1958). Knowing the value of *F does* tell us something about the contents of the box, since the knowledge rules out every theory about the contents that entails incompatible values of *F*. And the HD account of course requires acceptable theories about the contents to have such observable consequences and so to be capable of being ruled out by them. An indefinitely large number of mutually incompatible theories may indeed be left, all compatible with what is known of *F*; but that is not a problem peculiar to archaeology. It is an absolutely universal feature of our supposed knowledge of the external world.

Suppose I lift the lid of a literal black box and look inside. This is the process with which inspecting input and output is supposed to be contrasted; it is the process which is supposed to relieve the social anthropologist of the black box problem that the archaeologist has, since the former 'can observe the workings of the system at first hand' (Leach, 767). But still, even in the literal case, all I get is visual output from optical input. Suppose I put my hand in: still merely tactile output. Each test no doubt eliminates more conceivable theories about the contents of the box, but always an indefinite number remain (concerning, in the literal case, such things as hidden mirrors, false bottoms, etc.). The impossibility of ruling out by observation every alternative to a proposed theory is a commonplace in the philosophy of science (and indeed a problem still for any empiricist theory of knowledge). It is not an exciting new thesis about archaeology, nor does it give reason to suppose HD theories of prehistoric societies peculiarly incapable in principle of acquiring enough evidence to justify their acceptance and use in explaining the archaeological record.

Here a further objection may be raised, namely that the only evidence for archaeological theories is of the very kind that they are invoked to explain, i.e. the evidence of items in the archaeological record itself. Now the HD account certainly requires theories to be supported by independent evidence, on the basis of which what they explain could in principle have been predicted. (The connection with prediction is more complex when the theories are essentially statistical, as those of archaeology are likely to be; but the requirement that there should be independent evidence remains in any case.) Without evidence independent of what is to be explained, the purported explanation would be unacceptably *ad hoc*: which, it therefore seems, archaeological theory is doomed to be.

A partial reply to such an objection is that *some* of the archaeological record may suggest a theory which has further consequences testable against the rest of the record. Ideally of course the further consequences concern items not yet *in* the record, which are subsequently acquired precisely to test the theory, but this is not essential. Taking the record as a whole, the theory may then be said to unify it by giving a common explanation of previously unrelated data. In the same way Newton's gravitational theory gave a unified account of both celestial and terrestial motion, and its explaining each was taken as ground for accepting its explanation of the other. Such intellectual bootstrap operations are not in principle unacceptably *ad hoc* nor are they peculiar to archaeology; they are another corollary of theories inevitably going beyond all the data they can explain and against which they can be tested.

Certainly it would help if evidence of quite a different kind *could* be brought to bear on theories of prehistoric social structure. And the final argument I wish to consider is one deployed against the possibility of drawing evidence from facts about the structure of existing societies. This is the argument that rests most heavily on the premise that 'the intentionality of human action implies that, where human beings are concerned, we can never predict what will happen next . . . there is no law-like generalization which will allow anyone to . . . reconstruct the course of past history' (Leach, 764).

3. *People and laws*

Consider the claim that the actions of prehistoric people were intentional and so neither governable by laws of nature nor inferable from the observed actions of our contemporaries. Since we cannot ourselves observe the actions of our prehistoric ancestors, this claim is itself an inference; presumably from the observed intentional actions of our contemporaries and relying on the law of nature that all human actions of a certain kind are intentional and so . . . In short, if the claim is true it falls within the scope of its own scepticism. It cannot be coherently presented as a known fact about the past, nor even as something for which we could now have any evidence.

I do not deny, of course, that much human action is intentional. I deny merely that such action therefore cannot be governed by laws of nature. Consider a simple analogue of man's much publicised innate Chomskean capacity for endlessly original intentional language use (which is supposed to be evidence for the thesis I am here disputing (Leach, 763)): I have a pair of legs, which quite often take me on walks I have never taken before. These walks are (mostly!) intentional, original, in detail highly complex, and doubtless unexplainable in any crude terms of responses to specific stimuli. So I have an innate capacity for walking, provided in the genetic make-up which equipped me with legs, muscles and a controlling nervous system. So what? Who would infer from this that my motions cannot be governed by the laws of mechanics, of the conservation of energy, etc.? And if my *specific* motions are to be explained by my intentions, it still does not follow either that (*a*) intentions cannot be causes or themselves caused, or that (*b*) intentional action is not also susceptible of causal or other law-based HD explanation which need not refer to intentions at all.

There is not space to rehearse here the arguments against (*a*) and (*b*). Those interested may care to refer *inter alia* to Charles Taylor's (1970) retraction of his influential earlier arguments (1964) for (*b*). Certainly there is no consensus on (*a*) or (*b*) sufficient to rule out trying to use data from present societies to test hypotheses about the sorts of intentional action by which prehistoric societies might have left the items archaeology excavates. No doubt the data will always be flimsy, the tests inconclusive, the scope for imaginative alternative theories great. None of this reduces archaeological theorizing to the level of guesswork. The complexity of the subject and the relative paucity of data may well be part of what makes archaeology, like cosmology, endlessly fascinating and likely to be endlessly unsettled. But it is a great mistake to suppose that what is endlessly fascinating and unsettled therefore cannot be scientific. If that were so, there would be very few sciences.

REFERENCES

Binford, L.R. (1968) Archaeological perspectives. *In* Binford, L.R. and S.R. (eds.) *New Perspectives in Archaeology*. Chicago, Aldine.

Braithwaite, R.B. (1953) *Scientific Explanation.* Cambridge, University Press.

Carnap, R. (1966) *Philosophical Foundations of Physics.* New York, Basic Books.

Clarke, D.L. (1968) *Analytical Archaeology*. London, Methuen.

Feyerabend, P.K. (1962) Explanation, reduction and empiricism. *In* Feigl, H. and Maxwell, G. (eds.) *Minnesota Studies in the Philosophy of Science* vol. 3. Minnesota, University Press.

Hempel, C.G. (1958) The theoretician's dilemma. *In* Feigl, H., Scriven, M. and Maxwell, G. (eds.) *Minnesota Studies in the Philosophy of Science* vol. 2. Minnesota, University Press.

Hempel, C.G. (1966) *Philosophy of Natural Science.* Englewood Cliffs N.J., Prentice-Hall.

Kuhn, T.S. (1962) *The Structure of Scientific Revolutions.* Chicago, University Press.

Leach, E. (1972) Concluding Address. This volume, 761-71.

Nagel, E. (1961) *The Structure of Science.* New York, Harcourt, Brace & World.

Russell, B. (1914) *Our Knowledge of the External World.* New York, Open Court.

Sterud, G. (1972) A paradigmatic view of prehistory. This volume, 3-17.

Taylor, C. (1964) *The Explanation of Behaviour*. London, Routledge and Kegan Paul.

Taylor, C. (1970) The explanation of purposive behaviour *and* Reply. *In* Borger, R. and Cioffi, F. (eds.) *Explanation in the Behavioural Sciences.* Cambridge, University Press.

Winch, P. (1958) *The Idea of a Social Science.* London, Routledge and Kegan Paul.

ROBERT LAYTON

Social systems theory and a village community in France

Introduction

A system is a complex of interacting elements. The properties of a system cannot be explained simply by recourse to a study of the properties which its parts exhibit in isolation. Over time the relationships between the various parts of a system may change; the crucial characteristic of a system is not that the relationships between the parts remain constant, but that a change in the state of a certain element causes corresponding adjustments in other elements and in the relationships between them. Systems exist on many scales and with varying degrees of complexity. I propose in this paper to discuss the extent to which one may regard the social life of a single community as a total system. Although the changes discussed here occurred during what must, in archaeological terms, be an extremely short period of time, it is hoped that conclusions reached in this analysis will be relevant to the understanding of archaeological material.

The conclusions will be presented under two headings. I will attempt to determine first to what extent village life can be treated as a systematic whole; second, what are the crucial characteristics of a *social* system.

The notion that social interaction should be interpreted in a systematic fashion was clearly propounded by Emile Durkheim at the end of the 19th century. Throughout this French sociologist's writing runs the idea that the distinctive features of social life derive from the *association* of individuals; that in the association features emerge that cannot be explained by recourse to individual psychology. 'A whole' he wrote in his essay *The Rules of Sociological Method* (1895, English translation, 1938), 'is not identical with the sum of the parts . . . By reason of this principle, society is not a mere sum of individuals. Rather, the system formed by their association represents a specific reality which has its own characteristics'. The role of individual initiative, particularly in change, has thus been the subject of repeated debate, and it is a subject that will be discussed below. It was a point with respect to which Durkheim himself adopted a rather ambiguous position, arguing on the one hand that no individual could greatly modify the structure of his society; on the other that the deviant or criminal of one age points to the morality of the next.

In England, Durkheim's treatment of the systematic nature of social interaction was taken up by those anthropologists frequently collectively referred to as the *Functionalists.* It was an unfortunate tendency among these writers that, when expounding their argument, they were inclined to favour the comparison of a society with a rather different kind of system: the animal organism; a comparison that also confused the analysis of social change.

The clearest statement of this analogy is perhaps that presented by Radcliffe-Brown in his essay, 'On the concept of function in the social sciences' (Radcliffe-Brown, 1952:178-87). The animal organism, he writes, is an 'agglomeration' of cells and fluids arranged in relation to one another. Over a period of time the constituent cells are replaced by others, but the structure of the organism remains constant. The function of each process within the body is the contribution that it makes to the continued life of the organism as a whole. In social life human beings are linked by social relationships to form an integrated whole, the society. The function of each institutionalized pattern of activity is the contribution it makes to the continuing unity of the social aggregate. Radcliffe-Brown is here careful to point out that whereas, in the course of its lifetime, an animal organism does not generally undergo modification in its internal structure, a social system can be modified without in consequence losing its coherence or integrity. It seems true to say, however, that in stressing the systematic nature of both animal organism and human society, many forgot that these are not the same kind of system. The animal organism works to maintain its particular structure in the face of environmental change; the term used for this by biologists is *homeostasis.* The equilibrium theorist in social science has pointed out that in any society there is a set of norms, values and expectations protected by sanctions which tend to restrain deviance. For such theorists it is the normative patterns of interaction that assume prime significance. It is perhaps unfortunate that the recent reaction against this school of thought has led some people to minimize the significance of the patterns of interaction that give a social system its characteristic form at any one point in time.

The recent work of Easton, Buckley and others has evoked fresh interest in the existence and nature of social systems. Their ideas are well-summarized by Mackenzie (1967). Buckley had discussed the problems inherent in use of the organic analogy, suggesting that rather than look for parallels between a social system and an animal organism, greater similarities can be discovered between a social system and an animal *species* (Buckley, 1967). Both are distinguished by the fact that rather than tending to maintain a fixed structure in the face of a changing environment they frequently respond by undergoing internal modification. But Buckley stresses that even here there are important ways in which the two kinds of system differ. Natural selection is a random process: genetic mutations constantly occur but may or may not lead to variations in the phenotype that happen to be particularly appropriate to the contemporary environment. Appropriate mutations tend to be transmitted to succeeding generations. It is possible to talk of the exchange of genetic material as the transfer of a kind of information, and it is this exchange that gives an animal species its coherence as a system. Members of a human society also exchange information, but they exchange it in quite a different way: by direct observation of one another's behaviour, by speech, by non-verbal communication in gesture, and so on. Further, whichever of these forms the exchange takes, something quite different is involved here: pecple can learn from experience and they can communicate what they have learned. At least in some small degree, social change is not as random as natural selection: it involves a degree of deliberation and calculation on the part of the participants, however partially-informed the premisses of that deliberation may be. Actors can soon profit from their neighbours' experience. It is this fact that allows us to assess the significance of individual behaviour in change.

The village of Pellaport, in which I worked for nine months during 1969,* is situated in the northern French Jura, in the Department of Doubs. It has a population of a little over 250. For many centuries the economy of the region has been primarily one of dairy farming. In 1969 there were 22 farmers resident in the village. Each owned a small herd of dairy cattle (ranging from 3 to 20 animals). Nine-tenths of each farmer's land was under grass, some providing summer grazing for the cattle, some winter hay, for during six months of the year the cattle are housed continuously within their quarters in the large farm houses.

A most important aspect of social life in the area has been the existence of numerous small associations formed by neighbouring farmers who come together to pool their milk, jointly manufacturing cheeses for sale outside the region. The earliest written record of such an association occurs in a document dated 1264 (Lambert, 1953:175). Since the late 19th century the structure of these groups has been governed by French law, according to the regulations concerning the constitution of agricultural co-operatives. Further, there has long been a tendency towards more intensive agricultural

* This fieldwork was carried out from the University of Sussex, under the direction of F.G. Bailey. It was financed by a grant from the Social Science Research Council.

production; the smaller dairy associations coming together to construct better-equipped buildings and the farmers modernizing their techniques. The table below is taken from Daveau (1959:284); it illustrates the rate of this change, within the Department of Doubs, over a period of a century and a half.

	1811	1851	1903	1953
number of dairy associations	426	643	407	301
total weight of cheese manufactured in kilos x1,000	3,300	4,479	5,626	14,937

This paper, however, will deal only with developments that have taken place since the Second World War. During this period many people have left agriculture to find work in factories or offices in the towns and, at the same time, the size of each remaining agricultural household has decreased. Farmers have come to rely to a progressively greater extent upon agricultural machinery. The reasons for this are as follows. Since the late 1950s the markets available to French farmers have been saturated with agricultural goods. The producers have thus found it difficult to increase their incomes at a rate comparable to that achieved by industrial workers. Encouraged by the government many have therefore found other forms of employment. In order to make French agricultural produce more competitive the government has also promoted numerous technological innovations, working through the agency of extension workers based on Departmental *Chambres d'Agriculture.* Between 1954 and 1963 the number of farms in the Department of Doubs fell from 9,546 to 8,846; during approximately the same period the number of people engaged in agriculture dropped from 46,000 to 26,000. Yet these figures do not indicate a decline in the local importance of agriculture. As the children of former agriculturalists turn to work elsewhere many of the smaller farms have been absorbed by others. Subsidiary crops have been abandoned as farmers concentrate on the one activity to which the region is best suited. In 1952 there were 78,450 dairy cattle in the Department, producing on average 2,900 litres of milk per cow per year. By 1964 the number of dairy cattle had risen to 107,400; the annual milk yield to 3,000 litres per cow (figures cited from *Economie Rurale*, 1967-8).

Evidence of this process may be recognized at two levels: the technological and the social. It will be argued that there are certain parallels between these two aspects of change. Briefly, the pattern has been as follows. The farmers of the region have been exposed to agricultural innovations of various kinds: new techniques for animal breeding, new varieties of crops, machinery to perform tasks that otherwise would have to be carried out by hand. It will be shown how two of the available technological devices (the baler and the milking machine) allow the farmer to work more efficiently, and the factors which lead him to adopt such an innovation will be considered. There are other topics, such as the role of change agents in the region, or the status of those in the community who are the first to accept an innovation, which can only briefly be mentioned.* The second half of this paper will outline some of the social consequences of the changing economic pattern. In villages such as Pellaport, relatively close to an urban centre, the decline in agricultural employment has meant not only the emigration of villagers to the towns, but also that an increasing number of those *resident in the village* are no longer agriculturalists. In consequence a number of adjustments have been made necessary in the way that the community's affairs are administered, and it is in studying these that the systematic nature of social interaction in the village is most clearly revealed.

Technological Change

Aspects of technological change will be dealt with first. I will be concerned to assess both the significance of personal choice and the nature of the inter-relationship between the increasing size of the farm and the 'responses' provoked by the need to modernize one's techniques if this expansion is to continue.

There appear to be two ways in which a technological innovation may provide an improvement on existing practice. It may make it possible to carry out a particular process more rapidly or more thoroughly, or it may make possible the simultaneous performance of what were previously two separate tasks.

Most technological innovations introduced to Pellaport in recent years have proved advantageous in certain respects, but disadvantageous in others. The tractor, for instance, is more powerful than a horse or ox, but it needs to be controlled more rigorously. This may necessitate actually increasing the size of the farmer's labour force. If we are to understand the farmer's motives in accepting or rejecting this and other innovations we need to look at the way in which he himself has perceived the new trait; for he may be deterred by its manifest disadvantages, fail to exploit its benefits as fully as he might, or even be so overwhelmed by manifest benefits that he fails, until he has adopted the innovation, to recognize its drawbacks. We need also to study the circumstances in which the farmer reaches his decision; for what appears advantageous in one context may not seem so in another.

Some factors leading to the decision to mechanize

What prompts a farmer to buy a milking machine or a baler? There are many levels at which contributory causes may be recognized.

* There is more information on these topics in another paper to be published in *Debate and Compromise*, ed. F.G. Bailey. Oxford, Blackwell (*in press*).

Sometimes a technique ceases to seem satisfactory because the actor learns about available alternatives, hearing about a new device or seeing it being used by another. Often during the discussion of a novel agricultural technique the word *penible* (laborious) would be introduced into the discussion. It seemed to represent quite an important notion, for it is when a farmer comes to judge his present techniques *unnecessarily* laborious that he may set about looking for some alternative. One of the older farmers once complained that the young men nowadays expected to be able to stay in bed until five-thirty in the morning, whereas his father had always risen at three to milk the cattle, and at two-thirty if he had to feed the oxen before starting work in the fields. And now, he said, they don't even care to sow grain by hand because the seeds become embedded in the palms of their hands.

Temporary crises in the household may help to make tasks more laborious. When asked why he had purchased a milking machine, one farmer asserted that his motive had been the impending birth of his second child. With his wife temporarily withdrawn from the labour force he had found it impossible to milk all the cows alone, by hand. Another farmer explained that he had purchased his milking machine after his father retired from active work. Not having married, this man found his own labour insufficient to milk all the cows in the stable.

Yet such crises cannot wholly provide the motives for technological change. Behind them lies the constant pressure exerted on the farmer to expand his holding if it is to remain a viable proposition. The progression towards larger and more specialized exploitations is a continuous process, prompted by the gradually changing economic conditions in which the villagers find themselves. While many, when asked for their reasons for buying a milking machine, found them at the level of such crises in the domestic cycle as those discussed above, some explained their decision simply in terms of the fact that they had enlarged their dairy herd to such an extent that it was no longer possible to milk all by hand. It may be that, in a similar fashion, one can cope with the first childbirth, but that by the time the second is approaching the cattle have become too numerous for the farmer to milk all single-handed. Again, it may be feasible for a farmer to harvest 9 hectares of hay without a baler, but by the time he must gather in the produce of 18 hectares (if he is to keep his stable supplied throughout the winter) he would probably find that the fine weather had ended before all could be harvested by hand. If the farmer decides he can no longer work without a machine, it may not be that as the older farmer quoted above might have claimed he is becoming lazy, simply that his work-load has increased. It must, however, be stressed that a particular method may be practised throughout a range of conditions. The effect of continued agricultural expansion is simply to make the farmer's established mode of operation progressively less appropriate to its contemporary context. Often it appears that the role of the relatively superficial event cited by him as the cause of his decision was in reality something of a 'trigger' which finally obliged him to adjust his method of working, achieving a new equilibrium between the demands of production and agricultural technique. As will be seen below, similar observations may be made about change at the social level. Enquiry made it clear that different farmers had mechanized their stables at quite different points. The smallest stable equipped with a milking machine in 1969 contained 8 cows, the largest without one, 12. One farmer, who bought his machine in 1967, waited until he had 16 cows.

Perception, evaluation and communication

There are many ways in which a farmer may profit from the experience of his neighbours when he makes a decision concerning his own techniques. I cite one instance here. Local garage owners play an important role in promoting the diffusion of agricultural innovations. Rather than sell their wares with printed advertisements they tend to cultivate close personal relationships with the most advanced of their farmer-clients. One garage-owner asserted that no farmer would buy a piece of equipment until he had had an opportunity to experiment with it himself, and that he (the garage-owner) would therefore straight away demonstrate a new device to those whom he expected to be most interested, not waiting until enquiries about it reached him from the farmers.

When his old mechanical scythe broke during the hay harvest Nicolas Jouffroy, one of the young farmers in Pellaport, arranged to borrow a new, rotary scythe from his regular garage. He experimented with two rotary models during the summer of 1969, but eventually decided to purchase another of the older-fashioned reciprocating types such as he had used before. Although rotary scythes had been available in the region since 1966, he was the first of the villagers to experiment with them. During the course of his exploratory use of the new device one of his heifers gave premature birth to its first calf on the village's communal pasture. After the evening delivery of milk to the village dairy four other farmers accompanied Nicolas to the common to help him capture the heifer and recover the calf's body. Afterwards Nicolas invited them to his house for a drink, and the main topic of conversation was his rotary mower. How quickly, the others wanted to know, could it cut a strip of grass? How satisfactorily did it cope with uneven ground? Did it throw up earth and stones? How much did it cost? In revealing his experience Nicolas perhaps repaid the others for their help.

Such instances, however, raise the question of the degree to which the actors are perfectly informed of the consequences of their actions. To what extent do their decisions accord with what would seem rational in light of the apparent facts of the situation? The milking machine and baler will be discussed in some detail in order to examine this problem.

By 1969 nine of the twenty-two farmers in the village had already installed a milking machine in their stable. The first was purchased in 1962. The machine is designed to imitate the action of a calf suckling the teats. A metal cup, lined with rubber, fits over each of the cow's four teats. A tube passes from each into a small metal churn where the milk collects. From the churn runs an outlet pipe through which air is drawn, connected via a pipe running the length of the stable to an air pump. This pump creates a suction pressure that is intended to equal the pressure that would be exerted by a calf's mouth, and the pressure is applied to the teats alternately.

It is not only quicker to milk one's cows by machine; the figures I collected suggested that one gained at least as much, if not more, milk than when working by hand. The relative effectiveness of the two techniques can be estimated from the following table:

	Yield in kilos/minute	Average yield per cow in kilos	Average rate cows/hour
Milking by *hand**	0.65	4.7	9
Milking by *machine*†	1.28	5.8	13

* 54 cows in 7 stables
† 110 cows in 8 stables

However, despite the apparently greater effectiveness of the machine, this method involved the farmer and his wife in greater labour over cleaning equipment. Most washed the small churns into which the milk is drawn, the delivery pipes and the cups which fit over the cow's teats, at least once a day, often using specially boiled water, a scrubbing brush and soap. The pipes leading from the stable to the pump have also to be cleaned occasionally, and to do this a representative must come from the suppliers. The need to wash the complex equipment was frequently cited by those who continued to work by hand as a reason against purchasing a machine, particularly if they felt they had too few cows to make hand-milking unnecessarily laborious.

A further argument advanced in favour of hand-milking, one proposed both by those who continued with this technique and by those who had purchased a machine, was that by hand-milking a cow one obtained more milk. Yet, as I have noted, observation suggested that the opposite of what the villagers claimed was in fact the truth. In this instance it does seem demonstrable that actors reach their decisions on the basis of inaccurate information. The dairy records were consulted in order to discover how much milk had been produced by each stable during 1968. The division of each figure by the number of milch cows in that stable allows one to gain a more accurate impression of the relative yields gained by hand and by machine.

The results are shown in the following table:

Average yield per cow for those with a machine	3,116 kilos
Average yield per cow for those milking by hand	2,972 kilos

It has been suggested that those employing a milking machine may be those who also happen to use the most advanced techniques for feeding cattle, and that it is this which has led to their gaining more milk per cow. Whatever the truth of this, I would stress the fact that the villagers' contention that one gains significantly more milk by hand is not supported by these figures. One estimate, supplied by a farmer without a machine, was that 10 cows milked by hand would yield the same as 11 milked by machine. Another, provided by a man who already had a machine, was that 12 milked by hand would provide an equal quantity to 14 milked with the machine. Clearly those who believe this to be true may delay purchasing a machine until they find it impossible to continue working by hand, whereas in fact the extra yields apparently provided by the machine for a farmer with ten cows would cover its cost in about four years.*

The reason why it is quicker to milk cattle with the machine is not that each cow may separately be milked more rapidly; averages taken from two samples of 51 cows each revealed that it took 7 minutes to milk the average cow by hand, 6.75 minutes to milk it by machine. Time is gained because if one has two churns, two cows could be milked simultaneously by machine and a third, perhaps, by hand. Alternatively, the task of clearing out the stable can be performed while the machine is in operation. A farmer who fails to appreciate this fact will not exploit the machine to its fullest advantage. One villager had purchased a machine but, not having very many cows, had equipped it with only one churn. Despite the fact that he evidently expended less energy in milking than he would otherwise have done, this man failed to achieve a rate greater than 10 cows per hour; little better than the average performance of those who work by hand.

I turn now to the case of the baler, a device used for gathering mown hay from the fields. It packs the dried grass into large blocks which are then stacked on a trailer.

Those who harvested their hay by hand generally recruited a work

* The calculation is as follows. The cost of the milking machine is 3,000 F. The value of milk taken to the village dairy is approximately 0.50 F/kilo. Each cow appears to give an average yield of 150 kilos more per year when milked by machine. If a man has 10 cows it will take him $\frac{3000}{0.50 \times 150 \times 10} = 4$ years to recoup the cost of the machine.

force of four people. The hay was pitchforked onto a trailer towed behind the tractor. One person sits in the tractor seat, one pitchforks the hay onto the trailer and one stands on the trailer, receiving the hay and packing it down. The fourth person walks behind with a large rake, gathering the hay that has been missed by the pitchfork. Those who have purchased a baler generally reduce their work force to two. The baler now performs the task of picking up the hay from the field; it is towed between the tractor and the trailer. One man drives the tractor, the other stands on the trailer receiving and stacking the hay. The efficiency of the baler rendered use of the large rake unnecessary. The relative efficiency of the two techniques may be gauged from the following table:

	ares/trailer	minutes/trailer	ares/minute
By hand (2.5 hectares)	16	34	0.47
With baler (5.0 hectares)	39	23.5	1.60

Not only does the baler allow one to pack more hay onto a single trailer (thus necessitating fewer journeys back to the farmhouse), it also allows the gathering of hay to be carried out at a considerably faster rate. As was the case with the milking machine, however, fullest exploitation of its advantages demands a certain perception of how best to use the machine. I cite the case of one farmer who insisted on continued use of the large rake. Pierre had a work force of three: himself, his wife and his eldest daughter, aged about ten. The girl he put on the driving seat of the tractor, while he himself stood on the trailer to receive the hay. His wife was given the task of raking up loose hay which the baler had failed to gather. This arrangement turned out to be inefficient in two respects. First, his daughter was too small to do anything but grip the steering wheel of the tractor, and at the end of each run along the length of the field Pierre had to jump down to help her turn the tractor around. Second, his wife was repeatedly left behind in her attempts to rake up the few strands of loose hay that remained. He would evidently have done better had he adopted the arrangement employed by Nicolas Jouffroy, who put his wife in the tractor seat and decided to ignore the few strands of hay that were missed by the baler. If he noticed a relative large quantity still lying in the field, he simply instructed his wife to return in the opposite direction, gathering it with the baler. Nicolas was (on average) requiring only 18.5 minutes to fill a trailer, whereas it had taken Pierre 37.5 minutes; yet Nicolas apparently lost little hay in the process, since to fully load a trailer he required only 32 *ares* of land against Pierre's 30 *ares*.*

* My thanks are due to Mike Rowlands (who spent a month in the village helping to gather material) for the information on Pierre's methods. It should be noted, in Pierre's defence, that he encountered one or two other problems, not mentioned here, in gathering his hay.

Conclusion

The material presented in this section illustrated how the acceptance of innovation may follow a number of stimuli, their consequence being eventually to render the farmer's current techniques inappropriate to the context within which he operates. It has also been shown how actors may profit from others' experiments. Nevertheless, the importance of the actors' role in perceiving and evaluating their situation has been suggested in the evidence that some do not adopt what objectively would appear to be for them the most apt procedures.

Institutional change

Some of the social consequences of the changing occupational pattern will now be considered. The principles according to which the community administers its affairs will first be outlined. Having done this I will then discuss some of the changes that have taken place in the way that certain joint resources have been controlled.

The inhabitants of the village belong to a single *commune*, the smallest unit in French local administration. The internal affairs of each *commune* are administered by an elected council, whose size depends on the number of inhabitants contained in the *commune*. In Pellaport there are eleven councillors. There is an election once every six years, and the chosen eleven select a *Maire* from among themselves. The *Maire* acts as the local representative of the Central Government. Any national legislation that directly affects the *commune* must be put into effect by the *Maire*. Where the village's internal affairs are concerned, however, it is the municipal council that has final authority. Its members can instruct the *Maire* to put their decisions on the public affairs of the village into practice (Chapman, 1953:58-62).

With what activities is the council concerned? There is a large area (385 hectares) of communally-owned forest, the revenue from which provides an important part of the money that finances street-lighting, the pumping of drinking water to the village reservoir and other expenses. One of the council's responsibilities is to decide which trees should be felled each year (a task which in practice is delegated to a professional forester who lives in the village), and how best to spend the money which the sale of these trees brings in. The council is also responsible for arranging the allocation of a winter's supply of firewood from the forest to each household. In the past it also allocated strips of the communally-owned grassland that covers the higher level ground to each house, a resource that could either be mown for hay or grazed during the summer by cattle from the family stable. Certain tasks carried out on behalf of the community are paid for out of communal funds. Among these are such activities as the emptying of dustbins, the chopping of firewood to supply the church and village hall during the winter, and the breaking of stones to pave the tracks that cross the fields and forest. Any villager who wishes to perform one of these tasks submits a tender to the council, and the councillors choose from among those judged capable of performing the task, that man who asks for the lowest payment. This procedure is known as allocation *par soumission.*

The village dairy co-operative is structured according to a very similar set of principles and, as was noted above, its constitution is quite closely governed by French Law. The affairs of the association are managed by a committee of nine farmers. One third of the committee retires from office each year, and at the annual general meeting three new members are elected by a secret ballot. This committee chooses a president from among its members at the first committee meeting following the *reunion générale.* It allocates a number of tasks *par soumission*; work such as the loading of cheeses on to the lorry that comes from a wholesale warehouse in Lyons once a month. The committee is responsible for employing a dairy man to manufacture cheeses from the members' milk, and for the purchase of new equipment to be installed in the dairy building that stands at the centre of the village. Each member, on joining the association, must contribute a certain amount to the co-operative's capital. He may contribute more than the minimum required by law, but he remains entitled only to a single vote at meetings. The changing economic pattern, it will be remembered, has had two major consequences. Men have been obliged to specialize if they are successfully to participate in the market economy. No longer can a man combine a morning job in a factory in the nearby town with the running of a small farm; now he must either work or farm full-time. In consequence, as has been noted, many villagers are now no longer directly involved in agriculture. According to Daveau (1954:117) the councils of some villages in the Jura have as a result become divided into bitterly-opposed factions, farmers and non-farmers each pressing their particular interests. At the same time that this division increases, those who continue as farmers have been obliged to modernize their techniques, in order to increase the output of their exploitations. It is crucial to note that both these trends have been developing at a steady pace. The following table abstracts the figures for a few selected years from the local dairy association's records. Here the farmers of Pellaport are combined with those of the neighbouring hamlet of Montoiseau, who belong to the same co-operative.

	1948	1953	1958	1963	1968
number of members in co-op	46	43	40	35	31
total milk prod. in kilos	458,197	611,571	657,848	866,962	1,109,022

Nevertheless, despite the steadiness of this development, the accompanying adjustments in the pattern of village administration, like the modifications a farmer makes to his agricultural equipment, have been sporadic. I now consider a number of these changes.

During the forty or more years that followed the First World War a number of items of agricultural equipment were purchased by the municipal council, using a part of the income from the sale of trees in the communal forest. In recent years, however, it became increasingly clear that to spend funds to which the whole community had a right on items that would benefit only a fraction was not a justifiable policy. The municipal council therefore voted, during one of its quarterly meetings in 1966, to abolish the practice. If agricultural equipment has been jointly purchased since that date, it has been bought by a number of farmers who have come together as friends and agreed to share the cost on an informal basis.

The second administrative change I outline is that of the establishing of an agricultural co-operative in the village to control exploitation of the communally-owned pasture. For many years before the co-operative's formation in 1954, a large portion of the common had been grazed by the villagers' cattle. The municipal council hired a cow-herd (generally an elderly villager) to guard the cattle during the day, and each farmer paid him an agreed sum for his work. There were a number of reasons why this arrangement eventually became regarded as unsatisfactory. There were no fences around the common and in order to prevent his animals from straying into the surrounding fields or forest the herdsman had to keep them in one group. This prevented the cattle from seeking out the best grass. Because the common land lacked a water supply it was necessary to bring the animals back to the village cattle troughs at midday. Not only did the common receive no fertilizer, there was a constant tendency for its value to be further reduced by the spread of brushwood and the proliferation of mole hills. During the period between the First and Second World Wars some attempt was made to counter this when the dairy association arranged informally for each farmer to go in turn to clear a portion of the common land. Some did what was expected of them but some did not and gradually this rather inefficient arrangement was abandoned. Finally it may be noted that the portion of the commons being used as a source of hay was allocated to each household according to the number of *human* occupants. Since during the post-War period the size of the household was decreasing as consistently as the number of animals in the remaining stables rose this, too, was becoming an unsatisfactory method of exploiting the land.

Despite all these manifest disadvantages the farmers of the village persevered with the traditional arrangement until finally they were overtaken by a sudden crisis: in 1954 it was no longer possible to discover anyone willing to work all day at the task of cow-herd. At this point several of the younger farmers came together and announced their intention of forming a new co-operative. An inaugural meeting was held and those present drew up a set of regulations embodying all those required by the government, electing a committee of nine men to manage their affairs. Because the cattle could no longer be guarded all day the first task was to install a fence around the portion they had arranged to rent from the commune. Eight kilometres of fence were required in all, and the materials were purchased with money borrowed from communal funds. Once the fencing had been carried out it was necessary only to find someone willing to lead the cattle to and from the pasture. The co-operative undertook to pay him a lump sum drawn from the members' annual contributions. Later a pump and reservoir were installed to take water to the top of the hill, so that it would no longer be necessary to lead the cattle back at midday. A machine that could be towed behind a tractor was bought to spread chemical fertilizer and an arrangement made to purchase the necessary chemicals in bulk. The task of spreading the chemicals, together with those of clearing brushwood and molehills, have since been allocated *par soumission* by the co-operative's committee; a more effective arrangement than the informal one adopted between the Wars.

At the time of the co-operative's formation portions of the common land were still used as a source of hay but, as the number of animals which farmers wished to graze increased, the co-operative rented a progressively greater area. Finally the municipal council decided in 1967 to abolish the communal right to hay, and at this point the co-operative gained control of the entire common. It was agreed that non-farmers in the village who required small quantities of hay for their rabbits or the single cow they kept to supply the household with milk would be able to rent certain portions of common land, but now they, like the co-operative, would be required to pay a realistic rent, 'as though to another proprietor'. The present arrangement is generally felt to reduce any possibility of *jalousie* developing between the farmers and their non-agriculturalist neighbours, since all stand to gain equally from the money passing into communal funds as rent for the common land is collected.

Finally, for my third example, I want to turn back to an earlier period. Despite the antiquity of the dairy associations it was in many cases only after the Second World War that they were set up in their present form. At the beginning of the century the regional dairy economy suffered a decline; a trend which Daveau (1959:286) attributes to an increase in the number of cheeses imported from Switzerland. Many of the old associations decided at that time to relinquish control of the production and marketing of cheeses and instead to rent their buildings and equipment to an independant middleman who would buy their milk at an agreed price, accepting responsibility for the selling of the cheeses he manufactured. By 1929 almost two-thirds of the dairy associations in the Department of Doubs (among which was that of Pellaport) had adopted this new system. It proved, however, to be not without serious disadvantages, and eventually a rift developed between the farmers of the region and the men who processed their milk. For many the final crisis came during the German Occupation of the Second World War. The entrepreneur dairymen were quick to appreciate the profits that could be made by selling dairy produce on the Black Market and, being under no obligation to return any portion of their profits to the farmers, quickly amassed large sums of money. It was said in retrospect that many of these dairymen had arrived from Switzerland 'with their possessions in a pocket-handkerchief', yet a few years later were to be seen driving in large cars. As one French writer put it, 'cette fortune hâtivement acquise offusqua les paysans': this prematurely-acquired fortune outraged the local people (Lambert, 1953:176). After the Liberation, the men of many villages dismissed their local dairyman and restored control of cheese production to the dairy associations. Faced with a choice between two alternative procedures intended to achieve the same end one was selected and only later was it discovered that the chosen institution allowed too great a scope for the exploitation of the body of the community by a single man. As was true at the technological level, the villagers have thus at times failed fully to anticipate the outcome of a change instituted in the control of joint resources.

Conclusions

What conclusions may be drawn from this material? I believe, firstly, that the nature of the changes discussed here clearly demonstrates that the social activities of the community may be regarded as tending towards a systematic whole. Economic stimulus from the wider society has resulted in a changing occupational pattern, and this in turn has generated modifications both in social institutions and in the realm of agricultural technology.

But what kind of a system are we dealing with? Clearly, it is not a completely self-contained one, for it has been seen that certain of its parts (in particular the municipal council) are themselves parts of a wider whole (such, for example, as the French system of local administration). Many areas of village life: its principles of inheritance, the nature of the obligations incurred in marriage; these as well as the agricultural co-operatives are shaped by the village's participation in the French State.

One may in several respects directly compare the processes of recent change in the social and the technological spheres. When changes have been effected in the administration of the community's resources they have been built out of procedures required by the French State. It is in very much this way that the possibilities for technological change are to an important degree limited by the availability of equipment on the market. The few genuine instances of local innovation have not been of any very great consequence. Yet this should not be allowed to conceal the fact that individual initiative is significant, even in determining the direction of institutional change. The government does not *require* a community to administer any particular resource by means of a co-operative, it merely specifies the form that any extant co-operative must take. These recent political changes may thus be distinguished from those following the Revolution of 1789, since the earlier ones *imposed* both a new pattern of local administration, and a new Code of Civil Law upon the French. In as much as there is some choice so the processes by which decisions are made become significant. A comparison of Pellaport with neighbouring villages reveals that elsewhere other courses of action have been adopted: just as individual farmers are free to choose between a number of alternative methods in exploiting their farms, so different communities have adopted different policies. Of six communities in the immediate vicinity only three possess dairy co-operatives who control the production and marketing of their own cheese. The remaining three continue to rely on independant entrepreneurs, although in recent years any temptation on the entrepreneurs' part to exploit the farmers has been countered by the knowledge that they might soon be dismissed by dissatisfied clients. In three villages pasture co-operatives have been established, but in two the common land remains directly under the control of the municipal council. Indeed in one the common land was still (in 1969) unfenced and untreated with chemical fertilizers. In one of the surrounding communities a co-operative had been formed jointly to purchase agricultural equipment, but after a few years this association dissolved following a quarrel about how best to allocate the cost of repairs. The occurrence of such local experiments in administration is of great importance for, although in the past apparently inappropriate decisions have been reached concerning village policy, communities are able to profit from one another's experience. A conscious effort is made in this respect, villagers seeking information from kin and friends in neighbouring communities. This pattern may directly be compared with that of the exchange of information about technological innovations that occurs between farmers.

It may further be noted that in social, as in technological change, the kind of systematic relationship under study is not a *mechanical* one. Modification in the state of one component does not automatically provoke an immediate and quantifiably predictable response among the other parts of that system. Just as a farmer may continue to employ a progressively more outmoded technique until some relatively superficial crisis obliges him to make a change, so a community may persist with a certain procedure until conditions render it quite untenable. I have shown how, in Pellaport, it was evidently the impossibility of hiring a cow-herd that finally prompted the formation of the pasture co-operative, and how the era of the entrepreneur dairyman came to an end, in many communities, after their illicit dealings during the German Occupation. Von Bertalanffy has maintained that in any system 'a change in a certain element causes a change in *all other elements* and in the total system' (1950:146; my emphasis). In dealing with social systems it may be preferable to adopt a more cautious formulation, such as that proposed by Radcliffe-Brown, namely: 'It is a corollary of the hypothesis of the systematic connection of features of social life that changes in some features are *likely to* produce changes in other features' (1950:7; my emphasis). I do not believe that archaeologists should assume that a change in natural or social conditions *automatically* provokes 'responses' in any area of social life.

Finally, a point may be made *à propos* of the recent work of Frederik Barth, whose studies have encouraged anthropologists to interpret social change as the outcome of a process of rational decision-making by actors during a period when the conditions within which they operate undergo modification. The material presented in this paper suggests two reasons for being careful in one's reliance on such an assumption. In the first place, different actors, even within the same social milieu, evidently seek to maximize different ends. Some farmers apparently do not wish to enlarge their farms, even if others do. Perhaps they prefer the security of known procedures to the uncertainty of innovation. Secondly, the actors do not always, even when they change their patterns of behaviour, adopt what – objectively – appears the most rational means of achieving their chosen goal. This second point might be of interest to those archaeologists who assert that human behaviour is functionally adapted to the conditions of a people's physical environment. It must be emphasized that just as a failure correctly to assess the merits or disadvantages of a technological innovation may have serious consequences for the individual farmer, so the failure to perceive the outcome of a political innovation (and this was evidently the case in the initial decision to adopt independant entrepreneurs in the dairies of the Jura) may greatly limit the effectiveness with which a community utilizes its resources.

What one has demonstrated, by placing a local community within a wider context, is nothing more than the parameters of probable change. The prediction of what courses of action will actually be chosen would require a knowledge of the disposition of individual actors and an awareness of a multiplicity of contributing factors, smaller or greater in their individual impact, but all capable of affecting the actual course of change.

Acknowledgment

This paper has been revised in the light of discussion both at a seminar at University College, London, and at the Sheffield conference. I am particularly grateful to Professor M.G. Smith for his comments on the former occasion.

REFERENCES

Bertalanffy, L. von (1950) An outline of general systems theory. *British Journal of the Philosophy of Science* 1, 134-65.

Buckley, W. (1967) *Sociology and Modern Systems Theory.* Englewood Cliffs, N.J., Prentice-Hall.

Chapman, B. (1953) *Introduction to French Local Government.* London: Allen and Unwin.

Daveau, S. (1954) Une communauté Jurassienne au 18ieme siecle. *Revue de Geographie de Lyon,* 29, 117-29.

Daveau, S. (1959) *Les Régions Frontalières de la Montagne Jurassienne.* Lyon: Institut des Etudes Rhodaniennes de l'Université de Lyon, Memoires et Documents, 14.

Durkheim, E. (1938) *The Rules of Sociological Method.* New York: Free Press.

Economie Rurale (1967-8) *Tableaux de l'Agriculture France-Comtoise. 1ier et 2ième parties.* Chambres d'Agriculture de Franche-Comté, Service Interdépartemental d'Economie Rurale.

Lambert, R. (1953) Structure agraire et économie rurale du plateau de Levier. *Bulletin de l'Association des Géographes Français* 237-8, 170-8.

Mackenzie, W.J.M. (1967) *Politics and Social Science.* Harmondsworth, Middlesex, Penguin.

Radcliffe-Brown, A.R. (1952) *Structure and Function in Primitive Society.* London, Cohen and West.

J.D. EVANS

Islands as laboratories for the study of culture process

To the prehistorian interested in the problems of culture change in relation to archaeological evidence island communities may offer a number of significant advantages. These all stem essentially from the limitations imposed by this kind of habitat on the various forms of life which may be present. It makes for closed communities and tends to eliminate some of the variables which afflict the student of mainland groups, and whose effect is often so difficult to assess. Up to now, however, these qualities of island habitats seem to have been more fully recognized by natural scientists and anthropologists, by whom they have often been very successfully exploited, than by archaeologists.

1. As already indicated, the fundamental limitation of island life is the restrictions it imposes, more or less, on intercourse with groups living elsewhere. Islands, while they offer a home which is sheltered to a varying extent from some of the competitive pressures of life on the larger land masses, do this at the expense of isolating their living communities, whether plant, animal or human, in some measure from contact with neighbouring populations of the same kind. The degree to which such isolation actually occurs in particular instances will of course vary widely in accordance with a variety of factors, such as the nearness or remoteness of other islands or land masses, the climatic conditions obtaining in the area, and so on; but especially depending on the means of locomotion available to each species. Where human populations are involved, the last factor is closely linked to the prevailing technological level; not only that of the island communities themselves, of course, but to progress in this respect among the rest of the region, or even of the whole world.

It is true that other geographical factors, such as high mountain ranges, uncleared forests or undrained fens can be at least as effective as a stretch of salt water in producing barriers to free intercourse between human communities. Sometimes, indeed, they can be even more effective; but there are important differences, and the kind of isolation produced generally has a different quality. For though the sea divides and isolates one community from another, it can also be, in certain respects, a most effective medium of communication between them once adequate water transport becomes available. Even so, the extent to which advantage is taken of these possibilities will depend, in any particular instance, on a number of factors. Thus communication by sea may be restricted, by a combination of climatic and technological factors, to a few months in the year, as it was in the Mediterranean to a very late date, or the length of the voyage involved may be so great that contact is only likely to take place at relatively long intervals. In addition, cultural factors may be very important in determining the degree and nature of the contact which actually takes place.

Though naturally no hard and fast rule can be laid down, it is a resonable postulate that island communities are on the whole more open to some kinds of cultural contact than to others. For instance, though by no means immune, they are less likely than mainland ones to be affected by the kinds of contact which produce rapid and arbitrary cultural and ethnic change, such as mass immigration or hostile invasion. This applies especially before the appearance, in the area in which they are situated, of large and highly organized political groups with relatively complex technologies. On the other hand they are often open to cultural stimuli from a wide variety of sources, which may quite frequently include small accretions of population who may arrive either deliberately or by chance.

2. While the relative isolation of island communities makes it possible to study the development over long periods of human groups which have been unaffected by any radical interference from without, there is another characteristic of most islands which is also potentially most useful to the archaeologist. This is the limited range of resources which are likely to be available. It is helpful in two ways; first of all for the study of the ways in which any particular community has tried to adapt itself to the restrictions of its environment, its relative success or failure in making the best of what is available, and secondly because it can provide unequivocal evidence of contact with the outside world. Any island community is likely to feel the lack of a number of desirable things, as anyone who has lived or worked in one for any length of time must be aware, and it is highly likely that it will make some efforts to remedy these deficiencies if possible. From the archaeological standpoint what is important is that the restricted range of locally available resources often means that it is relatively easy to pick out objects made of substances which must have been brought from elsewhere, either as raw material or as finished products, and this is true also of animal and plant remains in so far as they survive. In this way we can build up a picture of the range of contacts available to a particular community at a given time, and even get some indication of the extent to which these were of real importance to it.

Conversely, many islands have special products which are in demand over a wide region, and the study of the distribution of these may give valuable evidence about the extent and nature of trade or other contacts in a particular area at a given time. The location of many of the most important deposits of obsidian in the Mediterranean region on islands is a striking instance of this. For a long time the potential value of this has been recognized by archaeologists, though it took the development of a reliable analytical technique by Cann and Renfrew for the full possibilities to be realized. There are many other instances which offer similar opportunities for carefully planned work of this kind.

3. Island communities often display a tendency towards the exaggerated development of some aspect of their culture, which is often connected with ceremonial. The isolation and relative security (and perhaps boredom) of island life can allow the continuance of trends which in a mainland environment are likely to be inhibited by various extraneous factors long before they can reach their logical conclusion. Particular biases then show up which may continue to become progressively more developed over a long period of uninterrupted community life. It is, for instance, a striking fact that a large number of island communities in many parts of the world have spent much time and energy in erecting extensive ceremonial and religious complexes, which they have gone on progressively elaborating and embellishing over a great many centuries.

4. Groups of islands lying relatively close to each other and with relatively easy communications one with another may provide information of special interest. This sort of situation gives an opportunity to study the related development of small discrete communities, to observe the mutual effect of their contacts, and to follow the development of differences between them. The Mediterranean area again provides a number of excellent examples for studies of this kind, notably the Cycladic islands, the Balearics and the group comprising Corsica, Sardinia and Elba, as well as other smaller groups.

While all the points just made are individually so well known as to rate more or less as commonplaces, it does not seem to me their collective implications have yet been fully seized on by archaeologists and consciously exploited. When the interest of prehistorians was largely concentrated, as it has chiefly been in the past, on reconstructing the broad outlines of cultural development, it was understandable that the archaeology of islands should have been somewhat neglected in favour of the larger land masses, and that they should have been regarded as mostly quiet and unimportant backwaters outside the main stream. While it is understandable that this should have been so, it is to be hoped that in the future more understanding will be displayed of the positive opportunities offered by these arbitrarily limited environments.

With the rise of the current interest in the mechanisms of cultural change among prehistoric communities and the limits of the interpretation of archaeological evidence the case is certainly altered. The potential of island habitats for the pursuit of 'archaeology as anthropology' is undoubtedly very considerable. By cutting out one or more of the variables with which we normally have to contend, islands offer us the possibility of in some sense conducting 'experiments'. By a careful choice of particular island communities for study in relation to any individual problem results commanding a higher degree of confidence may be arrived at than would be possible using mainland evidence, which is generally more open ended. In this sense, then, it is valid to regard every island which has at some time been the home of a human group as potentially a laboratory for the archaeologist, in very much the same way as the Galapagos group proved to be one for Darwin, and in which many others have since been used by other scientists.

In this discussion I have naturally been all along thinking chiefly in terms of relatively small islands, since in those with large areas some of the old uncertainties are quickly reintroduced. Britain, for instance, though it has always had a cultural history which is distinct from that of the Continent, is through its size and variety not otherwise well suited to the kind of laboratory role I have been describing, though some of the smaller islands around its coasts are. But it is not simply a question of size, and no arbitrary limit could reasonably be fixed for this; complexity of geographical and geological structure, the range of habitats and resources present, the size and structure of the population and its cultural diversity are all factors to be considered here. Finally, the nature of the problem to be investigated must be decisive, and it is up to each investigator to choose the most appropriate for his purposes.

PAUL ASHBEE

Culture and change in the Isles of Scilly

The Isles of Scilly lie 25 miles off and to the southwest of Land's End, Cornwall. At the present time five of the islands are inhabited, St. Mary's, the largest, St. Martin's, Tresco, Bryher and St. Agnes. There are forty-three smaller uninhabited islands of which about eighteen bear a mantle of vegetation. These range in size from Samson and Annet to the Eastern Isles and Northern Rocks. Rocky islets and reefs are adjacent to many of the main islands as well as extending in a south-westerly carpet from St. Agnes towards the Bishop's Rock lighthouse.

Scilly's highest land, 166 ft above O.D., is found at the northern end of St. Mary's. Almost all the larger islands have irregular coastlines ranging from exposed granite cairns and cliffs to sandy bays. Low spring tides expose considerable areas of sand, especially between Samson, Tresco and Bryher, as well as between St. Martin's and St. Mary's. On these exposed flats can be seen the remains of normally submerged field-walls, hut foundations and other features, for the islands, islets and rocks themselves are the remains of a considerable land-mass that may well have been two considerable islands until post-Roman times. Basically, these were parts of the Cornubian-Scillonian granite system and they may have been conjoined as recently as the Late Tertiary Period. It is thought (Harvey 1969) that the present flora and fauna derives in some measure from that of the eastern extremities of the greatly extended continent of Europe of immediate post-glacial times as well as from the shrinking elements of the Cornubian peninsula as it assumed its present form. Subsequent immigration, emigration and extinction during some ten millennia must also be taken into account.

Scillonian chamber tombs excited attention in the 18th century (Borlase 1756) and aspects of the islands' archaeology have been studied, from time to time, down to the present day. With exceptions (e.g. O'Neil 1949), published works have treated specific sites and situations and there has been little, if anything, of a synthetic character. This pattern of endeavour, together with unpublished documentation and the present writer's own excavations, does allow, however, the expression of a cultural sequence as well as providing patterns of evidence regarding a land and sea based subsistence economy.

The cultural sequence on the Isles of Scilly would seem to be, broadly, as follows:

c.2000-250 B.C.

A late neolithic society, with flint, stone, bone and antler equipment, making barrel, biconical and bucket-form pots, the upper half of which frequently bear varieties of stamped ornamentation. Eighteen habitation sites, some with the remains of stone-built huts, have been identified, while about eighty chamber tombs in regular cemeteries, termed 'entrance graves' are known, as are a number of cists. The rite was cremation, unurned or inurned, although, in one instance inhumation was practised. A bronze awl and pieces of an arm-band were in two chamber tombs: two massive bronze torques were seemingly found in a barrow; a socketed axe was a stray find.

c.250 B.C. – A.D. 250

Some four or five iron age sites with stone-built huts have produced quantities of pottery commensurate with that from the Cornish mainland and about four or five promontory forts have been identified.

A.D. c.250-400

Romano-British pottery both locally made and imported has been found at six sites and at one of these a demonstrable courtyard house has been excavated. Another yielded a great number of brooches and other bronze pieces, besides coins and pipe-clay figurines. It may have been of a ritual character. Burial was contracted inhumation in stone-built cists, often with brooches.

A.D. c.400-1000

Grass-marked pottery, imported and bar-lip wares have come from four or five sites. A number of ecclesiastical establishments, including one monastic enceinte, are a feature of this phase. An inscribed stone, some possible crosses and extended burials can also be considered.

A constantly recurring feature is the continuity of habitation to be found in certain places. At Halangy Porth, St. Mary's, the late neolithic settlement was abandoned because of the encroachment of blown sand and the same group moved up the hill into new buildings which were used through Iron Age, Roman and into post-Roman times. On Nor-Nour a similar pattern of continuity, into Roman times, can be seen within a closely-knit complex of stone buildings.

There must have been an initial *landnam* or 'breaking' of the Isles of Scilly. There is abundant evidence, in the form of pottery with grain impressions, broken-down ovens, great storage pots in pits and saddle querns, from the early phase of settlement down by the shore at Halangy Porth (Ashbee 1966:21) of an established neolithic mode of life which included domestic animals.

The settlement by Halangy Porth reflects, however, much more than a mere land-based economy. Land and sea merge, one into another, in the Scillonian scene and their inseparable dimensions are ever-present in the subsistence economy. Side by side with grain growing and the keeping of kine, swine and flocks or herds, there was gathering, catching and even hunting of the bounty of the sea. The gathering is attested by the enormous middens of limpet shells, a feature of almost every Scillonian habitation site, the catching, by fish bones in such middens, while at least one seal-hunting station has been found on St. Agnes.

Land farming, following the earlier patterns, persisted into later times. In the Halangy Down stone-built hutments and courtyard house numerous saddle and rotary querns have been found and the remains of corn-drying ovens uncovered, while an extensive field system is adjacent to the settlement. A huge midden of limpet shells with fish and domestic animal bones, as well as Romano-British pottery, was a feature of this phase of the site. Such middens are also a feature of post-Roman times and, indeed, limpet consumption persisted into the 19th century A.D.

Thus from an early stage, on the Isles of Scilly, a mixed land-sea subsistence economy both evolved and persisted. The importance of limpets is that they were an easily obtainable supply of protein over and above that which could be produced by a normal land-based economy. It is clearly impossible to say how many constituted a meal or how frequently they were eaten. Research upon these problems (Townsend 1967) has shown that to supply protein for a four-person family to American standards, 756 Scillonian limpets would be required daily. With the circumstances of the mixed economy that seem to have obtained on most Scillonian sites in mind, it would appear that limpet consumption was probably geared to the availability of other foodstuffs and modulated by the growth of limpets on specific shores. Indeed, the size of some midden shells may reflect controlled collecting circumstances. However, communities which consumed, at appropriate intervals, limpets for three or more millennia would doubtlessly have learned the lessons of over-exploitation of such a staple.

With the advantages of the land-sea economy it is even possible bearing in mind the relative profusion of early sites, both domestic and funerary, on the islands, that an above average population density could have obtained right through the 2nd and 1st millennium B.C. At the same time such self-containment could well have brought about what has been termed (Piggott 1965:17) a 'conserving' society. This means one of two things, first of all that the mode of life once established within the compass of the islands was deemed satisfactory and thus the communal consciousness was opposed to change or, secondly, that there was such a delicate adjustment to the habitat that this imposed a measure of social rigidity, so that change, other than in terms of material culture, was impossible. Presumably each circumstance affected the other and the result was at first a prolonged, stone-using, neolithic mode of life (for stray metal objects do not warrant the term 'bronze age'). This was followed by the later changes which, although involving iron and Romano-British and even post-Roman products, seems to have had little effect upon certain aspects of the basic stone technology nor the land-sea subsistence economy.

As Daniel (1968:34) has recently declared, we have during the past quarter century or so been living in a climate of thought which he defined as 'a kind of modified diffusionism'. In making an assessment of the record of material culture in the Isles of Scilly, its usages are difficult to avoid. Our envisagement of the advent of the first farmers, couched in terms of Humphrey Case's 'Neolithic explanations' (Case 1969) involves such thinking. In assessing the great number of urns from the Knackyboy chamber tomb O'Neil (1952:29) invoked both Dorset Deverel-Rimbury and Breton 'influence'. It is possible to see not unconvincing counterparts of the distinctive Scillonian chamber tombs in Brittany, on the Cornish Mainland, in the Tramore district of Southern Ireland, The Boyne Valley and distant Scotland. At a later stage promontory forts, pottery, courtyard houses, coins and cist-graves all give us links with Cornwall and beyond, although it must be observed that a large proportion of the 'Roman' brooches (Ashbee, 1955:16-24, Dudley 1967:28-30) remain obstinately Scillonian. Later still, grass-marked pottery, imported wares, bar-lip pottery and ecclesiastical establishments must all be seen as stimuli from without. Indeed, when the situation of Scilly is considered and the archaeological term 'trade' appealed to, such explanations do not appear unreasonable. Yet they appear as only a part of the story of man in Scilly: there are the questions of the subsistence economy plus the continual adjustments that must have been made in a changing island habitat down the years as well as the precise significance of the observable changes in the record of material culture. When these factors are taken into account, modified diffusionistic models, although not without value, are of limited utility.

The foregoing poses two questions, the nature of the employable concepts, constructs or models and the legitimate use that can be made of their apparatus in the Scillonian scene. These, which are inferential and intellectual, embody what we think synthetically about our selected material. It is my intention to consider something of the Scillonian archaeological record in terms of what could best be described as modified evolution.

In recent years archaeological thinking has moved to this mode in two ways. At particular and local levels much of neolithic and bronze age prehistory is explicable in terms of what I have called continuity (Ashbee 1960:154). It is best illustrated by Isobel Smith's treatment of neolithic pottery and Ian Longworth's (1961) patient work on Collared Urns. Clark (1966) has detailed the mechanics of the shift from the diffusionism of successive invasions. On a general and global basis Bohmers (1964) has argued for socio-genetic evolution, Daniel (1968) has boldly outlined the early emergences of agriculture and civilization, saying that we should think in terms of multi-linear evolution leading to synoecismic processes, while Clark (1970) sees us and our way of life as the product of natural selection.

If such thinking is to be applied to a circumscribed island situation such as Scilly there are, understandably, difficulties, not the least being the question of what is implied by culture change? For behind considerations of continuity there is the implication that human life continues, yet by what agency do the styles of pots, houses and burial arrangements change? Such considerations are not easy for they strike hard at cherished concepts, not the least being the equation of an archaeological 'culture' with a 'people' (Childe 1929:vi). Strike as one must, it should be remembered that Gordon Childe did say (1956:157) that whatever is diffused to another culture will not be assimilated unless it fits into the complex but flexible structure of the recipient culture. In the Isles of Scilly, one has this basic continuity changed by elements, both human and material, that were appropriate to the specific environment.

With all these considerations in mind one must review what I have called the cultural sequence of the Isles of Scilly in evolutionary terms, bearing in mind that this implies natural selection, the exploitation of those specific biological niches in which Charles Darwin saw his finches more than a century ago in the Galápagos.

The people who made landfall upon the Isles of Scilly in about 2000 B.C., were of Beaker stock as is suggested by flint industries, which include barbed-and-tanged arrowheads, some battle-axes, the bone points and bronze awl from a chamber tomb and, above all, their pottery. On their distinctive Scillonian ceramic products they developed characteristic systems of stamped ornamentation which includes so-called 'rouletting' in bands and zones. They built circular and sub-rectangular stone huts. Their chamber tombs, with circular drum-like cairns housed chambers which are rectangular, trapezoidal or coffin-shaped, sometimes with short passages. The cremation rites had been adapted from late neolithic sources. The circular cairn might be a stone version of a circular Beaker barrow and the stone chambers might equally be translations from timber mortuary houses, for such structures, in the earthen long barrow tradition, were a feature of many Beaker barrows. Their standing stones betoken similar processes.

Exploitation of the unique biological niche that the Isles of Scilly proffered resulted in the evolution of a stable land-sea subsistence economy which nurtured an above average population for almost two millennia.

Culture change, expressed in new forms of pottery and defensive earthworks, may have come about either by intercourse with the mainlands or by influxes of people who were assimilated into existent communities. Both are possible because there is continuity of settlement and even structure on several sites.

Roman times coincided with the beginnings of the process which broke up two large islands into something approaching their present form. Notwithstanding, the land-sea subsistence economy continued to sustain a population density above that of a commensurate area of inland mainland. Improved sea communications made the Isles of Scilly, in a sense, an extension of the Cornubian peninsula although, at all times, the basic subsistence economy, the product of the specific Scillonian environment, remained unchanged!

Curiously enough, Charles Darwin neglected the effects of territory as an evolutionary factor. It was left to Sir Arthur Keith (1949) to emphasize the part played by distinctive regions in the emergence of man. It may be that instead of considering the multiplicity of cultures, few of them conforming to the original concept of the term, that are a feature of our early archaeology, we should be thinking in terms of specific regions, the Southwest, Wessex and East Anglia, and examining the effects that these territories, and the environments that they offered, had upon the development of our early communities.

REFERENCES

Ashbee, P. (1955) The excavation of a cist-grave cemetery and associated structures, near Hughtown, St. Mary's, Isles of Scilly. *Archaeological Journal* **111**, 1-25.

Ashbee, P. (1960) *The Bronze Age Round Barrow in Britain.* London.

Ashbee, P. (1966) Excavations at Halangy Down, St. Mary's, Isles of Scilly. *Cornish Archaeology* **5**, 20-7.

Bohmers, A. (1964) Evolution and archaeology. *Palaeohistoria* **10**, 1-13.

Borlase, W. (1756) *Observations on the Ancient and Present State of the Islands of Scilly.* Oxford.

Case, H.J. (1969) Neolithic explanations. *Antiquity* **43**, 176-86.

Childe, V. (1929) *The Danube in Prehistory.* Oxford.

Childe, V. (1956) *Piecing together the Past.* London.

Clark, J.G.D. (1966) The invasion hypothesis in British archaeology. *Antiquity* **40**, 172-89.

Clark, J.G.D. (1970) *Aspects of Prehistory.* Los Angeles.

Daniel, G. (1968) *The First Civilisations.* London.

Dudley, D. (1967) Excavations on Nor'Nour in the Isles of Scilly, 1962-6. *Archaeological Journal* **124**, 1-64.

Harvey, L.A. (1969) The Marine flora and fauna of the Isles of Scilly. The Islands and their Ecology. *Journal of Natural History* 3.

Keith, A. (1949) *A New Theory of Human Evolution.* New York.

Longworth, I.H. (1961) The origins and development of the primary series in the Collared Urn tradition in England and Wales. *Proceedings of the Prehistoric Society* 27, 263-306.

O'Neil, B.H. St. J. (1949) *Isles of Scilly.* London, H.M.S.O.

O'Neil, B.H. St. J. (1952) The excavation of Knackyboy Cairn, St. Martin's, Isles of Scilly, 1948. *Antiquaries Journal* 32, 21-34.

Piggott, S. (1965) *Ancient Europe.* Edinburgh.

Townsend, M. (1967) The Common Limpet (*Patella vulgata*) as a source of protein. *Folia Biologica* 15, 343-51.

A.P. PHILLIPS

The evolutionary model of human society and its application to certain early farming populations of Western Europe

Introduction

The multi-linear evolutionary model of human society developed by Service (1962) is a useful tool for characterizing band and tribal societies. The first part of this paper will be devoted to a brief summary of the characteristics of the two types of society. It is generally assumed that most human groups of the palaeolithic would be organized in bands, and the majority of those of the neolithic in tribes. Sahlins and Service have produced possible explanations of how band societies evolved into tribal societies, but have offered no examples of the change. Harner (1970) has recently produced a model to explain such social change.

If one wishes to observe societies transforming themselves from bands to tribes in the archaeological record, theoretically the obvious place to look is the transition between the mesolithic and neolithic periods. Recent ethnographic studies (Harner 1970, Forge 1970) have suggested that population size is a critical factor in the change in social organization. On the basis of ethnographic observations, A. Forge has proposed, that a total population of 150 with 40 adult males was probably a critical size, above which new integrative bonds were necessary.

This paper presents estimates of population sizes on a number of French and Swiss sites and compares these estimates (plus artifactual and natural science evidence from each site) with Harner's model of social change, in order to identify possible prehistoric 'proto-tribes'.

Bands

Band societies have been principally characterized by E.R. Service (1962, 1966). 'A band is only an association, more or less residential, of nuclear families, ordinarily numbering 30-100 people, with affinal ties loosely allying it with one or a few other bands' (Service 1962:111). The custom of seeking a wife in a neighbouring band helps to keep the local peace, and the fact that it is usually the women who marry 'out' and reside in their husband's homes (virilocality) is related to male co-operation in hunting and offense-defence situations (Service 1962:75). (Although virilocality is not always the case in present-day bands, this is due, according to Service, to acculturation and loss of tradition). Within these small groups of people, habitually leading a wandering existence between zones of seasonal plenty, there is a basic egalitarianism (Service 1962:114). All the functions of the culture (economy, religion, political organization) are practised within the family group and status is only related to age and sex. The cross-cutting sodalities which bind a tribe are very poorly developed in patrilocal bands, and only slightly more so in composite bands (Service 1962:60). Most integration is achieved by kin obligations and ties, and subsistence resources are normally communally owned (Sanders and Marino 1970:5). Trade is generally not much developed.

Tribes

Service's view of a tribe is that it is 'an association of a much larger number of kinship segments which are each composed of families'; however, a tribe is not simply a collection of bands (1962:111). A tribe has a common culture, language and territory (Sanders and Marino 1970:6). The economically self-sufficient residential units of a tribe (often consisting of one or more descent groups or lineages) do not exist in total isolation from each other. They may be linked by such kinship sodalities as the clan, the kindred or the segmentary lineage, or by non-kinship sodalities such as age-grades, or warrior or ceremonial societies (Service 1962:116). Sharing of insignia and mythology are typical of non-kinship sodalities.

Sahlins has shown the assertive strength of the segmentary lineage as a kinship sodality (1961:326), and has claimed that such organization only appears fully-developed in an intertribal situation (1961:323). Sahlins emphasizes that tribes live in a perpetual state of warfare (1968:7). This hostility is often based on competition for land, and ideas of property and territorality seem to be strongly developed in tribes (Sahlins 1961:325; Watson and Watson 1969:95).

Although the tribe can act as a unit (usually offensively) under a leader, this is only a temporary appointment for the duration of the emergency, and tribes are ordinarily very weakly developed politically, with egalitarian status of individuals and no social stratification. Trade is quite brisk, without specific markets and entrepreneurs existing.

Origin of tribal societies

A number of models have been offered by ethnographers to suggest how bands may change into tribes. Service suggests that the larger populations created by the farming economy faced 'problems of consolidation', and that a tribe did not exist before such consolidation took place (1962:112). In a relatively free environment growing societies just divided and spread. In the face of competition, however, the 'better consolidated' groups would prevail. Thus the selective factors for tribal development were offense-defense requirements. The means of integration suggested by Service is the extension of sodalities (1962:115).

Harner (1970) proposes a 'natural resource scarcity' model and feels that the selective factor in societal change is most likely to be a sudden increase in population. He argues that in a purely hunting and gathering society pressure on the available resources is high, and social organization is tight – i.e. unilineal descent (see also Sahlins 1961:342); as more reliance can be placed on the products of farming, the pressure decreases and social organization relaxes (cognatic relationships), until successful agricultural economy permits a population build-up. At this point resources (agricultural and pastoral land) again become scarce, and there is a return to unilineality, and eventually to tighter forms of social and political cohesion (clans, stratification, chiefdoms, etc.). An increase in population precedes each 'stage' of social complexity (Harner 1970: Figs. 2-5).

Population estimates for early neolithic sites

Many of the following sites in France and Switzerland were occupied successively by mesolithic and early neolithic groups. An attempt is made to estimate their populations, based on the work of Naroll (1962) and Cook and Heizer (1968). Naroll, using a small but world-wide ethnographic sample, estimated that a prehistoric population would number one-tenth of the area in square metres occupied by its dwellings (1962:588). Cook and Heizer extrapolated from information about Californian Indian groups that a family of six persons usually occupied 12 m^2 floor space (= roofed dwelling area), but that each additional individual involved an increment of approximately 10 m^2 floor space (1962:588). The concept of 'floor space' can be extended to cover the internal area of caves under about 100 m^2 (Phillips 1972). This produces an estimated seven inhabitants for a cave just over 20 m^2, for instance, and ten inhabitants for a cave about 50 m^2 in area.

The stratigraphy of the Cova de l'Espérit (Pyrénées Orientales) (Abelanet and Charles 1964) had been badly disturbed before excavation, but palaeolithic and mesolithic material was found in Level III, and microlithic flint tools including segments of circles were associated in Level II with sherds bearing *Cardium* (cockle) and comb impressions and vertical cordons. The cave only measured 35 m^2 and might have housed eight people. The fauna included mussel and the 'dorade' fish, plus boar, badger, a small cervid and a ruminant, lots of rabbit, and some cattle and goat: however, the great majority of the fauna was wild. No signs of agriculture were found either in the form of flora or artifacts (no querns, etc.). The data from this cave are admittedly meagre, but they do follow Harner's model in that high dependance on hunting and gathering is associated with low numbers of people.

In Western France, a rock-shelter in the commune of Bellefonds (Vienne) contained a mesolithic level characterized by triangular lithic elements, surmounted by a level where pottery was associated with flint trapezes; there is a slow replacement of triangles by trapezes over time in the stratigraphic record (Patte, personal communication). The rock-shelter was very small (11 m^2) and probably housed only half a dozen people. The faunal remains from both the mesolithic and pottery levels consisted of wild animals (red deer, large cattle, boar, beaver) (Patte, in press, *Gallia Préhistoire*).

The lake-side dwelling of Burgäschi-See Süd in Central Switzerland provides a well-documented example of a small community, living in the open air and provided with pottery, but with a 90% proportion of wild to 10% domesticated fauna (Boessneck *et al.* 1963). The site is enclosed by a rectangular fence opening at several points, and contains two rectangular wooden houses and a small building described as a barn (Müller-Beck 1961). There is no prior mesolithic occupation on the site, although elsewhere in Switzerland mesolithic populations had lived by lakesides in oval huts (e.g. Fischerhäusern, Luzern-Ströbel 1938). The population of Burgäschi-See Süd has been calculated as approximately 25 individuals over 60-70 years (Müller-Beck 1961), and was sufficiently acculturated to use lots of wide, softly carinated bowls and taller jars, and to build rectangular houses, but depended very largely for its subsistence on wild products, both animal and plant. Their egalitarian organization is said to be shown by the numerous entrances to the compound, and since there is only one barn, apparently resources were shared communally.

While the French sites mentioned above (Cova de l'Espérit, Abri de Bellefonds) resemble Burgäschi-See Süd in their marked dependance on a hunting and gathering economy, it is unlikely that the tiny populations of the two caves were organized at anything more than the band level. However, the lengthy occupation of houses at a single spot by the Burgäschi-See Süd people indicates a more settled life than that of the average band, and this group may have been at Harner's level of low environmental pressure plus cognatic relationships.

In the south of France, continuity of population from the mesolithic to the neolithic is suggested at the Baume de Montclus (Gard) and Châteauneuf-les-Martigues (Bouches-du-Rhône) (Escalon de Fonton 1966-7:216, 233). There is a gradual evolution of the lithic industry at both sites, and the only intrusive element is *Cardium*-impressed pottery. This occurs in Level F6 at Châteauneuf, with the first true transverse arrowheads; however, some of the geometric pieces in the preceding Level C7 foreshadow the transverse arrowhead, and the scrapers and retouched blades of C7 and the preceding mesolithic levels continue into the levels with pottery. The continuity of lithic evolution suggests an acculturated and persistent population, which, based on site size (140 m^2) would consist of some eighteen persons. In the mesolithic levels there is a majority of rabbit, plus red deer, wild cattle, boar and wolf, and sheep (herded?), plus territorial and marine mollusca and fish and crab remains. In the pottery levels there is an increasing emphasis on sheep – now definitely domesticated – and bones of small domesticated cattle appear from level C6 onwards (Ducos 1958). There seems to have been a great emphasis on hunting in the mesolithic levels, which continued into the pottery levels; however, sheep herding increased in importance over time. Querns and grindstones are found from C6 onwards, and sickle blades are first indicated in C5 (Escalon de Fonton 1956). Wheat was found in earlier excavations (Courtin, personal communication). From the small population and the slowly developing dependance on agricultural products (only a few querns and sickles are indicated before F4), it seems unlikely that the inhabitants of Châteauneuf were organized beyond the band level.

'Proto - tribes'

In contrast to the early neolithic sites discussed above, the caves of the Middle Gorges of the Verdon river (dividing the departments of Var and Basses-Alpes) have mainly produced middle neolithic (Chasséen) artifacts. These sites, which are threatened by the construction of the dam of Sainte-Croix, have been excavated in the last ten or twelve years by C.N.R.S. personnel from Marseille. Jean Courtin has been the excavator of the neolithic levels. Full information about the caves appears in his thesis (Courtin 1969). However, not all the material has been analysed, and there is no information, for example, about floral and faunal remains from Grotte C (Var). However, querns were found there with the Chasséen pottery, and the 50 m^2 site could have housed ten people. The Abri du Jardin du Capitaine (Basses-Alpes) is a large rock-shelter at the water's edge, but Chasséen material is not found over the whole extent of the shelter, so the population at the period is difficult to estimate. Sickle blades were found at the site (Gagnière 1968:508-9). A tiny swallow-hole, the Aven de Vauclare (Basses-Alpes), too small for regular occupation, produced in addition to richly-decorated Chasséen pottery numerous querns and grinding stones (Gagnière 1963:345).

Another small site, Grotte G (Var) could probably have housed only five people in its 10 m^2 area; it contained two superimposed hearths, both with Chasséen pottery, and blades with sickle lustre are reported (Courtin 1961a). The faunal proportions are not known, but emmer, breadwheat, hulled barley, chickpea, broadbean, a vetchling and acorns have been identified. Dentalium and other marine shells were present (Courtin 1969).

The 50 m^2 Grotte Murée (Basses-Alpes) might have housed ten inhabitants; its Chasséen levels produced remains of emmer, bread-wheat, hulled barley and acorns, and 90% of the faunal remains were of domesticated species. Wild animals represented included the red deer and ibex, and shells of land snails and mussel were found in the cave. Four side-notched pebbles may indicate net fishing in the Verdon river.

Mid-way up the cliff wall on the far side of the Middle Gorges of the Verdon river lie the complex galleries of the Grotte de l'Eglise. The porch to the middle levels is 50 m^2 in area, and could have housed ten inhabitants. A number of hearths were found in the excavation (Courtin 1967), including one of river cobbles in Level 3, and two postholes, which unfortunately could not be made to reveal any structure, in Level 5. No grain or wild plants have yet been identified, but the faunal analysis indicates that 122 domesticated individuals and 15 wild individuals were represented. Most of the wild animals (red deer, boar, fox) come from the lower levels. Of the domesticated species, there is a majority of cattle in the lower levels, and a majority of sheep in the upper. Land snails and mussels have been found, plus pierced *Cardium* and *Cerithum* shells. Sickle blades and querns and grindstones suggest agriculture, and a notched pebble and double point in bone may have been used for fishing. A most unusual incised limestone figure, decorated with three notches and fish-scale incisions (perhaps used for tattooing?) was found in Level 6 (Courtin 1967: Fig. 8:5).

The Grotte de l'Eglise has an upper network, of which a 30 m^2 porch (eight inhabitants) was excavated in 1967-9. The results of faunal and floral analyses are not yet available, but it is known that carbonised grains and acorns were found, plus cattle, sheep-goat and rabbit bones. There were also land snails and mussels. Querns and sickle blades emphasize the agricultural interests of the inhabitants, and a double point in bone again may be a fishing implement. Hearths are found throughout the stratigraphy, plus a single post-hole, and a deep pit in Level 8. Although this porch may not have housed more than eight persons, there are at least two other porches of comparable size in the same network. In the galleries leading back into the hillside rayed sinuous designs are painted on the walls (Courtin 1961b); there is no definite proof that they were painted by Chasséen people. However, excavation in the clay at the base of the painted walls has revealed pits filled with Chasséen artifacts.

The data given above suggest that the Chasséen populations of these gorges relied strongly on domesticated species for their meat diet, and on wheats and barleys for plant food. However, the presence of acorns in a number of caves and the availability of fish in the river suggest at least some use of wild products. The sites are very small, but there is no reason to suppose that a number of them were not occupied simultaneously, giving a fairly large local population. Manipulation of the minimum number of individuals of each faunal species from the Grotte de l'Eglise, middle network suggests that 350 man-years of meat supply is represented (Phillips 1972).

An attribute analysis study of the pottery from the Verdon Valley has suggested that regional attribute clusters continued over time (time is indicated by stratigraphic provenance and C-14 dates from different levels and sites). This has been interpreted as a possible case of matrilocality, if the women were the potters (Phillips 1971). Residence after marriage is usually linked to the descent system: it is therefore postulated that the descent system was matrilineal, the more so since male artifacts (arrowheads) show no significant clustering of attributes on a regional level.

Chasséen sites normally produce very little in the way of personal ornaments – the usual finds are pierced bones of small rodents. The incised limestone figure found in the middle porch of the Grotte de l'Eglise is thus unusual, and it may represent the insignia of a sodality. Similarly, the cave paintings in the gallery of the Grotte de l'Eglise, upper network, may have been put there during some sort of ceremonial, also perhaps the work of a sodality.

The data presented above lead to the hypothesis that the inhabitants of the Verdon Valley Middle Gorges during the Chasséen period had an unilineal society and possibly sodalities, despite their relatively low numbers. There is no evidence of extreme population pressure, for instance in the founding of open-air villages locally (despite careful searches, no Chasséen sites have been found on the surrounding plateaux). Nor is there evidence of warfare, which Sahlins considers typical of tribal societies, in the form of defenses, or of skeletons bearing arrow-wounds. It is therefore suggested that the Chasséens of the Verdon Valley Middle Gorges were 'proto-tribesmen', whose descendants, if they multiplied rapidly, might develop the tribal institutions of which they already had the germs.

Conclusion

The model developed by Harner for societal change is a useful one, and it is not difficult to find examples of small hunting and gathering populations in Western European prehistory, people probably organized in unilineal bands, who apparently continue at that stage of societal organization after acquiring a few traits from local agriculturalists. With regard to Harner's stage of cognatic relationships, the data of the Burgäschi-See Süd site partially fit the model. The long-lived but small population probably imposed limited pressure upon local resources, and the several entrances to the compound suggest egalitarianism; nevertheless wild fauna and flora continue to be much more important than domesticated products. The data from the Chasséen sites in the Verdon Valley Middle Gorges also only partially fit Harner's model. Despite the apparent unilineal descent system and sodalities, there is no evidence of extreme population pressure or of warfare; for this reason the inhabitants have been described as 'proto-tribesmen'.

Harner's model is nevertheless valuable as a framework against which to measure studies of western European prehistoric society.

REFERENCES

Abelanet, J. and Charles, R.-P. (1964) Un site du Néolithique Ancien en Roussillon, La Cova de l'Espérit. *Cahiers Ligures de Préhistoire et d'Archéologie* 13, 177-206.

Barth, F. (1967) On the study of social change. *American Anthropologist* **69**, 661-9.

Boessneck, J., Jéquier, J.-P. and Stampfli, H.R. (1963) Seeberg, Burgäschisee-Süd: Die Tierreste. *Acta Bernensia* 2 (Teil 3). Bern.

Cook, S.F. and Heizer, R.F. (1968) Relationships among houses, settlement areas and population in aboriginal California. *In* Chang, K.C. (ed.) *Settlement Archaeology*, 79-116. Palo Alto: National Press Books.

Courtin, J. (1961a) La préhistoire recente de la Vallée du Verdon. *Cahiers Ligures de Préhistoire et d'Archéologie* **10**, 181-9.

Courtin, J. (1961b) Les peintures schématiques de la Grotte de l'Eglise (Var). *Revue d'Etudes Ligures* **25**, 186-95.

Courtin, J. (1967) La grotte de l'Eglise à Baudinard (Var). *Gallia Préhistoire* **10**, 282-300.

Courtin, J. (1969) Le Néolithique de la Provence (Thesis, Marseille: to be published 1972).

Ducos, P. (1958) Le gisement de Châteauneuf-les-Martigues (B-du-Rh); les mammifères et les problèmes de la domestication. *Bulletin du Musée d'Anthropologie Préhistorique de Monaco* **5**, 119-33.

Egloff, M. (1967) Huit niveaux archéologiques à l'Abri de la Cure (Baulmes, Canton de Vaud). *Urschweiz* **31** no. 4, 53-64.

Escalon de Fonton, M. (1956) Préhistoire de la Basse Provence. *Préhistoire* **XII.**

Escalon de Fonton, M. (1966-7) Origine et développement des civilisations néolithiques méditerranéennes en Europe occidentale. *Palaeohistoria* **12**, 209-48.

Forge, A. (1970) Oral communication.

Gagnière, S. (1963) Informations archéologiques. Circonscription des antiquités préhistoriques d'Aix-en-Provence. *Gallia Préhistoire* **6**, 337-69.

Gagnière, S. (1968) Informations archéologiques. Circonscription des antiquités préhistoriques de Provence-Côte d'Azur-Corse. *Gallia Préhistoire* **11**, 493-528.

Harner, M.J. (1970) Population pressure and the social evolution of agriculturalists. *Southwestern Journal of Anthropology* **26**, 67-86.

Müller-Beck, H. (1961) Prehistoric Swiss Lake Dwellers. *Scientific American* **205** no. 6, 138-47.

Naroll, R. (1962) Floor area and settlement population. *American Antiquity* **27**, 587-9.

Phillips, P. (1971) Attribute analysis and social structure of Chassey-Cortaillod-Lagozza populations. *Man* **6**, 341-52.

Phillips, P. (1972) Population, economy and society in the Chassey-Cortaillod-Lagozza cultures. *World Archaeology* **4**, 41-56.

Sahlins, M.D. (1961) The segmentary lineage: an organization of predatory expansion. *American Anthropologist* **63**, 322-45.

Sahlins, M.D. (1968) *Tribesmen* (Foundations of Modern Anthropology Series). Englewood Cliffs, N.J., Prentice-Hall.

Sanders, W.T. and Marino, J. (1970) *New World Prehistory* (Foundations of Modern Anthropology Series). Englewood Cliffs, N.J., Prentice-Hall.

Service, E.R. (1962) *Primitive Social Organization*. New York, Random House.

Service, E.R. (1966) *The Hunters* (Foundations of Modern Anthropology Series). Englewood Cliffs, N.J., Prentice-Hall.

Ströbel, R. (1938) *Die Pfahlbauten des Wauwilermooses*. Luzern.

Watson, R.A. and Watson, P.J., (1969) *Man and Nature*. An anthropological essay in human ecology. New York, Harcourt, Brace and World.

COLIN RENFREW

Monuments, mobilization and social organization in neolithic Wessex

> The structure of Neolithic societies in Western Europe may have been a great deal less egalitarian than the lack of differentiation in their artifacts might lead us to believe. (R.J.C. Atkinson 1961:299.)

The principal recorded sites of the neolithic period of south Britain are monumental: either funeral mounds sometimes more than 300 ft. long, or circular enclosures, with a bank and internal ditch, frequently more than 100 ft. in diameter. We know much less of settlement sites, or of more modest burial conventions. Yet the artifacts found are unimpressive: simple pottery, bone and stone tools, and some handsome axes, often of imported stone (Piggott 1954).

The general disparity between the megalithic monuments of western Europe as a whole – including both tombs and specialized structures, such as the alignments at Carnac or the edifice at Stonehenge – and the general level of material culture was one of the foundations of the 'modified diffusionism' of Montelius and Gordon Childe. It seemed to them, as to some extent it still seems today, paradoxical that monuments rivalling those of the civilized Orient should have been erected on the far fringes of barbarian Europe. One obvious solution was that the inspiration and the technical knowledge came from the east by what Childe saw as the 'sole unifying theme' of European prehistory, 'the irradiation of European barbarism by Oriental civilization' (Childe 1958:70). The megalithic tombs were sometimes explained by reference to megalithic missionaries, and (at a later date) 'the central Mediterranean provides the only outside source for the sophisticated approach to architecture exhibited at Stonehenge . . . Is it then any more incredible that the architect of Stonehenge should himself have been a Mycenaean, than that the monument should have been designed and erected, with all its unique and sophisticated detail, by mere barbarians?' (Atkinson 1960:165.)

The tree-ring calibration of radiocarbon dating has, however, made these views untenable (Renfrew 1970). Other explanations are needed for the monuments of prehistoric Britain, and indeed many writers have stressed that both the 'causewayed camps' of the early neolithic, and the 'henges' of the later neolithic are especially, almost uniquely British features. They can be discussed most profitably in local terms.

The changes for which some explanation is here desired are those seen in the neolithic of south Britain, and specifically in Wessex (Wiltshire and Dorset) which resulted in the construction of these monuments. In the first place there are the long burial mounds or 'barrows', generally earthen, of the early neolithic period. At the same time as those, probably before 4000 B.C. in calendar years, causewayed enclosures were constructed. Then, possibly later in the earlier neolithic period, there are the remarkable 'cursus' monuments – earthen banks sometimes running for several miles, and bounded by parallel ditches about 300 ft. apart.

Later in the neolithic, in the third millennium B.C. (in calendar years), very large henge monuments were constructed, of which Avebury is the most famous. Around the end of the later neolithic there were two prodigious building feats in this region – the construction in earth and chalk of the huge conical mound, Silbury Hill, which was at least three times the volume of the fluted 'pyramid' of the Olmecs at La Venta (cf. Heizer and Drucker 1968:52), and, a little later, the erection of the great sarsen structure at Stonehenge.

The difficult general question as to what constitutes an adequate 'explanation' for such changes and achievements will not be touched on here. It will be considered sufficient if the explanation or hypothesis:

(i) offers a framework in which the changes seem more intelligible

(ii) gives rise to logical consequences which can be tested in subsequent work.

Chiefdoms in neolithic Wessex

The explanatory model used here is a social one. It unites previous suggestions as to the function of some of the monuments and the organization of their construction. But as we shall see it goes further in relating their distribution to these other ideas, as well as to observed specialization in trade and religious practice.

Already six years ago, Isobel Smith (1965:19) rejected some earlier views about the 'causewayed camps', and elaborated a suggestion first made by Stuart Piggott (1954:29) and Richard Atkinson (cf. Case 1962:215), that 'the enclosure may have served as a centre or rallying-point for the population of a fairly wide area'.

> Such rallying points play an essential role in the lives of some contemporary communities living in a comparable stage of economic and technological development. Assembly of the scattered families or tribal units takes place at one or more intervals during the year, at the slack periods in the agricultural and/or stock-tending cycle, and affords opportunities for the transaction of the necessary business of tribal life. In addition to those matters which may come within the political field in its broader sense, such other matters can be attended to as the holding of initiation ceremonies, matchmaking and weddings, the exchange of stock and seed-corn and perhaps of more durable goods. Rites and ceremonies are performed to ensure the fertility of the flocks and herds and the growing of the corn, and finally to celebrate the harvest. Communal feasts are an inevitable accompaniment of such occasions, and some industrial activities may be undertaken, either because they are less tedious when performed to the accompaniment of a lively exchange of news and gossip, or because there is insufficient time at other seasons.

Miss Smith's further suggestion (1966:474) that there was a connection and a similarity in function between the early neolithic causewayed enclosures and the later neolithic henges has been discussed by Geoffrey Wainwright in the light of his recent discovery of wooden buildings in some of the larger henges. He compared these to the council houses of the Creek and Cherokee indians of the south-eastern United States and concluded that their function was communal rather than domestic (Wainwright 1970:38).

This useful discussion of the function of such monuments is supplemented by Atkinson's stimulating reflections on the social organization which produced Stonehenge (1960:166):

> The building of Stonehenge is . . . unlikely to have been the expression of the common will, but rather the fulfilment of a purpose imposed from above. Now in the rich and martially furnished Wessex graves we can admittedly see evidence of chieftainship, and the grouping of the graves in cemeteries may imply whole dynasties of chiefs. Yet the pattern of society which they represent is surely that of so many other heroic societies, in which clan wars with clan, and rival dynasties carry on a perpetual struggle for power. Under such conditions, can the construction of Stonehenge, involving the displacement of so many hundreds of men from their homes for so long, having been attempted, still less achieved? Surely not; for such great works can only be encompassed by a society at peace within itself. And in such a society of conflicting factions, how is peace imposed except from above?
>
> I believe, therefore, that Stonehenge itself is evidence for the concentration of political power, for a time at least, in the hands of a single man, who alone could create and maintain the conditions necessary for this great undertaking.

It is not necessary to agree with all of this to see that it does pose questions which in general have been much neglected. One point at present in doubt is whether the final structure of Stonehenge was in fact constructed during the rich Wessex early bronze age, of which

Atkinson writes, or in an earlier period, as Christopher Hawkes has recently suggested. Nor is Atkinson's notion of chiefly society very much like the one to be presented here. It is, rather, his realization of the social organisation involved in the investment of so much labour which is relevant. The same applies now to Silbury Hill, which a recent radiocarbon date would place as the contemporary or immediate senior of the pyramids of Egypt, just before 2500 B.C. in calendar years.

It is proposed here that the developments in neolithic Wessex be explained in terms of a developed social stratification in the society, resulting in the formation in or before the late neolithic period of what a number of American anthropologists have recently termed 'chiefdoms'. I am aware that this is now a fashionable concept, of limited meaning when used loosely, and yet have found it particularly apposite in the early bronze age Aegean (Renfrew 1972, chapter 18), a society paradoxically different, in many ways, from neolithic Britain.

Yet the old tripartite social classification of band/savagery, tribe/barbarism and state/civilization is no longer adequate to our needs. Between the relatively egalitarian tribal society which we may imagine for some early neolithic cultures of Europe – Starčevo perhaps, or Danubian I – and the civilizations of Crete, Mycenae, Classical Greece or Rome, there lies a considerable gap. In this same gap fall the stratified societies of Polynesia – which in Easter Island, Hawaii, Tonga, the Marquesas and elsewhere, likewise produced very impressive and large-scale monuments – and some of the tribes of the south-eastern United States, as well as many others.

This concept of chiefdom arose partly from Paul Kirchoff's notion of 'conical clan', and Raymond Firth's analysis of the 'ramages' of Polynesia. As Morton Fried put it (1957:1): 'One of the classic tasks in the quest for regularity is an attempt to derive the correlations of specific social institutions with other aspects of culture . . . The main concern is with the relations of social structure and economy'. The term has been well discussed by Elman R. Service (1962:142-77) and Marshall D. Sahlins (1968). A chiefdom is a ranked society, hierarchically arranged, sometimes in the form of a conical clan where the eldest descendent in the male line from the clan founder ranks highest, and the cadet branches are ranked in seniority after the main line.

> Chiefdoms are particularly distinguished from tribes by the presence of centres which coordinate economic, social and religious activities . . . The great change at chiefdom level is that specialization and redistribution are no longer merely adjunctive to a few particular endeavours, but continuously characterize a large part of the activity of the society. Chiefdoms are *redistributional societies* with a permanent central agency of coordination. Thus the central agency comes to have not only an economic role – however basic this factor in the origin of this type of society – but

> also serves additional functions which are social, political and religious. Once it is in existence, it can in other words, act to foster and preserve the integration of the society for the sake of integration alone. (Service 1962:143)

The proposal, then is that this affords an appropriate model for the late neolithic of Wessex. The following are brought out by Service and Sahlins as frequent features of chiefdoms, in addition to the defining ones of (1) a ranked society and (2) the redistribution of produce organized by the chief:

(3) greater population density
(4) increase in the total number in the society
(5) increase in the size of individual residence groups
(6) greater productivity
(7) more clearly defined territorial boundaries or borders
(8) a more integrated society with a greater number of sociocentric statuses
(9) centres which coordinate social and religious as well as economic activity
(10) frequent ceremonies and rituals serving wide social purposes
(11) rise of priesthood
(12) relation to a total environmental situation favouring specialization in production (and hence redistribution) – i.e. to some ecological diversity
(13) specialization, not only regional or ecological but also through the pooling of individual skills in large cooperative endeavours.
(14) Organization and deployment of public labour, sometimes for agricultural work (e.g. irrigation) and/or for building temples, temple mounds or pyramids.
(15) improvement in craft specialization
(16) potential for territorial expansion – associated with the 'rise and fall' of chiefdoms
(17) reduction of internal strife
(18) pervasive inequality of persons or groups in the society associated with permanent leadership, effective in fields other than the economic
(19) distinctive dress or ornament for those of high status
(20) no true government to back up decisions by legalized force.

The strength of the model is that it implies the conjoint occurrence of many of these features. We shall see that many are well documented in neolithic south Britain, while some others are conspicuously lacking.

Long barrows and territories of individual settlements

There are some 120 long barrows known from Wiltshire and Dorset (listed by Ashbee 1970). Most of them are of earth or chalk, sometimes covering the traces of a wooden 'mortuary house'. While in some cases this may have been accessible after the construction of the mound, it will not have stood for more than a couple of decades. After this the barrow was effectively 'unchambered'. There are in this area a number of barrows containing a stone chamber, which certainly was accessible for much longer, and may have been more expensive of labour to construct. For convenience they are included here with the more numerous 'unchambered' barrows.

Grinsell (1958, maps I to V) and others have emphasized how the prehistoric remains of Wessex cluster on the chalklands – the Marlborough Downs, the Salisbury Plain, Cranborne Chase and the Dorset Downs (Fig. 2). Ashbee has divided the Wessex barrows into five groups, corresponding to these topographic divisions, with separate groups for the east and west Salisbury plain. This is supported by an elementary isarithmic approach, and doubtless could be substantiated by other means, although the east and west Salisbury Plain groups are not well separated.

It has long been recognized that the long barrows sometimes occur in groups of two or three. There is a noted concentration in the region near Stonehenge (which was not itself begun, however, until later), and some lineation along chalk uplands in Cranborne Chase. But in the west Salisbury Plain at least, the spacing is such as to suggest that each barrow (or pair) may have been located in its own individual territory. Even accepting that some barrows have been destroyed, this is made plausible by the simple construction of Thiessen polygons (Fig. 1).

An important underlying assumption here is that all the barrows must have been functioning in some sense, although not necessarily for burial, at the same time – no doubt at the end of the early neolithic period – for such a conclusion to be valid. Atkinson has, by implication, suggested the contrary (Atkinson 1968), and his argument must be considered. He points out that on average six bodies only have been found within long barrows, and assumes that long barrows were being built over a period of ten centuries. His conclusion was that if the entire population was buried in such barrows, each barrow could have served a family of about six for about 25 years. On this model the population would be very small, and families would be moving from place to place, so that the ultimate distribution of barrows would reflect their wanderings, and in no sense the situation at any point in time. The notion of barrows reflecting territories would be inadmissable.

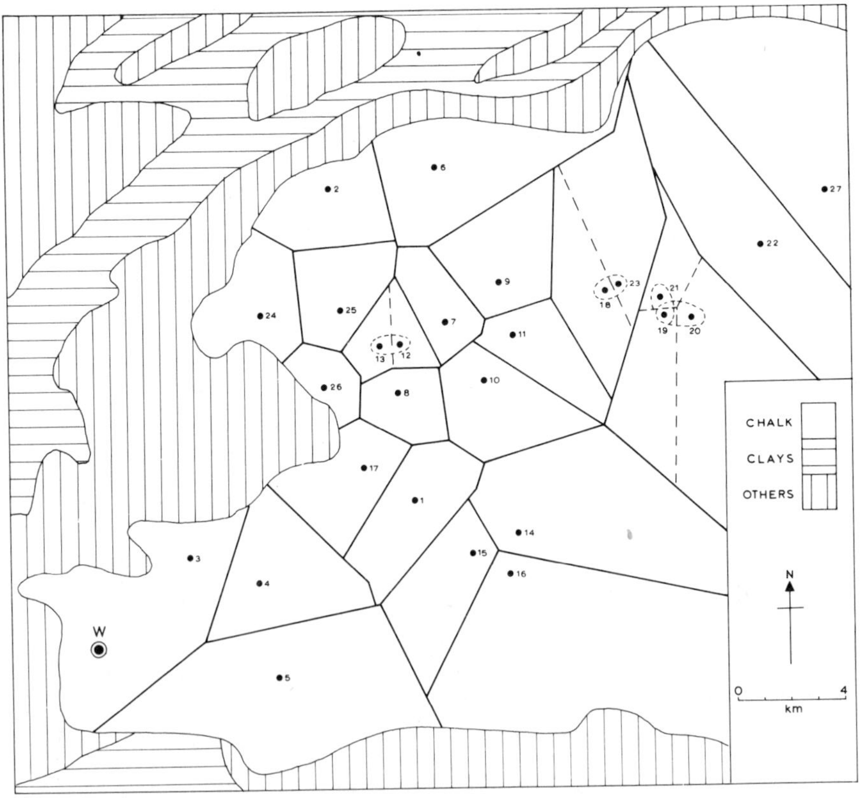

Figure 1 Locations of neolithic long barrows (indicated by dots) on the chalklands of the west Salisbury Plain, south Britain. By drawing unweighted Thiessen polygons the chalkland has been divided into 'territories' each with one barrow. (W indicates the enclosure at Whitesheet Hill). Data from Grinsell 1958 and Ashbee 1970.

However it is possible to counter that this argument sets the population impossibly low. A single family of six and their descendants, assuming the population did not increase, would, in 1000 years, given 25 years per generation, produce 240 dead, requiring (at 6 per barrow) 40 barrows. The barrows of Wessex would thus be the result of three families over this period. A mean population for early neolithic Wessex of 18 persons in more than 3000 sq.km. seems, however, too small – less than 0.01 per sq.km.

The inescapable alternative is that only some of the dead were buried in long barrows, and the others were disposed of by means which have left no trace, as is common in many communities. Indeed the practice of excarnation by exposure may well have operated for those whose bones were later interred in the barrows, since the remains were often altogether disarticulated. The barrow was used only for a few decades and then closed. But it would still have been an impressive monument subsequently, and a possible focus for the religious life of the community.

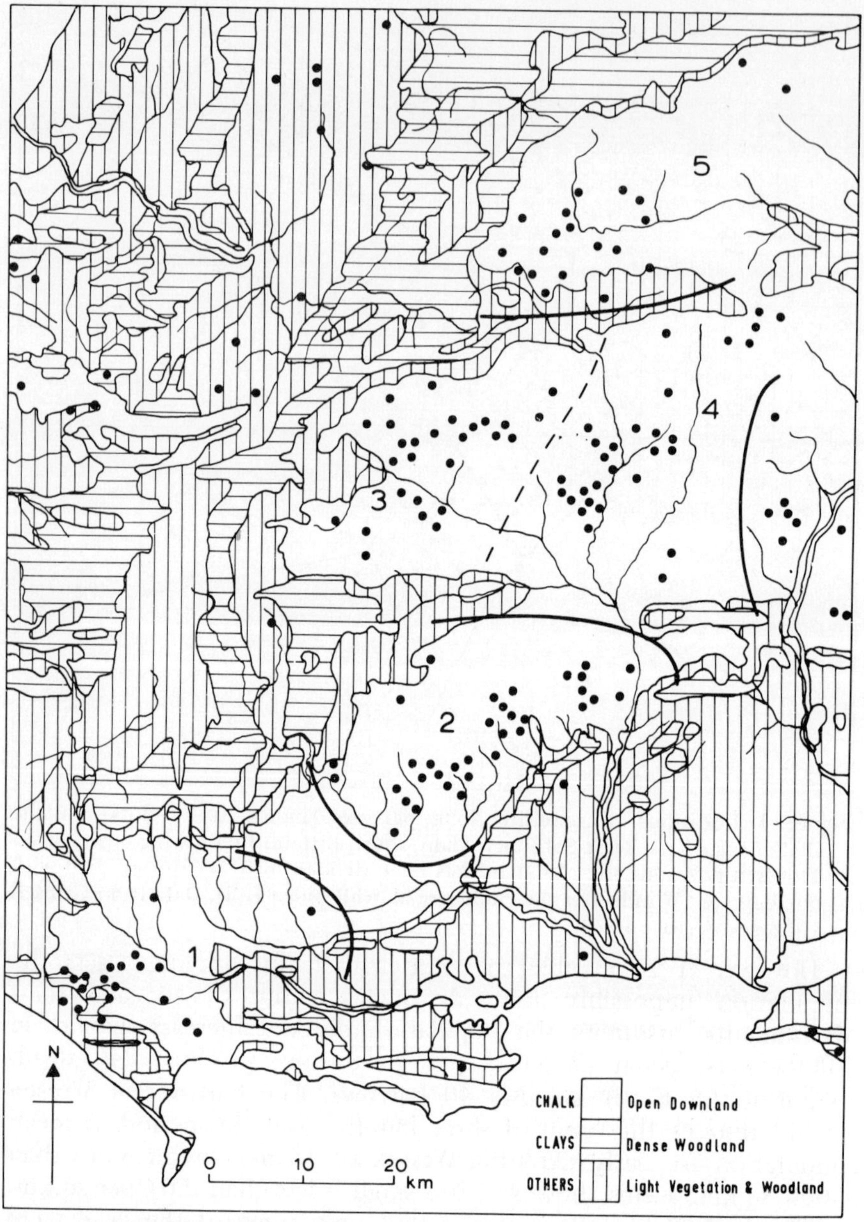

Figure 2 The principal groups of neolithic long barrows in Dorset and Wiltshire, as listed by Ashbee 1970.

It is possible that agriculture at this time was on a system of shifting cultivation. Soudský (1968)has described such a system in the loess lands of Czechoslovakia, where a community of about 125 persons occupied a total area of 2 square kilometres, shifting the location of the village every 15 years to one of four or five sites, and returning after 60 years or so at the beginning of a new cycle. Something of the same, initially in forest clearings, may be envisaged in

Wessex, although the groups may have been smaller – from 20 to 100 persons. The territories of roughly 10 sq.km. seen in Fig. 2, giving (on this hypothetical assumption) a total land area of 10 to 50 hectares per person should certainly have been adequate. The long barrow would be a permanent feature of the territory.

Ashbee has calculated that the Fussell's Lodge long barrow required 5000 man hours in its construction, or 500 man days. This is not a large figure and implies no supra-territorial organisation. No doubt the lineage in one territory might aid its neighbour in return for a good feast – and feasting was certainly part of the funeral ritual (Piggott 1954, 60). Such limited cooperation is known from many parts of the world in essentially egalitarian societies – 'family-oriented cooperative projects which are paid for in food given to the workers' (Heizer 1966: 828). It is not clear why only a favoured few should be buried in such a way, yet if the territorial argument is accepted, there were factors favouring the construction of a single barrow in each territory. In other words the existence of a barrow may have been a requirement of the community for social or religious reasons, rather than primarily a means of disposal of the dead. I am not aware of ethnographic parallels for the construction of such a monument soon after the colonization of new land, but perhaps they exist. Certainly the land surface beneath the South Street long barrow (Fowler and Evans 1967), as well as showing unexpected signs of ploughing, suggested only two clearances, separated by at least ten years, prior to its construction.

Larger monuments and chieftain territories

The different classes of neolithic monument in Wessex may be said to form a kind of hierarchy in terms of the manpower involved in their construction. It runs as follows.

(i) 10,000 man hours or less. Early neolithic unchambered long barrows. Barrows with stone chambers might take more than 5,000 hours, but could still be of this order.

(ii) About 100,000 man hours. Early neolithic causewayed enclosures. I estimate, using the formula proposed by Atkinson (1961:295) that the ditches and banks at Windmill Hill represent about 120,000 hours.

(iii) About 1 million man hours. The major henge monuments, of diameter greater than 600 ft., of which five are known in Wessex (Wainwright 1969; Burl 1969). Wainwright (1970:30) estimates 1.5 million man hours for Avebury and 0.9 million for Durrington Walls.

(iv) Over 10 million man hours. Silbury Hill and the completed cursus monuments (Dorset and Stonehenge cursus). Atkinson estimates a volume of 6.5 million cubic ft. of earth for the Dorset cursus (1955:9) which might suggest 9 million man-hours for its construction. He kindly indicates (personal communication) that he would tentatively estimate the minimum labour input for Silbury Hill at about 18 million man-hours. He makes also the important observation that, once begun, the process of construction was continuous, even though there were changes of plan.

(v) Over 30 million man-hours. Possibly Stonehenge III. Atkinson has estimated that the transport of the 81 sarsen stones for the final structure of Stonehenge, over a distance of 24 miles, would have taken 30 million man hours. The labour of dressing the stones is assessed at a further 500,000 hours, to which must be added the considerable effort of erecting the stones. If the recent suggestion be followed, however, that the stones of Stonehenge were transported to the Salisbury Plain by glacial action, the labour requirement for transport might be considerably reduced, and the labour involved in Stonehenge III might be no more, or indeed less, than that required for Silbury Hill.

This hierarchy of effort for the causewayed enclosures and long barrows is matched by one of distribution. Each of the areas of long barrows already distinguished has a single causeway camp (although the Marlborough Downs for some reason have three). (Fig. 3.)

Region	Total No. of long barrows	*(Stonebuilt barrows in brackets)*	Causewayed enclosures
Dorset Downs	20	(4)	Maiden Castle
Cranborne Chase	35	(0)	Hambledon Hill
West Salisbury Plain	27	(0)	Whitesheet
East Salisbury Plain	29	(0)	Robin Hood's Ball
Marlborough Downs	21	(16)	Windmill Hill
			Rybury
			? Knap Hill

If we accept that stone-built barrows involved more labour than earthen ones, the long barrow/camp ratio on the Marlborough Downs is partly explained. Two camps (Hambledon Hill and Whitesheet) lie at the western extreme of their chalkland, but they may well have included within their territory some of the clay and oolite lands to the west.

It is particularly interesting that this territorial division seems to persist into the later neolithic period, although the building of long barrows and the construction of causewayed camps had by then ceased. There are ten henge monuments in Britain with a diameter greater than 600 ft. Five of them are in Wessex. They related closely to the previous territories, and to the causewayed camps (cf. Smith 1971), (Fig. 4).

Region	*Henge*	*Diameter of Henge*	*Former Causewayed Enclosure*	*Greatest Diameter of Causewayed Enclosure*
Dorset Downs	Mount Pleasant	1200 ft.	Maiden Castle	1200 ft.
Cranborne Chase	Knowlton South	750 ft.	Hambledon Hill	1050 ft.
Salisbury Plain	Durrington Walls	1720 ft.	Robin Hood's Ball/Whitesheet	750/640 ft.
Vale of Pewsey	Marden	1700 ft.	Knap Hill/Rybury	650/520 ft.
Marlborough Downs	Avebury	1390 ft.	Windmill Hill	1270 ft.

The causewayed camp at Knap Hill, already noted as anomalous, does not find a corresponding major henge. Nor does Whitesheet, its territory apparently uniting with the east Salisbury Plain. The land which it may have served to the west could conceivably have come within the sphere of the four henges at Priddy, each of c. 500 ft. diameter.

There are of course other henges in Wessex, but they are all much smaller, less than 300 ft. in diameter except for the second henge at Knowlton and Stonehenge itself. There is no reason to suppose that all henges had the same function, and the special astronomical significance of Stonehenge is well known, so that we may reasonably distinguish these from the major henges.

The model applied

On the basis of the proposed model (itself admittedly hypothetical) we can assert that each early neolithic region served by a causewayed camp was the home of an emerging chiefdom. Each had on the average 20 long barrows, which might suggest a population of between 400 and 2000 persons. If we assume that one fifth of the population could be mobilised for public works for three months of the year, we have a potential annual work output of between 80,000 and 400,000 man hours. So a causewayed camp could be built in a single year.

It is just possible that the cursus at Dorchester in Oxfordshire was built during the early neolithic period (Atkinson, Piggott and Sandars 1951:63) and it would certainly present a problem if the same were true of the Dorset and Stonehenge cursus. For the Dorset cursus would then reflect at least 25 years work. But in fact we know that the Dorset cursus was built in at least two, and perhaps in several stages. Moreover Leach (1959:13) has rightly stressed that what seem today impressive and coherent achievements, reflecting perhaps the concept of a single mind, were often the result of accretions over

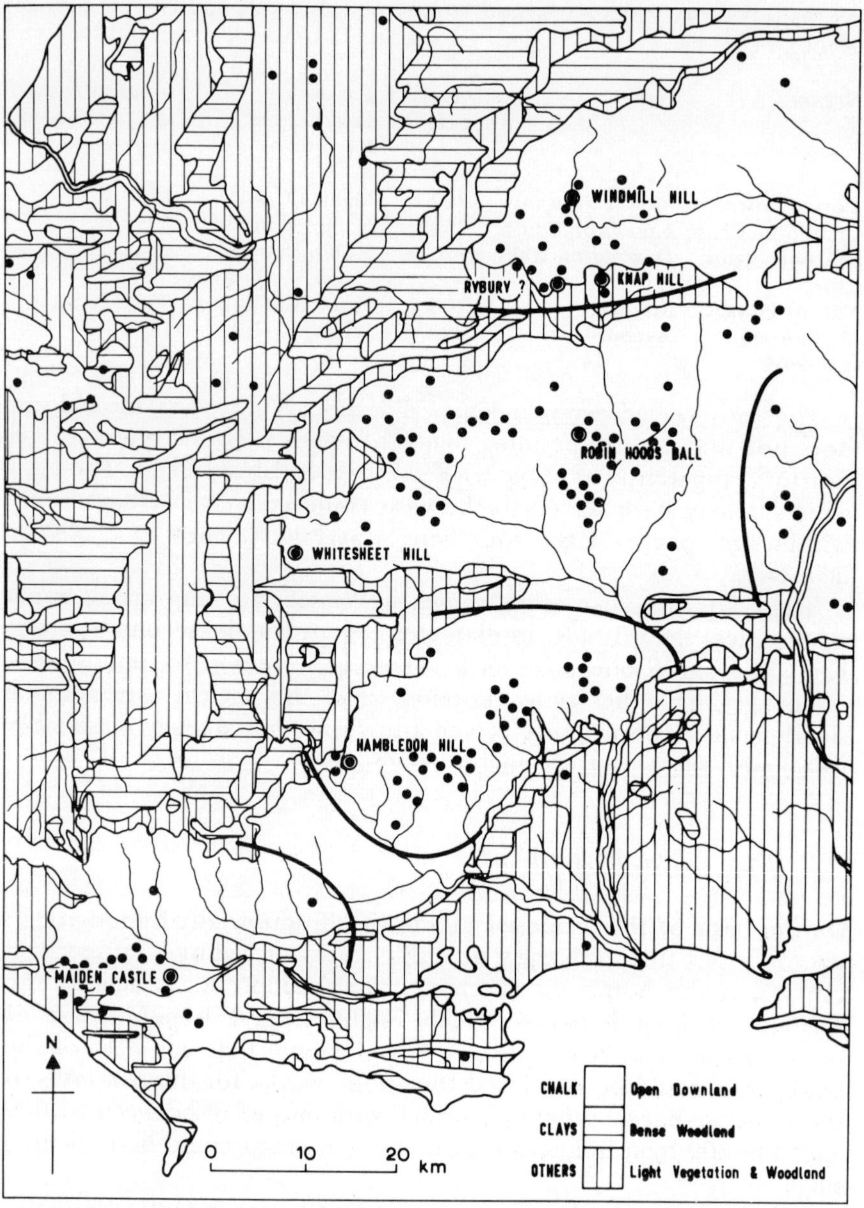

Figure 3 The neolithic causewayed enclosures of Dorset and Wiltshire in relation to the long barrows. Note that each of Ashbee's barrow groups is served by an enclosure.

many centuries. The same is true of Mediaeval cathedrals, and is of course now well documented for Stonehenge, although Silbury Hill was the result of a continuous process of construction. The early neolithic construction of cursus monuments would be more intelligible in these terms.

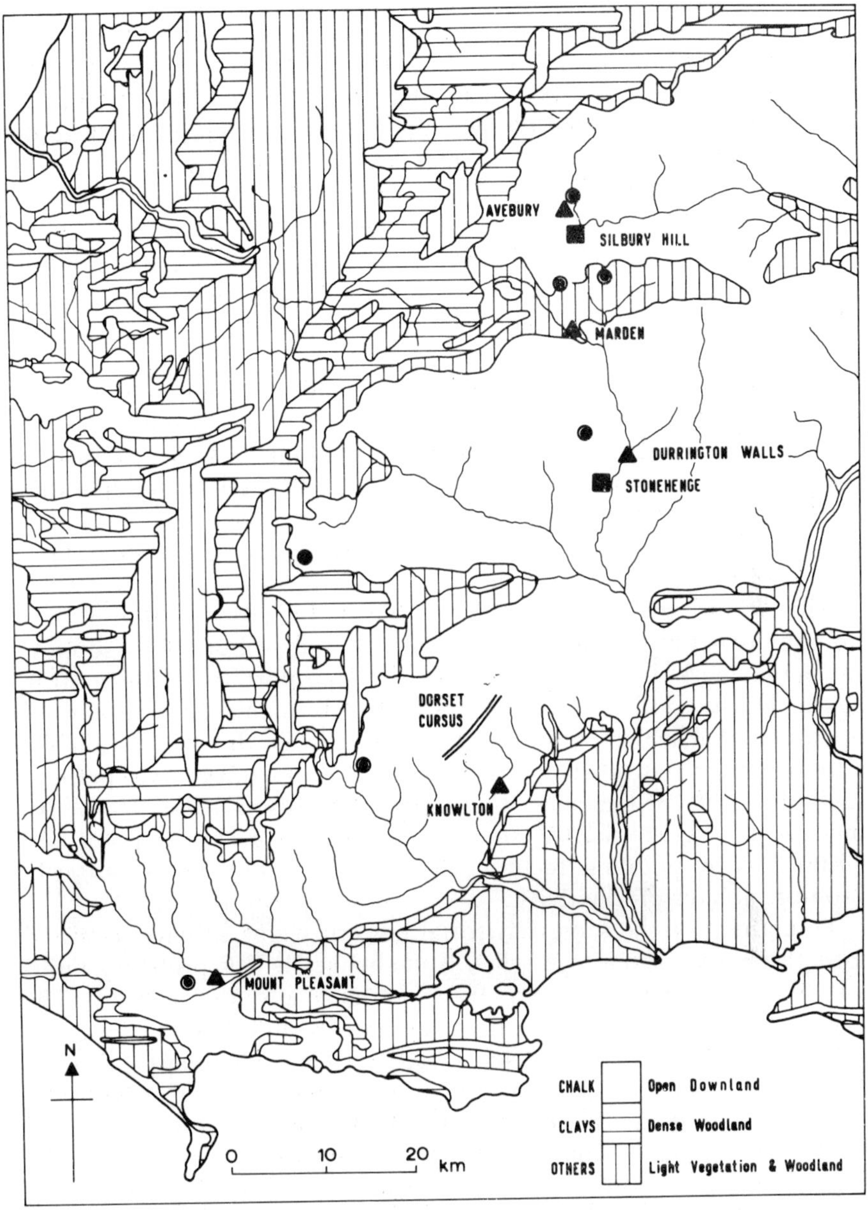

Figure 4 The major henge monuments of Dorset and Wiltshire (shown by triangles) in relation to the earlier neolithic enclosures (shown by circles). The large monuments at Stonehenge and Silbury Hill are also shown. Note that each area formerly served by a causewayed enclosure now has a major henge, except the west part of the Salisbury Plain, which is now apparently united with the eastern part.

Turning now to the late neolithic period, we are perhaps entitled to think in terms of an increased population and a more developed social hierarchy. For certainly the carrying capacity of the land should have been greater than the population estimated so far. If we were to take a figure of 10 per square kilometre, and 1,000, 1,400 and 1,000 sq.km. respectively for the Marlborough Downs, the Salisbury Plain and the Dorset chalklands, this would give us a total Wessex population of 34,000 persons. Each major henge would serve a population of about 5,000 persons, affording a possible annual mobilization of 1 million man hours. This was certainly sufficient to construct the henges. This was, of course, approximately the time of the supposed arrival of the 'Beaker Folk'. But until we know more of their settlement pattern and economy, it is preferable to think of their participating in the emerging social organization, rather than determining it.

For Silbury Hill, on the other hand, and especially Stonehenge III – for which the sarsen stones probably came from the Marlborough Downs anyway – we might well think in terms of further cooperation between the different regions, a 'confederation' like that of the Creek Indians in the eighteenth century. Or better, we might envisage the five Wessex chiefdoms coalescing into one greater chiefdom with five constituent tribes.

This would give a theoretical annual mobilization potential of 7 million man hours. But the concomitant redistribution to support the large work force would imply the transport of produce from south Dorset and the north Marlborough plains to the site of operations. Wheeled vehicles were not, it is thought, available, although river transport should not be ruled out since it was perhaps used for the Stonehenge bluestones (Atkinson 1960:107). An increase in the size of the social unit, beyond a certain point and without corresponding technological advance, does not necessarily promote greater productivity.

Something of the same territorial pattern seems to have persisted into the early bronze age when Stonehenge III was probably built, although the major henges were perhaps no longer used. The evidence then is from burials, single graves under round barrows, some of them exceedingly rich (Piggott 1938). Fleming (1971) has recently studied the distribution of these barrows and established four particularly dense concentrations of them, with densities well above 6 per square kilometre, in regions which may be related to the four invariant traditions already recognized (Fig. 5): Maiden Castle/Mount Pleasant; Hambledon Hill/Knowlton; Robin Hood's Ball/Durrington Walls; and Windmill Hill/Avebury (Fig. 4). There is a lesser concentration some way east of Marden, and another near Whitesheet. But what emerges above all is the great concentration in the Stonehenge area and this was clearly the most important burial region. The force of Fleming's elegant analysis is incontrovertible, but it is unnecessary to draw on the hypothesis of a predominantly pastoral economy. The old regional patterns are still visible, and the Wessex early bronze age population preferred to give influential

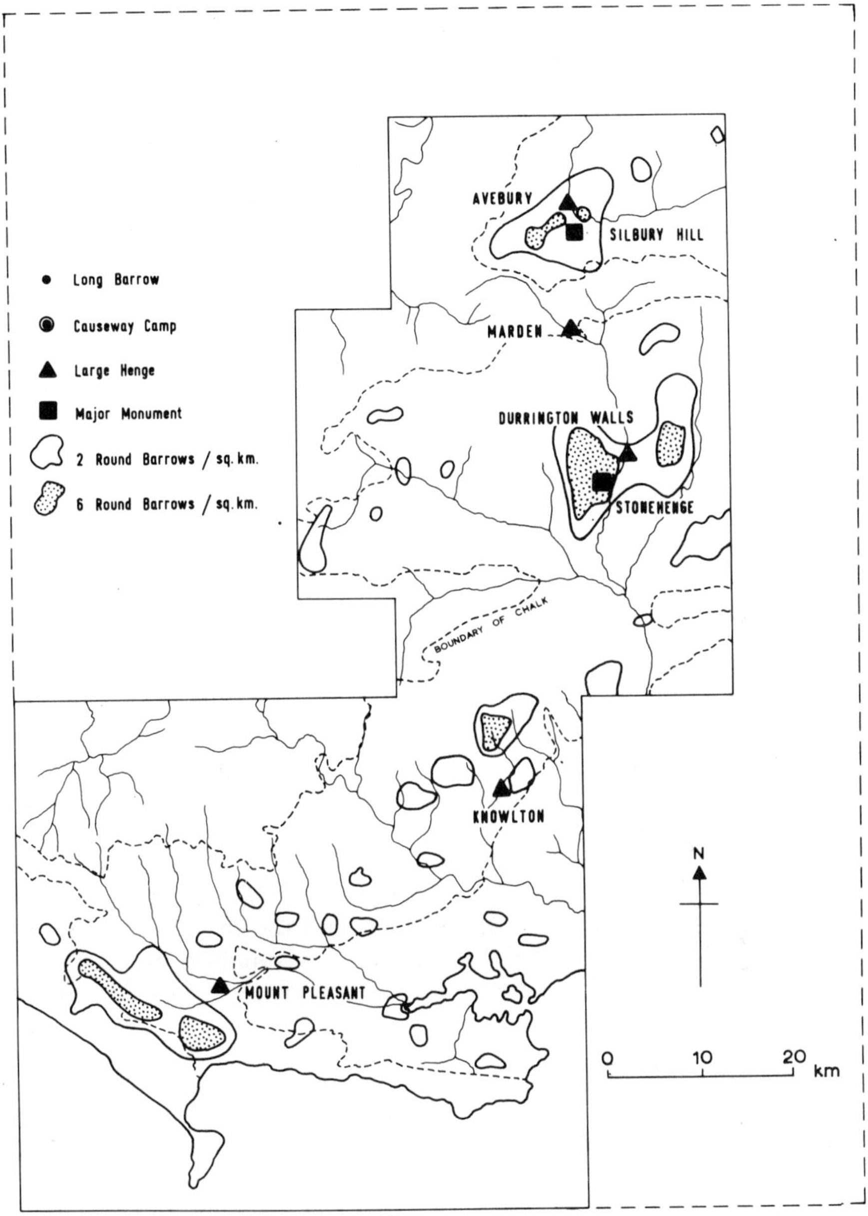

Figure 5 Distribution of the early bronze age round barrows on the chalklands of Dorset and Wiltshire (after Fleming 1971) in relation to the principal monuments of the late neolithic. The four main clusters suggest the persistence of regional divisions seen in figs. 2 to 4.

people burial near the centre of tribal areas, in the same way as they used to meet there at causewayed camps or henges. The special importance given to the Stonehenge area would support the tentative suggestion that the Salisbury Plain chief had by now become the paramount of a wider unit at the end of the neolithic.

On the basis of the field monuments of the successive phases in Wessex, a hypothetical picture has thus been constructed of emerging chiefdoms in the early neolithic, developing to full scale chiefdoms at the time of the henges, and possibly to a single unified chiefdom with four or five sub-regions at the time of Silbury Hill or Stonehenge III. This territorial pattern is still seen in the Wessex early bronze age (which may have been the period when Stonehenge III was constructed), but disappears from view in the later bronze age. (A surprisingly similar configuration re-emerges in the iron age, where it is documented by the hill forts. But occupation is by then no longer concentrated so exclusively upon the chalklands, so that a detailed comparison is not quite so striking.) It remains now to consider the relevance of the chiefdom model for features other than the distribution and scale of the monuments.

Specialization in the neolithic

Several of the salient features of chiefdoms listed earlier are implied in the preceding discussion, and indeed implicit in the monuments themselves. The organization of public labour (14) on such a scale necessitated some measure of redistribution (2) of food, and some central, organized control (9), at least during construction, presumably vested in an individual (1).

In addition, the very great number of early bronze age barrows compared with those of the neolithic is at least suggestive of an increased population density (3), although not an incontrovertible proof. We should expect this on *a priori* grounds anyway, following the introduction of a farming economy at the beginning of the neolithic (cf. Atkinson 1968:87). This, and the formation of larger territories documents an increase in the total numbers in the society (4). An increase in the size of individual residence groups (5) cannot yet be documented, although the central monuments increase in size.

One very important feature of the society not yet touched on is the existence of flint mines (Piggott 1954: 19 and 36 f.) some of which lie inside our area. With their deep shafts they do imply some specialization, although not necessarily full-time. A radiocarbon date from the Easton Down mines puts their use back into the earlier neolithic period, and there are very early dates from Cissbury in Sussex.

Craft specialisation (15) is implied here, sustained perhaps by the central organisation, for the large scale of the operation makes freelance activity unlikely. Similar specialization outside our area is indicated by the very wide distribution of axes of igneous stones (Piggott 1954:287 f.) originating in axe-factories in western Britain. Pottery was also traded over great distances (Peacock 1969), as no doubt were the flint axes themselves (Sieveking *et al.* 1970).

In the case of the flint mines, which are inside the chiefdom territory, it may be appropriate to speak of regional specialization within it, associated with redistribution (12). The mechanism for the movement or 'trade' of axes across territorial boundaries is less clear. Clark (1965) has suggested an inter-personal gift exchange, and this no doubt did occur. It would be possible also to suggest some additional and more highly organized mechanism for tribal exchange, using also the redistributive network already established within the territories by the chief for other produce.

The most obvious specialization, however, is in the use of some of the monuments themselves. Wainwright has written of the wooden rotundas in several of the larger henges (Wainwright 1970: cf. Piggott 1940) and very plausibly compared them with the council houses of the Creek and Cherokee Indians which are structually very similar (giving a wooden prototype for the stone rotunda at Stonehenge). It is not stretching the limits of proper ethnographic comparison too far to suggest that their function may likewise have been as 'centres which coordinate social and religious as well as economic activity' (9). Religious specialization is now hardly to be doubted at the stone circles of Stonehenge and Avebury, and Alexander Thom (1967) has shown how the observations of the sun and moon at such sites was part of a calendrical interest seen (perhaps later) over much of Britain, especially in the highland zone. Even if the megalithic unit of measure was related to the pace or span rather than to a fixed universal standard (Hammerton 1971), there can be no doubting the precision and geometrical skill with which they were laid out. Nor do we need to see an analogue computer in the Aubrey Holes to accept the long and careful observation needed to set up the Station Stones and the Heel Stone at Stonehenge. Specialist observers or 'seers', in effect a priesthood (11), were a feature of this society, as in many others which were not yet civilization-states. Obviously periodic ceremonies and rituals took place (10), perhaps associated, as in Polynesia (Sahlins 1958) with periodic distributions of produce.

Parallels for the pre-civilization monuments of neolithic Wessex are not hard to find in several parts of the world. The impressive earthworks of the Ohio/Hopewell culture and of the succeeding Temple Mound period offer a number of resemblances. And, as we have seen, the large chiefdoms of their Creek and Cherokee successors constructed council houses closely analogous to the wooden henge rotundas of Wessex.

Neolithic Wessex society indeed displays many of the features seen in chiefdoms elsewhere, and as Kaplan has stressed (1963:403): 'Just as we often underestimate the ability of many stateless societies to engage in large-scale communal production, so we often underestimate the high degree to which they are able to specialize their labour on a part-time basis'. There is no need to insist on full-time professionals for any of these enterprises, despite the skill displayed.

All of them were probably farmers as well, and there is no reason to suppose that anyone lived entirely from full-scale commercial enterprise or the 'profits' of trade in Wessex chiefdom society, which was still, at base, tribal.

Conclusions

It has been proposed that chiefdoms developed in Wessex during neolithic times. Using this notion, the size and distribution of the observed field monuments becomes intelligible, and they are seen as the natural counterpart of other features of the society.

The suggestion at once indicates some further approaches which, in a sense, could serve to 'test' the hypothesis. The first is the greater productivity (6) which is theoretically expected. If more settlements can be recognized and excavated, something further will be learned of farming methods. It may also be possible to follow up the intriguing suggestion of ploughing at this early time offered by the excavations at the South Street long barrow.

Secondly the predicted 'more clearly defined territorial boundaries or borders' (7) could be expected to have an influence both on artifact types and distributions. The recovery of more adequate pottery samples, again preferably by settlement excavation, and a systematic analysis, would be relevant here.

It should at once be admitted, however, that two important features of chiefdoms in some other areas are at present lacking. In the first place there is little evidence for ecological diversity (12). It may be that we should not regard the chiefdom territories as limited to the chalklands, although that is where their monuments lie, but imagine them as exploiting the heathlands on the sandy soils to the south and east, and the woodlands on the clays and oolitic soils to the west. If this could be demonstrated it would strengthen the application of the model.

Secondly, we have almost no direct evidence among the artifacts found (cf. Piggott 1954, *passim*) for personal ranking, as indicated by distinctive dress, ornament or possessions (18, 19). Only the beautifully worked jade axes and stone mace-heads, occasionally found, might indicate this. Dr. Isobel Smith (personal communication) kindly points out that two of the three jade axes found in any sort of context in south-west Britain were from causeway enclosures. Both were surface finds: one inside the enclosure on Hambledon Hill, the other from High Peak, Devon. One possibility is that such material signs as existed were of perishable materials. We could then argue that the finery of the Wessex early bronze age, seen in the rich burials, does not reflect a new attitude to personal ownership and display, but merely the greater opportunity for its expression offered by the development of metallurgy.

That would not be entirely convincing. It is wiser to admit that there may be different types of chiefdom society than to try to fit them all into the same mould. Otherwise the concept of chiefdom may becomy 'the ill-defined catchall' that Steward (1955:53) derides in the notion of 'tribal society'. To use the model of chiefdom for societies such as neolithic Wessex will be useful only so long as it establishes meaningful relationships between hitherto unrelated features of them, and suggests a search for new regularities in the material. Once it has done so, like the 'three age system' for the classification of artifacts, it will have to make way for, or be refined to yield, subtler and less inclusive concepts.

Acknowledgments

I am very grateful to Professor R.J.C. Atkinson and Dr. Isobel Smith for helpful criticisms of this paper.

REFERENCES

Ashbee, P. (1970) *The Earthen Long Barrow in Britain.* London, Dent.

Atkinson, R.J.C. (1955) The Dorset Cursus. *Antiquity* **29**, 4-9.

Atkinson, R.J.C. (1960) *Stonehenge.* London, Penguin.

Atkinson, R.J.C. (1961) Neolithic engineering. *Antiquity* **35**, 292-9.

Atkinson R.J.C. (1967) Silbury Hill. *Antiquity* **41**, 259-62.

Atkinson, R.J.C. Piggott, C.M. and Sandars, N.K. (1951) *Excavations at Dorchester, Oxon.* Oxford, Ashmolean Museum.

Atkinson, R.J.C. (1968) Old Mortality: some aspects of burial and population in neolithic England. In Coles, J.M. and Simpson, D.D.A. (eds.) *Studies in Ancient Europe, Essays Presented to Stuart Piggott.* Leicester, University Press, 83-94.

Burl, H.A.W. (1969) Henges: internal features and regional groups. *Archaeological Journal* **126**:1-28.

Case, H. (1962) Long barrows, chronology and causewayed camps. *Antiquity* **36**, 212-6.

Childe, V.G. (1958) Retrospect. *Antiquity* **32**, 69-74.

Clark, J.G.D. (1965) Traffic in stone axe and adze blades. *Economic History Review* **18**, 1-28.

Fleming, A. (1971) Territorial patterns in bronze age Wessex. *Proceedings of the Prehistoric Society* **37**, 138-66.

Fowler, P.J. and Evans, J.G. (1967) Plough-marks, lynchets and early fields. *Antiquity* **41**, 289-301.

Fried, M.H. (1957) The classification of corporate unilineal descent groups. *Journal of the Royal Anthropological Institute* **87**, 1-29.

Grinsell, L.V. (1958) *The Archaeology of Wessex.* London, Methuen.

Hammerton, M., (1971) The megalithic fathom: a suggestion. *Antiquity* **45**, 302.

Heizer, R.F. (1966) Ancient heavy transport, methods and achievements. *Science* **153**, 821-30.

Heizer, R.F. and Drucker, P. (1968) The La Venta fluted pyramid. *Antiquity* **42**, 52-6.

Kaplan, D. (1963) Men, monuments and political systems. *Southwestern Journal of Anthropology* **19**, 397-410.

Leach, E.R. (1951) Hydraulic society in Ceylon. *Past and Present* **15**, 2-26.

Peacock, D.P.S. (1969) Neolithic pottery production in Cornwall. *Antiquity* **43**, 145-9.

Piggott, S. (1938) The early bronze age in Wessex. *Proceedings of the Prehistoric Society* **4**, 52-106.

Piggott, S. (1940) Timber circles, a re-examination. *Archaeological Journal* **106**, 193-222.

Piggott, S. (1954) *The Neolithic Cultures of the British Isles*, Cambridge, University Press.

Renfrew, C. (1970) The tree-ring calibration of radiocarbon: an archaeological evaluation. *Proceedings of the Prehistoric Society* **36**, 280-311.

Renfrew, C. (1972) *The Emergence of Civilization, the Cyclades and the Aegean in the Third Millennium B.C.* London, Methuen.

Sahlins, M.D. (1958) *Social Stratification in Polynesia.* Seattle, University of Washington.

Sahlins, M.D. (1968) *Tribesmen.* Englewood Cliffs, Prentice Hall.

Service, E.R. (1962) *Primitive Social Organization.* New York, Random House.

Sieveking, G. de G., Craddock, P.T., Hughes, M.J., Bush, P. and Ferguson, J. (1970) Characterization of prehistoric flint mine products. *Nature* **228**, 251-4.

Smith, I.F. (1965) *Windmill Hill and Avebury, Excavations by Alexander Keiller 1925-1939.* Oxford, Clarendon.

Smith, I.F. (1966) Windmill Hill and its implications. *Palaeohistoria* **12**, 469-82.

Smith, I.F. (1971) Causewayed enclosures. *In* Simpson, D.D.A. (ed.) *Economy and Settlement in Neolithic and Early Bronze Age Britain and Europe.* Leicester, University Press.

Soudský, B. (1968) Criteria to distinguish cultural phases. Paper presented to the Research Seminar on Archaeology and Related Subjects. London, October 1968.

Steward, J.H. (1955) *Theory of Cultural Change.* Urbana, University of Illinois.

Thom, A. (1967) *Megalithic Sites in Britain.* Oxford, Clarendon.

Wainwright, G.J. (1969) A review of henge monuments in the light of recent research. *Proceedings of the Prehistoric Society* **35**, 112-33.

Wainwright, G.J. (1970) Woodhenges. *Scientific American* **223**, 30-7.

CHRISTOS DOUMAS

Grave types and related burial practices during the Cycladic early bronze age

The early bronze age in the Cyclades probably began during the 4th millennium B.C. and certainly endured throughout the 3rd millennium. Its existence was discovered towards the end of the last century, evidence being primarily derived from the excavation of cemeteries and graves. Early scholars designated the culture of this period in this area of the Aegean as Cycladic since it differed distinctly from chronologically parallel EBA cultures in the surrounding area. On the basis of its characteristic artifacts – pottery and marble vessels and marble figurines – three phases of the Early Cycladic were proposed; EC I, EC II, EC III. Although this subdivision was artificial and confusing it was universally accepted. Recently, on the same basis, Renfrew has distinguished three subcultures: Grotta-Pelos, Keros-Syros, Phylakopi City I, thus systematizing and amplifying our knowledge of the Early Cycladic. I prefer to use the term Pelos-Lakkoudhes rather than Grotta-Pelos because the early cemetery of Lakkhoudhes in Naxos has produced pottery forms hitherto unknown and of more primitive types, thus testifying a longer duration for this sub-culture.

The most characteristic forms for Pelos-Lakkoudhes pottery are spherical and cylindrical pyxides and funnel-necked jars standing upon a conical foot. This pottery is commonly decorated with incised rectilinear patterns usually arranged in a herring-bone motif. Marble vases are rare, the commonest form being a rectangular palette. Marble figurines are represented by a series of highly schematic forms and a small number of naturalistic types which appear towards the end of this phase.

The Keros-Syros phase of the Cycladic EBA is distinguished by the variety of forms both in pottery and marble vessels and by a high degree of technical achievement. Pyxides, jars, bowls, jugs, goblets, cups are shapes common in both pottery and marble and theriomorphic vases are also modelled in both materials. In addition to the incised patterns the pottery vessels are decorated with stamped curvilinear motifs and painted designs. Marble figurines are copious but are virtually all of the standardized folded-arm type.

The proliferation of pottery forms in the Phylakopi City I sub-culture is very marked. Incised decoration is limited to very few shapes whilst painted motifs are rather common. Marble vessels and figurines are quite rare, the latter being represented by highly schematic forms.

It is regrettable that the detailed study of cemeteries and graves – which yielded these artifacts – has advanced little. It is the aim of this paper to rectify this situation, for from a close examination of cemeteries and graves certain features recur, thus enabling one to formulate a model which has both practical and theoretical relevance.

Early scholars described EC cemeteries as extending on either flat or sloping areas in close proximity to settlements (Tsountas 1898:140-1; Stephanos 1903:53-4; 1904:57-8; Zapheiropoulos 1960:247); Tsountas noted that distinctions between graves in the same cemetery was achieved by grouping them in small clusters (1898:139-41; 1899:73-4). With regard to the individual graves, Tsountas, who was the first systematic excavator of Early Cycladic cemeteries, had classified them in two types: 'single' and 'double'. 'Double' graves were two-storied and the lower part served as an ossuary for earlier burials in the same tomb. He describes the 'single' graves thus, 'they usually consist of four upright and not very regular slabs; more rarely one of the sides, that is the one opposite the longest side is built of common stones' (1898:141-2). This was the classic typology for EC graves generally accepted (cf. Zervos 1957:25); although scholars have frequently given detailed descriptions of their plan and construction they have not embarked on any classification (Tsountas 1898:141-2; Stephanos 1905:216; Zervos 1957:25). Concerning the burials one gets the impression that multiple successive burials constituted an extremely rare phenomenon, the norm being one inhumation per grave (Tsountas 1898:143-4; Stephanos 1905:217).

Recent field-work has brought to light new evidence and prompted a more systematic study of the Cycladic EBA. In cemeteries extending on both flat and sloping areas the graves are supplied with a special construction on the capstone. An arrangement of white pebbles is found over graves dug in a flat area, as in the cemetery of Ayioi Anargyroi on Naxos. The graves dug in sloping ground are provided with a sort of platform supported by a small retaining wall made of rough stones embedded in clay. Such platforms are known from the cemeteries of Lakkoudhes and Akrotiri on Naxos. It is not known whether this construction over each grave was to serve as a marker or to weigh down the capstone. Irrespective of their siting some cemeteries exhibit clustering – the graves are clustered together in small groups separated from other groups usually by low rock eminences. Such cemeteries consist, as a rule, of cist-graves with all four sides lined with upright slabs (type A in the diagram). The cemetery of Chalandriani on Syros, where clustering is present but which consists of corbelled graves (type C) is an exceptional case. This local peculiarity may be due to the nonavailability of stone slabs or it may be that clustering is also the rule in cemeteries with corbelled tombs, but to extrapolate from one example is difficult. Whatever the grave type, in cemeteries where there is clustering there are only single burials. In graves of type A the body was accompanied with Pelos-Lakkoudhes objects whereas in type C graves the goods are of Keros-Syros culture.

In cemeteries where clustering is absent cist graves occur but with only three sides lined by stone slabs, the entrance being blocked by dry walling (type B). These graves are frequently multi-storied, served multiple burials and were furnished with Keros-Syros artifacts.

The change from grave type A to grave type B is directly associated with the change from single to multiple burials. It was more convenient to reopen the grave for each successive inhumation if the entrance was blocked with dry walling than to remove a flagstone. Perhaps clustering and multiple inhumations served the same purpose ostensibly, the marking off of groups of people from others. Since multiple burials are of Keros-Syros phase, which coincides with the appearance of nucleated villages in the Cyclades and probably an increase in population, this practice may have replaced clustering where the ground available for cemeteries was limited.

Multiple inhumation was also practised during the Phylakopi City I phase. The graves consisted of rock-cut chambers (type D) but since so few graves were excavated in Melos and all had been plundered it is not possible to discern whether they were clustered, indeed only some of these graves could definitely be assigned to this phase.

This model of grave types and related burial practices during the Cycladic EBA is expressed diagrammatically below.

At the practical level this model facilitates systematic excavation of cemeteries and graves since from the location of the cemetery the type of grave marker can be predicted and from the type of grave found their spatial arrangement in the cemetery, the number of burials and the kind of grave goods can all be ascertained. The model has theoretical implications as well for it is evident that concomitant with the expansion and diversification of the Early Cycladic culture in some spheres, as is apparent from the discussion of the artifacts, other features remained virtually unchanged during its entire duration. This is an important observation, for since an archaeologist relies almost entirely on material objects for information it is difficult to formulate a holistic view of the culture with which he is dealing. Too frequently the appearance of new forms and/or the disappearance of old ones is emphasized and utilized as a basis for theories of culture change. The concept of cultural development should not be neglected and in order to gain some insight into the processes involved and their interplay the existence of persistent features cannot be underestimated.

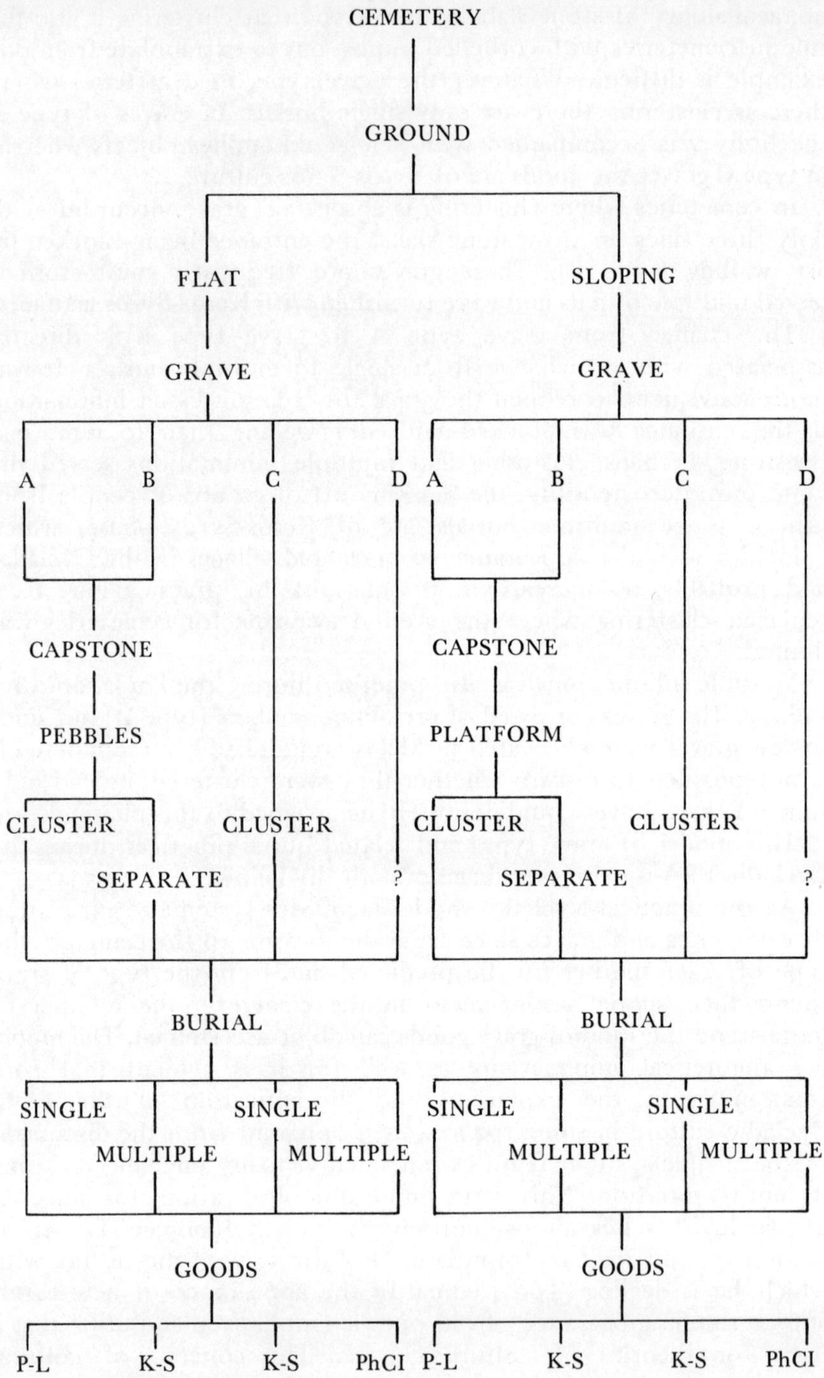

REFERENCES

Stephanos, K. (1903, 1904) Excavations in Naxos. *Praktika tes Archaiologikes Etaireias.*

Stephanos, K. (1905) Les tombeaux prémycéniens de Naxos. *Comptes rendus du Congrès International d'Archeologie, Athènes.*

Tsountas, C.·(1898, 1899) Kykladika. *Archeologike Ephemeris.*

Zapheiropoulos, N. (1960) Excavations in the Cyclades. *Archaiologikon Deltion.*

Zervos, C. (1957) *L'Art des Cyclades.* Paris.

KLAVS RANDSBORG

Wealth and social structure as reflected in bronze age burials - a quantitative approach

In Denmark, the central area of the so-called Nordic bronze age culture, hundreds of graves are known to us from the early bronze age barrows (Montelius Period I-III) (Broholm 1943). These graves – in which only a single person is buried – contain what looks like the personal equipment of the deceased: primarily weapons and jewellery made of bronze and gold. In the usual inhumation graves the artifacts are placed on the body itself.

The graves have been considered as representing either the interments of an 'upper class' or of the entire population (Moberg 1956), thus giving the following two alternative interpretations of the social structure:

(a) The society contains two main strata of which only the upper one is represented in the find material.
(b) The society contains no major social differences.

For supporters of either theory the stock of graves is quite homogeneous and no serious attempt has been made to describe the structure of the material. The women are normally believed to be 'equal' to the men, given the same kind of burial (Müller 1894:97:400).

As no metal is found naturally in the soil of Denmark, bronze and gold must have been imported and therefore of special value. In primitive societies the price of an object of costly material generally seems to be equivalent to the amount of material used. It is therefore of interest to know the weights of the equipment of bronze and gold from the graves, and to try to establish a quantitative approach to the problems of the social structure.

To produce basic data for this study (and for other investigations) the artifacts from the early bronze age in the National Museum (Copenhagen) – roughly 10,000 pieces – have been weighed. The finds were recorded with the necessary information on locality, reliability and category of the find, type and raw material of the artifacts, etc., plus a note on the physical state of preservation of each object graded in a scale from one to three. 944 of the grave finds were regarded as 'closed' and separated from the rest of the finds to be given the treatment briefly described below.

According to information on the groupings of the types of artifacts within the area and knowledge of the geographical distribution of the graves, Denmark was divided into five zones:

1. Island of Bornholm (in the Baltic)
2. The Danish Isles
3. Northeastern Jutland
4. Northwest Jutland
5. Southern Jutland

The find material was then arranged within the frame of the five geographical zones, the three periods (Period I, II and III) and the two sexes. 126 sexually indeterminable graves were now omitted. The deterioration of the bronze objects was taken as uniform and the information on the state of preservation has not so far been utilized. Special attention was paid to the presence or absence of gold, but unfortunately the rate of exchange between gold and bronze is unknown. (Contemporary Near Eastern sources put the ratio between gold and copper around 1:500-1000 (Heichelheim 1958:197 ff.).)

Histograms were made for the distributions of the weights of bronze (and gold) in the different groups of graves. An example is given in Fig. 1 for the male and female graves without gold of Zone 2, Period II. For the smaller groups containing gold histograms were made in two dimensions, so that the number in a square indicates the number of observations in the square, cf. the example in Fig. 2 for male and female graves of Zone 2, Period II. The distributions look irregular and they have a tendency to expose 'humps', in particular where the number of observations is high. It has not been possible to describe them with a simple well-known parametric family of distributions.

An identical tendency to humps is displayed by almost all groups without gold characterized by a reasonable number of observations. Therefore, it seems to be an essential property of these distributions and it would have been unfortunate to hide this fact. For the male graves three humps are observable, one around 0 g, one around 300-500 g, and one around 700-900 g.

The humps could be due to two reasons:

(a) The populations are heterogeneous.

(b) There are few objects in each grave and the weight of bronze in a grave is almost exclusively dependent on the kind of objects it contains.

If (b) is the reason and the populations are homogeneous, we might expect that the distribution of weight of one particular type of artifact would be unimodal and easy to describe. However, histograms for distributions of the types of object represented with a

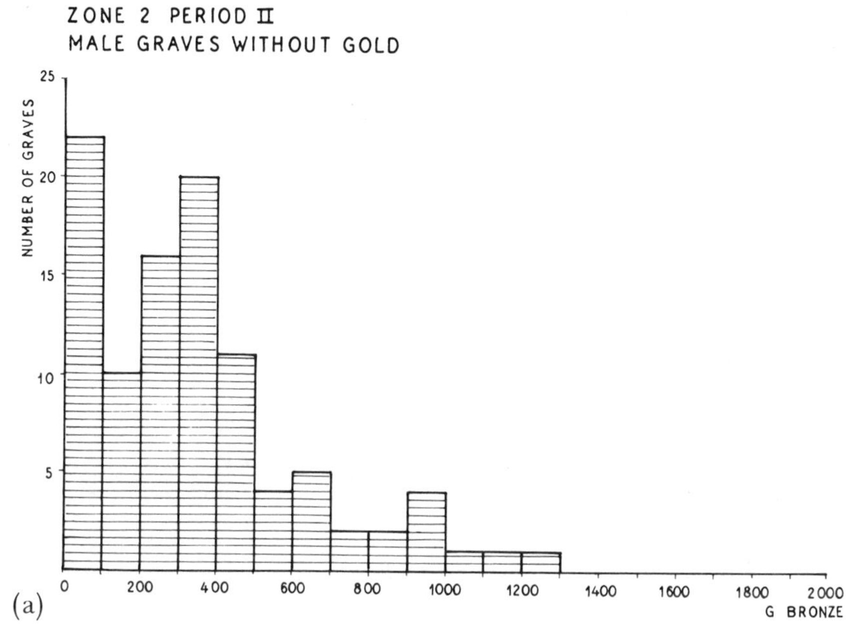

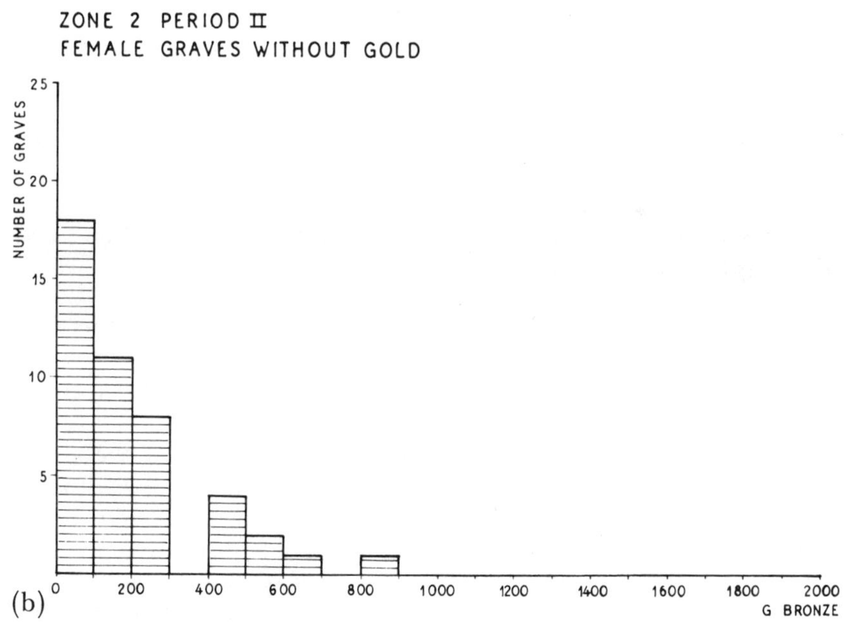

Figure 1 Frequency distribution of the weight of the bronze gravegoods (measured in grams) in graves with no golden gravegoods for a) male and b) female burials.

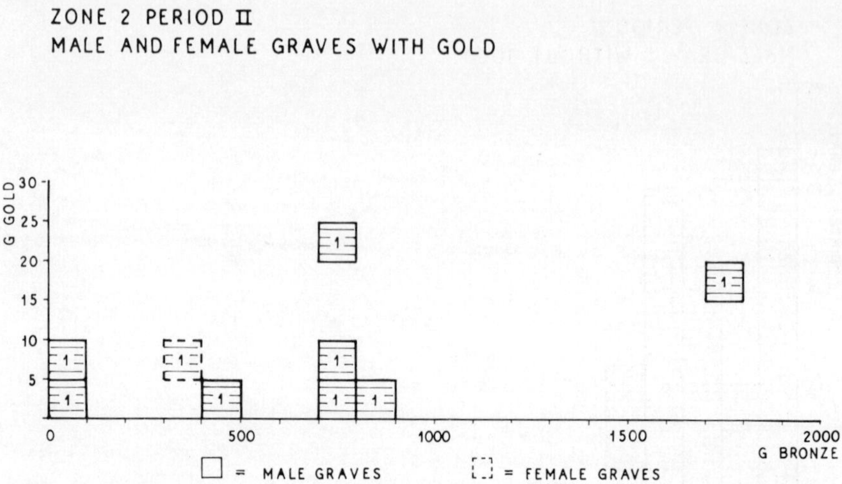

Figure 2 Plot of the weights of bronze and golden gravegoods in those graves which contain gold.

good number of observations also showed a very clear though minor tendency to expose humps.

The humps are therefore interpreted as being a result of heterogeneity within the populations of the particular zones and periods. We have different groups or kinds of graves, which we are not yet able to separate by means of independent information. (Four groups of wealth might thus have been in existence among the men. The fourth one, represented by the graves with gold, implies a low rate of exchange for bronze.)

In spite of this difficulty, the following main conclusions can be drawn from the grouping of the graves within zone, period and sex, and from the histograms:

(a) It is very clear that the graves containing gold generally are richer in bronze than the graves without gold. This result supports the basic theory of the bronze as a good indicator of wealth.

(b) The male graves generally contain more bronze – and more gold – than the female graves. The number of male graves equipped with objects of bronze and gold is also much higher than the number of the corresponding female interments: for the three periods together the ratio of male and female graves is 582:236. Thus, the woman's social status is probably lower than the man's.

(c) No female graves are known from Period I where the number of male graves is 22. In Period II the ratio between male and female graves is 268:98, in Period III 292:138. It should also be mentioned that the numbers of male and female graves containing gold in Period I are respectively 2 and 0, in Period II 25 and 4, and in Period III 64 and 24. The social status of the woman might have increased through the periods.

The conclusions (b) and (c) imply that the amount of metal generally reflects the social status – in terms of wealth – of the deceased. In support of this supposition the following observation should be added to conclusion (b). The twisted arm-rings of Period III occur in bronze in the female graves only. On the other hand, the golden specimens of the same type of ring are exclusively found in the male interments.

On the graves from Period II and III where the material seemed to be large enough another method of analysis was applied. Within each sex and period the graves were classified by zone and richness of the grave. The richness classes for the men of Period II were defined as 0-200 g, 200-400 g, 400-600 g, more than 600 g bronze, and graves containing gold. For the men of Period III the classes were 0-200 g, 200-400 g, more than 400 g bronze, and graves containing gold. For the women of both periods the classes were defined as 0-200 g, and more than 200 g bronze, plus graves containing gold.

Chi-square tests for homogeneity between the zones were performed. Homogeneity between zones was accepted in Period II for both sexes and heavily rejected in Period III also for both sexes. No zone was similar in the two periods, cf. the great amount of gold in the graves of Period III. This also reflects observations not yet mentioned from the histograms above. Considering the types of artifacts as well, Denmark is more heterogeneous in Period III than in Period II (Randsborg 1968).

In Period III, Zone 4 contains more rich male graves than poor ones (the numbers of graves ascribed to the four classes are respectively 11, 9, 33 and 25). This is in contradiction to all other zones. The female graves of the same period and zone do not show this pattern, which might underline the different social status of the sexes. The strange distribution of the male graves could further indicate the existence of a 'lower class' not represented in the find material. It is hard to believe that this structure of wealth can be shown by any society taken in total. More probably it is a phenomenon linked with an 'upper class' of a stratified society (Fried 1967:185 ff.). Also for this conclusion it is implied that the amount of metal in the graves generally reflects the wealth of the dead or of their milieu.

A lot of analytical problems, such as the deterioration of the bronze objects, so far remain unsolved. However, it is worth presenting a few preliminary results for further thought. In fact, a lot of thought is needed to comprehend the range of this method. Quite simple in itself, it might also prove applicable to other fields of archaeology than the nordic bronze age.

Acknowledgment

I am greatly indebted to Mr. Steen Andersson and Mr. Steffen Lauritzen, Institute of Mathematical Statistics, University of Copenhagen, who efficiently carried out the statistical work.

REFERENCES

Broholm, H.C. (1943) *Danmarks Bronzealder I.* København.

Heichelheim, F.M. (1958) *An Ancient Economic History I.* 2nd Ed. Leiden.

Moberg, C.-A. (1956) Till frågan om samhållsstrukturen i Norden under bronsåldern. *Fornvannen* 51, 65-79 (with a summary in English).

Müller, S. (1894-97) *Vor Oldtid.* København.

Randsborg, K. (1968) Von Periode II zu III, Chronologische Studien über die ältere Bronzezeit Südskandinaviens und Norddeutschlands. *Acta Archaeologica* XXXIX, 1-142.

ANDREW FLEMING

Models for the development of the Wessex culture

> They are assuredly, the single sepultures of kings, and great personages, buried during a considerable space of time, and that in peace. There are many groups of them together, and as family burial places; the variety of them, seems to indicate some note of difference in the persons there interr'd, well known in those ages. Probably the priests and laity were someway distinguished; as well as different orders and stations in them. (Stukeley 1740:43-4)

For a long time it has been accepted that the character and contents of the burial mounds of England ought to provide the prehistorian with insights into the society of their builders. However, looked at from this point of view, many assemblages found in graves are distinctly unpromising. A notable exception is the south English Wessex culture, defined by Piggott in 1938. As originally outlined the Wessex culture was a true culture in Childe's sense of the term, and its definition was not intended as an exercise in sociological reconstruction. Nonetheless, it can be argued that the Wessex culture, which is frequently characterized by rare archaeological types made from exotic materials, is best seen as a cross-cultural group which, with a little adjustment, can be seen to represent the 'richest' graves in contemporary southern England. This paper discusses the nature of Wessex society, as shown by the burial mounds and their contents, and goes on to consider models for the rise of such a society. Sites in italics are listed in an Appendix.

The nature of Wessex society

For the purposes of this paper I shall deal with 'rich' graves, defining as 'rich' those graves which contain a number of exotic materials, objects exhibiting skilled craftsmanship, or both of these things. Space prevents me from going into too much detail here; the list of graves which emerges is roughly coterminous with that originally produced by Piggott. In a perfect world, one might wish to produce a 'scale' of 'wealth', not a simple rich/poor dichotomy, but there are severe practical and interpretational difficulties here (see for instance Ucko, 1969).

The Wessex culture thus adjusted is characterized by burials, usually in or under round barrows, in an area to the south of a line drawn between the Severn Estuary and the Wash. Most of them are unsexed cremations, and in many cases these have not survived. This awkward fact has not prevented some workers from doing their own sexing, suggesting that graves with daggers belong to males, graves with ornaments to females. There seems to be no good reason why the wearing of daggers should have been confined to males (indeed, the so-called 'knife-daggers' are supposed to be characteristic of women's graves) even if the grave goods are seen as personal equipment; they might, of course, represent regalia, in which case this kind of sexing would be even less appropriate. Much the same remarks apply to the supposed correlation between ornaments and female graves. It is amusing to find Stukeley on the horns of this particular dilemma. A burial accompanied by both dagger and ornaments elicited the comment 'this person was an Heroin, for we found the head of her javelin in brass' (1740:44)

These burials included not only mature men, but sometimes children and young persons. A child of about 8 years of age is represented at *Easton Down,* children of about 15 years at *Stockbridge Down* and the *Mound of the Hostages, Tara,* an individual of 20 years at *Hengistbury Head*, and a person of about 21 years at *Ridgeway barrow no. 7.* Whether women were given rich burial is strictly unknown; the *Manton* burial was alleged to be that of an aged woman, apparently on the evidence of the skull, in 1907. Other contemporary barrow burials certainly included some women.

These 'rich' burials vary considerably in character. In central Wessex they are quite often found in cemeteries of up to 12 or 15 barrows, arranged in rows or clusters. These cemeteries include a high proportion of special barrow types (bell- and disc-barrows) and the simple bowl barrows are larger and higher than average. (Fleming, 1971b:147-8). Bell- and disc-barrows claim a larger share of rich burials than might be predicted from their relative numbers, and their distribution in southern England coincides with that of known Wessex graves and objects. Typical artifacts and barrows are found outside Wessex proper, in Somerset (Grinsell, 1939) Devon (Fox, 1948) Monmouthshire (Burgess, 1963) as well as West Sussex (Grinsell, 1940) and Norfolk (Clarke, 1960:73). At *Radley*, in Berkshire, a Wessex grave was found in a ploughed-out barrow just off the line of what looks from the air-photograph to be a classic Wessex linear cemetery.

Thus in many cases rich graves take their place beside more poorly furnished types, in complex, planned cemeteries. Sometimes, however, rich graves are found in specially large and apparently isolated mounds. Examples occur at *Hove* (approaching 60 metres in diameter) *Rillaton* (30 metres) *Hengistbury Head* (33 metres) and *Stanton Harcourt* (43 metres). In the Wessex heartland the *Upton Lovell Golden Barrow* and the *Manton* barrow fall into this category. Sometimes the individualistic appearance of these barrows is reinforced by their siting, which makes them dominate the local landscape; one thinks of *Clandon, Manton, Hammeldon* and *North Molton* and perhaps *Portsdown* if there was a barrow on this site. However, at *Hengistbury Head* the barrow which dominates the promontory is not the one which produced the rich grave goods.

There is a lot we would like to know about the correlation between barrow size and the richness of the goods found within. Outside central Wessex there does seem to be a rough correlation. In Wiltshire the situation is less certain. A passage from Colt Hoare's writings (1812-21, I:210) is illuminating:

> The history of this *tumulus*, which our learned Doctor would, for its superior size and beautiful form, have styled a KING BARROW, shows what little regard we ought to pay to system [perhaps a prophetic comment!] for here, at the vast depth of nearly 14 feet, we find only the deposit of an infant, accompanied by a simple drinking cup: whilst in no. 21, a mean and insignificant barrow, we discover articles of the greatest beauty and importance. The motto of *fronti nulla fides* may be justly and strictly applied to barrows; and the antiquary who makes them his study, must neither be disappointed in finding only a simple interment in the largest barrow, and the finest urns and most precious trinkets in the smallest.

Colt Hoare says the same thing elsewhere (ibid.:46, 166) and one cannot lightly dismiss his testimony. To summarize: Wessex interments are frequently found in large or special barrows, but the mere fact that a barrow is large does not necessarily imply that a richly furnished grave will be found within it. Nor were rich graves always central in, and primary to, their barrows. Colt Hoare usually gives the impression that most of those he found were set into the old land surface, and therefore were primary or satellite burials. But there are important exceptions, like the groups at the *Upton Lovell Golden Barrow, Clandon,* and *Ridgeway no. 7. Collingbourne Ducis 12* and *Collingbourne Kingston 8* have both produced Wessex secondaries (the latter in the berm of a bell-barrow). At *Hammeldon* the interment is clearly a satellite. *The Mound of the Hostages, Tara* produced a true Wessex grave which was secondary to the Passage Grave. At *Stockbridge* a cremation accompanied by rich grave goods was in the ditch of a round barrow containing a primary Beaker female inhumation. Finally, the *Easton Down* burial was part of a flat urnfield.

Thus the limited evidence for the character of the richer burials suggests diversified traditions, and that they may quite regularly be found in subordinate or inconspicuous positions.

Let us now turn to the nature of the Wessex objects. The best illustrations of the material may be found in Piggott (1938), Thurnam (1869) Ashbee (1960) and Annable and Simpson (1964). A few basic points will be mentioned here.

Firstly, few of the precious materials found in rich graves occur naturally in Wessex. Amber came from East Anglia or even further afield, copper and tin from at least Cornwall. Faience was probably manufactured at a coastal site not too far from copper or copper salts, as apparently in Scotland (Newton and Renfrew, 1970:263-4). Although a little gold might be obtainable from Sussex (J.J. Taylor personal communication), it seems likely that much of the Wessex material came from outside the zone of rich graves. The stone for battle-axes and mace-heads may also have originated from parts of the Highland Zone, although the possibility of transportation by ice should also be borne in mind.

Secondly, the skills represented seem to have developed in different areas and contexts. Dr. Joan Taylor (personal communication) suggests that the Wessex gold-smiths developed sheet-working from Beaker antecedents, and that the use of tiny nails came from Brittany (see also Briard, 1970). Even if faience was made in Britain, the technique must have been introduced from outside. The special daggers of Bush Barrow and Camerton-Snowshill types seem to be derived from ultimately central European traditions. Spacer-plate necklace craftsmanship must be native to northern Britain (Craw, 1929: Appendix D and figure 8). Amber-working, and the technique of V-perforation, were known among the preceding Beaker cultures, whilst work in shale, jet or lignite must have been almost a 'cottage industry' in northern England, to judge by the number of barrows which have produced waste of such working.

What is new and exciting about the objects of the Wessex culture is the way in which the different skills interacted, so that Wessex craftsmen learned to fit different materials together and to transfer decorative ideas from one substance to another. It would be no exaggeration to say that they became obsessed by the problems of fitting things together. Already the Beaker craftsmen had mastered the technique of fitting wooden hafts onto daggers, and they sometimes fitted bone pommels or bronze studs to these hafts (Annable and Simpson no. 114). The Wessex craftsmen went further. The *Bush Barrow* macehead, which combines soft limestone, bronze fitting-ring, wooden haft and bone insets, symbolizes this new confidence (Annable and Simpson nos. 174-5). Gold nails could be set into wooden hafts to produce complex geometric patterns, as at *Bush Barrow* (Annable and Simpson no. 169 and photo) or into amber, as at *Hammeldon* (Kendrick, 1937). Wooden boxes or other objects were sometimes provided with bronze sheet or stud decoration as with the 'shield' at the *Bush Barrow* (Annable and Simpson, nos. 171-3) or the box at *Winterbourne Stoke G.4* (Annable and

Simpson no. 222). Bone was used occasionally for awl handles (e.g. Annable and Simpson no. 264) or to form insets for complex dagger-pommels (Thomas 1966:fig.3).

The Wessex craftsmen mastered the techniques of coating conical shale buttons with gold sheet, of encasing amber discs in gold, and of combining several materials in the halberd-pendants – amber and metal at *Hengistbury Head*, gold, metal and wood at *Manton*, amber, gold and metal at *Wilsford G.8*. At the last-named site what may have been a cranial disc (Thomas, 1966:7) was half-covered in incised sheet gold.

The making of sheaths, too, was essentially an exercise in the art of fitting different materials together, and must have been a skilled and complicated craft. Sheaths which had been lined with cloth were found at *Wilsford G.56* and *Collingbourne Ducis G.4*. The most interesting example, from *Stanton Harcourt*, was made of wood with a leather covering, and included thin metal sheeting. At *Winterbourne Stoke G.4* the leather sheath had an outer covering of basketwork (Thomas, 1966:5). At *Bush Barrow* a wooden sheath was lined with undressed leather. (Thomas 1965:145.)

Incidentally, this interest in accurate fitting may well establish Stonehenge IIIa and IIIb as within this general tradition.

The Wessex craftsmen were also transferring decorative motifs from one material to another. The cross-motif was known from Beaker 'sun-discs' (e.g. Annable and Simpson no. 94), from the bases of one or two Southern Beakers (Clarke 1970:Figs 875, 1021, 1065) on northern Irish Food Vessels (Abercromby, 1912:Figs 241a, 245a, 285a, etc.) and from the bases of pygmy cups all over Britain (e.g. Annable and Simpson no. 449; Savory 1958:Figs. 4 and 5). It appears on the *Hammeldon* pommel as gold nails in amber, and in complex form on the base of the *Upton Lovell G.2(e)* button cap (Annable and Simpson no. 233), and on the *Clandon* lozenge plate. Dr. Joan Taylor has already pointed out (Coles and Taylor 1971) that the decorative techniques of the goldwork link such sites as *Clandon, Portsdown,* and *Cressingham* with central Wessex. The motif of multiple parallel lines links the daggers, the goldwork and the shale and amber cups from the southern part of the distributional area. The technique of multiple bands of gold on the *Wilsford G.8* halberd-pendant (Annable and Simpson no. 180) occurs on shale beads (e.g. *Manton*, Annable and Simpson no. 196). At *Upton Lovell G.2(e)* the decoration of the gold plate finds intriguing echoes in the complex-pattern spacer-plates from the same burial (Annable and Simpson nos. 227, 232).

Finally, the craftsmen's self-confidence is shown by the use of different materials to make the same object; thus there are cups of shale, amber and even gold, dagger pommels of bone, amber or gold, 'belt-hooks' of gold (Annable and Simpson no. 176) or bone (Annable and Simpson nos. 306, 313, 332) and so on.

A minor Wessex interest was miniaturization. This is shown by the halberd pendants, the small grooved dagger in bone from Crug-yr-Afan (Burgess 1963:plate II) the tiny lozenge plate from the *Bush Barrow* (Annable and Simpson no. 177) and the small bead, shaped like a battle-axe, from *Wilsford G.7* (Annable and Simpson no. 148).

Enough has been said to demonstrate the complex interdependence of Wessex craftsmanship. The craftsmen concerned must have been working in very close touch with one another. Some of them may have been given barrow burial with appropriate grave-goods (e.g. Wilsford G.58, Wilsford G.60, Upton Lovell G.2(a) and Collingbourne Kingston G.4 (Annable and Simpson nos. 211-8; 267-73; 242-62; 383-9).)

Having tried to describe the material and to keep interpretative statements as simple and uncontroversial as possible, I shall now discuss possible models for 'the rise of the Wessex culture'.

Views of the Wessex culture: historical perspective

Since 1938 there have really been two groups of origin theories. The first group concerns the question of where the Wessex leaders came from. Piggott's original idea was that 'a dominant and intrusive aristocracy' invaded from Brittany (Piggott, 1938:94). Others have preferred central Europe as the source area (e.g. Childe, 1957:320; Annable and Simpson 1964:21). More recently there has been a reaction against the invasion model. Clarke (1968:233) points out that much of the routine cultural equipment of the graves is a normal component of the Collared Urn culture. According to Coles and Taylor (1971:12) European Bronze Age groups were 'contributing ideas to a native population in a stage of culture process which could be called self-aggrandisement'.

The second group of theories concerns the origins of the Wessex wealth. Piggott (1938:94) suggested that the Wessex people were 'middlemen' on the metal route from Ireland. Most subsequent writers have agreed with this, although they were divided on whether the Wessex authorities were directly controlling exports of metal from Devon and Cornwall, or whether they were levying tolls on caravan routes across their territory from Wales or Ireland. All these ideas are based on the proposition that Wessex leaders controlled the export of metal to continental Europe, and that their prosperity followed directly from this.

Childe disagreed (1940:135). He says the Wessex culture evidently belongs to 'a small ruling class expending their accumulated surplus wealth on luxury trade with far-flung connexions. The basis of that wealth was presumably the farming and gathering activities of subject populations . . . the new chiefs could extort a surplus to barter for metals, amber and even Mediterranean beads and to support skilled artisans to work these imports'. Thus to Childe the basis of Wessex wealth was agricultural, and the surplus was extracted by conquest and subsequent exploitation of the victims.

To Piggott and his school, the possession of metal resources or the ability to levy tools on those carrying metal, facilitated the purchase of exotic materials and skilled craftsmen. For Childe, the economic and social setup in Wessex led to a concentration of skills and materials. The difference is a fundamental one.

Recently Renfrew has suggested that the development of the Wessex culture was a culture process phenomenon, and that the introduction of metallurgy in southern England had similar effects to those which accompanied its development in the Aegean (Renfrew 1968:285; 1971:14). He sees the critical variable as the introduction of a developed metallurgy and prestige products. Desire for the possession of these objects would have stimulated the growth of wealth and thus furthered the demand from them. Following Service, he describes this phenomenon, in the Aegean and in southern Britain, as 'the rise of chiefdoms' (1971:14).

I myself have put forward the hypothesis that the Wessex culture may represent that of mobile pastoralists, and that the political pattern might have been similar to that in parts of Africa where pastoralists dominated more settled arable farmers.

It is now time to consider how well these models fit the available facts, how far they can co-exist, and whether it will ever be possible to decide which one is more appropriate.

Intrusive chieftains from abroad

The problem with this model is that there is no substantial body of intrusive cultural equipment in Britain at this time. Secondly, the continental parallels which have been drawn for Wessex material do not point to any *one* area in Europe. Professor L. Klejn kindly informs me that composite migrations are known, but in this particular case it would be very hard to develop a convincing hypothesis encompassing two or more of the areas concerned – Switzerland, south-west Germany, the Rhineland, central Germany and Brittany. In any case, many Wessex artifacts have their roots firmly within Britain. In general, buttons were preferred to continental-style pins, battle-axes to halberds. The ideal necklace, including beads of faience, amber and shale, is a British concept. The ring-headed pin from *Collingbourne Ducis G.4* was wrapped in a cloth-lined sheath, not used to fasten clothes, suggesting a British re-interpretation of its function. On the whole the external conquest model fits the facts rather badly.

Conquest of Wessex from within Britain

As Clarke has pointed out (1970:224) part of the Wessex culture seems to represent a resurgence of Collared Urn traditions, and its rise may well coincide with the apparent expulsion of late Southern Beakers to regions outside central Wessex. Certainly when rich burials are accompanied by pottery it is almost always Collared Urns or the associated pygmy cups. These Urns are so stereotyped and so widespread that population movements of some sort must have played a part in establishing their distribution. Long and medium-distance movements have been detected, like those which gave rise to the Wessex Biconical pottery series (Calkin 1962:34-40) or the Hilversum urns (Smith 1961). In parts of northern England the Collared Urn users had settled on what must have been marginal land, and increasing economic difficulties may have forced them to seek a living elsewhere (Fleming 1971a).

The conquest theory is quite attractive for the following reason. In a society of subsistence cultivators there are few opportunities for the sustained aggrandisement of individuals or their families, even in situations where this is a socially approved activity. Labour is required to expand output, and this can normally only be obtained from the members of a man's immediate kinship group, with all the obligations this entails. The situation is much the same when labour is organized on a communal basis. Conquest of one group by another followed by political domination or actual enslavement, both backed by the threat of force, would change this situation immediately, and might result in the horizon of rich graves under discussion. The problem here is, how can one ever demonstrate conquest, using archaeological data?

The role of intrusive craftsmen

Various explanations have been given for the presence in Wessex of craftsmen originating elsewhere. The commonest one may be frivolously termed the 'take me to your leader' hypothesis. This postulates that metal prospectors and craftsmen were sent to Britain to barter their skills in exchange for prospecting concessions and export licences for metals. Unfortunately the main regions implied – central Germany and Brittany – are not short of metals; and to suppose that the inhabitants of the chalks and gravels of southern England were in control of Cornwall and areas further north and west would require rather special pleading. Economic imperialism from continental Europe does not explain why skills from within Britain also seem to have been attracted towards Wessex.

Some scholars envisage the entry of a few craftsmen as having generated the whole of the craftmanship complex outlined in the first half of this paper. For instance, Coles and Taylor suggest that 'two external elements are reflected in the Wessex Early Bronze Age graves, elements which somehow stimulated the production of different artifacts by the local population' (1971:13). This view overlooks the fact that Wessex itself is very badly supplied with raw materials. Craftsmen working here would need to be taking advantage of a pre-existing situation, in which territorial expansion, political dominance or alliances, or an economic network of some sort secured supplies of raw materials from outside. Wessex must have been able to offer attractive working conditions as well as materials. Thus there is every likelihood of craftsmen arriving in the wake of social and economic change, but little chance of their being able to stimulate or initiate it.

The rise of chiefdoms

It is possible that the rich graves under discussion symbolize the development of an increasingly acquisitive society, with intensified economic and social stratification. These changes would in turn stimulate trade and craftmanship, as individuals and groups vied with each other in displays of impressive possessions. David Clarke has expressed this very well (1970:233), describing the contrast between rich Beaker burials and the Wessex graves as essentially that of differing sets of prestige equipment. Emulation must certainly have played a part in Wessex society, and precious objects were imitated in poorer materials. Metal pins were copied in bone, and so were segmented faience beads. Some of the graves almost certainly imply political or religious power, not merely personal wealth. As Colt Hoare said of the Bush Barrow mace-head, 'I think we may not be too fanciful in considering it an article of consequence' (1812-21, I; 202).

If the dynamic, acquisitive individual could achieve great social status at this time, the fact is only partially reflected in the grave groups. Rich grave goods are quite often buried with young people whose competitive lives cannot have been long, and probably with women too; rich graves occur in insignificant and subordinate positions, and where they are primary they are usually integrated into a barrow cemetery. All this suggests that status had a hereditary basis, and that the wealth displayed in the graves might well be the property of a group as much as the personal wealth of the person concerned. The distinction is important, because as Veblen pointed out long ago (1925:153) the success of competing social groups does not necessarily imply the same social climate or value system as that of the emulative individual. On Salisbury Plain, the barrow cemeteries, each in its own area, each with roughly similar numbers of large and distinctive barrows, each with roughly the same proportion of rich and poor graves, suggest very strongly the co-existence of groups, each one of roughly equal status (see Piggott's map, 1951:Fig. 61). Probably the cemeteries here are those of related social groups which shared the use of this area for burial and perhaps summer grazing, but which still felt a powerful sense of separate identity within a system of shared social conventions. This may be a classic fission and fusion arrangement, similar to the one which I have postulated for some sections of British neolithic society (Fleming, 1972). In these circumstances, how far the 'chieftain' acquired or even 'owned' his wealth, as opposed to administering that of the group, must be a matter for debate.

Thus although the Wessex graves may display features which allow them to be pressed into service to illustrate Service's hypothetical 'chiefdom stage' – and his criteria, when deployed against archaeological evidence, allow considerable elasticity – it is doubtful whether the critical developments in the chiefdom's genesis were taking place at this time. Evidence of a ranked society, craft specialization, and considerable manpower organization is certainly available at an earlier period.

There are at least two more theoretical considerations which are important here. It is one thing to point out that all prehistorians make anthropologically-based assumptions. It is quite another to suggest that archaeological data should be made to fit different stages in a typological model of social evolution. As others have observed, archaeology should generate its own models, if possible. There are also grave dangers of circular argument, as anthropologists claim that archaeologists have validated their theories, while archaeologists fit their data into what seems a coherent and convenient frame of reference.

Secondly, it is clear that the concept of prehistory as a series of stages has become increasingly inappropriate, even the divisions are based on technology or economy, two areas in which prehistorians have felt reasonably confident. It is questionable whether archaeological data permit more confidence in the detection of a series of social stages.

The pastoral hypothesis

I have suggested elsewhere that the Wessex culture may have been pastoralist in nature (Fleming, 1971b). I do not insist on this theory – in any case, it is always impossible to demonstrate pure pastoralism beyond the possibility of contradiction – but it fits some of the facts fairly well. In the context of the present enquiry it would provide a mechanism for the development of increasing differentials in wealth. The relationship between the words *pecus* and *pecunia* (Latin), cattle and chattel, and *skot* (cattle) and *skotnitsa* (treasury) (Russian), are not coincidental. They reflect the fact that for pastoralists skill and luck enable groups and individuals to build up wealth, whereas amongst cereal farmers, weather and crop disease affect the whole community much more evenly. If animals are used as a medium of exchange, a skilled herdsman who has accumulated enough 'capital' can manipulate and live off the 'interest' much more readily than a cereal farmer who attempts to use grain in the same way. Furthermore, the grazier does not have the limitation of labour supply – indeed, the labour he saves can be profitably employed for military purposes, in acquiring and defending grazing land for this rather wasteful form of land use.

A shift towards pastoralism could have taken place within Wessex, and led to the buildup of economic and social stratification. It could also have occurred on the marginal lands in south-western or northern England, since the degeneration of the soils in those regions would inevitably have led to a decline in arable emphasis; land shortage would then have led to a predatory expansion. Thus the pastoralist theory and the conquest theory are not mutually exclusive, and might profitably be combined.

Further possibilities

As Vernon Reynolds' brilliant paper has shown (this volume) the discipline of ethology may provide us with some rewarding insight. It can be argued that, however élite groups and their leaders gain dominance, their ascendacy can only be maintained in population groups of any size by frequent conspicuous displays of status, eliciting 'followership behaviour' from subordinates. This is especially the case if the population is very mobile, dispersed, or subject to seasonal or other changes in density and composition. As Veblen said (1925:71) 'the means of communication and the mobility of the population . . . expose the individual to the observation of many persons who have no other means of judging his reputability then the display of goods (and perhaps of breeding) which he is able to make while he is under their direct observation.' When his subjects are strangers to him, the leader must impress them by a display of impressive possessions and an exaggerated life-style (and indeed, death-style). As Chance says (1967:505), among primates the subordinate animals pay an inordinate amount of attention to those more dominant in status. Their attention is attracted by objects like those under study in this paper, which are as much symbols of dominance as they are of wealth.

This viewpoint can be profitably extended to contemporary monuments (Fleming, in preparation). In primate troops, physical distance and social distance are closely related, and an animal's physical position within the group both reflects and reinforces his social role. In this connexion it is interesting that barrows share with dominant primates a tendency to be sited in positions where they are surrounded by space, for maximum visibility. Contemporary cemeteries are spaced out, with no suggestion of crowding, in the Stonehenge region (Piggott, 1951:Fig. 61); on the Dorset Ridgeway it has been plausibly suggested that the groups of barrows were deliberately sited for maximum intervisibility. (Royal Commission on Historical Monuments 1970). Very large, isolated barrows are also a fossilized record of the social space enjoyed by those buried in them. The two special types of barrows, bell-barrows and disc-barrows, which belong to the period of the rich graves, both have burial mounds which are separated by a berm and a circular platform respectively from the banks and internal ditches which surround them. These types of barrow may be devices for focussing attention by means of the creation of a clear intervening space between the onlooker and the object of his attention.

Another problem is whether these models deal adequately with the apparently centripetal drift of craftsmen's skills during the Wessex period. I do not feel that they do. It is tempting to suggest that in bronze age terms the period of the Wessex culture was a cultural climax (Kroeber 1948:134-6). To judge from similar and better-known historical situations, it would have corresponded to the life-span of one or more exceptionally gifted individuals, including perhaps a master gold-smith (Coles and Taylor, 1971). To suggest that another important figure may have been an energetic ruler with a magnetic personality is not to espouse the 'great man' theory of history in its crudest form, but to use the facts of more recent history in a predictive manner. To say that the role of the individual is always subordinate to the trend of culture process may be fashionable, but strictly speaking it is an undemonstrable proposition. If Sir Christopher Wren had died in infancy, London, as a grouping of archaeological monuments, would have looked rather different now; if the city fathers had accepted his offer to replan London after the Great Fire, it would have been changed out of all recognition. Whatever the general trends represented by the Wessex culture, the role of unknown individuals may have been very important.

Conclusions

I will not attempt to summarize these differing views, nor to choose between them. Given more excavation and a better chronology, it should be possible to test the hypotheses concerned with conquest and pastoralism, and to determine which of the external contacts are chronologically feasible. But our chronologies will never be fine enough to say which of a complex of factors came first, nor would the establishment of priority for any one element imply that this was a cause of the subsequent phenomena. The approaches concerned with social evolution and with ethology are really ways of looking at the data. They may seem plausible or implausible, but they are not readily testable. Does this make them useless? I believe that it does not, and I hope that others will agree. In these circumstances, can prehistoric research ever be a truly scientific discipline?

Acknowledgment

I would like to thank Paul Ashbee, Colin Renfrew and Joan Taylor in particular for useful and stimulating comments on this paper or on the approaches dealt with in it.

Appendix – Wessex graves mentioned in the text

Amesbury G.85, Wiltshire. *Wiltshire Archaeological Magazine* **45** (1930-2), 432-43.
Bush Barrow (Wilsford G.5), Wiltshire. Colt Hoare, Sir R. *Ancient Wiltshire* **I**, 202.
Clandon (Winterbourne St. Martin G.31), Dorset. *Proceedings of the Dorset Natural History and Archaeological Society* **58** (1936), 19-20.
Collingbourne Ducis G.4, Wiltshire. *Ancient Wiltshire*, **I**, 184.
Collingbourne Ducis G.12, Wiltshire. *Wiltshire Archaeological Magazine* **10** (1867), 91.
Collingbourne Kingston G.8, Wiltshire. *Wiltshire Archaeological Magazine* **56** (1955-6), 137-8.
Easton Down, Wiltshire. *Wiltshire Archaeological Magazine* **46** (1932-4), 218-24.
Hammeldon, Devon. *Transactions of the Devonshire Association* **5** (1872), 554-7.
Hengistbury Head I, Hampshire. Bushe-Fox, J.P. (1915) *Excavations at Hengistbury Head, Hampshire, in 1911-12*, 14-17.
Hove, Sussex. *Sussex Archaeological Collections* **9** (1857), 119-24.
Little Cressingham, Norfolk. *Proceedings of the Society of Antiquaries* **4** (1867-70), 456.
Manton (Preshute G.I.(a)), Wiltshire. *The Reliquary* **13** (1907), 28-46.
North Molton 17a or 17c, Devon. *Antiquaries Journal* **31** (1951), 25-9.
Portsdown, Portsmouth, Hampshire. *Proceedings of the Hampshire Field Club* **24** (1967), 20-41.
Radley, Berkshire. *Oxoniensia* **3** (1938), 35-6.
Ridgeway no. 7 (Weymouth G.8), Dorset. *Proceedings of the Dorset Natural History and Archaeological Society* **58** (1936), 20-1.
Rillaton, Cornwall. *Archaeological Journal* **24** (1867), 189-202.
Stanton Harcourt, Oxfordshire. *Oxoniensia* **10** (1945), 21-31.
Stockbridge Down, Hampshire. *Antiquaries Journal* **20** (1940), 39-47.
Tara, Mound of the Hostages, co. Meath, Ireland. *Proceedings of the Prehistoric Society* **21** (1955), 163-73.
Upton Lovell Golden Barrow (G.2(e)), Wiltshire. *Ancient Wiltshire* **I**, 98.
Wilsford G.7, Wiltshire. *Ancient Wiltshire* **I**, 202.
Wilsford G.8, Wiltshire. *Ancient Wiltshire* **I**, 201.
Wilsford G.56, Wiltshire. *Ancient Wiltshire* **I**, 207.
Winterbourne Stoke G.4, Wiltshire. *Ancient Wiltshire* **I**, 122.

REFERENCES

Abercromby, J. (1912) *A Study of the Bronze Age Pottery of Great Britain and Ireland.* Oxford, Clarendon Press.

Annable, F.K. and Simpson, D.D.A. (1964) *Guide Catalogue of the Neolithic and Bronze Age Collections in Devizes Museum.* Devizes, Wiltshire Archaeological and Natural History Society.

Ashbee, P. (1960) *The Bronze Age Round Barrow in Britain.* London, Phoenix House.

Briard, J. (1970) Les tumulus de l'age du bronze de Plouvorn-Plouzévédé (Finistère). *Bulletin de la Société Préhistorique Française* **67**, 372-85.

Burgess, C.B. (1963) Two grooved ogival daggers of the early bronze age from south Wales. *Bulletin of the Board of Celtic Studies* **20**, 75-94.

Calkin, J.B. (1962) The Bournemouth area in the middle and late bronze age with the 'Deverel-Rimbury' problem reconsidered. *Archaeological Journal* **119**, 1-65.

Chance, M.R.A. (1967) Attention structure as the basis of primate rank orders. *Man*, N.S. **2**, 503-18.

Childe, V.G. (1940) *Prehistoric Communities of the British Isles.* London, W. and Chambers, R.

Childe, V.G. (1957) *The Dawn of European Civilization.* London, Routledge and Kegan Paul.

Clarke, D.L. (1968) *Analytical Archaeology.* London, Methuen.

Clarke, D.L. (1970) *Beaker Pottery of Great Britain and Ireland.* Cambridge, University Press.

Clarke, R.R. (1960) *East Anglia.* London, Thames and Hudson.

Coles, J.M. and Taylor, H.H. (1971) The Wessex culture: a minimal view. *Antiquity* **45**, 6-13.

Colt Hoare, Sir R. (1812-21) *The Ancient History of South and North Wiltshire.* London.

Craw, J.H. (1929) On a jet necklace from a cist at Poltalloch, Argyll. *Proceedings of the Society of Antiquaries of Scotland* **63**, 154-89.

Fleming, A. (1971a) Bronze age agriculture on the marginal lands of northeast Yorkshire. *Agricultural History Review* **19**, 1-24.

Fleming, A. (1971b) Territorial patterns in bronze age Wessex. *Proceedings of the Prehistoric Society* **37**, 138-64.

Fleming, A. (1972) Vision and design: approaches to ceremonial monument typology. *Man* N.S. **7**.

Fox, A. (1948) The Broad Down (Farway) necropolis and the Wessex culture in Devon. *Proceedings of the Devonshire Archaeological Exploration Society*, 1-16.

Grinsell, L.V. (1939) Some rare types of round barrow on Mendip. *Proceedings of the Somerset Archaeological and Natural History Society* **85**, 151-61.

Grinsell, L.V. (1940) Sussex barrows; supplementary paper. *Sussex Archaeological Collections* **81**, 210-14.

Kendrick, T.D. (1937) The Hammeldon Down pommel. *Antiquaries Journal* **17**, 313-4.

Kroeber, A.L. (1948) *Anthropology: Culture Patterns and Processes* (paperback edition 1963). New York, Harcourt, Brace and World.

Newton, R.G. and Renfrew, A.C. (1970) British faience beads reconsidered. *Antiquity* **44**, 199-206.

Piggott, S. (1938) The early bronze age in Wessex. *Proceedings of the Prehistoric Society* **4**, 52-106.

Piggott, S. (1951) Stonehenge reviewed. *In* Grimes, W.F. (ed.) *Aspects of Archaeology in Britain and Beyond*, 274-92. London, H.W. Edwards.

Renfrew, A.C. (1968) Wessex without Mycenae. *Annual of the British School of Archaeology at Athens* **63**, 277-85.

Renfrew, A.C. (1971) Europe's creative barbarians. *The Listener* **85**, 12-15.

Royal Commission on Ancient and Historical Monuments (1970) *Dorset*, volume III. London, Her Majesty's Stationery Office.

Savory, H.N. (1958) A corpus of Welsh bronze age pottery. Part III. Pygmy cups. *Bulletin of the Board of Celtic Studies* **18**, 89-106.

Smith, I.F. (1961) An essay towards the reformation of the British bronze age. *Helinium* **1**, 97-118.

Stukeley, W. (1740) *Stonehenge, a Temple Restored to the British Druids*. London.

Taylor, J.J. (1971) The recent discovery of gold pins in the Ridgeway gold pommel. *Antiquaries Journal* **50**, 216-20.

Thomas, N. (1965) Review of Annable and Simpson, 1964. *Wiltshire Archaeological Magazine* **60**, 142-7.

Thomas, N. (1966) Notes on some early bronze age objects in Devizes Museum. *Wiltshire Archaeological Magazine* **61**, 1-8.

Thurnam, J. (1869) Ancient British barrows. *Archaeologia* **43**, 285-552.

Ucko, P.J. (1969) Ethnography and the archaeological interpretation of funerary remains. *World Archaeology* **1**, 262-77.

Veblen, T. (1925) *The Theory of the Leisure Class* (paperback edition 1970). London, Unwin Books.

Section 6: Movement, trade and contact, and their consequences

M.J. ROWLANDS

Modes of exchange and the incentives for trade, with reference to later European prehistory

The exchange of goods and services is a fundamental and universal aspect of human behaviour which pervades all patterns of social and cultural integration (Homans 1958). The view that social behaviour may be seen as an exchange of goods, material and non-material, stresses firstly that such transactions are usually unbalanced and denote degrees of dependence and obligation and are therefore basic to the understanding of many forms of social organization; and secondly that the movement of goods occurs in a social context, what Polanyi terms the 'embeddedness' of an economy and what Sahlins would appear to mean when he states 'a material transaction is usually a momentary episode in a continuous social relation'. (Polanyi 1957:243-70; Sahlins 1965a:135).

What is less clear, however, is the distinction between exchange carried out on a person to person basis in which the goods transferred are secondary to what they symbolize or reinforce, either for existing or 'hoped for' relationships; and an exchange of goods which has a manifest utilitarian function (need for raw materials, tools for production, etc.) and a latent socio-cultural function for levelling cultural differences and acting as a mechanism for wider socio-cultural integration. (Such a distinction does not appear to correspond with the comparison made by Mauss between two opposed systems of exchange based on gift and commerce (Mauss 1954:69-81).)

The term trade has been used loosely to describe the wider network of personal relationships whereby goods are acquired through exchange, devoid of social obligation, and carried on between groups on an extra-community and often extra-regional basis.

> In its beginning, commerce is an affair between ethnic groups; it does not take place between members of the same tribe or of the same community, but is in the oldest social communities, an external phenomenon being directed only towards foreign tribes. (Weber 1950:195)

A distinction is being tacitly drawn here between internal exchange based on reciprocity, and external exchange (extra-community/ tribal) based on gain. Alternatively, Sahlins would see this in tribal societies as a spatial continuum extending from generalized reciprocity (pure gift) within the community, village or lineage, to balanced reciprocity (one to one exchange) within the tribal sector, to negative reciprocity (barter, haggling) on the tribal periphery or in inter-tribal exchange (Sahlins 1965a:145-158).

The view of exchange as a continuum, with social distance equating roughly with spatial distance and both correlating with a decline in the moral sanctions controlling the social divisiveness of exchange, implies that it is in these peripheral areas, where goods and services are likely to move through mechanisms such as barter, that there is likely to be the greatest uncertainty as to the value of such commodities. The complexity of transactions is thus likely to be greater, particularly in cases where different exchange networks overlap and interpenetrate.

Weber's view that trade (for gain) is the means by which goods move across cultural and ethnic boundaries is very much in accordance with the archaeological use of the term. In prehistory, trade occurs between archaeological cultures and is recognized when objects characteristic of one cultural assemblage of artifacts are found in association with artifacts characteristic of another, roughly contemporary, cultural assemblage. The recognition of trade as the explanation for the movement of such objects, in contrast to other possible mechanisms, tends to depend on the number and quality of the objects and the consistency of their distribution to the extent that 'trade routes' or 'fall-off' rates can be distinguished. Alternatively *prima facie* cases for trade can be made where it is recognized that objects of a particular cultural assemblage were made of a material not found within the cultural area defined by the distribution of these assemblages. The next step is to look outside the culture area for likely sources of such material and find confirmation either through compositional studies, particularly in cases of unaltered raw material, or from supporting evidence of wider cultural exchange in objects and ideas.

Evidence for trade between different culture areas has been of considerable importance for supporting arguments relating to culture growth and for establishing relative chronologies. In a sense, such aims do not require understanding how or why trade occurred, but only the demonstration that it did occur. Thus, arguments for trade have centred principally on (a) similarities and dissimiliarities of artifact form in terms of style, technology, function; (b) whether morphologically similar objects are sufficiently contemporary with each other to allow for trade; (c) what sources of raw material could or could not have been exploited. As examples, in European prehistory, the trade of amber from the Baltic to the Aegean in the mid-2nd millenium B.C. has fluctuated on the basis of compositional studies from acceptance to rejection to acceptance again (Beck *et al.* 1971:235). The acceptance of a trade of faience beads from Egypt to Central Europe and the British Isles in the early-middle bronze age has recently come under attack (Newton and Renfrew 1970:199-206); and hopes of tracing the sources of copper and tin by analysing the composition of metal objects are receding at a rapid pace.

Modes of exchange

Most societies obtain goods and services for subsistence needs from beyond their immediate physical and social environment either by making direct trade expeditions and/or by entering into exchange with other groups. Subsistence oriented trade is an extension of domestic production and consumption, in which the goods obtained have 'use-value' and are not intended to be converted into capital profit or be used for further trading exploits. The trade is usually carried out seasonally, there are no specialist traders, no markets, no currency, and no set rates of exchange. In fact, material wealth cannot be accumulated since the reciprocal obligations of kinship and bridewealth will usually act as efficient mechanisms for the dissipation of any material 'gain' or 'profit' made by those involved in exchange. Since trade in these circumstances is tied to satisfying subsistence needs there is no reason to assume that it will generate a range of new activities in terms of specialized production or an internally differentiated economy dependent upon exchange.

Yet, complex networks can develop for the indirect exchange of a variety of goods due to the unequal capacity of different groups to enter into exchange for the same scarce commodity. The Busama of northeast New Guinea occupy coastal villages and participate in a local exchange network covering the Huon Gulf area. Their only surplus product is taro which has a low value since most of the other villages grow their own. The niche open to them is to trade with people in an ecologically poor zone to the south for pots which are highly valued elsewhere and which can then be used to trade with the rest of the Gulf for other commodities. In fact, because of their narrow exchange base, the Busama serve to articulate the southern and northern communities into a local network, yet are in too insecure a trading position to adopt a monopolistic or entrepreneurial role (Sahlins 1965b:107-14). Similarly, Miracle gives an account of Plateau Tonga 'entrepreneurs' who traded with ten different tribes up to distances of 300 miles for 30 different goods; he reveals as a starting mechanism their monopoly in the production of salt and a lack of local iron (Miracle 1959:34-50). The haphazard distribution of material resources and technical skills, therefore, is not merely an accident of nature, an environmental imponderable, that trade equalizes out. In the differential exploitation of natural resources there is reflected a definite pattern of selection for commodities with which one can enter into exchange. As an example of trading failure, Kooijman describes how people on the Sibil River (Star Mountains, West Irian) had to be content with poor quality stone axes from the Tabi River area because they had no suitable product nor were they in a suitable trading position to obtain one that could be exchanged for better axes circulating in the Moejoe area to the south (Kooijman 1962:15-44). As Harding says, in these circumstances the least important thing one can do with a pig is to eat it (Harding 1967:141).

Clearly an environment exists to trade for gain in such situations, yet it is unclear when and how it becomes possible to acquire goods for their 'exchange value' rather than their 'use value', allowing profits to be made either directly or after a series of conversions. The inbuilt discrepancies in the evaluation of goods and services, either spatially and/or between discrete spheres of exchange would appear to present the best opportunity for exploitation. Disparity in evaluation most frequently occurs between closed exchange networks separated by physical barriers, ecological boundaries, distance and the operation of different exchange mechanisms. Such a situation can promote the activities of the specialist trader operating in strategically well-placed communities who does not belong to any particular network but, by supplying bargaining skill and transport facilities, articulates communities in different exchange systems that would otherwise be widely separated from each other. Unlike trading expeditions or subsistence oriented trade, such commerce aims to 'buy and sell' goods under the best conditions depending on the most favourable time and place to carry out such transactions. The number of different activities generated for collecting, transporting and trading necessitates that it should form a specialist activity rather than be seasonal in nature. Sahlins has suggested an ecologic situation that might promote specialist trading, i.e. the advantage to those living in ecologically marginal areas of tapping the productive capacities of a number of more richly endowed communities (Sahlins 1965b:107-14). A study by Harding of the trade network of the Vitiaz St., separating the Bismarck archipelago from New Guinea, illustrates this principle in relation to the incentive for exchange for political prestige (Harding 1967:118-53, 238-5). Here, at the beginning of the century, three groups of island voyagers on Siassi, Bilibilli and Tami islands operated three overlapping exchange systems, along 1000 miles of coastline, which articulated several hundred coastal and island communities and their local exchange networks. Two exchange spheres, one in high value wealth objects and the other in low value, usually consumable, goods were operated, yet the goods contained in each sphere were not the same for each community, e.g.

pots made on the mainland were low value yet could be exchanged for high value goods in island communities. Thus, Siassi traders are able, by long distance trading, to convert from low value to high value and then convert the proceeds into a surplus of pigs which forms the material base for the status building rituals of the Siassian 'big-man' system. The point here is that trade for gain may be seen as a solution to the problem of a poor subsistence base and its deficiencies for supporting large-scale competitive feasting for prestige achievement; the feasts may be seen to have an economic function of redistributing wealth within each of the 'men's houses'. *In toto* it has a latent function of maintaining high population densities, a significant amount of interregional specialization and creating a form of regional economy; yet this would not equate with free exchange since no sector exists for individual gains to be used for further trading exploits. Trading for gain therefore will be inhibited because it is not sufficiently economic: it exists to supply the sociopolitical structure which each year syphons off the proceeds and requires the whole cycle to start all over again.

The freedom to trade is most easily satisfied when the agents of transaction are in a social position which frees them from prestation and social obligation. This is particularly true of minority ethnic groups whose lack of cultural integration allows such freedom and favours the exchange of information, the supervision of the transport of goods and the other arrangements necessary to establish a trade network. Cohen, for example, says that Islam has been associated with long-distance trading in West Africa because it provides a highly developed ideology for the establishment of 'a network of organized and highly interconnected communities, with their own political, social and economic institutions'. (In his study of the Hausa diaspora at Ibadan, Cohen remarks that all the butchers, without exception, have converted to Islam because only in this way can they participate in the cattle trade which extends from the Savanna to the forest zone (Cohen 1971:266-81).)

If it is in the articulation of local/regional networks that trading for gain is likely to be most advantageous, it is understandable that it has so often been seen to develop under external influence (usually European in the ethnographic present). Further, that it should be in the areas of intense exchange on the borders between complementary economic zones that exchange 'markets' and the use of mediums of exchange are most likely to appear. Clearly, such tendencies can encourage changes in the modes of production for the satisfaction of external trade. These could be associated with increasing internal economic differentiation/specialization, the development of internal markets for collecting food and raw materials (i.e. for the provisioning of the production of exchange goods), and internal distribution centres for the dispersal of imports. Meillassoux has distinguished between situations where lineage based societies participate in the circulation of goods for outside commerce without it involving a new social division of labour, specialization or a market economy and thus internal social change (Meillassoux 1971:67-76). He contrasts this to situations where a reorganization of subsistence activities occurs to maintain external trade through specialization, and where the relations of production are changed, and the distribution cycle within lineages and between lineage segments is broken. In the first situation various mechanisms may be adopted for the dissipation of accumulated wealth gained by individual lineage members acting as 'middlemen'. Alternatively, vertical rankings of discrete spheres of exchange could be seen as a means of neutralizing an accumulated wealth gained through middleman activities, with the aim of maintaining lineage solidarity. Thus, whilst each sphere allows the free circulation of goods, the implication is a restriction on exchange and the prevention of individuals converting low value goods into higher value goods. As Douglas has noted, such discrete spheres of exchange seem to occur most often in societies with ranked categories of status to support and serve to maintain those in privileged positions and deny the right of achieving a similar prestigious position to those without the adequate means (Douglas 1967:136-8). Alternatively, political control may be exercised over specialist production of goods for external exchange. For example, Basakata metalsmiths (Congo) are hierarchically ranked on the basis of the metalwork that they can produce (i.e. domestic tools to weapons to prestige objects), and the 'sale' of different categories of metalwork is limited by the status of the customer. Thus, tools were made for anyone, whilst a smith could refuse to make weapons for people of insufficient status since the bearing of arms was a sign of wealth. The production of parade objects and insignia could only be done by the master-smith who also happened to be the village chief (Maes 1930).

The disruptive tendencies of trading are inhibited not only by social and political mechanisms for the prevention of individual gain, but also by technical factors which affect the value of goods transported. Although goods can have an intrinsic value that may be expressed in a set of mutually accepted exchange rates with other goods in a network, desirability is not necessarily an absolute quality but can change in relation to factors like distance, mode of transport, freedom of exchange and accessibility to other exchange networks as alternative sources of goods. These are the factors that tend to define the limits of a network of exchange and the size of the field wherein fixed exchange rates are consistently accepted. Thus in many non-monetary economies, subsistence goods and particularly foodstuffs, that are widely available and do not travel well, tend to have a lower exchange value and a much narrower circuit of exchange (both in distance travelled and in their trade with other commodities) than durable, prestige or luxury items. The effect that the mode of transport available can have on the articulation of trade networks and the quantity of goods transported (and therefore their scarcity value) can be seen in West Africa where camels, mules and human porterage were used successively from the desert to the forest zone, thus breaking up the network into a series of relays, with each stage under the control of a different set of traders.

The idea that, in both monetary and non-monetary economies, different commodities will move with unequal ease depending on their desirability, implies that long distance trade will tend to be limited to luxury durables that will retain a consistently high value. Opportunities for gain, therefore, will be less for those in the centres of collection and distribution of goods than for those specialists who undertake the transport between these points. As seen, this sector is often found to be occupied by minority groups that are not integrated into any local social structure, or else it tends to be under some sort of state/political control. Limited freedom exists here for all to enter into free exchange and, typically, it is only when contact is made with large, world markets associated with massive technological changes for distribution of goods at high speed and in bulk that opportunities arise for large-scale involvement in production for trade.

Development of trade in later European prehistory

At this point, a tentative comparison will be made of the evidence for changes in trading patterns in later European prehistory from the bronze age to the end of the pre-Roman iron age. As a preliminary survey of the existing evidence, it is stressed that only a low level analysis has been attempted with the aim of contributing to the conceptual understanding of trade in this period and area, and emphasizing some implications for future research.

Gordon Childe postulated that a system of long distance trade routes existed in the European bronze age, forming a vast commercial network that was stimulated originally by the accumulated wealth and needs of the Minoan-Mycenaean 'civilization' of the Aegean (Childe 1958:162-73). The need for long distance trade in raw materials, particularly copper, tin, gold, amber and salt, was seen by Childe as a major socio-cultural integrative device which separated the bronze age from the neolithic in his techno-economic evolutionary sequence. The production of metalwork in this period was, by the nature of the skills and activities involved, a specialist activity rather than any sort of domestic occupation. A specific study of the metalwork of the middle bronze age of southern Britain suggests that smiths only worked seasonally when they would produce a stock of semi-finished implements. This stock could be used to meet a predicted demand at a time when smiths would be involved in subsistence activities and their time would be competed for by other tasks, (for example clearing fields, ploughing and harvesting). The limited spatial distribution of recurring assemblages of metalwork suggests a fairly static pattern of metalworking, implying that the craft was a dispersed occupation serving small settlement units, and predicts a dispersed lineage structure as a mode of organization (Rowlands: 1970). At the same time there is some evidence of specialization in production and more full-time working, particularly for the production of weapons, linked with the possession of particular technical skills in complex casting. Such specialist pieces are also found over a much wider area than more mundane metal types and it is possible to postulate a significant correlation between degree of specialization, the technical skill required to produce an object, and the distance travelled in trade by the finished metalwork product.

As far as raw materials are concerned, it is a geographical fact that no source of copper and tin occurs in the principal areas where metalworking was carried out. Raw materials would have had to be traded in by as much as two to three hundred miles, even if the nearest sources in Cornwall and North Devon were being exploited, with the additional possibility that sources in Ireland, Central Germany and the Alpine Foreland were being directly or indirectly tapped. There is no archaeological evidence for specialist groups of traders, markets or a currency system to articulate this trade; in fact the evidence points either to the presence of trading expeditions or to a form of subsistence oriented trade, with a weighting towards the latter since both raw materials – from a number of different sources – and finished products were in common circulation at this time.

The present evidence supports the hypothesis that during the bronze age Europe was connected by a number of inter-locking regional exchange networks, in which goods moved internally by such mechanisms as gift or redistribution and in the peripheral areas and between networks by barter and trade. A lack of independent evidence prevents, at the present time, an interpretation of the mechanisms which articulated these networks and which contributed to the long-distance exchange of goods, often in considerable quantities. In the light of the fact that previous explanations based on external stimuli (in the form of Aegean contacts) have now been disconfirmed, future research should lay greater stress on the mapping of these networks and their flows of goods and services, and the specification of imbalances in resources of raw materials and technical skills, and the differential capacity of individuals and communities to enter into exchange.

It is likely that this network of interlocking exchange spheres retained a high degree of coherence and stability during the

European bronze age. A major reorientation occurred at the beginning of the pre-Roman iron age when changes in the pattern and concentration of settlement and burial together with changes in technical skills reflect the consequences of the extraction and distribution of new raw materials such as iron and salt. These internal adjustments are accompanied by definite evidence for the expansion of trading interests into Central and Western Europe by the city states of Etruria and by the Greek colonies established in the Western Mediterranean. From entrepôt sites, such as Massalia (modern Marseilles), a limited category of luxury goods, including wine, oil, Black and Red Figure Wares and bronze vessels for the mixing, straining and serving of wine, were being traded into Central and Eastern France and Southern Germany. The stimulus behind this interest lay, if Strabo and Diodorus are to be believed, in the need to tap the internal traffic in copper, tin, gold, furs and slaves in order to supply the markets of the classical world with raw materials.

Two principal routes were developed: the first via Massalia up the Rhone-Saône corridor and through the Doubs valley into Eastern France and Southern Germany, or else, from Narbonne – at the mouth of the Aude – through the Garonne Valley to trading centres reputedly at Narbo and Corbilo. The second route, developed by the end of the 6th century B.C. with the expansion of the Etruscans into the Po valley of Northern Italy, connected the trading colony at Tarentum on the Adriatic to entrepôt centres at Adria and Spina in the Po Valley and thence over the Alpine passes into Central Europe. Involved in this trade were hinterland groups of native Celts, particularly Celto-Ligurians in Provence and the Middle Rhone valley, people of the Golasecca Culture (Lago Maggiore) in the Po Valley, and the Vento-Illyrians at the head of the Adriatic. Hecataeus has described the function of Celts as middlemen in the hinterland of Massalia and Herodotus described groups of Celts in the Upper Danube Valley who may have served in a similar middleman capacity.

The extent of the trade can be traced archaeologically by finds of metalwork and pottery of Greek and Etruscan manufacture often from rich, 'princely' burial contexts and settlement sites of Hallstatt D and Early La Tène date. At the Heuneburg, a large, defended settlement on the Upper Danube dating mainly to the 6th-5th centuries B.C., Mediterranean influence is seen in the use of air-dried clay bricks for the construction of one of the phases of fortification, the production of wheel-turned pottery, the use of donkeys for porterage, and the first evidence of the domesticated chicken in Europe. The settlement is associated with a cemetery of rich, 'princely' burials in which the grave contents included imports of pottery and bronze metalwork of Greek manufacture, whilst the presence of textiles made from Chinese silk in the Hohmichele indicates the richness and high value of goods being traded in from the classical world (Hundt 1968).

Although there is evidence of specialist craft activities being carried out, there is no evidence of the use of money or of a market economy. The quality and context of the imports from the classical world would suggest that long-distance trade was under some sort of political control. Centres like the Heuneburg, owing to their position on suitable communication routes, acted as collecting points for the siphoning off of goods from internal networks and the articulation of the latter with the trading colonies of Greece and Etruria. The accumulated wealth from such trade appears to have been monopolized by and helped to reinforce an existing social stratification and most probably affected the balance of political control in parts of Central Europe at this time.

Polanyi has suggested that the principle of a 'free exchange' market appeared first in Greece, notably Athens, by the 4th century B.C. (Polanyi 1957:64-94). If the spread of a market principle can be traced by the appearance of low value coins (particularly of bronze and tin alloy) in settlements, then the distribution of coins and die-links would suggest the adoption of a market principle in Central and Western Europe by the 1st century B.C. At first, this coinage is limited to complex, nucleated settlements which formed industrial centres for the production of iron, bronze, pottery and glass, and the political, economic and cultural foci of tribes and tribal alliances at the time of the Roman conquest of Gaul. Collis has shown how each of the major settlements (*oppida* in the strict sense) were in long-distance trade contact with each other – reflected in the disjointed distribution of pottery and metalwork and large numbers of low value coins – whilst each primary settlement was set in a local exchange network of secondary settlements and a hinterland zone from which raw materials and provisions could be acquired (Collis 1971:97-103).

Although oppida are widespread phenomena, it is possible to make certain postulates concerning the nature of the development of these political and economic aggregates of the European pre-Roman iron age, to which the term oppida should strictly refer. It might be useful, for example, to consider the introduction of coinage into Celtic Europe as a need for a common medium of exchange to articulate an increased exchange in luxury and prestige items with the developing market economies of the classical world. The expansion of a market sector in the economy of late La Tène could be one of the factors behind shifts in the position of the bases of political power and the development of the oppida as political and economic foci. The evidence would suggest that the use of money was at first limited to the articulation of trade between primary settlements and the Mediterranean world, whilst hinterland trade continued to be carried on by non-monetary principles. The appearance of coinage in open settlements, of apparent lower hierarchical status than oppida, during the late 1st century B.C.

implies the possible presence of specialized trading groups in the major settlements and the expansion of the market principle to include exchange within an internal exchange network. In fact, the archaeological evidence compares favourably with the predicted anthropological model of the gradual development of internal markets for the collection of raw materials and consumables and the redistribution of imports as a response to the requirements of external trade. If this is so, then it suggests that more fundamental changes were taking place, with the implication that the greater freedom to trade that a monetary currency allowed (unlike earlier trade contacts with the classical world when wealth accumulated was converted into prestige/luxury items for the support of the political structure) stimulated changes in the modes of production (particularly towards the development of an internally differentiated economy) and a new social division of labour. Such factors may well underlie the archaeological evidence for increasing social differentiation and changes in political centralization in the development towards urbanism in prehistoric Europe before and after the Roman conquest.

Conclusion

The paper has attempted to show that changes in patterns of trading activity in later European prehistory can be illuminated by using an explanatory framework derived from anthropological theory and ethnographic data. In the light of the data available, a largely conceptual and diachronic study has been attempted and it is felt that future research should concentrate on synchronic studies of trade mechanisms and the isolation of regional variations in trading patterns in European prehistory.

At this stage, the evidence does support the hypothesis that a significant change occurred from a subsistence oriented trade in the bronze age to an exchange oriented trade in the pre-Roman iron age, with a major turning point in the setting up of trading colonies in the Western Mediterranean and their success in connecting up the internal exchange networks of the European continent with the 'markets' of the classical world. It would seem that exchange oriented trade was at first limited to luxury items and was capitalized upon by those in favourable geographical positions. The ability to enter into free exchange with the introduction of a moneyed economy, stimulated the development of internal markets and is a factor of considerable significance for predicting the changes in the socio-economic infra-structure occurring at the time of the Roman conquest of Gaul in the latter part of the 1st century B.C.

REFERENCES

Beck, K. *et al.* (1971) Determination of the origin of Greek amber artifacts by computer classification of infra-red spectra. *In* Brill, R.G. (ed.) *Science and Archaeology*, Cambridge, Mass., Massachusetts Institute of Technology.
Childe, V.G. (1958) *The Prehistory of European Society.* Penguin.
Cohen, A. (1971) Cultural strategies in the organization of trading diasporas. *In* Meillassoux 1971, 266-81.
Collis, J.R. (1971) Markets and money. *In* Jesson, M. and Hill, D. (eds.) *The Iron Age and its Hill-forts. Papers presented to Sir Mortimer Wheeler.* University of Southampton Monograph Series 1.
Douglas, M.D. (1967) Primitive rationing, a study in controlled exchange. *In* Firth, R. (ed.) *Themes in Economic Anthropology* (ASA Monograph 6) 119-47.
Harding, T.G. (1967) *Voyagers of the Vitiaz Strait.* Washington.
Homans, G.C. (1958) Social behaviour as exchange. *American Journal of Sociology*, **62**, 597-606.
Hundt, H.J. (1969) Uber vorgeschichtliche Seidenfunde. *Jahrbuch des Römisch-Germanischen Zentralmuseum Mainz* **16**, 59-71.
Kooijman, S. (1962) Material aspects of the Star Mountain Culture. *Nova Guinea* **2**, 15-44.
Maes, J. (1930) La metallurgie chez les populations du Lac Leopold II-Luckenie, *Ethnologica* **4**.
Mauss, M. (1954) *The Gift.* London, Cohen and West.
Meillassoux, C. (1971) *The development of indigenous trade and markets in West Africa.* International African Institute, published by Oxford University Press.
Miracle, M.P. (1959) Plateau Tonga entrepreneurs in historical inter-regional trade. *Rhodes Livingstone Journal* **26**, 34-49.
Newton, R.G. and Renfrew, C. (1970) British faience beads reconsidered. *Antiquity* **44**, 199-206.
Polanyi, K., Ahrensberg, C. and Pearson, H. (eds.) (1957) *Trade and markets in the Early Empires.* Glencoe, Free Press.
Rowlands, M.J. (1970) A study of the metalworking industries of the Middle Bronze Age in Southern Britain. Unpublished Ph.D. thesis, University of London.
Sahlins, M.D. (1965a) On the sociology of primitive exchange. In *The Relevance of Models for Social Anthropology* (ASA Monograph 1) 139-236.
Sahlins, M.D. (1965b) Exchange value and the diplomacy of Primitive Trade. *In* Helm, J. (ed.) *Essays in Economic Anthropology* 95-129.
Weber, M. (1950) *General Economic History.* Glencoe, Free Press.

NORMAN HAMMOND

Models for Maya trade

This brief note considers the use of several simple models in the consideration of Classic Maya patterns of trade and exchange. The first is hierarchical. The exchange system in the Maya Area (Fig. 3) operated on three levels, the local, the regional and the external (Fig. 1). Local exchange consisted largely of inter-household and inter-hamlet transfer of surplus subsistence goods produced within the area. Such goods might include foodstuffs, domestic equipment, medicines and materials needed for religious observances.

In the Central Area, a tropical forested lowland, such goods could include corn, beans, root crops and breadnut grown in the *milpa* or around the house together with meat hunted in the forest as and when available; spices, dyes, herbs, medicinal plants, incense, and other products collected in the forest would also be exchanged, although they are desirable rather than basic subsistence materials, as would manufactured goods such as pottery, basketry and gourd containers.

Only in times of exceptional shortage would the basic subsistence products be exchanged beyond this local level, since their continuous local availability was the major *raison d'être* in the establishment and maintenance of settlement, but many of the gathered desirable products would have wider distribution. Such products as vanilla, cacao, and copal incense were universally desired in the Maya world, but produced in only a limited range of ecological niches. Within the 'region of control' or 'realm' under the suzerainty of any one major ceremonial centre a variety of niches would occur, each with its desirable resources. The realm of Lubaantún in the southeast of the Central Area (Fig. 2) has for instance, some ten zones ranging from high mountain ridges rich in game and minerals to offshore islands surrounded by marine resources. The products of all these zones would have been exchanged at the regional market, located at the major ceremonial centre (which would also act as a local-level market for the surrounding population); such markets are still common in Mesoamerica. This diversity of resources is characteristic of Rathje's

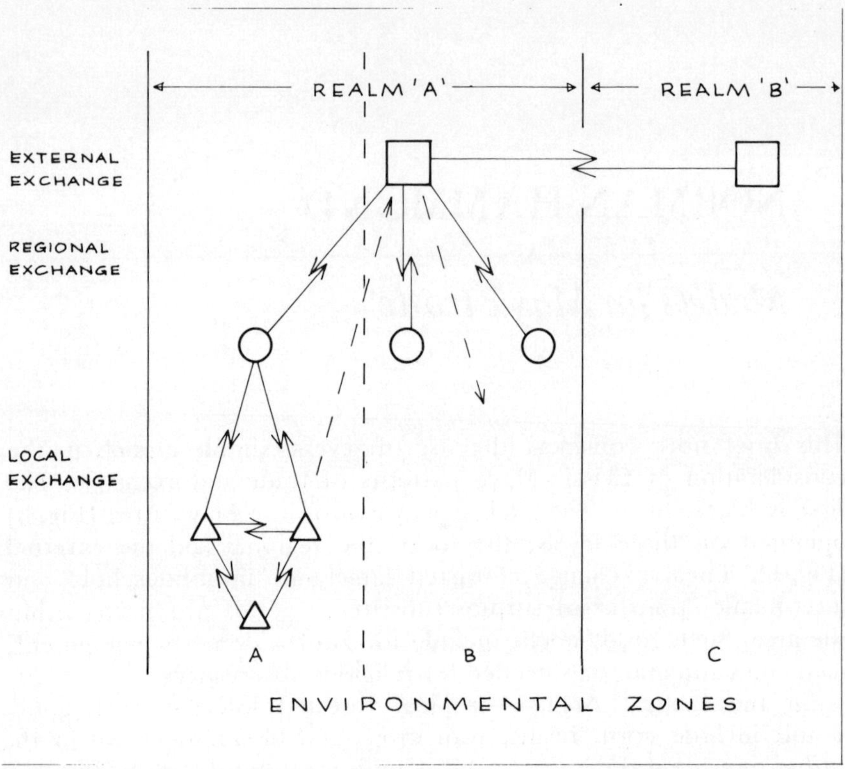

Figure 1 Representation of the exchange system operating in the Maya area.
△ = Hamlet
○ = Minor Ceremonial centre
□ = Major Ceremonial centre

'buffer zone', into which the realm of Lubaantún falls both geographically and economically (Rathje, this volume).

Some of the desirable goods were limited in occurrence not only within the realm but within the Maya Area as a whole, and would then be desired beyond the frontiers of the realm. This situation, of very restricted supply areas but widespread demand, is analogous to the endocrine system of the body, where the specialized products of different glands must be circulated throughout the organism by the vascular and lymphatic systems to maintain physical wellbeing. The ramifications of these physiological systems and movement through them can be followed by using a radioactive 'tracer', and an analogous device can be used to determine the spatial extent of an exchange system provided it is everywhere identifiable, widely distributed and of limited source. The routes by which the 'tracer' travels from its source to the main centres of distribution, in this case the major ceremonial centres, are the equivalent of the arteries, those by which it is distributed within the realm, of the smaller bloodvessels and capillaries. For the entire system to be traceable the

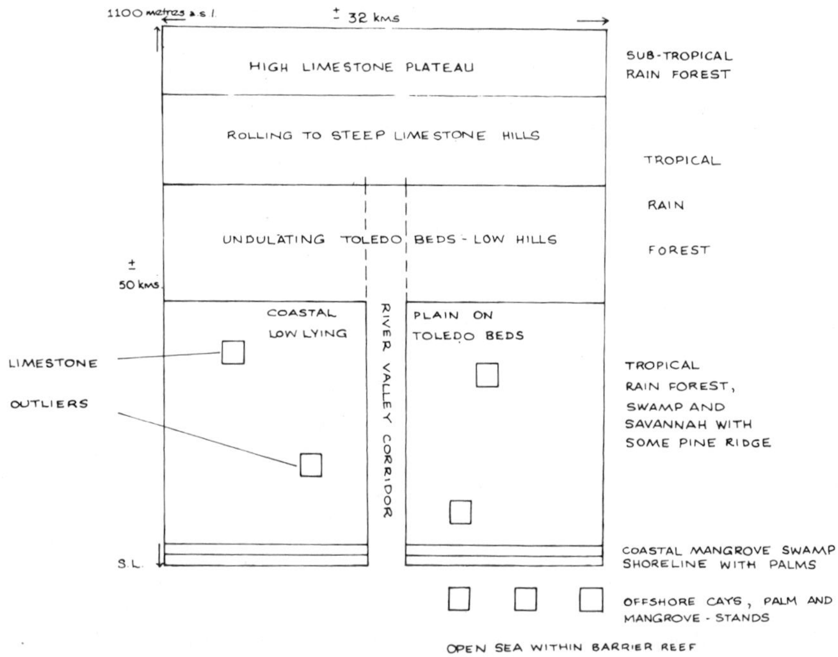

Figure 2 Environmental zones in the realm of Lubaantún, in the south-east of the Maya Central Area.

'tracer' must reach every section of society and therefore be a necessary and not a sumptuary product.

In the Maya area cacao, salt and obsidian fulfil this last condition, but only the latter is both identifiable and survives in archaeological deposits. Obsidian has already proved its value as a tracer in the Mediterranean and Middle East, as one of our hosts at Sheffield has ably shown (Renfrew, Dixon and Cann, 1966); a number of sources have been characterized in Mesoamerica, (Stross *et al.* 1968) but in the Maya area little attention has yet been paid to the implications. By examining the distribution of obsidians in the Maya area the skeleton of a Classic trade-route network can be assembled, and fleshed out by considering the evidence of other products and documentary sources.

We would expect the trade in any scarce product, including obsidian, to be (a) from areas of occurrence to areas of non-occurrence, (b) to the nearest areas from which other desirables can be obtained in return, and (c) aligned as far as possible from a competing (i.e. coeval) source of the same product, although ethnographic examples show that this qualifies as a rule at the expense of several exceptions.

The evidence of archaeology, ethnohistory and ethnography, illustrating successive states of the trade pattern in the Maya Area in its trajectory through time, indicates that the pattern has remained stable over a long period; this stability of demanded goods and sources of supply suggests that we may confidently extrapolate the documented later states back in time to add the dimension of perishable-product exchange to the imperishable-product trade pattern indicated by archaeological evidence.

The value of this approach, pioneered by Eric Thompson, may be seen from the fact that we have no archaeological evidence of the flourishing Postclassic export of honey, salt and embroidered textiles south from Yucatán in exchange for cacao beans and tropical forest products from the Central Area. Similarly the cacao trade from southern Belize in the Central Area up into the mountains of the Alta Verapaz is firmly attested by ethnographic and Colonial accounts that tell us the exact route followed, its stopping-places and the goods exchanged for cacao; this pattern is seen earlier in the distribution of Late Classic figurines, manufactured at Lubaantún in southern Belize and found or copied as far away as Cobán, but without the documentary evidence it would be difficult to explain.

In conditions such as these obsidian can successfully be used as a 'tracer' to determine the likely trade-routes of the Classic period. Most of the obsidian found in the Maya area comes from two sources in the highlands of Guatemala, El Chayal near Guatemala City and Ixtepeque/Papalhuapa near Asuncion Mita. The sources are some 80 airline km apart. The distribution of obsidian finds from the El Chayal source is in the highlands west of the source, in southern Belize around Lubaantún, in northeast Petén and along the Usumacinta, the last three areas all in the forest lowlands of the Central Area. Ixtepeque obsidian is found in the highlands east of the source, to the west at Kaminaljuyú, on the offshore cays of southern Belize, up the Belize River valley into northeast Petén, and in Yucatán.

These patterns suggest (Fig. 3) that Chayal obsidian was distributed overland, down the Chixoy or Pasión to the sites on the Usumacinta and in northeast Petén, and via the cacao route from the Alta Verapaz to southern Belize. Obsidian from Ixtepeque, on the other hand, seems to have been carried down the Motagua and up the east coast of Yucatán by canoe along the well-documented sea-route from the Ulua to Cozumel and the Gulf of Mexico (Thompson, 1970:chs. 1 and 5), taken inland in the Central Area along the major rivers of the Caribbean littoral and in the Northern Area on the documented overland routes from the coast to central Yucatán.

The obsidian distribution pattern for the Classic period thus accords with what we know of Maya trade routes for other products from documentary sources, confirming the assumed stability of the trade pattern through time. It also fulfils the three criteria enunciated previously: the trade is from areas of occurrence to those of non-occurrence, it is to areas where the range of resources is very different from that obtaining in the highlands, and its direction is

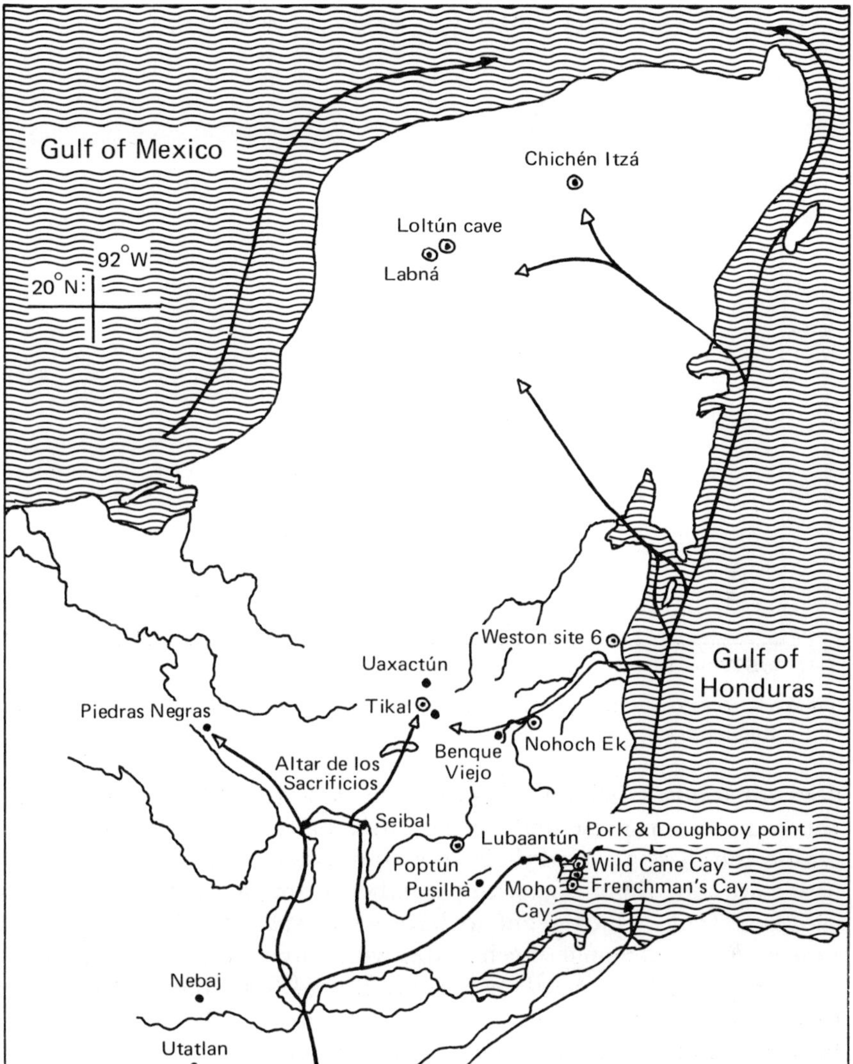

Figure 3 Patterns in the obsidian trade in the Maya area.

along the steepest *resource cline* (Fig. 4). The greater extent of the Ixtepeque network would seem to be due to the use of water transport, which on a cost-distance basis might well depict the Maya Area as a ring of land around an inland sea (as in fact such a map

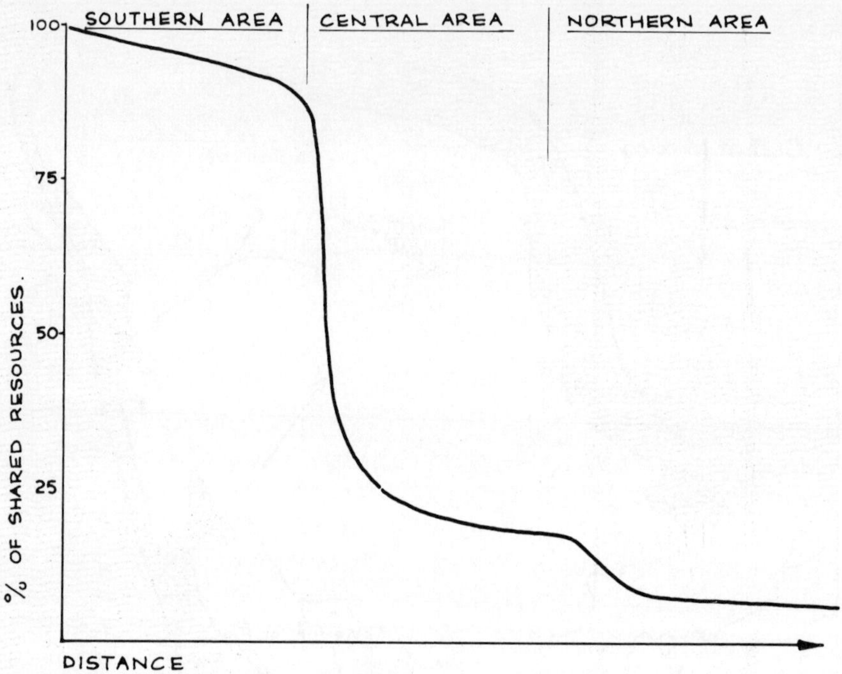

Figure 4 Resource cline for the Maya area, with an origin in the Southern Area highlands.

does for modern Britain). Thirdly, the trade is markedly away from the competition presented by the other source, suggesting that even within the Classic period their utilization was coeval (Park, 1929).

We are left, therefore, with a number of simple descriptive models of Maya trade which seem to have some validity: the hierarchical model of the exchange mechanism, with three levels rather than the two proposed by Sabloff and Tourtellot (1969); the analogy with physiology and use of a 'tracer' to demonstrate the stability of an historical trade pattern in the undocumented past; and the principle of exchange along the steepest resource cline, coupled with Park's principle of avoiding competition.

REFERENCES

Park, R.E. (1929) Urbanization as measured by newspaper circulation. *American Journal of Sociology* 35, 60-79.

Renfrew, C., Dixon, J.E. and Cann, J.R. (1966) Obsidian and Early Cultural Contact in the Near East. *Proceedings of the Prehistoric Society* **XXXII**, 30-72.

Sabloff, J.A. and Tourtellot, G. III (1969) Systems of exchange among the ancient Maya. Mimeographed. Peabody Museum, Harvard University. Presented at 68th Annual Meeting of the American Anthropological Association, New Orleans 1969. [A revised version has appeared in *American Antiquity*, 37, 126-35, since this article went to press].

Stross, F.H., Weaver, J.R., Wyld, A., Heizer, R.F. and Graham, J.A. (1968) Analysis of American obsidians by X-ray fluorescence and neutron activation analysis. *Contributions of the University of California Archaeological Research Facility*, no. 5, 59-79.

Thompson, J.E.S. (1970) *Maya History and Religion.* Norman.

BARBARA OTTAWAY

An analysis of cultural relations in neolithic north - central Europe based on copper ornaments

The objects which provided the material for this study are all the earliest copper ornaments found and reported in the literature in central Europe north of the Alps and the Carpathians: from Holland, Germany, Denmark, Sweden, Poland and Bohemia. 223 ornaments were recorded; beads and tubes which in some cases formed part of a complex ornament were not counted separately. The distribution map (Fig. 1) shows all the find sites down to, but excluding, the

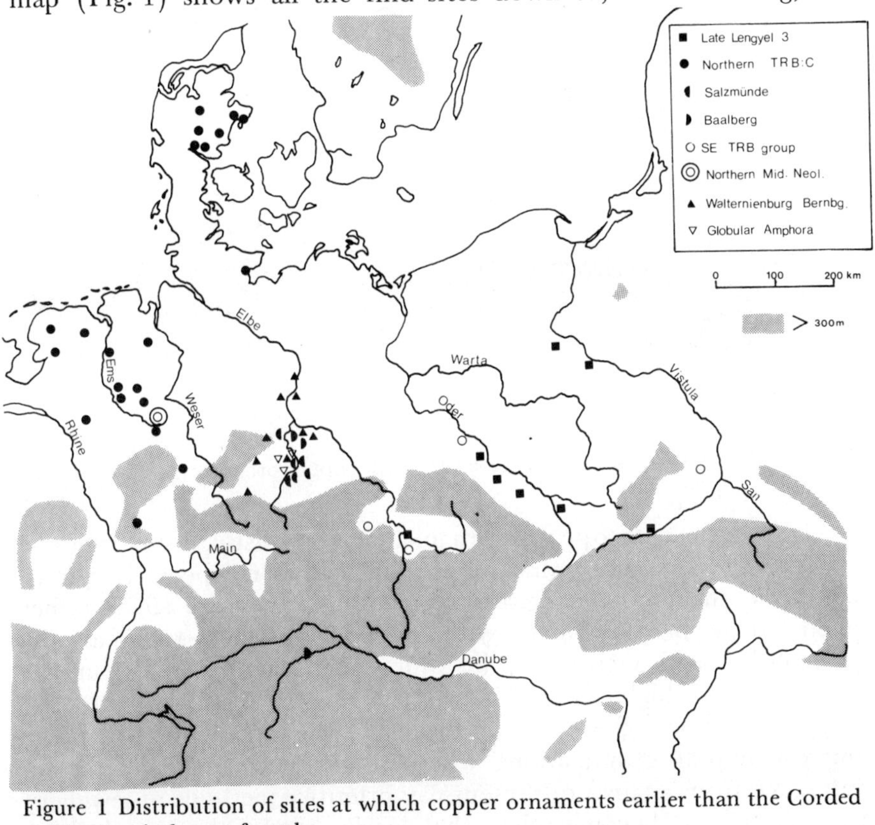

Figure 1 Distribution of sites at which copper ornaments earlier than the Corded Ware period were found.

Corded Ware period. The ornaments belonging to the Corded Ware period are mapped separately (Fig. 2) and are mainly concentrated around the Saale-Elbe area and in Bohemia. The area forms, in fact, a cultural unit with respect to copper ornaments since French and Swiss copper trinkets differ markedly in form as well as copper composition from those found in the area described above. The total period studied is about 1500 years: from *ca.* 3500 B.C. to 2000 B.C. These dates are based on C-14 measurements and are 'conventional', i.e. uncorrected.

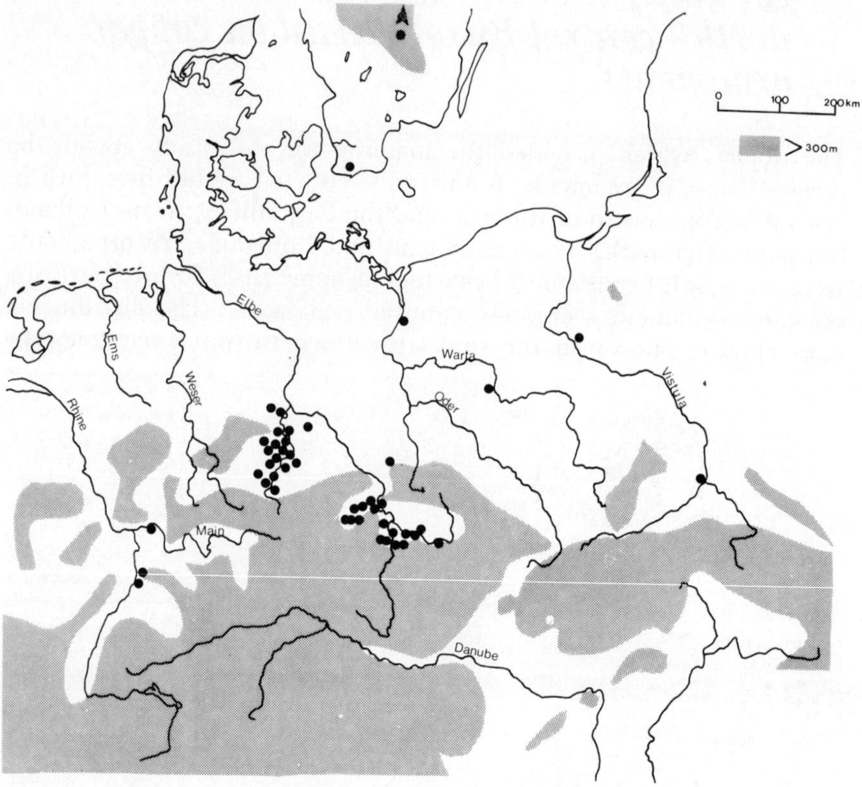

Figure 2 Distribution of Corded Ware sites with copper ornaments.

Eight basic categories of ornaments were distinguished: beads, tubes of sheet copper, spiral rings, spiral cylinders, spectacle spirals, pendants, sheet copper crescents and discs. They are all of rather plain shape if compared with previous periods such as the palaeolithic and mesolithic, in which manufacture of ornaments reached a very high standard indeed. However, if one investigates the possible methods of production of any of the ornaments – by using microstructural examinations wherever these are available or by inference from ancient or present-day primitive methods of jewellery manufacture, it becomes clear that hardly any of them could have been made in an 'amateur' way; even the most simple ornaments such as tubes of sheet copper or pendants required a knowledge of annealing, for instance.

It is important for the arguments advanced later in this paper to point out that the evidence is strongly against the possibility of any of these ornaments having been manufactured in northern Europe. Only 4 copper working sites are at present known, all of them in Poland or Bohemia. At only one of them is there unequivocal evidence of smelting, rather than simply re-melting of ingots, and at only one site (Cmielów) was any ornament found (a single bead). There is no evidence to suggest copper working in the Saale area during this period, or indeed until Corded Ware times, copper ornaments themselves being rather scarce in this area. It seems therefore that at least until well into Corded Ware all the ornaments which have been studied came from south of the Carpathian watershed.

Trace metal analyses exist for about 25% of the objects studied. It was possible to distinguish four main groups of copper from which the ornaments were made: native copper (copper group A) was taken to be any sample containing only one impurity or two impurities if one of them is silver, a criterion based on a study of the tables in Otto and Witter's Handbuch (Otto and Witter, 1952). Pure copper (group B) was defined as containing less than 0.1% of any impurity, where several of these are present; copper of this group is most likely to come from carbonates or copper sulphide ores. Group C is a fahlerz copper which contains more than 0.1% of arsenic and/or antimony. There are three clear-cut sub-groups of closely related analyses in this group, namely Ci: a group with relatively high arsenic and about 0.2% silver; Cii: a group which contains antimony but at most only a trace of arsenic (this is a very rare copper); and sub-group Ciii: a group containing about 0.5% arsenic but only a trace of silver (much less than in either Ci or Cii) and traces of other metals notably lead, nickel, bismuth and iron. Because all recorded ornaments from Denmark have this impurity pattern, group Ciii is called 'Danish' copper in this paper. The fourth group, D, comprises a small group of copper objects with impurities which are very mixed, although all are traceable to fahlerz ores. All ornaments of this group belong to Corded Ware finds.

The relationships between the copper groups were studied by simple matrix analysis (Tugby, 1969:635, Kendall, 1970:125), using first the cultural distribution as attributes and second the ornament categories (Fig. 3 top). In both cases the analysis showed a strong connection between copper groups A, B and Ciii. Group D was least closely connected to A. It has already been pointed out that D only occurred in Corded Ware sites; A (native copper) may be assumed to be the earliest. This was clearly established for Hungary, where in the cemetery Tiszapolgár-Basatanya all objects were of native copper

(Bognár-Kutzián 1963) and for Romania, to judge by the analyses in the tables of SAM II 3 (Junghans, Sangmeister and Schröder 1968). We may therefore infer that the matrix analysis has provided a seriation in time – the course of which is: native copper – followed by pure and 'Danish' copper – and these in turn succeeded by copper of group D. There was probably some overlap to a greater (minimal seriation Fig. 3, bottom) or lesser extent (optimal seriation, Fig. 3) but nevertheless there is a tendency with the lapse of time for the groups of copper to progress in the sequence above. The following maps illustrate that the groups of copper which were in use at earlier periods (Fig. 4) occur only very rarely in the Corded Ware period (Fig. 5).

	Cl	A	B	C3	C2	D
Cl						
A	1					
B	1	3				
C3	1	3	3			
C2	1	1	1	1		
D	1	0	0	0	1	

Cu-group/cultural group

	C2	D	C3	B	A	Cl
C2						
D	2					
C3	2	2				
B	2	2	4			
A	1	2	2	3		
Cl	1	2	1	2	2	

Cu-group/ornament type

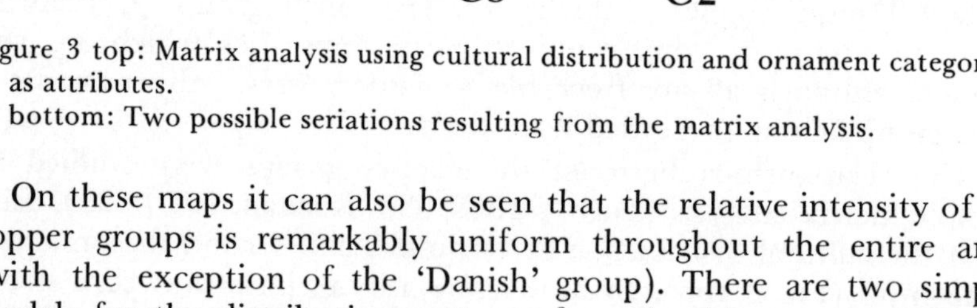

Figure 3 top: Matrix analysis using cultural distribution and ornament categories as attributes.
bottom: Two possible seriations resulting from the matrix analysis.

On these maps it can also be seen that the relative intensity of *all* copper groups is remarkably uniform throughout the entire area (with the exception of the 'Danish' group). There are two simple models for the distribution pattern of exotic objects: one proposes that if objects were distributed over a long period in time then the earliest objects would reach furthest, while the later ones would be concentrated nearer their origin. The second model proposes that earlier objects have a more limited distribution and are overtaken by

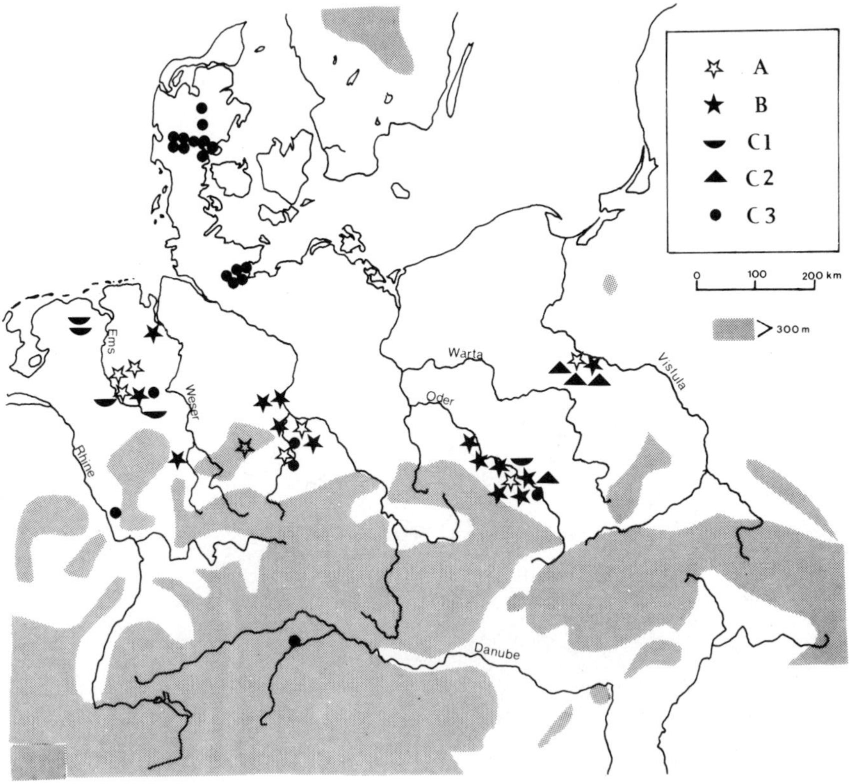

Figure 4 Distribution of early copper metal groups, before the Corded Ware period.

the more explosive expansion of later types of the objects. Neither of these models agrees with the distribution pattern found. The pattern rather seems to suggest that the cultural contacts – or trade – between northern central European areas and the producer(s) in south-east Europe were constant throughout the period since the earliest copper types reached just as far as any later type.

This is very interesting if we realize that although the contacts may have been at equal intensity throughout the period, the cultural groups inhabiting northern central Europe during this period were rather heterogeneous. This suggests that there was a constant stream of traders from the south-east who brought their ware along the edges of the northern plain and who probably made up the ornaments according to the demand of the customers: certain ornaments, such as sheet copper crescents, appear only west of the Elbe, whereas spectacle spirals, for instance, only occur east of the Elbe (map Fig. 6). Other ornament categories such as spiral rings and spiral cylinders are widely distributed in almost every part of the area studied. Also ornaments made of the earliest group of copper vary in

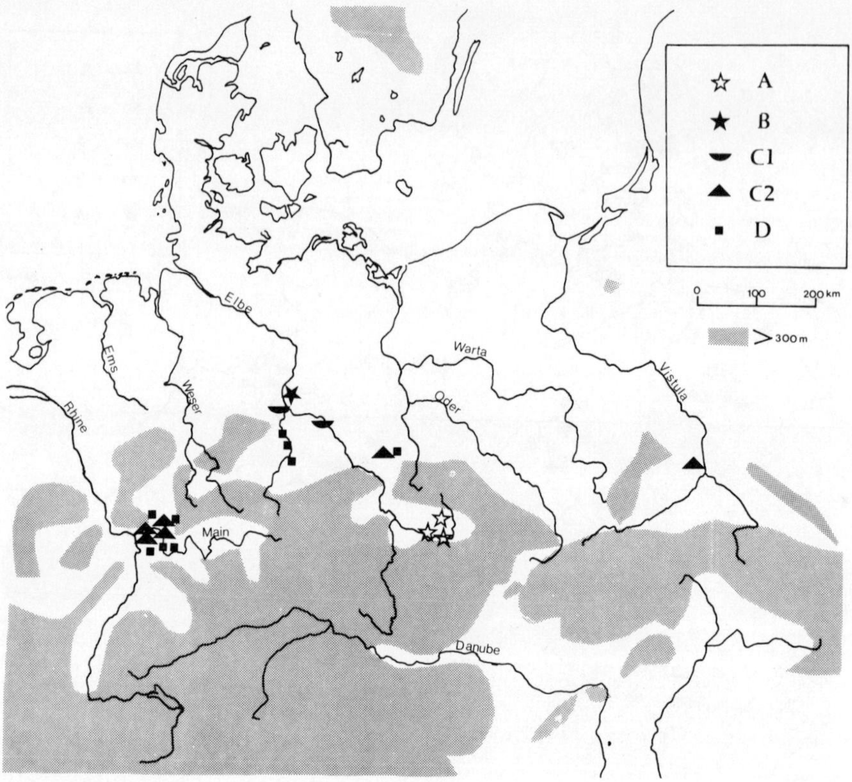

Figure 5 Distribution of copper groups in use during the Corded Ware period.

different regions: for instance, the earliest trinkets in north-west Germany were copper tubes, whereas in Poland they were spiral rings and – slightly later – spectacle spirals. This 'copper-dating' correlates with the association of these trinkets: north-west German ornaments belong to TRB:C, the Polish to late Lengyel; both are early cultures in relation to this study. At all events this may suggest that cultural contacts could persist undisturbed through several changes of 'culture', which are defined mainly by changes in pottery styles. We must be prepared to remember that the term 'culture' has a wider definition than this (cf. Childe, 1956:121).

Denmark presents a completely different pattern: here only one group of copper, 'Danish' copper, is used for all the ornaments, the occurrence is limited to the northern TRB:C period, and the types are almost exclusively spiral rings, spiral cylinders and discs. From this and other evidence which there is not space to discuss here, I have tentatively concluded that the inhabitants of Denmark in TRB:C times were themselves the agents who brought back the ornaments from a distant but presumably fairly specific source, as is suggested by the impurity pattern of a number of south-east

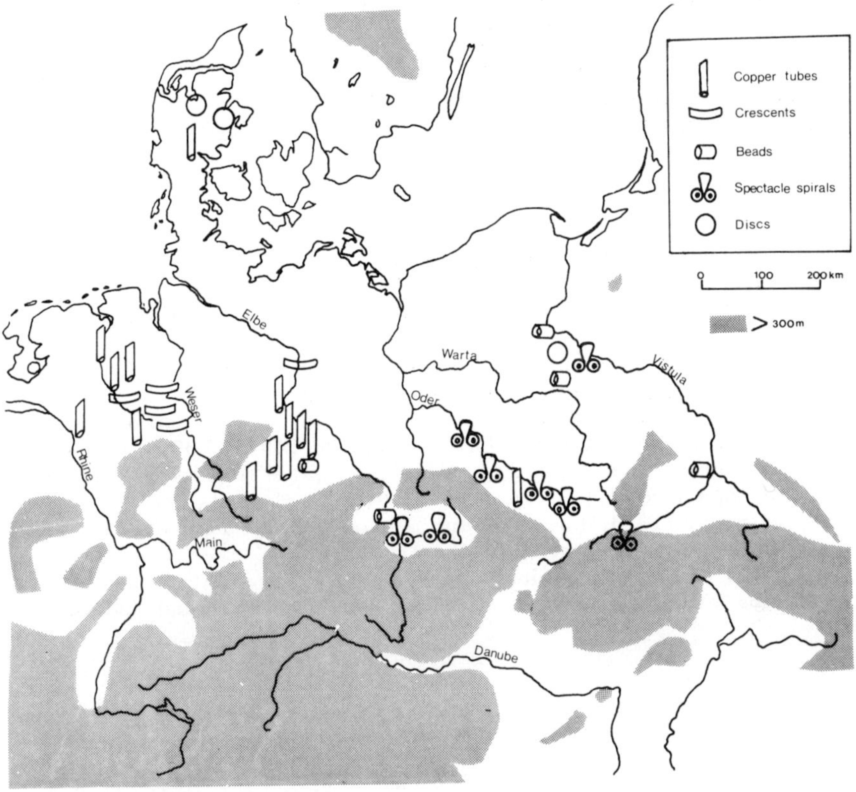

Figure 6 Distribution of some types of copper ornaments.

European metal finds and other evidence (cf. Randsborg, 1970:187). At the beginning of the northern Middle Neolithic there was a complete break in the relationship, from which one might infer that the inhabitants or the agents moved away from Jutland. Ornaments do not reappear there until well after the end of the era under discussion. A similar pattern of abrupt change is found in the north west German area of the TRB:C but not in Poland, or the Saale area.

Finally in Corded Ware a completely new group of copper appears and the old groups fade out. In addition there is also a marked shift in the distribution of the sites at which the ornaments have been found with the ornaments concentrating in two areas, the Saale and Bohemia (cf. Figs. 1 and 2). One must conclude that there was a more or less complete disruption of relationships with south-east Europe as far as copper imports are concerned. The evidence that ornament production in early Corded Ware periods is completely indigenous is rather weak, so that one cannot be sure whether relations of a different kind superseded those that disappeared. It is conceivable that Corded Ware or related people came to control the

Bohemian/Carpathian mountain passes, but it is difficult to assess the time scale of the discontinuity.

The material in this study will be treated in more detail in a forthcoming publication (Ottaway, *Proceedings of the Prehistoric Society*, in press).

REFERENCES

Bognár-Kutzián, I. (1963) The copper age cemetery of Tiszapolgár-Basatanya. *Archaeologia Hungarica*, N.S., 42.

Childe, V.G. (1956) *Piecing Together the Past.* London, Routledge and Kegan Paul.

Junghans, S., Sangmeister, E. and Schröder, M. (1968) *Kupfer und Bronze in der frühen Metallzeit Europas.* Berlin, Gebr. Mann.

Kendall, D.G. (1970) A mathematical approach to seriation. *Philosophical Transactions of the Royal Society of London* **269**, 125-35.

Otto, H. and Witter, W. (1952) *Handbuch der ältesten vorgeschichtlichen Metallurgie in Mitteleuropa.* Leipzig, Barth.

Randsborg, K. (1970) Eine kupferne Schmuckscheibe aus einem Dolmen in Jutland. *Acta Archaeologica* **XLI**, 181-90.

Tugby, D.J. (1969) Archaeology and Statistics. *In* Brothwell, D. and Higgs, E. (eds.) *Science in Archaeology* 635-48. London, Thames and Hudson.

RUTH D. WHITEHOUSE

The earliest towns in peninsular Italy

I begin with the hypotheses that there were towns or town-like communities in southeast Italy at least two centuries before the Greek colonies and that the earliest urban or 'para-urban' features appeared in the 13th century B.C. The communities I call towns were very small, usually less than one hectare in area, but they had an economy based on specialized manufacture and on trade; food was probably supplied in part by satellite communities in exchange for industrial products; there are indications of wealth, though no evidence that it was greatly concentrated; the settlements were surrounded by substantial stone defences. Renfrew (1969:158) uses the term 'urban' in a similar context and I shall do so here; if the term is inappropriate for these tiny communities, they are nonetheless 'proto-urban' in the specific sense that they reveal incipient urban traits and are the immediate ancestors of the indisputably urban settlements of the early iron age. Here my chief concern is with how this economic organization, however it is described, developed.

The 'urban' communities are exceptional among the late bronze age sites of the peninsula. Four locations supported sites of this type in the 13th or early 12th centuries B.C. They are all ports: Scoglio del Tonno at Taranto (Quagliati 1900; Säflund 1939); Leporano to the southeast, with two successive settlements, Porto Perone and Torre Saturo (Lo Porto 1963; 1964); Torre Castelluccia to the south (Lo Porto 1963:303, note 1); and Punta delle Terrare under modern Brindisi (Lo Porto 1968). Two other sites probably became urban later: Torre Guaceto north of Brindisi (Lo Porto 1968) and Coppa Nevigata, south of Manfredonia (Mosso 1900; Puglisi 1955). There are possible urban sites also at Egnazia and Torre a Mare (Peroni 1967:104) (Fig. 1). All. these sites are ports and most were established as undefended villages of the Apennine bronze age early in the second millennium B.C., though Torre Saturo and Torre Guaceto were established later and were urban from the start. Most of the sites subsequently supported important Greek or local iron age

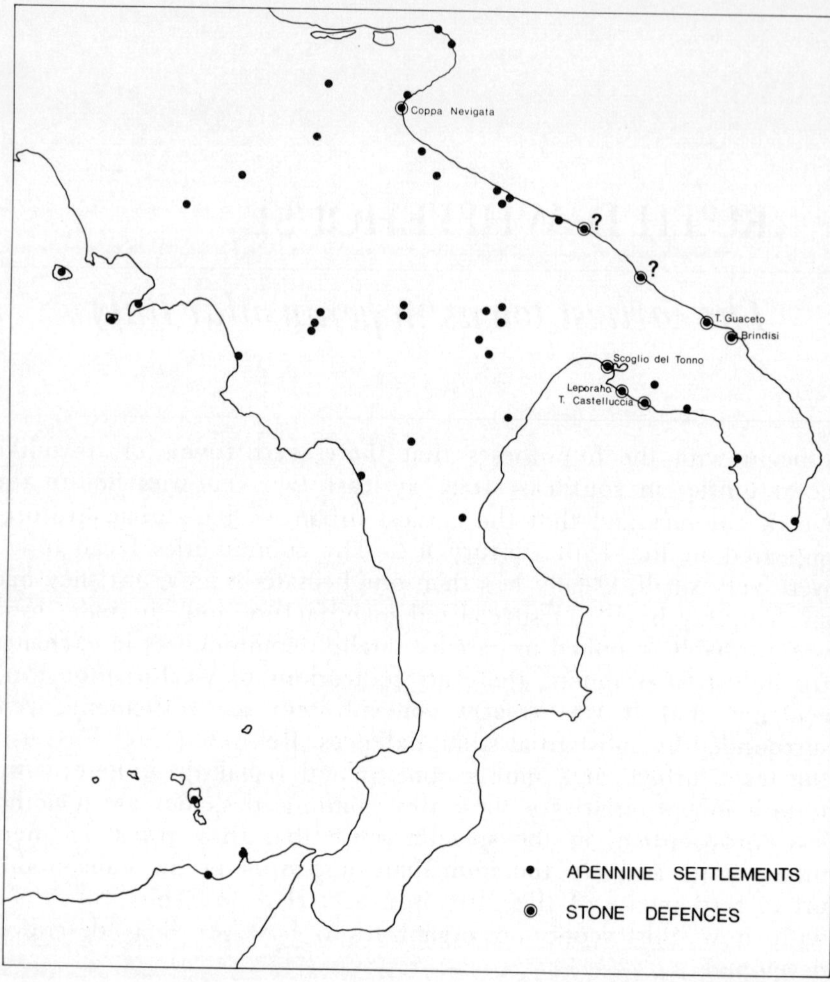

Figure 1 Sites mentioned in the text

centres. The admirable work of Lo Porto at Leporano (1963; 1964) has greatly elucidated Apulian prehistory and this account leans heavily on his results.

The appearance of urban traits

Trade

Trade with the Aegean is attested from the Middle Helladic period. In the L.H. I, II and IIIA phases the Aegean trade was shared with communities in Sicily, Lipari and Ischia; from the L.H. IIIB phase (13th century), however, the Apulian sites dominated this trade

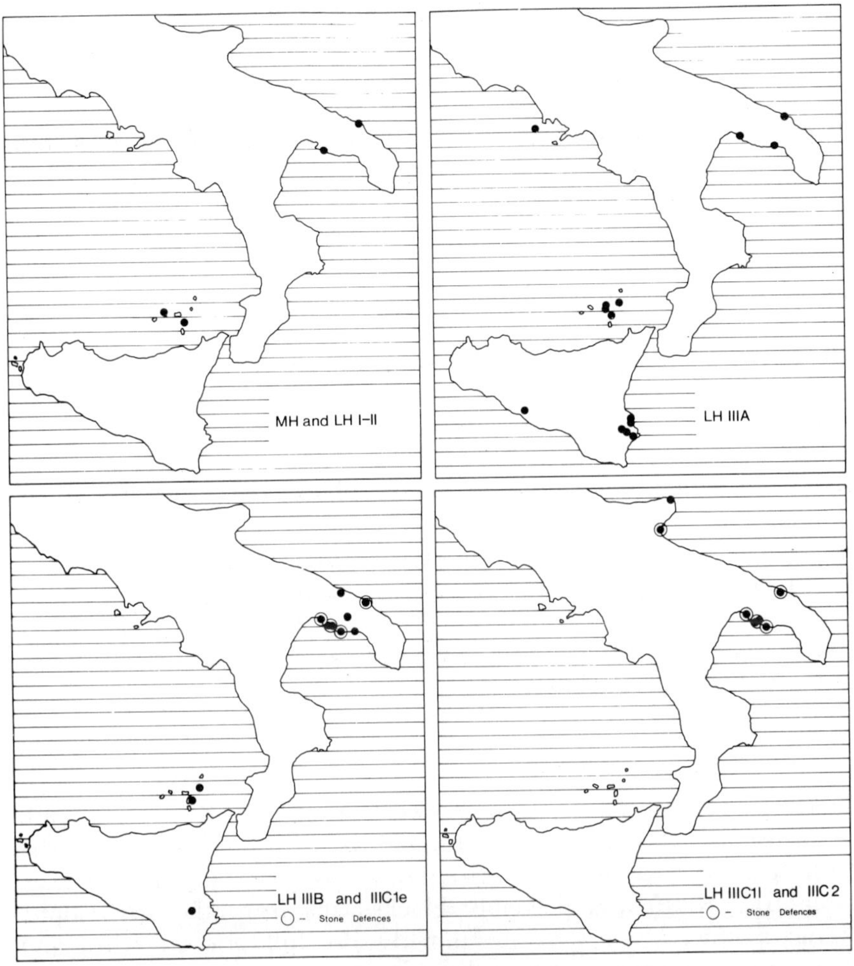

Figure 2 The distribution of Mycenaean pottery in southern Italy.

Phase	Porto Perone	Punta delle Terrare	Scoglio del Tonno	Torre Saturo	Torre Castelluccia	Coppa Nevigata	Torre Guaceto
M.H.	x						
L.H. I-II	x	x					
L.H. IIIA		x	x				
L.H. IIIB	x	x	x	x			
L.H. IIIC1	x		x	x	x		
L.H. IIIC2	x		x	x	x	x	x
Proto-Geom.			x	x			

Table 1 Aegean pottery on Apulian town sites.

(Fig. 2). Table I shows the occurrence of Mycenaean pottery on the urban sites.

Quantitively most of the trade belonged to L.H. IIIB and

Mycenaean finds from other Apulian sites (tombs, hoards and stray finds) are also mostly IIIB or early IIIC types. Thus trade with the Aegean was important in the 13th and early 12th centuries, until the fall of Mycenae. The small number of imported sub-Mycenaean (IIIC 2) sherds are thought to have come not from the Aegean, but from the other side of the Ionian Sea, from Ithaca or Cephalonia.

Trade with northern Italy is attested by, *inter alia*, finds of Terramara, Peschiera and Proto-Villanovan bronzes at Scoglio del Tonno, Porto Perone and Torre Castelluccia. The earliest of these are dated to the 14th century by Müller-Karpe (1959:34), but to the 13th by Sandars (1971:12). The north Italian communities of this date were more advanced than those of the peninsula; they were large, rich and show abundant evidence of industrial specialization; this economic organization, which can be considered 'urban' or 'proto-urban' in the sense that I have used the terms, was based on a highly developed bronze industry, and probably developed locally.

Thus the Apulian ports, though lacking local resources, were engaged in trade between the certainly urban Aegean communities and the urban or proto-urban settlements of the Po Valley.

After the fall of Mycenae the Aegean trade declined drastically and the important trade took place within the Adriatic itself; much of it was trans-Adriatic in nature.

Economic specialization

Specialist bronze smiths were active from the 13th or early 12th centuries (Scoglio del Tonno, Coppa Nevigata), potters from the 10th century (producing wheel-made painted 'Japygian Proto-geometric' Ware) and probably blacksmiths from the 9th (Coppa Nevigata). Merchants were presumably also full-time specialists and there may have been others, perhaps many.

Wealth

The existence of wealth is indicated, *inter alia*, by bronzes and Mycenaean pottery in tombs from the 13th century; as imported objects they must have been valuable. It must be remembered that southern Italy lacks local mineral resources and the abundance of bronze in sites of this period is itself a considerable indication of wealth.

By the 10th century hoards of bronze shaft-hole axes occur. These are sometimes considered, (rightly, I maintain), to be units of currency, indicating an economic organization appropriate to urban life (Peroni 1967:126-7; Sestieri 1969:270-5).

Fortifications

Defences *per se* do not, of course, indicate urban status, but in the south Italian context they occur only on the sites which also have evidence for abundant trading activities, economic specialization and the accumulation of wealth; as such they appear as part of a complex of traits which can be considered urban or proto-urban. Porto Perone was fortified during the 13th century B.C. The defences of the other sites are not dated archaeologically (or are not published), but they were all probably constructed in the 13th or 12th centuries.

Thus several urban features appeared in the 13th century and by the 10th urbanization had progressed both in internal complexity and external range.

The process of urbanization

Towns can arise through independent evolution or through contact with already urbanized regions. The earliest towns in the Old World arose in the alluvial valleys of Egypt, Mesopotamia, southern Iran and the Indus delta and rapidly developed into true cities. They are associated with intensified food production and high population densities. The economy depended on intensive food-production at home and on the importation of raw materials from abroad. The societies were rigidly stratified, with wealth and power concentrated in the hands of religious or political leaders.

While the diffusionist views of Childe dominated European prehistory, urbanization in Europe was thought to depend on the eastern civilizations (e.g. Childe 1956:176-8; 1958:150-61). Recently, however, Renfrew (1969:158-60) has suggested that the urbanization of the Aegean occurred without significant outside influence, though in an entirely different way to the eastern civilizations. There was no detectable intensification of food-production nor significant population increase; the causal factors were, Renfrew suggests, the development of metallurgy (creating new needs) and the consequent expansion of trade (increasing communications within the Aegean). Unlike the eastern cities, the Aegean towns could find initially all the raw materials they needed (including metal ores) within the area in which they arose, though additional sources were later sought abroad. Social stratification was much less rigid than in the eastern civilizations. Many authorities would reject Renfrew's interpretation, but if we accept it as possible, we have for consideration two different ways in which towns can arise independently.

There are also two ways in which urbanism can be acquired. It can be introduced by immigrants from already urban lands (whether peaceful colonists, as with the Greeks, or political overlords, as with the Romans). Alternatively, towns can arise through commerce with existing urban cultures, the secondary centres tapping enough of the wealth of the urban communities to allow them to develop an urban economy in their turn. It is by this process that Childe explained the rise of all towns in Europe before the Greek colonies.

While this brief account is necessarily incomplete, it provides sufficient scope for the present discussion. The four processes can be summarized as follows:

1. Independent development of towns on the basis of high population density, intensive food-production and external trade, as in the early civilizations.
2. Independent development of towns on the basis of increased internal trade following the invention of metallurgy, as perhaps in the Aegean bronze age.
3. Introduction of towns by immigrants, as with the Greeks and Romans in Europe.
4. Development of towns through commercial dependence on already urban cultures, as in zones adjacent to the early civilizations.

It remains to consider which of these processes best explains the rise of the Apulian townships. Any consideration of this question must aim at explaining the limited distribution of urban sites. Clearly the town sites had access to resources not available to contemporary sites elsewhere in the peninsula and the coastal nature of the distribution suggests that these may have been external resources accessible through maritime trade.

We may dismiss process 1: there is no evidence in southern Italy for a large population increase or a radical improvement in food production during the bronze age; moreover the area lacks the potential for really intensive food-production, which is necessary for this development.

I think we may dismiss also process 2. Although the urbanization of Apulia is associated with abundant evidence of trade, this cannot possibly be described as internal. The metal goods on which the economy depended were imported from the Po Valley (the ores coming ultimately from Tuscany and from Alpine sources). This is far outside the zone in which the towns arose. They were trading also with the Aegean, still farther afield. Moreover the Apulian communities could not, on the strength of their local resources, have afforded to buy many metal goods; I suggest that the external source on which they drew was the accumulated wealth of the urban communities of the east Mediterranean. What they offered in exchange was entrepôt commercial facilities with fine harbours strategically placed for trade up the Adriatic Sea; though *some* local commodities may also have been traded (e.g. the purple dye derived from *Murex* shells). Thus the Apulian towns certainly depended on trade, but not on internal trade within a self-sufficient system, as Renfrew has suggested for the Aegean bronze age.

The towns were in contact with the Mycenaean world. Were they established by Mycenaean colonists? I think not. Taylour (1958:81-136) described Scoglio del Tonno as a Mycenaean colony, but this interpretation depends on a reconstruction of the stratigraphy (Quagliati 1900; Säflund 1939) that is now generally rejected (e.g. Trump 1966:124). If, as is now thought, the Mycenaean wares were not found in an upper layer separated from the local Apennine pottery, the argument for a Mycenaean colony is weakened. The suggestion that the Mycenaean idols from this site, being religious in nature, were not trade objects, but belonged to actual settlers is unconvincing. The other Apulian sites were certainly native. I believe that though a few Mycenaean merchants may have settled in Apulian ports, they certainly did not introduce urban life.

We are left with the alternative that the Apulian townships arose through trade with the Aegean. The four early towns were certainly in contact with the Aegean in the 13th and early 12th centuries and at this period no site in peninsular Italy without Mycenaean contacts shows any urban characteristics. In the following centuries the situation changed: the Aegean trade had dwindled to nearly nothing though there was still some contact with Mycenaean communities in northwest Greece. By this stage it was the flourishing trade within the Adriatic and Ionian Seas that supported the urban economy of the Apulian ports and indeed allowed it to expand. However, this development seems to have been dependent on the previous urbanization of the area through contact with the Aegean, since even as late as the 10th century there were no towns in peninsular Italy outside the Adriatic littoral.

My argument here is much compressed, but to me the evidence seems clear. Although I am loth to present so unfashionable a view, I believe that southern Italy provides a classic example of the diffusion of urbanism propounded by Childe. I believe that the Apulian townships arose as a direct result of trade with the Aegean world and that they would not have arisen without it.

REFERENCES

Childe, V.G. (1956) *Man Makes Himself.* London.

Childe, V.G. (1958) *The Prehistory of European Society.* London.

Lo Porto, F.G. (1963) Leporano (Taranto). La stazione protostorica di Porto Perone. *Notizie degli Scavi.* Ser. 8, 17, 280-380.

Lo Porto, F.G. (1964) Satyrion (Taranto). Scavi e ricerche nel luogo del più antico insediamento laconico in Puglia. *Notizie degli Scavi.* Ser. 8. 18, 177-279.

Lo Porto, F.G. (1968) Una nuova stazione protostorica a Brindisi. *Atti della XI e XII Riunione Scientifica del Istituto Italiano di Preistorica e Protostoria,* Florence, 99-101.

Mosso, A. (1909) Stazione preistorica di Coppa Nevigata presso Manfredonia. *Monumenti Antichi* 19, 305-96.

Müller-Karpe, H. (1959) *Beiträge zur Chronologie der Urnenfelderzeit nördlich und südlich der Alpen.* Berlin.

Peroni, R. (1967) *Archeologia della Puglia preistorica.* Rome.

Puglisi, S.M. (1955) Industria microlitica nei livelli a ceramica impressa di Coppa Nevigata. *Rivista di Scienze Preistoriche* **10**, 19-37.

Quagliati, Q. (1900) Taranto. Relazione degli scavi archeologici allo Scoglio del Tonno presso la città. *Notizie degli Scavi.* 411-64.

Renfrew, C. (1969) Trade and Culture Process in European Prehistory. *Current Anthropology* **10** 151-69.

Säflund, G. (1939) Punta del Tonno. *Dragma. Martino P. Nilsson.*

Sandars, N. (1971) From Bronze Age to Iron Age: a sequel to a sequel. *In* Boardman, J., Brown, M.A. and Powell, T.G.E. (eds.) *The European Community in Later Prehistory*, 3-29. London.

Sestieri, A.M.B. (1969) Ripostigli di bronzi dell'Italia meridionale: scambi fra le due sponde dell'Adriatico. *Bullettino di Paletnologia Italiana* **78**, 259-77.

Taylour, Lord W. (1958) *Mycenaean Pottery in Italy and Adjacent Areas.* Cambridge.

Trump, D.H. (1966) *Central and Southern Italy before Rome.* London.

ROBIN M. DERRICOURT

Classification and culture change in late Post-Pleistocene South Africa

South Africa presents an important laboratory for the testing of models and hypotheses concerning culture change and culture configurations. Significant information is available from historic and traditional sources on subjects with which archaeology is also concerned; these include hunter-gatherers and nomadic pastoralists as well as their interactions with more settled cultivators.

A conventional picture has emerged from history and tradition of three independant groups in the pre-European settlement of South Africa: Bushmen hunters, Hottentot pastoralists and Bantu mixed farmers. For each of these groups certain linguistic, physical and technological attributes were assumed. Processes visible to European settlers were taken to have been the norm (Derricourt, in press), and traditional African oral histories which tend to concentrate on the ruling dynasties with the familiar pattern of temporal telescoping (Wilson 1970) have been used to assume a predominant factor of population migration of Bantu peoples (Huffman 1970).

Archaeology

All archaeologists in South Africa use a two-fold division for the Post-Pleistocene into later stone age (L.S.A.), thought to represent hunter-gatherers (Clark 1959), and iron age. The established divisions of the L.S.A. (Goodwin and van Riet Lowe 1929) are now coming under increasing criticism (Inskeep 1967) and partial replacement (Sampson 1970). The lack of reliable area sequences puts our L.S.A. taxonomy into a state of flux; attempts to use individual L.S.A. traits to hypothesize population spreads (Goodwin 1947) are unconvincing. Iron age studies are still in early stages (Inskeep 1969) though much recent work awaits publication. Radiocarbon dates for the iron age have been extended back to A.D. 400 ± 60, but little has been revealed concerning the relations of L.S.A. and iron age in individual areas.

A pattern has emerged of iron age origins being linked with Bantu migrations to suggest an invasion of iron-working Bantu-speaking negroes with a mixed farming economy, and argument has developed over the date of this invasion. 'Hottentot' cultural traits have been interpreted as either diffusion from this group or an independent invasion. This assumption is less convincing when we examine the distribution of individual traits.

Physical type

Major differences have in general been assumed between a 'negroid' type and a 'bush-boskop' (khoisaniform) type for Post-Pleistocene skeletal material. This assumption of pure racial types has led to the utilization of the concept of active hybridization to explain the many skeletal finds that deviate from the type form (Stern and Singer 1967), with subjective estimates of the degree of racial admixture.

Historically it is difficult to see the difference between the hunters and the herders on the basis of physical type: the distinctions drawn by early writers do not bear internal consistency (Wilson & Thompson 1969:ix). Tobias (1955) notes that the 'Hottentots' are not a physically homogenous group, and a search for skeletal material of confirmed Hottentot and Bushman social origin (Stern and Singer 1967) found only a small and invalid sample of 4 and 8 males respectively, and here the only difference visible was an overall larger cranial size in the Hottentot.

Samples of human skeletal material in archaeological context are disappointingly few. Many skeletons of iron age and unconfirmed context have bush-boskop and negro features admixed (Wilson and Thompson 1969:147). The site of Mapungubwe in the northern Transvaal had a fully iron age culture (metalworking, mixed farming, pottery and stone walling) (Fouché 1937) associated with which were skeletal finds of bush-boskop type (Galloway 1959). Views that the material is other than iron age (Gardner 1963) cannot be seen as valid (Fagan 1964).

Language

Westphal (1963) sees as separate language groups Bush, Kwadi, Hottentot and Bantu, but observes that one cannot claim an identity of these groups with groupings distinguished on other criteria. He suggests a Hottentot (language) expansion in South Africa from a base within it.

The clicks of modern Xhosa are derived from non-Bantu languages (Harinck 1969:150) suggesting long interaction between Bantu and

Khoi. Word borrowing, seemingly from Khoi to Xhosa, has been noted (ibid:151) including terms connected with cattle, and Khoi names occur as far north as Mzimvubu in the Transkei; Wilson (1969:80-1) suggests intermarriage between Khoi and Bantu-speakers is responsible for this mixture. Harinck (1969:53) suggests a period of interaction between the two linguistic groups from 500-700 years ago.

It has further been noted that the negroid Dama hunters of South West Africa speak a Hottentot language (Wilson and Thompson 1969:ix).

Economy

It is clear from historical considerations that language, economic and physiological groups in South Africa do not coincide, despite traditional assumptions (Wilson and Thompson 1969:40 ff). The negroid Dama hunters are one example. Historical evidence shows that the herders and cultivators supplemented their diet with hunting and collecting, while the origins of the sheep which many Bushmen possess today remain uncertain. Historically the Khoi had fat-tailed sheep and cattle, and the Nama also had goats from trade with a Sotho group. Nguni and Sotho had a wide range of animal and plant domesticants.

Ehret (1967, 1968) has used linguistic evidence of the names of domestic animals to suggest that South Africa's sheep were introduced by people with a central Sudanic language. He also argues that cattle were introduced at least to the northern part of the area before Bantu-speakers who acquired them from local Khoi. He somewhat overreaches his data by tying the spread of all livestock to the Central Sudanic people; it seems that Khoi and Nguni cattle may well have come from different sources (Wilson 1969).

Archaeological evidence for domestic plants is poor. A form of sorghum is known at Klipriviersberg in the Transvaal (R.J. Mason, pers. comm.) and both sorghum and a bean type (*Vigna sinensis*) at Mapungubwe (Fouché 1937). No domestic animal bones are known from late stone age sites or from any site in the 'Hottentot' area of the western Cape. Welbourne (1971) has provided analysis of animal food resources on Transvaal iron age sites, and shows the presence of cattle, sheep, goat, dog and domestic fowl in sites whose proportion of meat from domestic rather than hunted fauna varies from less than 20% to 90%. The presence of domestic animals at numerous iron age sites is indirectly given by stone wall structures: indirect evidence of domestic plants is, however, less easy to confirm.

Rock paintings show domestic cattle and sheep, as do some engravings (Willcox 1965, Fock 1971). The art has been used to hypothesize a northern immigration for the sheep independent from contact with the South African iron age (Cooke 1965, Willcox

1966), and though such a claim is often used to support the 'Hottentot migration' theory such a claim oversteps the evidence.

There is thus no certainty that all iron age sites possessed domestic plants; and very little evidence that the domestic animals known historically among 'Hottentots' were derived from Bantu-speakers or iron age people in South Africa.

Technology

It has long been noted that at the end of late stone age sequences pottery was often present, and until recently it was possible to suggest that techniques for its manufacture spread from direct contact with iron age people (Phillipson 1969:42). Hottentots and sometimes Bushmen were historically associated with pottery making (Schofield 1948). Recently, however, radiocarbon dates for ceramic late stone age contexts have dramatically altered the picture. These show the presence of pottery at Bonteberg in 100 B.C. ± 95 (Grindley *et al.* 1970); a date immediately before the introduction of pottery at Robberg at A.D. 20 ± 60 (Vogel 1970; Inskeep pers. comm.), both sites in the southwest Cape. The overall picture of radiocarbon dates and archaeological sequences for South Africa suggests the possibility that the first pottery in South Africa was in the south and west and that a spread of the technique took place from there independently of iron age acculturation.

The historical picture (Goodwin 1956; Wilson and Thompson 1969) indicates that the herders had the use of copper and iron but there is no evidence that they had knowledge of smelting. Few L.S.A. contexts show any metal or contact with metal workers (Fagan 1967; Clark 1959:204; Humphries and Maggs 1970). The records show the rarity and great value of metals among the herders – but this situation is also seen among some of the early cultivators (Wilson and Thompson 1969:80-1). This picture is borne out by the rarity of metal and the absence of slag on many iron age sites. Since historically it is known that certain groups of Africans acted as specialist smiths and traders over a wide area, it would seem probable that some iron age communities may have had the same relation to metal as the herders: users but not smelters. Recent claims for middle stone age association with iron ore mining (Dart and Beaumont 1971) and for late stone age mining (Vogel 1970) must await fuller publication.

	1	2	3	4	5	6	7	8
1 Race								
2 Language	NO							
3 Self-classification	?	?						
4 Pottery	NO	NO	NO					
5 Metal use	NO	NO	NO	NO				
6 Metal smelting	NO	NO	NO	NO	NO			
7 Domestic animals	NO	NO	NO	NO	?	NO		
8 Domestic plants	NO	NO?	?	NO	NO	NO?	NO	

Table 1 Presence of high correlation between variables in societies of late Post-Pleistocene South Africa.

Conclusions

We can thus see that none of the major variables of human societies in late Post-Pleistocene South Africa can be correlated absolutely with any other, and most combinations clearly do not correlate highly (Table 1). That major population movements took place in later South African prehistory is undeniable; but the linking of variables in causative models of population replacement and borrowing from invaders is not acceptable. Classification and temporal reconstruction may be made from each of a number of measurable variables, each of great significance to culture process, as well as from the social classification of the people involved. Archaeology's role is to investigate the static and dynamic structures of such configurations, to observe the degree of correlation and multivariate patterning without prior assumptions of causality. With the use of historical, anthropological and related data in test areas we may hope to expand such descriptive model-building into interpretation and explanation in terms of social process.

REFERENCES

Clark, J.D. (1959) *The prehistory of southern Africa.* London, Penguin.

Cooke, C.K. (1965) Evidence of human migrations from the rock art of Southern Rhodesia. *Africa* 35, 263-85.

Dart, R.A. and Beaumont, P.B. (1971) On a further radiocarbon date from ancient mining in southern Africa. *South African Journal of Science* 67, 10-11.

Derricourt, R.M. in press. The origin of the South African Iron Age. *Actes du VIIe Congrès panafricain de prehistoire et des études du quaternaire.* Addis Ababa.

Ehret, C. (1967) Cattle-keeping and milking in eastern and southern African history – the linguistic evidence. *Journal of African History* 8, 1-17.

Ehret, C. (1968) Sheep and central Sudanic peoples in southern Africa. *Journal of African History* 9, 213-21.

Fagan, B.M. (1964) The Greefswald sequence: Bambandyanalo and Mapungubwe. *Journal of African History* 4, 337-61.

Fagan, B.M. (1967) Radiocarbon dates for sub-Saharan Africa: IV. *Journal of African History* 7, 495-506.

Fock, G.J. (1971) Occurrence of domestic cattle on rock engravings. Paper read at conference of the South African Association for the Advancement of Science.

Fouché, L. (ed.) (1937) *Mapungubwe*. Cambridge, University Press.

Galloway, A. (1959) *The skeletal remains of Bambandyanalo*. Johannesburg, Witwatersrand University Press.

Gardner, G.A. (1963) *Mapungubwe II*. Pretoria, University of Pretoria.

Goodwin, A.J.H. (1947) The bored stones of South Africa. *Annals of the South African Museum* 37, 1-210.

Goodwin, A.J.H. (1956) Metal working among the early Hottentots. *South African Archaeological Bulletin* 11, 46-51.

Goodwin, A.J.H. and van Riet Lowe, C. (1929) The Stone Age cultures of South Africa. *Annals of the South African Museum* 27, 1-289.

Grindley, J.R., Speed, E. and Maggs, T. (1970) The age of the Bonteberg Shelter deposits, Cape Peninsular. *South African Archaeological Bulletin* 25, 24.

Harinck, G. (1969) Interaction between Xhosa and Khoi: emphasis on the period 1620-1750. *In* Thompson, L. (ed.) *African societies in Southern Africa* 145-69. London, Heinemann.

Huffman, T. (1970) The early Iron Age and the spread of the Bantu. *South African Archaeological Bulletin* 25, 3-21.

Humphries, A.J.B. and Maggs, T.M. O'C. (1970) Further graves and cultural material from the bank of the Riet River. *South African Archaeological Bulletin* 25, 116-26.

Inskeep, R.R. (1967) The Late Stone Age in Southern Africa. *In* Bishop, W.W. and Clark, J.D. (eds.) *Background to Evolution in Africa*, 557-82. Chicago, University of Chicago.

Inskeep, R.R. (1969) The archaeological background. *In* Wilson and Thompson 1969: 1-39.

Phillipson, D.W. (1969) Early iron-using peoples of Southern Africa. *In* Thompson, L. (ed.) *African societies in Southern Africa*, 24-49. London, Heinemann.

Sampson, C.G. (1970) *The Smithfield industrial complex: further field results.* National Museum, Bloemfontein. Memoir 5.

Schofield, J.F. (1948) *Primitive pottery*. Cape Town: South African Archaeological Society. Handbook 3.

Stern, J.T. and Singer, R. (1967) Quantitative morphological distinction between Bushman and Hottentot skulls: a preliminary report. *South African Archaeological Bulletin* 22 (1967), 103-11.

Tobias, P.V. (1955) Physical anthropology and somatic origins of the Hottentots. *African Studies* 14, 1-15.

Vogel, J.C. (1970) Groningen radiocarbon dates IX. *Radiocarbon* 12, 444-71.

Welbourne, R.G. (1971) Provisional assessment of Transvaal Iron Age economies. In *University of the Witwatersrand Department of Archaeology Occasional Papers* 6, 76-84.

Westphal, E.O.J. (1963) The linguistic prehistory of Southern Africa. *Africa* 33, 237-65.

Willcox, A.R. (1965) Petroglyphs of domestic animals. *South African Archaeological Bulletin* 20, 214.

Willcox, A.R. (1966) Sheep and sheep-herders in South Africa. *Africa* 36, 432-8.

Wilson, M. (1969) Changes in social structure in southern Africa. *In* Thompson, L. (ed.) *African Societies in Southern Africa*, 71-85. London, Heinemann.

Wilson, M. (1970) *The thousand years before Van Riebeeck*. Sixth Raymond

Dart lecture. Johannesburg, Witwatersrand University Press.
Wilson, M. and Thompson, L. (ed.) 1969. *Oxford History of South Africa I.* London, Oxford University Press.

R.A. CROSSLAND

Factors affecting language change

1. Prehistoric language

Language is an essential component in human culture, and must have become so at an early point in the evolution of *Homo sapiens*, if not in that of his hominid predecessors. Change in it may be expected, *prima facie*, to be either the consequence of other changes in the culture of a community or the cause of them; and any regularity or patterning in its changes should be of interest to those whose primary study is a feature of human social behaviour other than language, or material culture. The disadvantageous special situation of the linguist is that the activity which he studies has left no material product or reflection (on one possible exception see 7a below) before the development of writing in some areas and its adoption in others. If he makes deductions about language in pre-literate periods, he must work by introspection ('intuition') or analogy; even the conclusions of comparative linguistics about prehistoric languages should be treated as probable only in proportion to their compatibility with phenomena observed in historical periods.

2. Deductions about prehistoric communities from linguistic evidence

'Humanologists' (*sit venia ioco*; 'anthropologist' has specialized sense) other than linguists should find the following kinds of deduction from linguistic phenomena of interest.

(a) Deduction, if feasible, about the point in human physical or social evolution at which 'speech' became a feature of behaviour.

(b) Possible correlations between types of languages (however categorized) and types of society and patterns of material culture, or both.

(c) Patterns of manner and rate of change of languages, whether they can be shown to be universal, or different specific responses to defined non-linguistic stimuli or features of environment.

(d) Deductions from comparative linguistic evidence about the society or material culture of particular (late) prehistoric communities ('linguistic palaeontology').

3. *Linguistic evidence in reconstruction of prehistoric events*

Linguistic evidence might contribute to reconstruction of the prehistory of an area in the following ways.

(a) It might indicate stability of population in it in a late prehistoric period:

(i) if the area's earliest known language had features known to be characteristic of the languages of communities which have been genetically isolated (or nearly so) in historical periods.

(ii) if linguistic comparison indicated differentiation of a a language in the area late in prehistory, and a maximum or minimum duration, or both, can be established for the kind of differentiation indicated.

(b) 'Linguistic palaeontology' may indicate features of material culture for the late prehistoric population of the area which may be compared with, and might supplement, the findings of archaeology. If a duration can be deduced for the late prehistoric linguistic differentiation which occurred in the area (see 2, d), then the culture indicated by linguistic comparison might be roughly dated.

(c) Otherwise, linguistic evidence might indicate the extent to which the population of the area was divided into 'communities' or 'ethne' ('peoples', 'tribes' etc.) in cases where the material evidence did not indicate this; i.e. 'communities' may be differentiated by language without differing in traits of culture which are reflected in differences in non-perishable artifacts; reconstruction of the prehistoric language-pattern of an area might indicate the division of its population into 'communities' in cases where archaeology did not.

4. *Comparative linguistics*

Much of the contribution that linguistics may make to prehistory rests on comparison.

(a) The basic hypothesis of 'comparative linguistics' is that certain patterns of similarity and difference within sets of languages are best explained as resulting from dialectal differentiation of a prehistoric language (the concepts of a 'language' and of the essential homogeneity of a particular language need definition, but appear to admit of it). The hypothesis does not specify the social events which led to or accompanied the linguistic differentiation.

(b) The validation of the hypothesis depends on:

(i) Analogy; the processes by which, for example Latin developed into the Romance languages and French into its modern dialects in historical periods can be established (with certain gaps in the record); *prima facie*, it may be assumed that similar differentiation produced the patterns of correspondence, similar to those found e.g. among the Romance languages and among the dialects of French, which are observed in other groups of apparently cognate dialects or languages, whose putative 'ancestor' is not recorded. However, the social conditions in which the differentiation of the Romance languages, among other historical 'families', took place were different from those in which language-families of earlier origin differentiated.

(ii) Certain changes in speech habits, at least in pronunciation, appear to be one-way (i.e. the reverse change is not attested; see Hoenigswald 1966); hypotheses of differentiation which assume such changes in explaining patterns of correspondence are likely to be correct. Analogical argument is involved here to the extent that human articulatory behaviour is assumed to have been the same in late prehistoric periods as in historical.

5. The time-scale of linguistic change: 'lexico-statistics' ('glotto-chronology')

In view of 3b, a deduction about language differentiation will be most useful if its approximate duration can be estimated. Estimates have been based on (a) general analogical impression; (b) attempts to establish average rate of change in vocabulary in languages by statistical methods, with analogical assumption that the rate determined obtained in prehistoric times as well as in historical (Swadesh 1952; 1956). Objections to the hypotheses of 'lexicostatistics', and difficulties encountered in attempting it, are as follows (cf. Plath 1963:33-8; Polomé 1964; Haas 1966).

(a) The total vocabularies of historical languages seem manifestly to have changed at different rates in different social circumstances; especially according to the intensity and nature of the contact between the community which has spoken a language under study and other language-communities (Sweeney 1968; Crossland 1971: 232-4).

(b) The definition of 'basic' vocabulary, of words for simple 'fundamental' objects and concepts, allegedly little affected by contact with a linguistically alien population, seems arbitrary.

(c) Almost all observation of divergence of genetically related languages in vocabulary involves comparison of earlier languages (or diachronic dialects) known only from written sources with later ones which may be spoken, known in writing, or both. In such cases a literary tradition, keeping an early language or dialect in use alongside a later vernacular, or at least maintaining archaic usage, may have affected a normal rate of change in vocabulary. Moreover, the texts in an ancient language often have specialized or restricted vocabulary, so that accurate observation of the loss in 'basic' vocabulary between it and a later cognate will be impossible.

Analogues likely to indicate average rate of change in vocabulary (whatever its degree of variation) in the languages of non-literate peoples may be expected from:

(i) Studies of differentiation of the languages of such peoples in historical times, if any have been recorded by literates over a few centuries.

(ii) Cases in which the development of one language within a 'family', or the differentiation of one group within it, is documented over a period of some centuries, while another clearly related group may be assumed to have developed unaffected by the influence of literary or other archaic dialects (Bynon and Bynon 1970).

(iii) Cases where the beginning of a process of linguistic differentiation may be dated by non-linguistic (usually archaeological) evidence; this may be possible for the great majority of the languages of the Australian aborigines (Wurm 1962; McBryde 1968; Mulvaney 1969); also for the Uto-Aztecan family in northern central America, and perhaps the Turkic family and the Polynesian sub-family (Voegelin, Voegelin and Hale 1961: 1-8; Troike 1969; Grace 1964; Green 1966; Pawley 1966; Groube 1971).

At present, it is comparison of the Semitic and 'Hamitic' languages that seems likely to yield the longest time span of linguistic prehistory. Akkadian is already well differentiated from other Semitic languages when first known c. 2500 B.C. A date of at least a thousand years earlier may well be suggested for unitary proto-Semitic; and one at least a millennium before that for the 'ancestor' of the Semitic group, Ancient Egyptian and languages which have been classed as 'Hamitic' (Diakonov (D'yakonov) 1965; Bynon and Bynon 1970).

6. Factors affecting rate of differentiation: some impressions

Analogical deductions for prehistoric periods from the development and cross-influencing of languages of literate communities may well be misleading. 'Impressionistic' conclusions from what is observed about those of non-literate historical peoples would seem a little less hazardous, though the unsoundness of assuming that surviving 'primitives' necessarily preserve the culture-patterns of prehistoric late palaeolithic or neolithic peoples is well known.

(a) Specialized nomads or hunters who range over extensive territories apparently tend to use mutually intelligible or closely related languages over wide regions; examples are the Eskimo and the Turkic-speaking peoples; the typological similarity of Turkic, Mongol and Uralic is suggestive; and Australian aborigine languages are reported to show, with a few exceptions, graduated variation in vocabulary across the Australian sub-continent (Wurm 1962).

(b) The languages of communities that are isolated by natural obstacles, and live in a way that requires little travel or contact with other communities, seem in some cases to be grossly differentiated and dissimilar over quite small regions. This is reported of Papua (Wurm 1962).

(c) In all cases, however, the alternative explanation should be considered; this is that peoples who speak cognate languages over a wide region have extended over it relatively recently; while those who speak dissimilar languages have been static for longer.

7. Language in relatively early prehistoric periods

A.C. Renfrew in a recent paper (1970) invited linguists to speculate whether any known language might have continued in use essentially unchanged since the mesolithic. 'Essentially unchanged' required definition (see Crossland 1970a). But speculation suggests:

(a) E.H. Lenneberg's findings, that humans inherit the ability to acquire a language if exposed to normal stimuli in childhood, would seem to answer in the affirmative the question whether men were using systems of oral communication that would be regarded as 'languages' so early (Lenneberg 1967: 227-70). Also of interest is the suggestion that laterality in manual operations evolved in association with the capacity for speech, and that evidence for it in artifacts may indicate that men used systematic speech as early as the upper palaeolithic (Semeonov 1965).

(b) It seems doubtful whether speech passed through a stage in which the language of a particular community was more 'fluid' or 'unstable' than those of historical periods, in the sense that there was greater individual to individual variation in usage, or more rapid change in it between generations. 'Speech' presumably developed by parallel evolution, with large numbers of human (or possible hominid) communities developing systems of articulatory signals which became gradually more specific in reference and at the same time more extensive in the range of references and directives that could be communicated. Some preceding system of oral communication may well have been common to the species, or each of a small number of systems might have been used by a large division of it. C.S. Coon's average 'breeding unit' of 500-600 deduced for food-gatherers (Coon 1963:100-2) would seem to be one of a size likely to develop more sophisticated oral communication. It seems likely that after a certain point of elaboration in size and specificity of the vocabulary of signals or words had been reached (apart from greater complexity in other respects) communication within the 'unit' would only have been effective if communicatory behaviour became very regular. From this point, differentiation between the 'languages' of 'units' would have been natural, though contact and need for intercourse between 'units', where they were present, would have been an inhibiting factor.

(c) In principle, the earliest known language of an area may have had a continuous development (see Crossland 1970a) since the mesolithic. Among linguistic evidence, only indications of prehistoric language-differentiation in an area, together with analogical indication of an extremely slow average speed for such a change (if forthcoming; see above, 5) might imply it.

(d) Alternative indication might be: exceptional idiosyncrasy of a language in comparison with others; non-linguistic evidence for genetic or cultural stability in an area since the mesolithic; or the two phenomena in combination. The unusual features of the Tibeto-Burman languages and

Chinese (quite probably forming a single family) set beside the alleged continuity of some physical features in Mongoloid populations from the palaeolithic (Coon 1963: 454-60) might provide an example.

L.S. Klejn (in comment sent to the Seminar) put the question of how to decide when a language which may be considered to have had a continuous development during a given period as regards certain of its features, or in view of a literary tradition, 'becomes "another language" '. He takes as example assessment of the difference between the language of the Russian chronicles (12th century A.D.), and Modern Russian. The former is essentially unintelligible to Russians today (Frunkina 1965; Frunkina and Dobrovich 1971). He notes that in general a speaker of a language cannot understand a text in a related idiom if more than 30% of the basic vocabulary in it (e.g. of the 2500 or so words of highest frequency in normal vernacular speech) is different from his own. In non-literate societies, it is presumably only differences between 'diachronic dialects' of four generations at the most that will be of any importance in normal communication (though older dialects may be maintained in use by oral tradition for religious or other special purposes). Only changes which produce within such a time-span differences of usage which make older and younger speakers mutually unintelligible will have practical consequences. The social pressure of need to communicate will presumably prevent change at a rate which might have that result. But average rate of linguistic change does not appear to have been nearly rapid enough for it ever to have been a real possibility. In literate societies tradition and education appear to have slowed rate of change in vernacular language to some extent (Crossland 1970b; 1971:232-3). In contemporary 'advanced' (urban and industrial) societies, technical and other specialized vocabulary appears to be changing more quickly, but it is too early yet to judge whether rate of change of basic vocabulary has accelerated. The conclusion would seem to be that apparent retention of one or a few items of vocabulary in a historical language over a few millennia does not prove that the language had a long prehistoric period of slow development, in stable social conditions. Since average rate of change of vocabulary seems to have been sufficient to have produced almost complete change of the vocabulary of any language which had a continuous development from the mesolithic to historical times, occasional long survival of a particular item might be fortuitous.

C.M. Nelson suggested (referring to current research by W. Gibbons at Yale University) that the similarity of stone artifacts over a large part of Africa and Eurasia in the lower palaeolithic and their diversity in the upper palaeolithic indicate that language came into use at the end of the former period or cultural phase. The argument is that only the development of speech (systems of articulatory communication of a certain complexity) would have made it possible for men to share experience with tools and design new types, and that the necessary ability to symbolize would have evolved in parallel with it. The only hope of putting speculation about the 'origin of language' on a sounder basis (and it should not be over-estimated) would seem to lie in further studies of the oral communication of young children and primates. For the present, it may be worth suggesting that the transmission of information and skills across generations may not have been the primary function of language in its earlier stages of development, important as it was later, and noting that such transmission has been largely by visual teaching even in historical times. Language may well have developed in the first place as more effective systems of synchronic oral communication within hunting groups. A further suggestion of L.S. Klejn's should be noted here; that 'typochronology' might be developed: a study of rates of change in culture patterns and their relation to rates of change in languages.

8. Conclusions

Linguistic research which might be specially valuable for general study of culture-change would seem to be:

1. Typological comparison of language of surviving 'primitive' communities in different parts of the world, aimed at establishing whether any features of speech correlate with their other patterns of behaviour;
2. Further investigation of the results of 'lexico-statistics', especially their consistency, in cases where language differentiation can be observed or be deduced to have occurred over a time-span either known, or deducible with useful accuracy, say to within five hundred years.

REFERENCES

Bergsland, K. and Vogt, H. (1962) On the validity of glottochronology. *Current Anthropology* 3, 115-53.

Bynon, T. and Bynon, J. (1970) *Proceedings of the Colloquium on Hamito-Semitic Comparative Linguistics*, London (in press).

Coon, C.S. (1963) *The Origin of Races.* London.

Crossland, R.A. (1970a) Comment on Renfrew, A.C.; Problems in the general correlation of archaeological and linguistic strata in prehistoric Greece; the model of autochthonous origin. *In* Crossland, R.A. and Birchall, A. (eds.) *Bronze Age Migrations in the Aegean* (London, in press).

Crossland, R.A. (1970b) Retrospect and prospects in Aegean prehistory: the linguistic data. *In* Crossland, R.A. and Birchall, A. (eds.) *Bronze Age Migrations in the Aegean.*

Crossland, R.A. (1971) The position in the Indo-European language-family of Thracian and Phrygian and their possible close cognates. *Studia Balcanica*

5 (Georgiev, V.I., ed., *L'ethnogénèse des peuples balkaniques*), 225-36.

Diakonov (D'yakonov), I.M. (1965) *Semito-Hamitic languages: an essay in classification.* Moscow.

Frunkina, R.M. (1965) Ponimanie teksta v usobiyakh organichennovo znaniya slovarya. *Nauchno tekhicheskaya informastsiya* 1965/4.

Frunkina, R.M. and Dobrovich, A. (1971) Kak luzirobat' Simenova? *Znanie-Gila* 1971/1.

Grace, G.W. (1964) Movement of the Malayo-Polynesians 1500 B.C.-A.D. 500: the linguistic evidence. *Current Anthropology* 5, 361-8.

Green, R.C. (1966) Linguistic subgrouping within Polynesia: the implications of prehistoric settlement. *Journal of the Polynesian Society* 75, 6-38.

Groube, L.M. (1971) Tonga, 'Lapita' pottery and Polynesian origins. *Journal of the Polynesian Society*, **80**, 278-316.

Haas, M.R. (1966) Historical linguistics and the genetic relationship of languages. *In* Sebeok, T.A. (ed.) *Current trends in linguistics* **III**, 116-52. The Hague.

Hoenigswald, H.M. (1966) Criteria for the subgrouping of languages. *In* Birnbaum, H. and Puhvel, J. (eds.) *Ancient Indo-European dialects*, 1-12. Berkeley and Los Angeles.

Hymes, D.H. (1960) Lexicostatistics so far. *Current Anthropology* **1**, 3-44.

Lenneberg, E.H. (1967) *Biological Foundations of Language.* New York, London. Sidney.

McBryde, I. (1966) Radiocarbon dates for northern New South Wales. *Antiquity* **40**, 285-92.

Mulvaney, D.J. (1969) *The Prehistory of Australia.* London.

Pawley, A. (1966) Polynesian languages: a subgrouping based on shared innovations in morphology. *Journal of the Polynesian Society* **75**, 39-64.

Plath, W. (1963) Mathematical linguistics; *In* Mohrmann, C. (ed.) *Trends in European and American linguistics* 1930-1960, 21-57. Utrecht.

Polomé, E. (1964) Considérations sur la valeur des données lexicostatistiques. *In* van Windekens, A.J. and Pop, S. (eds.) *Comm. et rapports du Ier congres int. de dialectologie généralc I*, 1962. Louvain.

Rabin, C. (1970) Lexicostatistics and the internal divisions of Semitic; *In* Bynon, T. and Bynon, J. (eds.) *Proceedings of the Colloquium on Hamito-Semitic Comparative Linguistics.*

Renfrew, A.C. (1970) Problems in the general correiation of archaeological and linguistic strata in prehistoric Greece: the model of autochthonous origin; *In* Crossland, R.A. and Birchall, A. (eds.) *Bronze Age Migrations in the Aegean.*

Semeonov, V. and Thompson, M.W. (translator) (1965) *Prehistoric Technology.* London.

Swadesh, M. (1952) Lexicostatistic dating of prehistoric ethnic contacts. *Proceedings of the American Philosophical Society* **96**, 452-63.

Swadesh, M. (1956) Towards greater accuracy in lexicostatistic dating. *International Journal of American Linguistics* **21**, 121-37.

Sweeney, W.D. (1968) Linguistic influences on the glotto-chronology rate: literacy, isolation, borrowing. *Godišnak Filozofskog Fakulteta u Novom Sadu* **11**, 445-73.

Troike, R.C. (1969) The glottochronology of six Turkic languages. *International Journal of American Linguistics* **35**, 183-91.

Voegelin, C.F., Voegelin, F.M. and Hale, K.L. (1961) Typological and comparative grammar of Uto-Aztecan: I (Phonology). *International Journal of American Linguistics* **28**, 1: *Supplement* (= *Indiana University Publications in Anthropology and Linguistics: Memoire* 17).

Wurm, S.A. (1964) The present state of New Guinea (non-Melanesian or Papuan) and Australian linguistics. *In* Lunt, H.G. (ed.) *Proceedings of the IXth International Congress of Linguistics*, 1962. 575-9. The Hague.

J. CARNOCHAN

Lexicostatistics and African languages

The languages of Africa have little documented history, many of them none at all, even for comparatively modern times, and any account of the past of the peoples speaking these languages is inevitably of a rather speculative nature. In time no doubt, such extra-linguistic sources as archaeology will furnish much more information than up to the moment, but some indications concerning the history and prehistory – if such a distinction is valid – of the area have resulted from comparative linguistic studies based mainly on the state of the languages in the twentieth century, although there is a small amount of information available from earlier periods. The work of Meinhof and Westermann in this field is well known, and more recently Greenberg (1963) and Guthrie (1968) have made important contributions, using what may be called the traditional methods. Greenberg has worked in Africa, investigating linguistic problems and collecting language data, but of course no one individual could have personal knowledge of all the languages concerned, and in his classification he has had to rely largely on the published and unpublished work of others. His classification is far-ranging and bold, and has not found universal acceptance among other scholars in the field, who feel that he should perhaps have proceeded rather more cautiously. Guthrie's work concerns just the Bantu languages, an immense undertaking in itself, and he has been able to rely very much on the data of his own personal field research, which should make for the maximum internal consistency of the whole project. He is, however, extremely cautious in putting forward theoretical statements about the pre-history of the Bantu peoples on the basis of the results of linguistic comparison. The work of both these scholars and of many others has been along the lines of historical comparative linguistics, and important though their findings are, they do not give a sufficient estimation for archaeologists, anthropologists and historical linguists who need to know at what date certain changes in the language took place, and how such changes can be correlated with other changes in the culture.

Linguistic phenomena have provided many examples of regularity, regularity of grammatical forms, of morphology and syntax, regularity of phonological structure, regularity of change due to the operation over time of sound laws. Were there other forms of regularity to be investigated, such as the replacement of vocabulary items? As long ago as 1916, Sapir had pointed out 'The greater the degree of linguistic differentiation within a stock the greater is the period of time that must be assumed for the development of such differentiation'. The analysis of decay products in mineral samples permits the calculation of the earth's crust. Similarly, analyses of morpheme decay products should provide an absolute chronology for lexical history (Lees, 1953, 114). Swadesh extended Sapir's principle, and (1950, 1952) advanced the theory that items of the vocabulary of a language, or of part of that vocabulary decay and are replaced at a fixed rate, and he invented the statistical method to show this, which he called glottochronology. In 1953, Robert Lees sought to establish the validity of the techniques involved by applying them to thirteen sets of data, English, Spanish, French, German, Coptic, Athenian, Cypriot, Chinese, Swedish, Italian, Portuguese, Rumanian and Catalan. He used Swadesh's list of 215 English words, translating them into 'the most common colloquial term' for each language tested, but for two stages of each language, one older and one more recent, there being an independent way of dating the vocabulary of both stages. The items of one stage were compared with those of the other by specialists in the language family involved, and the pairs were marked as cognate, non-cognate, or indeterminate. From the number of cognates, the retention rate of items was calculated, the time lapse was known independently, and from these two sets of figures, the rate of retention per thousand years was calculated for each language, the scatter being from 76% (for Coptic) to 85.4% (for both German and Swedish), with a mean of 80.5%. 'We take this to mean that on the average about 81% of the basic-root-morphemes of a language will survive as cognates after a thousand years, for all languages, at all times.' Such claims have not passed without challenge. Fodor (1961) tested the validity of glottochronology on the basis of the Slavonic languages, Old Church Slavonic, Bulgarian, Macedonian, Serbocroatian, Slovenian, Russian, Ukranian, Byelorussian, Czech, Slovak, Polish, Kashub, Lower Lusatian, Upper Lusatian and Polab, and unlike some, he published the whole of his findings and his data. Summing up, he says: 'The method of glottochronology is not suitable as a means of revealing genetic relationships between the languages and for establishing the time depth of the separation from the parent language. The assumption that the basic vocabularies of the languages change at an equal rate over a long period does not hold water. The most permanent layer of the basic vocabulary on which the investigations rest cannot be determined with a general validity for all the languages of the world; it would have to be modified for every language family. No general principle can be set up for establishing sameness, each case requiring an individual evaluation; and the decisions in favour or against a word may be equally correct. Many different results can be attained in any investigation . . . The results of all investigations performed with the method of glottochronology are illusory and unreliable even if they happen to agree with the correct results obtained by other means.' He does not wish, however, to discard the method altogether; 'Provided it does not claim to reveal genetic relationships, lexicostatistics may be very usefully employed for the sub-grouping of the languages, because the dialects can well be distinguished by its exact methods.'

Glottochronology makes indeed four basic assumptions, as set out by Sarah C. Gudschinsky (1956).

1. Some parts of the vocabulary of any language are assumed, on empirical evidence, to be much less subject to change than other parts. This basic core vocabulary includes such items as terms for pronouns, numerals, body parts, geographical features etc. Swadesh showed this (1951:13) by reference to French loan words in English.
2. The rate of retention of vocabulary items in the basic core of relatively stable vocabulary is constant through time. Complete empirical evidence that the rate of loss is constant through time is still lacking since the assumption has not been checked for a time span greater than 2,200 years.
3. The rate of loss of basic vocabulary is approximately the same in all languages.
4. If the percentage of true cognates within the core vocabulary is known for any pair of languages, the length of time that has elapsed since the two languages began to diverge from a single parent language can be computed, provided that there are no interfering factors through migrations, conquests, or other social contacts which slowed or speeded the divergence.

In the field of African languages, glottochronology would seem to offer an attractive method of arriving at a time depth scale, and some applications of the techniques have been made. Swadesh himself and Evangelina Arana with John T. Bendor-Samuel and W.A.A. Wilson published *A preliminary glottochronology of Gur Languages* (1966). Diagnostic word lists using the Swadesh first 100 words were prepared for forty-five languages of the Gur group, spoken in West Africa, and the results of the experiment suggested some re-classification of the languages compared with the traditional method. Bendor-Samuel and Wilson accepted Swadesh's findings in general, even though they criticised details of his method, suggesting that he was rather more liberal in his assessment of cognates than they might have been, and thus in some cases giving a reduced time depth. The procedure followed in the identification of cognates 'based on the experience of Swadesh, is one designed to permit rapid work and to keep down errors, both those of excessive boldness, and those of excessive caution'.

In another paper, Kay Williamson presented to the West African Language Conference an account of the Izi-Ekpeye language group. The best known of these is Igbo, and her glottochronological method suggested that there is considerably more diversity between the units than was thought, while there is a classic position geographically, with a greater degree of correspondence between these units closer together, and more divergence from those further away.

In Africa the greatest need is still for more descriptive studies of the languages, and this would lead to some of the criticisms made by Fodor with regard to Slavonic and glottochronology being at least partially removed from work on African languages about which little is still known.

REFERENCES

Fodor, I. (1961) The validity of glottochronology on the basis of the Slavonic languages, *Studia Slavonica*, Tomus VII fasciculus 4, 295-346.

Greenberg, J.H. (1963) *The Languages of Africa*. Mouton.

Gudschinsky, S.C. (1956) The ABCs of lexicostatistics (glottochronology), *Word* 12, no. 2, 175-210.

Guthrie, (1968) *Comparative Bantu*.

Hymes, D.H. (1960) Lexicostatistics so far, *Current Anthropology* 1, 3-44.

Lees, B. (1953) The basia of glottochronology, *Language* 29, no. 2 (part 1), 113-27.

Swadesh, M. (1950) Salish internal relationships, *International Journal of American Linguistics*, 16, 157-67.

Swadesh, M. (1951) Diffusional cumulation and archaic residue as historical explanations, *Southwestern Journal of Anthropology* 7, 1-21.

Swadesh, M. (1952) Lexicostatistic dating of prehistoric ethnic contacts, *Proceedings of the American Philosophical Society* 96, 452-63.

Swadesh, M. (1955) Towards greater accuracy in lexicostatistic dating, *International Journal of Applied Linguistics* 21, 121-37.

Swadesh, M., Arana, E., Bendor-Samuel, T. and Wilson, W.A.A. (1966) A preliminary glottochronology of Gur languages, *Journal of West African Languages* III, no. 2, 27-65.

Williamson, K. (1969) The Izi-Ekpeye language group. Paper to the W.A. Language conference.

Section 7: Systems theory, law and the multivariate analysis of change

FRED PLOG

Laws, systems of law, and the explanation of observed variation

For several years, archaeologists have been discussing and debating the appropriate role of laws and operational procedures in their discipline. Whatever effect this discussion has had on the discipline, it has clearly not led us much closer to the use of laws, or operational procedures attuned to the discovery of laws, in our work. This paper is an attempt to recapitulate some of the issues that led to the initial concern with laws and their discovery and use, to restate my own ideas concerning these issues, and to detail some of the reasons why we are still so frequently confounded in our search for laws.

The issues

No single consideration motivated the many archaeologists who during the last decade, began to discuss laws, explanation and operational procedures and to argue that the lack of concern for these topics was creating problems in doing archaeology. However, a few issues were most critical.

First, the sociology of archaeology made increasingly difficult the kind of communication which had for many decades served to secure archaeologists' confidence in their colleagues' work. Where a few dozen years earlier archaeologists working in the same area or on the same problem met each other with some frequency, the day of the face to face archaeological gathering was over. No archaeologist is capable of interacting with all of the other archaeologists whose ideas affect his work. The confidence gained in such interaction had and still has a great effect on one's willingness to rely upon the research results of others. But as the number of practising archaeologists grew and face to face interaction became less frequent some other standard for assessing the adequacy of the work of others seemed desirable. We needed and still need a set of ideas for assessing when the propositions that archaeologists advance should be deemed verified or usable and when they should not.

Second, comparative studies became more frequent and more important for the discipline. Reading such studies, it was evident to many archaeologists that the discipline needed a good deal more standardization in the techniques of observation and reporting that archaeologists were using. Some of the apparent differences and similarities in the prehistory of two areas under examination seemed as much the product of similarities and differences in the kinds of data that the archaeologists recorded and/or the analytic techniques they used as of any real similarity or difference in the archaeological record. In the same way, it was sometimes simply impossible for a third party to compare the prehistory of two regions because the archaeological work done in them was so different. A more sharply defined problem focus plus agreement on a set of verification procedures seemed a likely solution to this problem also.

Third, these same comparative studies raised serious questions about the bases for comparison archaeologists were using. Regularities in the evolution of prehistoric societies seemed not to be found at the level of facts or events. The context in which domesticates, for example, were adopted proved remarkably varied as did the effect of their adoption on the society in question. At best, event-centred treatments of evolution led to endless discussion over how many events had to be similar before the sequences were similar, how many had to be different before they were declared different. If regularities were not to be found at the level of events, then they might exist at the level of processes – linked series of events. And, in other sciences, regularities in processes are called laws. In this way some archaeologists were led to a concern with the issues under discussion.

A fourth factor that led to a concern with these issues was the increase in archaeological dabbling in areas where discussions of laws and operational procedures were characteristic and important. Evolution, statistics, and mathematics are all examples. As archaeologists began to use ideas sets – theoretical or operational – where discussions of laws and testing were important, the issues that motivated the discussion became important to us also. As a result of the use of these techniques, laws or generalizations were proposed. The area of dwelling units was said to have a determinant relationship with the number of individuals inhabiting the unit. But, multiple formulae for the same relationship soon appeared. How was the archaeologist to know when a relationship was valid for everyone and when for only a few?

Finally, some archaeologists were greatly bothered by the endless involvement of archaeologists and anthropologists in borrowing ideas from other disciplines and the concomitant lack of commitment to developing a set of concepts uniquely attuned to the practice of their own discipline. The pattern of borrowing carried on at its current intensity would involve archaeology in an endless series of fads, not infrequently based on rather inaccurate interpretations of the concepts in question. Archaeology needed both a rigorous method for evaluating the utility of these borrowed concepts and a stimulus to beginning the construction of its own body of concepts – operational and theoretical.

One position

Stimulated by many of these issues, I have tried to define my own position with respect to laws and, more broadly, explanation. I offer no universal definition of explanation because I think that archaeologists and for that matter philosophers of science and scientists generally have in mind three related but rather different activities or contexts when they speak of explanation.

In a first or formal context, explanation is the process of constructing valid arguments. This is explanation in the sense of a concern for Aristotelean logic or the Hempel-Oppenheim model (Hempel 1966). A concern with explanation in this context is a concern with the kinds of propositions of which an argument is composed and the relationships that must exist between the propositions if the argument is to be considered valid. For the archaeologists, these issues reduce to a simpler desire – to know when an argument concerning the occurrence of some prehistoric event is valid and when it is only seemingly so.

In a second context, a substantive one, explanation is the process of accounting for the patterned variation of some topic phenomenon or variable. The explanation for this phenomenon is its place in a system of variables with a defined relationship between the causal variables such that changes in the topic phenomenon can be predicted. Techniques such as multiple regression provide the investigator with yardsticks indicating how much of the observed variation has been accounted for and how much hasn't. If used correctly, they also tell the investigators in what ways his formulations are successful and in what ways they are not. They tell us how closely we are approaching the goal of constructing a model that accurately predicts the pattern of variation in the phenomena with which we are concerned.

Thirdly, explanation is used in an operational context where it refers to the process of doing research. It is a definition of ways for arriving at valid arguments or predictive models. I have argued that such a process has the following structure:

Definition of problem
Formulation of hypotheses
Operationalization of hypotheses
Collection of data
Analysis

Testing
Evaluation

This is a model of the structure of doing research. I certainly do not deny that research is a process: that we are continually revising some portions of the design while explicitly performing others – that, for example, our experience in formulating hypotheses leads us to see and define problems in new ways.

But the model does have an internal logic. Without a problem, some observed variation that he wishes to explain, the investigator has no idea what propositions he should attempt to evaluate. Without hypotheses, formulations of potential explanations to the problem, research cannot be planned so as to guarantee that appropriate data will be collected. Operations without problems or hypotheses involve the investigator in doing methodology for the sake of methodology – in mindlessly using statistical or analytical techniques for the sake of demonstrating that they can be used – in generating typologies for the sake of generating typologies and so on.

The existence of an internal logic does not of course ensure success. But, it is more probable that research based on a rigorous design will produce the desired results than the typical alternative, waiting around for a moment of brilliant insight.

I do not believe that research can be successful unless the investigator is concerned with explanation in all three of these contexts. One can build formally elegant arguments that have no predictive powers and cannot be tested. One can build models with unbelievable predictive powers that offer no insight into the topic phenomenon because the investigator has no idea why they work, what arguments underly their operation. And, one can do fantastically rigorous research that is devoid of either substantive or formal meaning.

The response

The response of archaeologists to the discussion of explanation has been both heartening and disheartening. There is probably a great deal more concern for regularities and for techniques of verifying propositions than there was a decade ago. But there is also a good deal of further discussion that promises to do very little for archaeology. The vast majority of the responses that I have seen and heard to papers that I and others have published focus on three points: there are other interpretations of the work of the philosophers whose works are being interpreted, other philosophers have different and competing ideas, and there are other definitions of crucial terms such as law and hypothesis. All of these points are perfectly correct. However, they are generally stated in an absurdly *ad hominem* or my-source-knows-more-than-your-source fashion that totally misses the issue of whether a particular set of ideas is useful for doing archaeology.

There has also been a great deal of healthy discussion that focuses on the problem of doing archaeology.

What is most disappointing, from my own perspective, is the blithe ignorance that some archaeologists continue to demonstrate toward the issues that have been raised. For example, conceptual borrowing continues – almost all archaeologists are now doing ecology and calling themselves ecologists. Terms are borrowed from ecology and general systems theory and uttered as blessings from the Bible. More critically, the terms are often flagrantly misused or misrepresented. *Deviation amplification*, a perfectly useful term for conceptualizing a change situation, is used as an *explanation* for particular sequences of change. Ecosystem becomes the holy word of archaeological research, and one gets the impression that it holds the same status in ecology. Such proves not to be the case. Ecosystem is to ecology as culture area is to anthropology, a way of dealing with a range of very general and large scale problems. Other schools of ecology (e.g. Levins 1969) focus on problems quite distinct from those hung on an ecosystem frame. And, not surprisingly, ecologists have their processual and non-processual and mathematical and non-mathematical camps, each with distinctive approaches and idea sets. Yet, the way that this discipline has been represented to archaeologists, this rich diversity is scarcely evident – there is only one true style of ecology, the ecosystem style. The kind of rigour in evaluating concepts and propositions that some archaeologists have sought to introduce is badly needed still in the area of conceptual borrowing.

Why we overlook regularities

Perhaps some of the dissatisfaction with the concept of laws stems from the failure of those who say they exist to produce them immediately – 'If there are laws, show us some'. I do not see this as a crucial issue. Anthropology is full of statements of regularity which, if verified, ought to be considered laws. Moreoever, there are publications that have collected together many of the regularities, empirical generalizations, and law-like statements that social scientists have produced (Miller 1965, Berelson and Steiner 1968). These too are potential laws, propositions wanting further systematic testing.

Turning to the issue of generating laws and law-like propositions, there are a number of good reasons why an investigator might encounter difficulty even if he already believed that laws existed and were useful and wished to discover them.

First, there is no reason to assume that the fashion in which we have learned to view the archaeological record is susceptible to treatment as a body of laws. Our ideas of what is relevant and what is not in an archaeological task – what sort of data we will collect, what sort of attributes we will record – have been shaped by the whole history of archaeology. These data and attributes will not necessarily be the ones that can be used in creating laws. For example, the Greeks were perfectly capable of creating a typology of matter that operated in terms of varying contents of fire, water, and earth. It was a real typology and was consistent with the then extant knowledge concerning matter. However, it did not prove to offer the required insight into patterned variation in the physical universe. Its application produced anomalies as well as insights. Later typologies were developed in terms more akin to what we now call elements, but they keyed on attributes of these elements that were not susceptible to law-like treatment – colour and weight, for example. The typology that ultimately proved useful – Mendeleev's periodic table – did identify the critical attributes. This typology is not used because a convention of physicists and chemists decided to use it. It is used because it works. It offered new insights into the structure of the elements, reasons for their behaviour with respect to each other, and predictions that as yet undiscovered elements would and should be found.

Again, not every attribute of an element is subject to such systematization. Not every attribute of a site or an artifact is either. We have no way of knowing whether the attributes on which we currently focus are the most useful ones or not, but the extent to which they are subject to systematization is certainly one good clue. In other words, the search for regularities is one mechanism for separating less from more useful attributes of our data.

Even if we knew that we were looking at the right attributes, we would have to be concerned with how we were using these attributes, with the kinds of variables we used them to create. Science has always achieved its successes in explaining variation or variables, not in explaining constants. 'If it doesn't vary, you're not going to explain it' is a simple but oft violated dictum. In fact, archaeology has a long history of trying to deal with some of its best variables as constants.

Diffusion is perhaps the most classic of examples. Diffusion is a process that occurred in the past and occurs today. But, it does not have and has not had any characteristic or constant pattern as archaeologists have fought so hard to assume. Rates of diffusion or the adoption of innovation are highly varied both in space and in time. Even if we imagine that the pattern illustrated at the right edge of line A in Fig. 1 is the one that archaeologists typically observe, there are many ways of arriving at this configuration. Line A illustrates the pattern that archaeologists usually envisage. But line B where the artifact achieves a wide distribution over an area and then is adopted with particular rapidity in some areas, is also possible. So are the other alternatives illustrated. If it is the case that the pattern of line A is the one most characteristically produced by the interaction of variation in the spatial and temporal rates of artifact adoption, this fact is itself worth explaining. But no explanation, no laws, no understanding will be derived if archaeologists simply assume that characteristic configurations are constants and not the result of the regular interaction of some behavioural variables.

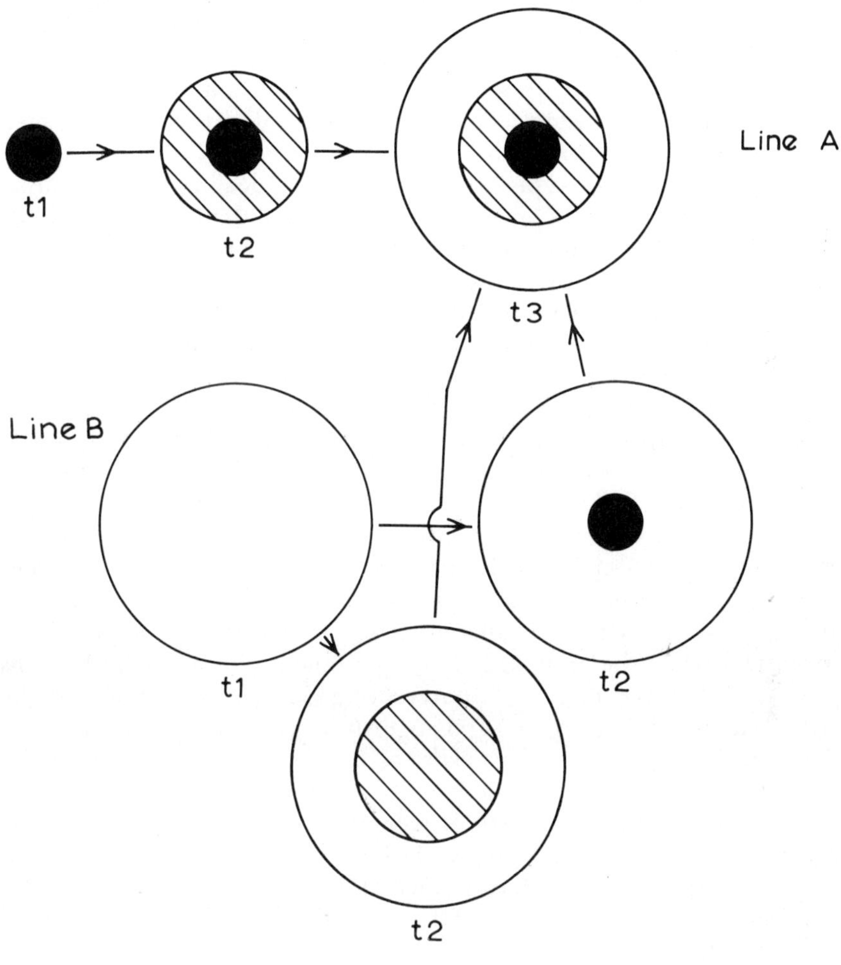

Figure 1 Alternative spatial patterns for the diffusion of an innovation observed at three points in time.

The same problem exists when we substitute categories for continua. Sometimes this occurs because we do not perceive the continuum, but other times it is the product of laziness. It is much easier to deal with a particular variable as a finite number of categories rather than an almost infinite number of points on a continuum. But, in so doing, the investigator is systematically underestimating and oversimplifying the variability with which he is dealing. The long history of science demonstrates rather clearly that sciences do not begin to formulate laws and regularities until they are using continuous rather than categorical variables. Alternatively, legitimate laws rarely involve categorical variables and almost always involve continuous ones.

Even with the right attributes and variables, there are still problems in achieving laws. Sciences have been successful in formulating laws when they began to deal principally with temporal and only incidentally with spatial variability. We talk about processes as linked series of events. There is a school of anthropology called evolutionism. But the scholars associated with both of these concepts are most typically seen to be dealing with spatial, cross-sectional and synchronic variation rather than temporal, longitudinal, and diachronic variation. It makes no sense to talk about laws of process or laws of change and then to use static data in attempting to discover them.

Many social scientists have learned this lesson but find longitudinal data difficult to obtain. Collecting it often requires studies that are longer than the lifetime of any individual. Archaeologists deal with longitudinal data all the time. If the archaeological record is anything, it is a record of change. But, what do we do with our record of change? We try to force it into a static model.

When archaeologists deal with time, their characteristic practice is to break time into a series of units, phases or whatever. These studies are most successful when the variation within the units is minimized and that between units is maximized. This attempt is in turn most successful when the units demarcate periods of relative stability. This procedure has the effect of representing periods of stability as the critical units while periods of change show as no more than the lines that separate the units. If we claim to be interested in process, this is a queer practice to follow (and yet one that follows rather directly from the ecosystem concept). If we are to understand processes, we will do so only by representing variations in populations, resources or whatever as having a continuous trajectory over time, not by representing them as a series of static units that just happen to come one after the other.

If one looks carefully at the laws of natural science, it is evident that they are statements of tendency, not of outcome. Water seeks its own level. This does not mean that everywhere in nature inter-connected containers of water will have actually the same level. A variety of forces may interfere with this tendency: if the level of one container is below the base of another, all of the water will flow to the former. To the extent that chronologies force us to look at the outcome of periods of change rather than the changes as they occur, they direct our attention away from the laws of process that we seek.

The problems discussed so far concern first and foremost the fashion in which we perceive and conceptualize our data. There are still problems in the way that we use that data. The old warning about the difference between correlation and causation is worth repeating. Anyone who has extensively employed multiple regression or other multivariate techniques is aware that it is possible in many instances to construct multiple models that predict patterned variation in a topic variable with equal accuracy. Successful predictions, fantastically high correlations do not necessarily point to laws. They do only when accompanied by a valid argument.

The most basic problem is one which a concern for explanation should solve. We too frequently tend to work either principally with data, introducing theory only to the extent required to make the data seem sensible, or we work principally with theory, using data only to the extent necessary to make the theories seem supported. Neither of these alternatives can be the legitimate goal of our research. Observed variation is automatically the touchstone of our work – we deal with data. But a concern with regularities is equally vital because it is in regularities and not in data that knowledge is systematized.

An example

I have no doubts that I cannot successfully escape from this paper without defending the proposition that anthropology does in fact have laws. Two of the more obvious of these are the Law of Cultural Dominance and the Law of Evolutionary Potential as discussed by Sahlins and Service (1960). These laws, I argue, are valid in any processual context that one might choose to observe, and are valid far beyond the contexts in which Sahlins and Service discuss them.

The Law of Cultural Dominance simply put states that: Those cultural systems which most effectively harness the energy sources of a given environment will grow at the expense of less effective systems.

The Law of Evolutionary Potential states that: The more specialized a cultural system the lower the probability of its advancement to the next evolutionary stage; the more generalized the cultural system the greater the probability of advancement.

Each of these formulations contains a pair of critical variables. The Law of Evolutionary Potential relates the extent of specialization-generalization that characterizes a cultural system to the probability of its evolving further. The Law of Cultural Dominance relates the effectiveness of energy capture to the extent of growth.

As these propositions stand, they are quite limited in scope; they fail to transcend the bounds of rather dogmatic Whitean evolutionism. However, we need not leave them in so limited a state.

Taking first the Law of Cultural Dominance, one may observe that this statement about whole cultural systems very closely parallels a Skinnerian-Homansian statement about the behaviour of individuals: the more a given item of behaviour is rewarded, the more likely it is to be copied or repeated. All of the various scholars concerned have developed evidence to indicate the validity of their respective propositions. Successful behaviour patterns are abandoned or those who practice them are selected against – die or are forced out of the behavioural context.

In the case of the Law of Evolutionary Potential, the problem is the evolutionary stage concept. Not all cases of change involve changes in evolutionary stages. But we do know, in rather simple fashion, that the greater the range of behaviour represented in a cultural system, the greater the probability that the system contains some behaviour that would be appropriate given a change in the conditioning environment.

Let us examine the operation of these laws in a specific behavioural context. Suppose we are studying a series of prehistoric communities that seem to have practised a mixed hunting-gathering and agricultural subsistence strategy. Given that human behaviour is varied, it should not be our expectation that every community and every individual in each community practised precisely the same mix of hunting, gathering and agriculture. From a normative viewpoint, one might say that the communities were predominently agricultural. But, to make such a statement would do great violence to any more systemic approaches, approaches that allow for variability in human behaviour.

It might be discovered that for the group of these communities the average mix of the two subsistence strategies is 60% agriculture, 40% hunting-gathering. But, there is variation about this mean as in A of Fig. 2. Neither the mean nor the range of variation is a simple existential fact. The subsistence strategy practised by the communities is related to the environmental conditions in which the communities exist. It is important here to recall the old dictum that societies don't adapt to means, they adapt to variation. Just as behaviour, environmental variables vary. In the short run, they have a mean and some variation about the mean. In the long run, rather substantial changes in both mean and range of variation are possible.

One might ask two questions about the curve: why does the mean occur where it occurs? Why does the curve cover the range that it covers? In answering the questions, we can point to two processes that occur in any behavioural situation: variety generating processes and variety reducing processes. Variety is continually being generated in any behavioural situation. It occurs when: individuals invent new ways of accomplishing an old end, individuals come in contact with individuals or groups from other societies where the same end is met differently, individuals are mal-socialized, mis-learn the desired way

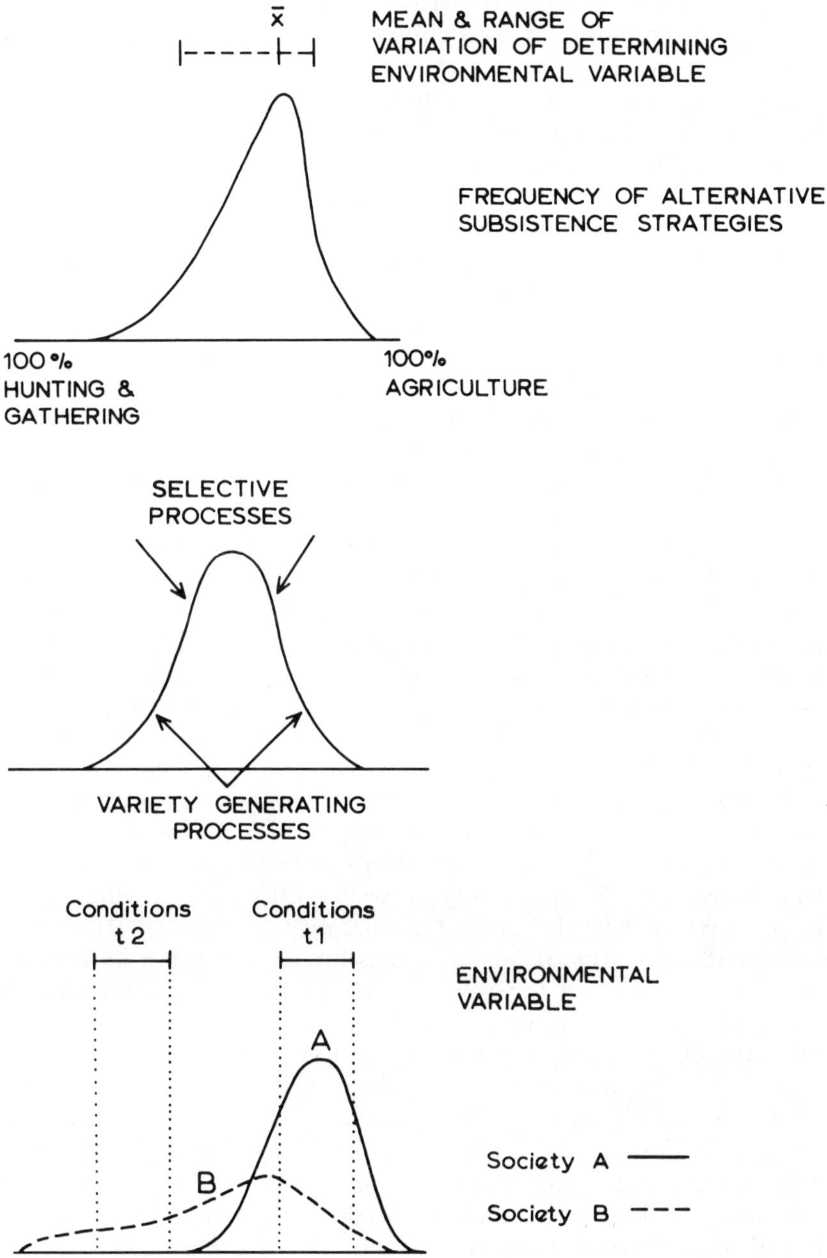

Figure 2 Operation of the laws.

of meeting an end, and individuals are unable to follow normal patterns for meeting the end and choose near alternatives. All of these events are commonplace in any behavioural situation and have the effect of producing varied behaviour within that situation. This variation may be represented either as explicit practised behavioural alternatives or simply as ideas about alternative courses of behaviour.

But variety generation does not cause the variety represented within a system to expand endlessly. There are selective pressures. Behavioural strategies that are absolutely unsuccessful in meeting environmental contingencies will be abandoned or those practising them will die out. Strategies that are more successful will grow – because their practitioners will produce more viable offspring – and will be copied. This is the rationale for our restated Law of Cultural Dominance: the more successful a behavioural strategy in meeting its determining environmental contingency, the more frequent its repetition. In marked contrast with so much evolutionary dogma, the restated law recognizes both the importance of the environmental conditions – mean and range – and the historically derived and equally varied behaviour on which they are acting.

The Law of Evolutionary Potential is useful in comparing the responses of two populations to the same environmental change. Continuing the example of subsistence, suppose two populations with the same mean strategy but very different ranges are faced with a long term environmental shift in a critical variable. It is more probable that the society with the more varied strategies will have a number of individuals or communities who are already practicing the strategy. This does not mean that the more specialized society will not survive, only that the adjustment will be easier for the less specialized one.

Proponents of this law often ignore another factor that has an important effect on the situation: population. It has been assumed up to this point that the populations were of approximately equal size. If there is a great disparity, however, one would predict that the larger society has the greater probability of survival. With more individuals, the risk of adjustment is lower per capita. Moreover, if the same segment of the behavioural curve fell within the tolerable range of the new conditions, the larger society would actually have more people practising the desirable strategy.

It is for this reason that in dealing with any natural laboratory situation investigators should not expect to find single laws that cover variation in the topic phenomenon. In nature, physical or behavioural, more than one law is generally operating in producing any given pattern of variation and explanations will consequently be found in systems of laws, not individual laws. This is why it is so difficult to predict accurately what any individual or group will do next. An investigator may perceive only some of the factors that are affecting behaviour.

In any case, the laws that we have been discussing make sense in terms of our most basic commonsensical notions about behaviour. Any brief examination would show that these propositions or nearly identical statements are explicitly and implicitly used in many of the social sciences. They do systematize our knowledge of process and can be used in making predictions about observed patterns of variation. (They would not, however, prove useful by themselves in predicting outcome). They are, in short, regularities or laws.

Summary

To the extent that we seek to systematize the knowledge of the past that we acquire, and especially to the extent that we seek to systematize knowledge of process, archaeologists need to be concerned with formulating and testing laws. It makes no sense, however, to deal with such laws without continual reference to the patterns of variation that they were created to explain. And in dealing with natural laboratory situations, it is vital to remember that we observe outcomes not processes, and that these outcomes are probably to be understood only in terms of relatively complex systems of laws.

To those who remain unconvinced of the existence of laws, I add one final note. To date, no mature science has failed to find laws that explain patterns of variation in the phenomena it studies. Moreover, the advent of laws is rarely a question of the discovery of a total new set of ideas so much as making precise, explicit, and systematized that which some preferred to leave as a body of unstated assumptions.

REFERENCES

Berelson, B. and Steiner, G.A. (1964) *Human Behaviour: an Inventory of Scientific Findings.* New York, Harcourt, Brace and World.

Hempel, C.G. (1966) *Philosophy of Natural Science.* Englewood Cliffs, N.J., Prentice Hall.

Miller, G. (1965) Living systems: cross-level hypotheses. *Behavioural Science* **10**, no. 4, 38-411.

Sahlins, M.D. and Service, E.R. (eds.) (1960) *Evolution and Culture.* Ann Arbor, University of Michigan.

E. GARY STICKEL and
JOSEPH L. CHARTKOFF

The nature of scientific laws and their relation to law-building in archaeology

Introduction

There has been an increasing concern among archaeologists over the past several years on the topic of whether we can formulate valid laws pertaining to cultural processes and past human behaviour. The present conference is an example of that interest. One may also make reference to Binford and Binford (1968), Clarke (1968:638-641), Carniero (1970), Fritz and Plog (1970) and Watson, Le Blanc and Redman (1971). While many professionals remain sceptical and pessimistic, many others now acknowledge that a major goal of archaeology is the discovery and explication of those general principles or laws which would account for past human behaviour and the evolution of societies. Given this goal, it becomes quite important that archaeologists have a clear understanding of what is meant by the term 'law'. It also places a burden on the archaeologist to strive for clarity and precision in the presentation of laws which purport to be adequate explanations for phenomena.

Today archaeology has a fair degree of control over its data (fairly comprehensive though not complete), and it is at present attempting to formulate its own organizational principles and theoretical underpinnings. A review of archaeological literature, however, reveals no clear idea as to what laws of science or nature are, nor what their properties are. The purpose of this paper is to explore and describe the properties and characteristics of scientific laws as a preliminary step in the development of laws specifically for archaeology. This study is intended as a tool for those who want to design their law-like formulations according to guide-lines suggested by philosophers of science.

Properties of laws

All scientific laws possess certain qualities in common which make it possible to discuss the nature of laws in general. Laws may be considered statements which relate variables or phenomena in nature to each other and which describe the processes involved in these relationships. The following properties or characteristics can be ascribed to the various kinds of scientific laws (after Nagel 1961:47-78):

1. They are spatially and temporally universal as prescribed by the limitations and qualification in their statements. That is, whenever and wherever the conditions described by the law exist, the relationship(s) described by the law should also occur. From this property, laws can be used to predict phenomena not already known or discovered.
2. They possess both *necessary* and *sufficient* conditions. Necessary conditions are those which *permit* relationships to exist, or which make the predicted outcome possible or likely. Sufficient conditions are those which *produce* the predicted outcome. The specification of necessary conditions defines the scope of the phenomena (variables) with which the law deals whereas the specification of sufficient conditions deals with the magnitude or intensity of the processes which effect the variables.
3. Laws must possess the property of validity. Only statements which are syntactically or structurally correct, and which also have been rigorously tested with positive results, can be accepted as valid laws. This is not to say that a law must be eternally perfect, incapable of amendment or later disproof based on new discoveries (cf. Hempel 1966).
4. Laws must deal with variables which are spatially and temporally contiguous. A law must state all significant variables in a relationship from cause to effect. If all the variables do not form a continuous structure in space or time, it is presumed that a significant variable remains yet to be described, and the statement is inadequate.
5. In addition to the above, causal laws have a temporal aspect in that the causes precede the effects in the cause-and-effect relationship. They also have an asymmetrical aspect in that the causes can produce the effects, but the effects cannot produce the causes. In other words, in a set of variables presented by a law, no one variable can be both a causal variable and an effect variable.

Some writers have stated that a law is a statement of constant association, conjunction, covariation, or correlation of certain variables which holds true for all times and places (see Clarke 1968:638, and Fritz and Plog 1970:405, for examples). Laws do possess this characteristic but they are more than that. A law of nature is a statement concerning relationships (including variables and processes) in the external world defined and justified by a set of considerations. Such considerations include, (1) syntactical considerations relating to the form of law-like statements (*our note:* rules of proper wording and organization of ideas); (2) the logical relations of statements to other statements in a system of explanation; (3) the functions assigned to law-like statements in a scientific inquiry; and (4) the cognitive attitudes manifested toward a statement because of the nature of the available evidence (*our note:* in terms of the sociology of ideas, a proposed law must be fit against the current state of knowledge). (Nagel 1961:68; also cf. Hempel 1966). This brief synopsis outlines the characteristics of scientific laws in general. These properties must be distinguished from the possible variation in the kinds of laws which can be formulated.

Kinds of laws

In order to propose a law, one must construct a statement which possesses all the essential qualities of laws except that of demonstrated validity. Such statements can be termed 'law-like statements'. These statements should be modelled after any one of the types of laws which have been recognized by philosophers of science. Each of the several kinds of laws has its own specific properties and its own specific applications, so the choice of an appropriate model depends upon the kind of law needed. Nagel (1961) has outlined the major forms of laws in science (see Table 1).

1. *Causal laws.* Causal laws relate two or more variables in a specified determinate relationship and explain why the stated relationship must hold true. They are generally the kind of law used in causal or deductive-nomological explanations (Hempel 1966:51; Rudner 1966:63).

2. *Statistical or Probabilistic laws.* These are laws which predict the likelihood of an event or relationship between variables.

3. *Determinable Properties laws.* Such laws define useful and meaningful types of things by adequate description of essential attributes. Fritz and Plog (1970) state that many classifications of artifacts in archaeology assume law-like status; if so, they would assume the form of determinable properties laws.

4. *Functional Dependence laws.* These laws prescribe the nature of the functional interdependence of phenomena. According to Nagel (1961:77), they may be classified into two subtypes: (1) numerical laws which lack a time element in them, such as Boyle's Law . . . which is not a causal law . . . as it . . . does not assert for example that a change in the temperature is followed (or preceded) by some change in the volume or in the pressure, it asserts only that a change

in T is concurrent with changes in p or V or in both, and (2) numerical laws which have a time element in them (e.g. Galileo's law for freely falling bodies in a vacuum), also called 'dynamical laws' (Nagel 1961:78).

5. *Developmental or Historical laws.* Such laws are those which describe sequential changes of phenomena and which account for their changes over time.

TABLE I: KINDS OF LAWS

Kinds of Laws	*Examples from Science* (after Nagel 1961)	*Potential or Actual Archaeological Examples*
1. Causal laws.	1. Laws of Quantum Mechanics.	1. Binford's 'tension zone' hypothesis for the origin of food production. (Binford 1968)
2. Statistical or Probabilistic laws.	2. Hardy-Weinberg Law of genetics.	2. Carniero's (1970) 'A quantitative law in anthropology'.
3. Determinable Properties laws.	3. The atomic elements.	3. Semenov's (1964) *Prehistoric Technology.*
4. Functional Dependence laws. a. with time element.	4a. Galileo's laws for freely falling bodies in a vacuum; The Second Law of Thermodynamics.	4a. Deetz and Dethlefsen's (1965) 'Doppler Effect' and archaeological diffusion; Steno's Law.
b. without time element.	4b. Boyle's Law; Venturi's Principle.	4b. Naroll's (1962) relationship relationship between floor space and population size; Cook and Heizer's (1968) relationship between house size, settlement size and population size.
5. Developmental or Historical laws.	5. Principle of Biological Evolution; Marx's Economic Theory of History.	5. Adam's (1966) *The Evolution of Urban Society;* White's (1943) *Energy and the Evolution of Culture.*

Such laws may be developed for any area of archaeological research. For example, some archaeologists are particularly concerned at this time with the problem of deriving laws to explain stability and change of past socio-cultural systems. If one wishes such an explanation to be stated as a causal law, he must state his argument in the form of a syllogism in which the related phenomena to be explained are described, a cover law-like statement is cited, following which it is convincingly shown that the relationships of the phenomena are accounted for by the general law. Such procedures must be used in order for archaeology to obtain its own explanatory laws.

Laws must be distinguished from empirical generalizations or from accidental generalizations which may resemble several forms of laws in some attributes, but which do not meet all the defined requirements of laws. They may lack several qualities: demonstrated validity, necessary and sufficient conditions, asymmetry, universality, or contiguity (cf. Hempel 1966:49-56; Nagel 1961:47-78). Regarding archaeology, laws must be distinguished from traditional models of cultural reconstruction (Bordes 1968 for example). Such models, as they presently exist in the literature, are plausible constructs but they are not adequate explanations nor do they contain laws. Such models may correctly order prehistoric developments but they do not explain anything in themselves. They especially do not explain why phenomena became ordered in the fashion described. They therefore cannot be used as substitutes for causal explanations. Causal explanations, as previously discussed, account for relationships among phenomena by reference to causal laws. It should be possible to construct models of cultural reconstruction which incorporate in their structures sets of causal laws, in which case such models would assume the status of explanations.

The foremost example of a commonly used archaeological model is the Three Age System which (in modified form) is still referred to in the literature of European archaeology. This model, albeit crude, enables an excavator immediately to place gross dates on certain archaeological data as well as to recognize other pertinent facts concerning the data (e.g. imported trade items, the type of food economy, or the presence of certain technological capabilities). Although this system has some predictive value, it hardly contains any explanations for the changes in the archaeological record upon which it is based. If, however, an evolutionary model contained principles which provided the reasons for cultural systems developing, adapting, or perishing in the manner in which they did, the principles would stand as proposed laws and the model would serve as a proposed explanation for the course of prehistory. The proposed laws would purport to explain how and why various causal factors affected the operation of cultural systems. They would also specify the degree and form of structural and functional adjustment made by both successful and non-successful systems throughout the transformation of human cultural history.

The derivation of laws

Archaeology today has at best a few poorly derived or recognized laws, whereas many other fields of science have substantial development in this area. This situation has prompted a number of archaeologists to look to these other fields for concepts which they might apply to archaeological data. It may be felt that the use of laws from other fields is inappropriate or methodologically unsound, but philosophers of science disagree (cf. Kaplan 1964:4). It is a legitimate procedure for archaeologists to borrow such knowledge from other fields if it is relevant to the solution of archaeological problems. For example, Steno's Law, which concerns stratigraphy and sequences of deposition, was borrowed from geology more than a century ago. There should be a distinction made, however, between archaeological laws derived from other disciplines and laws derived from archaeology itself. Fritz and Plog (1970), for example, imply that many of the typological concepts now in use in archaeology are in fact laws themselves or are based on intuitively acknowledged laws. If these 'laws' were verified, they could attain the status of determinable properties laws. Separately, Carniero (1970) has proposed a law of prehistory which states that 'The degree of regularity in the relative order of development of any two traits in a sequence is directly proportional to the evolutionary distance between them'. His formulation does not meet all the specific requirements of a law and therefore cannot qualify as a legitimate law at this time. But although his formulation is not yet an acceptable law, it is an encouraging sign that scholars are thinking increasingly in terms of the formulation of archaeological laws.

The ways in which laws may be derived have been suggested in part by Platt (1964) in his discussion of profitable scientific reasoning (see Fig. 1). Platt has analysed fields (e.g. molecular biology and high-energy physics) which have made much progress in explanation, and he has concluded that they share a reliance on inductive inference, which he calls 'strong inference . . . just the simple and old fashioned method of inductive inference which goes back to Francis Bacon' (Platt 1964:347 .) His 'strong inference' combines deductive and inductive reasoning in practice. Knowledge of the data base of an inquiry suggests both problem areas which require explanation and possible test situations. Also, a general knowledge of the operation of systems helps indicate possible causal relationships among variables. A methodology of testing which seeks to exclude possible relationships from actual causation efficiently discards incorrect or misleading correlations. Such a procedure isolates correlations which support a proposed law and at the same time provides for a degree of closure or circumscribes those phenomena to which the law pertains. Strong inference, then, is basically an open-minded attitude which will initially consider several possible relationships and interpretations and rigorously exclude all which cannot be substantiated by impartial and replicable tests.

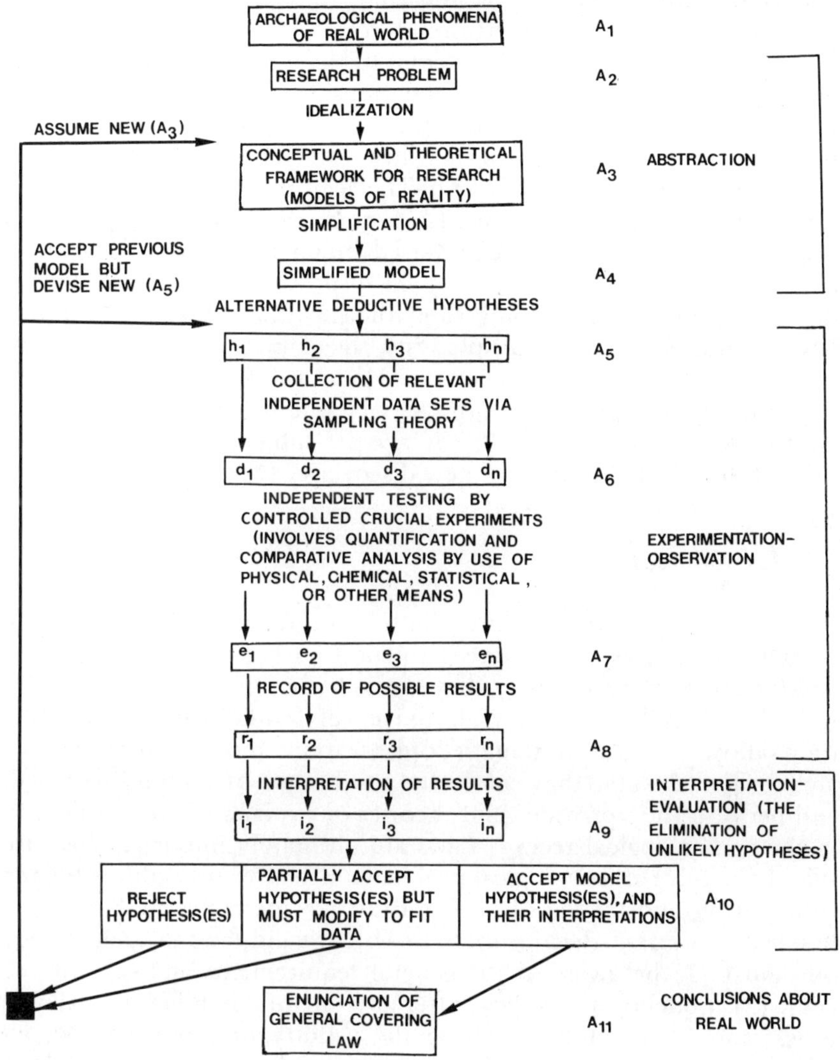

Figure 1 A procedural model for establishing archaeological laws (cf. Platt 1964; Clarke 1968:36; Haggett 1965:20).

Validation of proposed laws

One of the properties of laws, as previously mentioned, is that of validity. Validity cannot be built into proposed laws when they are formulated. It can only be established through testing. Until tests have substantiated it, a stated relationship between variables is only *law-like.* It is not yet a law, even though the statement possesses all other characteristics of laws.

Proposed laws may be tested with positive results, but positive test results do not necessarily demonstrate the validity of the law-like statement. Positive or confirming results may be produced for reasons which are entirely incidental to the proposed law. Premature inferences may be based on correlations which are coincidental or irrelevant. To accept positive test results as confirmation of a proposed law is what has been called 'the fallacy of affirming the consequent' (Hempel 1966:7-8). The legitimate procedure for the validation of law-like statements involves the attempt to reject or disprove the proposal through varied independent tests. The more that a law-like statement cannot be disproved or rejected through different kinds of tests, the greater the likelihood that the proposed law is valid. Even with multiple tests, the validation of any given law remains a relative quality because (1) the validity of any given law depends upon the nature of the law and the nature of the confirmatory evidence, and (2) all laws are subject to being amended, limited, or rejected in light of new discoveries (Nagel 1961:65-6).

Conclusions

It should no longer be an issue whether or not archaeology is capable of generating laws. It is more germane to ask why laws are needed and (assuming they are) how they are to be obtained. Laws are of use to archaeology because they are universally and objectively testable, they allow for the systematic organization and interpretation of archaeological data, they allow for prediction of the undiscovered, and because they provide valid theories or explanations of variability in the archaeological record. Laws are ultimately important because they help solve archaeological problems. Effective procedures for the formulation and testing of laws is thus of wide concern. This paper has tried to stress that in order to obtain valid laws in archaeology one must (1) be aware of the general requirements and qualities of laws, (2) model proposed laws after any one of a number of available types, and (3) carefully establish the validity of proposed laws by varied testing procedures. Also, the quest for archaeological laws must not be hindered by obsolete notions of what constitutes archaeological research. Any information from any field should be considered if it is relevant to the solution of an archaeological problem.

REFERENCES

Adams, R. McC. (1966) *The Evolution of Urban Society*. Chicago, Aldine.
Binford, L.R. (1968) Post-Pleistocene adaptations, *In* Binford, L.R. and S.R.

(eds.) *New Perspectives in Archaeology*. Chicago, Aldine.
Binford, L.R. and S.R. (eds.) (1968) *New Perspectives in Archaeology*. Chicago, Aldine.
Bordes, F.B. (1968) *The Old Stone Age*. New York, McGraw-Hill.
Carniero, R.L. (1970) A quantitative law in anthropology. *American Antiquity* 35, no. 4, 492-4.
Clarke, D.L. (1968) *Analytical Archaeology*. London, Methuen.
Cook, S.F. and Heizer, R.F. (1968) Relationships among houses, settlement areas, and population in aboriginal California, *In* Chang, K.C. (ed.) *Settlement Archaeology*, 79-116. Palo Alto, California, National Press.
Deetz, J. and Dethlefsen, E. (1965) The Doppler effect and archaeology: a consideration of the spatial aspects of seriation, *Southwestern Journal of Anthropology* 21, 196-206.
Fritz, K. and Plog, F. (1970) The nature of archaeological explanation. *American Antiquity* 35, no. 4, 405-12.
Haggett, P. (1965) *Locational Analysis in Human Geography*. New York, St. Martin's Press.
Hempel, C. (1966) *Philosophy of Natural Science*. Englewood Cliffs, N.J., Prentice-Hall.
Kaplan, A. (1964) *The Conduct of Inquiry*. San Francisco, Chandler.
Nagel, E. (1961) *The Structure of Science: Problems in the Logic of Scientific Explanation*. New York, Harcourt, Brace and World.
Naroll, R. (1962) Floor area and settlement pattern. *American Antiquity* 27, 587-9.
Platt, J. (1964) Strong Inference. *Science* 146, no. 3642, 347-53.
Rudner, R.S. (1966) *Philosophy of Social Science*. Englewood Cliffs, N.J., Prentice-Hall.
Semenov, S.A. (1964) *Prehistoric Technology*. Trans. M.W. Thompson. London, Cory, Adams and Mackay.
Watson, P.J., Le Blanc, S.A. and Redman, C.L. (1971) *Explanation in Archaeology, an Explicitly Scientific Approach*. New York, Columbia University.
White, A. (1943) Energy and the evolution of culture. *American Anthropologist* 45, no. 3, 335-56.

JOHN J. WOOD and R.G. MATSON

Two models of sociocultural systems and their implications for the archaeological study of change

Introduction

Social scientists seem to agree on the systematic nature of society and culture: however, we think it is fair to say that there is some disagreement on the nature of the systematic relationships, how they are articulated with their environment, and how they change. In this paper we shall review just two models of sociocultural systems and examine the implications of each for the archaeological study of change. We do not wish to deal with explanation in the abstract at this time.

We believe that there are several important reasons for examining the assumptions and methodological implications of these models (cf. Kushner 1970). First, a paradigm or model suggests which problems are to be studied and how one goes about studying them. Kuhn emphasizes this point in his study of paradigmatic revolutions in the history of science (1962). The accepted paradigms of established sciences, in Kuhn's view, direct the endeavours of each field of inquiry toward a narrow and specific set of research goals. Both Kuhn and Kaplan (1964) have implied that science or knowledge does not advance with the last decimal place; it surges forward when new models or new ideas are found to be helpful in understanding observations which are incongruent with established paradigms. But we cannot count on the inevitability or pervasiveness of useful models since there are normative as well as cognitive reasons for acceptance or rejection of ideas. Thus the usefulness of competing models may vary widely.

It has been suggested many times (perhaps too many times) that the social and behavioural sciences are less 'developed' than the more traditional disciplines. In Kuhn's terms these sciences are pre-paradigmatic in that they do not yet have an established paradigm which guides the research of the majority. In sciences with widely accepted paradigms, the main controversies typically deal with methodological questions, while in pre-paradigmatic disciplines the arguments tend to centre on conflicting models without coming to grips with the underlying issues. Even if the extant models of sociocultural systems do not have the consensus of paradigms in other fields we are still faced with the conclusion that models can and do determine the direction and goals of research.

It is for these reasons that we believe that the assumptions and implications of models of sociocultural systems should be examined carefully. We intend to show that there are important differences in the two models we are considering here. Hopefully we shall come to grips with some of the underlying issues in the process.

The first model we shall consider is the homeostatic model which has been explicitly formulated – though not in sociocultural terms – by W. Ross Ashby (1954, 1962, et passim) and presented, in preliminary fashion, for prehistorians by James N. Hill (1970, 1971). Some of the assumptions of the homeostatic model, such as the requisite 'steady-state' articulation of variables, are implicit in the works of other prehistorians whom Kushner calls 'processual functionalists', implying that they are in the same camp with sociological and anthropological functionalists (1970:129-30).

With Buckley (1967, 1968), we shall call the second view of sociocultural systems under consideration the complex adaptive system model. We are not aware of any general applications of the complex adaptive system model in anthropology, although several anthropologists, including some prehistorians, have explicitly or implicitly espoused a similar view of sociocultural systems; for example, see Geertz (1963:10), Vayda and Rappaport (1968:486), Rappaport (1971:131), Sahlins (1964), and Flannery (1968). Our presentation is based mainly on the works of Buckley, Campbell (1959, 1965), von Bertalanffy (1962), and Maruyama (1963).

Both models are cast in the terminology of 'modern systems theory' (Buckley 1968). Consequently, the analytical focus is a system, usually defined as a set of elements standing in non-trivial interaction, and its environment, or a set of all elements, a change in whose relationships affects the system together with all elements whose relationships are changed by the behaviour of the system. The differences between the two models lie in the specification of the nature of the relationships among the elements of the system, how a system is articulated with its environment, and how a system changes.

The homeostatic model

Originally (Cannon 1939), homeostasis referred to: '. . . the ensemble of organic regulations which act to maintain the steady states of the organism and are effectuated by regulating mechanisms in such a way that they do not occur necessarily in the same, and often in opposite, direction to what a corresponding external change would cause according to physical laws' (von Bertalanffy 1962:17); for example, the maintenance of body temperature through negative feedback. W. Ross Ashby is largely responsible for extending the concept by equating homeostasis with organic self-regulation and adaptation in general (1954, 1962, et passim).

Ashby's view of a dynamic, homeostatic system is best seen by starting with his conception of the 'machine with input' (1962). A machine is 'defined by a set S of internal states, a set I of input or surrounding states, and a mapping, f say, of the product set I x S into S' (ibid.: 111). Organization of the parts of a system, defined by its states S and its input I, is specified by the mapping, and, if the mapping changes, the organization changes. Although Ashby clearly indicates that there is no absolutely 'good' organization (good is relative to the context), he states that an organization 'is judged "good" if and only if it acts so as to keep an assigned set of variables, the "essential" variables, within assigned limits' (ibid.: 112); hence, homeostatasis can cover both self-regulation and adaptation (cf. Ashby 1954:57ff).

Change in an 'Ashby machine' occurs as follows: 'We start with the set S of states, and assume that f (the mapping) changes, to g say. So we really have a *variable*, α (t) say, a function of the time that had at first the value f and later the value g. This change, as we have just seen, cannot be ascribed to any cause in the set S; so it must have come from some outside agent, acting on the system S as input' (1962:114, parentheses ours). Ashby's model, then, directs our attention to 'external' sources of change and to an understanding of adaptation as a process which maintains 'essential' variables within limits. We now turn to a consideration of self-organization and evolution in Ashby's framework.

It is Ashby's position that: 'no system can correctly be said to be self-organizing, and since use of the phrase "self-organizing" tends to perpetuate a fundamentally confused and inconsistent way of looking at the subject, the phrase is probably better allowed to die out' (ibid.: 114). However, he does concede that in one sense a system may have the 'appearance of' self-organization: 'If the system is to be in some sense "*self*-organizing", the "self" must be enlarged to include this variable α (see above), and, to keep the whole bounded, the cause of α's change must be in S (or α)' (ibid.: 114, first parenthesis ours).

We are to understand evolution, speaking generally, as the consequence of the observation that: '*every isolated determinate dynamic system obeying unchanging laws will develop "organisms" that are adapted to their "environments"*' (ibid.:115). This argument is explained by the 'fact' that systems, for the most part, go to equilibrium, and, in the process, selection occurs. When a dynamic system, characterized by unchanging laws, goes to equilibrium, Ashby says: 'You will find that the states or forms now in being are peculiarly able to survive against the changes induced by the laws. Split the equilibrium in two, call one part "organism" and the other part "environment": you will find that this "organism" is peculiarly able to survive against the disturbances from the "environment". The *degree* of adaptation and complexity that this organism can develop is bounded only by the size of the whole dynamic system and by the time over which it is allowed to progress toward equilibrium' (1962:116).

We have quoted at some length from Ashby's homeostatic model, even though it is not explicitly a model of sociocultural systems, because, in our view, Hill's (1970, 1971) 'theoretical framework for explaining organizational change' is not essentially different.

Hill (1970, 1971) shares with Ashby the view that: 'We can choose to study any set of systemically articulated variables . . . The only requirement is that if they are to qualify as *systems*, not only must the variables be systematically articulated, but the formal nature of this articulation must be regulated (maintained in steady-state) by homeostatic processes.' (1971:407g, cf. Ashby 1954:15, et passim). Hill is further interested in the dynamic aspects of systems; that is, how the structure of a system 'operates in both space and time'. 'In order to explain change in a system', Hill says, 'we must first be able to isolate the homeostatic mechanisms that are operating to maintain *stability* in the particular component or aspect of the society we are interested in. We only explain change when we can show why these regulatory process fail to operate successfully in given cases . . . Change has only occurred if the character of the equational description of the system is altered' (1971:407). In Hill's view, 'the source of change is *always* external to the system *in question* (ibid.:407). Specifically:

> Systemic change results from matter-energy and information exchanges with other systems (natural or social) which exceeds the degree of variation that can be adequately buffered (regulated) by established homeostatic mechanisms within the system. When these negative feedback processes fail, we have a situation in which positive feedback . . . occurs, thus amplifying the deviation from 'normal' and resulting in systemic change. This process will continue until new homeostatic mechanisms are brought into play to restore a steady state at a new level of systemic articulation . . . (ibid.:407-8)

The methodological implications and the research goals suggested by the homeostatic model are clear. Hill nicely summarizes some of them in the conclusion of his 1970 report where he lists the factors necessary to explain change as follows:

1. A functional (mathematical) description of the system and its homeostatic processes prior to change.

2. Isolation of the extra-systemic inputs promoting change; and demonstration of the failure of homeostatic mechanisms to cope with the inputs.
3. Demonstration that 'new' variables and homeostatic mechanisms have been selected for, which stabilize the system at a different level (Hill 1970:13, cf. 1971:408).

The archaeological study of change in the viewpoint of the homeostatic model must start with the description of the more or less stable, adaptive homeostatic mechanisms in the system in question, which, as Hill indicates, must take into account both time and space. Then we are directed to look outside of the system for the sources of change which 'overload' the homeostatic (regulatory) mechanisms thereby changing the nature of the relations among the variables (as opposed to simple state regulation). The process of selection leads to a new set of homeostatic mechanisms which stabilize the system at a new level. Thus systemic change in the prehistoric record should be charactérized, in the long run, by periods of stability separated by periods of change.

Hill does not indicate how selection takes place. We have seen Ashby's position on selection above, but in fairness to Hill, we do not wish to imply that he holds the same view. On the other hand, although Hill does not deal with the problem of self-organization, his insistence that the source of change must be external to the system in question leads us to believe that he, like Ashby, excludes the possibility of self-organizing systems.

The complex adaptive system model

A complex adaptive system is first an *open* system. There are at least two fundamental consequences of assuming the primacy of openness. First: 'That a system is *open* means, not simply that it engages in interchanges with the environment, but that this interchange is *an essential factor* underlying the system's viability, its reproductive ability or continuity, and its ability to change' (Buckley 1967:50). In von Bertalanffy's words, our attention is directed toward 'dynamic interaction within multivariable systems' (1962:17). Second, because open systems may be characterized as importing 'negative entropy' (von Bertalanffy 1962:16), information generated by interactions among system elements may result in changes in the elements themselves which in turn affect the nature of the system (cf. Whyte 1965). Therefore, an open system may be self-differentiating and self-organizing; feedback may elaborate or change relationships (amplify deviation) as well as contribute to stability (counteract deviation).

Maruyama (1963) calls the processes which tend to contribute to stability, morphostasis, and the processes which tend to elaborate or change, morphogenesis. In the terminology of Maruyama, the complex adaptive system model is designed to help understand morphogenesis; although, as we shall see, the model can easily encompass processes contributing to stability.

In Buckley's 'Abstract Model of Morphogenesis' (1967:62-6), distinguishable differences in the ensemble comprising the environment are regarded as variety; relatively stable relationships among the elements are called constraints; and where there is an equal probability of any element being associated with any other element, we speak of the absence of constraint. With these concepts in mind, we can do no better than to quote Buckley (1967:63) extensively regarding the nature of morphogenesis:

> In these terms, then, the paradigm underlying the evolution of more and more complex adaptive systems begins with the fact of a potentially changing environment characterized by constrained variety and an adaptive system or organization whose persistence and elaboration to higher levels depends upon a successful mapping of some of the environmental variety and constraints into its own organization on at least a semi-permanent basis. This means that an adaptive system – whether biological, psychological, or sociocultural – must manifest 1) some degrees of 'plasticity' and 'sensitivity' or *tension* vis-a-vis its environment such that it carries on a constant interchange with environmental events, acting on and reacting to them; 2) some source of mechanisms providing for *variety*, to act as a potential pool of adaptive variability to meet the problem of mapping new or more detailed variety and constraints in a changeable environment; 3) a set of *selective* criteria or mechanisms against which the 'variety pool' may be sifted into those variations in the organization or system that more closely map the environment and those that do not; and 4) an arrangement for *preserving and/or propagating* these successful mappings. (cf. Campbell 1959, 1965)

The morphogenic aspect of the complex adaptive system model holds the promise of providing us with a conceptual base for further understanding the fundamental elaborations and changes in the course of the evolution of sociocultural systems. As stated earlier, the model does not at the same time preclude the study and explication of processes leading to and maintaining stability.

Hall and Fagen (1956:87) tell us that: 'A system is stable with respect to certain of its variables if these variables tend to remain within defined limits'; that we should 'Note that a system may be stable in some respects and unstable in others'; and that 'An adaptive system maintains stability for all those variables which must, for favorable operation, remain with limits'. The processes leading to or maintaining stability can be described as deviation-counteracting and/or homeostatic (in the sense of Cannon's original definition). However, the nature of stability in the viewpoint of the complex adaptive system model, as we see it, is an empirical question.

An adaptive system may indeed be stable in some respects for its continued viability. We would call these more or less stable relationships, structure. But structure, in our viewpoint, is an aspect of the organization of the system (cf. Buckley 1967:82-84). The concept of organization, according to Ashby (1962), must include the essential features of 'conditionality' and 'constraint'. 'As soon as the relation between two entities A and B becomes conditional on C's value or state', Ashby says, 'then a necessary component of organization is present' (1962:108). Moreover, conditionality is a matter of degree. For a set of variables to be organized, there also must be: '*constraint* in the product-space of possibilities'; which is to say, there must be: 'some correlation between what happens at A and what at B. If, for a given event at A, all possible events may occur at B, then there is no communication from A to B and no constraint over the possible (A, B) – couples that can occur' (Ashby 1962:109). We should like to add, with Buckley (1967:82-4), that the interdependence of the variables (constraint) also must be a matter of degree. So structure consists of the demonstrably stable, relatively constrained, highly conditional relationships among variables in the organization of the system. Logically, then, we can see that structure is also a matter of degree.

Degrees of freedom in organization are extremely important for they provide a significant source of variety for the adaptive process. Buckley reminds us that: *'Persistence or continuity of an adaptive system may require, as a necessary condition, change in its structure*, the degree of change being a complex function of the internal state of the system, the state of its relevant environment, and the nature of the interchange between the two' (1968:493).

In the opening paragraph of this section we stated that an open system may be self-organizing. Now, with an understanding of some of the basic concepts of the complex adaptive system model, we turn to an exposition of how a complex adaptive system may be self-organizing.

We can look at self-organization in two different ways. First, the relationships among some variables in the organization may be more or less independent, as we have seen above. In an ongoing system the nature of these relationships may change from relative independence to conditionality through the formation of 'connections' among the variables (cf. Ashby 1962:113). Short-term, emergent properties of sociocultural systems, such as political activity, might be said to be self-organizing in this respect. Long-term organizational changes may have their roots in this type of self-organization, providing, of course, that the conditionality is selected for.

The second way of looking at self-organization is also suggested by Ashby (1962). We recall in our discussion of the homeostatic model that a system may be said to be self-organizing if the system includes, in addition to its set of states, a variable 'mapping' which is a function of time. We recall also that the organization changes if the 'mapping' changes. In the complex adaptive system model, the mapping of environmental variety and constraint is explicitly considered to be an aspect of the organization of the system (Buckley 1967:63ff); consequently, any morphogenic process, such as deviation-amplification, could generate changes in the mapping 'channels' and thus give rise to self-organization, again subject to selection.

The methodological implications and the research goals suggested by the complex adaptive system model are relatively clear, although they are not as axiomatic as those suggested by the homeostatic model. The complex adaptive system model assumes non-trivial interaction (some degree of conditionality and constraint) among the elements comprising the system; however, the relationships do not have to be regulated by homeostatic processes to qualify as a system. A description of the organization of a system would include an account of the relative conditionality and constraint among the variables over time and space.

Systemic change is considered to be an ongoing process and stability is considered to be an empirical question. The study of the evolution of sociocultural systems is the study of the evolution of ecosystems as systems; that is, there is no implicit conceptual division between sociocultural systems and their environment. Changes occur as the result of the *interchanges* between the system and its relevant environment (natural or social), and they may be initiated 'internally' as well as 'externally'. In Buckley's words: 'We recall that the model assumes an ongoing system of interacting components with an internal source of tension, the whole engaged in continuous transaction with its varying external and internal environment, such that the latter tend to become selectively "mapped" into its structure in some way . . .' (1967:128) and: 'Both stability and change are a function of the same set of variables, which must include both the internal state of the system and the state of its significant environment, along with the nature of the interchange between the two' (1968:510).

Summary and conclusions

In the introduction we indicated that there were three major areas of difference between the homeostatic model and the complex adaptive system model: (1) the nature of the relationships among the variables; (2) how a system is articulated with its environment; and (3) how a system changes. Before drawing our conclusions, let us recapitulate and compare briefly the two models in these three areas.

The homeostatic model presupposes that the variables comprising the system must be regulated by homeostatic mechanisms in order to qualify as a system. Conditionality and constraint are the only requisites for defining a system in the complex adaptive system model. The homeostatic model is obviously designed to study structure, while the complex adaptive system model focuses on organization.

By insisting that the source of change is external to the system in question, the homeostatic model poses an implicit dichotomy between a sociocultural system and its environment. The system and environment are articulated only through inputs from the environment (with respect to systemic change) or, at best, by the coupling of two or more 'Ashby machines'. The complex adaptive system model is an open system model; hence, it is the *relationship* between the sociocultural system and the environment that is most important, since, for continued viability and change, the sociocultural system must map some of the variety and constraints of its relevant environment into its organization.

Systemic change in the viewpoint of the homeostatic model occurs when extra-systemic input overloads the homeostatic mechanisms which define the system so that the nature of the relationships among the variables changes. After some oscillation, the system is stabilized at a new homeostatic level. Both change and stability are the result of the same set of variables in the complex adaptive system model; so, change may be initiated 'internally' or 'externally'. The system changes continuously through the adaptive process of successive mappings of environmental and systemic variety and constraint into its organization. Implicitly, some parts of the system may change more rapidly than others, and these rates of change may vary spatially and temporally.

Although both models are designed to study long-term systemic change (evolution), it is clear that the questions asked and the explanations proffered can be quite different. In concluding our review of the two models and their implications for the archaeological study of change, we should like to offer our opinions on the relative merits of each.

We suggest that the homeostatic model is little more than a restatement, in systems terminology, of the functionalist, organismic model in sociology and anthropology (cf. Buckley 1967:11-17). It is a little more than a restatement because it is designed to study systemic change – a problem that has plagued functionalists for some time (see Cancian 1960). So it is not surprising to find many of the assumptions of the homeostatic model in the literature of prehistory preceding the formal statement of the model as we have presented it here. In fact, we suggest that some implicit variety of the homeostatic model is close to being the dominant model in the field. How common, for example, are statements like: 'It is suggested that changes in the ecological setting of any given system are the prime causitive situations activating processes of cultural change' (Binford 1964:440)? Ecological setting usually can be equated with environment in the sense that changes originate outside of the system. If we insist that change come from outside of the system, we run the risk of a self-fulfilling prophecy; that is, if we look hard enough for a changing environmental variable, we shall surely find one.

Some form of steady-state articulation of variables is usually implied in our definitions of phases, periods, stages, etc. In some cases it is an explicit guiding assumption (see Kushner 1970). We commonly read that the prehistory of a region is characterized by periods of stability (equilibrium) separated by periods of change (e.g. Clark 1952:7). How different is this view from the idea of progression from one homeostatic level to another in the course of systemic change? Further, if it is true, that sociocultural systems are frequently characterized by continuing positive feedback (deviation, amplifying) processes as Rappaport (1971:131) and Flannery (1968) have suggested, then the homeostatic model would seem to be singularly inappropriate to deal with these situations.

The complex adaptive system model is by no means perfect; there are many things still left unsaid. It is nevertheless, a reasonable, potentially fruitful alternative to the homeostatic model. The latter is nicely axiomatic, and, as such, it promises to be an advance over the naively functional approach characteristic of much of past archaeological methodology. But does it ask the questions that we want to answer? We think that it asks only some of them. The complex adaptive system model is more general; with it we are prepared to include all facets of system operation.

It should be clear at this point that there are important differences in the two models and that these differences can: (1) lead us to ask different questions; (2) define different research goals; and (3) suggest different explanations. In the final analysis a choice will have to be made, if not between these two models, then between others. We hope the choice will be made for cognitive rather than normative reasons.

REFERENCES

Ashby, W.R. (1954) *Design for a Brain.* New York, John Wiley 1962. Principles of the self-organizing system. *In* Buckley 1968, 108-18.

Bertalanffy, L. von (1962) General system theory – a critical review. *In* Buckley 1968, 11-30.

Binford, L.R. (1964) A consideration of archaeological research design. *American Antiquity* 29, 425-41.

Buckley, W. (1967) *Sociology and Modern Systems Theory.* New Jersey, Prentice-Hall.

Buckley, W. (1968) (ed.) *Modern Systems Research for the Behavioural Scientist.* Chicago, Aldine.

Campbell, D.T. (1959) Methodological suggestions from a comparative psychology of knowledge. *Inquiry* 2, 159-82.

Campbell, D.T. (1965) Variation and selective retention in socio-cultural Evolution. *In* Barringer, H.R., Blanksten, G.I. and Mack, R. (eds.) *Social Change in Developing Areas.* Cambridge, Schenkman.

Cancian, F. (1960) Functional analysis of change. *American Sociological Review* 25, 818-27.

Cannon, W.B. (1939) Self-regulation of the the body. *In* Buckley 1968, 256-9.
Clark, J.G.D. (1952) *Prehistoric Europe, the Economic Basis.* London, Methuen.
Flannery, K.V. (1968) Archaeological systems theory and early Mesoamerica. *In* Meggers, B. (ed.) *Anthropological Archaeology in the Americas.* Washington D.C., Anthropological Society of Washington.
Geertz, C. (1963) *Agricultural Involution: the Process of Ecological Change in Indonesia.* Berkeley, University of California Press.
Hall, A.D. and Fagen, R.E. (1956) Definition of a system. *In* Buckley 1968, 81-92.
Hill, J.N. (1970) School of American Research advanced seminar. *Newsletter* vol. 11, no. 10, 12-13. American Anthropological Association.
Hill, J.N. (1971) Seminar on the explanation of prehistoric organizational change. *Current Anthropology* 12, 406-8.
Kaplan, A. (1964) *The Conduct of Inquiry.* San Francisco, Chandler.
Kuhn, T.S. (1962) The structure of scientific revolutions. In *International Encyclopedia of Unified Science* vol. 2 no. 2. Chicago, University Press.
Kushner, G. (1970) A consideration of some processual designs for archaeology as anthropology. *American Antiquity* 35, 125-32.
Maruyama, M. (1963) The second cybernetics: deviation-amplifying mutual causal processes. *American Scientist* 51, 164-79.
Rappaport, R.A. (1971) The flow of energy in an agricultural society. *Scientific American* 224, no. 3, 116-32.
Sahlins, M.D. (1964) Culture and environment: the study of cultural ecology. *In* Tax, S. (ed.) *Horizons of Anthropology*, 132-47. Chicago, Aldine.
Vayda, A.P. and Rappaport, R.A. (1968) Ecology, cultural and non-cultural. *In* Clifton, J.A. (ed.) *Introduction to Cultural Anthropology* 476-97. Boston, Houghton Mifflin.
Whyte, L.L. (1965) *Internal Factors in Evolution.* New York, George Braziller.

R.J.C. MUNTON

Systems analysis: a comment

Implicit in much scientific work is a form of reductivism which assumes that a system can be most satisfactorily analysed and understood through the separate study of its parts. Systems analysis attempts to refute this assumption by demonstrating that the interdependence or interconnectedness of the parts is such that it is impossible to predict their individual behaviour outside the context of the system to which they belong. Consequently, a systems view requires more than the mere specification of the parts (elements); it necessitates an understanding of their place and function within the whole (for further discussion see Klejn, this volume). Study is focused therefore on the flows or links between the parts and not the attributes of the separate parts. Moreover, as a time-dependent concept the system represents an appropriate conceptual framework within which to examine change.

Systems analysis should be distinguished from General Systems Theory. The latter, stemming from the work of Ashby (1958), von Bertalanffy (1956), Boulding (1956) and the Society for General Systems Research (founded 1955-6), attempts to construct general theories relating to systems irrespective of the real world situations to which the systems refer. Its value lies in the development of such concepts as feed-back, equilibrium and homeostasis (see the papers in Buckley 1968; Emery 1969), and the manner in which it suggests analogies between physical, biological and social systems. Systems analysis, on the other hand, is concerned with operationalising the systemic approach. Its potential value in the solution of many problems in the social sciences is now generally acknowledged (see, for example, Ackerman 1963; Buckley 1967; Harvey 1969:447; Johnson *et al.* 1964; Miller 1965; Wilbanks and Symanski 1968), although few questions in prehistory have been investigated in these terms (exceptions include Flannery 1968; Harris 1969). Two main uses of systems analysis may be recognized. Where data are incomplete or models difficult to validate a systems framework is usually employed simply to provide an enhanced understanding of a complex problem, as in this volume (see the papers by Layton, Rathje, Wood and Matson). Alternatively, where well-defined management objectives exist the primary aim may be to manipulate the system to improve, or even to optimize, its efficiency (Dent and Anderson 1971; McLoughlin and Webster 1970; Watt 1968). Needless to say, not all problems are susceptible to the systemic approach.

A closed system consists of a set of elements and a set of relationships or links between them. All social systems, however, are open systems, that is they also have links with an environment external to the system. For conceptual and analytical purposes some boundary has to be drawn between the system and its environment. Debate frequently arises over its definition, except in the most obvious of situations such as possibly around an island or other isolated community, as well as over the specification of those elements of the environment, theoretically infinite in number, that are relevant. There are no absolute rules by which these problems of definition and specification may be resolved, but common sense and data availability should indicate when the time and effort committed to a further increase in the complexity and scope of the system outweighs the value of the increased precision derived from the more complicated analysis. Further consideration of this issue is largely unfruitful outside the specific contexts of the problems under discussion. More importantly, system definition requires the researcher to be explicit as to his reasoning for the inclusion of some elements and the exclusion of others.

All systems represent an abstraction of that part of the real world under investigation, but this kind of simplification does not return systems analysis to that form of reductivism referred to earlier. Systems analysis accepts the complexity of the real world, and the need to investigate it in its own right, and employs models that attempt to account parsimoniously for as much of that complexity as possible. A system therefore represents only a conceptual framework for the investigation of a particular problem and should not be accorded a real world existence of its own. This also means however, that the amount of data collected and the scale of study can reflect the problem, the elements of a system at one scale even representing the whole system as another. For example, a systemic model of the settlement pattern of Roman Britain might have each town as an element, whilst a more detailed study of the internal structure of a single town might view the town itself as the system with each house as an element within it.

Critical to this discussion is the availability of data. Inevitably there is a tendency to emphasize those aspects of the system for which data exist or are of greater reliability. Equally inevitably this will bias the results of any analysis and it may be more useful to accept a crude model that relates directly to the problem under investigation than to adopt a sophisticated model adjusted to meet data requirements. The degree to which the model can reasonably be adjusted to account for data variability is a subjective decision, but if the researcher is satisfied that the system as he defines it will generate new questions or create new insights into existing problems then he can reasonably proceed. Acceptability of the findings must relate to standards prevailing in the discipline, for whilst it is desirable to strive for accuracy of measurement and analysis it is quite as unrealistic to expect archaeologists working with their fragmentary record to reach the level of explanation demanded by anthropologists studying aspects of life in the contemporary world as it is to expect anthropologists to reach the level of explanation demanded by physicists experimenting with laboratory controlled situations.

Associated with the different levels of explanation that can be achieved by archaeologists and anthropologists are different kinds of systemic model. Data derived from the archaeological record alone only permit the development of 'morphological systems' (Chorley and Kennedy 1971), systems described simply in terms of the structural relationships between their constituent elements, whose strength and direction are commonly revealed by correlation analysis. In studies of contemporary situations it may be possible to describe the relationships in terms of the magnitude of their energy exchanges or information flows. This represents a higher order of measurement than that indicated by the correlation bond, which at best only suggests the nature of the functional relationships existing between the elements. Such higher order systems have been termed 'cascading systems' (Chorley and Kennedy 1971), and many of their analysts believe that a primary function of their work is to elucidate as fully as possible the flows between the elements. This is not to suggest that the description of the flows is the ultimate aim of most investigations. Most hope to further our understanding of the relationships between the system inputs and system outputs thereby elaborating on the storage structure of the system itself. Depending on the problem under investigation, it may be unnecessary to acquire a detailed knowledge of the structure of the system provided change in output can be predicted from change in input, although without closer examination it may be impossible to isolate weak links in the system's structure, essential if its efficiency is to be increased.

Attempts are currently being made to measure in detail energy flows within primitive agricultural (Rappaport 1971) and hunting (Foote and Greer-Wootten 1968; Kemp 1971) communities. These communities have been selected because of the relative ease of recording their energy exchanges with the biosphere and because of the limited amount of energy they import from outside their agricultural or hunting systems. The communities' limited technologies have resulted in social organizations well adapted to the available energy resources of the biosphere, and so are particularly suited to this kind of investigation. It would be quite possible, if very laborious, to measure energy exchanges within more advanced societies, but because of their more complex social organization and more highly developed technologies their behaviour does not reflect the same degree of dependence on the energy resources of the biosphere as that of more primitive communities. Consequently, social scientists have often found it more useful to develop notions relating to the flow and exchange of information, or because of the difficulty of measuring information surrogates for it such as cash or goods, in their investigations of the structure and behaviour of modern societies (for a critical review see Rapaport 1956). For example, theories of information flow and exchange have been developed in the contexts of innovation diffusion studies (Brown 1968; Hägerstrand 1966; Rogers 1962), and the links between regions and between sectors of economies evaluated systemically through input-output analysis (see, for example, Leontieff 1965; Isard 1960).

The apparent impossibility of reducing energy and information to a common measure within a single system has been commented upon (Cooke 1971). Further consideration of this question is necessary, otherwise the links between change in the physical environment and change in social organization may never be fully understood, especially where the organization of society is only indirectly related to energy exchanges in the biosphere. Scientists in the physical and biological sciences usually describe systems by reference to energy exchange, cultural constraints being regarded as external to the system. Likewise, social scientists who analyse systems by means of information flow normally treat the biosphere simply as an external constraint that reduces choice. Neither approach overcomes the problem, because then 'the laws connecting the parts of the environment to each other are often incommensurate with those connecting parts of the organization to each other, or even those that govern the exchanges' (Emery and Trist 1969:23).

For the present, systems encompassing both flows of energy and information will have to be described in a more abstract form, normally by mathematical functions. This will tend to obscure a number of important considerations. First, information is much more difficult to define and measure than energy, largely as a result of its very variable quality, and surrogates such as cash, whilst easier to measure, are only relevant in specific situations. Second, natural systems are dominated by negative feedback, that is they have a built-in self-regulating function (homeostasis) which minimizes change in the state of the system as a result of external stimuli. Social systems, on the other hand, are frequently characterized by positive feedback, that is they tend to amplify change in a particular direction once it has begun to take place. The continued concentration of services in a central place, because of the external economies each service derives from the presence of others, is a case in point. Social systems would therefore appear to have the ability to stimulate change internally whilst major external forces may be necessary to destroy the homeostatic functioning of natural systems. However, once certain thresholds are crossed natural systems can also reflect cumulative change, as progressive soil erosion demonstrates. Third, social systems infrequently operate within the same time-space dimensions as biological systems. The spatial distribution of man's activities, particularly where these are tightly defined by institutional boundaries, such as those around private property, rarely coincide with the boundaries of biological systems (Caldwell 1970). This is aptly demonstrated by pollution, the ecological effects of which almost always extend beyond the boundaries of the source – firm or country – of the pollutant. Likewise, the rate at which man exploits the energy resources of natural systems is often out of step with their regenerative capacity. Unless this is recognized before the homeostatic controls of the natural system are exceeded breakdown in the natural system, and perhaps the social system as well, will result.

It is clear that the archaeological record can only be examined as a series of morphological systems. Nevertheless, the structures of these systems reflect their responses or adjustments to the cascading systems to which they were once linked. Whilst the notion of equifinality, which points out that similar morphological systems can result from different processes or historical sequences, suggests caution over predicting process from a study of structure or form, a systemic approach, because it focuses attention on the links between elements rather than on the attributes of the separate elements, can lead to the asking of new questions of the archaeological record. Equally important, anthropologists can analyse primitive communities in the contemporary world in terms of either morphological or cascading systems, as well as investigating the relationships between these two types of system. Change resulting from different feedback processes can also be recorded and when this information is combined with that extracted from the archaeological record our understanding of the processes of change in prehistory should be substantially enhanced.

REFERENCES

Ackerman, E.A. (1963) Where is a research frontier? *Annals of the Association of American Geographers* 53, 429-40.

Ashby, W.R. (1958) *An Introduction to Cybernetics.* New York, Wiley.

Bertalanffy, L. von (1956) General system theory. *General Systems* 1, 1-10.

Boulding, K.E. (1956) General systems theory: the skeleton of science. *Management Science* 1, 197-208.

Buckley, L. (1967) *Sociology and Modern Systems Theory.* New Jersey, Prentice-Hall.

Buckley, L. (ed.) (1968) *Modern Systems Research for the Behavioural Scientist: a sourcebook.* Chicago, Aldine.

Caldwell, L.K. (1970) The ecosystem as a criterion for public land policy. *Natural Resources Journal* **10**, 203-21.

Chorley, R.J. and Kennedy, B.A. (1971) *Physical Geography: a systems approach.* London, Prentice-Hall.

Cooke, R.U. (1971) Systems and physical geography. *Area* **3**, 212-6.

Dent, J.B. and Anderson, J.R. (eds.) (1971) *Systems Analysis in Agricultural Management.* Sydney, Wiley.

Emery, F.E. (ed.) (1969) *Systems Thinking.* Harmondsworth, Middlesex, Penguin.

Emery, F.E. and Trist, E.L. (1965) The causal texture of organizational environments. *Human Relations* **18**, 21-32.

Flannery, K.V. (1968) Archaeological systems theory and early Mesoamerica. *In* Meggers, B.J. (ed.) *Anthropological Archaeology in the Americas*, 67-87. Washington D.C. Anthropological Society of Washington.

Foote, D.C. and Greer-Wootten, B. (1968) An approach to systems analysis in cultural geography. *Professional Geographer* **20**, 86-91.

Hägerstrand, T. (1966) Aspects of the spatial structure of social communication and the diffusion of information. *Papers and Proceedings of the Regional Science Association* (European Session) **16**, 27-42.

Harris, D.R. (1969) Agricultural systems, ecosystems and the origins of agriculture. *In* Ucko, P.J. and Dimbleby, G.W. (eds.) *The Domestication and Exploitation of Plants and Animals.* London, Duckworth.

Harvey, D.W. (1969) *Explanation in Geography.* ch. 23, 447-80. London, Edward Arnold.

Isard, W. (1960) *Methods of Regional Analysis: an introduction to regional science.* Cambridge, Mass., M.I.T. Press.

Johnson, R.A., Kast, F.E. and Rosenzweig, J.E. (1964) Systems theory and management. *Management Science* **10**, 367-84.

Kemp, W.B. (1971) The flow of energy in a hunting society. *Scientific American* **224**, 105-15.

Klejn, L.S. (1972) Marxism, the systemic approach, and archaeology. This volume.

Layton, R. (1972) Some consequences of economic change in a French village. This volume.

Leontieff, W.W. (1965) The structure of the United States economy. *Scientific American*, Offprint no.624.

McLoughlin, J.B. and Webster, J.N. (1970) Cybernetic and general system approaches to urban and regional research: a review of the literature. *Environment and Planning* **2**, 369-408.

Miller, J.G. (1965) Living systems: basic concepts. *Behavioural Science* **10**, 193-239; Living systems: structure and process. ibid. 337-79; Living systems: cross-level hypotheses. ibid. 380-411.

Rapaport, A. (1956) The promise and pitfalls of information theory. *Behavioural Science* **1**, 303-9.

Rappaport, R.A. (1971) The flow of energy in an agricultural society. *Scientific American* **224**, 116-32.

Rathje, W.L. (1972) Models for mobile Maya: a variety of constraints. This volume.

Rogers, E.M. (1962) *Diffusion of Innovations.* New York, Free Press of Glencoe.

Watt, K.E.F. (1968) *Ecology and Resource Management, A Quantitative Approach.* New York, McGraw-Hill.

Wilbanks, T.J. and Symanski, R. (1968) What is systems analysis? *Professional Geographer* **20**, 81-5.

Wood, J.J. and Matson, R.G. (1972) Two models of socio-cultural systems and their implications for the archaeological study of change. This volume.

LEO S. KLEJN

Marxism, the systemic approach, and archaeology

1. The three general approaches

A sequential approach to the understanding of material remains was characteristic of archaeology, as of a number of other disciplines, in the late 18th and the 19th century. It was expressed in Winckelmann's concept of 'styles', in Thomsen's Three Age System and in the evolutionary constructions of de Mortillet and Montelius. Chronological sequence was the main axis of consideration, unilinear development the main inference, and the comparison of elements the main method. Later on the principles of this approach were retained in the stadialistic theory ('theory of stageness', 'teoriya stadialnosti'). However, very widely in the late 19th and in the first half of the 20th century this general approach changed as another – distributional – moved the emphasis from development in time to that of spread in space. This is easily seen in the constructions of the American taxonomic-archaeologists of the interwar period and in a number of archaeological conceptions: migrationism, diffusionism, geographical determinism (the ecological school) – and is visible also in the 'settlement archaeology' concept of the post-war years.

If followed logically then to ask whether it is possible to combine both approaches. The question, and attempts to solve it, became popular for a short time among the American taxonomist archaeologists as well as in Soviet archaeology not long ago. But to solve the question appeared to be an arduous task. The resulting schemes remained mechanistic, and in each the component parts were somewhat artificially stuck together.

A further change in the principles used in the consideration of various subject materials may be discerned in the second half of the 20th century in many disciplines: in biology, linguistics, philosophy etc. The understanding developed, that the elements, and the relations and connections between them, isolated for analysis and for separate study did not yield the totality of the data needed in order to know the world – try as we might thereafter to put them together, to sum them, and to synthesize anew. A special study of their actual and general interconnection, in systems, was required.

The world was always systemic. Natural selection was working already, from the very beginning of animate nature, and artificial selection at least from the neolithic period. But Darwin, the man who was to seize on the existence and the importance of natural selection, did not appear until the development of free competition in human society had made the idea of 'struggle for life' a natural one for the human mind (Bernal, 1956:33, 37, 360, 371). Similarly, the idea of a large complex system not reducible to the sum of its parts, the idea of a specific approach to the study of the world as an organized, ordered and structured whole, was steadily developing under the influence of the emergence of enormous and highly autonomous systems, whose control was difficult: in modern production, technology, war and politics.

Of course, the concept of system has long been known in science, and the problems of ordering, seriating and systematizing materials were solved many times, but until recently students have tried to bypass the problem of studying a system as a whole. They tried to reduce the study of systemic objects to a study of non-systemic ones, or to change the revelation of the inner characters of a system to a description of its outer parameters (Sadovsky, 1965:173-6).

The systemic approach did not drop from the clouds. It was long developing in the sciences and although not following any teleological lines, it emerged in time to service and to make intelligible those big systems which were to appear by the middle of the 20th century. Yet now, in retrospect, we can recognize some theoretical discoveries in the science of the past as important steps towards the systemic approach, although they may only be by-products from the point of view of the main stream of scientific advance, as it was then conceived.

It has been noted in the literature that many of the ideas of the systemic approach were anticipated by Marx in his study of the economic system of capitalism and by Lenin in his study of imperialism (Sadovsky, 1965:177-8; Godelier 1966; Novik 1969). This should not be surprising if we remember the above example of the importance of human political-economic relations as a model for the understanding of the entire world. Recently it has been noted how unjustly Bogdanov's 'tectology' (Bogdanov, 1912, 1921) was so indiscriminately rejected and forgotten. Lenin who strongly and rightly criticized Bogdanov for the relativism and mechanicism of his approach (Lenin 1958-65, vol. 18) nevertheless stressed the value of some of Bogdanov's concrete scientific propositions (Lenin 1958-65, vol. 4:35-43). Quite a number of propositions of cybernetics and of the general theory of systems, which are especially close to Ross Ashby's ideas, are contained in Bogdanov's 'tectology' (Setrov, 1967, 1970). Even the founder of the general theory of systems, Bertalanffy himself, postponed for twenty years the publication of his conclusions because of the unfavourable climate in the scientific world. He ventured to publish them only much later, in post-war times (Bertalanffy, 1962:2-3).

2. *Towards the systems approach in biology*

In biology, the classical branch of science for the general theory of systems, the development leading to the systemic approach has been examined by Khailov, by Kremyansky and by Sadovsky.

Later, students had first turned to the analytical study of similarities. The ordering in terms of morphological similarities led to the discovery of a new system – the *species.* Arrangement of species by their degree of complexity became a basis for an idea of phylogenetic linkage: evolution. The *phylogenetic* system reflected only past connections, fixed in relict materials. As a result of a departure from the purely evolutionist approach, students were now able to pay attention to real, actual, currently operating connections within the species. While remaining the main object of study, the species has since been considered as a *genetic* system in the light of Mendel's *population* studies, with its adaptive adjustments, and so on. In its turn, this study guided scholars to consider the connections of the species with the environment, and brought the system of *biocoenosis* and then of *biogeocoenosis* (ecosystem) under the object of science. However this study too appeared limited and mechanistic. The development of several one-sided and mutually exclusive points of view on the subject stimulated a search for ways to achieve more integral and more comprehensive notions (Khailov 1970).

As Kremyansky has shown, a vast group of '*organicist*' theories has appeared in the twentieth century, having discovered anew the great truth of Plato: 'the whole is bigger than the sum of its parts', together with the accompanying understanding that the parts taken outside the whole may lose some important characters. These theories were fighting against *neovitalism*, and against *mechanicism* with its accompanying reductionism, i.e. the attempt to reduce the comprehension of higher forms to an additive analysis of lower forms: sociology to biology, biology to chemistry and physics, and these to mechanics. But the organicists were working very differently: some from idealistic standpoints, others from materialistic positions. The former were in the majority, and, trying to consider the parts only from the position of the whole, (i.e. the lower forms from the standpoint of the higher ones) often tended to ignore the importance of these lower forms and with them the material substratum of the system. Bertalanffy's *Theory of Open Systems*, and then his *General Theory of Systems*, arose from the circle of organicist theories. From the same circle developed the *Theory of Structure Levels* by Brown and Sellars, and the *Theory of Integration Levels* by Gerard, Emmerson, Novikov and others. The latter is seen by Kremyansky as especially important in combining the advantages of both approaches: the organicist and mechanicist, holistic and reductionist. So precedents were being created for examining both aspects of the system at once: the higher level and the lower one (Kremyansky 1969, 16-142). Such bipolar variety of the systemic approach has been recognized by some Soviet authors as a special trend: *integratism* (Engelgardt 1971).

Sadovsky has shown, in a series of articles, how numerous, different and unconformable are the contemporary varieties of the systemic approach in biology and in other sciences. In Bertalanffy's view the principle of *equifinality* of systems must take first place. It emphasizes the integral characters, deeming monosemantic, one-channelled and one-directional determinism, with its rigid causal connection, to be insufficient. In Ross Ashby's view the idea of *homeostasis* is prominent: it stresses how complicated is the interrelation of the system with the environment. For Ashby the problem is not to comprehend or open the mechanism operating in the system but to consider the system as a Black Box and to present in a mathematical form the connection of the input restraint and the output signal, indeed to construct a mathematical model of the system (Sadovsky 1962, 1965, 1970; Blauberg, Sadovsky and Yudin 1970). These conceptions are criticized by Sadovsky as attempts to bypass the main task of the systemic approach, namely to penetrate into the inside of the system. How one could dissect it into its components without losing its integral character? Sadovsky views both the teleological description arising from the equifinality principle of Bertalanffy and the Black Box model of Ashby as inadequate attempts, for in both these conceptions the system is not opened and dissected, but is examined only on the outside, from the standpoint of its behaviour as a whole (Sadovsky 1970:436). He concludes that a developed theory of systems, and an adequate methodology and logic for the systemic approach, have not yet been constructed (Sadovsky 1965:168). To him the most promising way of solving this problem seems to be to work out a strategy for investigating *structures* (Sadovsky 1970:436-42). In his view the work of Zinoviev, who proposed a logical formalization for the integral examination of multiple connections within the system (Zinoviev 1959:1960), is an important step in this direction. It was noted, however, that Zinoviev proceeded only to formalize the functional connections, but that these are not system forming (Blauberg, Sadovsky and Yudin 1970:41-2). Summing up their review of the present state of science, Blauberg, Sadovsky and Yudin conclude: 'We cannot yet speak today of a united Theory of Systems' (ibid.:27).

3. Towards the systems approach in archaeology

Thus, in noting a tendency towards a new general approach in archaeology – toward a systemic approach – we must be ready from the very beginning for a situation in which marked differences will become visible behind the similarity and unity of some of the general principles. The 'systemic and multivariate' approach of Binford will appear as only one variety of the systemic approach in archaeology. The argument about the contrary trends – pluralism and monism, materialism and idealism and so on – will probably continue within the framework of the new, systemic approach, just as it was itself developed in the milieu of the preceding general approaches.

Tracing in retrospect the evolution of archaeology, we can now observe that there were early developments towards the systemic approach and that those developments took different parallel courses. We may say that there is evident in archaeology a certain general line of discoveries of increasingly complicated and less obvious systems, much like the line revealed in biology.

The first object of study in archaeology was the *artifact* which in itself is not as a rule a system (or better to say, not a complex system) in nature. Systemic comprehension proceeded as the focus turned to problems of reconstruction, and as the interest shifted from the artifact to the *feature* and the *pattern* and to the *site* as a whole. The example of Pompeii, for instance, shows that this shift took place rather late. This was the main road to the discovery of systems in archaeology. The study of formal similarities among artifacts within each class of things with a single functional purpose led to discovery of the '*type*' system, and on the basis of such similarities between things of different classes the '*style*' system was discovered. Without tending to biologization and the equation of archaeological systems with biological ones, we may nevertheless note the concept of 'type' taking a place in the history of our discipline analagous to that which belonged in biology to the concept 'species'. As in biology (and not without its influence) further developments led to the discovery of the phylogenetic ties between types. The '*typological sequence*' appeared to be the mainstay of the phylogenetic system. The attempt to strengthen the application of this system (and to convert it into a *chronological system*) stimulated Montelius to study parallel sequences and to discover the system '*assemblage*' (*sicherer Fund, geschlossener Fund*). The shift to the study of such associational connections, which was necessary to establish the duration of each type, has led in archaeology to the substitution of the distributive approach for the sequentional one, and the growing attention to the distribution, combination and mutual influence of types. In the course of studying these connections the system *'archaeological culture'* was revealed – many times, from different sides, and was formalized in different concept-definitions: *chronological, chorological, stylistic,* and *combination-typological.* The proper understanding of the unity of all these notions of archaeological culture was delayed until our own time (Klejn 1970, 1971, 1972b). The quite evident importance of this system stretched its formal limits from the very beginning, and incited archaeologists to go out beyond the borders of archaeology. Hence, from the very time of the discovery of this system, the search for such a way out was prosecuted, and attempts were made to include archaeological cultures in some more extensive *non-archaeological systems – 'ethnos', 'social-economic formation', 'eco-system', 'society'* (*'social organism', 'social group'* etc.). These attempts in their different ways may be recognized as early moves towards the systemic approach. In this sense the activity of the British ecologist school, for instance (the trend from archaeological culture to the ecosystem) may also be considered, like other aspects, as leading in the same direction.

The way out of the restricting framework of archaeological culture was sought also in another direction, which also leads to the systemic approach – the direction of a purely archaeological broadening of the horizon. Migrationists and diffusionists revealed the genetic ties of cultures, and thus more extensive archaeological systems appeared – groups of cultures (*Kulturkreise*). The American taxonomists united cultures in large blocks on the basis of purely external formal connections. The stadialists (adepts of the 'theory of stageness') bound cultures together into systems (*'stadia' i.e. stages*) according to levels of development ('synstadial' phenomena). Gradually a notion of the universal interconnection of all the cultures in the world was developing.

This principle was suggested from two mutually opposite sides and, of course, in two different versions. On the one hand it was advanced by Marxist archaeologists and historians, and on the other, by the Anglo-Saxon indeterminists, the adepts of the 'contextual' trend in archaeology.

To Marxist scholars this principle was a realization of one of the fundamental demands of materialistic dialectics, namely the study of the real world in its universal interconnection and interdependence. In the works of Soviet historians this interdependence was presumably considered as causal connection, and elaborated not only in the diachronic aspect – as the system of common history (Zhukov 1955:V-VIII) – but also in its synchronic aspect – as the system of world history (Porshnev 1967, 1969). Lenin enjoined us 'to consider each question by asking how did a particular phenomenon in history appear, which main stages was this phenomenon going through' (Lenin 1958-65, vol. 39:67). He noted, too: 'In order really to know an object, one must to comprehend it, study all its aspects, all its connections and possibilities. We shall never reach this perfectly, but the examination from all sides will protect us from errors and from insensitivity' (Lenin 1958-65, vol. 42:290). In the works of Marxist scholars the history of mankind is presented as an integral whole, bound together by the logic of historical development. This view is altogether contrary to Toynbee's 'local civilizations' conception. From the first steps of Soviet archaeology its representatives tried to consider each large archaeological phenomenon as a link in a long chain of historical development, as a result of a logical resolution of some previous events, also as a basis for some following ones, and indeed as a focus of various connections in the present. The creators of the 'stadialist theory' ('theory of stageness') in the '20s and '30s had already studied archaeological materials in this way. Their work suffered from hyperschematization, although undoubtedly they tried to comprehend each archaeological phenomenon looking at it from the standpoint of the whole. Indeed their historical approach permitted them to consider each complicated cultural phenomenon as a result of an increase in organization, as a transition to a higher level of integration, and, consequently, to discern in this phenomenon, in this new order, the old, more simple elements, i.e. to avoid losing the material substratum from view. From the 'stadialist theory' a straight road leads to Childe's conception of the 'Neolithic and Urban revolutions', and this conception in one form or another has stimulated and been reflected in many modern notions – from Braidwood and Masson to Adams and Binford.

Another approach developed by the indeteminist trend in archaeology was the principle of integrity and of common interconnection. W. Taylor, in his *Study of archaeology* formulated objections to formal isolation, to the study of artifacts out of the context of their concrete assemblages, and of the environment. Instead, he declared the principle of studying archaeological materials in their concrete historic context (Taylor 1948). This trend to concreteness is based on a belief that each historical event or cultural phenomenon is unique, that culture is not determined by any regularities, and that the entire process is directed only by the free will of individuals, by individual choices and decisions, whose combinations are accidental and unpredictable. Causes of events can be valid only for each given case. In accordance with this the 'locality' was proclaimed by Taylor's followers, to be the main object of study, for in it, to their mind, all aspects of culture are focussed best, concreteness is ensured and the trustworthiness is evident (Chang 1967:231-2). It was on this base that 'settlement archaeology' appeared (Chang 1968; Willey 1968:52). The 'locality' is set off against all other systems and the entire culture of mankind appeared to be the context in which the locality must be seen, without intermediate instances between. Developing these ideas Daniel has written that it is necessary to pass from studying cultures to studying culture (Daniel 1950:246).

Others, too, reject the study of cultures (Müller-Karpe 1966:187; Renfrew 1969:153).

Evidently this is quite another path to the systemic approach. Going this way it is necessary to overcome some significant obstacles, for in the 'contextual' conception there are some principles acting against the systemic approach. Just this difficulty gave rise to the critical questioning of Binford and his adherents. Among archaeologists they were the first to recognize, and clearly to declare, that the goal and inevitable result of modern methodological reconstruction in archaeology must be the systemic approach.

4. Localities and cultures

Is the entire culture of the world in itself one system only, since all mankind is one collective or one body? The problem is not so simple. The connections between human groups are not only direct and visible. The indirect and unconscious connections are also significant: prehistoric tribes not only fought or confederated, they also limited each other's free space for settlement, blocked the roads to distant sources of raw materials or to wanted territories, and so on. A change in one region may lead to consequences in different distant regions.

However, in the full network of cultural connections and relations we should see discreteness, with boundaries of various rank importance. And among the entities of different rank it is important to single out those recognizable as the main ones, since inside them the most important process of cultural development occur. A long cultural development of a single locality would be inconceivable; analogous phenomena in physical anthropology (the existence of isolated micropopulations) are considered anomalous. On the other hand *Kulturkreise* are the product more of common descent or common environment than real, actual development through contact (trade or exchange was not of paramount importance for prehistoric society). So a culture remains the central object.

But the processes of development proceed in time; to liken them to Markovian chains is problematic, and the systemic approach presupposes also an initial consideration from the viewpoint of the whole, i.e. proceeding from the integral process to its stages. We must deal with chronological rows of mutually interacting cultures. Such rows I propose to call '*sequentions*'. Sequentions appear as stratigraphic-chronological columns in each cultural-geographical region – I call such sequentions '*columnar sequentions*' or '*pillars*'. However, in real life, processes of cultural development did not proceed in cultural sequentions but in *genetic sequention.* By genetic sequention I understand a row of interconnected cultures tied by direct genetic succession. In other words, the archaeological material is given us in columnar sequences, and it is our task as archaeologists to convert it to genetic sequences. The important problems of migration, diffusion, autochthonous development and so on in archaeology can be considered as the way to approach this task. But the genetic development of cultures was not simple or unilinear: the crossing processes postulated by Rostovtsev and by the school of Marr played an important role. The roots of almost every culture stretch simultaneously into different preceding cultures, and each culture may be simultaneously a link in different genetic sequentions. Instead of a genealogical tree or some kind of a bamboo grove of genetic sequentions we must deal with a network. In this sense (through the agency of cultures and sequences) the entire culture of the world tends to become a single systemic object of study. This tendency has been strengthened through to the common occurrences of many regularities which united, for instance, the development of American and Old World cultures in the period when intercontinental contacts hardly existed.

Since the American 'contextualists' and the British hypersceptics advocate indeterminism and uniqueness of events, and since they doubt the existence of regularities, they quite naturally reject the possibility of recovering regular connections between different spheres of culture, between archaeological objects and past events and ideas. The possibilities of verifying hypotheses appear minimal, and only flat empiricism is left as the destiny of archaeology.

However, the systemic approach presupposes multiple interconnections of elements within a system, a dense network of connections with keen sensitivity to partial changes, and the plurality of recurrence of such changes. On this Binford bases the possibility of the verification of hypotheses and his preference for the hypothetico-deductive method (Binford 1968). One should add that the interpretation of archaeological objects as systems presupposes the recognition of some order in them, some organization, i.e. a *regularity of connections.* This makes the basis for the application of the hypothetico-deductive method wider and stronger. The principles of the systemic approach as advocated by Binford found methodical expression in multivariate, tool-kit or factor analysis, and these methods bring good results in concrete research. The most important of these results to my mind is the discovery of *new systems* as an archaeological reality, namely the male and female *fractions (subcultures)* within a culture, detectable by differences in their behaviour (Deetz 1965; 1968).

Yet despite the value of these methodological principles, the systemic approach may not be reduced to them. It is much wider.

5. The principles of the systemic approach

(i) Proceeding from the Soviet philosophers' now general notions on the systemic approach, *the principle of entirety* must be named first of all. The description of elements and the revealing of separate connections between them is no longer sufficient: the existence of each within the system must now be also taken into account. In other words those properties of the elements and their connections are also considered which are engendered by the characters of the whole, and which can neither be caught nor comprehended outside the whole. This principle in archaeology is often stated as a *principle of complexity*, and by complexity archaeologists have quite often understood *completeness*, i.e. the need to take into account all the elements and all the connections. This is vulgarization. The essence of the principle lies in the search for those properties and characters imposed on all the elements and on all the connections by the system within which they are included.

Manifestations of this principle in archaeology may be very various. At one time the dating of an assemblage after its latest artifact (terminus post quem) was considered the most accurate possible method. Today we are able to build chronological systems in which, through intercrossing chronological relations and a plurality of connections, types and assemblages receive narrower datings than separately (Shchukin 1967, 1970). In defining the ethnical status of those buried in barrows of the 9th-11th centuries some things (weapons) were formerly held as less important, others (fibulae, torques with amulets) as more important elements of the burial custom, but the ethnical status of each single grave was discussed separately, individually. Today we try to divide the entirety of the graves of that time into large series on the basis of totality of attributes. We try to define the ethnic position of each such series, considering the latter as a whole after summing many signals, both differential (i.e. taking graves individually) and integral (i.e. on the basis of the total series as a whole, e.g. through comparison of the area with preserved place names, or with the data from narrative sources etc.). Here even assemblages having no clear individual ethnic signals at all may yet receive an ethnic definition (Klejn, Lebedev, Nazarenko 1970:232-8, 243-8; Bulkin 1970).

In archaeology there is one very modern phenomenon which clearly opposes this principle, namely the placing of hope on the salvation through natural-scientific methods and their power in solving cardinal archaeological problems. The grounds for this hope consists on the one hand in a passion for successes of the natural sciences and their techniques, and on the other hand in a mistrust of archaeology's own methods, which are sociological and humanitarian in nature. This is a crisis of faith. In some archaeologists' minds, archaeology must become simply a natural science and work almost entirely with naturalist methods, incorporating them as its own (Kolchin, 1965: Fig. 1; 1970). No doubt a number of the concrete tasks of the archaeologist will soon pass to a laboratory (chronology for instance, the provenance of raw materials, technology). However, the attempts to dissect all archaeological problems into parts so as to reduce them to problems to be solved by natural-scientific methods, constitute a kind of reductionism (cf. Klejn 1969-70), which risks forgetting the specific integrative problems of archaeology and ignoring the principle of integrity. On the other hand the reaction of some archaeologists, usually the senior ones, to the modern reductionism often comes to a full denial of the fruitfulness of such analysis, and of the applicability of natural-scientific and mathematical methods to archaeology at all. Integrity is then equated with insubstantial humanitarianism, and the reductionist way of study is fully rejected (Hawkes 1968; cf. Agrawal 1970). These scholars forget that the greatest successes of modern biology were nevertheless obtained through the reductionist approach, or more exactly, that branch of it which does not limit itself to the dissection of the complex into its simplest elements but researches their integration and the new situations that arise from this integration (Engelgardt 1971). For archaeology this means studying (with a previous dissection of elements and their formalization) processes of integration and reorganization of its main systems, namely cultures. The leading aspect here is two-fold: first in relating the problem of the origin of the properties of the whole to the properties of the elements (i.e. speaking of cultures, to the interaction of cultures, types, extra-cultural factors etc.) and secondly, in illuminating the problem of the birth of the characters of the elements by considering the properties of the whole. It might be better, supplementing the *principle of entirety* with the *principle of reduction*, to combine them into a united *principle of integration.*

(ii) The second important principle of the systemic approach is the *contextual* one. Philosophers formulate it thus: the study of a system is inseparable from the study of the conditions of its existence. In a distorted and narrowed form this principle has been advanced by the proponents of the ecologist and contextualist schools. In the latter it easily reaches absurd extremes, undermining the basis of science. Indeed, if all conclusions are valid only for each concrete context, then science is not needed. In the Marxist mind, the essence of the principle lies in the study of each system, (in archaeology, for instance, each culture), without tearing it away from those other systems with which it is connected, i.e. other cultures, economics, ecology etc. This means keeping constantly in mind the possibility of explaining changes in the system by means of the influences of its environment. This is connected with a demand not to limit the study at the borders of a single system or a single kind of system. In Soviet archaeology there is already a long tradition of this kind, although in the past the application of this tradition was sometimes narrowed by some unwarranted limitations (as, for example, on the influences of other cultures – this was too easily labelled as diffusionism). It might be better to speak not of a contextual principle but of a *principle of concreteness.*

(iii) The third principle of the systemic view is the *multivariate approach*: one and the same material may possess various characters, parameters, functions and building principles, according to the view point taken. The systemic approach claims to cover the total range of the aspects, to take into account all possible points of view, to include them all unseparated and matched in a single survey. In Binford's multivariate methodology this principle has been achieved by means of the equation of all the possible parameters and functions (Binford and Binford 1966); proponents of numerical taxonomy make the same claim (Culberg 1968; 1970; Clarke 1968:512-46); Renfrew considered the interaction of various factors in the cultural process likely (Renfrew 1969, 1970). But in such understanding the structural organization of the system is ignored.

(iv) Yet the *structural organization* is also a principle of the systemic approach, and not the least of them; it is connected with the functioning of elements and parts. To consider a culture as a system means to the Marxist mind differentiating its elements, following their *position* in the structural hierarchy of the culture. The dependence of the functions of elements on those elements' position within a system was the main idea of Propp (1928; 1946).

To David Clarke everything depends on the quantity of the elements, to other workers the internal qualitative potentials of the elements are also important. But let us look at some examples. European clothing, weapons and customs diffused into Russia even before Peter the Great; these weapons were even then better than Russian ones, whereas the wig, I think, has no evident advantages in comparison with one's own hair. Peter's personal passion for them would not have influenced the entire country unless he had become tsar. The import of fibulae to the population of the Oka basin in the middle of the first millennium A.D. had no results – fibulae were understood as ornaments. By breaking the pins, people made them into necklaces, which were added to old local ornaments. The same fibulae when acquired by the population of the neighbouring south zone were understood as fastenings, and in this position and function they became a source for some local sequences of fibula types, and in a certain measure changed the appearance of local clothing. The results of innovation depend not only on its own quantitative and qualitative characters but also on the position of the changing elements within the culture. On this depends whether the culture will remain the same after incorporating this innovation, or if the innovation will lead to a general transformation of the whole culture.

In terms of the systemic approach this is realized by means of management or by a control set. In a narrow view this set consists of special elements and functions: machinery for codifying, transmitting and deciphering organization-bearing information. In a wide view the stable interconnection and *hierarchical subordination* of subsystems and their elements within a system must also be included. Childe showed well the important consequences which sprang from the introduction of copper and bronze into a system of stone age culture (Childe 1930:1-12). I doubt, however, whether the introduction of spiral motifs into the pottery decoration of this culture, for instance, is comparable.

An interesting idea put forward by Müller-Karpe was that the introduction of ceramics was connected with an important transformation of prehistoric man's mentality: the desire to keep supplies appeared, indicating a primitive planning economy (Müller-Karpe 1970:13-14, 19). But this psychical transformation has no other root than the influence of new economic possibilities: not only the introduction of ceramics but also the appearance of a significant surplus from new, and more productive methods. (It is hardly accidental that ceramics appear at practically the same time as the widespread introduction of cattle-breeding and agriculture). The appearance of ceramics and other economic innovations may indeed be explained independently of supposed psychical changes. The example shows why Marxist archaeologists admit the leading role of the *production factor* in changes of the cultural system. Today Marxist archaeologists pay more attention than formerly to the significance of the conditions in which this factor becomes apparent, to influences of other economical factors (e.g. trade/exchange), to the role of the geographic environment, to the reciprocal actions of the political and ideological substructures, and to the complexity and indirectness of connections within the cultural system, but the primacy of the production factor in our beliefs is not shaken.

(v) The principle of *immanent* development, proclaimed long since in Marxism (development as a result of the struggle between internal contradictions), is now acknowledged as one of the most important principles in the systemic approach. It consists in admitting that our main objects are *self-organizing* systems. This means that the source of the main transformations of a system is supposed to be within the system itself. Here we mean not any transformations, but specifically those which raise a system onto a higher level of integration (by a leap) and which may be considered as processes of emergence of new qualitative states – neolithic, civilization, animal style, military democracy, urban settlement and so on. We may say, for instance, that we find embryos of all the distinctive components of neolithic life in a previous state of the stone age. If we consider them all only statically, and suppose the only quantitative accumulation possible to be endlessly the same, then we must seek the stimulus for their integration only outside the system. But Marxist dialectics teach us to see the dynamics of development as a neutral state of things, since it is rooted in a struggle of internal contradictions. We have learned to search culture trajectories (in David Clarke's terms), and to consider quantitative accumulation as discrete, as having certain *a priori* limits beyond which the quantitative accumulation results in qualitative leaps. In such a picture the recognition of an outside stimulus is possible and thinkable but it is not necessary. Quite a contrary view to this has recently been suggested, however, by a Symposium of adherents of Binfordian thought (Hill 1971:407-8).

6. *Law, fact and system*

In order to explain the similarity of many results (cf. Bertalanffy's equifinality) or repetition in cultural history we must suppose the existence of some *regularities*, and hence some determinism of the transformation processes of archaeological systems. It was earlier usual to seek, in our material, manifestations of single-minded mechanistic determinism, of a firm causal connection of phenomena, and indeed to assume, so to speak, the *monosemantism* of an archaeological fact. Each archaeological fact seemed able to have one and only one reasonable explanation, and two similar facts might have one and the same explanation (e.g. rich graves are the graves of the rich). Now it has become fashionable to reject all determinism, to believe that all the events are conditioned only by the free will of individuals, to proclaim the uniqueness of every archaeological phenomenon. Accordingly the archaeological fact is invested with an endless plurality of possible meanings, i.e. becomes *asemantic.* I think the healthy mean would be to admit the *polysemantic determinism* of cultural processes, with a limited freedom of choice, likening a regularity to a river which has a stream and a direction, and an estuary with a width and banks (Klejn 1971). The archaeological fact is thus polysemantic: behind a single fact may be hidden one of a number of meanings. Their number is limited, and the task of an archaeologist consists of finding specific criteria for a choice. This is possible by setting the fact in new situations and considering it in system terms.

We are able to ascertain in precisely which cases the richness of a grave is connected with a specific cause in prehistoric ideology – e.g. the childrens' graves of Häusler (Häusler 1968) – and in what cases with the richness of the buried person, e.g. when we state a correlation with the insignia of power, the inclusion of several sets of ornaments and so on (Klejn 1967). The inclusion of a fact in a system does not enlarge the polysemantism of the fact; rather it lessens it. The more complicated a system becomes, the smaller is the number of possible meanings of each fact. But, at the same time, it becomes more difficult to comprehend the construction of this system and to reveal the regularities of its construction.

7. Models in archaeology

The study of complex systems has raised in science the problem of *models*. This is not here simply a fashionable word introduced into science merely to rejuvenate old procedures. A model is an object (it may be a systemic one) which is similar to another one and which is studied instead because the latter is too complicated or inaccessible. In operations with models the main thing is the choice of a model (or rather of *the* model) and the conditions and rules for transferring the result received onto the object modelled. Renfrew with good reason suggested that it is necessary for archaeologists to use the concept of model more exactly and it might be well to follow the usage of this term accepted among natural scientists; I must add, and among Soviet philosphers, too – cf. Uemov 1962; Shtoff 1963, 1966; Glinsky *et al.* 1965; Novik 1965; etc. Models express 'as-if-thinking' (Renfrew 1968). However, Renfrew overlooks the fact that neither Piggott's nor his own understanding actually corresponds to 'as-if-thinking'. Piggott had used the term 'model' to designate general approaches to explanation, or the types of the logical structure of explanation, and to emphasize the stereotyped nature of the concrete realizations of each such approach for a given period. To him: 'after one model' means 'after one cliché' (Piggott 1959:1-6; also Neustupný 1967). David Clarke tautologically calls every hypothesis and every scheme a model. This may be correct in the frame of gnoseology (epistemology), but what insight does such a wide usage offer for archaeology? The more wide and all-embracing we make a scientific concept, the narrower is its applicability. Besides, it might be better not to confuse as do Clarke and Trigger (Clarke 1968: 32-40; Trigger 1969) the application of models in meta-archaeological explanation, the archaeologist's activity, and their use in the explanation of the archaeological materials. Renfrew following Daniel (Daniel 1964) designates by the term 'model' general conceptions, large explanatory hypotheses applied to the series of uniform (or not very uniform) occurrences. The intention here was to emphasize the relativity and shakiness of these conceptions ('they all are merely models' in the sense: 'artificial schemes, speculative constructions'). Renfrew has suggested another meaning: any mathematical formula approximating one or another actual row of interconnected values measured. This is a model on the lines of Ashby. Does it help to comprehend a system? No, it helps only to describe adequately the connection of the external characters of a system. Does such a model express 'as-if-thinking'? To a very small extent it does, for limiting ourselves by a procedure we deal *as if* more complex internal connections of these characters do not exist. But they do!

Besides mathematical models, two kinds of model perfectly expressing 'as-if-thinking' are applicable in archaeology.

(i) David Clarke has indicated the correspondence of many archaeological systems to Ashby's Very Big Black Box in which there is ample room for a very complex mechanism. To Ashby and Clarke the only way out consists in gathering together the separate details of this mechanism before or after their functioning. Within the box we will try gropingly to construct a model for them *isomorphic* to that mechanism and able to behave similarly. Clarke notices, however, that in an integral mechanism there appear some properties which were not characteristic of its elements alone and which depend on the mode of integration. He adds that of one and the same collection of elements when assembled together one may form mechanisms with different properties. He merely states this obstacle, but gives no solution.

In order to comprehend very complex mechanisms in archaeological systems we seek or build *simpler* models of these mechanisms taking into account only some of their important properties – these are the first kind of model. They may be of different types.

(a) One of the possibilities is to build a *homomorphic model* acting like the system under study, as concerns the features which interest us. Thus, in order to comprehend the transformation of the Sarmatian culture of the North Pontic region under the influence of Roman-Hellenic culture we may imagine the result as a mechanical aggregate or as a chemical solution, or again as an alloy of two metals (with new properties not seen in either), or indeed as a hybrid (with a combination of new and old properties) and so on. All these examples would be homomorphic models of the cultural admixture. Each is built on a single feature; they are therefore over-simplifying and as such useful only for the sake of visual demonstration. But more appropriate models of this kind are conceivable.

(b) Another possibility is to find, among the elements of the mechanism under study, those which reflect the most important and interesting integral processes and properties, although in micro-realization. In other words, to find among the parts of the complex system the minimal one in which the integral properties of the whole system are still found, and then to extend some aspects of the resultant data to the whole system. Thus, in the assemblage of the so-called Novotcherkassk Hoard (the Khokhlach barrow) there are many gold plaques of local, Sarmatian manufacture. Some of these plaques imitate the decoration of an imported Roman askos found in the same assemblage, and some others from the same assemblage are a divergent modification of these. This may show how the Sarmatian craftsmen mastered and transformed the new motifs, and we receive a sort of *cellular model* for more complex processes of cultural crossing. These were models of the first kind.

(ii) The models of the other kind must facilitate the understanding of those processes and structures which are inaccessible to direct study. These models have a special importance in archaeology since archaeological systems are simply the preserved remains of active cultural systems living long ago. The other parts of these systems are not preserved, and so are inaccessible now for direct study. David Clarke has likened this archaeological problem to Ashby's situation with the Incompletely Observed Black Box. He suggests a search for other (previous and subsequent) states of the same system by defining its trajectory and the trajectories of its parts. This implies, as a matter of fact, the use of these states of the system as models (trajectorial models) of the state under study, with extra- and interpolative corrections. Alas, these model states also are observed only in fragments. However, if we admit that in the organization of a given system regularities are seen which are characteristic of the organization of a number of other systems, then the possibilities of a search for models are enlarged by considering actual living, and therefore more completely observable systems. In order to reveal the place of the archaeological objects under study in the once living systems now long defunct and how these systems looked, how they were constructed, we must find living models, i.e. similar living systems, employing similar objects, and study them. This new statement of the question differs fundamentally from the old search for ethnographic parallels by virtue of the complete scope of the kinds of *ethnographic parallels* now sought, by a trend to compare whole systems instead of isolated elements, and, above all, by the intention to find suitable criteria for the appropriate comparison of systems, an important step towards the understanding of systems. The problems arising will be further considered in two forthcoming articles (Klejn 1972a, 1973).

REFERENCES

Agrawal, D.P. (1970) Archaeology and the Luddites. *Antiquity* 44, 115-9.

Bernal, J. (1956) *Nauka v istorii obshchestva (Science in the History of Society).* Moscow, Inostrannaya literatura.

Bertalanffy, L. von. (1962) General System Theory; a critical review. *General Systems* 7, 1-20.

Binford, L.R. and S.R. (1966) A preliminary analysis of functional variability in the Mousterian of Levallois facies. *American Anthropologist* **68**, 508-12.

Binford, L.R. (1968) Archaeological perspectives. *In* Binford, S.R. and L.R. (eds.) *New Perspectives in Archaeology*, 5-32. Chicago, Aldine.

Blauberg, I.V., Sadovsky, V.N. and Yudin, E.G. (1970) Sistemnyj podkhod v sovremennoy nauke. *Problemy metodologii sistemnogo issledovaniya.* (The systemic approach in the contemporary science. *Methodological Problems of Systemic Research.*) 7-48. Moscow, Mysl.

Bogdanov, A. (1912) *Vseobshchaya organizacionnaya nauka, (Tektologiya), (Universal Organizational Science (Tektology))*, ch. I. St. Petersburg, Prometey. (2nd ed. 1925, Moscow-Leningrad.)

Bogdanov, A. (1912, 1921) *Ocherki vseobshchey organizacionnoy nauki (An Outline of Universal Organizational Science)*. Samara, Samproletkult.

Bulkin, V.A. (1970) Tipy pogrebalnogo obryada v kurganakh Gnezdovskogo megilnika. *Statistiko-kombinatornyye metody v arkheologii.* (Types of burial custom in the barrows of the Gnozdovo cemetery. *Statistical-combinatorial Methods in Archaeology*). 207-10. Moscow, Nauka.

Chang, K.C. (1967) Major aspects of interrelationship of archaeology and ethnology. *Current Anthropology* **8**, 225-50.

Chang, K.C. (ed.) (1968) *Settlement Archaeology.* Palo Alto, California, National Press.

Childe, V.G. (1930) *The Bronze Age*. Cambridge, University Press.

Clarke, D.L. (1968) *Analytical Archaeology*. London, Methuen.

Culberg, C. (1968) *On artifact analysis.* A study in the systematics and classification of a Scandinavian Early Bronze Age Material . . . (Acta Archaeological Lundensia, ser. in 4°, no. 7). Lund-Bonn.

Culberg, C. (1970) Reply on comments. *Norwegian Archaeological Review* 3, 50-721.

Daniel, G.E. (1950) *A Hundred Years of Archaeology*. London, Duckworth.

Daniel, G.E. (1964) The personality of Wales. In *Culture and Environment: Essays in Honour of Sir Cyril Fox*, 7-23. London, Routledge and Kegan Paul.

Deetz, J. (1965) *The Dynamics of Stylistic Change in Arikara Ceramics*. Urbana, University of Illinois, Series in Anthropology, no. 4.

Deetz, J. (1968) The inference of residence and descent rules from archaeological data. *In* Binford, S.R. and L.R. (eds.) *New Perspectives in Archaeology*, 4-8. Chicago, Aldine.

Engelgardt, V. (1971) Integratism – put' ot prostogo k slozhnomu. (Integratism – the way from the simple to the complex). *Nauka i zhizn'* **5**, 8-15.

Glinsky, B.A. *et al.* (1965) *Modelirovaniye kak metod nauchnogo issledovaniya. (Modelling as a Method of Scientific Research).* Izdatelstvo Moskovskogo Universiteta.

Godelier, M. (1966) *Rationalité et irrationalité en economie.* Paris, Maspero.

Häusler, A. (1968) Kritische Bemerkungen zum Versuch soziologischer Deutungen ur-und frühgeschichtlicher Gräberfelder – erläutert am Beispiel des Gräberfeld von Hallstatt. *Ethnographisch-Archäologische Zeitschrift* **9**, 1, 1-30.

Hawkes, J. (1968) The proper study of mankind. *Antiquity* **42**, 255-62.

Hill, J.N. (1971) Seminar on the explanation of prehistoric organizational change. *Current Anthropology* **12**, 406-8.

Khailov, K.M. (1970) Sistemy i sistematizaciya v biologii. *Problemy metodologii sistemnogo issledovaniya.* (Systems and systematization in biology. *Methodological Problems of Systemic Research*). 127-45. Moscow, Mysl.

Klejn, L.S. (1967) Reiche Katakombengräber. *Ethnographisch-Archäologische Zeitschrift* **8**, 4, 210-34.

Klejn, L.S. (1969-70) Ostayus' arkheologom. Traktat o krizise gumanitarnosti v arkheologii i yego svyazi s upspekhami yestestvennykh i tochnykh nauk. (I remain an archaeologist. A treatise on the crisis of the humanitarian approach in archaeology and the crisis' association with the successes of the natural and exact sciences.) *Znanie-sila* 1969, 2, 26-7; 1970, 2, 33-4.

Klejn, L.S. (1970) Problema opredeleniya arkheologischeskoy Kultury. (The problem of definition of archaeological culture.) *Sovyetskaya Arkhologiya* 2, 37-51, 298-302.

Klejn, L.S. (1971) Was ist archäologishe Kultur? *Ethnographisch-Archäologishe Zeitschrift* 12, 4:210-34.

Klejn, L.S. (1972a) Why exception? A rejoinder. *Current Anthropology* 12 (in press).

Klejn, L.S. (1972b) The concept of culture in modern archaeology. *In* Ehrich, R.W. (ed.) *Theory and Method in Contemporary Archaeology.* The Flagstaff Symposium. (in press).

Klejn, L.S. (1973) Major aspects of interrelationship of archaeology and ethnology. *Current Anthropology* 14 (in press).

Klejn, L.S., Lebedev, G.S. and Nazarenko, V.A. (1970) Normanskie drevnosti Kievskoy Rusi na sovremennom etape arkheologischeskogo izucheniya. *Istoricheskie svyazi Skandinavii i Rossii IX-XX vv.* (The Viking antiquities of the Kiever Rus' in the present state of archaeological knowledge. *The Historical Ties of Scandinavia and Russia in IX-XX cent.*) 226-52. Leningrad, Nauka.

Kolchin, B.A. (1965) Arkheologiya i yestestvennye nauki. *Materialy i issledovaniya po arkheologii SSSR.* (Archaeology and the natural sciences. *Materials and Studies in the Archaeology of the USSR.*) **129**, 7-26.

Kolchin, B.A. (1970) Integraciya nauk i arkheologiya. *Leninskie idei v izuchenii istorii pervobytnogo obshchestva, rabovladeniva i feodalizma.* (The integration of sciences and archaeology. *Lenin's Ideas in the Study of Prehistoric Society, Slave Owning and Feudalism.*) 34-49. Moscow, Nauka.

Kolman, E. (1968) Yestiche raz o chuvstue mery (Once more on the sense of the right measure). *In* Berg, A.I. and Kolman, E. (eds.) *Kibernetika ozhidaemaya i kibernetika neozhidannaya* (Cybernetics expected and cybernetics unexpected). 61-75. Moscow, Nauka.

Kremyansky, V.I. (1969) *Strukturnye urovni zhivoy materii. (The Structural Levels of Living Matter).* Moscow, Nauka.

Lenin, V.I. (1958-65) *Polnoe sobranie sochineniy (The Complete Works)*, vol. 1-55. Moscow, Gospolitizdat.

Müller-Karpe, H. (1966) *Handbuch der Vorgèschichte.* I. München, Beck.

Müller-Karpe, H. (1970) *Die Geshichtliche Bedeutung des Neolithikums.* Wiesbaden, Steiner (Sitzungsberichte der Wissenschaftlichen Gesellschaft an der Johann Wolfgang Goethe-Universität Frankfurt/Main, 9, no. 1).

Neustupný, E. (1967) *Zäkladni prehistorické modely. Dějiny a současnost,* **II**, 4, 32-4.

Novik, B.I. (1965) *O modelirovanii slozhnykh sistem. (On the modelling of Complex Systems.)* Moscow, Mysl.

Novik, B.I. (1969) *Filosofskie idei Lenina i kibernetika.* (Lenin's philosophical ideas and cybernetics.) Moscow, Znanie.

Piggott, S. (1959) *Approach to Archaeology.* Black and Harvard University Press.

Porshnev, B.F. (1967) Odin iz predstaviteley amerkanskoy shkoly istorii mexhdunarodnykh otnosheniy – Raymon Aron. *Ot Alaski do Ognennoy Zemli.* (One of the representatives of the American school of the history of international relations – Raymond Aron. *From Alaska to Terra del Fuego.*) Moscow.

Porshnev, B.F. (1969) Myslima li istoriya odnoy strany? *Istoricheskaya nauka i nekotorye problemy sovremennosti.* (Is a history of a single land thinkable? *The Historical Sciences and Some Problems of Contemporaneity*.) 301-25. Moscow, Nauka.

Propp, V. Ya. (1928) *Morfologia skaski (The Morphology of the Fairy-Tale)* (Voprosy poetiki, XII).

Propp, V. Ya. (1946) *Istoricheskie korni volshebnoy skaski. (The Historical Roots of the Fairy-tale.)* Leningrad Universitet.

Renfrew, C. (1968) Models in prehistory. *Antiquity* **42**, 132-4.

Renfrew, C. (1969) Trade and culture process in European prehistory. *Current Anthropology* **10**, 151-69.

Renfrew, C. (1970) Reply to comments. *Current Anthropology* **11**, 173-5.

Sadovsky, V.N. (1965) Metodologicheskie problemy issledovaniya objektov, predstavlayushchikh soboy sistemy. *Sociologiya v SSSR*, t.I. (The methodological problems of the study of objects as systems. *Sociology in the U.S.S.R.* Vol. I.) 164-92. Moscow, Mysl.

Sadovsky, V.N. (1970) Logiko-metodologicheskiy analiz 'obshchey teorii sistem' L. von Bertalanffy. *Problemy metodologii sistemnogo issledovaniya.* (The logical-methodological analysis of the General Theory of Systems of L. von Bertallanffy, in *Methodological Problems of Systemic Research*) 411-42. Moscow, Mysl.

Setrov, M.I. (1967) Ob obshchikh elementakh tektologii A. Bogdanova, kibernetiki i teorii sistem. *Uchenye zapiski kafedr obshchostvennykh nauk yuzov g. Leningrada*, vyp. VII. Filosofiya. (On the common elements of A. Bogdanov's tectology, cybernetics, and the theory of systems. *Academic Transactions of the Chairs of Social Sciences of the Colleges of Leningrad*, VIII. Philosophy.) Leningrad, Izdatelstvo Leningraskogo Universiteta.

Setrov, M.I. (1970) Princip sistemnosti i yego osnovnye ponyatiya. *Problemy Metodologii sistemnogo issledovaniya.* (The systemic principle and its main concepts. *Problems in the Methodology of Systemic Research.*) 49-63. Moscow, Mysl.

Shchukin, M.B. (1967) O trekh datirovkakh chernyakhovskoy kultury. (On the three datings of the Chernyakhovo culture.) *Kratkie soobshcheniya Instituta arkheologii* **112**, 8-13. Moscow.

Shchukin, M.B. (1970) K voprosu o khronologii chernyakhovskikh pamyatnikov Srednego Podneprovya. (On the question of the chronology of the Chernyakhovian sites of the Middle Dniepr basin.) *Kratkie soobshcheniya Instituta arkheologii* **121**, 104-13. Moscow.

Shtoff, V.A. (1963) *Rol modeley v poznanii (The significance of models in cognition).* Leningrad, Izdatelstvo Leningradskogo Universiteta.

Shtoff, V.A. (1966) *Modelirovanie i filosofiya. (Modelling and philosophy.)* Moscow-Leningrad, Nauka.

Taylor, W.W. (1948) *A Study of Archaeology.* (Memoir no. 69. *American Anthropologist* **50** (3), part 2.)

Trigger, B.G. (1969) More on models. *Antiquity* **43**, 59-61.

Uemov, A.I. (1962) Analogiya i model (Analogy and model.) *Voprosy filosofii* 3, 138-45.

Willey, G.R. (1968) One hundred years of American archaeology. *In* Brew, J.O. (ed.) *One Hundred Years of Anthropology*, 26-53. Cambridge, Mass., Harvard University Press.

Zhukov, E.M. (ed.) (1955) *Vsemirnaya istoriya. (World History, I)* vol. I. Moscow, Gospolitizdat.

Zinoviev, A.A. (1959) Logicheskoe stroenie znaniy o svyazyakh. *Logicheskie issledovaniya.* (The logical structure of the knowledge of connections. *Logical Studies*) 113-38. Moscow, Izdatelstvo Akadedemii Nauk SSSR.

Zinoviev, A.A. (1962) *Logika vyskazyvaniy i teoriya vyvoda. (The Logic of Statements and the Theory of Inference.)* Moscow, Izdatelstvo Akademii Nauk SSSR.

JACK GOODY

Correlation and causal inference: a case study

In thinking of the relationship between human institutions, we constantly speak in vaguely casual terms. We discuss various *causes* of the French Revolution, or maintain that the Protestant ethic was *the crucial factor* in the development of capitalism; or see divorce rates as *depending* upon the strength of the sibling bond; or matrilateral cross-cousin marriage as *implying* certain structural arrangements. In all these cases we not only recognize an association between two or more factors but we also impute, however tentatively, a vectorial element, a direction.

Comparative sociology (in which I include social anthropology), however, has had little time for causal analysis. Partly this has been the result of the kind of data with which it is dealing, and the kinds of method which it is able to use; here the absence of diachronic data and of the experimental method are of critical importance. But Radcliffe-Brown has also argued that relationships can be analyzed more accurately in terms of co-variation rather than cause, since 'it is the system as a whole which is involved in cause' (1957:42). This approach, which displays a holistic bias, smacks too much of making a virtue out of a necessity; we still continue to think and act in causal terms, which can be dropped from the social sciences only to their detriment, though the appropriate place for their introduction must always be a matter of assessment.

In the social sciences, the problem of cause is twofold. It is not simply a matter of establishing direction but of weighting the different factors. Arguments which centre upon dismissing one cause, or type of causes, in order to establish another (e.g. social versus biological) are of limited usefulness; we need to know the relative influence of a variety of factors on a particular situation; or alternatively we need to examine a variety of consequences of a particular factor. The problem is not one of rejection or acceptance but of measurement and judgment.

The other main problem is one of proof. Hypotheses that account for a set of data are not hard to come by; it is selecting between the alternatives that is a major stumbling block. Do we have to choose on the basis of fashion? Or are there other ways of sifting the proposed theories?

In this paper we try to use one such technique that has been applied to more rigorously collected data than we have at our disposal. We recognize the limitations of this material but it has seemed worth while using these techniques as a method of exploring their possibilities.

The data is derived from a paper* entitled 'Inheritance, property and marriage in Africa and Eurasia' (Goody, 1969) where an attempt was made to show the social institutions that were significantly associated with modes of inheriting (or more strictly devolving) property. The method used was cross-cultural comparison by means of the *Ethnographic Atlas* (Murdock 1967) and the hypotheses to be tested were naturally limited by the information available from that source.

The central hypothesis concerned the concomitants of the transmission of property to both males and females, that is, diverging devolution. This form of transmission was thought to be associated with a greater degree of control over the marriages of women since under this system they are often 'bearers of property'. An index of this control over marriage is shown by the prohibition on pre-marital sex and by forms of in-marriage, that is, by endogamy and by father's brother's daughter's marriage: all of these four variables are coded in the *Atlas*. For in these systems of devolution a man endows all his daughters (either at their marriage by dowry or at his death by inheritance) as well as his sons: he is consequently concerned to see that they marry 'well', in a social and economic sense, and so maintain their position in society. The complex nature of conjugal property is such that each pair forms a kind of corporation (or enters into a specific arrangement), and a premium is therefore placed on monogamous unions rather than polygynous marriages; or, if plural marriage is allowed, then it is likely to involve a distinction between those women married with property ('wives') and those married without ('concubines'). It was also suggested that property-bearing women would influence the pattern of residence because where they acted as sole heirs to a landed estate, the husband would tend to join his wife's family rather than vice versa, a feature described as alternative residence. Finally, the system of direct inheritance within

*This paper is a summary presentation of an article entitled 'Causal inferences concerning inheritance and property', which appeared in *Human Relations*, (1971:294-314); the joint authors are Jack Goody, Barrie Irving and Nicky Tahany. I have included here some sections from that part of the paper for which I was primarily responsible. Further implications relating to Boserup's hypothesis about the role of female farming have been developed in a subsequent paper (with Joan Buckley).

the nuclear family, of which diverging devolution is a type, seemed likely to be associated with kinds of kinship terminology that isolate the sibling group from 'cousins', that is to say, the Eskimo and descriptive terms for persons of ego's own generation.

These variables, all of which are coded in the *Atlas*, were seen as dependent upon diverging devolution. But diverging devolution in turn appeared to depend upon certain specific conditions, namely, the existence of social groups which attempt to retain property within their own ranks. While these forms of stratification are found in complex states, they depend primarily upon the attainment of a certain level of productivity through an intensive use of agricultural resources, by plough, irrigation or other means, which meant that productive property was often in relatively short supply. These linked hypotheses, which together formed a theory concerning the development of and association between certain elements of social organization, were subjected to numerical testing on the data coded in the *Atlas*.

Analytic procedures

The form in which the data was earlier presented (Goody 1969) can be described as an 'implications model'. Correlations were established using the available data and these associations were discussed in terms of the general hypothesis concerning the role of diverging devolution and its influence on other facets of social organization.

Is it possible to test these assumptions and to go further than the kind of diffuse, untestable and infinitely arguable proposition which usually represents the limit of historical and sociological research? Social scientists have recently been encouraged by Simon (1954), Blalock (1960a; 1960b; 1964) and others to try, and these authors have suggested various statistical techniques that might be appropriate for testing causal inferences on non-experimental data.

In this paper we devise a causal model based on the data from the *Ethnographic Atlas*. We first construct a matrix of correlations of the variables involved, which is presented graphically in Fig. 1. From this, we cluster the most closely related variables, and proceed to construct a series of plausible models. The method of path analysis enables us to test each of these arrangements and to reject those which are mathematically inconsistent.

A model may be logically consistent in mathematical terms and yet be theoretically meaningless. Hence, its viability must consist in a combination of theoretical and statistical consistency. In cases where the causal relationships are uncertain (as with the correlations already established), path analysis may be used to find the logical consequences of any particular hypothesis in terms of the available data.

I cannot here go into the details of the procedures used; they can be obtained from the original article and from a variety of other sources, for example, Boudon's paper in the recent collection on method in cultural anthropology, edited by Naroll and Cohen (1970). What we have tried to do is to make them available to the social scientist with little mathematical skill. But I do want to comment briefly on the interpretation of the data. By and large our analysis supports the critical role of plough and intensive agriculture, which has long been assumed by prehistorians (e.g. Childe, 1954; Hole and Flannery, 1967). It suggests the ways in which these changes were connected with the appearance in Babylonia of the type of inheritance I describe as 'diverging devolution' and its associated features of social organization (Driver and Miles, 1952). In other words the model, tested by a comparative survey using ethnographic data and subjected to the techniques of linkage and path analysis, helps to associate changes in the productive systems, detectable by archaeological means, with developments in the sphere of 'family law' and social organization.

Conclusion

'The purpose of path analysis', wrote Duncan, 'is to determine whether a proposed set of interpretations is consistent throughout' (1966:15). The results of applying the combined method of path and linkage analysis support a causal model derived from the original hypothesis. The relative positions of some of the dependent variables undergo some alterations. Nevertheless, the overall trend is to confirm the important implications of diverging devolution. Meanwhile, the relationship with advanced agriculture makes it possible to introduce a vectorial factor into the analysis of certain elements of social structure in a way that is consistent with the evidence provided by history and archaeology. The convergence of ideas from different branches of knowledge provides valuable support for the conclusions derived from any one particular field.

In conclusion, this paper represents the same kind of mixture of theoretical and methodological interests which informs path analysis itself. We offer it neither as God's truth nor yet as hocus pocus, but as a contribution to the solution of problems concerning the development of human institutions. We realize that each of the steps we have taken is surrounded by a diversity of opinion; some prefer non-hierarchical linkages; others doubt the validity of using path analysis with dichotomous variables; others prefer Q to phi in such cases. However, we are prepared to proceed 'as if' the procedures applied to the data, on the grounds that most model building in the social sciences is either cruder or more evasive than the techniques adopted here.

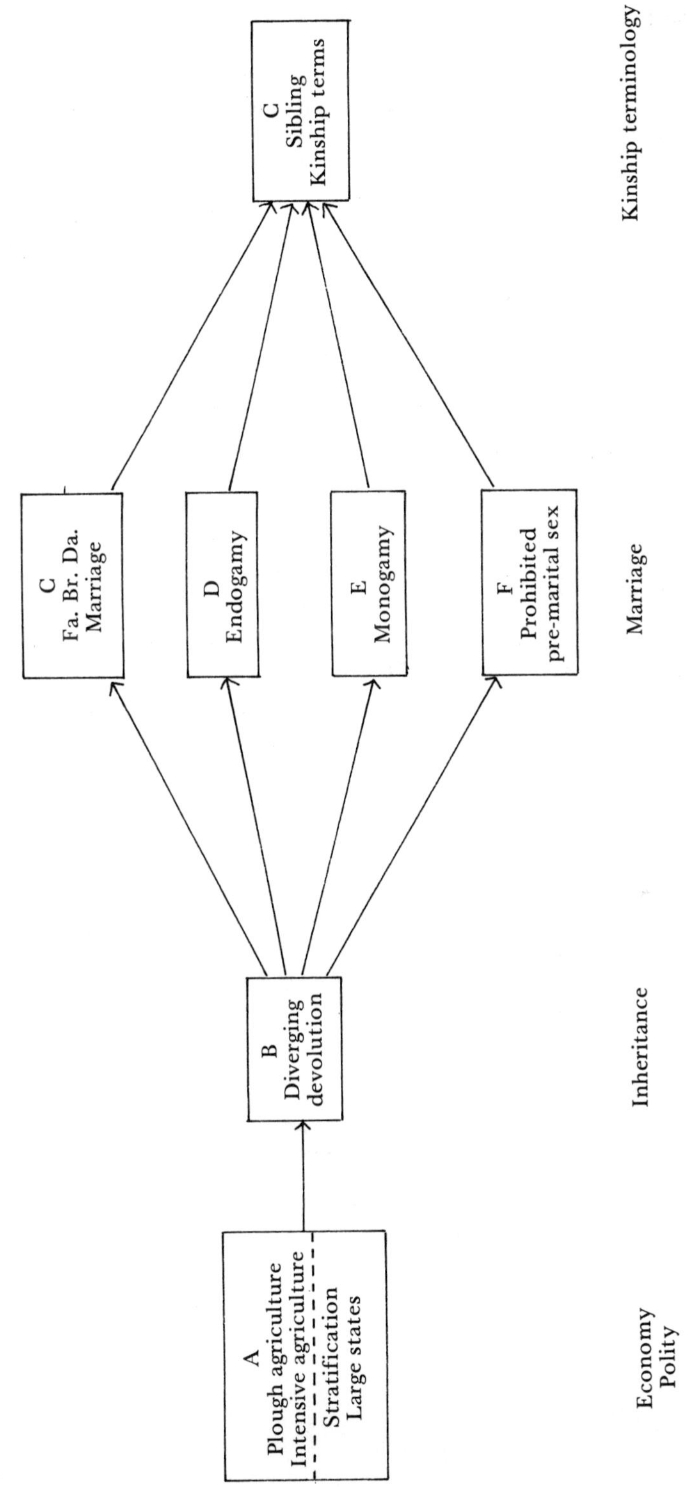

Figure 1 Final Causal Model for Path Analysis.

REFERENCES

Blalock, H.M. (1960a) *Social Statistics*. New York, McGraw-Hill.

Blalock, H.M. (1960b) Correlational analysis and causal inference. *American Anthropologist* 62, 624-31.

Blalock, H.M. (1964) *Causal Inferences in Non-Experimental Research*. Chapel Hill, University of North Carolina Press.

Boudon, R. (1970) A method of linear causal analysis – dependence analysis. *In* Naroll, R. and Cohen, R. (eds.) *A Handbook of Method in Cultural Anthropology*. New York, Natural History Press.

Childe, V.G. (1964) *What Happened in History?* London, Penguin Books (first ed. 1942).

Driver, G.R. and Miles, J.C. (1952) *The Babylonian Laws*. Oxford, Clarendon Press.

Duncan, O.D. (1966) Path analysis: sociological examples. *American Journal of Sociology* 72, 1-16.

Goody, J. (1969) Inheritance, property, and marriage in Africa and Eurasia. *Sociology* 3, 55-76.

Hole, F. and Flannery, K.V. (1967) The prehistory of southwestern Iran: a preliminary report. *Proceedings of the Prehistoric Society* 33, 147-206.

Murdock, G.P. (1967) Ethnographic Atlas. *Ethnology* 6, 106-236.

Radcliffe-Brown, A.R. (1957) *A Natural Science of Society*. Glencoe, Illinois, The Free Press.

Simon, H.A. (1954) Spurious correlation: a causal interpretation. *Journal of the American Statistical Association* 49, 467-79.

CHARLES L. REDMAN

Multivariate approach to understanding changes in an early farming community in southeast Anatolia

The methods of archaeological investigation and analysis must be co-ordinated with the researcher's concept of his subject matter. The subject matter of archaeology is the residue of man's ancient behavioural patterns. In order to organize one's interpretations, archaeologists have often conceived of these behavioural patterns as forming a heuristic composite called culture. Depending on the type of analysis one wishes to pursue, past behaviour can be considered in terms of individual activity sets or the combination of these interrelated activities, i.e., a culture. The perspective through which one views culture directly affects the models to explain change, hypotheses to be tested, and methods that should be employed. I propose that a systems view of culture is both productive of insights and a good approximation of reality. In this perspective culture is defined as an interdependent series of subsystems of activities participated in by the prehistoric people (Binford 1965; Flannery 1967). The archaeologist recognizes these subsystems of activities by the patterning of their artifactual remains preserved in the archaeological record.

If one accepts this systems approach to culture, then it is necessary to examine the archaeological record in a manner that will emphasize the interdependence and patterning of the prehistoric behaviour that has resulted in the present form of the residues. In order to accomplish this, methods of investigation and analysis must be adopted which will recognize the great variability and complexity of socio-cultural systems. Some system theorists would replace the preference for the simpler explanations exemplified by Occam's razor with a dictum that 'systems are complex until proven otherwise' (Watson, LeBlanc, and Redman 1971). Single cause explanations should not be pursued by ignoring other relevant evidence. One cannot condone simplicity in the face of inaccuracy.

The basic proposition put forth in this paper is the explicit formulation of methods of analysis that are appropriate to the hypotheses being tested. The two examples outlined here represent different aspects of this problem. The first involves utilizing the proper variables in making measurements to test a specific hypothesis. The second is a more general multivariate approach to drawing inferences on the relative diversity of activities in the different phases of occupation of a prehistoric community.

Data for both of these examples are drawn from the early village site of Çayönü, in southeastern Turkey. This information was collected during three excavation seasons by the Joint Prehistoric Project of the University of Istanbul and the Oriental Institute of the University of Chicago directed by Halet Çambel and Robert J. Braidwood. The recovered data is currently being analysed with a series of distributional and multivariate statistics. It is extremely important to understand the various changes occurring at the site of Çayönü because its prehistoric occupation spans the transition in subsistence from a primary reliance on hunting and collecting to a major dependence on domesticated plants and animals (Braidwood, Çambel, Redman, and Watson 1971). The transition, coupled with very substantial architecture and the earliest known evidence for worked copper, make Çayönü an exciting laboratory for testing processual hypotheses. The excavated levels were divided into five stratigraphic phases based on observations made during and after their excavation. Though these phases ary utilized as analytical units, it has not yet been concluded whether they are continuous or chronologically distinct. Available radiocarbon dates (Libby half-life, uncorrected) indicate that the prehistoric occupations at Çayönü fall within the range of 6500 to 7500 B.C.

The first hypothesis to be examined is the relative amount of obsidian brought to Çayönü during its different occupational phases by some kind of trading network (moderate distance). The Çayönü data adds an interesting case to the already considerable research conducted on obsidian trading in the Near East (Renfrew, Dixon, Cann 1966; G. Wright 1969). Preliminary analyses of the excavated artifacts from Çayönü reveal a progressively increasing proportion of obsidian to flint pieces in each of the five phases of occupation (see Fig. 1). Though there is variation within each phase, the total value for the ratio of obsidian to flint pieces increases markedly with each successive stratigraphic phase (phase 1 = .05, phase 2 = .20, phase 3 = .52, phase 4 = .98, and phase 5 = 1.02).

The values for this ratio provide an interesting measure of the relative importance of raw materials for utilized tools, but an insufficient measure of the availability of obsidian brought through a trading network. Other related variables must be taken into account if a measure appropriate to the trading hypothesis is to be calculated. By measuring the average weight per piece of obsidian and the average number of pieces per cubic metre excavated in each phase,

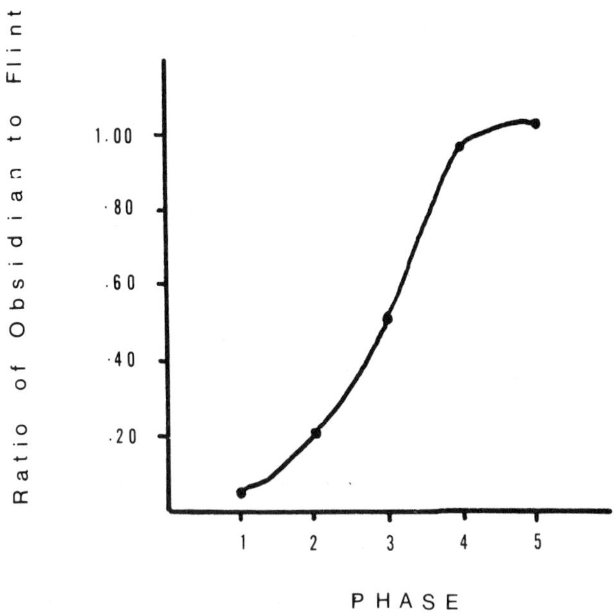

Figure 1 Relative number of obsidian and flint pieces found in each occupational phase at Çayonu.

one can compute the average weight of obsidian per cubic metre. Approximate information on the horizontal distribution of each occupation within the site can be obtained through an intensive systematic surface collection (Redman and Watson 1970). Combining this data with the different stratigraphic excavations of Çayönü, one can estimate with reasonable accuracy the area and depth of each phase and hence the number of cubic metres preserved of each stratigraphic phase.

In Fig. 2 I have incorporated both of these estimates to yield the total weight of obsidian contained in each phase for the total site of Çayönü. Whereas the ratio of obsidian to flint pieces shows a steady increase throughout the occupation of the site, the total weight of obsidian on the site increases only through the first four phases, and falls sharply in the fifth and final preceramic phase. This is because the average weight per piece is one third as much in phase five as in phase four (3.8 versus 1.2 grams) and the relative density of pieces per cubic metre is only one-half, while the area and volume of occupation debris remain relatively constant during phases four and five.

It is possible to further one's understanding of this decrease in the amount of obsidian at Çayönü by examining the shifting ratios of tool types during the last phases. The proportion of obsidian pieces that are cores and core fragments reflects the importance of manufacturing new tools versus reutilization of existing and broken

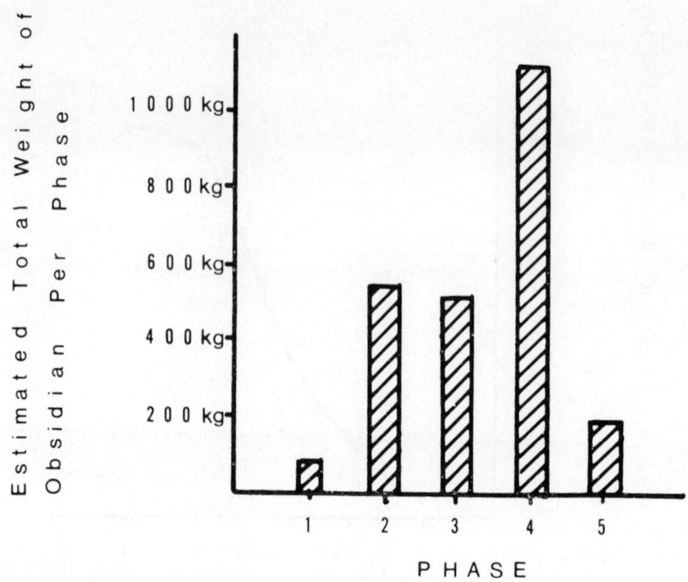

Figure 2 Estimated total weight of obsidian contained in each occupational phase at Çayönü.

pieces. This value remains relatively constant during the first four phases at Çayönü, varying between 5.8% and 7.0%. The proportion of obsidian cores and core fragments falls sharply in the fifth phase to 3.5% which reflects a decline in the manufacturing of new tools. The difference in the results of the methods used in Figs. 1 and 2 for measuring the quantity of obsidian, and the added insight gained from the proportion of cores, are clear illustrations of the fact that one must be certain to collect all of the relevant data and utilize the proper measures for the hypothesis in question.

In addition to testing hypotheses with the distributional analysis of the Çayönü material a series of multivariate statistics are being used to describe the complex assemblage in a simplified manner and to elicit insights into the changes in the systemic structures of the community. Factor analysis was selected as the primary multivariate statistical technique for use with the Çayönü artifacts because it is suited to the assumptions and systems perspective of the research (Cowgill 1968; Harman 1967). Factor analysis is a method of explaining the relationships among numerous variables in terms of simpler relations yet emphasizing the interrelated nature of the assemblage. This is done by examining the covariational patterning of the input variables and then approximating them with a smaller number of hypothetical variables, or factors. Each factor is interpreted as reflecting a possible tool kit or complex of tools that were used by the prehistoric occupants (Binford and Binford 1966). Factor analysis determines which excavation units were decisive in the formation of the factors and prints these values as factor scores. I suggest that these scores reflect where the tool kits were being used, or what may be interpreted as the different activity areas of the site.

The factor analysis of the chipped stone artifacts from Çayönü utilized a varimax rotation and an input of the raw counts of artifacts divided into 125 categories from 157 excavation units. The categories are types defined on the basis of material from various sites in the Near East. By examining the diminishing eigenvalues, a solution with eighteen factors was selected for analysis. The factors seem to reflect reasonable clusters of tool types. Six of the factors were composed of flint types only, six of obsidian types only, and six were mixed flint and obsidian. Five general functional types could be assigned to the factors: manufacturing of blades or flakes, general utility, scraping, points, and pieces with sheen.

The results of a factor analysis are applicable to the formulation or testing of models based on a systemic view of culture. The distribution of factor scores for each of the factors, or tool kits during each of the chronological phases offers a useful measure of the number of different activities being performed and the relative importance of each. In this way it is possible to determine whether activities were limited in their temporal span or occurred in every phase. Fig. 3 shows the proportion of high scores for each of the factors separated into the five stratigraphic phases on the site. The graph indicates that in the first phase at Çayönü there were a relatively limited number of activities involving chipped stone. This agrees with the faunal and floral data that imply it was a hunting and collecting community with no agriculture. The lack of any large scale architecture implies that it might have been only a seasonal encampment. Phases two and three have a broader, even distribution of activities reflecting the functioning of a more substantial community. There is the possibility of experimentation with agriculture during these phases in addition to the hunting and collecting pursuits. In phases four and five there is a shift to fewer activities with some being more important than others. This may be attributed to an increasing dependence on agriculture and specialization occurring in these phases.

These changes in distribution of factor scores can be represented quantitatively by a coefficient of variability (J. Wright 1937; Whallon 1968). I employ the following modification of this statistic: $C = 1 - \frac{2(p-c)}{p(n-1)}$, where p equals one hundred per cent, n equals the possible number of categories (eighteen factors), and c equals the cumulative percentage taking the largest categories first. This coefficient is a measure of the dispersion or specialization of activities and varies from 0.0, or an even distribution of all activities in all categories, to 1.0, which implies that all activity is centred in one category. Phase one shows a high value (.81) and reflects the

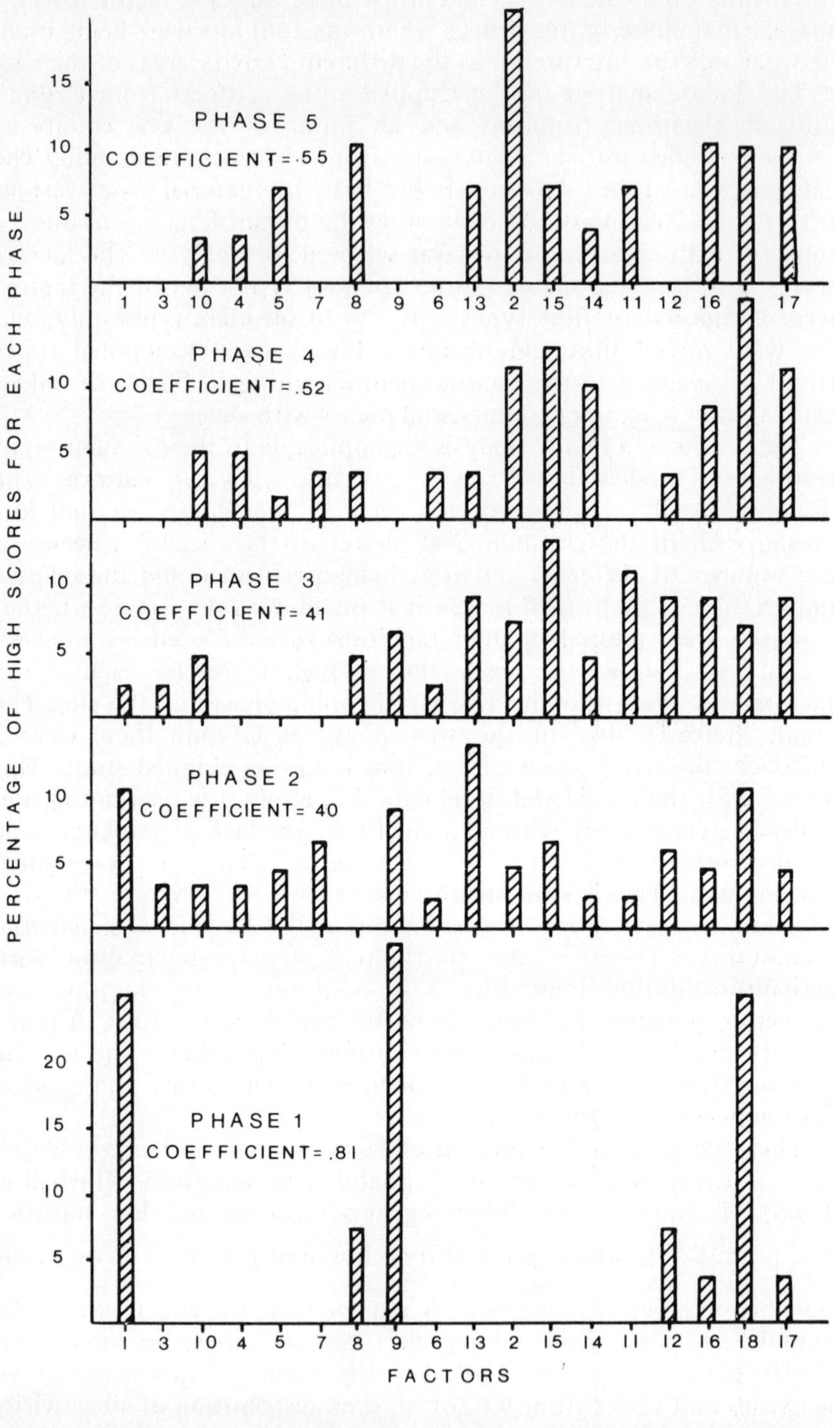

Figure 3 Histograms of high factor scores in each phase of the prehistoric sequence at Çayonu.

high intensity of only a few activities. Phase two (.40) and three (.41) are characterized by diversity of activities with none predominating. Phases four (.52) and five (.55) show an increase in the importance of some activities at the cost of others. The quantitative values of this statistic confirm the subjective evaluation of Fig. 3, that the earliest phases are characterized by few activities, the middle phases by many, and the later phases by a re-emerging specialization, perhaps accompanying the effective employment of agriculture.

Being an inductive technique, the results of a factor analysis should be confirmed with independent tests on other data. This is currently being done with other categories of artifacts, such as bone tools, ground stone, and clay pieces. The basic pattern of maximum diversity of activities during the second and third phases is generally reaffirmed by these results.

A multivariate statistic such as factor analysis is useful because it incorporates information from numerous variables simultaneously. This is in accord with system theory's assumption of the interrelatedness of behavioural patterns. By investigating the proportionate distribution of activities in each occupation level it is possible to derive a more meaningful view of structural changes in the community than by examining changes in proportions of individual tool types. The examples described in this paper are attempts to devise measuring and analytical methods appropriate to the specific hypotheses being tested and more generally to a multivariate approach to culture change. By continued efforts to formulate relevant and precise research strategies, it will be possible to increase the scope and reliability of models of cultural change.

REFERENCES

Binford, L.R. (1965) Archaeological systematics and the study of culture process. *American Antiquity* 31 (2), 203-10.

Binford, L.R. and S.R. (1966) A preliminary analysis of functional variability in the Mousterian of Levallois facies. *In* Clark, J.D. and Howell, F.C. (eds.) *Recent Studies in Palaeoanthropology* (American Anthropologist **68**, no. 2, part 2, 238-95).

Braidwood, R.J., Çambel, H., Redman, C.L. and Watson, P.J. (1971) Beginnings of village-farming communities in southeastern Turkey. *Proceedings of the National Academy of Sciences* **68**, 1236-40.

Cowgill, G. (1968) Archaeological applications of factor, cluster, and proximity analysis. *American Antiquity* **33**, 367-75.

Flannery, K.V. (1967) Culture history v. culture process: a debate in American archaeology. *Scientific American* **217** (2), 119-22.

Harman, H.H. (1967) *Modern Factor Analysis.* Chicago, University Press.

Redman, C.L. and Watson, P.J. (1970) Systematic, intensive surface collection. *American Antiquity* **35**, 279-91.

Renfrew, C., Dixon, J.E. and Cann, J.R. (1966) Obsidian and early culture contact in the Near East. *Proceedings of the Prehistoric Society* **32**, 30-72.

Watson, P.J., LeBlanc, S.A. and Redman, C.L. (1971) *Explanation in Archae-*

ology: An Explicitly Scientific Approach. New York, Columbia University Press.

Whallon, R.C. (1968) Investigations of late prehistoric social organization in New York. *In* Binford, S.R. and L.R. (eds.) *New Perspectives in Archaeology*, 223-44. Chicago, Aldine.

Wright, G. (1969) *Obsidian Analyses and Prehistoric Near Eastern Trade: 7500 to 3500 B.C.* Anthropological Papers no. 37. Museum of Anthropology, University of Michigan.

Wright, J.K. (1937) Some measures of distributions. *Annals of the Association of American Geographers* 27, 177-211.

EVŽEN NEUSTUPNÝ

Factors determining the variability of the Corded Ware culture

It is increasingly accepted that the traditional methods of archaeology, known and practised since the time of the great Scandinavian archaeologists in the last century and the beginnings of the present one, have exhausted their potential. While in parts of the world archaeologically not yet well known, such methods can still offer much new information, in other regions they cause the stagnation of both archaeology and prehistory. The best demonstration of this is that in some cases archaeological knowledge has not notably increased in recent decades despite the rapidly growing volume of archaeological evidence available.

The central problem of modern archaeology and prehistory has two aspects. One is the search for structures among the archaeological data; the other is the construction of models able to explain those structures, i.e. to give them some meaning for contemporary humanity. I have tried to show elsewhere that prehistorical models cannot be obtained through archaeology alone but must be derived from outside. The construction of such models should become as scientific a procedure as their testing by means of archaeological finds – this being the major point of our disagreement with some of the so-called process-oriented archaeologists for whom models (or hypotheses) seem to come from heaven or, at best, from common sense.

The generation of archaeological structures can in part be accomplished by so-called multivariate techniques. These have now been widely used in many parts of the world although often their potentialities have not been fully exploited. Even if a configuration in several dimensions is obtained, only one of these is usually used and explained. Among the few exceptions, the best perhaps is the analysis of Mousterian assemblages by the Binfords. But if only one dimension is used, the multivariate technique becomes just a simple seriation, which in most cases yields nothing more than chronological ordering.

I have recently performed a series of multivariate analyses of archaeological finds from various periods, and report here on one of them concerning the variability of the Corded Ware culture of Bohemia. This late eneolithic culture (ca. 2900 to 2450 B.C.) is known exclusively from graves. Some 300 sites have been recorded from Bohemia alone, and several hundreds from neighbouring regions. I selected 134 well excavated graves from all over Bohemia and 120 graves from a single cemetery (Vikletice) in the northwest. Ten major types (or group of types) have been examined: (1) beakers B, (2) handled jugs C, (3) ovoid pots D, (4) beakers with lugs E, (5) small cups without handles J, (6) cups with one handle P, (7) cups with two handles or lugs N, (8) stone hammer-axes and/or maces HA/DK, (9) stone axes B1, and (10) ornaments Or. The reason for this selection as well as the details of the methods used will be described elsewhere. Factor analysis, principal components and cluster analysis were applied, all yielding similar results. The results of the factor analysis will be discussed here in more detail.

As two independent samples from the same population were available it was possible to select factors appearing in both, which could consequently be supposed to be of real significance. Three such factors occurred, all of them typically bipolar. They represent, however, a minimum number of meaningful dimensions since each of the samples could, at least theoretically, include more than a single unique factor. The three factors taken together accounted only for about one half of the total variance of the samples and, in view of the small number of graves used in the analyses, random variance must be enormous. The rotated factors common to both the samples have been summarized in Table 1.

At least three formal structures have thus been generated, each consisting of ten types, and the next task is to devise models able to explain them. In this simple example, our previous knowledge of the Corded Ware culture is very helpful, so that we need not reproduce the whole process of forming the models. This is a problem I have tried to tackle elsewhere.

Despite the fact that the samples did not offer any direct and explicit information on the sex of persons interred with the ten types, the first type was clearly recognized as reflecting cultural sexual dimorphism. The highest positive loadings are associated with ornaments, the negative loadings with weapons and axes – typical male equipment. Some of the pottery types included in the sample are also more typically associated with one of the sexes. This was found to be equally true of other types of vessels, and even of some types of decoration not included in the multivariate sample.

Amphorae decorated with engraved patterns, for example, are frequent in graves of women, while amphorae with some other types of decoration occur indiscrimately with remains both of men and women. The results of this multivariate analysis can fortunately be verified, at least in the case of the first factor, by very simple means,

Table 1

	Factor 1				Factor 2				Factor 3		
	CW & V	V	CW		CW & V	V	CW		CW & V	V	CW
Bl	.44	.36	.41	B	.33	.44	.26	E	.50	.54	.47
HA/DK	.42	.52	.40	Bl	.25	.28	.28	Bl	.21	.30	.17
B	.23	.33	.13	J	.22	.12	.20	C	.19	.07	.31
E	.16	.20	.09	HA/DK	.12	.05	.19	D	.06	.03	.06
C	.14	.13	.22	E	.01	–.02	.10	HA/DK	.05	.12	–.05
N	–.05	.06	–.10	Or	–.01	–.11	–.06	P	.02	.03	–.02
P	–.11	–.24	.04	P	–.08	–.-4	–.35	N	.02	–.02	.09
D	–.22	–.24	–.14	C	–.30	–.33	–.30	J	.00	–.05	–.01
J	–.48	–.40	–.52	N	–.54	–.61	–.40	Or	–.04	–.06	–.06
Or	–.54	–.27	–.74	D	–.67	–.70	–.64	B	–.59	–.53	–.61

CW — Bohemian Corded Ware from sites other than Vikletice

V — Corded Ware from Vikletice

namely the simple correlation coefficient of each of our types with the position of the skeleton on its right side (males) or the left side (females). It also agrees with the results obtained by physical anthropologists directly on the skeletons. Few reliable determinations of sex on this basis, however, are available.

The second factor can be identified as the chronological coordinate. The types with high positive loadings are characteristic of the early phase of the Bohemian Corded ware, while those on the opposite end belong to the late phase of the culture. The types, however, have been defined so generally that no exact chronology can be derived from this factor.

The third factor, which appears in both independent samples, is something of a surprise. A comparison with the first two factors shows clearly that it is neither sexual nor chronological. The strongest opposition is between beakers (B) and lugged beakers (E), although these two types are in fact chronologically almost exclusive.

A possible explanation, which has to be tested on a wider sample, is that this factor selects male equipment, sorting it chronologically. This may be the reason why nearly all the types except beakers, lugged beakers, stone axes (and possibly hammer-axes and jugs) have insignificant loadings in respect of this factor. The reason for this phenomenon, however, would be different with various types: with the hammer-axes it would be caused by their chronological position between the two poles (in other words: they were equally typical for both the early and late phases of the Bohemian Corded Ware), while with the 'female' types the near-zero loading would be caused by their irrevelance in respect to the factor.

The exponents of traditional archaeology could argue that the above statements could have been achieved without complicated mathematical methods. But we can show that this view is not correct. Dr. Buchvaldek studied the Bohemian Corded Ware culture by traditional methods intensively for almost a quarter of a century. After so many years of thorough examination of several hundreds of Corded Ware graves he could only state that weapons and stone axes were typical of male graves while ornaments and small cups (J) represented graves of women. He did not discover that other goods, predominently pottery, also differed according to the sex of the deceased. Although he originally set up a more or less correct chronological scheme for Bohemian Corded Ware, he later abandoned it in favour of ethnical speculations, and considered the types divided by our bipolar factor two as manifestations of two different ethnical units. He did not recognize at all that anything like our third factor might have been of importance.

In addition to discovering clear structures among the data, the method has at the same time been able to quantify them. There are some differences in the two samples we studied and a good explanation can be found for most of the observed discrepancies.

Some very rare types have intentionally been included (such as, for example, the cups with one handle P, of which only 8 and 2 instances respectively occur in the two samples). These proved to be the least stable elements. This phenomenon limits the extension of the method to the study of more types (and sub-types), at least as far as samples of small size are concerned.

The scientific study of the Bohemian Corded Ware culture has only just begun and the data included in this analysis represent only a small fraction of the still undeciphered information contained in the finds. Nevertheless, some important new aspects can already be stated. First, the first factor reveals a large-scale cultural sexual dimorphism which can perhaps be put as follows: there were two distinct subcultures in the Corded Ware culture, one male and the other female. It is possible that a stronger polarization could be obtained by using sub-types instead of our general types.

The analysis did not reveal any age groupings, though the Corded Ware cemeteries quite often include graves of juveniles, i.e. graves of individuals aged approximately 12 years and onwards. This may suggest that these individuals, according to our modern standards children, were treated as adults in the late eneolithic. This question, however, must be investigated in the course of future research, as simple analysis of variance has shown that graves of the children class are significantly smaller than those of adults. Further detailed research may discover a weak age sub-culture not discernible by our generalizing methods.

If our interpretation of the third factor is right, we have to suggest that the beaker was an important item among the grave goods to which some special significance was attributed (together perhaps with other associated types not mentioned here) by the Corded Ware people.

The findings show that the main dividing criterion in the Corded Ware society was sex. This, of course, is not simply a natural division but a social one. Otherwise one could hardly explain why the male and the female sub-cultures differ not only in ornaments, tools and weapons but in pottery form and decoration also. On the other hand, if age sub-cultures existed at all, they were weak. This situation contrasts with that of many other prehistoric cultures, where graves of men and women differ solely in personal ornaments, tools and weapons, and where there is a marked difference between the graves of children and those of adults. All these facts offer a deeper insight into this particular prehistoric society. By applying such methods to more diverse material one can perhaps discover a greater number of social structures and even tackle the problem of the real nature of social evolution in prehistory.

Acknowledgment

The author is grateful to Mr Jan Kaspar from the Centre of Numerical Mathematics at the Charles University in Prague for writing the necessary computer programs.

REFERENCES

Buchvaldek, M. (1967) *Die Schnurkeramik in Böhmen.* Prague.

Buchvaldek, M. and Koutecký, D. (1970) *Vikletice, ein schnurkeramisches Gräberfeld.* Prague.

Neustupný, E. (1967a) Základni prehistorické modely. *Dèhiny a soucasnost* IX-4: 32-4.

Neustupný, E. (1967b) *K pocatkum patriarchátu ve stredni Evrope*, Prague, Academia.

WILLIAM L. RATHJE

Models for mobile Maya: a variety of constraints

1. Introduction

Archaeological models of change within cultural systems are 'synthetic systems' that isolate and define the dynamic relationship between variables critical to the processes of change. These abstract models can be used to predict the behaviour through time of the material remains of extant or extinct cultural systems. If the patterns developed from the synthetic systems replicate patterns on the ground, the synthetic systems are retained and expanded. If not, new models are constructed.

This paper will construct synthetic systems that generate parameters of change within and between Lowland Classic Maya (800 B.C. – A.D. 900) cultural systems. The material remains patterns generated from the synthetic systems will be tested by comparison with Lowland Classic Maya burial patterns through the use of a Material Culture/Social Mobility model.

2. Variety and constraints

All systems produce patterned variety. Constraints describe the interaction parameters of the variables that produce patterned variety. The concepts of 'variety' and 'constraints', as outlined by Ashby (1968) can be utilized to structure the internal interaction parameters of the components of synthetic cultural systems.

Variety, for the purposes of this paper, can simply be defined as the potential number of arrangements of distinct elements in a system. Thus, for each specific application of the concept of variety, the 'elements' must be defined. Once variety is identified, the constraints upon that variety can be isolated. Constraints control variety. For example, the elements of variety can be defined as six men (A,B,C,D,E,F). One aspect of variety is the potential number of ways the six men can be placed in a single file (after Ashby 1968 and

Luebbermann, personal communication). With no constraints there would be a variety of 720 possible orderings (ABCDEF, BACDEF, CBADEF, DCBAEF, etc.). A slight constraint would be applied if the men were ordered by eye colour, blue (left) to brown (right). If A, B and C have blue eyes and D, E and F have brown eyes, there are still 36 potential orderings (ABC/DEF, ACB/DEF, ACB/DFE, etc.). The constraint of ordering the men by absolute height, tall to short, is severe and allows no variety in the way the men are placed in a file. 'The intensity of the constraint is thus shown by the reduction it causes in the number of possible arrangements', i.e. in variety (Ashby 1968:130).

3. A definition of variety within cultural systems

This paper will attempt to describe the effect of some of the constraints upon the variety within Lowland Classic Maya cultural systems through time. Variety within cultural systems, for present purposes, is defined as the number of different arrangements of specific households and small kin groups (the 'elements') possible within economic, social, religious, political and other status hierarchies.

In order to test for variety it is assumed that measurements of 'Mobility potential' (cf. section 14) are measures of the amount of variety within cultural systems. If the constraints on variety are minimized, then the potential for mobility within status hierarchies is maximized and a large number of arrangements of households will be possible and will actually occur through time. If constraints on variety are maximized, then mobility potential is minimized and only a limited number of arrangements will be possible and will actually occur through time. Mobility potential varies directly with the amount of variety within a cultural system, i.e. increased mobility potential means more variety through time.

4. Culture change: variable and constant constraints

Both variable and constant constraints set the parameters of 'possible arrangements'. Within complex cultural systems many sources of constraint, such as population size and technology, vary directly with changes in variety. Population size has been hypothesized to be one important constraint which effected the variety within Classic Maya cultural systems (Rathje 1970, 1971a, in press). This hypothesis accurately predicted that, other factors constant, in each Classic Maya system where population increased, the mobility potential (variety) decreased. However, the relationship of mobility potential at specific times between specific Classic Maya systems could not be predicted by population constraints alone.

Some important constraints upon complex cultural systems, such as ecological variety and geographic position, often remain constant as others vary. In any consideration of change the constraints that remain constant upon systems, as well as the constraints that vary, must be defined. By constructing a model of constant constraints (basic resource, ecological and geographic) on specific Lowland Maya cultural systems, parameters of change within and between systems can be predicted that supplement the parameters predicted by variable constraints.

5. Constant constraints: Pan-Lowland Constraint 1

Some of the most critical constraints in any cultural system occur at the interface of environment and technology. Every household (the minimum production-consumption unit, i.e. nuclear family, extended family, etc.) needs basic resources to efficiently exploit a given eco-zone. Basic resources are defined as those which are present archaeologically, ethnohistorically, and ethnographically, in every household in a specific subsistence configuration – in this case the maize agriculture and/or silviculture complex. At least three resources were basic enough to the standard efficiency of Classic Maya subsistence patterns to be imported to all parts of the Maya Lowlands in all time periods: igneous or hard stone metates for grinding corn, razor sharp obsidian tools, and salt (cf. Rathje 1971a and 1971b for the rationale behind the selection of these resources; for a similar definition and use of 'basic resource' see Fried 1967:52, 186-7, 191 and Leone 1968:43, 126-8).

Most areas of highland Mesoamerica are not far from one or more sources of these essentials. In the Central Maya Lowlands (Fig. 1), however, they are few and far between. Basic household tools and condiments were imported everywhere in the lowlands in quantity and over considerable distances (Rathje 1971a:57-67). The lack of variety in basic resources was a constant constraint (Constraint 1) on lowland cultural systems. Although Constraint 1 (basic resources) applied to the entire lowlands, its effect was not the same throughout. It was acted upon by other constant constraints that occurred differentially in the Central Maya Lowlands.

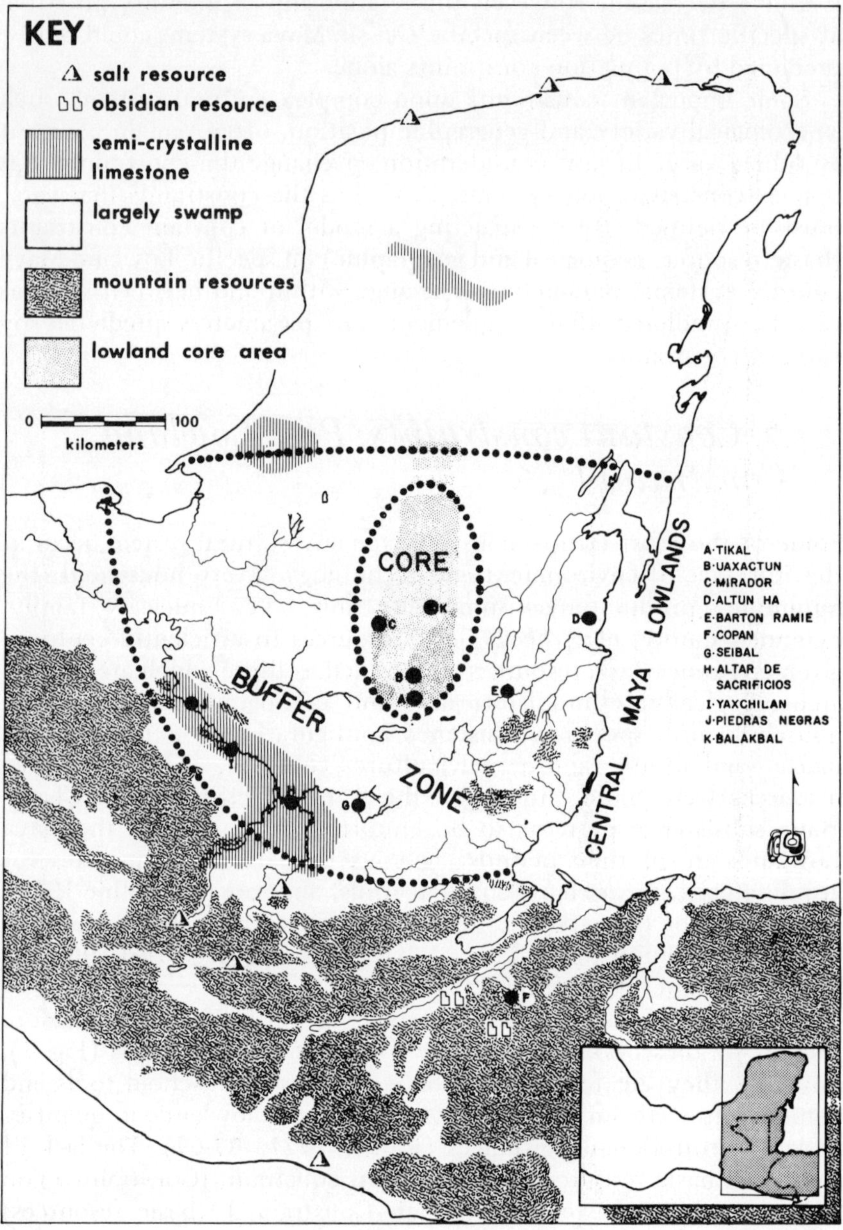

Figure 1 The Central Maya lowlands.

6. The core/buffer zone dichotomy of constant constraints

A model of sectors within the Central Maya Lowlands can be based on differential constraints upon cultural systems. These constraints take the form of differences in ecological variety and geographic limitations. Large lowland areas in Mesoamerica can be divided into two parts (Fig. 1): (1) The outer *buffer zone* borders highland resource areas and contains or borders major bulk-transport systems (rivers and the Atlantic Ocean). The clustering of tropical rainforest with several other eco-zones creates general ecological variety throughout the buffer zone. (2) The inner *core* area is landlocked and sequestered from highland resources by the buffer zone. Tropical rainforest is the only major eco-system in the core and general ecological variety is minimal.

This division is between areas with relatively easy access to, and areas with restricted access to, basic resources. It is also between an area with one major ecological configuration, and an area where that one and several others cluster. The core and the buffer zone impose different constraints upon complex cultural systems.

7. Core constant constraints

In the core Constraint 1 interacted with two additional constraints upon the variety within cultural systems. Constraint 2 upon core systems was limited ecological variety. Constraint 3 was the core's isolated geographic position (spatial distance from basic resources) and the total lack of bulk-transport systems. Constraint 1 (basic resources) required that non-local commodities be imported from the buffer zone and/or highland resource areas. Constraint 2 (ecological) and 3 (geographic) severely limited the potential variety of resource exchange interactions.

Constraint 3 (geographic) narrowed the variety of exchange interactions to 'long-distance' trade carried out by complex resource procurement organizations. Long-distance trade was not merely an extension of face-to-face exchanges common in highland market systems (Chapman 1957:115; Thompson 1964). In pre-mule days the upper limit a single cargador could carry into large lowland areas was 100 lbs., i.e. two metates and six manos. The difficulties of consistently supplying large inland areas were considerable. The core's geographic position, translated into transport of goods, time investments, and the dangers of long distance travel selected against independent household procurement efforts. Because of Constraint 3 (geographic), the prerequisites of successful procurement of resources were capital accumulation and complex organization for security and leadership far above that which a single household could muster.

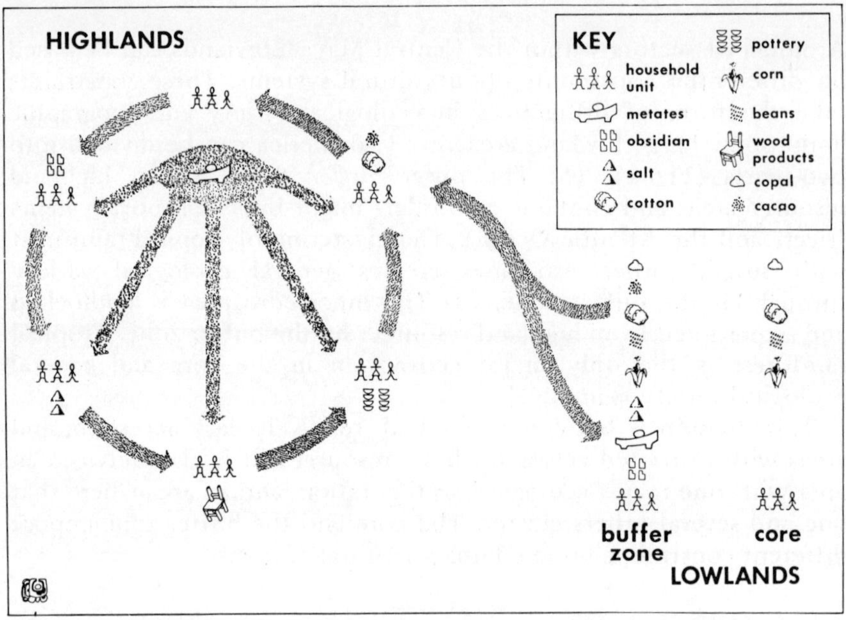

Figure 2 A model of the exchange potential of natural resources between highland, *buffer zone*, and *core* areas.

Traders need items with exchange potential. All core resources were duplicated in the buffer zone so that there was little potential for core/buffer zone trade in natural resources. Highland markets for lowland products could be more easily supplied by buffer zone neighbours than by core long-distance traders. Thus, there was little potential for exchange of core natural resources for other basic commodities (Fig. 2). Constraint 2 (ecological) selected for the development of scarce 'artificial' resources.

If complex organization is necessary to procure resources, then community ceremonial interaction and luxury paraphernalia are equally necessary to maintain local core stratification and organization (cf. Flannery 1968:100; Fried 1967:32; Rappaport 1967:105-7; Binford 1962). The products and services that reinforced community integration and complex organizations were recognized as 'artificial' scarce resources with exchange potential. Constraint 2 (ecological) selected for complex organizations and resource concentration to produce trade items through support of craft specialization (ceremonial paraphernalia – polychrome pottery, decorated textiles, carved wooden objects, featherwork, etc.) and esoteric knowledge production (calendrics, glyphic writing, stone carving, etc.). The production of such commodities for long-distance exchange was also beyond the capacity of individual households and reinforced the need for complex resource concentration and procurement systems (Fig. 3).

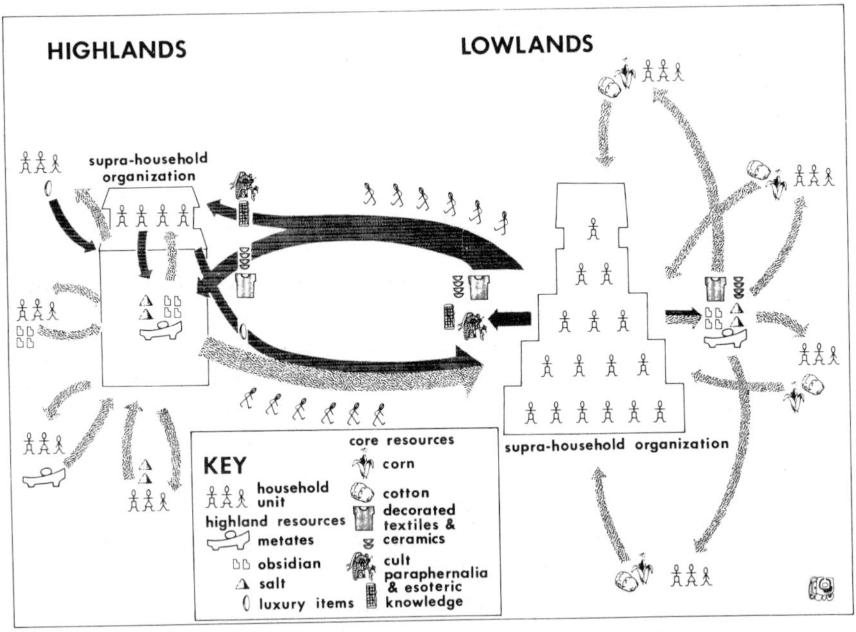

Figure 3 A model of the exchange functions of the *core*'s cult organization.

For trade in basic resources to reach every household consistently, goods and authority, extracted at the expense of every household had to be concentrated within a highly organized procurement system. Constraint 1 (basic resources), Constraint 2 (ecological) and Constraint 3 (geographic) selected for lowland development in socio-political interaction and organization (cf. Sahlins 1958, 1963; Fried 1967). The core ceremonial centre provided the supra-household capital, organizational potential, and integration of scattered population for successful resource procurement and redistribution. The ceremonial centre/sustaining area system was the minimal unit of autonomous economics (cf. Leone 1968:127-8) (for tests of this construct see Rathje 1971a, 1971b).

8. *The synthetic core cultural system*

From the constraints discussed above, a 'synthetic' core cultural system can be described (Fig. 4). CH represents the minimum core production-consumption unit – the individual household. CH_1 represents all of the subsistence households in the sustaining area of one ceremonial system. To move through the system, start at CH_1 when a harvest is collected. The arrows in the diagram stand for actions or processes.

Action Set 1 represents the consumption and storage of part of the harvest. This process provided the nutrition and the resources to be invested in gaining subsistence from the limited set of core natural resources. In the core Constraint 2, the availability of the same limited range of ecological variety to all, placed constraints upon the amount of resulting variety in return on investments of labour and capital. Action Set 1 is the only basic viable investment opening for household resources independent of the complex resource procurement organization, System A.

Trade as an extension of the lowland core environment required that individual household resources be concentrated. Thus, a major part of the household harvest was invested in System A_1. Action Set 2 represents the process of resource concentration as households invested in the ceremonial centre system's functions. The actions supported, especially craft production and other aspects of long-distance trade, required a constant influx of resources to be manipulated by a few individuals.

Action Set 3 represents craft production. Action Set 4 represents public conspicuous consumption (stelae construction, temples, palaces, etc.). Action Set 5 stands for the local distribution of local craft items. These action sets provided the trappings indicative of a successful procurement organization. The Vector of Sets 3, 4 and 5 culminated in lavish burials and other complex ritual potlatches which produced community integration and distribution of local craft items that *supported* status networks and filtered down as a strong positive feedback to the small investor. It is assumed in the system that the return (economic, social, political, etc.) on individual household investments was relatively proportional to the original investment. Action Set 6 represents strong ideological and sociological investment returns and investment incentives in the form of social status, status items, and ideological cohesion. Action Set 6 continually reactivated Action Set 2.

Some of the resources invested in System A_1 went directly into supporting bearers, merchants, trade routes, and trade factories. Those craft items that did not follow Action Set 5 followed Action Set 7 and were exchanged for highland and buffer zone resources. Two kinds of resources were procured – basic resources and exotic resources. The exotic items followed Action Set 9 to local redistribution in Action Set 6. The basic resources, for the most part, followed Action Set 11. These basic commodities (salt, obsidian, metates) formed the second part of the prerequisites to production and maintenance of CH_1. Action Set 11 also continually reactivated Action Set 2. Investment in both Action Set 1 and Action Set 2, System A_1, was essential to the survival of the local household.

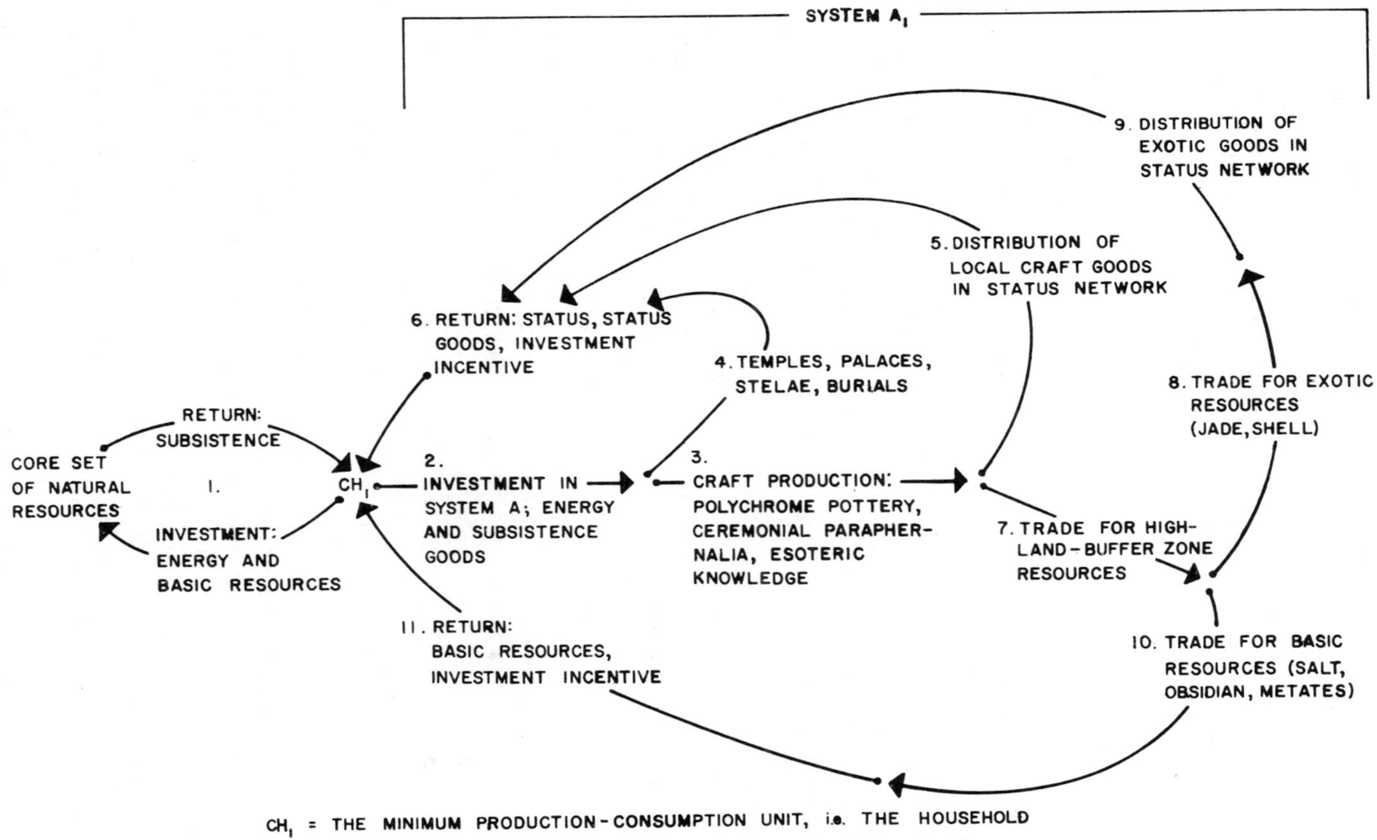

Figure 4 Classic Maya core ceremonial centre — individual household system

9. Buffer zone constant constraints

Constraints 2 (ecological) and 3 (geographic) are not severe in the buffer zone. The buffer zone abuts highland resource areas, trade routes and the Atlantic Ocean, which at the time of the Conquest was a major means of bulk transportation (Thompson 1964, 1970). Several navigable river systems (the Usumacinta, Pasion, Chixoy, Hondo, Belize, New, etc.) run through the buffer zone. The tropical rainforest in the buffer zone is broken by clusters of other eco-zones (alluvial, riverine, ocean, etc.). The ecological variety provides rainforest products (cotton, copal, dyes, etc.), cacao and other alluvial products, and marine shell and fish – all with high exchange potential in highland resource areas.

Thus, the geographic position and ecological variety of the buffer zone placed few constraints upon highland/buffer zone trade interactions. As a result, the effect of Constraint 1 (basic resources) upon buffer zone systems was rather limited. This situation was expressed in the wide range of variation in socio-political organization that occurred in the buffer zone. Complex organizations developed with the first settlements in, and until the 'collapse' were maintained throughout, the core (cf. W. Coe 1963). Unlike the core, the variaton in socio-political organizations within the buffer zone was great. Some systems were poorly developed in the Early Classic, but rivalled core systems in complexity in the Late Classic (i.e. Yaxchilan and Piedras Negras on the Usumacinta River and Copan on the Copan River in Honduras – Fig. 1). However, many areas, especially in Belize and around Lake Izabal, remained devoid of major ceremonial centre systems (cf. Willey *et al.* 1965).

10. The buffer zone synthetic system

Complex systems that did develop in the buffer zone functioned somewhat like the core's System A_1. However, BZH_1 (buffer zone households) had the potential of investing resources in additional action sets created by ecological variety and access to the highlands (Fig. 5). The core Action Set 1 was replaced by Action Set 1′, 1″, and 1‴. The core had a limited range of natural resources available to most households. In the buffer zone several ecological zones were within reach of most households. For example, Altun Ha (Fig. 1) is located one mile inland from the Belize coast. Exploitation of seafood and/or exotic resources, estuary exploitation, and slash-and-burn agriculture are all possible subsistence (Action Set 1′, 1″, 1‴) activities. A variety in avenues of investment created a potential for differential returns on investments.

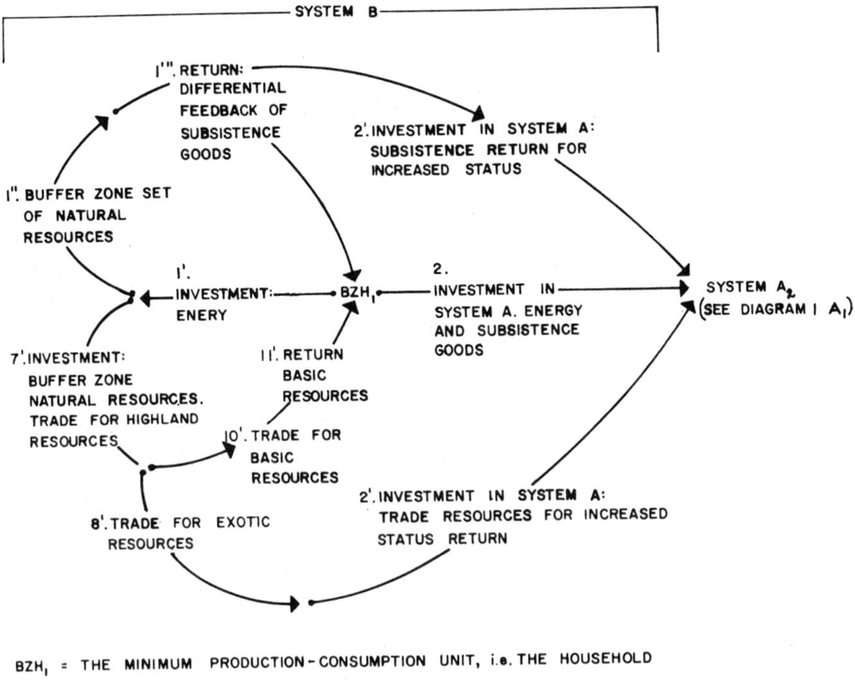

Figure 5 The test implications of core/buffer zone synthetic systems.

Additional action sets also provided the buffer zone with the potential for independent procurement efforts. Due to differential resource distribution, bulk-transport systems, and proximity to the highlands, households and small kin groups had the potential to independently collect local natural resources and exchange them for highland products (Fig. 2). Exchanges could have been made in the highlands or locally along buffer zone-highland trade routes. Action Sets 7′, 8′ and 11′ in System B are alternatives to the actions in System A_2. Thus, additional differential returns on investment were possible independent of System A_2.

System A_2 functioned as a social, political and ceremonial interaction sphere as well as a procurement organization. Households invested in System A_2 for social, political, and ceremonial returns as well as for ease of resource procurement. System B merely provided an alternative for obtaining a variety of investment returns independent of System A_2. Many of System B's returns were invested in Actions Sets 2 and 2′ to obtain new status positions within System A_2's hierarchies.

11. The law of requisite variety and synthetic systems' test implications

The parameters of variety in the core and buffer zone cultural systems, defined in terms of the number of possible arrangements of households within status hierarchies, can be predicted. The predictions can be generated from the core and buffer zone synthetic systems and from the *law of requisite variety*: variety is required to create or destroy variety (Ashby 1968).

From the core area/buffer zone model it can be deduced that constant constraints affected the parameters of social mobility potential (internal variety) within Classic Maya systems. Because of Constraint 3 (geographic), core area households could not independently procure basic commodities. Status hierarchies (which by definition involved differential access to resources) developed as a prerequisite of basic resource procurement. To obtain resources households were forced to invest heavily in highly stratified systems (System A_1) which concentrated resources in ways that constrained social mobility potential and reinforced the established order. Because of Constraint 2, a limited ecological range available to all, differential distribution of resources based upon differential investment in a variety of eco-zones was minimized. In sum, the core area lacked ecological variety and variety in trade interactions. From the law of requisite variety it follows that core systems lacked internal variety, i.e. mobility potential.

In the buffer zone ecological variety, spatial position, and bulk-transport systems allowed variety in subsistence investment and variety in trade interactions. Households had the potential of changing economic statuses outside of System A_2 and then using that change to transform social and political statuses within System A_2. From the law of requisite variety it follows that because the buffer zone systems had more ecological and trade interaction variety than core systems, buffer zone systems should have more internal variety than core systems, i.e. more mobility potential than core systems.

The test implication of core and buffer zone synthetic systems states that: given relatively similar fluctuations in variable constraints in the core and buffer zone systems, through time there will be more variety within buffer zone systems than within core systems.

12. A model of social mobility

The ability of the core and buffer zone synthetic systems to predict accurately the parameters of variety can be briefly tested by using Classic Maya burials and a Material Culture/Social Mobility model (for a more detailed explanation of the model see Rathje 1971a:74-107).

A *social identity* is a culturally distinguished social position or category (Goodenough 1969; Keesing 1967). Adult, male, priest, distributor of goods in Ceremony X, are all separate social identities. A *social persona* is the composite of several identities appropriate to a given social intereaction, such as: adult, male, chief priest of God Z, and distributor of goods in dealing with adult male worshippers at Ceremony X.

The following *mobile* and *non-mobile* constructs do not exist in reality. Their sharp contrast is helpful in comparing differences in emphasis among real systems. In non-mobile systems social identities are not easily interchanged. The general status level of identities is consistent within social persona. For example, the nobles in highly stratified Western Chou China manipulated bronze urns in rites for their ancestors. These acts were not only based on elite kin and religious statuses, but also validated elite political authority and economic interactions. When a Chou noble manipulated a bronze vessel, his political, economic, religious, and kinship identities were all employed in an elite social persona (Cheng 1963:XXX; Reischauer and Fairbank 1958:51, 61).

In non-mobile systems specific identities tend to co-occur in replicated sets. If Family A in a non-mobile system monopolized political positions, then each member of Family A is either a political leader or a potential political leader (subject to age and sex restrictions, i.e. adult male). There will be no potential or actual political leader who is not an adult male member of Family A. No potential or actual political leader will do anything that an adult male member of Family A does not do. In overt behaviour the two identities directly co-vary. Non-elite social persona do not include elite social identities. Each adult male member of Family B is neither a political leader nor a potential political leader. Thus, social identities in non-mobile societies tend to occur in mutually exclusive, consistently replicated sets.

In a mobile social system which by definition means that individuals can potentially change their positions in a number of hierarchies, specific genealogical and other identities will not directly co-vary with one another. An adult male who has the general political identity 'leader' may be a member of Family A or Family B or Family C. As a result of a certain amount of independent assortment, the general status level of identities in individual social persona is not always consistent. For example, among the Basoga Bantu there are situations in which high-level political leaders hold low-level positions within kinship authority systems (Fallers 1965). The social identities that comprise social persona in a mobile system are changeable and often incongruous at any one time.

13. A Material Culture / Social Mobility model

To apply the above model to past cultures, it must be translated into material culture terms. For efficient social interactions, the individuals involved must inform each other of their respective social identities (Goodenough 1969; Binford 1962, 1971). Material culture will vary in form and distribution characteristics in direct relation to the form and distribution characteristics of hierarchically ranked social identities. Variation in material symbol distribution will be used in the following tests.

Symbol distribution

In mobile systems material symbols will not directly co-vary in social persona clusters. In a system responsive to individual achievements numerous symbols will be acquired and manipulated in small-scale increments. For example, specific family and political leadership identities and their symbols may sort relatively independently (Fig. 6-3, 6-2). In non-mobile systems material symbols will significantly co-vary in sets. Symbols will be acquired and manipulated in clusters. For example, specific family and political leader symbols will directly co-vary. Leadership symbols will be associated with the symbols of one family and not with the symbols of other families (Figs. 6-1, 6-4).

14. Mobility potential

Two systems can be described as mobile or non-mobile by comparing the amount of independent assortment versus significant co-variation of identify symbols in social persona (regardless of the symbols' 'subjective' status). Such Material Culture/Social Mobility characterizations do not directly measure mobility. They describe the potential for expressing identity mobility within the material culture distributions of a system (Shimkin, personal communication). *This 'mobility potential' is assumed to be responsive to the actual amount of variety within a system* (cf. section 3). This measure for comparing two cultural systems can only be applied within bounds. The symbol clusters studied must be shown to relate to relatively complete individual or family group social persona. Cluster proveniences, or 'scenes', must be equivalent and potential artifact inventories must be comparable in both systems.

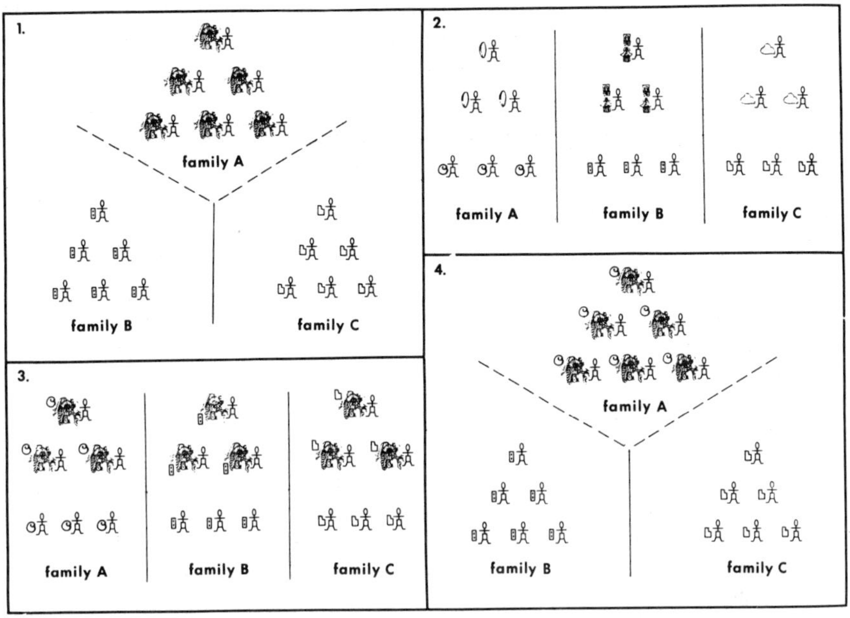

Figure 6, 1-4 are four social identity allocation systems and associated distributions of material symbols. The headdress represents a political leadership identity. The three symbols in the top half of Segment 2 each represent both a political leadership and a specific family identity. The other symbols each represent specific family identity symbols. Segments 2 and 3 represent mobile systems: segments 1 and 4 are non-mobile systems.

15. Classic Maya burials: Statistic 1 and Statistic 2

Classic Maya burials represent social persona clusters and provide an array of data relevant to the Material Culture/Social Mobility model (Rathje 1971a:108-15). Throughout the Maya lowlands the ranges of artifacts from which burial assemblages could be drawn were similar. To employ the social mobility model, individual symbol units were created; 58 variable categories were defined (Table 1). Each of the 58 variables was given a numerical loading based on a subjective ordering. The number of occurrences of each variable in a burial was multiplied by that variable's loadings. The results were summed to obtain Statistic 1 for each burial. Each Statistic 1 score is, therefore, the product of the kind and quantity of all the variables present in a burial.

Since Statistic 1 is based on a subjective loading of variables, Statistic 2 was developed as an independent description of a burial's contents. For Statistic 2 each of the 58 variables was given an objective numerical loading as a function of the rarity of its occurrence in a total sample of 1009 Classic Maya burials, i.e. the fewer occurrences the higher the loading (Table 1). Statistic 2 was then obtained for each burial by the same procedure as Statistic 1.

Table 1: The Loadings of the 58 Variables*

		Statistic 1	Statistic 2
01	Facial Ornaments	58	0.32
02	Ceremonial Paraphernalia	57	0.72
03	Pendants	56	0.58
04	Stingray Spines	55	0.81
05	Unworked Shell	54	0.46
06	Body Ornamentation	53	0.10
07	Bead Necklaces	52	0.24
08	Figurines	51	3.57
09	Tubes	50	2.63
10	Associated Carvings	49	0.09
11	Blades	48	2.22
12	Unidentified Objects	47	2.56
13	Utilitarian Objects	46	0.50
14	Seated Humans	45	1.04
15	Standing Humans	44	1.07
16	Head-only Humans	43	1.14
17	Reclining Humans	42	8.33
18	Real Glyphs	41	0.12
19	Pseudo Glyphs	40	0.96
20	Deities	39	2.17
21	Jaguars	38	2.43
22	Birds	37	1.53
23	Snakes	36	3.70
24	Deer	35	5.00
25	Dog-like Animals	34	4.00
26	Monkeys	33	6.66
27	Frogs	32	9.09
28	Aquatic Animals	31	4.54
29	Fruits	30	7.69
30	Miscellaneous	29	1.29
31	Shell Count	28	0.16
32	Type of Shell Count	27	0.34
33	Jade Count	26	0.19
34	Other Stone Count	25	0.54
35	Type of Other Stone Count	24	0.56
36	Obsidian Count	23	0.68
37	Flint Count	22	0.89
38	Bone Count	21	0.40
39	Clay Count	20	2.04
40	Pottery Count	19	0.07
41	Polychrome Pottery	18	0.26
42	Relief Pottery	17	0.36
43	Filed Teeth	16	0.25
44	Ceremonial Pottery	15	2.43
45	Legged Flat-bottom Dishes	14	1.06
46	Vases	13	0.54
47	Deep Bowls	12	0.13

* For definitions of each of the variables see Rathje 1971a: Appendix F.

		Statistic 1	Statistic 2
48	Legged Round-bottom Bowls/Dishes	11	2.70
49	Deep Full Bowls	10	1.13
50	Medium Bowls	09	0.59
51	Shallow Bowls/Dishes	08	1.44
52	Shallow Flat-bottom Dishes	07	0.71
53	Incurving Bowls	06	1.33
54	Restricted Bowls	05	2.70
55	Miniature Cups	04	1.56
56	Miniature Jars	03	3.51
57	Ollas	02	1.06
58	Monochrome Pottery	01	0.14

16. *Describing mobility potential*

A *mobility potential profile* was obtained by plotting the statistics for a Set (defined by date and provenience) of burials on logarithmic paper. The burials were ordered along the X axis on the basis of ascending Y (Statistic 1 or 2) value. Burials with no grave goods were excluded. The burials were spaced to make the X axis length of each set comparable. The plotted points were then connected to form a graph, or profile. The Statistic values were normalized so that each graph was the same height and only differences in profile form were recorded. This operation made differences in the range and internal variation of social persona present in a given set of burials clear (Fig. 7).

KEY TO BURIAL ILLUSTRATIONS

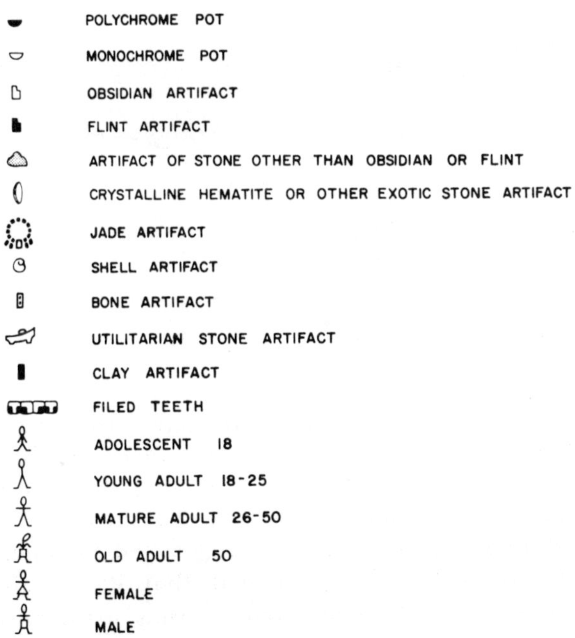

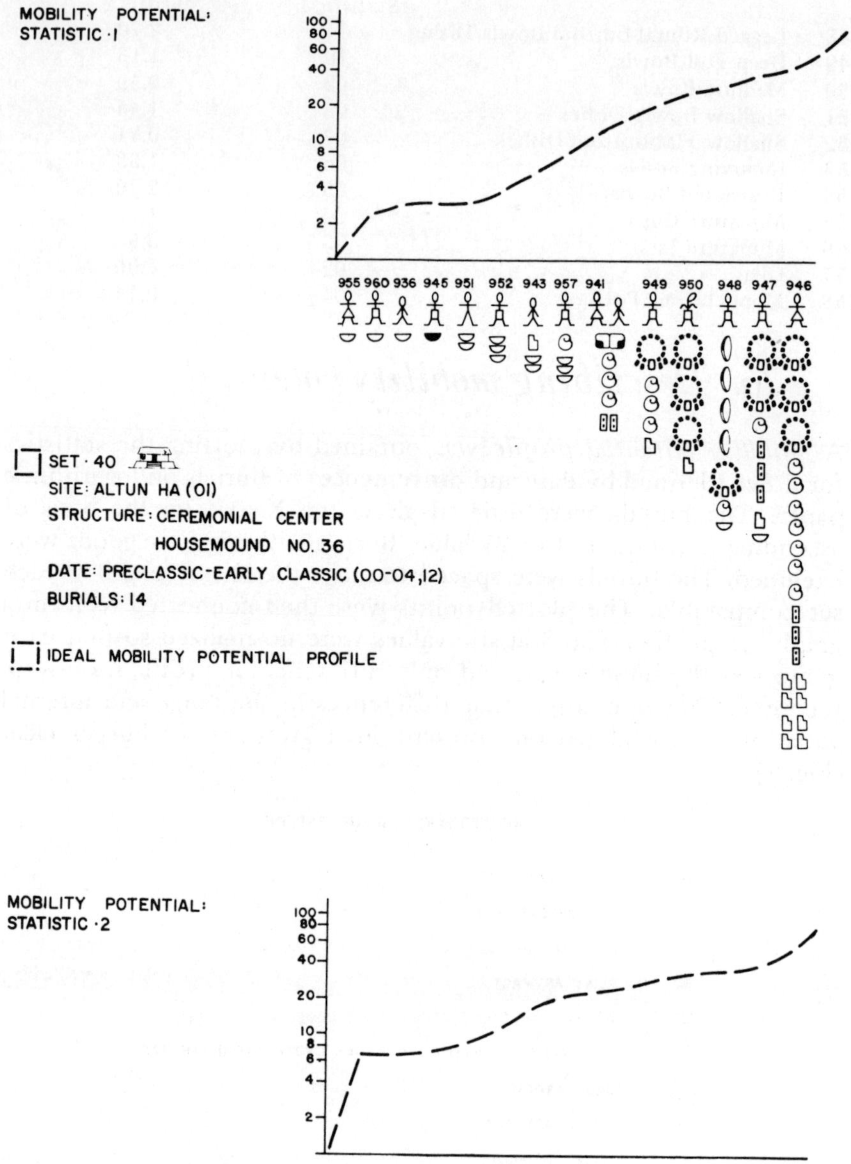

Figure 7 The burial set profiles for Set 40.

In any status system the number of holders of specific identities generally decreases exponentially as the identities become more advantaged, i.e. 1000 household constituents, 100 priests, 10 chief priests, 1 high priest. In addition, it was obvious from the data that the burial statistic values (i.e. material social persona) increased exponentially. It is therefore assumed that if a profile forms a continuum of statuses in a consistently rising exponential slope, it reflects the relative independent sorting of social identities and social identity symbols in a mobile system (cf. Set 40, Figs. 8 and 10). If the rising graph forms plateaus, it reflects the significant co-variation of symbols in non-mobile identity clusters (cf. Set 47, Figs 9 and 10). Profiles were compared and rated as mobile or non-mobile by the following method.

Experiments were made in an attempt to evaluate objectively the relative social mobility potential (internal variety) represented in two burial sets and their graphs. Set 40 clearly had a high social mobility potential (as defined by this paper); Set 47 had a low social mobility potential (Figs. 8 and 9). A fourth power exponential curve fitted between the end points of the graph was found to best fit the *mobile* graph (40) and still deviate greatly from the *non-mobile* graph (47) (Fig. 10).

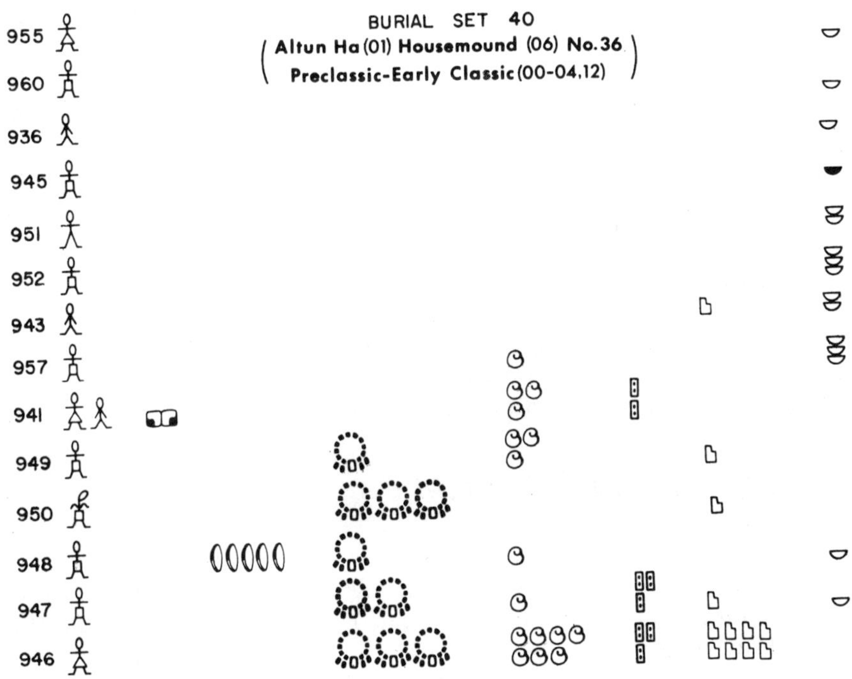

Figure 8 The burials in Set 40.

The 'ideal' profile was arbitrarily fitted to both the Statistic 1 and Statistic 2 profiles. The differences between the observed (real) and expected ('ideal') values of all of the burials in a set were summed. The number of burials in a profile was divided into the sum to normalize the result and make it comparable to those from sets with different numbers of burials. The final statement is the average deviation between a profile and an 'ideal' mobile exponential continuum connecting its high and low points – the *greater* the

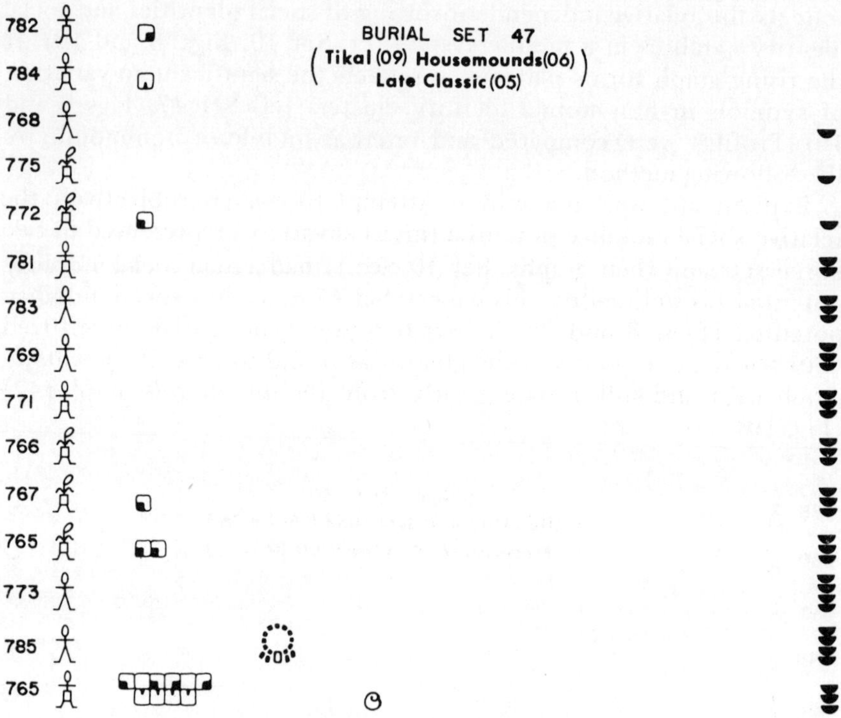

Figure 9 The burials in Set 47.

deviation the *less* the mobility potential. Thus, Set 40 (Statistic 1 rating 5.78; Statistic 2 rating 9.13) is more mobile than Set 47 (Statistic 1 rating 20.04; Statistic 2 rating 23.30) (Fig. 10).

17. *The burial sample*

Housemound burial sets will be compared to test the core and buffer zone synthetic systems (for more detailed tests see Rathje 1971a, in press). Burial data, although minimal, is available from six Central Maya Lowlands sites.

Although the core sites, Tikal and Uaxactun, are large, the housemound sample from both sites is only forty-one burials (Wauchope 1934, Smith 1950, Haviland 1963). When more of the Tikal burial data is made public a more thorough test will be possible. Until then, preliminary statements by Haviland (1963) and W. Coe (1965) indicate that the published Tikal burials (Haviland 1963) are typical examples of the unpublished burials.

Four buffer zone sites have produced housemound burial sites. David M. Pendergast (personal communication) has excavated over 200 housemound burials at the small ceremonial centre of Altun Ha, near the coast of Belize (British Honduras). Barton Ramie is a rural

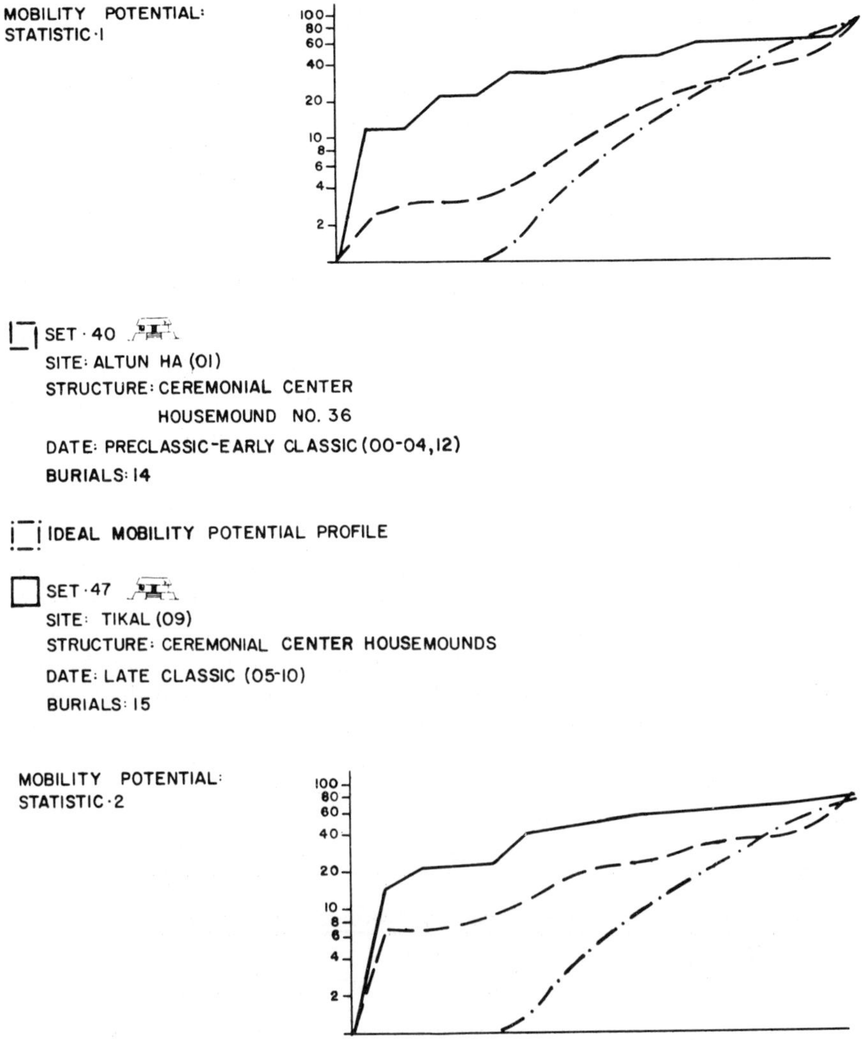

Figure 10 A comparison of mobile (Set 40) and non-mobile (Set 47) burial set profiles.

housemound site several kilometres inland in Belize on the Belize River. No major ceremonial centres have been found near Barton Ramie. One hundred and four burials in the buffer zone sample are from Barton Ramie (Willey *et al.* 1965). Fifty housemound burials come from the ceremonial centre of Altar de Sacrificios (A.L. Smith, personal communication), located at the junction of the Usumacinta, Pasion, and Chixoy Rivers. Gair Tourtellot (personal communication) excavated twenty-five housemound burials at Seibal, a ceremonial centre on the Pasion River. The Statistic 1 and 2 rating or each burial are available in Rathje 1971a.

18. Expanded test implications

At this point the test implications should be elaborated. The model of constant constraints on change states that: given the relatively similar fluctuations in variable constraints in the core and buffer zone systems, through time there will be more variety, i.e. a higher mobility potential, within the buffer zone systems than within core systems.

To make the test more interesting an additional prediction can be added. Population has been hypothesized to be a variable constraint upon variety within Classic Maya cultural systems. At all of the sites to be considered below, population increased from the Preclassic to the Late Classic (Rathje 1971a:145-51). Thus, it can be predicted that at each site variety, i.e. mobility potential, decreased through time.

For the following test Tikal and Uaxactun will represent core systems; Barton Ramie, Altun Ha, Altar de Sacrificios, and Seibal will represent buffer zone systems. By combining constant and variable constraints in synthetic systems, predictions can be generated which outline the paramters of change within Classic Maya cultural systems. The test implication of these synthetic systems then becomes: Through time variety (mobility potential) will decrease in core and buffer zone Classic Maya cultural systems; however, given relatively similar fluxuations of variable constraints on cultural systems in both areas, at any one time *buffer zone systems will have more variety than core systems* (Fig. 11).

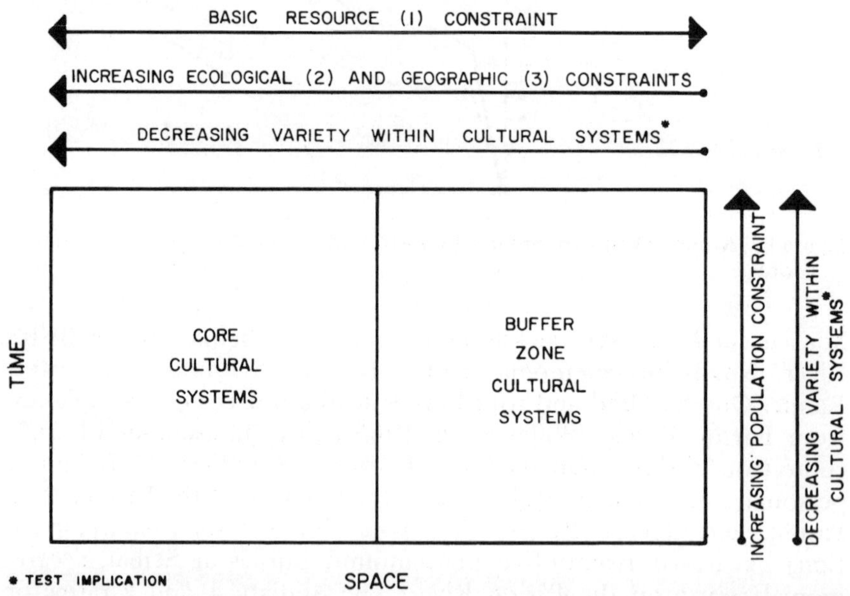

Figure 11 Classic Maya buffer zone ceremonial centre – individual household system.

19. *The test*

Due to small sample sizes and obvious sampling error, the mobility potential ratings are only tentative indicators of mobility potential. However, when these indicators consistently follow test implications, they may be considered tentative confirmation of the predictive power of the synthetic systems that generated them.

Preclassic/Early Classic household mobility potential

Even though the numbers of burials are small, both Statistics consistently agree that each of the three buffer zone housemound burial sets has more mobility potential (a lower Statistic rating) than the core set (Table 2).

Table 2: Central Lowland Maya Household Mobility Potential

			Statistic 1	Statistic 2
Preclassic/Early Classic Household Mobility Potential				
CORE:	Set 54	Uaxactun/Tikal (7)[1]	15.48[2]	15.73
BUFFER ZONE:	Set 55	Barton Ramie (14)	6.36	8.54
	Set 12	Altun Ha (58)	7.32	8.57
	Set 143	Altar de Sacrificios (22)	6.15	6.58
Late Classic Household Mobility Potential				
CORE:	Set 22	Uaxactun/Tikal (26)	18.05	12.55
	Set 47	Tikal (15)	20.04	23.30
	Set 166	Uaxactun (10)	14.80	10.80
BUFFER ZONE:	Set 56	Barton Ramie (50)	11.99	12.45
	Set 69	Altun Ha (111)	11.30	7.78
	Set 149	Altar de Sacrificios (37)	9.26	10.74
	Set 148	Seibal (19)	7.81	9.70

1. This figure is the number of burials in each set. The burials that make up each set are listed in Rathje 1971a, Appendix G.
2. A high Statistic rating indicates a small mobility potential, a low Statistic rating indicates a large mobility potential.

Late Classic household mobility potential

Statistic 1 ratings totally confirmed the test implications. Each of four buffer zone sets has more variety than Tikal or Uaxactun, separately or combined. The Statistic 2 ratings support the test implications also. However, the Statistic 2 rating of the Barton Ramie housemound set is higher than the rating of the Uaxactun housemound set, indicating less mobility potential at Barton Ramie.

If the sets are compared by pairs within specific time periods by Statistic 1 and Statistic 2 separately, there are thirty specific predictions involved in the test (Table 3). Twenty-nine out of the thirty are confirmed.

Table 3: Core/Buffer Zone Mobility Potential Predictions

KEY:	PCL/ECL	=	Preclassic/Early Classic (800 B.C.-A.D. 600)
	LCL	=	Late Classic (600 A.D.-900 A.D.)
	S1	=	Statistic 1 Rating
	S2	=	Statistic 2 Rating
	>	=	is greater than, i.e. has LESS mobility potential than
	UAX	=	Uaxactun (Core)
	TIK	=	Tikal (Core)
	B.R.	=	Barton Ramie (Buffer Zone)
	A.H.	=	Altun Ha (Buffer Zone)
	A.S.	=	Altar de Sacrificios (Buffer Zone)
	SEI	=	Seibal (Buffer Zone)
	*	=	CORRECT prediction
	†	=	INCORRECT prediction

1.	PCL/ECL	UAX/TIK	S1	>	PCL/ECL	B.R.	S1	*	15.48	>	6.36
2.	PCL/ECL	UAX/TIK	S2	>	PCL/ECL	B.R.	S2	*	15.73	>	8.54
3.	PCL/ECL	UAX/TIK	S1	>	PCL/ECL	A.H.	S	*	15.48	>	7.32
4.	PCL/ECL	UAX/TIK	S2	>	PCL/ECL	A.H.	S2	*	15.73	>	8.57
5.	PCL/ECL	UAX/TIK	S1	>	PCL/ECL	A.S.	S1	*	15.48	>	6.15
6.	PCL/ECL	UAX/TIK	S2	>	PCL/ECL	A.S.	S2	*	15.73	>	6.58
7.	LCL	UAX/TIK	S1	>	LCL	B.R.	S1	*	18.05	>	11.99
8.	LCL	UAX/TIK	S2	>	LCL	B.R.	S2	*	12.55	>	12.45
9.	LCL	UAX/TIK	S1	>	LCL	A.H.	S1	*	18.05	>	11.30
0.	LCL	UAX/TIK	S1	>	LCL	A.H.	S2	*	12.55	>	7.78
11.	LCL	UAX/TIK	S1	>	LCL	A.S.	S1	*	18.05	>	9.26
12.	LCL	UAX/TIK	S2	>	LCL	A.S.	S2	*	12.55	>	10.74
13.	LCL	UAX/TIK	S1	>	LCL	SEI	S1	*	18.05	>	7.81
14.	LCL	UAX/TIK	S2	>	LCL	SEI	S2	*	12.55	>	9.70
15.	LCL	TIK	S1	>	LCL	B.R.	S1	*	20.04	>	11.99
16.	LCL	TIK	S2	>	LCL	B.R.	S2	*	23.30	>	12.45
17.	LCL	TIK	S1	>	LCL	A.H.	S1	*	20.04	>	11.30
18.	LCL	TIK	S2	>	LCL	A.H.	S2	*	23.30	>	7.78
19.	LCL	TIK	S1	>	LCL	A.S.	S1	*	20.04	>	9.26
20.	LCL	TIK	S2	>	LCL	A.S.	S2	*	23.30	>	10.74
21.	LCL	TIK	S1	>	LCL	SEI	S1	*	20.04	>	7.81
22.	LCL	TIK	S2	>	LCL	SEI	S2	*	23.30	>	9.70
23.	LCL	UAX	S1	>	LCL	B.R.	S1	*	14.80	>	11.99
24.	LCL	UAX	S2	>	LCL	B.R.	S2	†	10.80	<	12.45
25.	LCL	UAX	S1	>	LCL	A.H.	S1	*	14.80	>	11.30
26.	LCL	UAX	S2	>	LCL	A.H.	S2	*	10.80	>	7.78
27.	LCL	UAX	S1	>	LCL	A.S.	S1	*	14.80	>	9.26
28.	LCL	UAX	S2	>	LCL	A.S.	S2	*	10.80	>	10.74
29.	LCL	UAX	S1	>	LCL	SEI	S1	*	14.80	>	7.81
30.	LCL	UAX	S2	>	LCL	SEI	S2	*	10.80	>	9.70

Household mobility potential through time

Within four sites it is possible to calculate Statistic 1 and Statistic 2 measures for two time periods: Preclassic/Early Classic and Late Classic. If Statistics 1 and 2 are considered separately, eight predictions can be made (Table 4). Six of the eight predictions that mobility potential decreases as population increases were confirmed.

Table 4: Preclassic/Early Classic-Late Classic Mobility Potential Predictions

KEY: See Table 3
* = CORRECT prediction
† = INCORRECT prediction

1.	LCL	UAX/TIK	S1	>	PCL/ECL	UAX/TIK	S1	*	18.05	>	15.48
2.	LCL	UAX/TIK	S2	>	PCL/ECL	UAX/TIK	S2	†	12.35	<	15.73
3.	LCL	B.R.	S1	>	PCL/ECL	B.R.	S1	*	11.99	>	6.36
4.	LCL	B.R.	S2	>	PCL/ECL	B.R.	S2	*	12.45	>	8.54
5.	LCL	A.H.	S1	>	PCL/ECL	A.H.	S1	*	11.30	>	7.32
6.	LCL	A.H.	S2	>	PCL/ECL	A.H.	S2	†	7.78	<	8.57
7.	LCL	A.S.	S1	>	PCL/ECL	A.S.	S1	*	9.26	>	6.15
8.	LCL	A.S.	S2	>	PCL/ECL	A.S.	S2	*	10.74	>	6.58

20. *Conclusions*

Two synthetic systems have been constructed to define some of the dynamic relationships between variables critical to the parameters of change. The concepts of 'variety', variable and constant constraints and the law of requisite variety were employed to make the parameters of variety within Classic Maya cultural systems predictable through time and space. The predictions generated from the synthetic systems were compared with Classic Maya burial data and tentatively seem to be much more accurate than could be expected by chance alone.

In conclusion, it would seem that at any one point in time a system has only one specific arrangement of elements and, therefore, no variety. Variety as seen by changes in the configurations of the elements in a system occurs only through the medium of time. Archaeology is the study of the variety in cultural systems through time. The empirical relationship between the concept of variety and archaeological data can be quantified. Thus, the parameters placed on variety by constraints can be predicted and the predictions can be tested. Because all archaeological problems can be phrased in terms of variety and constraints (for another example cf. Luebbermann n.d.), the law of requisite variety is a powerful deductive concept in the construction of synthetic systems. The utility of the concepts of variety and constraint and the law of requisite variety, like other aspects of General Systems Theory, transcend both specific data and specific problems. In constructing archaeological models the concept of variety would seem to order conceptual schema by delimiting empirical evidence to certain areas of concern which are worthy of testing. If this is true, the concept of variety might be profitably utilized in areas other than the Maya Lowlands.

Acknowledgment

Many of the aspects of this paper's approach to models of culture change developed directly from reading W. Ross Ashby (1956, 1968) and from discussions with H.A. Luebbermann, Jr. The statistical measurement of mobility potential was devised by Richard G. Sanders, Jr. and Lawrence Manire. Unpublished burial material, constructive criticisms, and encouragement were freely given by Gordon R. Willey, David M. Pendergast, A. Ledyard Smith, and Gair Tourtellot. The illustrations were drawn by C. Sternberg, S. Burstein, W. Rathje and L. Irwin. The manuscript was edited with gusto by Susan Luebbermann. Several portions of this paper were prepared through the aid of the Wenner-Gren Foundation for Anthropological Research, the National Science Foundation, and the Bowditch Exploration Fund. The opportunity to present this paper was made possible by Kent C. Day.

REFERENCES

Ashby, W.R. (1956) *An Introduction to Cybernetics.* London, Chapman and Hall.

Ashby, W.R. (1968) Variety, constraint, and the Law of Requisite Variety. *In* Buckley, W. (ed.) *Modern Systems Research for the Behavioural Scientist.* Chicago, Aldine.

Binford, L.R. (1962) Archaeology as anthropology. *American Antiquity* **28**, 217-25.

Binford, L.R. (1971) Mortuary practices: their study and their potential. *In* Brown, J.A. (ed.) *Approaches to the Social Dimensions of Mortuary Practices.* Memoirs of the Society for American Archaeology, no. 25.

Chapman, A.M. (1957) Port of trade enclaves in Aztec and Maya civilization. *In* Polyani, K., Arensberg, C.M. and Pearson, H.W. (eds.) *Trade and Market in the Early Empires.* New York, The Free Press.

Cheng, T. (1963) *Archaeology in China: Chou China.* Cambridge, Heffer.

Coe, W.R. (1965) Tikal, Guatemala and the emergent Maya Civilization. *Science* 1962. *Estudios de Cultura Maya* 3, 41-64.

Coe, W.R. (1965) Tikal, Guatemala,and the emergent Maya Civilization. *Science* 147, 1401-19.

Fallers, L.A. (1965) *Bantu Bureaucracy: a Century of Political Evolution among the Basoga of Uganda.* Chicago, University Press.

Fried, M.H. (1967) *The Evolution of Political Society: an Essay in Political Anthropology.* New York, Random House.

Goodenough, W.H. (1969) Rethinking 'status' and 'role': toward a general model of the cultural organization of social relationships. *In* Tyler, S.A. (ed.) *Cognitive Anthropology*. New York, Holt, Rinehart and Winston.

Haviland, W.A. (1963) *Excavation of Small Structures in the Northeast Quadrant of Tikal, Guatemala.* Unpublished doctoral dissertation, Department of Anthropology, University of Pennsylvannia, Philadelphia.

Keesing, R.M. (1967) Toward an ethnographic theory of 'roles'. Manuscript. Peabody Museum Library, Cambridge.

Leone, M.P. (1968) *Economic Autonomy and Social Distance: Archaeological Evidences.* Unpublished doctoral dissertation, Department of Anthropology, University of Arizona, Tucson.

Luebbermann, H.A. Jr. (n.d.) Aztec game theory. Manuscript. Arizona State Museum Library. University of Arizona.

Pendergast, D.M. (1969) *Altun Ha: a Guidebook to the Ancient Maya Ruins.* The Government of British Honduras (Belize).

Rappaport, R.A. (1967) *Pigs for the Ancestors: Ritual in the Ecology of a New Guinea People.* Yale University Press.

Rathje, W.L. (1970) Socio-political implications of Lowland Maya burials: methodology and tentative hypotheses. *World Archaeology* **1**, 359-74.

Rathje, W.L. (1971a) *Lowland Classic Maya socio-political Organization: Degree and Form in Time and Space.* Unpublished doctoral dissertation, Department of Anthropology, Harvard University.

Rathje, W.L. (1971b) The origin and development of Lowland Classic Maya civilization. *American Antiquity* **36**, 275-85.

Rathje, W.L. In press. Classic Maya development and denouement. *In* Culbert, T.P. (ed.) A volume on the collapse of Classic Maya civilization. University of New Mexico Press.

Reischauer, E.O. and Fairbank, J.K. (1958) *East Asia: the Great Tradition.* Boston, Houghton Mifflin.

Sahlins, M.D. (1958) *Social Stratification in Polynesia.* Seattle, University of Washington Press.

Sahlins, M.D. (1963) Poor man, rich man, big-man, chief: political types in Melanesia and Polynesia. *Comparative Studies in Society and History* **5**, 285-303.

Smith, A.L. (1950) *Uaxactun, Guatemala: Excavations of 1931-7.* Carnegie Institution of Washington, Publication no. 588.

Thompson, J.E.S. (1964) Trade relations between the Maya highlands and lowlands. *Estudios de Cultura Maya* **4**, 13-49.

Thompson, J.E.S. (1970) *Maya History and Religion.* University of Oklahoma Press.

Wauchope, R. (1934) *House Mounds of Uaxactun, Guatemala.* Carnegie Institution of Washington, Publication 436. Contributions to American archaeology, vol. 2, no. 7.

Willey, G.R., Bullard, W.R. Jr., Class, J.B. and Clifford, J.C. (1965) *Prehistoric Maya settlements in the Belize Valley.* Peabody Museum Papers, vol. 54.

Concluding Address

EDMUND LEACH

Concluding Address

In preparing these final comments I was far from clear as to what role I was expected to fill in the proceedings of the Seminar. Before the presentation of this paper we already had one and a half hours of 'final discussion' so that it cannot be that I was supposed to attempt the impossible by 'summing up'. Perhaps it was that, in accordance with the prevailing behaviourist ethos of this Seminar, I had been subjected to a stimulus-reponse experiment. Having been stimulated, I will duly respond.

Right at the beginning of our proceedings we had a considerable discussion as to whether Professor Binford's dreams might rate as data for scientific investigation and I have to confess that a good deal of data from my own murky sub-conscious were floating to the surface during the three days of discussion. In the second session Gene Sterud suggested that archaeologists are only now beginning to break out of the paradigm with which they operated in the latter part of the 19th century and he glossed that suggestion in the final discussion. The general proposition seems to have been born out by our proceedings. All the way along contributors were making remarks that could only make sense if you were to take as given a unilinear theory of social development of a kind which the social anthropologists finally abandoned about forty years ago. As far as social anthropology is concerned, I appreciate your difficulty as archaeologists; you would like to use the data of ethnography to give flesh and blood to your archaeological remnants. Used with great discretion, I believe that ethnographic evidence can in fact help you to do this; but far too many of the participants at the Seminar seemed to think that the analogies between ethnographic society and archaeological society are direct . . . i.e. that 'primitive' societies from the 20th century can be treated as fossilised survivals from proto-historical or even palaeolithic times. This is a very 19th-century idea.

Clearly a shift in paradigm is taking place, but it is less drastic than some participants seem to think. Professor Binford's remark that 'behaviour is the by-product of the interaction of a cultural repertoire with the environment' may be proto-typical of the 'new' archaeology but to a social anthropologist it reads like a quotation from Malinowski writing at the time when naive functionalism was at its peak – that is to say about 1935.

Do not misunderstand me. Functionalism is 'old hat' in social anthropology; it is 'new style' in archaeology. This is not a matter for denigration. Paradigms in this Kuhnian sense are neither good nor bad; they are just different. It may well be that a functionalist paradigm will prove more useful and enduring in archaeology than it has done in social anthropology; I cannot tell. But I am in a personal difficulty because I have myself become allergic to 'functionalism' and the various other 'isms' that go with it – e.g. positivism, behaviourism and so on. Correspondingly the paradigm which is currently high fashion among the social anthropologists, namely that of structuralism, has not as yet caught up with the archaeologists at all. Don't worry, it will! But meanwhile interdisciplinary communication is rather difficult.

Incidentally, one relevant aspect of Kuhn's thesis about scientific revolutions was not noted in our discussions. It is this. When there is a shift of paradigm the principal upholders of an established orthodoxy never change their views. Justification in terms of scientific methodology is in part self-deception, for when the figures turn out wrong the true believer will always reshuffle the figures; when contrary evidence turns up he throws doubt upon the credentials of the investigator. New paradigms eventually become dominant only because old men die and young men espouse new ideas. But there is nothing intrinsically meritorious about new ideas; science, as such, is neutral. In the course of the three days of the Seminar we saw some evidence of the validity of Kuhn's analysis. It seems plain that several of the more prominent and scientifically committed members are prepared to go to the stake in defence of beliefs which they came to accept long before they started to investigate the evidence. Whenever someone lets slip the phrase: 'We have been able to show' – or some equivalent form of words – you may be sure that you are in the presence of Kuhnian man.

As I hinted earlier, one of the major differences between the functionalist paradigm – which some archaeologists are beginning to use but which the social anthropologists have now mostly abandoned – and the structuralist paradigm which I myself now take for granted, is that functionalist proto-man is a tool-maker whereas structuralist proto-man is a user of language.

At this point I should like to elaborate some of the things which were said in passing by Professor Crossland in the presentation of his paper. The essence of language is not that it consists of words or sounds but that is syntactically ordered. I would define language as an arrangement of information elements capable of being transmitted from a sender to a receiver against a background of noise – i.e. random interference. In this very general sense, language is not confined to verbal language but, even so, all languages which convey *human* information are necessarily structures *like* verbal languages. This is demonstrably the case. Ritual performances, dancing, music and so forth can all be shown to possess grammatical structure which is strictly analogous to that of the grammatical structure of verbal utterance.

Because this is so, and because structuralist social anthropologists emphasize the communication aspect of human culture, they pay much greater attention to ritual symbolism than did their functionalist predecessors, who tended to concentrate on economics. I have been interested to observe that the 'new' functionalist archaeology likewise concentrates on the economic and demographic aspects of prehistoric society to the neglect of the religious aspects. Presumably this bias will persist until such time as you are overwhelmed by structuralist fashion.

But to go back to language. Following Chomsky's very far-reaching but questionable assertions concerning the universality of major features of verbal grammar there has, of late, been a vast amount of research into the way that children first learn to speak. Renneberg's work has already been mentioned; but there is a great deal else besides. The conclusion seems inescapable that some features of the coding and decoding procedures, which allow us to embody meaningful utterances in sound patterns imposed on the breath and then understand what is said, must be innate in man. These procedures are so complicated that they must have required an immensely long period of evolutionary development. Indeed, since experimental chimpanzees, such as Washoe, seem to share a rudimentary truncated form of these special coding/decoding capacities we must suppose that our speech making capacity is the outcome of several *million* years of evolutionary development.

The relevance of this observation is that the making and decoding of speech utterances is an activity wholly *unlike* the trigger-response reaction which functionalists tend to regard as typical of all animal behaviour including human behaviour. Human speech is not simply imitative, nor is it simple repetitive; it is a creative activity and infinitely original. Although every individual has only a limited linguistic competence he can, and very frequently does, make entirely new statements. What I was saying, in speaking these words, had never been said before in the history of the world. This originality of utterance is a characteristically human activity; no other animal, so far as we know, is capable of anything even remotely similar.

Our human capacity for original speech creativity is closely related to creativity in non-verbal forms; it is linked with human consciousness and human intentionality. This creativity implies that we are not just part of the natural world governed by 'natural laws'. We have a unique human capability to engage in 'work' (*praxis*), and when we work we alter the state of our surroundings intentionally. The archaeologist's reflections about the processes of culture change should take account of this fact.

The intentionality of human action implies that, where human beings are concerned, we can never predict what will happen next. We now understand natural physical forces so well that we can send men to the moon, and before they ever start we can predict within an accuracy of seconds just when they will splash down after their return. Yet with all the computer gadgetry in the world one cannot predict with any confidence what the exchange rate between Sterling and U.S. Dollars will be tomorrow morning . . . that is a measure of the difference between matters which are governed by natural laws and matters which are governed by human intention.

The proper analogy for human behaviour is not natural law – of a physical kind – but a game of chess. The field of play and the rules of the game are laid out in advance but the way the game is played out is unpredictable.

What is the relevance of that? My point is that the task of the archaeologist is to dig up and analyse the residues of the past. By all means let all the resources of science be used to improve techniques so that a more and more accurate record is obtained of what these residues really are, when they came into existence and so on. But do please recognize the limitations of the archaeologist. As soon as you go beyond asking 'What' questions, such as: 'What is the nature of my material?' and start asking 'How' and 'Why' questions, such as 'How did this deposit come into existence?', 'Why does my series of deposits change over time?', or, by analogy, 'How was the prehistoric game of social chess played out?', then you are moving away from verifiable fact into the realm of pure speculation. This does not mean that the archaeologist should not speculate, but he needs to understand what he is doing and when he is doing it. In speculative areas of this sort, because the subject is dealing with *human* materials, there are no intrinsic probabilities, and science and statistics can give no answers at all. Just as there is no 'law-like generalization' which will enable anyone to predict what I am going to say next when I am speaking, so there is no law-like generalization which will allow one to predict the future course of history or to reconstruct the course of past history. One can of course pick up ideas by looking for ethnographic parallels . . . but do not deceive yourselves. History does not repeat itself; the closest ethnographic parallel to an archaeological situation can do no more than offer an illustration of what is possible. It can never exemplify the probable.

I can make my point in a different way by resort to a model. The word model was included in the general title of our seminar and it has recurred very frequently in the course of our discussions. It is a word which, in vernacular speech, has many different meanings. For example just now at Christmas time, if you go into a toy shop and ask for a 'model aeroplane', you are liable to be offered one of two quite different things: one is an object that looks like an aeroplane but does not fly; the other does *not* look like a 'real' aeroplane but will fly. Here in this seminar the word 'model' has become oddly confused with the two quite separate concepts of 'hypothesis' and of 'law', but discussion has been further confused by some uncertainty as to whether contributors wanted a model that worked or simply something that looked like the real thing . . . but didn't work.

Anyway, my own use of the word 'model' is rather different. It is simply a heuristic device, a drawing on the blackboard, an aid to thinking about complex phenomena.

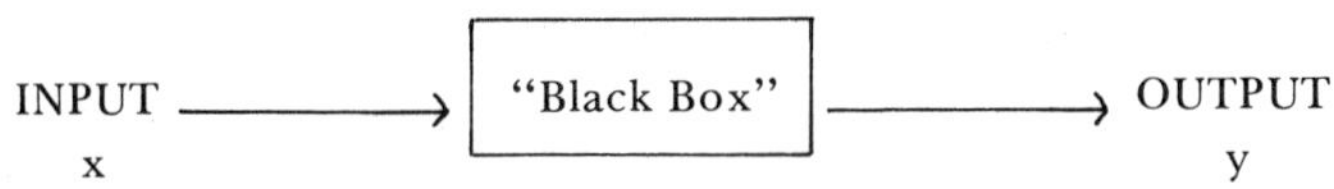

$$y = F(x)$$

Figure 1

Fig. 1 represents a Black Box. A Black Box is any imaginary mechanism, the workings of which cannot be investigated. Notionally we can observe the input (x) to the Black Box and also the output (y). This may show us that the relationship between y and x is ordered and not random, i.e. that $y = F(x)$. In such circumstances we cannot infer with any confidence whatsoever what goes on inside the Black Box. There will ordinarily be an indefinitely large number of possible forms of mechanism inside the Black Box which might produce the observed results. It is true that if the investigator postulates that there is one and only one solution, he can then produce an inferential interpretation of what is going on which will carry a great deal of conviction . . . until it turns out to be wrong, as is currently happening in particle physics! But if, as is the case with social systems, it is known that there are no unique solutions, then nothing whatever can be inferred about the mechanism of F simply by observing the patterning of y and x.

Fig. 2 represents an elaboration of Fig. 1, in which the Black Box is conceived of as a closed social system existing in prehistoric time. x is the work pattern of that society as generated by its ecological interaction with its physical environment; y is the archaeological residue discovered by the field archaeologist in the 20th century. It is to the credit of the 'new' archaeologists that they appreciate much more clearly than their predecessors that relationship between x and

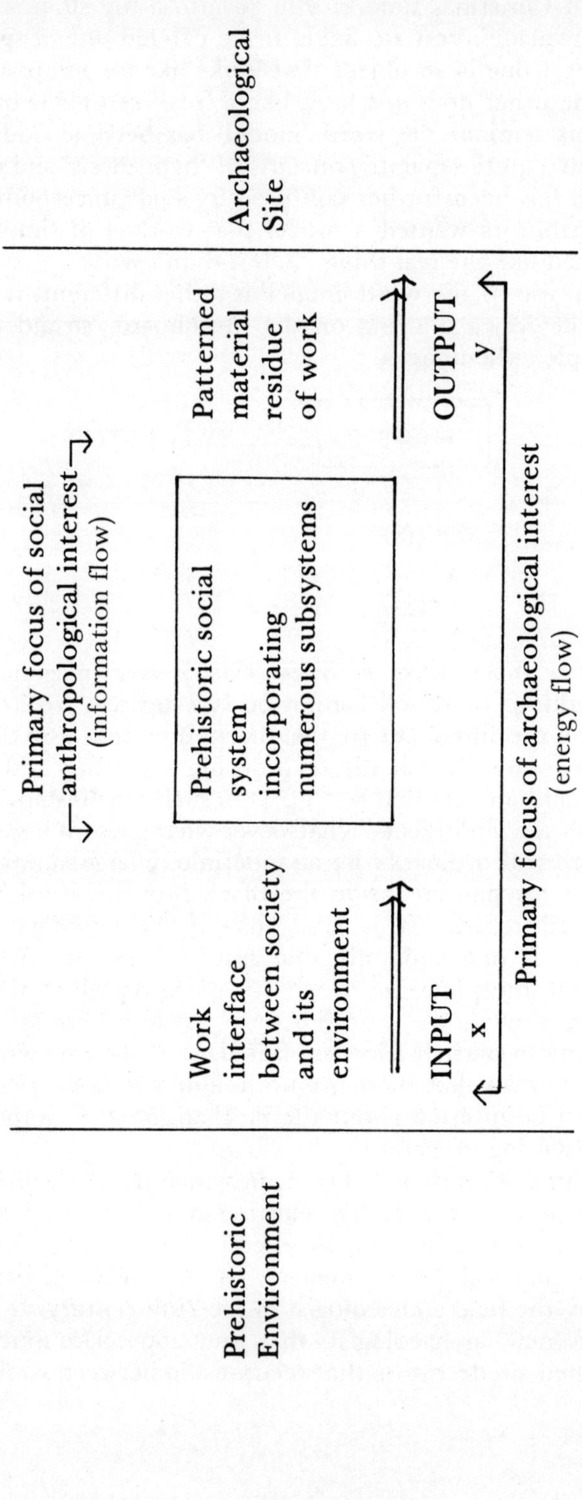
Prehistoric Environment
Work interface between society and its environment
INPUT x
Primary focus of social anthropological interest
(information flow)
Prehistoric social system incorporating numerous subsystems
Primary focus of archaeological interest
(energy flow)
Patterned material residue of work
OUTPUT y
Archaeological Site

Figure 2

y is complex rather than simple and that it is difficult, perhaps even impossible, to infer patterns in x from a study of patterns in y. But at the same time these same 'new' archaeologists – and I am thinking here of Professor Binford's contributions to our present discussions – give the impression that they are naively optimistic. They appear to believe that, given sufficient scientific ingenuity and sufficient wealth of ethnographic parallels, they will not only be able to make inferences about x from a study of y, but further they will then be able to extend the study of x to a point at which they can reconstruct the structure of the internal organization of the Black Box itself.

This is an illusion. There are always an indefinitely large number of alternative ways in which particular human social systems might be adapted to meet particular ecological and demographic situations. It is quite untrue that forms of social organization are somehow 'determined' by the environmental situation and the cultural repertoire with which a particular group is equipped to encounter that environment.

We had a case in point earlier in the seminar. Colin Renfrew produced a map of henge sites of the neolithic period in southern England and suggested that they should be treated as a single system rather than isolated items. Fair enough. But he then went on to argue that this must imply that the political regime in this part of the map at the relevant period was one of 'chiefdoms'. As we have seen the social anthropologists in this audience were quite unimpressed by the second half of Renfrew's suggestion; . . . ethnographic parallels suggest at least half a dozen alternative possibilities and none of them need be right. That does not mean that they should not be used as guesses; but the highly speculative nature of such reconstructions needs to be appreciated.

My diagram models bring out another point. In this seminar there has been a good deal of talk about the need for ethnographer-social anthropologists on the one hand and archaeologists on the other to collaborate in order to achieve their common goals. Certainly I favour collaboration, but we need to recognize that the goals are not really common. The data of archaeology are the residues of ancient social systems and the most that the archaeologists can hope for is he may be able to establish, with reasonable confidence, the work pattern that produced those residues – he can hope to generate x by observing y; but the *contents* of the Black Box, social organization as the social anthropologist understands that term, must for ever remain a mystery. In contrast, the ethnographer-social anthropologist has no Black Box problem; he can observe the workings of the system at first hand, and that is always the focal point of *his* interest. y, which forms the data of archaeology, does not fall within the purview of the social anthropologist at all. The two fields of enquiry are thus much less closely linked than is sometimes supposed.

But although I am insisting that archaeological speculations about the workings of the sociological Black Box can never rate better than 'well informed guesses' I would still argue that such guessing is an essential activity for any archaeologist. All I am saying is that you should recognize your guesses for what they are, and not delude yourselves into thinking that, by resort to statistics and computers, you can convert your guesses into scientifically established facts.

I agree with those archaeologists who have been insisting that, in the last analysis, archaeology must be concerned with people rather than with things. You would not be interested in the objects and places which you investigate at all unless they had, in the past, been either made or modified by human work. But are you really capable of studying 'people'?. I realize that archaeologists are very well aware of the paucity of their evidence and that they take legitimate pride in the ingenuity with which they apply scientific procedures so as to make the most of such evidence as they have. That is fine, but all the ingenuity in the world will not replace the evidence that is lost and gone for ever, and you need to be on your guard against persuading yourselves that you have discovered more than is actually discoverable. It seems to me that the wise archaeologist should steer away from trying to do the kind of social anthropology which the professional social anthropologist knows to be quite impossible.

You may think that warnings of this sort are quite unnecessary. I am not so sure. During the first day of the seminar I was assured by Professor Binford that he could prove from the archaeological record that there have been human societies in the past in which gift exchange played no part. This struck me as a surprising claim. If it were valid it would remove at a stroke the one law-like generalization which has any significance in the whole of sociological theory. But Professor Binford's threat does not alarm me. In contemporary ethnographic situations the vast majority of all gift exchanges consist of swapping identical highly perishable gifts – on the principle that if I stand you a glass of beer you will give me one back. Such transactions will leave no trace, and negative evidence for such activity in the archaeological record can have no significance whatsoever.

I appreciate that the new archaeology, being functionalist and behaviourist, is practical, down to earth and scientific, so that its practitioners tend to be rather disdainful of symbolic non-rational human activity. It is consistent with this that practically every paper in the seminar has been concerned with problems of economic subsistence, settlement patterns, demography. Religious rituals have scarcely been mentioned. John Alexander's safety pins were the nearest we ever came to talking about symbolic value as distinct from utilitarian economic value. And of course, if one is really convinced that the development of human society is governed by natural laws and the monocausal responses to economic pressures, this is all very sensible. Yet to a social anthropologist it somehow seems very odd. In present-day ethnographic situations the problems of day-to-day survival seldom loom very large. Sometimes (but by no means always) subsistence activities take up a great deal of working time but, except in times of food crisis, they tend to be taken very much for granted. What matters, in the minds of the actors, is religion and politics. Archaeologists who concentrate their attention exclusively on the kitchen aspects of the garbage pit are certainly missing a lot.

Let me try to give an illustration of how complicated these matters may be. 'Explanation', or if you prefer it 'insight', is not limited to the identification of cause and effect.

The publication of Max Weber's *The Protestant Ethic and the Spirit of Capitalism* in 1905 started an intellectual storm among historians and sociologists which has been going on ever since. Weber claimed that there was a demonstrable association between the location of innovating capitalism in the period 1600-1750 and concentrations of Calvinistic puritanism; he did not propound a cause and effect relationship, though others have sometimes done so. The facts have been vigorously disputed but in some countries anyway the evidence seems clear and striking. What sort of 'explanation' should we look for: is this a case where economic forces had a causal influence on non-rational values, or did non-rational values have a causal influence on economic forces? Much of the academic debate over the past 65 years has focussed on just this issue. But now that the facts are coming to be better understood the issue of 'cause' fades into the background. What really happens? The English pattern runs something like this. The families which got themselves involved in the industrial revolution from 1750 onwards were families which had managed to accumulate capital over the previous century but had not allowed it to set frozen in landed assets. The conditions for such accumulation had been created at the beginning of the 17th century by scientific, technical and educational innovations. But, as we know from an observation of what has happened recently in Asia and elsewhere, technical innovation which creates the conditions for capital accumulation also tends to favour a Malthusian upsurge of population, which in turn frustrates the generation of industrial 'take-off'. However, in England, in the relevant social classes at the relevant period, i.e. 1620-1750, there was no upsurge of population. Standards of living increased dramatically but the population remained the same. This in turn seems to be associated with a very late age of marriage for women and an unusually low rate of illegitimacy. In short, it seems that by round about means, the puritan sexual ethic functioned as a system of birth control.

The point of my example is to show that, when the facts of

history are known *in detail*, 'explanations' which are in any way adequate are always enormously complicated. They always contain an intricate mixture of demographic facts, economic forces, and religious and political ideology. No one parameter can be picked out as being in causal relationship towards all the rest.

It seems probable that this was just as true in proto-historical times as it was in historical times and an archaeology, which seeks to eliminate ideology just because it is inaccessible, is resorting to 'explanations' which are in no way connected with 'what happened in history'.

I am very far from wanting to suggest that there can be no feedback at all between the social anthropologists and the ethnographers on the one hand and the archaeologists on the other, but it does seem to me that many archaeologists have quite a wrong impression about the *kind* of cross fertilization of ideas that might take place. Let me illustrate this point.

Some of those who have been talking about early palaeolithic cultures have been suggesting that once you get back to about 25,000 B.C. you may be dealing with 'men' who were undifferentiated in culture and undifferentiated in language; yet those who argue in this fashion still seem to think that the 20th-century activities of present day Eskimos and Australian Aborigines can be, in some sense, 'relevant' for the interpretation of the residues of such hypothetical proto-human social systems. You can't have it both ways. Clearly if we go back far enough in time we shall come to a period at which the societies of proto-men were pre-human. But either the men of 40,000 years ago (or whatever other baseline is chosen) were true men 'like us' or they were not. *If* they were like us, then a recognition of cultural difference by the people themselves was a key factor which accounted for a vast amount of their observable behaviour . . . for this is true of *all* human societies of the present day . . . human behaviour in Belfast at the present time is a case in point. But if they were *not* like us in this respect, then social anthropology has nothing whatever to contribute, and dragging in analogies from the Eskimo and the Australian Aborigines is just a red herring and, from the archaeologist's point of view, a piece of self-deception.

On the other hand, where you are dealing with real men of real history who lie, as it were, only just out of sight so far as normal historical records are concerned – Norman Hammond's material concerning the Maya for example, or the very intensive archaeological research which is currently in progress all over the Pacific – then close collaboration between archaeologist and social anthropologist is not only possible but quite essential, if *either* side is to contribute anything significant to history. This job of collaboration is disconcertingly and unexpectedly difficult. Archaeology shows that most of what the social anthropologist thought he knew about the life style of 18th-century Maori is plainly wrong, yet the social anthropologist's evidence is almost equally disturbing for the archaeologist. Even so *some* joint progress has been made.

Effective collaboration need not imply harmonious agreement. On the contrary, it can mostly proceed only as dialectic. The social anthropologist will always be telling the archaeologist that his simple mono-causal explanations are preposterously simplistic and that, for every possibility which comes to the archaeologists's mind, ethnography suggests a dozen alternatives. The archaeologist in turn can repeatedly bring the social anthropologist's speculations to a full stop by showing that it wasn't so. The short run interaction in each case is negative. Both sides can help curb the wilder speculative guesses of the other. But speculation in itself is highly desirable. Let me go back to Mr Case's remarks in our first session when he was talking about the role of insight in relation to scientific discovery. Computers and similar gadgetry have their proper place in archaeological method, but do not forget that in the past real progress in your subject, as in mine, has always originated in an inspired guess.

Index of Authors

General and Site Index